Archie

1000 PAGE COMICS HOOPLA

Archie ®
1000 PAGE COMICS HOOPLA

Publisher / Co-CEO: **Jon Goldwater**
Co-CEO: Nancy Silberkleit
President: Mike Pellerito
Co-President / Editor-In-Chief: Victor Gorelick
Chief Creative Officer: Roberto Aguirre-Sacasa
Chief Operating Officer: William Mooar
Chief Financial Officer: Robert Wintle
Senior Vice President – Publicity & Marketing: Alex Segura
Director of Book Sales & Operations: Jonathan Betancourt
Production Manager: Stephen Oswald
Lead Designer: Kari McLachlan
Associate Editor: Carlos Antunes
Editorial Assistant / Proofreader: Jamie Lee Rotante

Published by Archie Comic Publications, Inc.
629 Fifth Avenue, Suite 100, Pelham, NY 10803-1242

First Printing.   Printed in U.S.A.   ISBN: 978-1-68255-974-1

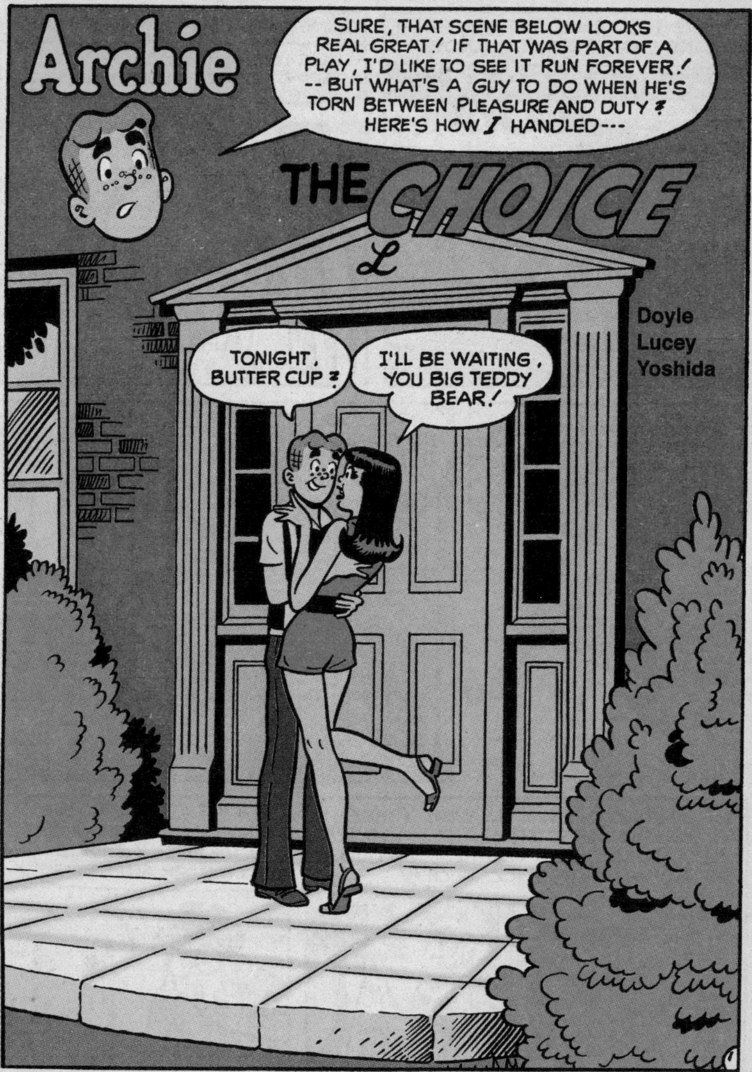
Archie
SURE, THAT SCENE BELOW LOOKS REAL GREAT! IF THAT WAS PART OF A PLAY, I'D LIKE TO SEE IT RUN FOREVER! -- BUT WHAT'S A GUY TO DO WHEN HE'S TORN BETWEEN PLEASURE AND DUTY? HERE'S HOW I HANDLED---
THE CHOICE
Doyle
Lucey
Yoshida
TONIGHT, BUTTER CUP?
I'LL BE WAITING, YOU BIG TEDDY BEAR!
1

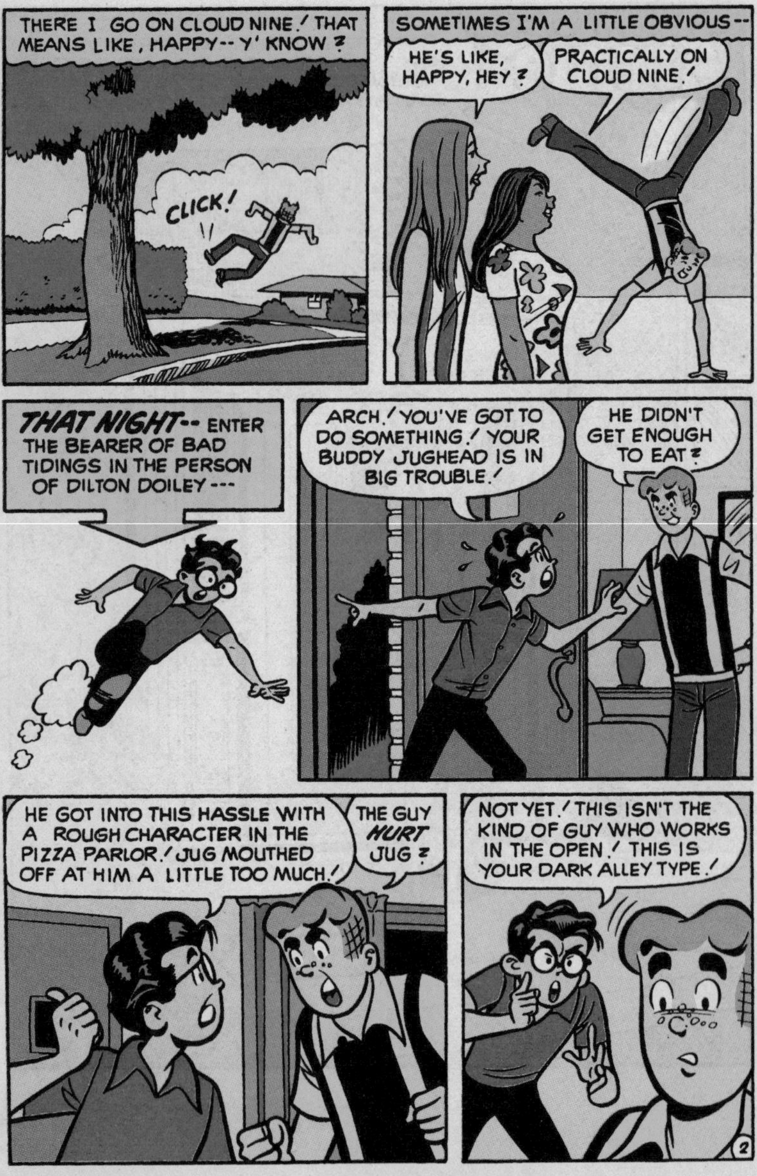

THERE I GO ON CLOUD NINE! THAT MEANS LIKE, HAPPY-- Y' KNOW?
CLICK!
SOMETIMES I'M A LITTLE OBVIOUS--
HE'S LIKE, HAPPY, HEY?
PRACTICALLY ON CLOUD NINE!
THAT NIGHT-- ENTER THE BEARER OF BAD TIDINGS IN THE PERSON OF DILTON DOILEY---
ARCH! YOU'VE GOT TO DO SOMETHING! YOUR BUDDY JUGHEAD IS IN BIG TROUBLE!
HE DIDN'T GET ENOUGH TO EAT?
HE GOT INTO THIS HASSLE WITH A ROUGH CHARACTER IN THE PIZZA PARLOR! JUG MOUTHED OFF AT HIM A LITTLE TOO MUCH!
THE GUY HURT JUG?
NOT YET! THIS ISN'T THE KIND OF GUY WHO WORKS IN THE OPEN! THIS IS YOUR DARK ALLEY TYPE!
2

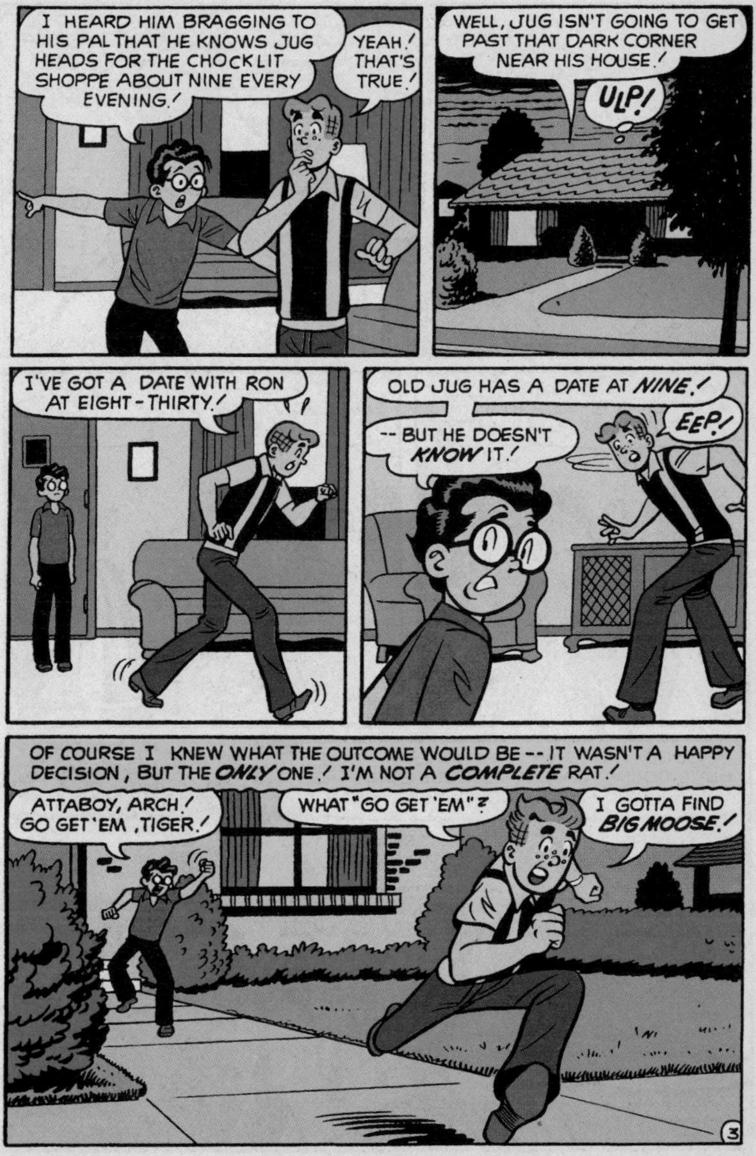
I HEARD HIM BRAGGING TO HIS PAL THAT HE KNOWS JUG HEADS FOR THE CHOCKLIT SHOPPE ABOUT NINE EVERY EVENING!
YEAH! THAT'S TRUE!
WELL, JUG ISN'T GOING TO GET PAST THAT DARK CORNER NEAR HIS HOUSE!
ULP!
I'VE GOT A DATE WITH RON AT EIGHT-THIRTY!
OLD JUG HAS A DATE AT NINE!
-- BUT HE DOESN'T KNOW IT!
EEP!
OF COURSE I KNEW WHAT THE OUTCOME WOULD BE -- IT WASN'T A HAPPY DECISION, BUT THE ONLY ONE! I'M NOT A COMPLETE RAT!
ATTABOY, ARCH! GO GET 'EM, TIGER!
WHAT "GO GET 'EM"?
I GOTTA FIND BIG MOOSE!
3

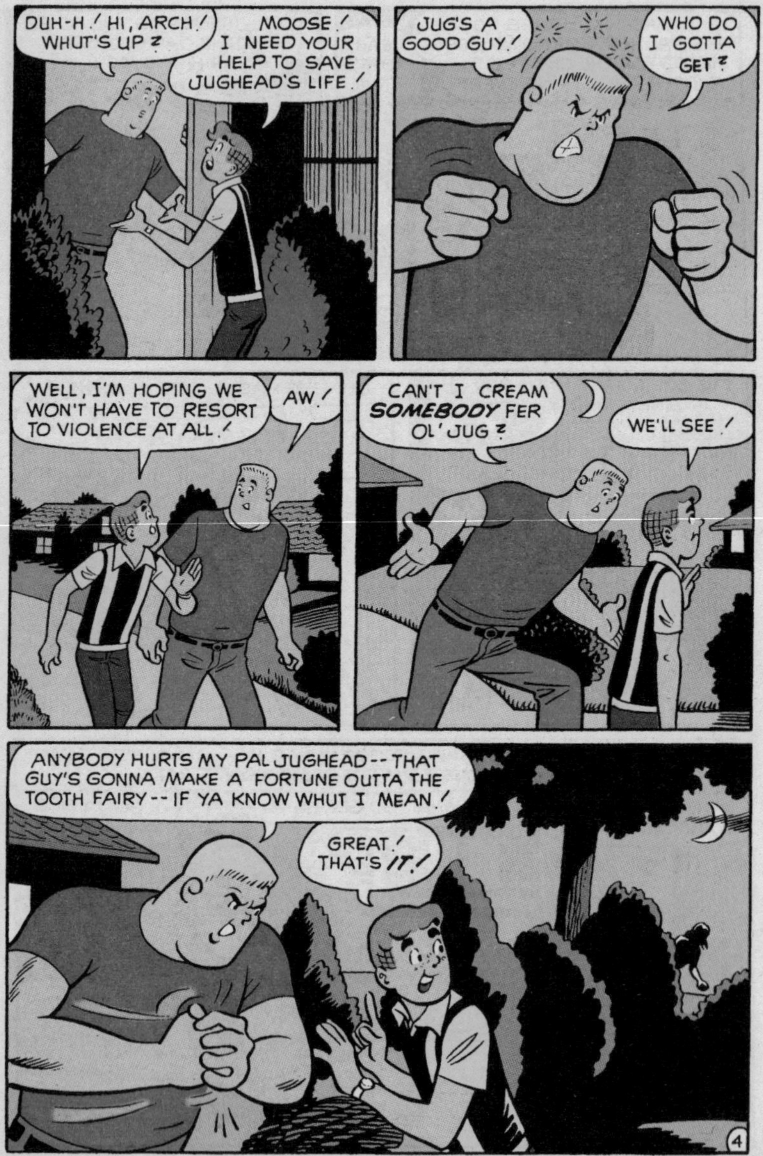
DUH-H! HI, ARCH! WHUT'S UP?
MOOSE! I NEED YOUR HELP TO SAVE JUGHEAD'S LIFE!
JUG'S A GOOD GUY!
WHO DO I GOTTA GET?
WELL, I'M HOPING WE WON'T HAVE TO RESORT TO VIOLENCE AT ALL!
AW!
CAN'T I CREAM *SOMEBODY* FER OL' JUG?
WE'LL SEE!
ANYBODY HURTS MY PAL JUGHEAD-- THAT GUY'S GONNA MAKE A FORTUNE OUTTA THE TOOTH FAIRY-- IF YA KNOW WHUT I MEAN!
GREAT! THAT'S *IT*!
4

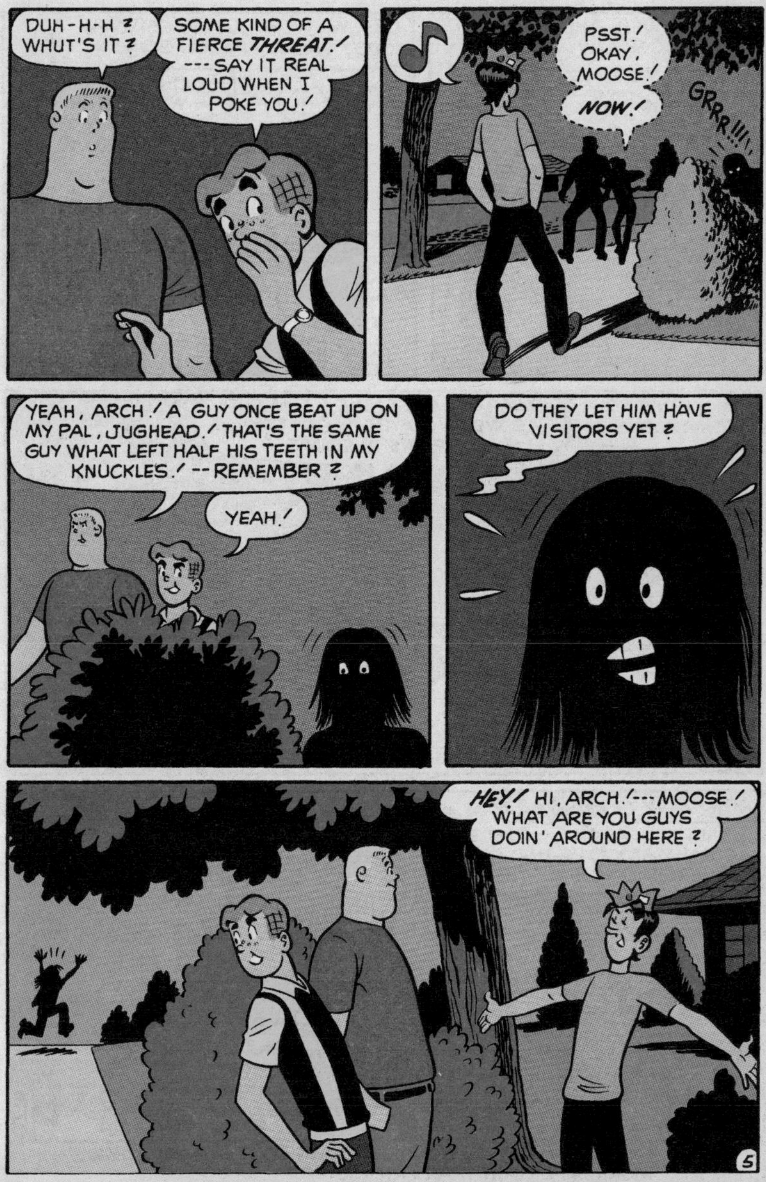
DUH-H-H? WHUT'S IT?
SOME KIND OF A FIERCE THREAT! --- SAY IT REAL LOUD WHEN I POKE YOU!
PSST! OKAY, MOOSE!
NOW!
GRRR!!!!
YEAH, ARCH! A GUY ONCE BEAT UP ON MY PAL, JUGHEAD! THAT'S THE SAME GUY WHAT LEFT HALF HIS TEETH IN MY KNUCKLES! --REMEMBER?
YEAH!
DO THEY LET HIM HAVE VISITORS YET?
HEY! HI, ARCH!---MOOSE! WHAT ARE YOU GUYS DOIN' AROUND HERE?
5

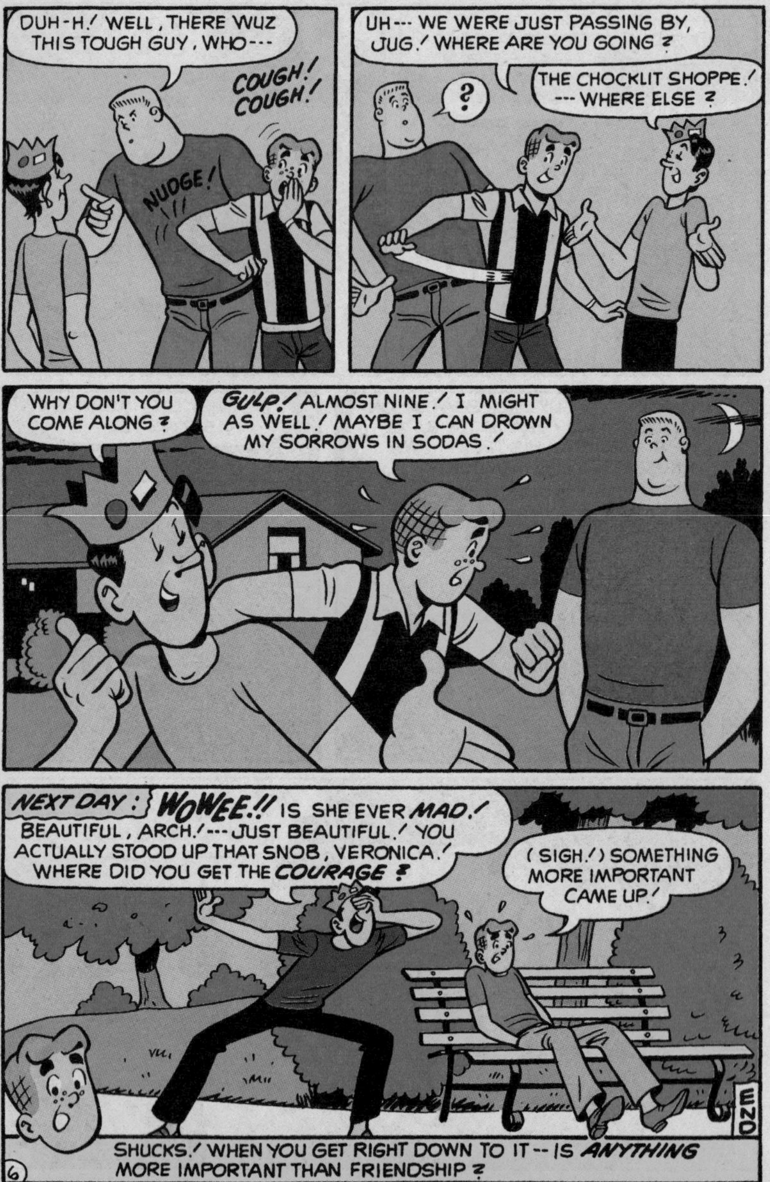
DUH-H.! WELL, THERE WUZ THIS TOUGH GUY, WHO---
COUGH! COUGH!
NUDGE!
UH--- WE WERE JUST PASSING BY, JUG.! WHERE ARE YOU GOING ?
?
THE CHOCKLIT SHOPPE.! --- WHERE ELSE ?
WHY DON'T YOU COME ALONG ?
GULP! ALMOST NINE.! I MIGHT AS WELL.! MAYBE I CAN DROWN MY SORROWS IN SODAS.!
NEXT DAY:
WOWEE.!! IS SHE EVER MAD.! BEAUTIFUL, ARCH.!--- JUST BEAUTIFUL.! YOU ACTUALLY STOOD UP THAT SNOB, VERONICA.! WHERE DID YOU GET THE COURAGE ?
(SIGH.!) SOMETHING MORE IMPORTANT CAME UP.!
END
SHUCKS.! WHEN YOU GET RIGHT DOWN TO IT -- IS ANYTHING MORE IMPORTANT THAN FRIENDSHIP ?

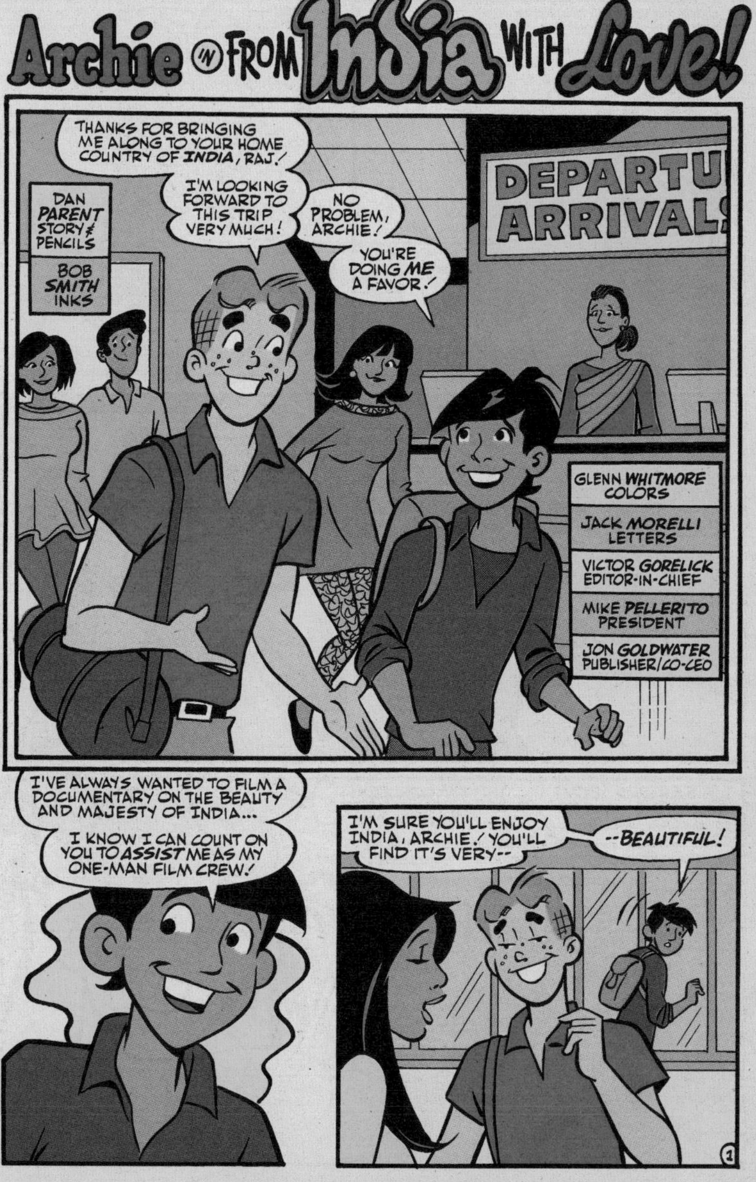

Archie in FROM India WITH Love!
THANKS FOR BRINGING ME ALONG TO YOUR HOME COUNTRY OF INDIA, RAJ!
I'M LOOKING FORWARD TO THIS TRIP VERY MUCH!
NO PROBLEM, ARCHIE!
YOU'RE DOING ME A FAVOR!
DAN PARENT STORY & PENCILS
BOB SMITH INKS
DEPARTU
ARRIVAL
GLENN WHITMORE COLORS
JACK MORELLI LETTERS
VICTOR GORELICK EDITOR-IN-CHIEF
MIKE PELLERITO PRESIDENT
JON GOLDWATER PUBLISHER/CO-CEO
I'VE ALWAYS WANTED TO FILM A DOCUMENTARY ON THE BEAUTY AND MAJESTY OF INDIA...
I KNOW I CAN COUNT ON YOU TO ASSIST ME AS MY ONE-MAN FILM CREW!
I'M SURE YOU'LL ENJOY INDIA, ARCHIE! YOU'LL FIND IT'S VERY--
--BEAUTIFUL!
1

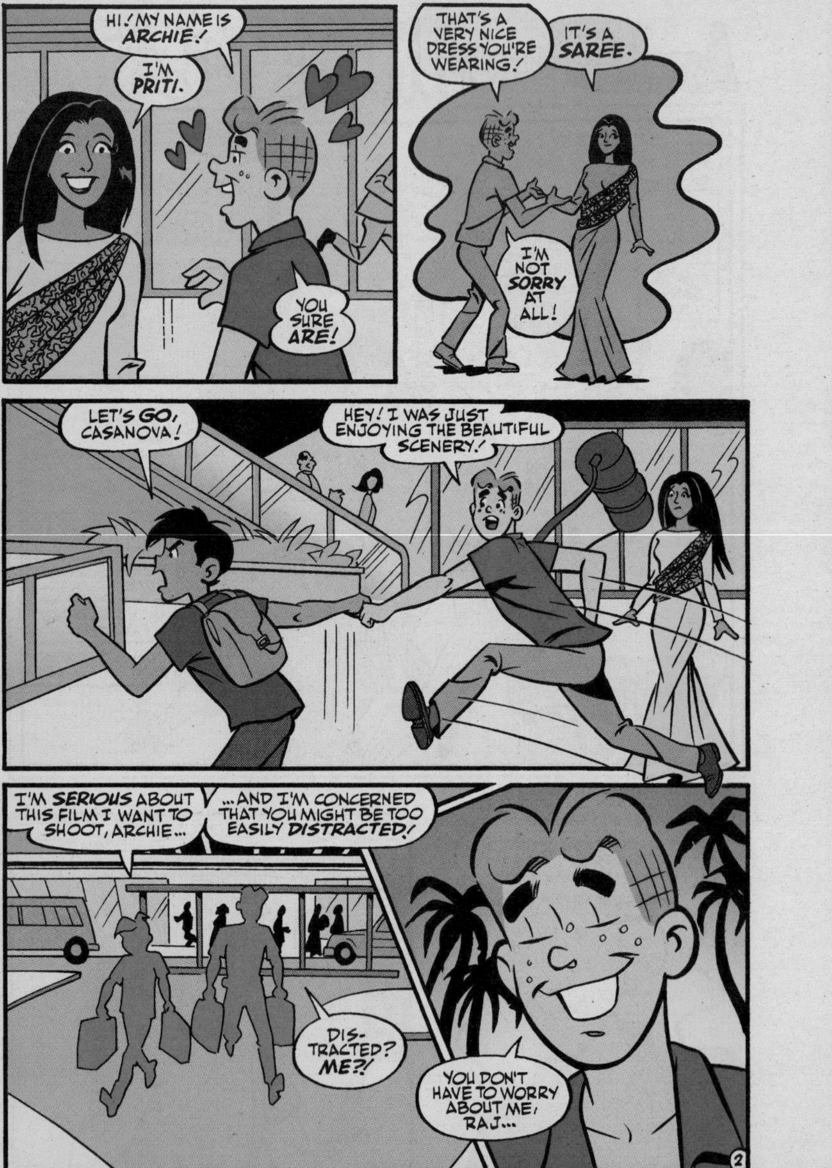
HI! MY NAME IS ARCHIE!
I'M PRITI.
YOU SURE ARE!
THAT'S A VERY NICE DRESS YOU'RE WEARING!
IT'S A SAREE.
I'M NOT SORRY AT ALL!
LET'S GO, CASANOVA!
HEY! I WAS JUST ENJOYING THE BEAUTIFUL SCENERY!
I'M SERIOUS ABOUT THIS FILM I WANT TO SHOOT, ARCHIE...
...AND I'M CONCERNED THAT YOU MIGHT BE TOO EASILY DISTRACTED!
DIS-TRACTED? ME?!
YOU DON'T HAVE TO WORRY ABOUT ME, RAJ...
2

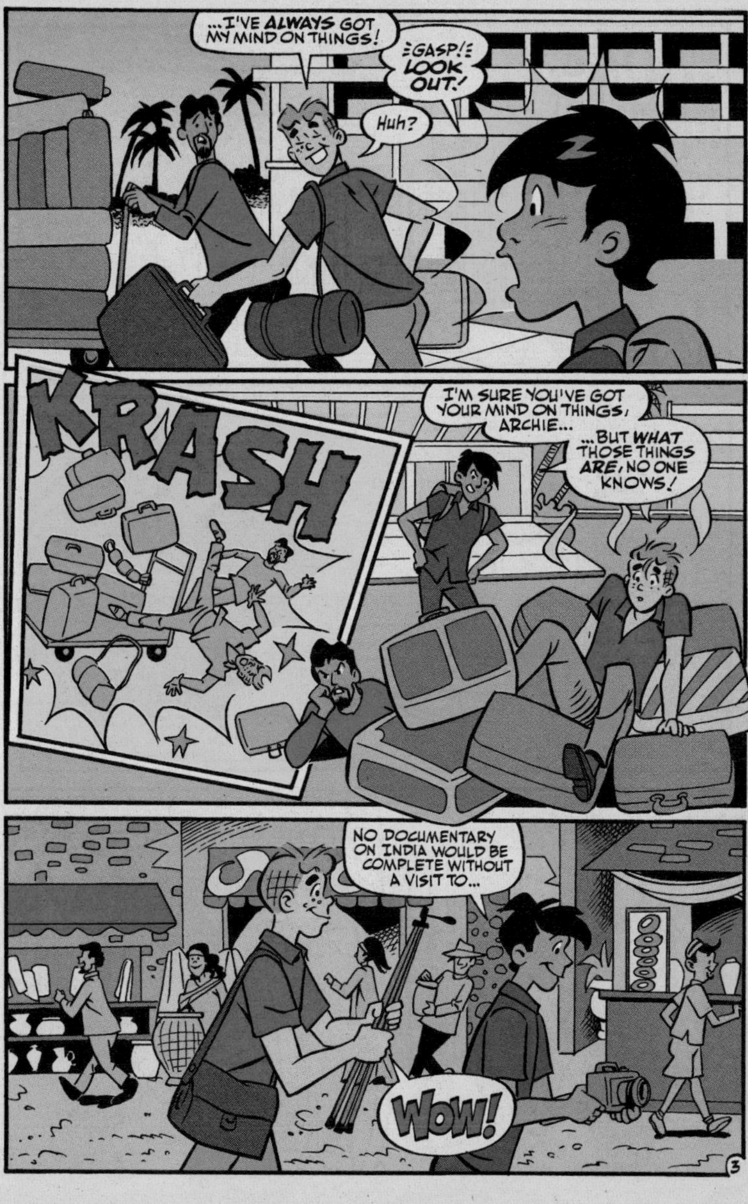

...I'VE ALWAYS GOT MY MIND ON THINGS!
GASP! LOOK OUT!
Huh?
KRASH
I'M SURE YOU'VE GOT YOUR MIND ON THINGS, ARCHIE...
...BUT WHAT THOSE THINGS ARE, NO ONE KNOWS!
NO DOCUMENTARY ON INDIA WOULD BE COMPLETE WITHOUT A VISIT TO...
WOW!

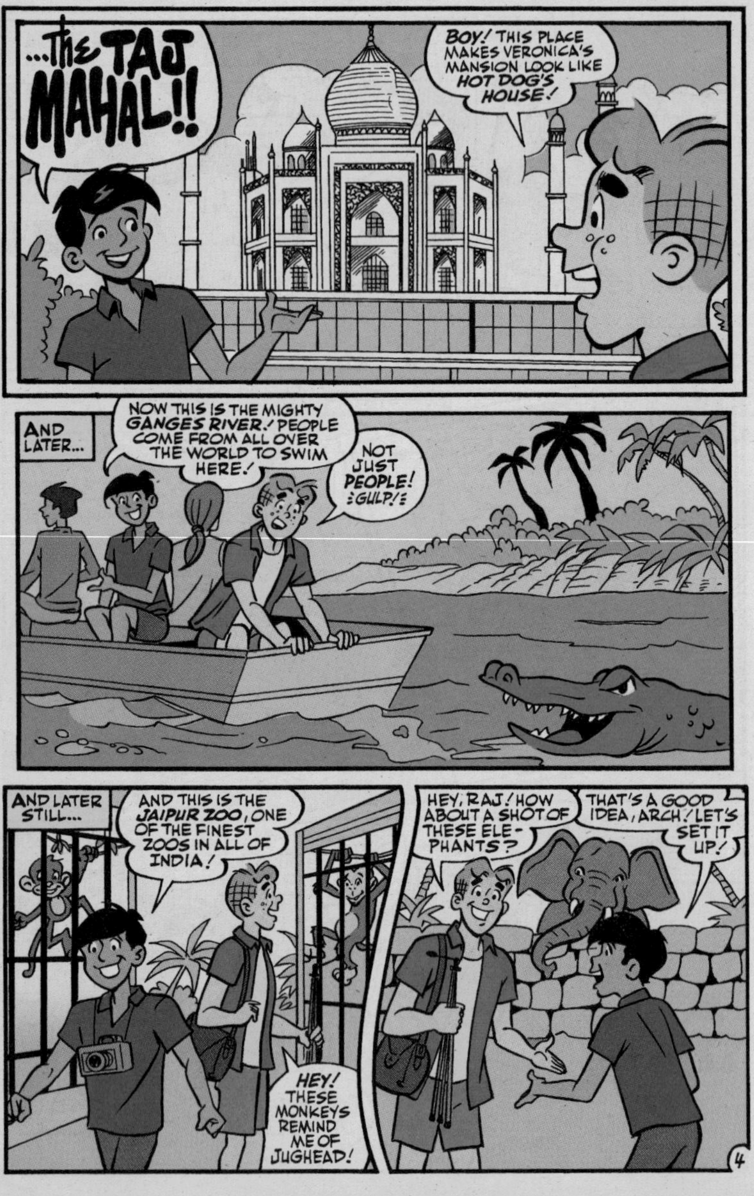
...THE TAJ MAHAL!!
BOY! THIS PLACE MAKES VERONICA'S MANSION LOOK LIKE HOT DOG'S HOUSE!
AND LATER...
NOW THIS IS THE MIGHTY GANGES RIVER! PEOPLE COME FROM ALL OVER THE WORLD TO SWIM HERE!
NOT JUST PEOPLE! GULP!
AND LATER STILL...
AND THIS IS THE JAIPUR ZOO, ONE OF THE FINEST ZOOS IN ALL OF INDIA!
HEY! THESE MONKEYS REMIND ME OF JUGHEAD!
HEY, RAJ! HOW ABOUT A SHOT OF THESE ELE-PHANTS?
THAT'S A GOOD IDEA, ARCH! LET'S SET IT UP!
4

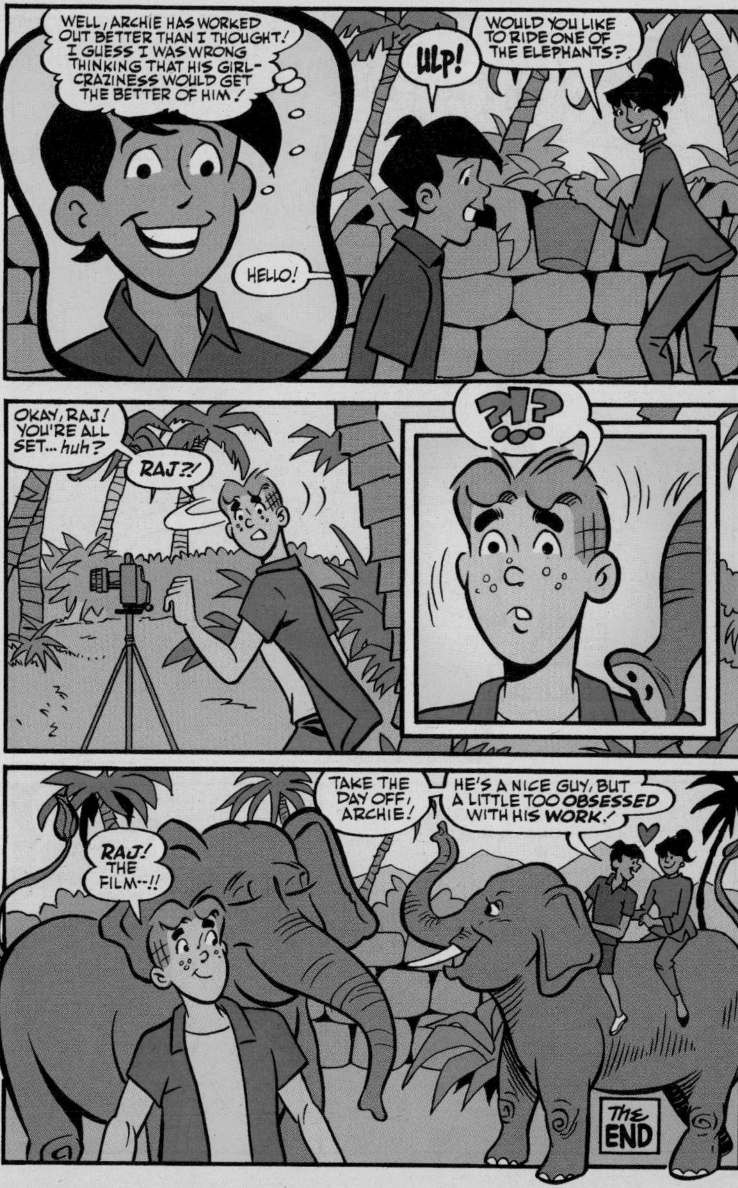
WELL, ARCHIE HAS WORKED OUT BETTER THAN I THOUGHT! I GUESS I WAS WRONG THINKING THAT HIS GIRL-CRAZINESS WOULD GET THE BETTER OF HIM!
HELLO!
ULP!
WOULD YOU LIKE TO RIDE ONE OF THE ELEPHANTS?
OKAY, RAJ! YOU'RE ALL SET... huh?
RAJ?!
?!?
RAJ! THE FILM--!!
TAKE THE DAY OFF, ARCHIE!
HE'S A NICE GUY, BUT A LITTLE TOO OBSESSED WITH HIS WORK!
THE END

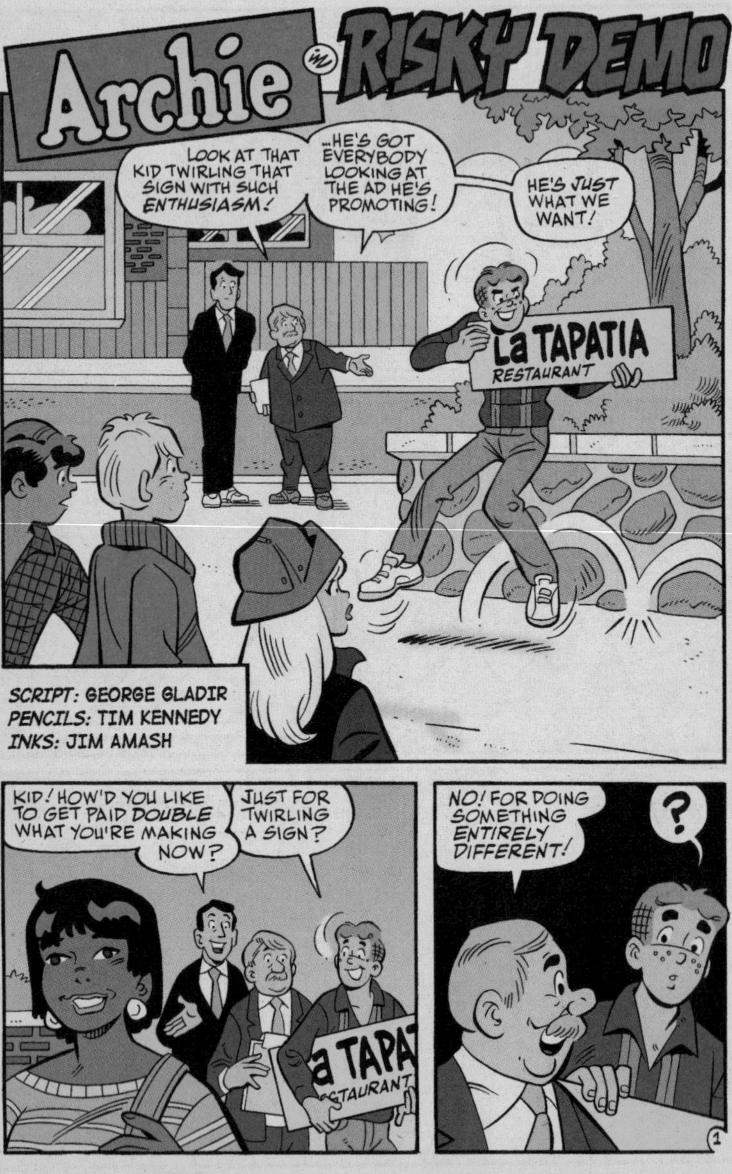
Archie in RISKY DEMO
LOOK AT THAT KID TWIRLING THAT SIGN WITH SUCH ENTHUSIASM!
..HE'S GOT EVERYBODY LOOKING AT THE AD HE'S PROMOTING!
HE'S JUST WHAT WE WANT!
La TAPATIA RESTAURANT
SCRIPT: GEORGE GLADIR
PENCILS: TIM KENNEDY
INKS: JIM AMASH
KID! HOW'D YOU LIKE TO GET PAID DOUBLE WHAT YOU'RE MAKING NOW?
JUST FOR TWIRLING A SIGN?
NO! FOR DOING SOMETHING ENTIRELY DIFFERENT!
?

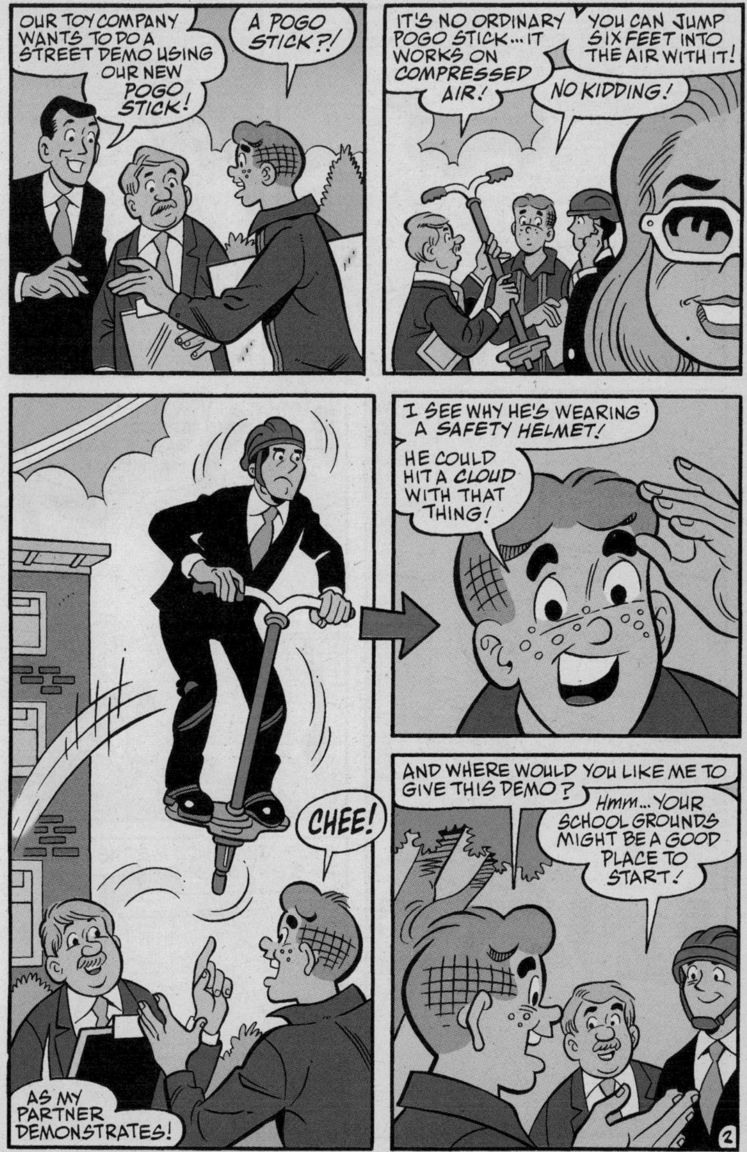

OUR TOY COMPANY WANTS TO DO A STREET DEMO USING OUR NEW POGO STICK!
A POGO STICK?!
IT'S NO ORDINARY POGO STICK... IT WORKS ON COMPRESSED AIR!
YOU CAN JUMP SIX FEET INTO THE AIR WITH IT!
NO KIDDING!
CHEE!
AS MY PARTNER DEMONSTRATES!
I SEE WHY HE'S WEARING A SAFETY HELMET!
HE COULD HIT A CLOUD WITH THAT THING!
AND WHERE WOULD YOU LIKE ME TO GIVE THIS DEMO?
Hmm... YOUR SCHOOL GROUNDS MIGHT BE A GOOD PLACE TO START!
2

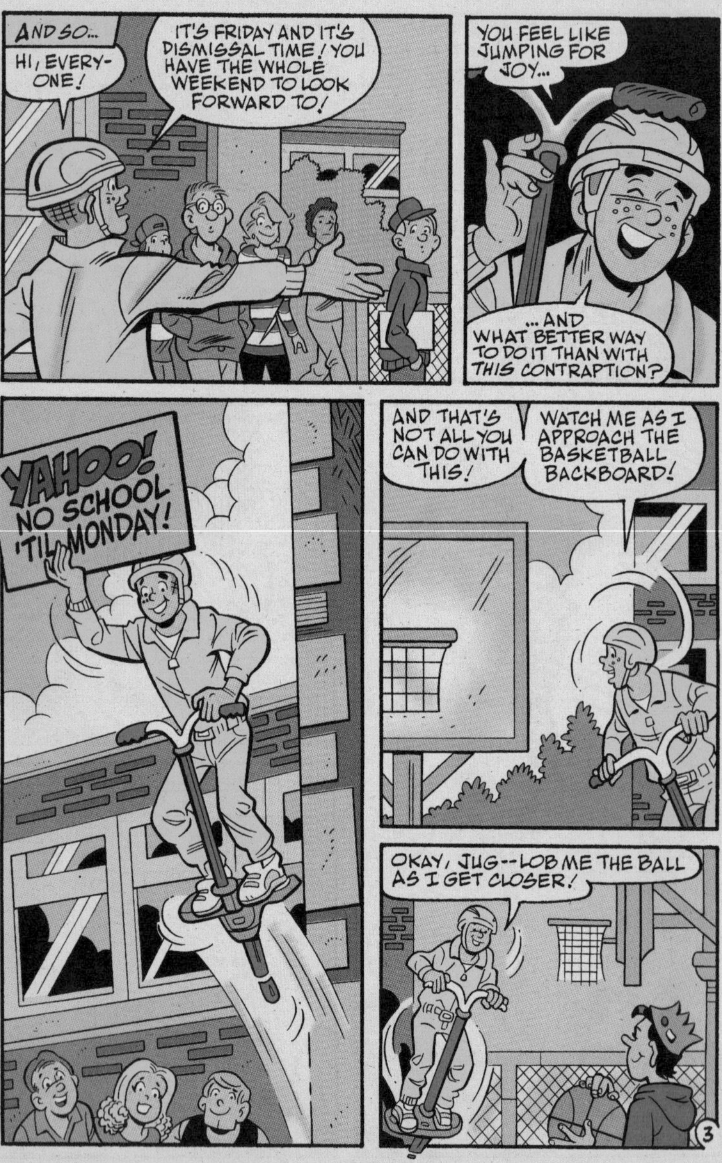
AND SO...
HI, EVERY-ONE!
IT'S FRIDAY AND IT'S DISMISSAL TIME! YOU HAVE THE WHOLE WEEKEND TO LOOK FORWARD TO!
YOU FEEL LIKE JUMPING FOR JOY...
...AND WHAT BETTER WAY TO DO IT THAN WITH THIS CONTRAPTION?
YAHOO! NO SCHOOL 'TIL MONDAY!
AND THAT'S NOT ALL YOU CAN DO WITH THIS!
WATCH ME AS I APPROACH THE BASKETBALL BACKBOARD!
OKAY, JUG--LOB ME THE BALL AS I GET CLOSER!
3

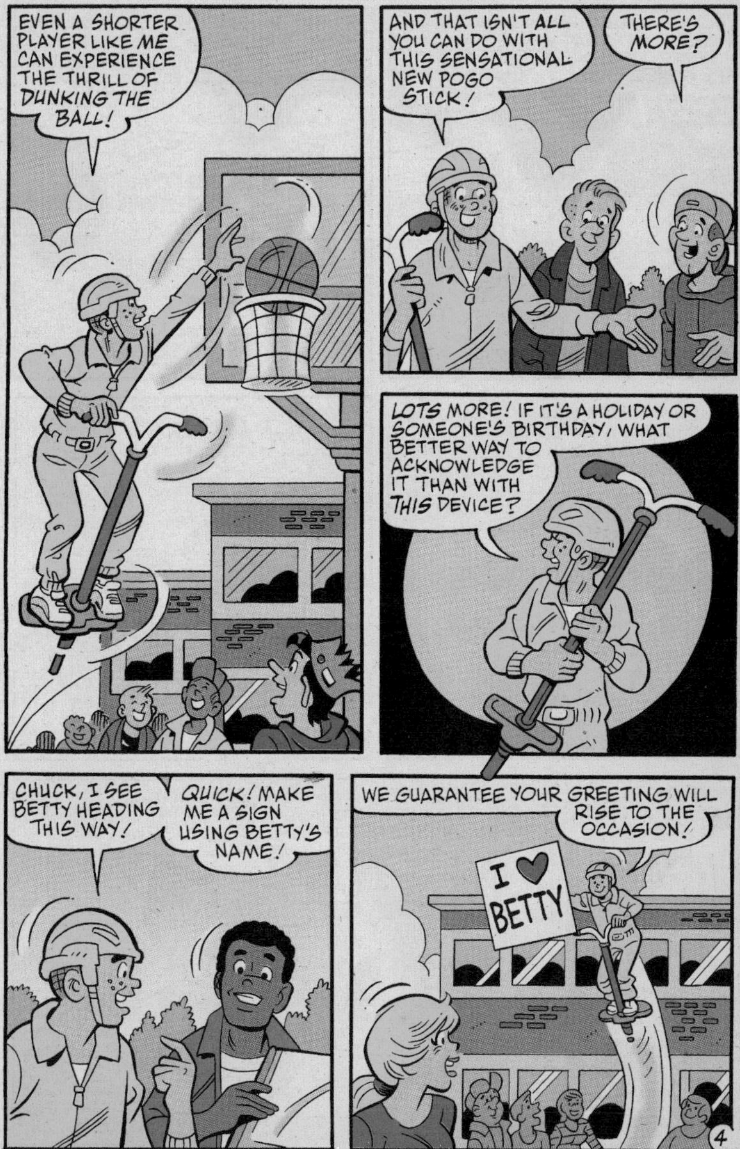
EVEN A SHORTER PLAYER LIKE ME CAN EXPERIENCE THE THRILL OF DUNKING THE BALL!
AND THAT ISN'T ALL YOU CAN DO WITH THIS SENSATIONAL NEW POGO STICK!
THERE'S MORE?
LOTS MORE! IF IT'S A HOLIDAY OR SOMEONE'S BIRTHDAY, WHAT BETTER WAY TO ACKNOWLEDGE IT THAN WITH THIS DEVICE?
CHUCK, I SEE BETTY HEADING THIS WAY!
QUICK! MAKE ME A SIGN USING BETTY'S NAME!
WE GUARANTEE YOUR GREETING WILL RISE TO THE OCCASION!
I ♥ BETTY
4

ARCHIE, I JUST HEARD ABOUT YOUR POGO STUNT THAT HONORED BETTY THE OTHER DAY!

YEAH! WASN'T THAT SOMETHING?

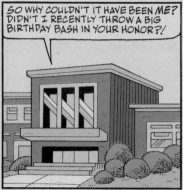

SO WHY COULDN'T IT HAVE BEEN *ME*? DIDN'T I RECENTLY THROW A BIG BIRTHDAY BASH IN YOUR HONOR?!

YOU CAN'T EVEN *BEGIN* TO IMAGINE HOW HUMILIATED I FEEL....TO BE IGNORED BY YOU IN FRONT OF THE ENTIRE STUDENT BODY!!

YES... B-BUT—

YES, BUT *NOTHING!*

KLONK

SIR, THERE'S AN ARCHIE ANDREWS TO SEE YOU!

Oh, THAT'S THE BOY WHO WE HIRED A FEW DAYS AGO TO DEMONSTRATE OUR NEW POGO STICK!

SEND HIM RIGHT IN, PLEASE!

TOTS UNLIMITED

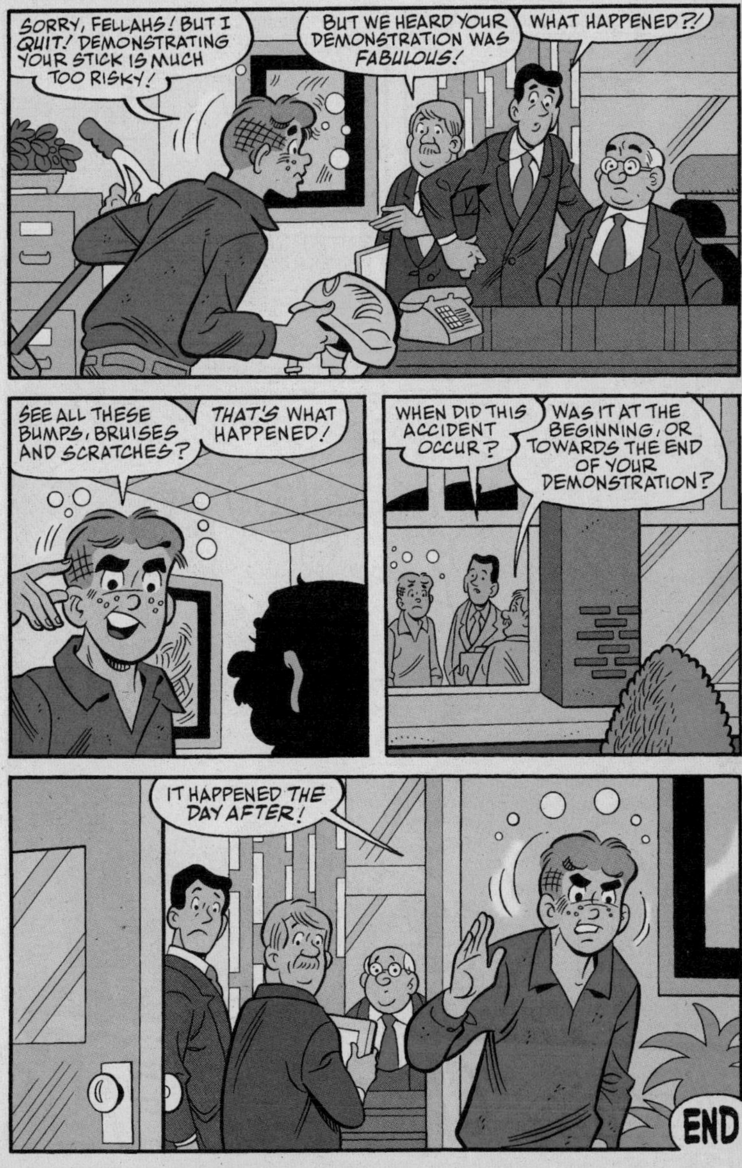

SORRY, FELLAHS! BUT I QUIT! DEMONSTRATING YOUR STICK IS MUCH TOO RISKY!
BUT WE HEARD YOUR DEMONSTRATION WAS FABULOUS!
WHAT HAPPENED?!
SEE ALL THESE BUMPS, BRUISES AND SCRATCHES?
THAT'S WHAT HAPPENED!
WHEN DID THIS ACCIDENT OCCUR?
WAS IT AT THE BEGINNING, OR TOWARDS THE END OF YOUR DEMONSTRATION?
IT HAPPENED THE DAY AFTER!
END

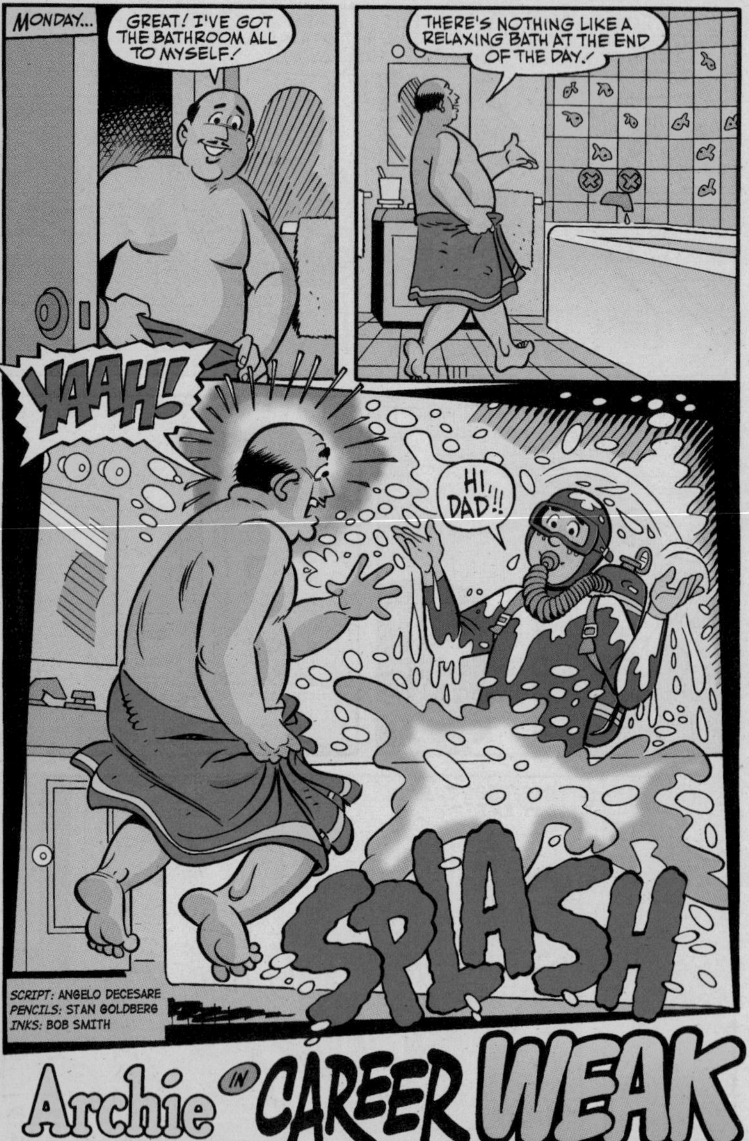
MONDAY...
GREAT! I'VE GOT THE BATHROOM ALL TO MYSELF!
THERE'S NOTHING LIKE A RELAXING BATH AT THE END OF THE DAY!
YAAH!
HI, DAD!!
SPLASH
SCRIPT: ANGELO DECESARE
PENCILS: STAN GOLDBERG
INKS: BOB SMITH
Archie IN CAREER WEAK

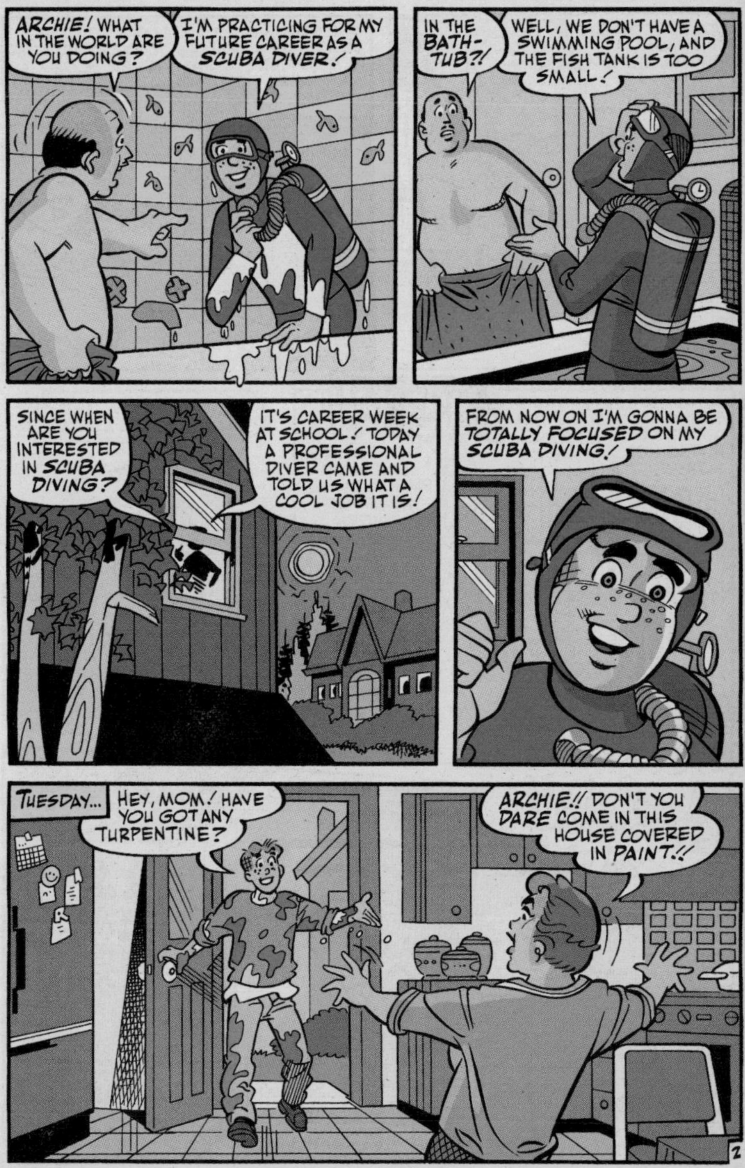
ARCHIE! WHAT IN THE WORLD ARE YOU DOING?
I'M PRACTICING FOR MY FUTURE CAREER AS A SCUBA DIVER!
IN THE BATH-TUB?!
WELL, WE DON'T HAVE A SWIMMING POOL, AND THE FISH TANK IS TOO SMALL!
SINCE WHEN ARE YOU INTERESTED IN SCUBA DIVING?
IT'S CAREER WEEK AT SCHOOL! TODAY A PROFESSIONAL DIVER CAME AND TOLD US WHAT A COOL JOB IT IS!
FROM NOW ON I'M GONNA BE TOTALLY FOCUSED ON MY SCUBA DIVING!
TUESDAY...
HEY, MOM! HAVE YOU GOT ANY TURPENTINE?
ARCHIE!! DON'T YOU DARE COME IN THIS HOUSE COVERED IN PAINT!!
2

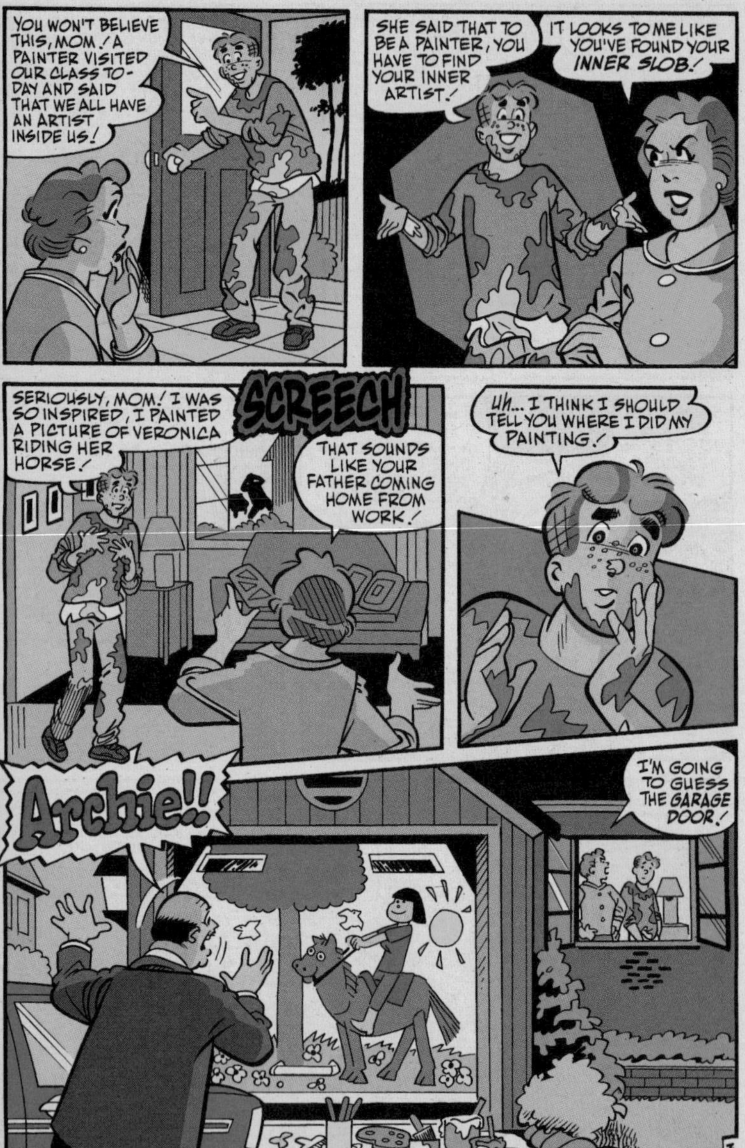
YOU WON'T BELIEVE THIS, MOM! A PAINTER VISITED OUR CLASS TO-DAY AND SAID THAT WE ALL HAVE AN ARTIST INSIDE US!
SHE SAID THAT TO BE A PAINTER, YOU HAVE TO FIND YOUR INNER ARTIST!
IT LOOKS TO ME LIKE YOU'VE FOUND YOUR INNER SLOB!
SERIOUSLY, MOM! I WAS SO INSPIRED, I PAINTED A PICTURE OF VERONICA RIDING HER HORSE!
SCREECH
THAT SOUNDS LIKE YOUR FATHER COMING HOME FROM WORK!
UH... I THINK I SHOULD TELL YOU WHERE I DID MY PAINTING!
ARCHIE!!
I'M GOING TO GUESS THE GARAGE DOOR!
3

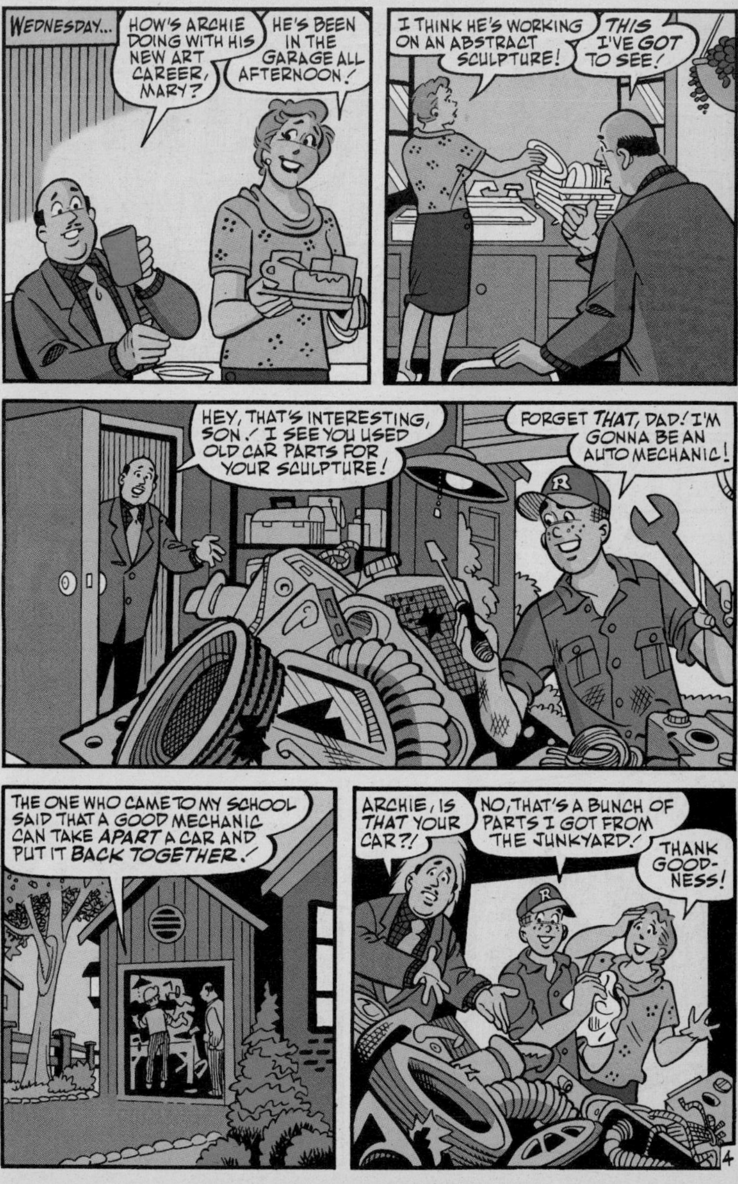
WEDNESDAY...
HOW'S ARCHIE DOING WITH HIS NEW ART CAREER, MARY?
HE'S BEEN IN THE GARAGE ALL AFTERNOON!
I THINK HE'S WORKING ON AN ABSTRACT SCULPTURE!
THIS I'VE GOT TO SEE!
HEY, THAT'S INTERESTING, SON! I SEE YOU USED OLD CAR PARTS FOR YOUR SCULPTURE!
FORGET THAT, DAD! I'M GONNA BE AN AUTO MECHANIC!
THE ONE WHO CAME TO MY SCHOOL SAID THAT A GOOD MECHANIC CAN TAKE APART A CAR AND PUT IT BACK TOGETHER!
ARCHIE, IS THAT YOUR CAR?!
NO, THAT'S A BUNCH OF PARTS I GOT FROM THE JUNKYARD!
THANK GOOD-NESS!
4

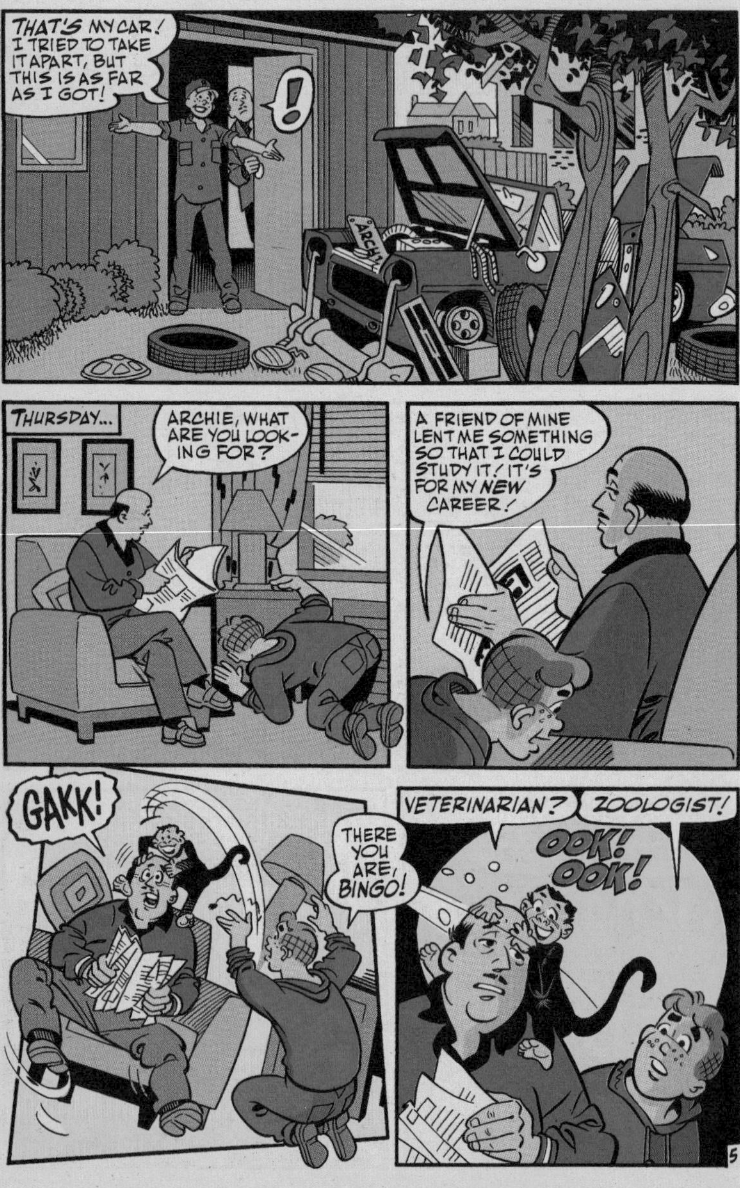
THAT'S MY CAR! I TRIED TO TAKE IT APART, BUT THIS IS AS FAR AS I GOT!
!
ARCHIE
THURSDAY...
ARCHIE, WHAT ARE YOU LOOKING FOR?
A FRIEND OF MINE LENT ME SOMETHING SO THAT I COULD STUDY IT! IT'S FOR MY NEW CAREER!
GAKK!
THERE YOU ARE, BINGO!
VETERINARIAN?
ZOOLOGIST!
OOK! OOK!

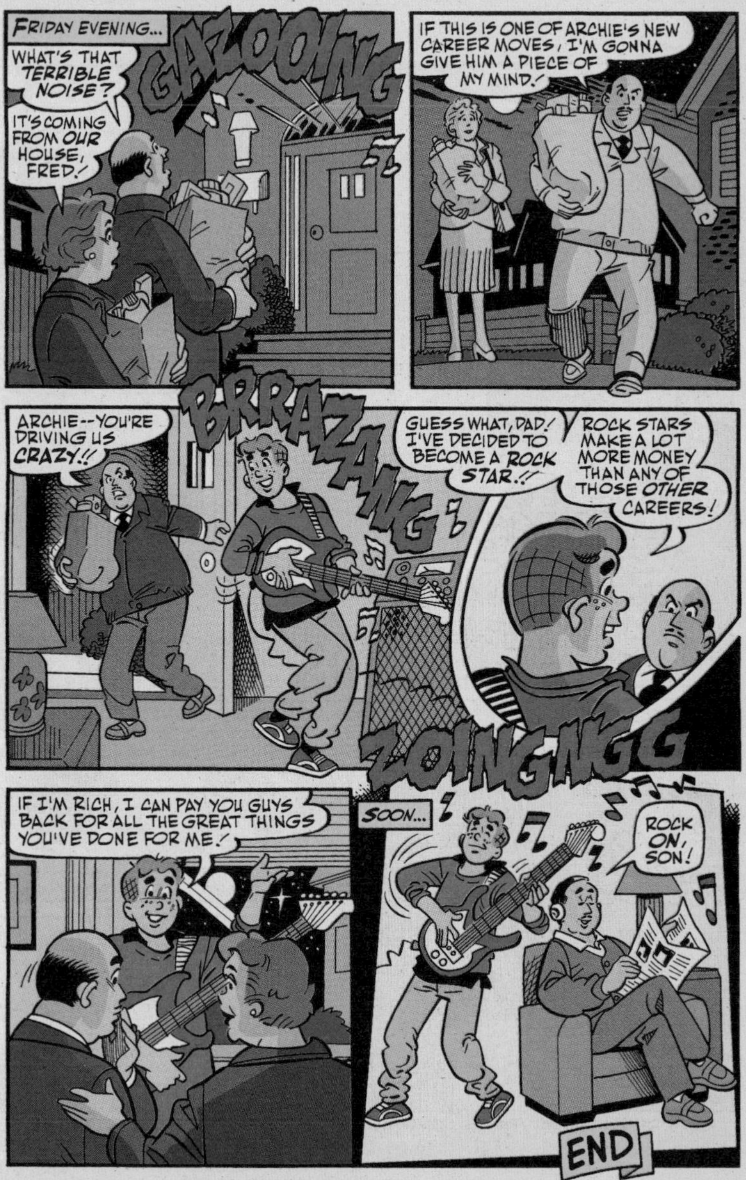

FRIDAY EVENING...
GAZOOING
WHAT'S THAT TERRIBLE NOISE?
IT'S COMING FROM OUR HOUSE, FRED!
IF THIS IS ONE OF ARCHIE'S NEW CAREER MOVES, I'M GONNA GIVE HIM A PIECE OF MY MIND!
BRRAZANG
ARCHIE--YOU'RE DRIVING US CRAZY!!
GUESS WHAT, DAD! I'VE DECIDED TO BECOME A ROCK STAR!!
ROCK STARS MAKE A LOT MORE MONEY THAN ANY OF THOSE OTHER CAREERS!
ZOINGNGG
IF I'M RICH, I CAN PAY YOU GUYS BACK FOR ALL THE GREAT THINGS YOU'VE DONE FOR ME!
SOON...
ROCK ON, SON!
END

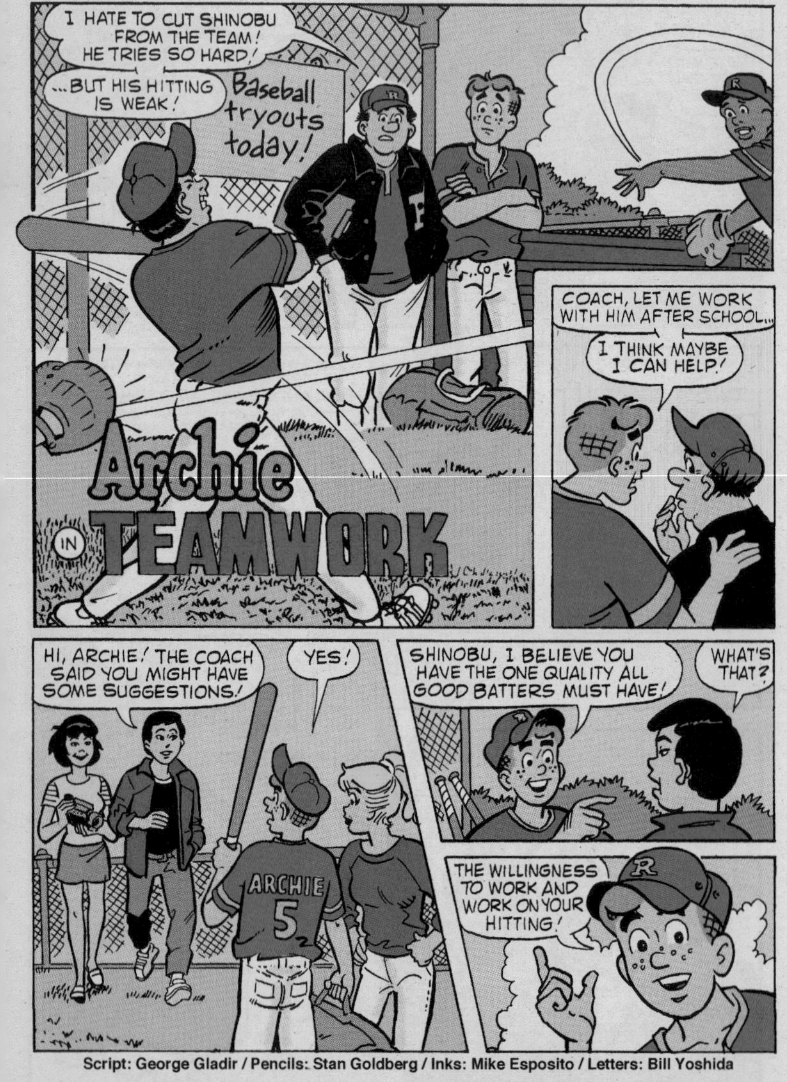
I HATE TO CUT SHINOBU FROM THE TEAM! HE TRIES SO HARD!
...BUT HIS HITTING IS WEAK!
Baseball tryouts today!
Archie
IN TEAMWORK
COACH, LET ME WORK WITH HIM AFTER SCHOOL...
I THINK MAYBE I CAN HELP!
HI, ARCHIE! THE COACH SAID YOU MIGHT HAVE SOME SUGGESTIONS!
YES!
ARCHIE 5
SHINOBU, I BELIEVE YOU HAVE THE ONE QUALITY ALL GOOD BATTERS MUST HAVE!
WHAT'S THAT?
THE WILLINGNESS TO WORK AND WORK ON YOUR HITTING!

Script: George Gladir / Pencils: Stan Goldberg / Inks: Mike Esposito / Letters: Bill Yoshida

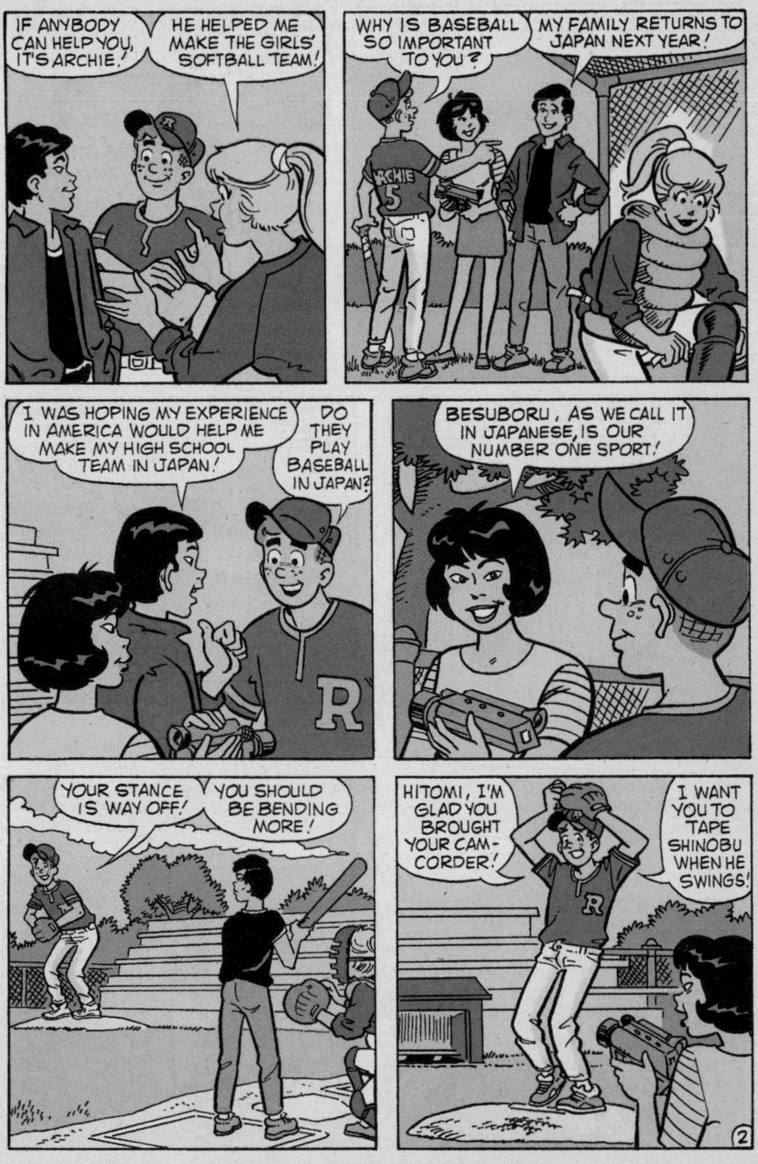
IF ANYBODY CAN HELP YOU, IT'S ARCHIE!
HE HELPED ME MAKE THE GIRLS' SOFTBALL TEAM!
WHY IS BASEBALL SO IMPORTANT TO YOU?
MY FAMILY RETURNS TO JAPAN NEXT YEAR!
ARCHIE
5
I WAS HOPING MY EXPERIENCE IN AMERICA WOULD HELP ME MAKE MY HIGH SCHOOL TEAM IN JAPAN!
DO THEY PLAY BASEBALL IN JAPAN?
BESUBORU, AS WE CALL IT IN JAPANESE, IS OUR NUMBER ONE SPORT!
YOUR STANCE IS WAY OFF!
YOU SHOULD BE BENDING MORE!
HITOMI, I'M GLAD YOU BROUGHT YOUR CAM-CORDER!
I WANT YOU TO TAPE SHINOBU WHEN HE SWINGS!
2

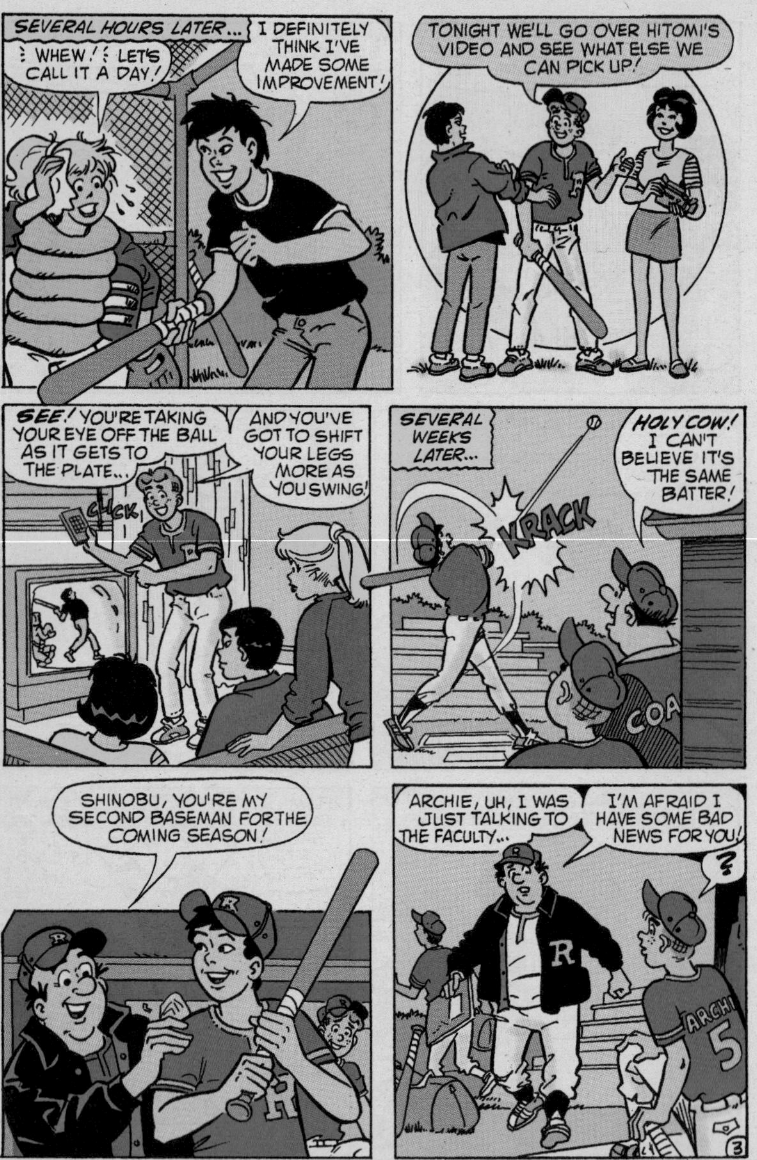
SEVERAL HOURS LATER...
WHEW! LET'S CALL IT A DAY!
I DEFINITELY THINK I'VE MADE SOME IMPROVEMENT!
TONIGHT WE'LL GO OVER HITOMI'S VIDEO AND SEE WHAT ELSE WE CAN PICK UP!
SEE! YOU'RE TAKING YOUR EYE OFF THE BALL AS IT GETS TO THE PLATE...
AND YOU'VE GOT TO SHIFT YOUR LEGS MORE AS YOU SWING!
CLICK
SEVERAL WEEKS LATER...
KRACK
HOLY COW! I CAN'T BELIEVE IT'S THE SAME BATTER!
COA
SHINOBU, YOU'RE MY SECOND BASEMAN FOR THE COMING SEASON!
ARCHIE, UH, I WAS JUST TALKING TO THE FACULTY...
I'M AFRAID I HAVE SOME BAD NEWS FOR YOU!
?
ARCHIE 5
3

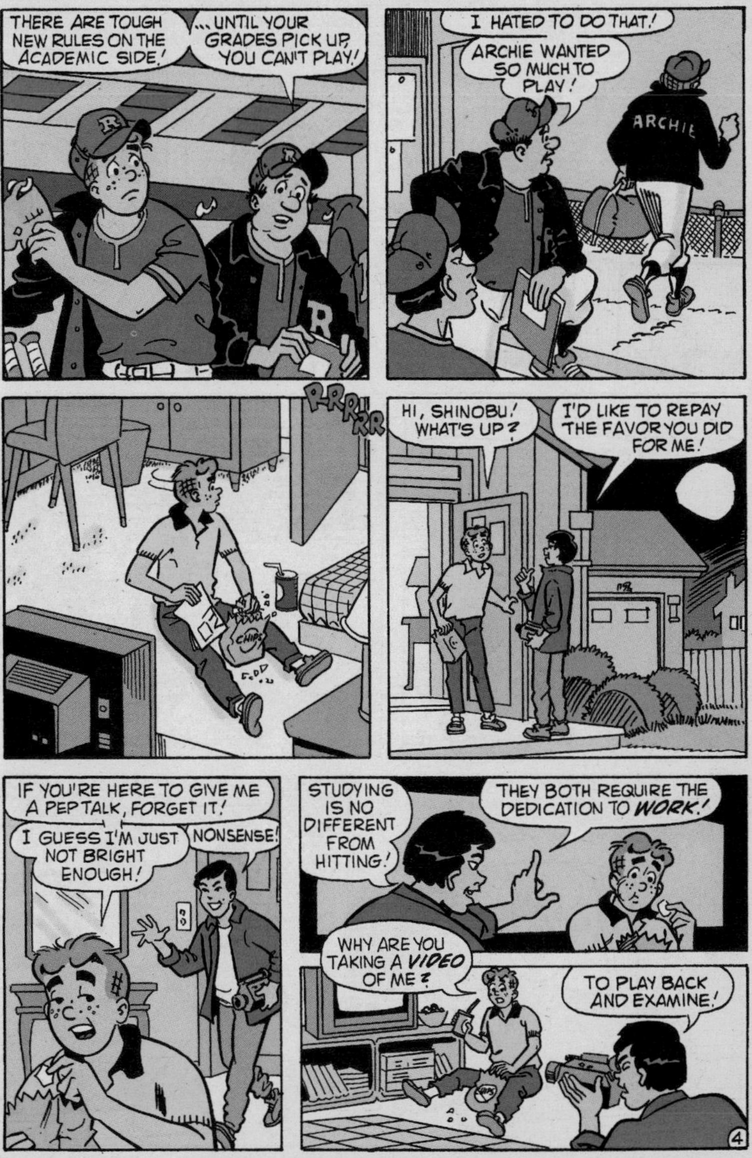
THERE ARE TOUGH NEW RULES ON THE ACADEMIC SIDE!
...UNTIL YOUR GRADES PICK UP, YOU CAN'T PLAY!
I HATED TO DO THAT!
ARCHIE WANTED SO MUCH TO PLAY!
ARCHIE
RRRRRR
HI, SHINOBU! WHAT'S UP?
I'D LIKE TO REPAY THE FAVOR YOU DID FOR ME!
IF YOU'RE HERE TO GIVE ME A PEP TALK, FORGET IT!
I GUESS I'M JUST NOT BRIGHT ENOUGH!
NONSENSE!
STUDYING IS NO DIFFERENT FROM HITTING!
THEY BOTH REQUIRE THE DEDICATION TO WORK!
WHY ARE YOU TAKING A VIDEO OF ME?
TO PLAY BACK AND EXAMINE!
4

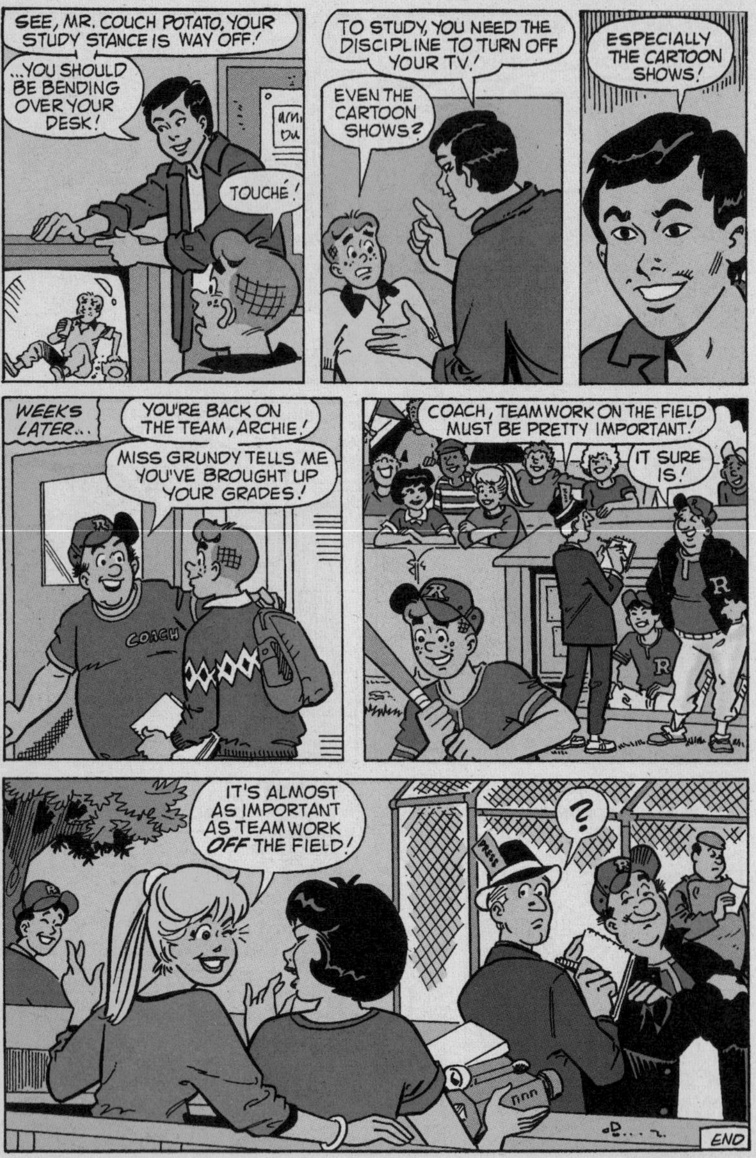

SEE, MR. COUCH POTATO, YOUR STUDY STANCE IS WAY OFF!
...YOU SHOULD BE BENDING OVER YOUR DESK!
TOUCHÉ!
TO STUDY, YOU NEED THE DISCIPLINE TO TURN OFF YOUR TV!
EVEN THE CARTOON SHOWS?
ESPECIALLY THE CARTOON SHOWS!
WEEKS LATER...
YOU'RE BACK ON THE TEAM, ARCHIE!
MISS GRUNDY TELLS ME YOU'VE BROUGHT UP YOUR GRADES!
COACH
COACH, TEAMWORK ON THE FIELD MUST BE PRETTY IMPORTANT!
IT SURE IS!
IT'S ALMOST AS IMPORTANT AS TEAMWORK OFF THE FIELD!
?
PRESS
END

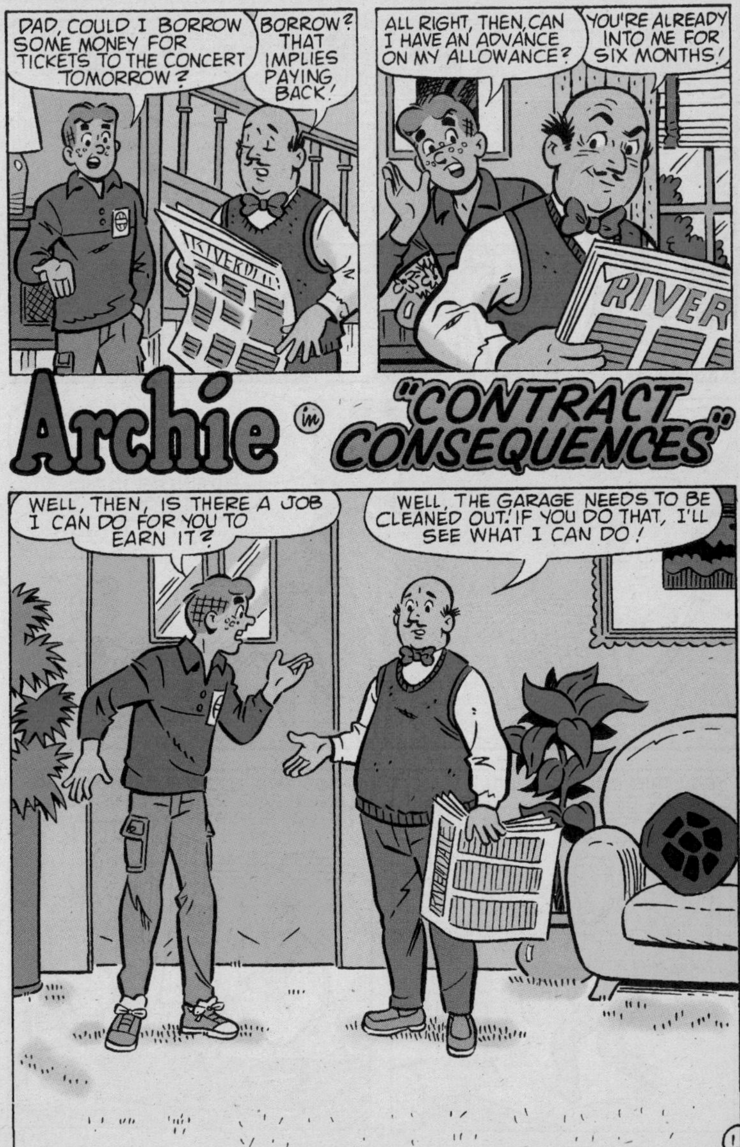
DAD, COULD I BORROW SOME MONEY FOR TICKETS TO THE CONCERT TOMORROW?
BORROW? THAT IMPLIES PAYING BACK!
ALL RIGHT, THEN, CAN I HAVE AN ADVANCE ON MY ALLOWANCE?
YOU'RE ALREADY INTO ME FOR SIX MONTHS!
Archie in "CONTRACT CONSEQUENCES"
WELL, THEN, IS THERE A JOB I CAN DO FOR YOU TO EARN IT?
WELL, THE GARAGE NEEDS TO BE CLEANED OUT! IF YOU DO THAT, I'LL SEE WHAT I CAN DO!
1

Script: Hal Smith / Pencils: Chic Stone / Inks: Rudy Lapick / Letters: Bill Yoshida / Colors: Barry Grossman

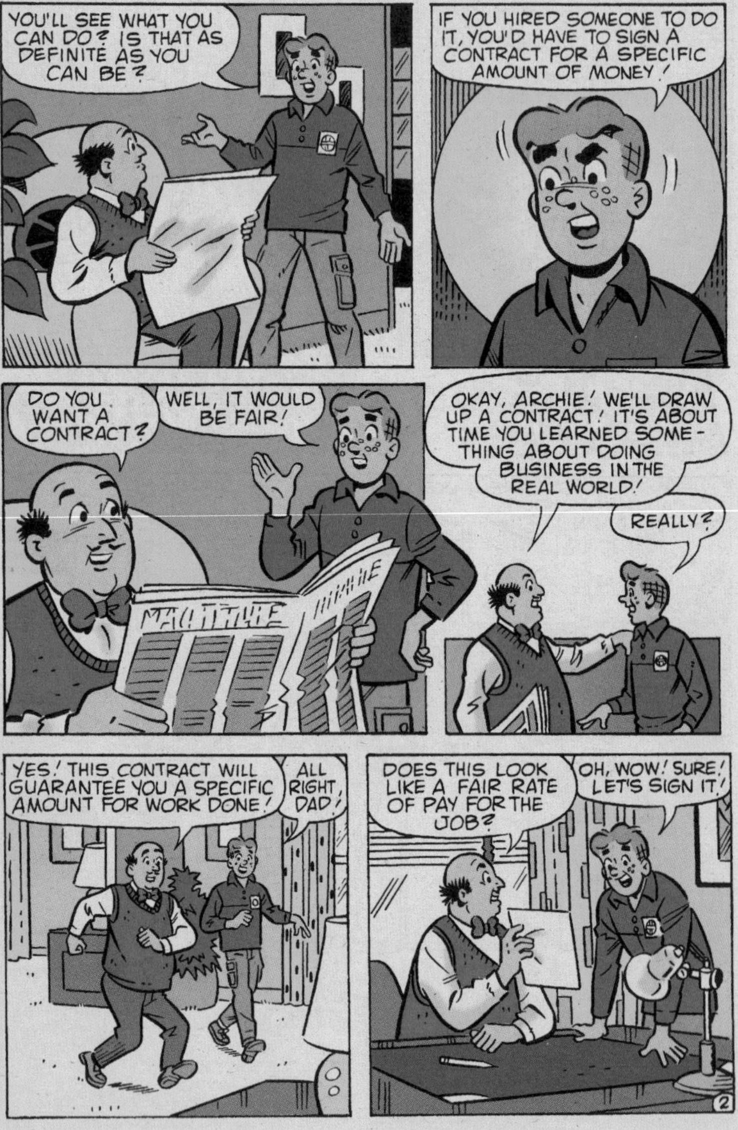
YOU'LL SEE WHAT YOU CAN DO? IS THAT AS DEFINITE AS YOU CAN BE?
IF YOU HIRED SOMEONE TO DO IT, YOU'D HAVE TO SIGN A CONTRACT FOR A SPECIFIC AMOUNT OF MONEY!
DO YOU WANT A CONTRACT?
WELL, IT WOULD BE FAIR!
OKAY, ARCHIE! WE'LL DRAW UP A CONTRACT! IT'S ABOUT TIME YOU LEARNED SOME-THING ABOUT DOING BUSINESS IN THE REAL WORLD!
REALLY?
YES! THIS CONTRACT WILL GUARANTEE YOU A SPECIFIC AMOUNT FOR WORK DONE!
ALL RIGHT, DAD!
DOES THIS LOOK LIKE A FAIR RATE OF PAY FOR THE JOB?
OH, WOW! SURE! LET'S SIGN IT!
2

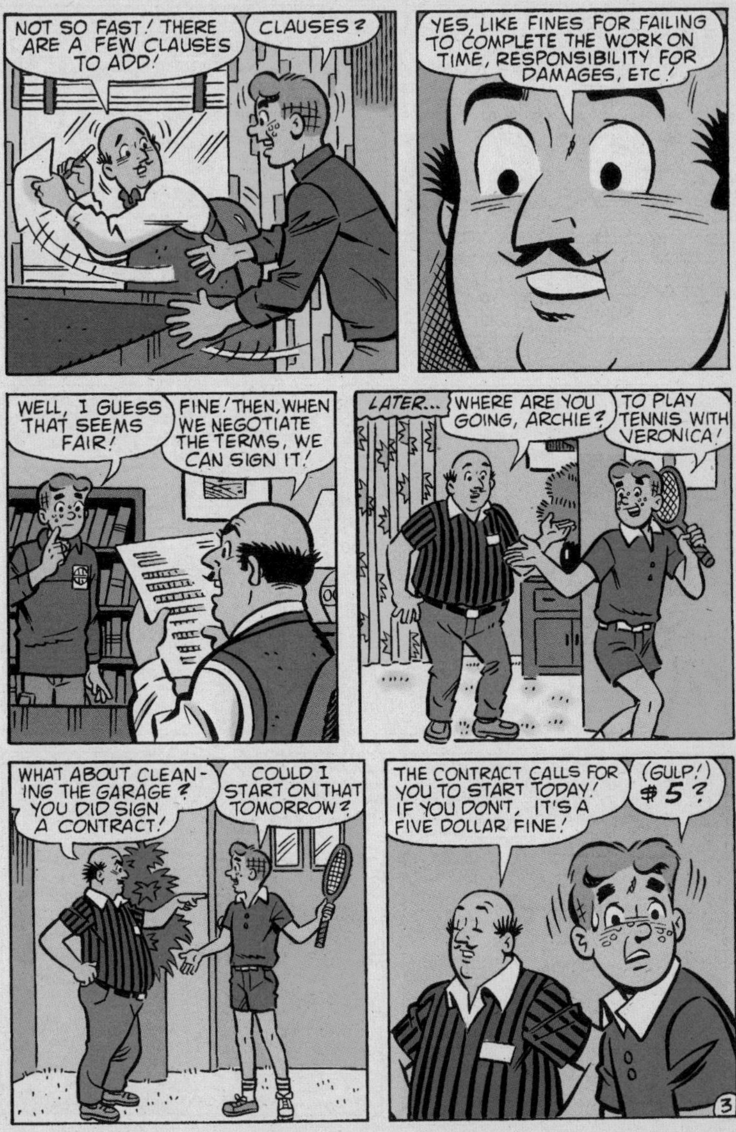
NOT SO FAST! THERE ARE A FEW CLAUSES TO ADD!
CLAUSES?
YES, LIKE FINES FOR FAILING TO COMPLETE THE WORK ON TIME, RESPONSIBILITY FOR DAMAGES, ETC!
WELL, I GUESS THAT SEEMS FAIR!
FINE! THEN, WHEN WE NEGOTIATE THE TERMS, WE CAN SIGN IT!
LATER...
WHERE ARE YOU GOING, ARCHIE?
TO PLAY TENNIS WITH VERONICA!
WHAT ABOUT CLEANING THE GARAGE? YOU DID SIGN A CONTRACT!
COULD I START ON THAT TOMORROW?
THE CONTRACT CALLS FOR YOU TO START TODAY! IF YOU DON'T, IT'S A FIVE DOLLAR FINE!
(GULP!) $5?
3

VERONICA: THAT WAS A GREAT GAME, ARCHIE! WANT TO PLAY AGAIN TOMORROW?

ARCHIE: I CAN'T! IT'S COSTING ME $5 A DAY!

THE NEXT DAY...

MR. ANDREWS: HOW'S IT GOING, ARCHIE?

ARCHIE: GREAT, DAD! JUG'S BEEN HELPING ME!

MR. ANDREWS: YOU'RE SUBCONTRACTING? I DIDN'T AGREE TO PAY FOR THAT!

MR. ANDREWS: YOU'LL HAVE TO PAY HIM OUT OF YOUR WAGES!

JUGHEAD: PAY?! DID SOMEONE SAY PAY?

PAY?

ARCHIE: ER...LOOK, JUG, I THINK I CAN HANDLE THE REST OF THIS JOB BY MYSELF! THANKS FOR YOUR HELP! I'LL PAY YOU WHEN I GET PAID!

JUGHEAD: OKAY, BOSS!

LATER—

CRASH!

PAINT

4

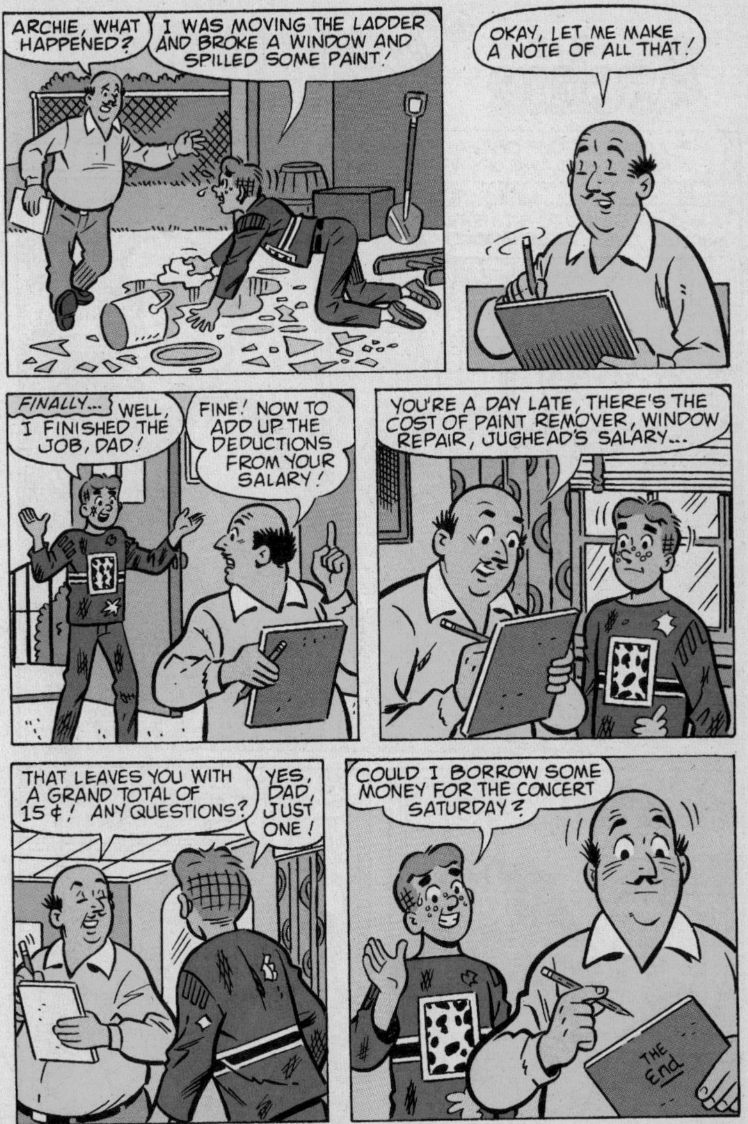
ARCHIE, WHAT HAPPENED?
I WAS MOVING THE LADDER AND BROKE A WINDOW AND SPILLED SOME PAINT!
OKAY, LET ME MAKE A NOTE OF ALL THAT!
FINALLY...
WELL, I FINISHED THE JOB, DAD!
FINE! NOW TO ADD UP THE DEDUCTIONS FROM YOUR SALARY!
YOU'RE A DAY LATE, THERE'S THE COST OF PAINT REMOVER, WINDOW REPAIR, JUGHEAD'S SALARY...
THAT LEAVES YOU WITH A GRAND TOTAL OF 15¢! ANY QUESTIONS?
YES, DAD, JUST ONE!
COULD I BORROW SOME MONEY FOR THE CONCERT SATURDAY?
THE End

Archie in The WILD ONES

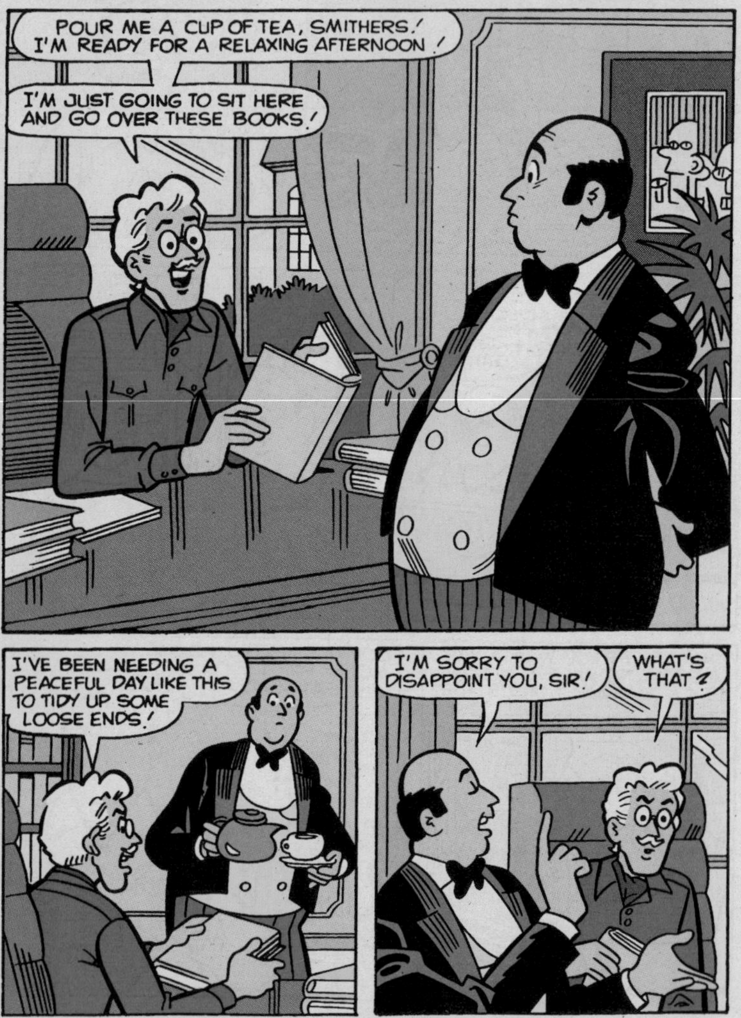

POUR ME A CUP OF TEA, SMITHERS! I'M READY FOR A RELAXING AFTERNOON!
I'M JUST GOING TO SIT HERE AND GO OVER THESE BOOKS!
I'VE BEEN NEEDING A PEACEFUL DAY LIKE THIS TO TIDY UP SOME LOOSE ENDS!
I'M SORRY TO DISAPPOINT YOU, SIR!
WHAT'S THAT?

Script: Frank Doyle / Art: Stan Goldberg / Letters: Bill Yoshida

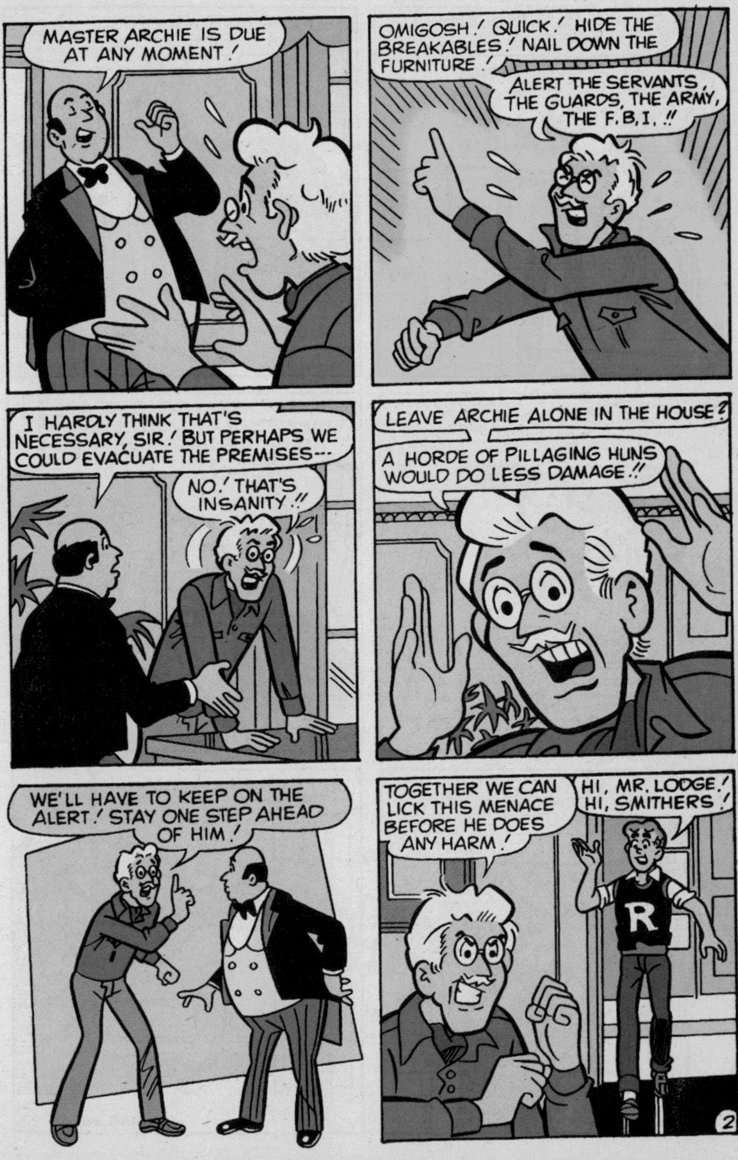
MASTER ARCHIE IS DUE AT ANY MOMENT!
OMIGOSH! QUICK! HIDE THE BREAKABLES! NAIL DOWN THE FURNITURE!
ALERT THE SERVANTS, THE GUARDS, THE ARMY, THE F.B.I.!!
I HARDLY THINK THAT'S NECESSARY, SIR! BUT PERHAPS WE COULD EVACUATE THE PREMISES---
NO! THAT'S INSANITY!!
LEAVE ARCHIE ALONE IN THE HOUSE?
A HORDE OF PILLAGING HUNS WOULD DO LESS DAMAGE!!
WE'LL HAVE TO KEEP ON THE ALERT! STAY ONE STEP AHEAD OF HIM!
TOGETHER WE CAN LICK THIS MENACE BEFORE HE DOES ANY HARM!
HI, MR. LODGE! HI, SMITHERS!
R
2

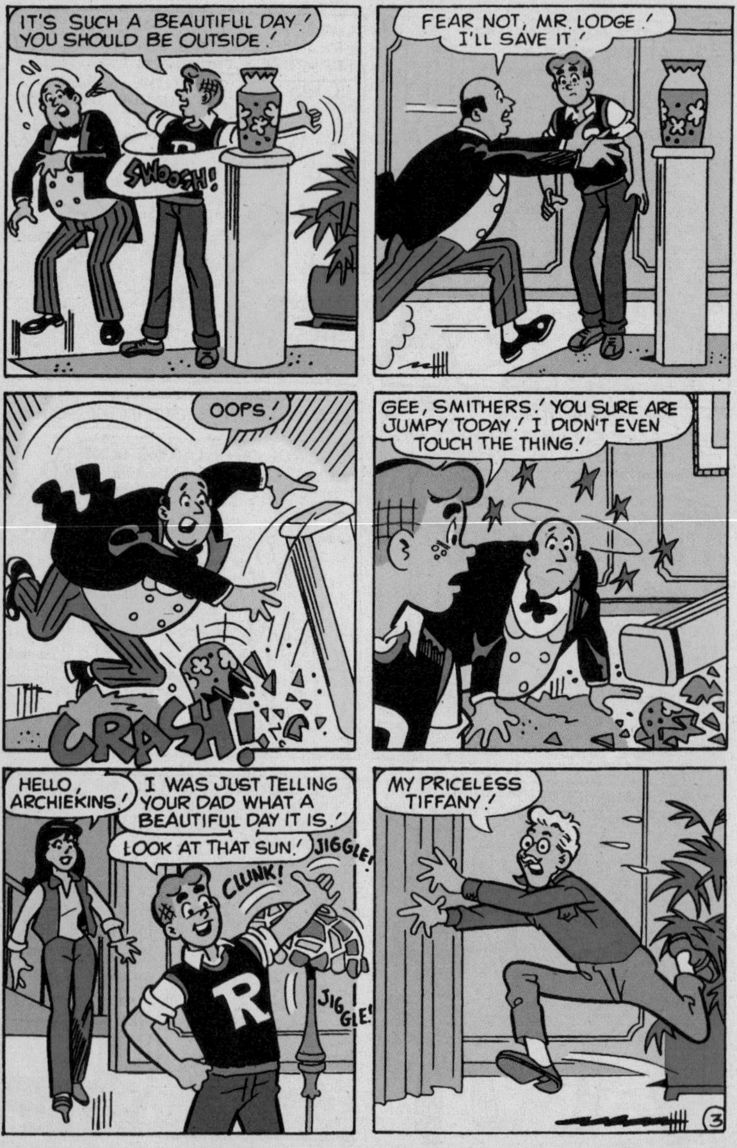
IT'S SUCH A BEAUTIFUL DAY! YOU SHOULD BE OUTSIDE!
SWOOSH!
FEAR NOT, MR. LODGE! I'LL SAVE IT!
OOPS!
CRASH!
GEE, SMITHERS! YOU SURE ARE JUMPY TODAY! I DIDN'T EVEN TOUCH THE THING!
HELLO, ARCHIEKINS!
I WAS JUST TELLING YOUR DAD WHAT A BEAUTIFUL DAY IT IS!
LOOK AT THAT SUN!
JIGGLE!
CLUNK!
JIGGLE!
MY PRICELESS TIFFANY!
3

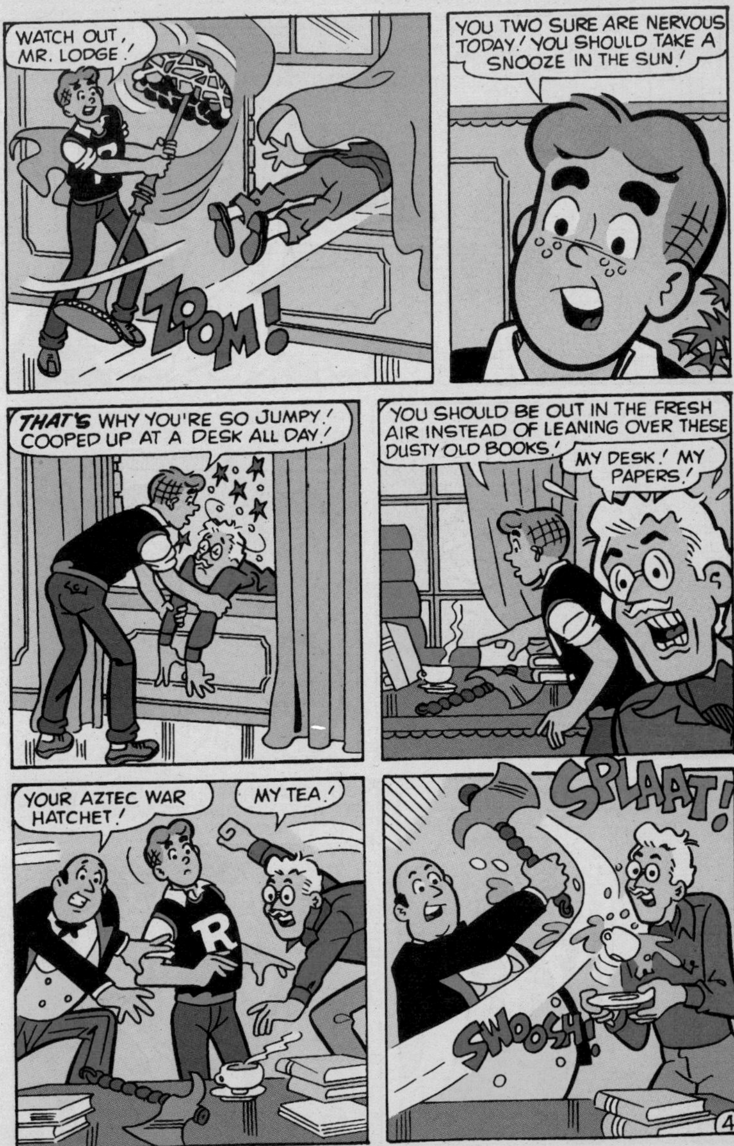
WATCH OUT, MR. LODGE!
ZOOM!
YOU TWO SURE ARE NERVOUS TODAY! YOU SHOULD TAKE A SNOOZE IN THE SUN!
THAT'S WHY YOU'RE SO JUMPY! COOPED UP AT A DESK ALL DAY!
YOU SHOULD BE OUT IN THE FRESH AIR INSTEAD OF LEANING OVER THESE DUSTY OLD BOOKS!
MY DESK! MY PAPERS!
YOUR AZTEC WAR HATCHET!
MY TEA!
R
SPLAAT!
SWOOSH!
4

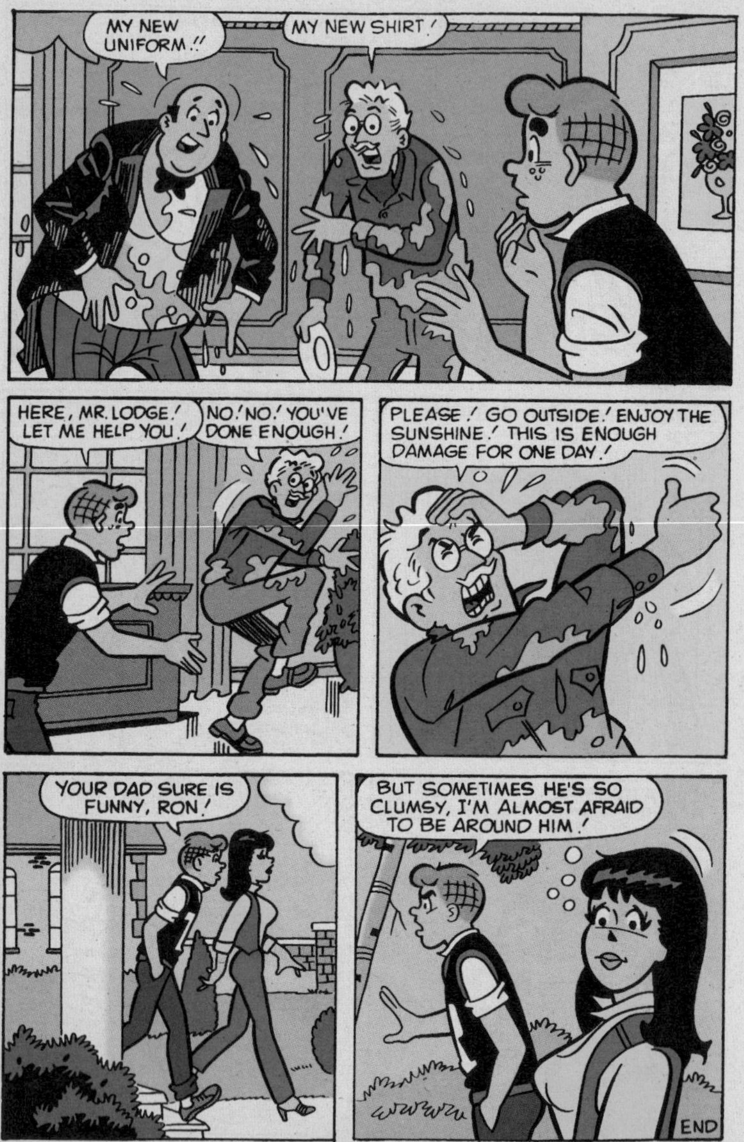
MY NEW UNIFORM.!!
MY NEW SHIRT!
HERE, MR. LODGE! LET ME HELP YOU!
NO! NO! YOU'VE DONE ENOUGH!
PLEASE! GO OUTSIDE! ENJOY THE SUNSHINE! THIS IS ENOUGH DAMAGE FOR ONE DAY!
YOUR DAD SURE IS FUNNY, RON!
BUT SOMETIMES HE'S SO CLUMSY, I'M ALMOST AFRAID TO BE AROUND HIM!
END

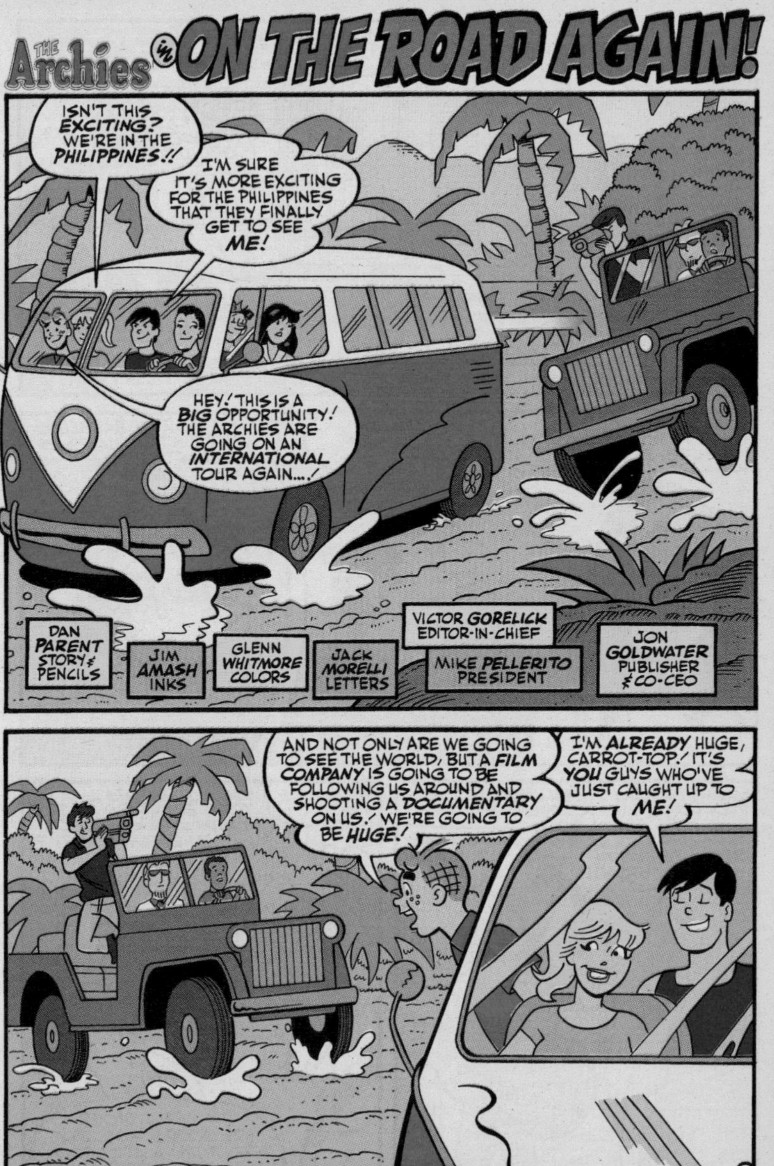

THE Archies in ON THE ROAD AGAIN!
ISN'T THIS EXCITING? WE'RE IN THE PHILIPPINES!!
I'M SURE IT'S MORE EXCITING FOR THE PHILIPPINES THAT THEY FINALLY GET TO SEE ME!
HEY! THIS IS A BIG OPPORTUNITY! THE ARCHIES ARE GOING ON AN INTERNATIONAL TOUR AGAIN....!
DAN PARENT STORY & PENCILS
JIM AMASH INKS
GLENN WHITMORE COLORS
JACK MORELLI LETTERS
VICTOR GORELICK EDITOR-IN-CHIEF
MIKE PELLERITO PRESIDENT
JON GOLDWATER PUBLISHER & CO-CEO
AND NOT ONLY ARE WE GOING TO SEE THE WORLD, BUT A FILM COMPANY IS GOING TO BE FOLLOWING US AROUND AND SHOOTING A DOCUMENTARY ON US! WE'RE GOING TO BE HUGE!
I'M ALREADY HUGE, CARROT-TOP! IT'S YOU GUYS WHO'VE JUST CAUGHT UP TO ME!
1

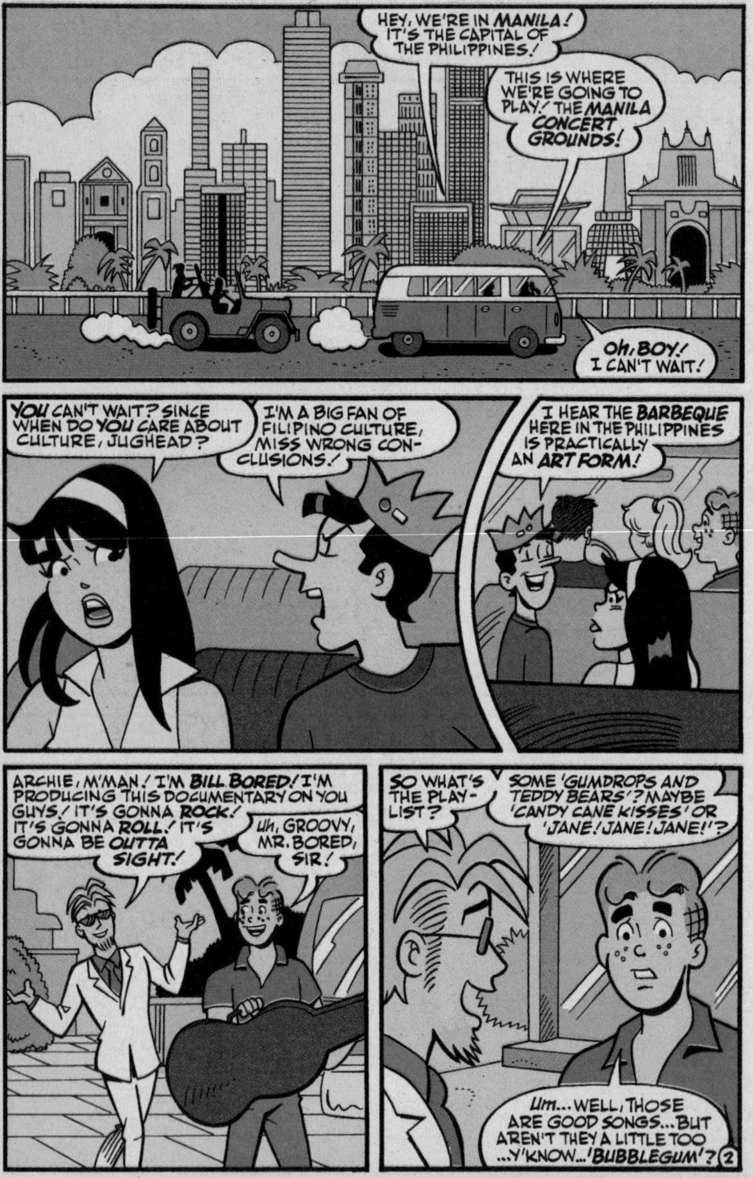
HEY, WE'RE IN MANILA! IT'S THE CAPITAL OF THE PHILIPPINES!
THIS IS WHERE WE'RE GOING TO PLAY! THE MANILA CONCERT GROUNDS!
OH, BOY! I CAN'T WAIT!
YOU CAN'T WAIT? SINCE WHEN DO YOU CARE ABOUT CULTURE, JUGHEAD?
I'M A BIG FAN OF FILIPINO CULTURE, MISS WRONG CONCLUSIONS!
I HEAR THE BARBEQUE HERE IN THE PHILIPPINES IS PRACTICALLY AN ART FORM!
ARCHIE, M'MAN! I'M BILL BORED! I'M PRODUCING THIS DOCUMENTARY ON YOU GUYS! IT'S GONNA ROCK! IT'S GONNA ROLL! IT'S GONNA BE OUTTA SIGHT!
UH, GROOVY, MR. BORED, SIR!
SO WHAT'S THE PLAY-LIST?
SOME 'GUMDROPS AND TEDDY BEARS'? MAYBE 'CANDY CANE KISSES' OR 'JANE! JANE! JANE!'?
UM... WELL, THOSE ARE GOOD SONGS... BUT AREN'T THEY A LITTLE TOO ...Y'KNOW...'BUBBLEGUM'?
2

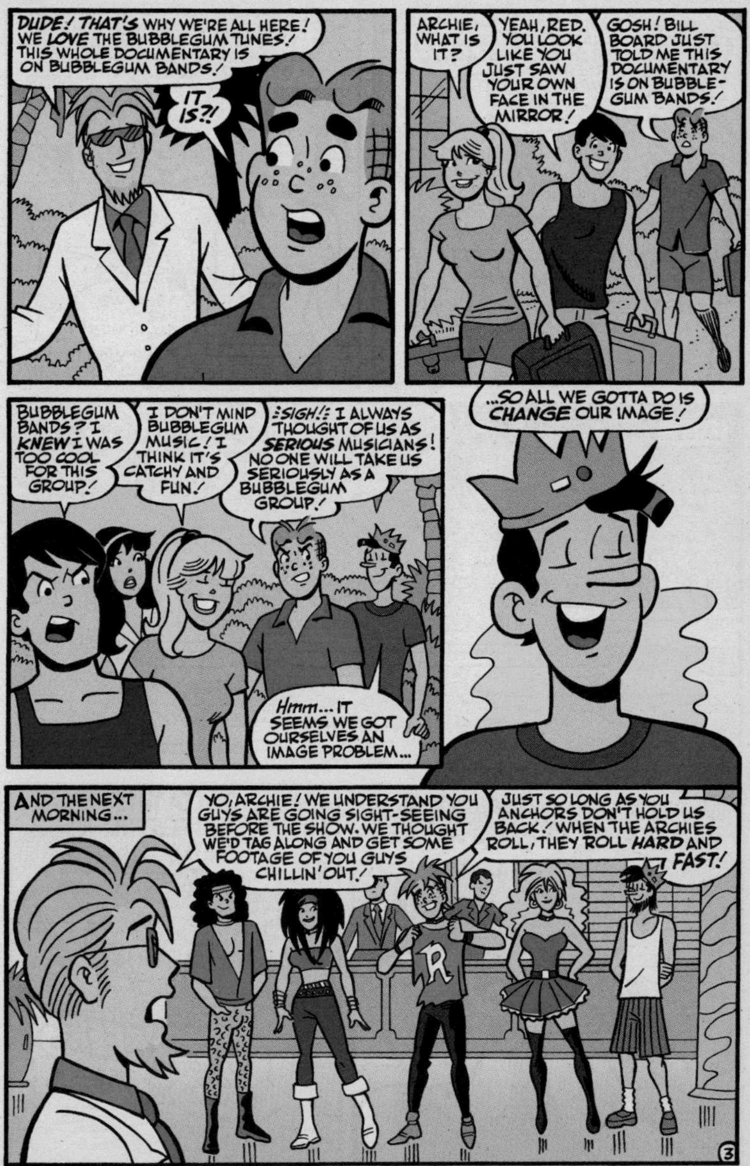
DUDE! THAT'S WHY WE'RE ALL HERE! WE LOVE THE BUBBLEGUM TUNES! THIS WHOLE DOCUMENTARY IS ON BUBBLEGUM BANDS!
IT IS?!
ARCHIE, WHAT IS IT?
YEAH, RED. YOU LOOK LIKE YOU JUST SAW YOUR OWN FACE IN THE MIRROR!
GOSH! BILL BOARD JUST TOLD ME THIS DOCUMENTARY IS ON BUBBLE-GUM BANDS!
BUBBLEGUM BANDS? I KNEW I WAS TOO COOL FOR THIS GROUP!
I DON'T MIND BUBBLEGUM MUSIC! I THINK IT'S CATCHY AND FUN!
SIGH! I ALWAYS THOUGHT OF US AS SERIOUS MUSICIANS! NO ONE WILL TAKE US SERIOUSLY AS A BUBBLEGUM GROUP!
Hmm... IT SEEMS WE GOT OURSELVES AN IMAGE PROBLEM...
...SO ALL WE GOTTA DO IS CHANGE OUR IMAGE!
AND THE NEXT MORNING...
YO, ARCHIE! WE UNDERSTAND YOU GUYS ARE GOING SIGHT-SEEING BEFORE THE SHOW. WE THOUGHT WE'D TAG ALONG AND GET SOME FOOTAGE OF YOU GUYS CHILLIN' OUT!
JUST SO LONG AS YOU ANCHORS DON'T HOLD US BACK! WHEN THE ARCHIES ROLL, THEY ROLL HARD AND FAST!
R

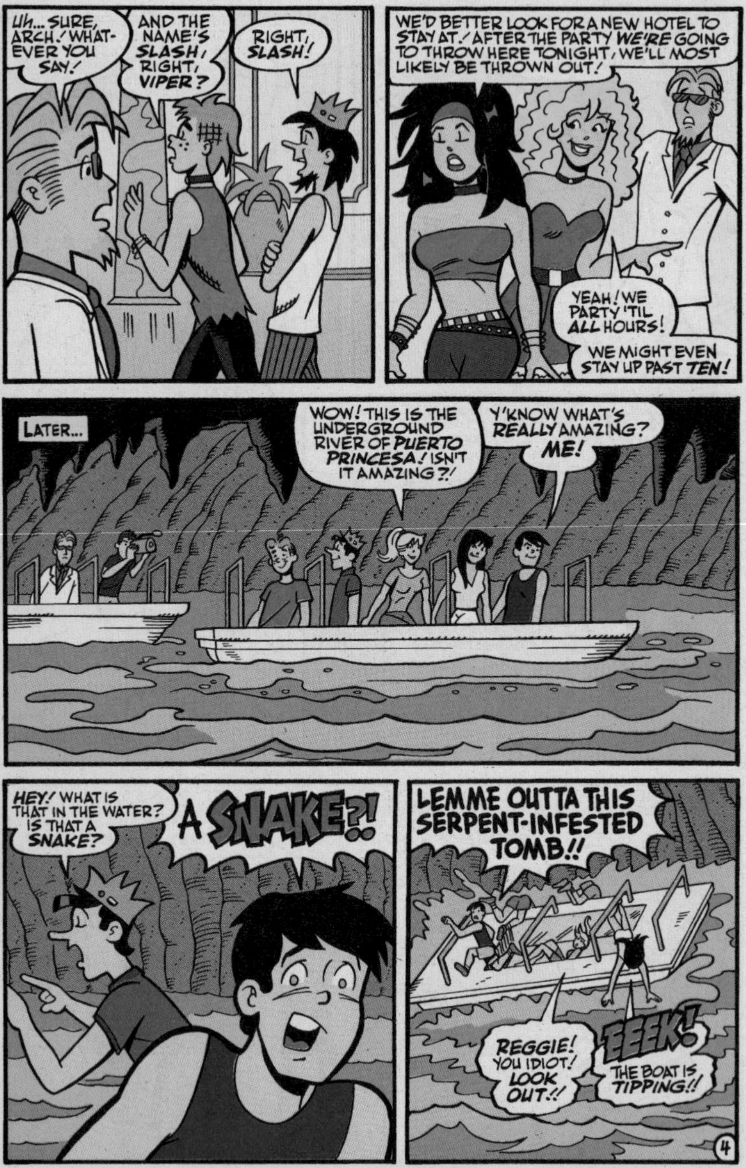

UH... SURE, ARCH! WHATEVER YOU SAY!
AND THE NAME'S SLASH, RIGHT, VIPER?
RIGHT, SLASH!
WE'D BETTER LOOK FOR A NEW HOTEL TO STAY AT! AFTER THE PARTY WE'RE GOING TO THROW HERE TONIGHT, WE'LL MOST LIKELY BE THROWN OUT!
YEAH! WE PARTY 'TIL ALL HOURS!
WE MIGHT EVEN STAY UP PAST TEN!
LATER...
WOW! THIS IS THE UNDERGROUND RIVER OF PUERTO PRINCESA! ISN'T IT AMAZING?!
Y'KNOW WHAT'S REALLY AMAZING? ME!
HEY! WHAT IS THAT IN THE WATER? IS THAT A SNAKE?
A SNAKE?!
LEMME OUTTA THIS SERPENT-INFESTED TOMB!!
REGGIE! YOU IDIOT! LOOK OUT!!
EEEK!
THE BOAT IS TIPPING!!
4

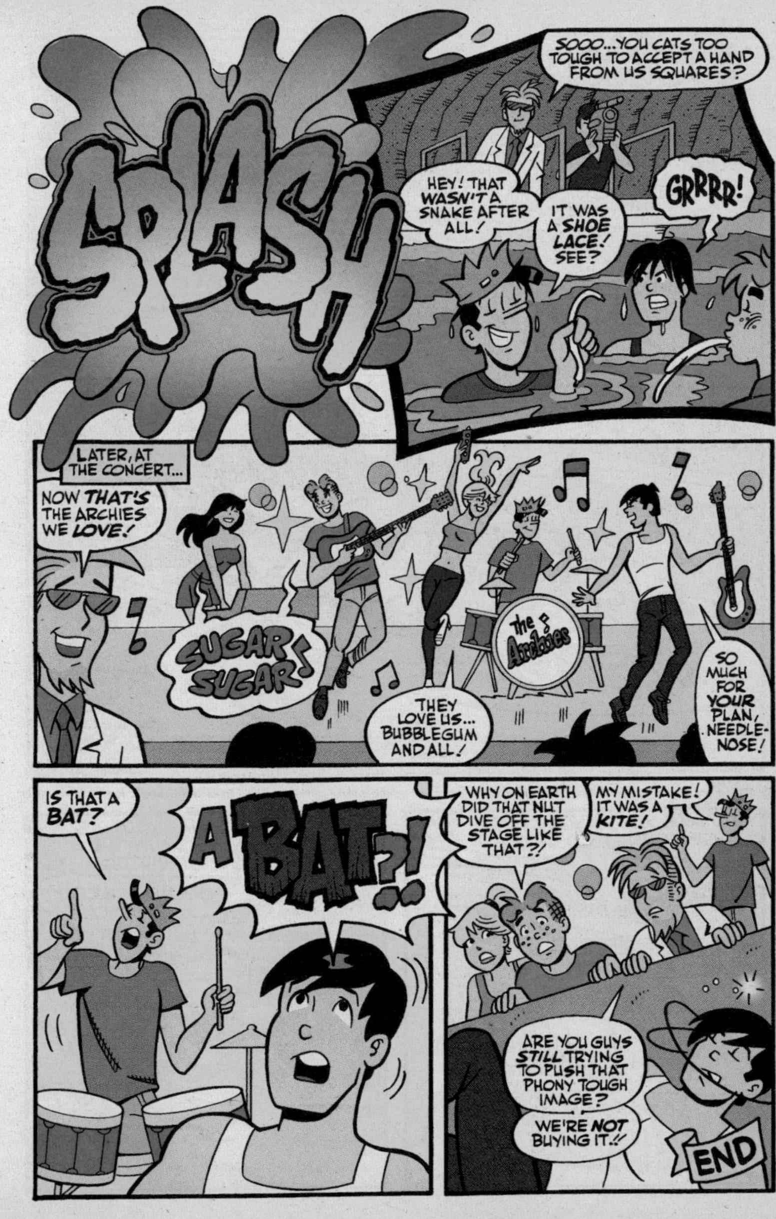
SPLASH
SOOO...YOU CATS TOO TOUGH TO ACCEPT A HAND FROM US SQUARES?
HEY! THAT WASN'T A SNAKE AFTER ALL!
IT WAS A SHOE LACE! SEE?
GRRRR!
LATER, AT THE CONCERT...
NOW THAT'S THE ARCHIES WE LOVE!
SUGAR SUGAR
the Archies
THEY LOVE US... BUBBLEGUM AND ALL!
SO MUCH FOR YOUR PLAN, NEEDLE-NOSE!
IS THAT A BAT?
A BAT?!
WHY ON EARTH DID THAT NUT DIVE OFF THE STAGE LIKE THAT?!
MY MISTAKE! IT WAS A KITE!
ARE YOU GUYS STILL TRYING TO PUSH THAT PHONY TOUGH IMAGE?
WE'RE NOT BUYING IT.!!
END

Betty and Veronica (IN) "SPRING BREAK"

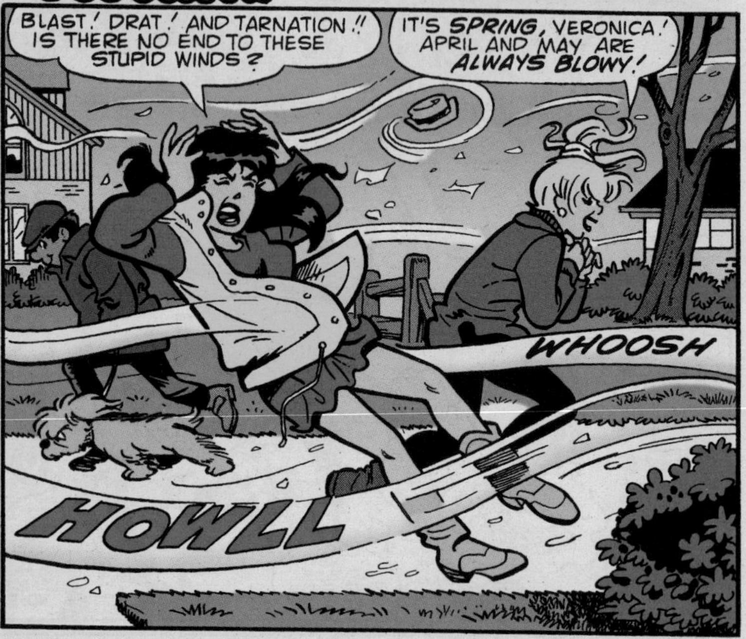
BLAST! DRAT! AND TARNATION!! IS THERE NO END TO THESE STUPID WINDS?
IT'S SPRING, VERONICA! APRIL AND MAY ARE ALWAYS BLOWY!
WHOOSH
HOWLL

Script: Frank Doyle / Pencils: Dan DeCarlo / Inks: Henry Scarpelli / Letters: Bill Yoshida / Colors: Barry Grossman

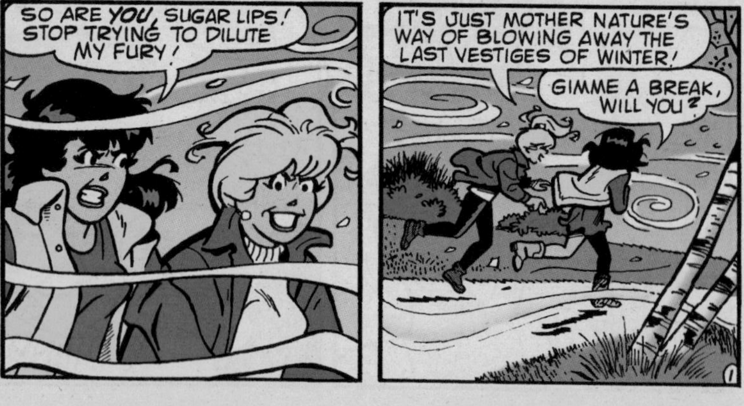
SO ARE YOU, SUGAR LIPS! STOP TRYING TO DILUTE MY FURY!
IT'S JUST MOTHER NATURE'S WAY OF BLOWING AWAY THE LAST VESTIGES OF WINTER!
GIMME A BREAK, WILL YOU?

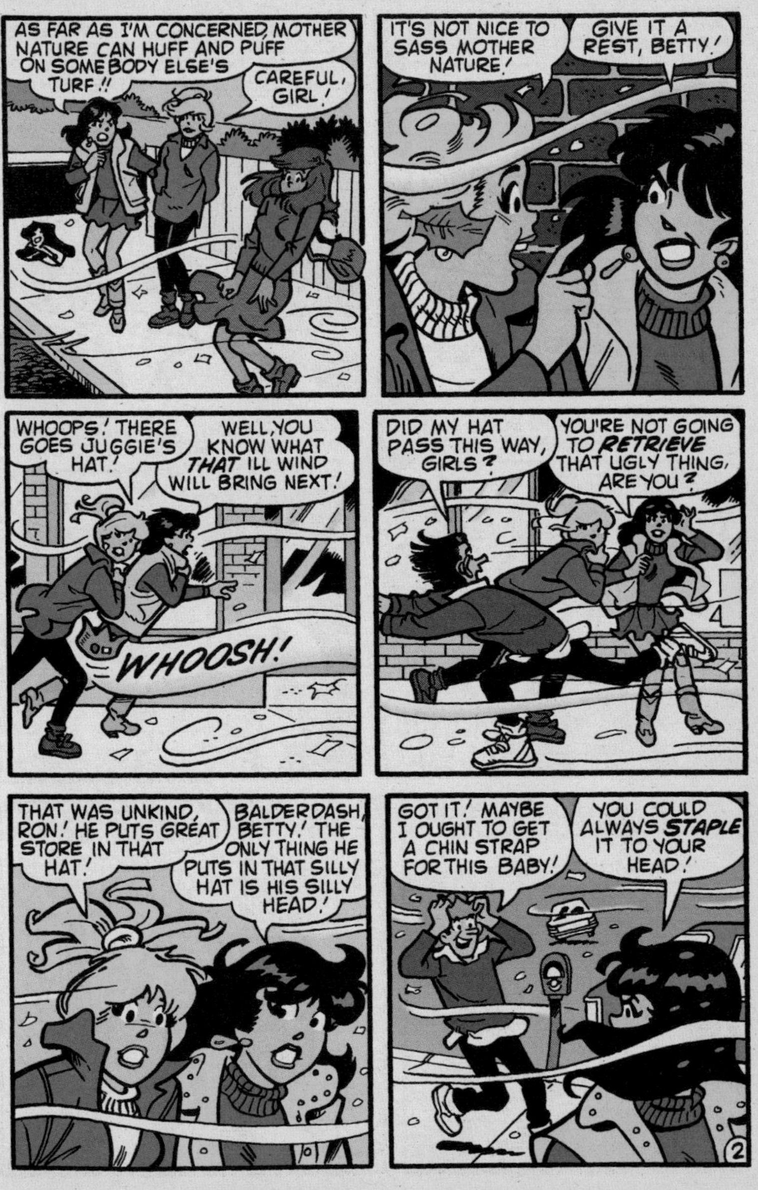
AS FAR AS I'M CONCERNED, MOTHER NATURE CAN HUFF AND PUFF ON SOMEBODY ELSE'S TURF!!
CAREFUL, GIRL!
IT'S NOT NICE TO SASS MOTHER NATURE!
GIVE IT A REST, BETTY!
WHOOPS! THERE GOES JUGGIE'S HAT!
WELL, YOU KNOW WHAT THAT ILL WIND WILL BRING NEXT!
WHOOSH!
DID MY HAT PASS THIS WAY, GIRLS?
YOU'RE NOT GOING TO RETRIEVE THAT UGLY THING, ARE YOU?
THAT WAS UNKIND, RON! HE PUTS GREAT STORE IN THAT HAT!
BALDERDASH, BETTY! THE ONLY THING HE PUTS IN THAT SILLY HAT IS HIS SILLY HEAD!
GOT IT! MAYBE I OUGHT TO GET A CHIN STRAP FOR THIS BABY!
YOU COULD ALWAYS STAPLE IT TO YOUR HEAD!
2

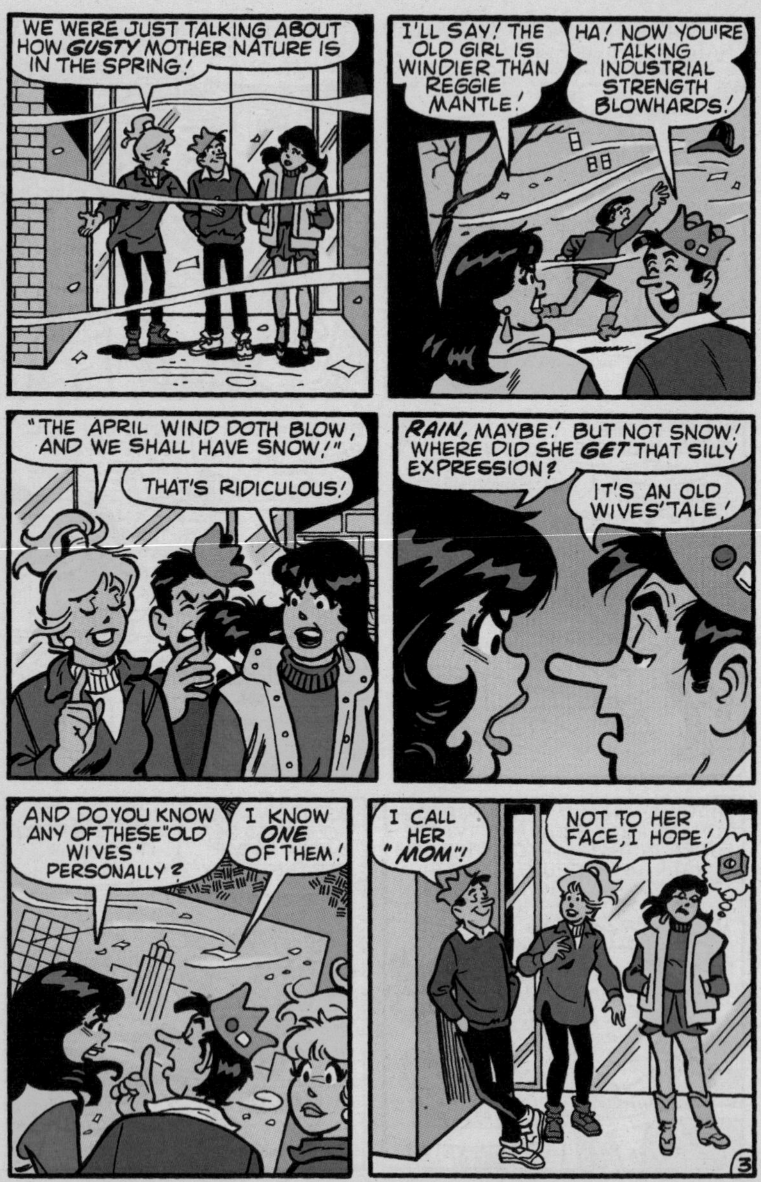
WE WERE JUST TALKING ABOUT HOW GUSTY MOTHER NATURE IS IN THE SPRING!
I'LL SAY! THE OLD GIRL IS WINDIER THAN REGGIE MANTLE!
HA! NOW YOU'RE TALKING INDUSTRIAL STRENGTH BLOWHARDS!
"THE APRIL WIND DOTH BLOW, AND WE SHALL HAVE SNOW!"
THAT'S RIDICULOUS!
RAIN, MAYBE! BUT NOT SNOW! WHERE DID SHE GET THAT SILLY EXPRESSION?
IT'S AN OLD WIVES' TALE!
AND DO YOU KNOW ANY OF THESE "OLD WIVES" PERSONALLY?
I KNOW ONE OF THEM!
I CALL HER "MOM"!
NOT TO HER FACE, I HOPE!
3

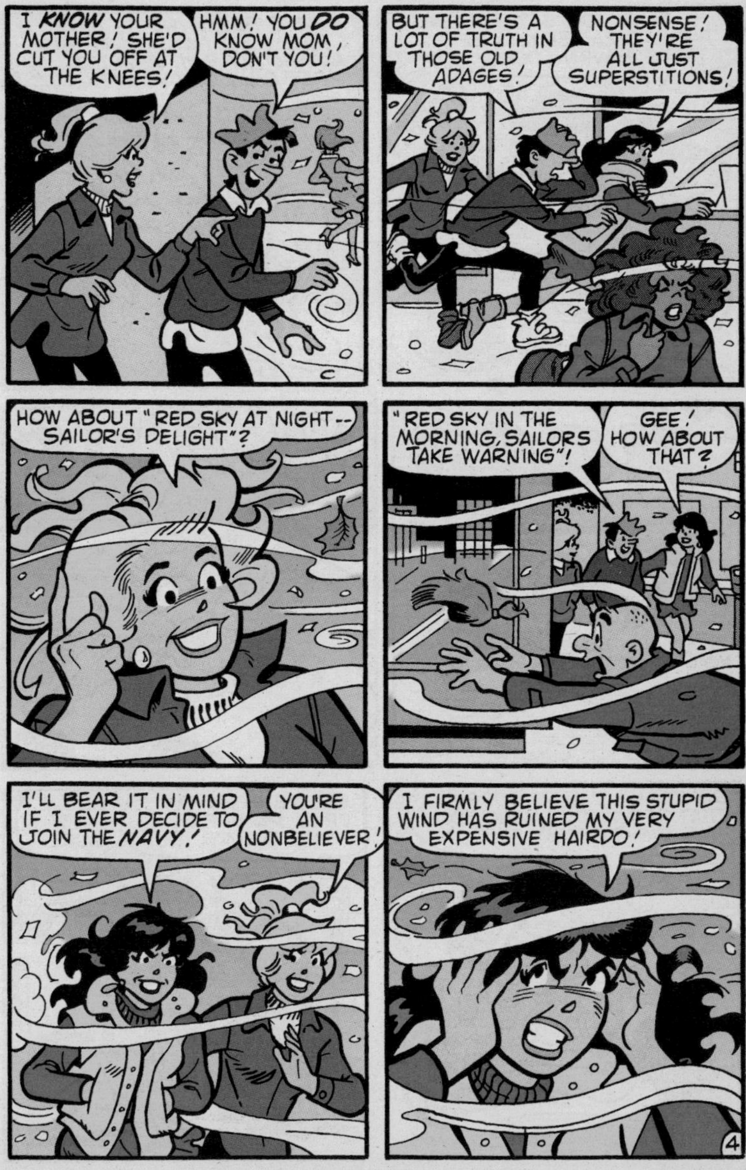

I KNOW YOUR MOTHER! SHE'D CUT YOU OFF AT THE KNEES!
HMM! YOU DO KNOW MOM, DON'T YOU!
BUT THERE'S A LOT OF TRUTH IN THOSE OLD ADAGES!
NONSENSE! THEY'RE ALL JUST SUPERSTITIONS!
HOW ABOUT "RED SKY AT NIGHT-- SAILOR'S DELIGHT"?
"RED SKY IN THE MORNING, SAILORS TAKE WARNING"!
GEE! HOW ABOUT THAT?
I'LL BEAR IT IN MIND IF I EVER DECIDE TO JOIN THE NAVY!
YOU'RE AN NONBELIEVER!
I FIRMLY BELIEVE THIS STUPID WIND HAS RUINED MY VERY EXPENSIVE HAIRDO!
4

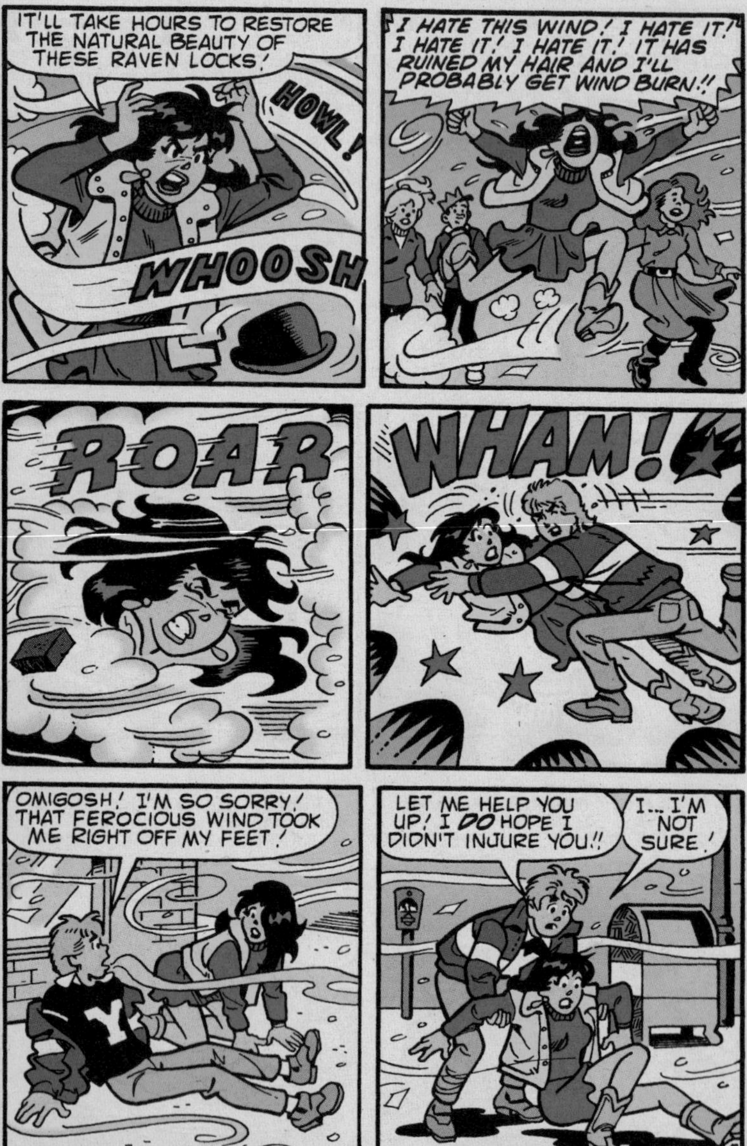
IT'LL TAKE HOURS TO RESTORE THE NATURAL BEAUTY OF THESE RAVEN LOCKS!
HOWL!
WHOOSH
I HATE THIS WIND! I HATE IT! I HATE IT! I HATE IT! IT HAS RUINED MY HAIR AND I'LL PROBABLY GET WIND BURN!!
ROAR
WHAM!!
OMIGOSH! I'M SO SORRY! THAT FEROCIOUS WIND TOOK ME RIGHT OFF MY FEET!
Y
LET ME HELP YOU UP! I DO HOPE I DIDN'T INJURE YOU!!
I... I'M NOT SURE!
5

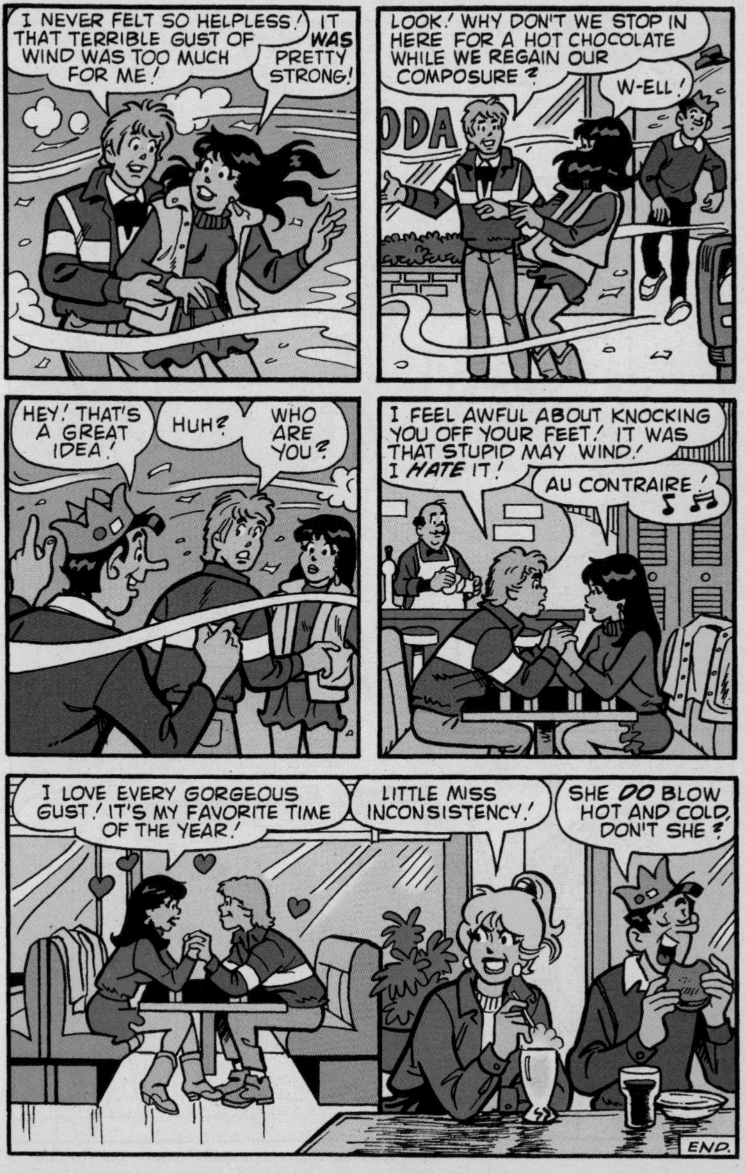
I NEVER FELT SO HELPLESS! THAT TERRIBLE GUST OF WIND WAS TOO MUCH FOR ME!
IT WAS PRETTY STRONG!
LOOK! WHY DON'T WE STOP IN HERE FOR A HOT CHOCOLATE WHILE WE REGAIN OUR COMPOSURE?
W-ELL!
ODA
HEY! THAT'S A GREAT IDEA!
HUH?
WHO ARE YOU?
I FEEL AWFUL ABOUT KNOCKING YOU OFF YOUR FEET! IT WAS THAT STUPID MAY WIND! I HATE IT!
AU CONTRAIRE!
I LOVE EVERY GORGEOUS GUST! IT'S MY FAVORITE TIME OF THE YEAR!
LITTLE MISS INCONSISTENCY!
SHE DO BLOW HOT AND COLD, DON'T SHE?
END.

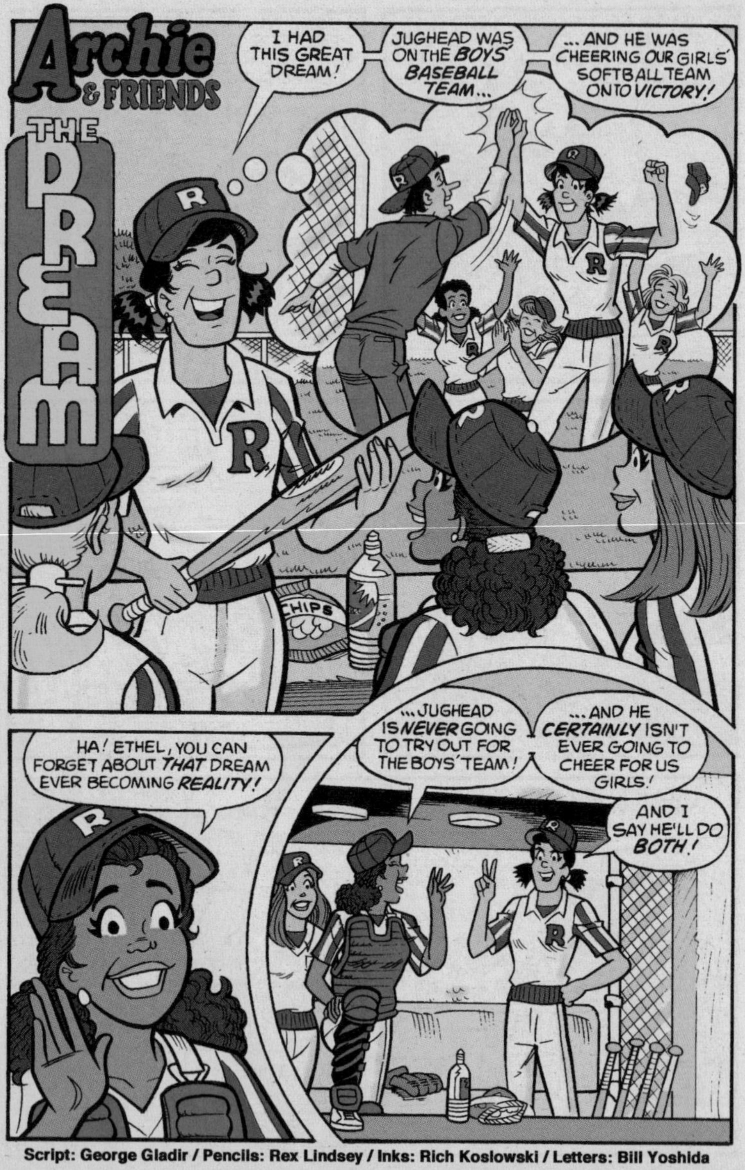
Archie & FRIENDS
THE DREAM
I HAD THIS GREAT DREAM!
JUGHEAD WAS ON THE BOYS' BASEBALL TEAM...
... AND HE WAS CHEERING OUR GIRLS' SOFTBALL TEAM ONTO VICTORY!
CHIPS
HA! ETHEL, YOU CAN FORGET ABOUT THAT DREAM EVER BECOMING REALITY!
...JUGHEAD IS NEVER GOING TO TRY OUT FOR THE BOYS' TEAM!
...AND HE CERTAINLY ISN'T EVER GOING TO CHEER FOR US GIRLS!
AND I SAY HE'LL DO BOTH!

Script: George Gladir / Pencils: Rex Lindsey / Inks: Rich Koslowski / Letters: Bill Yoshida

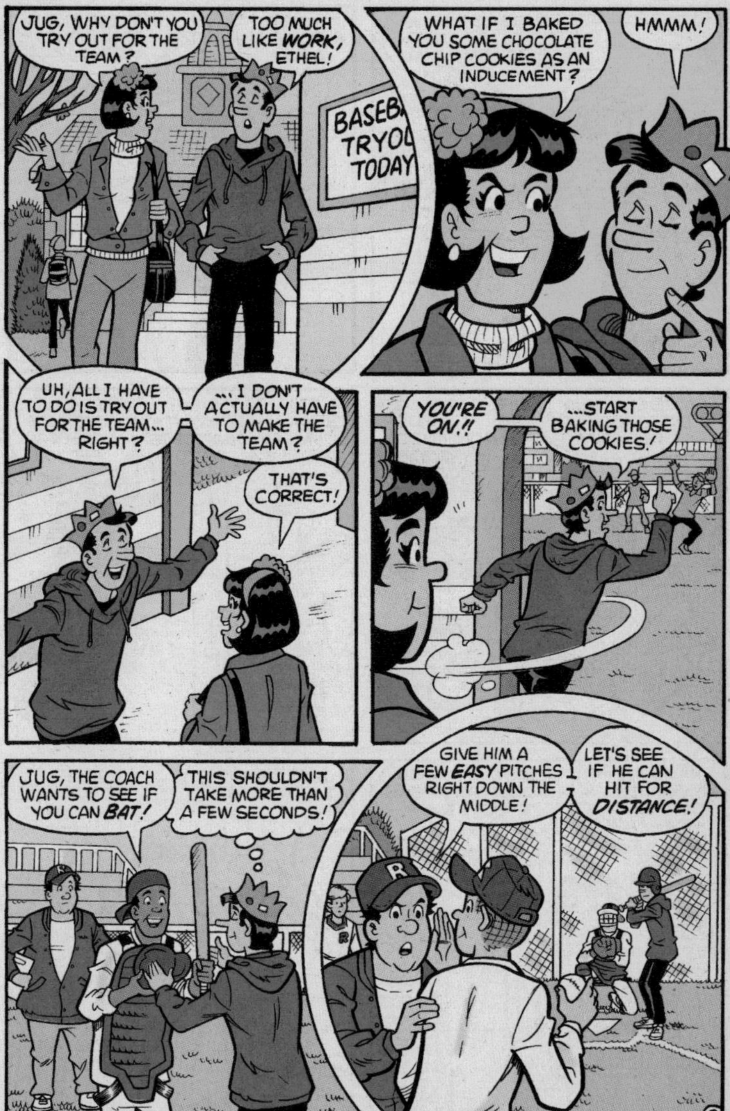
JUG, WHY DON'T YOU TRY OUT FOR THE TEAM?
TOO MUCH LIKE WORK, ETHEL!
BASEB TRYO TODAY
WHAT IF I BAKED YOU SOME CHOCOLATE CHIP COOKIES AS AN INDUCEMENT?
HMMM!
UH, ALL I HAVE TO DO IS TRY OUT FOR THE TEAM... RIGHT?
...I DON'T ACTUALLY HAVE TO MAKE THE TEAM?
THAT'S CORRECT!
YOU'RE ON!!
...START BAKING THOSE COOKIES!
JUG, THE COACH WANTS TO SEE IF YOU CAN BAT!
THIS SHOULDN'T TAKE MORE THAN A FEW SECONDS!
GIVE HIM A FEW EASY PITCHES RIGHT DOWN THE MIDDLE!
LET'S SEE IF HE CAN HIT FOR DISTANCE!
2

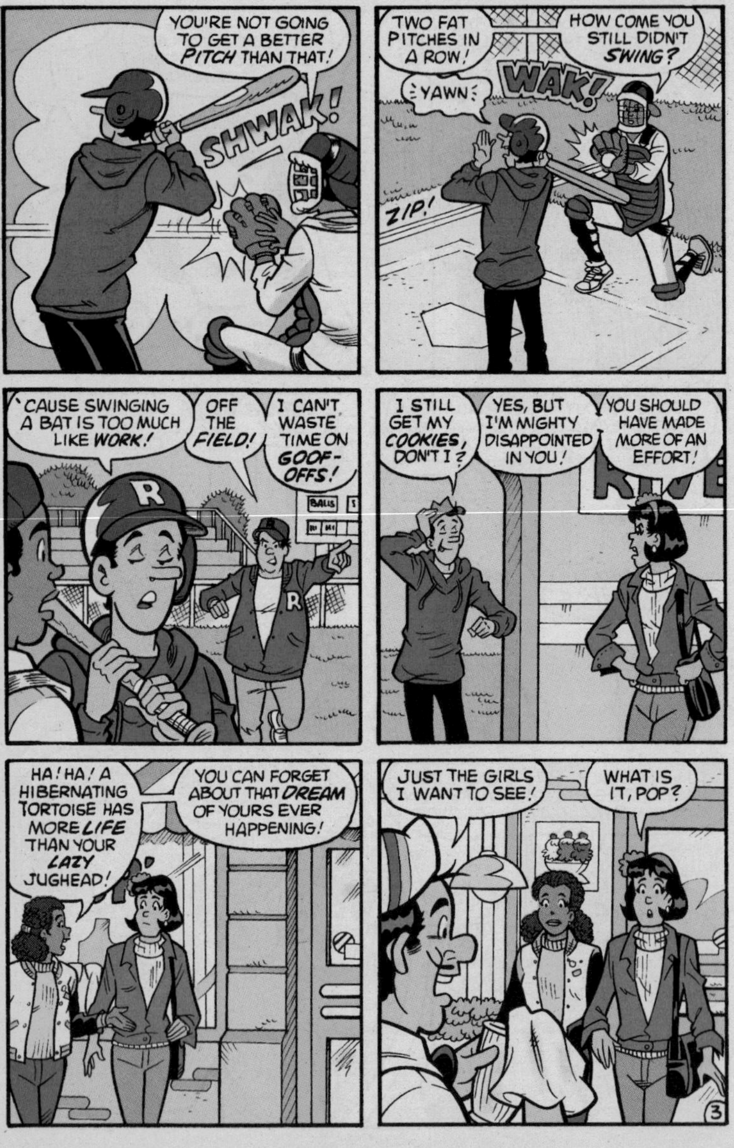
YOU'RE NOT GOING TO GET A BETTER PITCH THAN THAT!
SHWAK!
TWO FAT PITCHES IN A ROW!
YAWN
HOW COME YOU STILL DIDN'T SWING?
WAK!
ZIP!
'CAUSE SWINGING A BAT IS TOO MUCH LIKE WORK!
OFF THE FIELD!
I CAN'T WASTE TIME ON GOOF-OFFS!
I STILL GET MY COOKIES, DON'T I?
YES, BUT I'M MIGHTY DISAPPOINTED IN YOU!
YOU SHOULD HAVE MADE MORE OF AN EFFORT!
HA! HA! A HIBERNATING TORTOISE HAS MORE LIFE THAN YOUR LAZY JUGHEAD!
YOU CAN FORGET ABOUT THAT DREAM OF YOURS EVER HAPPENING!
JUST THE GIRLS I WANT TO SEE!
WHAT IS IT, POP?
3

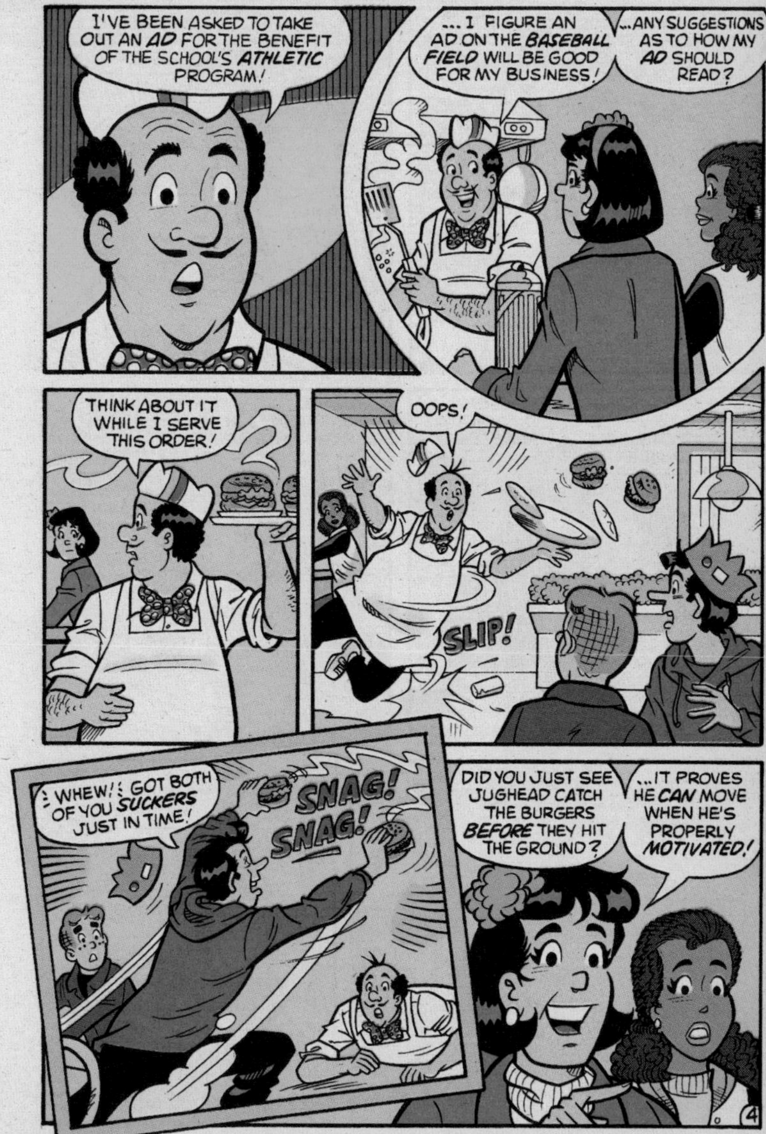
I'VE BEEN ASKED TO TAKE OUT AN AD FOR THE BENEFIT OF THE SCHOOL'S ATHLETIC PROGRAM!
... I FIGURE AN AD ON THE BASEBALL FIELD WILL BE GOOD FOR MY BUSINESS!
...ANY SUGGESTIONS AS TO HOW MY AD SHOULD READ?
THINK ABOUT IT WHILE I SERVE THIS ORDER!
OOPS!
SLIP!
WHEW! GOT BOTH OF YOU SUCKERS JUST IN TIME!
SNAG!
SNAG!
DID YOU JUST SEE JUGHEAD CATCH THE BURGERS BEFORE THEY HIT THE GROUND?
...IT PROVES HE CAN MOVE WHEN HE'S PROPERLY MOTIVATED!
4

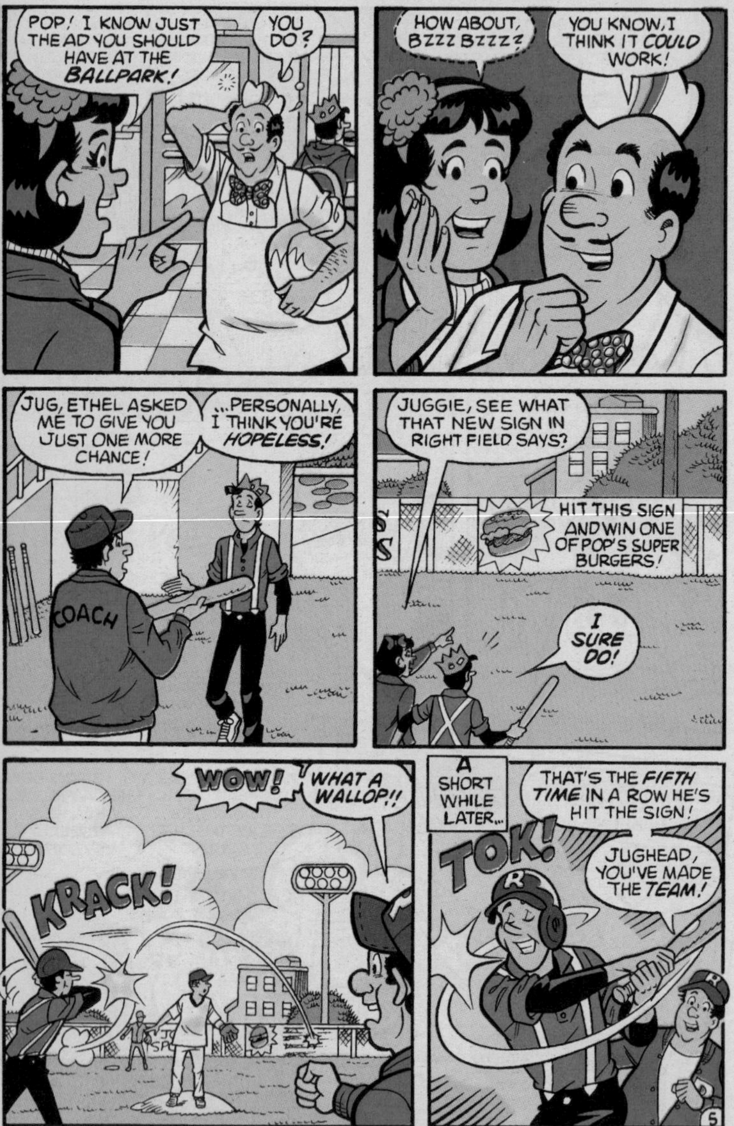
POP! I KNOW JUST THE AD YOU SHOULD HAVE AT THE BALLPARK!
YOU DO?
HOW ABOUT, BZZZ BZZZ?
YOU KNOW, I THINK IT COULD WORK!
JUG, ETHEL ASKED ME TO GIVE YOU JUST ONE MORE CHANCE!
...PERSONALLY, I THINK YOU'RE HOPELESS!
COACH
JUGGIE, SEE WHAT THAT NEW SIGN IN RIGHT FIELD SAYS?
HIT THIS SIGN AND WIN ONE OF POP'S SUPER BURGERS!
I SURE DO!
WOW!
WHAT A WALLOP!!
KRACK!
A SHORT WHILE LATER...
THAT'S THE FIFTH TIME IN A ROW HE'S HIT THE SIGN!
TOK!
JUGHEAD, YOU'VE MADE THE TEAM!
5

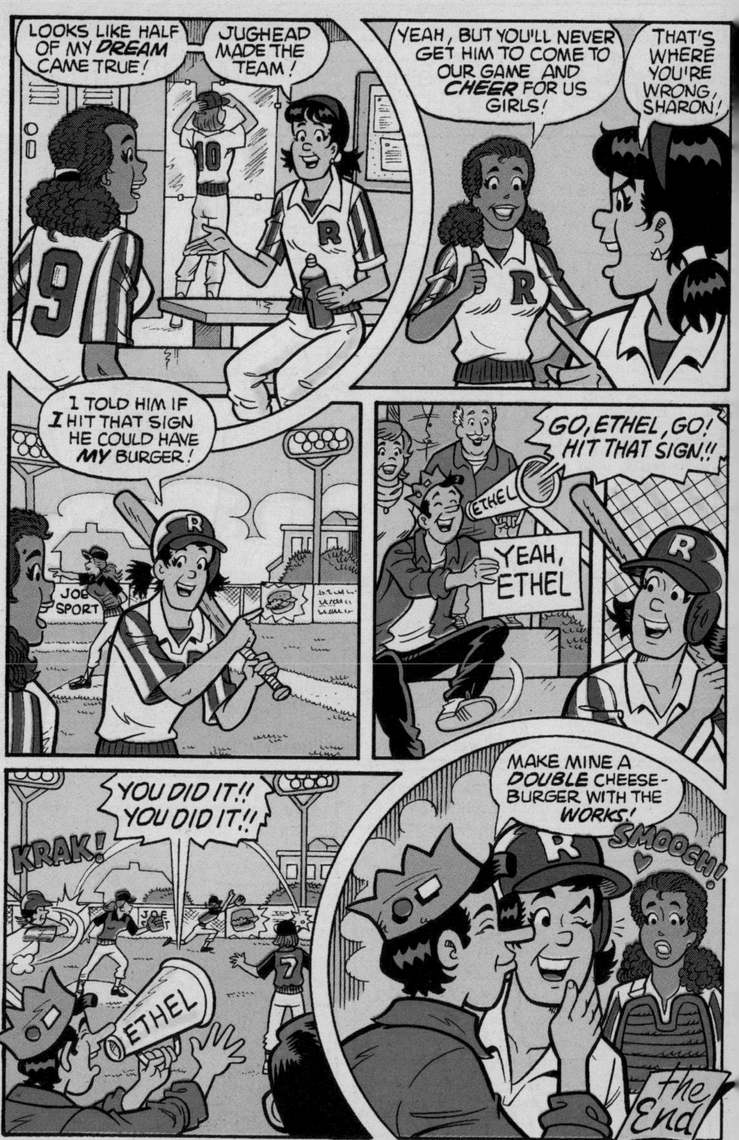
LOOKS LIKE HALF OF MY DREAM CAME TRUE!
JUGHEAD MADE THE TEAM!
10
9
R
YEAH, BUT YOU'LL NEVER GET HIM TO COME TO OUR GAME AND CHEER FOR US GIRLS!
THAT'S WHERE YOU'RE WRONG, SHARON!
I TOLD HIM IF I HIT THAT SIGN HE COULD HAVE MY BURGER!
JOE SPORT
GO, ETHEL, GO! HIT THAT SIGN!!
ETHEL
YEAH, ETHEL
KRAK!
YOU DID IT!! YOU DID IT!!
ETHEL
7
MAKE MINE A DOUBLE CHEESE-BURGER WITH THE WORKS!
SMOOCH!
the End

Betty in SPRING CLEANING

(WHEW!) IT WAS A NASTY, NASTY CHORE, BUT I'M GLAD IT'S FINISHED!

THIS OLD HOUSE HAS NEVER LOOKED SO CLEAN, HUH, MOM?

MOM

BEST CLEANER

Webb / Goldberg / Lowe / Yoshida

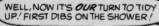

WELL, NOW IT'S *OUR* TURN TO TIDY UP! FIRST DIBS ON THE SHOWER!

HEY!!

MOM

WOW, I NEVER KNEW HOUSECLEANING COULD BE SUCH A WORKOUT! PHEW!

RIVERDALE

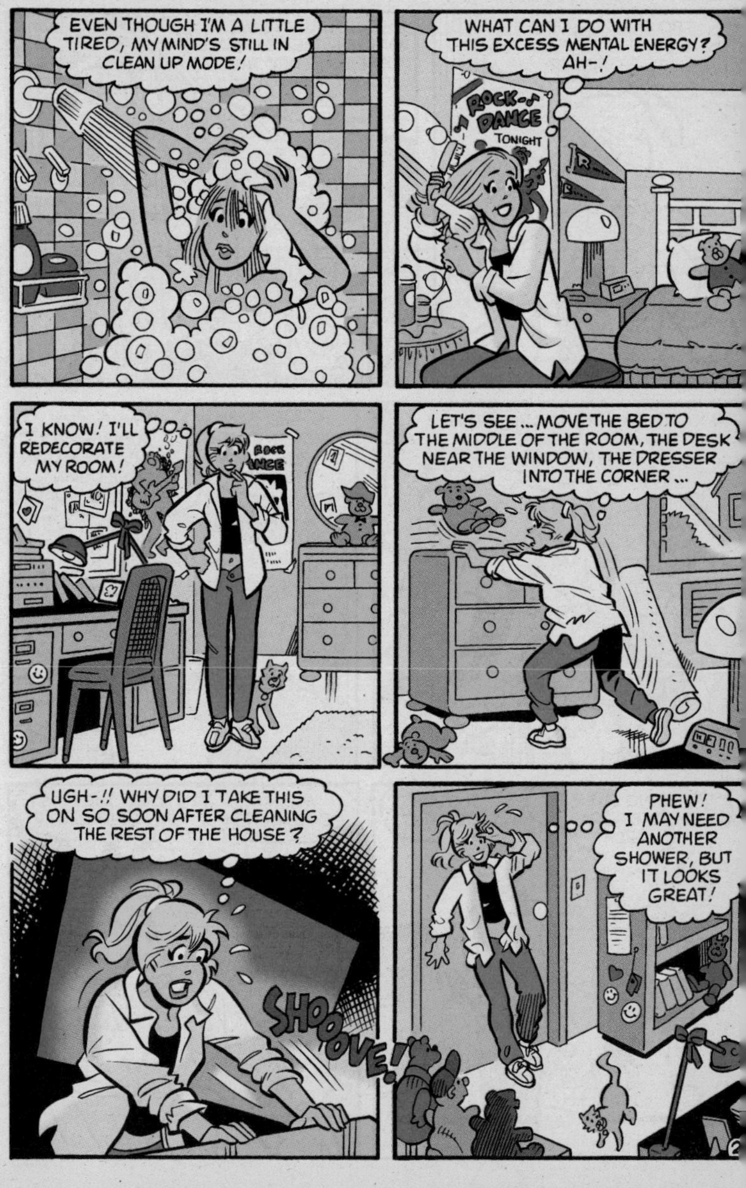
EVEN THOUGH I'M A LITTLE TIRED, MY MIND'S STILL IN CLEAN UP MODE!
WHAT CAN I DO WITH THIS EXCESS MENTAL ENERGY? AH-!
ROCK-A DANCE TONIGHT
I KNOW! I'LL REDECORATE MY ROOM!
LET'S SEE ... MOVE THE BED TO THE MIDDLE OF THE ROOM, THE DESK NEAR THE WINDOW, THE DRESSER INTO THE CORNER ...
UGH-!! WHY DID I TAKE THIS ON SO SOON AFTER CLEANING THE REST OF THE HOUSE?
SHOOOVE!
PHEW! I MAY NEED ANOTHER SHOWER, BUT IT LOOKS GREAT!

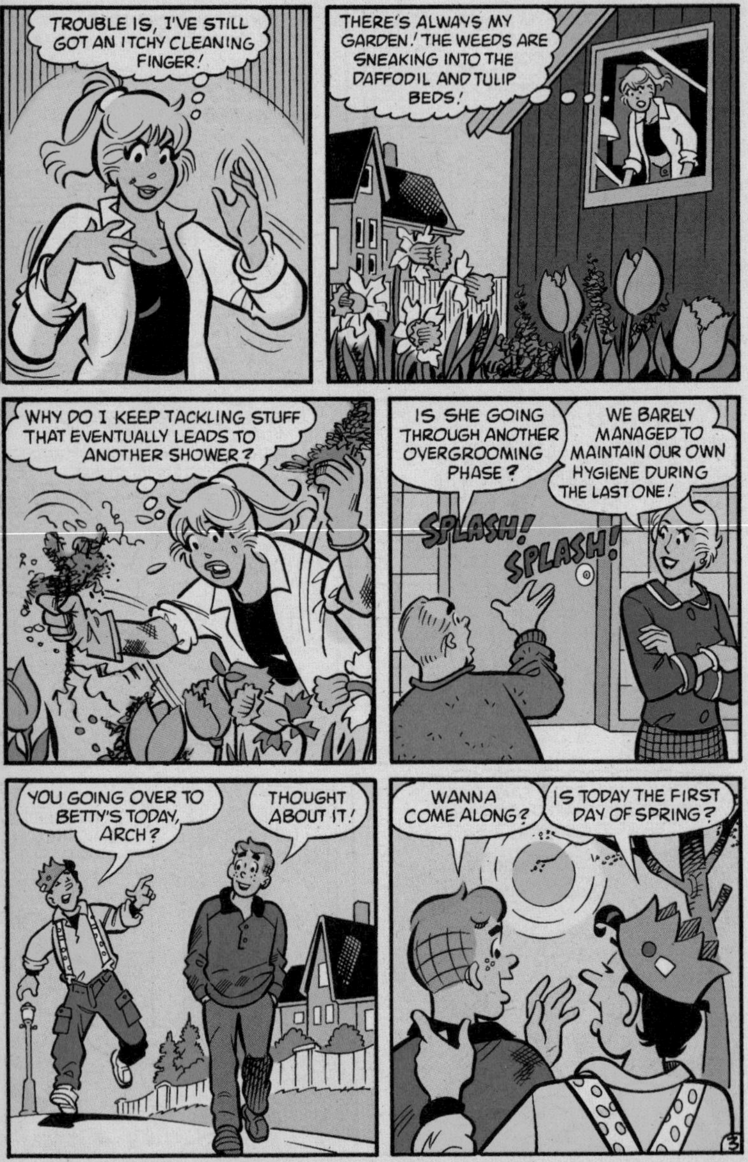
TROUBLE IS, I'VE STILL GOT AN ITCHY CLEANING FINGER!
THERE'S ALWAYS MY GARDEN! THE WEEDS ARE SNEAKING INTO THE DAFFODIL AND TULIP BEDS!
WHY DO I KEEP TACKLING STUFF THAT EVENTUALLY LEADS TO ANOTHER SHOWER?
IS SHE GOING THROUGH ANOTHER OVERGROOMING PHASE?
WE BARELY MANAGED TO MAINTAIN OUR OWN HYGIENE DURING THE LAST ONE!
SPLASH!
SPLASH!
YOU GOING OVER TO BETTY'S TODAY, ARCH?
THOUGHT ABOUT IT!
WANNA COME ALONG?
IS TODAY THE FIRST DAY OF SPRING?
3

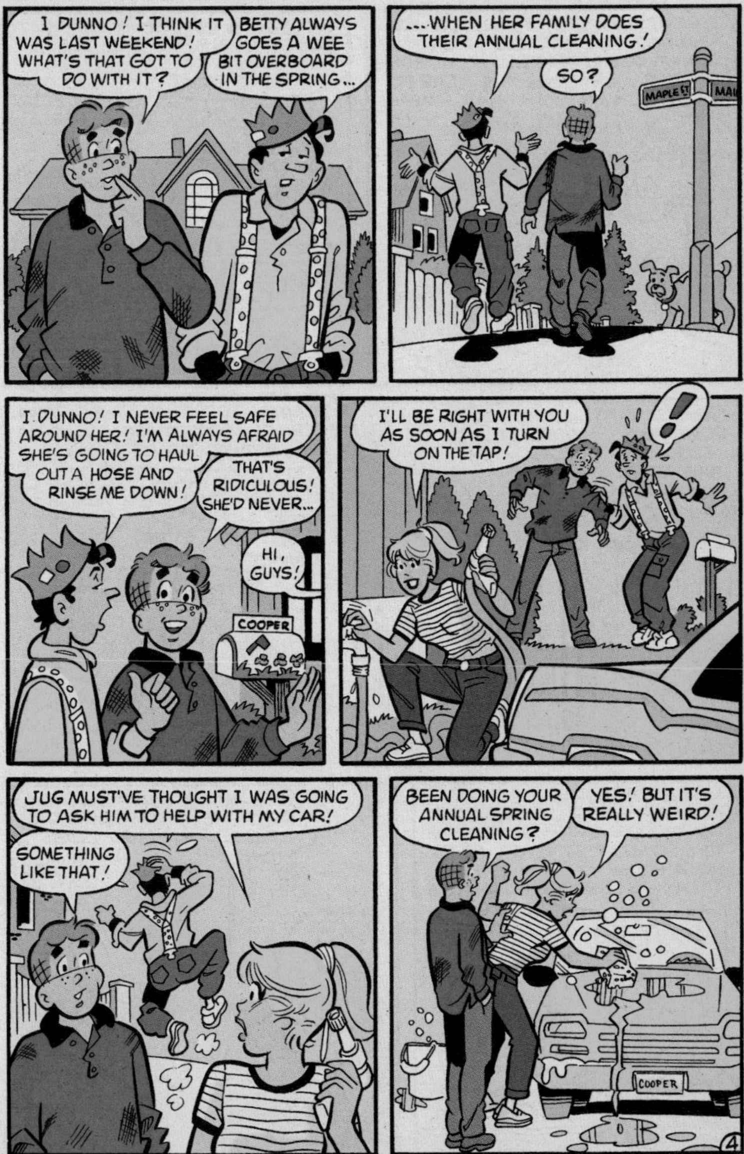
I DUNNO! I THINK IT WAS LAST WEEKEND! WHAT'S THAT GOT TO DO WITH IT?
BETTY ALWAYS GOES A WEE BIT OVERBOARD IN THE SPRING...
....WHEN HER FAMILY DOES THEIR ANNUAL CLEANING!
SO?
MAPLE ST
I DUNNO! I NEVER FEEL SAFE AROUND HER! I'M ALWAYS AFRAID SHE'S GOING TO HAUL OUT A HOSE AND RINSE ME DOWN!
THAT'S RIDICULOUS! SHE'D NEVER...
HI, GUYS!
COOPER
I'LL BE RIGHT WITH YOU AS SOON AS I TURN ON THE TAP!
!
JUG MUST'VE THOUGHT I WAS GOING TO ASK HIM TO HELP WITH MY CAR!
SOMETHING LIKE THAT!
BEEN DOING YOUR ANNUAL SPRING CLEANING?
YES! BUT IT'S REALLY WEIRD!
COOPER

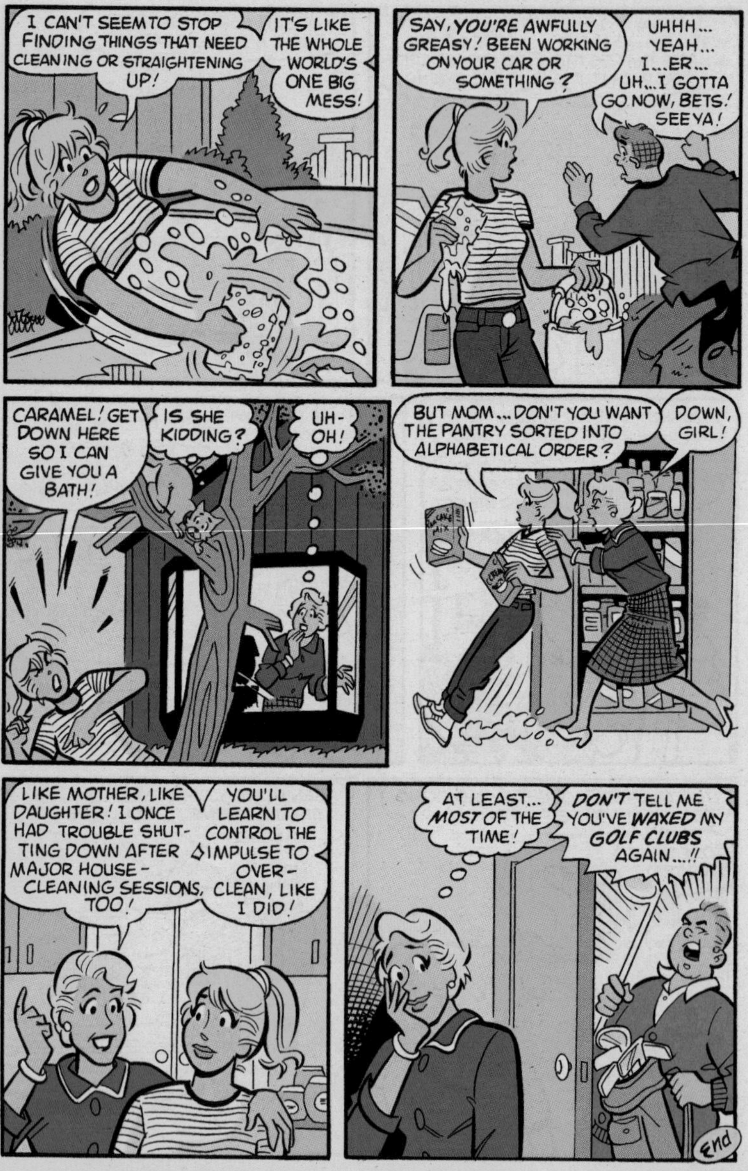

I CAN'T SEEM TO STOP FINDING THINGS THAT NEED CLEANING OR STRAIGHTENING UP!
IT'S LIKE THE WHOLE WORLD'S ONE BIG MESS!
SAY, YOU'RE AWFULLY GREASY! BEEN WORKING ON YOUR CAR OR SOMETHING?
UHHH... YEAH... I...ER... UH...I GOTTA GO NOW, BETS! SEE YA!
CARAMEL! GET DOWN HERE SO I CAN GIVE YOU A BATH!
IS SHE KIDDING?
UH-OH!
BUT MOM... DON'T YOU WANT THE PANTRY SORTED INTO ALPHABETICAL ORDER?
DOWN, GIRL!
PANCAKE MIX
LIKE MOTHER, LIKE DAUGHTER! I ONCE HAD TROUBLE SHUTTING DOWN AFTER MAJOR HOUSE-CLEANING SESSIONS, TOO!
YOU'LL LEARN TO CONTROL THE IMPULSE TO OVER-CLEAN, LIKE I DID!
AT LEAST... MOST OF THE TIME!
DON'T TELL ME YOU'VE WAXED MY GOLF CLUBS AGAIN...!!
End

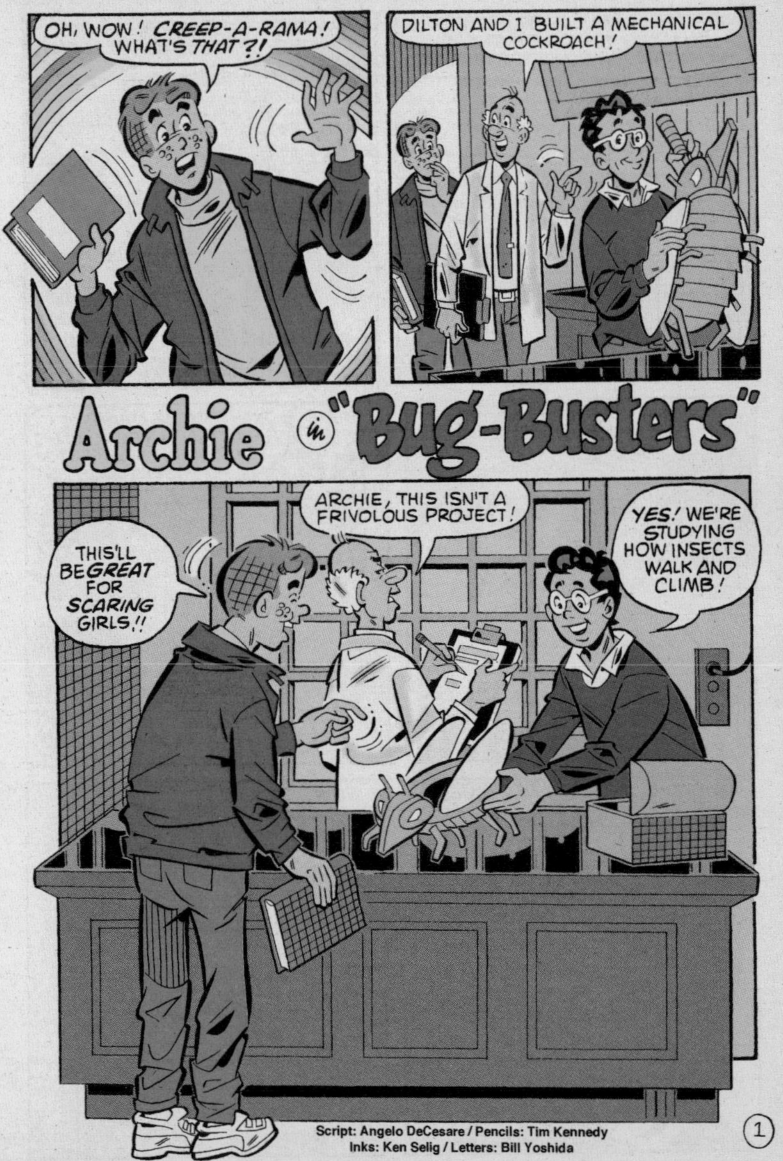
OH, WOW! CREEP-A-RAMA! WHAT'S THAT?!
DILTON AND I BUILT A MECHANICAL COCKROACH!
Archie in "Bug-Busters"
THIS'LL BE GREAT FOR SCARING GIRLS!!
ARCHIE, THIS ISN'T A FRIVOLOUS PROJECT!
YES! WE'RE STUDYING HOW INSECTS WALK AND CLIMB!
Script: Angelo DeCesare / Pencils: Tim Kennedy
Inks: Ken Selig / Letters: Bill Yoshida
1

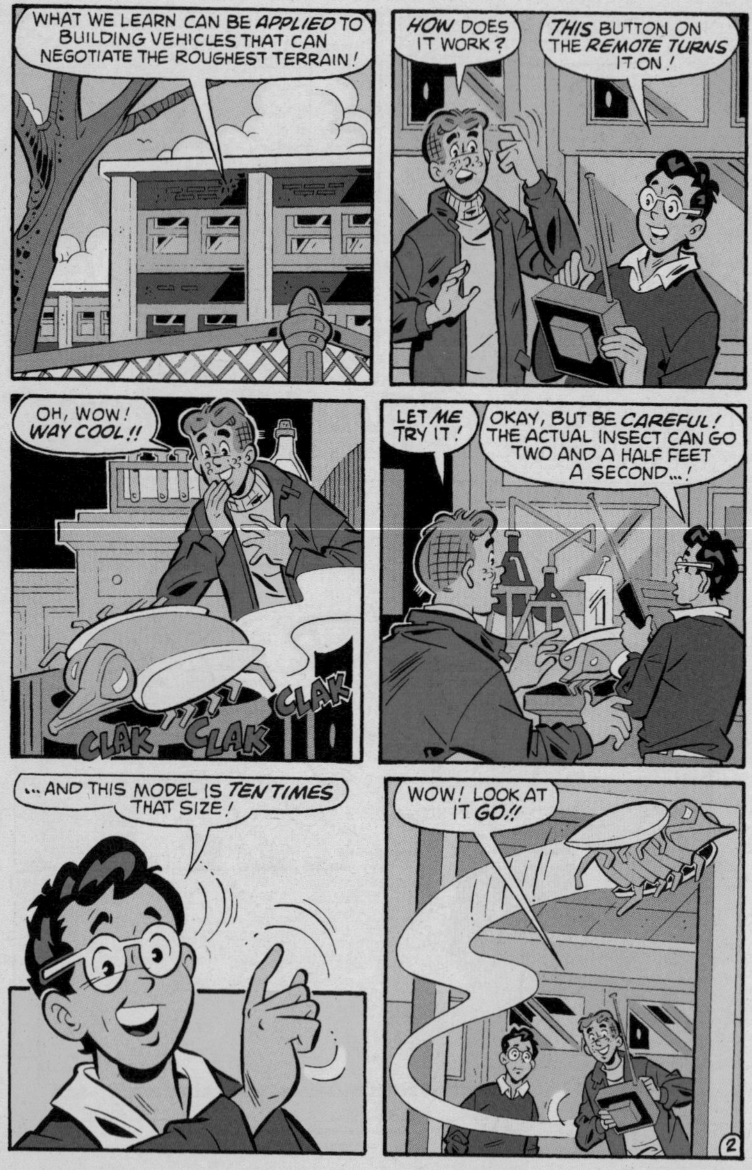
WHAT WE LEARN CAN BE APPLIED TO BUILDING VEHICLES THAT CAN NEGOTIATE THE ROUGHEST TERRAIN!
HOW DOES IT WORK?
THIS BUTTON ON THE REMOTE TURNS IT ON!
OH, WOW! WAY COOL!!
CLAK CLAK CLAK
LET ME TRY IT!
OKAY, BUT BE CAREFUL! THE ACTUAL INSECT CAN GO TWO AND A HALF FEET A SECOND...!
...AND THIS MODEL IS TEN TIMES THAT SIZE!
WOW! LOOK AT IT GO!!
2

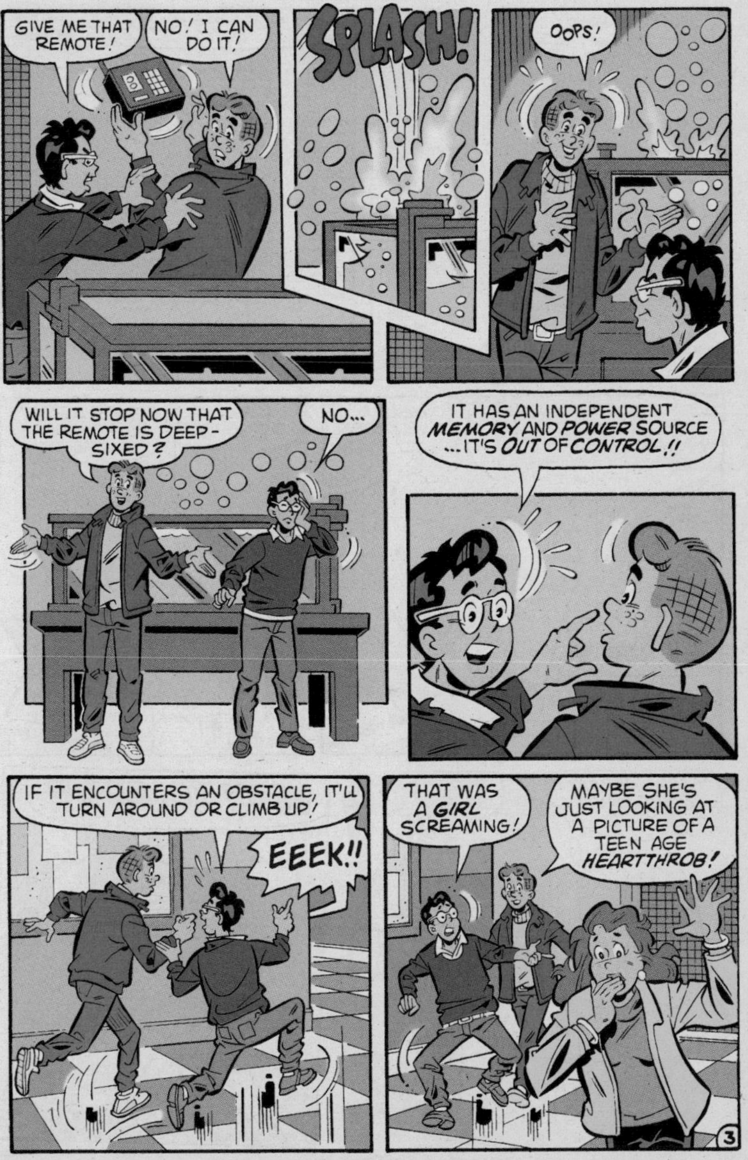
GIVE ME THAT REMOTE!
NO! I CAN DO IT!
SPLASH!
OOPS!
WILL IT STOP NOW THAT THE REMOTE IS DEEP-SIXED?
NO...
IT HAS AN INDEPENDENT MEMORY AND POWER SOURCE ...IT'S OUT OF CONTROL!!
IF IT ENCOUNTERS AN OBSTACLE, IT'LL TURN AROUND OR CLIMB UP!
EEEK!!
THAT WAS A GIRL SCREAMING!
MAYBE SHE'S JUST LOOKING AT A PICTURE OF A TEEN AGE HEARTTHROB!
3

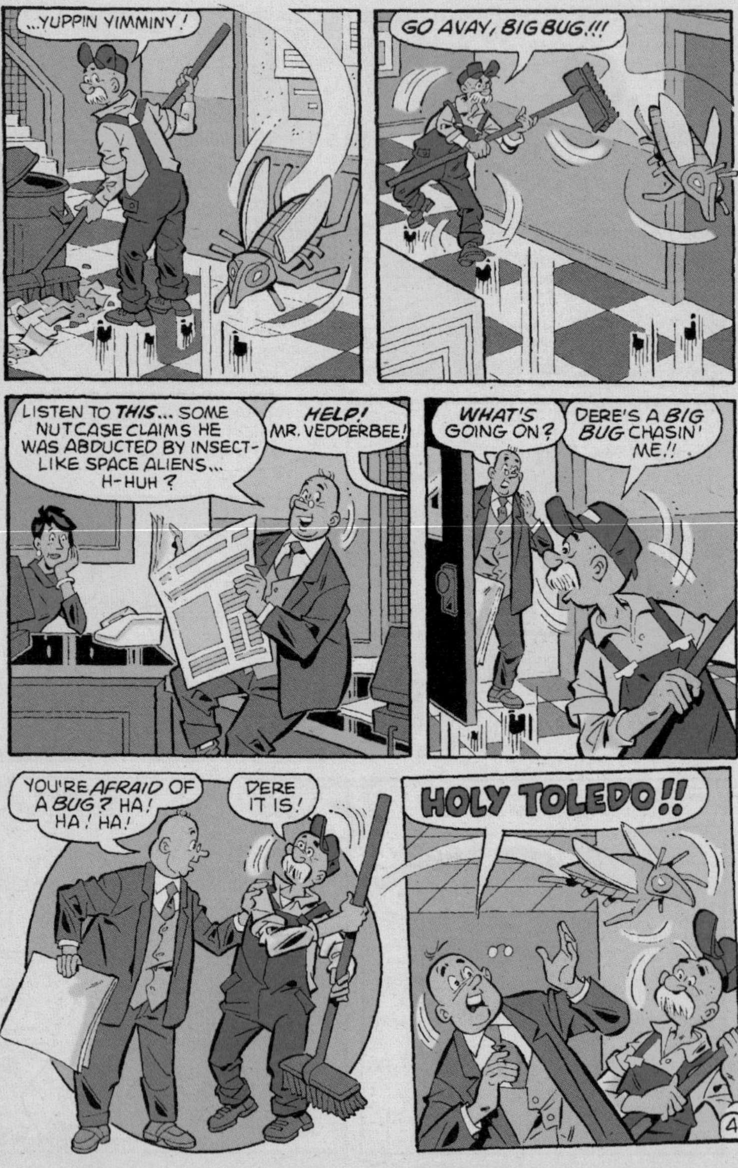

...YUPPIN YIMMINY!
GO AVAY, BIG BUG!!!
LISTEN TO THIS... SOME NUTCASE CLAIMS HE WAS ABDUCTED BY INSECT-LIKE SPACE ALIENS... H-HUH?
HELP! MR. VEDDERBEE!
WHAT'S GOING ON?
DERE'S A BIG BUG CHASIN' ME!!
YOU'RE AFRAID OF A BUG? HA! HA! HA!
DERE IT IS!
HOLY TOLEDO!!
4

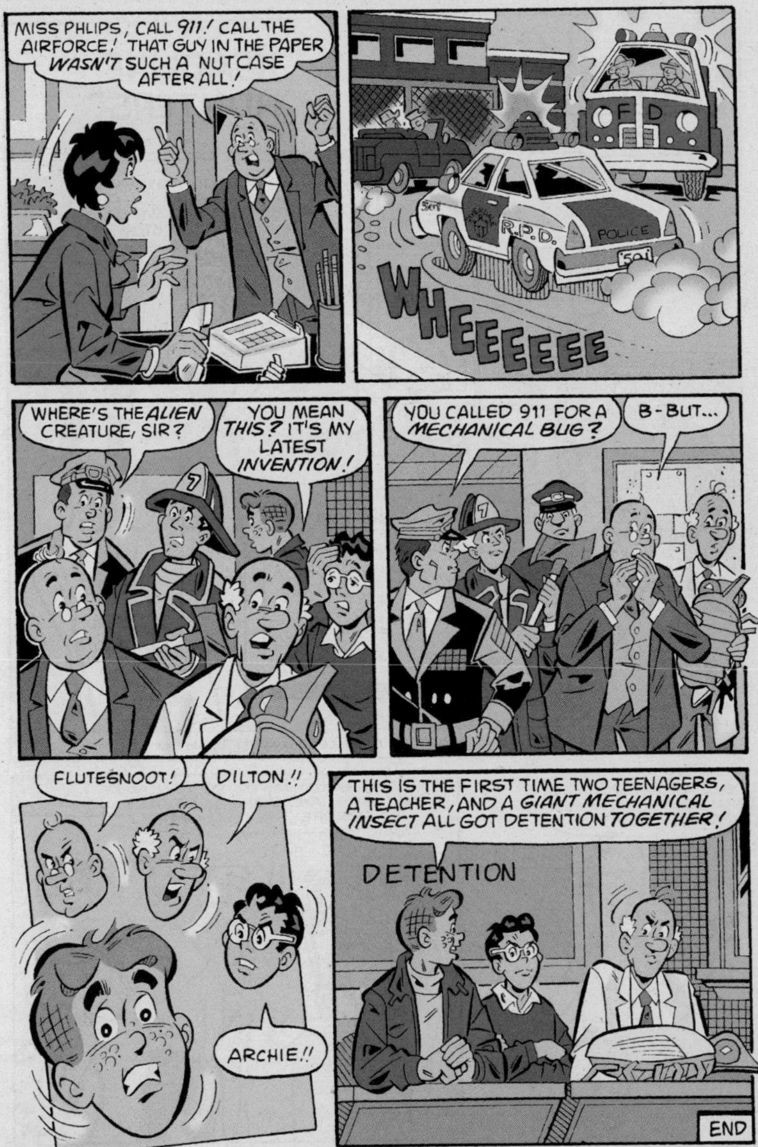
MISS PHLIPS, CALL 911! CALL THE AIRFORCE! THAT GUY IN THE PAPER WASN'T SUCH A NUTCASE AFTER ALL!
FD
R.P.D.
POLICE
WHEEEEEEE
WHERE'S THE ALIEN CREATURE, SIR?
YOU MEAN THIS? IT'S MY LATEST INVENTION!
YOU CALLED 911 FOR A MECHANICAL BUG?
B-BUT...
FLUTESNOOT!
DILTON!!
ARCHIE!!
THIS IS THE FIRST TIME TWO TEENAGERS, A TEACHER, AND A GIANT MECHANICAL INSECT ALL GOT DETENTION TOGETHER!
DETENTION
END

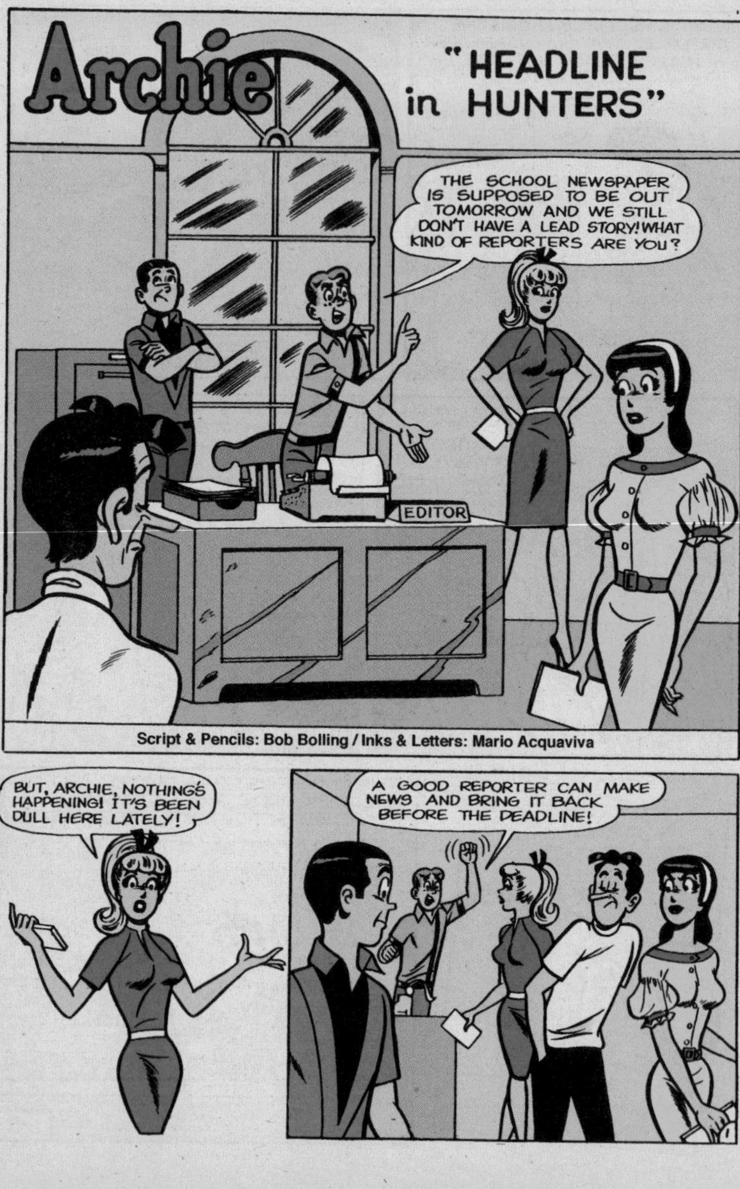
Archie
"HEADLINE in HUNTERS"
THE SCHOOL NEWSPAPER IS SUPPOSED TO BE OUT TOMORROW AND WE STILL DON'T HAVE A LEAD STORY! WHAT KIND OF REPORTERS ARE YOU?
EDITOR
Script & Pencils: Bob Bolling / Inks & Letters: Mario Acquaviva
BUT, ARCHIE, NOTHING'S HAPPENING! IT'S BEEN DULL HERE LATELY!
A GOOD REPORTER CAN MAKE NEWS AND BRING IT BACK BEFORE THE DEADLINE!
1

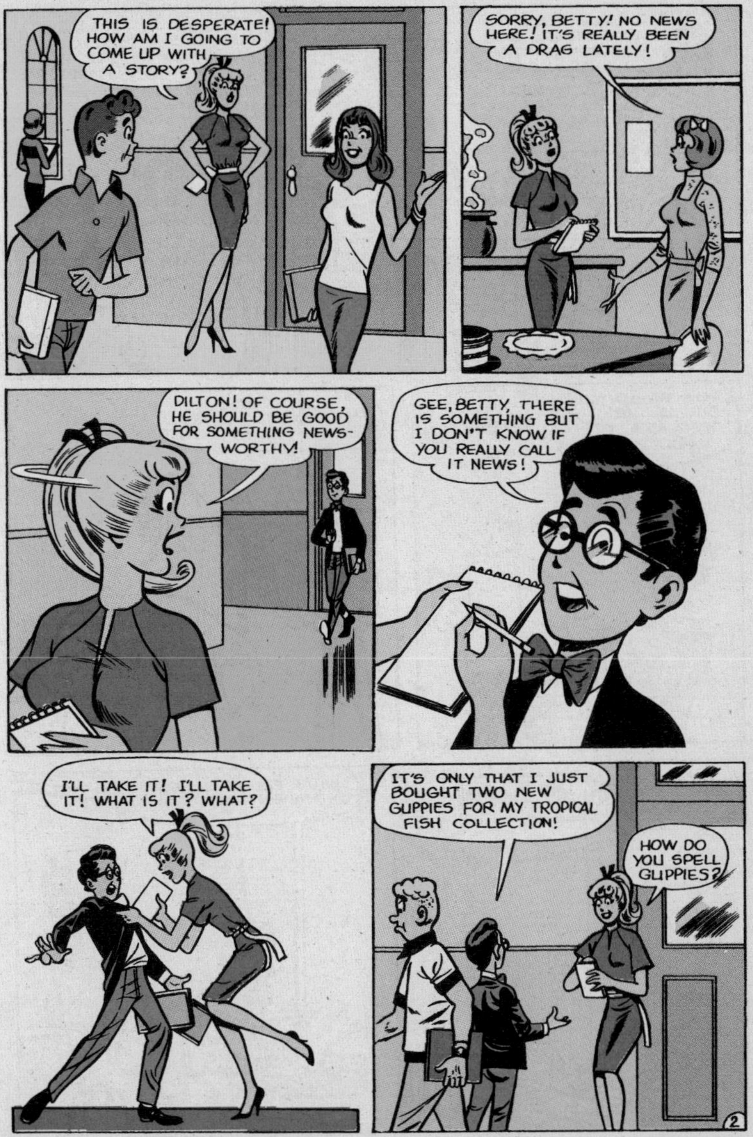

THIS IS DESPERATE! HOW AM I GOING TO COME UP WITH A STORY?
SORRY, BETTY! NO NEWS HERE! IT'S REALLY BEEN A DRAG LATELY!
DILTON! OF COURSE, HE SHOULD BE GOOD FOR SOMETHING NEWS-WORTHY!
GEE, BETTY, THERE IS SOMETHING BUT I DON'T KNOW IF YOU REALLY CALL IT NEWS!
I'LL TAKE IT! I'LL TAKE IT! WHAT IS IT? WHAT?
IT'S ONLY THAT I JUST BOUGHT TWO NEW GUPPIES FOR MY TROPICAL FISH COLLECTION!
HOW DO YOU SPELL GUPPIES?
2

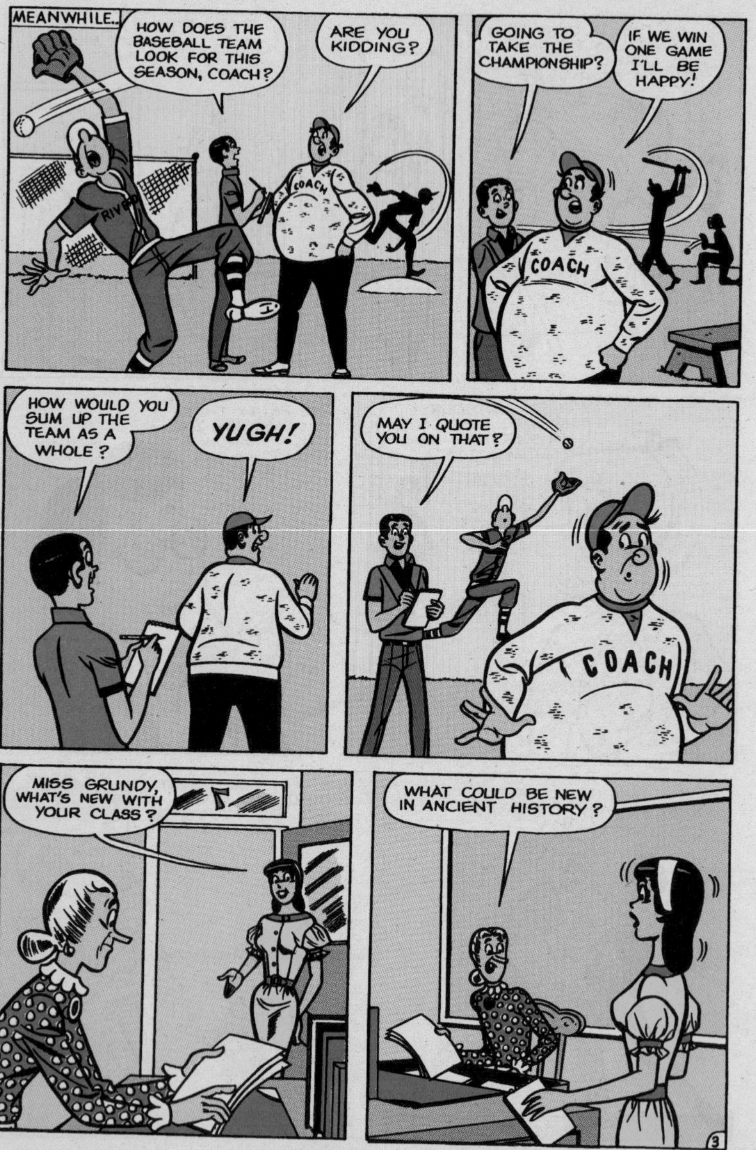

MEANWHILE..
HOW DOES THE BASEBALL TEAM LOOK FOR THIS SEASON, COACH?
ARE YOU KIDDING?
GOING TO TAKE THE CHAMPIONSHIP?
IF WE WIN ONE GAME I'LL BE HAPPY!
HOW WOULD YOU SUM UP THE TEAM AS A WHOLE?
YUGH!
MAY I QUOTE YOU ON THAT?
MISS GRUNDY, WHAT'S NEW WITH YOUR CLASS?
WHAT COULD BE NEW IN ANCIENT HISTORY?

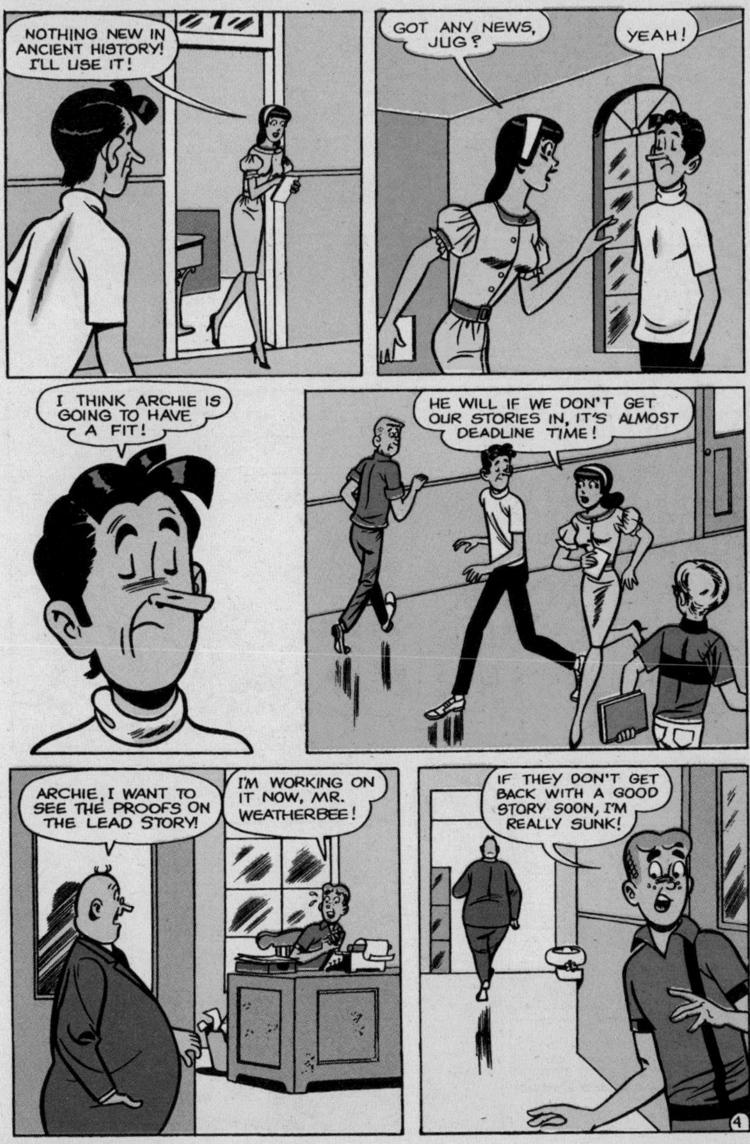
NOTHING NEW IN ANCIENT HISTORY! I'LL USE IT!
GOT ANY NEWS, JUG?
YEAH!
I THINK ARCHIE IS GOING TO HAVE A FIT!
HE WILL IF WE DON'T GET OUR STORIES IN, IT'S ALMOST DEADLINE TIME!
ARCHIE, I WANT TO SEE THE PROOFS ON THE LEAD STORY!
I'M WORKING ON IT NOW, MR. WEATHERBEE!
IF THEY DON'T GET BACK WITH A GOOD STORY SOON, I'M REALLY SUNK!
4

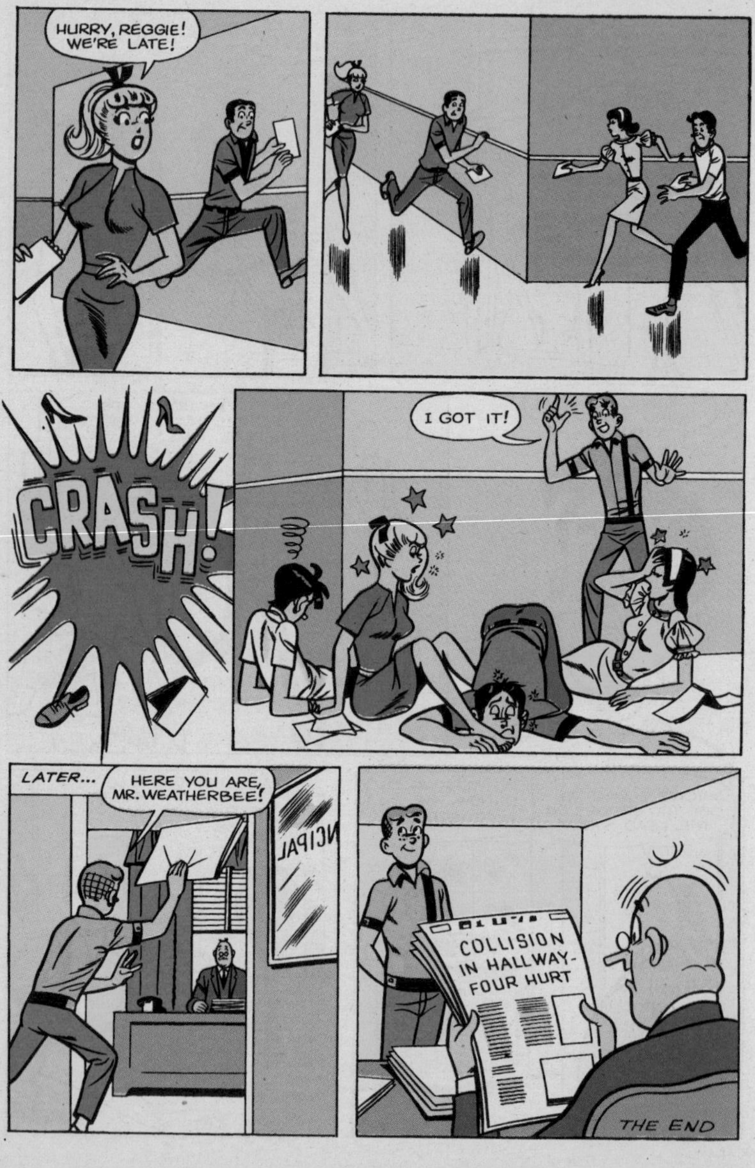
HURRY, REGGIE! WE'RE LATE!
CRASH!
I GOT IT!
LATER...
HERE YOU ARE, MR. WEATHERBEE!
NCIPAL
COLLISION IN HALLWAY- FOUR HURT
THE END

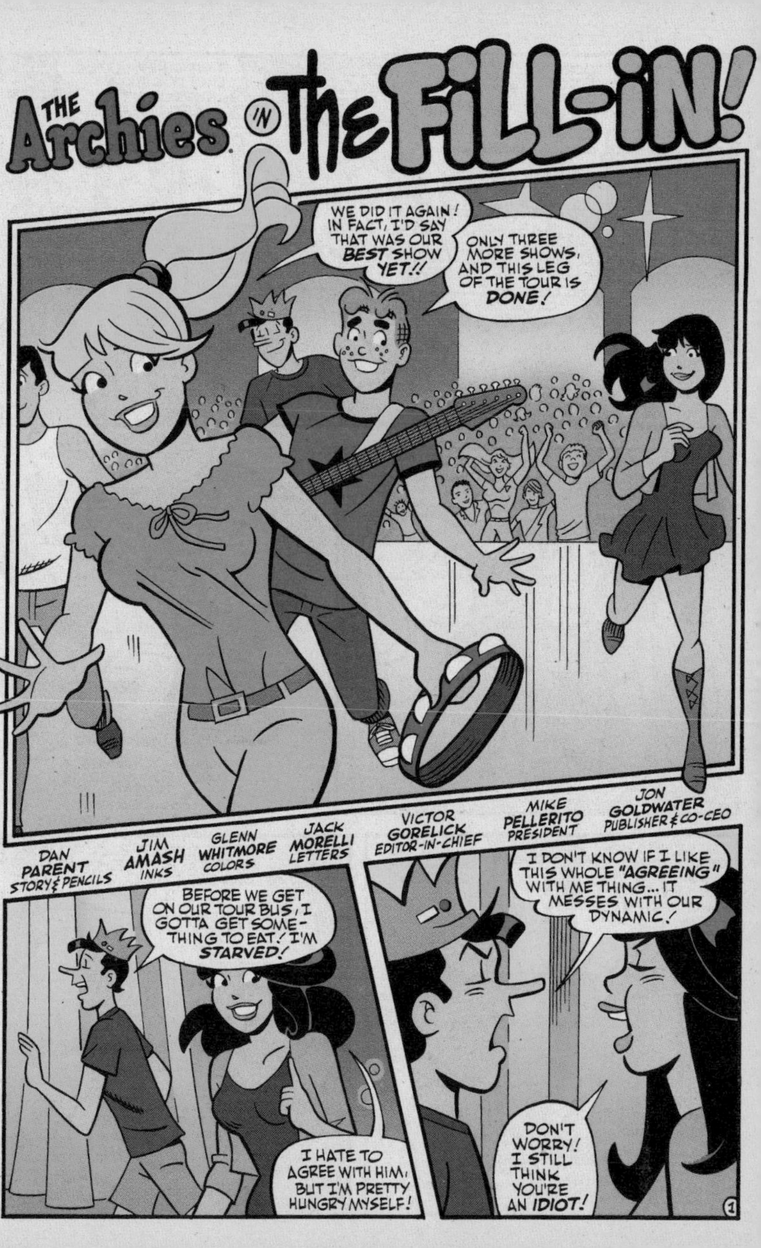
THE Archies IN The FILL-IN!
WE DID IT AGAIN! IN FACT, I'D SAY THAT WAS OUR BEST SHOW YET!!
ONLY THREE MORE SHOWS, AND THIS LEG OF THE TOUR IS DONE!
DAN PARENT STORY & PENCILS
JIM AMASH INKS
GLENN WHITMORE COLORS
JACK MORELLI LETTERS
VICTOR GORELICK EDITOR-IN-CHIEF
MIKE PELLERITO PRESIDENT
JON GOLDWATER PUBLISHER & CO-CEO
BEFORE WE GET ON OUR TOUR BUS, I GOTTA GET SOME-THING TO EAT! I'M STARVED!
I HATE TO AGREE WITH HIM, BUT I'M PRETTY HUNGRY MYSELF!
I DON'T KNOW IF I LIKE THIS WHOLE "AGREEING" WITH ME THING... IT MESSES WITH OUR DYNAMIC!
DON'T WORRY! I STILL THINK YOU'RE AN IDIOT!
1

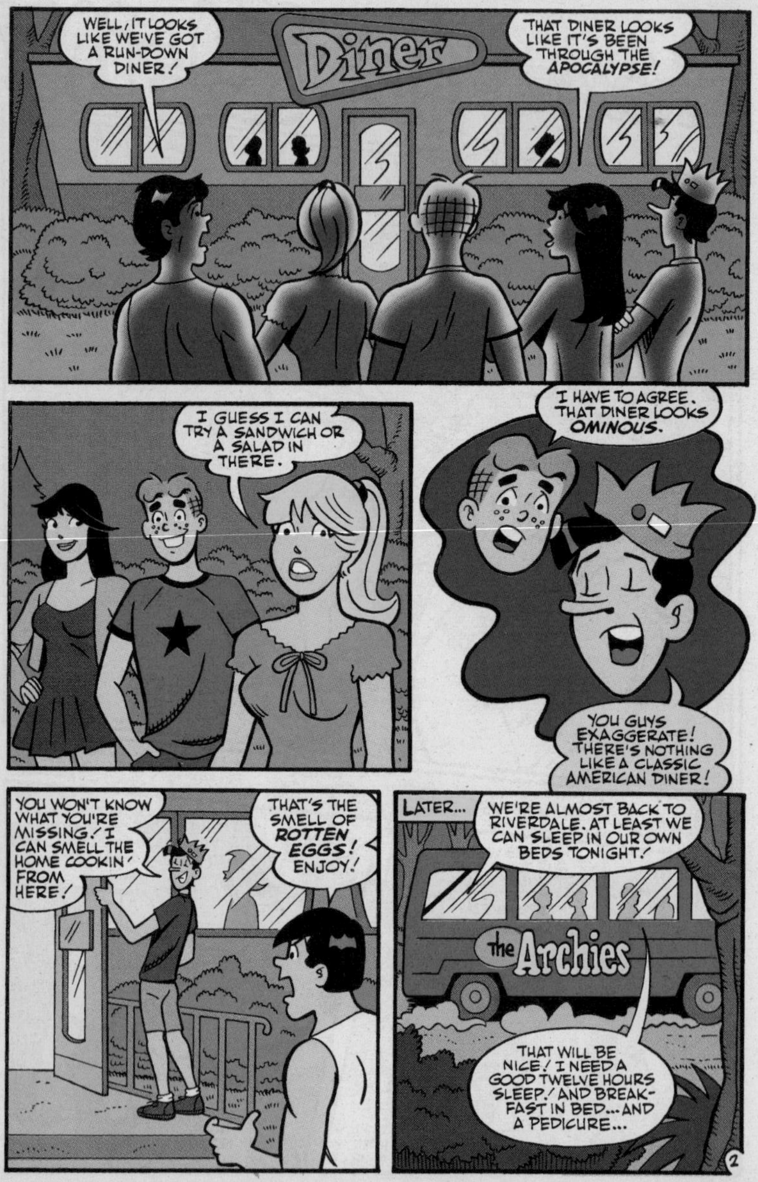

WELL, IT LOOKS LIKE WE'VE GOT A RUN-DOWN DINER!
Diner
THAT DINER LOOKS LIKE IT'S BEEN THROUGH THE APOCALYPSE!
I GUESS I CAN TRY A SANDWICH OR A SALAD IN THERE.
I HAVE TO AGREE. THAT DINER LOOKS OMINOUS.
YOU GUYS EXAGGERATE! THERE'S NOTHING LIKE A CLASSIC AMERICAN DINER!
YOU WON'T KNOW WHAT YOU'RE MISSING! I CAN SMELL THE HOME COOKIN' FROM HERE!
THAT'S THE SMELL OF ROTTEN EGGS! ENJOY!
LATER...
WE'RE ALMOST BACK TO RIVERDALE. AT LEAST WE CAN SLEEP IN OUR OWN BEDS TONIGHT!
the Archies
THAT WILL BE NICE! I NEED A GOOD TWELVE HOURS SLEEP! AND BREAK-FAST IN BED... AND A PEDICURE...

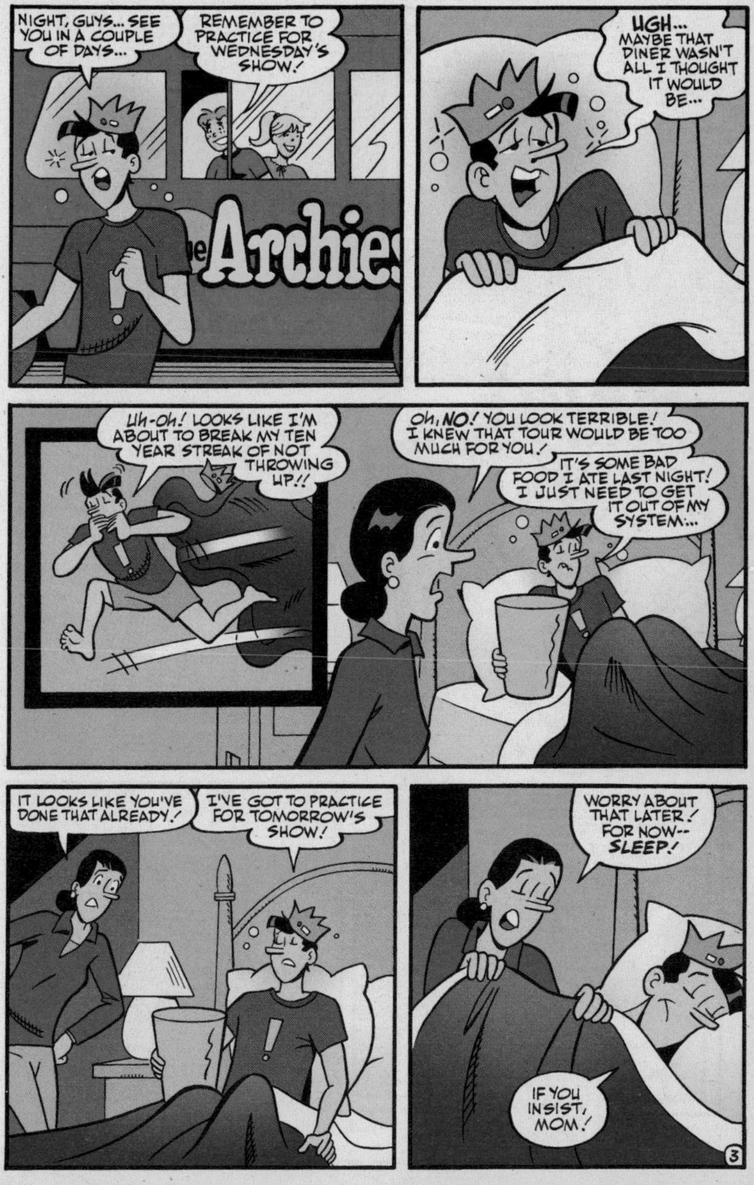
NIGHT, GUYS... SEE YOU IN A COUPLE OF DAYS...
REMEMBER TO PRACTICE FOR WEDNESDAY'S SHOW!
The Archies
UGH... MAYBE THAT DINER WASN'T ALL I THOUGHT IT WOULD BE...
Uh-oh! LOOKS LIKE I'M ABOUT TO BREAK MY TEN YEAR STREAK OF NOT THROWING UP!!
Oh, NO! YOU LOOK TERRIBLE! I KNEW THAT TOUR WOULD BE TOO MUCH FOR YOU!
IT'S SOME BAD FOOD I ATE LAST NIGHT! I JUST NEED TO GET IT OUT OF MY SYSTEM...
IT LOOKS LIKE YOU'VE DONE THAT ALREADY!
I'VE GOT TO PRACTICE FOR TOMORROW'S SHOW!
WORRY ABOUT THAT LATER! FOR NOW-- SLEEP!
IF YOU INSIST, MOM!
3

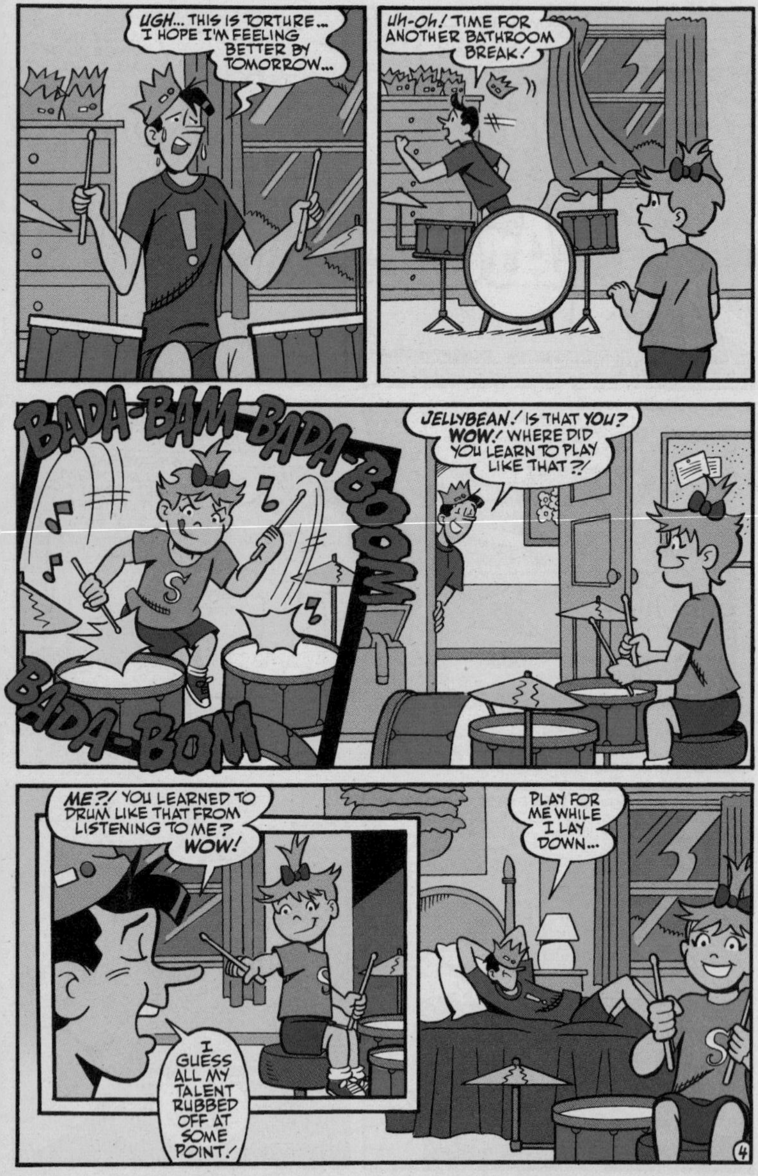

UGH... THIS IS TORTURE... I HOPE I'M FEELING BETTER BY TOMORROW...
UH-OH! TIME FOR ANOTHER BATHROOM BREAK!
BADA-BAM BADA-BOOM
BADA-BOM
JELLYBEAN! IS THAT YOU? WOW! WHERE DID YOU LEARN TO PLAY LIKE THAT?!
ME?! YOU LEARNED TO DRUM LIKE THAT FROM LISTENING TO ME? WOW!
I GUESS ALL MY TALENT RUBBED OFF AT SOME POINT!
PLAY FOR ME WHILE I LAY DOWN...
4

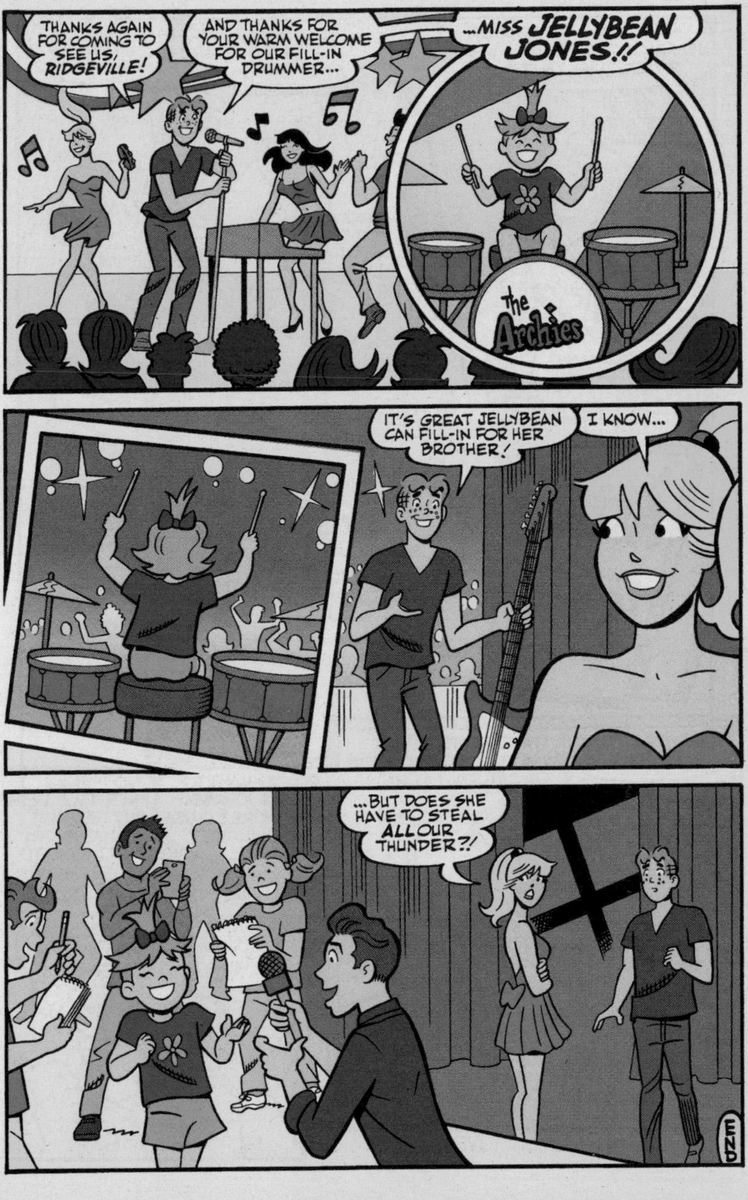
THANKS AGAIN FOR COMING TO SEE US, RIDGEVILLE!
AND THANKS FOR YOUR WARM WELCOME FOR OUR FILL-IN DRUMMER...
...MISS JELLYBEAN JONES!!
The Archies
IT'S GREAT JELLYBEAN CAN FILL-IN FOR HER BROTHER!
I KNOW...
...BUT DOES SHE HAVE TO STEAL ALL OUR THUNDER?!
END

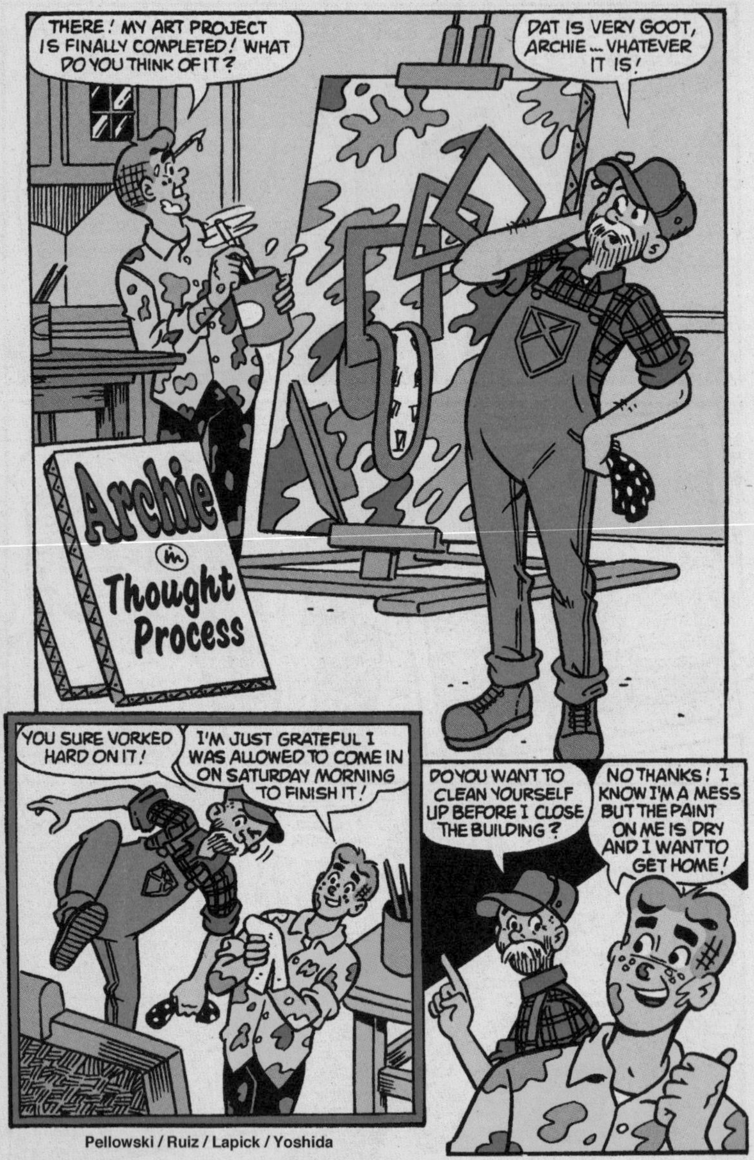
THERE! MY ART PROJECT IS FINALLY COMPLETED! WHAT DO YOU THINK OF IT?
DAT IS VERY GOOT, ARCHIE ... VHATEVER IT IS!
Archie in Thought Process
YOU SURE VORKED HARD ON IT!
I'M JUST GRATEFUL I WAS ALLOWED TO COME IN ON SATURDAY MORNING TO FINISH IT!
DO YOU WANT TO CLEAN YOURSELF UP BEFORE I CLOSE THE BUILDING?
NO THANKS! I KNOW I'M A MESS BUT THE PAINT ON ME IS DRY AND I WANT TO GET HOME!

Pellowski / Ruiz / Lapick / Yoshida

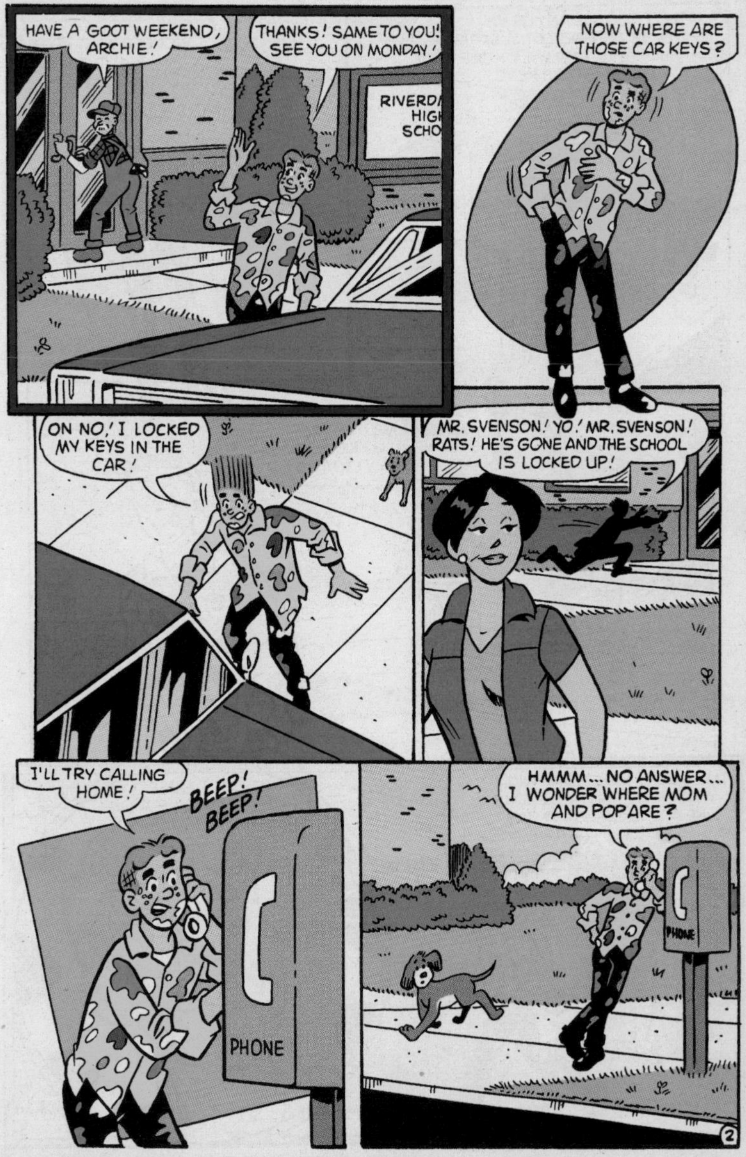
HAVE A GOOT WEEKEND, ARCHIE!
THANKS! SAME TO YOU! SEE YOU ON MONDAY!
RIVERDA HIGH SCHO
NOW WHERE ARE THOSE CAR KEYS?
ON NO! I LOCKED MY KEYS IN THE CAR!
MR. SVENSON! YO! MR. SVENSON! RATS! HE'S GONE AND THE SCHOOL IS LOCKED UP!
I'LL TRY CALLING HOME!
BEEP! BEEP!
PHONE
HMMM... NO ANSWER... I WONDER WHERE MOM AND POP ARE?
PHONE
2

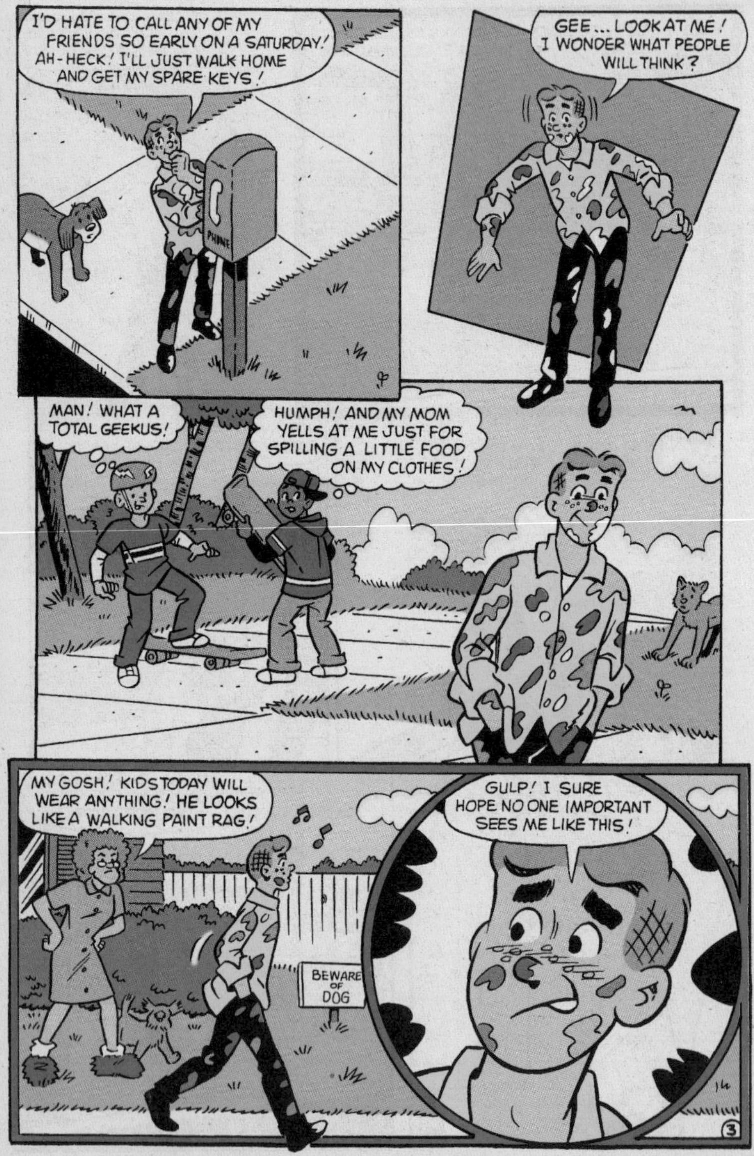

I'D HATE TO CALL ANY OF MY FRIENDS SO EARLY ON A SATURDAY! AH-HECK! I'LL JUST WALK HOME AND GET MY SPARE KEYS!
PHONE
GEE... LOOK AT ME! I WONDER WHAT PEOPLE WILL THINK?
MAN! WHAT A TOTAL GEEKUS!
HUMPH! AND MY MOM YELLS AT ME JUST FOR SPILLING A LITTLE FOOD ON MY CLOTHES!
MY GOSH! KIDS TODAY WILL WEAR ANYTHING! HE LOOKS LIKE A WALKING PAINT RAG!
BEWARE OF DOG
GULP! I SURE HOPE NO ONE IMPORTANT SEES ME LIKE THIS!
3

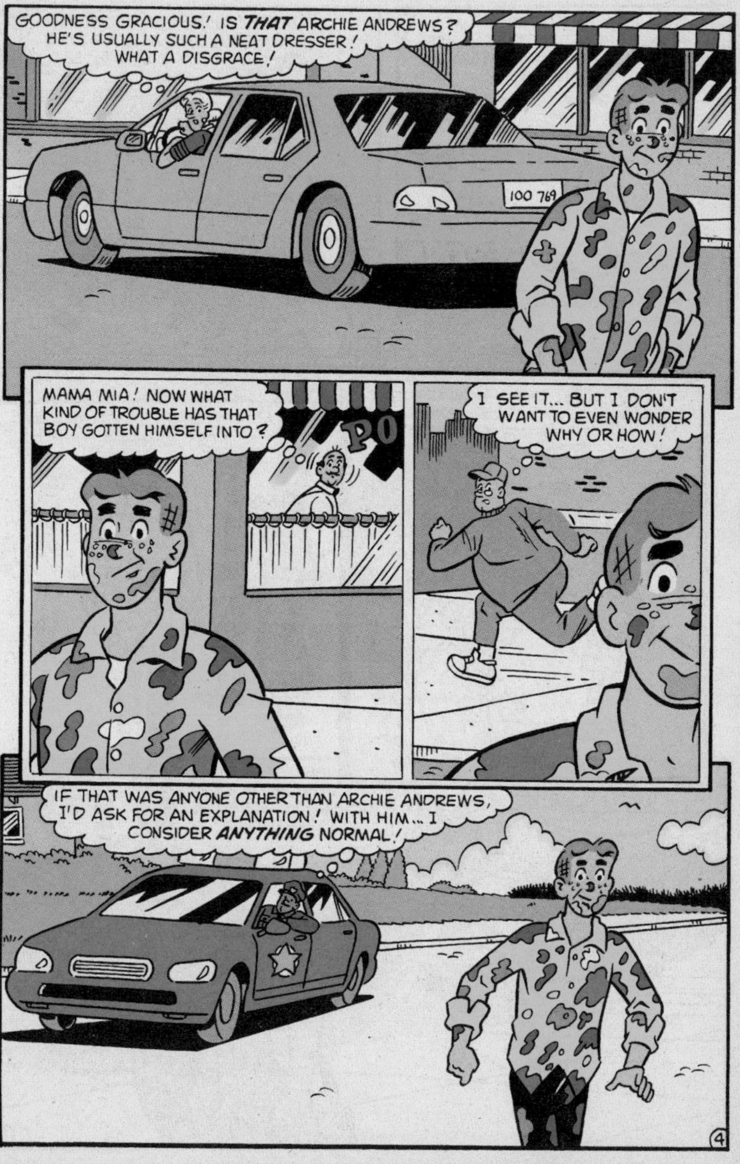
GOODNESS GRACIOUS! IS THAT ARCHIE ANDREWS? HE'S USUALLY SUCH A NEAT DRESSER! WHAT A DISGRACE!
100 769
MAMA MIA! NOW WHAT KIND OF TROUBLE HAS THAT BOY GOTTEN HIMSELF INTO?
PO
I SEE IT... BUT I DON'T WANT TO EVEN WONDER WHY OR HOW!
IF THAT WAS ANYONE OTHER THAN ARCHIE ANDREWS, I'D ASK FOR AN EXPLANATION! WITH HIM... I CONSIDER ANYTHING NORMAL!
4

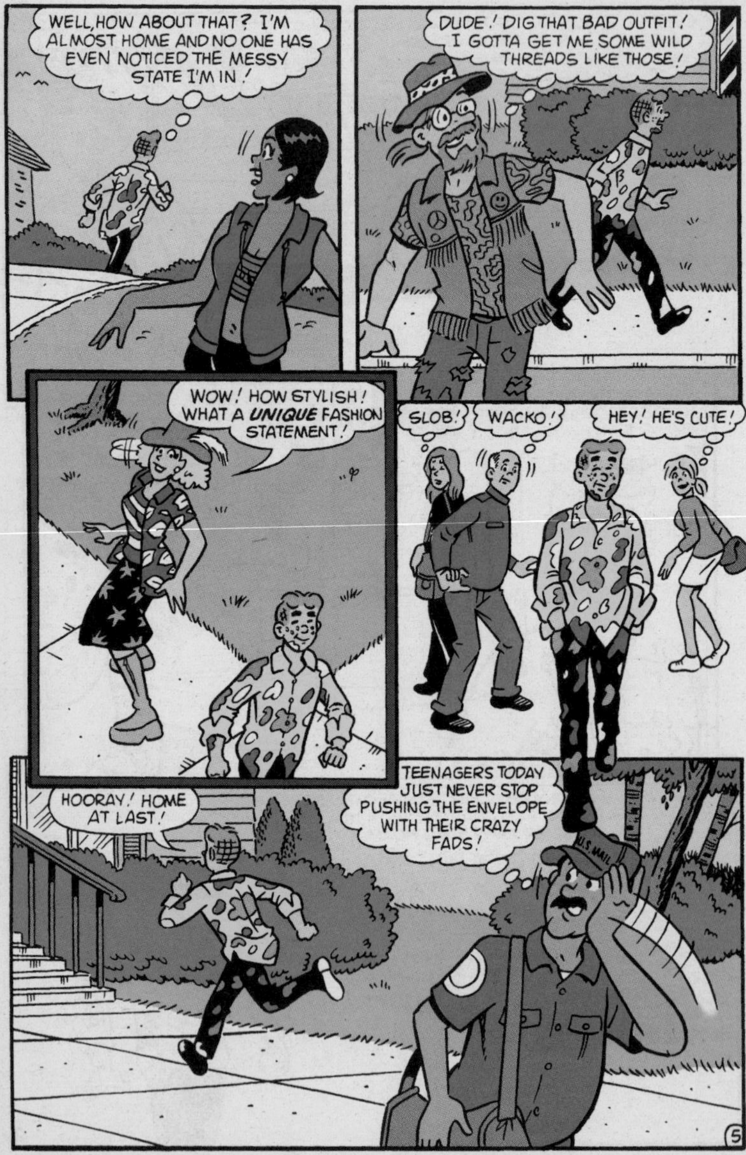
WELL, HOW ABOUT THAT? I'M ALMOST HOME AND NO ONE HAS EVEN NOTICED THE MESSY STATE I'M IN!
DUDE! DIG THAT BAD OUTFIT! I GOTTA GET ME SOME WILD THREADS LIKE THOSE!
WOW! HOW STYLISH! WHAT A *UNIQUE* FASHION STATEMENT!
SLOB!
WACKO!
HEY! HE'S CUTE!
HOORAY! HOME AT LAST!
TEENAGERS TODAY JUST NEVER STOP PUSHING THE ENVELOPE WITH THEIR CRAZY FADS!
U.S. MAIL
5

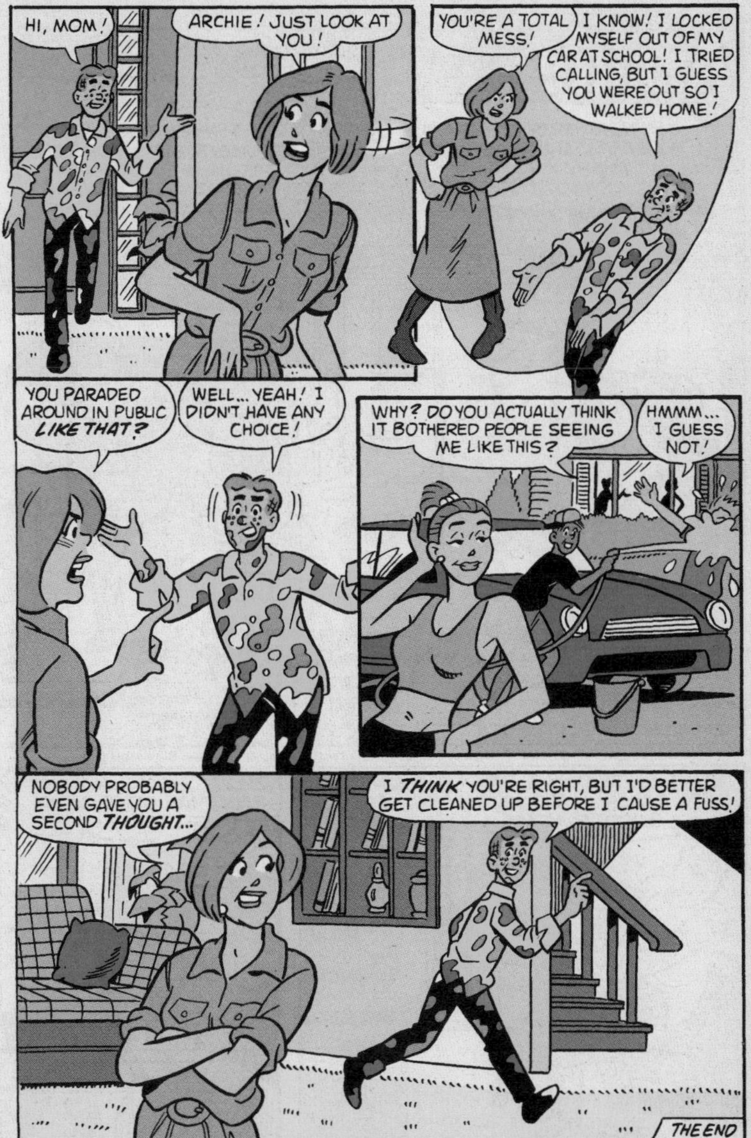
HI, MOM!
ARCHIE! JUST LOOK AT YOU!
YOU'RE A TOTAL MESS!
I KNOW! I LOCKED MYSELF OUT OF MY CAR AT SCHOOL! I TRIED CALLING, BUT I GUESS YOU WERE OUT SO I WALKED HOME!
YOU PARADED AROUND IN PUBLIC LIKE THAT?
WELL... YEAH! I DIDN'T HAVE ANY CHOICE!
WHY? DO YOU ACTUALLY THINK IT BOTHERED PEOPLE SEEING ME LIKE THIS?
HMMM... I GUESS NOT!
NOBODY PROBABLY EVEN GAVE YOU A SECOND THOUGHT...
I THINK YOU'RE RIGHT, BUT I'D BETTER GET CLEANED UP BEFORE I CAUSE A FUSS!
THE END

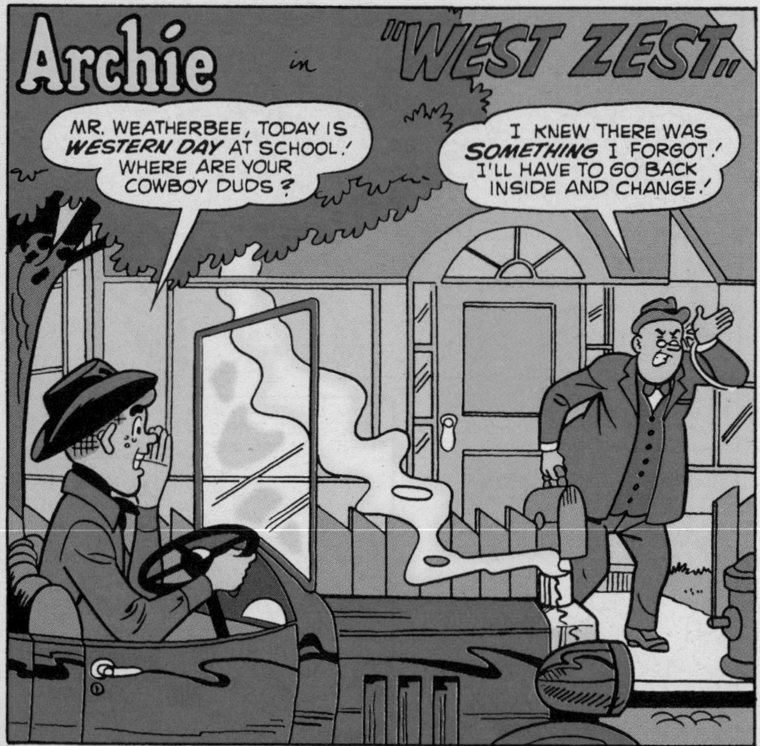
Archie in
"WEST ZEST"
MR. WEATHERBEE, TODAY IS WESTERN DAY AT SCHOOL! WHERE ARE YOUR COWBOY DUDS?
I KNEW THERE WAS SOMETHING I FORGOT! I'LL HAVE TO GO BACK INSIDE AND CHANGE!

Script: George Gladir / Pencils: Bob Bolling / Inks: Rudy Lapick / Letters: Bill Yoshida

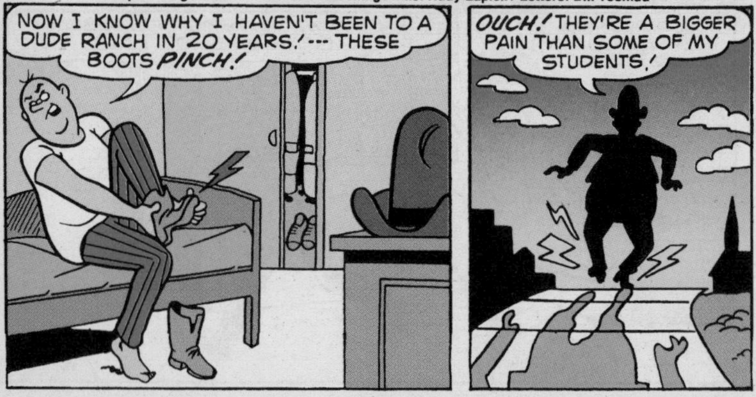
NOW I KNOW WHY I HAVEN'T BEEN TO A DUDE RANCH IN 20 YEARS! --- THESE BOOTS PINCH!
OUCH! THEY'RE A BIGGER PAIN THAN SOME OF MY STUDENTS!

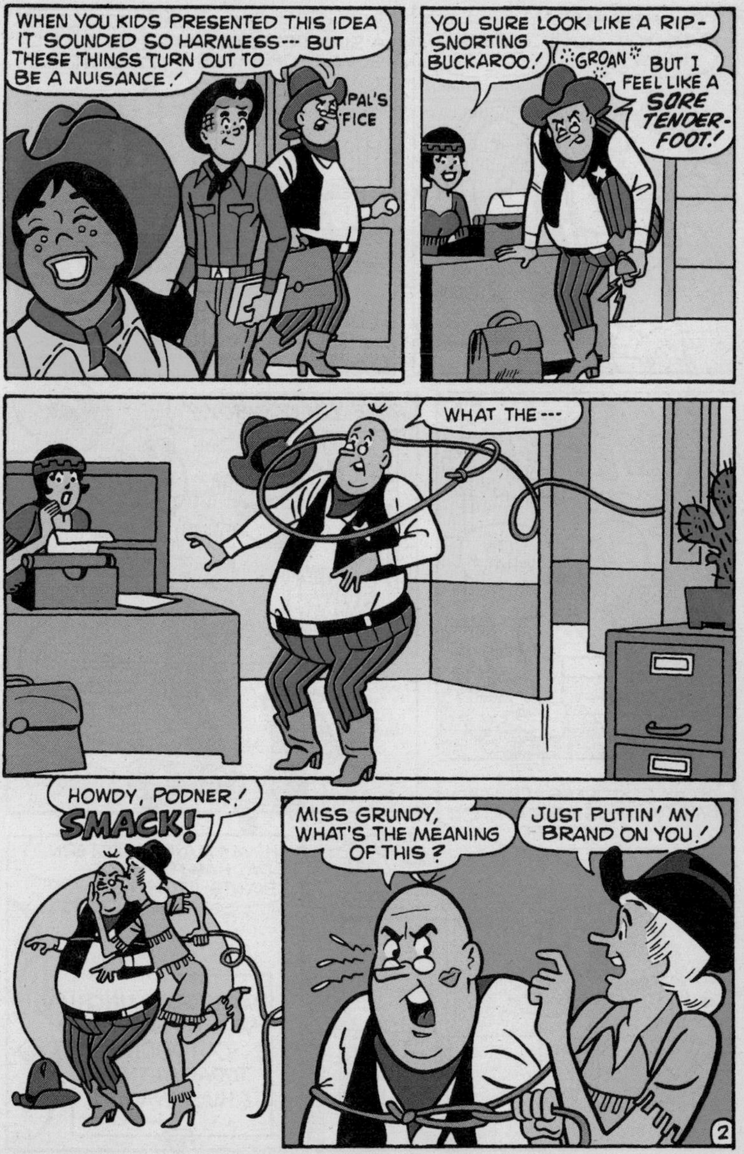
WHEN YOU KIDS PRESENTED THIS IDEA IT SOUNDED SO HARMLESS--- BUT THESE THINGS TURN OUT TO BE A NUISANCE!
PAL'S FICE
YOU SURE LOOK LIKE A RIP-SNORTING BUCKAROO!
GROAN
BUT I FEEL LIKE A SORE TENDER-FOOT!
WHAT THE---
HOWDY, PODNER!
SMACK!
MISS GRUNDY, WHAT'S THE MEANING OF THIS?
JUST PUTTIN' MY BRAND ON YOU!
2

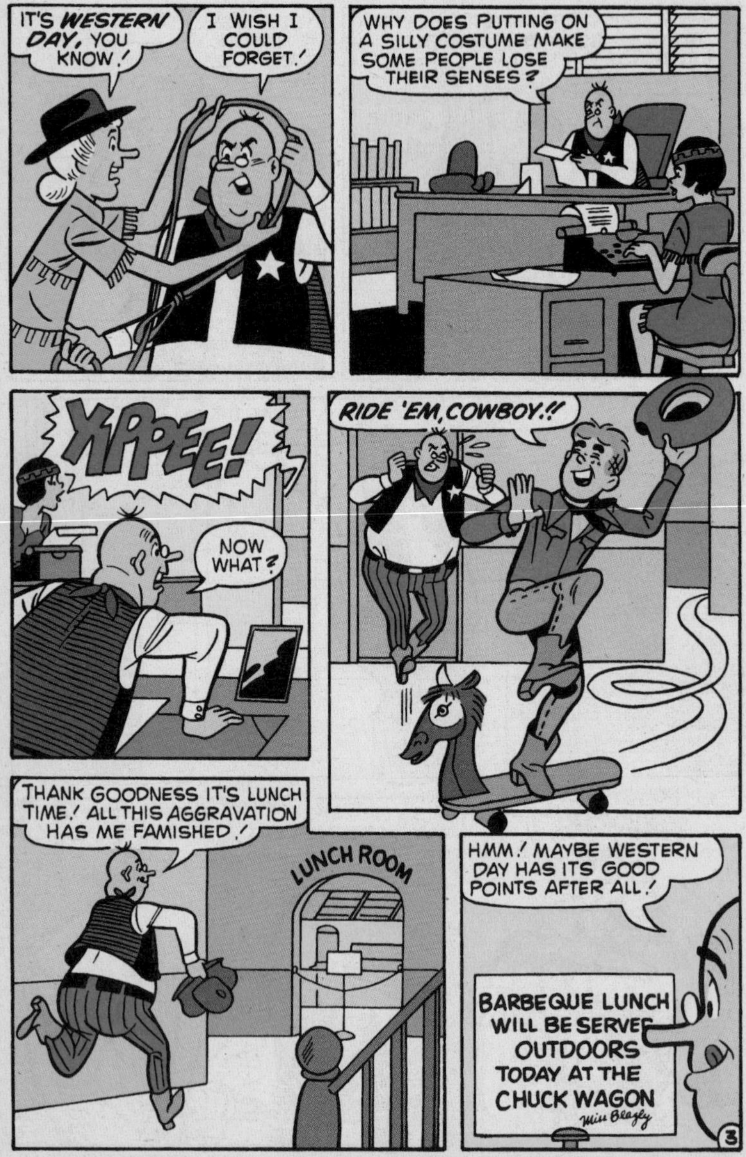

IT'S WESTERN DAY, YOU KNOW!
I WISH I COULD FORGET!
WHY DOES PUTTING ON A SILLY COSTUME MAKE SOME PEOPLE LOSE THEIR SENSES?
YIPPEE!
NOW WHAT?
RIDE 'EM, COWBOY!!
THANK GOODNESS IT'S LUNCH TIME! ALL THIS AGGRAVATION HAS ME FAMISHED!
LUNCH ROOM
HMM! MAYBE WESTERN DAY HAS ITS GOOD POINTS AFTER ALL!
BARBEQUE LUNCH WILL BE SERVED OUTDOORS TODAY AT THE CHUCK WAGON
Miss Beazly
3

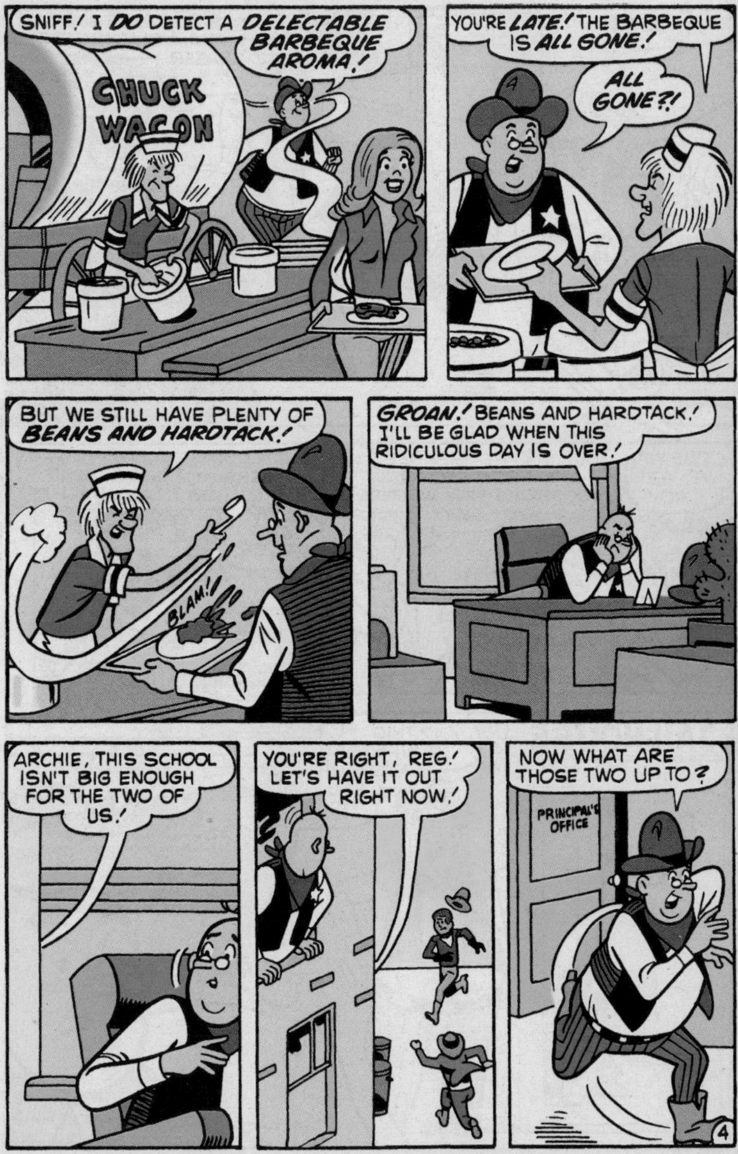
SNIFF! I DO DETECT A DELECTABLE BARBEQUE AROMA!
CHUCK WAGON
YOU'RE LATE! THE BARBEQUE IS ALL GONE!
ALL GONE?!
BUT WE STILL HAVE PLENTY OF BEANS AND HARDTACK!
BLAM!
GROAN! BEANS AND HARDTACK! I'LL BE GLAD WHEN THIS RIDICULOUS DAY IS OVER!
ARCHIE, THIS SCHOOL ISN'T BIG ENOUGH FOR THE TWO OF US!
YOU'RE RIGHT, REG! LET'S HAVE IT OUT RIGHT NOW!
NOW WHAT ARE THOSE TWO UP TO?
PRINCIPAL'S OFFICE

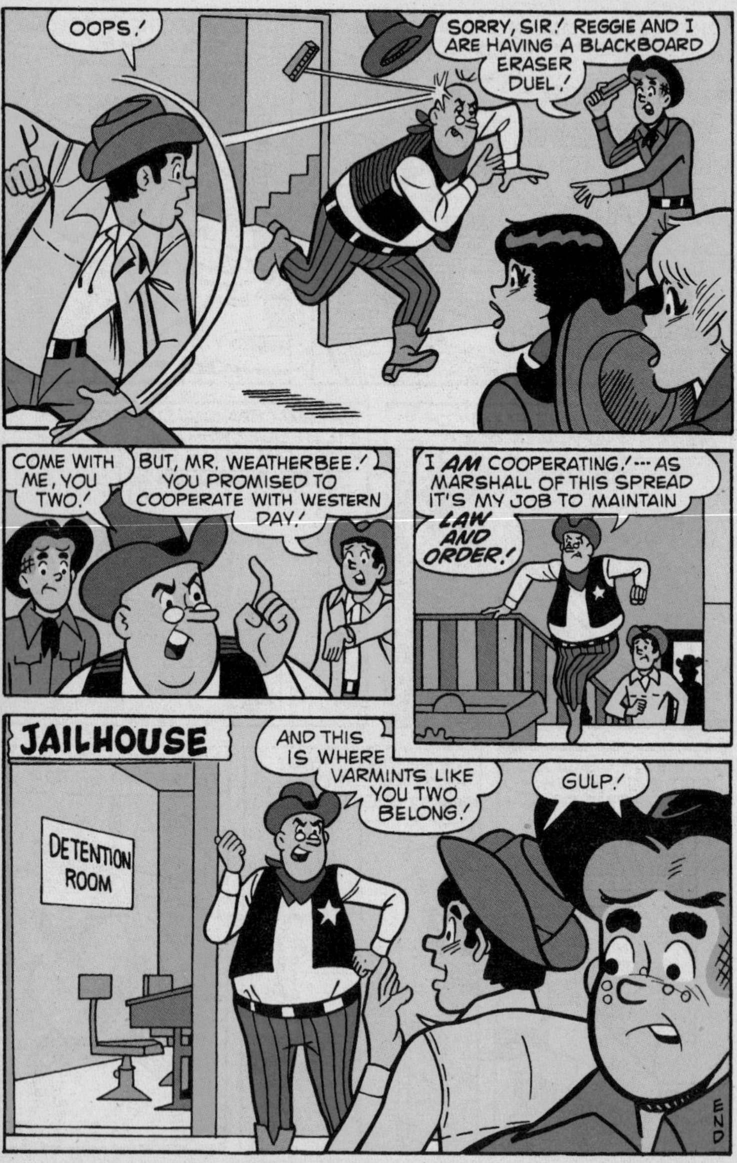
OOPS.!
SORRY, SIR.! REGGIE AND I ARE HAVING A BLACKBOARD ERASER DUEL.!
COME WITH ME, YOU TWO.!
BUT, MR. WEATHERBEE.! YOU PROMISED TO COOPERATE WITH WESTERN DAY.!
I AM COOPERATING.! --- AS MARSHALL OF THIS SPREAD IT'S MY JOB TO MAINTAIN LAW AND ORDER.!
JAILHOUSE
DETENTION ROOM
AND THIS IS WHERE VARMINTS LIKE YOU TWO BELONG.!
GULP.!
END

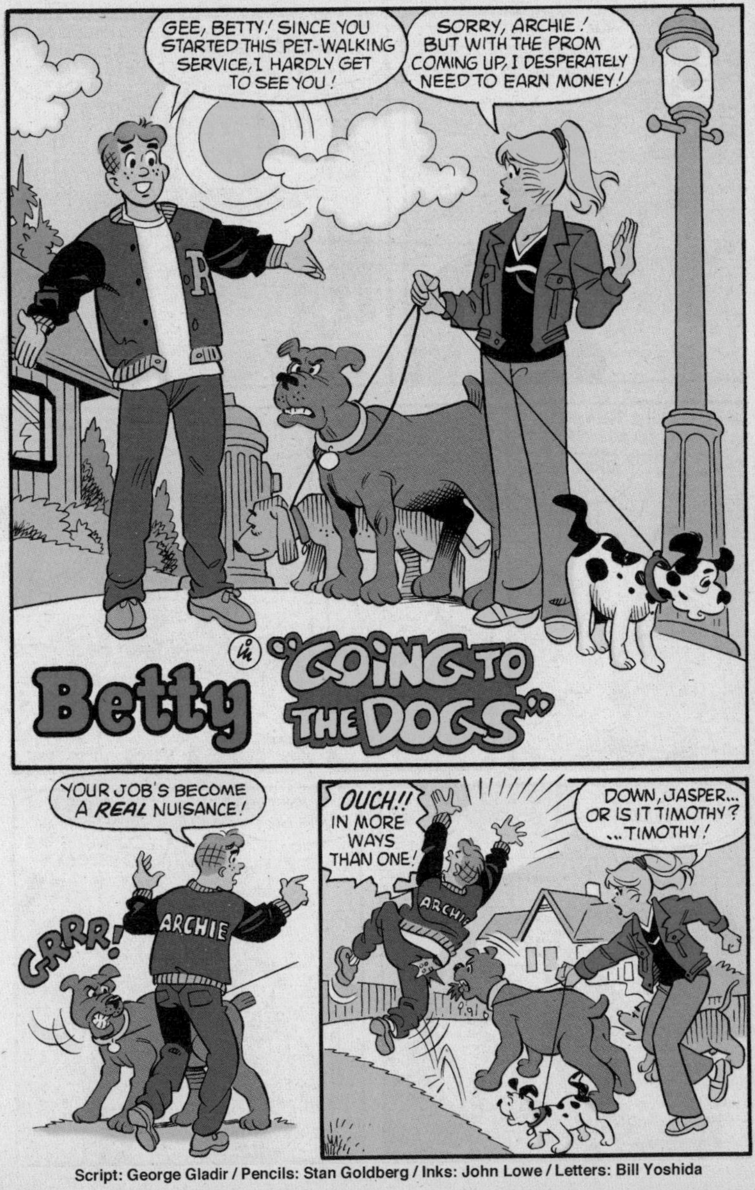
GEE, BETTY! SINCE YOU STARTED THIS PET-WALKING SERVICE, I HARDLY GET TO SEE YOU!
SORRY, ARCHIE! BUT WITH THE PROM COMING UP, I DESPERATELY NEED TO EARN MONEY!
Betty in "GOING TO THE DOGS"
YOUR JOB'S BECOME A REAL NUISANCE!
ARCHIE
GRRRR!
OUCH!! IN MORE WAYS THAN ONE!
ARCHIE
DOWN, JASPER... OR IS IT TIMOTHY? ...TIMOTHY!

Script: George Gladir / Pencils: Stan Goldberg / Inks: John Lowe / Letters: Bill Yoshida

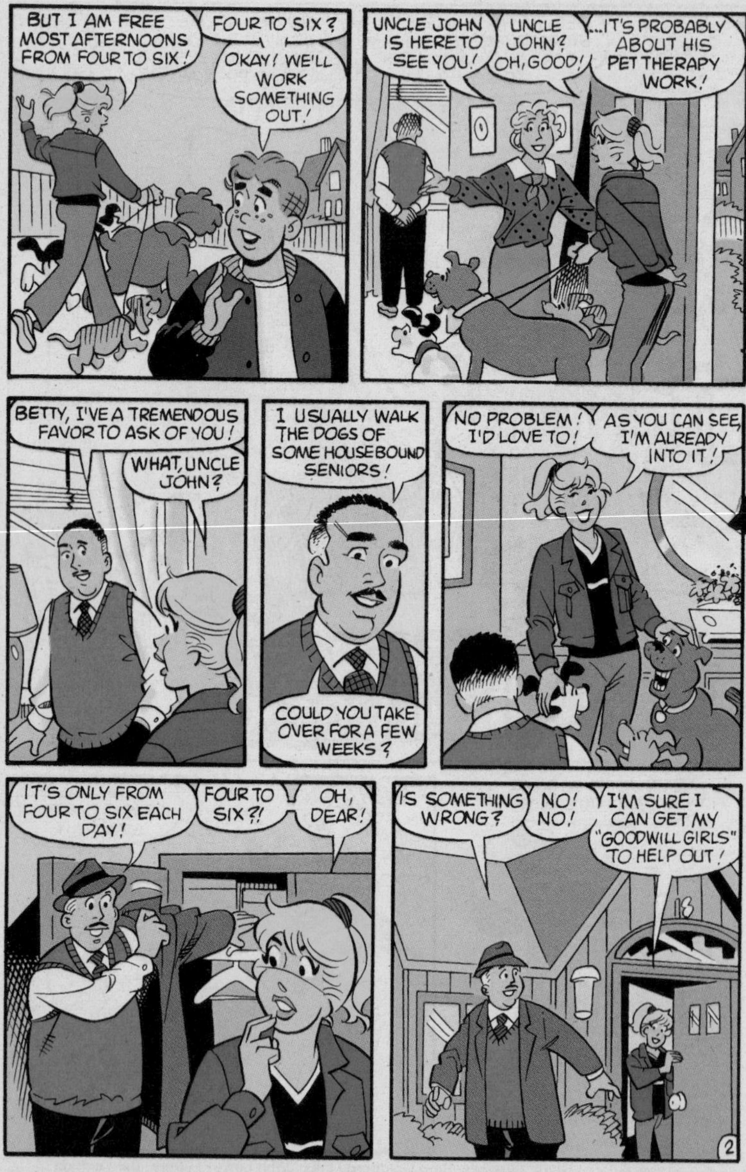
BUT I AM FREE MOST AFTERNOONS FROM FOUR TO SIX!
FOUR TO SIX?
OKAY! WE'LL WORK SOMETHING OUT!
UNCLE JOHN IS HERE TO SEE YOU!
UNCLE JOHN? OH, GOOD!
...IT'S PROBABLY ABOUT HIS PET THERAPY WORK!
BETTY, I'VE A TREMENDOUS FAVOR TO ASK OF YOU!
WHAT, UNCLE JOHN?
I USUALLY WALK THE DOGS OF SOME HOUSEBOUND SENIORS!
COULD YOU TAKE OVER FOR A FEW WEEKS?
NO PROBLEM! I'D LOVE TO!
AS YOU CAN SEE, I'M ALREADY INTO IT!
IT'S ONLY FROM FOUR TO SIX EACH DAY!
FOUR TO SIX?!
OH, DEAR!
IS SOMETHING WRONG?
NO! NO!
I'M SURE I CAN GET MY "GOODWILL GIRLS" TO HELP OUT!
18
2

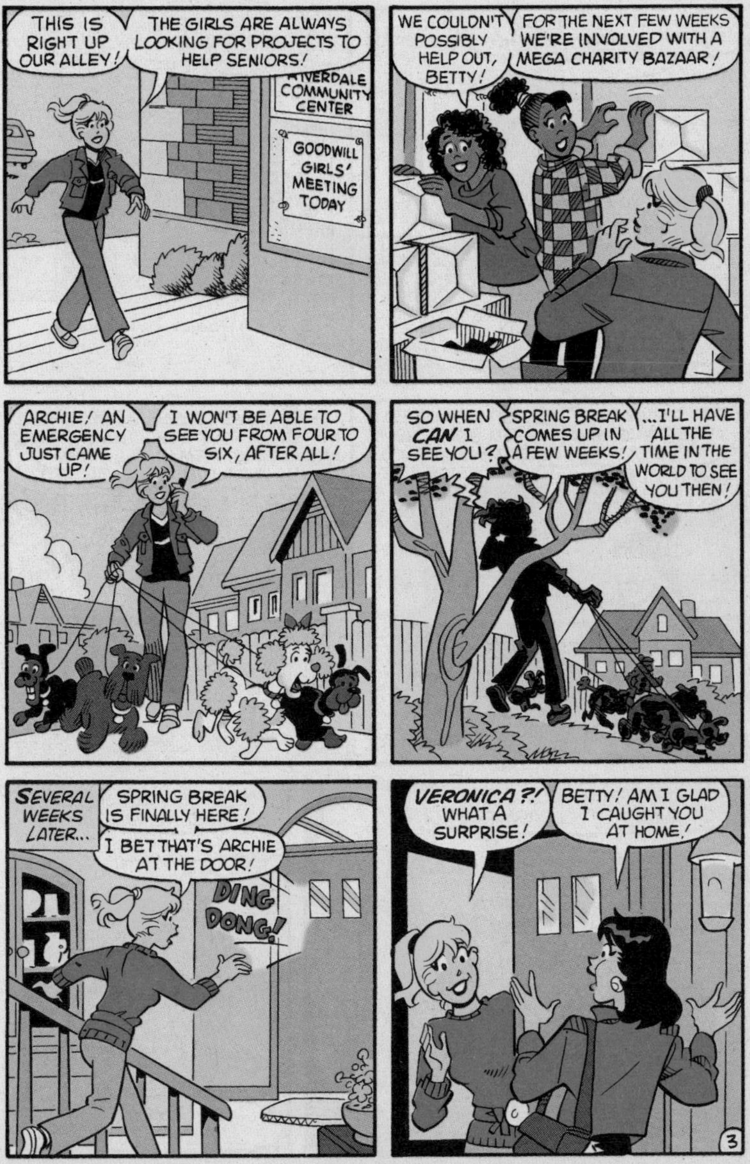
THIS IS RIGHT UP OUR ALLEY!
THE GIRLS ARE ALWAYS LOOKING FOR PROJECTS TO HELP SENIORS!
COMMUNITY CENTER
GOODWILL GIRLS' MEETING TODAY
WE COULDN'T POSSIBLY HELP OUT, BETTY!
FOR THE NEXT FEW WEEKS WE'RE INVOLVED WITH A MEGA CHARITY BAZAAR!
ARCHIE! AN EMERGENCY JUST CAME UP!
I WON'T BE ABLE TO SEE YOU FROM FOUR TO SIX, AFTER ALL!
SO WHEN CAN I SEE YOU?
SPRING BREAK COMES UP IN A FEW WEEKS!
...I'LL HAVE ALL THE TIME IN THE WORLD TO SEE YOU THEN!
SEVERAL WEEKS LATER...
SPRING BREAK IS FINALLY HERE!
I BET THAT'S ARCHIE AT THE DOOR!
DING DONG!
VERONICA?! WHAT A SURPRISE!
BETTY! AM I GLAD I CAUGHT YOU AT HOME!
3

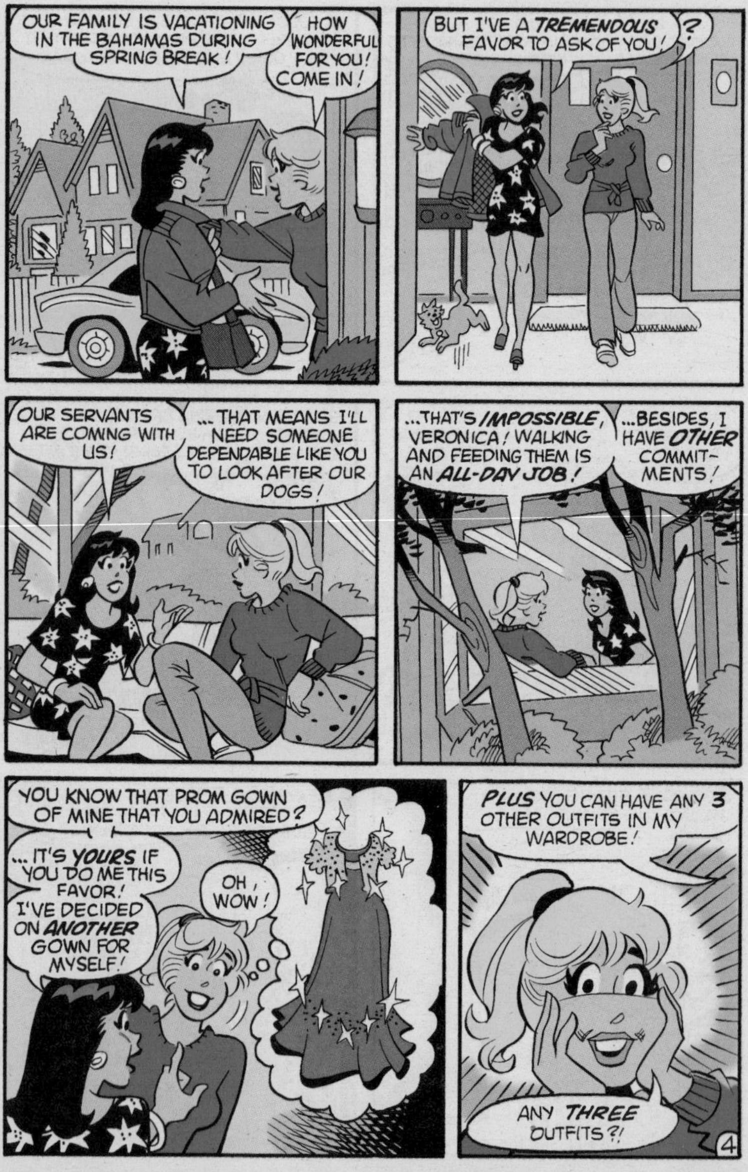
OUR FAMILY IS VACATIONING IN THE BAHAMAS DURING SPRING BREAK!
HOW WONDERFUL FOR YOU! COME IN!
BUT I'VE A TREMENDOUS FAVOR TO ASK OF YOU!
?
OUR SERVANTS ARE COMING WITH US!
...THAT MEANS I'LL NEED SOMEONE DEPENDABLE LIKE YOU TO LOOK AFTER OUR DOGS!
...THAT'S IMPOSSIBLE, VERONICA! WALKING AND FEEDING THEM IS AN ALL-DAY JOB!
...BESIDES, I HAVE OTHER COMMIT-MENTS!
YOU KNOW THAT PROM GOWN OF MINE THAT YOU ADMIRED?
...IT'S YOURS IF YOU DO ME THIS FAVOR! I'VE DECIDED ON ANOTHER GOWN FOR MYSELF!
OH, WOW!
PLUS YOU CAN HAVE ANY 3 OTHER OUTFITS IN MY WARDROBE!
ANY THREE OUTFITS?!

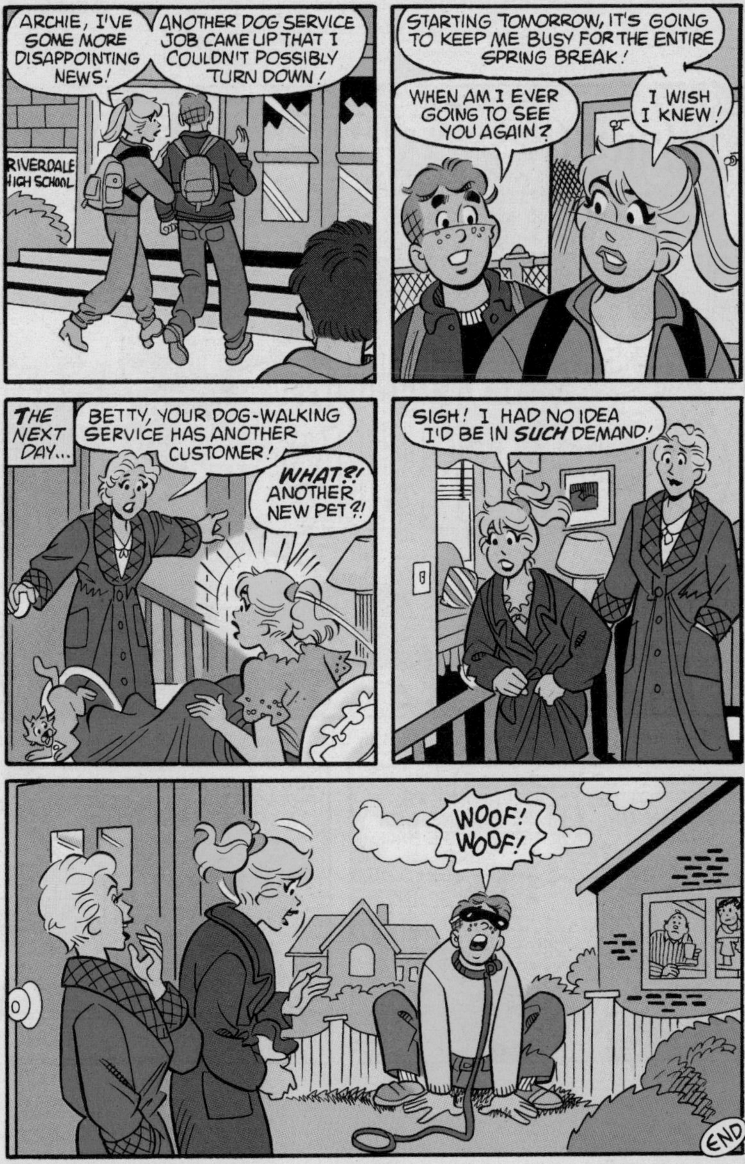

ARCHIE, I'VE SOME MORE DISAPPOINTING NEWS!
ANOTHER DOG SERVICE JOB CAME UP THAT I COULDN'T POSSIBLY TURN DOWN!
RIVERDALE HIGH SCHOOL
STARTING TOMORROW, IT'S GOING TO KEEP ME BUSY FOR THE ENTIRE SPRING BREAK!
WHEN AM I EVER GOING TO SEE YOU AGAIN?
I WISH I KNEW!
THE NEXT DAY...
BETTY, YOUR DOG-WALKING SERVICE HAS ANOTHER CUSTOMER!
WHAT?! ANOTHER NEW PET?!
SIGH! I HAD NO IDEA I'D BE IN SUCH DEMAND!
WOOF! WOOF!
END

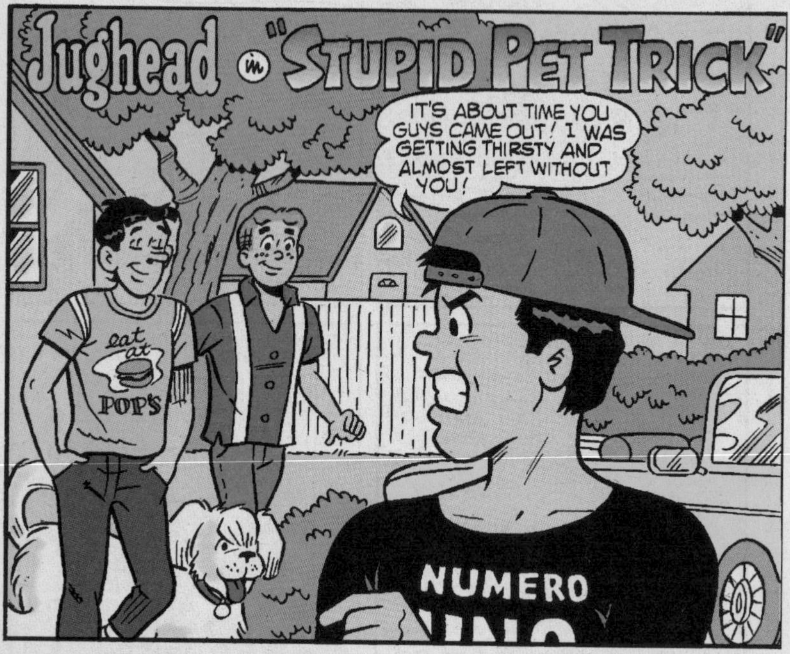
Jughead in "STUPID PET TRICK"
IT'S ABOUT TIME YOU GUYS CAME OUT! I WAS GETTING THIRSTY AND ALMOST LEFT WITHOUT YOU!
eat at POP'S
NUMERO

Script: Mike Pellowski / Pencils: Dan Parent / Inks: Rudy Lapick / Letters: Bill Yoshida / Colors: Frank Gagliardo

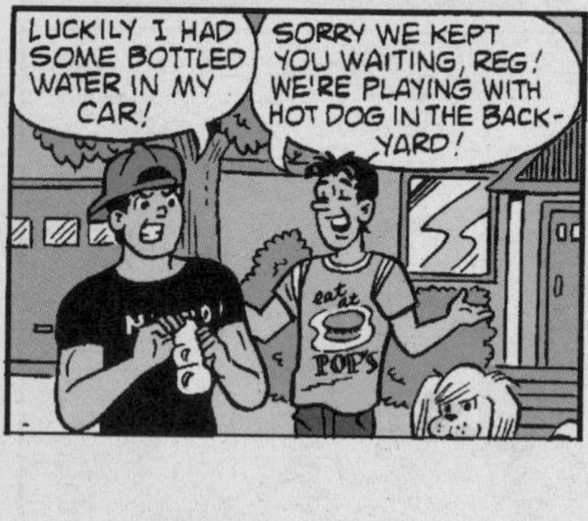
LUCKILY I HAD SOME BOTTLED WATER IN MY CAR!
SORRY WE KEPT YOU WAITING, REG! WE'RE PLAYING WITH HOT DOG IN THE BACK-YARD!
eat at POP'S

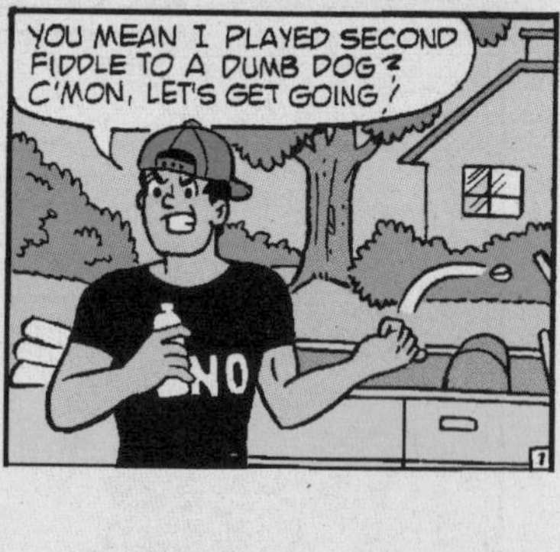
YOU MEAN I PLAYED SECOND FIDDLE TO A DUMB DOG? C'MON, LET'S GET GOING!
1

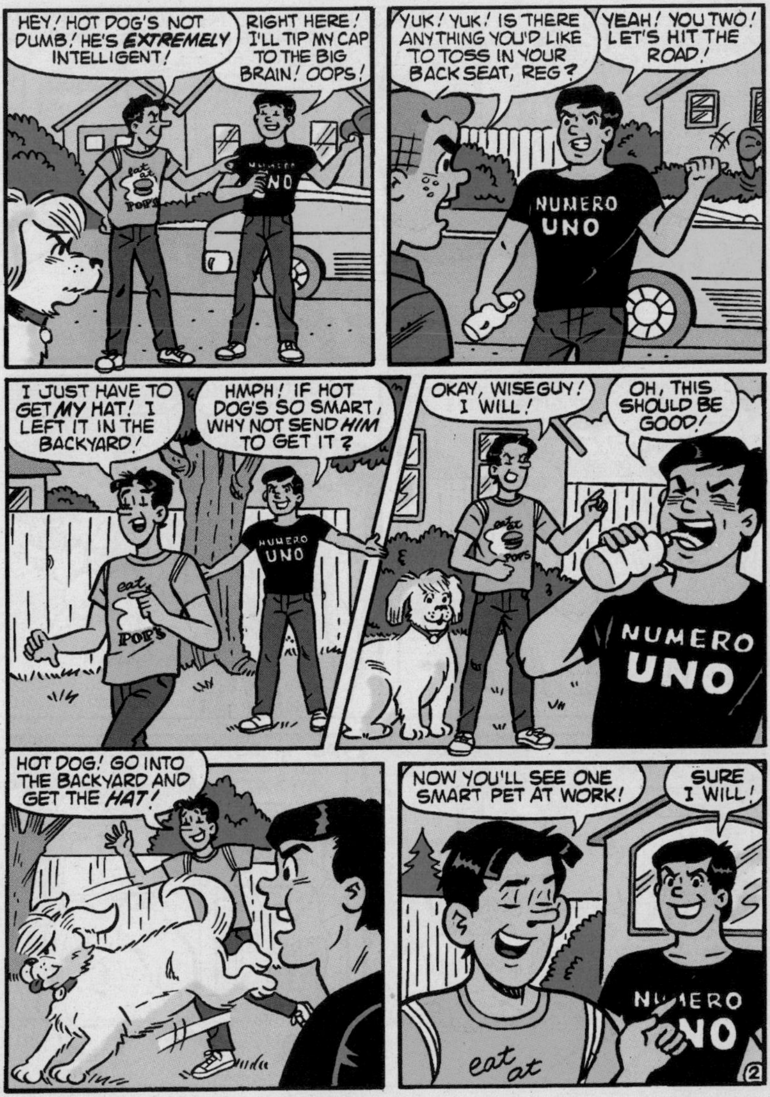
HEY! HOT DOG'S NOT DUMB! HE'S EXTREMELY INTELLIGENT!
RIGHT HERE! I'LL TIP MY CAP TO THE BIG BRAIN! OOPS!
NUMERO UNO
eat at POP'S
YUK! YUK! IS THERE ANYTHING YOU'D LIKE TO TOSS IN YOUR BACK SEAT, REG?
YEAH! YOU TWO! LET'S HIT THE ROAD!
NUMERO UNO
I JUST HAVE TO GET MY HAT! I LEFT IT IN THE BACKYARD!
HMPH! IF HOT DOG'S SO SMART, WHY NOT SEND HIM TO GET IT?
OKAY, WISEGUY! I WILL!
OH, THIS SHOULD BE GOOD!
NUMERO UNO
HOT DOG! GO INTO THE BACKYARD AND GET THE HAT!
NOW YOU'LL SEE ONE SMART PET AT WORK!
SURE I WILL!
2

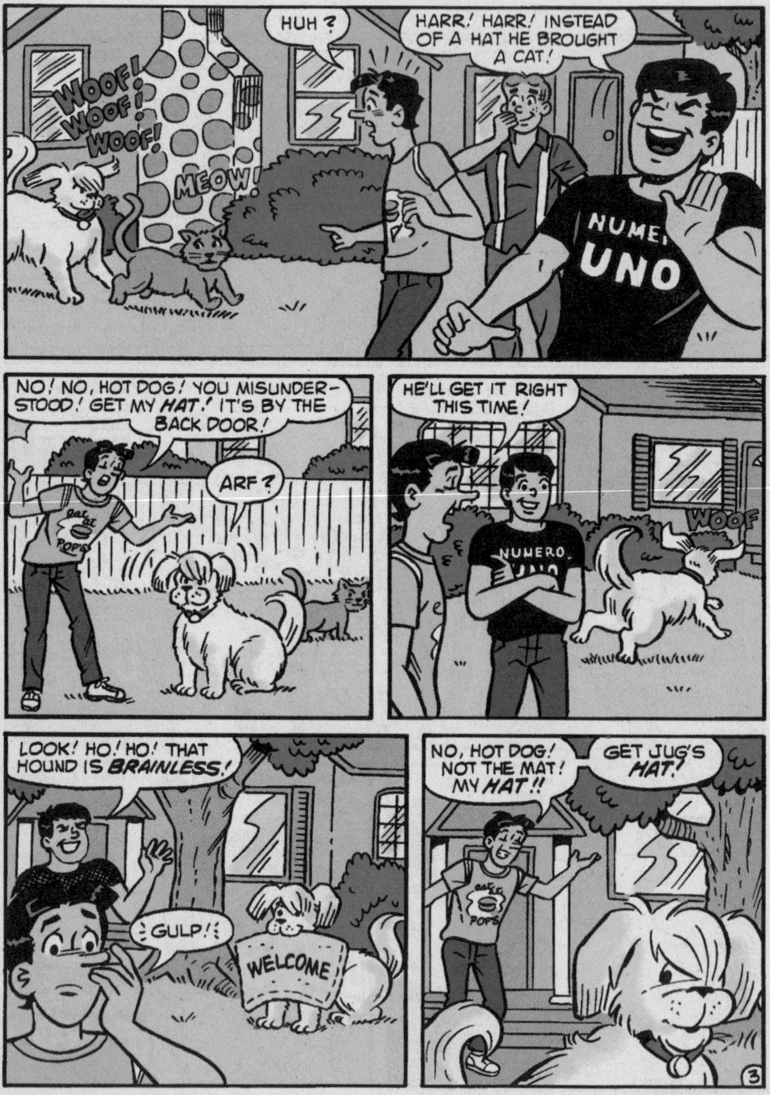

WOOF! WOOF! WOOF!
MEOW!
HUH ?
HARR! HARR! INSTEAD OF A HAT HE BROUGHT A CAT!
NUMERO UNO
NO! NO, HOT DOG! YOU MISUNDERSTOOD! GET MY HAT! IT'S BY THE BACK DOOR!
ARF ?
HE'LL GET IT RIGHT THIS TIME!
NUMERO UNO
WOOF
LOOK! HO! HO! THAT HOUND IS BRAINLESS!
GULP!
WELCOME
NO, HOT DOG! NOT THE MAT! MY HAT!!
GET JUG'S HAT!
3

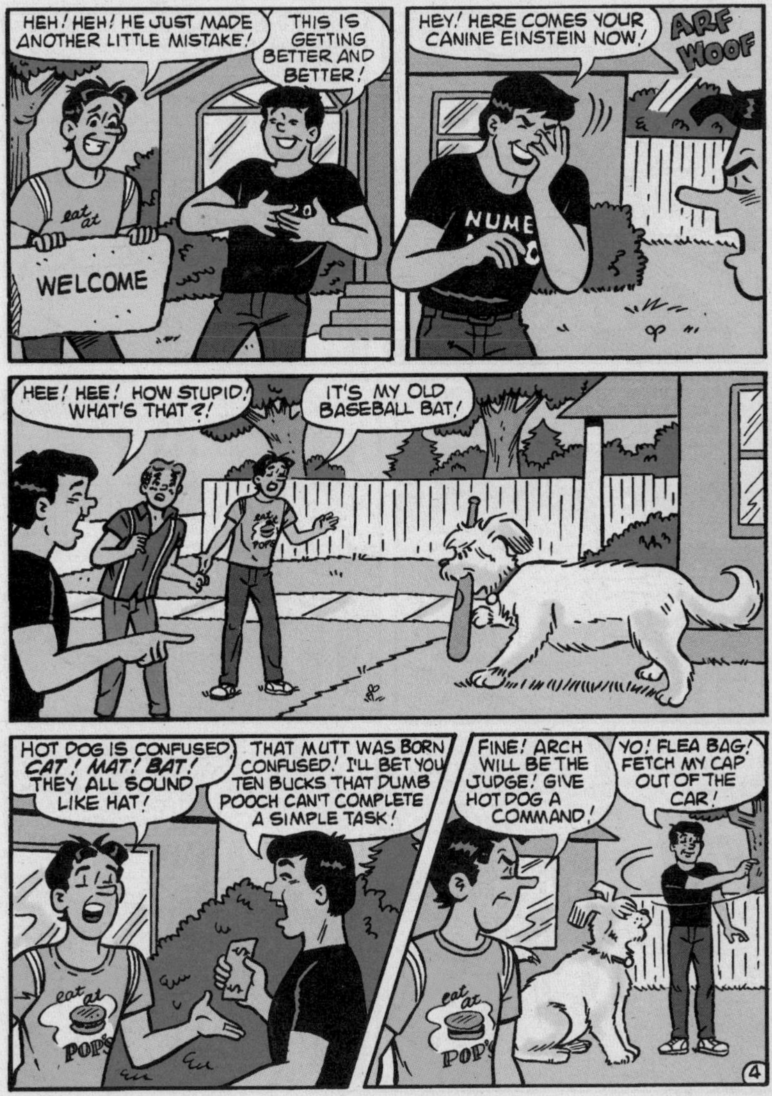

HEH! HEH! HE JUST MADE ANOTHER LITTLE MISTAKE!
THIS IS GETTING BETTER AND BETTER!
WELCOME
HEY! HERE COMES YOUR CANINE EINSTEIN NOW!
ARF
WOOF
HEE! HEE! HOW STUPID! WHAT'S THAT?!
IT'S MY OLD BASEBALL BAT!
HOT DOG IS CONFUSED! CAT! MAT! BAT! THEY ALL SOUND LIKE HAT!
THAT MUTT WAS BORN CONFUSED! I'LL BET YOU TEN BUCKS THAT DUMB POOCH CAN'T COMPLETE A SIMPLE TASK!
FINE! ARCH WILL BE THE JUDGE! GIVE HOT DOG A COMMAND!
YO! FLEA BAG! FETCH MY CAP OUT OF THE CAR!
4

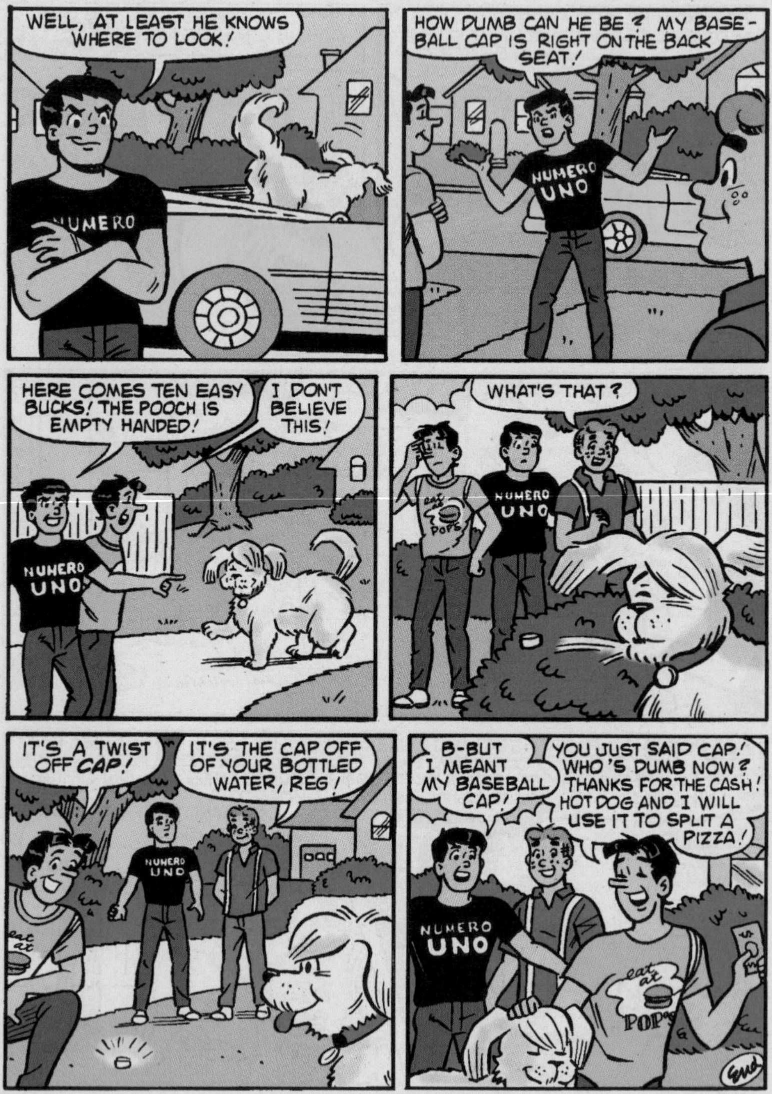
WELL, AT LEAST HE KNOWS WHERE TO LOOK!
NUMERO
HOW DUMB CAN HE BE? MY BASEBALL CAP IS RIGHT ON THE BACK SEAT!
NUMERO UNO
HERE COMES TEN EASY BUCKS! THE POOCH IS EMPTY HANDED!
I DON'T BELIEVE THIS!
NUMERO UNO
WHAT'S THAT?
NUMERO UNO
IT'S A TWIST OFF CAP!
IT'S THE CAP OFF OF YOUR BOTTLED WATER, REG!
NUMERO UNO
B-BUT I MEANT MY BASEBALL CAP!
YOU JUST SAID CAP! WHO'S DUMB NOW? THANKS FOR THE CASH! HOT DOG AND I WILL USE IT TO SPLIT A PIZZA!
NUMERO UNO
eat at POP'S
END

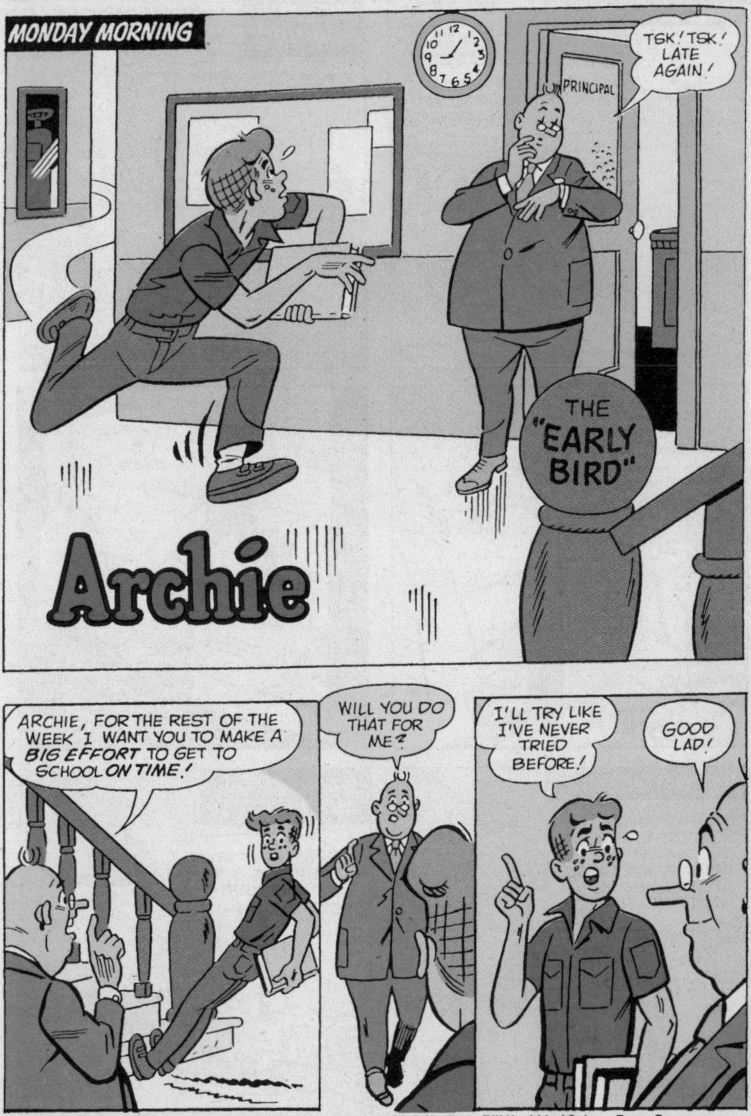
MONDAY MORNING
TSK! TSK! LATE AGAIN!
PRINCIPAL
THE "EARLY BIRD"
Archie
ARCHIE, FOR THE REST OF THE WEEK I WANT YOU TO MAKE A BIG EFFORT TO GET TO SCHOOL ON TIME!
WILL YOU DO THAT FOR ME?
I'LL TRY LIKE I'VE NEVER TRIED BEFORE!
GOOD LAD!
Script: George Gladir / Pencils: Bob Bolling / Inks: Rudy Lapick / Letters: Bill Yoshida / Colors: Barry Grossman

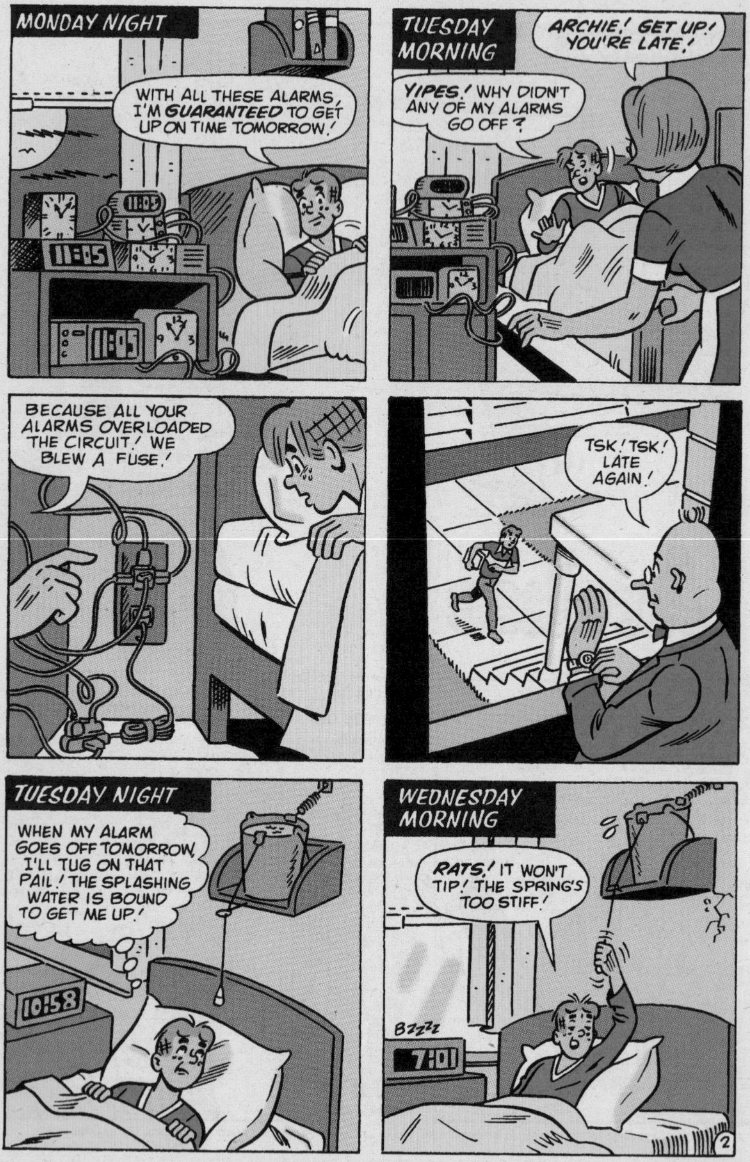
MONDAY NIGHT
WITH ALL THESE ALARMS, I'M GUARANTEED TO GET UP ON TIME TOMORROW!
TUESDAY MORNING
ARCHIE! GET UP! YOU'RE LATE!
YIPES! WHY DIDN'T ANY OF MY ALARMS GO OFF?
BECAUSE ALL YOUR ALARMS OVERLOADED THE CIRCUIT! WE BLEW A FUSE!
TSK! TSK! LATE AGAIN!
TUESDAY NIGHT
WHEN MY ALARM GOES OFF TOMORROW, I'LL TUG ON THAT PAIL! THE SPLASHING WATER IS BOUND TO GET ME UP!
10:58
WEDNESDAY MORNING
RATS! IT WON'T TIP! THE SPRING'S TOO STIFF!
BZZZZ
7:01
2

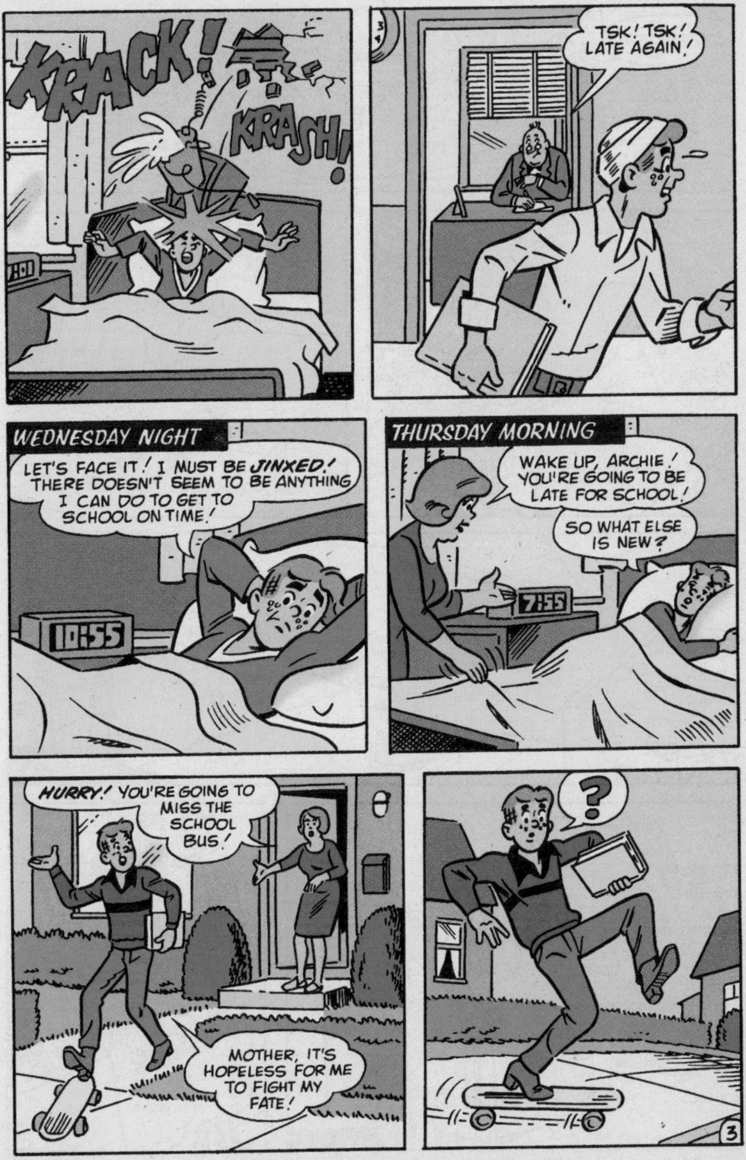
KRACK!
KRASH!
TSK! TSK! LATE AGAIN!
WEDNESDAY NIGHT
LET'S FACE IT! I MUST BE JINXED! THERE DOESN'T SEEM TO BE ANYTHING I CAN DO TO GET TO SCHOOL ON TIME!
10:55
THURSDAY MORNING
WAKE UP, ARCHIE! YOU'RE GOING TO BE LATE FOR SCHOOL!
SO WHAT ELSE IS NEW?
7:55
HURRY! YOU'RE GOING TO MISS THE SCHOOL BUS!
MOTHER, IT'S HOPELESS FOR ME TO FIGHT MY FATE!
?
3

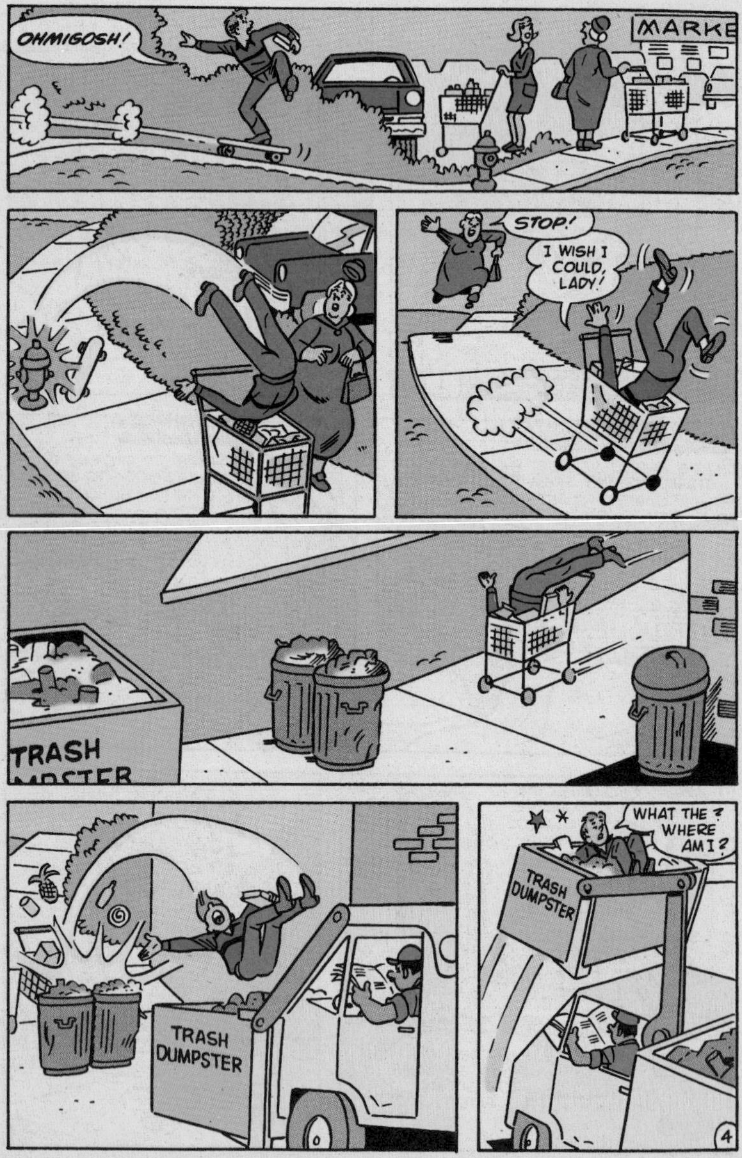

OHMIGOSH!
MARKE
#1
STOP!
I WISH I COULD, LADY!
TRASH
DUMPSTER
TRASH
DUMPSTER
TRASH
DUMPSTER
WHAT THE ?
WHERE AM I?

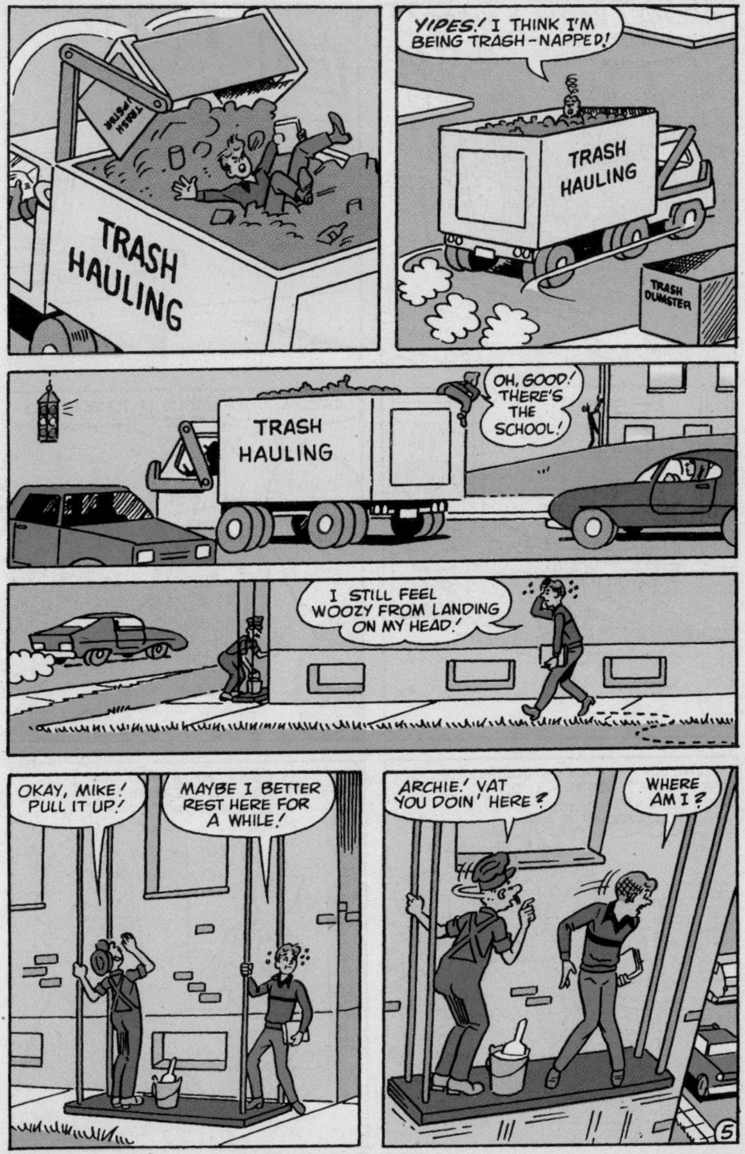
TRASH UPSTIRE
TRASH HAULING
YIPES! I THINK I'M BEING TRASH-NAPPED!
TRASH HAULING
TRASH DUMSTER
TRASH HAULING
OH, GOOD! THERE'S THE SCHOOL!
I STILL FEEL WOOZY FROM LANDING ON MY HEAD!
OKAY, MIKE! PULL IT UP!
MAYBE I BETTER REST HERE FOR A WHILE!
ARCHIE! VAT YOU DOIN' HERE?
WHERE AM I?
5

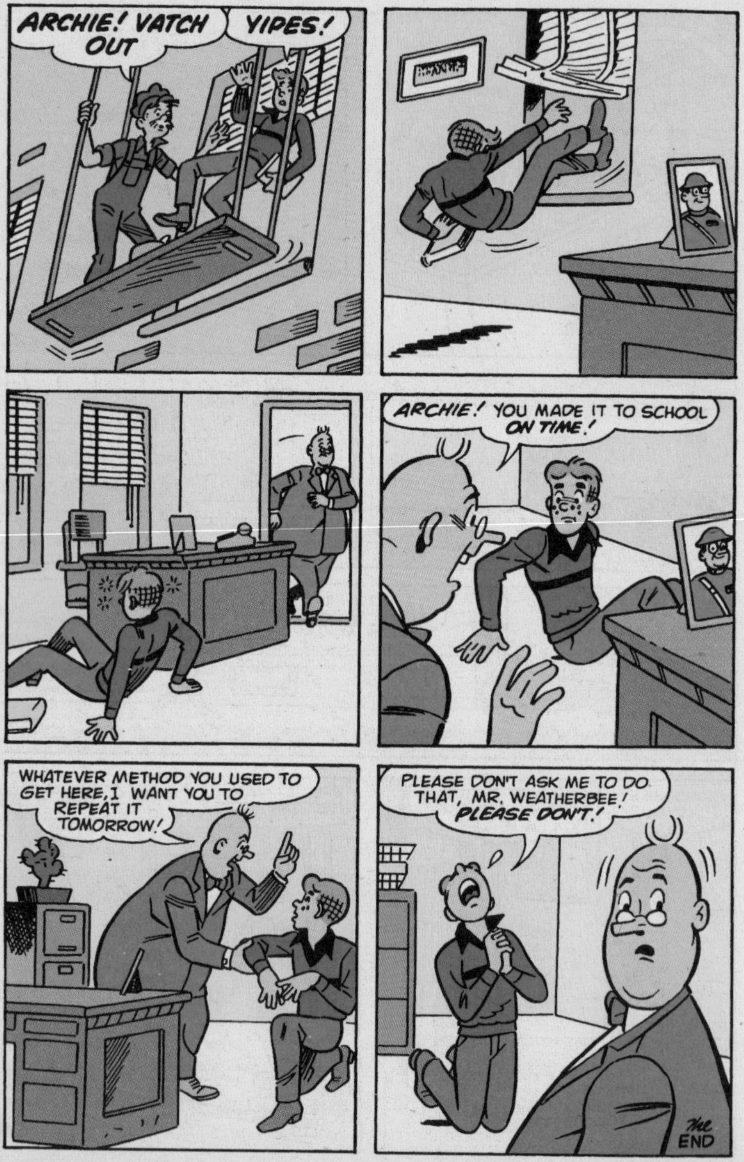
ARCHIE! VATCH OUT
YIPES!
ARCHIE! YOU MADE IT TO SCHOOL ON TIME!
WHATEVER METHOD YOU USED TO GET HERE, I WANT YOU TO REPEAT IT TOMORROW!
PLEASE DON'T ASK ME TO DO THAT, MR. WEATHERBEE! PLEASE DON'T!
END

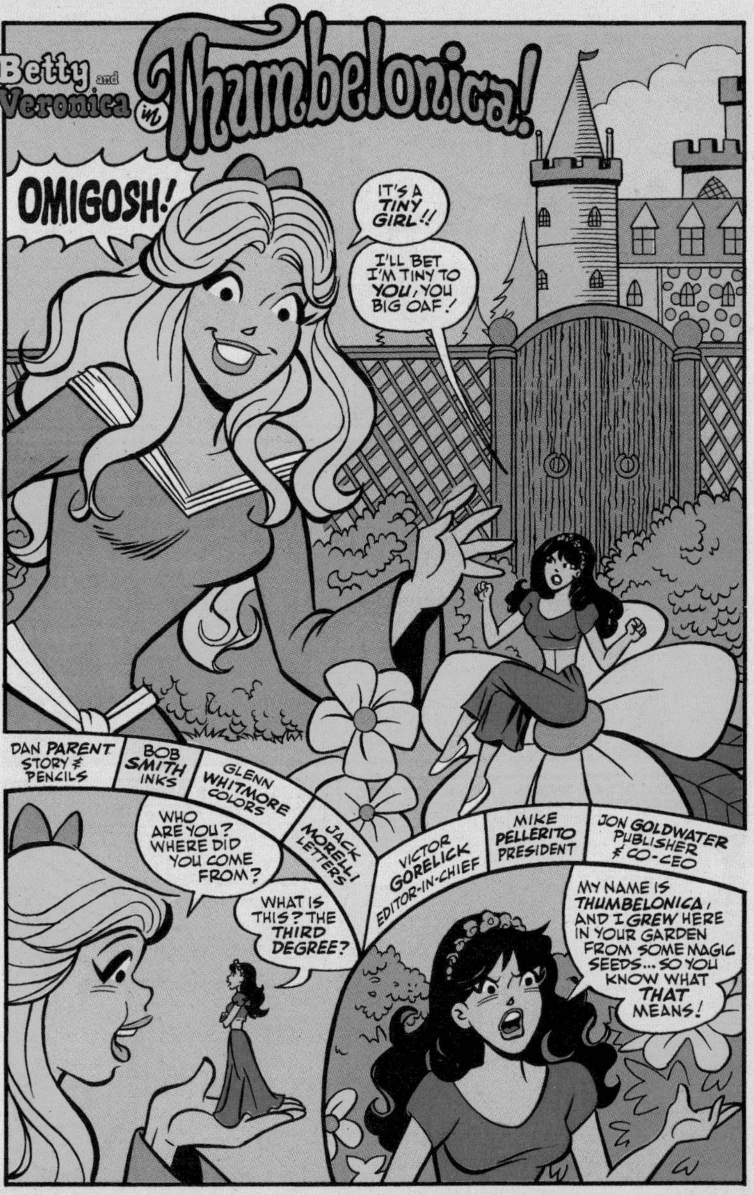
Betty and Veronica in Thumbelonica!
OMIGOSH!
IT'S A TINY GIRL!!
I'LL BET I'M TINY TO YOU, YOU BIG OAF!
DAN PARENT STORY & PENCILS
BOB SMITH INKS
GLENN WHITMORE COLORS
JACK MORELLI LETTERS
VICTOR GORELICK EDITOR-IN-CHIEF
MIKE PELLERITO PRESIDENT
JON GOLDWATER PUBLISHER & CO-CEO
WHO ARE YOU? WHERE DID YOU COME FROM?
WHAT IS THIS? THE THIRD DEGREE?
MY NAME IS THUMBELONICA, AND I GREW HERE IN YOUR GARDEN FROM SOME MAGIC SEEDS... SO YOU KNOW WHAT THAT MEANS!

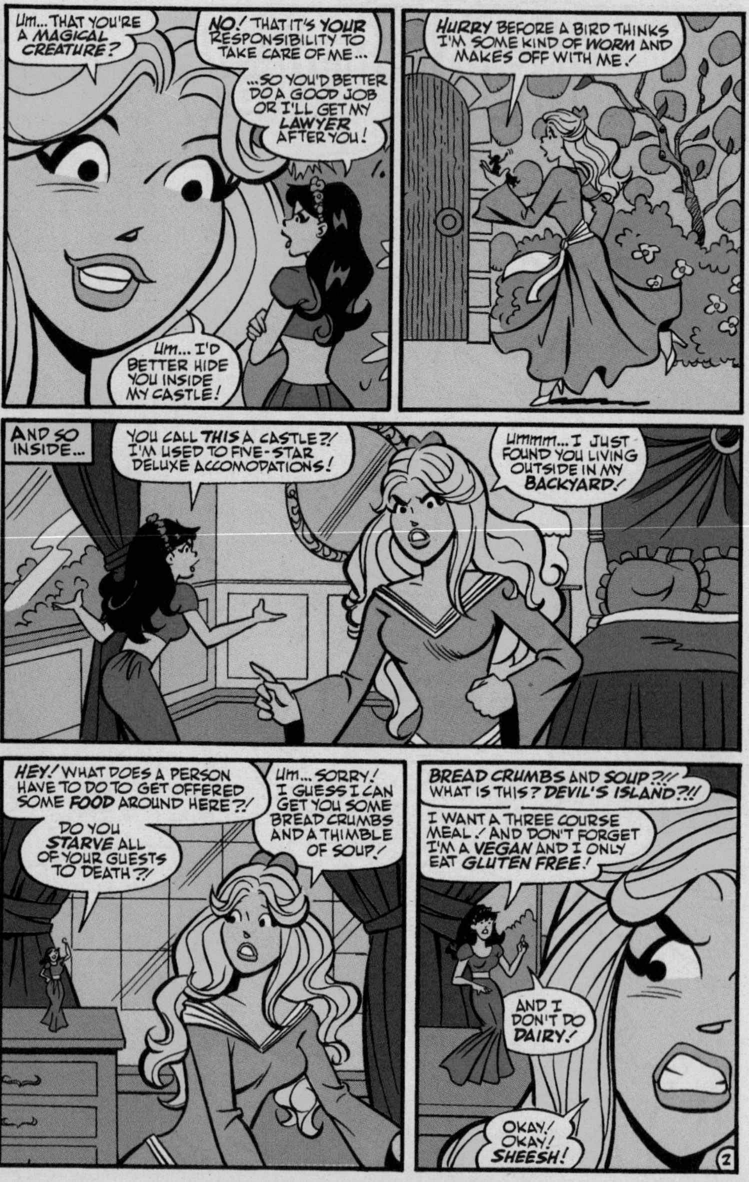
UM... THAT YOU'RE A MAGICAL CREATURE?
NO! THAT IT'S YOUR RESPONSIBILITY TO TAKE CARE OF ME...
...SO YOU'D BETTER DO A GOOD JOB OR I'LL GET MY LAWYER AFTER YOU!
UM... I'D BETTER HIDE YOU INSIDE MY CASTLE!
HURRY BEFORE A BIRD THINKS I'M SOME KIND OF WORM AND MAKES OFF WITH ME!
AND SO INSIDE...
YOU CALL THIS A CASTLE?! I'M USED TO FIVE-STAR DELUXE ACCOMODATIONS!
UMMMM... I JUST FOUND YOU LIVING OUTSIDE IN MY BACKYARD!
HEY! WHAT DOES A PERSON HAVE TO DO TO GET OFFERED SOME FOOD AROUND HERE?!
DO YOU STARVE ALL OF YOUR GUESTS TO DEATH?!
UM... SORRY! I GUESS I CAN GET YOU SOME BREAD CRUMBS AND A THIMBLE OF SOUP!
BREAD CRUMBS AND SOUP?!! WHAT IS THIS? DEVIL'S ISLAND?!!
I WANT A THREE COURSE MEAL! AND DON'T FORGET I'M A VEGAN AND I ONLY EAT GLUTEN FREE!
AND I DON'T DO DAIRY!
OKAY! OKAY! SHEESH!

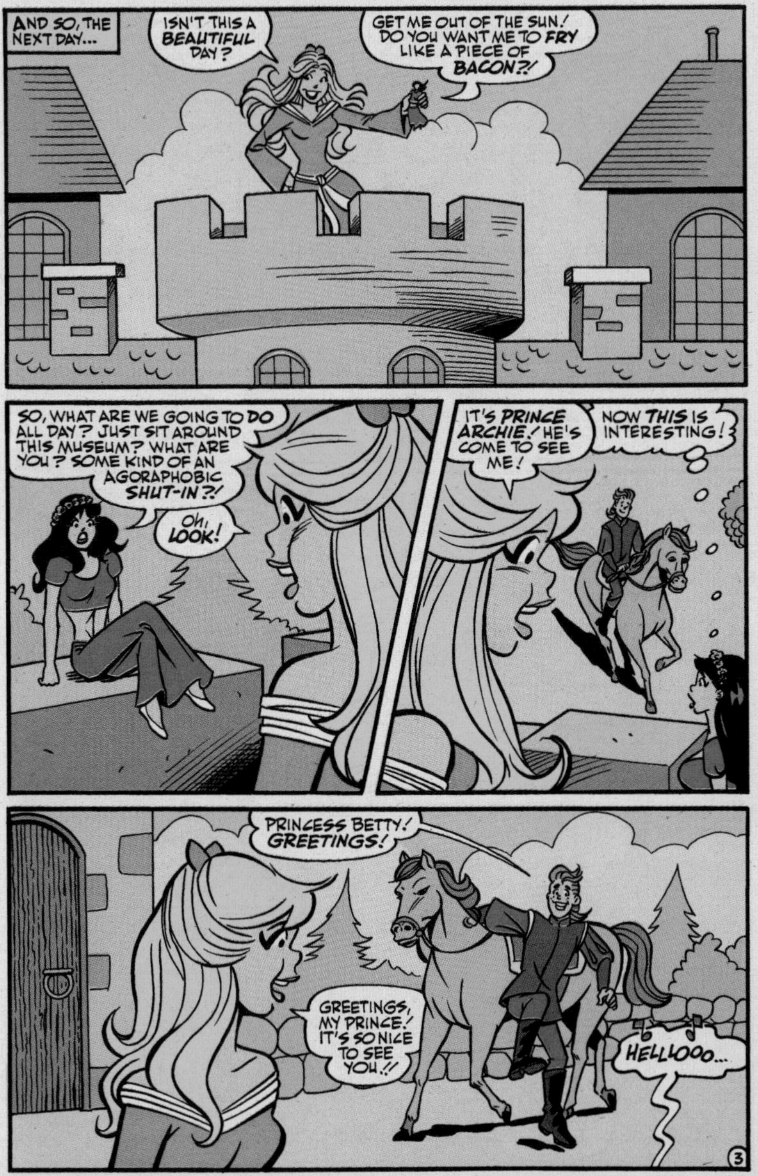
AND SO, THE NEXT DAY...
ISN'T THIS A BEAUTIFUL DAY?
GET ME OUT OF THE SUN! DO YOU WANT ME TO FRY LIKE A PIECE OF BACON?!
SO, WHAT ARE WE GOING TO DO ALL DAY? JUST SIT AROUND THIS MUSEUM? WHAT ARE YOU? SOME KIND OF AN AGORAPHOBIC SHUT-IN?!
OH, LOOK!
IT'S PRINCE ARCHIE! HE'S COME TO SEE ME!
NOW THIS IS INTERESTING!
PRINCESS BETTY! GREETINGS!
GREETINGS, MY PRINCE! IT'S SO NICE TO SEE YOU!!
HELLOOO...
3

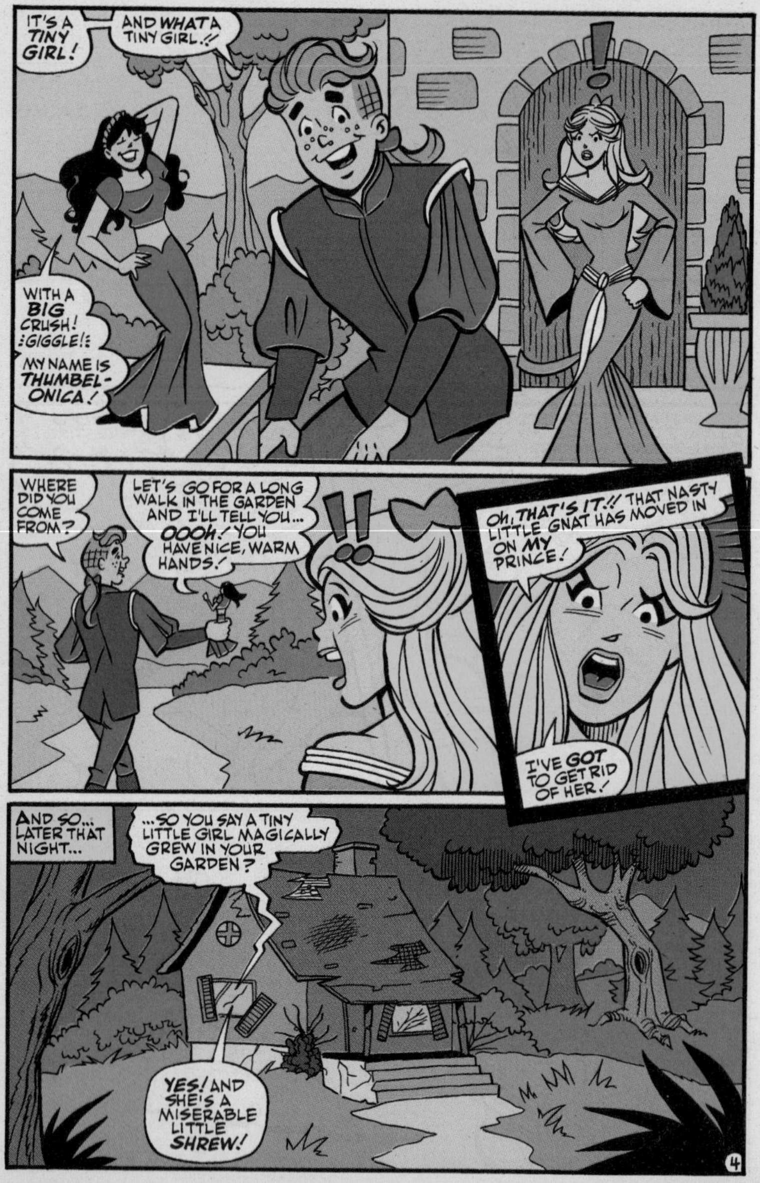

IT'S A TINY GIRL!
AND WHAT A TINY GIRL.!!
WITH A BIG CRUSH! :GIGGLE!:
MY NAME IS THUMBEL-ONICA!
WHERE DID YOU COME FROM?
LET'S GO FOR A LONG WALK IN THE GARDEN AND I'LL TELL YOU... OOOh! YOU HAVE NICE, WARM HANDS!
Oh, THAT'S IT!! THAT NASTY LITTLE GNAT HAS MOVED IN ON MY PRINCE!
I'VE GOT TO GET RID OF HER!
AND SO... LATER THAT NIGHT...
...SO YOU SAY A TINY LITTLE GIRL MAGICALLY GREW IN YOUR GARDEN?
YES! AND SHE'S A MISERABLE LITTLE SHREW!
4

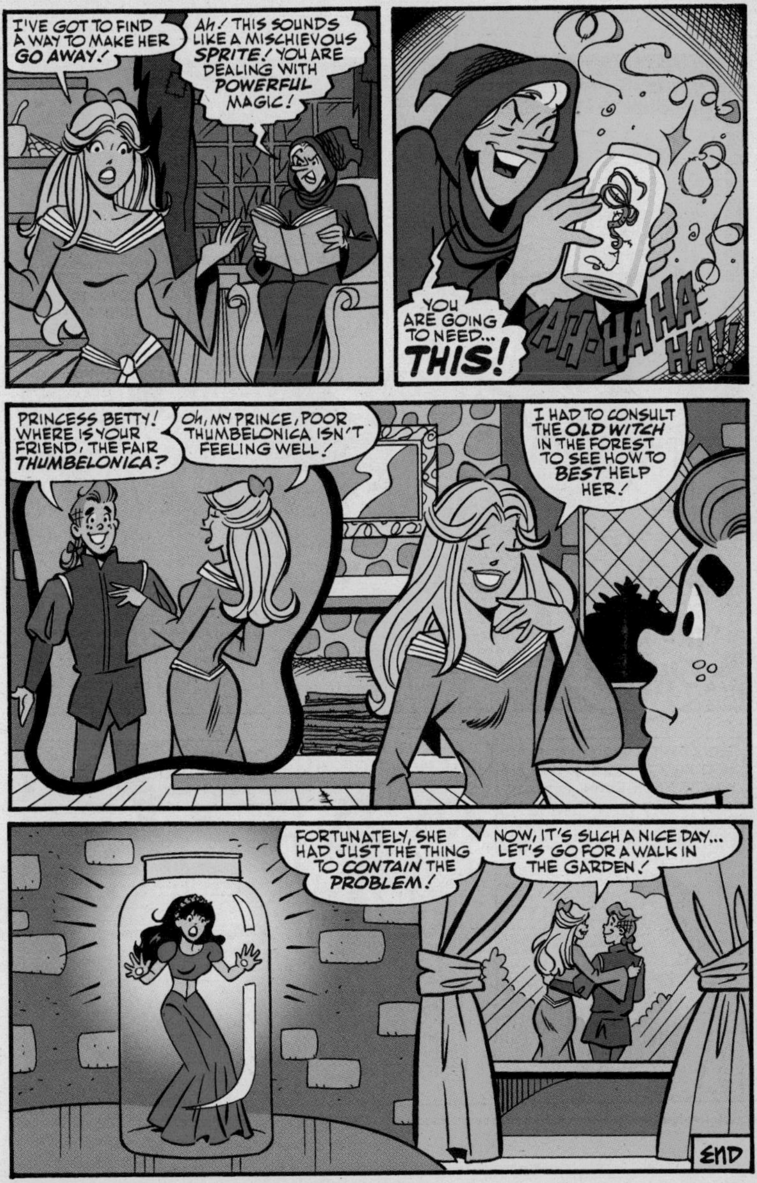
I'VE GOT TO FIND A WAY TO MAKE HER GO AWAY!
Ah! THIS SOUNDS LIKE A MISCHIEVOUS SPRITE! YOU ARE DEALING WITH POWERFUL MAGIC!
YOU ARE GOING TO NEED... THIS!
AH-HAHAHA HA!!
PRINCESS BETTY! WHERE IS YOUR FRIEND, THE FAIR THUMBELONICA?
Oh, MY PRINCE, POOR THUMBELONICA ISN'T FEELING WELL!
I HAD TO CONSULT THE OLD WITCH IN THE FOREST TO SEE HOW TO BEST HELP HER!
FORTUNATELY, SHE HAD JUST THE THING TO CONTAIN THE PROBLEM!
NOW, IT'S SUCH A NICE DAY... LET'S GO FOR A WALK IN THE GARDEN!
END

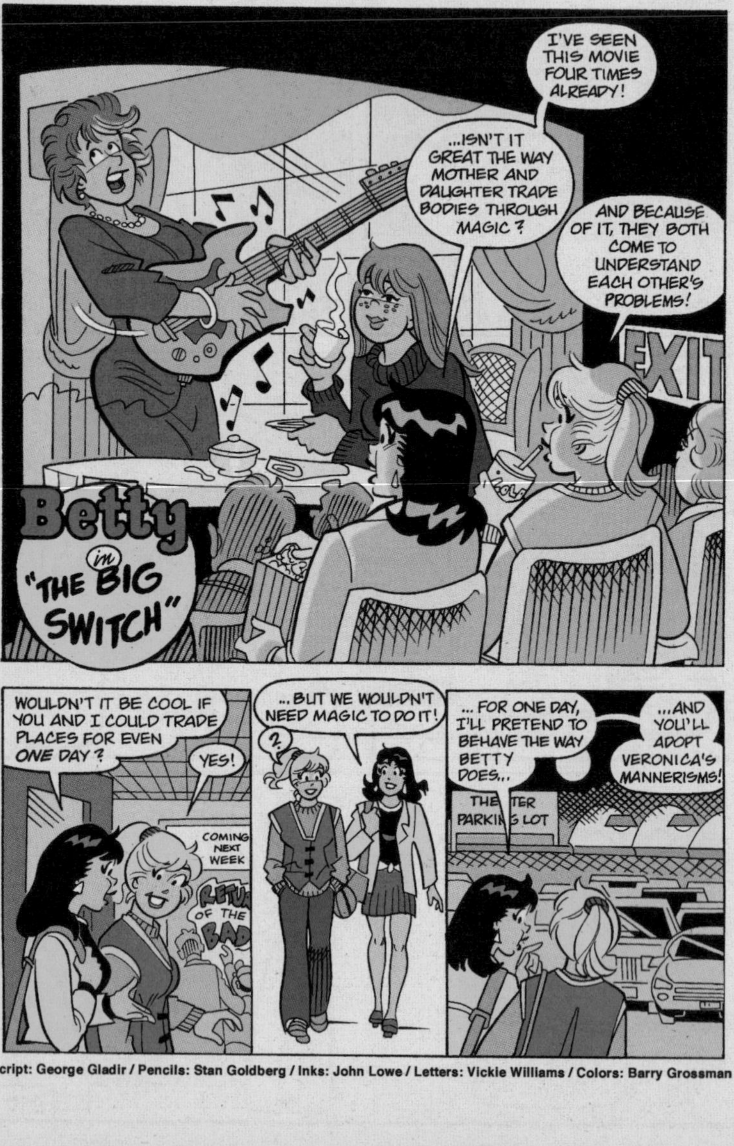
Betty in "THE BIG SWITCH"
I'VE SEEN THIS MOVIE FOUR TIMES ALREADY!
...ISN'T IT GREAT THE WAY MOTHER AND DAUGHTER TRADE BODIES THROUGH MAGIC?
AND BECAUSE OF IT, THEY BOTH COME TO UNDERSTAND EACH OTHER'S PROBLEMS!
EXIT
WOULDN'T IT BE COOL IF YOU AND I COULD TRADE PLACES FOR EVEN ONE DAY?
YES!
COMING NEXT WEEK
OF THE
... BUT WE WOULDN'T NEED MAGIC TO DO IT!
?
... FOR ONE DAY, I'LL PRETEND TO BEHAVE THE WAY BETTY DOES...
...AND YOU'LL ADOPT VERONICA'S MANNERISMS!
PARKING LOT

Script: George Gladir / Pencils: Stan Goldberg / Inks: John Lowe / Letters: Vickie Williams / Colors: Barry Grossman

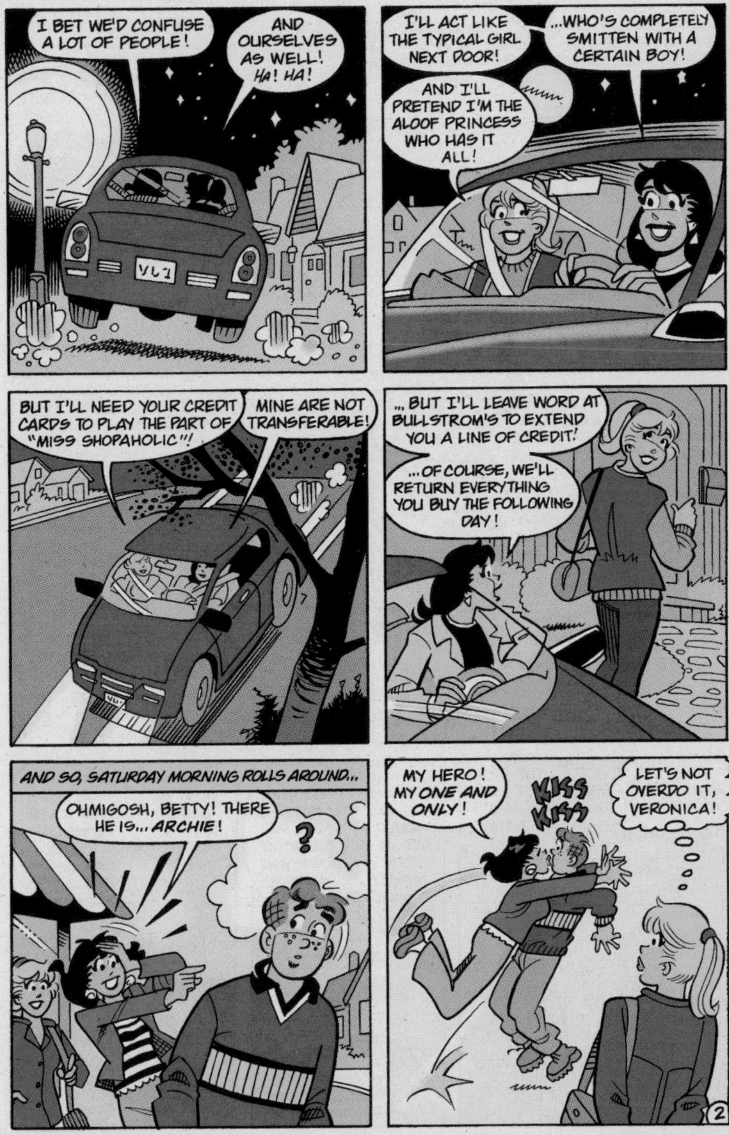
I BET WE'D CONFUSE A LOT OF PEOPLE!
AND OURSELVES AS WELL! HA! HA!
I'LL ACT LIKE THE TYPICAL GIRL NEXT DOOR!
...WHO'S COMPLETELY SMITTEN WITH A CERTAIN BOY!
AND I'LL PRETEND I'M THE ALOOF PRINCESS WHO HAS IT ALL!
BUT I'LL NEED YOUR CREDIT CARDS TO PLAY THE PART OF "MISS SHOPAHOLIC"!
MINE ARE NOT TRANSFERABLE!
... BUT I'LL LEAVE WORD AT BULLSTROM'S TO EXTEND YOU A LINE OF CREDIT!
...OF COURSE, WE'LL RETURN EVERYTHING YOU BUY THE FOLLOWING DAY!
AND SO, SATURDAY MORNING ROLLS AROUND...
OHMIGOSH, BETTY! THERE HE IS... ARCHIE!
?
MY HERO! MY ONE AND ONLY!
KISS KISS
LET'S NOT OVERDO IT, VERONICA!
2

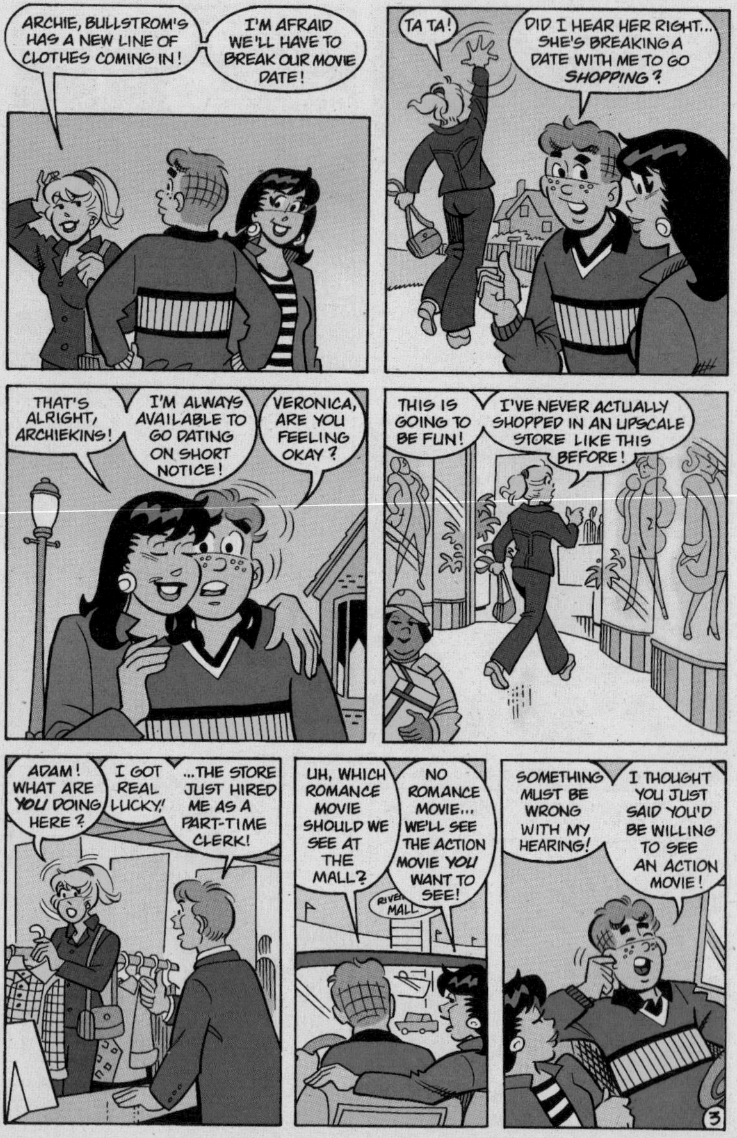
ARCHIE, BULLSTROM'S HAS A NEW LINE OF CLOTHES COMING IN!
I'M AFRAID WE'LL HAVE TO BREAK OUR MOVIE DATE!
TA TA!
DID I HEAR HER RIGHT... SHE'S BREAKING A DATE WITH ME TO GO SHOPPING?
THAT'S ALRIGHT, ARCHIEKINS!
I'M ALWAYS AVAILABLE TO GO DATING ON SHORT NOTICE!
VERONICA, ARE YOU FEELING OKAY?
THIS IS GOING TO BE FUN!
I'VE NEVER ACTUALLY SHOPPED IN AN UPSCALE STORE LIKE THIS BEFORE!
ADAM! WHAT ARE YOU DOING HERE?
I GOT REAL LUCKY!
...THE STORE JUST HIRED ME AS A PART-TIME CLERK!
UH, WHICH ROMANCE MOVIE SHOULD WE SEE AT THE MALL?
NO ROMANCE MOVIE... WE'LL SEE THE ACTION MOVIE YOU WANT TO SEE!
SOMETHING MUST BE WRONG WITH MY HEARING!
I THOUGHT YOU JUST SAID YOU'D BE WILLING TO SEE AN ACTION MOVIE!
3

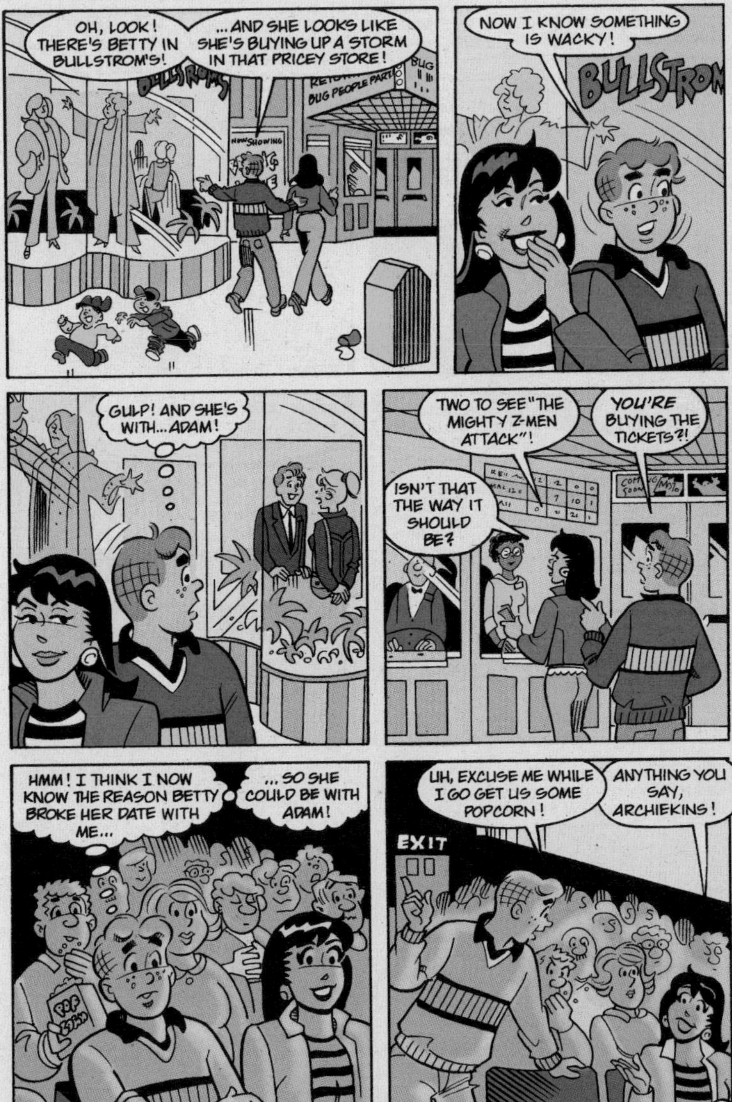
OH, LOOK! THERE'S BETTY IN BULLSTROM'S!
...AND SHE LOOKS LIKE SHE'S BUYING UP A STORM IN THAT PRICEY STORE!
BUG PEOPLE PART
NOW SHOWING
NOW I KNOW SOMETHING IS WACKY!
BULLSTROM
GULP! AND SHE'S WITH... ADAM!
TWO TO SEE "THE MIGHTY Z-MEN ATTACK"!
YOU'RE BUYING THE TICKETS?!
ISN'T THAT THE WAY IT SHOULD BE?
HMM! I THINK I NOW KNOW THE REASON BETTY BROKE HER DATE WITH ME...
...SO SHE COULD BE WITH ADAM!
UH, EXCUSE ME WHILE I GO GET US SOME POPCORN!
ANYTHING YOU SAY, ARCHIEKINS!
EXIT
4

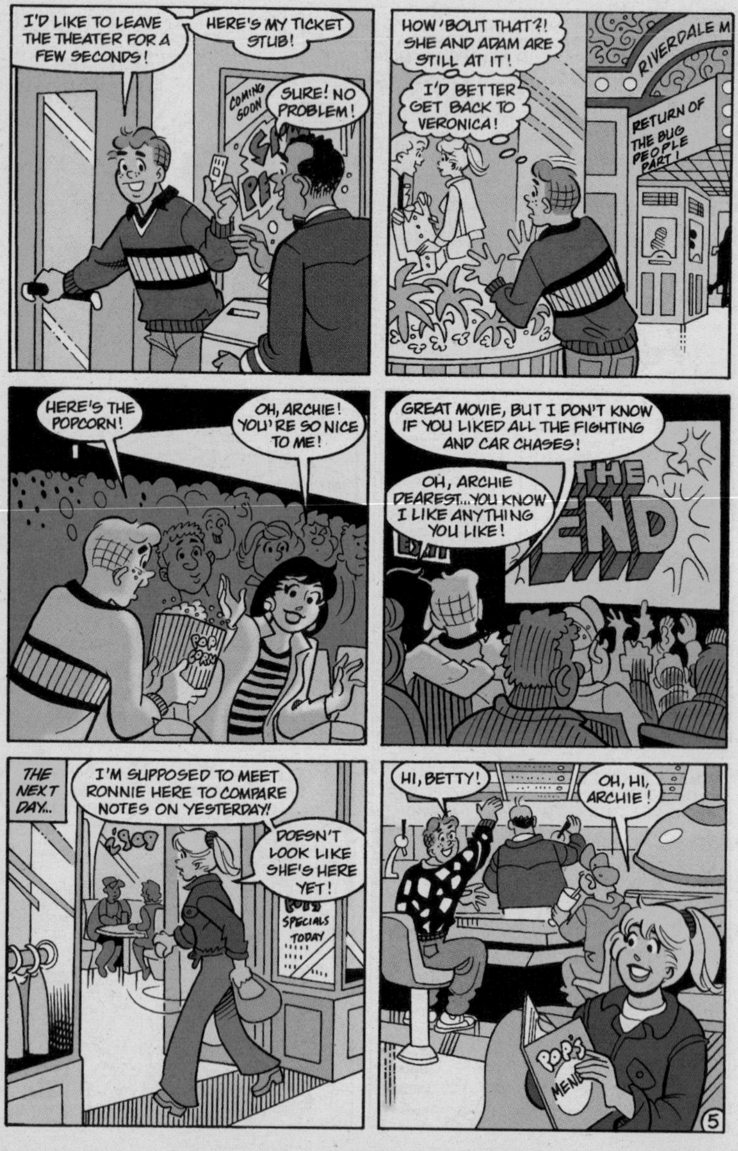
I'D LIKE TO LEAVE THE THEATER FOR A FEW SECONDS!
HERE'S MY TICKET STUB!
COMING SOON
SURE! NO PROBLEM!
HOW 'BOUT THAT?! SHE AND ADAM ARE STILL AT IT!
I'D BETTER GET BACK TO VERONICA!
RIVERDALE M
RETURN OF THE BUG PEOPLE PART I
HERE'S THE POPCORN!
OH, ARCHIE! YOU'RE SO NICE TO ME!
POP CORN
GREAT MOVIE, BUT I DON'T KNOW IF YOU LIKED ALL THE FIGHTING AND CAR CHASES!
OH, ARCHIE DEAREST...YOU KNOW I LIKE ANYTHING YOU LIKE!
THE END
THE NEXT DAY...
I'M SUPPOSED TO MEET RONNIE HERE TO COMPARE NOTES ON YESTERDAY!
DOESN'T LOOK LIKE SHE'S HERE YET!
POP'S
SPECIALS TODAY
HI, BETTY!
OH, HI, ARCHIE!
POP'S MENU

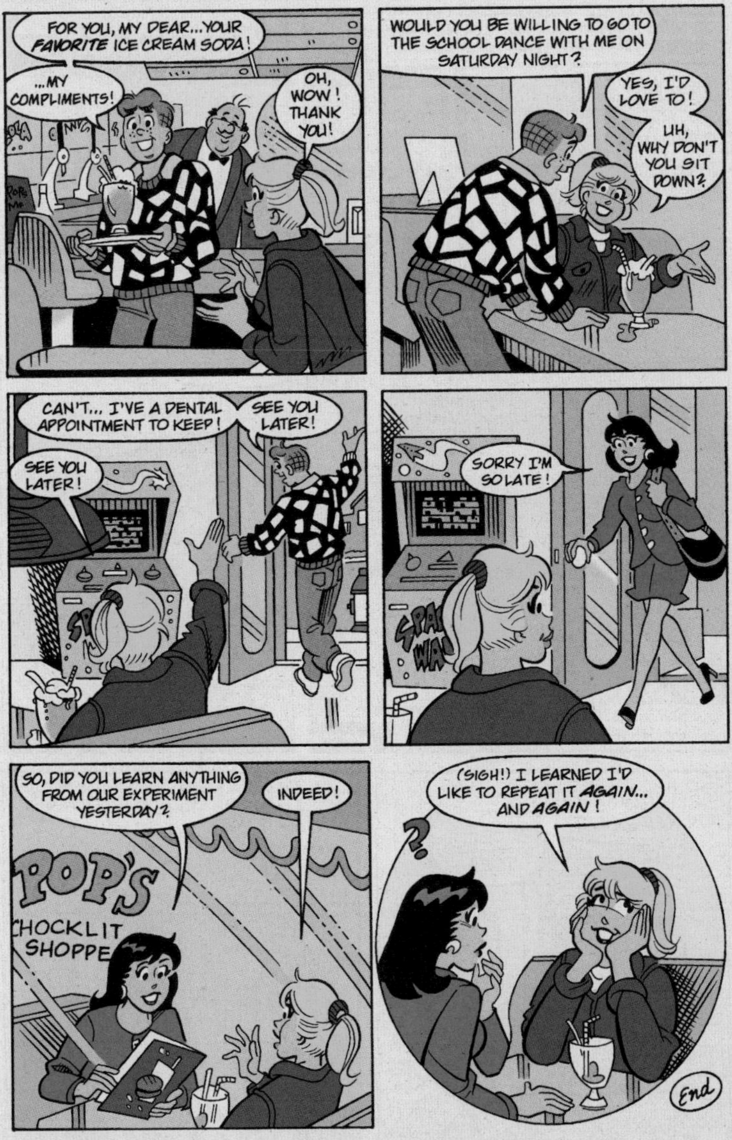
FOR YOU, MY DEAR...YOUR FAVORITE ICE CREAM SODA!
...MY COMPLIMENTS!
OH, WOW! THANK YOU!
WOULD YOU BE WILLING TO GO TO THE SCHOOL DANCE WITH ME ON SATURDAY NIGHT?
YES, I'D LOVE TO!
UH, WHY DON'T YOU SIT DOWN?
CAN'T... I'VE A DENTAL APPOINTMENT TO KEEP!
SEE YOU LATER!
SEE YOU LATER!
SORRY I'M SO LATE!
SO, DID YOU LEARN ANYTHING FROM OUR EXPERIMENT YESTERDAY?
INDEED!
POP'S
CHOCKLIT SHOPPE
(SIGH!) I LEARNED I'D LIKE TO REPEAT IT AGAIN... AND AGAIN!
End

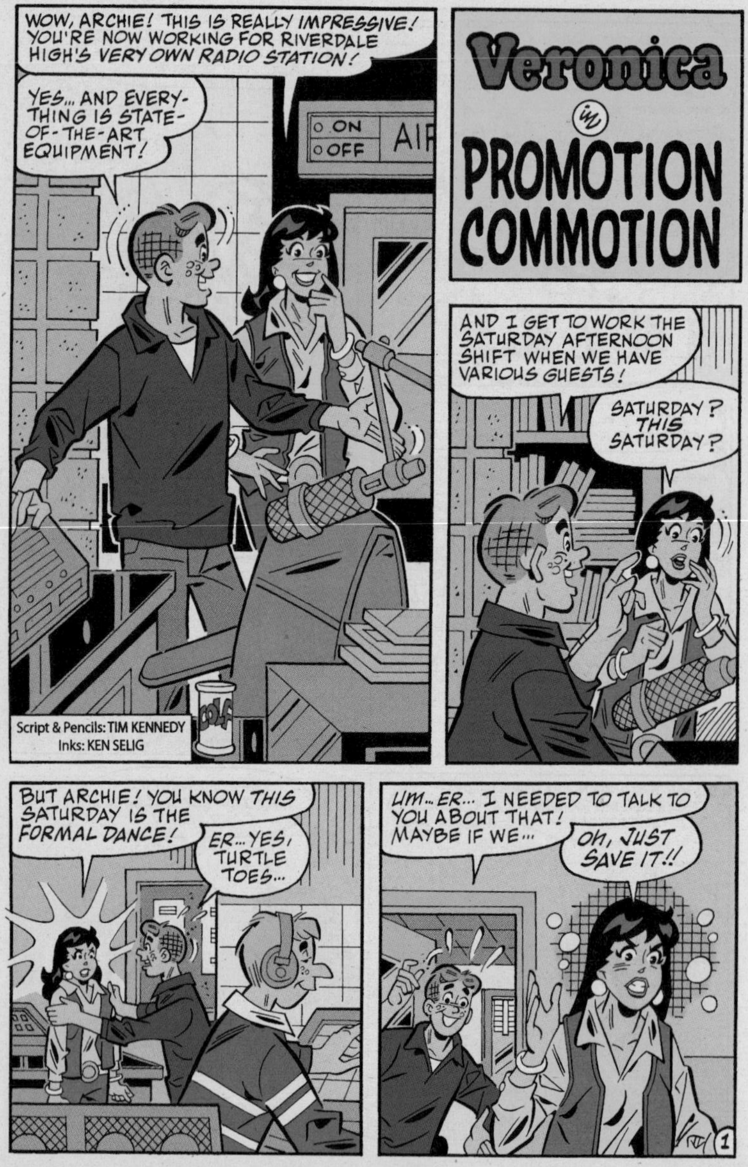
WOW, ARCHIE! THIS IS REALLY IMPRESSIVE! YOU'RE NOW WORKING FOR RIVERDALE HIGH'S VERY OWN RADIO STATION!
YES... AND EVERY-THING IS STATE-OF-THE-ART EQUIPMENT!
ON
OFF
AIR
Veronica
in
PROMOTION COMMOTION
Script & Pencils: TIM KENNEDY
Inks: KEN SELIG
AND I GET TO WORK THE SATURDAY AFTERNOON SHIFT WHEN WE HAVE VARIOUS GUESTS!
SATURDAY? THIS SATURDAY?
BUT ARCHIE! YOU KNOW THIS SATURDAY IS THE FORMAL DANCE!
ER... YES, TURTLE TOES...
UM... ER... I NEEDED TO TALK TO YOU ABOUT THAT! MAYBE IF WE...
OH, JUST SAVE IT!!

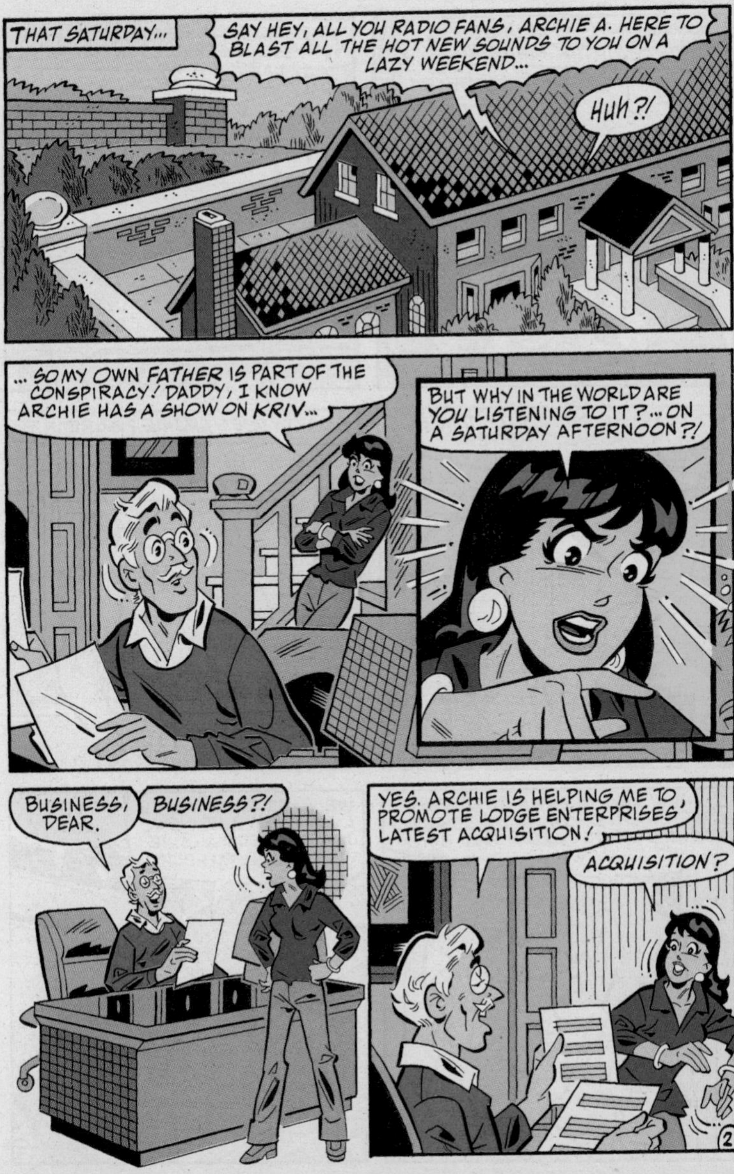
THAT SATURDAY...
SAY HEY, ALL YOU RADIO FANS, ARCHIE A. HERE TO BLAST ALL THE HOT NEW SOUNDS TO YOU ON A LAZY WEEKEND...
Huh?!
... SO MY OWN FATHER IS PART OF THE CONSPIRACY! DADDY, I KNOW ARCHIE HAS A SHOW ON KRIV...
BUT WHY IN THE WORLD ARE YOU LISTENING TO IT? ... ON A SATURDAY AFTERNOON?!
BUSINESS, DEAR.
BUSINESS?!
YES. ARCHIE IS HELPING ME TO PROMOTE LODGE ENTERPRISES' LATEST ACQUISITION!
ACQUISITION?
2

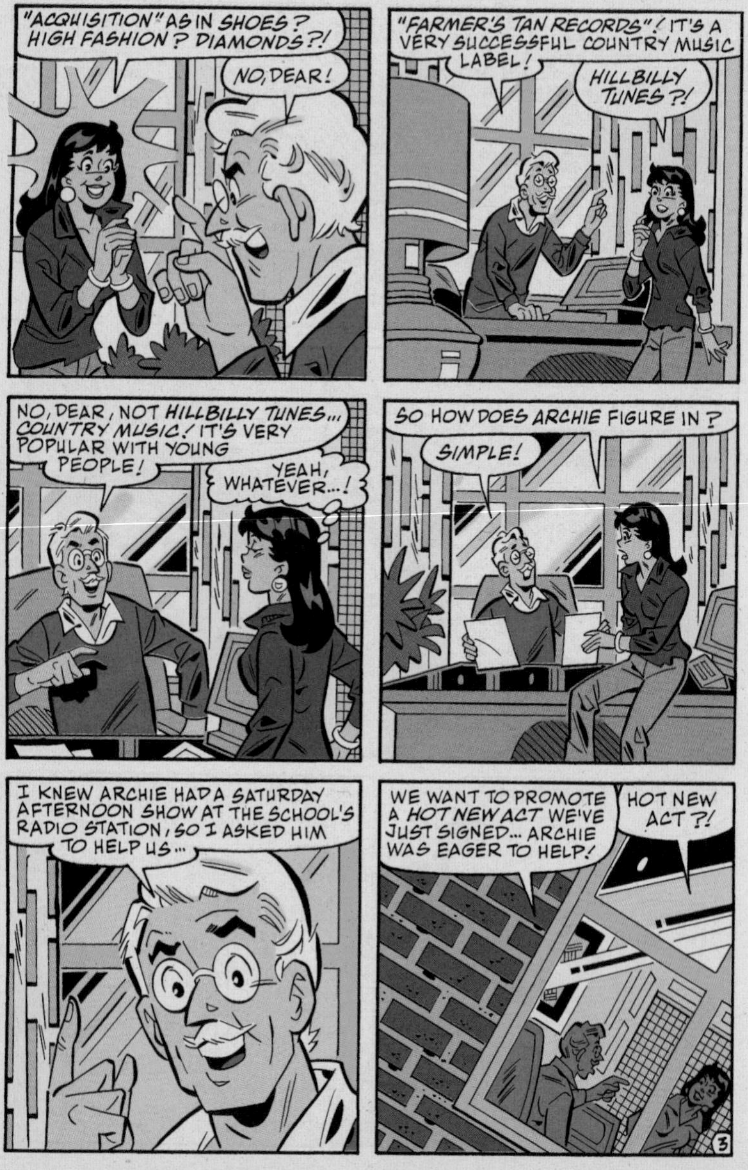
"ACQUISITION" AS IN SHOES? HIGH FASHION? DIAMONDS?!
NO, DEAR!
"FARMER'S TAN RECORDS"! IT'S A VERY SUCCESSFUL COUNTRY MUSIC LABEL!
HILLBILLY TUNES?!
NO, DEAR, NOT HILLBILLY TUNES... COUNTRY MUSIC! IT'S VERY POPULAR WITH YOUNG PEOPLE!
YEAH, WHATEVER...!
SO HOW DOES ARCHIE FIGURE IN?
SIMPLE!
I KNEW ARCHIE HAD A SATURDAY AFTERNOON SHOW AT THE SCHOOL'S RADIO STATION, SO I ASKED HIM TO HELP US...
WE WANT TO PROMOTE A HOT NEW ACT WE'VE JUST SIGNED... ARCHIE WAS EAGER TO HELP!
HOT NEW ACT?!
3

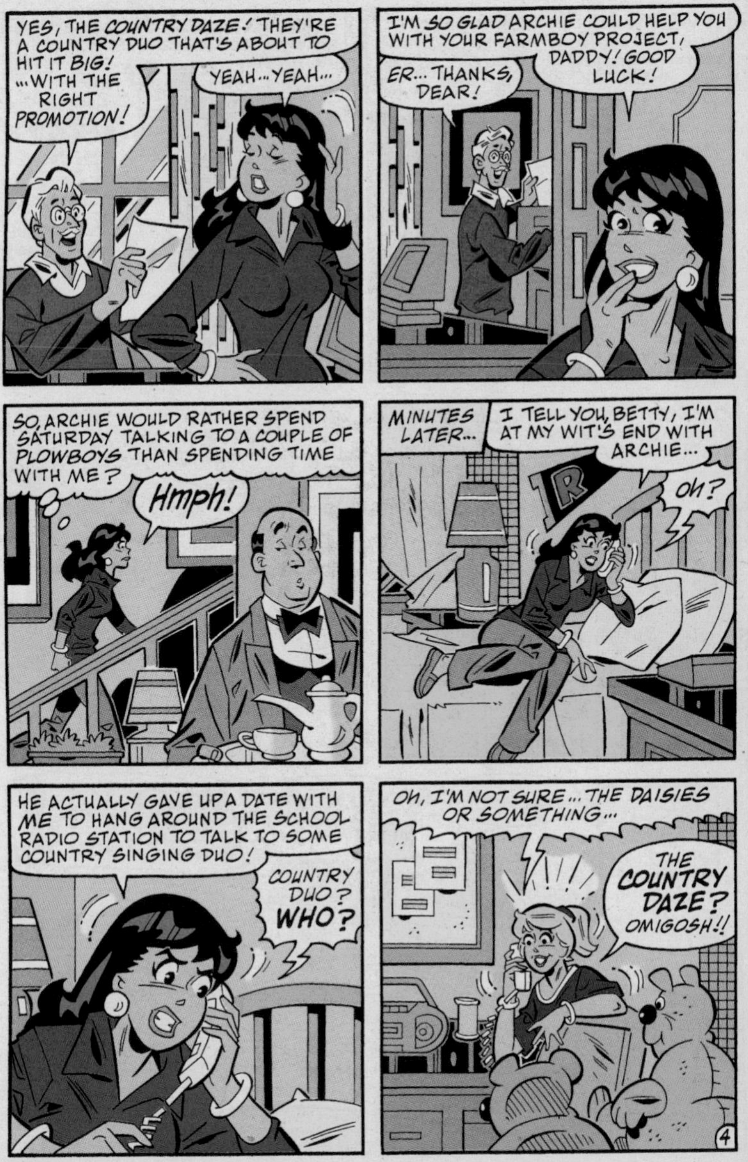
YES, THE COUNTRY DAZE! THEY'RE A COUNTRY DUO THAT'S ABOUT TO HIT IT BIG! ...WITH THE RIGHT PROMOTION!
YEAH...YEAH...
I'M SO GLAD ARCHIE COULD HELP YOU WITH YOUR FARMBOY PROJECT, DADDY! GOOD LUCK!
ER... THANKS, DEAR!
SO, ARCHIE WOULD RATHER SPEND SATURDAY TALKING TO A COUPLE OF PLOWBOYS THAN SPENDING TIME WITH ME?
Hmph!
MINUTES LATER...
I TELL YOU, BETTY, I'M AT MY WIT'S END WITH ARCHIE...
Oh?
HE ACTUALLY GAVE UP A DATE WITH ME TO HANG AROUND THE SCHOOL RADIO STATION TO TALK TO SOME COUNTRY SINGING DUO!
COUNTRY DUO? WHO?
Oh, I'M NOT SURE... THE DAISIES OR SOMETHING...
THE COUNTRY DAZE? OMIGOSH!!
4

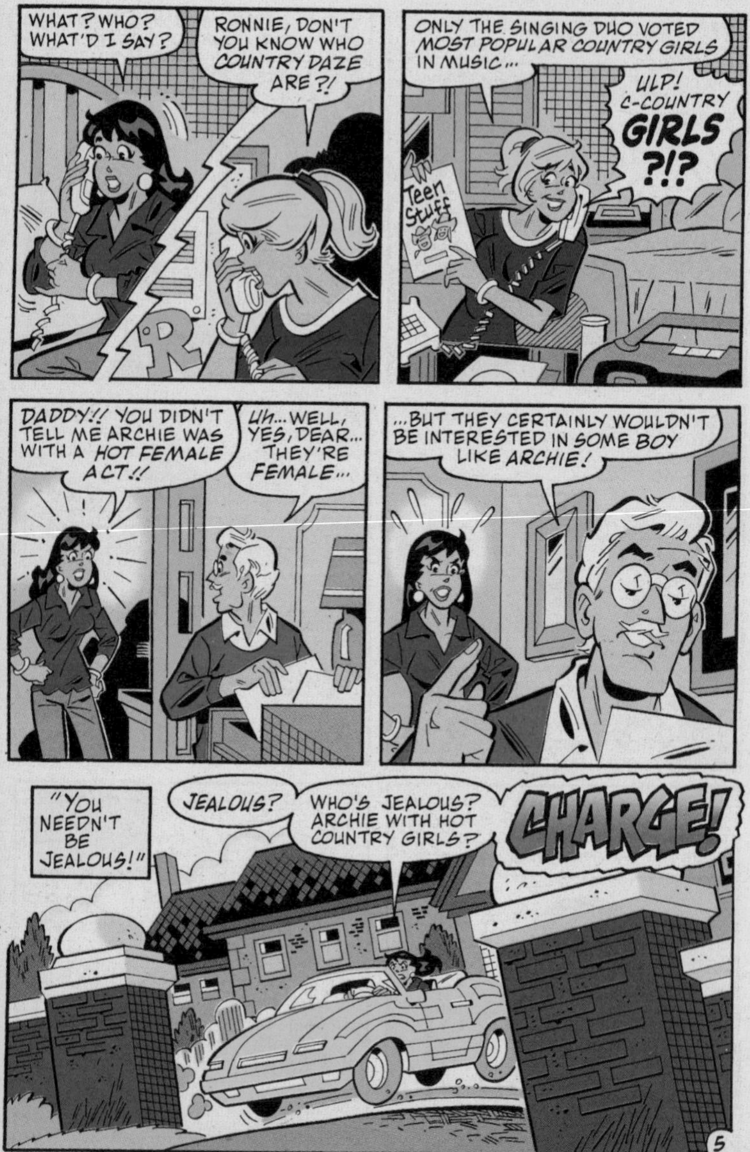
WHAT? WHO? WHAT'D I SAY?
RONNIE, DON'T YOU KNOW WHO COUNTRY DAZE ARE?!
ONLY THE SINGING DUO VOTED MOST POPULAR COUNTRY GIRLS IN MUSIC...
ULP! C-COUNTRY GIRLS ?!?
Teen Stuff
DADDY!! YOU DIDN'T TELL ME ARCHIE WAS WITH A HOT FEMALE ACT!!
UH... WELL, YES, DEAR... THEY'RE FEMALE...
...BUT THEY CERTAINLY WOULDN'T BE INTERESTED IN SOME BOY LIKE ARCHIE!
"YOU NEEDN'T BE JEALOUS!"
JEALOUS?
WHO'S JEALOUS? ARCHIE WITH HOT COUNTRY GIRLS?
CHARGE!

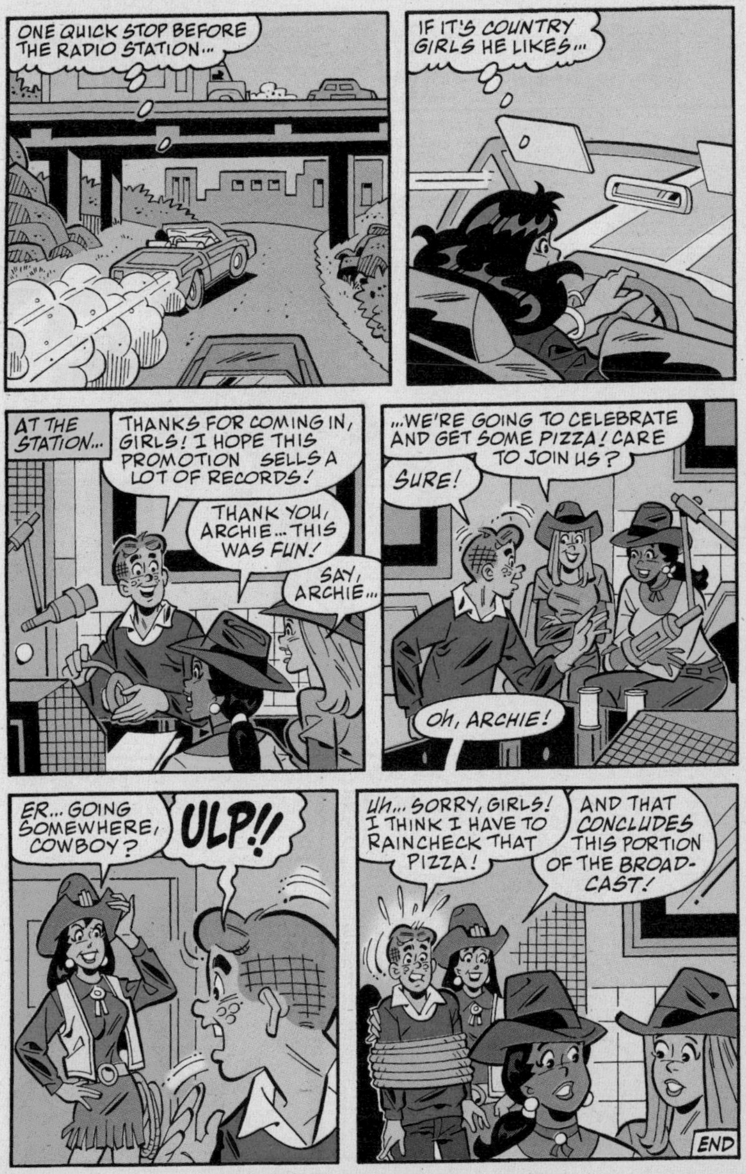
ONE QUICK STOP BEFORE THE RADIO STATION...
IF IT'S COUNTRY GIRLS HE LIKES...
AT THE STATION...
THANKS FOR COMING IN, GIRLS! I HOPE THIS PROMOTION SELLS A LOT OF RECORDS!
THANK YOU, ARCHIE... THIS WAS FUN!
SAY, ARCHIE...
...WE'RE GOING TO CELEBRATE AND GET SOME PIZZA! CARE TO JOIN US?
SURE!
Oh, ARCHIE!
ER... GOING SOMEWHERE, COWBOY?
ULP!!
Uh... SORRY, GIRLS! I THINK I HAVE TO RAINCHECK THAT PIZZA!
AND THAT CONCLUDES THIS PORTION OF THE BROADCAST!
END

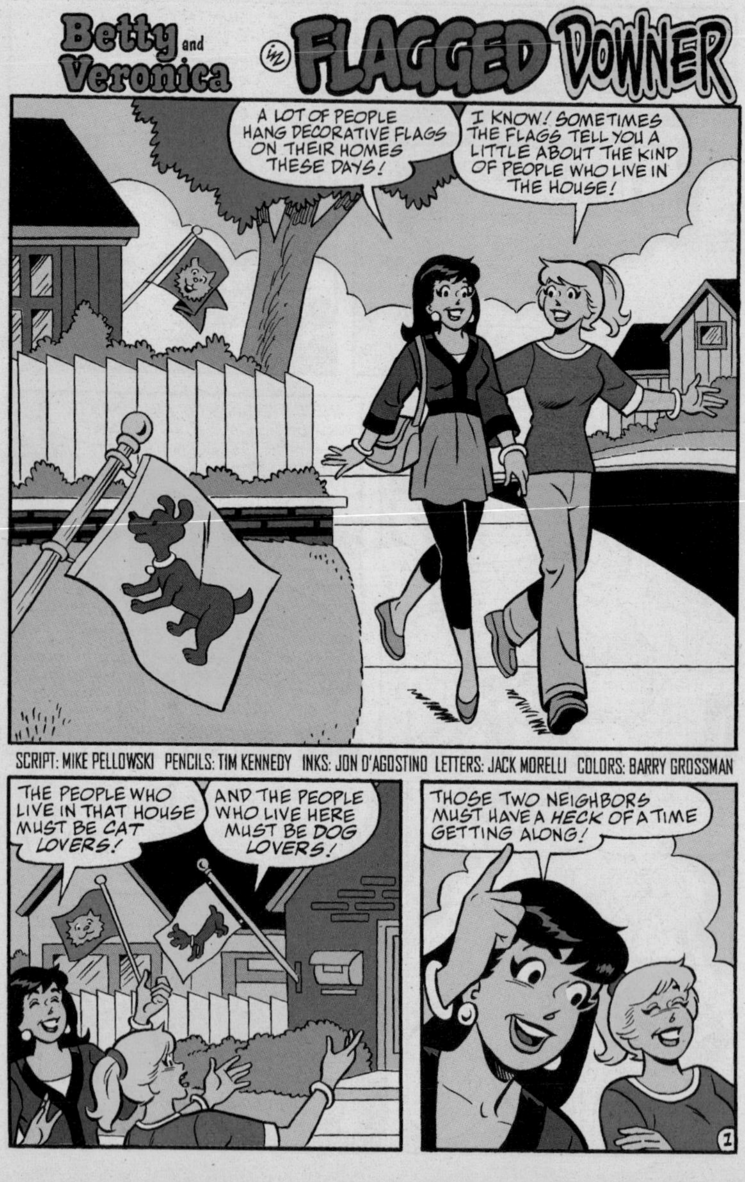

Betty and Veronica in FLAGGED DOWNER
A LOT OF PEOPLE HANG DECORATIVE FLAGS ON THEIR HOMES THESE DAYS!
I KNOW! SOMETIMES THE FLAGS TELL YOU A LITTLE ABOUT THE KIND OF PEOPLE WHO LIVE IN THE HOUSE!
SCRIPT: MIKE PELLOWSKI PENCILS: TIM KENNEDY INKS: JON D'AGOSTINO LETTERS: JACK MORELLI COLORS: BARRY GROSSMAN
THE PEOPLE WHO LIVE IN THAT HOUSE MUST BE CAT LOVERS!
AND THE PEOPLE WHO LIVE HERE MUST BE DOG LOVERS!
THOSE TWO NEIGHBORS MUST HAVE A HECK OF A TIME GETTING ALONG!
1

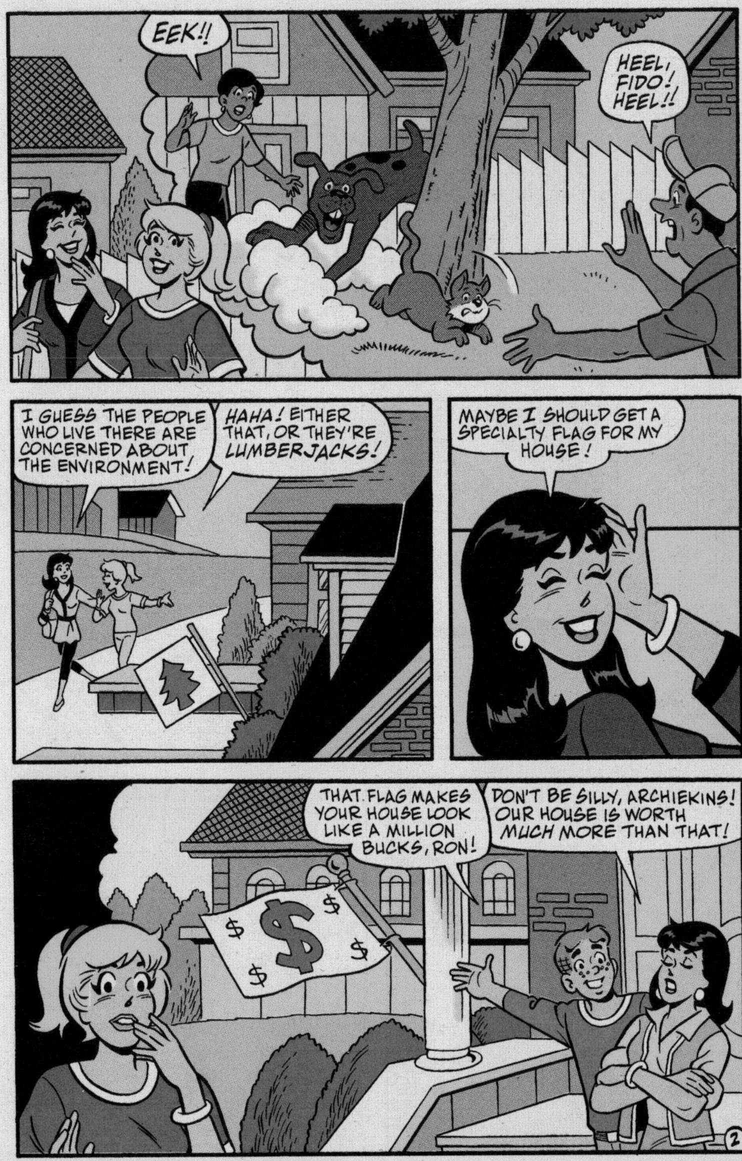
EEK!!
HEEL, FIDO! HEEL!!
I GUESS THE PEOPLE WHO LIVE THERE ARE CONCERNED ABOUT THE ENVIRONMENT!
HAHA! EITHER THAT, OR THEY'RE LUMBERJACKS!
MAYBE I SHOULD GET A SPECIALTY FLAG FOR MY HOUSE!
THAT FLAG MAKES YOUR HOUSE LOOK LIKE A MILLION BUCKS, RON!
DON'T BE SILLY, ARCHIEKINS! OUR HOUSE IS WORTH MUCH MORE THAN THAT!
2

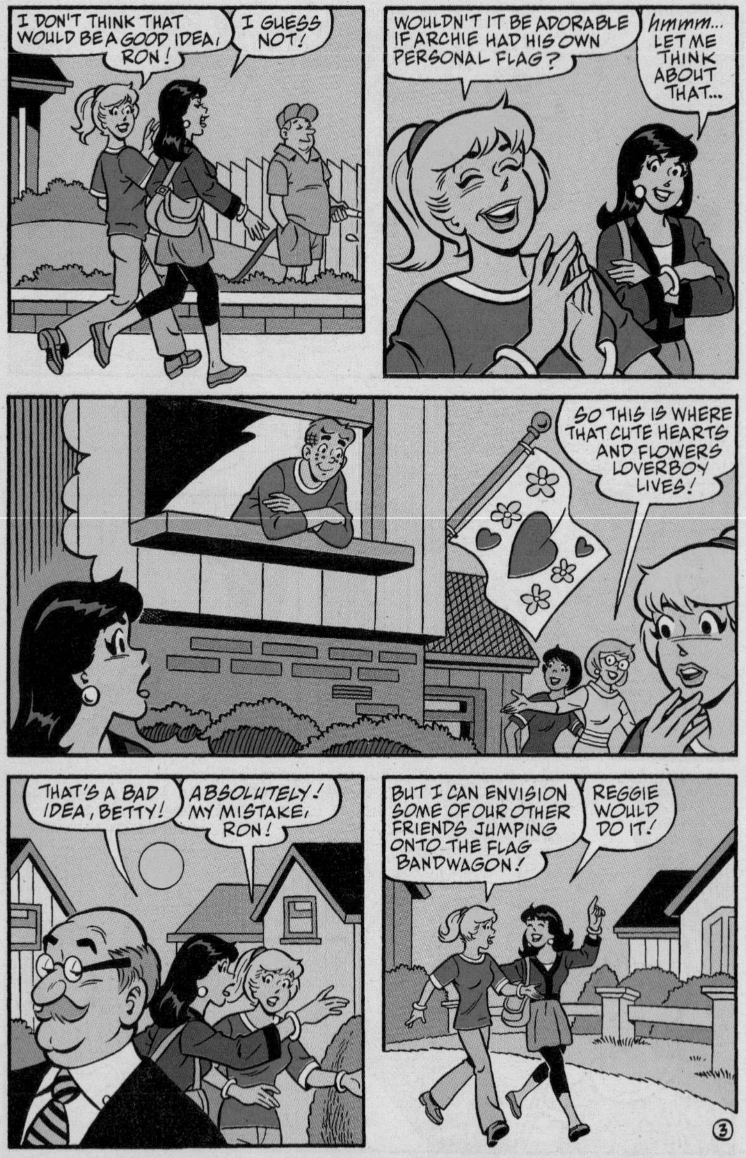
I DON'T THINK THAT WOULD BE A GOOD IDEA, RON!
I GUESS NOT!
WOULDN'T IT BE ADORABLE IF ARCHIE HAD HIS OWN PERSONAL FLAG?
hmmm... LET ME THINK ABOUT THAT...
SO THIS IS WHERE THAT CUTE HEARTS AND FLOWERS LOVERBOY LIVES!
THAT'S A BAD IDEA, BETTY!
ABSOLUTELY! MY MISTAKE, RON!
BUT I CAN ENVISION SOME OF OUR OTHER FRIENDS JUMPING ONTO THE FLAG BANDWAGON!
REGGIE WOULD DO IT!
3

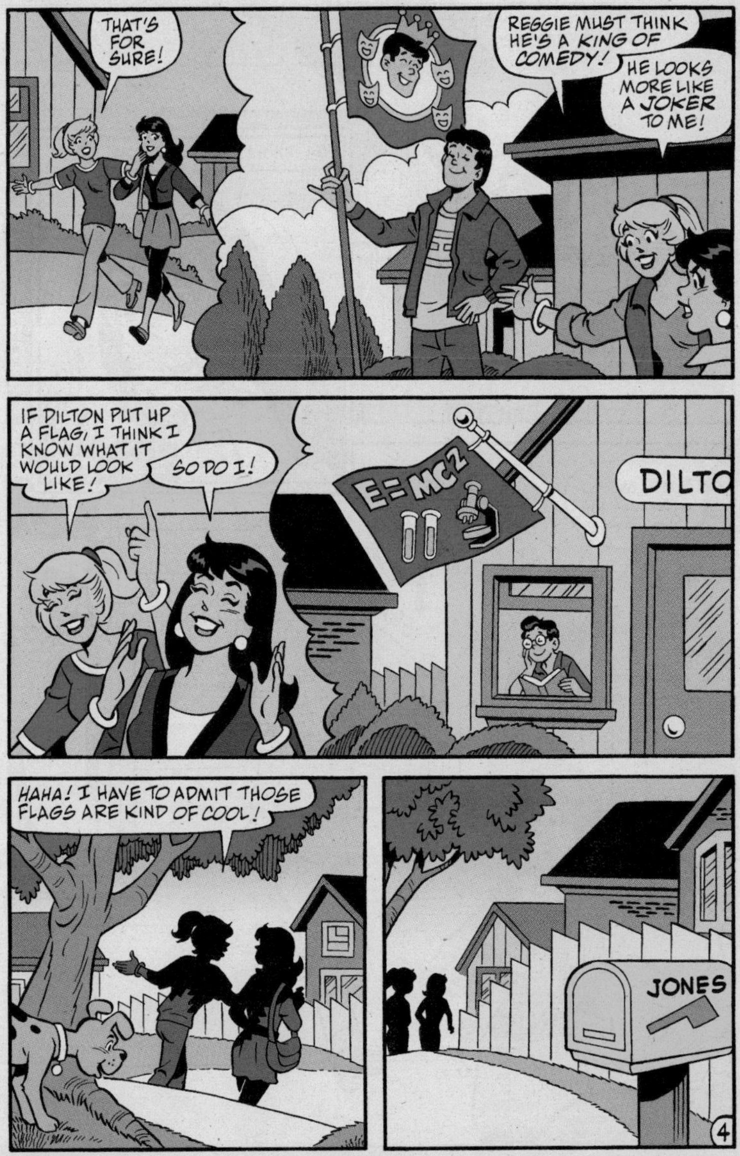
THAT'S FOR SURE!
REGGIE MUST THINK HE'S A KING OF COMEDY!
HE LOOKS MORE LIKE A JOKER TO ME!
IF DILTON PUT UP A FLAG, I THINK I KNOW WHAT IT WOULD LOOK LIKE!
SO DO I!
E=MC2
DILTO
HAHA! I HAVE TO ADMIT THOSE FLAGS ARE KIND OF COOL!
JONES
4

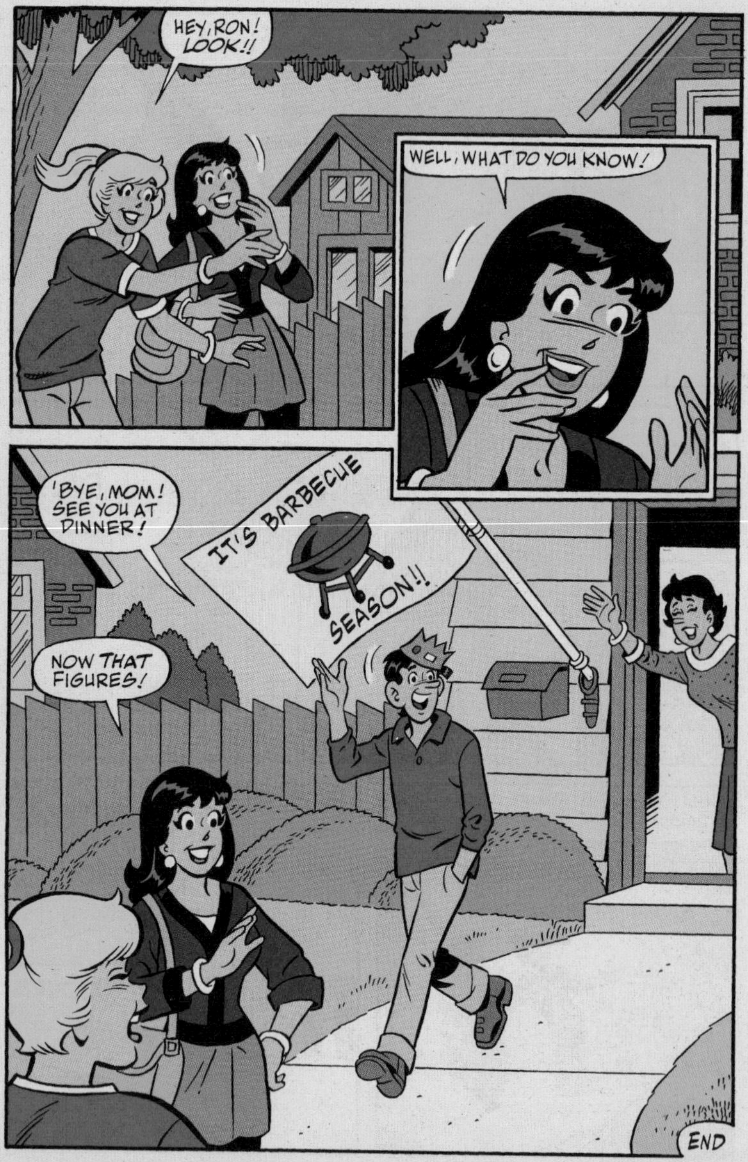
HEY, RON! LOOK!!
WELL, WHAT DO YOU KNOW!
'BYE, MOM! SEE YOU AT DINNER!
IT'S BARBECUE SEASON!!
NOW THAT FIGURES!
END

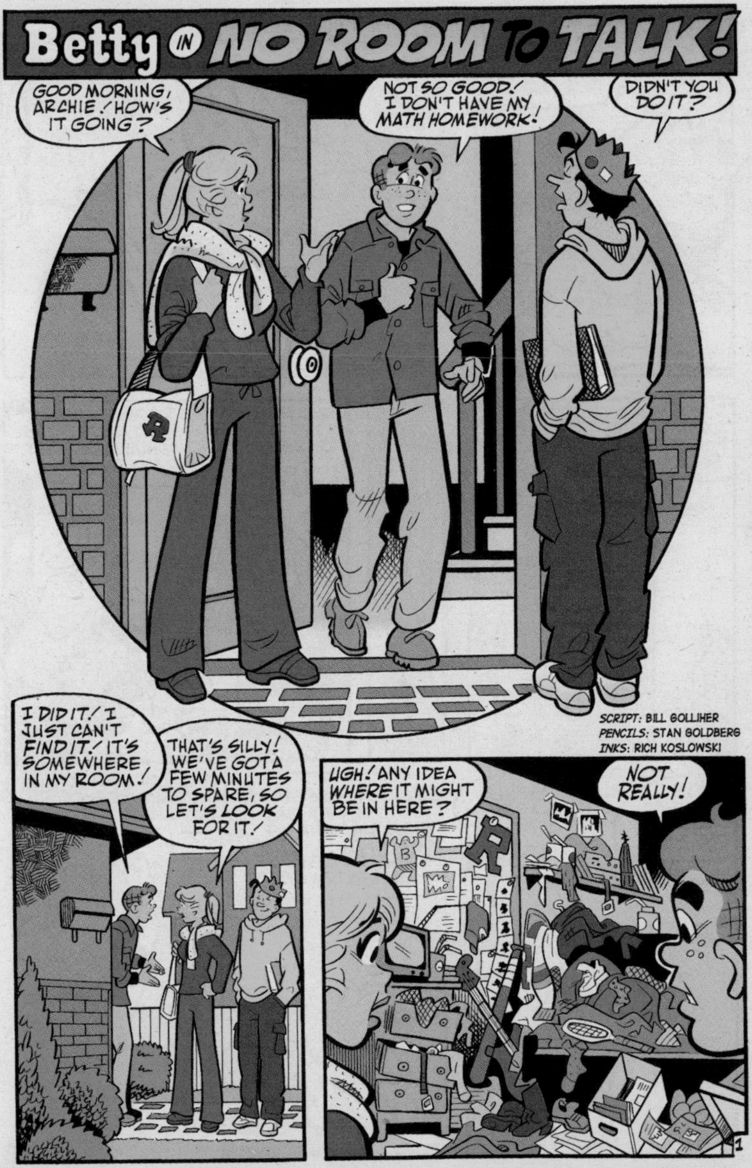
Betty IN NO ROOM TO TALK!
GOOD MORNING, ARCHIE! HOW'S IT GOING?
NOT SO GOOD! I DON'T HAVE MY MATH HOMEWORK!
DIDN'T YOU DO IT?
I DID IT! I JUST CAN'T FIND IT! IT'S SOMEWHERE IN MY ROOM!
THAT'S SILLY! WE'VE GOT A FEW MINUTES TO SPARE, SO LET'S LOOK FOR IT!
SCRIPT: BILL GOLLIHER
PENCILS: STAN GOLDBERG
INKS: RICH KOSLOWSKI
UGH! ANY IDEA WHERE IT MIGHT BE IN HERE?
NOT REALLY!

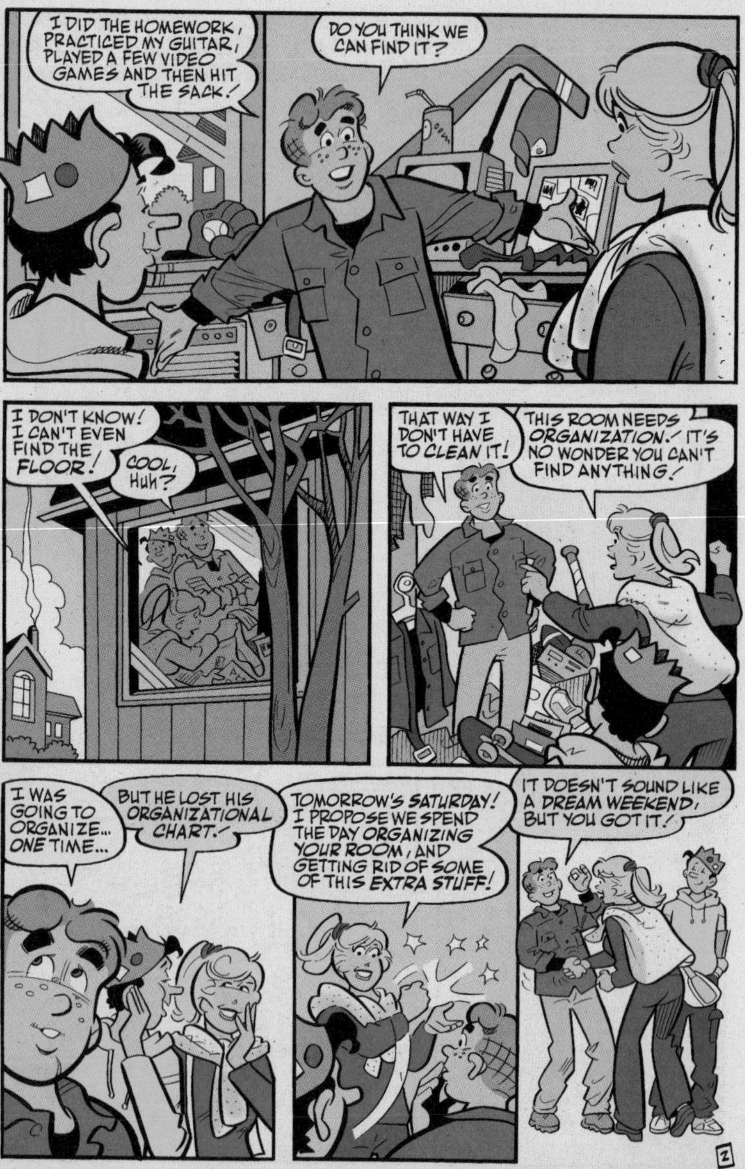
I DID THE HOMEWORK, PRACTICED MY GUITAR, PLAYED A FEW VIDEO GAMES AND THEN HIT THE SACK!
DO YOU THINK WE CAN FIND IT?
I DON'T KNOW! I CAN'T EVEN FIND THE FLOOR!
COOL, HUH?
THIS ROOM NEEDS ORGANIZATION! IT'S NO WONDER YOU CAN'T FIND ANYTHING!
THAT WAY I DON'T HAVE TO CLEAN IT!
I WAS GOING TO ORGANIZE... ONE TIME...
BUT HE LOST HIS ORGANIZATIONAL CHART!
TOMORROW'S SATURDAY! I PROPOSE WE SPEND THE DAY ORGANIZING YOUR ROOM, AND GETTING RID OF SOME OF THIS EXTRA STUFF!
IT DOESN'T SOUND LIKE A DREAM WEEKEND, BUT YOU GOT IT!

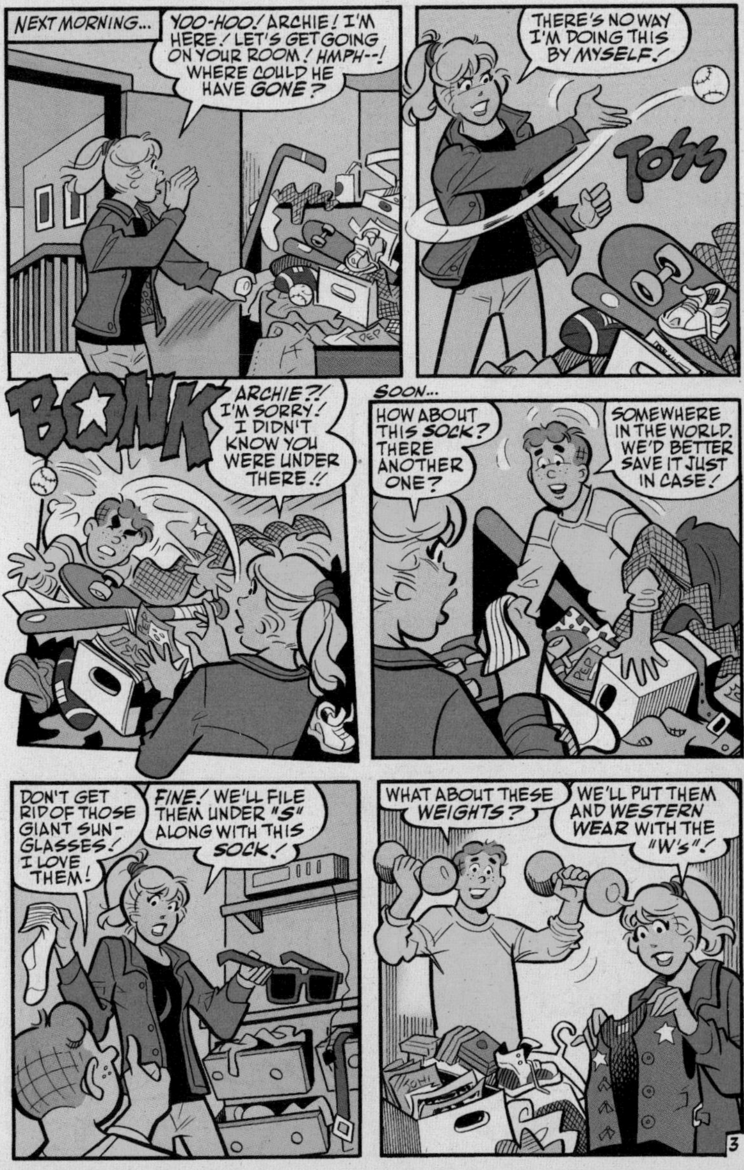

NEXT MORNING...
YOO-HOO! ARCHIE! I'M HERE! LET'S GET GOING ON YOUR ROOM! HMPH--! WHERE COULD HE HAVE GONE?
THERE'S NO WAY I'M DOING THIS BY MYSELF!
TOSS
BONK
ARCHIE?! I'M SORRY! I DIDN'T KNOW YOU WERE UNDER THERE!!
SOON...
HOW ABOUT THIS SOCK? THERE ANOTHER ONE?
SOMEWHERE IN THE WORLD. WE'D BETTER SAVE IT JUST IN CASE!
DON'T GET RID OF THOSE GIANT SUN-GLASSES! I LOVE THEM!
FINE! WE'LL FILE THEM UNDER "S" ALONG WITH THIS SOCK!
WHAT ABOUT THESE WEIGHTS?
WE'LL PUT THEM AND WESTERN WEAR WITH THE "W's"!

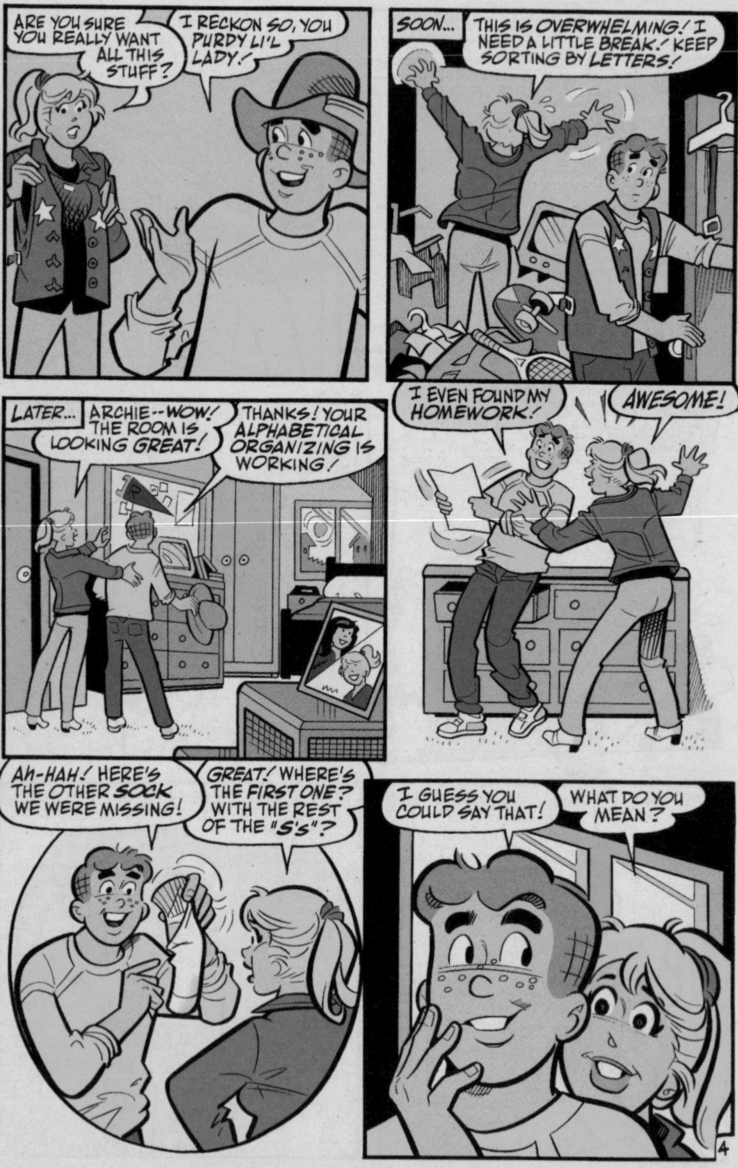
ARE YOU SURE YOU REALLY WANT ALL THIS STUFF?
I RECKON SO, YOU PURDY LI'L LADY!
SOON...
THIS IS OVERWHELMING! I NEED A LITTLE BREAK! KEEP SORTING BY LETTERS!
LATER...
ARCHIE--WOW! THE ROOM IS LOOKING GREAT!
THANKS! YOUR ALPHABETICAL ORGANIZING IS WORKING!
I EVEN FOUND MY HOMEWORK!
AWESOME!
AH-HAH! HERE'S THE OTHER SOCK WE WERE MISSING!
GREAT! WHERE'S THE FIRST ONE? WITH THE REST OF THE "S's"?
I GUESS YOU COULD SAY THAT!
WHAT DO YOU MEAN?
4

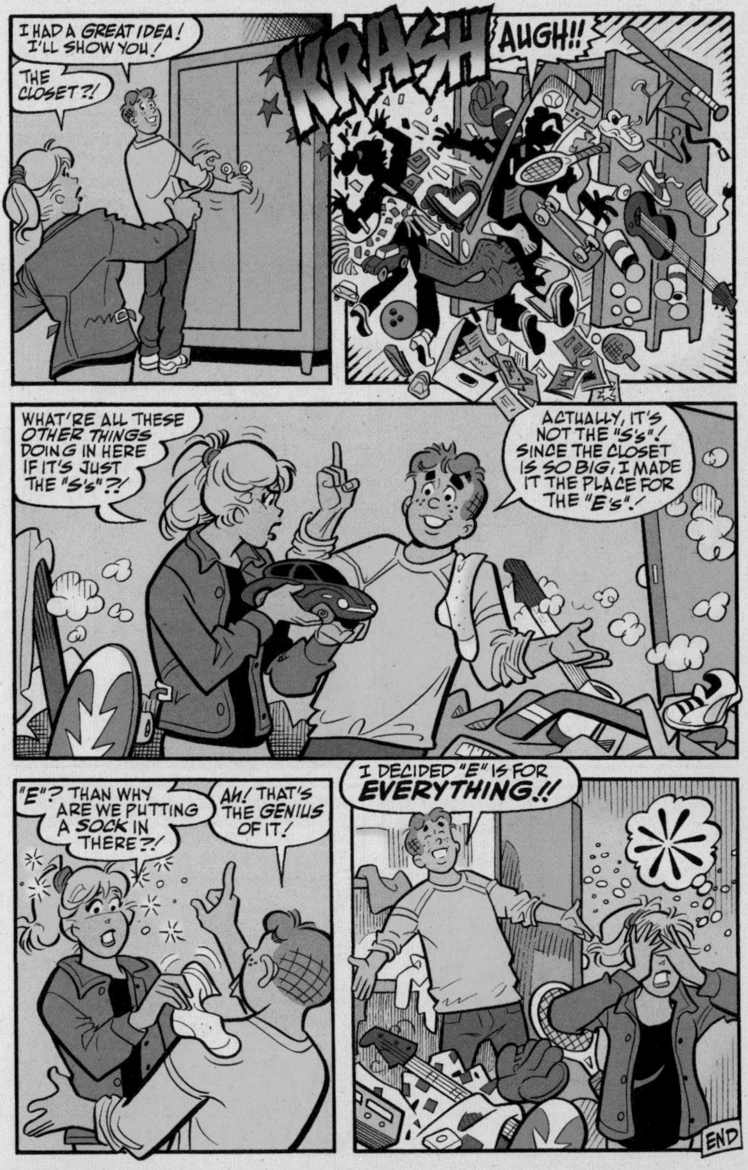
I HAD A GREAT IDEA! I'LL SHOW YOU!
THE CLOSET?!
KRASH
AUGH!!
WHAT'RE ALL THESE OTHER THINGS DOING IN HERE IF IT'S JUST THE "S's"?!
ACTUALLY, IT'S NOT THE "S's"! SINCE THE CLOSET IS SO BIG, I MADE IT THE PLACE FOR THE "E's"!
"E"? THAN WHY ARE WE PUTTING A SOCK IN THERE?!
AH! THAT'S THE GENIUS OF IT!
I DECIDED "E" IS FOR EVERYTHING!!
END

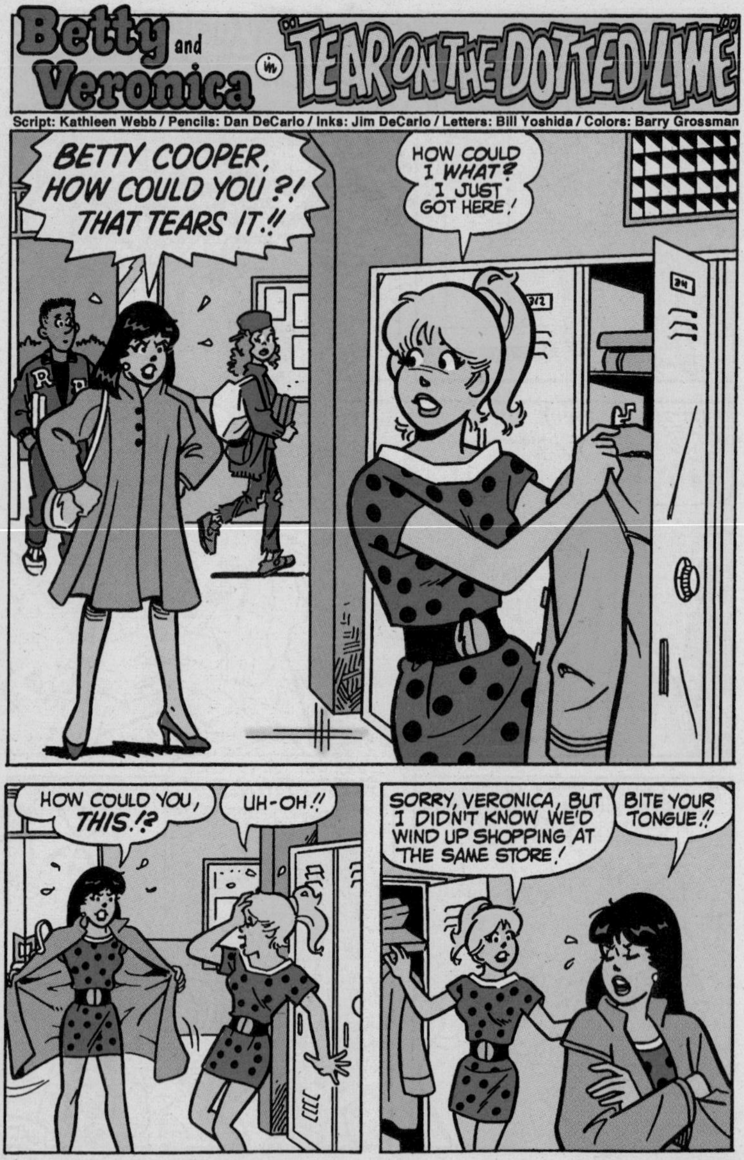

Betty and Veronica in "TEAR ON THE DOTTED LINE"
Script: Kathleen Webb / Pencils: Dan DeCarlo / Inks: Jim DeCarlo / Letters: Bill Yoshida / Colors: Barry Grossman
BETTY COOPER, HOW COULD YOU ?! THAT TEARS IT.!!
HOW COULD I WHAT? I JUST GOT HERE!
HOW COULD YOU, THIS.!?
UH-OH.!!
SORRY, VERONICA, BUT I DIDN'T KNOW WE'D WIND UP SHOPPING AT THE SAME STORE!
BITE YOUR TONGUE.!!

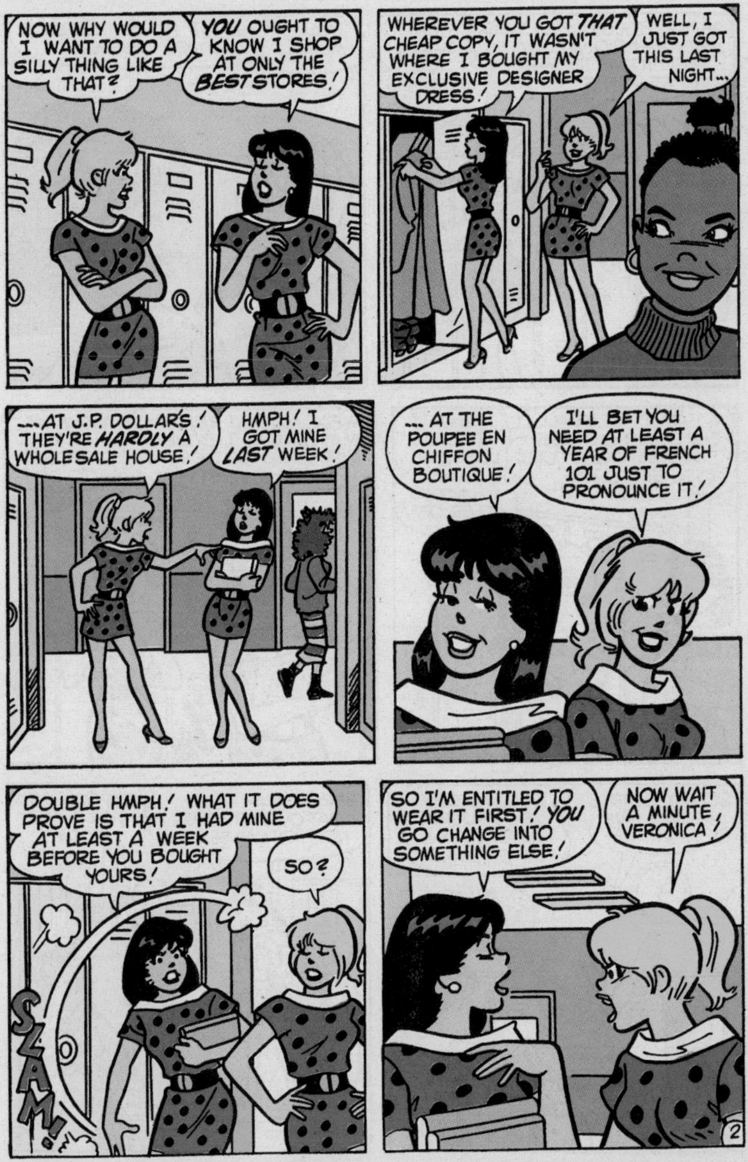
NOW WHY WOULD I WANT TO DO A SILLY THING LIKE THAT?
YOU OUGHT TO KNOW I SHOP AT ONLY THE BEST STORES!
WHEREVER YOU GOT THAT CHEAP COPY, IT WASN'T WHERE I BOUGHT MY EXCLUSIVE DESIGNER DRESS!
WELL, I JUST GOT THIS LAST NIGHT...
...AT J.P. DOLLAR'S! THEY'RE HARDLY A WHOLESALE HOUSE!
HMPH! I GOT MINE LAST WEEK!
...AT THE POUPEE EN CHIFFON BOUTIQUE!
I'LL BET YOU NEED AT LEAST A YEAR OF FRENCH 101 JUST TO PRONOUNCE IT!
DOUBLE HMPH! WHAT IT DOES PROVE IS THAT I HAD MINE AT LEAST A WEEK BEFORE YOU BOUGHT YOURS!
SO?
SLAM!
SO I'M ENTITLED TO WEAR IT FIRST! YOU GO CHANGE INTO SOMETHING ELSE!
NOW WAIT A MINUTE, VERONICA!
2

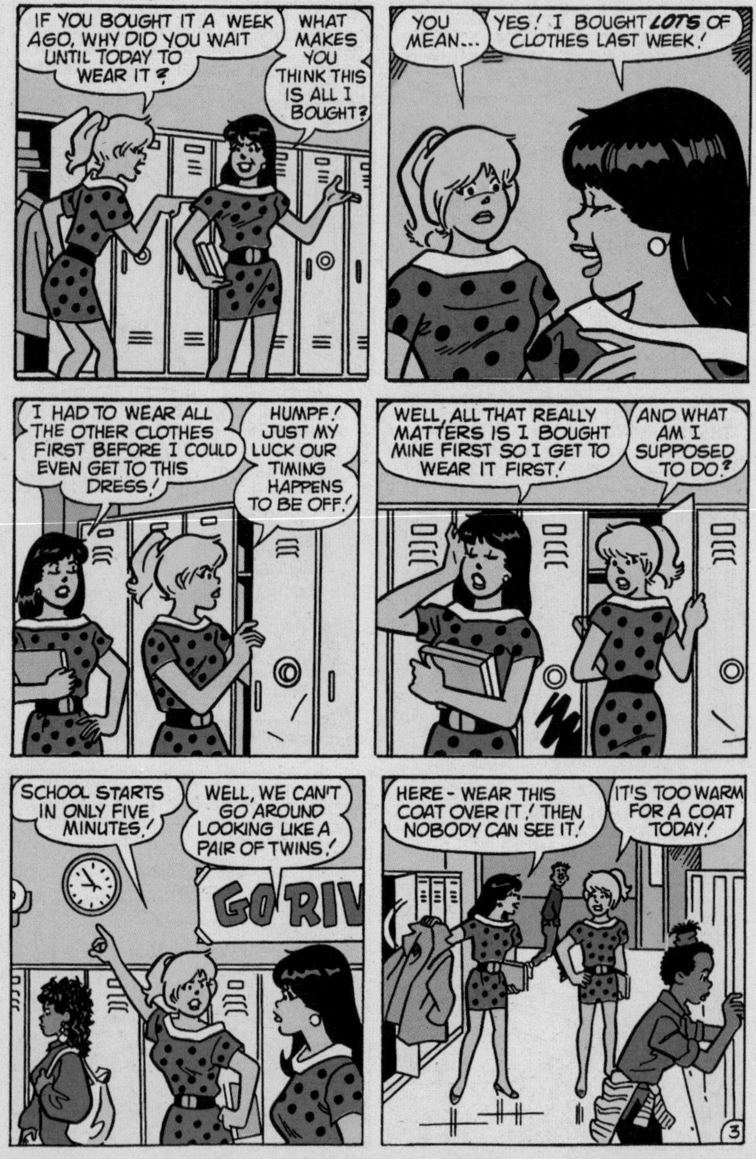

IF YOU BOUGHT IT A WEEK AGO, WHY DID YOU WAIT UNTIL TODAY TO WEAR IT?
WHAT MAKES YOU THINK THIS IS ALL I BOUGHT?
YOU MEAN...
YES! I BOUGHT LOTS OF CLOTHES LAST WEEK!
I HAD TO WEAR ALL THE OTHER CLOTHES FIRST BEFORE I COULD EVEN GET TO THIS DRESS!
HUMPF! JUST MY LUCK OUR TIMING HAPPENS TO BE OFF!
WELL, ALL THAT REALLY MATTERS IS I BOUGHT MINE FIRST SO I GET TO WEAR IT FIRST!
AND WHAT AM I SUPPOSED TO DO?
SCHOOL STARTS IN ONLY FIVE MINUTES!
WELL, WE CAN'T GO AROUND LOOKING LIKE A PAIR OF TWINS!
GO RIV
HERE - WEAR THIS COAT OVER IT! THEN NOBODY CAN SEE IT!
IT'S TOO WARM FOR A COAT TODAY!
3

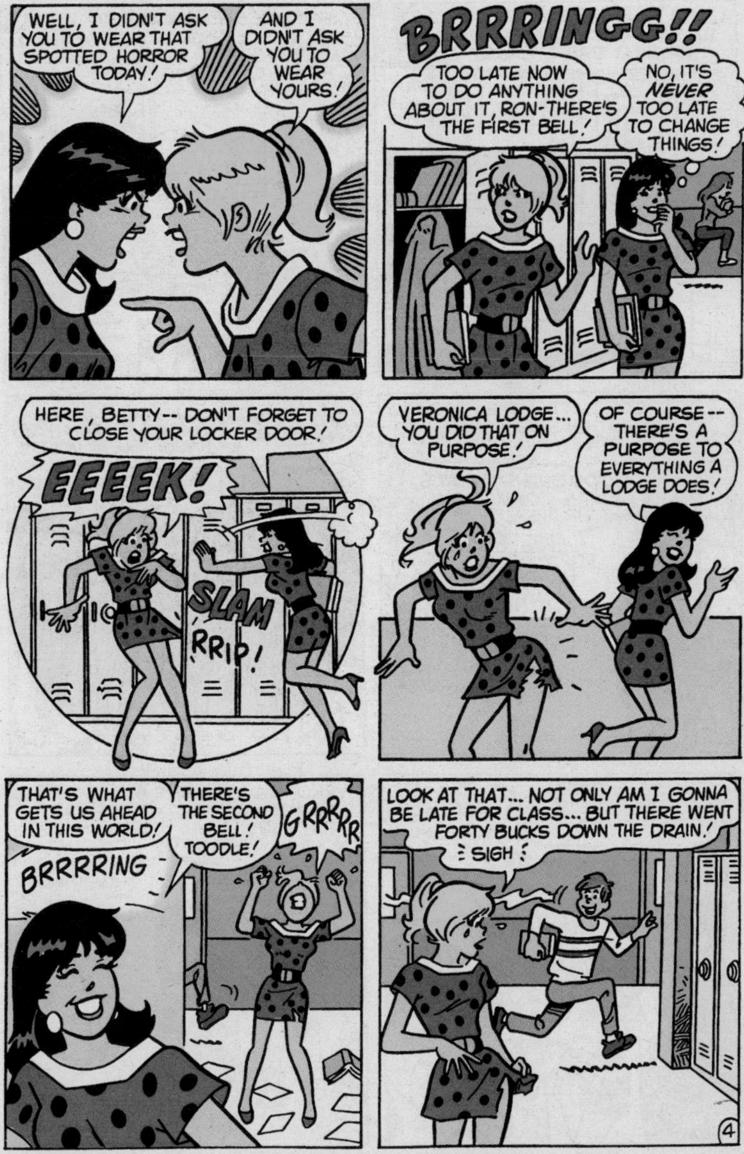
WELL, I DIDN'T ASK YOU TO WEAR THAT SPOTTED HORROR TODAY!
AND I DIDN'T ASK YOU TO WEAR YOURS!
BRRRINGG!!
TOO LATE NOW TO DO ANYTHING ABOUT IT, RON-THERE'S THE FIRST BELL!
NO, IT'S NEVER TOO LATE TO CHANGE THINGS!
HERE, BETTY-- DON'T FORGET TO CLOSE YOUR LOCKER DOOR!
EEEEK!
SLAM
RRIP!
VERONICA LODGE... YOU DID THAT ON PURPOSE!
OF COURSE-- THERE'S A PURPOSE TO EVERYTHING A LODGE DOES!
THAT'S WHAT GETS US AHEAD IN THIS WORLD!
BRRRRING
THERE'S THE SECOND BELL! TOODLE!
GRRRRR
LOOK AT THAT... NOT ONLY AM I GONNA BE LATE FOR CLASS... BUT THERE WENT FORTY BUCKS DOWN THE DRAIN!
SIGH
4

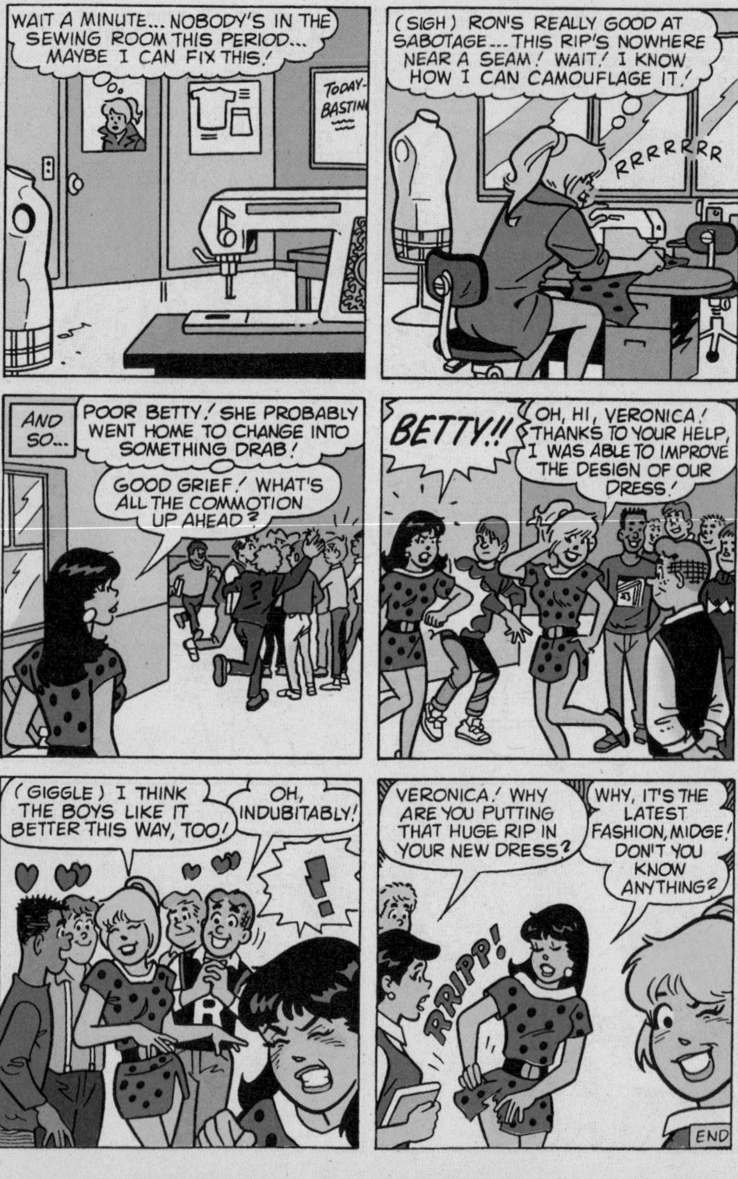
WAIT A MINUTE... NOBODY'S IN THE SEWING ROOM THIS PERIOD... MAYBE I CAN FIX THIS!
TODAY- BASTIN
(SIGH) RON'S REALLY GOOD AT SABOTAGE... THIS RIP'S NOWHERE NEAR A SEAM! WAIT! I KNOW HOW I CAN CAMOUFLAGE IT!
RRRRRRRR
AND SO...
POOR BETTY! SHE PROBABLY WENT HOME TO CHANGE INTO SOMETHING DRAB!
GOOD GRIEF! WHAT'S ALL THE COMMOTION UP AHEAD?
BETTY!!
OH, HI, VERONICA! THANKS TO YOUR HELP, I WAS ABLE TO IMPROVE THE DESIGN OF OUR DRESS!
(GIGGLE) I THINK THE BOYS LIKE IT BETTER THIS WAY, TOO!
OH, INDUBITABLY!
!
R
VERONICA! WHY ARE YOU PUTTING THAT HUGE RIP IN YOUR NEW DRESS?
WHY, IT'S THE LATEST FASHION, MIDGE! DON'T YOU KNOW ANYTHING?
RRIPP!
END

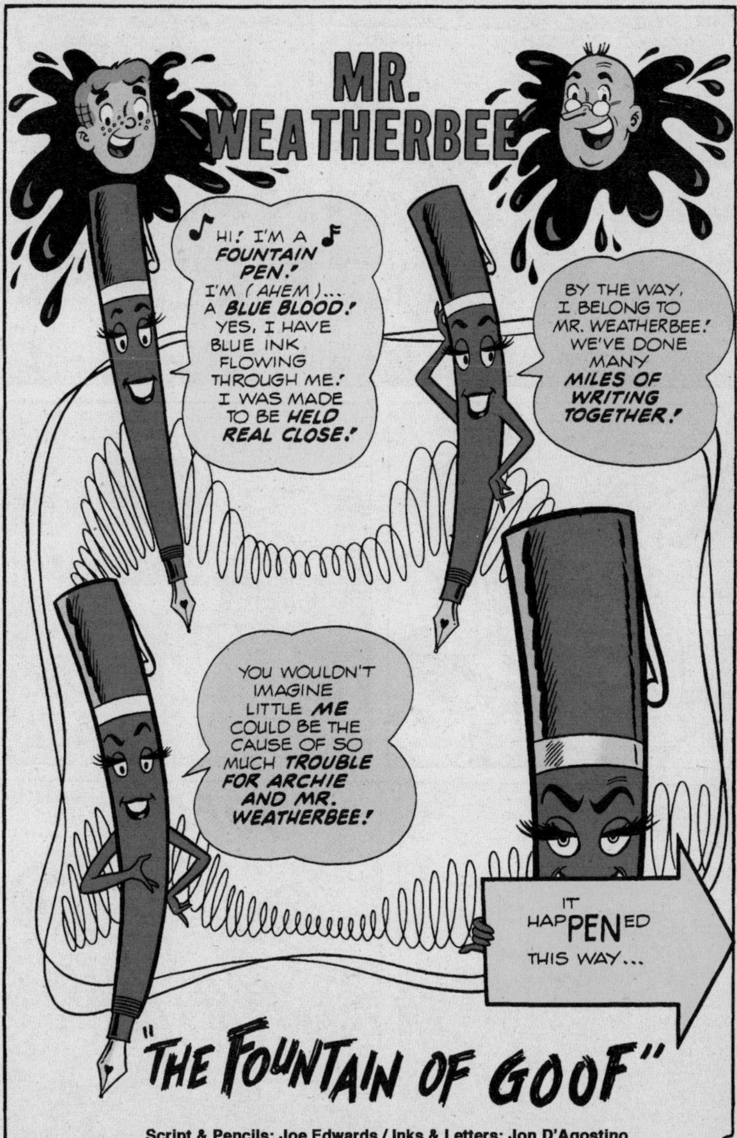

MR. WEATHERBEE
HI! I'M A FOUNTAIN PEN! I'M (AHEM)... A BLUE BLOOD! YES, I HAVE BLUE INK FLOWING THROUGH ME! I WAS MADE TO BE HELD REAL CLOSE!
BY THE WAY, I BELONG TO MR. WEATHERBEE! WE'VE DONE MANY MILES OF WRITING TOGETHER!
YOU WOULDN'T IMAGINE LITTLE ME COULD BE THE CAUSE OF SO MUCH TROUBLE FOR ARCHIE AND MR. WEATHERBEE!
IT HAPPENED THIS WAY...
"THE FOUNTAIN OF GOOF"
Script & Pencils: Joe Edwards / Inks & Letters: Jon D'Agostino

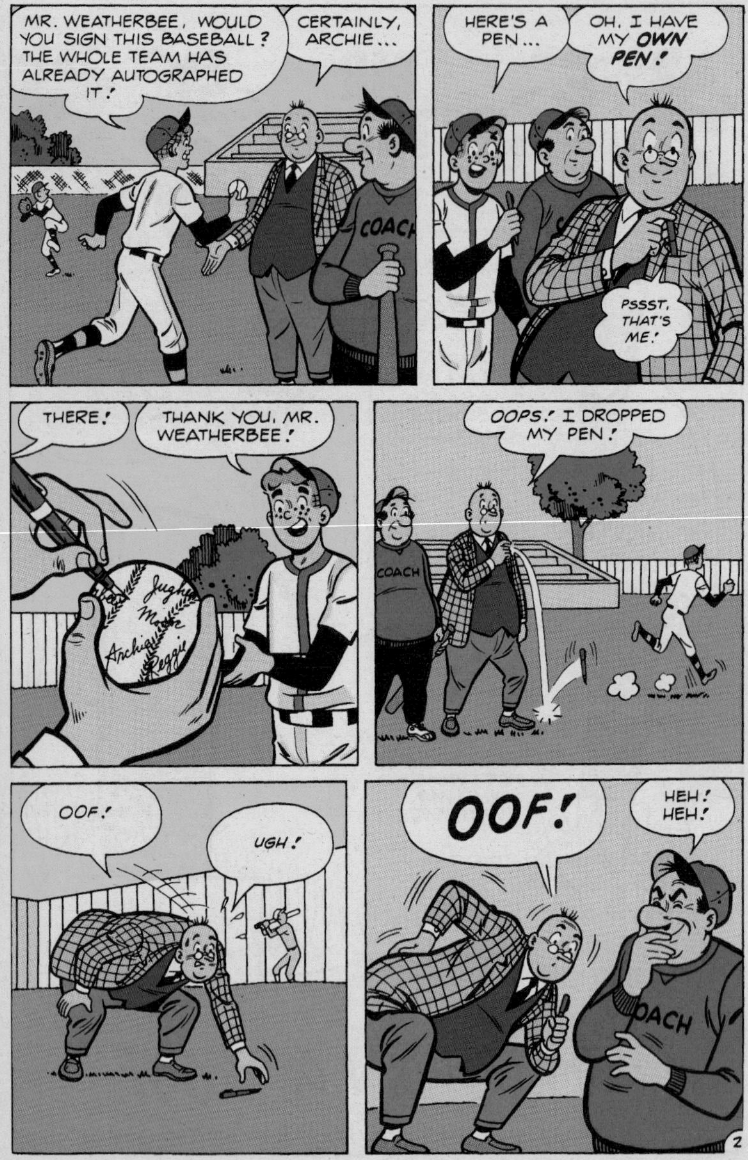
MR. WEATHERBEE, WOULD YOU SIGN THIS BASEBALL? THE WHOLE TEAM HAS ALREADY AUTOGRAPHED IT!
CERTAINLY, ARCHIE...
COACH
HERE'S A PEN...
OH, I HAVE MY **OWN PEN!**
PSSST, THAT'S ME!
THERE!
THANK YOU, MR. WEATHERBEE!
Archie
OOPS! I DROPPED MY PEN!
COACH
OOF!
UGH!
OOF!
HEH! HEH!
2

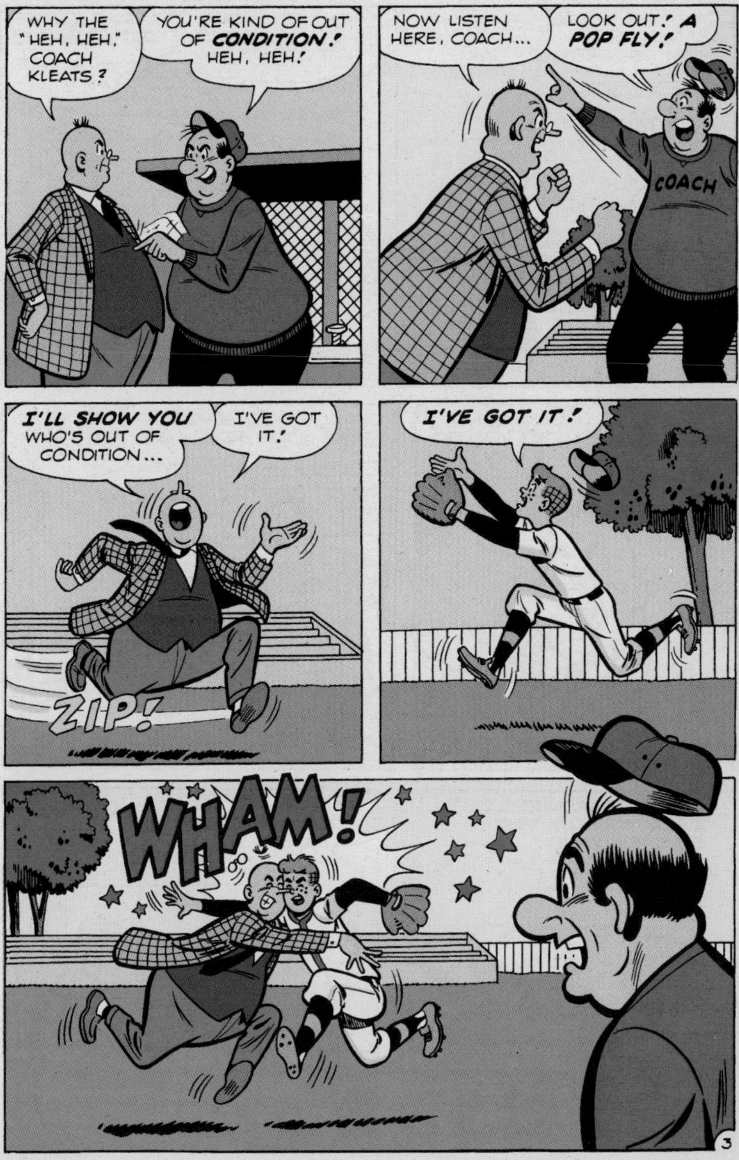

WHY THE "HEH, HEH," COACH KLEATS ?
YOU'RE KIND OF OUT OF CONDITION! HEH, HEH!
NOW LISTEN HERE, COACH...
LOOK OUT! A POP FLY!
COACH
I'LL SHOW YOU WHO'S OUT OF CONDITION...
I'VE GOT IT!
ZIP!
I'VE GOT IT!
WHAM!

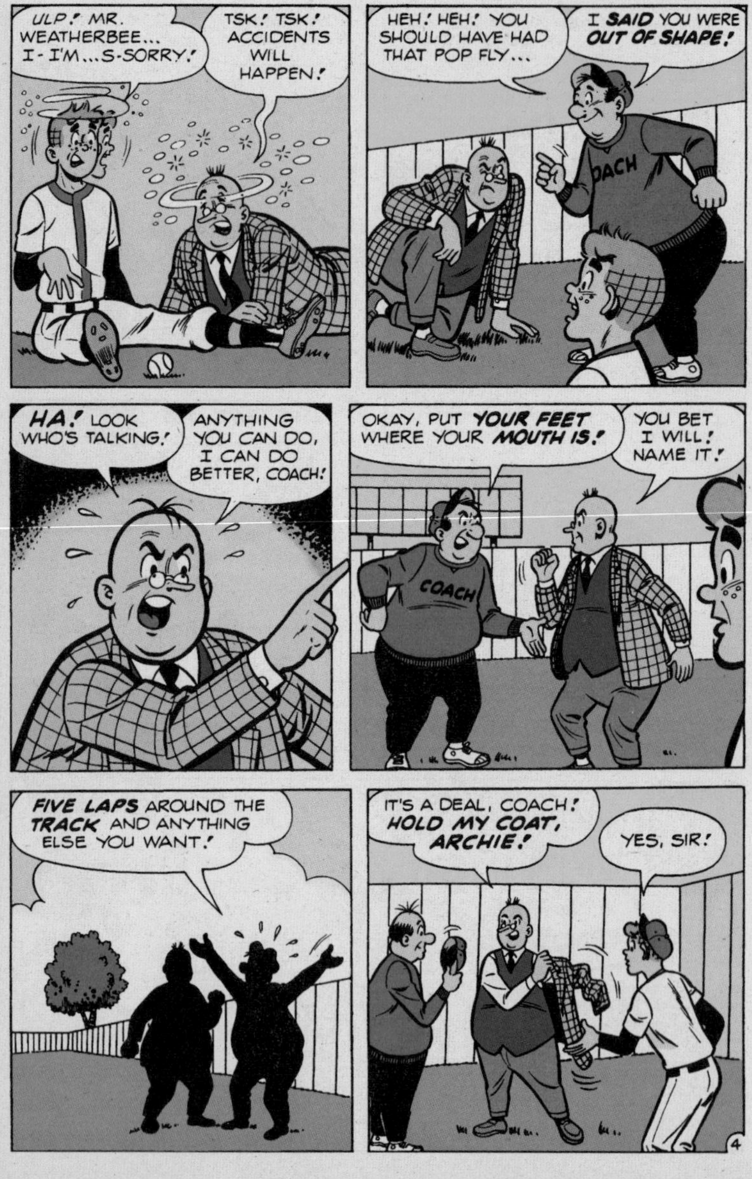
ULP! MR. WEATHERBEE... I-I'M...S-SORRY!
TSK! TSK! ACCIDENTS WILL HAPPEN!
HEH! HEH! YOU SHOULD HAVE HAD THAT POP FLY...
I SAID YOU WERE OUT OF SHAPE!
COACH
HA! LOOK WHO'S TALKING!
ANYTHING YOU CAN DO, I CAN DO BETTER, COACH!
OKAY, PUT YOUR FEET WHERE YOUR MOUTH IS!
YOU BET I WILL! NAME IT!
COACH
FIVE LAPS AROUND THE TRACK AND ANYTHING ELSE YOU WANT!
IT'S A DEAL, COACH! HOLD MY COAT, ARCHIE!
YES, SIR!
4

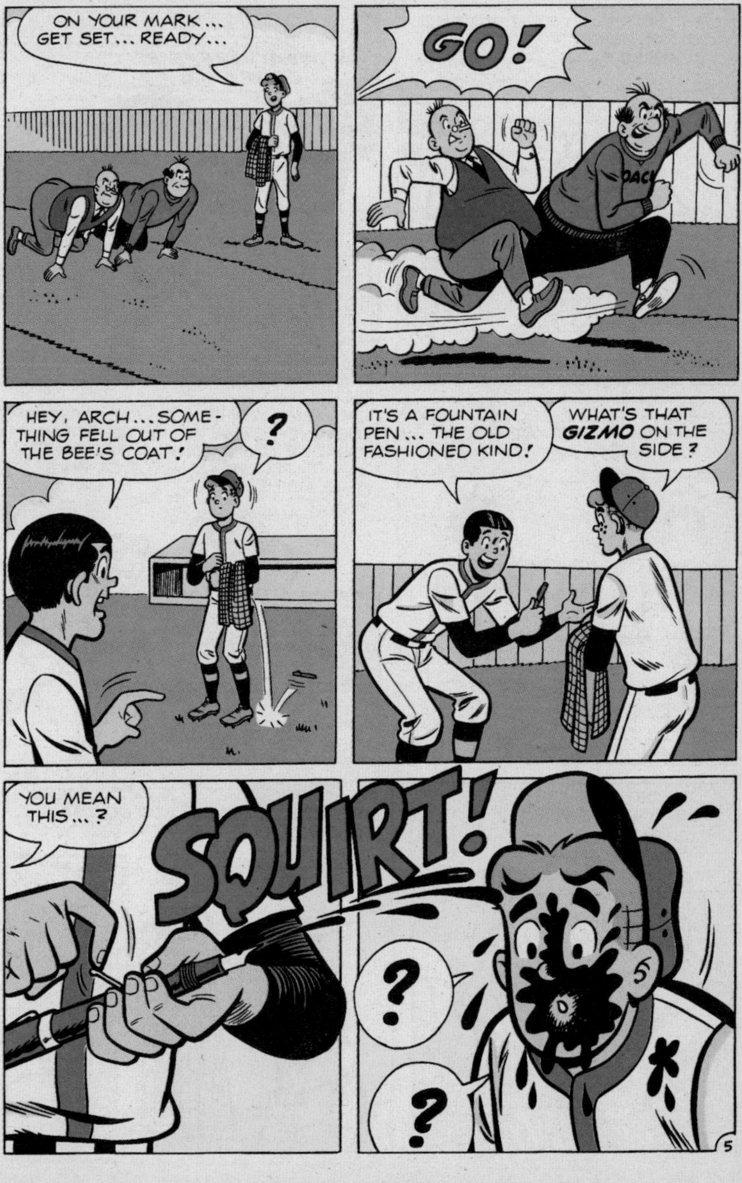
ON YOUR MARK... GET SET... READY...
GO!
HEY, ARCH...SOME-THING FELL OUT OF THE BEE'S COAT!
?
IT'S A FOUNTAIN PEN... THE OLD FASHIONED KIND!
WHAT'S THAT GIZMO ON THE SIDE?
YOU MEAN THIS...?
SQUIRT!
?
?

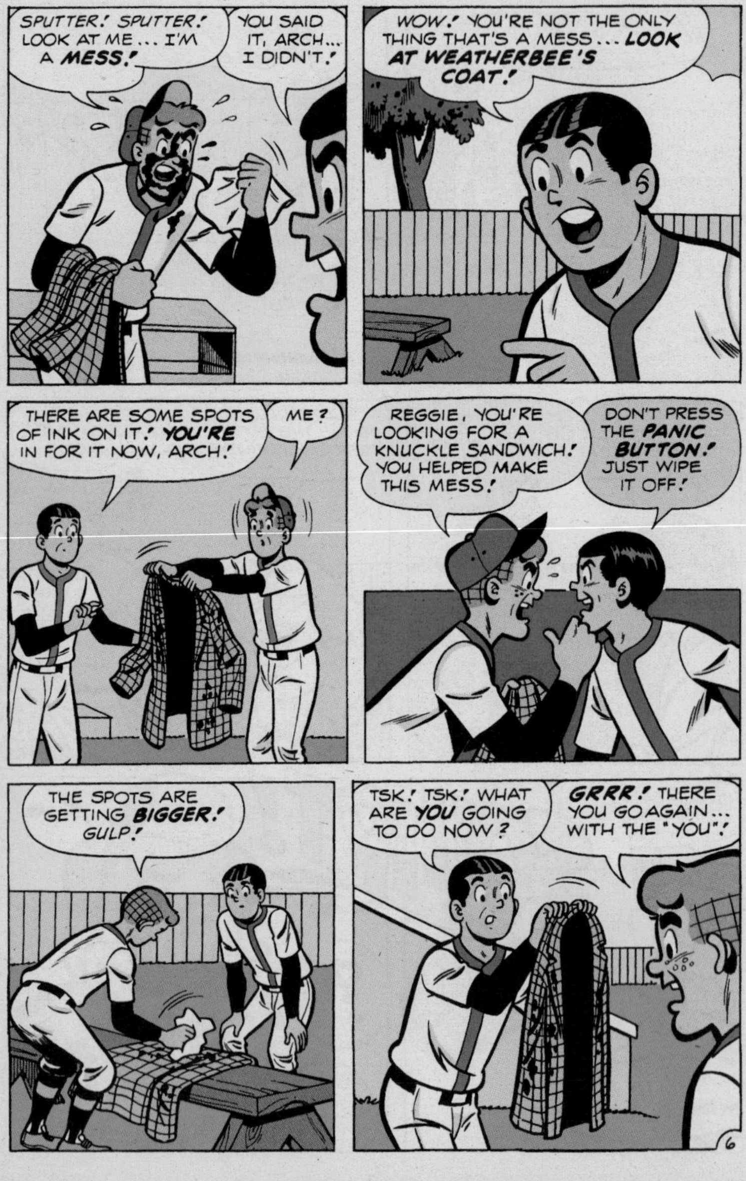
SPUTTER! SPUTTER! LOOK AT ME... I'M A MESS!
YOU SAID IT, ARCH... I DIDN'T!
WOW! YOU'RE NOT THE ONLY THING THAT'S A MESS... LOOK AT WEATHERBEE'S COAT!
THERE ARE SOME SPOTS OF INK ON IT! YOU'RE IN FOR IT NOW, ARCH!
ME?
REGGIE, YOU'RE LOOKING FOR A KNUCKLE SANDWICH! YOU HELPED MAKE THIS MESS!
DON'T PRESS THE PANIC BUTTON! JUST WIPE IT OFF!
THE SPOTS ARE GETTING BIGGER! GULP!
TSK! TSK! WHAT ARE YOU GOING TO DO NOW?
GRRR! THERE YOU GO AGAIN... WITH THE "YOU"!
6

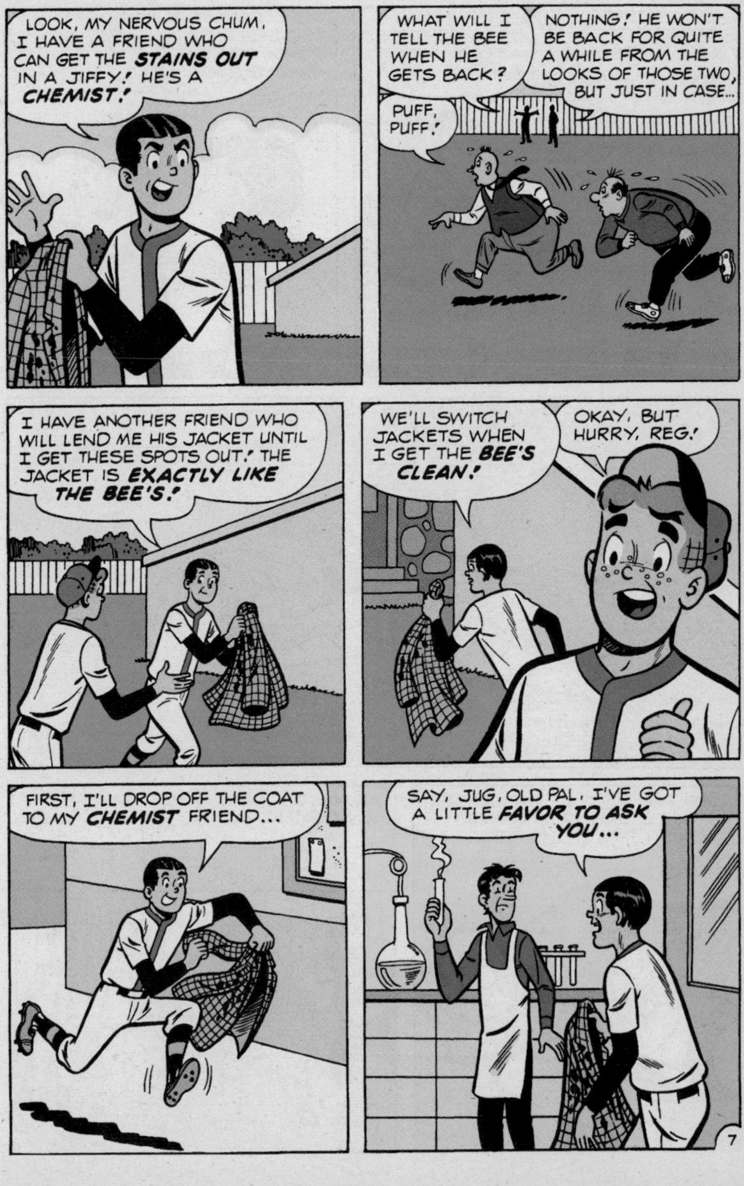
LOOK, MY NERVOUS CHUM, I HAVE A FRIEND WHO CAN GET THE STAINS OUT IN A JIFFY! HE'S A CHEMIST!
WHAT WILL I TELL THE BEE WHEN HE GETS BACK?
NOTHING! HE WON'T BE BACK FOR QUITE A WHILE FROM THE LOOKS OF THOSE TWO, BUT JUST IN CASE...
PUFF, PUFF!
I HAVE ANOTHER FRIEND WHO WILL LEND ME HIS JACKET UNTIL I GET THESE SPOTS OUT! THE JACKET IS EXACTLY LIKE THE BEE'S!
WE'LL SWITCH JACKETS WHEN I GET THE BEE'S CLEAN!
OKAY, BUT HURRY, REG!
FIRST, I'LL DROP OFF THE COAT TO MY CHEMIST FRIEND...
SAY, JUG, OLD PAL, I'VE GOT A LITTLE FAVOR TO ASK YOU...

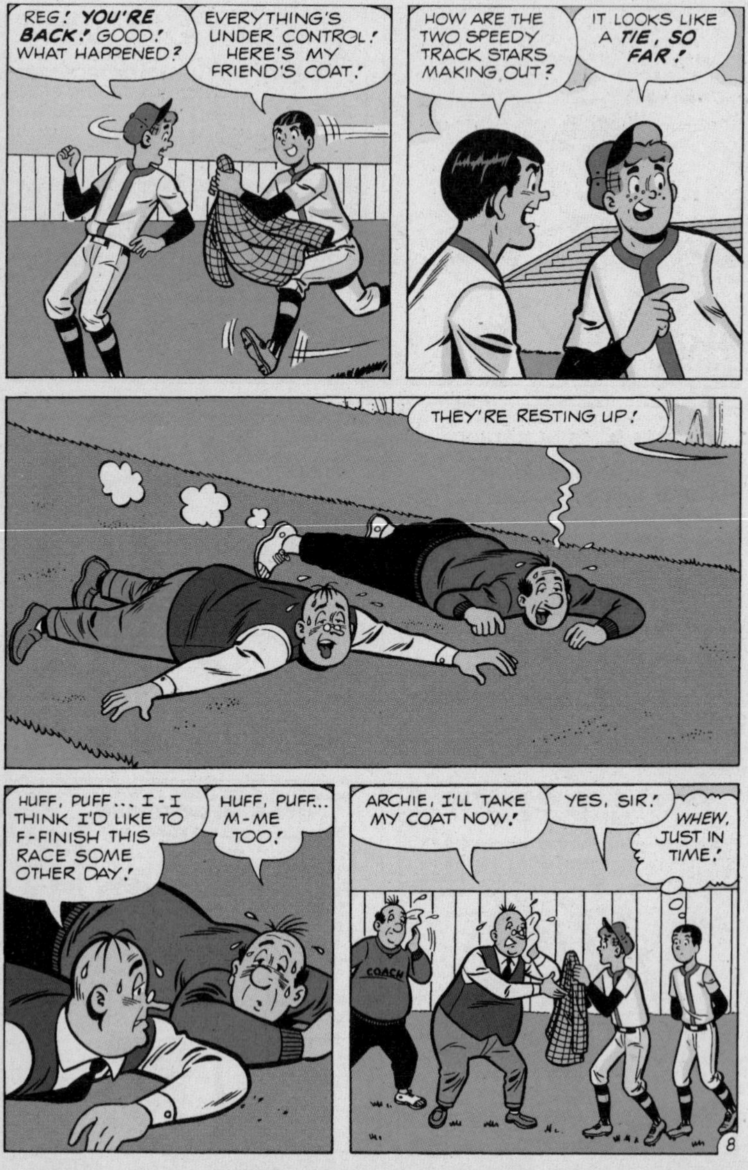
REG! YOU'RE BACK! GOOD! WHAT HAPPENED?
EVERYTHING'S UNDER CONTROL! HERE'S MY FRIEND'S COAT!
HOW ARE THE TWO SPEEDY TRACK STARS MAKING OUT?
IT LOOKS LIKE A TIE, SO FAR!
THEY'RE RESTING UP!
HUFF, PUFF... I-I THINK I'D LIKE TO F-FINISH THIS RACE SOME OTHER DAY!
HUFF, PUFF... M-ME TOO!
ARCHIE, I'LL TAKE MY COAT NOW!
YES, SIR!
WHEW, JUST IN TIME!
COACH
8

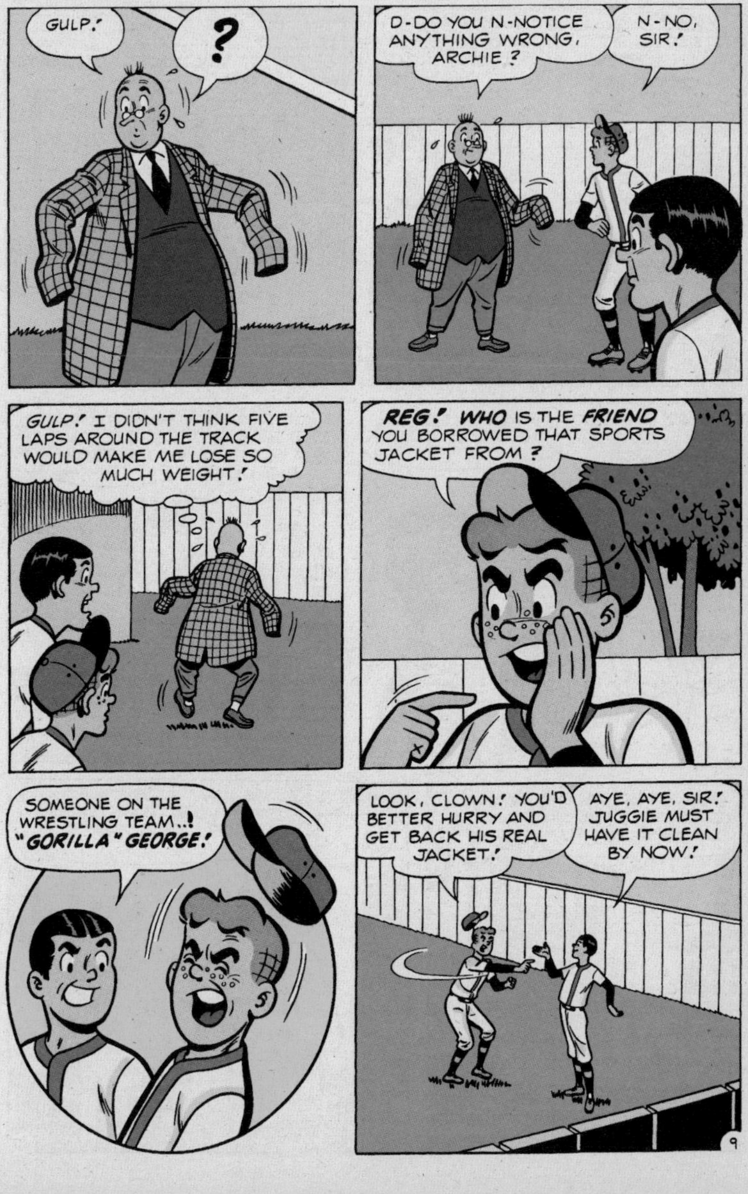
GULP!
?
D-DO YOU N-NOTICE ANYTHING WRONG, ARCHIE?
N-NO, SIR!
GULP! I DIDN'T THINK FIVE LAPS AROUND THE TRACK WOULD MAKE ME LOSE SO MUCH WEIGHT!
REG! WHO IS THE FRIEND YOU BORROWED THAT SPORTS JACKET FROM?
SOMEONE ON THE WRESTLING TEAM..! "GORILLA" GEORGE!
LOOK, CLOWN! YOU'D BETTER HURRY AND GET BACK HIS REAL JACKET!
AYE, AYE, SIR! JUGGIE MUST HAVE IT CLEAN BY NOW!

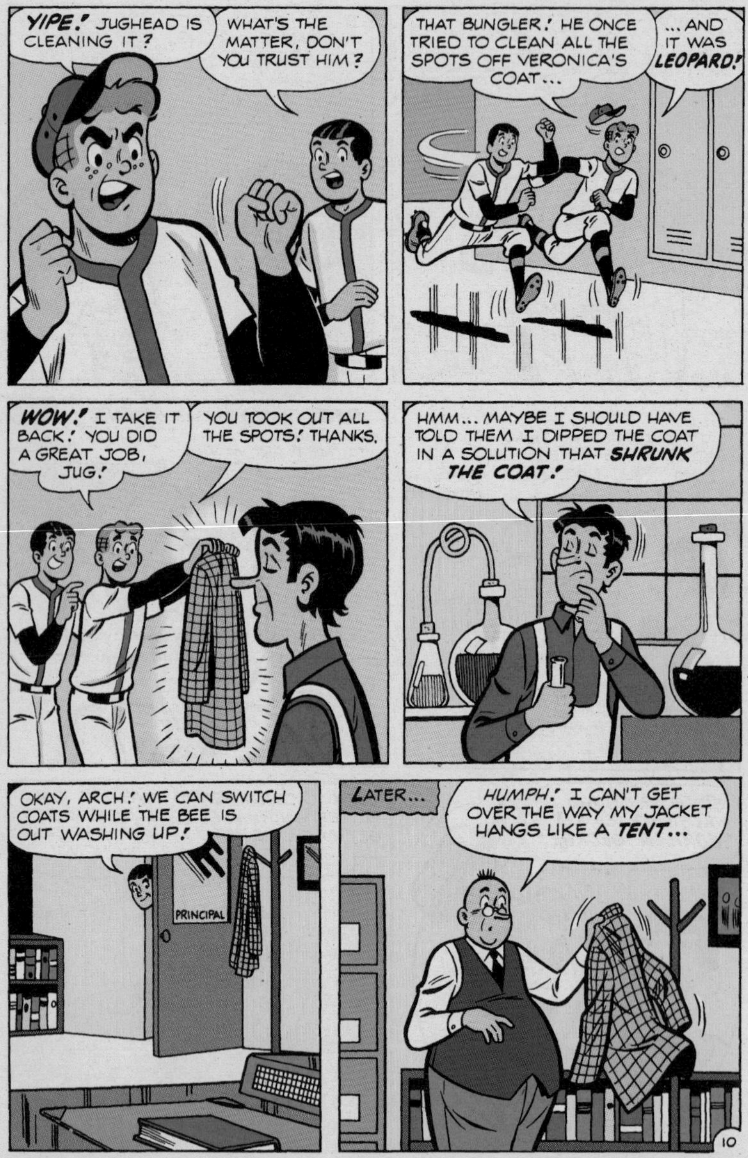
YIPE! JUGHEAD IS CLEANING IT?
WHAT'S THE MATTER, DON'T YOU TRUST HIM?
THAT BUNGLER! HE ONCE TRIED TO CLEAN ALL THE SPOTS OFF VERONICA'S COAT...
...AND IT WAS LEOPARD!
WOW! I TAKE IT BACK! YOU DID A GREAT JOB, JUG!
YOU TOOK OUT ALL THE SPOTS! THANKS.
HMM... MAYBE I SHOULD HAVE TOLD THEM I DIPPED THE COAT IN A SOLUTION THAT SHRUNK THE COAT!
OKAY, ARCH! WE CAN SWITCH COATS WHILE THE BEE IS OUT WASHING UP!
PRINCIPAL
LATER...
HUMPH! I CAN'T GET OVER THE WAY MY JACKET HANGS LIKE A TENT...
10

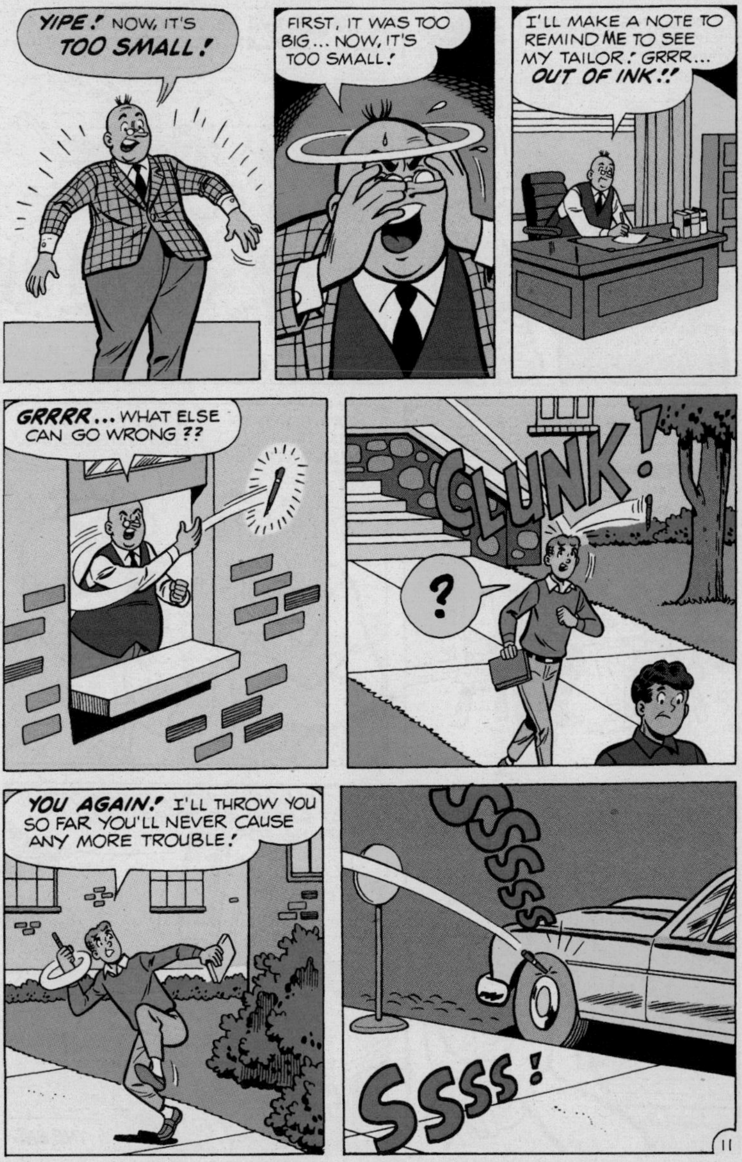
YIPE! NOW, IT'S TOO SMALL!
FIRST, IT WAS TOO BIG... NOW, IT'S TOO SMALL!
I'LL MAKE A NOTE TO REMIND ME TO SEE MY TAILOR! GRRR... OUT OF INK!!
GRRRR... WHAT ELSE CAN GO WRONG ??
CLUNK!
?
YOU AGAIN! I'LL THROW YOU SO FAR YOU'LL NEVER CAUSE ANY MORE TROUBLE!
SSSSSS
SSSS!

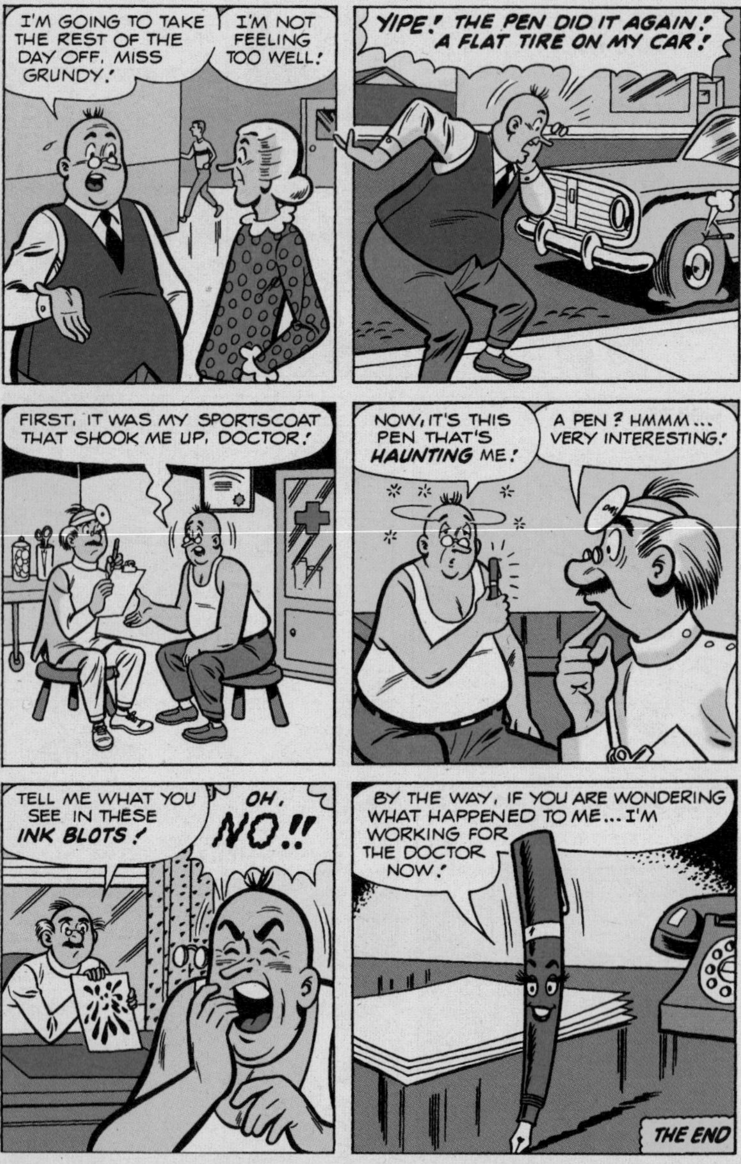

I'M GOING TO TAKE THE REST OF THE DAY OFF, MISS GRUNDY!
I'M NOT FEELING TOO WELL!
YIPE! THE PEN DID IT AGAIN! A FLAT TIRE ON MY CAR!
FIRST, IT WAS MY SPORTSCOAT THAT SHOOK ME UP, DOCTOR!
NOW, IT'S THIS PEN THAT'S HAUNTING ME!
A PEN ? HMMM... VERY INTERESTING!
TELL ME WHAT YOU SEE IN THESE INK BLOTS!
OH, NO!!
BY THE WAY, IF YOU ARE WONDERING WHAT HAPPENED TO ME... I'M WORKING FOR THE DOCTOR NOW!
THE END

Archie in "TODAY'S KIDS"

Mary: OH, FRED! I'VE CALLED THE POLICE, THE HOSPITAL AND ALL OF ARCHIE'S FRIENDS!

Mary: NO ONE KNOWS *WHERE* HE IS! AND IT'S A *SCHOOL NIGHT!*

Fred: HE NEVER STAYS OUT THIS LATE— EVEN ON A *WEEKEND!* TODAY'S KIDS, THEY JUST DON'T *CARE...* JUST WAIT'LL I GET MY *HANDS* ON HIM--!

WAP!

Mary: FRED, YOU KNOW YOU DON'T *MEAN* THAT!

Fred: YOU'RE *RIGHT,* MARY! YOU'RE *RIGHT!* IT'S JUST SO--!

Script: Rich Margopoulos / Pencils: Rex Lindsey / Inks: Rudy Lapick / Letters: Bill Yoshida

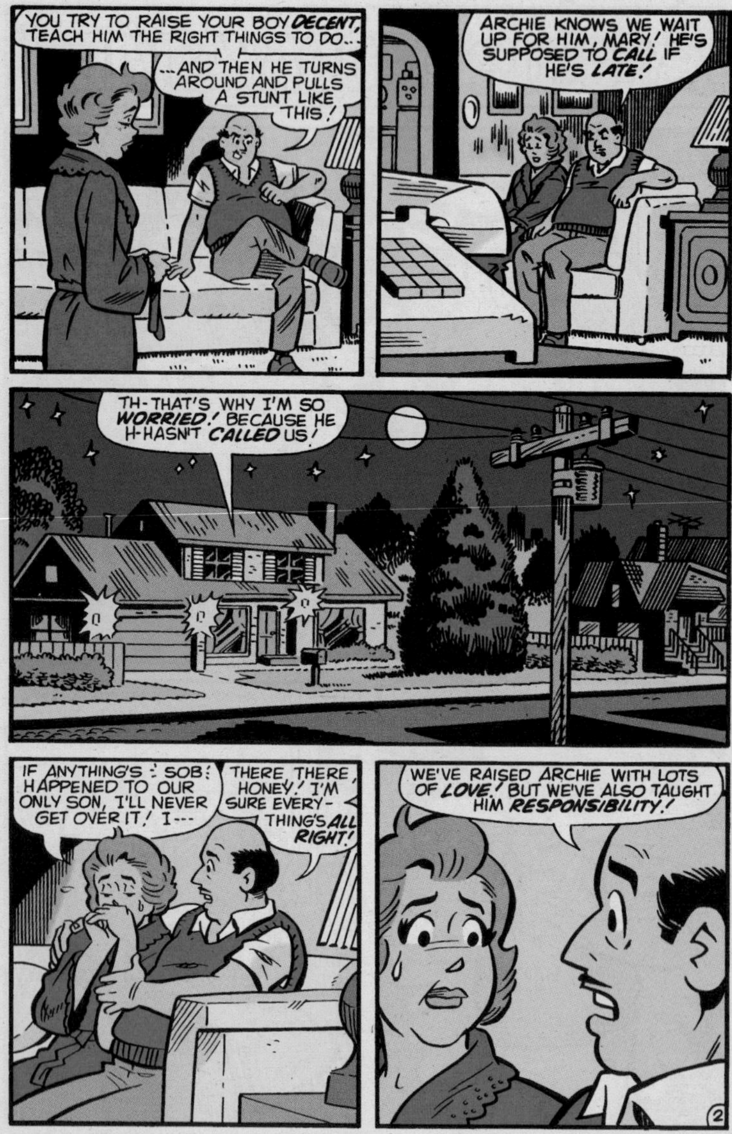
YOU TRY TO RAISE YOUR BOY DECENT, TEACH HIM THE RIGHT THINGS TO DO...
...AND THEN HE TURNS AROUND AND PULLS A STUNT LIKE THIS!
ARCHIE KNOWS WE WAIT UP FOR HIM, MARY! HE'S SUPPOSED TO CALL IF HE'S LATE!
TH-THAT'S WHY I'M SO WORRIED! BECAUSE HE H-HASN'T CALLED US!
IF ANYTHING'S - SOB! - HAPPENED TO OUR ONLY SON, I'LL NEVER GET OVER IT! I---
THERE THERE, HONEY! I'M SURE EVERYTHING'S ALL RIGHT!
WE'VE RAISED ARCHIE WITH LOTS OF LOVE! BUT WE'VE ALSO TAUGHT HIM RESPONSIBILITY!

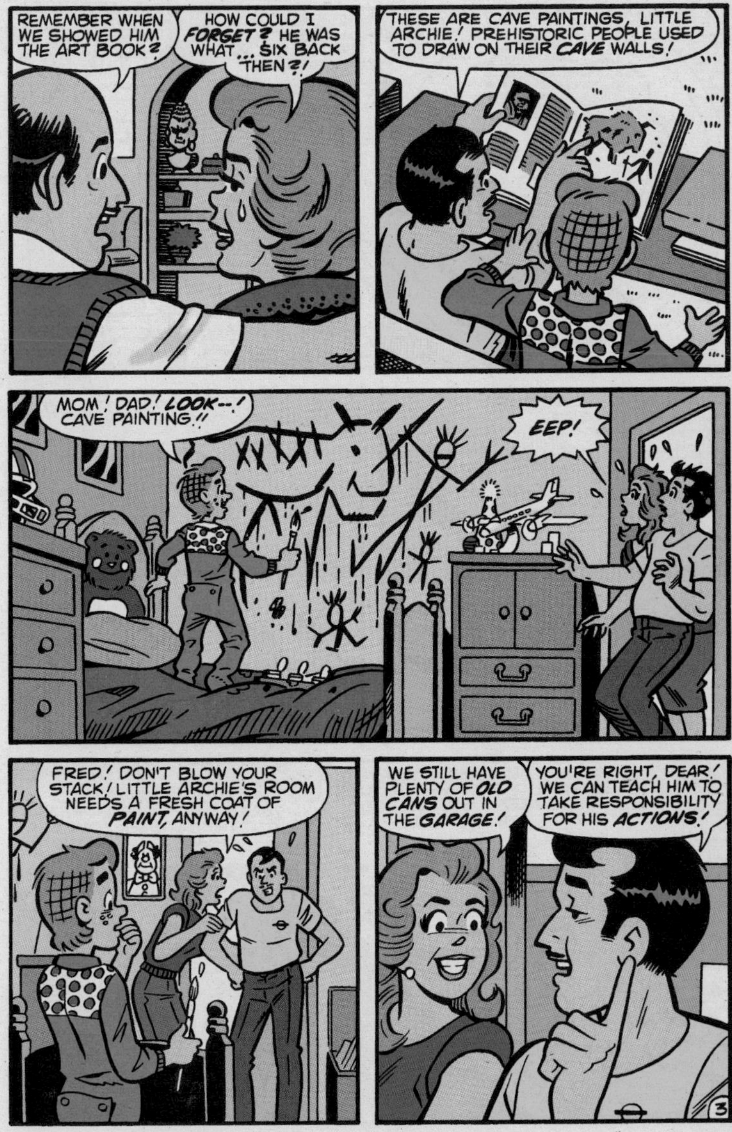
REMEMBER WHEN WE SHOWED HIM THE ART BOOK?
HOW COULD I FORGET? HE WAS WHAT... SIX BACK THEN?!
THESE ARE CAVE PAINTINGS, LITTLE ARCHIE! PREHISTORIC PEOPLE USED TO DRAW ON THEIR CAVE WALLS!
MOM! DAD! LOOK--! CAVE PAINTING!!
EEP!
FRED! DON'T BLOW YOUR STACK! LITTLE ARCHIE'S ROOM NEEDS A FRESH COAT OF PAINT, ANYWAY!
WE STILL HAVE PLENTY OF OLD CANS OUT IN THE GARAGE!
YOU'RE RIGHT, DEAR! WE CAN TEACH HIM TO TAKE RESPONSIBILITY FOR HIS ACTIONS!
3

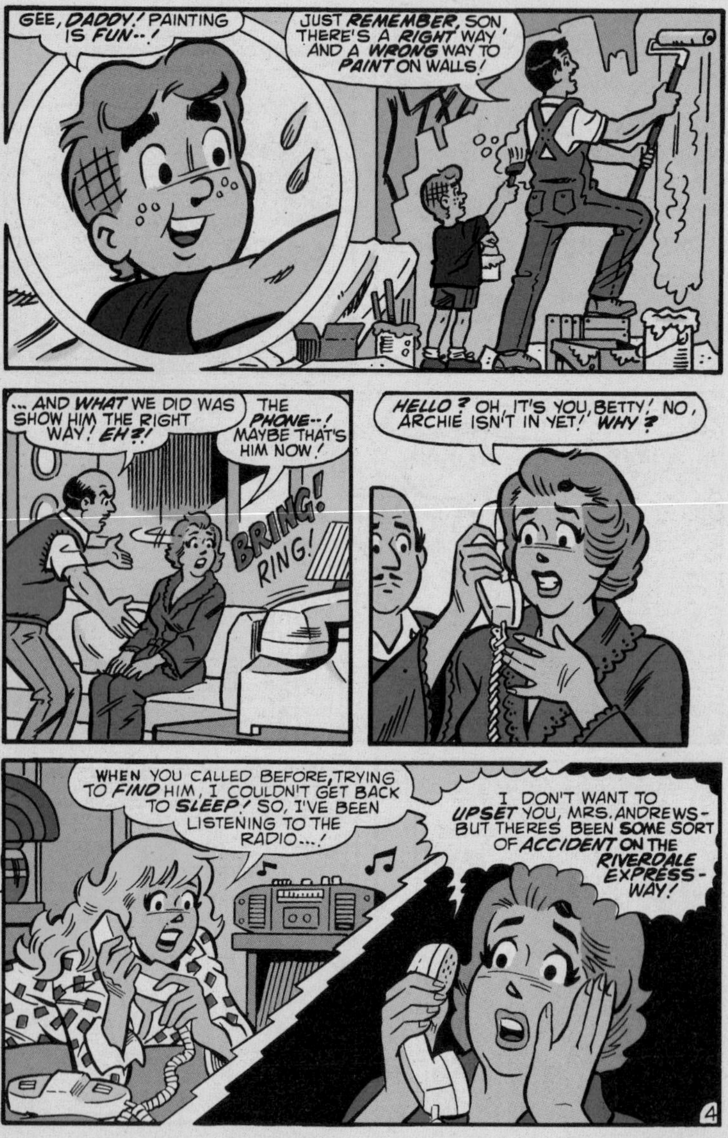
GEE, DADDY! PAINTING IS FUN--!
JUST REMEMBER, SON THERE'S A RIGHT WAY AND A WRONG WAY TO PAINT ON WALLS!
... AND WHAT WE DID WAS SHOW HIM THE RIGHT WAY! EH?!
THE PHONE--! MAYBE THAT'S HIM NOW!
BRING! RING!
HELLO? OH, IT'S YOU, BETTY! NO, ARCHIE ISN'T IN YET! WHY?
WHEN YOU CALLED BEFORE, TRYING TO FIND HIM, I COULDN'T GET BACK TO SLEEP! SO, I'VE BEEN LISTENING TO THE RADIO...!
I DON'T WANT TO UPSET YOU, MRS. ANDREWS-BUT THERES BEEN SOME SORT OF ACCIDENT ON THE RIVERDALE EXPRESS-WAY!
4

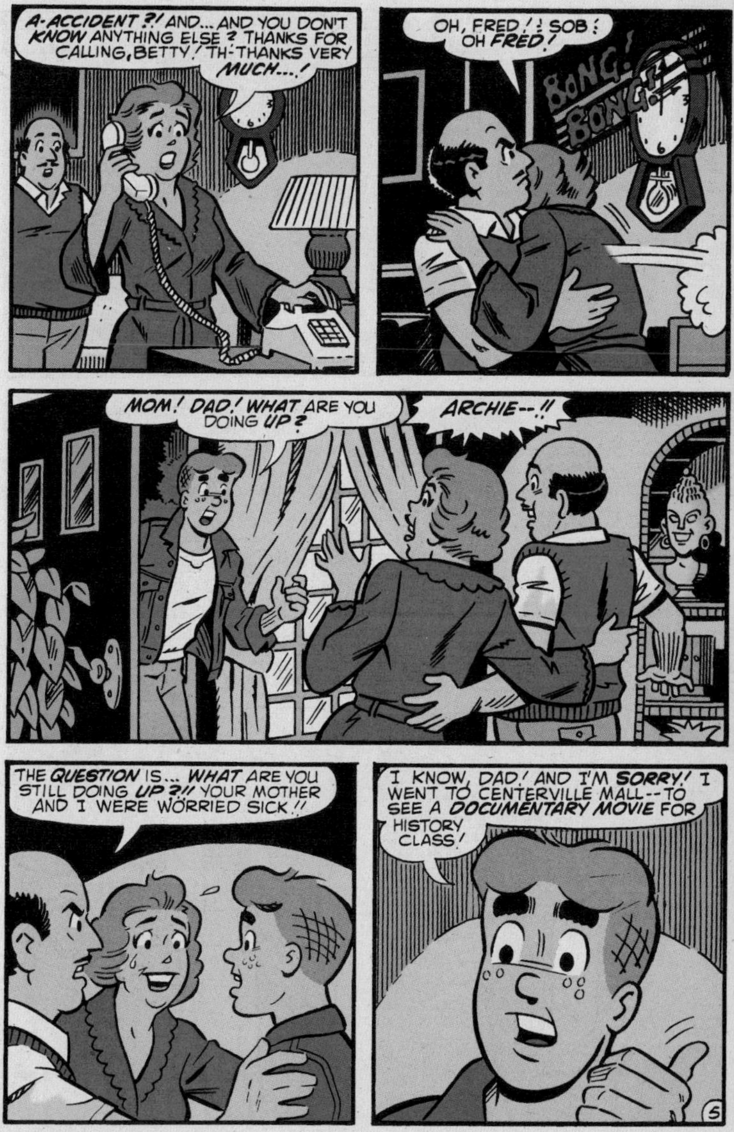

A-ACCIDENT?! AND... AND YOU DON'T KNOW ANYTHING ELSE? THANKS FOR CALLING, BETTY! TH-THANKS VERY MUCH...!
OH, FRED!! SOB! OH FRED!
BONG! BONG!!
MOM! DAD! WHAT ARE YOU DOING UP?
ARCHIE--!!
THE QUESTION IS... WHAT ARE YOU STILL DOING UP?!! YOUR MOTHER AND I WERE WORRIED SICK!!
I KNOW, DAD! AND I'M SORRY! I WENT TO CENTERVILLE MALL--TO SEE A DOCUMENTARY MOVIE FOR HISTORY CLASS!
5

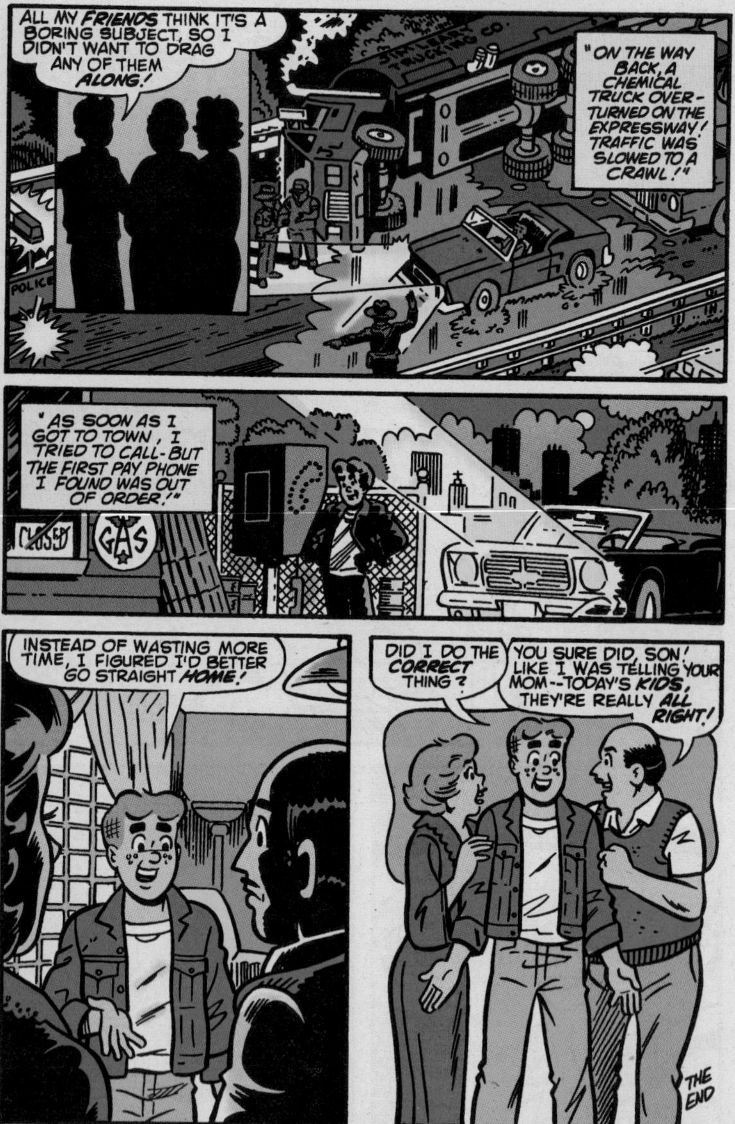
ALL MY FRIENDS THINK IT'S A BORING SUBJECT, SO I DIDN'T WANT TO DRAG ANY OF THEM ALONG!
"ON THE WAY BACK, A CHEMICAL TRUCK OVER-TURNED ON THE EXPRESSWAY! TRAFFIC WAS SLOWED TO A CRAWL!"
POLICE
"AS SOON AS I GOT TO TOWN, I TRIED TO CALL-BUT THE FIRST PAY PHONE I FOUND WAS OUT OF ORDER!"
CLOSED
GAS
INSTEAD OF WASTING MORE TIME, I FIGURED I'D BETTER GO STRAIGHT HOME!
DID I DO THE CORRECT THING?
YOU SURE DID, SON! LIKE I WAS TELLING YOUR MOM--TODAY'S KIDS, THEY'RE REALLY ALL RIGHT!
THE END

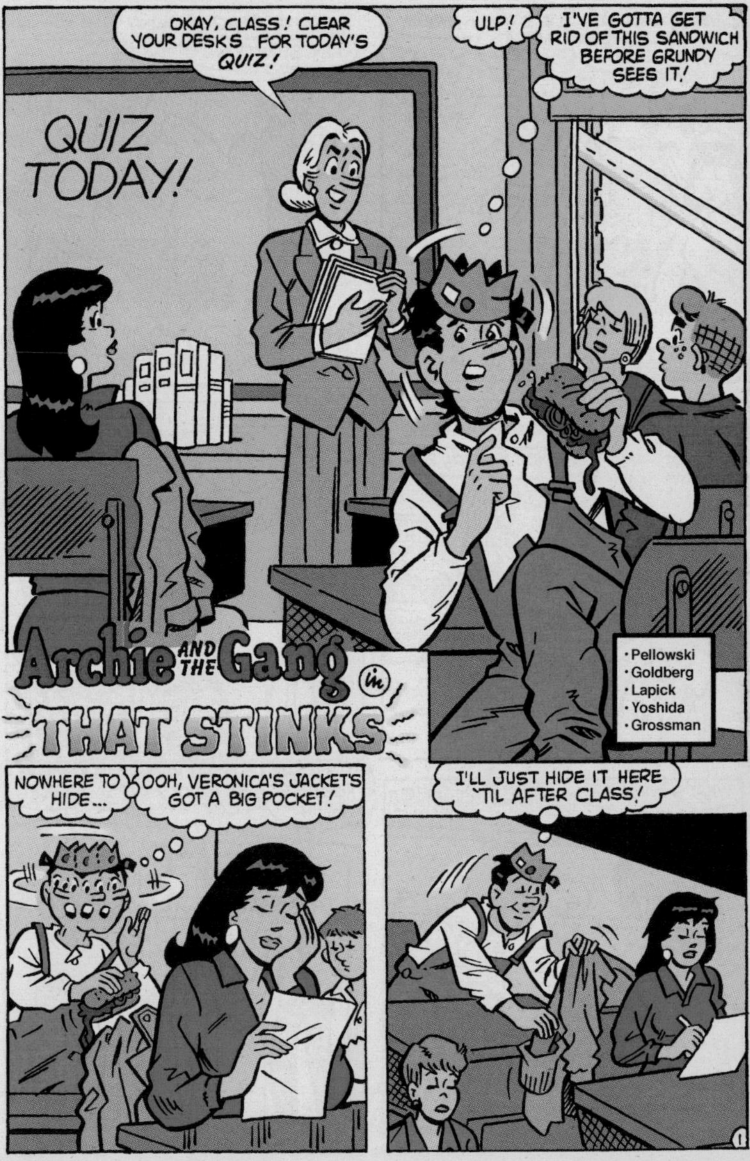

OKAY, CLASS! CLEAR YOUR DESKS FOR TODAY'S QUIZ!
QUIZ TODAY!
ULP!
I'VE GOTTA GET RID OF THIS SANDWICH BEFORE GRUNDY SEES IT!
Archie AND THE Gang in
THAT STINKS
•Pellowski
•Goldberg
•Lapick
•Yoshida
•Grossman
NOWHERE TO HIDE...
OOH, VERONICA'S JACKET'S GOT A BIG POCKET!
I'LL JUST HIDE IT HERE 'TIL AFTER CLASS!
1

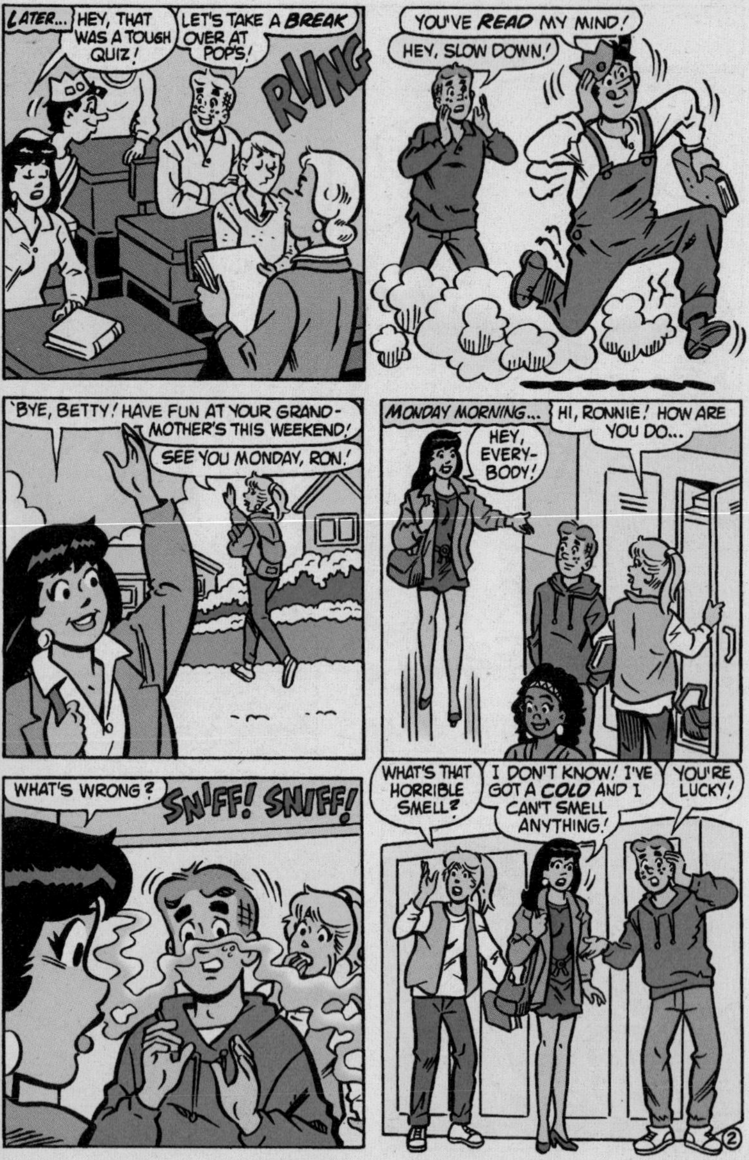
LATER...
HEY, THAT WAS A TOUGH QUIZ!
LET'S TAKE A BREAK OVER AT POP'S!
RIING
YOU'VE READ MY MIND!
HEY, SLOW DOWN!
'BYE, BETTY! HAVE FUN AT YOUR GRAND-MOTHER'S THIS WEEKEND!
SEE YOU MONDAY, RON!
MONDAY MORNING...
HEY, EVERY-BODY!
HI, RONNIE! HOW ARE YOU DO...
WHAT'S WRONG?
SNIFF! SNIFF!
WHAT'S THAT HORRIBLE SMELL?
I DON'T KNOW! I'VE GOT A COLD AND I CAN'T SMELL ANYTHING!
YOU'RE LUCKY!
2

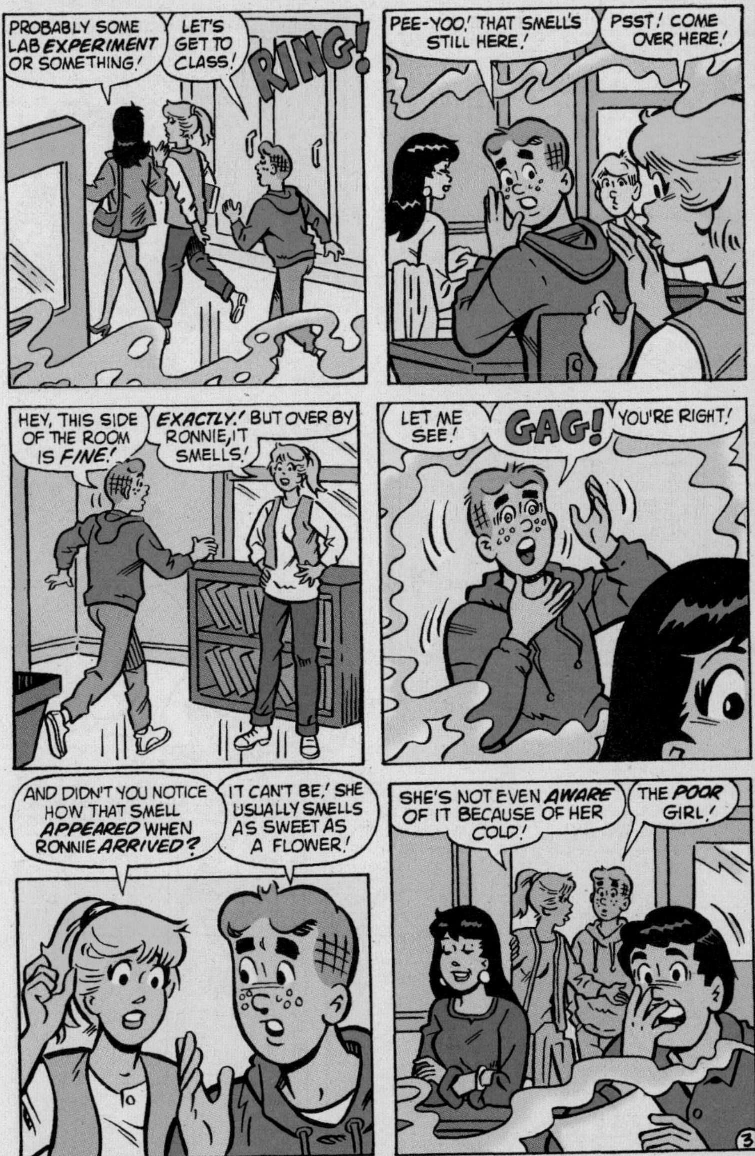
PROBABLY SOME LAB EXPERIMENT OR SOMETHING!
LET'S GET TO CLASS!
RING!
PEE-YOO! THAT SMELL'S STILL HERE!
PSST! COME OVER HERE!
HEY, THIS SIDE OF THE ROOM IS FINE!
EXACTLY! BUT OVER BY RONNIE, IT SMELLS!
LET ME SEE!
GAG!
YOU'RE RIGHT!
AND DIDN'T YOU NOTICE HOW THAT SMELL APPEARED WHEN RONNIE ARRIVED?
IT CAN'T BE! SHE USUALLY SMELLS AS SWEET AS A FLOWER!
SHE'S NOT EVEN AWARE OF IT BECAUSE OF HER COLD!
THE POOR GIRL!
3

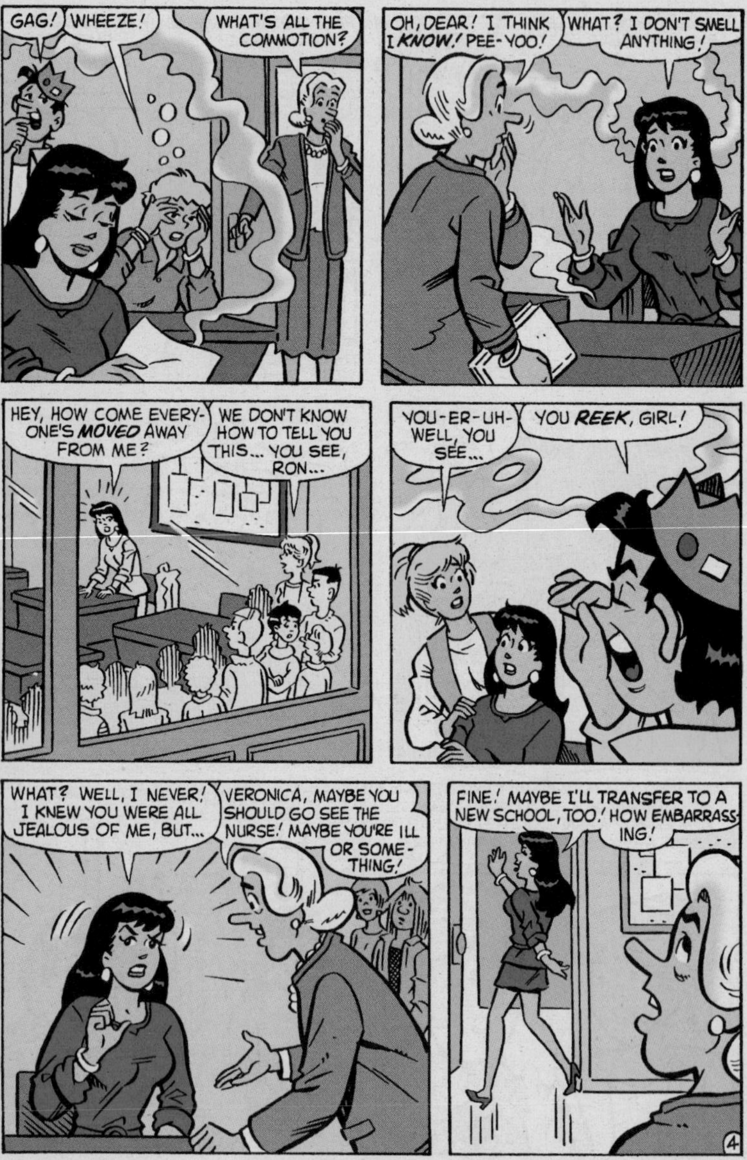
GAG!
WHEEZE!
WHAT'S ALL THE COMMOTION?
OH, DEAR! I THINK I KNOW! PEE-YOO!
WHAT? I DON'T SMELL ANYTHING!
HEY, HOW COME EVERYONE'S MOVED AWAY FROM ME?
WE DON'T KNOW HOW TO TELL YOU THIS... YOU SEE, RON...
YOU-ER-UH-WELL, YOU SEE...
YOU REEK, GIRL!
WHAT? WELL, I NEVER! I KNEW YOU WERE ALL JEALOUS OF ME, BUT...
VERONICA, MAYBE YOU SHOULD GO SEE THE NURSE! MAYBE YOU'RE ILL OR SOMETHING!
FINE! MAYBE I'LL TRANSFER TO A NEW SCHOOL, TOO! HOW EMBARRASSING!
4

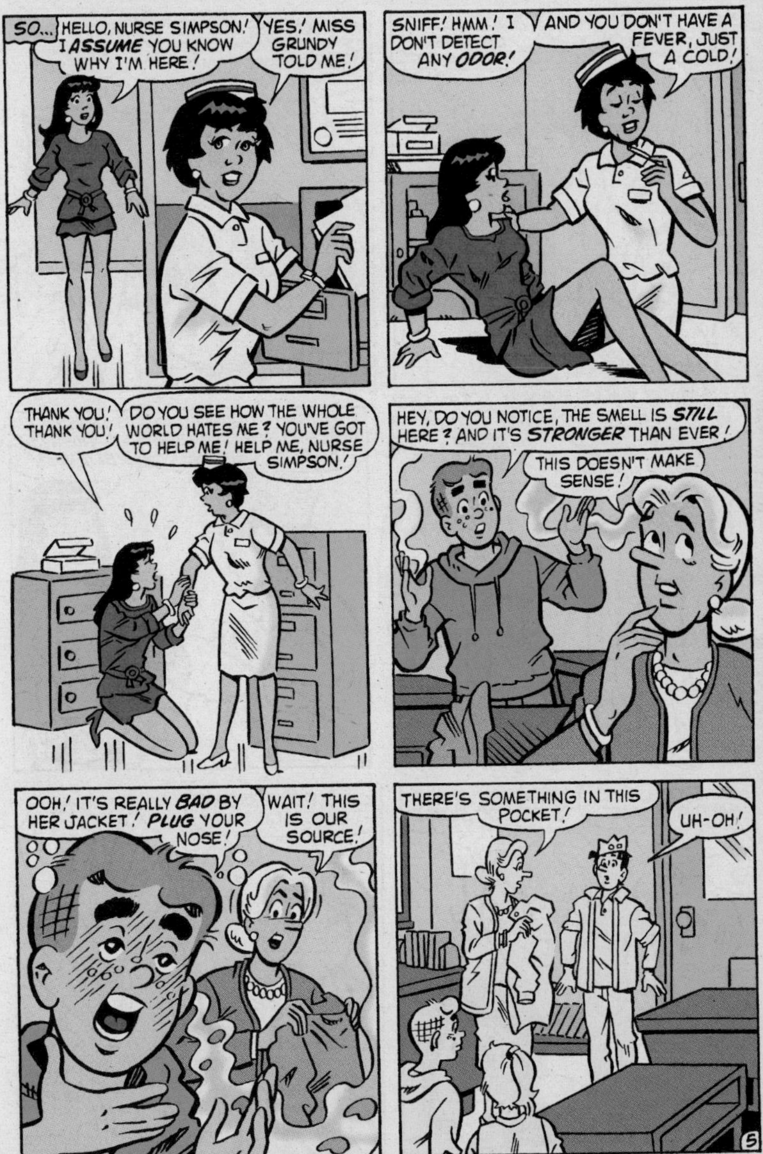

SO...
HELLO, NURSE SIMPSON! I ASSUME YOU KNOW WHY I'M HERE!
YES! MISS GRUNDY TOLD ME!
SNIFF! HMM! I DON'T DETECT ANY ODOR!
AND YOU DON'T HAVE A FEVER, JUST A COLD!
THANK YOU! THANK YOU!
DO YOU SEE HOW THE WHOLE WORLD HATES ME? YOU'VE GOT TO HELP ME! HELP ME, NURSE SIMPSON!
HEY, DO YOU NOTICE, THE SMELL IS STILL HERE? AND IT'S STRONGER THAN EVER!
THIS DOESN'T MAKE SENSE!
OOH! IT'S REALLY BAD BY HER JACKET! PLUG YOUR NOSE!
WAIT! THIS IS OUR SOURCE!
THERE'S SOMETHING IN THIS POCKET!
UH-OH!
5

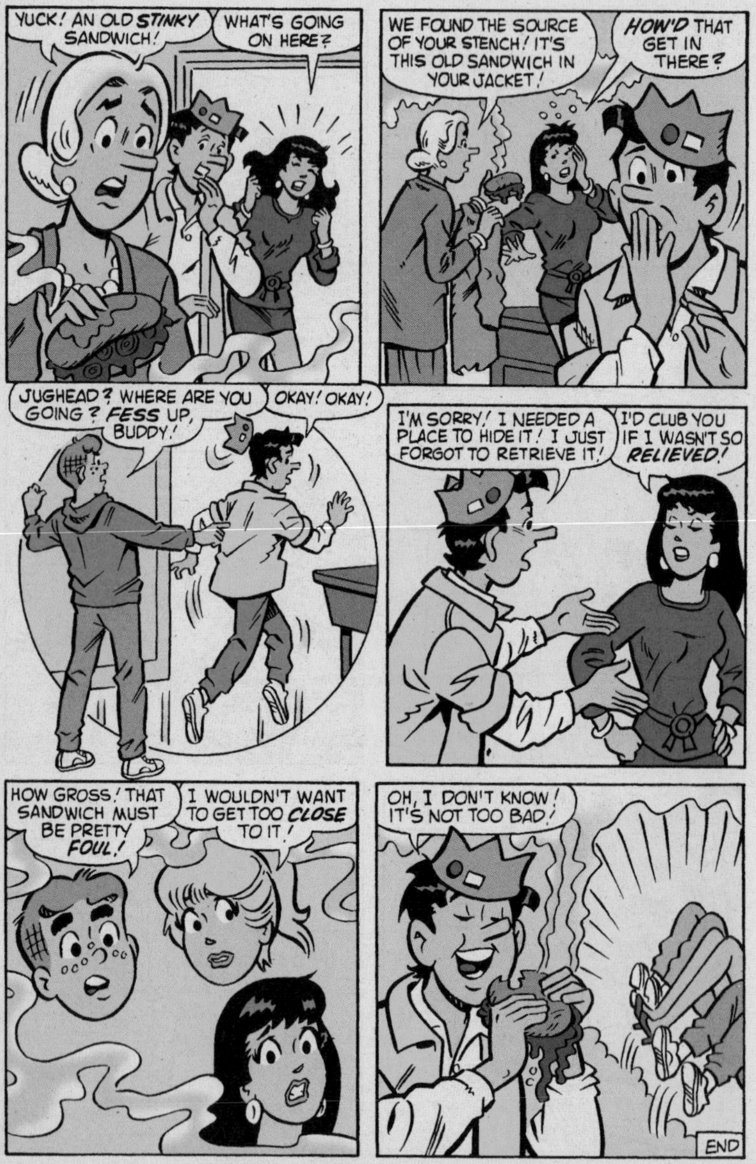
YUCK! AN OLD STINKY SANDWICH!
WHAT'S GOING ON HERE?
WE FOUND THE SOURCE OF YOUR STENCH! IT'S THIS OLD SANDWICH IN YOUR JACKET!
HOW'D THAT GET IN THERE?
JUGHEAD? WHERE ARE YOU GOING? FESS UP, BUDDY!
OKAY! OKAY!
I'M SORRY! I NEEDED A PLACE TO HIDE IT! I JUST FORGOT TO RETRIEVE IT!
I'D CLUB YOU IF I WASN'T SO RELIEVED!
HOW GROSS! THAT SANDWICH MUST BE PRETTY FOUL!
I WOULDN'T WANT TO GET TOO CLOSE TO IT!
OH, I DON'T KNOW! IT'S NOT TOO BAD!
END

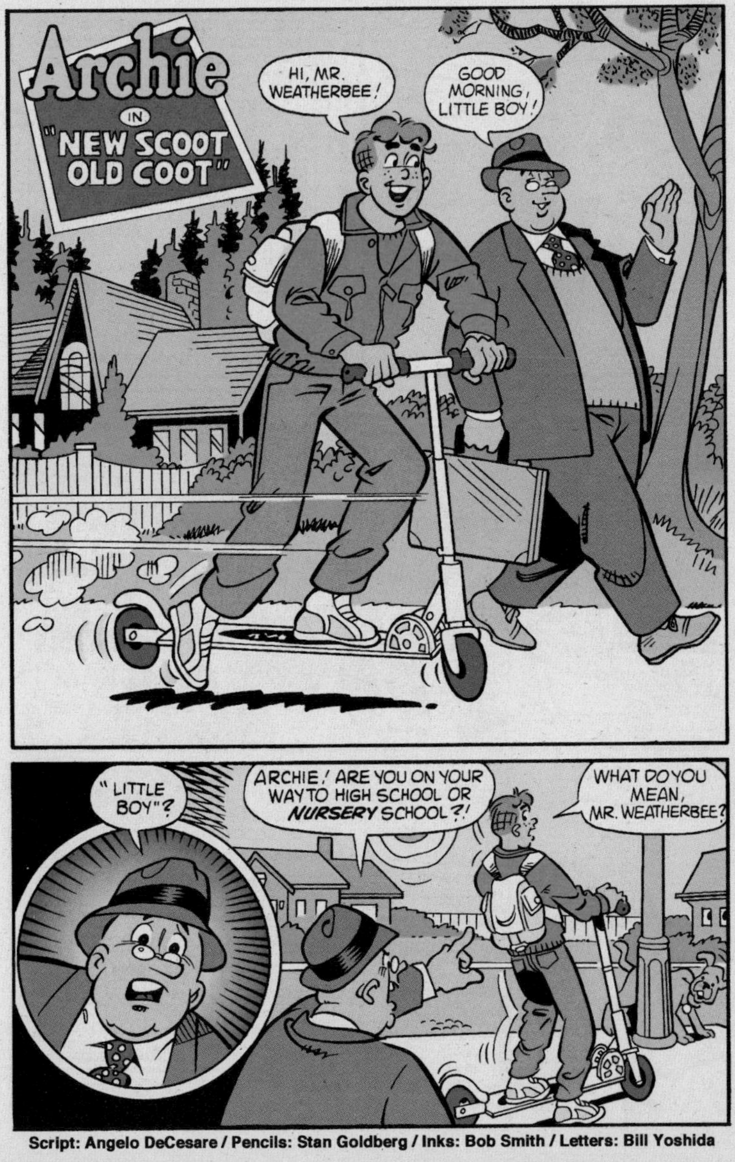
Archie
IN
"NEW SCOOT OLD COOT"
HI, MR. WEATHERBEE!
GOOD MORNING, LITTLE BOY!
"LITTLE BOY"?
ARCHIE! ARE YOU ON YOUR WAY TO HIGH SCHOOL OR *NURSERY* SCHOOL?!
WHAT DO YOU MEAN, MR. WEATHERBEE?

Script: Angelo DeCesare / Pencils: Stan Goldberg / Inks: Bob Smith / Letters: Bill Yoshida

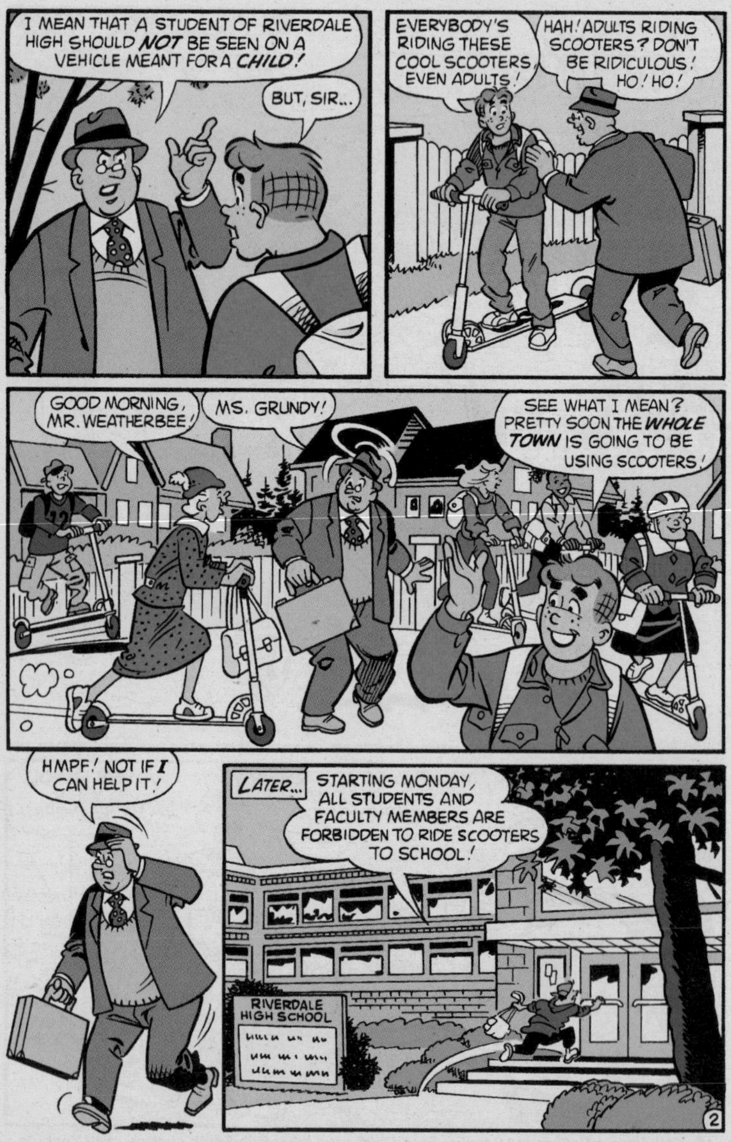
I MEAN THAT A STUDENT OF RIVERDALE HIGH SHOULD NOT BE SEEN ON A VEHICLE MEANT FOR A CHILD!
BUT, SIR...
EVERYBODY'S RIDING THESE COOL SCOOTERS, EVEN ADULTS!
HAH! ADULTS RIDING SCOOTERS? DON'T BE RIDICULOUS! HO! HO!
GOOD MORNING, MR. WEATHERBEE!
MS. GRUNDY!
SEE WHAT I MEAN? PRETTY SOON THE WHOLE TOWN IS GOING TO BE USING SCOOTERS!
HMPF! NOT IF I CAN HELP IT!
LATER...
STARTING MONDAY, ALL STUDENTS AND FACULTY MEMBERS ARE FORBIDDEN TO RIDE SCOOTERS TO SCHOOL!
RIVERDALE HIGH SCHOOL
2

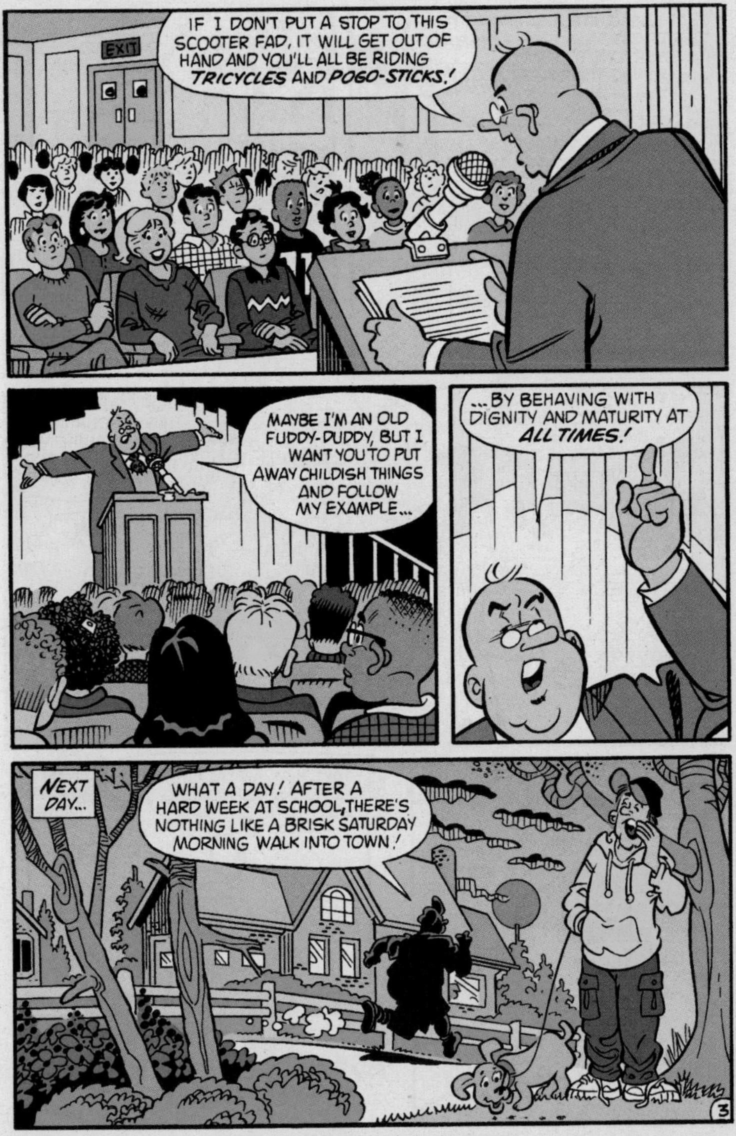
IF I DON'T PUT A STOP TO THIS SCOOTER FAD, IT WILL GET OUT OF HAND AND YOU'LL ALL BE RIDING TRICYCLES AND POGO-STICKS!
EXIT
MAYBE I'M AN OLD FUDDY-DUDDY, BUT I WANT YOU TO PUT AWAY CHILDISH THINGS AND FOLLOW MY EXAMPLE...
...BY BEHAVING WITH DIGNITY AND MATURITY AT ALL TIMES!
NEXT DAY...
WHAT A DAY! AFTER A HARD WEEK AT SCHOOL, THERE'S NOTHING LIKE A BRISK SATURDAY MORNING WALK INTO TOWN!
3

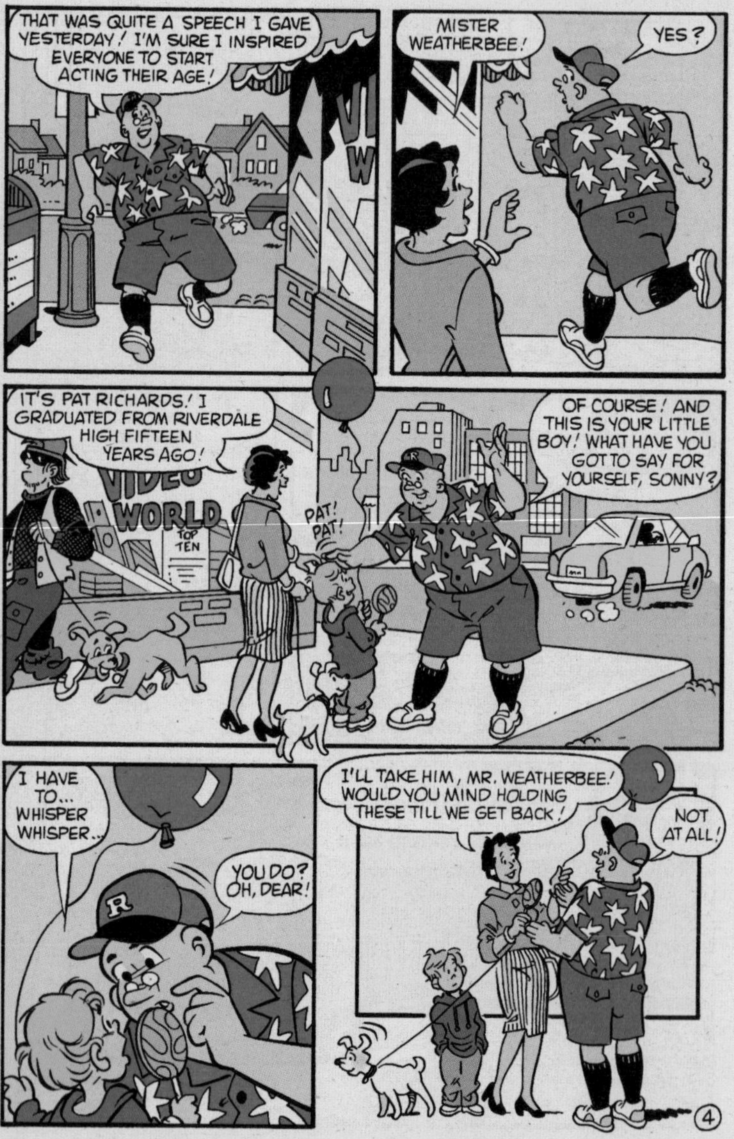
THAT WAS QUITE A SPEECH I GAVE YESTERDAY! I'M SURE I INSPIRED EVERYONE TO START ACTING THEIR AGE!
MISTER WEATHERBEE!
YES?
IT'S PAT RICHARDS! I GRADUATED FROM RIVERDALE HIGH FIFTEEN YEARS AGO!
VIDEO WORLD
TOP TEN
PAT! PAT!
OF COURSE! AND THIS IS YOUR LITTLE BOY! WHAT HAVE YOU GOT TO SAY FOR YOURSELF, SONNY?
I HAVE TO... WHISPER WHISPER...
YOU DO? OH, DEAR!
I'LL TAKE HIM, MR. WEATHERBEE! WOULD YOU MIND HOLDING THESE TILL WE GET BACK!
NOT AT ALL!

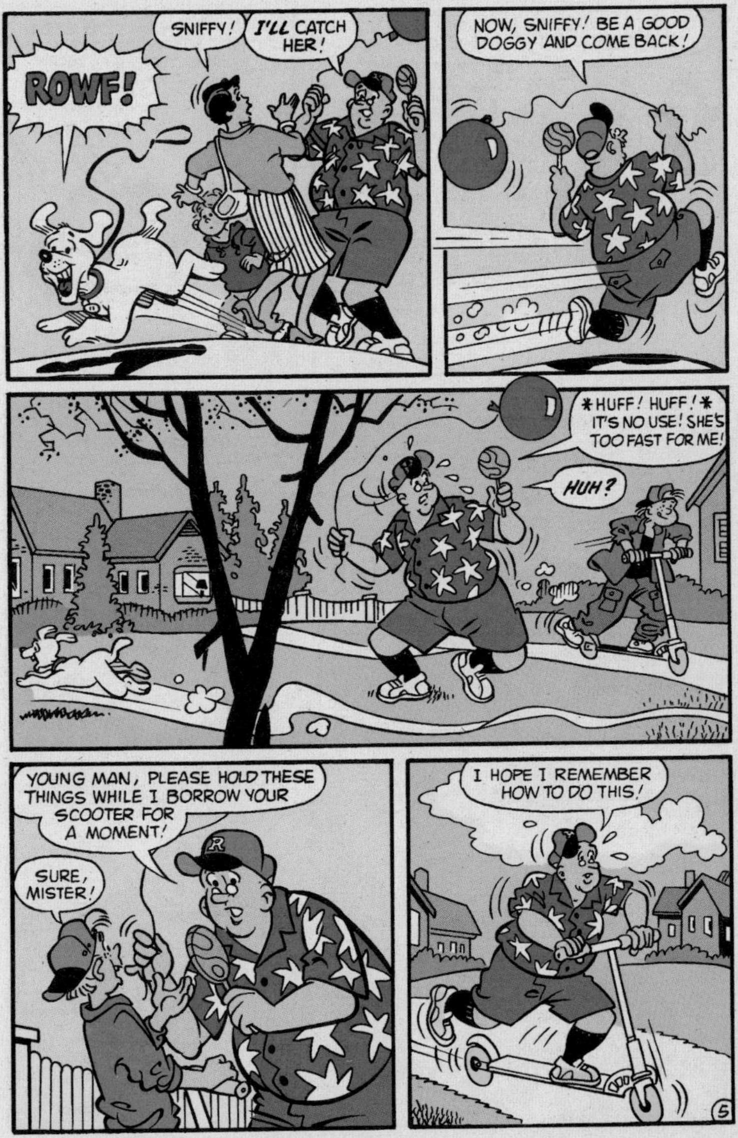

ROWF!
SNIFFY!
I'LL CATCH HER!
NOW, SNIFFY! BE A GOOD DOGGY AND COME BACK!
HUFF! HUFF! IT'S NO USE! SHE'S TOO FAST FOR ME!
HUH?
YOUNG MAN, PLEASE HOLD THESE THINGS WHILE I BORROW YOUR SCOOTER FOR A MOMENT!
SURE, MISTER!
I HOPE I REMEMBER HOW TO DO THIS!
5

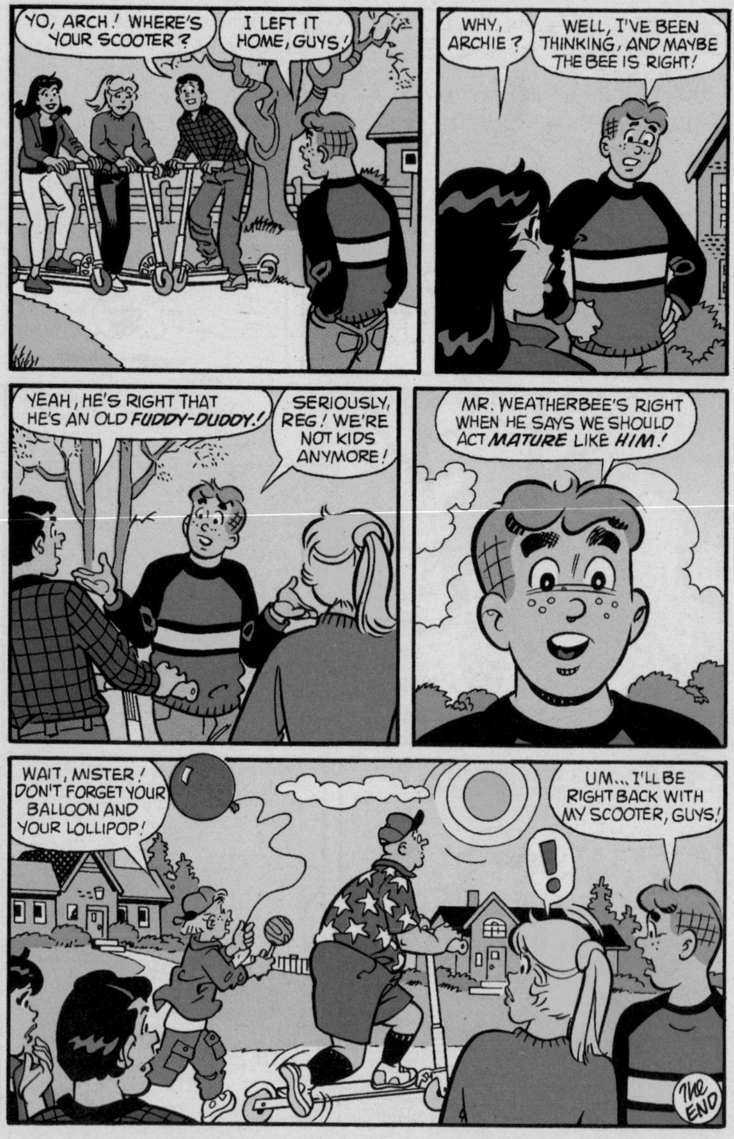
YO, ARCH! WHERE'S YOUR SCOOTER?
I LEFT IT HOME, GUYS!
WHY, ARCHIE?
WELL, I'VE BEEN THINKING, AND MAYBE THE BEE IS RIGHT!
YEAH, HE'S RIGHT THAT HE'S AN OLD FUDDY-DUDDY!
SERIOUSLY, REG! WE'RE NOT KIDS ANYMORE!
MR. WEATHERBEE'S RIGHT WHEN HE SAYS WE SHOULD ACT MATURE LIKE HIM!
WAIT, MISTER! DON'T FORGET YOUR BALLOON AND YOUR LOLLIPOP!
!
UM... I'LL BE RIGHT BACK WITH MY SCOOTER, GUYS!
THE END

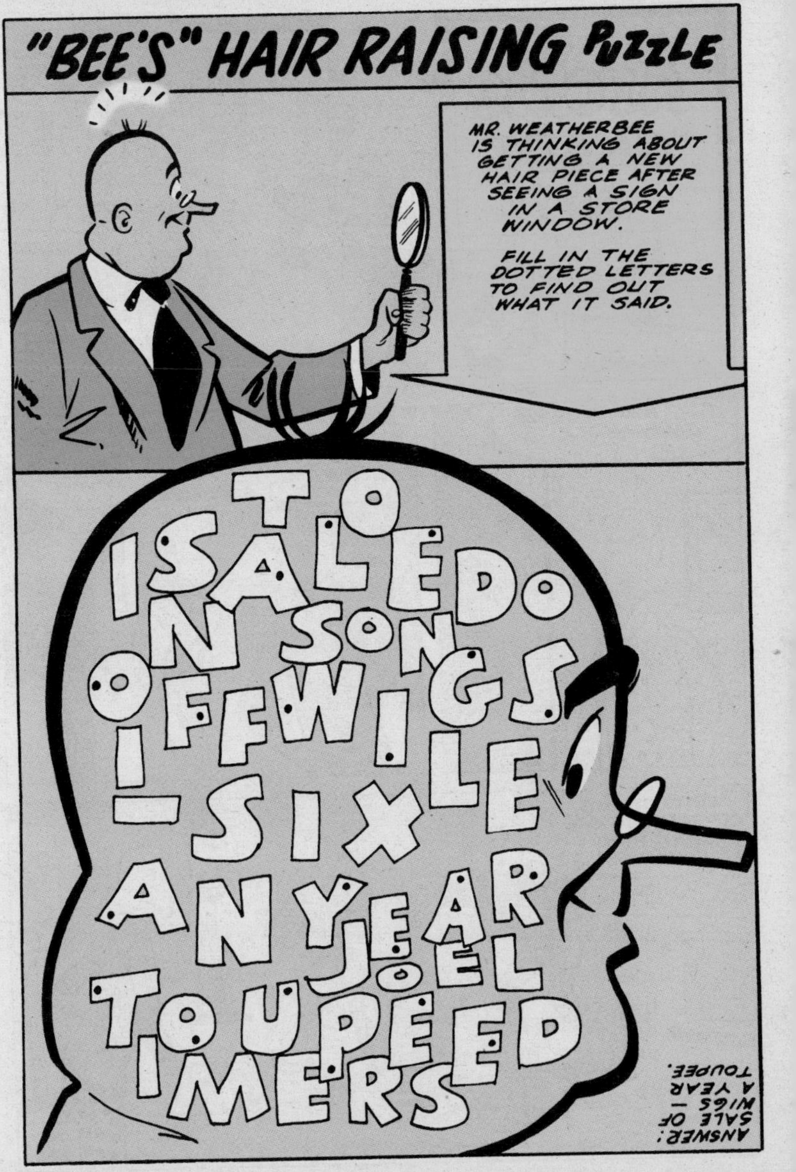
"BEE'S" HAIR RAISING PUZZLE
MR. WEATHERBEE IS THINKING ABOUT GETTING A NEW HAIR PIECE AFTER SEEING A SIGN IN A STORE WINDOW.
FILL IN THE DOTTED LETTERS TO FIND OUT WHAT IT SAID.
ANSWER: SALE OF WIGS — A YEAR TOUPEE.

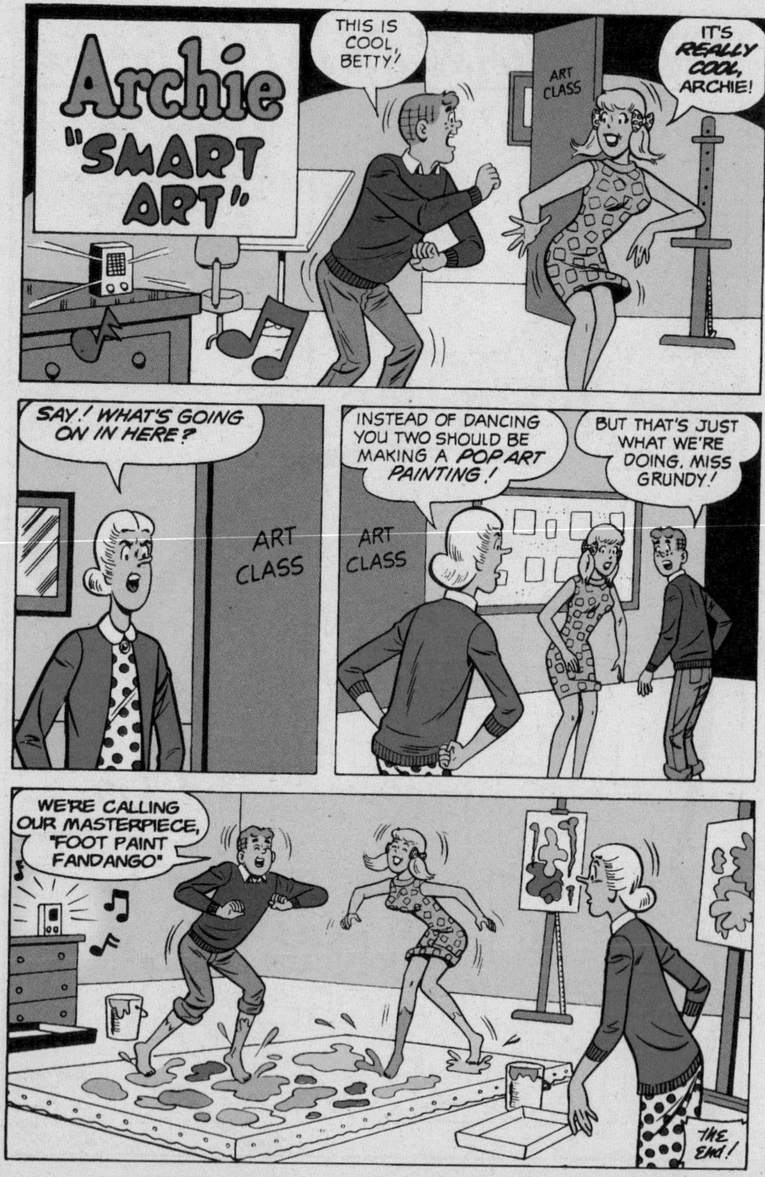
Archie
"SMART ART"
THIS IS COOL, BETTY!
IT'S REALLY COOL, ARCHIE!
ART CLASS
SAY! WHAT'S GOING ON IN HERE?
ART CLASS
INSTEAD OF DANCING YOU TWO SHOULD BE MAKING A POP ART PAINTING!
BUT THAT'S JUST WHAT WE'RE DOING, MISS GRUNDY!
ART CLASS
WE'RE CALLING OUR MASTERPIECE, "FOOT PAINT FANDANGO"
THE END!

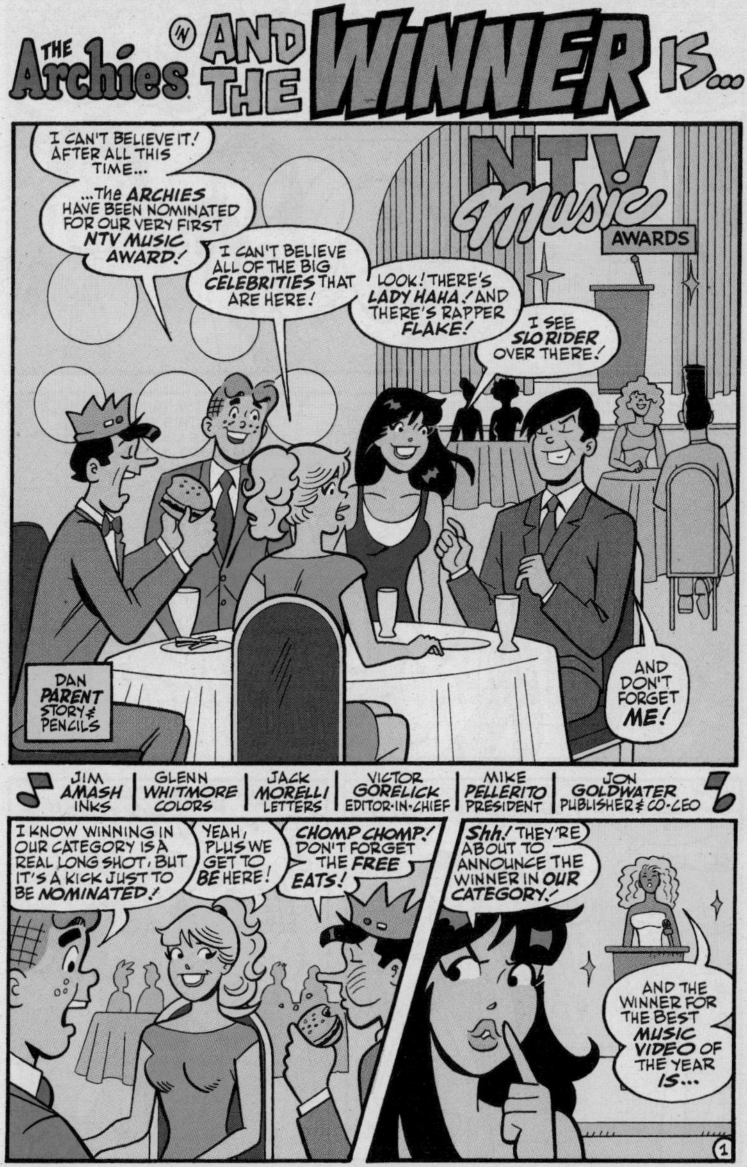

THE Archies IN AND THE WINNER IS...
I CAN'T BELIEVE IT! AFTER ALL THIS TIME...
...The ARCHIES HAVE BEEN NOMINATED FOR OUR VERY FIRST NTV MUSIC AWARD!
I CAN'T BELIEVE ALL OF THE BIG CELEBRITIES THAT ARE HERE!
LOOK! THERE'S LADY HAHA! AND THERE'S RAPPER FLAKE!
I SEE SLO RIDER OVER THERE!
NTV Music AWARDS
AND DON'T FORGET ME!
DAN PARENT STORY & PENCILS
JIM AMASH INKS
GLENN WHITMORE COLORS
JACK MORELLI LETTERS
VICTOR GORELICK EDITOR-IN-CHIEF
MIKE PELLERITO PRESIDENT
JON GOLDWATER PUBLISHER & CO-CEO
I KNOW WINNING IN OUR CATEGORY IS A REAL LONG SHOT, BUT IT'S A KICK JUST TO BE NOMINATED!
YEAH, PLUS WE GET TO BE HERE!
CHOMP CHOMP! DON'T FORGET THE FREE EATS!
Shh! THEY'RE ABOUT TO ANNOUNCE THE WINNER IN OUR CATEGORY!
AND THE WINNER FOR THE BEST MUSIC VIDEO OF THE YEAR IS...
1

...The Archies!!

Jughead: Huh?!

Veronica: WE WON! I CAN'T BELIEVE IT! WE *WON!*

Betty: QUICK! LET'S GET ON STAGE SO SOMEONE CAN TAKE MY PICTURE ACCEPTING THE AWARD!

Betty: C'MON REGGIE! HURRY!

Reggie: HANG ON! I'M TRYING TO LINE UP THIS SHOT SO IT LOOKS LIKE *MARIAH SCARY* IS IN THE PIC WITH ME!

Archie: WOW! I--I CAN'T BELIEVE THIS!!

Archie: ON BEHALF OF THE *ARCHIES*, I'D JUST LIKE TO SAY THA--

YO! YO! *YO!* HOLD UP! *HOLD UP!!*

2

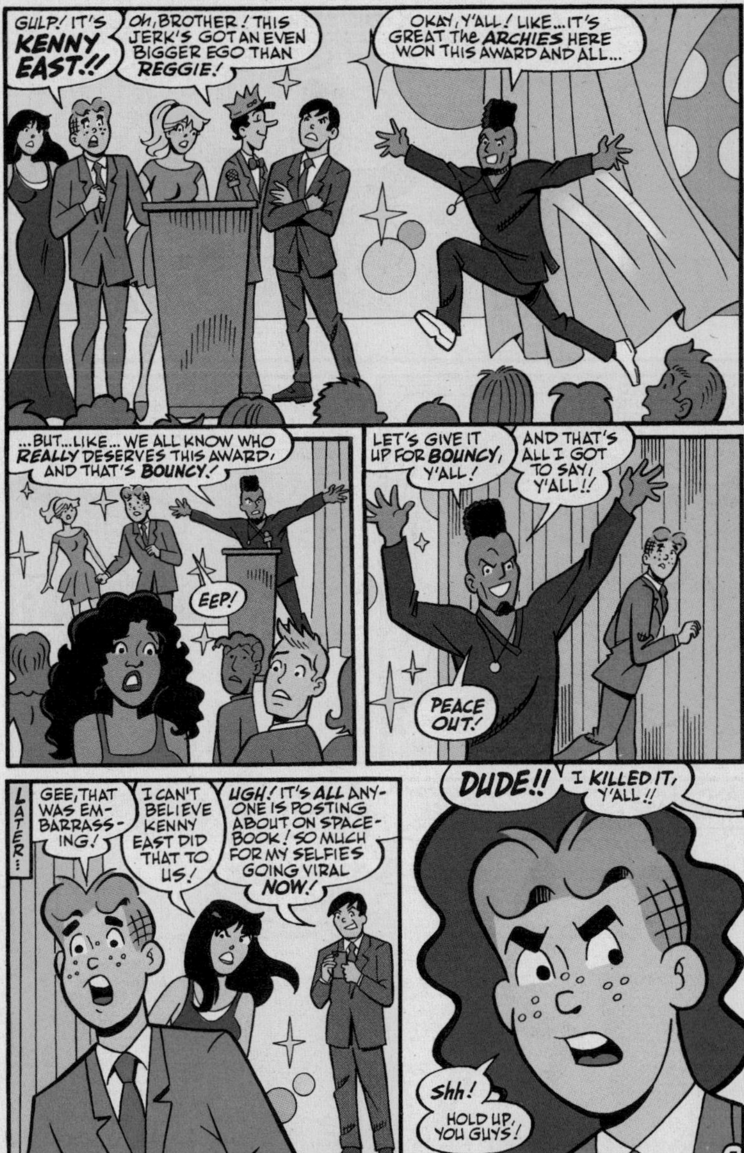
GULP! IT'S KENNY EAST!!!
Oh, BROTHER! THIS JERK'S GOT AN EVEN BIGGER EGO THAN REGGIE!
OKAY, Y'ALL! LIKE...IT'S GREAT THE ARCHIES HERE WON THIS AWARD AND ALL...
...BUT...LIKE... WE ALL KNOW WHO REALLY DESERVES THIS AWARD, AND THAT'S BOUNCY!
EEP!
LET'S GIVE IT UP FOR BOUNCY, Y'ALL!
AND THAT'S ALL I GOT TO SAY, Y'ALL!!
PEACE OUT!
LATER...
GEE, THAT WAS EM-BARRASS-ING!
I CAN'T BELIEVE KENNY EAST DID THAT TO US!
UGH! IT'S ALL ANY-ONE IS POSTING ABOUT ON SPACE-BOOK! SO MUCH FOR MY SELFIES GOING VIRAL NOW!
DUDE!!
I KILLED IT, Y'ALL!!
Shh!
HOLD UP, YOU GUYS!

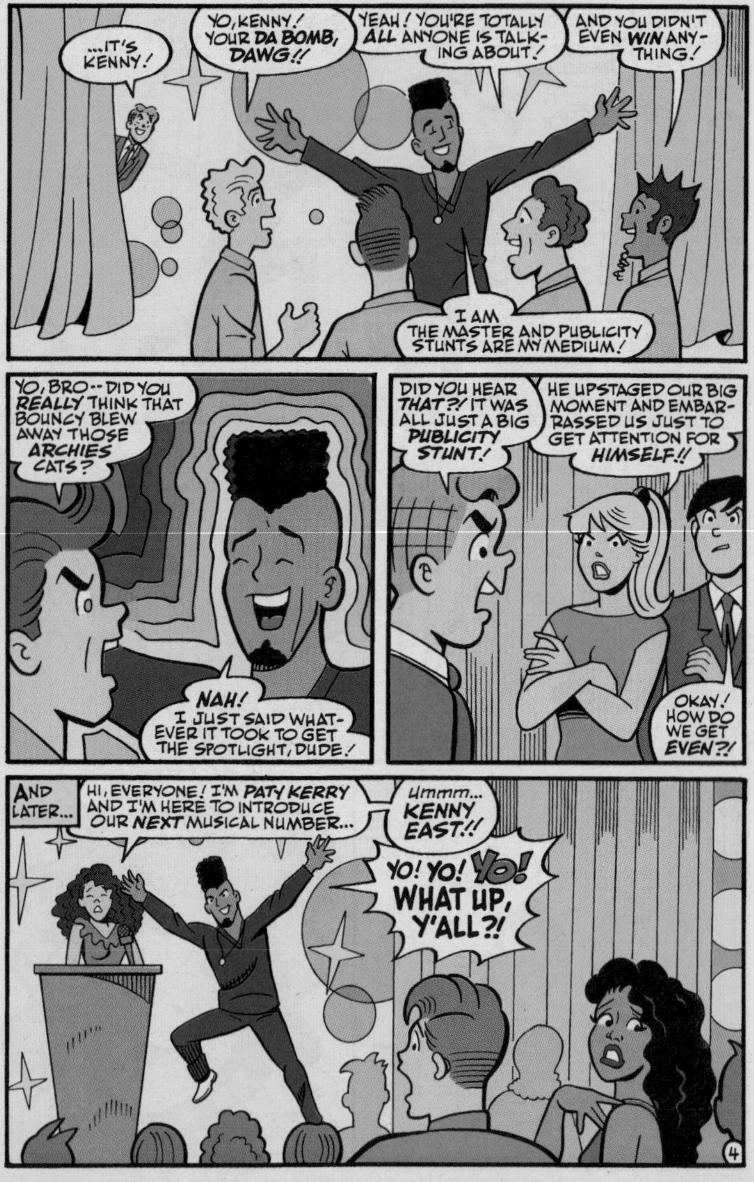
...IT'S KENNY!
YO, KENNY! YOUR DA BOMB, DAWG!!
YEAH! YOU'RE TOTALLY ALL ANYONE IS TALKING ABOUT!
AND YOU DIDN'T EVEN WIN ANYTHING!
I AM THE MASTER AND PUBLICITY STUNTS ARE MY MEDIUM!
YO, BRO-- DID YOU REALLY THINK THAT BOUNCY BLEW AWAY THOSE ARCHIES CATS?
NAH! I JUST SAID WHATEVER IT TOOK TO GET THE SPOTLIGHT, DUDE!
DID YOU HEAR THAT?! IT WAS ALL JUST A BIG PUBLICITY STUNT!
HE UPSTAGED OUR BIG MOMENT AND EMBARRASSED US JUST TO GET ATTENTION FOR HIMSELF!!
OKAY! HOW DO WE GET EVEN?!
AND LATER...
HI, EVERYONE! I'M PATY KERRY AND I'M HERE TO INTRODUCE OUR NEXT MUSICAL NUMBER...
Ummm... KENNY EAST!!
YO! YO! YO! WHAT UP, Y'ALL?!
4

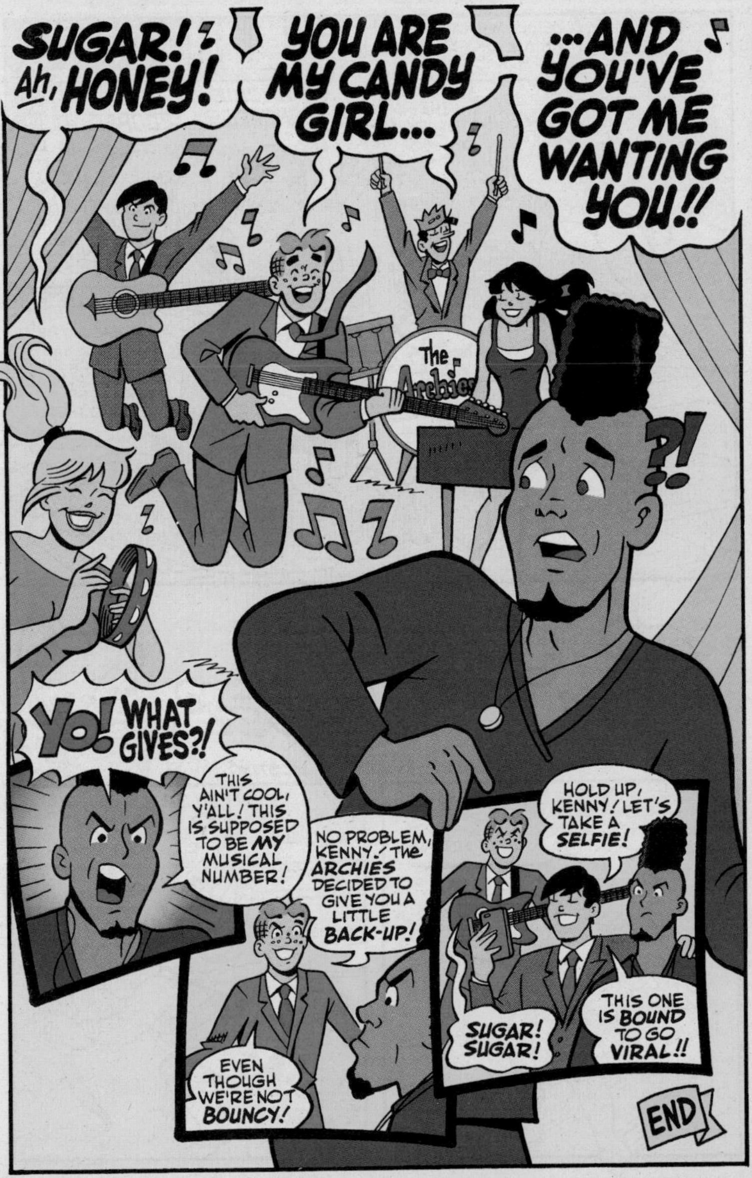
SUGAR! Ah, HONEY!
YOU ARE MY CANDY GIRL...
...AND YOU'VE GOT ME WANTING YOU!!
The Archies
?!
YO! WHAT GIVES?!
THIS AIN'T COOL, Y'ALL! THIS IS SUPPOSED TO BE MY MUSICAL NUMBER!
NO PROBLEM, KENNY! THE ARCHIES DECIDED TO GIVE YOU A LITTLE BACK-UP!
EVEN THOUGH WE'RE NOT BOUNCY!
HOLD UP, KENNY! LET'S TAKE A SELFIE!
SUGAR! SUGAR!
THIS ONE IS BOUND TO GO VIRAL!!
END

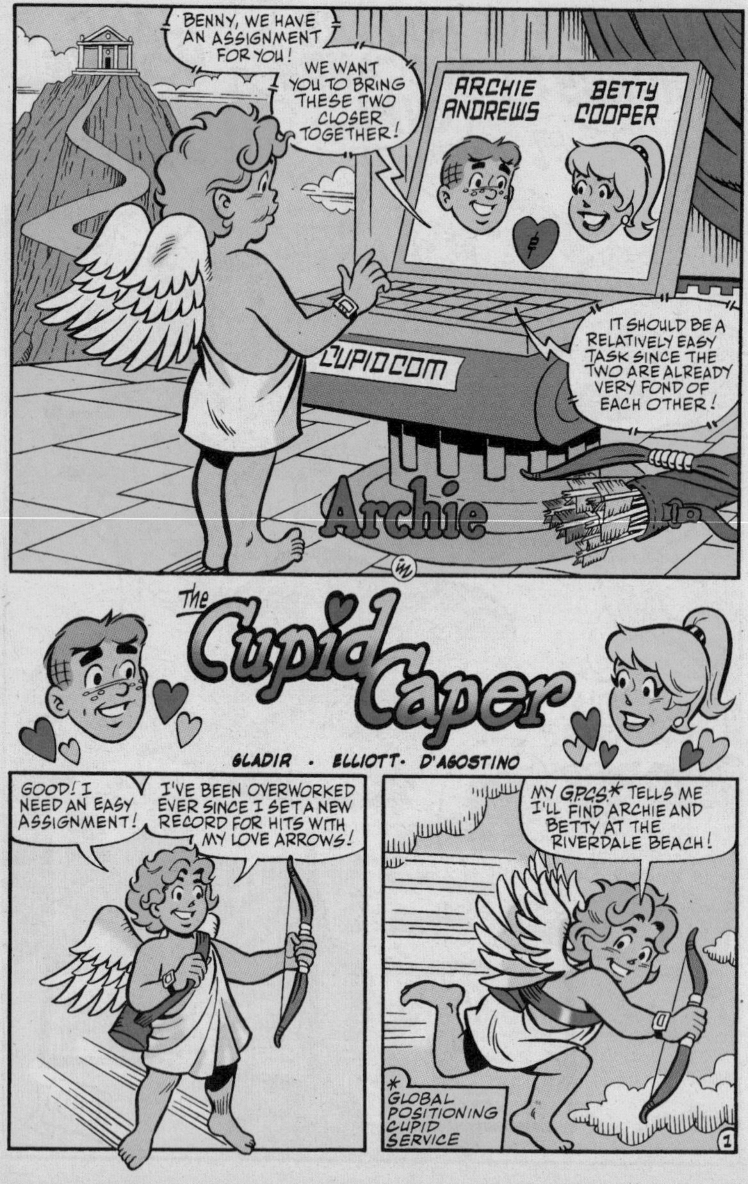
BENNY, WE HAVE AN ASSIGNMENT FOR YOU!
WE WANT YOU TO BRING THESE TWO CLOSER TOGETHER!
ARCHIE ANDREWS
BETTY COOPER
IT SHOULD BE A RELATIVELY EASY TASK SINCE THE TWO ARE ALREADY VERY FOND OF EACH OTHER!
CUPIDCOM
Archie
The Cupid Caper
GLADIR · ELLIOTT · D'AGOSTINO
GOOD! I NEED AN EASY ASSIGNMENT!
I'VE BEEN OVERWORKED EVER SINCE I SET A NEW RECORD FOR HITS WITH MY LOVE ARROWS!
MY G.P.C.S.* TELLS ME I'LL FIND ARCHIE AND BETTY AT THE RIVERDALE BEACH!
* GLOBAL POSITIONING CUPID SERVICE
1

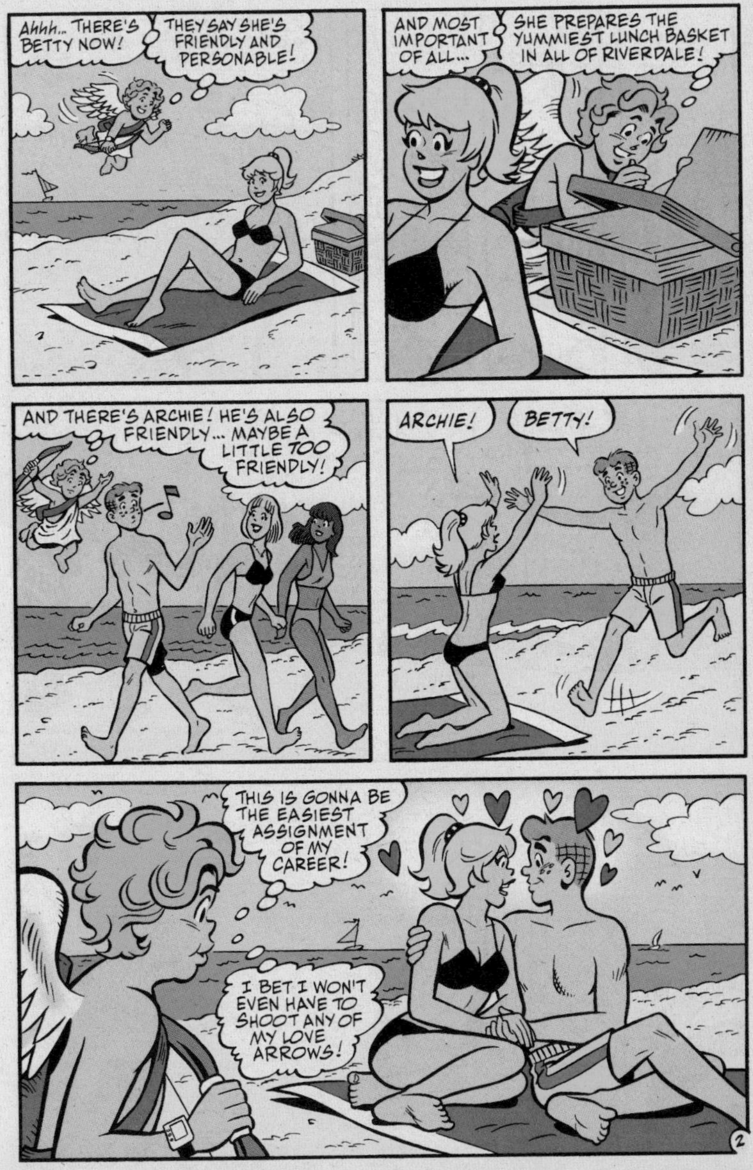

AHHH... THERE'S BETTY NOW!
THEY SAY SHE'S FRIENDLY AND PERSONABLE!
AND MOST IMPORTANT OF ALL...
SHE PREPARES THE YUMMIEST LUNCH BASKET IN ALL OF RIVERDALE!
AND THERE'S ARCHIE! HE'S ALSO FRIENDLY... MAYBE A LITTLE TOO FRIENDLY!
ARCHIE!
BETTY!
THIS IS GONNA BE THE EASIEST ASSIGNMENT OF MY CAREER!
I BET I WON'T EVEN HAVE TO SHOOT ANY OF MY LOVE ARROWS!

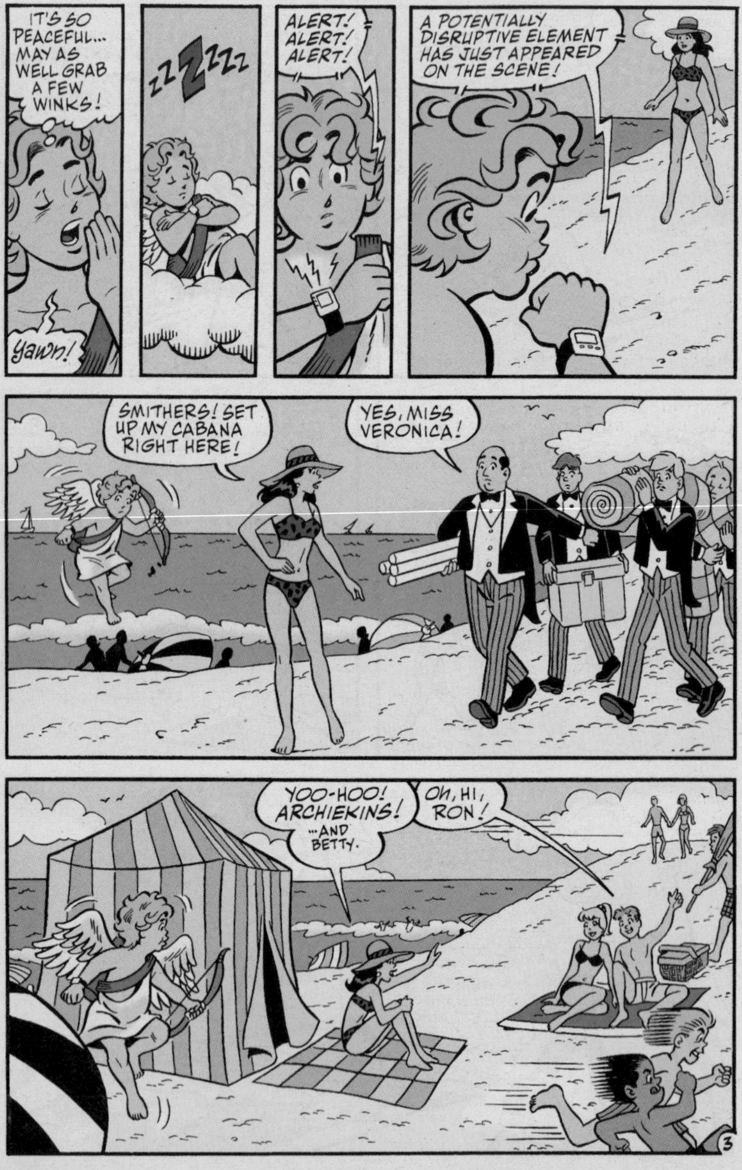
IT'S SO PEACEFUL... MAY AS WELL GRAB A FEW WINKS!
Yawn!
zzZzzz
ALERT! ALERT! ALERT!
A POTENTIALLY DISRUPTIVE ELEMENT HAS JUST APPEARED ON THE SCENE!
SMITHERS! SET UP MY CABANA RIGHT HERE!
YES, MISS VERONICA!
YOO-HOO! ARCHIEKINS! ...AND BETTY.
Oh, HI, RON!
3

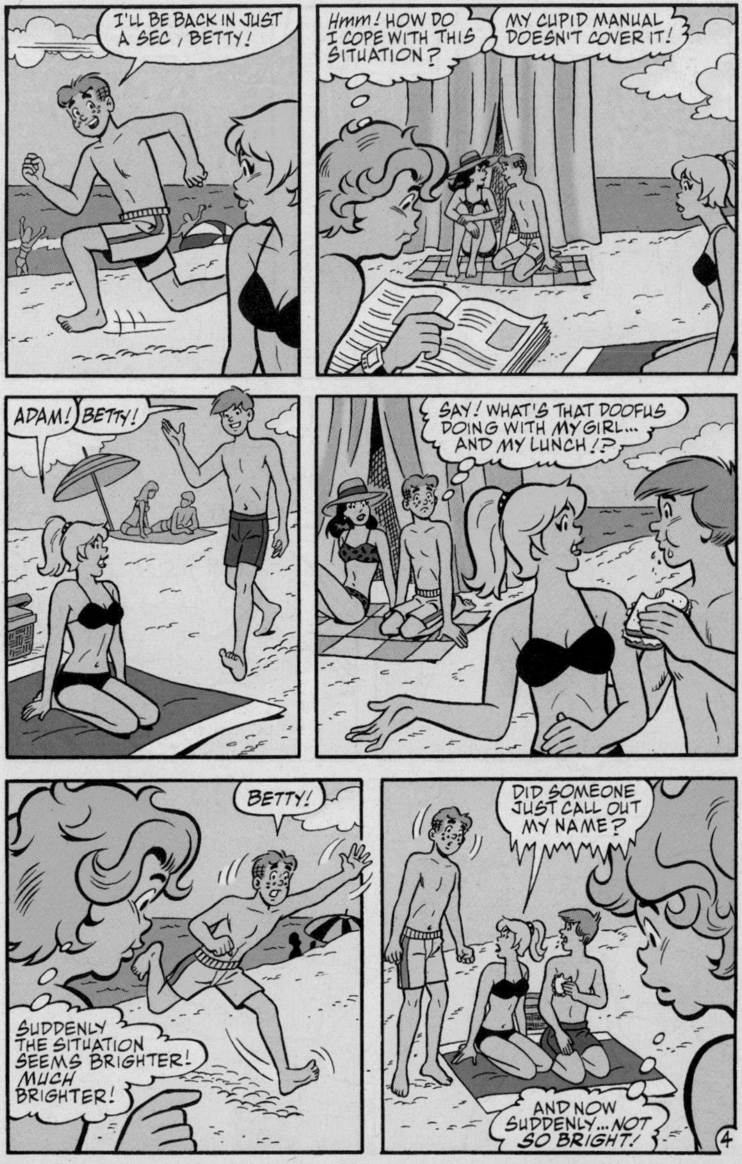
I'LL BE BACK IN JUST A SEC, BETTY!
Hmm! HOW DO I COPE WITH THIS SITUATION?
MY CUPID MANUAL DOESN'T COVER IT!
ADAM!
BETTY!
SAY! WHAT'S THAT DOOFUS DOING WITH MY GIRL... AND MY LUNCH!?
BETTY!
SUDDENLY THE SITUATION SEEMS BRIGHTER! MUCH BRIGHTER!
DID SOMEONE JUST CALL OUT MY NAME?
AND NOW SUDDENLY... NOT SO BRIGHT!
4

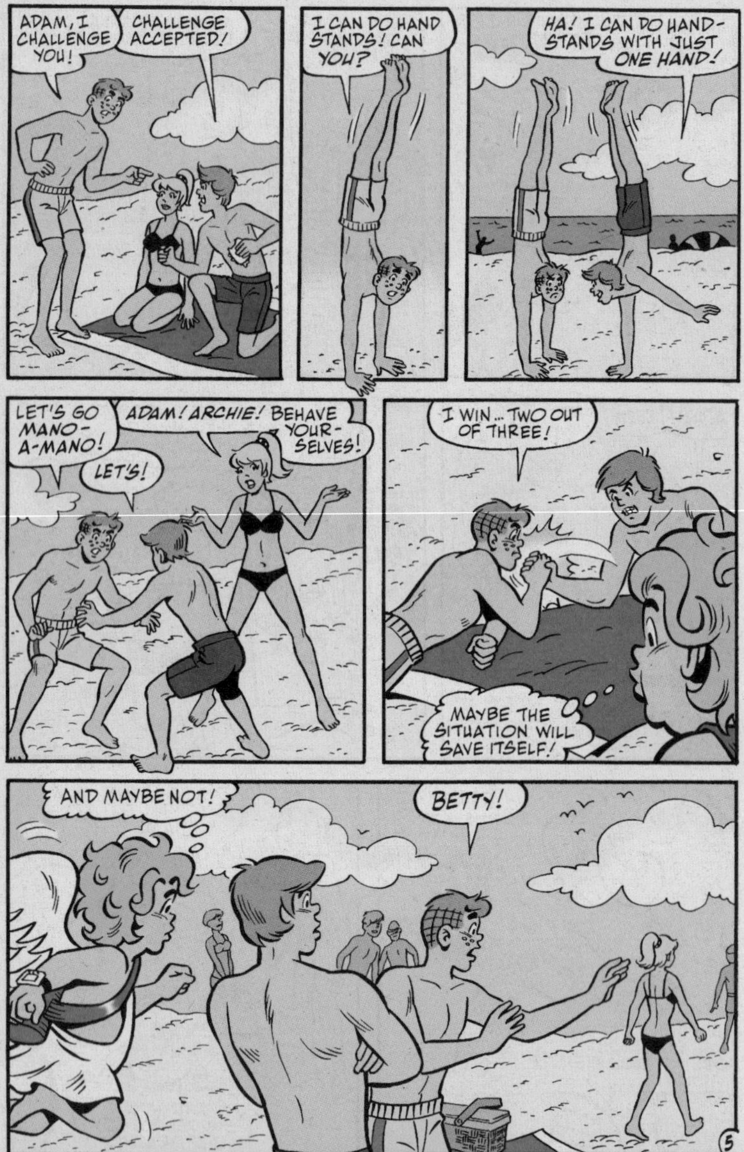
ADAM, I CHALLENGE YOU!
CHALLENGE ACCEPTED!
I CAN DO HAND STANDS! CAN YOU?
HA! I CAN DO HAND-STANDS WITH JUST ONE HAND!
LET'S GO MANO-A-MANO!
LET'S!
ADAM! ARCHIE! BEHAVE YOUR-SELVES!
I WIN... TWO OUT OF THREE!
MAYBE THE SITUATION WILL SAVE ITSELF!
AND MAYBE NOT!
BETTY!

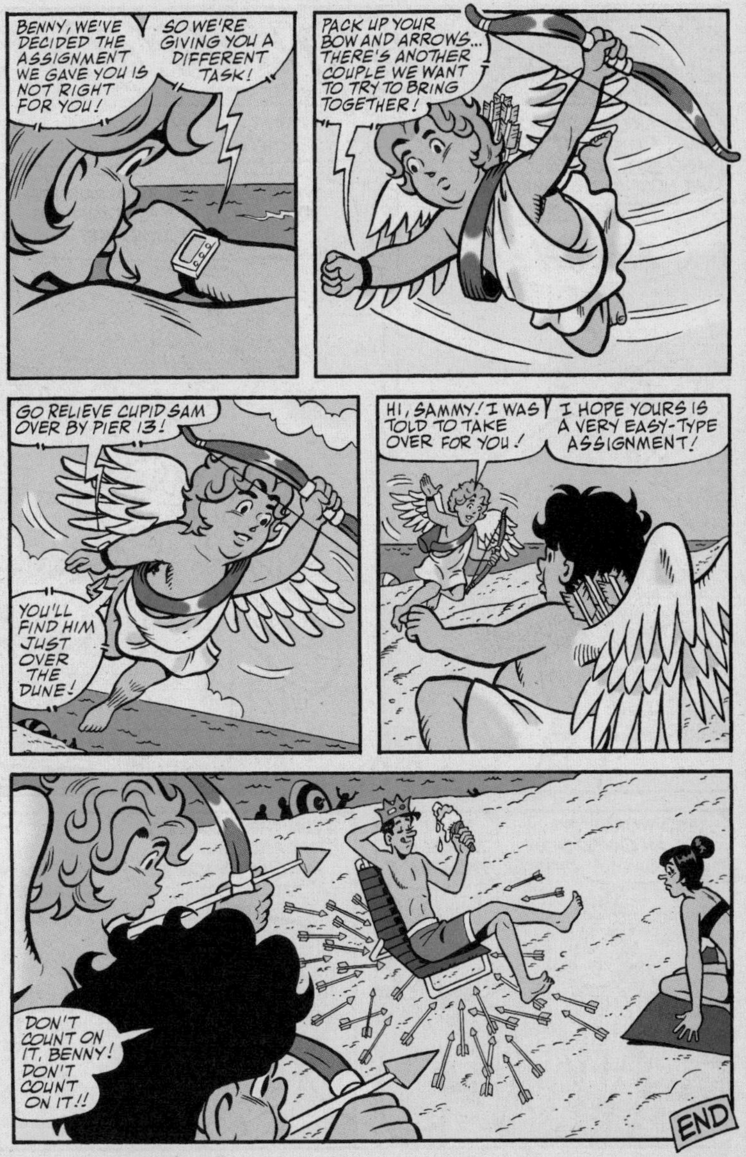
BENNY, WE'VE DECIDED THE ASSIGNMENT WE GAVE YOU IS NOT RIGHT FOR YOU!
SO WE'RE GIVING YOU A DIFFERENT TASK!
PACK UP YOUR BOW AND ARROWS... THERE'S ANOTHER COUPLE WE WANT TO TRY TO BRING TOGETHER!
GO RELIEVE CUPID SAM OVER BY PIER 13!
YOU'LL FIND HIM JUST OVER THE DUNE!
HI, SAMMY! I WAS TOLD TO TAKE OVER FOR YOU!
I HOPE YOURS IS A VERY EASY-TYPE ASSIGNMENT!
DON'T COUNT ON IT, BENNY! DON'T COUNT ON IT!!
END

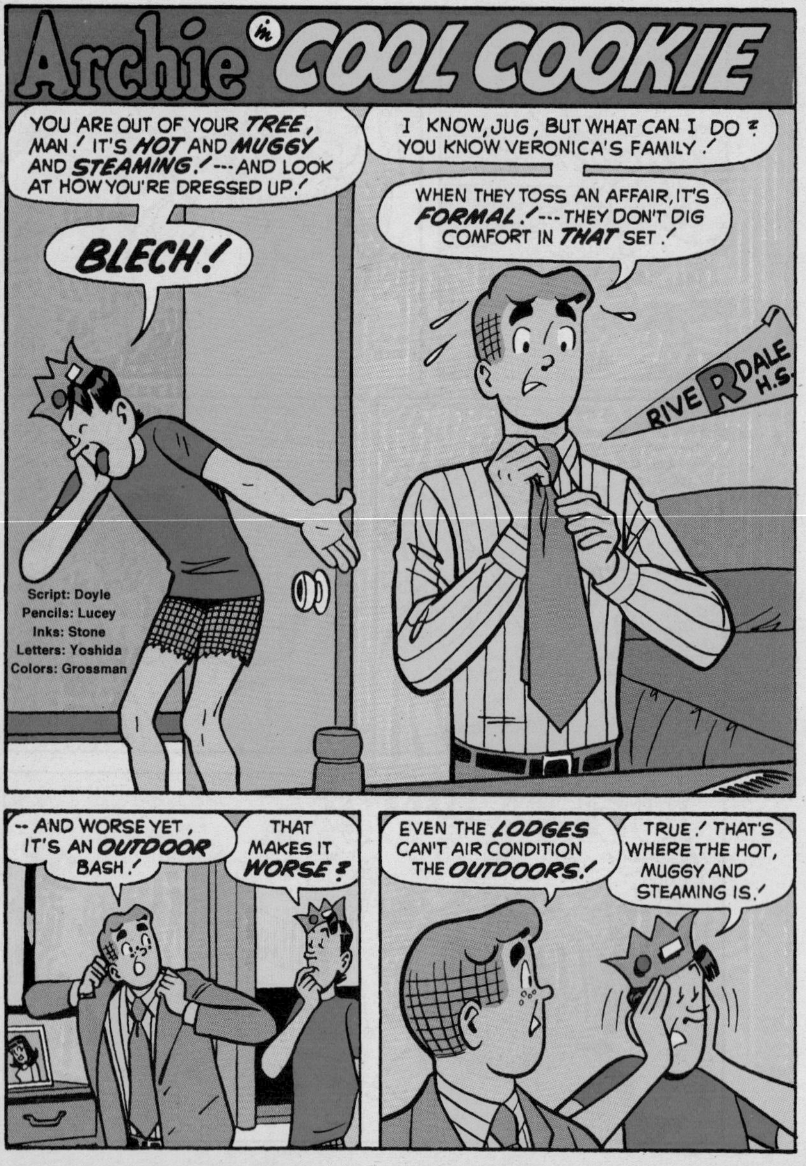

Archie in COOL COOKIE
YOU ARE OUT OF YOUR TREE, MAN.! IT'S HOT AND MUGGY AND STEAMING.! --- AND LOOK AT HOW YOU'RE DRESSED UP.!
BLECH!
I KNOW, JUG, BUT WHAT CAN I DO? YOU KNOW VERONICA'S FAMILY.!
WHEN THEY TOSS AN AFFAIR, IT'S FORMAL.! --- THEY DON'T DIG COMFORT IN THAT SET.!
RIVERDALE H.S.
Script: Doyle
Pencils: Lucey
Inks: Stone
Letters: Yoshida
Colors: Grossman
-- AND WORSE YET, IT'S AN OUTDOOR BASH.!
THAT MAKES IT WORSE?
EVEN THE LODGES CAN'T AIR CONDITION THE OUTDOORS.!
TRUE.! THAT'S WHERE THE HOT, MUGGY AND STEAMING IS.!

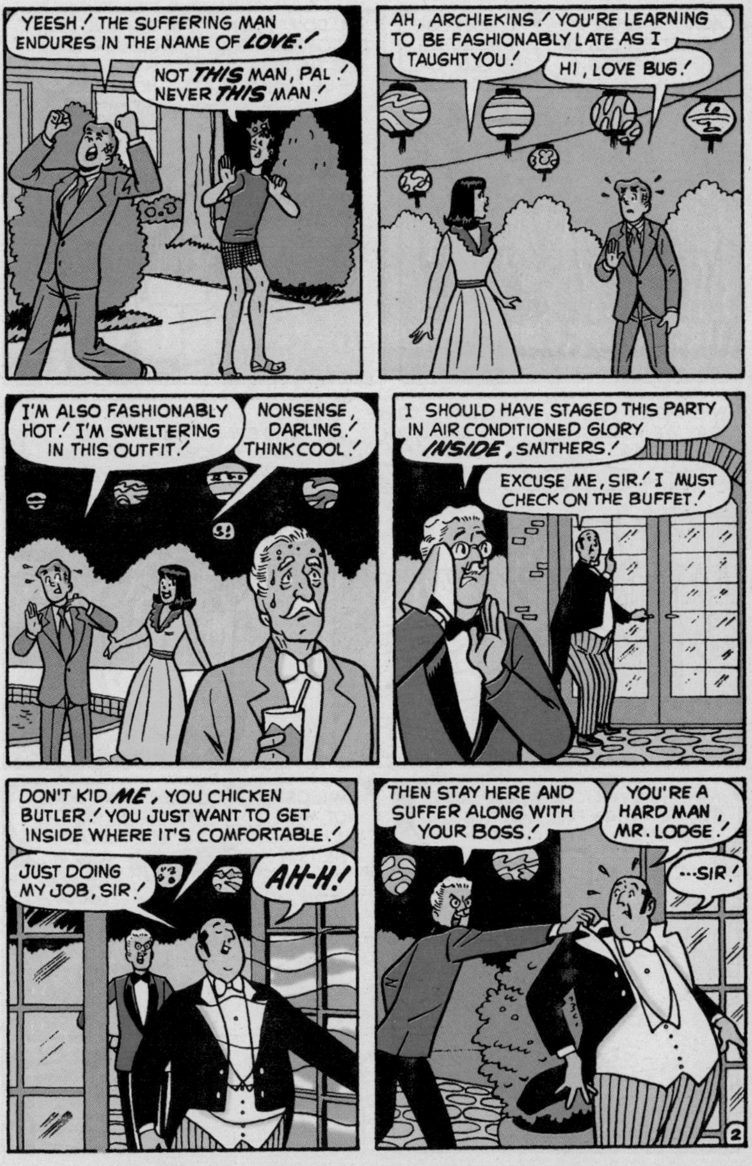
YEESH! THE SUFFERING MAN ENDURES IN THE NAME OF LOVE!
NOT THIS MAN, PAL! NEVER THIS MAN!
AH, ARCHIEKINS! YOU'RE LEARNING TO BE FASHIONABLY LATE AS I TAUGHT YOU!
HI, LOVE BUG!
I'M ALSO FASHIONABLY HOT! I'M SWELTERING IN THIS OUTFIT!
NONSENSE, DARLING! THINK COOL!
I SHOULD HAVE STAGED THIS PARTY IN AIR CONDITIONED GLORY INSIDE, SMITHERS!
EXCUSE ME, SIR! I MUST CHECK ON THE BUFFET!
DON'T KID ME, YOU CHICKEN BUTLER! YOU JUST WANT TO GET INSIDE WHERE IT'S COMFORTABLE!
JUST DOING MY JOB, SIR!
AH-H!
THEN STAY HERE AND SUFFER ALONG WITH YOUR BOSS!
YOU'RE A HARD MAN, MR. LODGE!
...SIR!

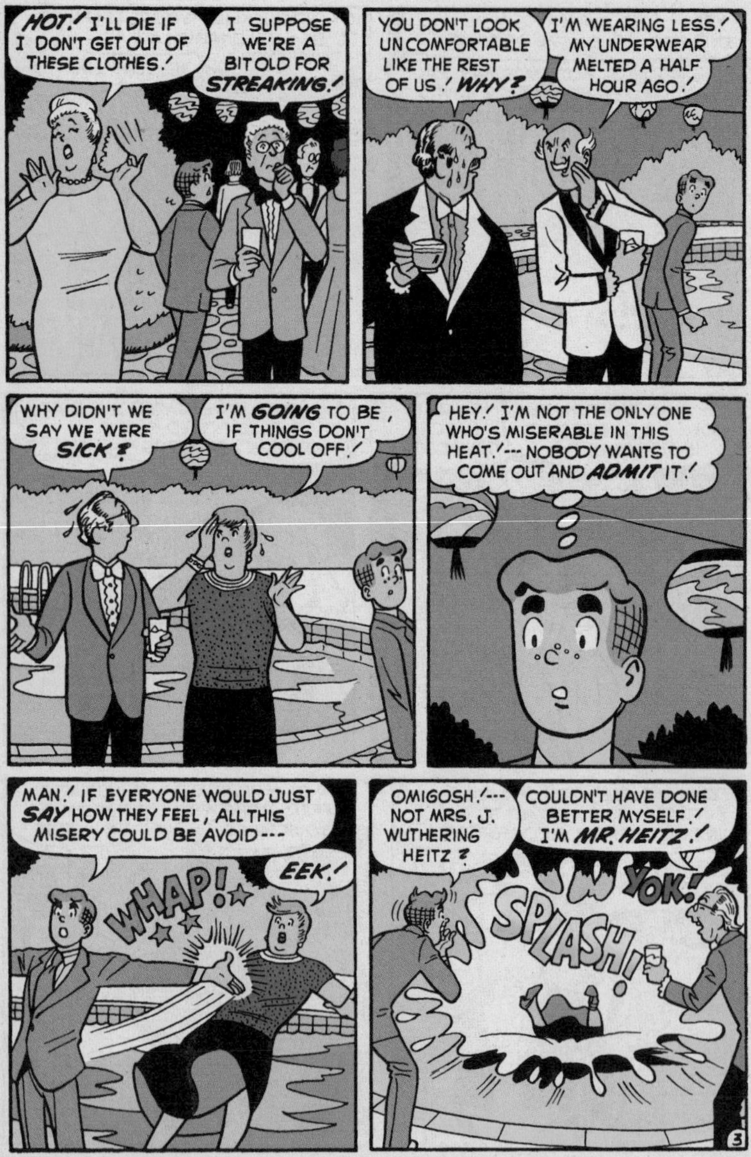
HOT! I'LL DIE IF I DON'T GET OUT OF THESE CLOTHES!
I SUPPOSE WE'RE A BIT OLD FOR STREAKING!
YOU DON'T LOOK UNCOMFORTABLE LIKE THE REST OF US! WHY?
I'M WEARING LESS! MY UNDERWEAR MELTED A HALF HOUR AGO!
WHY DIDN'T WE SAY WE WERE SICK?
I'M GOING TO BE, IF THINGS DON'T COOL OFF!
HEY! I'M NOT THE ONLY ONE WHO'S MISERABLE IN THIS HEAT!--- NOBODY WANTS TO COME OUT AND ADMIT IT!
MAN! IF EVERYONE WOULD JUST SAY HOW THEY FEEL, ALL THIS MISERY COULD BE AVOID---
WHAP!
EEK!
OMIGOSH!--- NOT MRS. J. WUTHERING HEITZ?
COULDN'T HAVE DONE BETTER MYSELF! I'M MR. HEITZ!
YOK!
SPLASH!
3

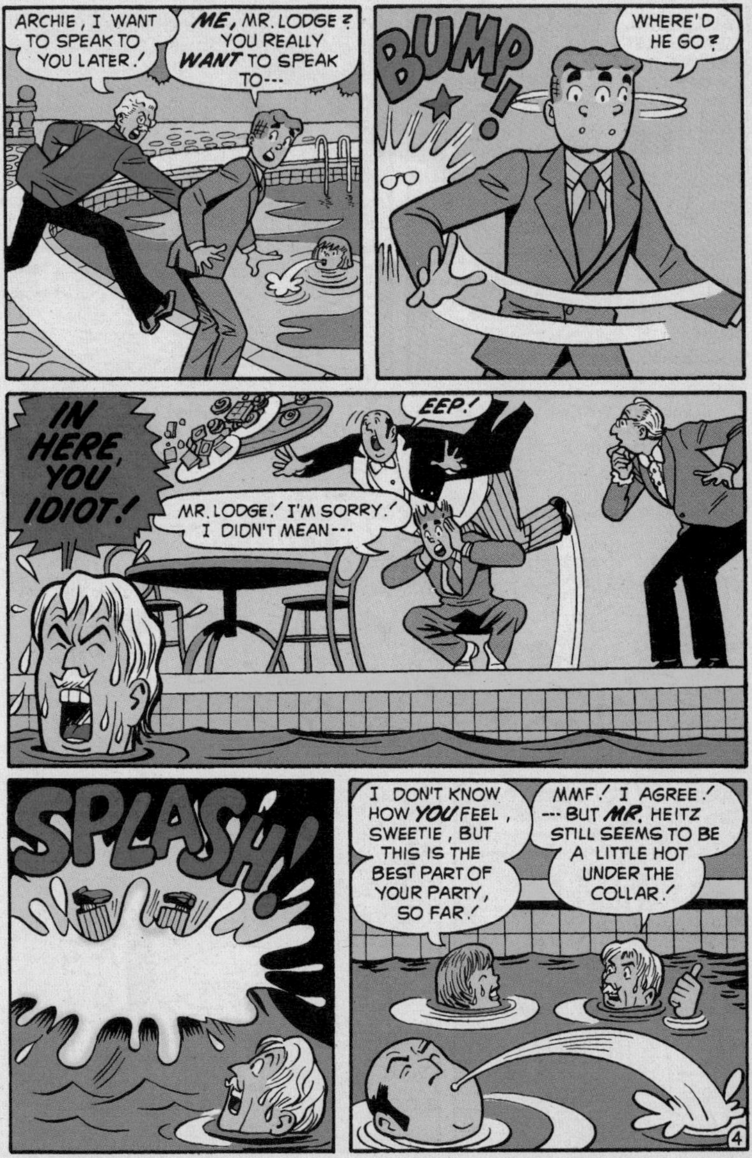
ARCHIE, I WANT TO SPEAK TO YOU LATER!
ME, MR. LODGE? YOU REALLY WANT TO SPEAK TO---
BUMP!
WHERE'D HE GO?
IN HERE, YOU IDIOT!
EEP!
MR. LODGE! I'M SORRY! I DIDN'T MEAN---
SPLASH!
I DON'T KNOW HOW YOU FEEL, SWEETIE, BUT THIS IS THE BEST PART OF YOUR PARTY, SO FAR!
MMF! I AGREE! --- BUT MR. HEITZ STILL SEEMS TO BE A LITTLE HOT UNDER THE COLLAR!
4

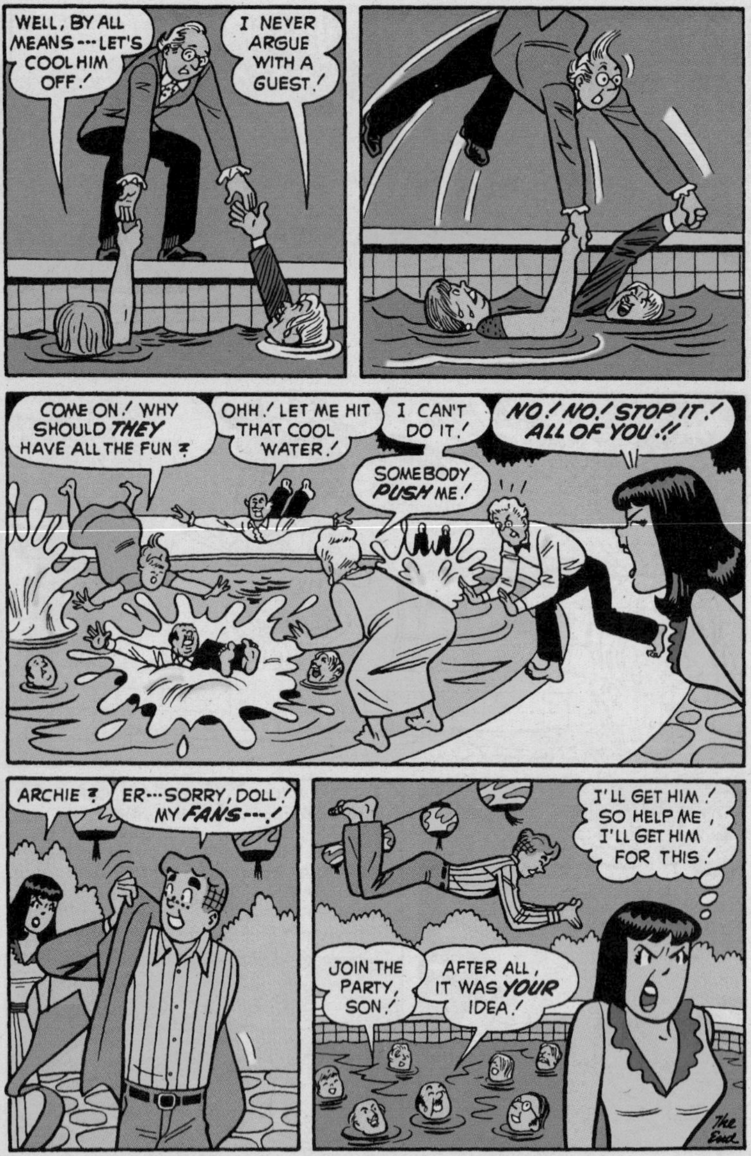
WELL, BY ALL MEANS---LET'S COOL HIM OFF!
I NEVER ARGUE WITH A GUEST!
COME ON! WHY SHOULD THEY HAVE ALL THE FUN?
OHH! LET ME HIT THAT COOL WATER!
I CAN'T DO IT!
SOMEBODY PUSH ME!
NO! NO! STOP IT! ALL OF YOU!!
ARCHIE?
ER---SORRY, DOLL! MY FANS---!
I'LL GET HIM! SO HELP ME, I'LL GET HIM FOR THIS!
JOIN THE PARTY, SON!
AFTER ALL, IT WAS YOUR IDEA!
The End

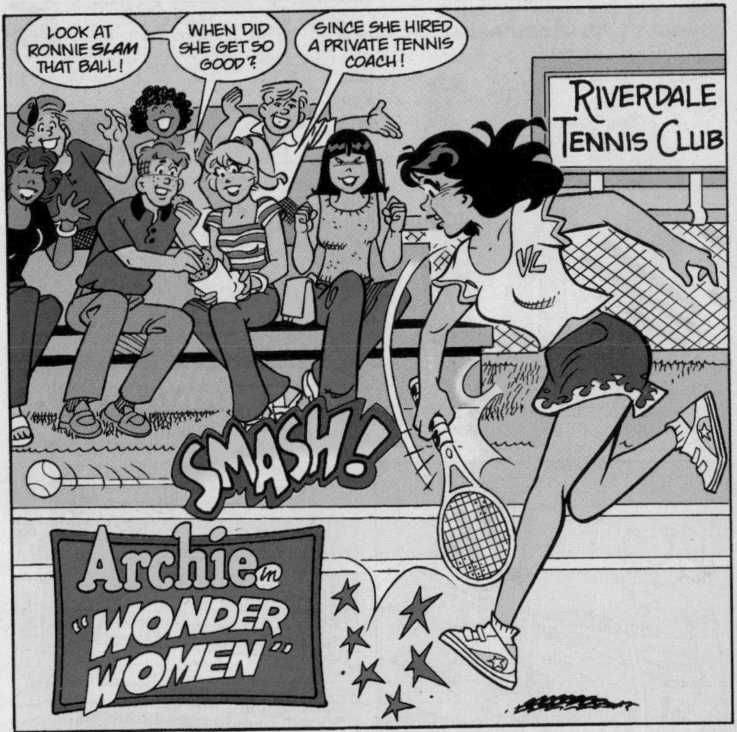
LOOK AT RONNIE SLAM THAT BALL!
WHEN DID SHE GET SO GOOD?
SINCE SHE HIRED A PRIVATE TENNIS COACH!
RIVERDALE TENNIS CLUB
VL
SMASH!
Archie in
"WONDER WOMEN"

Script: George Gladir / Pencils: Stan Goldberg / Inks: Bob Smith / Letters: Vickie Williams / Colors: Barry Grossman

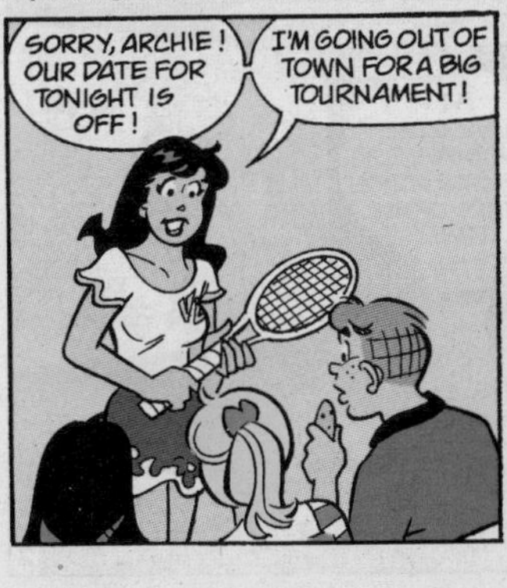
SORRY, ARCHIE! OUR DATE FOR TONIGHT IS OFF!
I'M GOING OUT OF TOWN FOR A BIG TOURNAMENT!

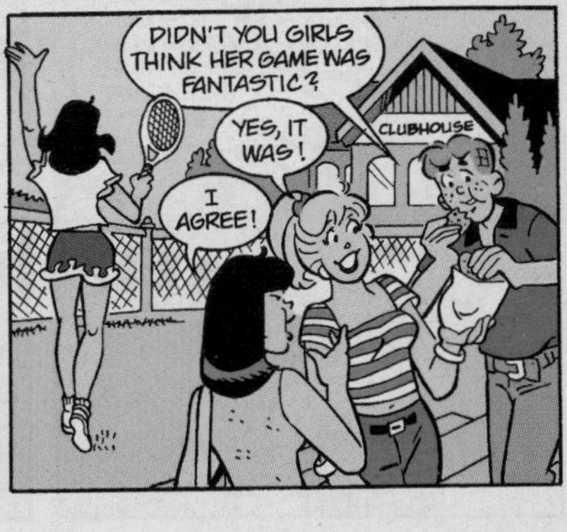
DIDN'T YOU GIRLS THINK HER GAME WAS FANTASTIC?
CLUBHOUSE
YES, IT WAS!
I AGREE!

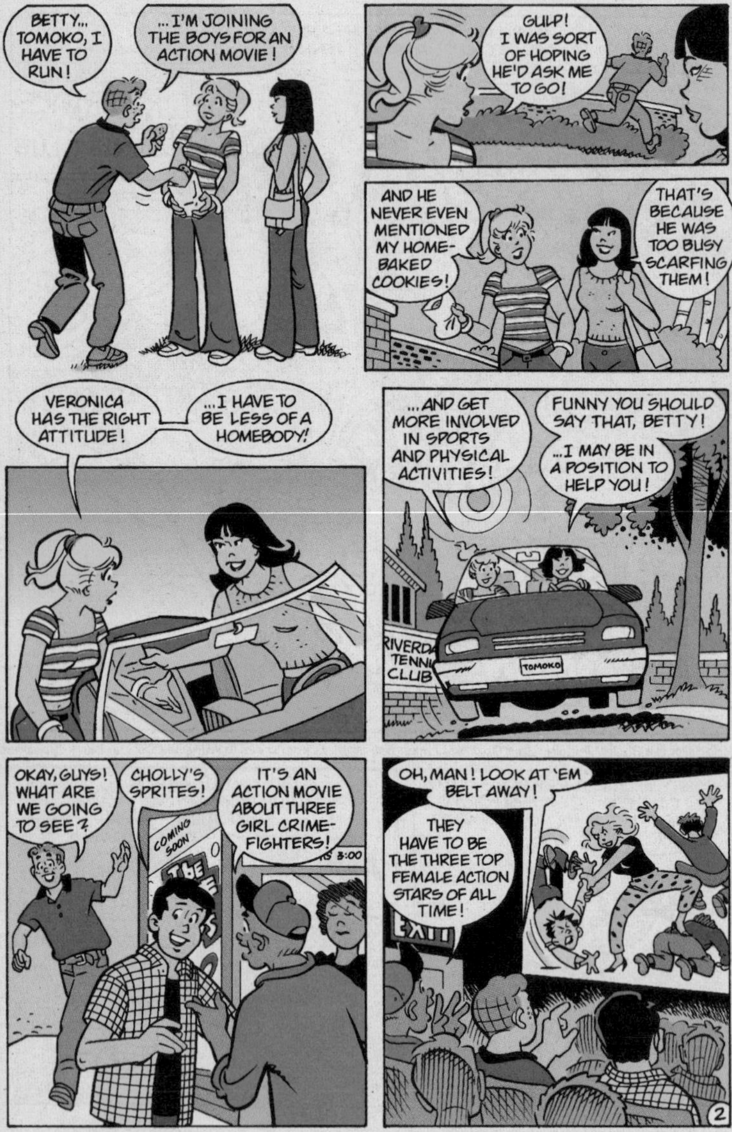
BETTY... TOMOKO, I HAVE TO RUN!
...I'M JOINING THE BOYS FOR AN ACTION MOVIE!
GULP! I WAS SORT OF HOPING HE'D ASK ME TO GO!
AND HE NEVER EVEN MENTIONED MY HOME-BAKED COOKIES!
THAT'S BECAUSE HE WAS TOO BUSY SCARFING THEM!
VERONICA HAS THE RIGHT ATTITUDE!
...I HAVE TO BE LESS OF A HOMEBODY!
...AND GET MORE INVOLVED IN SPORTS AND PHYSICAL ACTIVITIES!
FUNNY YOU SHOULD SAY THAT, BETTY!
...I MAY BE IN A POSITION TO HELP YOU!
RIVERDA TENNI CLUB
TOMOKO
OKAY, GUYS! WHAT ARE WE GOING TO SEE?
CHOLLY'S SPRITES!
IT'S AN ACTION MOVIE ABOUT THREE GIRL CRIME-FIGHTERS!
COMING SOON
OH, MAN! LOOK AT 'EM BELT AWAY!
THEY HAVE TO BE THE THREE TOP FEMALE ACTION STARS OF ALL TIME!
EXIT
2

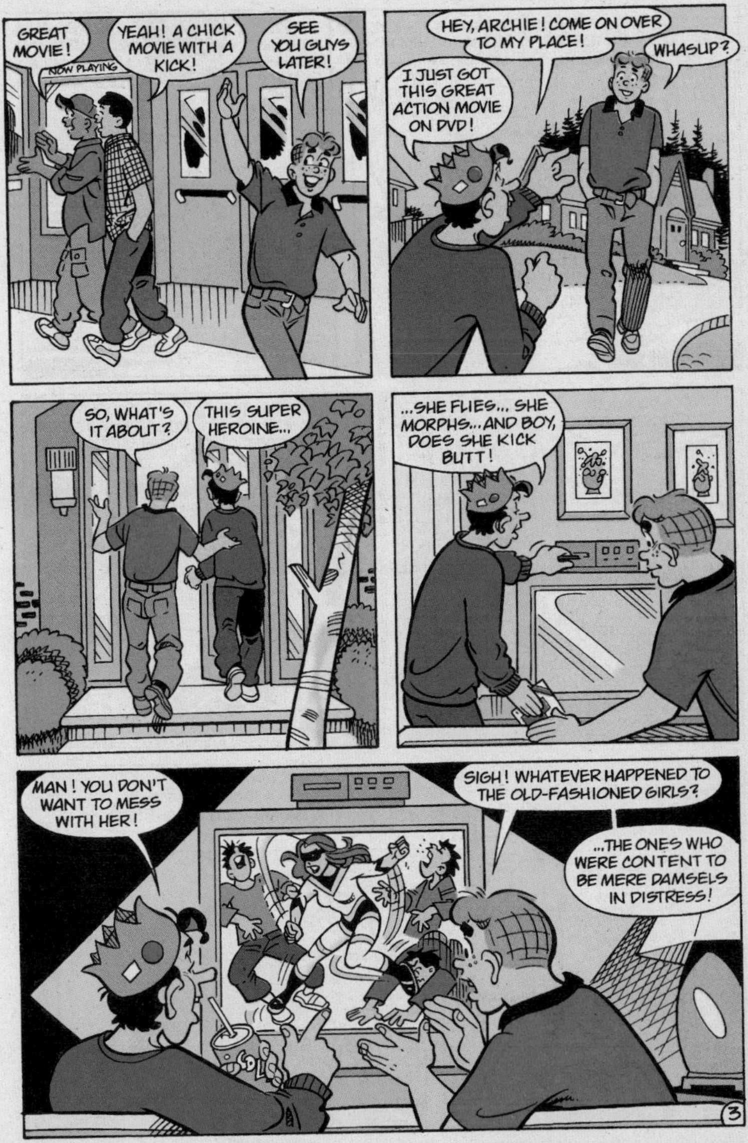
GREAT MOVIE!
NOW PLAYING
YEAH! A CHICK MOVIE WITH A KICK!
SEE YOU GUYS LATER!
HEY, ARCHIE! COME ON OVER TO MY PLACE!
WHASUP?
I JUST GOT THIS GREAT ACTION MOVIE ON DVD!
SO, WHAT'S IT ABOUT?
THIS SUPER HEROINE...
...SHE FLIES... SHE MORPHS... AND BOY, DOES SHE KICK BUTT!
MAN! YOU DON'T WANT TO MESS WITH HER!
SIGH! WHATEVER HAPPENED TO THE OLD-FASHIONED GIRLS?
...THE ONES WHO WERE CONTENT TO BE MERE DAMSELS IN DISTRESS!
3

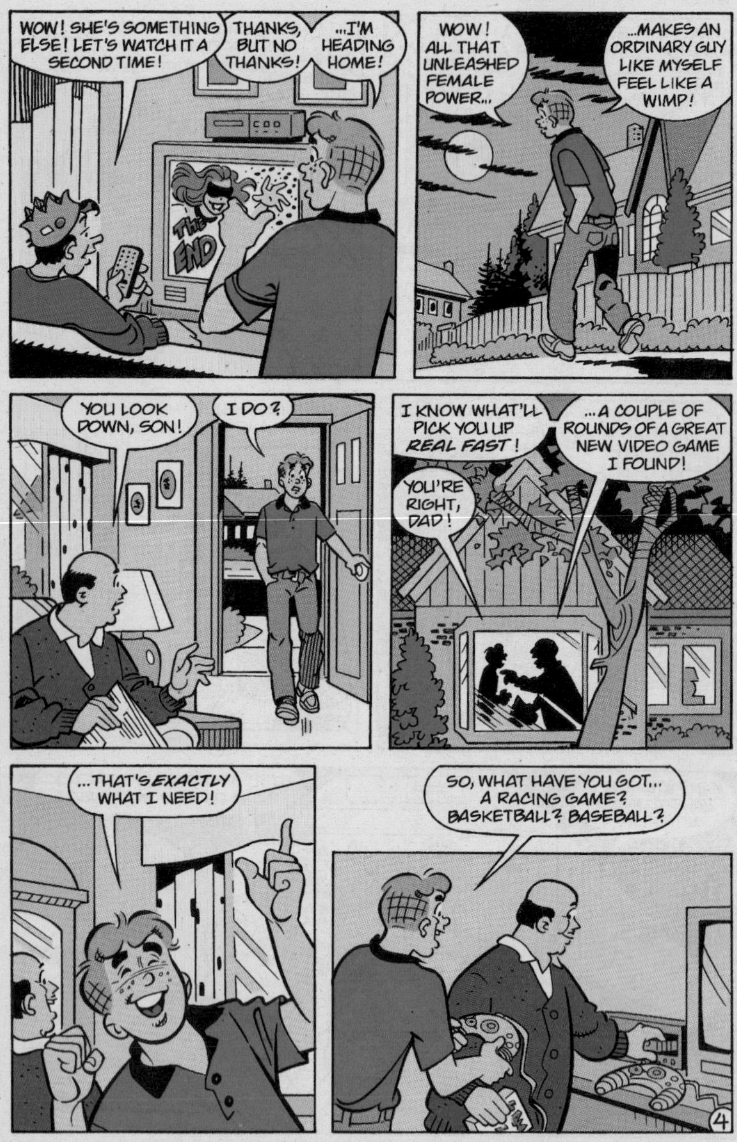
WOW! SHE'S SOMETHING ELSE! LET'S WATCH IT A SECOND TIME!
THANKS, BUT NO THANKS!
...I'M HEADING HOME!
THE END
WOW! ALL THAT UNLEASHED FEMALE POWER...
...MAKES AN ORDINARY GUY LIKE MYSELF FEEL LIKE A WIMP!
YOU LOOK DOWN, SON!
I DO?
I KNOW WHAT'LL PICK YOU UP REAL FAST!
...A COUPLE OF ROUNDS OF A GREAT NEW VIDEO GAME I FOUND!
YOU'RE RIGHT, DAD!
...THAT'S EXACTLY WHAT I NEED!
SO, WHAT HAVE YOU GOT... A RACING GAME? BASKETBALL? BASEBALL?
4

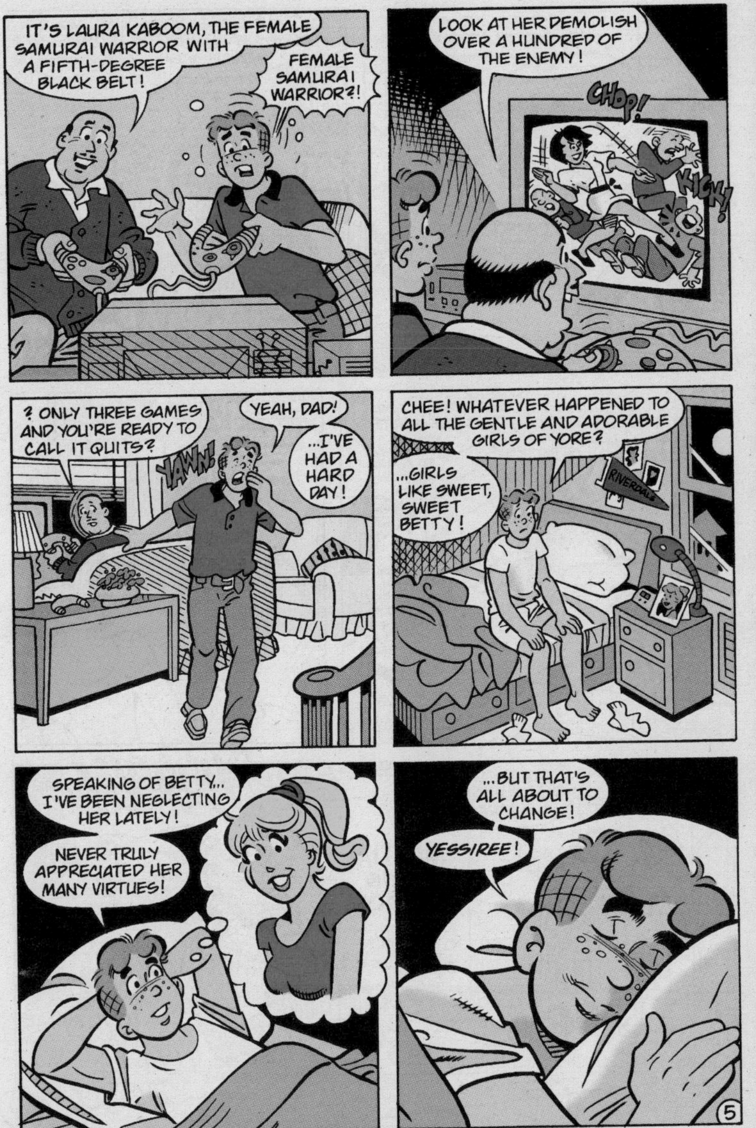
IT'S LAURA KABOOM, THE FEMALE SAMURAI WARRIOR WITH A FIFTH-DEGREE BLACK BELT!
FEMALE SAMURAI WARRIOR?!
LOOK AT HER DEMOLISH OVER A HUNDRED OF THE ENEMY!
CHOP!
KICK!
? ONLY THREE GAMES AND YOU'RE READY TO CALL IT QUITS?
YEAH, DAD!
YAWN!
...I'VE HAD A HARD DAY!
CHEE! WHATEVER HAPPENED TO ALL THE GENTLE AND ADORABLE GIRLS OF YORE?
...GIRLS LIKE SWEET, SWEET BETTY!
RIVERDALE
SPEAKING OF BETTY... I'VE BEEN NEGLECTING HER LATELY!
NEVER TRULY APPRECIATED HER MANY VIRTUES!
...BUT THAT'S ALL ABOUT TO CHANGE!
YESSIREE!

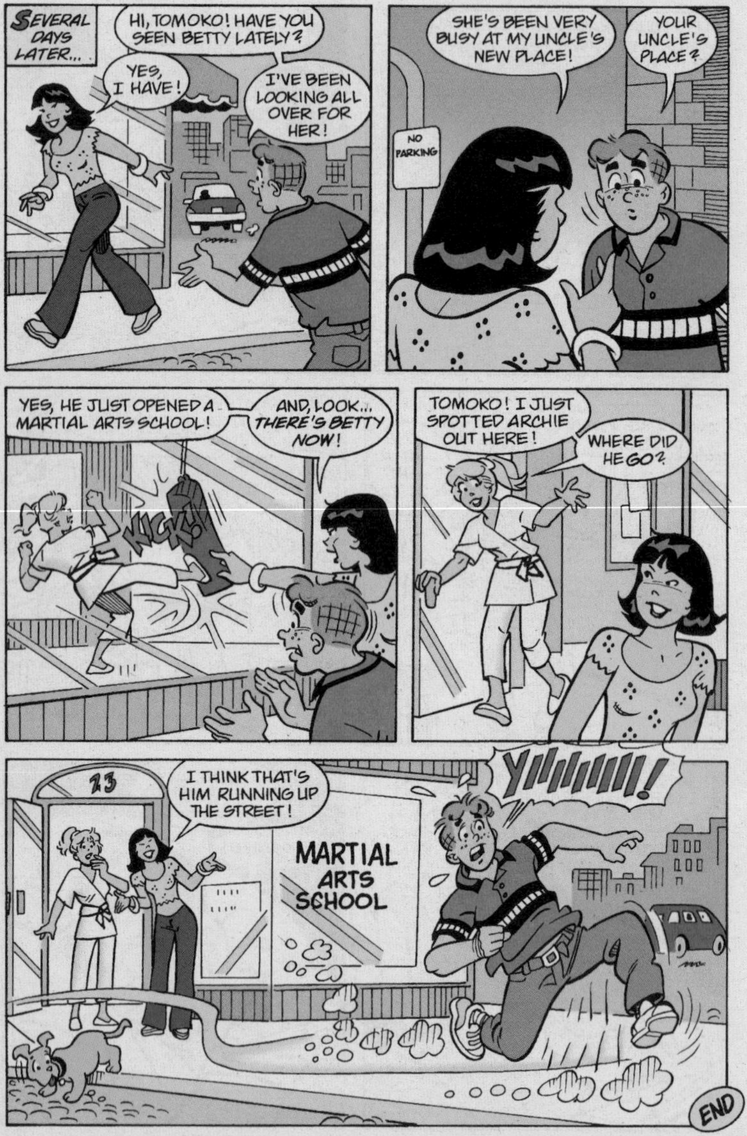
SEVERAL DAYS LATER...
HI, TOMOKO! HAVE YOU SEEN BETTY LATELY?
YES, I HAVE!
I'VE BEEN LOOKING ALL OVER FOR HER!
SHE'S BEEN VERY BUSY AT MY UNCLE'S NEW PLACE!
YOUR UNCLE'S PLACE?
NO PARKING
YES, HE JUST OPENED A MARTIAL ARTS SCHOOL!
AND, LOOK... THERE'S BETTY NOW!
KICK!
TOMOKO! I JUST SPOTTED ARCHIE OUT HERE!
WHERE DID HE GO?
23
I THINK THAT'S HIM RUNNING UP THE STREET!
MARTIAL ARTS SCHOOL
YIIIIIIII!
END

Archie in "THRILL THRALL"

Gladir / DeCarlo Jr. / J. DeCarlo / Yoshida / Grossman

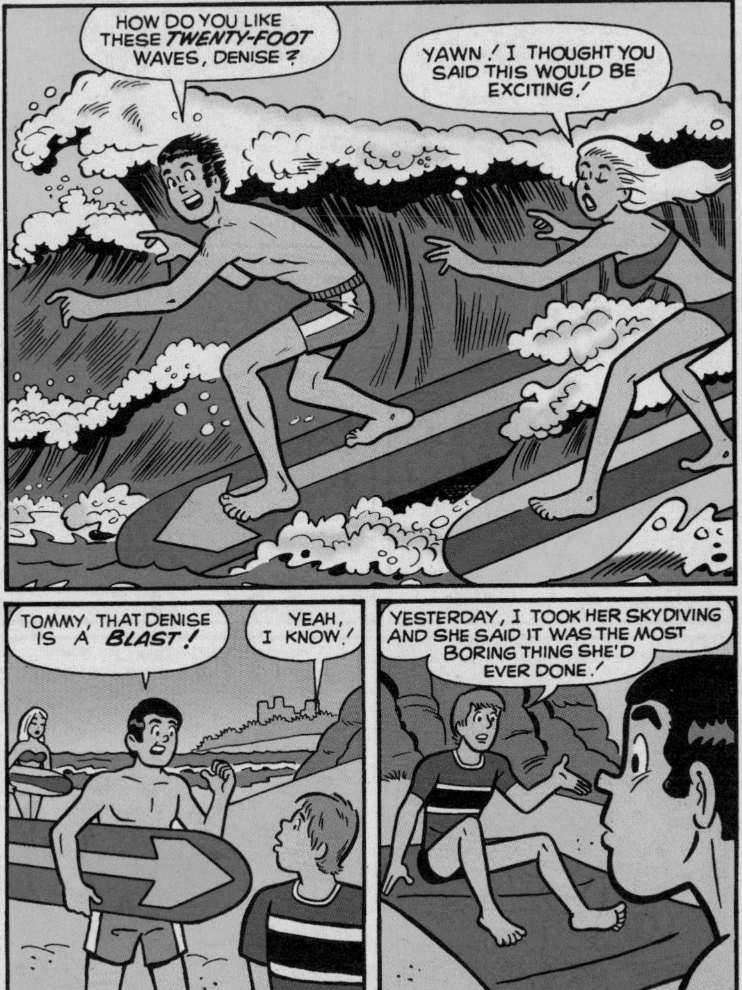

HOW DO YOU LIKE THESE *TWENTY-FOOT* WAVES, DENISE ?
YAWN ! I THOUGHT YOU SAID THIS WOULD BE EXCITING !
TOMMY, THAT DENISE IS A *BLAST* !
YEAH, I KNOW !
YESTERDAY, I TOOK HER SKYDIVING AND SHE SAID IT WAS THE MOST BORING THING SHE'D EVER DONE !
1

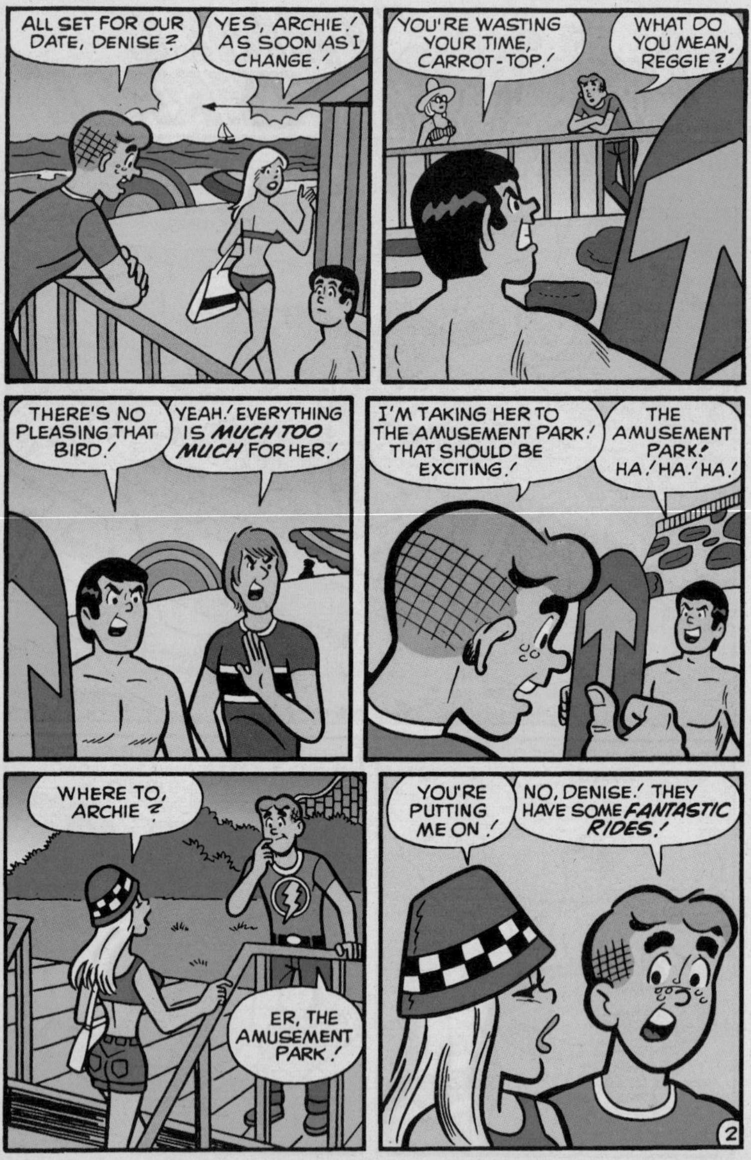
ALL SET FOR OUR DATE, DENISE?
YES, ARCHIE! AS SOON AS I CHANGE!
YOU'RE WASTING YOUR TIME, CARROT-TOP!
WHAT DO YOU MEAN, REGGIE?
THERE'S NO PLEASING THAT BIRD!
YEAH! EVERYTHING IS *MUCH TOO MUCH* FOR HER!
I'M TAKING HER TO THE AMUSEMENT PARK! THAT SHOULD BE EXCITING!
THE AMUSEMENT PARK! HA! HA! HA!
WHERE TO, ARCHIE?
ER, THE AMUSEMENT PARK!
YOU'RE PUTTING ME ON!
NO, DENISE! THEY HAVE SOME *FANTASTIC RIDES!*
2

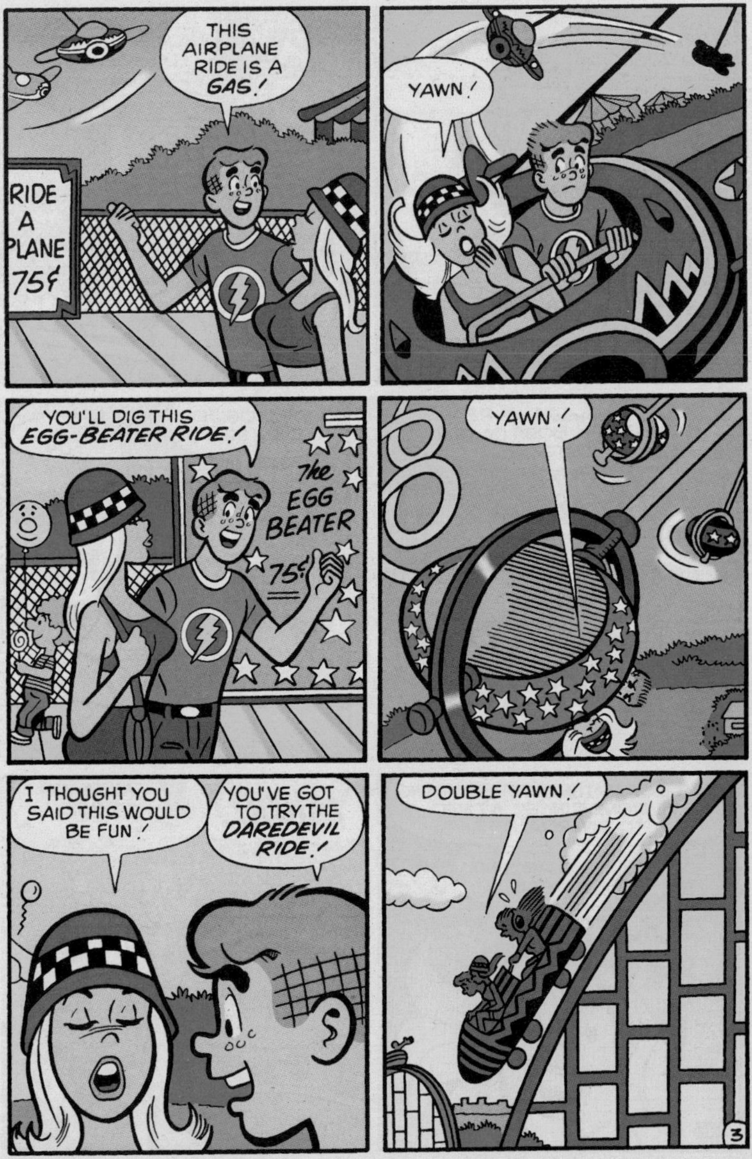
THIS AIRPLANE RIDE IS A GAS!
RIDE A PLANE 75¢
YAWN!
YOU'LL DIG THIS EGG-BEATER RIDE!
The EGG BEATER 75¢
YAWN!
I THOUGHT YOU SAID THIS WOULD BE FUN!
YOU'VE GOT TO TRY THE DAREDEVIL RIDE!
DOUBLE YAWN!
3

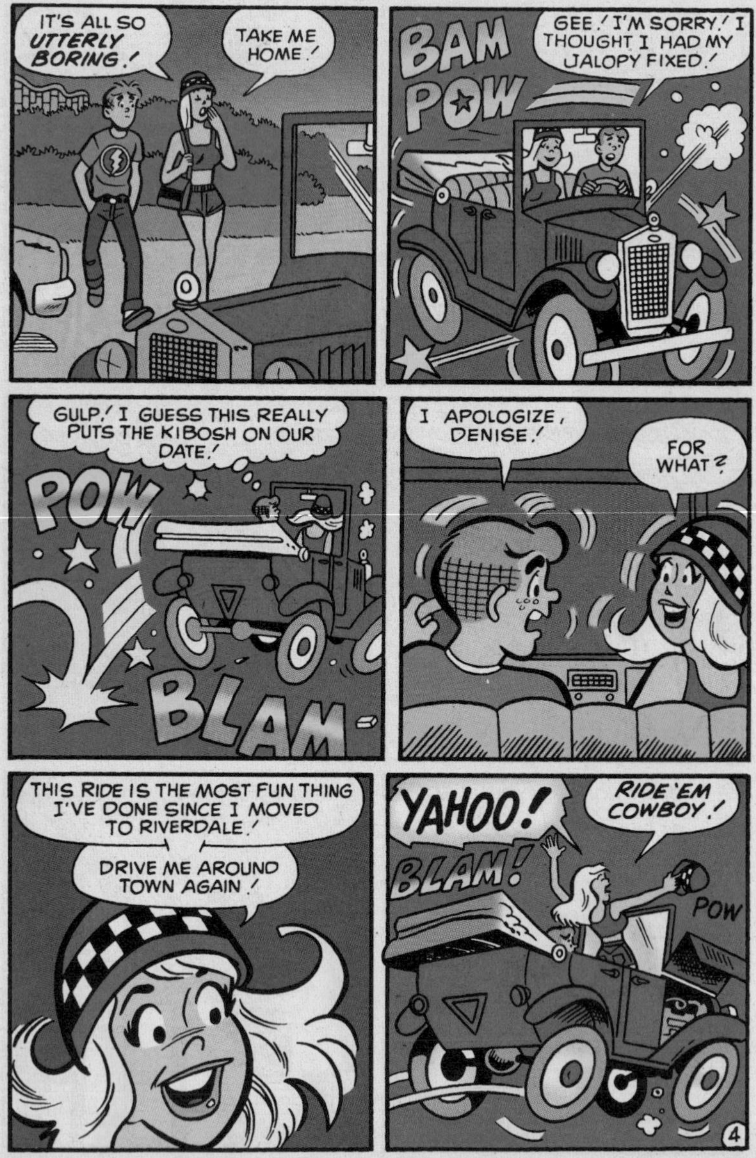
IT'S ALL SO UTTERLY BORING!
TAKE ME HOME!
BAM
POW
GEE! I'M SORRY! I THOUGHT I HAD MY JALOPY FIXED!
GULP! I GUESS THIS REALLY PUTS THE KIBOSH ON OUR DATE!
POW
BLAM
I APOLOGIZE, DENISE!
FOR WHAT?
THIS RIDE IS THE MOST FUN THING I'VE DONE SINCE I MOVED TO RIVERDALE!
DRIVE ME AROUND TOWN AGAIN!
YAHOO!
RIDE 'EM COWBOY!
BLAM!
POW
4

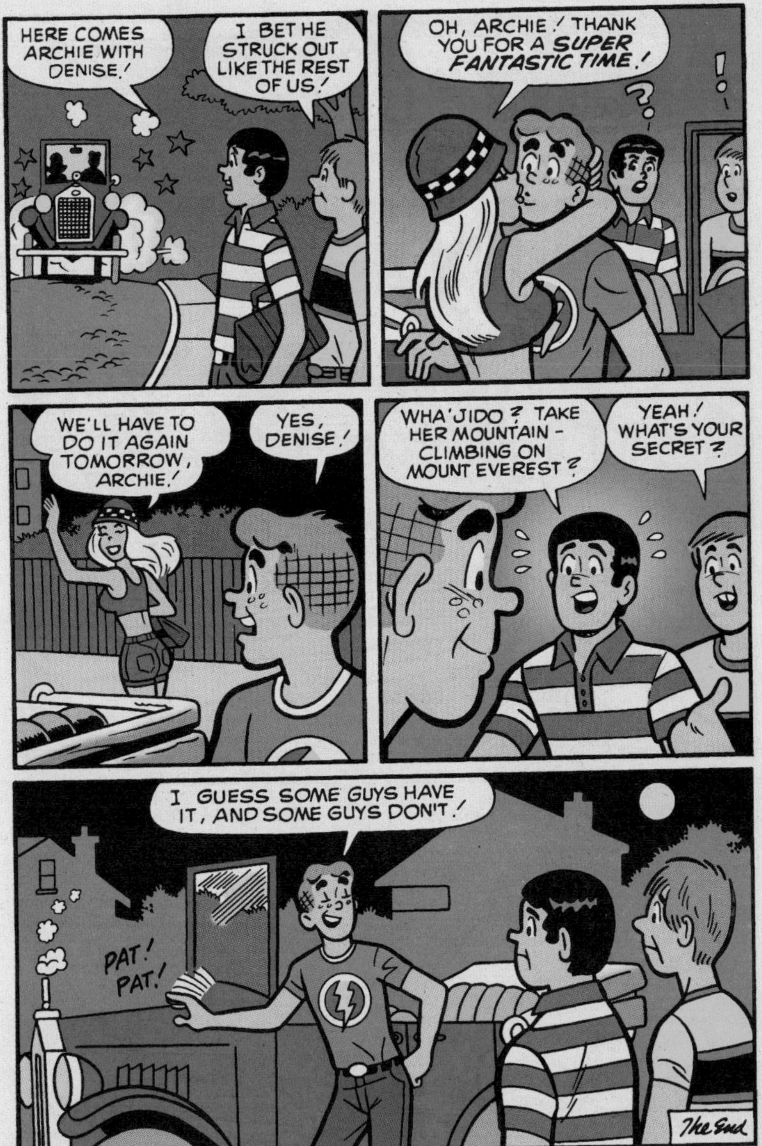
HERE COMES ARCHIE WITH DENISE!
I BET HE STRUCK OUT LIKE THE REST OF US!
OH, ARCHIE! THANK YOU FOR A SUPER FANTASTIC TIME!
?
!
WE'LL HAVE TO DO IT AGAIN TOMORROW, ARCHIE!
YES, DENISE!
WHA'JIDO? TAKE HER MOUNTAIN-CLIMBING ON MOUNT EVEREST?
YEAH! WHAT'S YOUR SECRET?
I GUESS SOME GUYS HAVE IT, AND SOME GUYS DON'T!
PAT! PAT!
The End

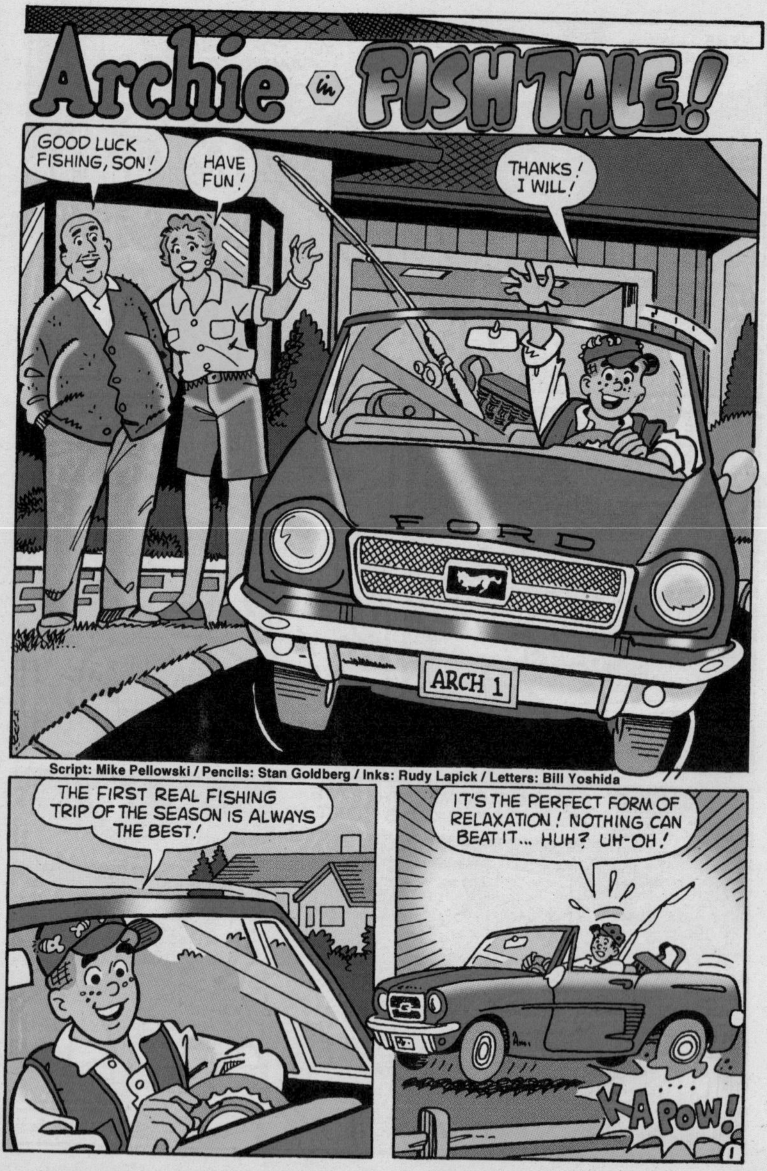
Archie in FISH TALE!
GOOD LUCK FISHING, SON!
HAVE FUN!
THANKS! I WILL!
FORD
ARCH 1
Script: Mike Pellowski / Pencils: Stan Goldberg / Inks: Rudy Lapick / Letters: Bill Yoshida
THE FIRST REAL FISHING TRIP OF THE SEASON IS ALWAYS THE BEST!
IT'S THE PERFECT FORM OF RELAXATION! NOTHING CAN BEAT IT... HUH? UH-OH!
KA POW!

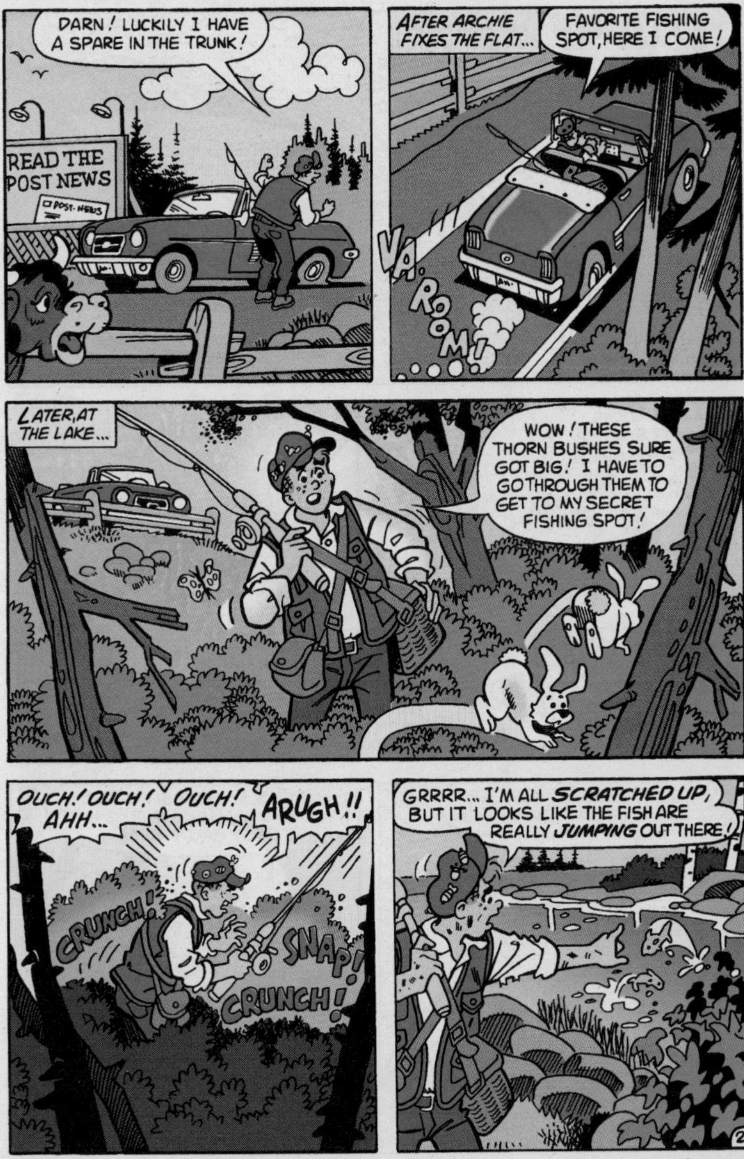
DARN! LUCKILY I HAVE A SPARE IN THE TRUNK!
READ THE POST NEWS
POST NEWS
AFTER ARCHIE FIXES THE FLAT...
FAVORITE FISHING SPOT, HERE I COME!
VA-ROOM!
LATER, AT THE LAKE...
WOW! THESE THORN BUSHES SURE GOT BIG! I HAVE TO GO THROUGH THEM TO GET TO MY SECRET FISHING SPOT!
OUCH! OUCH! OUCH! AHH...
ARUGH!!
CRUNCH!
SNAP!
CRUNCH!
GRRRR... I'M ALL SCRATCHED UP, BUT IT LOOKS LIKE THE FISH ARE REALLY JUMPING OUT THERE!
2

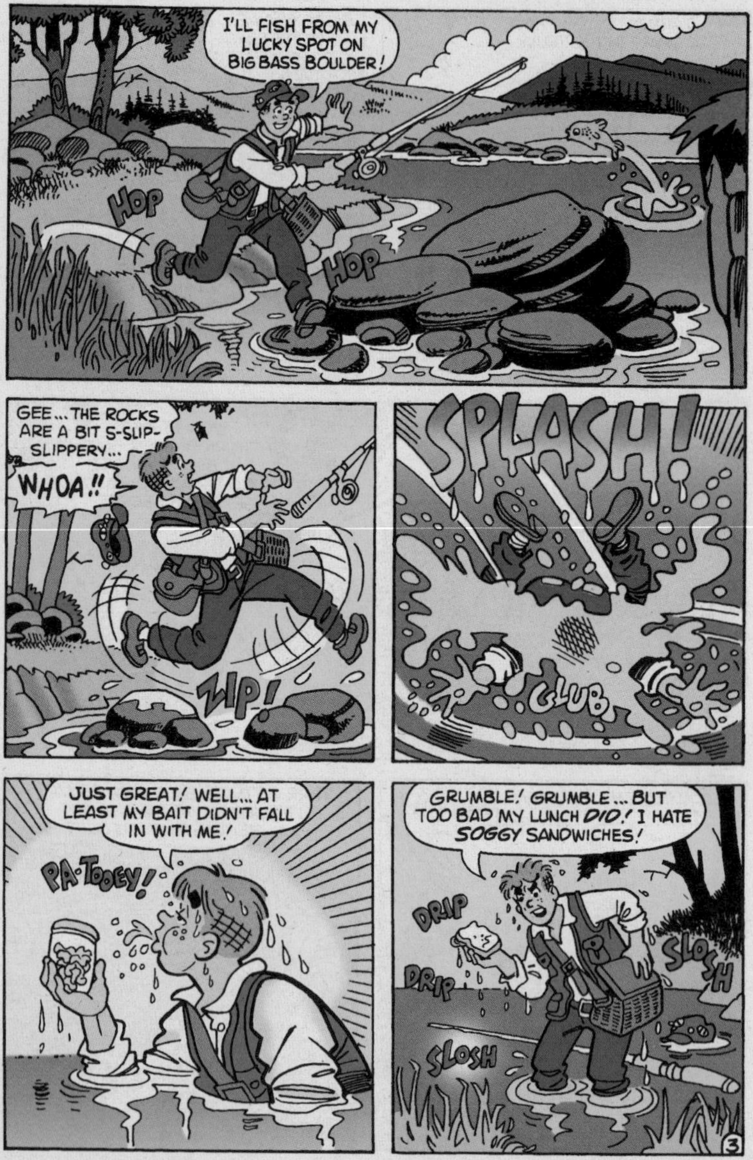
I'LL FISH FROM MY LUCKY SPOT ON BIG BASS BOULDER!
HOP
HOP
GEE... THE ROCKS ARE A BIT S-SLIP-SLIPPERY...
WHOA!!
ZIP!
SPLASH!
GLUB
JUST GREAT! WELL... AT LEAST MY BAIT DIDN'T FALL IN WITH ME!
PA-TOOEY!
GRUMBLE! GRUMBLE... BUT TOO BAD MY LUNCH DID! I HATE SOGGY SANDWICHES!
DRIP
DRIP
SLOSH
SLOSH
3

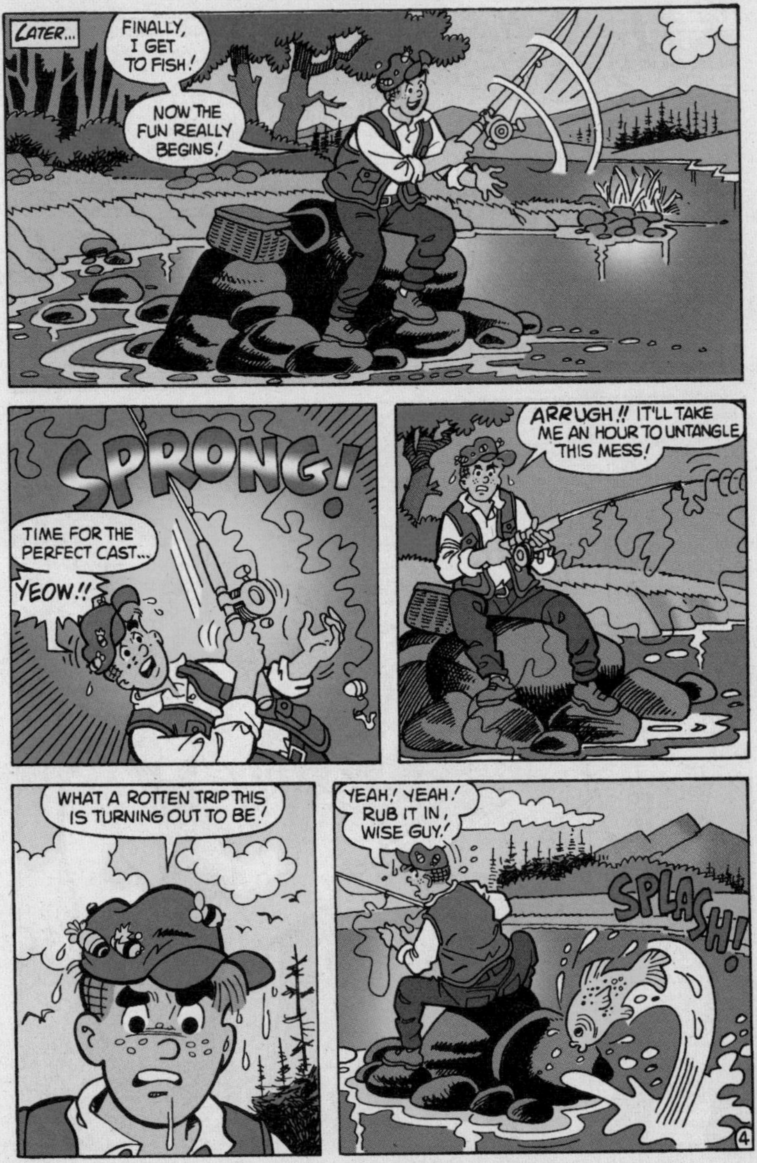
LATER...
FINALLY, I GET TO FISH!
NOW THE FUN REALLY BEGINS!
SPRONG!
TIME FOR THE PERFECT CAST...
YEOW!!
ARRUGH!! IT'LL TAKE ME AN HOUR TO UNTANGLE THIS MESS!
WHAT A ROTTEN TRIP THIS IS TURNING OUT TO BE!
YEAH! YEAH! RUB IT IN, WISE GUY!
SPLASH!
4

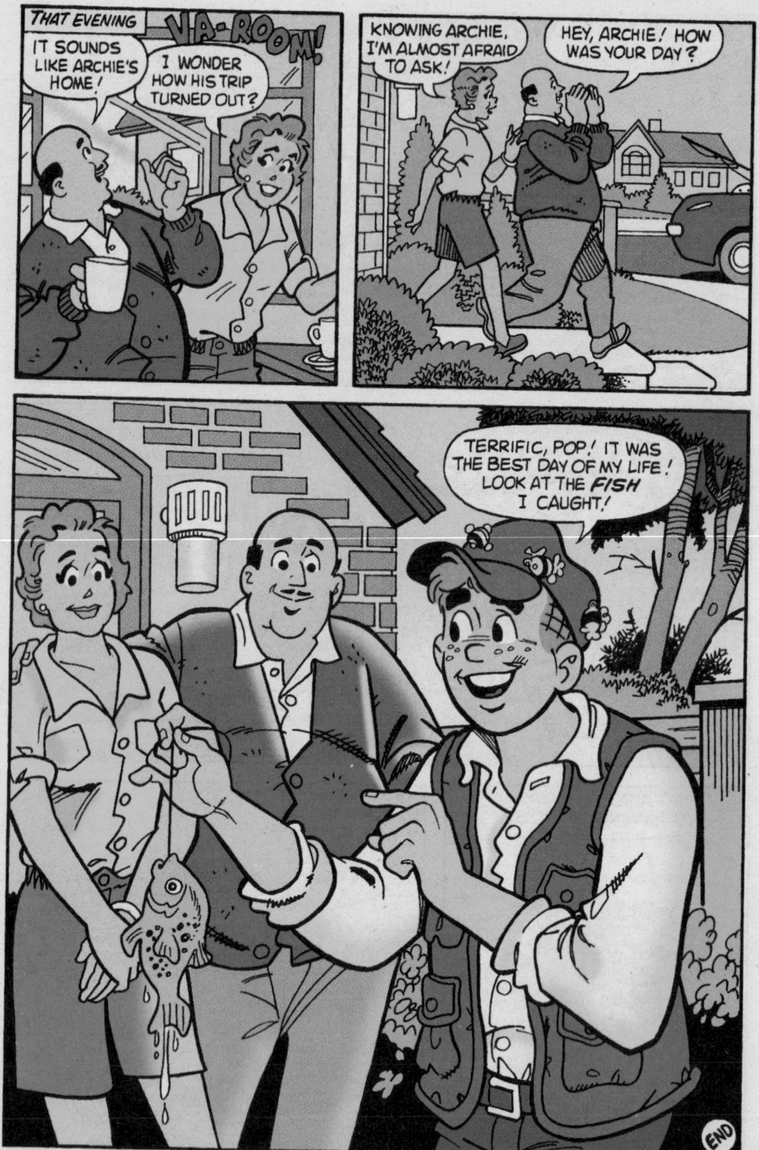
THAT EVENING
VA-ROOM!
IT SOUNDS LIKE ARCHIE'S HOME!
I WONDER HOW HIS TRIP TURNED OUT?
KNOWING ARCHIE, I'M ALMOST AFRAID TO ASK!
HEY, ARCHIE! HOW WAS YOUR DAY?
TERRIFIC, POP! IT WAS THE BEST DAY OF MY LIFE! LOOK AT THE FISH I CAUGHT!
END

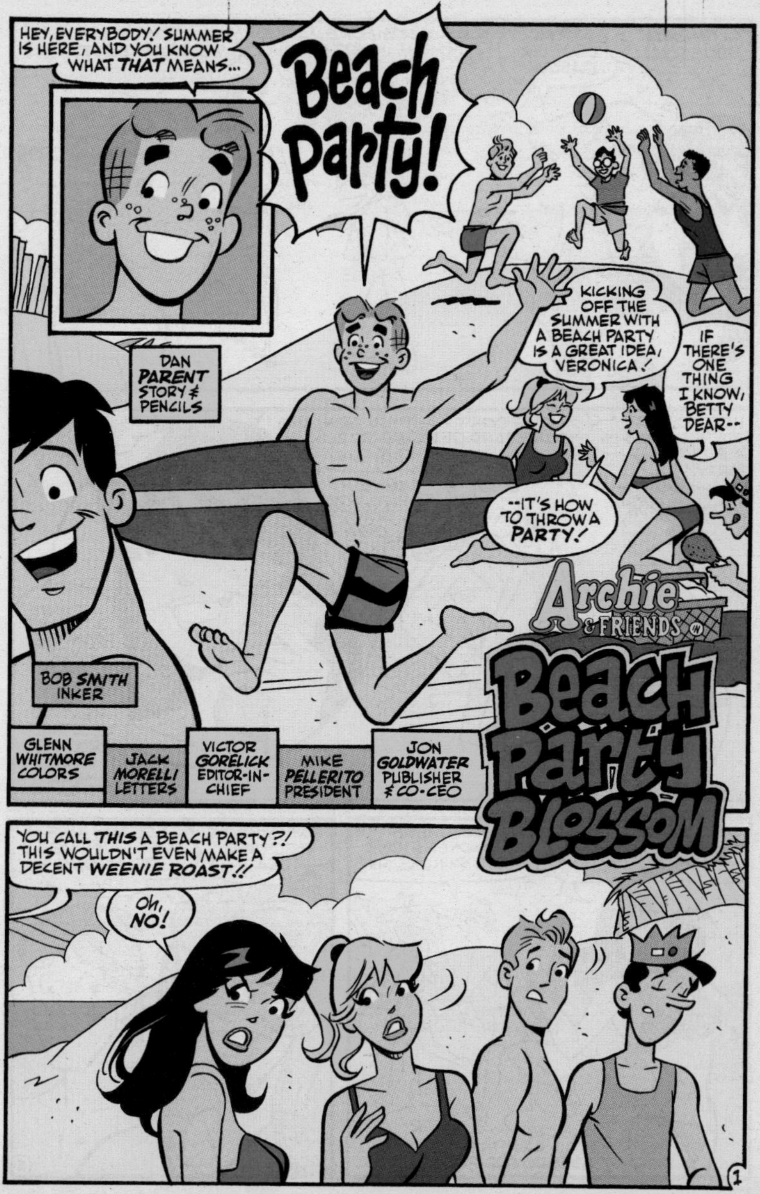
HEY, EVERYBODY! SUMMER IS HERE, AND YOU KNOW WHAT THAT MEANS...
Beach Party!
KICKING OFF THE SUMMER WITH A BEACH PARTY IS A GREAT IDEA, VERONICA!
IF THERE'S ONE THING I KNOW, BETTY DEAR--
--IT'S HOW TO THROW A PARTY!
DAN PARENT STORY & PENCILS
BOB SMITH INKER
GLENN WHITMORE COLORS
JACK MORELLI LETTERS
VICTOR GORELICK EDITOR-IN-CHIEF
MIKE PELLERITO PRESIDENT
JON GOLDWATER PUBLISHER & CO-CEO
Archie & FRIENDS in
Beach Party Blossom
YOU CALL THIS A BEACH PARTY?! THIS WOULDN'T EVEN MAKE A DECENT WEENIE ROAST!!
Oh, NO!
1

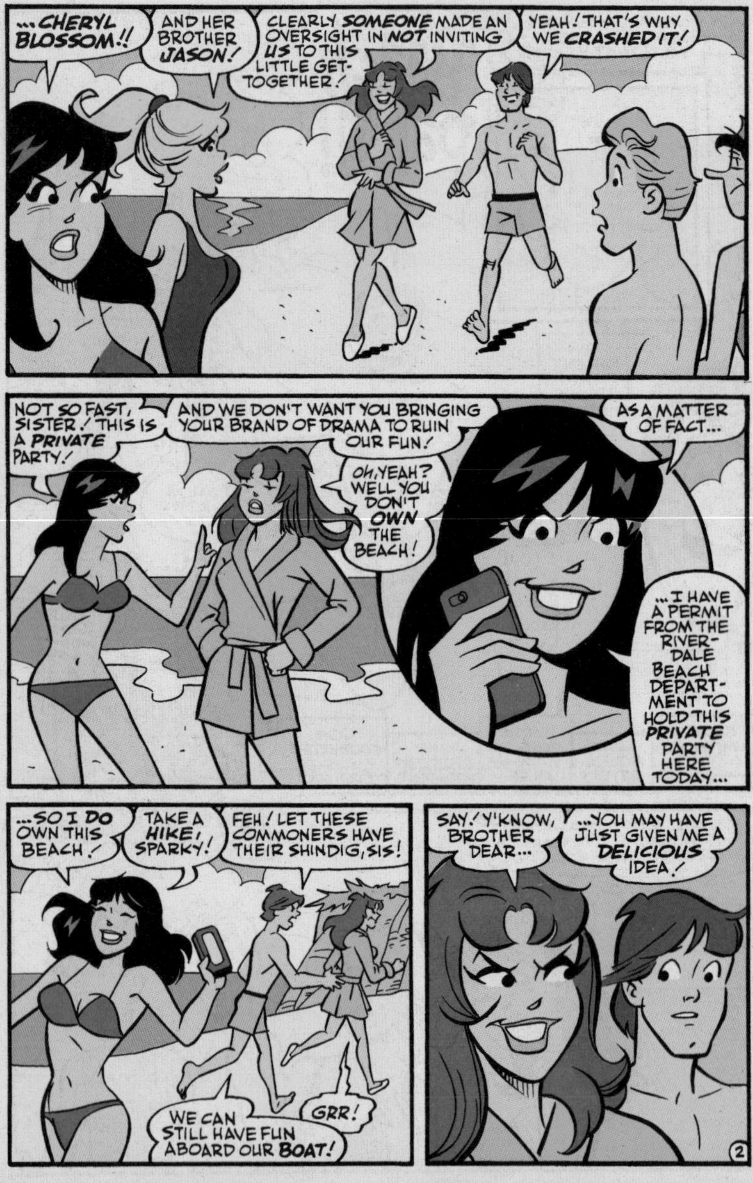
...CHERYL BLOSSOM!!
AND HER BROTHER JASON!
CLEARLY SOMEONE MADE AN OVERSIGHT IN NOT INVITING US TO THIS LITTLE GET-TOGETHER!
YEAH! THAT'S WHY WE CRASHED IT!
NOT SO FAST, SISTER! THIS IS A PRIVATE PARTY!
AND WE DON'T WANT YOU BRINGING YOUR BRAND OF DRAMA TO RUIN OUR FUN!
OH, YEAH? WELL YOU DON'T OWN THE BEACH!
AS A MATTER OF FACT...
...I HAVE A PERMIT FROM THE RIVER-DALE BEACH DEPART-MENT TO HOLD THIS PRIVATE PARTY HERE TODAY...
...SO I DO OWN THIS BEACH!
TAKE A HIKE, SPARKY!
FEH! LET THESE COMMONERS HAVE THEIR SHINDIG, SIS!
GRR!
WE CAN STILL HAVE FUN ABOARD OUR BOAT!
SAY! Y'KNOW, BROTHER DEAR...
...YOU MAY HAVE JUST GIVEN ME A DELICIOUS IDEA!
2

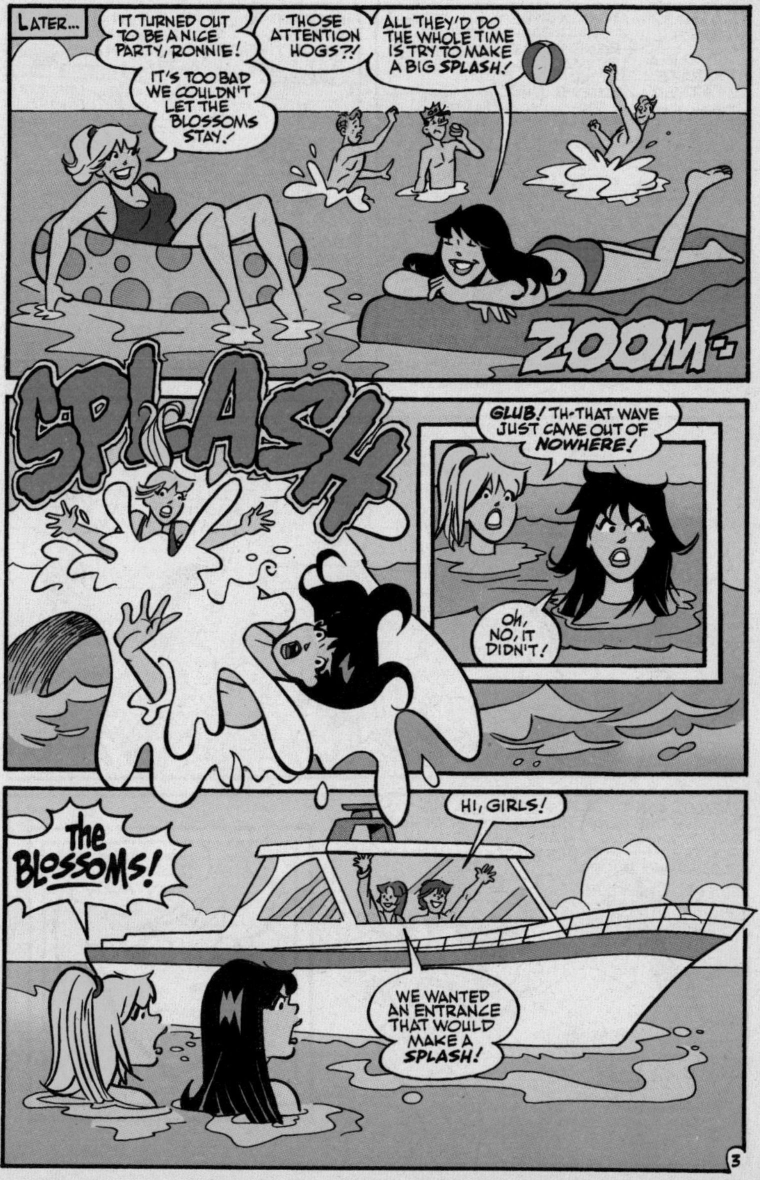
LATER...
IT TURNED OUT TO BE A NICE PARTY, RONNIE!
IT'S TOO BAD WE COULDN'T LET THE BLOSSOMS STAY!
THOSE ATTENTION HOGS?!
ALL THEY'D DO THE WHOLE TIME IS TRY TO MAKE A BIG SPLASH!
ZOOM
SPLASH
GLUB! TH-THAT WAVE JUST CAME OUT OF NOWHERE!
OH, NO, IT DIDN'T!
THE BLOSSOMS!
HI, GIRLS!
WE WANTED AN ENTRANCE THAT WOULD MAKE A SPLASH!
3

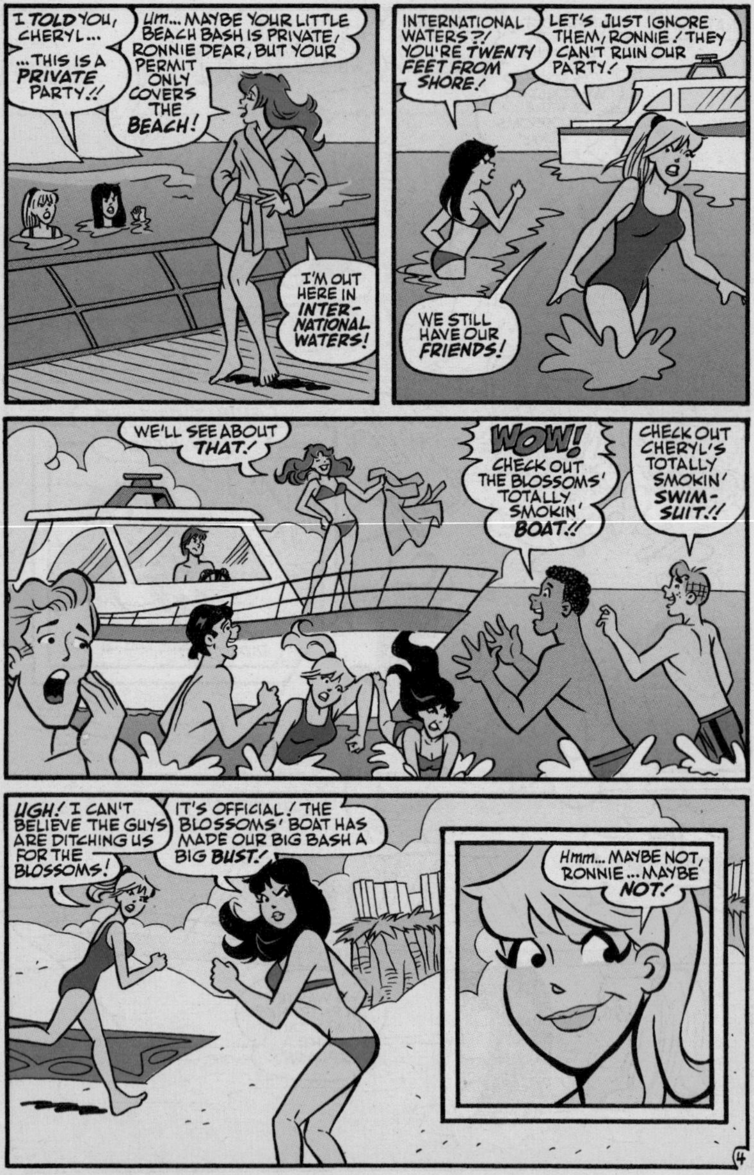
I TOLD YOU, CHERYL...
...THIS IS A PRIVATE PARTY!!
UM... MAYBE YOUR LITTLE BEACH BASH IS PRIVATE, RONNIE DEAR, BUT YOUR PERMIT ONLY COVERS THE BEACH!
I'M OUT HERE IN INTERNATIONAL WATERS!
INTERNATIONAL WATERS?! YOU'RE TWENTY FEET FROM SHORE!
LET'S JUST IGNORE THEM, RONNIE! THEY CAN'T RUIN OUR PARTY!
WE STILL HAVE OUR FRIENDS!
WE'LL SEE ABOUT THAT!
WOW! CHECK OUT THE BLOSSOMS' TOTALLY SMOKIN' BOAT!!
CHECK OUT CHERYL'S TOTALLY SMOKIN' SWIM-SUIT!!
UGH! I CAN'T BELIEVE THE GUYS ARE DITCHING US FOR THE BLOSSOMS!
IT'S OFFICIAL! THE BLOSSOMS' BOAT HAS MADE OUR BIG BASH A BIG BUST!
Hmm... MAYBE NOT, RONNIE... MAYBE NOT!
4

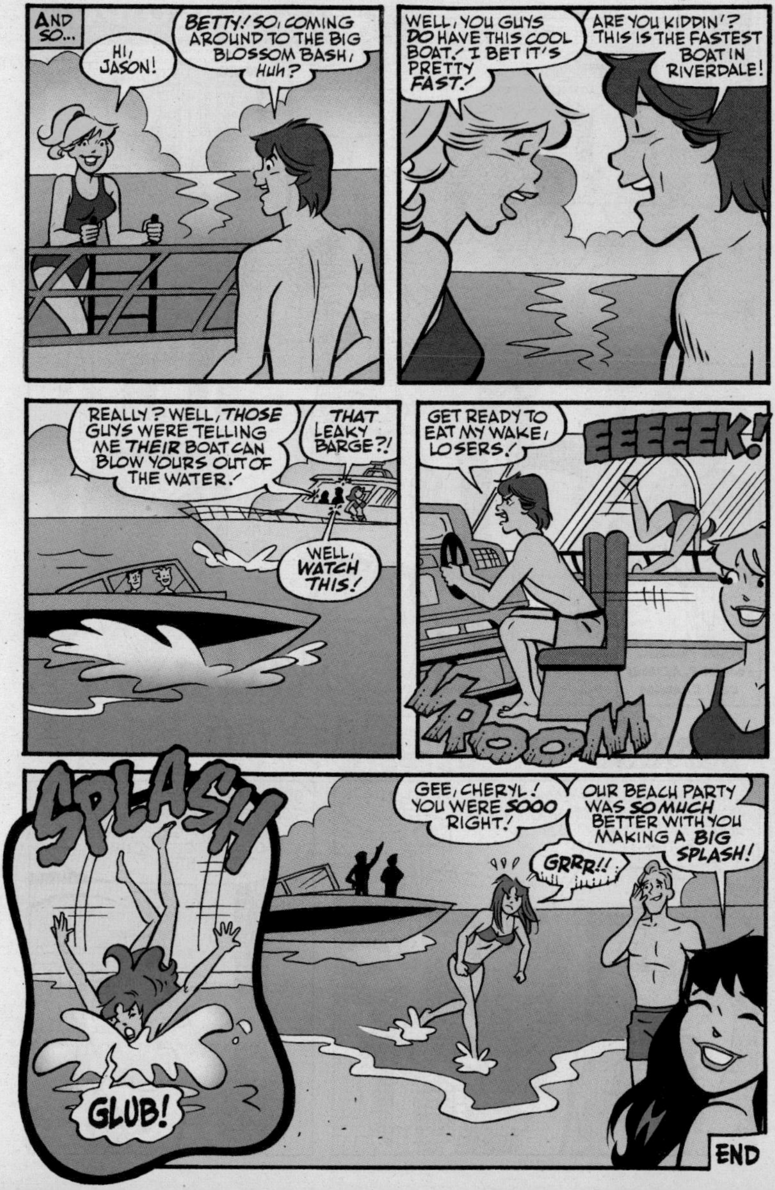
AND SO...
HI, JASON!
BETTY! SO, COMING AROUND TO THE BIG BLOSSOM BASH, Huh?
WELL, YOU GUYS DO HAVE THIS COOL BOAT! I BET IT'S PRETTY FAST!
ARE YOU KIDDIN'? THIS IS THE FASTEST BOAT IN RIVERDALE!
REALLY? WELL, THOSE GUYS WERE TELLING ME THEIR BOAT CAN BLOW YOURS OUT OF THE WATER!
THAT LEAKY BARGE?!
WELL, WATCH THIS!
GET READY TO EAT MY WAKE, LOSERS!
EEEEEK!
VROOOM
SPLASH
GLUB!
GEE, CHERYL! YOU WERE SOOO RIGHT!
OUR BEACH PARTY WAS SO MUCH BETTER WITH YOU MAKING A BIG SPLASH!
GRRR!!
END

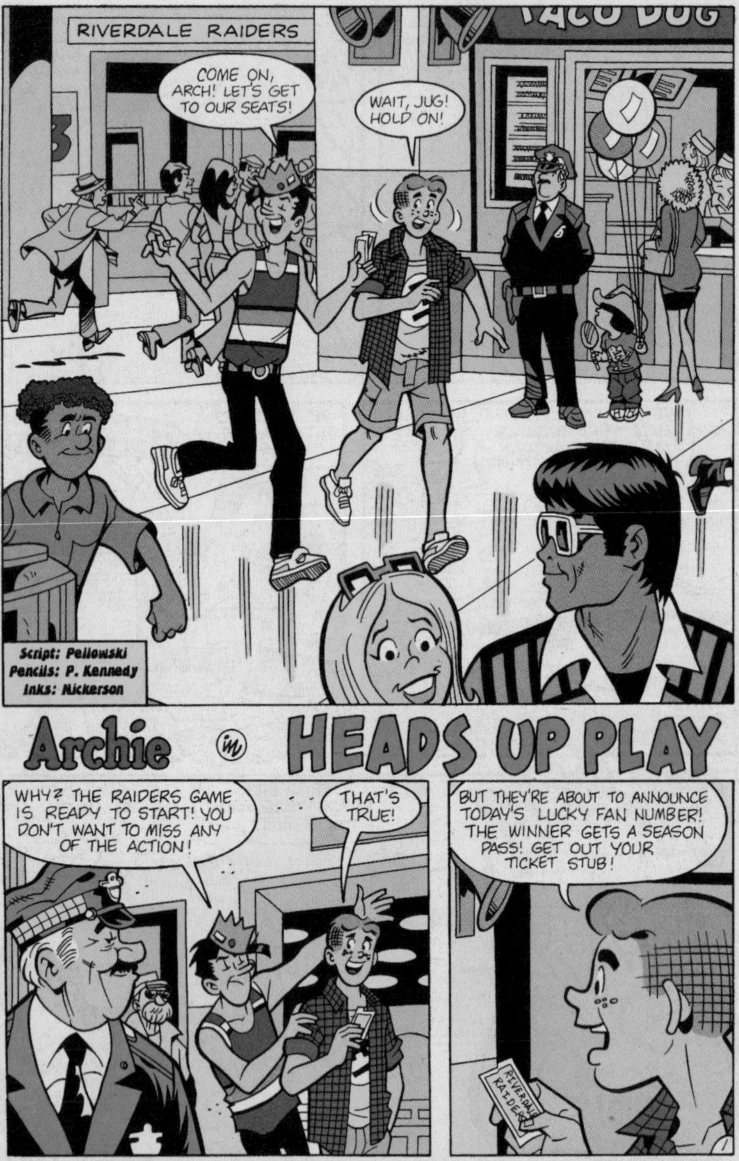

RIVERDALE RAIDERS
TACO DOG
COME ON, ARCH! LET'S GET TO OUR SEATS!
WAIT, JUG! HOLD ON!
Script: Pellowski
Pencils: P. Kennedy
Inks: Nickerson
Archie in HEADS UP PLAY
WHY? THE RAIDERS GAME IS READY TO START! YOU DON'T WANT TO MISS ANY OF THE ACTION!
THAT'S TRUE!
BUT THEY'RE ABOUT TO ANNOUNCE TODAY'S LUCKY FAN NUMBER! THE WINNER GETS A SEASON PASS! GET OUT YOUR TICKET STUB!
RIVERDALE RAIDERS

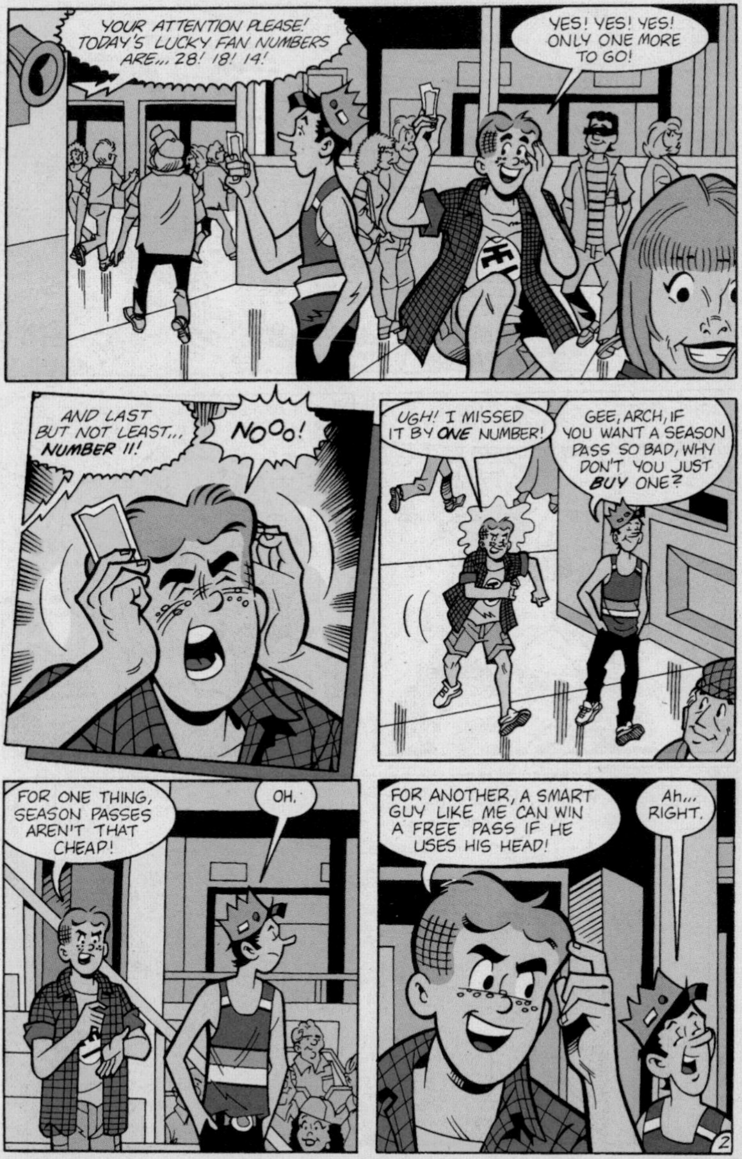
YOUR ATTENTION PLEASE! TODAY'S LUCKY FAN NUMBERS ARE... 28! 18! 14!
YES! YES! YES! ONLY ONE MORE TO GO!
AND LAST BUT NOT LEAST... NUMBER 11!
NOOO!
UGH! I MISSED IT BY ONE NUMBER!
GEE, ARCH, IF YOU WANT A SEASON PASS SO BAD, WHY DON'T YOU JUST BUY ONE?
FOR ONE THING, SEASON PASSES AREN'T THAT CHEAP!
OH.
FOR ANOTHER, A SMART GUY LIKE ME CAN WIN A FREE PASS IF HE USES HIS HEAD!
Ah... RIGHT.
2

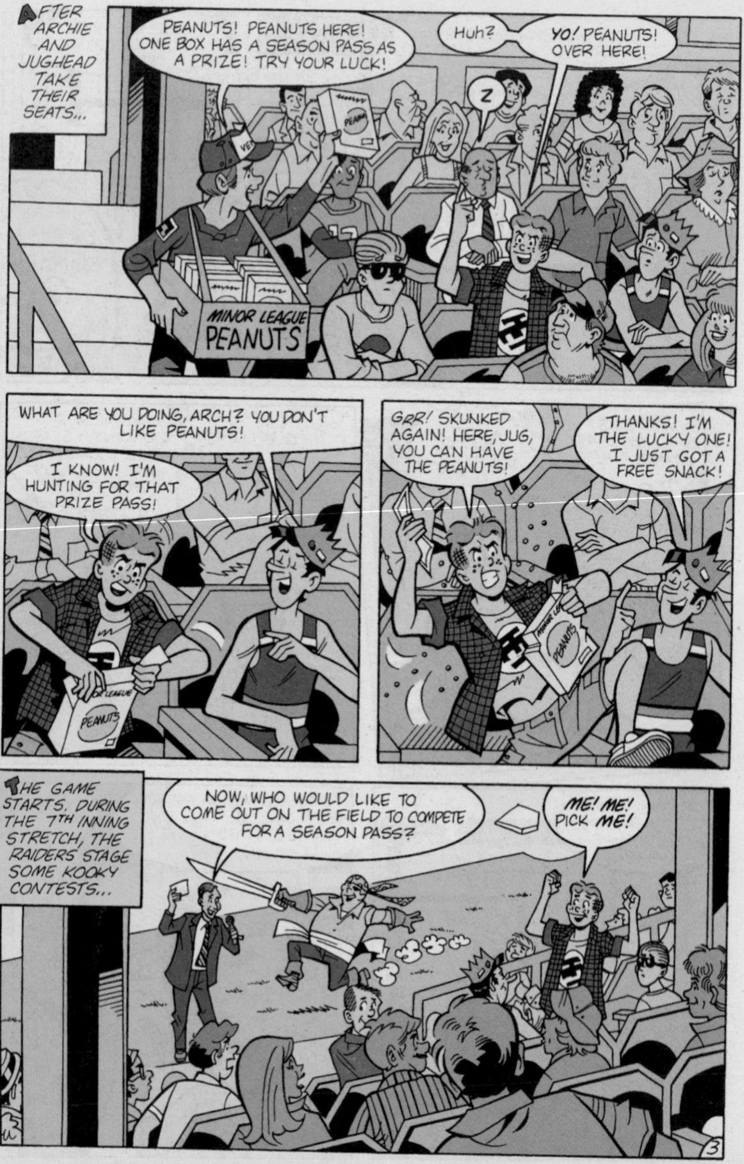
AFTER ARCHIE AND JUGHEAD TAKE THEIR SEATS...
PEANUTS! PEANUTS HERE! ONE BOX HAS A SEASON PASS AS A PRIZE! TRY YOUR LUCK!
Huh?
YO! PEANUTS! OVER HERE!
Z
MINOR LEAGUE PEANUTS
WHAT ARE YOU DOING, ARCH? YOU DON'T LIKE PEANUTS!
I KNOW! I'M HUNTING FOR THAT PRIZE PASS!
GRR! SKUNKED AGAIN! HERE, JUG, YOU CAN HAVE THE PEANUTS!
THANKS! I'M THE LUCKY ONE! I JUST GOT A FREE SNACK!
THE GAME STARTS. DURING THE 7TH INNING STRETCH, THE RAIDERS STAGE SOME KOOKY CONTESTS...
NOW, WHO WOULD LIKE TO COME OUT ON THE FIELD TO COMPETE FOR A SEASON PASS?
ME! ME! PICK ME!

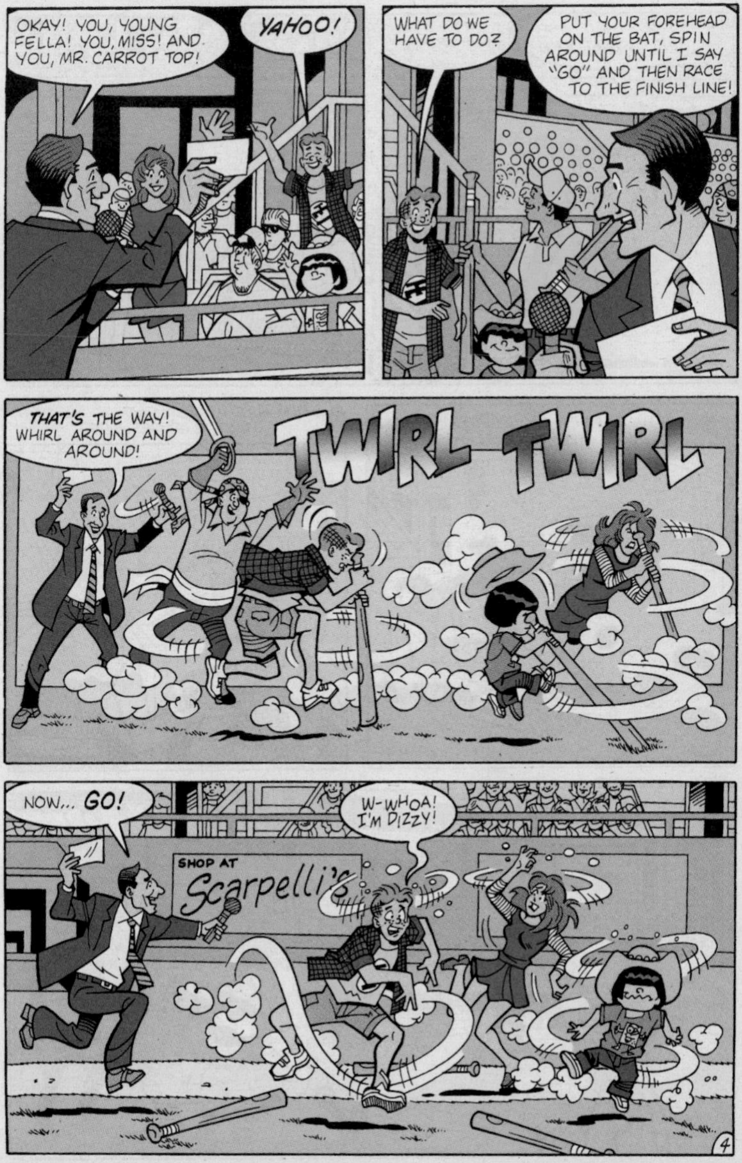
OKAY! YOU, YOUNG FELLA! YOU, MISS! AND. YOU, MR. CARROT TOP!
YAHOO!
WHAT DO WE HAVE TO DO?
PUT YOUR FOREHEAD ON THE BAT, SPIN AROUND UNTIL I SAY "GO" AND THEN RACE TO THE FINISH LINE!
THAT'S THE WAY! WHIRL AROUND AND AROUND!
TWIRL TWIRL
NOW... GO!
W-WHOA! I'M DIZZY!
SHOP AT Scarpelli's

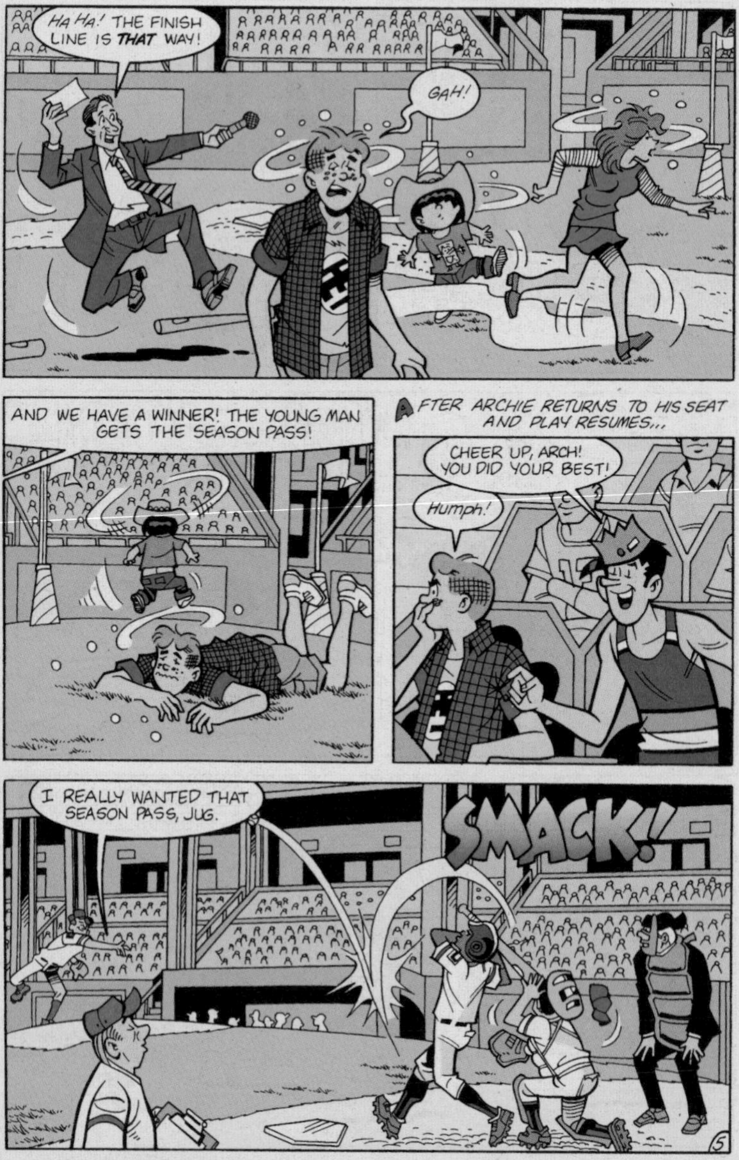
HA HA! THE FINISH LINE IS THAT WAY!
GAH!
AND WE HAVE A WINNER! THE YOUNG MAN GETS THE SEASON PASS!
AFTER ARCHIE RETURNS TO HIS SEAT AND PLAY RESUMES...
CHEER UP, ARCH! YOU DID YOUR BEST!
Humph!
I REALLY WANTED THAT SEASON PASS, JUG.
SMACK!!
5

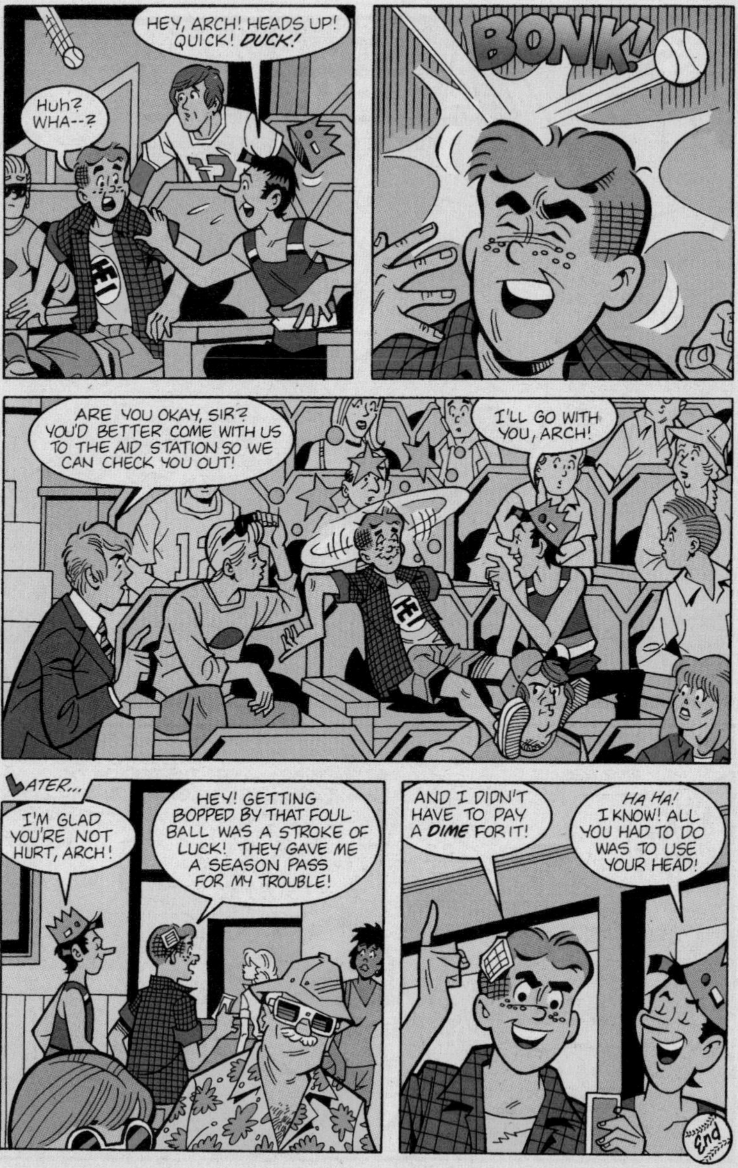
HEY, ARCH! HEADS UP! QUICK! DUCK!
Huh? WHA--?
BONK!
ARE YOU OKAY, SIR? YOU'D BETTER COME WITH US TO THE AID STATION SO WE CAN CHECK YOU OUT!
I'LL GO WITH YOU, ARCH!
LATER...
I'M GLAD YOU'RE NOT HURT, ARCH!
HEY! GETTING BOPPED BY THAT FOUL BALL WAS A STROKE OF LUCK! THEY GAVE ME A SEASON PASS FOR MY TROUBLE!
AND I DIDN'T HAVE TO PAY A DIME FOR IT!
HA HA! I KNOW! ALL YOU HAD TO DO WAS TO USE YOUR HEAD!
End

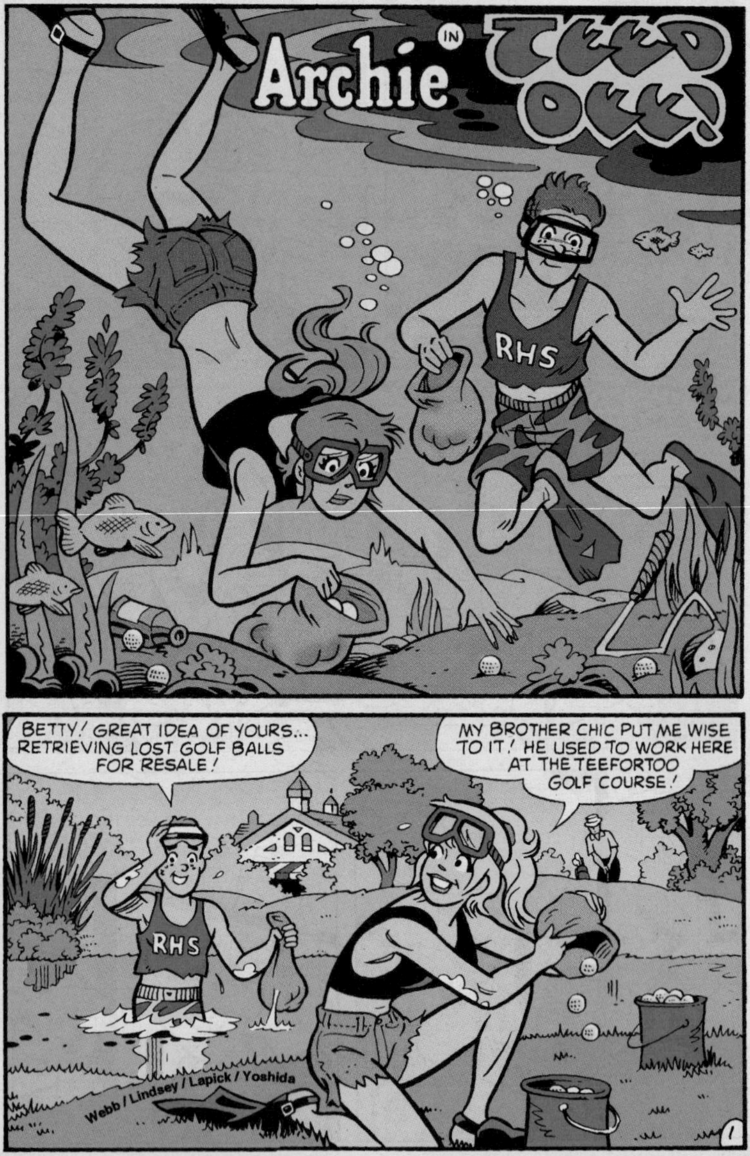
Archie
IN
TEED OFF!
BETTY! GREAT IDEA OF YOURS... RETRIEVING LOST GOLF BALLS FOR RESALE!
MY BROTHER CHIC PUT ME WISE TO IT! HE USED TO WORK HERE AT THE TEEFORTOO GOLF COURSE!
RHS
Webb / Lindsey / Lapick / Yoshida
1

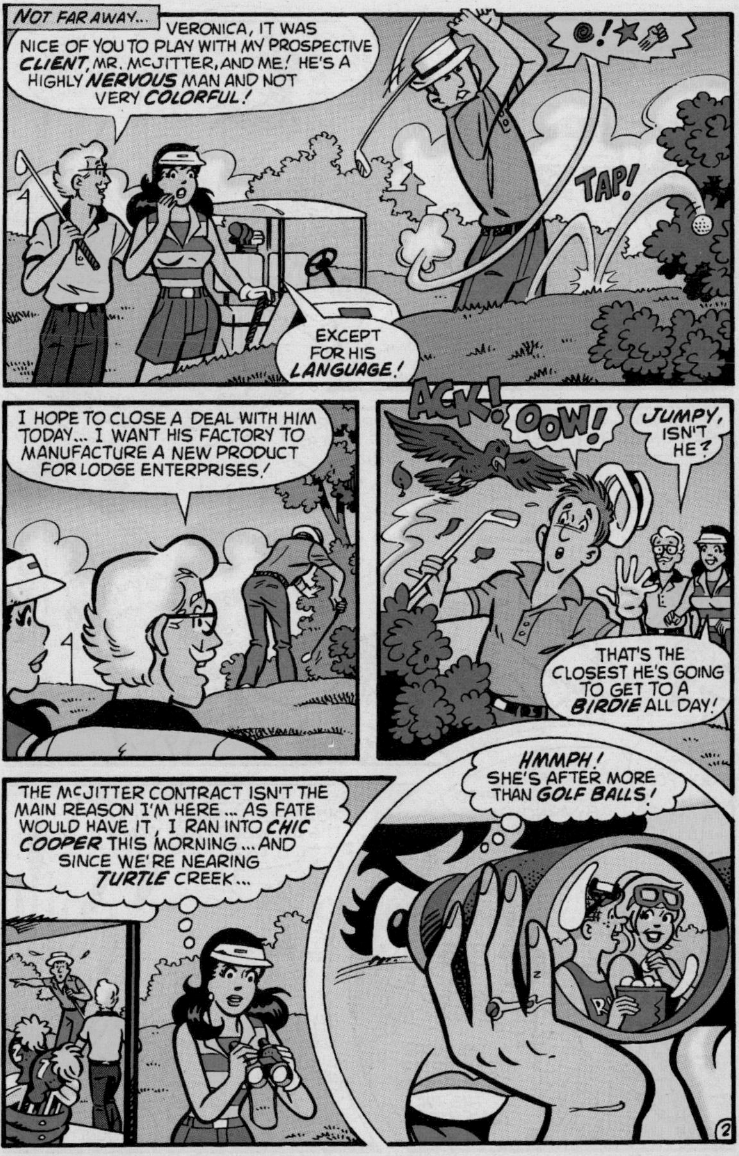
NOT FAR AWAY...
VERONICA, IT WAS NICE OF YOU TO PLAY WITH MY PROSPECTIVE CLIENT, MR. McJITTER, AND ME! HE'S A HIGHLY NERVOUS MAN AND NOT VERY COLORFUL!
@!★
TAP!
EXCEPT FOR HIS LANGUAGE!
I HOPE TO CLOSE A DEAL WITH HIM TODAY... I WANT HIS FACTORY TO MANUFACTURE A NEW PRODUCT FOR LODGE ENTERPRISES!
ACK!
OOW!
JUMPY, ISN'T HE?
THAT'S THE CLOSEST HE'S GOING TO GET TO A BIRDIE ALL DAY!
THE McJITTER CONTRACT ISN'T THE MAIN REASON I'M HERE ... AS FATE WOULD HAVE IT, I RAN INTO CHIC COOPER THIS MORNING ... AND SINCE WE'RE NEARING TURTLE CREEK...
HMMPH! SHE'S AFTER MORE THAN GOLF BALLS!
2

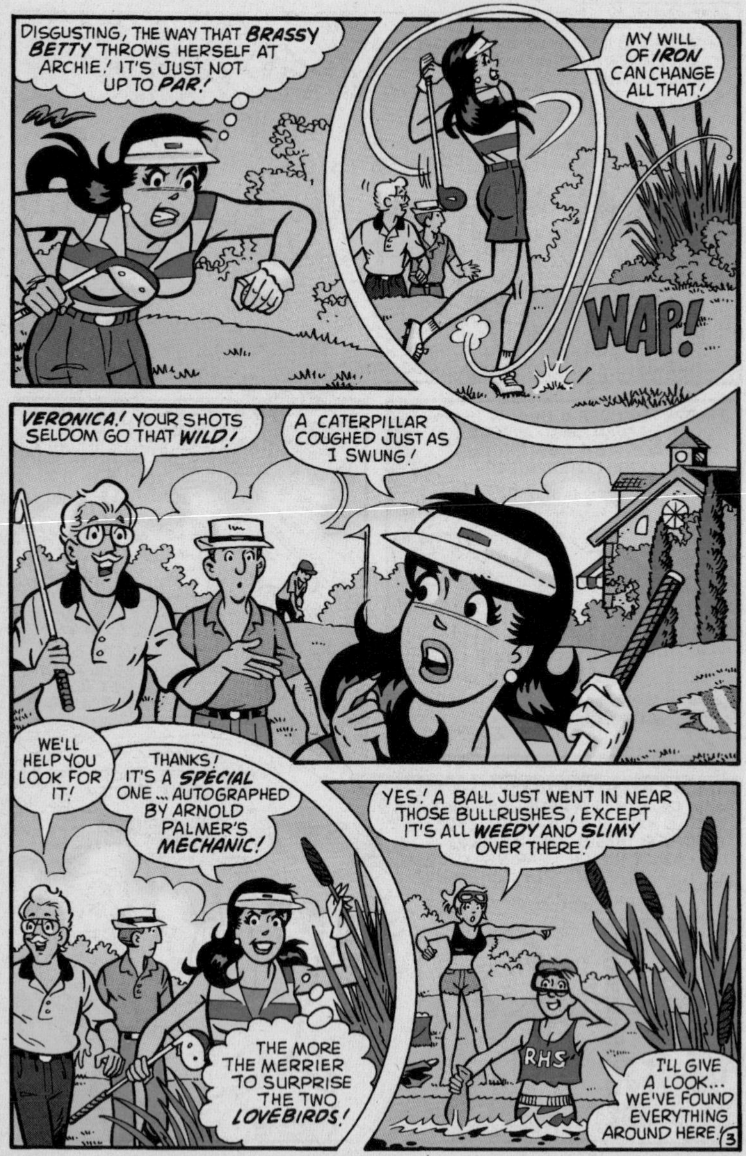
DISGUSTING, THE WAY THAT BRASSY BETTY THROWS HERSELF AT ARCHIE! IT'S JUST NOT UP TO PAR!
MY WILL OF IRON CAN CHANGE ALL THAT!
WAP!
VERONICA! YOUR SHOTS SELDOM GO THAT WILD!
A CATERPILLAR COUGHED JUST AS I SWUNG!
WE'LL HELP YOU LOOK FOR IT!
THANKS! IT'S A SPECIAL ONE ... AUTOGRAPHED BY ARNOLD PALMER'S MECHANIC!
THE MORE THE MERRIER TO SURPRISE THE TWO LOVEBIRDS!
YES! A BALL JUST WENT IN NEAR THOSE BULLRUSHES, EXCEPT IT'S ALL WEEDY AND SLIMY OVER THERE!
RHS
I'LL GIVE A LOOK... WE'VE FOUND EVERYTHING AROUND HERE!
3

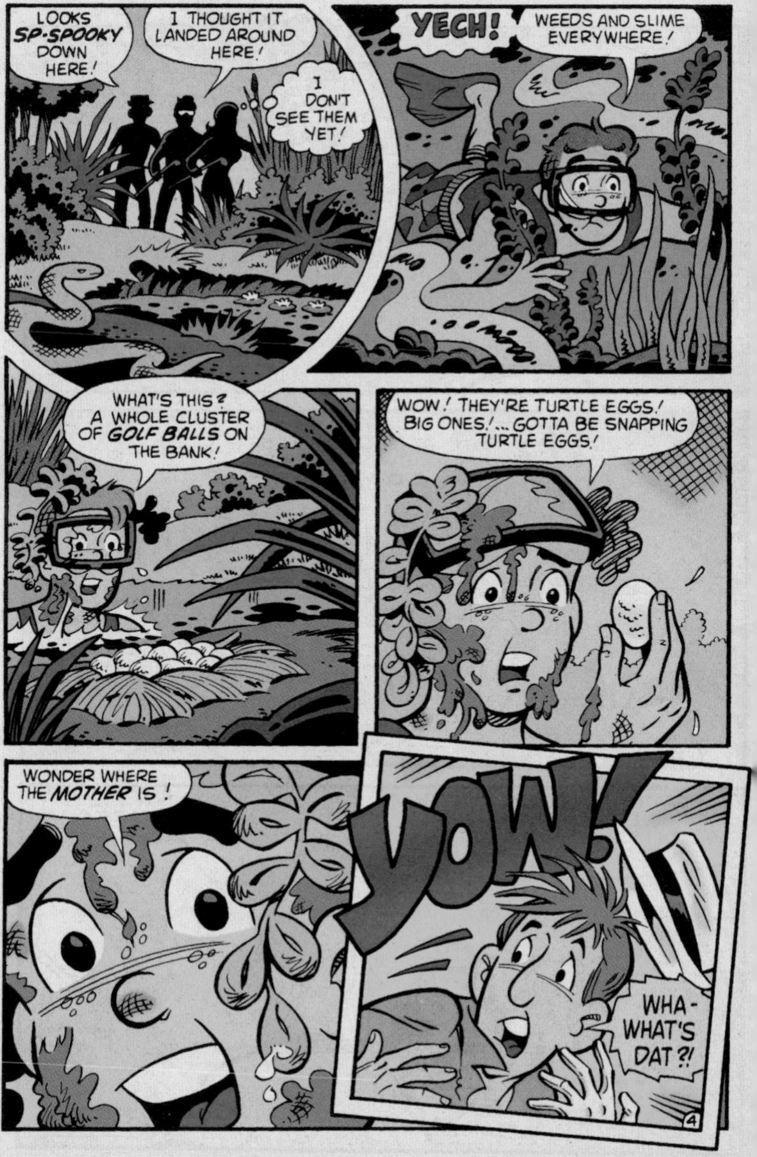
LOOKS SP-SPOOKY DOWN HERE!
I THOUGHT IT LANDED AROUND HERE!
I DON'T SEE THEM YET!
YECH!
WEEDS AND SLIME EVERYWHERE!
WHAT'S THIS? A WHOLE CLUSTER OF GOLF BALLS ON THE BANK!
WOW! THEY'RE TURTLE EGGS! BIG ONES!... GOTTA BE SNAPPING TURTLE EGGS!
WONDER WHERE THE MOTHER IS!
YOW!
WHA-WHAT'S DAT?!
4

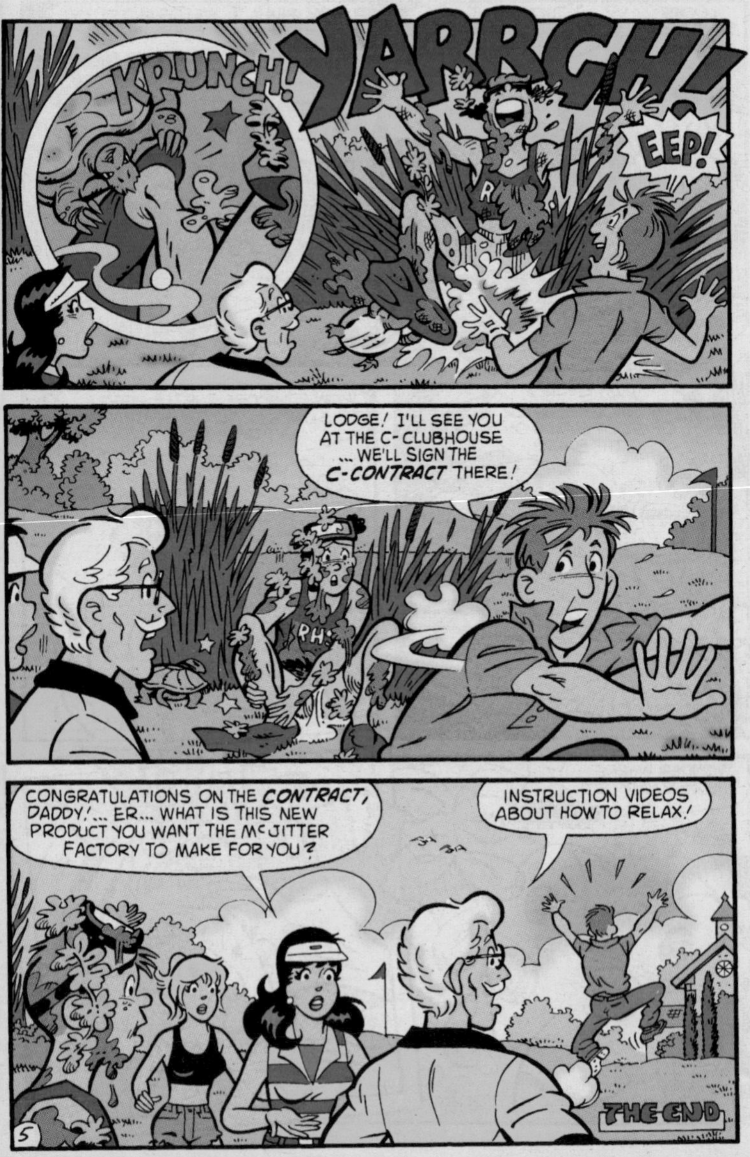
KRUNCH!
YARRGH!
EEP!
LODGE! I'LL SEE YOU AT THE C-CLUBHOUSE ... WE'LL SIGN THE C-CONTRACT THERE!
CONGRATULATIONS ON THE CONTRACT, DADDY!... ER... WHAT IS THIS NEW PRODUCT YOU WANT THE McJITTER FACTORY TO MAKE FOR YOU?
INSTRUCTION VIDEOS ABOUT HOW TO RELAX!
THE END
5

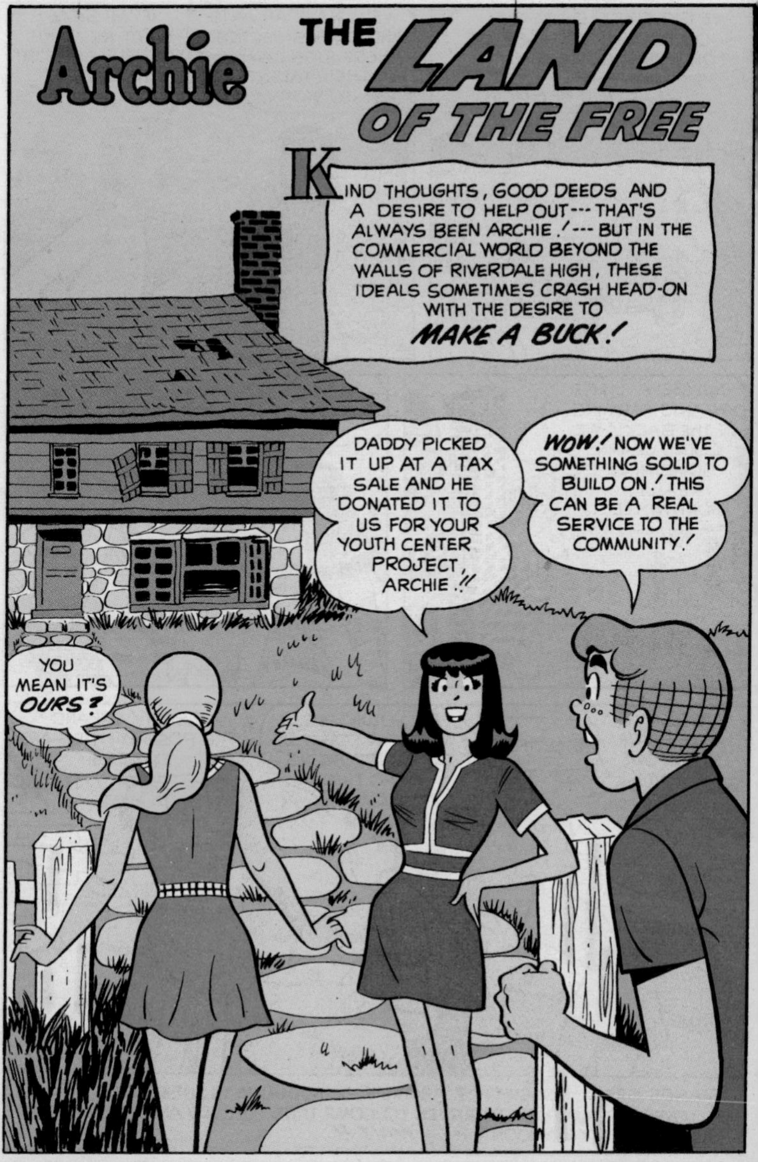
Archie
THE LAND OF THE FREE
KIND THOUGHTS, GOOD DEEDS AND A DESIRE TO HELP OUT--- THAT'S ALWAYS BEEN ARCHIE!--- BUT IN THE COMMERCIAL WORLD BEYOND THE WALLS OF RIVERDALE HIGH, THESE IDEALS SOMETIMES CRASH HEAD-ON WITH THE DESIRE TO MAKE A BUCK!
DADDY PICKED IT UP AT A TAX SALE AND HE DONATED IT TO US FOR YOUR YOUTH CENTER PROJECT, ARCHIE!!
WOW! NOW WE'VE SOMETHING SOLID TO BUILD ON! THIS CAN BE A REAL SERVICE TO THE COMMUNITY!
YOU MEAN IT'S OURS?

Script: Frank Doyle / Pencils: Harry Lucey / Inks: Chic Stone / Letters: Bill Yoshida / Colors: Barry Grossman

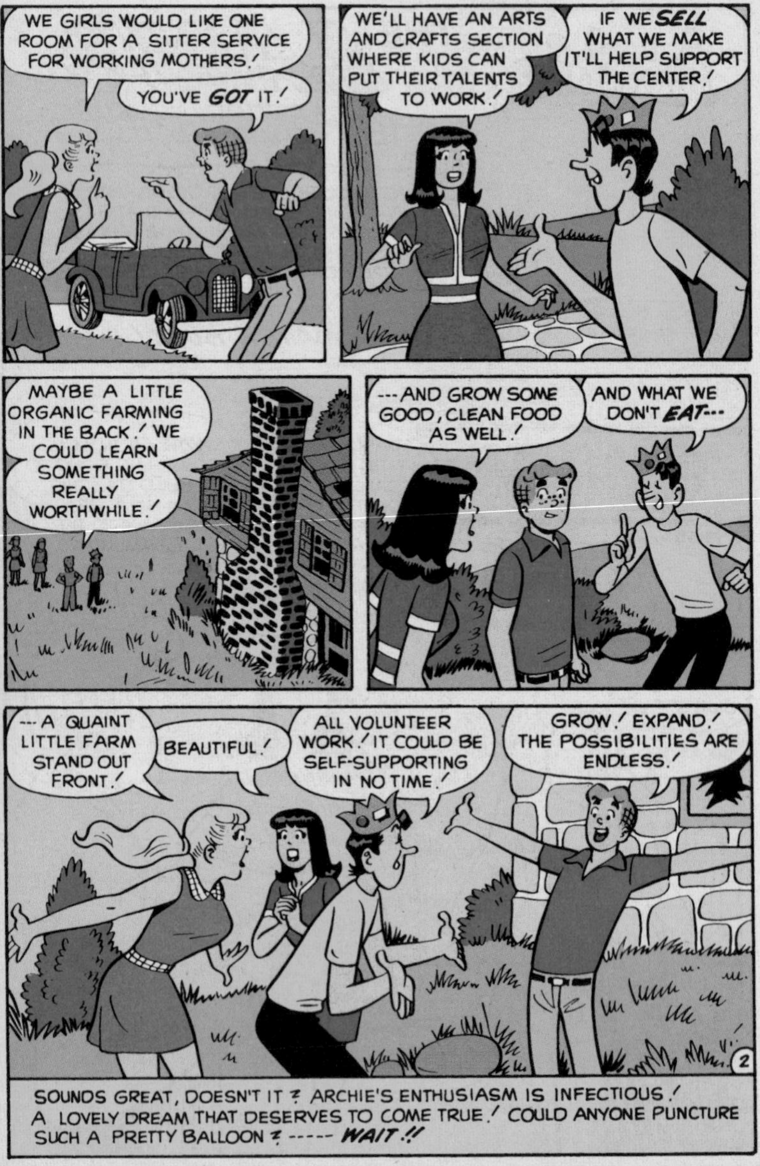
WE GIRLS WOULD LIKE ONE ROOM FOR A SITTER SERVICE FOR WORKING MOTHERS!
YOU'VE GOT IT!
WE'LL HAVE AN ARTS AND CRAFTS SECTION WHERE KIDS CAN PUT THEIR TALENTS TO WORK!
IF WE SELL WHAT WE MAKE IT'LL HELP SUPPORT THE CENTER!
MAYBE A LITTLE ORGANIC FARMING IN THE BACK! WE COULD LEARN SOMETHING REALLY WORTHWHILE!
---AND GROW SOME GOOD, CLEAN FOOD AS WELL!
AND WHAT WE DON'T EAT---
---A QUAINT LITTLE FARM STAND OUT FRONT!
BEAUTIFUL!
ALL VOLUNTEER WORK! IT COULD BE SELF-SUPPORTING IN NO TIME!
GROW! EXPAND! THE POSSIBILITIES ARE ENDLESS!
2
SOUNDS GREAT, DOESN'T IT? ARCHIE'S ENTHUSIASM IS INFECTIOUS! A LOVELY DREAM THAT DESERVES TO COME TRUE! COULD ANYONE PUNCTURE SUCH A PRETTY BALLOON? ----- WAIT!!

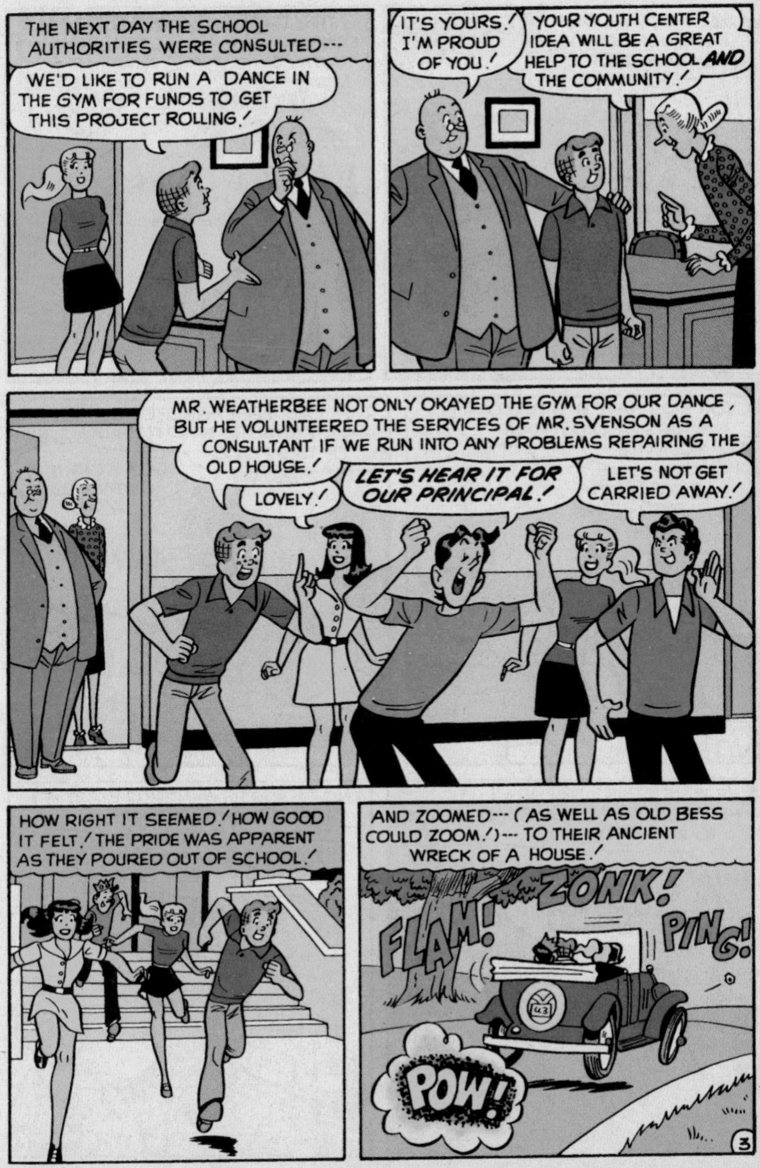
THE NEXT DAY THE SCHOOL AUTHORITIES WERE CONSULTED---
WE'D LIKE TO RUN A DANCE IN THE GYM FOR FUNDS TO GET THIS PROJECT ROLLING!
IT'S YOURS! I'M PROUD OF YOU!
YOUR YOUTH CENTER IDEA WILL BE A GREAT HELP TO THE SCHOOL AND THE COMMUNITY!
MR. WEATHERBEE NOT ONLY OKAYED THE GYM FOR OUR DANCE, BUT HE VOLUNTEERED THE SERVICES OF MR. SVENSON AS A CONSULTANT IF WE RUN INTO ANY PROBLEMS REPAIRING THE OLD HOUSE!
LOVELY!
LET'S HEAR IT FOR OUR PRINCIPAL!
LET'S NOT GET CARRIED AWAY!
HOW RIGHT IT SEEMED! HOW GOOD IT FELT! THE PRIDE WAS APPARENT AS THEY POURED OUT OF SCHOOL!
AND ZOOMED--- (AS WELL AS OLD BESS COULD ZOOM!)--- TO THEIR ANCIENT WRECK OF A HOUSE!
ZONK!
FLAM!
PING!
POW!
3

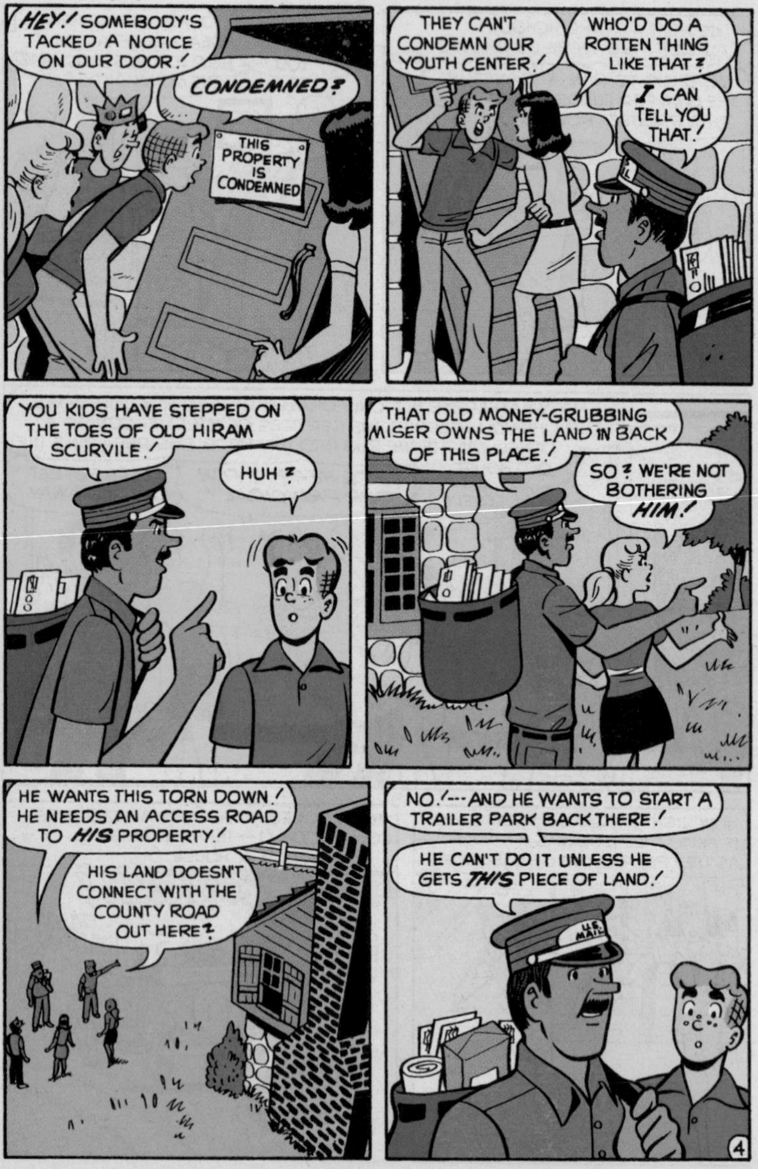
HEY! SOMEBODY'S TACKED A NOTICE ON OUR DOOR!
CONDEMNED?
THIS PROPERTY IS CONDEMNED
THEY CAN'T CONDEMN OUR YOUTH CENTER!
WHO'D DO A ROTTEN THING LIKE THAT?
I CAN TELL YOU THAT!
YOU KIDS HAVE STEPPED ON THE TOES OF OLD HIRAM SCURVILE!
HUH?
THAT OLD MONEY-GRUBBING MISER OWNS THE LAND IN BACK OF THIS PLACE!
SO? WE'RE NOT BOTHERING HIM!
HE WANTS THIS TORN DOWN! HE NEEDS AN ACCESS ROAD TO HIS PROPERTY!
HIS LAND DOESN'T CONNECT WITH THE COUNTY ROAD OUT HERE?
NO!---AND HE WANTS TO START A TRAILER PARK BACK THERE!
HE CAN'T DO IT UNLESS HE GETS THIS PIECE OF LAND!
U.S. MAIL
4

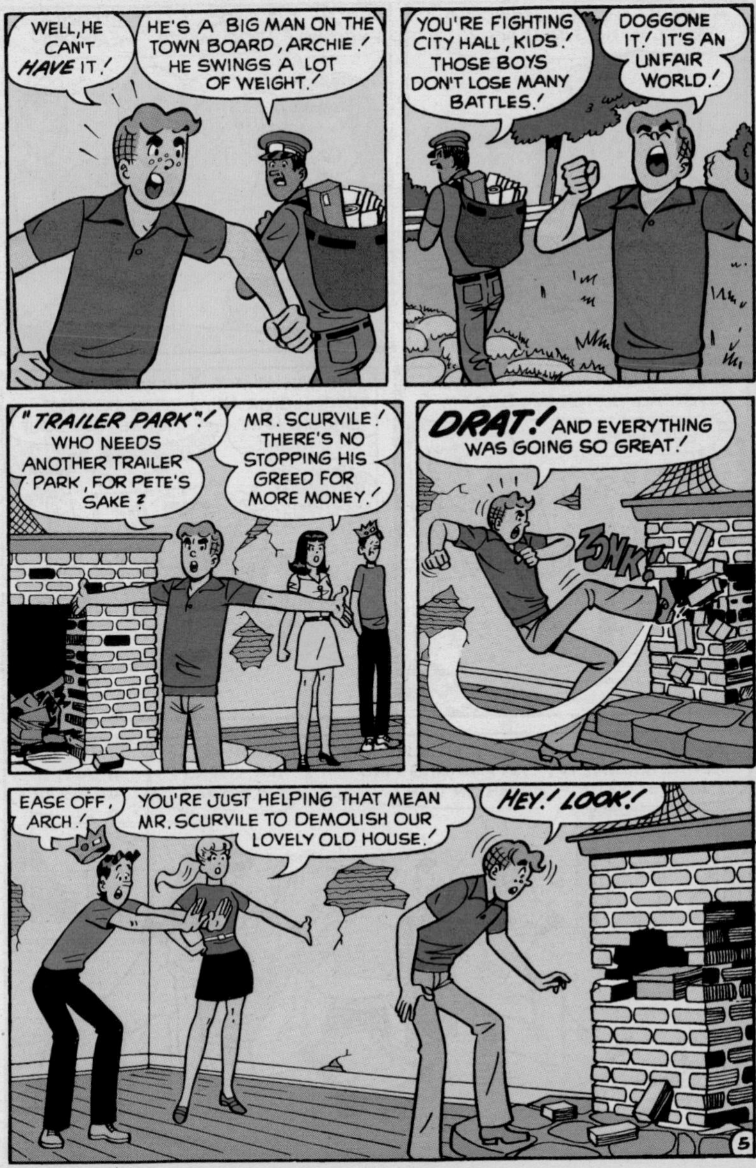

WELL, HE CAN'T *HAVE* IT!
HE'S A BIG MAN ON THE TOWN BOARD, ARCHIE! HE SWINGS A LOT OF WEIGHT!
YOU'RE FIGHTING CITY HALL, KIDS! THOSE BOYS DON'T LOSE MANY BATTLES!
DOGGONE IT! IT'S AN UNFAIR WORLD!
"*TRAILER PARK*"! WHO NEEDS ANOTHER TRAILER PARK, FOR PETE'S SAKE?
MR. SCURVILE! THERE'S NO STOPPING HIS GREED FOR MORE MONEY!
DRAT! AND EVERYTHING WAS GOING SO GREAT!
ZONK!
EASE OFF, ARCH!
YOU'RE JUST HELPING THAT MEAN MR. SCURVILE TO DEMOLISH OUR LOVELY OLD HOUSE!
HEY! LOOK!

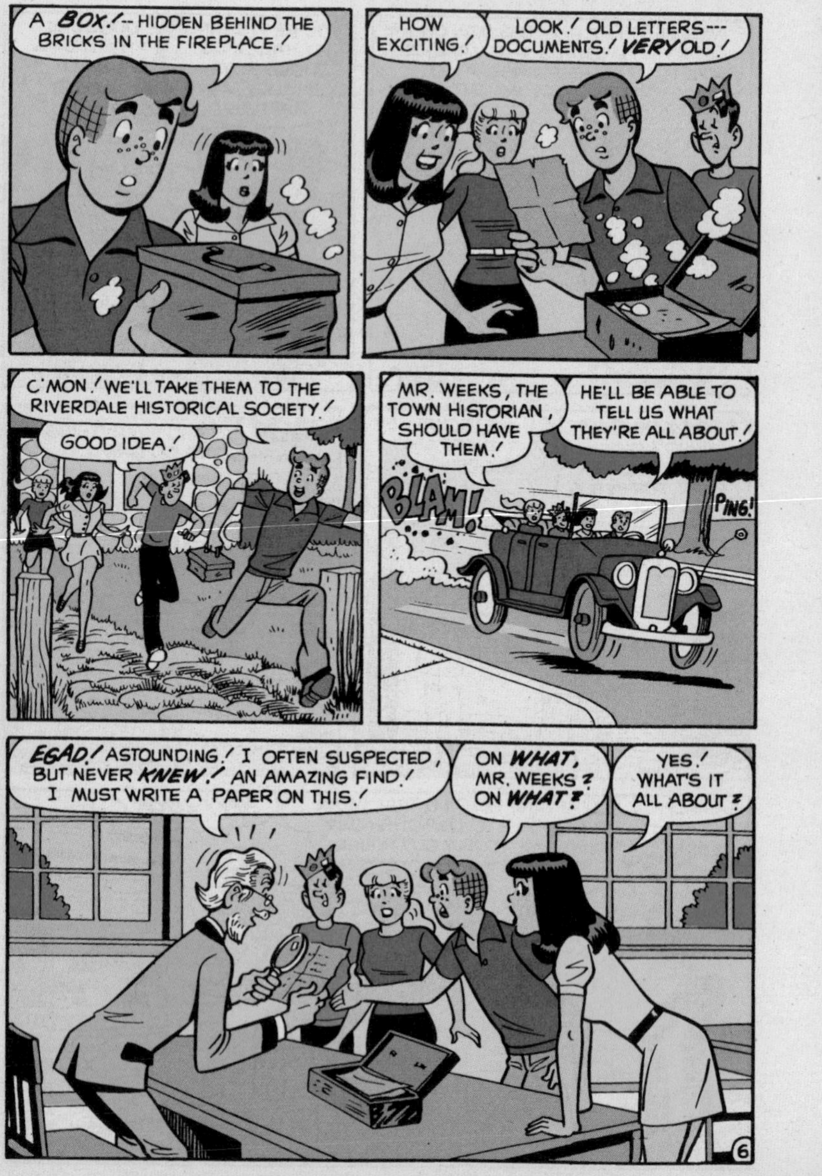

A BOX!--HIDDEN BEHIND THE BRICKS IN THE FIREPLACE!
HOW EXCITING!
LOOK! OLD LETTERS---DOCUMENTS! VERY OLD!
C'MON! WE'LL TAKE THEM TO THE RIVERDALE HISTORICAL SOCIETY!
GOOD IDEA!
MR. WEEKS, THE TOWN HISTORIAN, SHOULD HAVE THEM!
HE'LL BE ABLE TO TELL US WHAT THEY'RE ALL ABOUT!
BLAM!
PING!
EGAD! ASTOUNDING! I OFTEN SUSPECTED, BUT NEVER KNEW! AN AMAZING FIND! I MUST WRITE A PAPER ON THIS!
ON WHAT, MR. WEEKS? ON WHAT?
YES! WHAT'S IT ALL ABOUT?
6

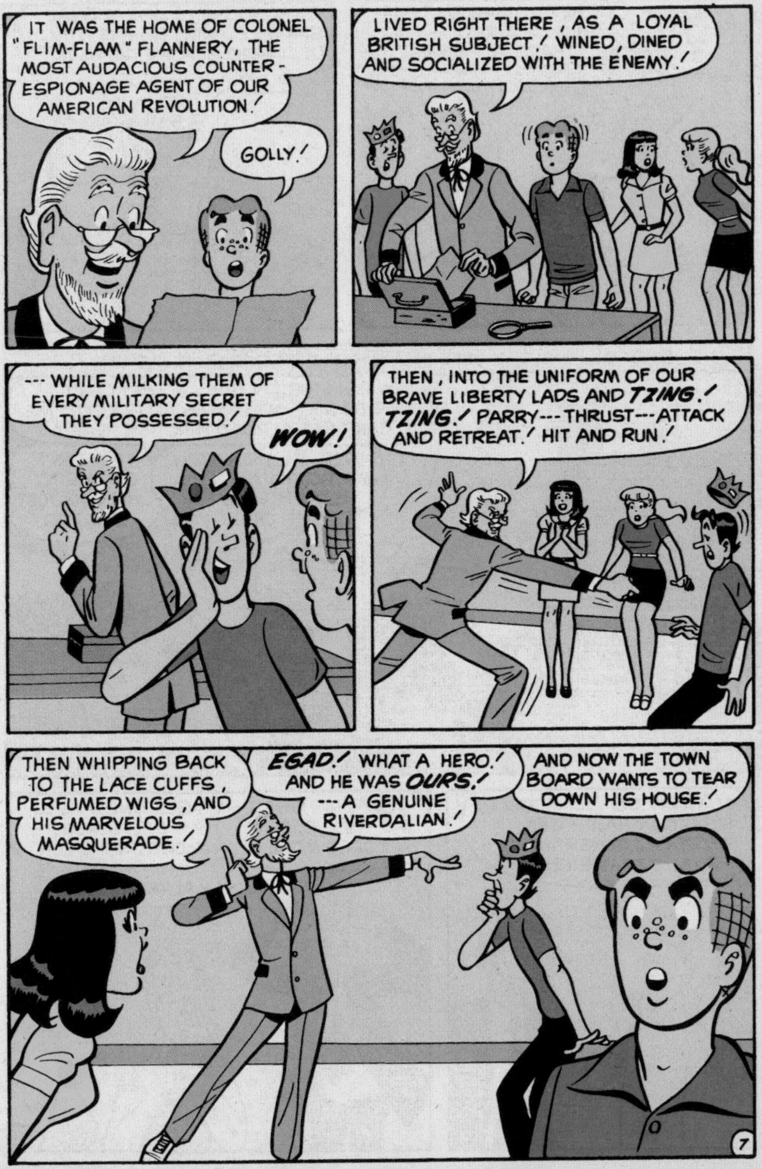
IT WAS THE HOME OF COLONEL "FLIM-FLAM" FLANNERY, THE MOST AUDACIOUS COUNTER-ESPIONAGE AGENT OF OUR AMERICAN REVOLUTION!
GOLLY!
LIVED RIGHT THERE, AS A LOYAL BRITISH SUBJECT! WINED, DINED AND SOCIALIZED WITH THE ENEMY!
--- WHILE MILKING THEM OF EVERY MILITARY SECRET THEY POSSESSED!
WOW!
THEN, INTO THE UNIFORM OF OUR BRAVE LIBERTY LADS AND TZING! TZING! PARRY---THRUST---ATTACK AND RETREAT! HIT AND RUN!
THEN WHIPPING BACK TO THE LACE CUFFS, PERFUMED WIGS, AND HIS MARVELOUS MASQUERADE!
EGAD! WHAT A HERO! AND HE WAS OURS! --- A GENUINE RIVERDALIAN!
AND NOW THE TOWN BOARD WANTS TO TEAR DOWN HIS HOUSE!
7

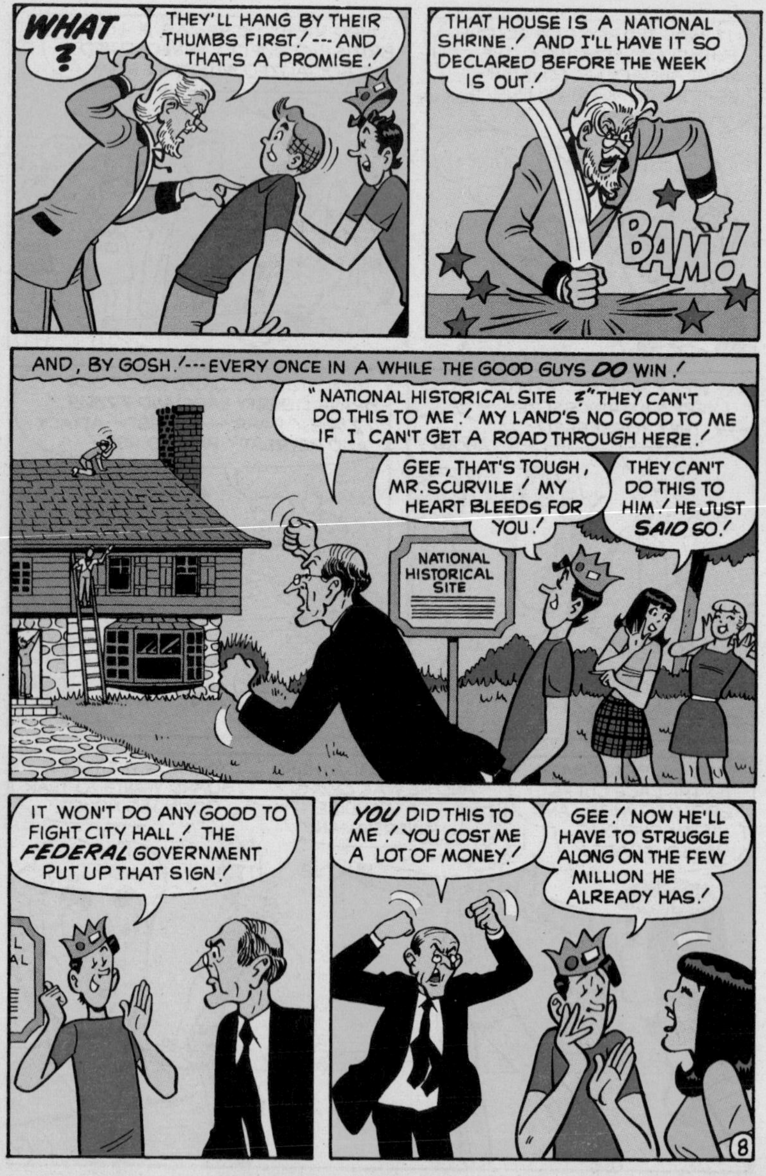
WHAT ?
THEY'LL HANG BY THEIR THUMBS FIRST! --- AND THAT'S A PROMISE!
THAT HOUSE IS A NATIONAL SHRINE! AND I'LL HAVE IT SO DECLARED BEFORE THE WEEK IS OUT!
BAM!
AND, BY GOSH! --- EVERY ONCE IN A WHILE THE GOOD GUYS DO WIN!
"NATIONAL HISTORICAL SITE ?" THEY CAN'T DO THIS TO ME! MY LAND'S NO GOOD TO ME IF I CAN'T GET A ROAD THROUGH HERE!
GEE, THAT'S TOUGH, MR. SCURVILE! MY HEART BLEEDS FOR YOU!
THEY CAN'T DO THIS TO HIM! HE JUST SAID SO!
NATIONAL HISTORICAL SITE
IT WON'T DO ANY GOOD TO FIGHT CITY HALL! THE FEDERAL GOVERNMENT PUT UP THAT SIGN!
YOU DID THIS TO ME! YOU COST ME A LOT OF MONEY!
GEE! NOW HE'LL HAVE TO STRUGGLE ALONG ON THE FEW MILLION HE ALREADY HAS!
8

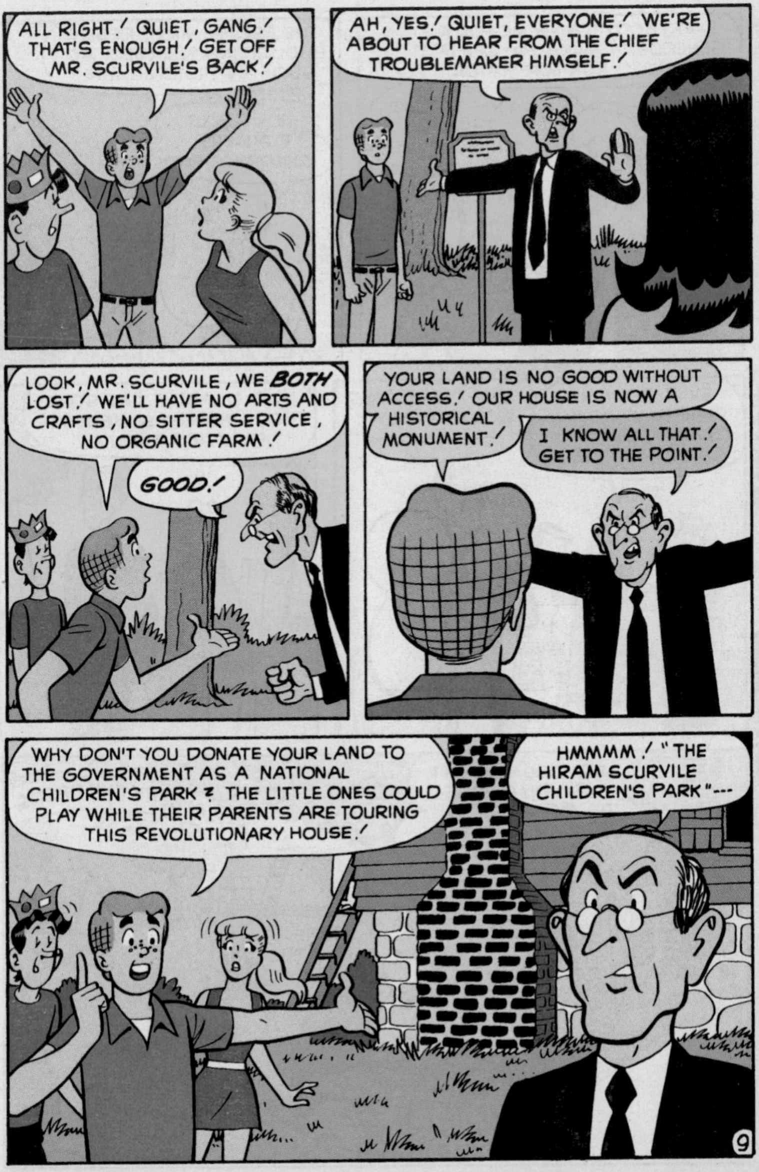
ALL RIGHT! QUIET, GANG! THAT'S ENOUGH! GET OFF MR. SCURVILE'S BACK!
AH, YES! QUIET, EVERYONE! WE'RE ABOUT TO HEAR FROM THE CHIEF TROUBLEMAKER HIMSELF!
LOOK, MR. SCURVILE, WE BOTH LOST! WE'LL HAVE NO ARTS AND CRAFTS, NO SITTER SERVICE, NO ORGANIC FARM!
GOOD!
YOUR LAND IS NO GOOD WITHOUT ACCESS! OUR HOUSE IS NOW A HISTORICAL MONUMENT!
I KNOW ALL THAT! GET TO THE POINT!
WHY DON'T YOU DONATE YOUR LAND TO THE GOVERNMENT AS A NATIONAL CHILDREN'S PARK? THE LITTLE ONES COULD PLAY WHILE THEIR PARENTS ARE TOURING THIS REVOLUTIONARY HOUSE!
HMMMM! "THE HIRAM SCURVILE CHILDREN'S PARK"---
9

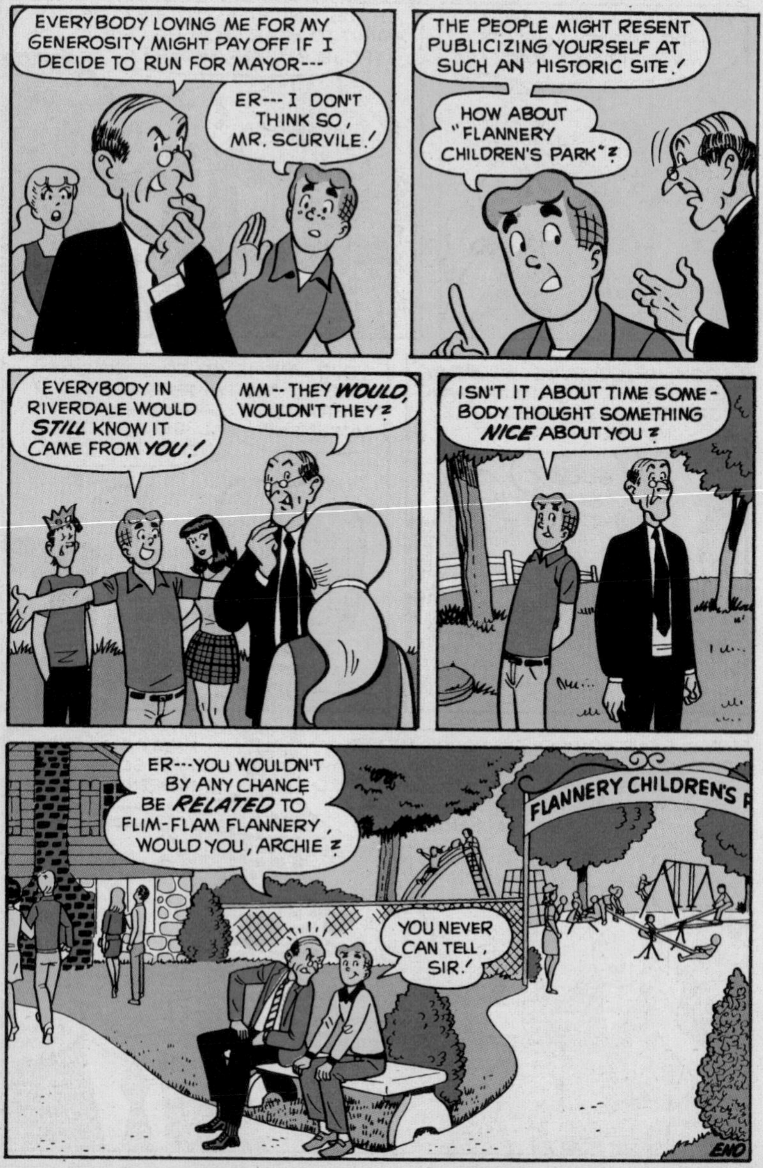
EVERYBODY LOVING ME FOR MY GENEROSITY MIGHT PAY OFF IF I DECIDE TO RUN FOR MAYOR---
ER--- I DON'T THINK SO, MR. SCURVILE!
THE PEOPLE MIGHT RESENT PUBLICIZING YOURSELF AT SUCH AN HISTORIC SITE!
HOW ABOUT "FLANNERY CHILDREN'S PARK"?
EVERYBODY IN RIVERDALE WOULD STILL KNOW IT CAME FROM YOU!
MM-- THEY WOULD, WOULDN'T THEY?
ISN'T IT ABOUT TIME SOMEBODY THOUGHT SOMETHING NICE ABOUT YOU?
ER---YOU WOULDN'T BY ANY CHANCE BE RELATED TO FLIM-FLAM FLANNERY, WOULD YOU, ARCHIE?
FLANNERY CHILDREN'S
YOU NEVER CAN TELL, SIR!
ENO

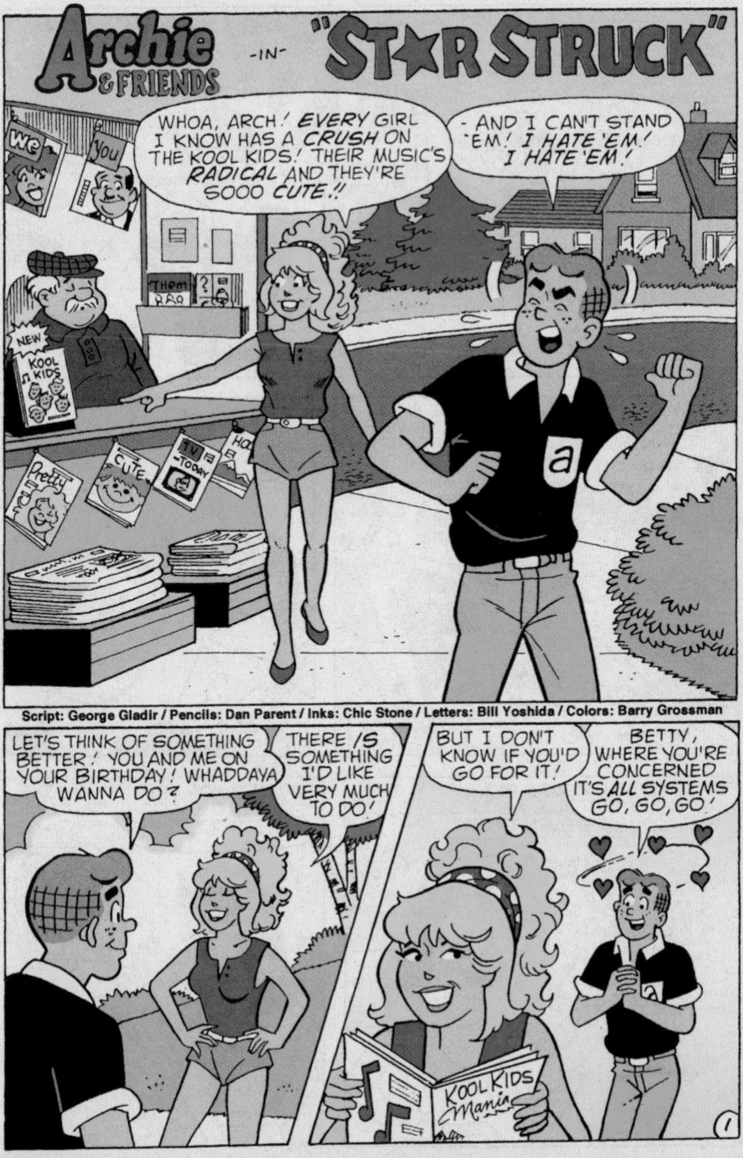
Archie & FRIENDS
-IN-
"ST★R STRUCK"
WHOA, ARCH! EVERY GIRL I KNOW HAS A CRUSH ON THE KOOL KIDS! THEIR MUSIC'S RADICAL AND THEY'RE SOOO CUTE!!
-AND I CAN'T STAND 'EM! I HATE 'EM! I HATE 'EM!
NEW
KOOL KIDS
We
You
Them
Pretty
CUTE
TV TODAY
Script: George Gladir / Pencils: Dan Parent / Inks: Chic Stone / Letters: Bill Yoshida / Colors: Barry Grossman
LET'S THINK OF SOMETHING BETTER! YOU AND ME ON YOUR BIRTHDAY! WHADDAYA WANNA DO?
THERE IS SOMETHING I'D LIKE VERY MUCH TO DO!
BUT I DON'T KNOW IF YOU'D GO FOR IT!
BETTY, WHERE YOU'RE CONCERNED IT'S ALL SYSTEMS GO, GO, GO!
KOOL KIDS Mania
1

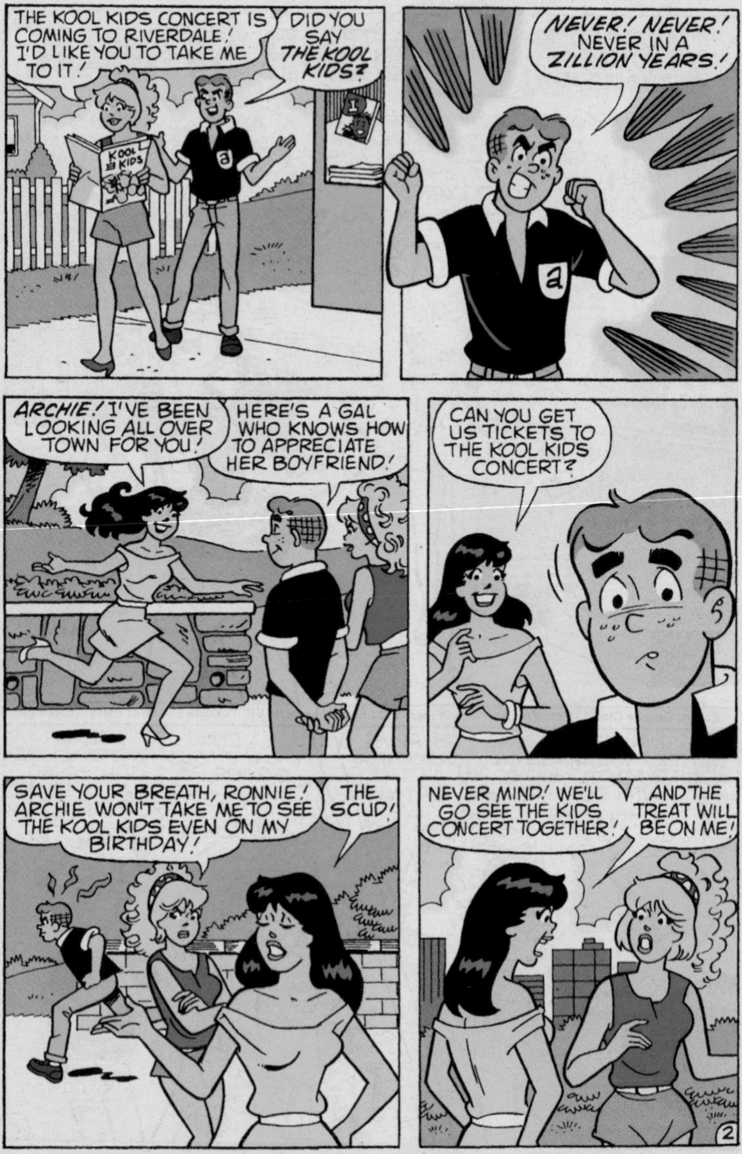
THE KOOL KIDS CONCERT IS COMING TO RIVERDALE! I'D LIKE YOU TO TAKE ME TO IT!
DID YOU SAY THE KOOL KIDS?
KOOL KIDS
NEVER! NEVER! NEVER IN A ZILLION YEARS!
ARCHIE! I'VE BEEN LOOKING ALL OVER TOWN FOR YOU!
HERE'S A GAL WHO KNOWS HOW TO APPRECIATE HER BOYFRIEND!
CAN YOU GET US TICKETS TO THE KOOL KIDS CONCERT?
SAVE YOUR BREATH, RONNIE! ARCHIE WON'T TAKE ME TO SEE THE KOOL KIDS EVEN ON MY BIRTHDAY!
THE SCUD!
NEVER MIND! WE'LL GO SEE THE KIDS CONCERT TOGETHER!
AND THE TREAT WILL BE ON ME!
2

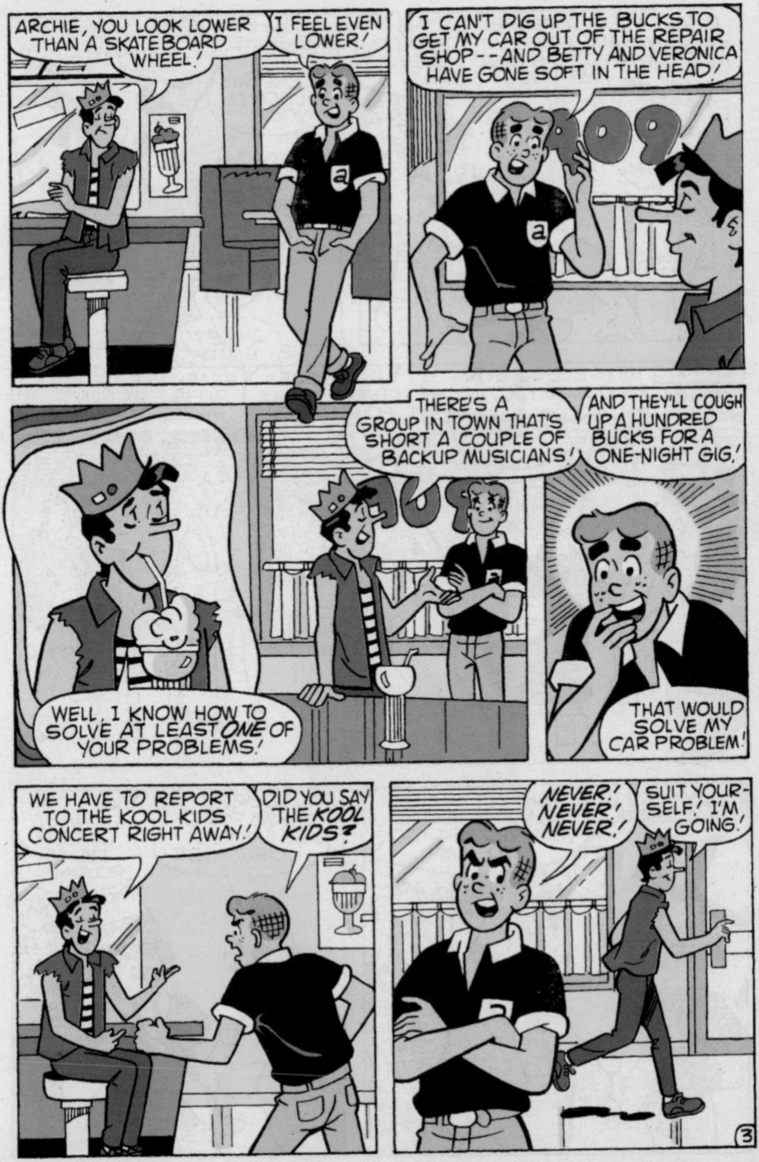
ARCHIE, YOU LOOK LOWER THAN A SKATEBOARD WHEEL!
I FEEL EVEN LOWER!
I CAN'T DIG UP THE BUCKS TO GET MY CAR OUT OF THE REPAIR SHOP--AND BETTY AND VERONICA HAVE GONE SOFT IN THE HEAD!
WELL, I KNOW HOW TO SOLVE AT LEAST ONE OF YOUR PROBLEMS!
THERE'S A GROUP IN TOWN THAT'S SHORT A COUPLE OF BACKUP MUSICIANS!
AND THEY'LL COUGH UP A HUNDRED BUCKS FOR A ONE-NIGHT GIG!
THAT WOULD SOLVE MY CAR PROBLEM!
WE HAVE TO REPORT TO THE KOOL KIDS CONCERT RIGHT AWAY!
DID YOU SAY THE KOOL KIDS?
NEVER! NEVER! NEVER!
SUIT YOURSELF! I'M GOING!
3

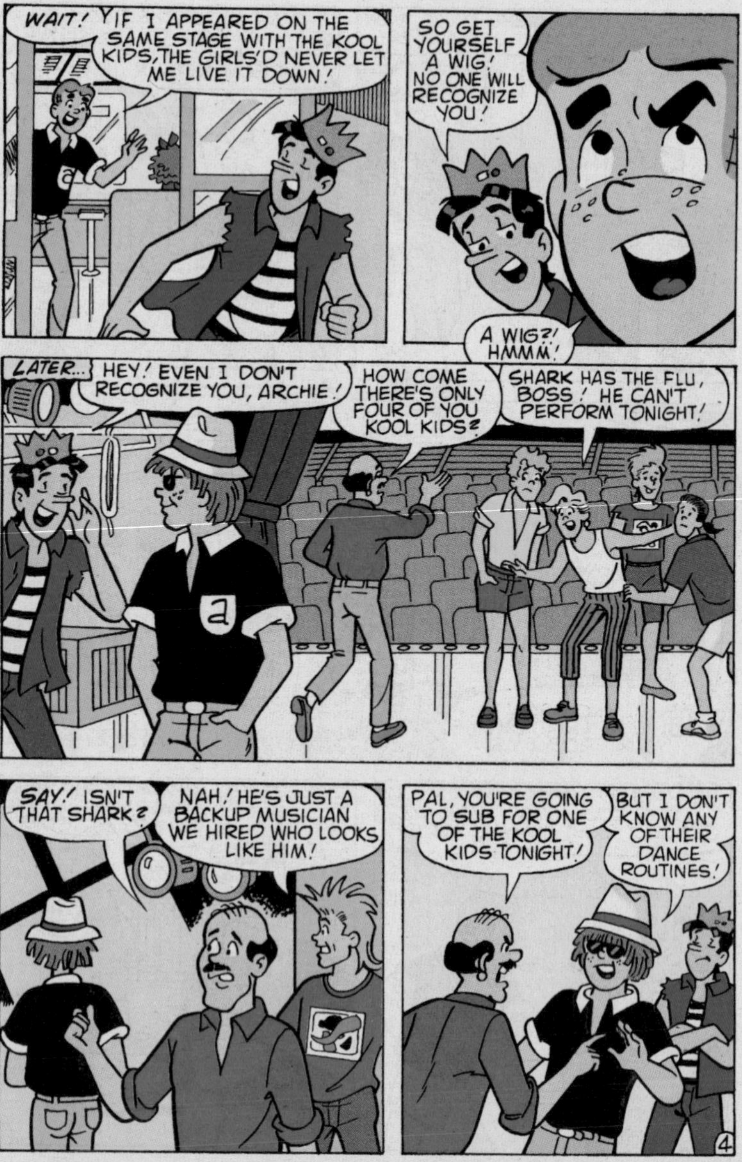
WAIT!
IF I APPEARED ON THE SAME STAGE WITH THE KOOL KIDS, THE GIRLS'D NEVER LET ME LIVE IT DOWN!
SO GET YOURSELF A WIG! NO ONE WILL RECOGNIZE YOU!
A WIG?! HMMM!
LATER...
HEY! EVEN I DON'T RECOGNIZE YOU, ARCHIE!
HOW COME THERE'S ONLY FOUR OF YOU KOOL KIDS?
SHARK HAS THE FLU, BOSS! HE CAN'T PERFORM TONIGHT!
SAY! ISN'T THAT SHARK?
NAH! HE'S JUST A BACKUP MUSICIAN WE HIRED WHO LOOKS LIKE HIM!
PAL, YOU'RE GOING TO SUB FOR ONE OF THE KOOL KIDS TONIGHT!
BUT I DON'T KNOW ANY OF THEIR DANCE ROUTINES!
4

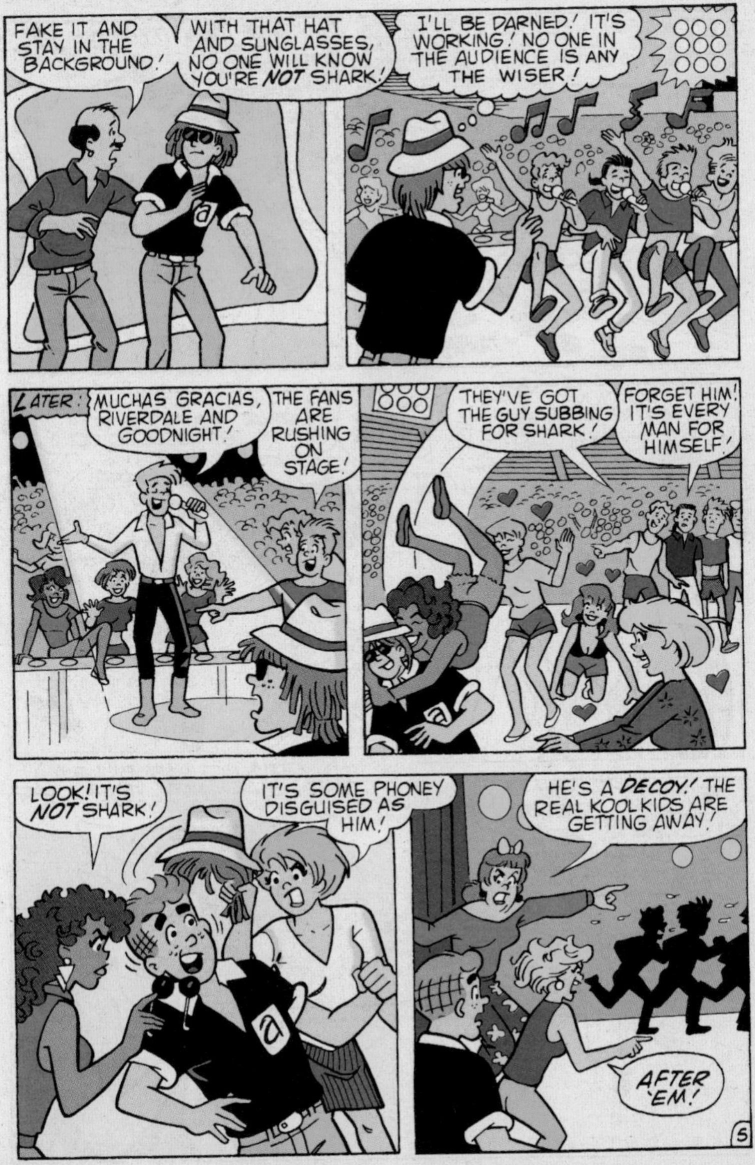

FAKE IT AND STAY IN THE BACKGROUND!
WITH THAT HAT AND SUNGLASSES, NO ONE WILL KNOW YOU'RE NOT SHARK!
I'LL BE DARNED! IT'S WORKING! NO ONE IN THE AUDIENCE IS ANY THE WISER!
LATER:
MUCHAS GRACIAS, RIVERDALE AND GOODNIGHT!
THE FANS ARE RUSHING ON STAGE!
THEY'VE GOT THE GUY SUBBING FOR SHARK!
FORGET HIM! IT'S EVERY MAN FOR HIMSELF!
LOOK! IT'S NOT SHARK!
IT'S SOME PHONEY DISGUISED AS HIM!
HE'S A DECOY! THE REAL KOOL KIDS ARE GETTING AWAY!
AFTER 'EM!

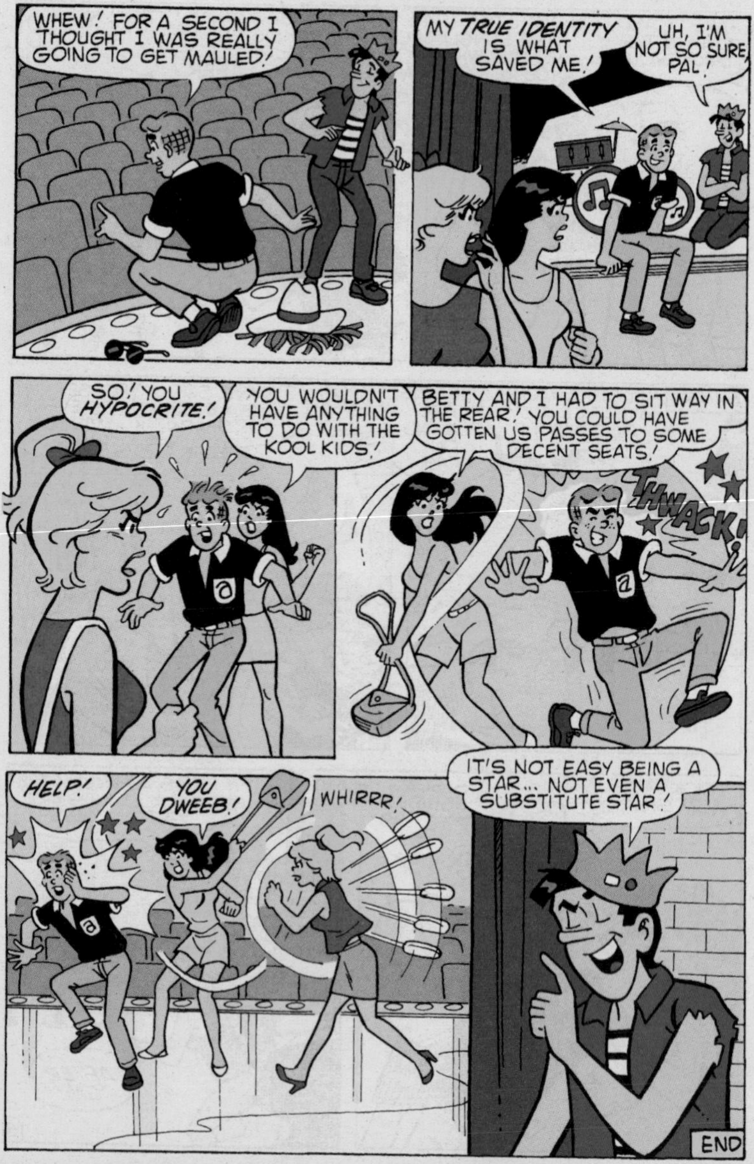
WHEW! FOR A SECOND I THOUGHT I WAS REALLY GOING TO GET MAULED!
MY TRUE IDENTITY IS WHAT SAVED ME!
UH, I'M NOT SO SURE, PAL!
SO! YOU HYPOCRITE!
YOU WOULDN'T HAVE ANYTHING TO DO WITH THE KOOL KIDS!
BETTY AND I HAD TO SIT WAY IN THE REAR! YOU COULD HAVE GOTTEN US PASSES TO SOME DECENT SEATS!
THWACK!
HELP!
YOU DWEEB!
WHIRRR!
IT'S NOT EASY BEING A STAR... NOT EVEN A SUBSTITUTE STAR!
END

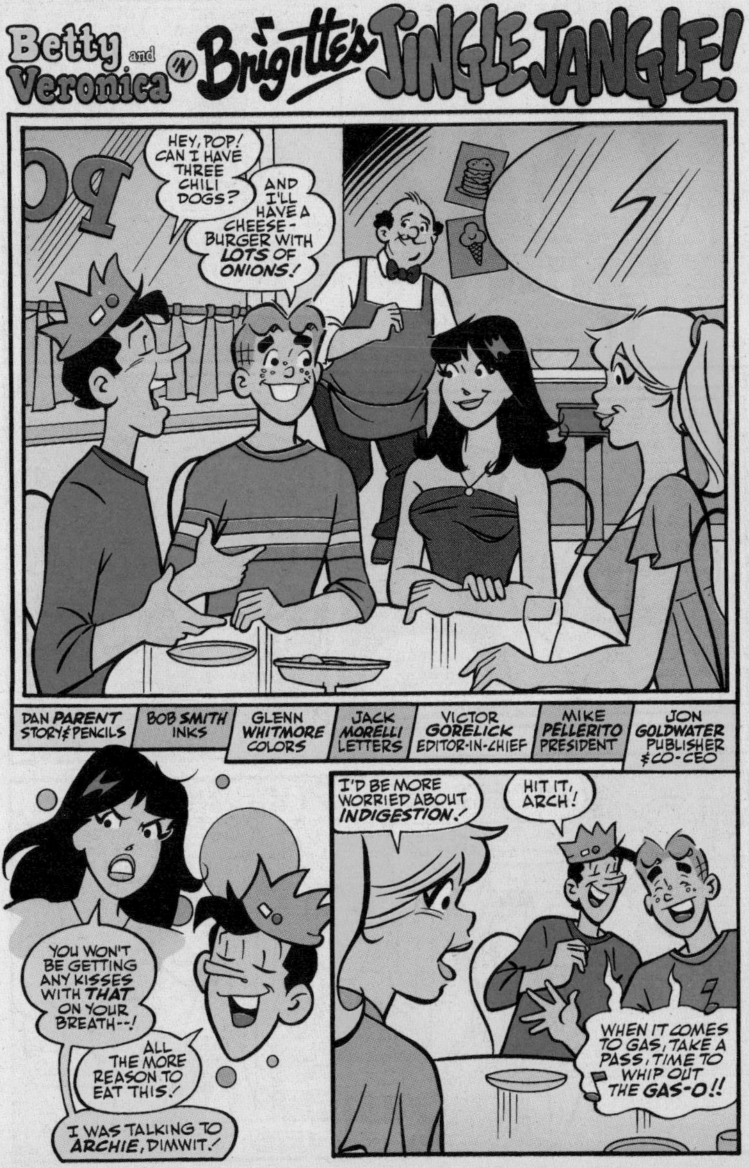
Betty and Veronica in Brigitte's JINGLE JANGLE!
HEY, POP! CAN I HAVE THREE CHILI DOGS?
AND I'LL HAVE A CHEESE-BURGER WITH LOTS OF ONIONS!
DAN PARENT STORY & PENCILS
BOB SMITH INKS
GLENN WHITMORE COLORS
JACK MORELLI LETTERS
VICTOR GORELICK EDITOR-IN-CHIEF
MIKE PELLERITO PRESIDENT
JON GOLDWATER PUBLISHER & CO-CEO
YOU WON'T BE GETTING ANY KISSES WITH THAT ON YOUR BREATH--!
ALL THE MORE REASON TO EAT THIS!
I WAS TALKING TO ARCHIE, DIMWIT!
I'D BE MORE WORRIED ABOUT INDIGESTION!
HIT IT, ARCH!
WHEN IT COMES TO GAS, TAKE A PASS, TIME TO WHIP OUT THE GAS-O!!

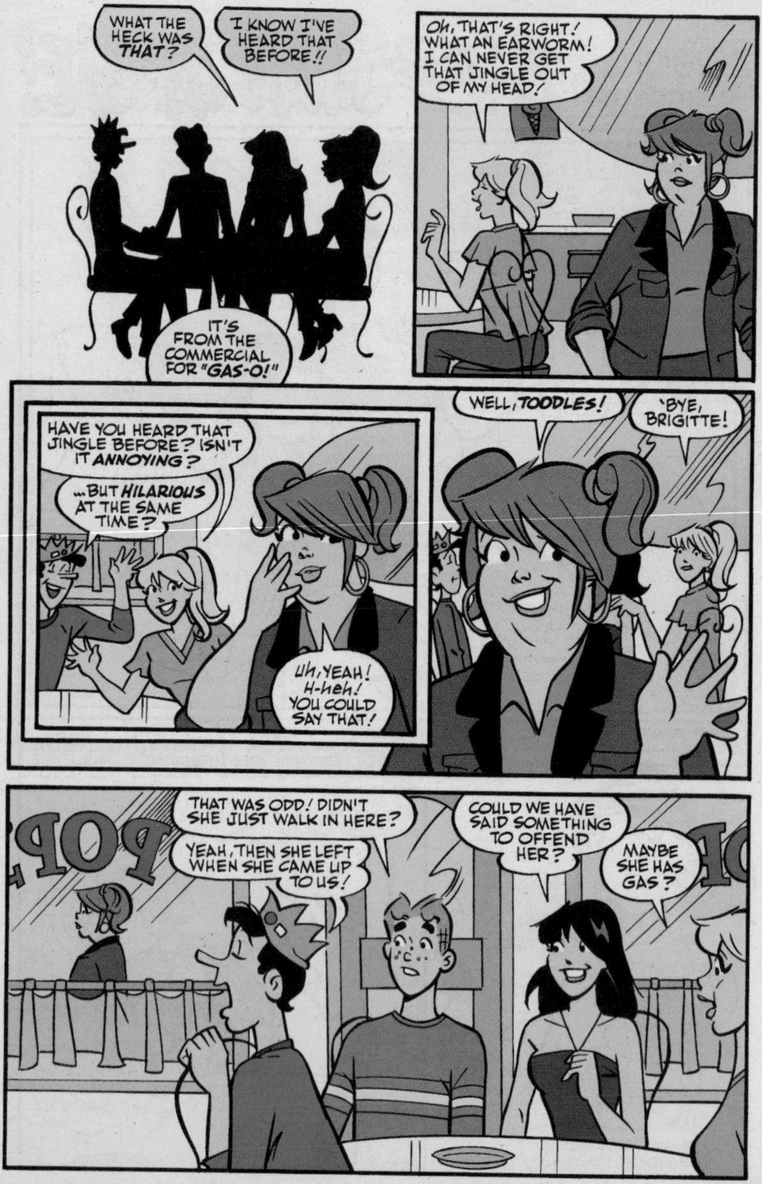
WHAT THE HECK WAS *THAT*?
I KNOW I'VE HEARD THAT BEFORE!!
IT'S FROM THE COMMERCIAL FOR "*GAS-O!*"
Oh, THAT'S RIGHT! WHAT AN EARWORM! I CAN NEVER GET THAT JINGLE OUT OF MY HEAD!
HAVE YOU HEARD THAT JINGLE BEFORE? ISN'T IT *ANNOYING*?
...BUT *HILARIOUS* AT THE SAME TIME?
Uh, YEAH! *H-heh!* YOU COULD SAY THAT!
WELL, *TOODLES*!
'BYE, BRIGITTE!
THAT WAS ODD! DIDN'T SHE JUST WALK IN HERE?
YEAH, THEN SHE LEFT WHEN SHE CAME UP TO US!
COULD WE HAVE SAID SOMETHING TO OFFEND HER?
MAYBE SHE HAS GAS?

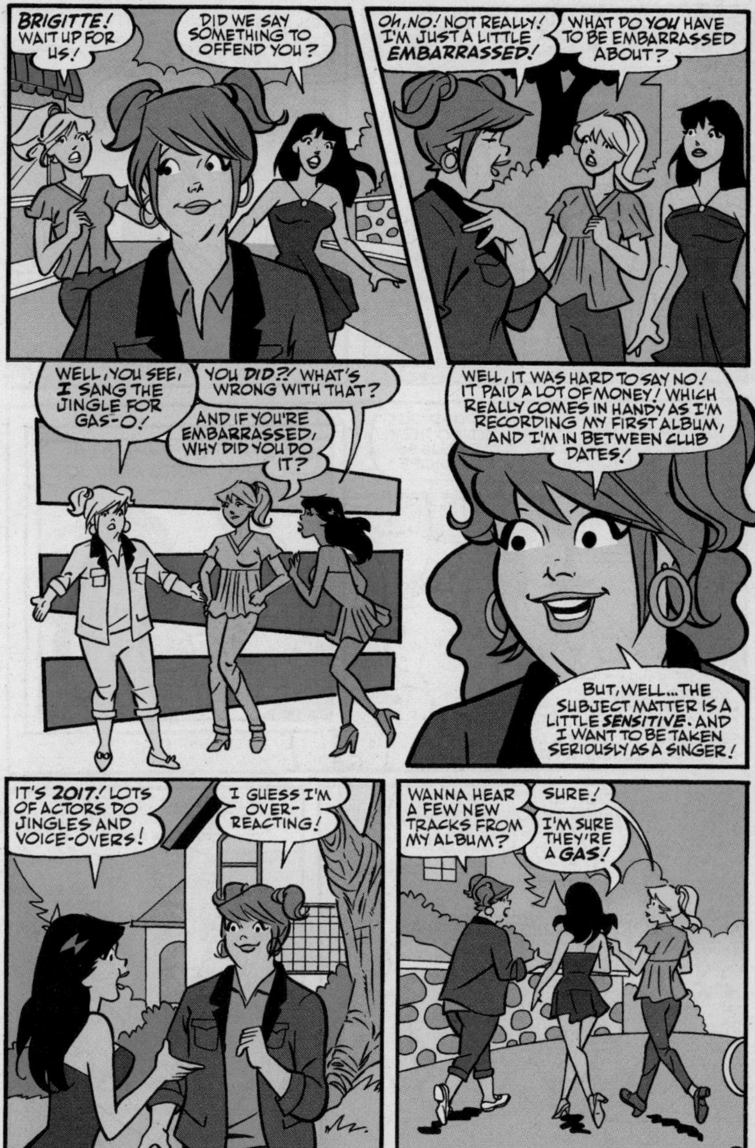
BRIGITTE! WAIT UP FOR US!
DID WE SAY SOMETHING TO OFFEND YOU?
OH, NO! NOT REALLY! I'M JUST A LITTLE EMBARRASSED!
WHAT DO YOU HAVE TO BE EMBARRASSED ABOUT?
WELL, YOU SEE, I SANG THE JINGLE FOR GAS-O!
YOU DID?! WHAT'S WRONG WITH THAT?
AND IF YOU'RE EMBARRASSED, WHY DID YOU DO IT?
WELL, IT WAS HARD TO SAY NO! IT PAID A LOT OF MONEY! WHICH REALLY COMES IN HANDY AS I'M RECORDING MY FIRST ALBUM, AND I'M IN BETWEEN CLUB DATES!
BUT, WELL... THE SUBJECT MATTER IS A LITTLE SENSITIVE. AND I WANT TO BE TAKEN SERIOUSLY AS A SINGER!
IT'S 2017! LOTS OF ACTORS DO JINGLES AND VOICE-OVERS!
I GUESS I'M OVER-REACTING!
WANNA HEAR A FEW NEW TRACKS FROM MY ALBUM?
SURE!
I'M SURE THEY'RE A GAS!

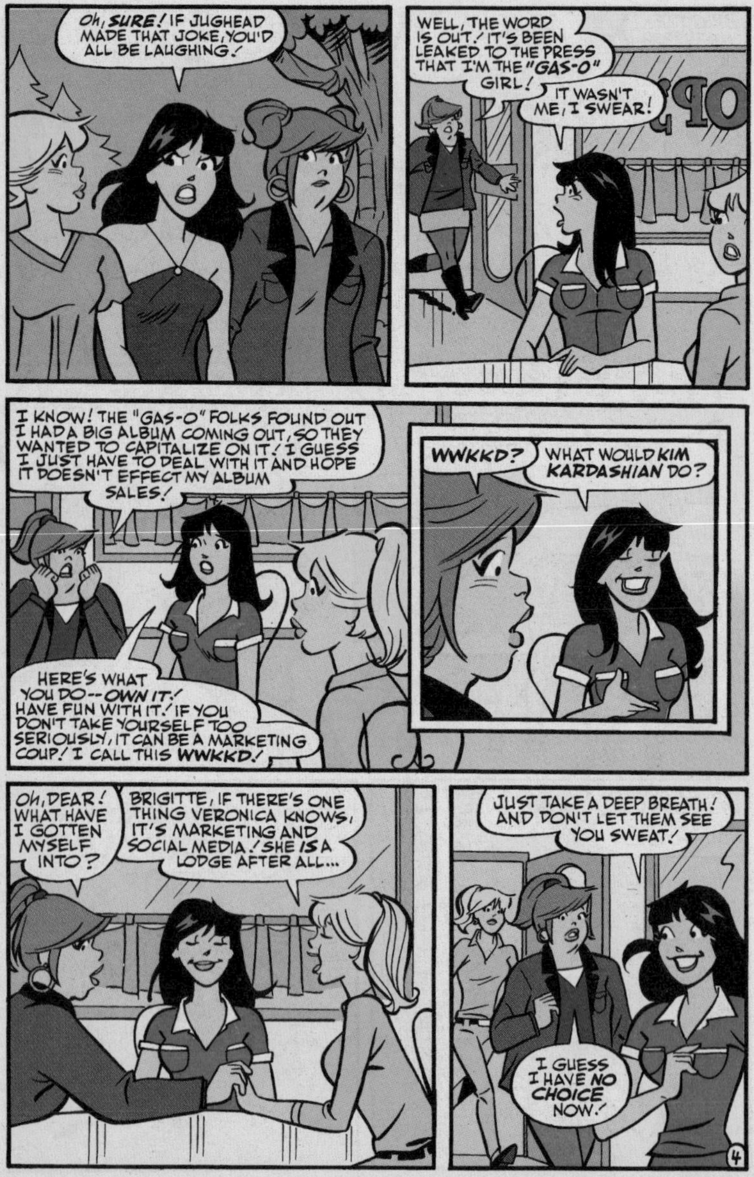

Oh, SURE! IF JUGHEAD MADE THAT JOKE, YOU'D ALL BE LAUGHING!
WELL, THE WORD IS OUT! IT'S BEEN LEAKED TO THE PRESS THAT I'M THE "GAS-O" GIRL!
IT WASN'T ME, I SWEAR!
I KNOW! THE "GAS-O" FOLKS FOUND OUT I HAD A BIG ALBUM COMING OUT, SO THEY WANTED TO CAPITALIZE ON IT! I GUESS I JUST HAVE TO DEAL WITH IT AND HOPE IT DOESN'T EFFECT MY ALBUM SALES!
HERE'S WHAT YOU DO--OWN IT! HAVE FUN WITH IT! IF YOU DON'T TAKE YOURSELF TOO SERIOUSLY, IT CAN BE A MARKETING COUP! I CALL THIS WWKKD!
WWKKD?
WHAT WOULD KIM KARDASHIAN DO?
Oh, DEAR! WHAT HAVE I GOTTEN MYSELF INTO?
BRIGITTE, IF THERE'S ONE THING VERONICA KNOWS, IT'S MARKETING AND SOCIAL MEDIA! SHE IS A LODGE AFTER ALL...
JUST TAKE A DEEP BREATH! AND DON'T LET THEM SEE YOU SWEAT!
I GUESS I HAVE NO CHOICE NOW!
4

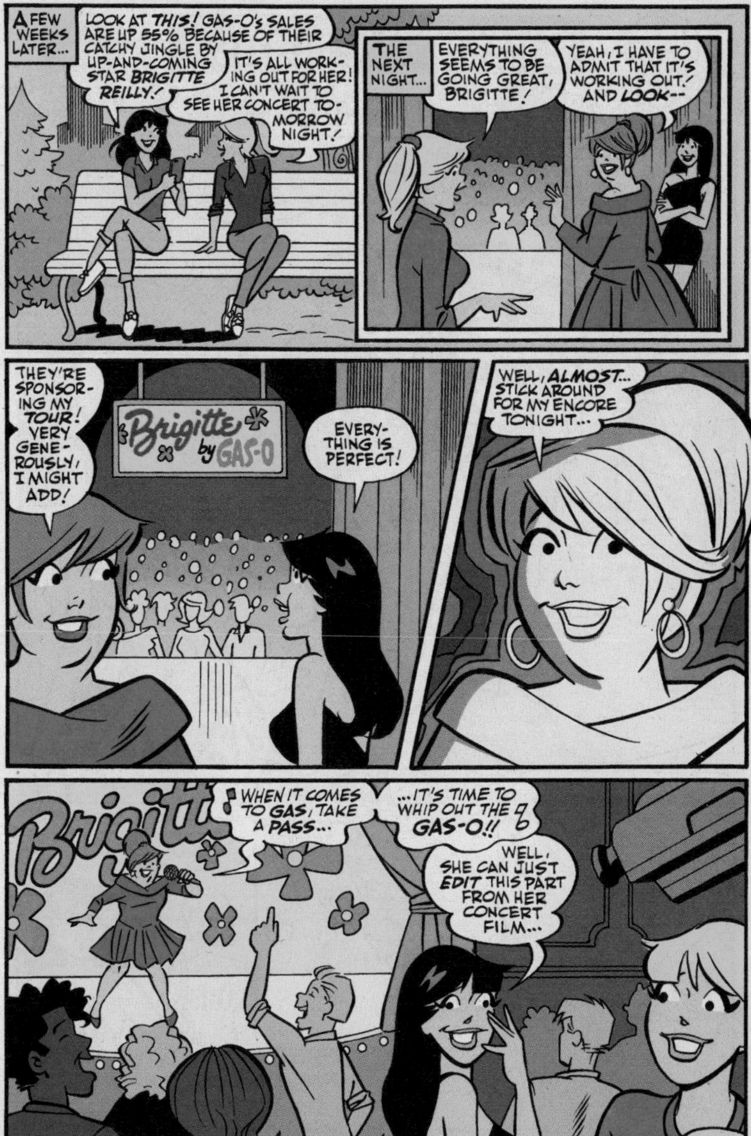
A FEW WEEKS LATER...
LOOK AT THIS! GAS-O's SALES ARE UP 55% BECAUSE OF THEIR CATCHY JINGLE BY UP-AND-COMING STAR BRIGITTE REILLY!
IT'S ALL WORKING OUT FOR HER! I CAN'T WAIT TO SEE HER CONCERT TOMORROW NIGHT!
THE NEXT NIGHT...
EVERYTHING SEEMS TO BE GOING GREAT, BRIGITTE!
YEAH, I HAVE TO ADMIT THAT IT'S WORKING OUT! AND LOOK--
THEY'RE SPONSORING MY TOUR! VERY GENEROUSLY, I MIGHT ADD!
Brigitte by GAS-O
EVERYTHING IS PERFECT!
WELL, ALMOST... STICK AROUND FOR MY ENCORE TONIGHT...
WHEN IT COMES TO GAS, TAKE A PASS...
...IT'S TIME TO WHIP OUT THE GAS-O!!
WELL, SHE CAN JUST EDIT THIS PART FROM HER CONCERT FILM...
END

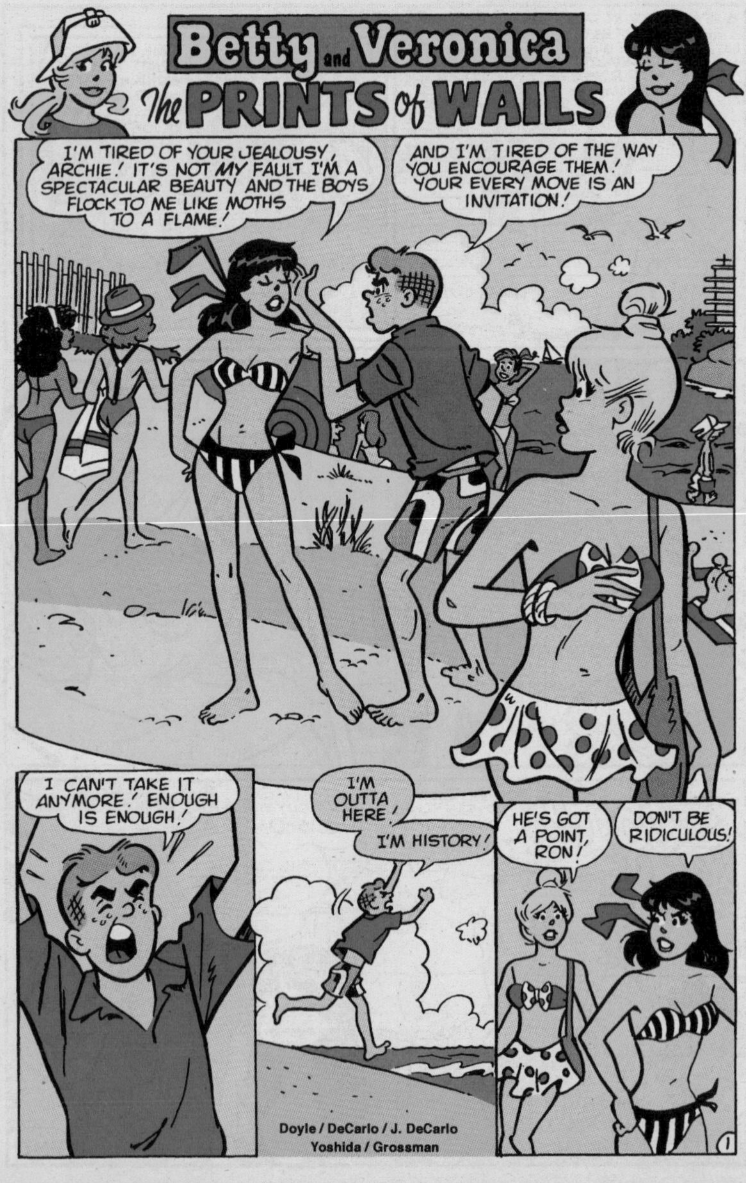
Betty and Veronica
The PRINTS of WAILS
I'M TIRED OF YOUR JEALOUSY, ARCHIE! IT'S NOT MY FAULT I'M A SPECTACULAR BEAUTY AND THE BOYS FLOCK TO ME LIKE MOTHS TO A FLAME!
AND I'M TIRED OF THE WAY YOU ENCOURAGE THEM! YOUR EVERY MOVE IS AN INVITATION!
I CAN'T TAKE IT ANYMORE! ENOUGH IS ENOUGH!
I'M OUTTA HERE!
I'M HISTORY!
Doyle / DeCarlo / J. DeCarlo
Yoshida / Grossman
HE'S GOT A POINT, RON!
DON'T BE RIDICULOUS!
1

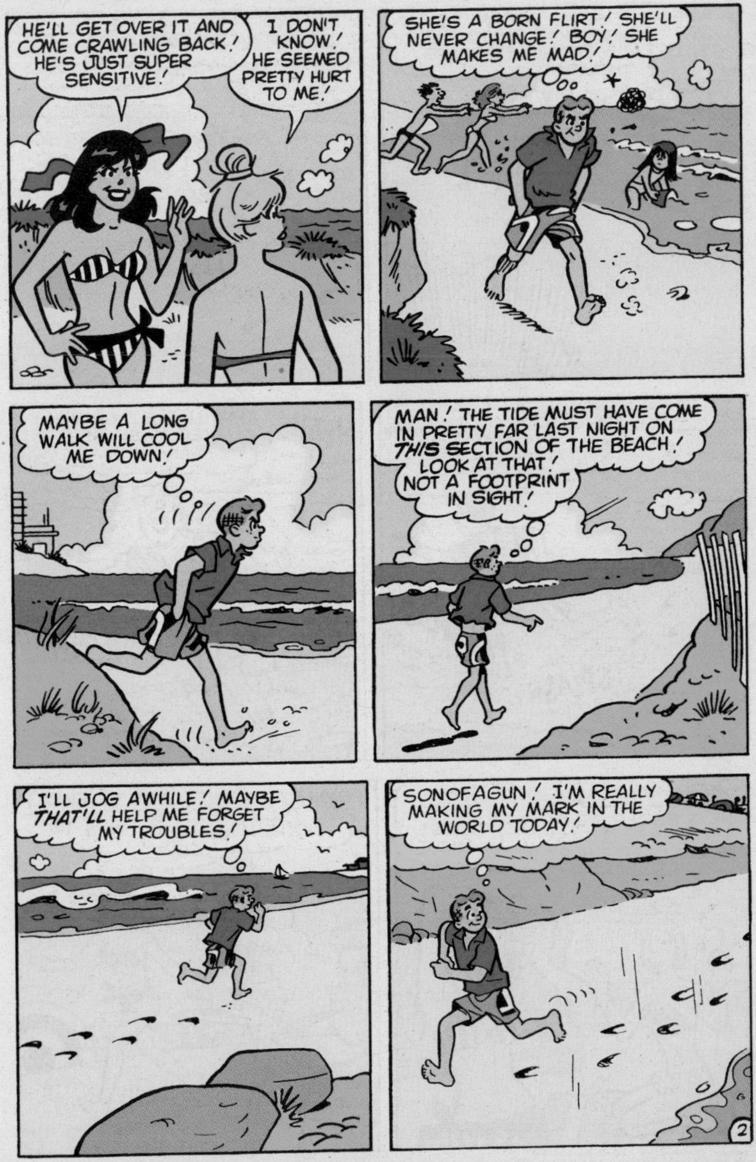

HE'LL GET OVER IT AND COME CRAWLING BACK! HE'S JUST SUPER SENSITIVE!
I DON'T KNOW! HE SEEMED PRETTY HURT TO ME!
SHE'S A BORN FLIRT! SHE'LL NEVER CHANGE! BOY! SHE MAKES ME MAD!
MAYBE A LONG WALK WILL COOL ME DOWN!
MAN! THE TIDE MUST HAVE COME IN PRETTY FAR LAST NIGHT ON *THIS* SECTION OF THE BEACH! LOOK AT THAT! NOT A FOOTPRINT IN SIGHT!
I'LL JOG AWHILE! MAYBE *THAT'LL* HELP ME FORGET MY TROUBLES!
SONOFAGUN! I'M REALLY MAKING MY MARK IN THE WORLD TODAY!

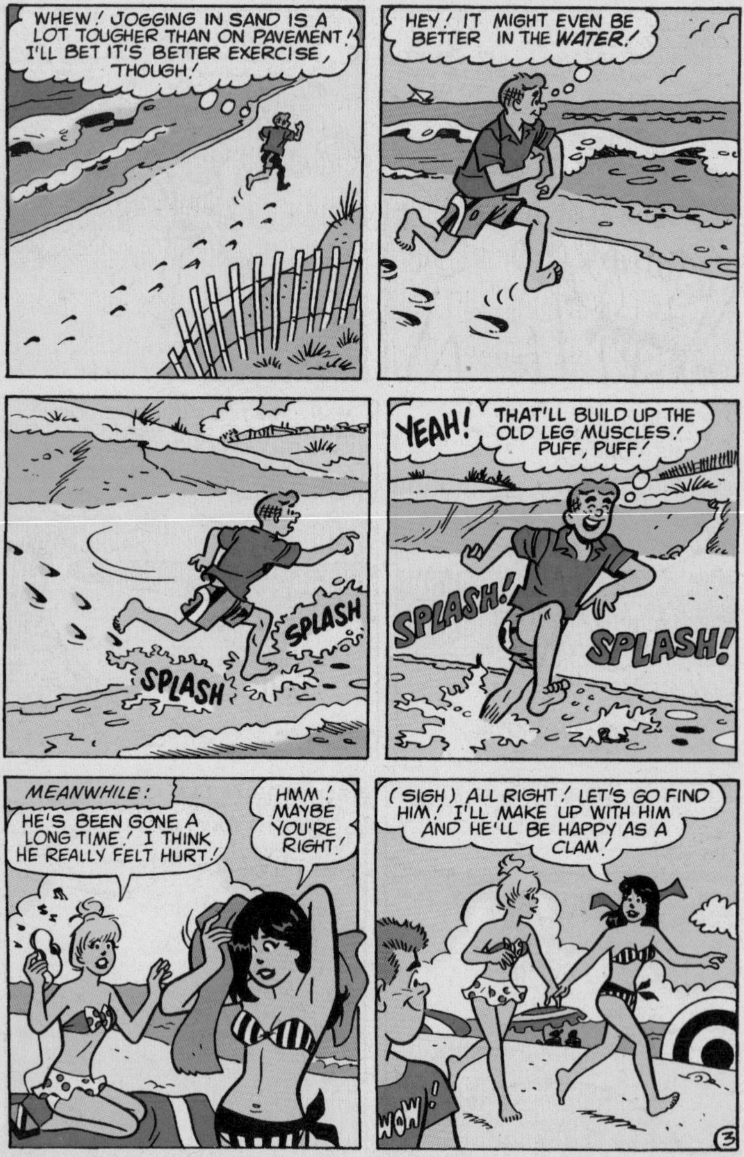

WHEW! JOGGING IN SAND IS A LOT TOUGHER THAN ON PAVEMENT! I'LL BET IT'S BETTER EXERCISE, THOUGH!
HEY! IT MIGHT EVEN BE BETTER IN THE WATER!
SPLASH
SPLASH
YEAH! THAT'LL BUILD UP THE OLD LEG MUSCLES! PUFF, PUFF!
SPLASH!
SPLASH!
MEANWHILE:
HE'S BEEN GONE A LONG TIME! I THINK HE REALLY FELT HURT!
HMM! MAYBE YOU'RE RIGHT!
(SIGH) ALL RIGHT! LET'S GO FIND HIM! I'LL MAKE UP WITH HIM AND HE'LL BE HAPPY AS A CLAM!
WOW!
3

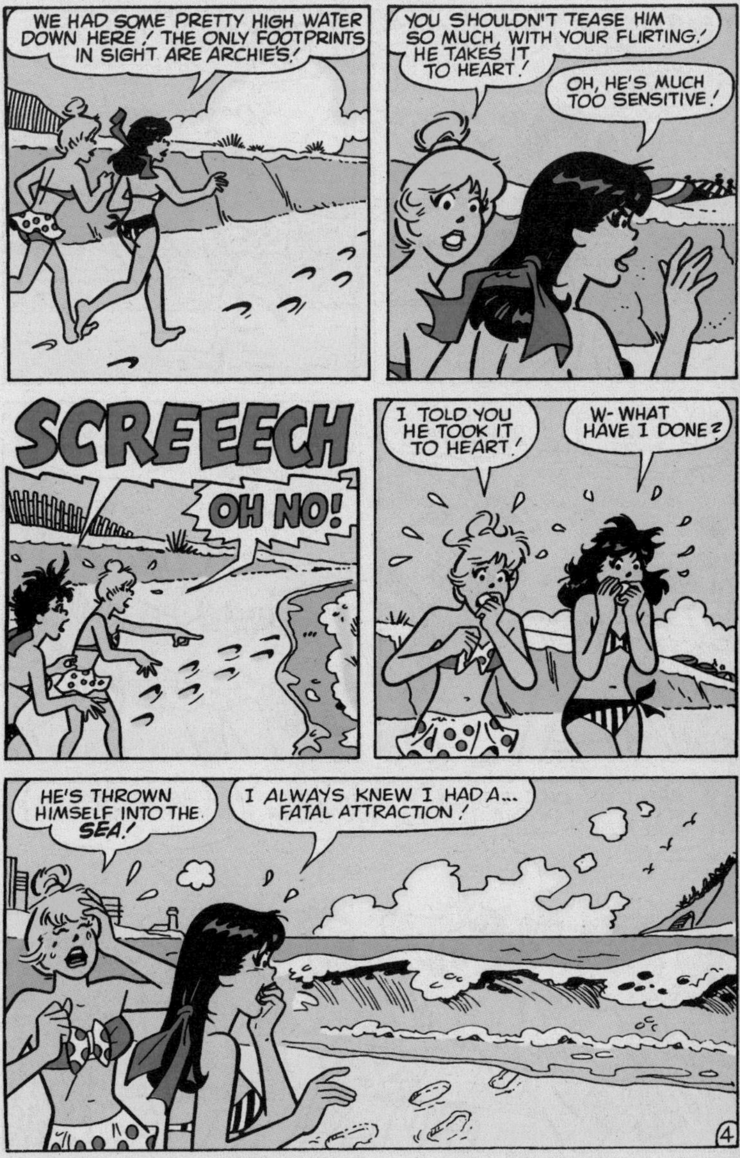
WE HAD SOME PRETTY HIGH WATER DOWN HERE! THE ONLY FOOTPRINTS IN SIGHT ARE ARCHIE'S!
YOU SHOULDN'T TEASE HIM SO MUCH, WITH YOUR FLIRTING! HE TAKES IT TO HEART!
OH, HE'S MUCH TOO SENSITIVE!
SCREEECH
OH NO!
I TOLD YOU HE TOOK IT TO HEART!
W- WHAT HAVE I DONE?
HE'S THROWN HIMSELF INTO THE SEA!
I ALWAYS KNEW I HAD A... FATAL ATTRACTION!
4

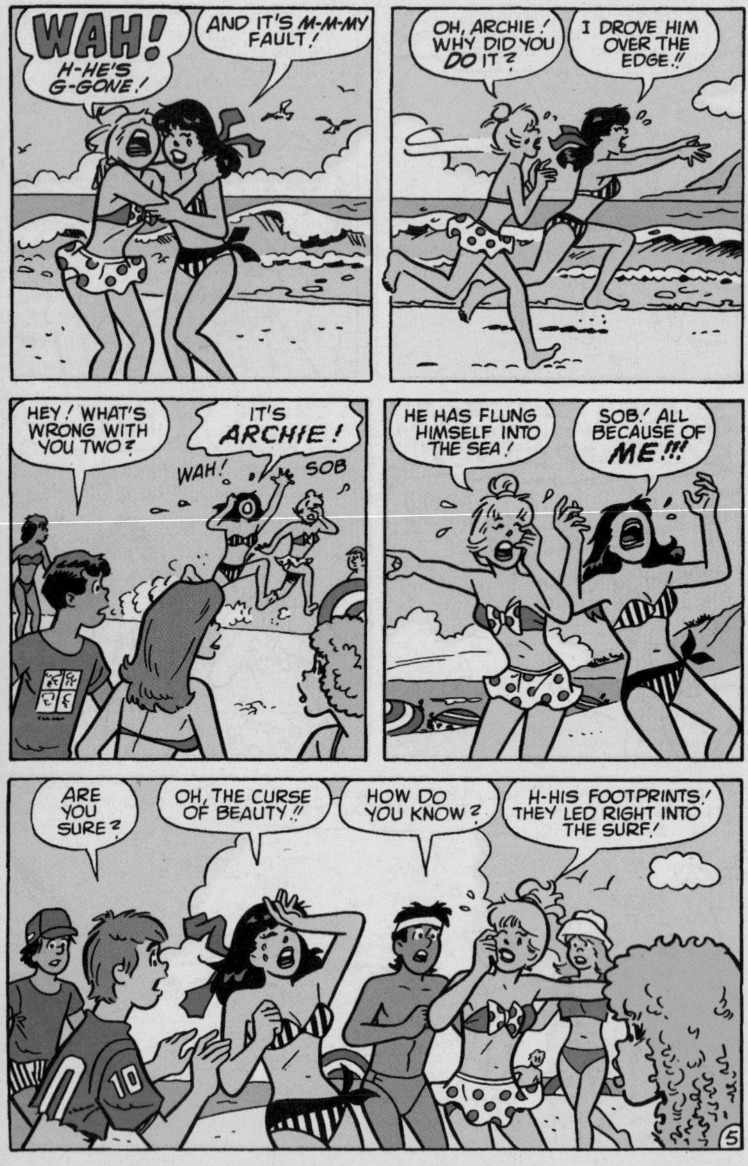

WAH! H-HE'S G-GONE!
AND IT'S M-M-MY FAULT!
OH, ARCHIE! WHY DID YOU DO IT?
I DROVE HIM OVER THE EDGE!!
HEY! WHAT'S WRONG WITH YOU TWO?
IT'S ARCHIE!
WAH!
SOB
HE HAS FLUNG HIMSELF INTO THE SEA!
SOB! ALL BECAUSE OF ME!!!
ARE YOU SURE?
OH, THE CURSE OF BEAUTY!!
HOW DO YOU KNOW?
H-HIS FOOTPRINTS! THEY LED RIGHT INTO THE SURF!
10
5

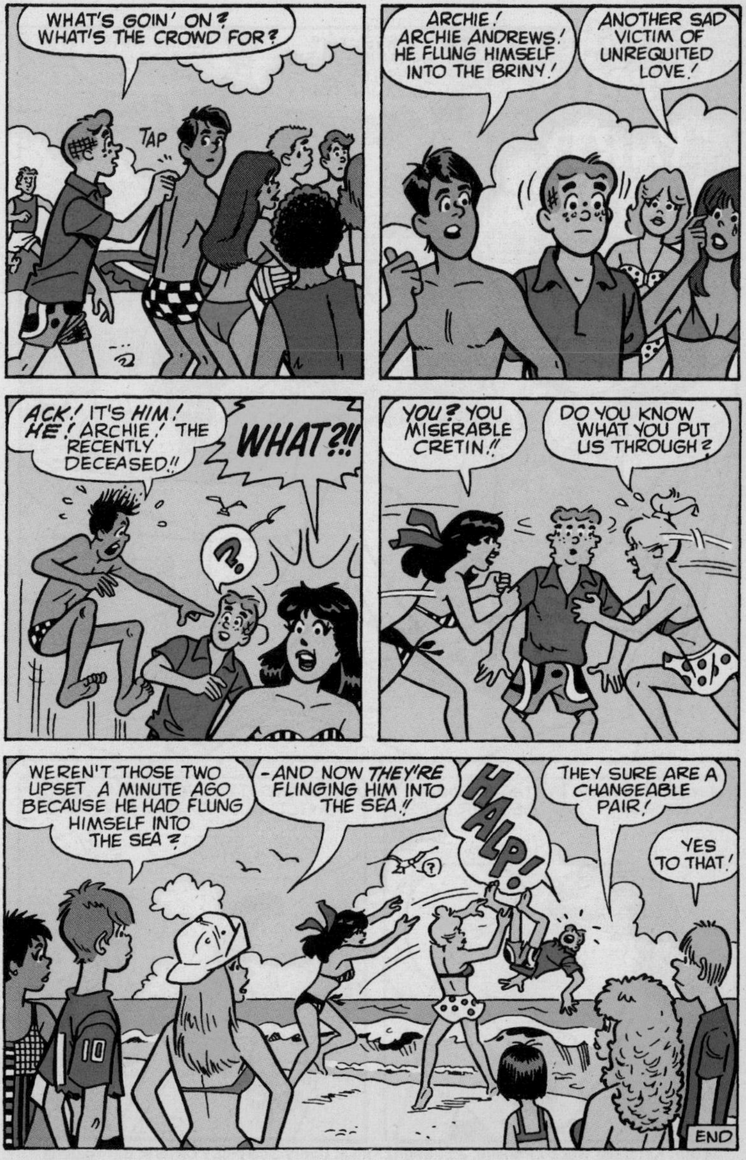
WHAT'S GOIN' ON? WHAT'S THE CROWD FOR?
TAP
ARCHIE! ARCHIE ANDREWS! HE FLUNG HIMSELF INTO THE BRINY!
ANOTHER SAD VICTIM OF UNREQUITED LOVE!
ACK! IT'S HIM! HE! ARCHIE! THE RECENTLY DECEASED!!
WHAT?!!
?
YOU? YOU MISERABLE CRETIN!!
DO YOU KNOW WHAT YOU PUT US THROUGH?
WEREN'T THOSE TWO UPSET A MINUTE AGO BECAUSE HE HAD FLUNG HIMSELF INTO THE SEA?
-AND NOW THEY'RE FLINGING HIM INTO THE SEA!!
HALP!
THEY SURE ARE A CHANGEABLE PAIR!
YES TO THAT!
END

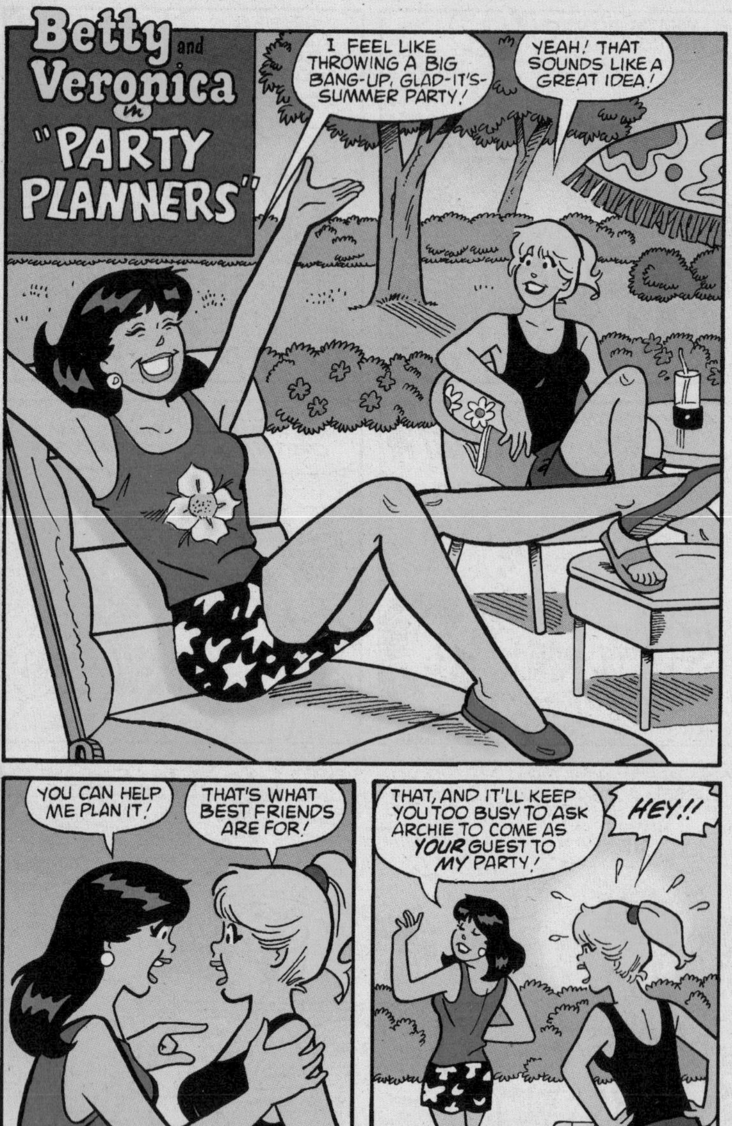
Betty and Veronica in "PARTY PLANNERS"
I FEEL LIKE THROWING A BIG BANG-UP, GLAD-IT'S-SUMMER PARTY!
YEAH! THAT SOUNDS LIKE A GREAT IDEA!
YOU CAN HELP ME PLAN IT!
THAT'S WHAT BEST FRIENDS ARE FOR!
THAT, AND IT'LL KEEP YOU TOO BUSY TO ASK ARCHIE TO COME AS YOUR GUEST TO MY PARTY!
HEY!!

Script: Kathleen Webb / Pencils: Jeff Shultz / Inks: Henry Scarpelli / Letters: Bill Yoshida

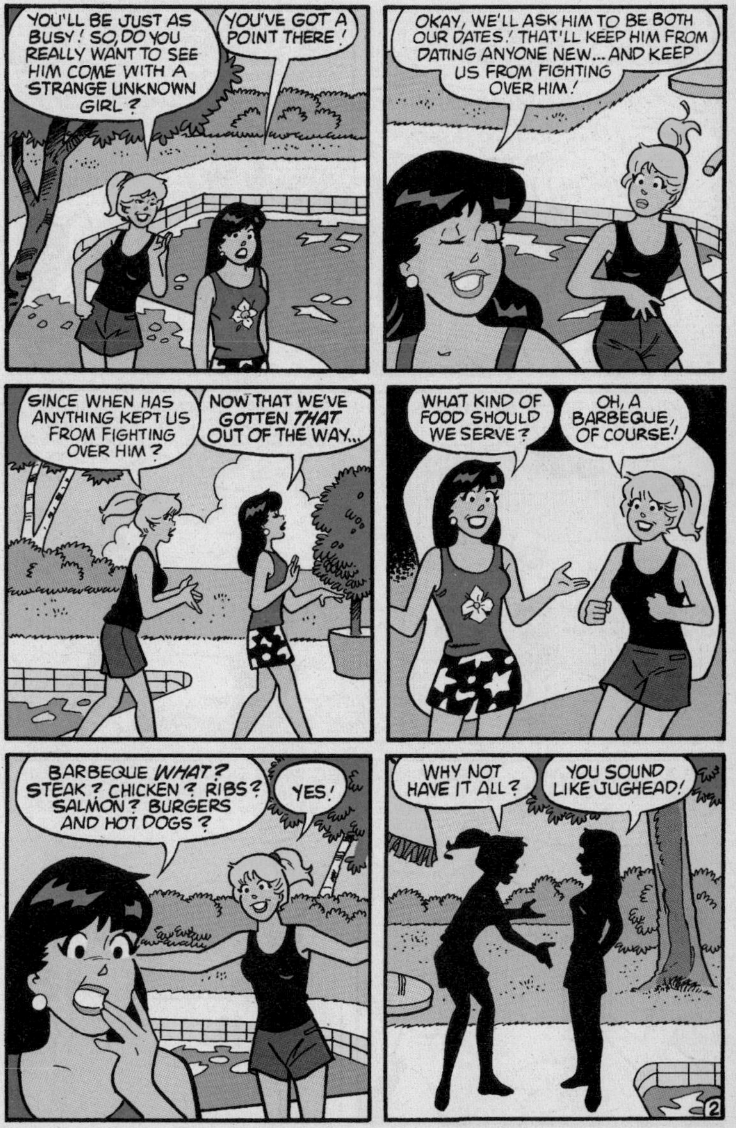
YOU'LL BE JUST AS BUSY! SO, DO YOU REALLY WANT TO SEE HIM COME WITH A STRANGE UNKNOWN GIRL?
YOU'VE GOT A POINT THERE!
OKAY, WE'LL ASK HIM TO BE BOTH OUR DATES! THAT'LL KEEP HIM FROM DATING ANYONE NEW... AND KEEP US FROM FIGHTING OVER HIM!
SINCE WHEN HAS ANYTHING KEPT US FROM FIGHTING OVER HIM?
NOW THAT WE'VE GOTTEN *THAT* OUT OF THE WAY...
WHAT KIND OF FOOD SHOULD WE SERVE?
OH, A BARBEQUE, OF COURSE!
BARBEQUE *WHAT?* STEAK? CHICKEN? RIBS? SALMON? BURGERS AND HOT DOGS?
YES!
WHY NOT HAVE IT ALL?
YOU SOUND LIKE JUGHEAD!
2

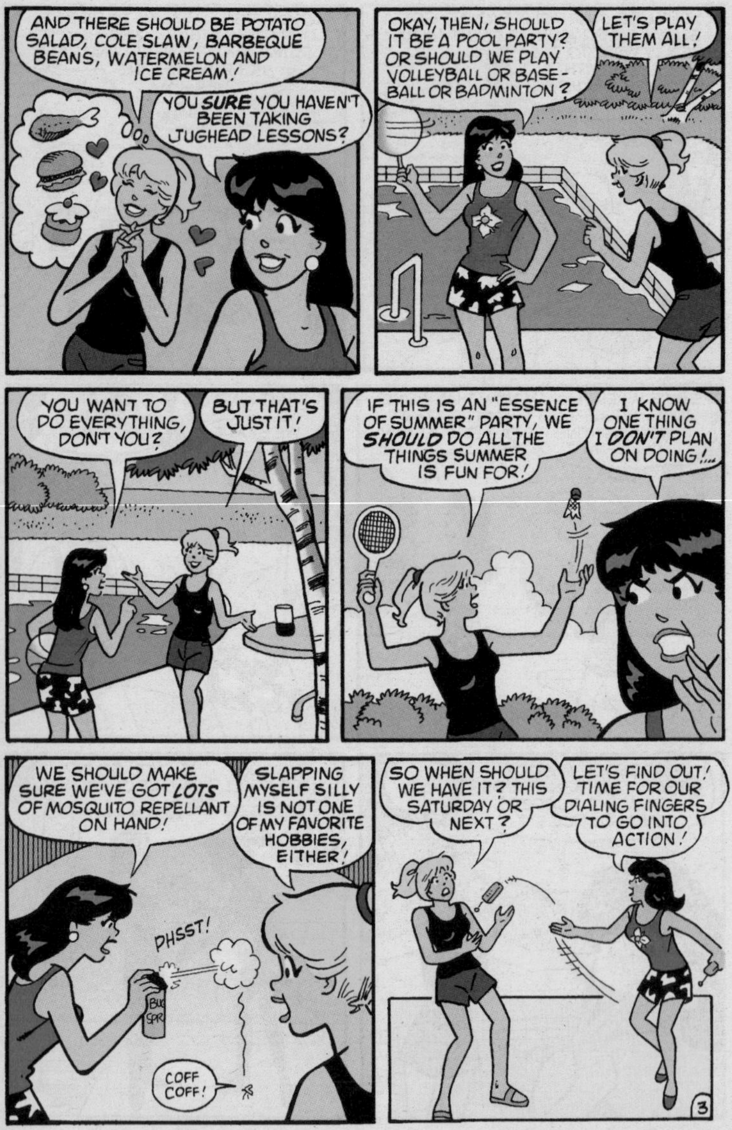
AND THERE SHOULD BE POTATO SALAD, COLE SLAW, BARBEQUE BEANS, WATERMELON AND ICE CREAM!
YOU SURE YOU HAVEN'T BEEN TAKING JUGHEAD LESSONS?
OKAY, THEN, SHOULD IT BE A POOL PARTY? OR SHOULD WE PLAY VOLLEYBALL OR BASE-BALL OR BADMINTON?
LET'S PLAY THEM ALL!
YOU WANT TO DO EVERYTHING, DON'T YOU?
BUT THAT'S JUST IT!
IF THIS IS AN "ESSENCE OF SUMMER" PARTY, WE SHOULD DO ALL THE THINGS SUMMER IS FUN FOR!
I KNOW ONE THING I DON'T PLAN ON DOING!...
WE SHOULD MAKE SURE WE'VE GOT LOTS OF MOSQUITO REPELLANT ON HAND!
SLAPPING MYSELF SILLY IS NOT ONE OF MY FAVORITE HOBBIES, EITHER!
PHSST!
COFF COFF!
SO WHEN SHOULD WE HAVE IT? THIS SATURDAY OR NEXT?
LET'S FIND OUT! TIME FOR OUR DIALING FINGERS TO GO INTO ACTION!
3

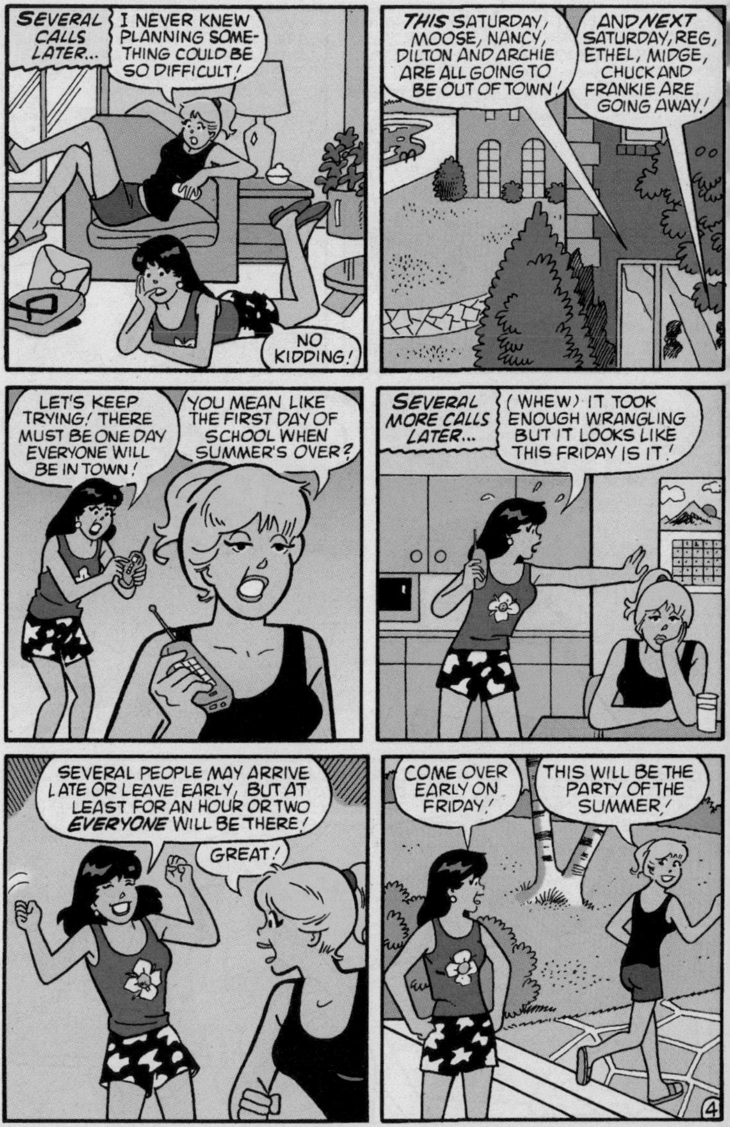
SEVERAL CALLS LATER...
I NEVER KNEW PLANNING SOMETHING COULD BE SO DIFFICULT!
NO KIDDING!
THIS SATURDAY, MOOSE, NANCY, DILTON AND ARCHIE ARE ALL GOING TO BE OUT OF TOWN!
AND NEXT SATURDAY, REG, ETHEL, MIDGE, CHUCK AND FRANKIE ARE GOING AWAY!
LET'S KEEP TRYING! THERE MUST BE ONE DAY EVERYONE WILL BE IN TOWN!
YOU MEAN LIKE THE FIRST DAY OF SCHOOL WHEN SUMMER'S OVER?
SEVERAL MORE CALLS LATER...
(WHEW) IT TOOK ENOUGH WRANGLING BUT IT LOOKS LIKE THIS FRIDAY IS IT!
SEVERAL PEOPLE MAY ARRIVE LATE OR LEAVE EARLY, BUT AT LEAST FOR AN HOUR OR TWO EVERYONE WILL BE THERE!
GREAT!
COME OVER EARLY ON FRIDAY!
THIS WILL BE THE PARTY OF THE SUMMER!
4

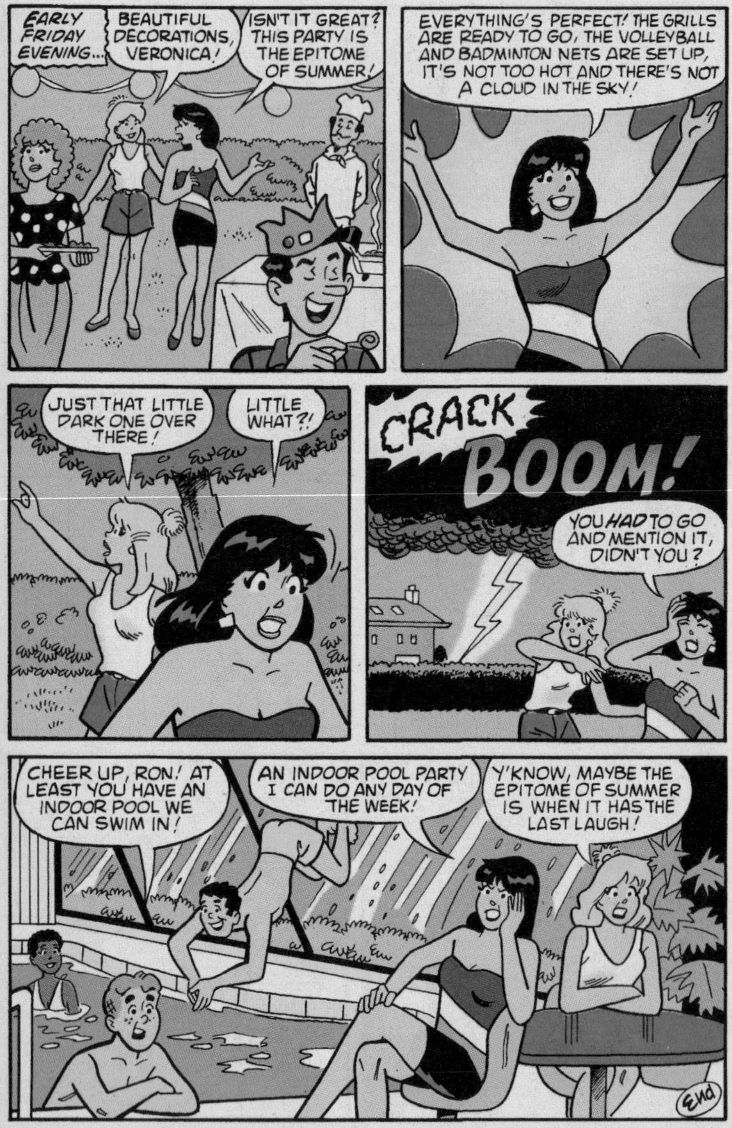
EARLY FRIDAY EVENING...
BEAUTIFUL DECORATIONS, VERONICA!
ISN'T IT GREAT? THIS PARTY IS THE EPITOME OF SUMMER!
EVERYTHING'S PERFECT! THE GRILLS ARE READY TO GO, THE VOLLEYBALL AND BADMINTON NETS ARE SET UP, IT'S NOT TOO HOT AND THERE'S NOT A CLOUD IN THE SKY!
JUST THAT LITTLE DARK ONE OVER THERE!
LITTLE WHAT?!
CRACK
BOOM!
YOU HAD TO GO AND MENTION IT, DIDN'T YOU?
CHEER UP, RON! AT LEAST YOU HAVE AN INDOOR POOL WE CAN SWIM IN!
AN INDOOR POOL PARTY I CAN DO ANY DAY OF THE WEEK!
Y'KNOW, MAYBE THE EPITOME OF SUMMER IS WHEN IT HAS THE LAST LAUGH!
End

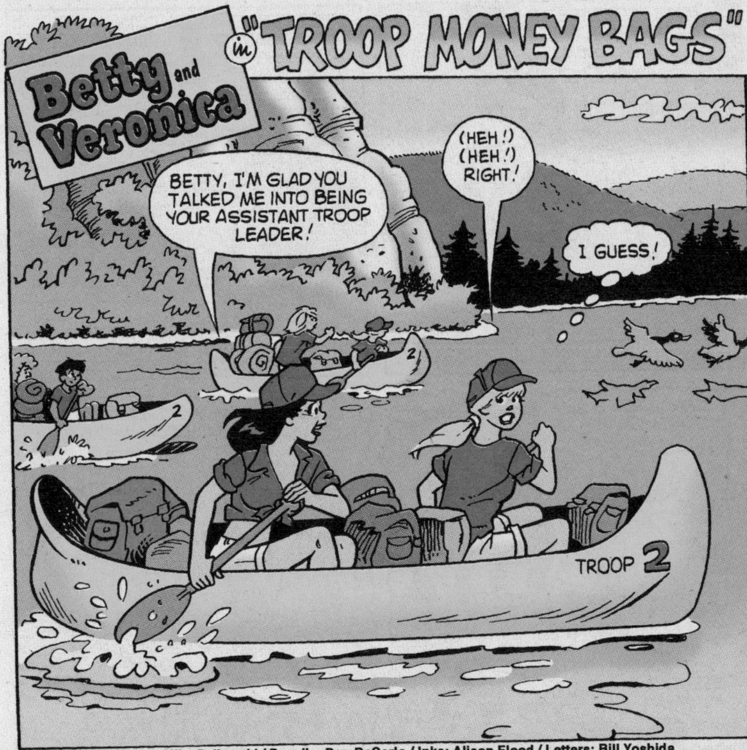
Betty and Veronica
in "TROOP MONEY BAGS"
BETTY, I'M GLAD YOU TALKED ME INTO BEING YOUR ASSISTANT TROOP LEADER!
(HEH!) (HEH!) RIGHT!
I GUESS!
TROOP 2

Script: Mike Pellowski / Pencils: Dan DeCarlo / Inks: Alison Flood / Letters: Bill Yoshida

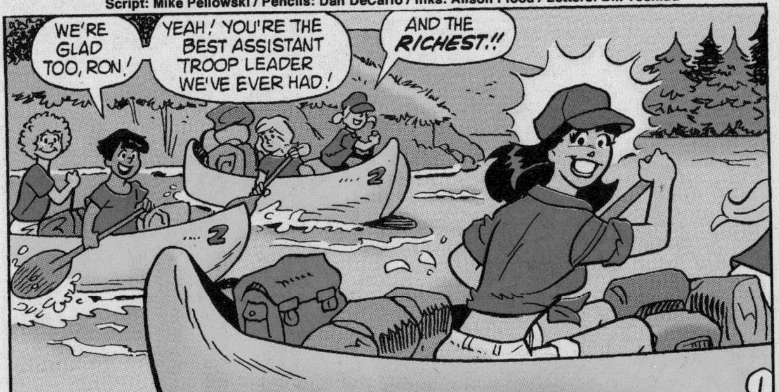
WE'RE GLAD TOO, RON!
YEAH! YOU'RE THE BEST ASSISTANT TROOP LEADER WE'VE EVER HAD!
AND THE RICHEST!!

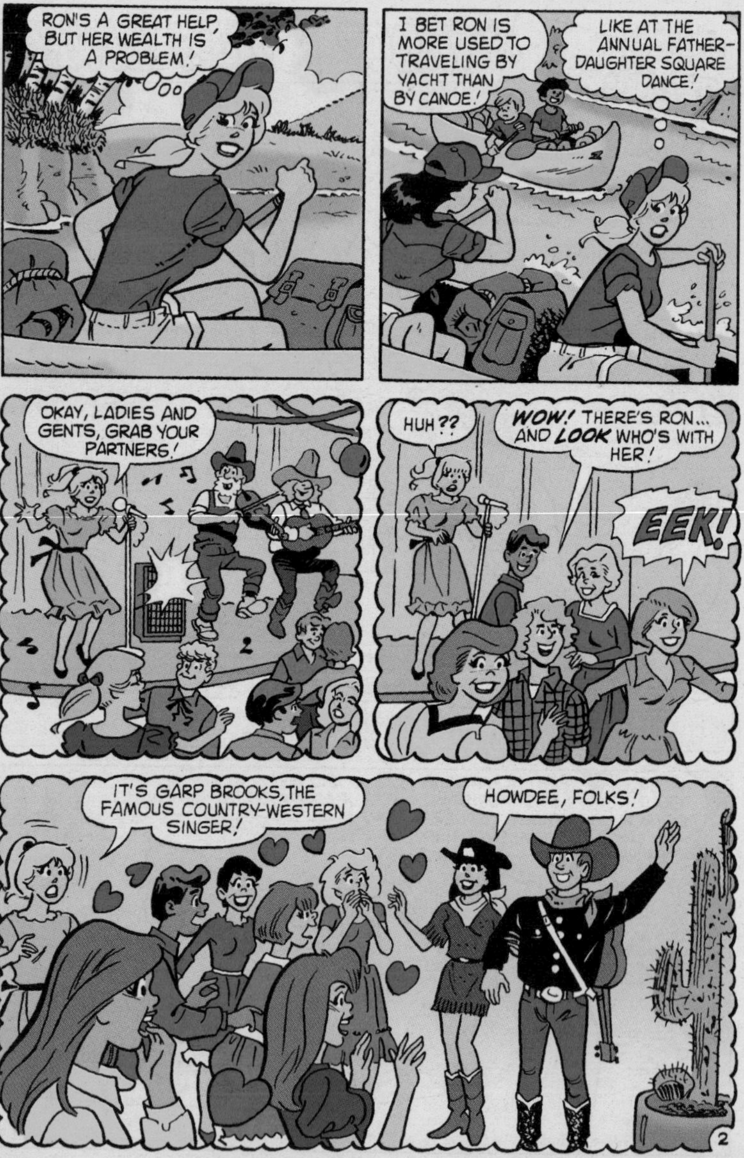
RON'S A GREAT HELP, BUT HER WEALTH IS A PROBLEM!
I BET RON IS MORE USED TO TRAVELING BY YACHT THAN BY CANOE!
LIKE AT THE ANNUAL FATHER-DAUGHTER SQUARE DANCE!
OKAY, LADIES AND GENTS, GRAB YOUR PARTNERS!
HUH??
WOW! THERE'S RON... AND LOOK WHO'S WITH HER!
EEK!
IT'S GARP BROOKS, THE FAMOUS COUNTRY-WESTERN SINGER!
HOWDEE, FOLKS!

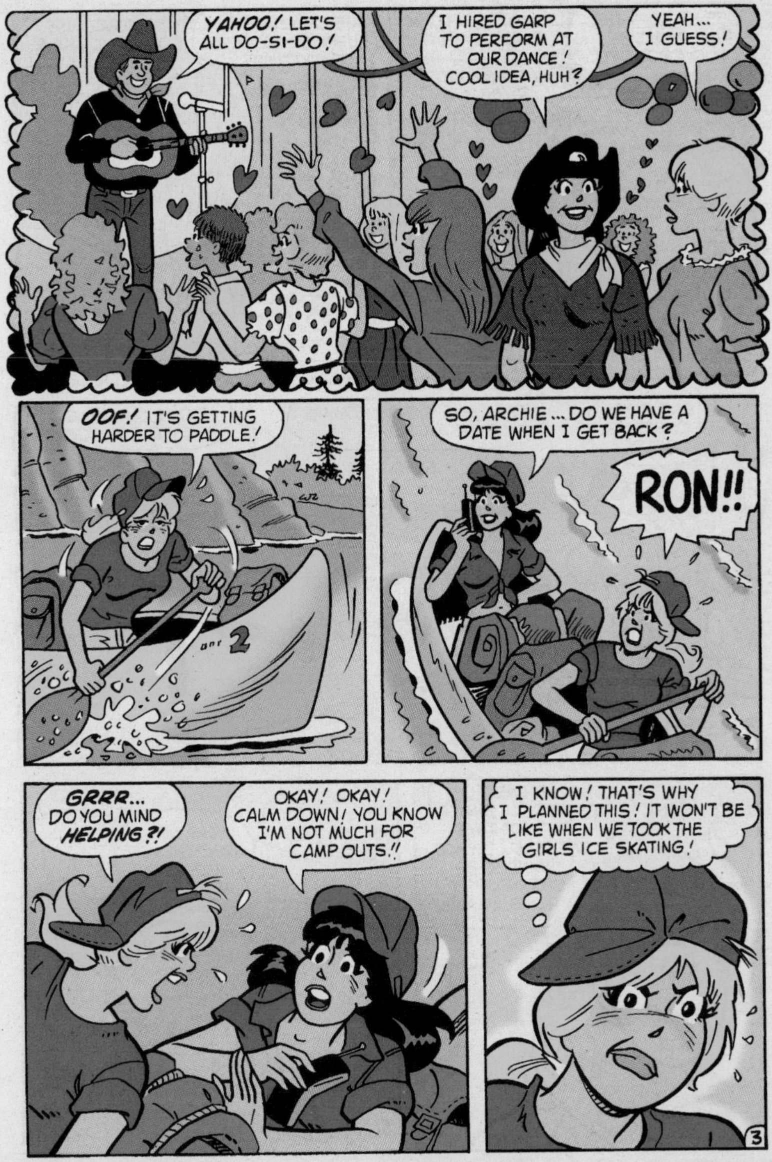
YAHOO! LET'S ALL DO-SI-DO!
I HIRED GARP TO PERFORM AT OUR DANCE! COOL IDEA, HUH?
YEAH... I GUESS!
OOF! IT'S GETTING HARDER TO PADDLE!
SO, ARCHIE ... DO WE HAVE A DATE WHEN I GET BACK?
RON!!
GRRR... DO YOU MIND HELPING?!
OKAY! OKAY! CALM DOWN! YOU KNOW I'M NOT MUCH FOR CAMP OUTS!!
I KNOW! THAT'S WHY I PLANNED THIS! IT WON'T BE LIKE WHEN WE TOOK THE GIRLS ICE SKATING!
3

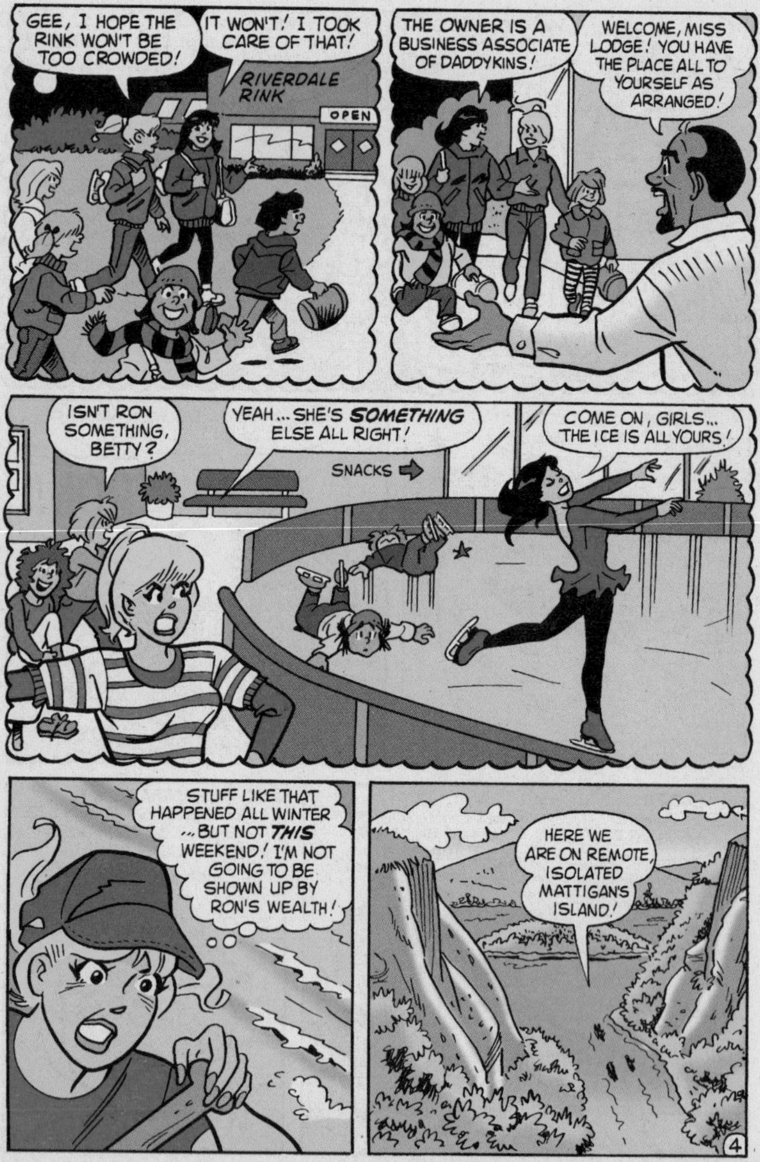
GEE, I HOPE THE RINK WON'T BE TOO CROWDED!
IT WON'T! I TOOK CARE OF THAT!
RIVERDALE RINK
OPEN
THE OWNER IS A BUSINESS ASSOCIATE OF DADDYKINS!
WELCOME, MISS LODGE! YOU HAVE THE PLACE ALL TO YOURSELF AS ARRANGED!
ISN'T RON SOMETHING, BETTY?
YEAH ... SHE'S SOMETHING ELSE ALL RIGHT!
SNACKS
COME ON, GIRLS... THE ICE IS ALL YOURS!
STUFF LIKE THAT HAPPENED ALL WINTER ... BUT NOT THIS WEEKEND! I'M NOT GOING TO BE SHOWN UP BY RON'S WEALTH!
HERE WE ARE ON REMOTE, ISOLATED MATTIGAN'S ISLAND!

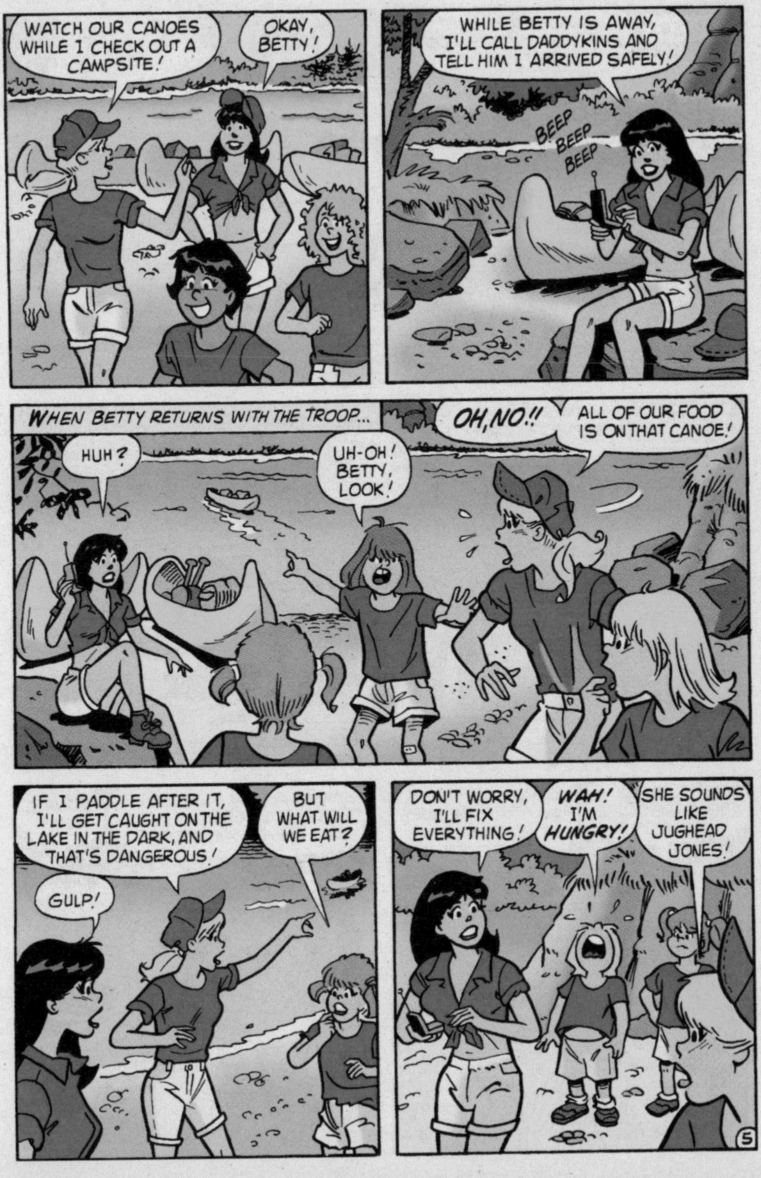
WATCH OUR CANOES WHILE I CHECK OUT A CAMPSITE!
OKAY, BETTY!
WHILE BETTY IS AWAY, I'LL CALL DADDYKINS AND TELL HIM I ARRIVED SAFELY!
BEEP BEEP BEEP
WHEN BETTY RETURNS WITH THE TROOP...
HUH?
UH-OH! BETTY, LOOK!
OH, NO!!
ALL OF OUR FOOD IS ON THAT CANOE!
IF I PADDLE AFTER IT, I'LL GET CAUGHT ON THE LAKE IN THE DARK, AND THAT'S DANGEROUS!
BUT WHAT WILL WE EAT?
GULP!
DON'T WORRY, I'LL FIX EVERYTHING!
WAH! I'M HUNGRY!
SHE SOUNDS LIKE JUGHEAD JONES!
5

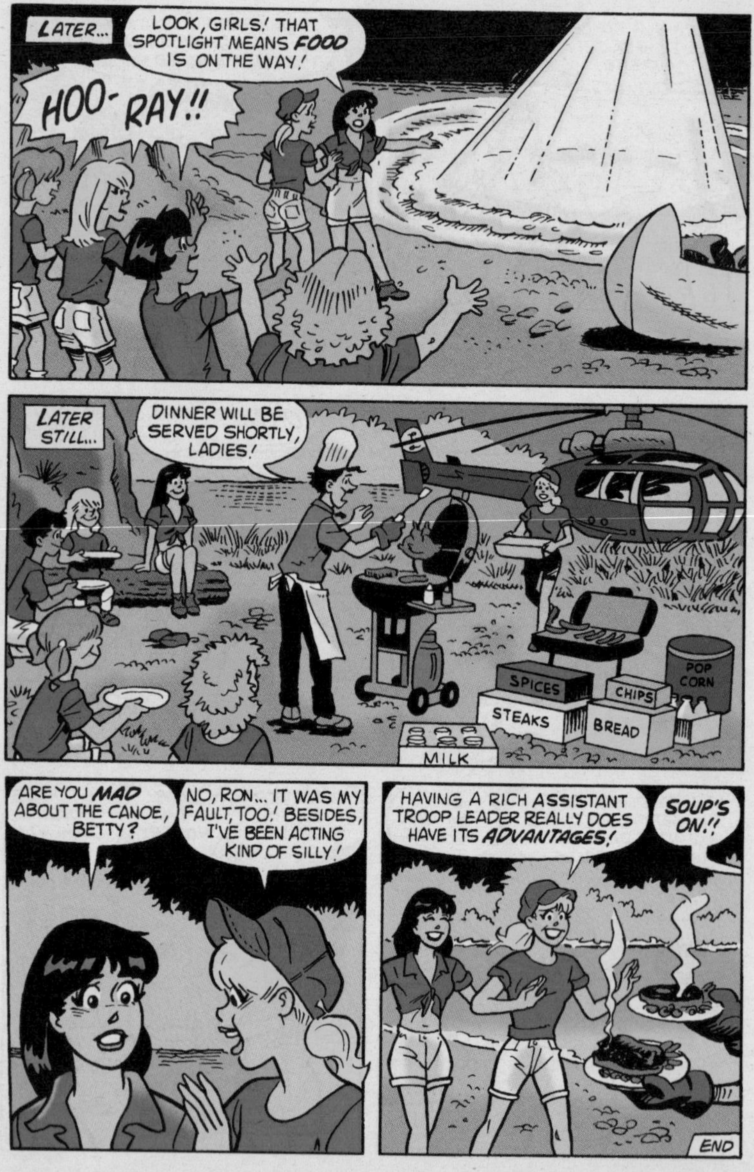
LATER...
LOOK, GIRLS! THAT SPOTLIGHT MEANS FOOD IS ON THE WAY!
HOO-RAY!!
LATER STILL...
DINNER WILL BE SERVED SHORTLY, LADIES!
SPICES
CHIPS
POP CORN
STEAKS
BREAD
MILK
ARE YOU MAD ABOUT THE CANOE, BETTY?
NO, RON... IT WAS MY FAULT, TOO! BESIDES, I'VE BEEN ACTING KIND OF SILLY!
HAVING A RICH ASSISTANT TROOP LEADER REALLY DOES HAVE ITS ADVANTAGES!
SOUP'S ON!!
END

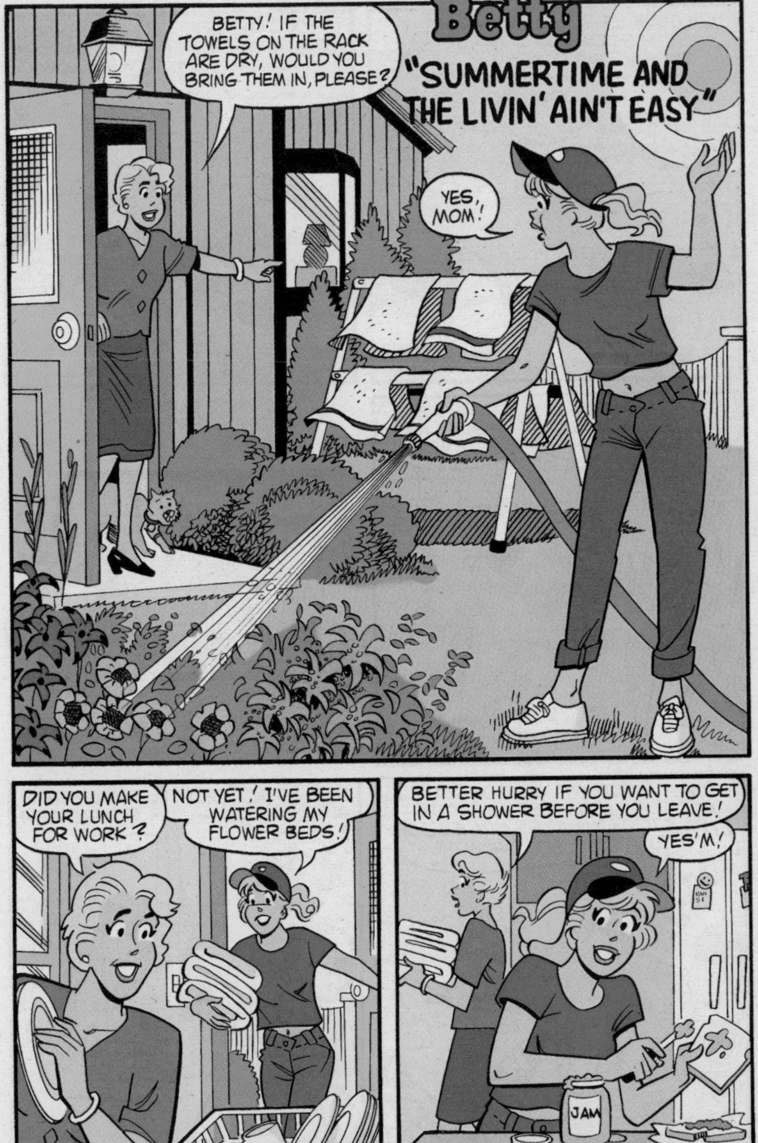
Betty
"SUMMERTIME AND THE LIVIN' AIN'T EASY"
BETTY! IF THE TOWELS ON THE RACK ARE DRY, WOULD YOU BRING THEM IN, PLEASE?
YES, MOM!
DID YOU MAKE YOUR LUNCH FOR WORK?
NOT YET! I'VE BEEN WATERING MY FLOWER BEDS!
BETTER HURRY IF YOU WANT TO GET IN A SHOWER BEFORE YOU LEAVE!
YES'M!
JAM

Script: Kathleen Webb / Pencils: Stan Goldberg / Inks: John Lowe / Letters: Bill Yoshida

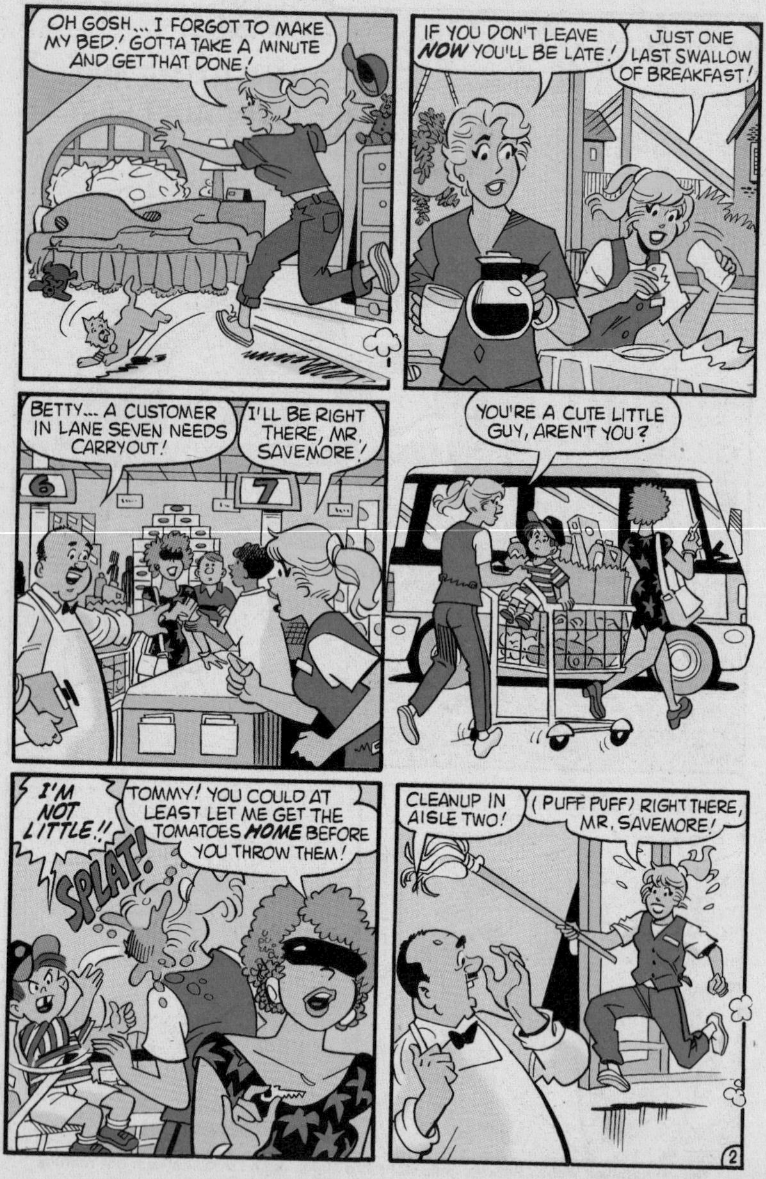
OH GOSH... I FORGOT TO MAKE MY BED! GOTTA TAKE A MINUTE AND GET THAT DONE!
IF YOU DON'T LEAVE NOW YOU'LL BE LATE!
JUST ONE LAST SWALLOW OF BREAKFAST!
BETTY... A CUSTOMER IN LANE SEVEN NEEDS CARRYOUT!
I'LL BE RIGHT THERE, MR. SAVEMORE!
6
7
YOU'RE A CUTE LITTLE GUY, AREN'T YOU?
I'M NOT LITTLE!!
TOMMY! YOU COULD AT LEAST LET ME GET THE TOMATOES HOME BEFORE YOU THROW THEM!
SPLAT!
CLEANUP IN AISLE TWO!
(PUFF PUFF) RIGHT THERE, MR. SAVEMORE!

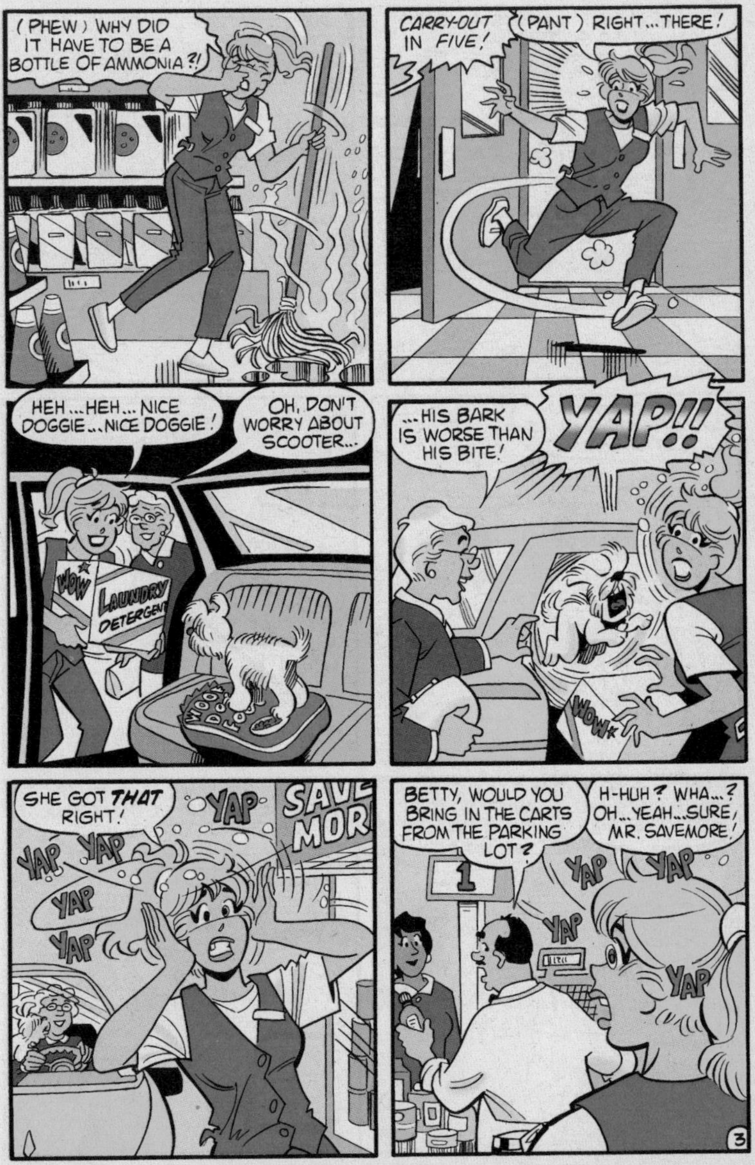

(PHEW) WHY DID IT HAVE TO BE A BOTTLE OF AMMONIA ?!
CARRY-OUT IN FIVE!
(PANT) RIGHT... THERE!
HEH... HEH... NICE DOGGIE... NICE DOGGIE!
OH, DON'T WORRY ABOUT SCOOTER...
WOW
LAUNDRY DETERGENT
...HIS BARK IS WORSE THAN HIS BITE!
YAP!!
WOW
SHE GOT THAT RIGHT!
YAP
YAP
YAP
YAP
YAP
BETTY, WOULD YOU BRING IN THE CARTS FROM THE PARKING LOT?
H-HUH? WHA...? OH... YEAH... SURE, MR. SAVEMORE!
YAP
YAP
YAP
YAP
1
3

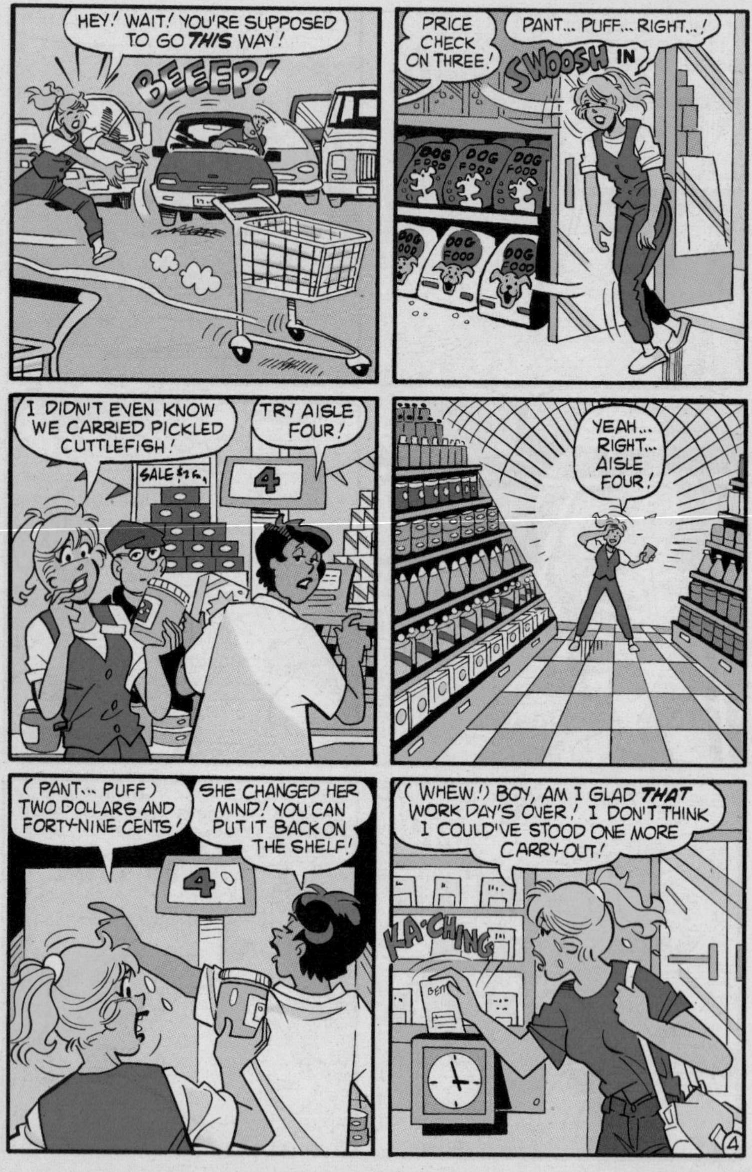
HEY! WAIT! YOU'RE SUPPOSED TO GO THIS WAY!
BEEEP!
PRICE CHECK ON THREE!
PANT... PUFF... RIGHT...!
SWOOSH IN
DOG FOOD
I DIDN'T EVEN KNOW WE CARRIED PICKLED CUTTLEFISH!
TRY AISLE FOUR!
4
YEAH... RIGHT... AISLE FOUR!
(PANT... PUFF) TWO DOLLARS AND FORTY-NINE CENTS!
SHE CHANGED HER MIND! YOU CAN PUT IT BACK ON THE SHELF!
4
(WHEW!) BOY, AM I GLAD THAT WORK DAY'S OVER! I DON'T THINK I COULD'VE STOOD ONE MORE CARRY-OUT!
KA-CHING
4

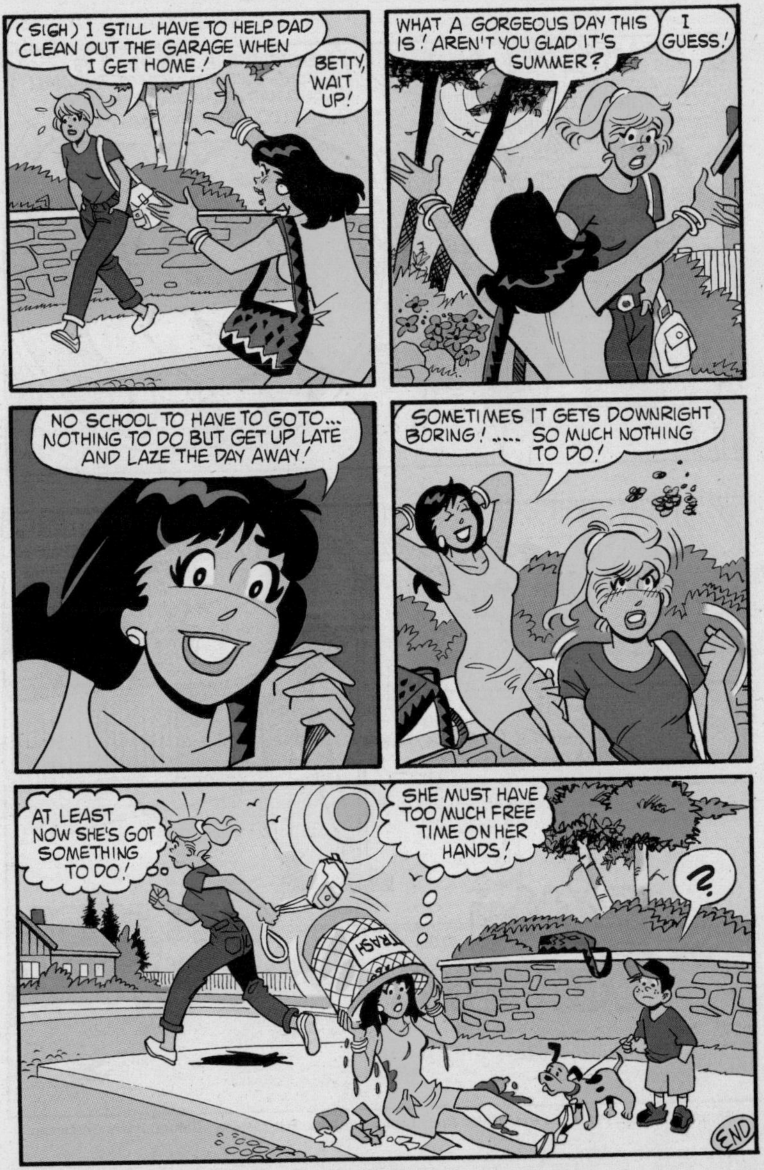
(SIGH) I STILL HAVE TO HELP DAD CLEAN OUT THE GARAGE WHEN I GET HOME!
BETTY, WAIT UP!
WHAT A GORGEOUS DAY THIS IS! AREN'T YOU GLAD IT'S SUMMER?
I GUESS!
NO SCHOOL TO HAVE TO GO TO... NOTHING TO DO BUT GET UP LATE AND LAZE THE DAY AWAY!
SOMETIMES IT GETS DOWNRIGHT BORING! ..... SO MUCH NOTHING TO DO!
AT LEAST NOW SHE'S GOT SOMETHING TO DO!
SHE MUST HAVE TOO MUCH FREE TIME ON HER HANDS!
TRASH
?
END

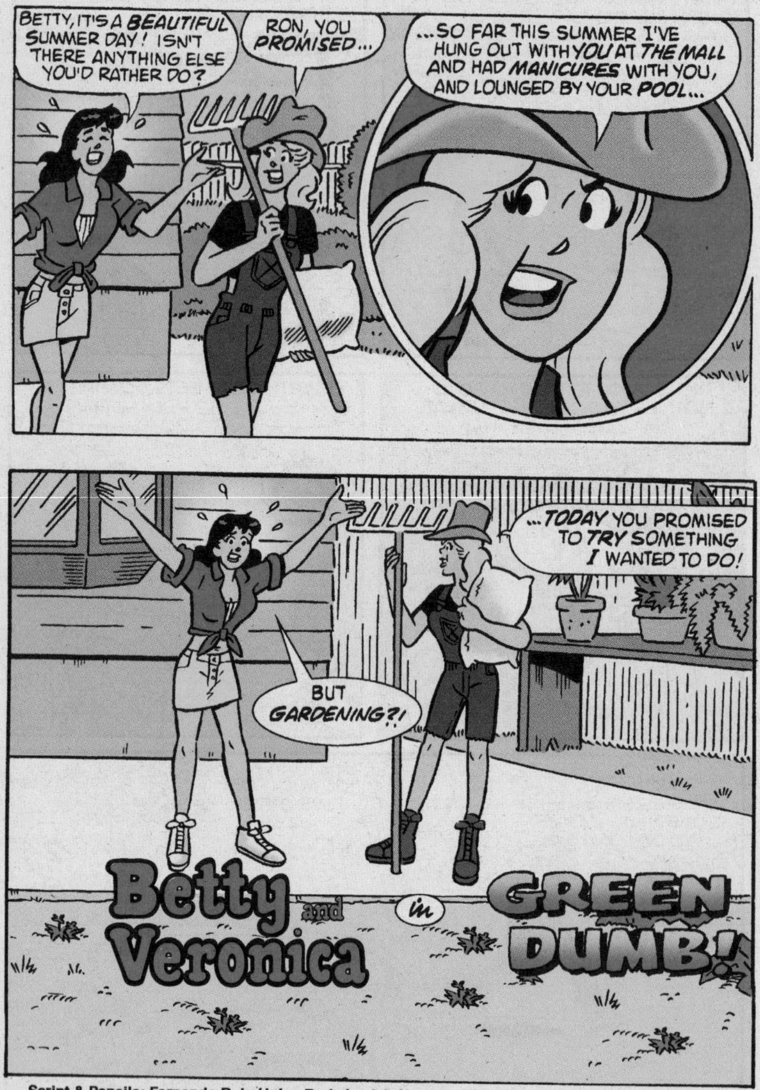
BETTY, IT'S A BEAUTIFUL SUMMER DAY! ISN'T THERE ANYTHING ELSE YOU'D RATHER DO?
RON, YOU PROMISED...
...SO FAR THIS SUMMER I'VE HUNG OUT WITH YOU AT THE MALL AND HAD MANICURES WITH YOU, AND LOUNGED BY YOUR POOL...
...TODAY YOU PROMISED TO TRY SOMETHING I WANTED TO DO!
BUT GARDENING?!
Betty and Veronica in GREEN DUMB!

Script & Pencils: Fernando Ruiz / Inks: Rudy Lapick / Letters: Bill Yoshida / Colors: Barry Grossman

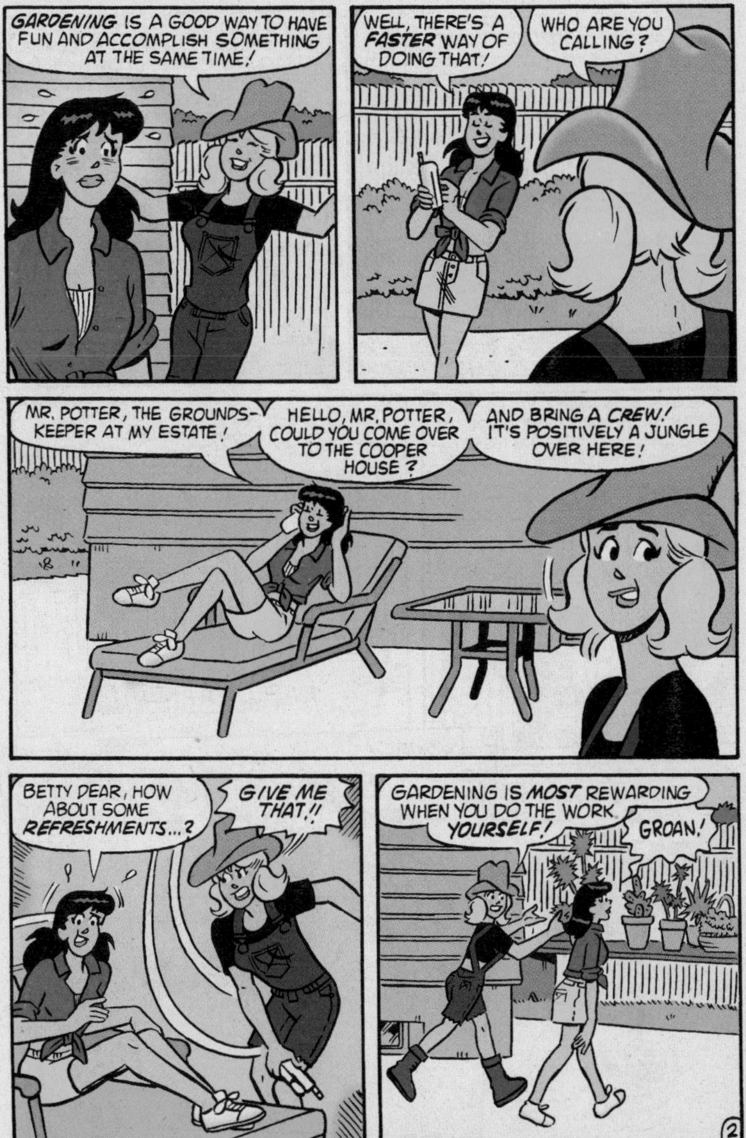
GARDENING IS A GOOD WAY TO HAVE FUN AND ACCOMPLISH SOMETHING AT THE SAME TIME!
WELL, THERE'S A FASTER WAY OF DOING THAT!
WHO ARE YOU CALLING?
MR. POTTER, THE GROUNDS-KEEPER AT MY ESTATE!
HELLO, MR. POTTER, COULD YOU COME OVER TO THE COOPER HOUSE?
AND BRING A CREW! IT'S POSITIVELY A JUNGLE OVER HERE!
BETTY DEAR, HOW ABOUT SOME REFRESHMENTS...?
GIVE ME THAT!!
GARDENING IS MOST REWARDING WHEN YOU DO THE WORK YOURSELF!
GROAN!
2

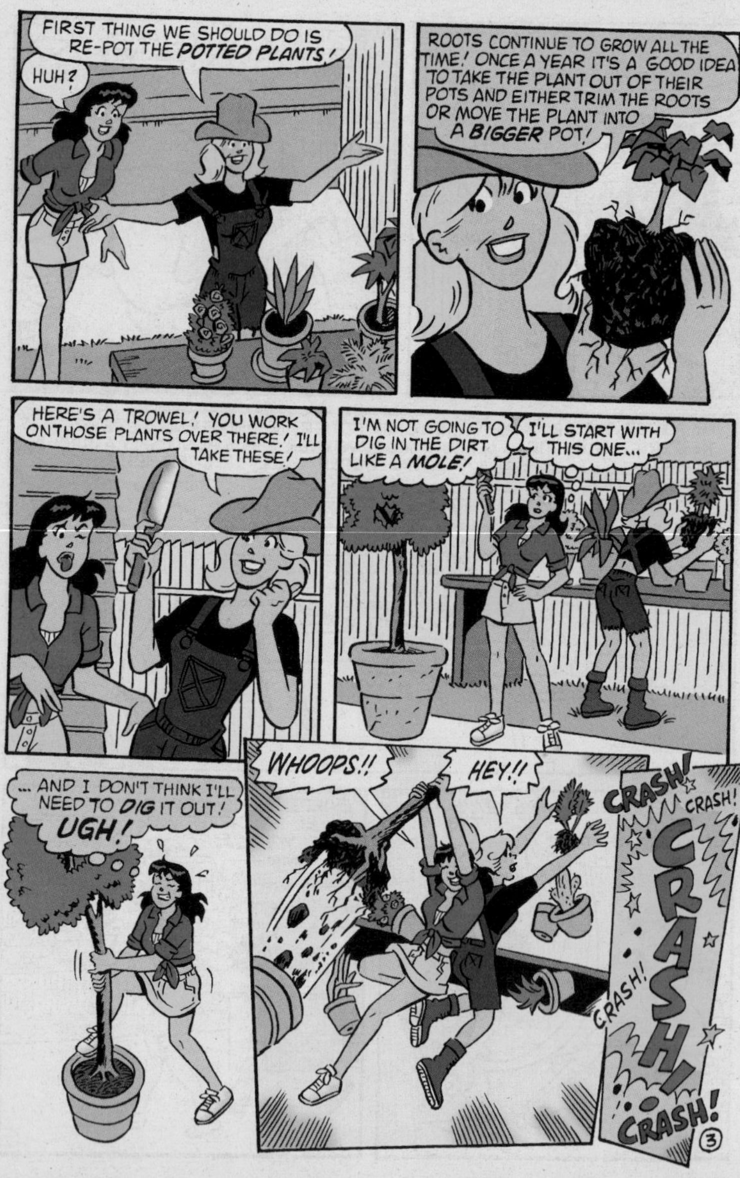
FIRST THING WE SHOULD DO IS RE-POT THE POTTED PLANTS!
HUH?
ROOTS CONTINUE TO GROW ALL THE TIME! ONCE A YEAR IT'S A GOOD IDEA TO TAKE THE PLANT OUT OF THEIR POTS AND EITHER TRIM THE ROOTS OR MOVE THE PLANT INTO A BIGGER POT!
HERE'S A TROWEL! YOU WORK ON THOSE PLANTS OVER THERE! I'LL TAKE THESE!
I'M NOT GOING TO DIG IN THE DIRT LIKE A MOLE!
I'LL START WITH THIS ONE...
... AND I DON'T THINK I'LL NEED TO DIG IT OUT! UGH!
WHOOPS!!
HEY!!
CRASH!
CRASH!
CRASH!
CRASH!
CRASH!
CRASH!
3

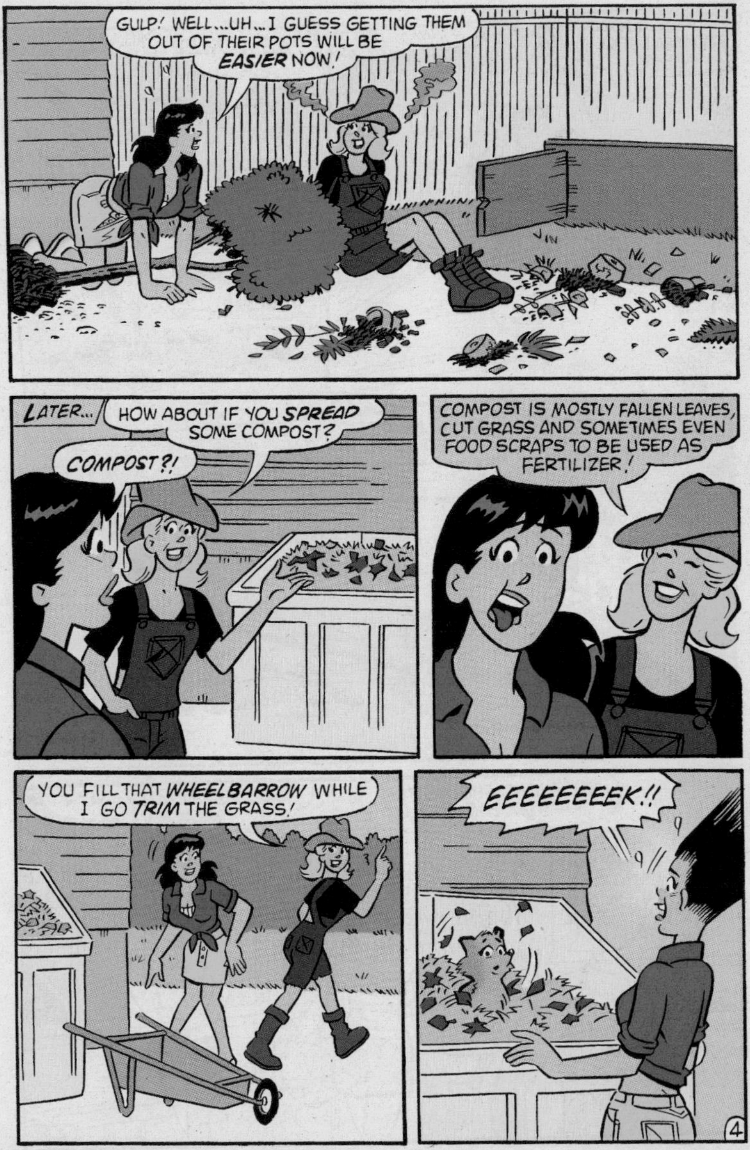

GULP! WELL...UH...I GUESS GETTING THEM OUT OF THEIR POTS WILL BE EASIER NOW!
LATER...
HOW ABOUT IF YOU SPREAD SOME COMPOST?
COMPOST?!
COMPOST IS MOSTLY FALLEN LEAVES, CUT GRASS AND SOMETIMES EVEN FOOD SCRAPS TO BE USED AS FERTILIZER!
YOU FILL THAT WHEELBARROW WHILE I GO TRIM THE GRASS!
EEEEEEEEK!!
4

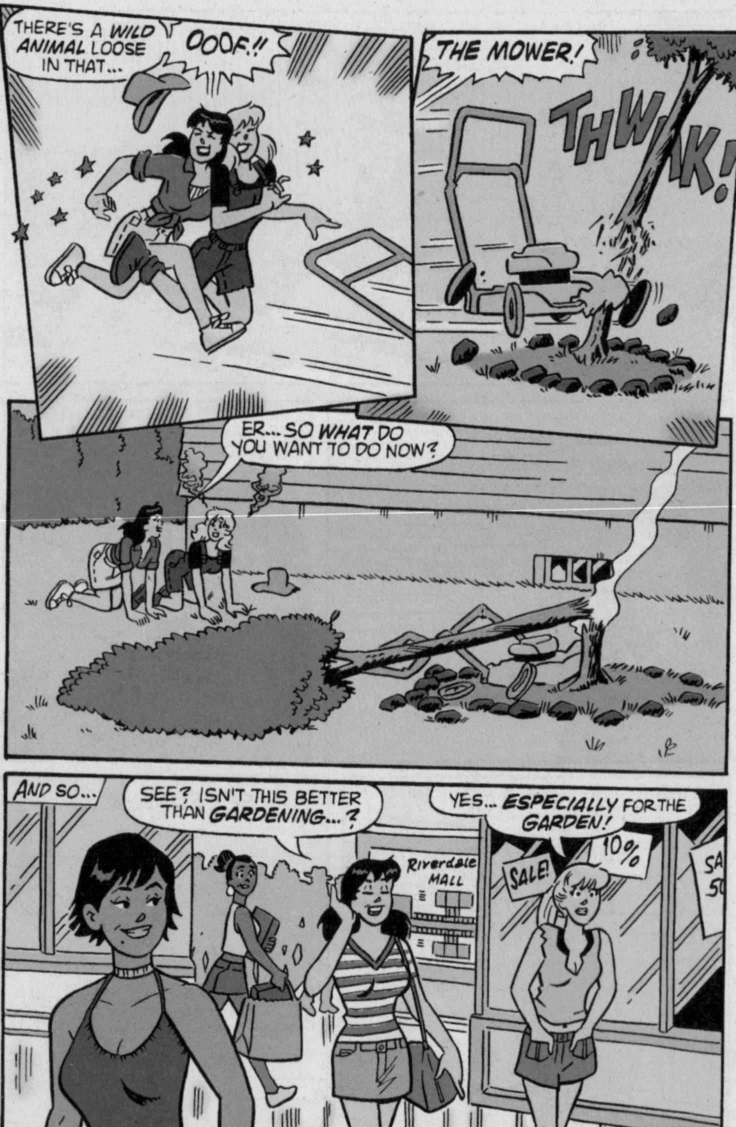
THERE'S A WILD ANIMAL LOOSE IN THAT...
OOOF.!!
THE MOWER!
THWAK!
ER... SO WHAT DO YOU WANT TO DO NOW?
AND SO...
SEE? ISN'T THIS BETTER THAN GARDENING...?
YES... ESPECIALLY FOR THE GARDEN!
Riverdale MALL
SALE!
10%
END

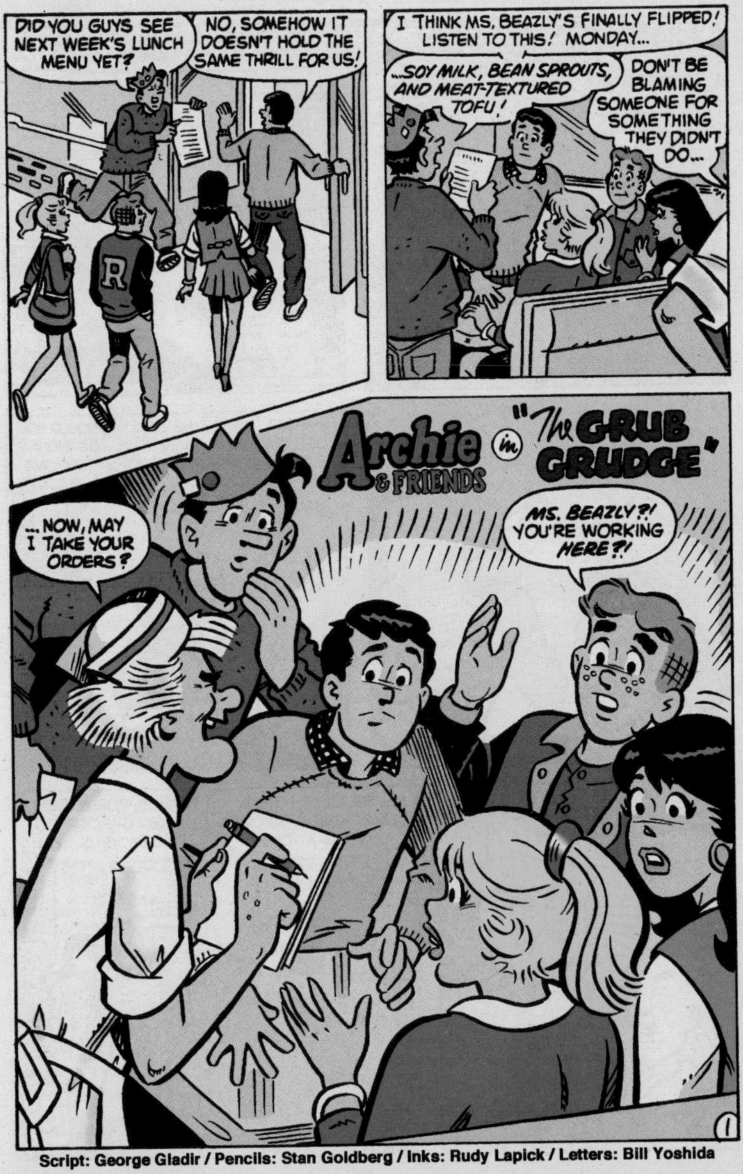

DID YOU GUYS SEE NEXT WEEK'S LUNCH MENU YET?
NO, SOMEHOW IT DOESN'T HOLD THE SAME THRILL FOR US!
I THINK MS. BEAZLY'S FINALLY FLIPPED! LISTEN TO THIS! MONDAY...
...SOY MILK, BEAN SPROUTS, AND MEAT-TEXTURED TOFU!
DON'T BE BLAMING SOMEONE FOR SOMETHING THEY DIDN'T DO...
Archie & FRIENDS in "The GRUB GRUDGE"
...NOW, MAY I TAKE YOUR ORDERS?
MS. BEAZLY?! YOU'RE WORKING HERE?!
1

Script: George Gladir / Pencils: Stan Goldberg / Inks: Rudy Lapick / Letters: Bill Yoshida

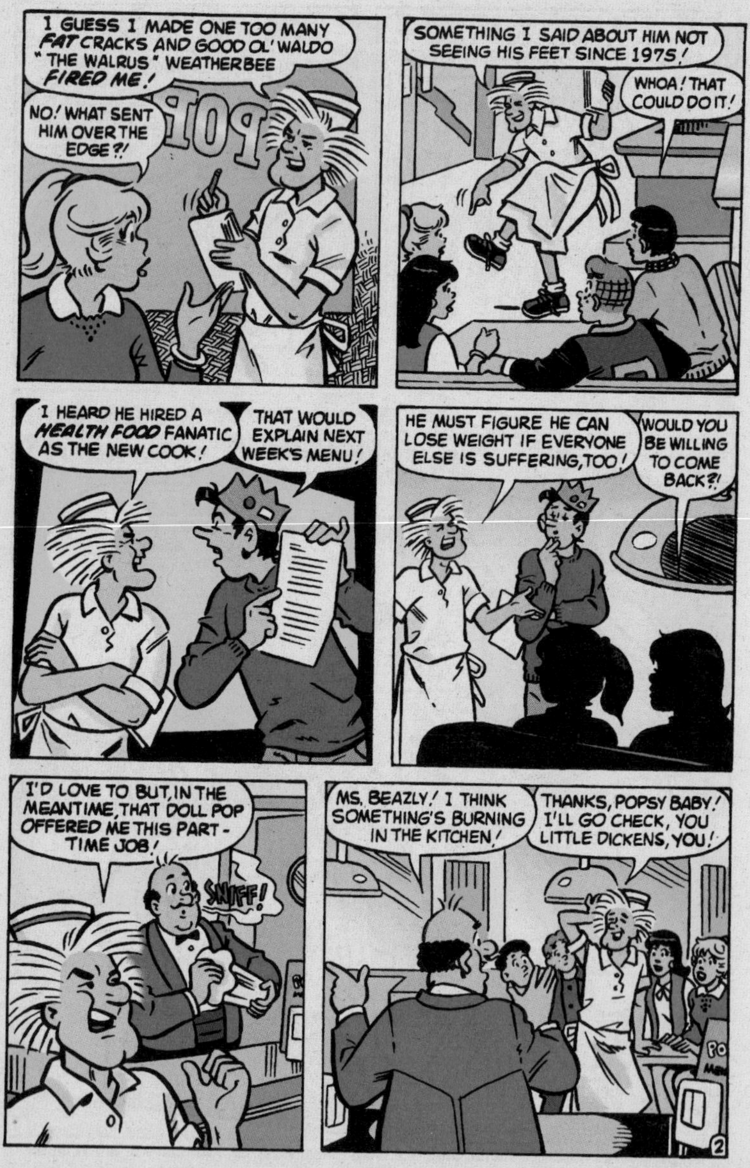

I GUESS I MADE ONE TOO MANY FAT CRACKS AND GOOD OL' WALDO "THE WALRUS" WEATHERBEE FIRED ME!
NO! WHAT SENT HIM OVER THE EDGE?!
POP
SOMETHING I SAID ABOUT HIM NOT SEEING HIS FEET SINCE 1975!
WHOA! THAT COULD DO IT!
I HEARD HE HIRED A HEALTH FOOD FANATIC AS THE NEW COOK!
THAT WOULD EXPLAIN NEXT WEEK'S MENU!
HE MUST FIGURE HE CAN LOSE WEIGHT IF EVERYONE ELSE IS SUFFERING, TOO!
WOULD YOU BE WILLING TO COME BACK?!
I'D LOVE TO BUT, IN THE MEANTIME, THAT DOLL POP OFFERED ME THIS PART-TIME JOB!
SNIFF!
MS. BEAZLY! I THINK SOMETHING'S BURNING IN THE KITCHEN!
THANKS, POPSY BABY! I'LL GO CHECK, YOU LITTLE DICKENS, YOU!
2

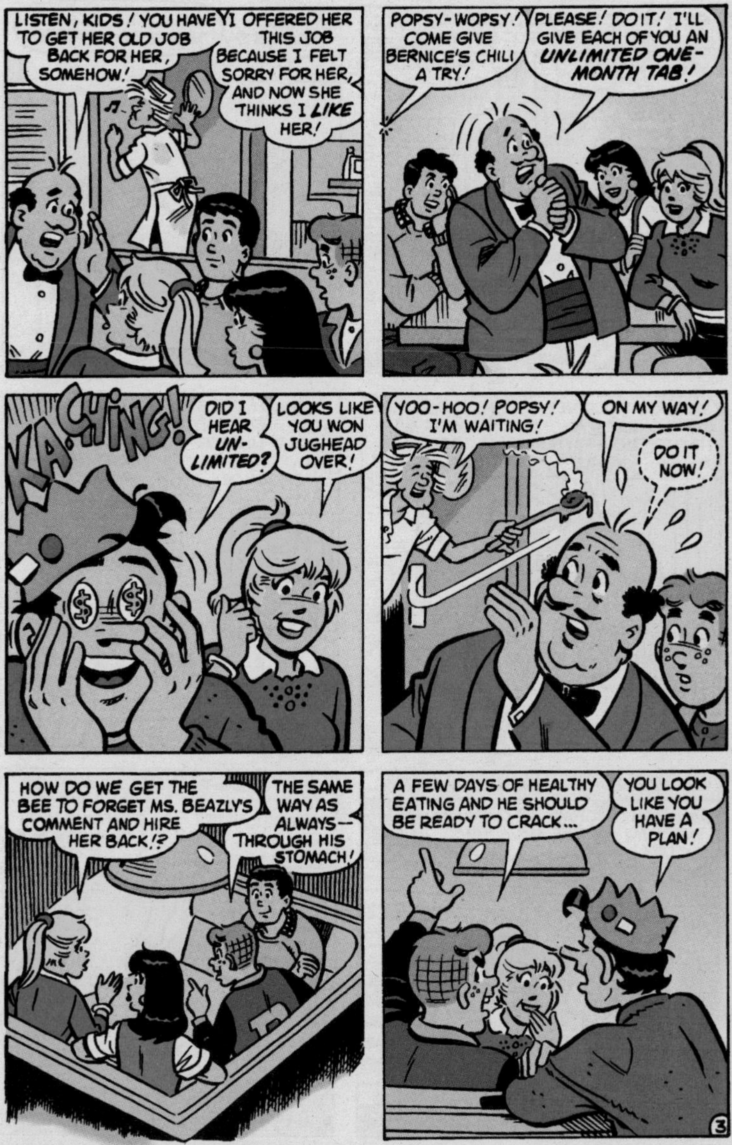
LISTEN, KIDS! YOU HAVE TO GET HER OLD JOB BACK FOR HER, SOMEHOW!
I OFFERED HER THIS JOB BECAUSE I FELT SORRY FOR HER, AND NOW SHE THINKS I LIKE HER!
POPSY-WOPSY! COME GIVE BERNICE'S CHILI A TRY!
PLEASE! DO IT! I'LL GIVE EACH OF YOU AN UNLIMITED ONE-MONTH TAB!
KA-CHING!
DID I HEAR UN-LIMITED?
LOOKS LIKE YOU WON JUGHEAD OVER!
YOO-HOO! POPSY! I'M WAITING!
ON MY WAY!
DO IT NOW!
HOW DO WE GET THE BEE TO FORGET MS. BEAZLY'S COMMENT AND HIRE HER BACK!?
THE SAME WAY AS ALWAYS-- THROUGH HIS STOMACH!
A FEW DAYS OF HEALTHY EATING AND HE SHOULD BE READY TO CRACK...
YOU LOOK LIKE YOU HAVE A PLAN!
3

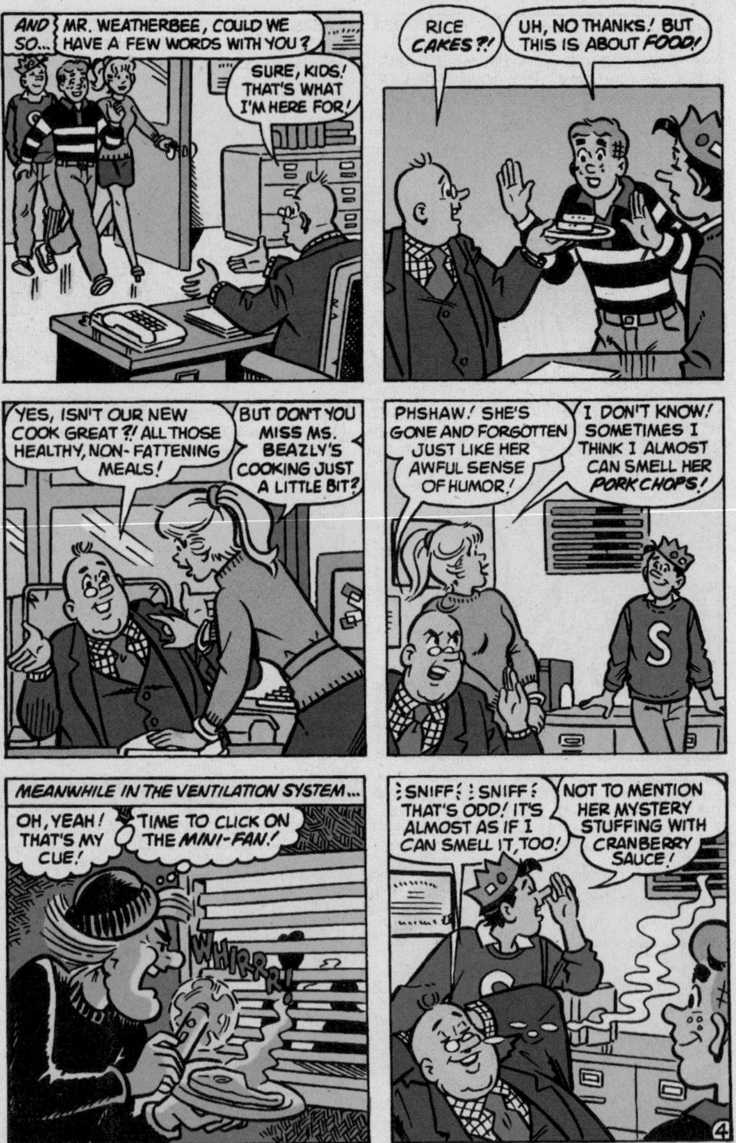
AND SO...
MR. WEATHERBEE, COULD WE HAVE A FEW WORDS WITH YOU?
SURE, KIDS! THAT'S WHAT I'M HERE FOR!
RICE CAKES?!
UH, NO THANKS! BUT THIS IS ABOUT FOOD!
YES, ISN'T OUR NEW COOK GREAT?! ALL THOSE HEALTHY, NON-FATTENING MEALS!
BUT DON'T YOU MISS MS. BEAZLY'S COOKING JUST A LITTLE BIT?
PHSHAW! SHE'S GONE AND FORGOTTEN JUST LIKE HER AWFUL SENSE OF HUMOR!
I DON'T KNOW! SOMETIMES I THINK I ALMOST CAN SMELL HER PORK CHOPS!
MEANWHILE IN THE VENTILATION SYSTEM...
OH, YEAH! THAT'S MY CUE!
TIME TO CLICK ON THE MINI-FAN!
WHIRRR!
SNIFF! SNIFF! THAT'S ODD! IT'S ALMOST AS IF I CAN SMELL IT, TOO!
NOT TO MENTION HER MYSTERY STUFFING WITH CRANBERRY SAUCE!
4

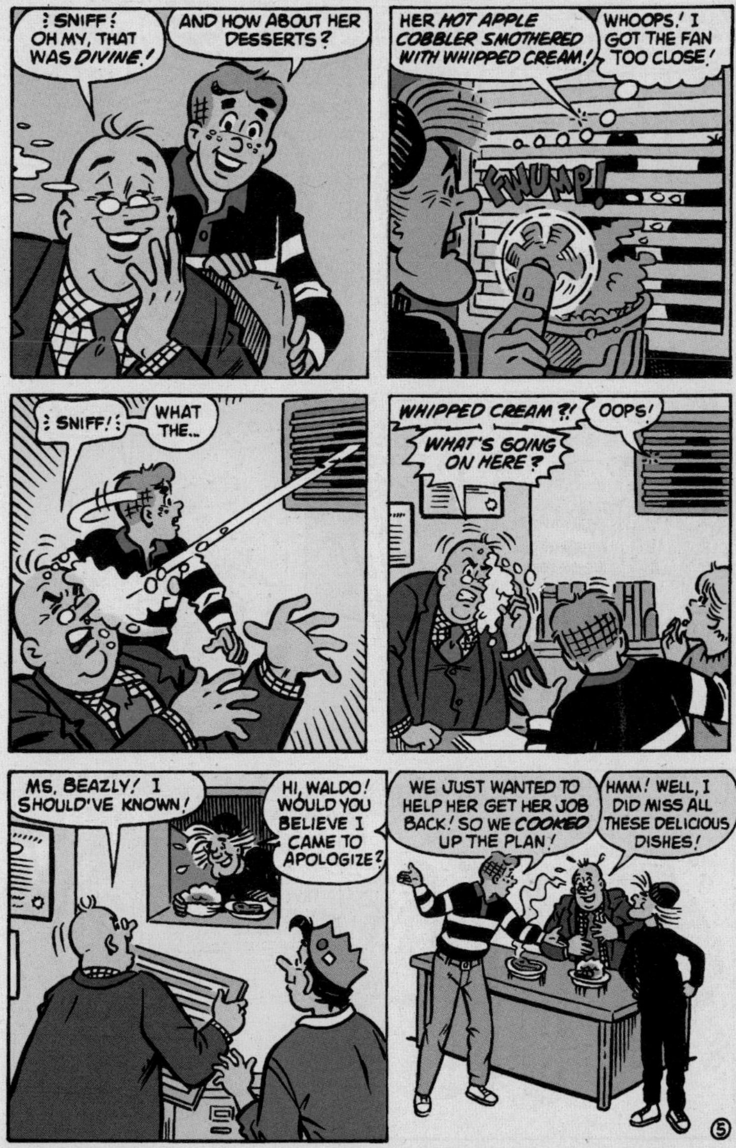

SNIFF! OH MY, THAT WAS DIVINE!
AND HOW ABOUT HER DESSERTS?
HER HOT APPLE COBBLER SMOTHERED WITH WHIPPED CREAM!
WHOOPS! I GOT THE FAN TOO CLOSE!
FWUMP!
SNIFF!
WHAT THE...
WHIPPED CREAM?!
WHAT'S GOING ON HERE?
OOPS!
MS. BEAZLY! I SHOULD'VE KNOWN!
HI, WALDO! WOULD YOU BELIEVE I CAME TO APOLOGIZE?
WE JUST WANTED TO HELP HER GET HER JOB BACK! SO WE COOKED UP THE PLAN!
HMM! WELL, I DID MISS ALL THESE DELICIOUS DISHES!
5

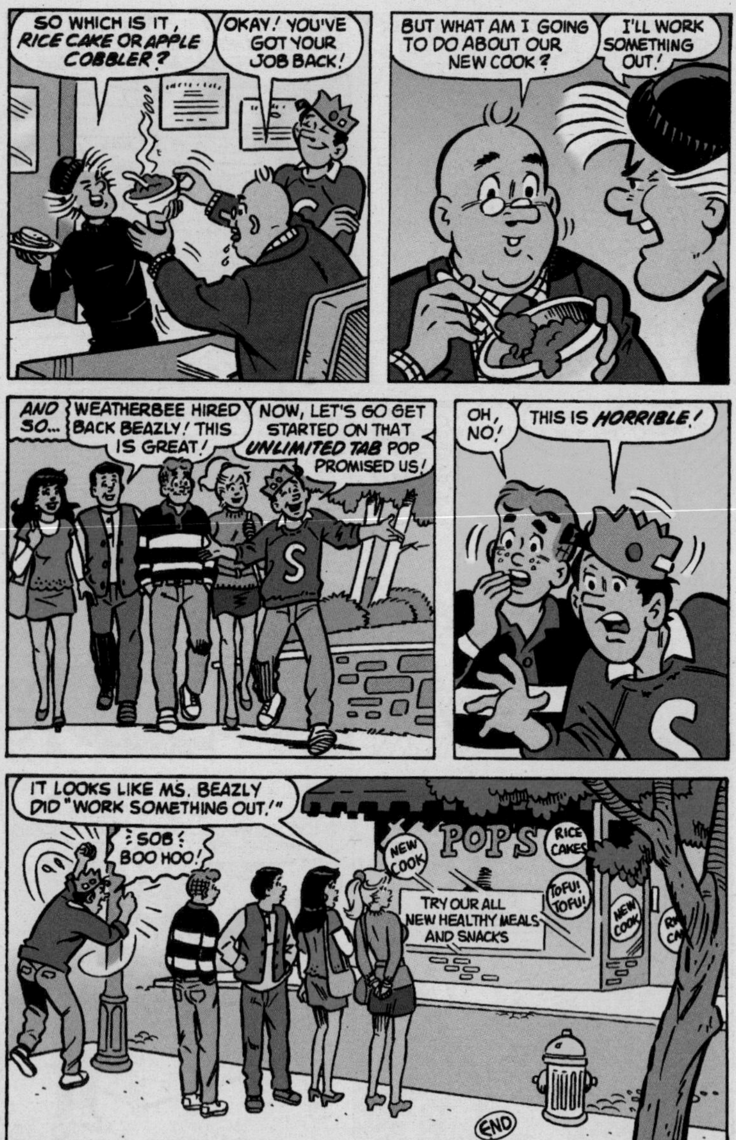
SO WHICH IS IT, RICE CAKE OR APPLE COBBLER?
OKAY! YOU'VE GOT YOUR JOB BACK!
BUT WHAT AM I GOING TO DO ABOUT OUR NEW COOK?
I'LL WORK SOMETHING OUT!
AND SO...
WEATHERBEE HIRED BACK BEAZLY! THIS IS GREAT!
NOW, LET'S GO GET STARTED ON THAT UNLIMITED TAB POP PROMISED US!
OH, NO!
THIS IS HORRIBLE!
IT LOOKS LIKE MS. BEAZLY DID "WORK SOMETHING OUT!"
SOB BOO HOO!
POP'S
NEW COOK
RICE CAKES
TOFU! TOFU!
TRY OUR ALL NEW HEALTHY MEALS AND SNACKS
NEW COOK
END

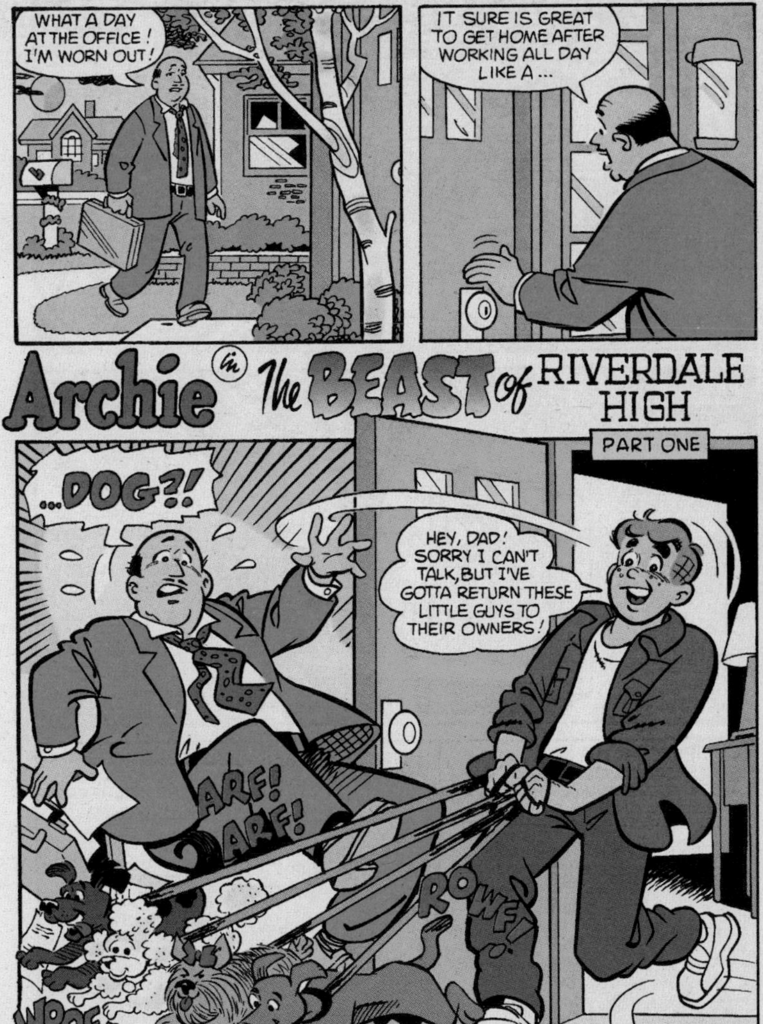
WHAT A DAY AT THE OFFICE! I'M WORN OUT!
IT SURE IS GREAT TO GET HOME AFTER WORKING ALL DAY LIKE A ...
Archie in The BEAST of RIVERDALE HIGH
PART ONE
...DOG?!
HEY, DAD! SORRY I CAN'T TALK, BUT I'VE GOTTA RETURN THESE LITTLE GUYS TO THEIR OWNERS!
ARF! ARF!
ROWF!
WOOF! WOOF!

Script: Angelo DeCesare / Pencils: Stan Goldberg / Inks: Bob Smith / Letters: Bill Yoshida / Colors: Barry Grossman

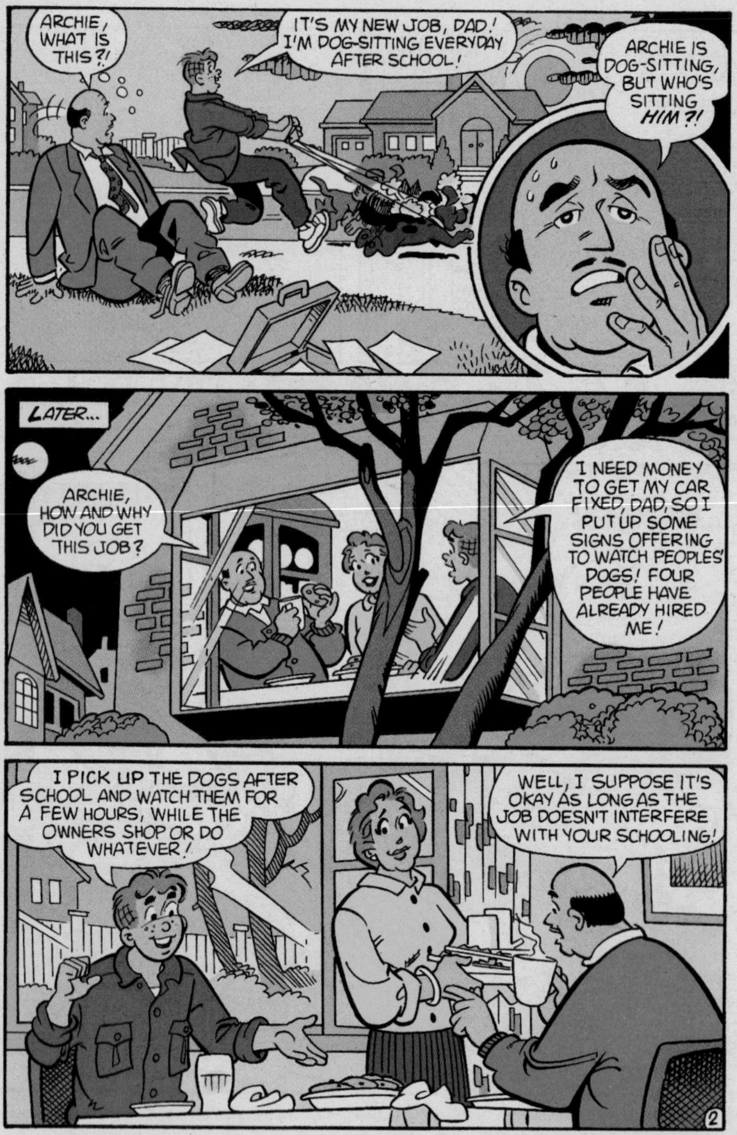
ARCHIE, WHAT IS THIS?!
IT'S MY NEW JOB, DAD! I'M DOG-SITTING EVERYDAY AFTER SCHOOL!
ARCHIE IS DOG-SITTING, BUT WHO'S SITTING HIM?!
LATER...
ARCHIE, HOW AND WHY DID YOU GET THIS JOB?
I NEED MONEY TO GET MY CAR FIXED, DAD, SO I PUT UP SOME SIGNS OFFERING TO WATCH PEOPLES' DOGS! FOUR PEOPLE HAVE ALREADY HIRED ME!
I PICK UP THE DOGS AFTER SCHOOL AND WATCH THEM FOR A FEW HOURS, WHILE THE OWNERS SHOP OR DO WHATEVER!
WELL, I SUPPOSE IT'S OKAY AS LONG AS THE JOB DOESN'T INTERFERE WITH YOUR SCHOOLING!
2

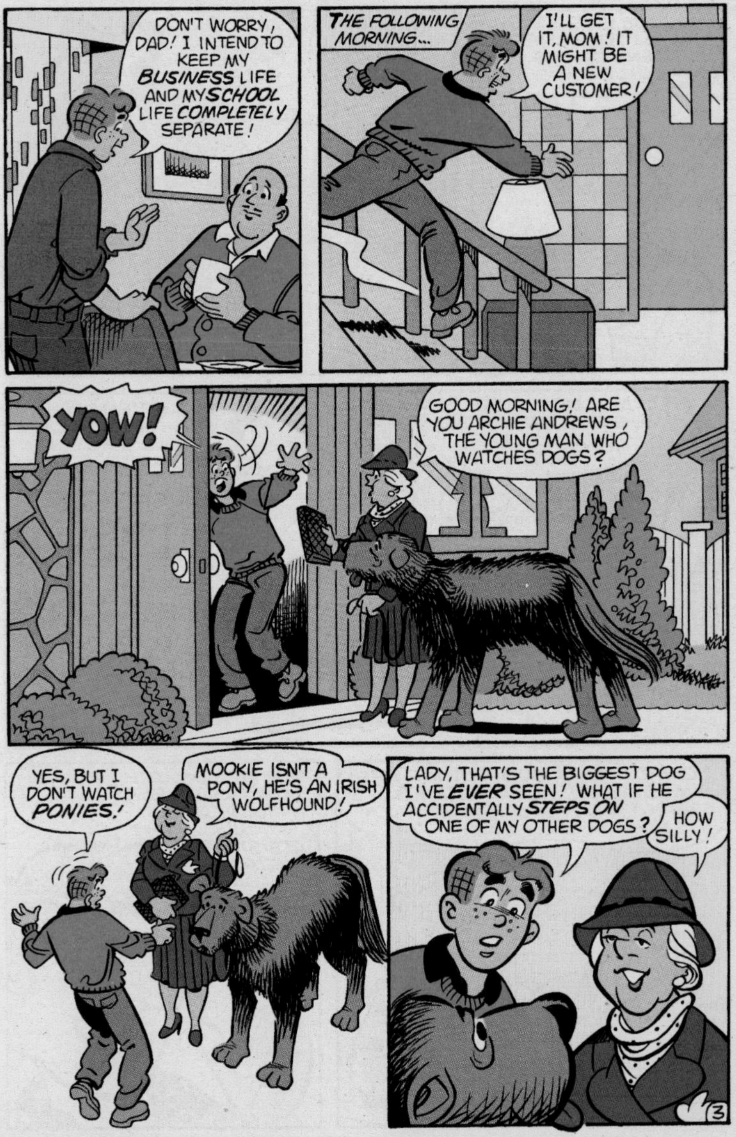
DON'T WORRY, DAD! I INTEND TO KEEP MY BUSINESS LIFE AND MY SCHOOL LIFE COMPLETELY SEPARATE!
THE FOLLOWING MORNING...
I'LL GET IT, MOM! IT MIGHT BE A NEW CUSTOMER!
YOW!
GOOD MORNING! ARE YOU ARCHIE ANDREWS, THE YOUNG MAN WHO WATCHES DOGS?
YES, BUT I DON'T WATCH PONIES!
MOOKIE ISN'T A PONY, HE'S AN IRISH WOLFHOUND!
LADY, THAT'S THE BIGGEST DOG I'VE EVER SEEN! WHAT IF HE ACCIDENTALLY STEPS ON ONE OF MY OTHER DOGS?
HOW SILLY!
3

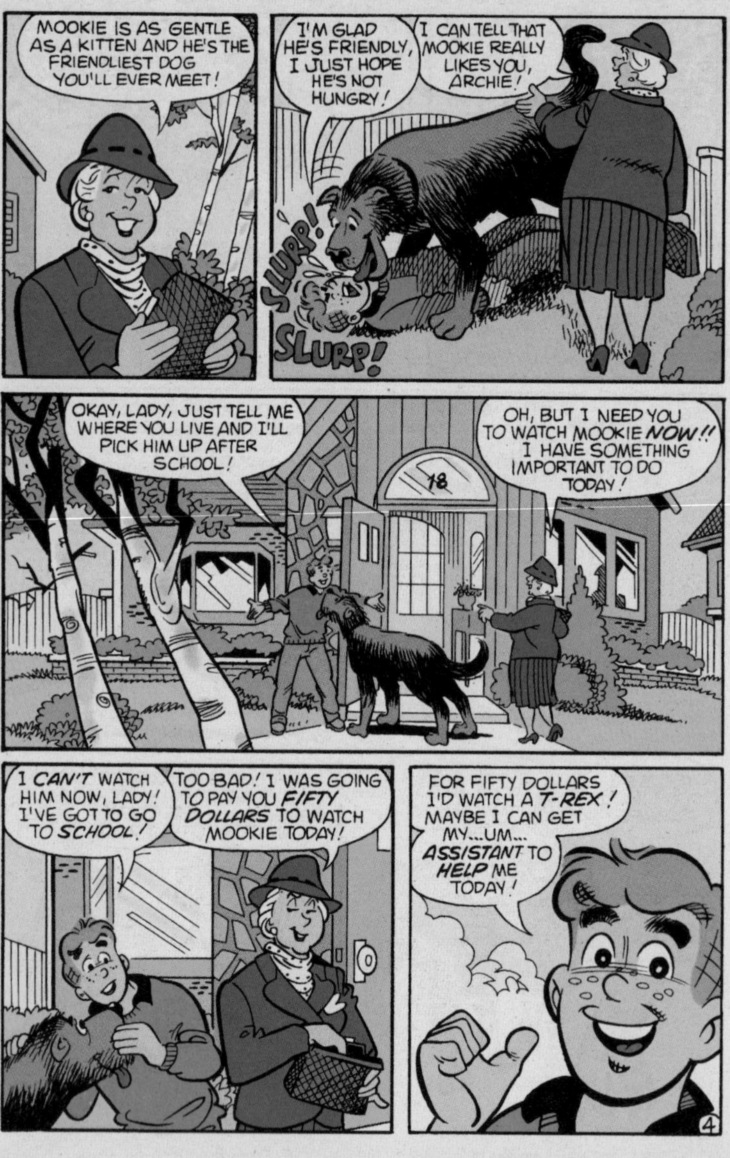
MOOKIE IS AS GENTLE AS A KITTEN AND HE'S THE FRIENDLIEST DOG YOU'LL EVER MEET!
I'M GLAD HE'S FRIENDLY, I JUST HOPE HE'S NOT HUNGRY!
I CAN TELL THAT MOOKIE REALLY LIKES YOU, ARCHIE!
SLURP!
SLURP!
OKAY, LADY, JUST TELL ME WHERE YOU LIVE AND I'LL PICK HIM UP AFTER SCHOOL!
OH, BUT I NEED YOU TO WATCH MOOKIE NOW!! I HAVE SOMETHING IMPORTANT TO DO TODAY!
18
I CAN'T WATCH HIM NOW, LADY! I'VE GOT TO GO TO SCHOOL!
TOO BAD! I WAS GOING TO PAY YOU FIFTY DOLLARS TO WATCH MOOKIE TODAY!
FOR FIFTY DOLLARS I'D WATCH A T-REX! MAYBE I CAN GET MY...UM... ASSISTANT TO HELP ME TODAY!
4

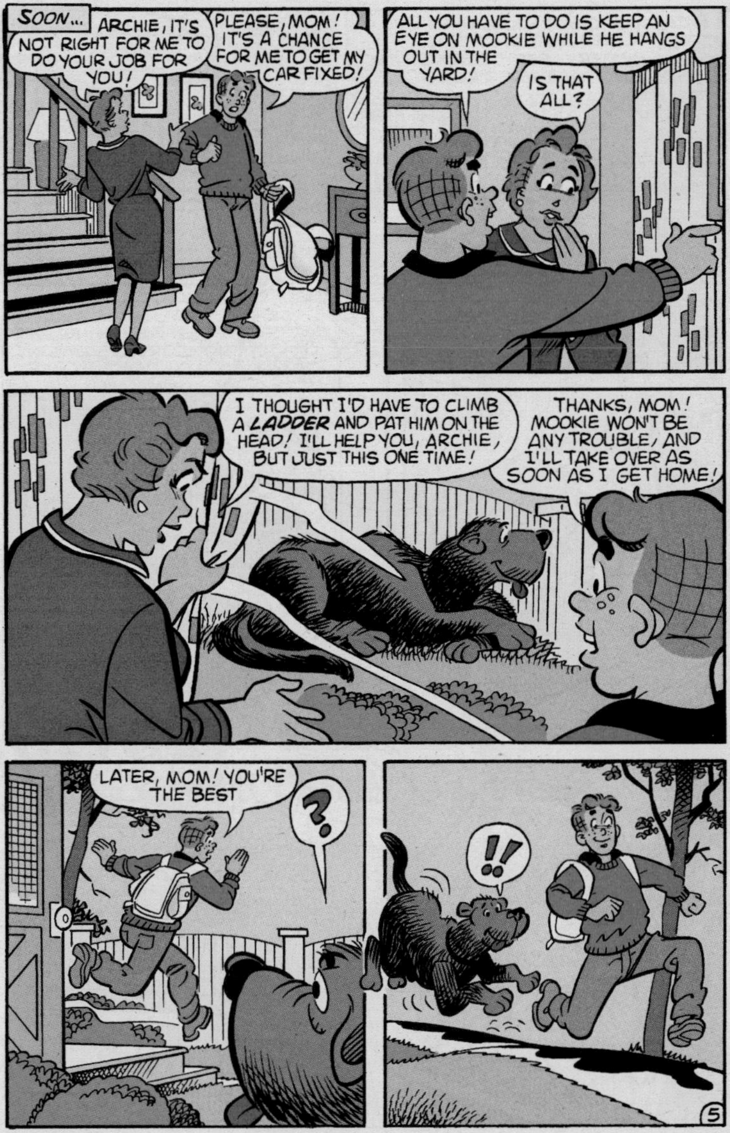
SOON...
ARCHIE, IT'S NOT RIGHT FOR ME TO DO YOUR JOB FOR YOU!
PLEASE, MOM! IT'S A CHANCE FOR ME TO GET MY CAR FIXED!
ALL YOU HAVE TO DO IS KEEP AN EYE ON MOOKIE WHILE HE HANGS OUT IN THE YARD!
IS THAT ALL?
I THOUGHT I'D HAVE TO CLIMB A LADDER AND PAT HIM ON THE HEAD! I'LL HELP YOU, ARCHIE, BUT JUST THIS ONE TIME!
THANKS, MOM! MOOKIE WON'T BE ANY TROUBLE, AND I'LL TAKE OVER AS SOON AS I GET HOME!
LATER, MOM! YOU'RE THE BEST
?
!!
5

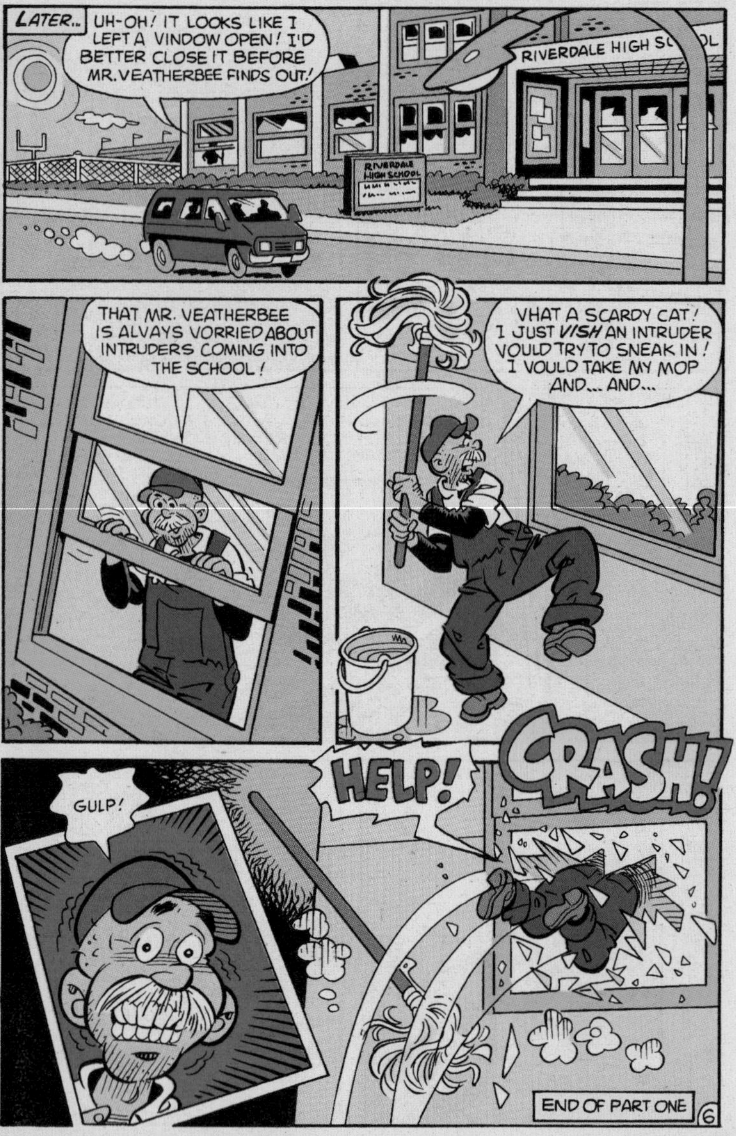
LATER...
UH-OH! IT LOOKS LIKE I LEFT A VINDOW OPEN! I'D BETTER CLOSE IT BEFORE MR. VEATHERBEE FINDS OUT!
RIVERDALE HIGH SCHOOL
RIVERDALE HIGH SCHOOL
THAT MR. VEATHERBEE IS ALVAYS VORRIED ABOUT INTRUDERS COMING INTO THE SCHOOL!
VHAT A SCARDY CAT! I JUST VISH AN INTRUDER VOULD TRY TO SNEAK IN! I VOULD TAKE MY MOP AND... AND...
GULP!
HELP!
CRASH!
END OF PART ONE
6

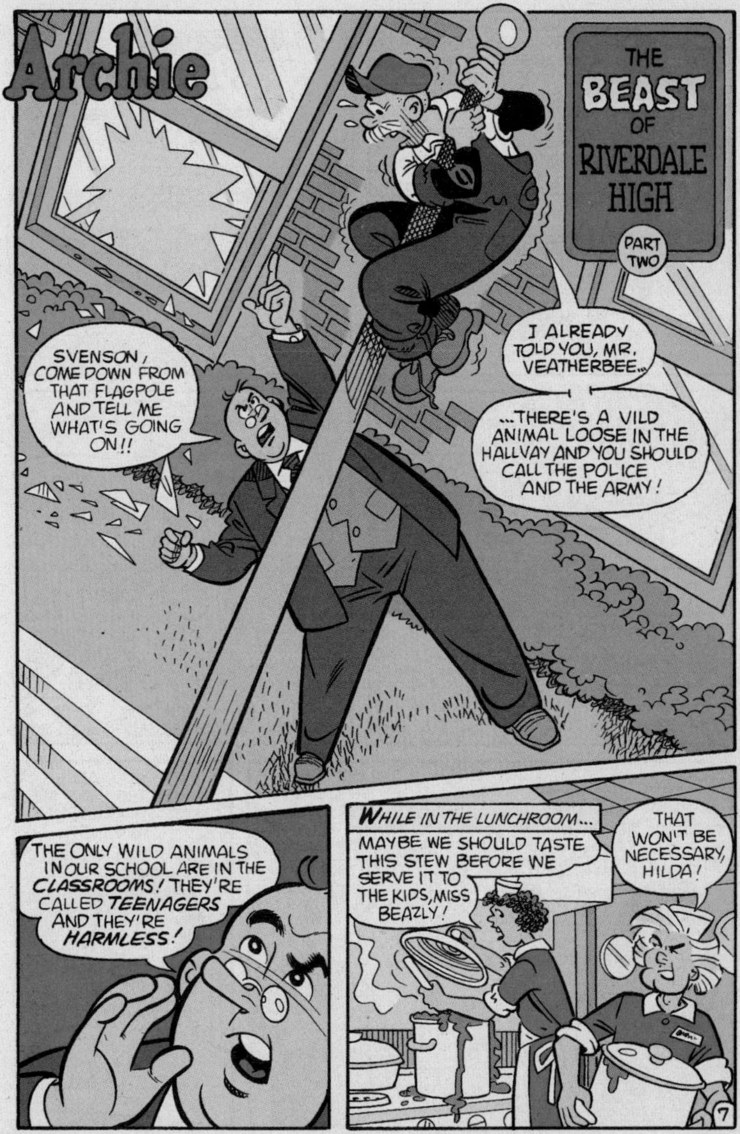
Archie
THE BEAST OF RIVERDALE HIGH
PART TWO
SVENSON, COME DOWN FROM THAT FLAGPOLE AND TELL ME WHAT'S GOING ON!!
I ALREADY TOLD YOU, MR. VEATHERBEE...
...THERE'S A VILD ANIMAL LOOSE IN THE HALLVAY AND YOU SHOULD CALL THE POLICE AND THE ARMY!
THE ONLY WILD ANIMALS IN OUR SCHOOL ARE IN THE CLASSROOMS! THEY'RE CALLED TEENAGERS AND THEY'RE HARMLESS!
WHILE IN THE LUNCHROOM...
MAYBE WE SHOULD TASTE THIS STEW BEFORE WE SERVE IT TO THE KIDS, MISS BEAZLY!
THAT WON'T BE NECESSARY, HILDA!

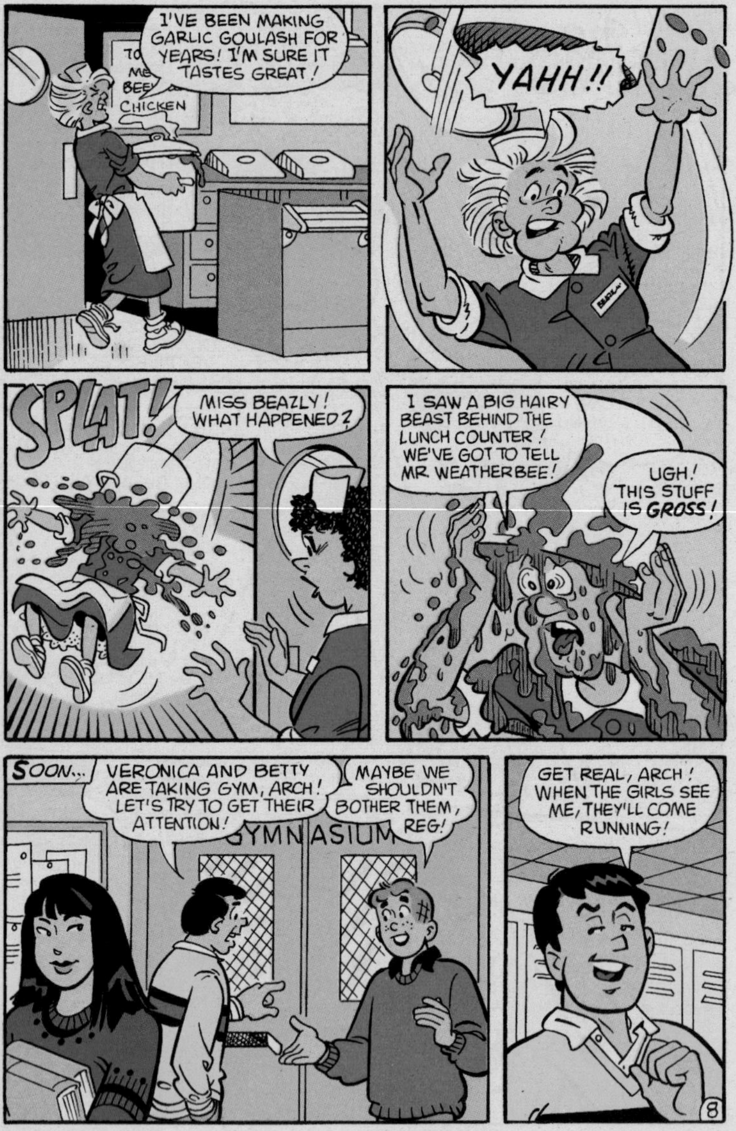
I'VE BEEN MAKING GARLIC GOULASH FOR YEARS! I'M SURE IT TASTES GREAT!
CHICKEN
YAHH!!
SPLAT!
MISS BEAZLY! WHAT HAPPENED?
I SAW A BIG HAIRY BEAST BEHIND THE LUNCH COUNTER! WE'VE GOT TO TELL MR. WEATHERBEE!
UGH! THIS STUFF IS GROSS!
SOON...
VERONICA AND BETTY ARE TAKING GYM, ARCH! LET'S TRY TO GET THEIR ATTENTION!
MAYBE WE SHOULDN'T BOTHER THEM, REG!
GYMNASIUM
GET REAL, ARCH! WHEN THE GIRLS SEE ME, THEY'LL COME RUNNING!
8

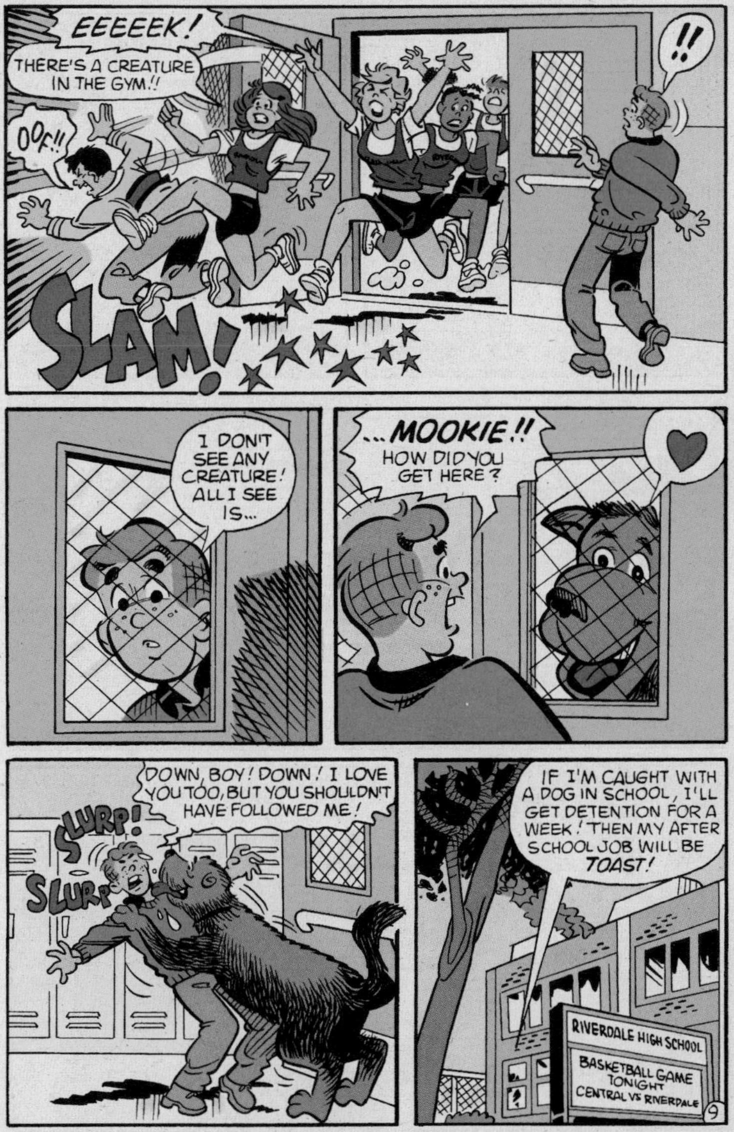
EEEEEK!
THERE'S A CREATURE IN THE GYM!!
OOF!!
SLAM!
!!
I DON'T SEE ANY CREATURE! ALL I SEE IS...
...MOOKIE!! HOW DID YOU GET HERE?
DOWN, BOY! DOWN! I LOVE YOU TOO, BUT YOU SHOULDN'T HAVE FOLLOWED ME!
SLURP!
SLURP
IF I'M CAUGHT WITH A DOG IN SCHOOL, I'LL GET DETENTION FOR A WEEK! THEN MY AFTER SCHOOL JOB WILL BE TOAST!
RIVERDALE HIGH SCHOOL
BASKETBALL GAME TONIGHT
CENTRAL VS RIVERDALE

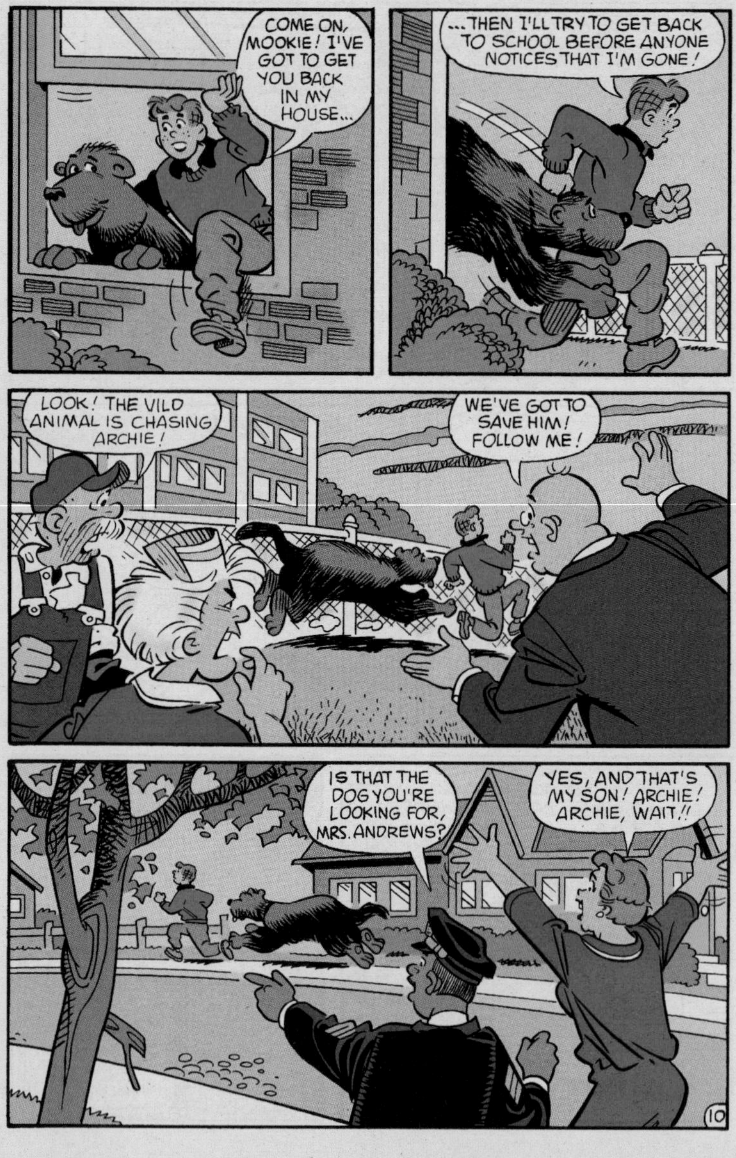
COME ON, MOOKIE! I'VE GOT TO GET YOU BACK IN MY HOUSE...
...THEN I'LL TRY TO GET BACK TO SCHOOL BEFORE ANYONE NOTICES THAT I'M GONE!
LOOK! THE VILD ANIMAL IS CHASING ARCHIE!
WE'VE GOT TO SAVE HIM! FOLLOW ME!
IS THAT THE DOG YOU'RE LOOKING FOR, MRS. ANDREWS?
YES, AND THAT'S MY SON! ARCHIE! ARCHIE, WAIT!!
10

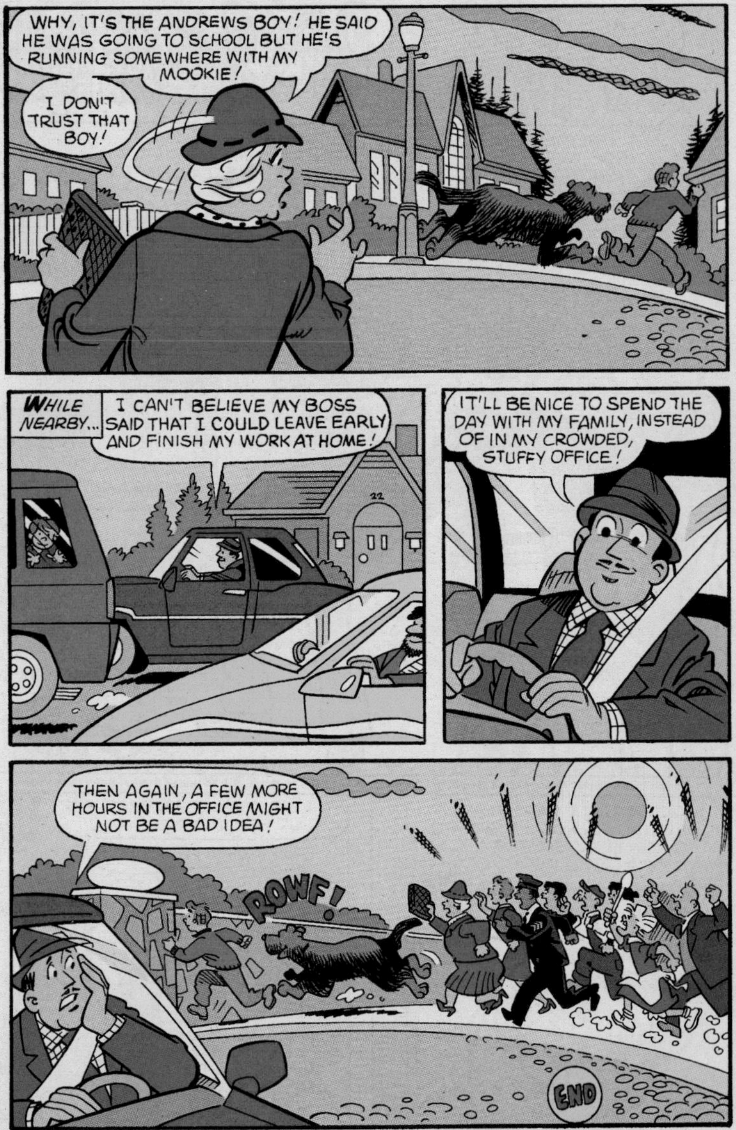

WHY, IT'S THE ANDREWS BOY! HE SAID HE WAS GOING TO SCHOOL BUT HE'S RUNNING SOMEWHERE WITH MY MOOKIE!
I DON'T TRUST THAT BOY!
WHILE NEARBY...
I CAN'T BELIEVE MY BOSS SAID THAT I COULD LEAVE EARLY AND FINISH MY WORK AT HOME!
22
IT'LL BE NICE TO SPEND THE DAY WITH MY FAMILY, INSTEAD OF IN MY CROWDED, STUFFY OFFICE!
THEN AGAIN, A FEW MORE HOURS IN THE OFFICE MIGHT NOT BE A BAD IDEA!
ROWF!
END

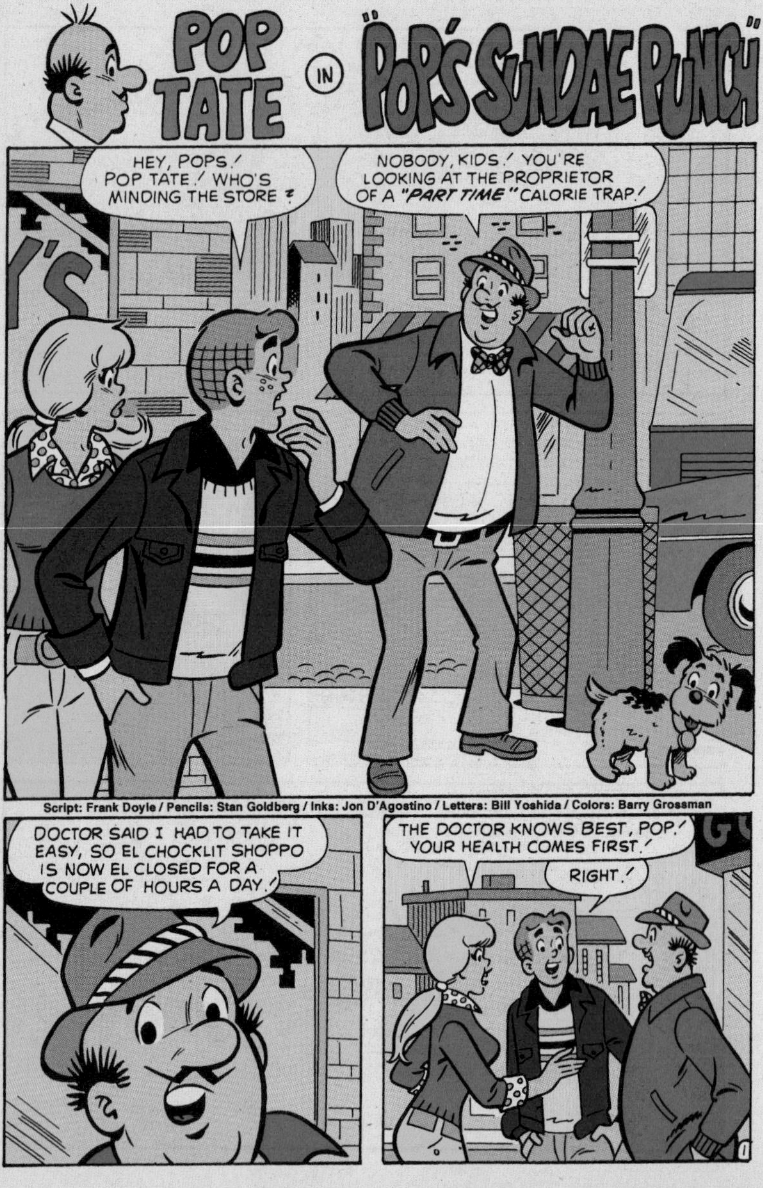
POP TATE IN "POP'S SUNDAE PUNCH"
HEY, POPS! POP TATE! WHO'S MINDING THE STORE ?
NOBODY, KIDS! YOU'RE LOOKING AT THE PROPRIETOR OF A "PART TIME" CALORIE TRAP!
Y'S
Script: Frank Doyle / Pencils: Stan Goldberg / Inks: Jon D'Agostino / Letters: Bill Yoshida / Colors: Barry Grossman
DOCTOR SAID I HAD TO TAKE IT EASY, SO EL CHOCKLIT SHOPPO IS NOW EL CLOSED FOR A COUPLE OF HOURS A DAY!
THE DOCTOR KNOWS BEST, POP! YOUR HEALTH COMES FIRST!
RIGHT!
1

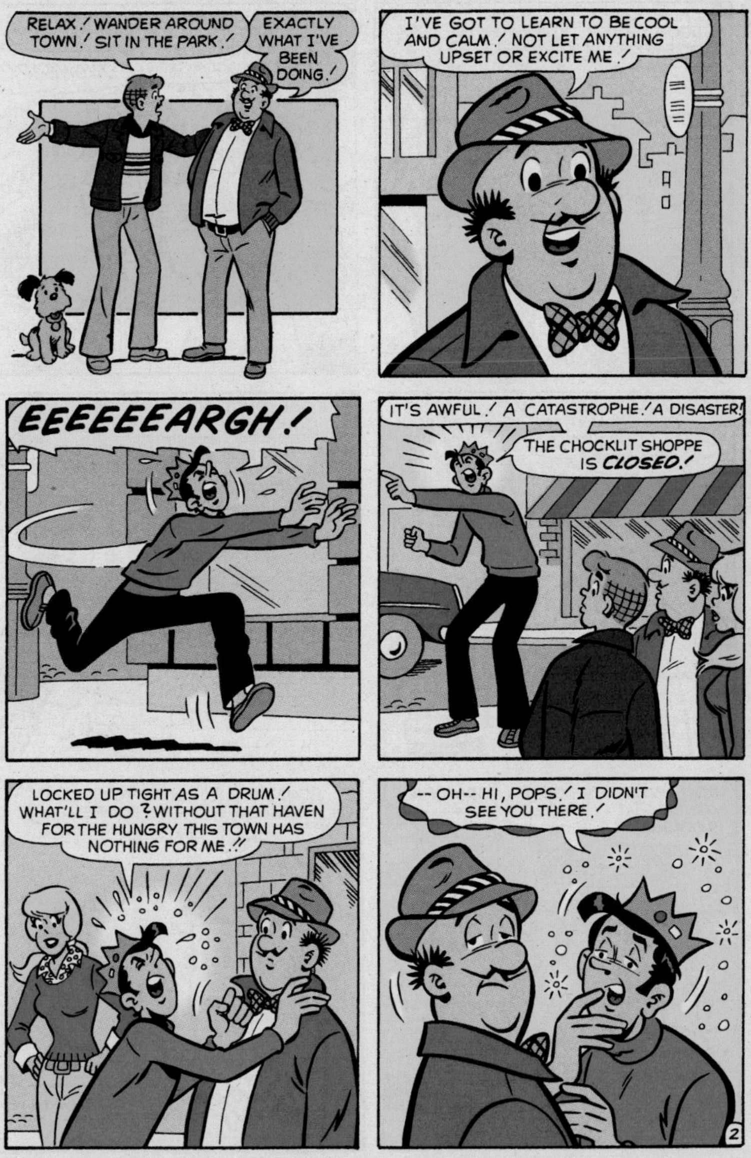
RELAX.! WANDER AROUND TOWN.! SIT IN THE PARK.!
EXACTLY WHAT I'VE BEEN DOING.!
I'VE GOT TO LEARN TO BE COOL AND CALM.! NOT LET ANYTHING UPSET OR EXCITE ME.!
EEEEEEEARGH!
IT'S AWFUL.! A CATASTROPHE.! A DISASTER!
THE CHOCKLIT SHOPPE IS CLOSED.!
LOCKED UP TIGHT AS A DRUM.! WHAT'LL I DO? WITHOUT THAT HAVEN FOR THE HUNGRY THIS TOWN HAS NOTHING FOR ME.!!
-- OH-- HI, POPS.! I DIDN'T SEE YOU THERE.!
2

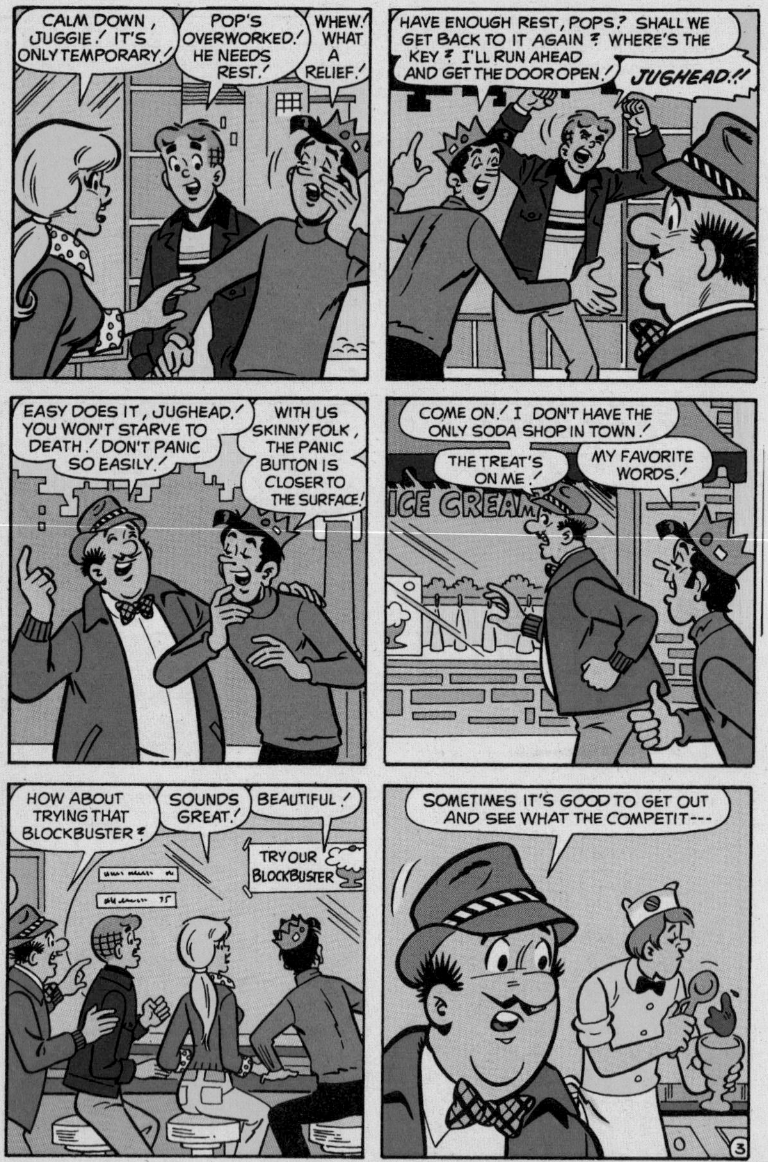

CALM DOWN, JUGGIE! IT'S ONLY TEMPORARY!
POP'S OVERWORKED! HE NEEDS REST!
WHEW! WHAT A RELIEF!
HAVE ENOUGH REST, POPS? SHALL WE GET BACK TO IT AGAIN? WHERE'S THE KEY? I'LL RUN AHEAD AND GET THE DOOR OPEN!
JUGHEAD!!
EASY DOES IT, JUGHEAD! YOU WON'T STARVE TO DEATH! DON'T PANIC SO EASILY!
WITH US SKINNY FOLK, THE PANIC BUTTON IS CLOSER TO THE SURFACE!
COME ON! I DON'T HAVE THE ONLY SODA SHOP IN TOWN!
THE TREAT'S ON ME!
MY FAVORITE WORDS!
ICE CREAM
HOW ABOUT TRYING THAT BLOCKBUSTER?
SOUNDS GREAT!
BEAUTIFUL!
TRY OUR BLOCKBUSTER
SOMETIMES IT'S GOOD TO GET OUT AND SEE WHAT THE COMPETIT---

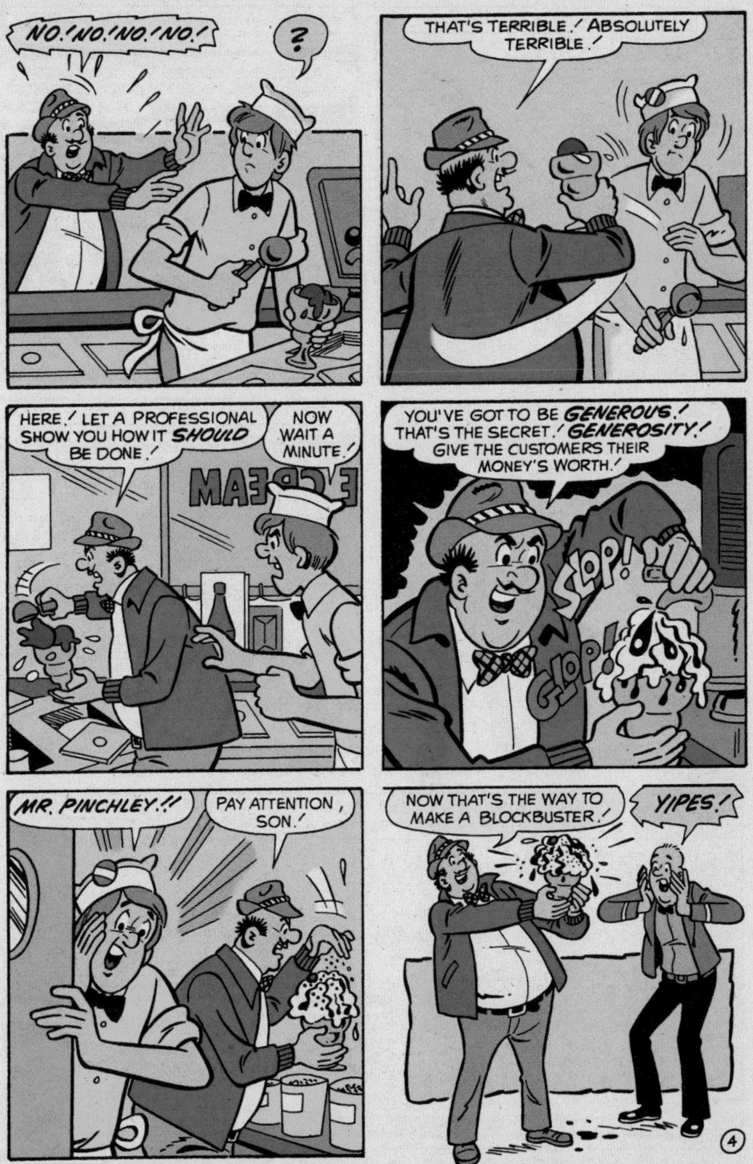
NO.! NO.! NO.! NO.!
?
THAT'S TERRIBLE.! ABSOLUTELY TERRIBLE.!
HERE.! LET A PROFESSIONAL SHOW YOU HOW IT SHOULD BE DONE.!
NOW WAIT A MINUTE.!
YOU'VE GOT TO BE GENEROUS.! THAT'S THE SECRET.! GENEROSITY.! GIVE THE CUSTOMERS THEIR MONEY'S WORTH.!
SLOP!
GLOP!
MR. PINCHLEY.!!
PAY ATTENTION, SON.!
NOW THAT'S THE WAY TO MAKE A BLOCKBUSTER.!
YIPES.!

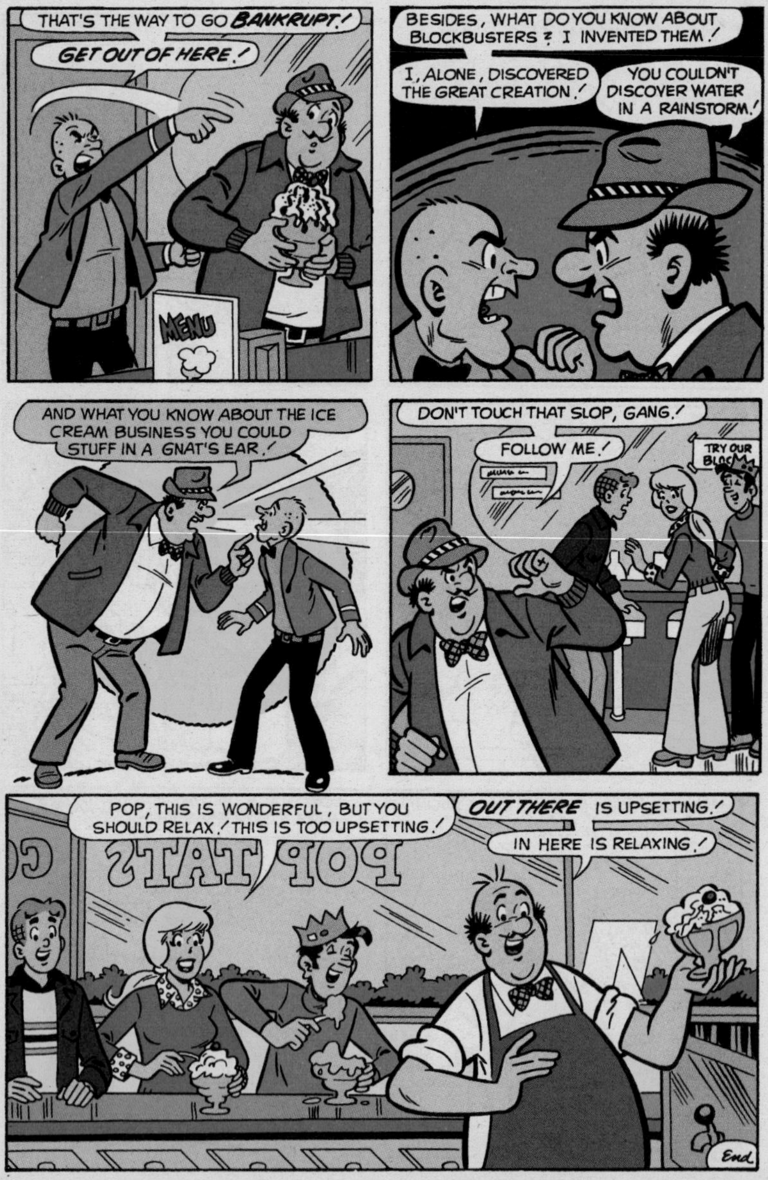

THAT'S THE WAY TO GO BANKRUPT!
GET OUT OF HERE!
MENU
BESIDES, WHAT DO YOU KNOW ABOUT BLOCKBUSTERS? I INVENTED THEM!
I, ALONE, DISCOVERED THE GREAT CREATION!
YOU COULDN'T DISCOVER WATER IN A RAINSTORM!
AND WHAT YOU KNOW ABOUT THE ICE CREAM BUSINESS YOU COULD STUFF IN A GNAT'S EAR!
DON'T TOUCH THAT SLOP, GANG!
FOLLOW ME!
TRY OUR
POP, THIS IS WONDERFUL, BUT YOU SHOULD RELAX! THIS IS TOO UPSETTING!
OUT THERE IS UPSETTING!
IN HERE IS RELAXING!
End

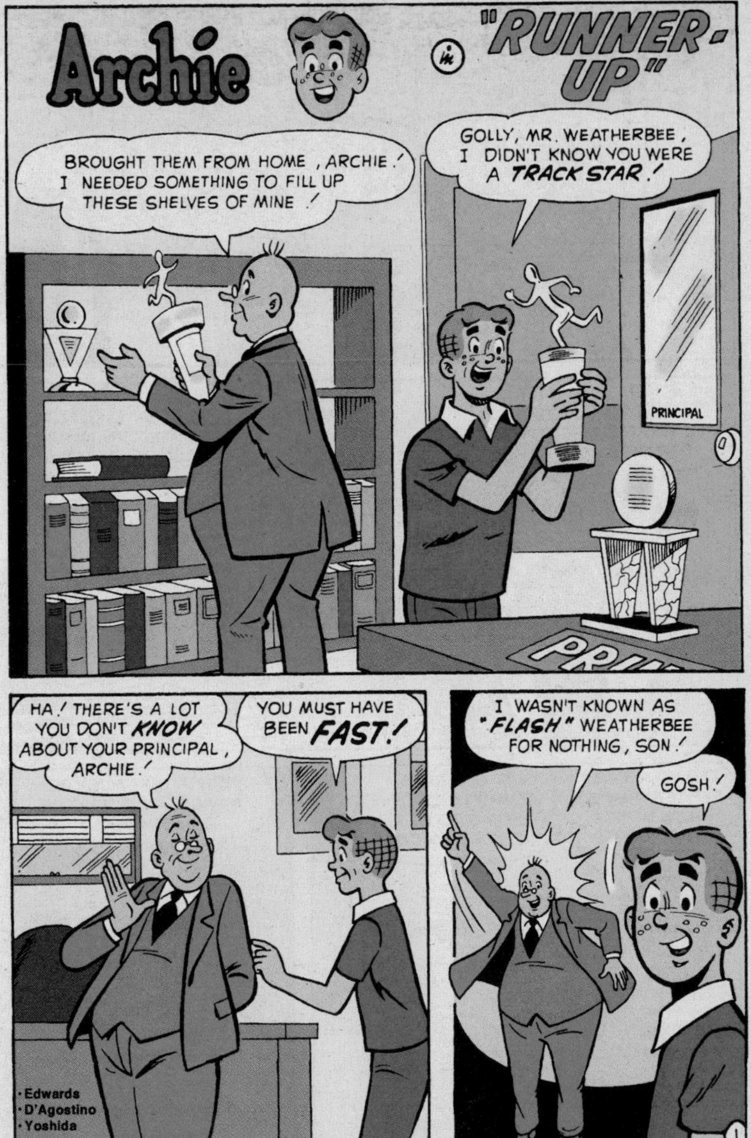
Archie
in
"RUNNER-UP"
BROUGHT THEM FROM HOME, ARCHIE! I NEEDED SOMETHING TO FILL UP THESE SHELVES OF MINE!
GOLLY, MR. WEATHERBEE, I DIDN'T KNOW YOU WERE A TRACK STAR!
PRINCIPAL
HA! THERE'S A LOT YOU DON'T KNOW ABOUT YOUR PRINCIPAL, ARCHIE!
YOU MUST HAVE BEEN FAST!
I WASN'T KNOWN AS "FLASH" WEATHERBEE FOR NOTHING, SON!
GOSH!
•Edwards
•D'Agostino
•Yoshida
1

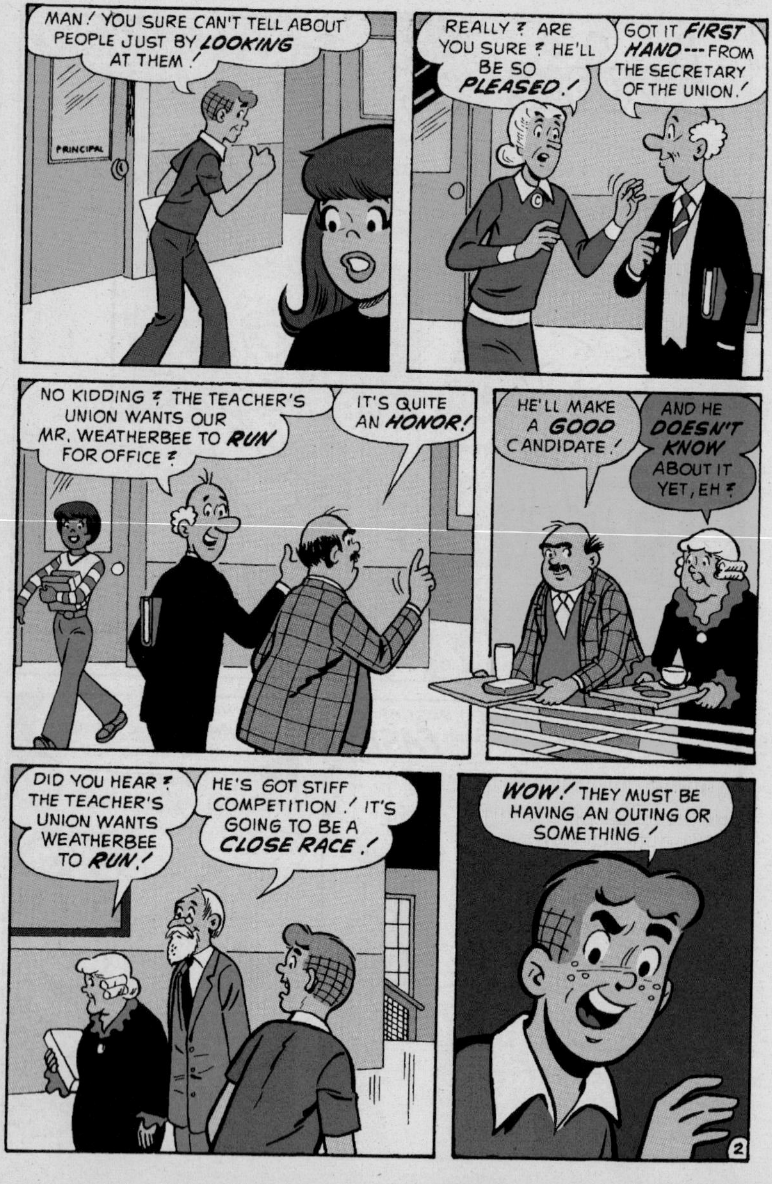
MAN! YOU SURE CAN'T TELL ABOUT PEOPLE JUST BY LOOKING AT THEM!
PRINCIPAL
REALLY? ARE YOU SURE? HE'LL BE SO PLEASED!
GOT IT FIRST HAND--- FROM THE SECRETARY OF THE UNION!
NO KIDDING? THE TEACHER'S UNION WANTS OUR MR. WEATHERBEE TO RUN FOR OFFICE?
IT'S QUITE AN HONOR!
HE'LL MAKE A GOOD CANDIDATE!
AND HE DOESN'T KNOW ABOUT IT YET, EH?
DID YOU HEAR? THE TEACHER'S UNION WANTS WEATHERBEE TO RUN!
HE'S GOT STIFF COMPETITION! IT'S GOING TO BE A CLOSE RACE!
WOW! THEY MUST BE HAVING AN OUTING OR SOMETHING!
2

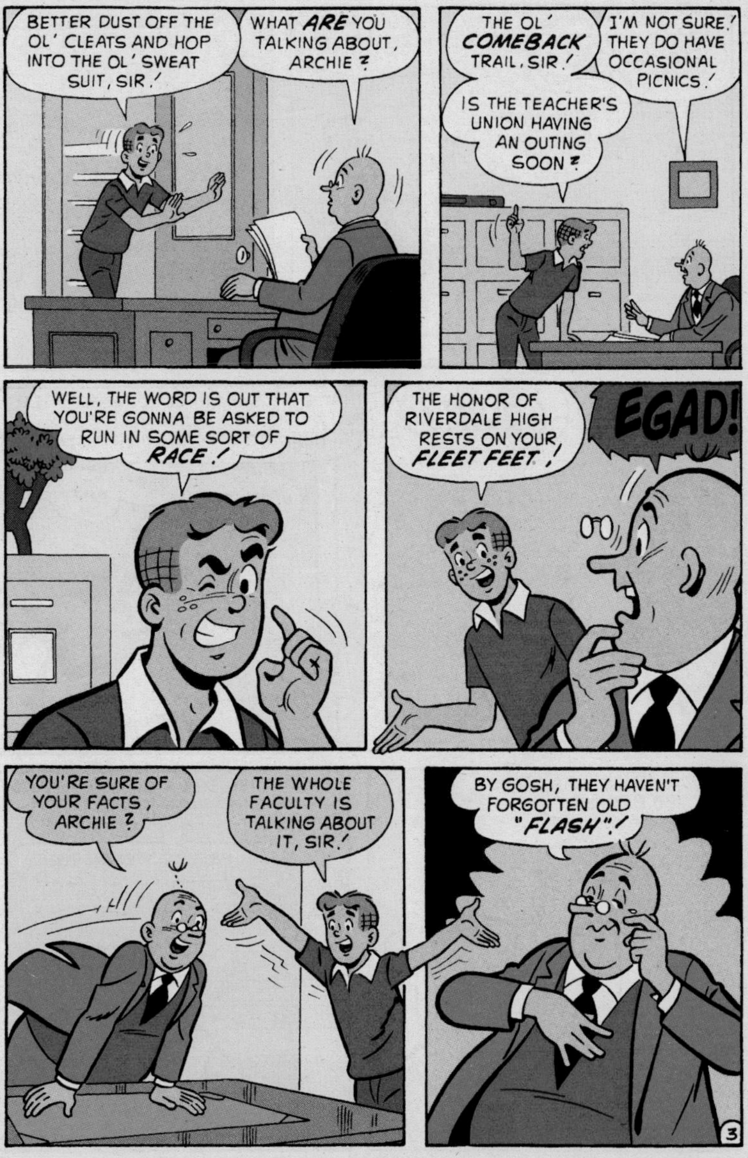
BETTER DUST OFF THE OL' CLEATS AND HOP INTO THE OL' SWEAT SUIT, SIR.!
WHAT ARE YOU TALKING ABOUT, ARCHIE ?
THE OL' COMEBACK TRAIL, SIR.!
IS THE TEACHER'S UNION HAVING AN OUTING SOON ?
I'M NOT SURE.! THEY DO HAVE OCCASIONAL PICNICS.!
WELL, THE WORD IS OUT THAT YOU'RE GONNA BE ASKED TO RUN IN SOME SORT OF RACE.!
THE HONOR OF RIVERDALE HIGH RESTS ON YOUR FLEET FEET.!
EGAD!
YOU'RE SURE OF YOUR FACTS, ARCHIE ?
THE WHOLE FACULTY IS TALKING ABOUT IT, SIR.!
BY GOSH, THEY HAVEN'T FORGOTTEN OLD "FLASH".!
3

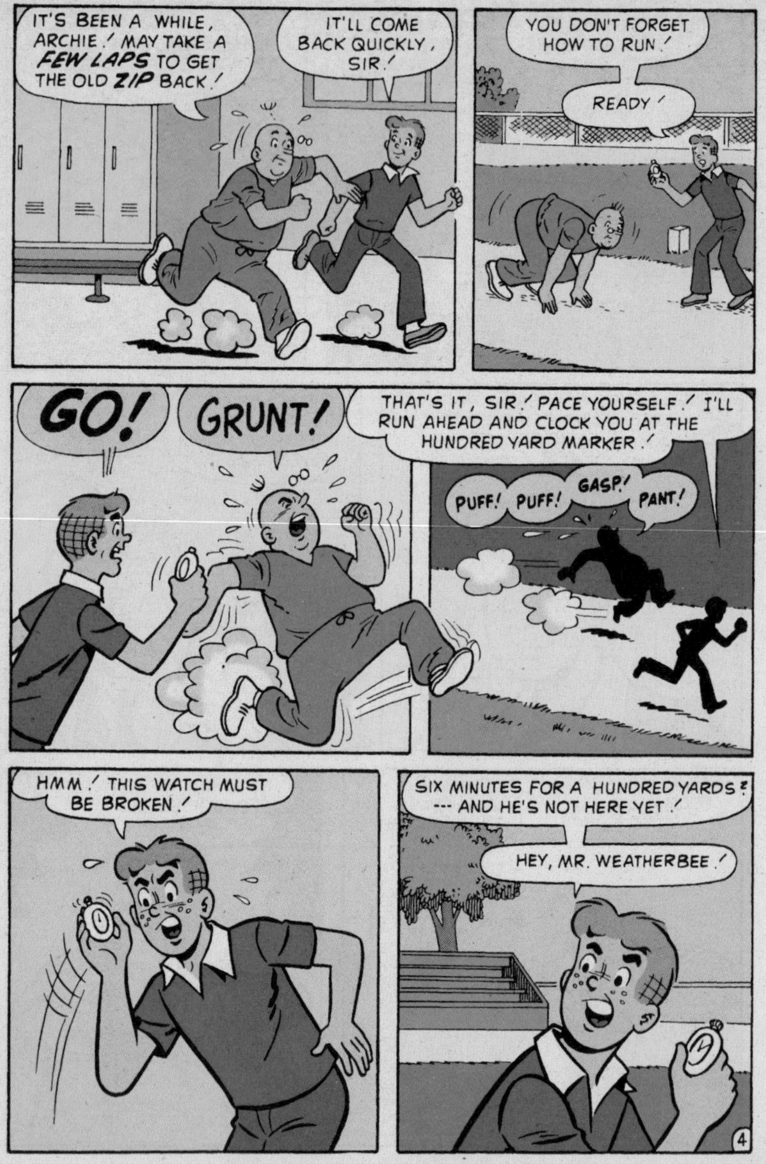

IT'S BEEN A WHILE, ARCHIE! MAY TAKE A FEW LAPS TO GET THE OLD ZIP BACK!
IT'LL COME BACK QUICKLY, SIR!
YOU DON'T FORGET HOW TO RUN!
READY!
GO!
GRUNT!
THAT'S IT, SIR! PACE YOURSELF! I'LL RUN AHEAD AND CLOCK YOU AT THE HUNDRED YARD MARKER!
PUFF! PUFF! GASP! PANT!
HMM! THIS WATCH MUST BE BROKEN!
SIX MINUTES FOR A HUNDRED YARDS? --- AND HE'S NOT HERE YET!
HEY, MR. WEATHERBEE!
4

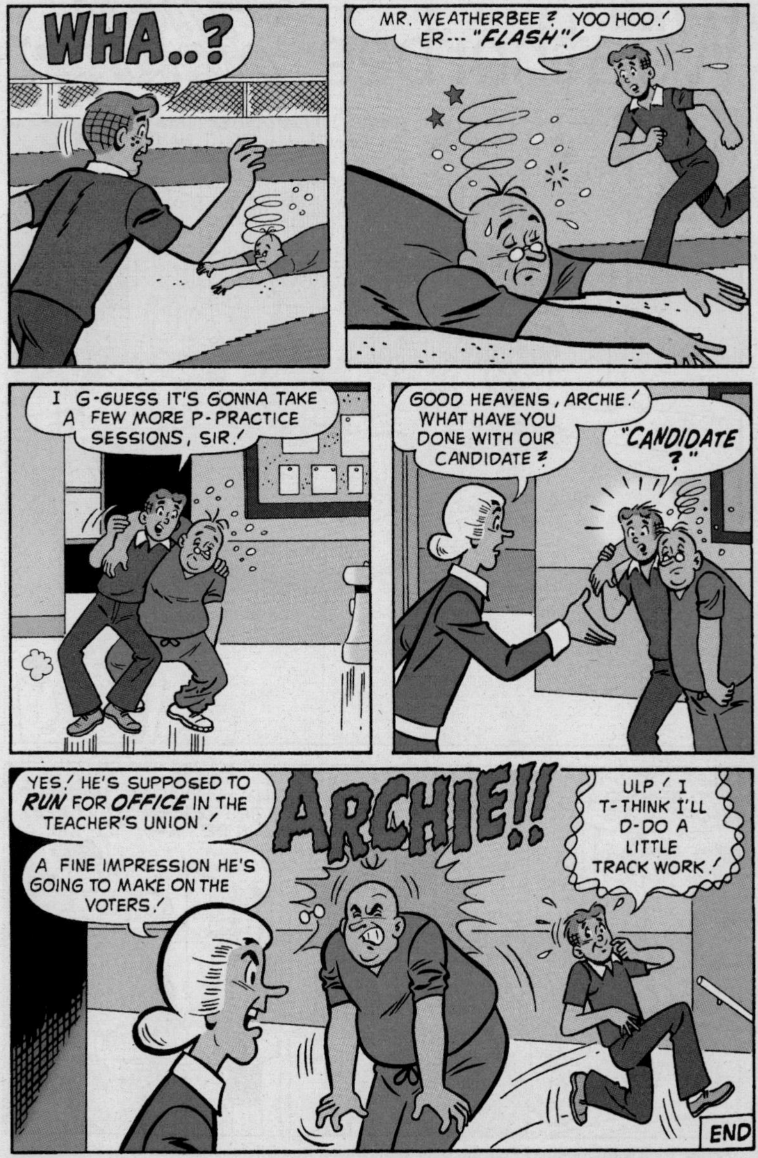

WHA..?
MR. WEATHERBEE? YOO HOO! ER--- "FLASH"!
I G-GUESS IT'S GONNA TAKE A FEW MORE P-PRACTICE SESSIONS, SIR!
GOOD HEAVENS, ARCHIE! WHAT HAVE YOU DONE WITH OUR CANDIDATE?
"CANDIDATE?"
YES! HE'S SUPPOSED TO RUN FOR OFFICE IN THE TEACHER'S UNION!
A FINE IMPRESSION HE'S GOING TO MAKE ON THE VOTERS!
ARCHIE!!
ULP! I T-THINK I'LL D-DO A LITTLE TRACK WORK!
END

Mr. Weatherbee in "High Marks"

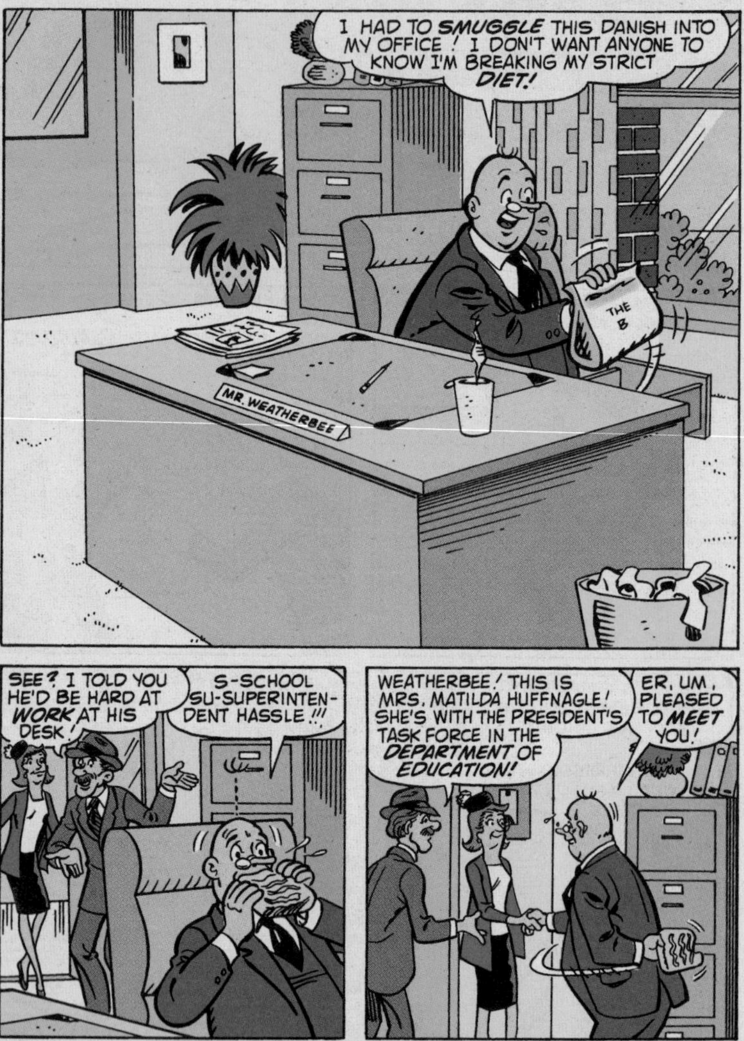
I HAD TO SMUGGLE THIS DANISH INTO MY OFFICE! I DON'T WANT ANYONE TO KNOW I'M BREAKING MY STRICT DIET!
THE B
MR. WEATHERBEE
SEE? I TOLD YOU HE'D BE HARD AT WORK AT HIS DESK!
S-SCHOOL SU-SUPERINTEN-DENT HASSLE!!!
WEATHERBEE! THIS IS MRS. MATILDA HUFFNAGLE! SHE'S WITH THE PRESIDENT'S TASK FORCE IN THE DEPARTMENT OF EDUCATION!
ER, UM, PLEASED TO MEET YOU!

Script: Rich Margopoulos / Pencils: Chic Stone / Inks: Rod Ollerenshaw / Letters: Bill Yoshida

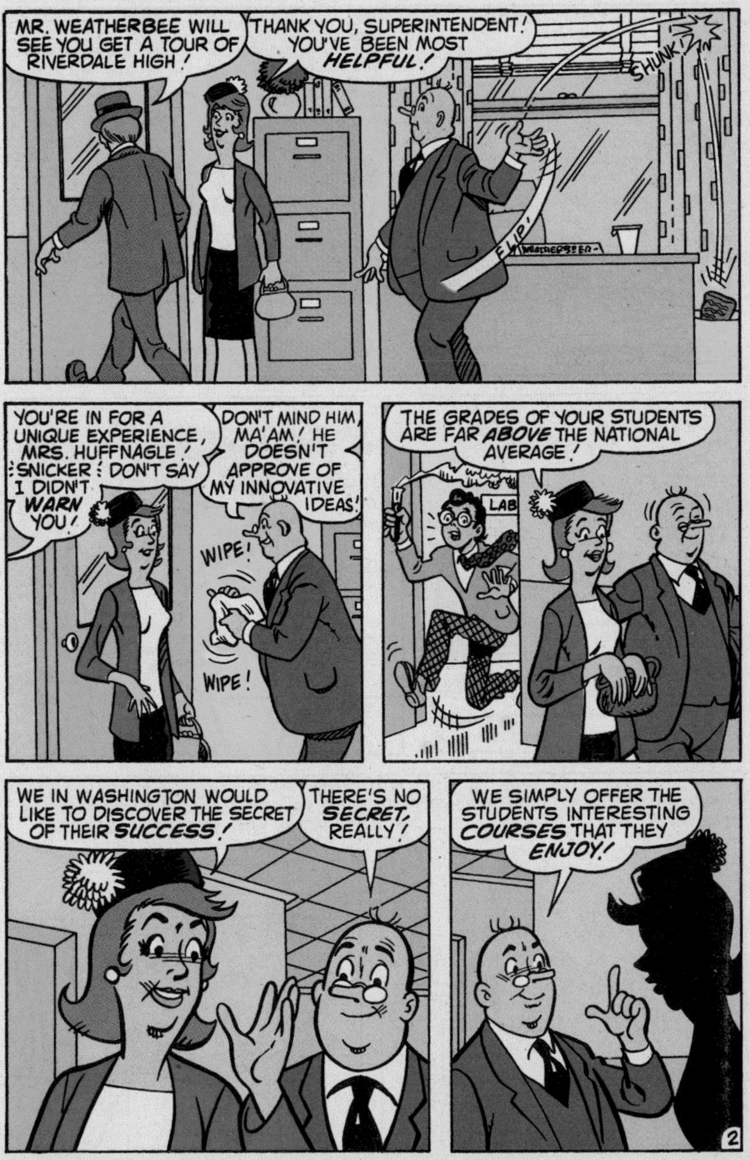
MR. WEATHERBEE WILL SEE YOU GET A TOUR OF RIVERDALE HIGH!
THANK YOU, SUPERINTENDENT! YOU'VE BEEN MOST HELPFUL!
SHUNK!
FLIP!
YOU'RE IN FOR A UNIQUE EXPERIENCE, MRS. HUFFNAGLE! :SNICKER: DON'T SAY I DIDN'T WARN YOU!
DON'T MIND HIM, MA'AM! HE DOESN'T APPROVE OF MY INNOVATIVE IDEAS!
WIPE!
WIPE!
THE GRADES OF YOUR STUDENTS ARE FAR ABOVE THE NATIONAL AVERAGE!
LAB
WE IN WASHINGTON WOULD LIKE TO DISCOVER THE SECRET OF THEIR SUCCESS!
THERE'S NO SECRET, REALLY!
WE SIMPLY OFFER THE STUDENTS INTERESTING COURSES THAT THEY ENJOY!
2

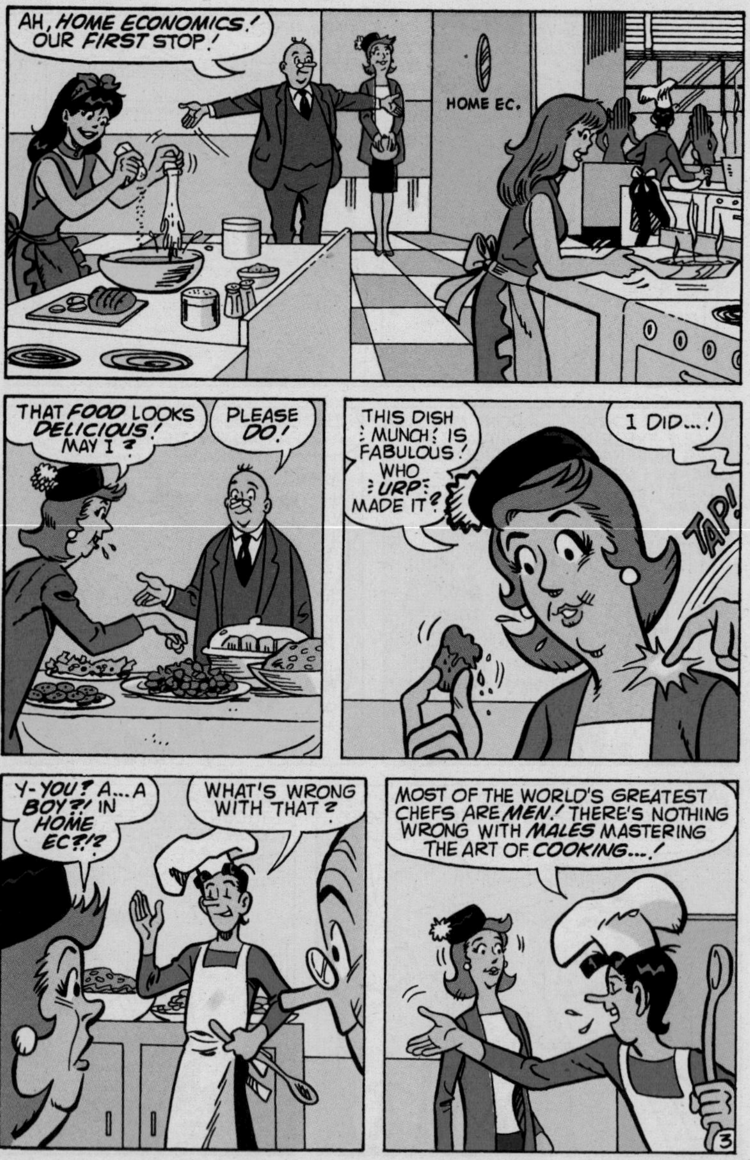
AH, HOME ECONOMICS! OUR FIRST STOP!
HOME EC.
THAT FOOD LOOKS DELICIOUS! MAY I?
PLEASE DO!
THIS DISH ⁝MUNCH⁝ IS FABULOUS! WHO ⁝URP⁝ MADE IT?
I DID...!
TAP!
Y-YOU? A... A BOY?! IN HOME EC?!?
WHAT'S WRONG WITH THAT?
MOST OF THE WORLD'S GREATEST CHEFS ARE MEN! THERE'S NOTHING WRONG WITH MALES MASTERING THE ART OF COOKING...!
3

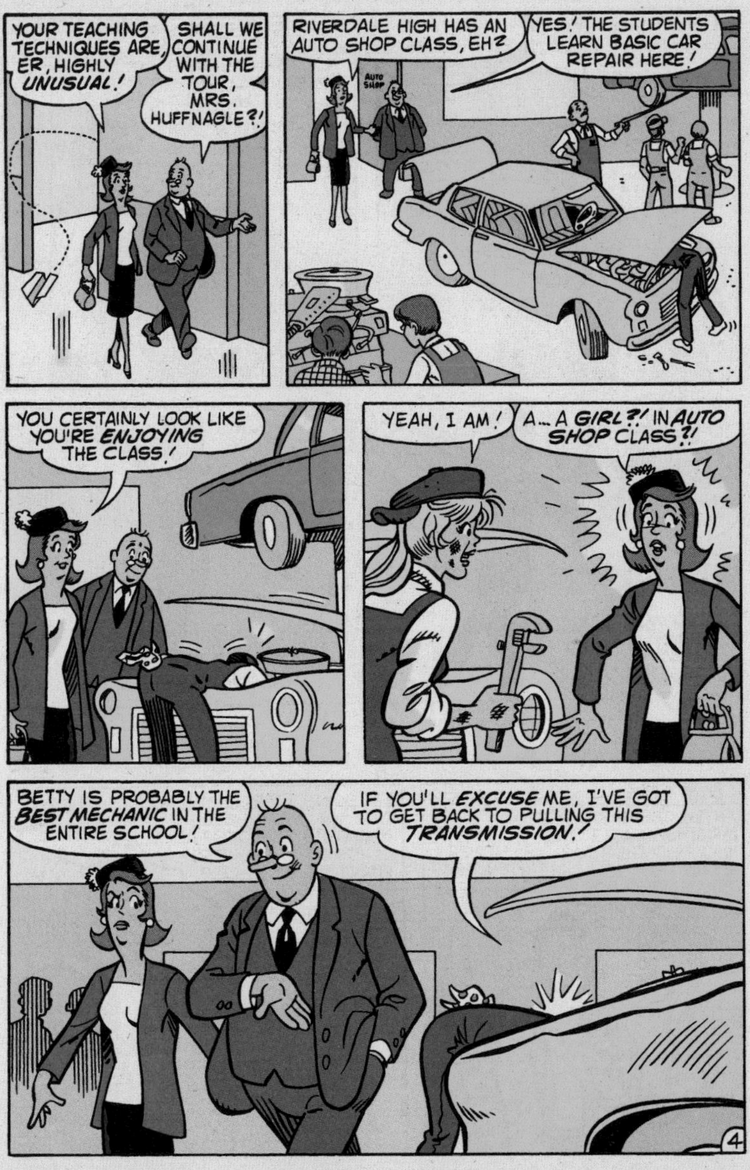
YOUR TEACHING TECHNIQUES ARE, ER, HIGHLY UNUSUAL!
SHALL WE CONTINUE WITH THE TOUR, MRS. HUFFNAGLE?!
RIVERDALE HIGH HAS AN AUTO SHOP CLASS, EH?
YES! THE STUDENTS LEARN BASIC CAR REPAIR HERE!
AUTO SHOP
YOU CERTAINLY LOOK LIKE YOU'RE ENJOYING THE CLASS!
YEAH, I AM!
A... A GIRL?! IN AUTO SHOP CLASS?!
BETTY IS PROBABLY THE BEST MECHANIC IN THE ENTIRE SCHOOL!
IF YOU'LL EXCUSE ME, I'VE GOT TO GET BACK TO PULLING THIS TRANSMISSION!
4

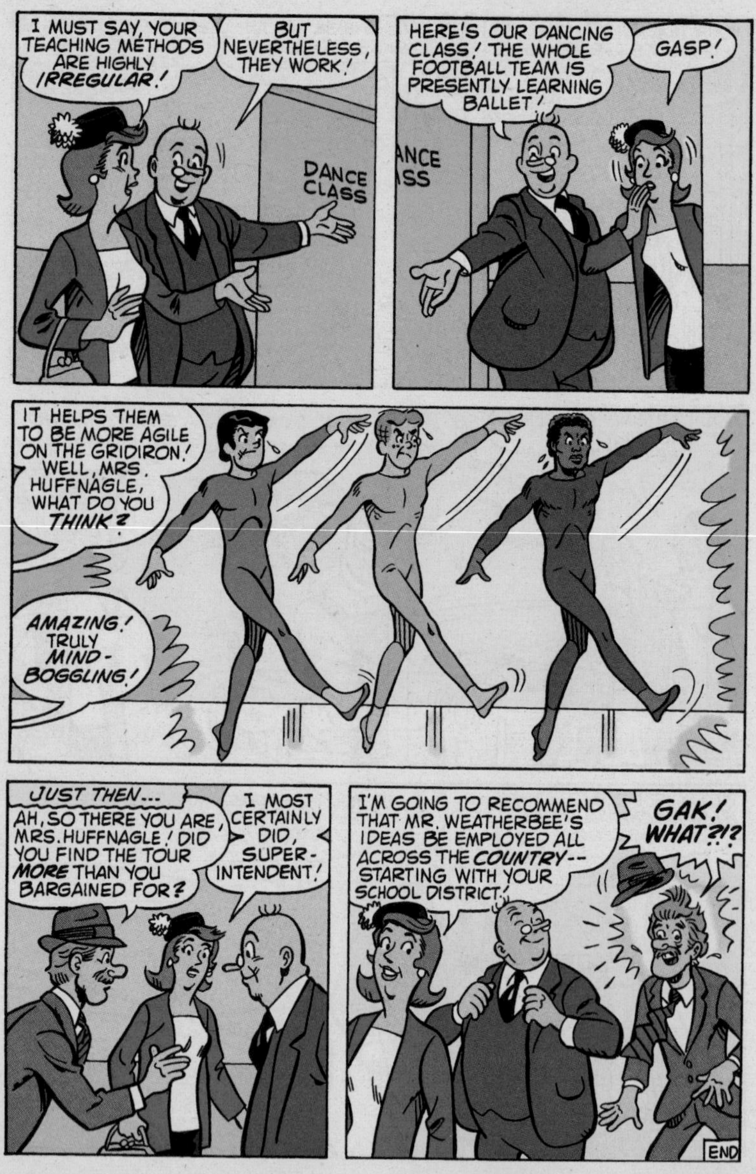
I MUST SAY, YOUR TEACHING METHODS ARE HIGHLY IRREGULAR!
BUT NEVERTHELESS, THEY WORK!
DANCE CLASS
HERE'S OUR DANCING CLASS! THE WHOLE FOOTBALL TEAM IS PRESENTLY LEARNING BALLET!
GASP!
ANCE ASS
IT HELPS THEM TO BE MORE AGILE ON THE GRIDIRON! WELL, MRS. HUFFNAGLE, WHAT DO YOU THINK?
AMAZING! TRULY MIND-BOGGLING!
JUST THEN...
AH, SO THERE YOU ARE, MRS. HUFFNAGLE! DID YOU FIND THE TOUR MORE THAN YOU BARGAINED FOR?
I MOST CERTAINLY DID, SUPER-INTENDENT!
I'M GOING TO RECOMMEND THAT MR. WEATHERBEE'S IDEAS BE EMPLOYED ALL ACROSS THE COUNTRY-- STARTING WITH YOUR SCHOOL DISTRICT!
GAK! WHAT?!?
END

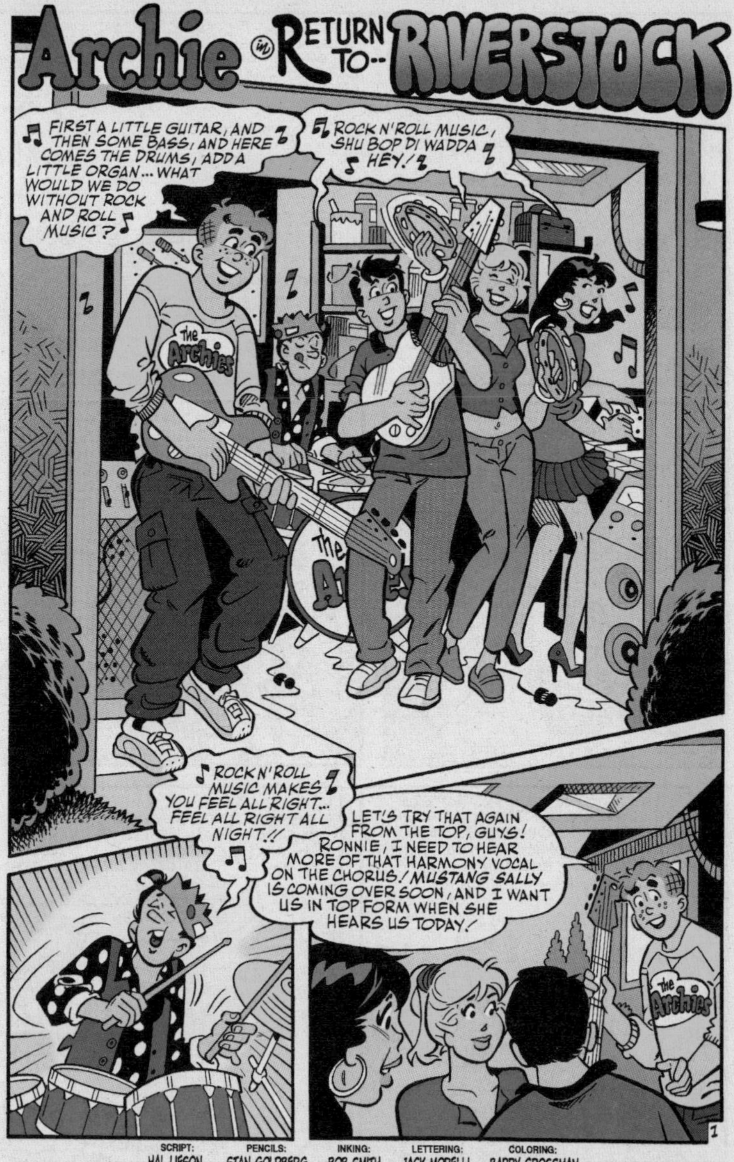

SCRIPT: HAL LIFSON PENCILS: STAN GOLDBERG INKING: BOB SMITH LETTERING: JACK MORELLI COLORING: BARRY GROSSMAN

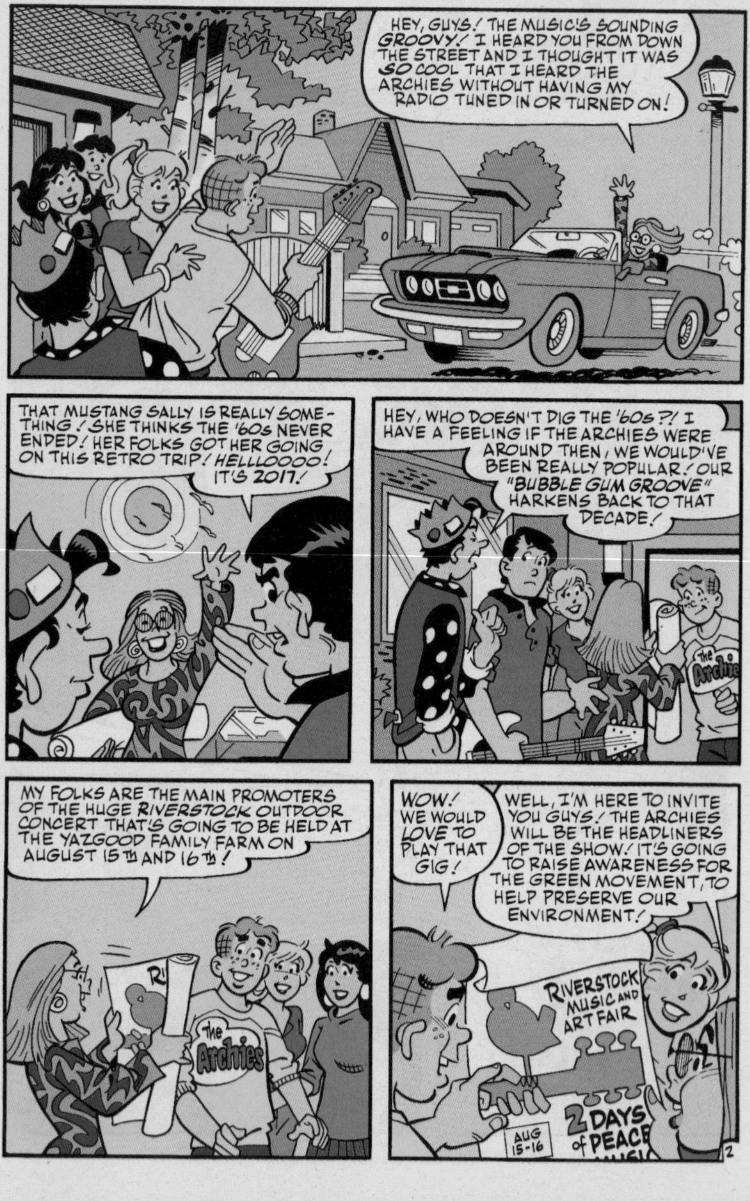
HEY, GUYS! THE MUSIC'S SOUNDING GROOVY! I HEARD YOU FROM DOWN THE STREET AND I THOUGHT IT WAS SO COOL THAT I HEARD THE ARCHIES WITHOUT HAVING MY RADIO TUNED IN OR TURNED ON!
THAT MUSTANG SALLY IS REALLY SOMETHING! SHE THINKS THE '60s NEVER ENDED! HER FOLKS GOT HER GOING ON THIS RETRO TRIP! HELLLOOOO! IT'S 2017!
HEY, WHO DOESN'T DIG THE '60s?! I HAVE A FEELING IF THE ARCHIES WERE AROUND THEN, WE WOULD'VE BEEN REALLY POPULAR! OUR "BUBBLE GUM GROOVE" HARKENS BACK TO THAT DECADE!
The Archies
MY FOLKS ARE THE MAIN PROMOTERS OF THE HUGE RIVERSTOCK OUTDOOR CONCERT THAT'S GOING TO BE HELD AT THE YAZGOOD FAMILY FARM ON AUGUST 15TH AND 16TH!
The Archies
WOW! WE WOULD LOVE TO PLAY THAT GIG!
WELL, I'M HERE TO INVITE YOU GUYS! THE ARCHIES WILL BE THE HEADLINERS OF THE SHOW! IT'S GOING TO RAISE AWARENESS FOR THE GREEN MOVEMENT, TO HELP PRESERVE OUR ENVIRONMENT!
RIVERSTOCK MUSIC AND ART FAIR
AUG 15-16
2 DAYS of PEACE
2

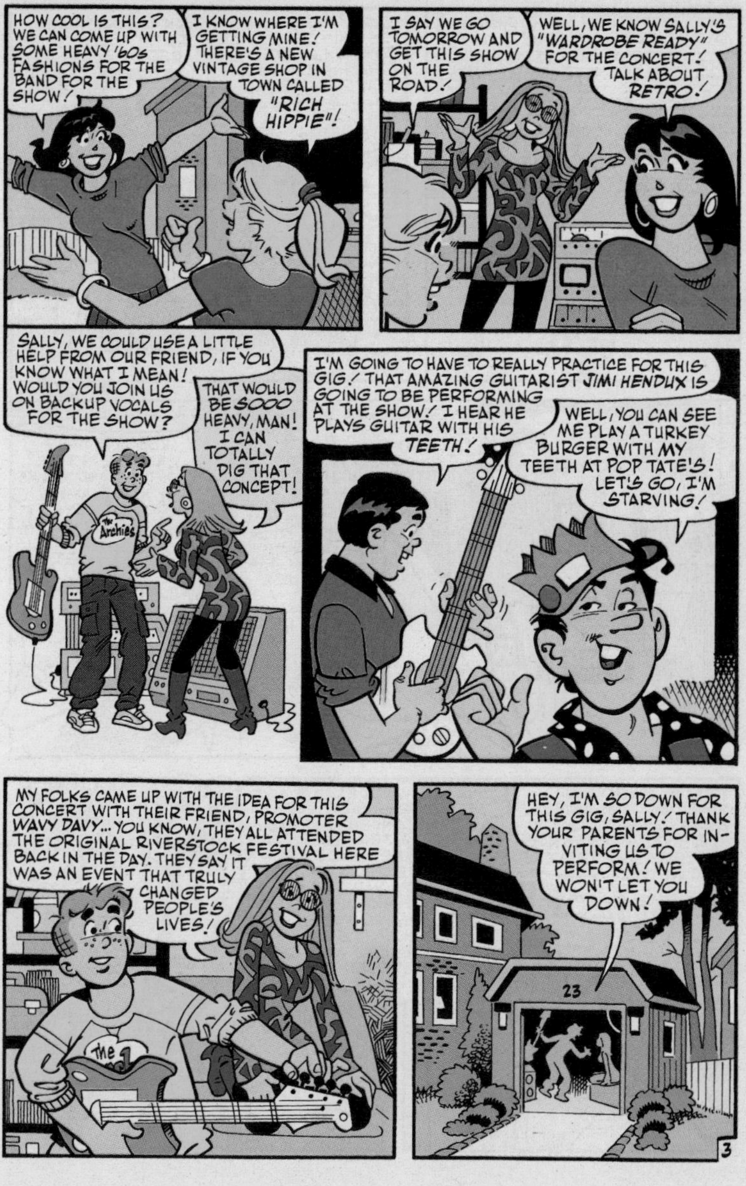
HOW COOL IS THIS? WE CAN COME UP WITH SOME HEAVY '60s FASHIONS FOR THE BAND FOR THE SHOW!
I KNOW WHERE I'M GETTING MINE! THERE'S A NEW VINTAGE SHOP IN TOWN CALLED "RICH HIPPIE"!
I SAY WE GO TOMORROW AND GET THIS SHOW ON THE ROAD!
WELL, WE KNOW SALLY'S "WARDROBE READY" FOR THE CONCERT! TALK ABOUT RETRO!
SALLY, WE COULD USE A LITTLE HELP FROM OUR FRIEND, IF YOU KNOW WHAT I MEAN! WOULD YOU JOIN US ON BACKUP VOCALS FOR THE SHOW?
THAT WOULD BE SOOO HEAVY, MAN! I CAN TOTALLY DIG THAT CONCEPT!
The Archies
I'M GOING TO HAVE TO REALLY PRACTICE FOR THIS GIG! THAT AMAZING GUITARIST JIMI HENDUX IS GOING TO BE PERFORMING AT THE SHOW! I HEAR HE PLAYS GUITAR WITH HIS TEETH!
WELL, YOU CAN SEE ME PLAY A TURKEY BURGER WITH MY TEETH AT POP TATE'S! LET'S GO, I'M STARVING!
MY FOLKS CAME UP WITH THE IDEA FOR THIS CONCERT WITH THEIR FRIEND, PROMOTER WAVY DAVY... YOU KNOW, THEY ALL ATTENDED THE ORIGINAL RIVERSTOCK FESTIVAL HERE BACK IN THE DAY. THEY SAY IT WAS AN EVENT THAT TRULY CHANGED PEOPLE'S LIVES!
HEY, I'M SO DOWN FOR THIS GIG, SALLY! THANK YOUR PARENTS FOR INVITING US TO PERFORM! WE WON'T LET YOU DOWN!
23

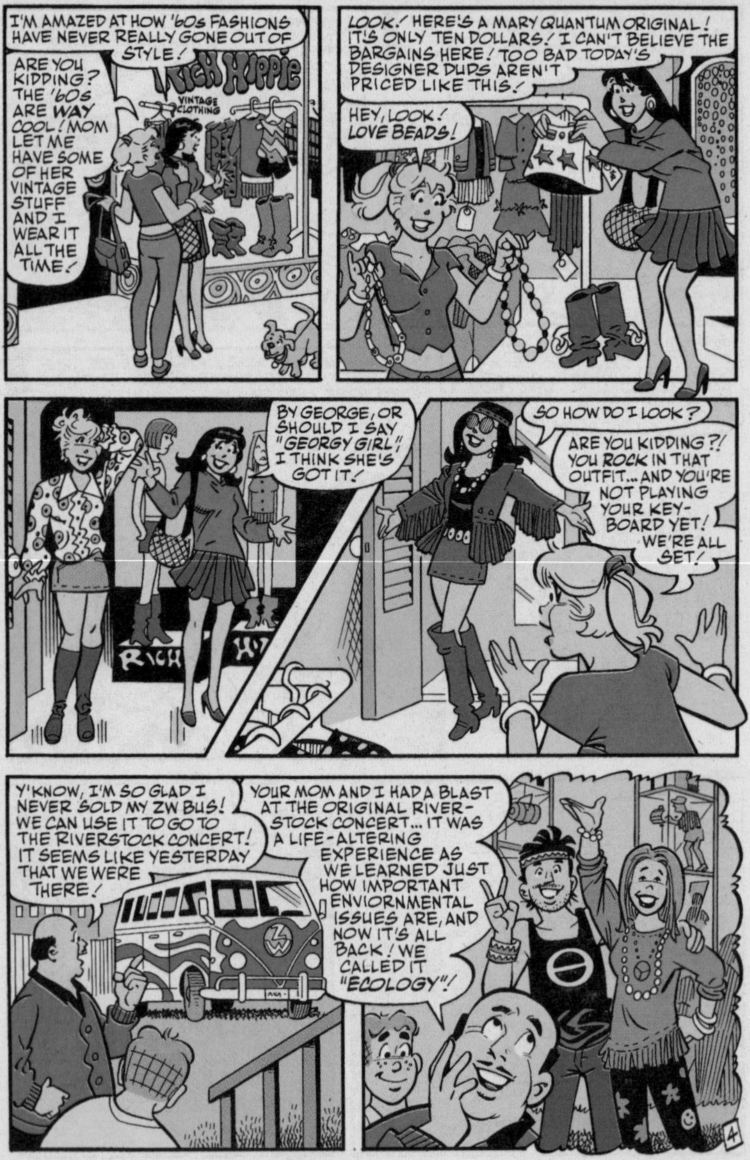
I'M AMAZED AT HOW '60s FASHIONS HAVE NEVER REALLY GONE OUT OF STYLE!
ARE YOU KIDDING? THE '60s ARE WAY COOL! MOM LET ME HAVE SOME OF HER VINTAGE STUFF AND I WEAR IT ALL THE TIME!
Rich Hippie
VINTAGE CLOTHING
LOOK! HERE'S A MARY QUANTUM ORIGINAL! IT'S ONLY TEN DOLLARS! I CAN'T BELIEVE THE BARGAINS HERE! TOO BAD TODAY'S DESIGNER DUDS AREN'T PRICED LIKE THIS!
HEY, LOOK! LOVE BEADS!
BY GEORGE, OR SHOULD I SAY "GEORGY GIRL", I THINK SHE'S GOT IT!
SO HOW DO I LOOK?
ARE YOU KIDDING?! YOU ROCK IN THAT OUTFIT... AND YOU'RE NOT PLAYING YOUR KEY-BOARD YET! WE'RE ALL SET!
Y'KNOW, I'M SO GLAD I NEVER SOLD MY ZW BUS! WE CAN USE IT TO GO TO THE RIVERSTOCK CONCERT! IT SEEMS LIKE YESTERDAY THAT WE WERE THERE!
YOUR MOM AND I HAD A BLAST AT THE ORIGINAL RIVER-STOCK CONCERT... IT WAS A LIFE-ALTERING EXPERIENCE AS WE LEARNED JUST HOW IMPORTANT ENVIORNMENTAL ISSUES ARE, AND NOW IT'S ALL BACK! WE CALLED IT "ECOLOGY"!
4

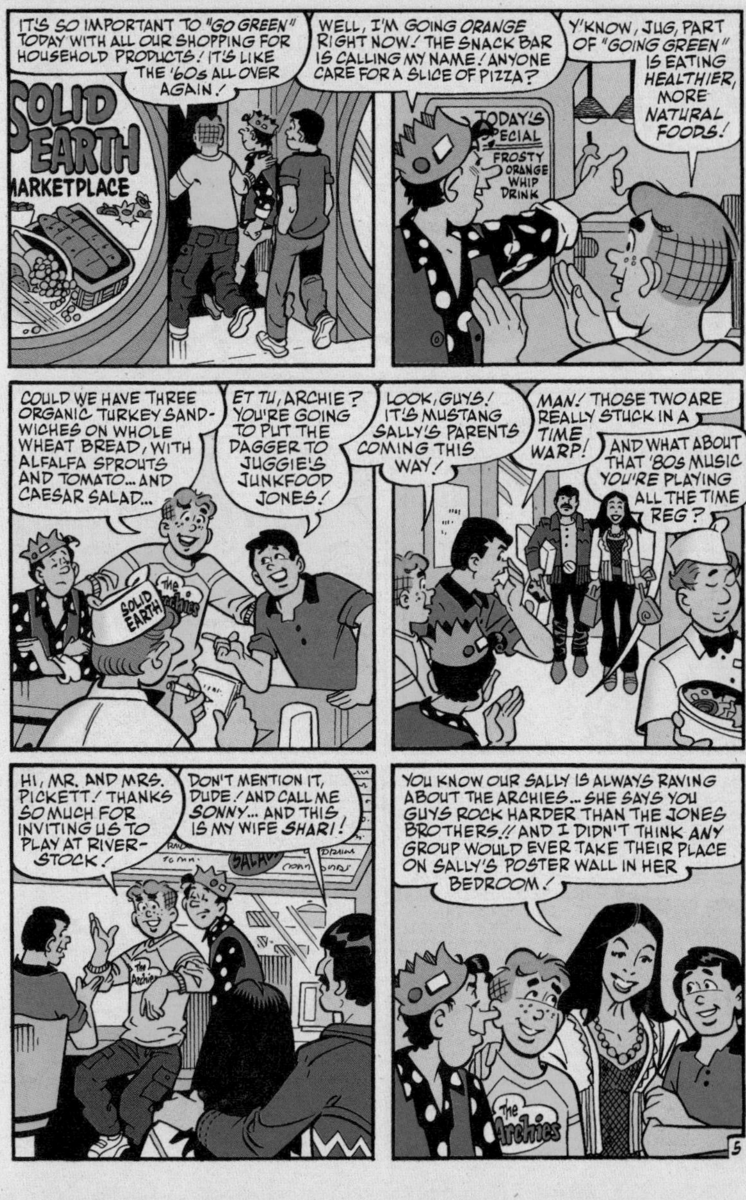

IT'S SO IMPORTANT TO "GO GREEN" TODAY WITH ALL OUR SHOPPING FOR HOUSEHOLD PRODUCTS! IT'S LIKE THE '60s ALL OVER AGAIN!
SOLID EARTH MARKETPLACE
WELL, I'M GOING ORANGE RIGHT NOW! THE SNACK BAR IS CALLING MY NAME! ANYONE CARE FOR A SLICE OF PIZZA?
Y'KNOW, JUG, PART OF "GOING GREEN" IS EATING HEALTHIER, MORE NATURAL FOODS!
TODAY'S SPECIAL
FROSTY ORANGE WHIP DRINK
COULD WE HAVE THREE ORGANIC TURKEY SANDWICHES ON WHOLE WHEAT BREAD, WITH ALFALFA SPROUTS AND TOMATO... AND CAESAR SALAD...
ET TU, ARCHIE? YOU'RE GOING TO PUT THE DAGGER TO JUGGIE'S JUNKFOOD JONES!
SOLID EARTH
The Archies
LOOK, GUYS! IT'S MUSTANG SALLY'S PARENTS COMING THIS WAY!
MAN! THOSE TWO ARE REALLY STUCK IN A TIME WARP!
AND WHAT ABOUT THAT '80s MUSIC YOU'RE PLAYING ALL THE TIME REG?
HI, MR. AND MRS. PICKETT! THANKS SO MUCH FOR INVITING US TO PLAY AT RIVER-STOCK!
DON'T MENTION IT, DUDE! AND CALL ME SONNY... AND THIS IS MY WIFE SHARI!
The Archies
YOU KNOW OUR SALLY IS ALWAYS RAVING ABOUT THE ARCHIES... SHE SAYS YOU GUYS ROCK HARDER THAN THE JONES BROTHERS!! AND I DIDN'T THINK ANY GROUP WOULD EVER TAKE THEIR PLACE ON SALLY'S POSTER WALL IN HER BEDROOM!
The Archies

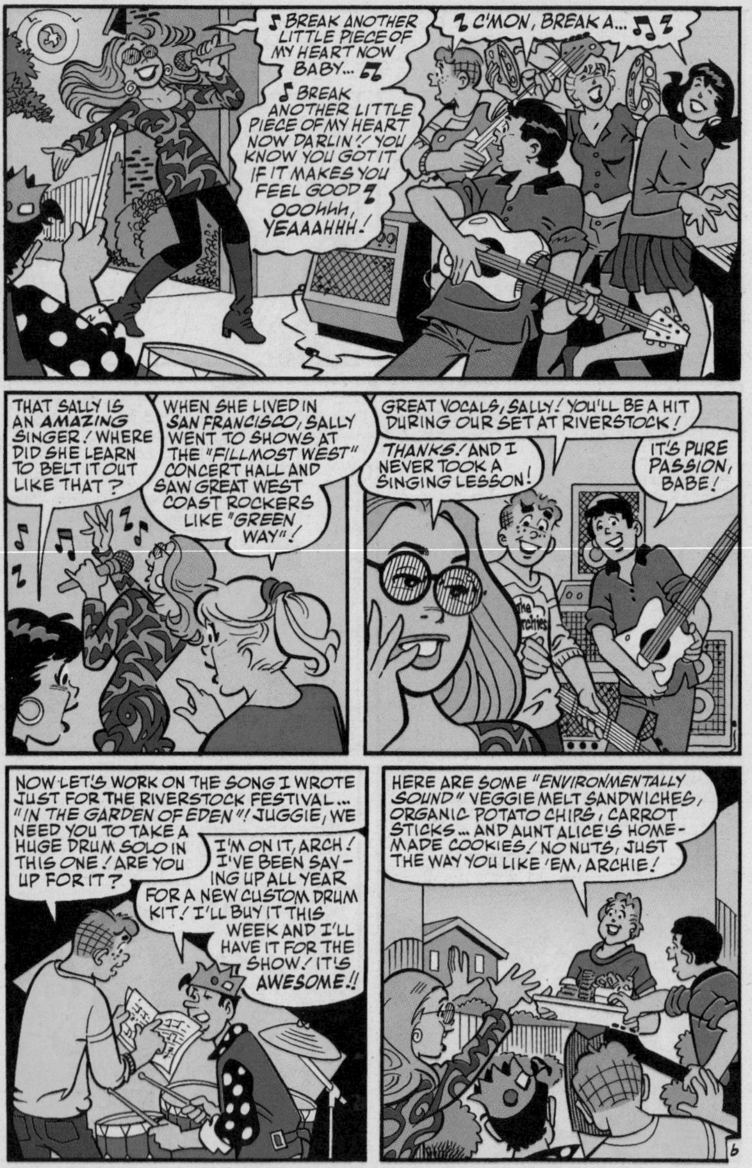
BREAK ANOTHER LITTLE PIECE OF MY HEART NOW BABY...
BREAK ANOTHER LITTLE PIECE OF MY HEART NOW DARLIN'! YOU KNOW YOU GOT IT IF IT MAKES YOU FEEL GOOD OOOhhh, YEAAAHHH!
C'MON, BREAK A...
THAT SALLY IS AN AMAZING SINGER! WHERE DID SHE LEARN TO BELT IT OUT LIKE THAT?
WHEN SHE LIVED IN SAN FRANCISCO, SALLY WENT TO SHOWS AT THE "FILLMOST WEST" CONCERT HALL AND SAW GREAT WEST COAST ROCKERS LIKE "GREEN WAY"!
GREAT VOCALS, SALLY! YOU'LL BE A HIT DURING OUR SET AT RIVERSTOCK!
THANKS! AND I NEVER TOOK A SINGING LESSON!
IT'S PURE PASSION, BABE!
NOW LET'S WORK ON THE SONG I WROTE JUST FOR THE RIVERSTOCK FESTIVAL... "IN THE GARDEN OF EDEN"! JUGGIE, WE NEED YOU TO TAKE A HUGE DRUM SOLO IN THIS ONE! ARE YOU UP FOR IT?
I'M ON IT, ARCH! I'VE BEEN SAVING UP ALL YEAR FOR A NEW CUSTOM DRUM KIT! I'LL BUY IT THIS WEEK AND I'LL HAVE IT FOR THE SHOW! IT'S AWESOME!!
HERE ARE SOME "ENVIRONMENTALLY SOUND" VEGGIE MELT SANDWICHES, ORGANIC POTATO CHIPS, CARROT STICKS... AND AUNT ALICE'S HOME-MADE COOKIES! NO NUTS, JUST THE WAY YOU LIKE 'EM, ARCHIE!

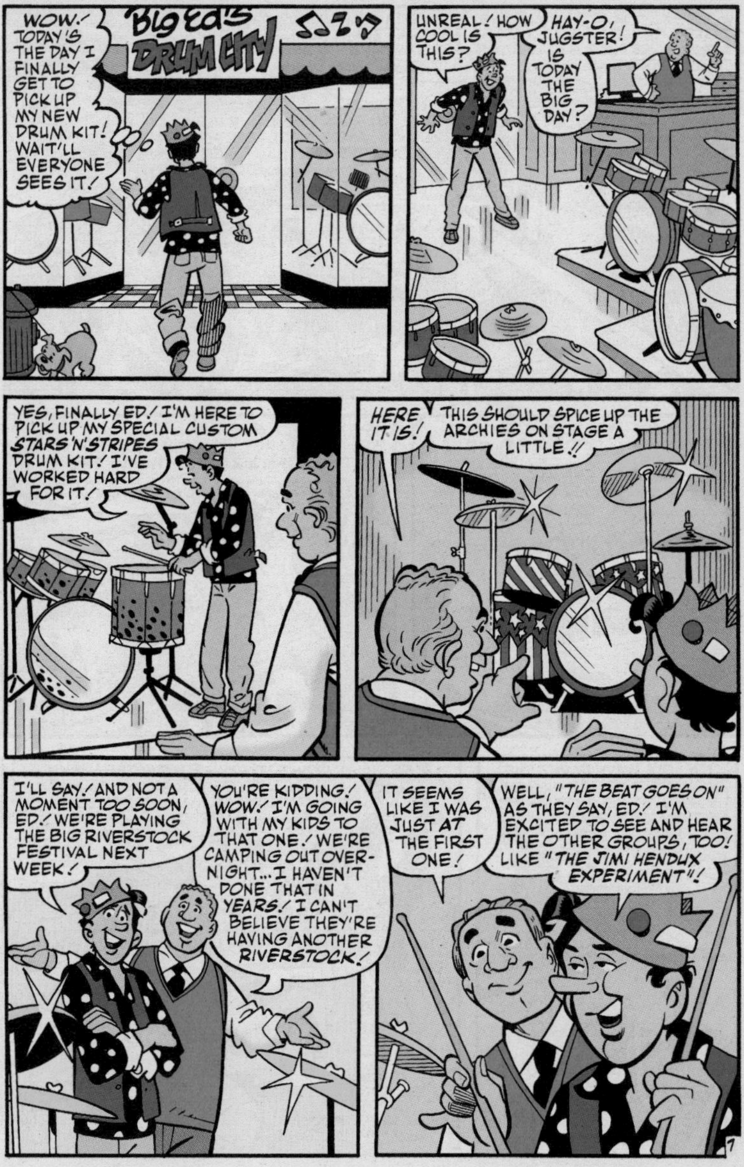
Big Ed's DRUM CITY
WOW! TODAY'S THE DAY I FINALLY GET TO PICK UP MY NEW DRUM KIT! WAIT'LL EVERYONE SEES IT!
UNREAL! HOW COOL IS THIS?
HAY-O, JUGSTER! IS TODAY THE BIG DAY?
YES, FINALLY ED! I'M HERE TO PICK UP MY SPECIAL CUSTOM STARS 'N' STRIPES DRUM KIT! I'VE WORKED HARD FOR IT!
HERE IT IS!
THIS SHOULD SPICE UP THE ARCHIES ON STAGE A LITTLE!!
I'LL SAY! AND NOT A MOMENT TOO SOON, ED! WE'RE PLAYING THE BIG RIVERSTOCK FESTIVAL NEXT WEEK!
YOU'RE KIDDING! WOW! I'M GOING WITH MY KIDS TO THAT ONE! WE'RE CAMPING OUT OVER-NIGHT... I HAVEN'T DONE THAT IN YEARS! I CAN'T BELIEVE THEY'RE HAVING ANOTHER RIVERSTOCK!
IT SEEMS LIKE I WAS JUST AT THE FIRST ONE!
WELL, "THE BEAT GOES ON" AS THEY SAY, ED! I'M EXCITED TO SEE AND HEAR THE OTHER GROUPS, TOO! LIKE "THE JIMI HENDUX EXPERIMENT"!

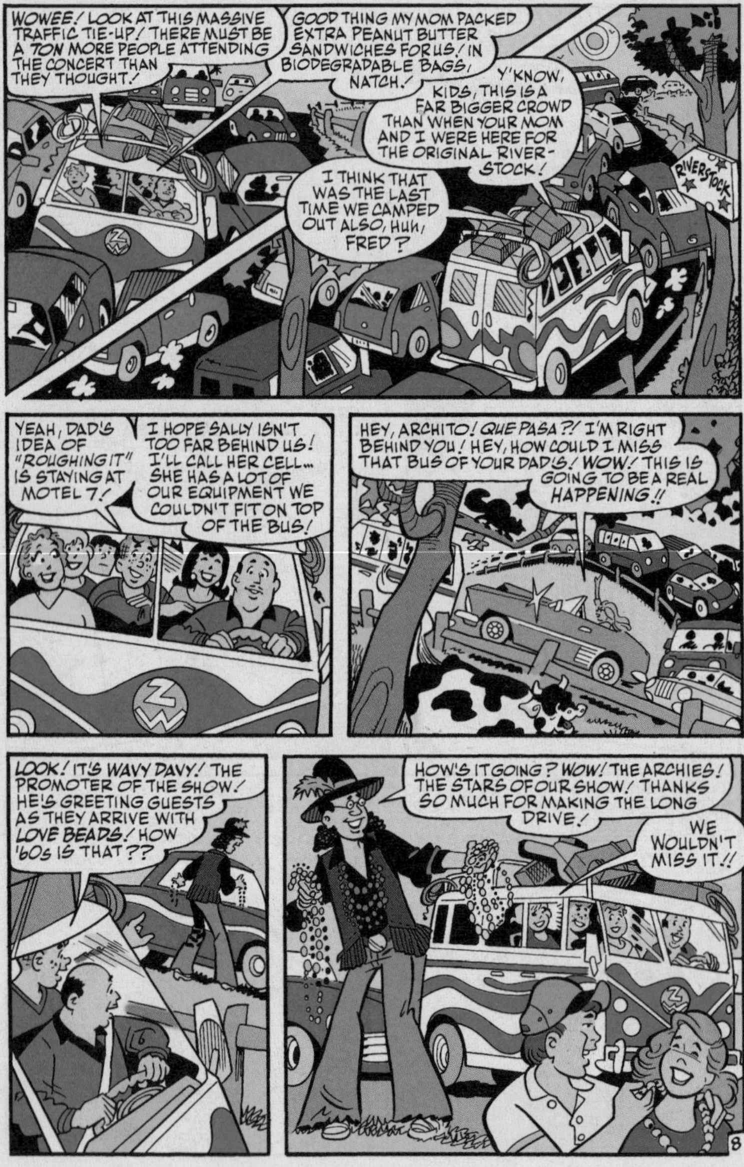
WOWEE! LOOK AT THIS MASSIVE TRAFFIC TIE-UP! THERE MUST BE A TON MORE PEOPLE ATTENDING THE CONCERT THAN THEY THOUGHT!
GOOD THING MY MOM PACKED EXTRA PEANUT BUTTER SANDWICHES FOR US! IN BIODEGRADABLE BAGS, NATCH!
Y'KNOW, KIDS, THIS IS A FAR BIGGER CROWD THAN WHEN YOUR MOM AND I WERE HERE FOR THE ORIGINAL RIVER-STOCK!
I THINK THAT WAS THE LAST TIME WE CAMPED OUT ALSO, HUH, FRED?
RIVERSTOCK
YEAH, DAD'S IDEA OF "ROUGHING IT" IS STAYING AT MOTEL 7!
I HOPE SALLY ISN'T TOO FAR BEHIND US! I'LL CALL HER CELL... SHE HAS A LOT OF OUR EQUIPMENT WE COULDN'T FIT ON TOP OF THE BUS!
HEY, ARCHITO! QUE PASA?! I'M RIGHT BEHIND YOU! HEY, HOW COULD I MISS THAT BUS OF YOUR DAD'S! WOW! THIS IS GOING TO BE A REAL HAPPENING!!
LOOK! IT'S WAVY DAVY! THE PROMOTER OF THE SHOW! HE'S GREETING GUESTS AS THEY ARRIVE WITH LOVE BEADS! HOW '60s IS THAT??
HOW'S IT GOING? WOW! THE ARCHIES! THE STARS OF OUR SHOW! THANKS SO MUCH FOR MAKING THE LONG DRIVE!
WE WOULDN'T MISS IT!!

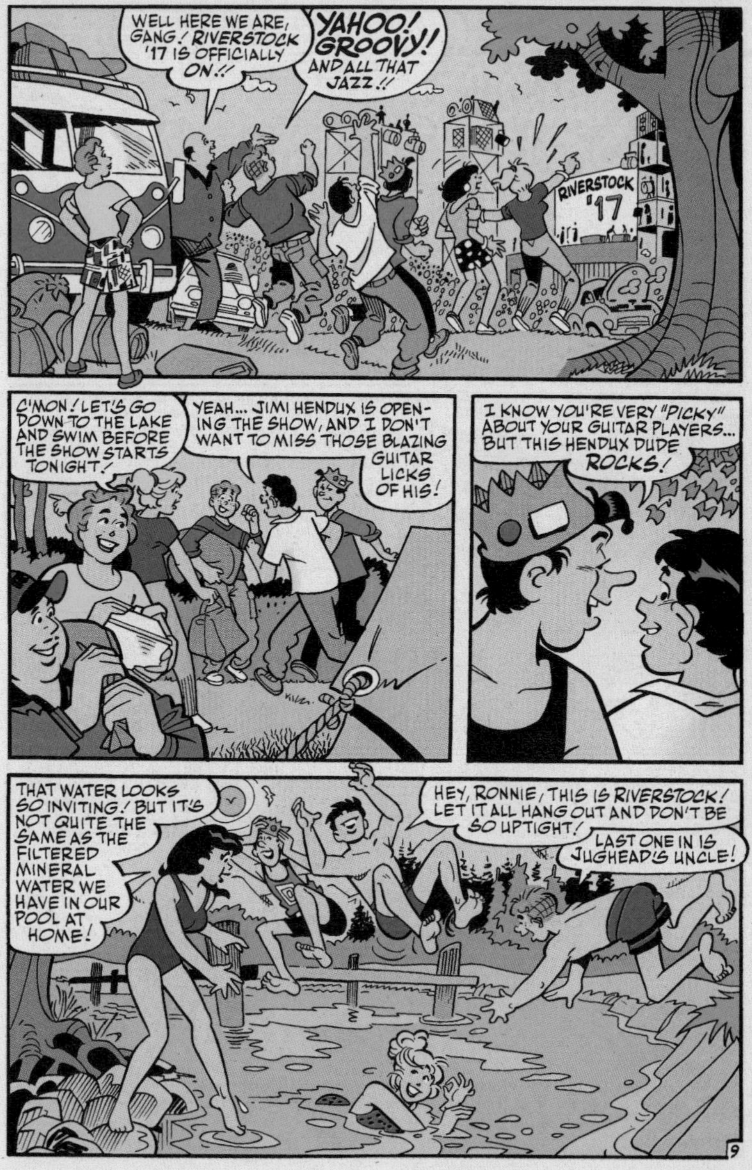
WELL HERE WE ARE, GANG! RIVERSTOCK '17 IS OFFICIALLY ON!!
YAHOO! GROOVY! AND ALL THAT JAZZ!!
RIVERSTOCK '17
C'MON! LET'S GO DOWN TO THE LAKE AND SWIM BEFORE THE SHOW STARTS TONIGHT!
YEAH... JIMI HENDUX IS OPENING THE SHOW, AND I DON'T WANT TO MISS THOSE BLAZING GUITAR LICKS OF HIS!
I KNOW YOU'RE VERY "PICKY" ABOUT YOUR GUITAR PLAYERS... BUT THIS HENDUX DUDE ROCKS!
THAT WATER LOOKS SO INVITING! BUT IT'S NOT QUITE THE SAME AS THE FILTERED MINERAL WATER WE HAVE IN OUR POOL AT HOME!
HEY, RONNIE, THIS IS RIVERSTOCK! LET IT ALL HANG OUT AND DON'T BE SO UPTIGHT!
LAST ONE IN IS JUGHEAD'S UNCLE!

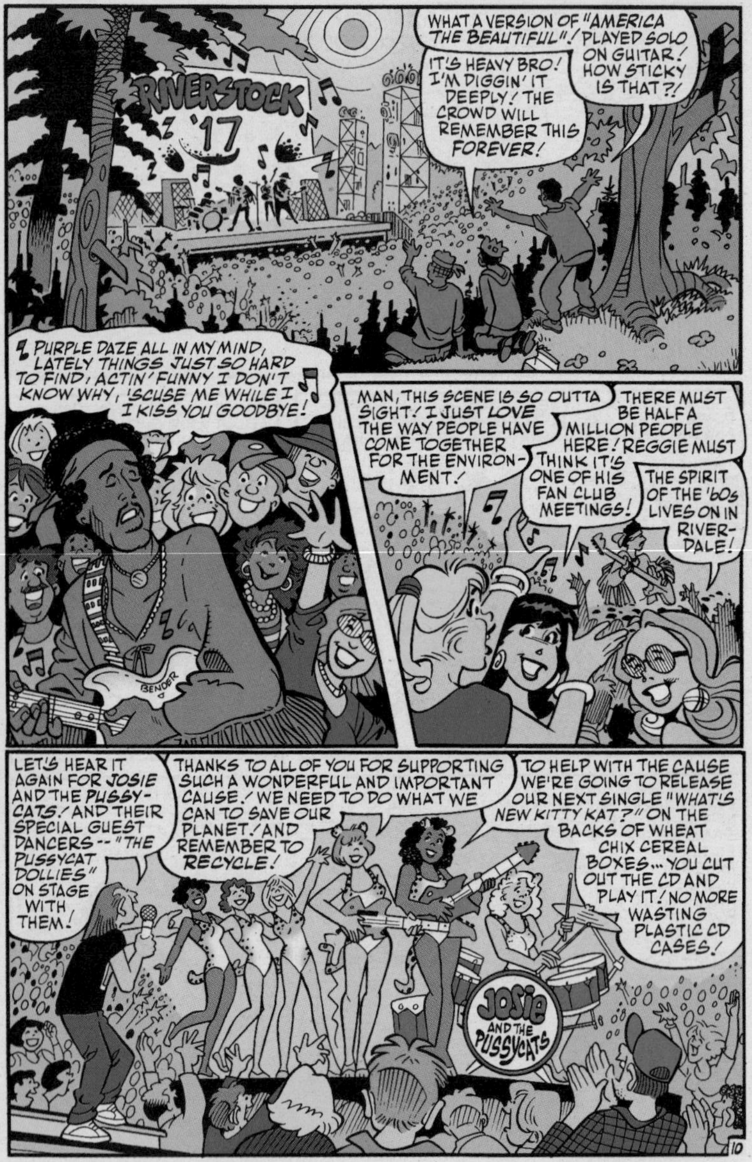
RIVERSTOCK '17
WHAT A VERSION OF "AMERICA THE BEAUTIFUL"! PLAYED SOLO ON GUITAR! HOW STICKY IS THAT?!
IT'S HEAVY BRO! I'M DIGGIN' IT DEEPLY! THE CROWD WILL REMEMBER THIS FOREVER!
PURPLE DAZE ALL IN MY MIND, LATELY THINGS JUST SO HARD TO FIND; ACTIN' FUNNY I DON'T KNOW WHY, 'SCUSE ME WHILE I I KISS YOU GOODBYE!
BENDER
MAN, THIS SCENE IS SO OUTTA SIGHT! I JUST LOVE THE WAY PEOPLE HAVE COME TOGETHER FOR THE ENVIRON-MENT!
THERE MUST BE HALF A MILLION PEOPLE HERE! REGGIE MUST THINK IT'S ONE OF HIS FAN CLUB MEETINGS!
THE SPIRIT OF THE '60s LIVES ON IN RIVER-DALE!
LET'S HEAR IT AGAIN FOR JOSIE AND THE PUSSY-CATS! AND THEIR SPECIAL GUEST DANCERS -- "THE PUSSYCAT DOLLIES" ON STAGE WITH THEM!
THANKS TO ALL OF YOU FOR SUPPORTING SUCH A WONDERFUL AND IMPORTANT CAUSE! WE NEED TO DO WHAT WE CAN TO SAVE OUR PLANET! AND REMEMBER TO RECYCLE!
TO HELP WITH THE CAUSE WE'RE GOING TO RELEASE OUR NEXT SINGLE "WHAT'S NEW KITTY KAT?" ON THE BACKS OF WHEAT CHIX CEREAL BOXES... YOU CUT OUT THE CD AND PLAY IT! NO MORE WASTING PLASTIC CD CASES!
JOSIE AND THE PUSSYCATS

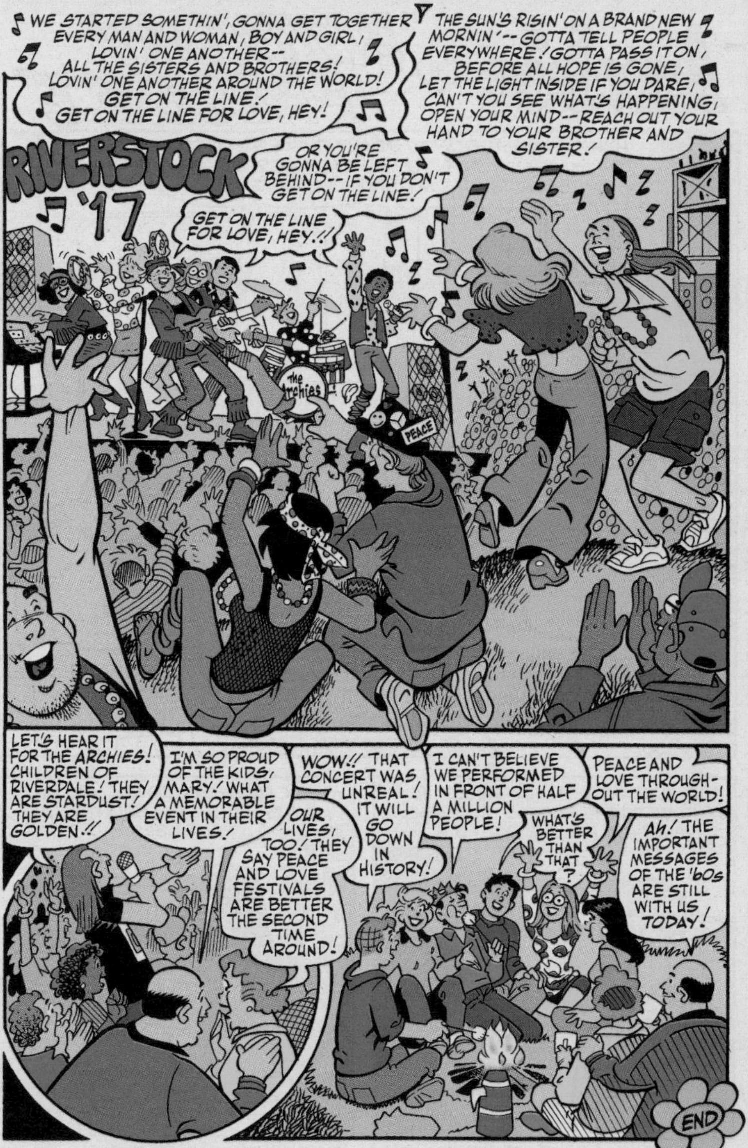
WE STARTED SOMETHIN', GONNA GET TOGETHER EVERY MAN AND WOMAN, BOY AND GIRL, LOVIN' ONE ANOTHER-- ALL THE SISTERS AND BROTHERS! LOVIN' ONE ANOTHER AROUND THE WORLD! GET ON THE LINE! GET ON THE LINE FOR LOVE, HEY!
THE SUN'S RISIN' ON A BRAND NEW MORNIN'-- GOTTA TELL PEOPLE EVERYWHERE! GOTTA PASS IT ON, BEFORE ALL HOPE IS GONE, LET THE LIGHT INSIDE IF YOU DARE, CAN'T YOU SEE WHAT'S HAPPENING, OPEN YOUR MIND-- REACH OUT YOUR HAND TO YOUR BROTHER AND SISTER!
RIVERSTOCK '17
OR YOU'RE GONNA BE LEFT BEHIND-- IF YOU DON'T GET ON THE LINE!
GET ON THE LINE FOR LOVE, HEY!!
PEACE
LET'S HEAR IT FOR THE ARCHIES! CHILDREN OF RIVERDALE! THEY ARE STARDUST! THEY ARE GOLDEN!!
I'M SO PROUD OF THE KIDS, MARY! WHAT A MEMORABLE EVENT IN THEIR LIVES!
OUR LIVES, TOO! THEY SAY PEACE AND LOVE FESTIVALS ARE BETTER THE SECOND TIME AROUND!
WOW!! THAT CONCERT WAS UNREAL! IT WILL GO DOWN IN HISTORY!
I CAN'T BELIEVE WE PERFORMED IN FRONT OF HALF A MILLION PEOPLE!
WHAT'S BETTER THAN THAT?
PEACE AND LOVE THROUGHOUT THE WORLD!
AH! THE IMPORTANT MESSAGES OF THE '60s ARE STILL WITH US TODAY!
END

Archie in "BIRTHDAY PRESENCE"

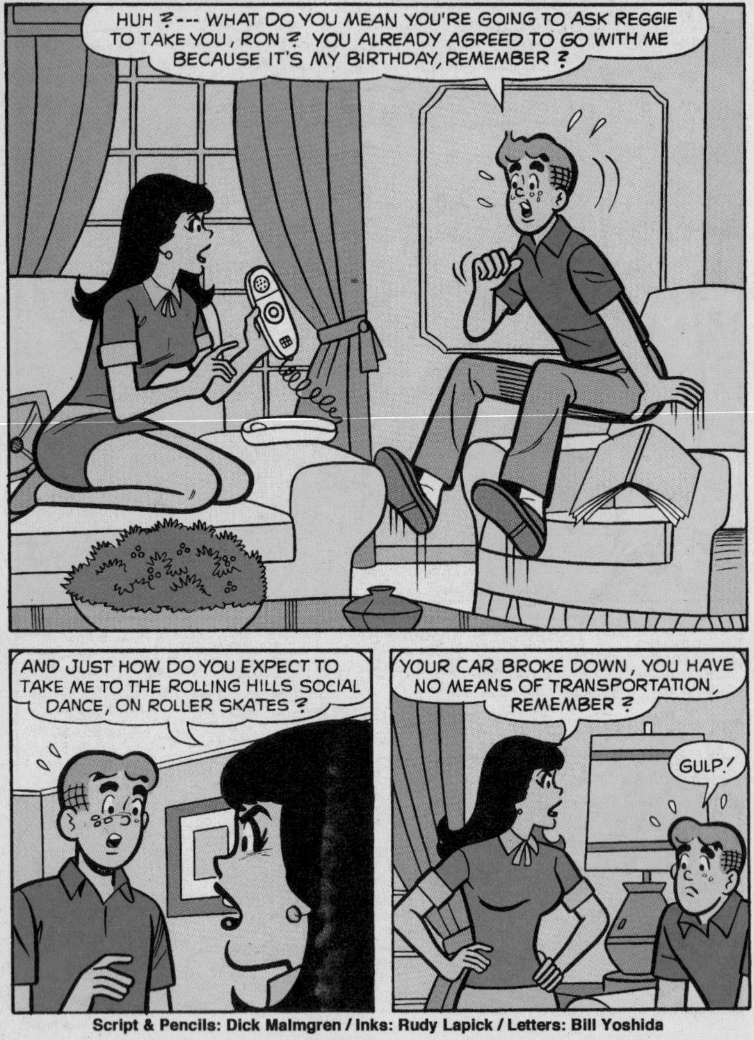
HUH ?--- WHAT DO YOU MEAN YOU'RE GOING TO ASK REGGIE TO TAKE YOU, RON ? YOU ALREADY AGREED TO GO WITH ME BECAUSE IT'S MY BIRTHDAY, REMEMBER ?
AND JUST HOW DO YOU EXPECT TO TAKE ME TO THE ROLLING HILLS SOCIAL DANCE, ON ROLLER SKATES ?
YOUR CAR BROKE DOWN, YOU HAVE NO MEANS OF TRANSPORTATION, REMEMBER ?
GULP!

Script & Pencils: Dick Malmgren / Inks: Rudy Lapick / Letters: Bill Yoshida

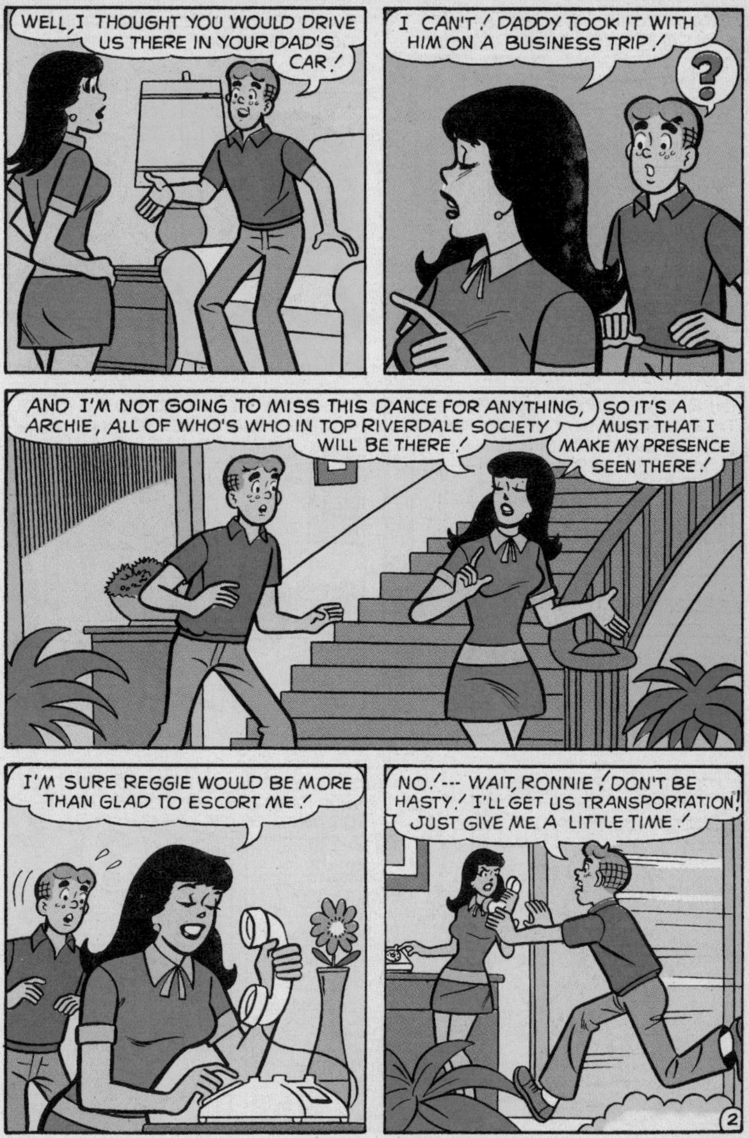
WELL, I THOUGHT YOU WOULD DRIVE US THERE IN YOUR DAD'S CAR!
I CAN'T! DADDY TOOK IT WITH HIM ON A BUSINESS TRIP!
?
AND I'M NOT GOING TO MISS THIS DANCE FOR ANYTHING, ARCHIE, ALL OF WHO'S WHO IN TOP RIVERDALE SOCIETY WILL BE THERE!
SO IT'S A MUST THAT I MAKE MY PRESENCE SEEN THERE!
I'M SURE REGGIE WOULD BE MORE THAN GLAD TO ESCORT ME!
NO!--- WAIT, RONNIE! DON'T BE HASTY! I'LL GET US TRANSPORTATION! JUST GIVE ME A LITTLE TIME!
2

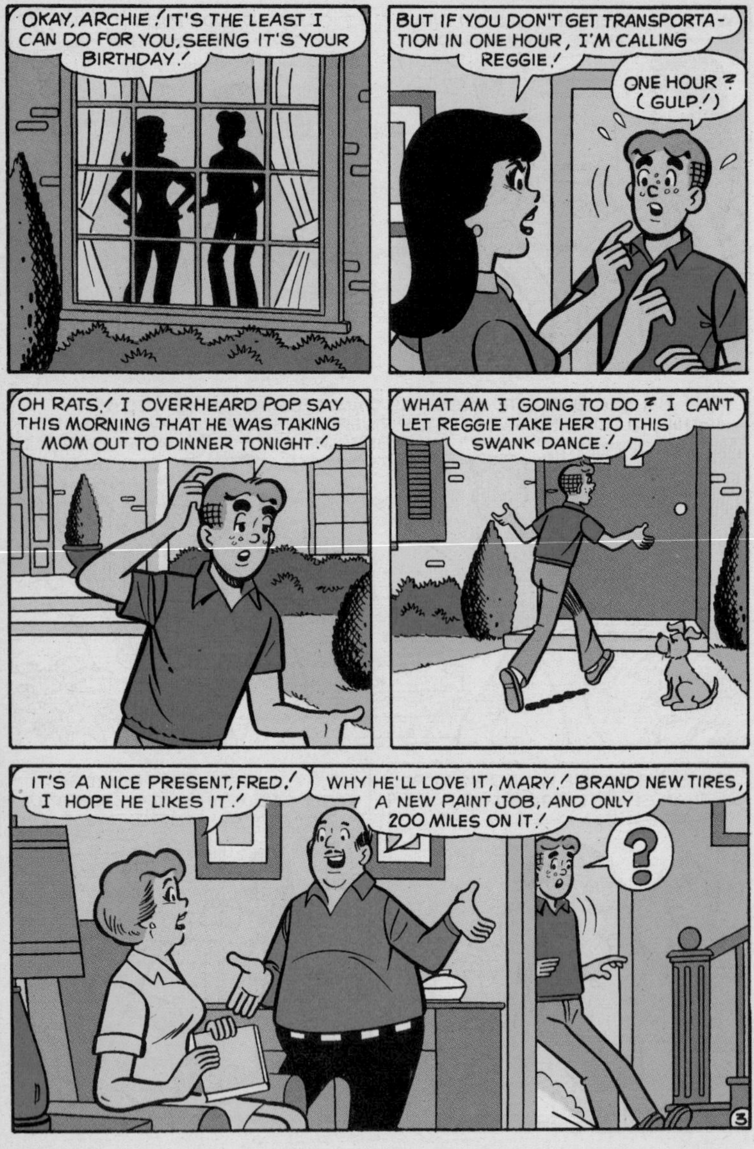
OKAY, ARCHIE! IT'S THE LEAST I CAN DO FOR YOU, SEEING IT'S YOUR BIRTHDAY!
BUT IF YOU DON'T GET TRANSPORTATION IN ONE HOUR, I'M CALLING REGGIE!
ONE HOUR? (GULP!)
OH RATS! I OVERHEARD POP SAY THIS MORNING THAT HE WAS TAKING MOM OUT TO DINNER TONIGHT!
WHAT AM I GOING TO DO? I CAN'T LET REGGIE TAKE HER TO THIS SWANK DANCE!
IT'S A NICE PRESENT, FRED! I HOPE HE LIKES IT!
WHY HE'LL LOVE IT, MARY! BRAND NEW TIRES, A NEW PAINT JOB, AND ONLY 200 MILES ON IT!
?
3

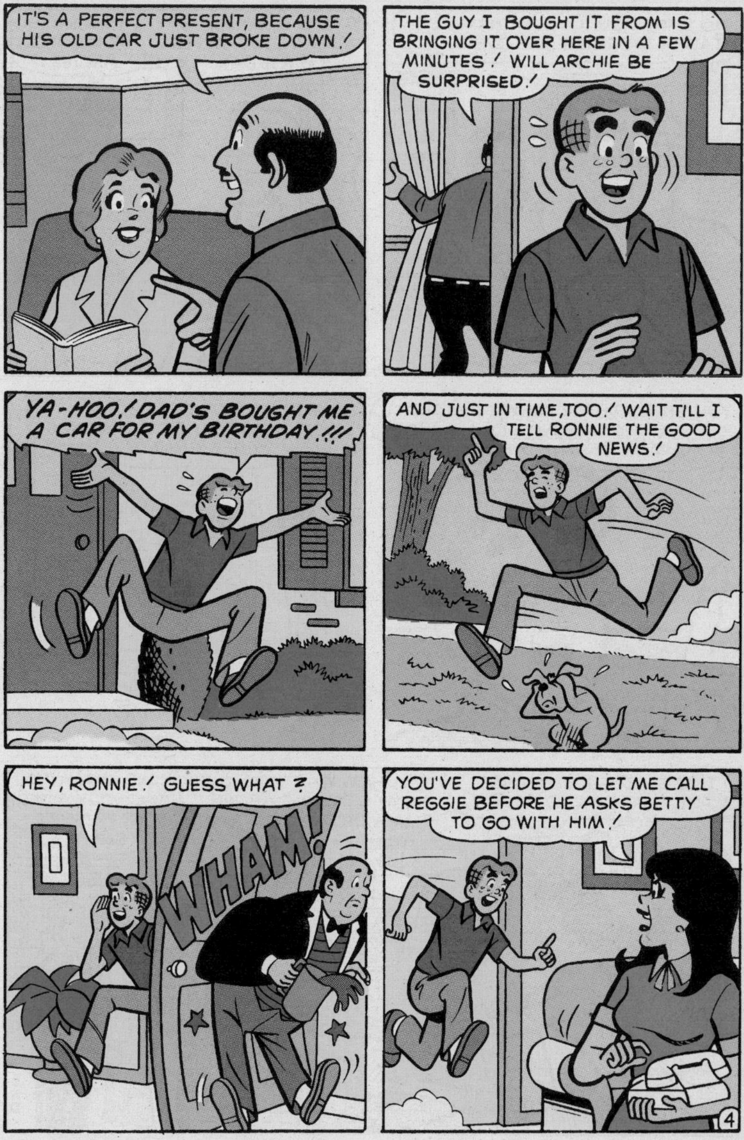
IT'S A PERFECT PRESENT, BECAUSE HIS OLD CAR JUST BROKE DOWN!
THE GUY I BOUGHT IT FROM IS BRINGING IT OVER HERE IN A FEW MINUTES! WILL ARCHIE BE SURPRISED!
YA-HOO! DAD'S BOUGHT ME A CAR FOR MY BIRTHDAY!!!
AND JUST IN TIME, TOO! WAIT TILL I TELL RONNIE THE GOOD NEWS!
HEY, RONNIE! GUESS WHAT?
WHAM!
YOU'VE DECIDED TO LET ME CALL REGGIE BEFORE HE ASKS BETTY TO GO WITH HIM!
4

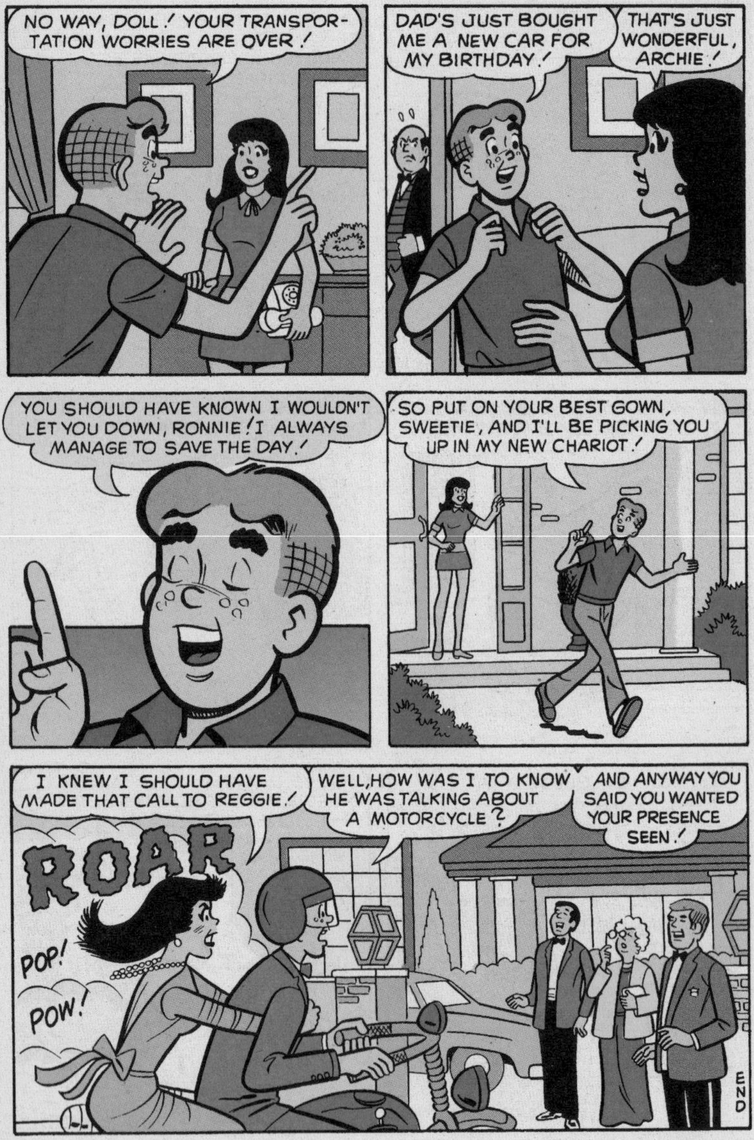
NO WAY, DOLL! YOUR TRANSPORTATION WORRIES ARE OVER!
DAD'S JUST BOUGHT ME A NEW CAR FOR MY BIRTHDAY!
THAT'S JUST WONDERFUL, ARCHIE!
YOU SHOULD HAVE KNOWN I WOULDN'T LET YOU DOWN, RONNIE! I ALWAYS MANAGE TO SAVE THE DAY!
SO PUT ON YOUR BEST GOWN, SWEETIE, AND I'LL BE PICKING YOU UP IN MY NEW CHARIOT!
I KNEW I SHOULD HAVE MADE THAT CALL TO REGGIE!
WELL, HOW WAS I TO KNOW HE WAS TALKING ABOUT A MOTORCYCLE?
AND ANYWAY YOU SAID YOU WANTED YOUR PRESENCE SEEN!
ROAR
POP!
POW!
END

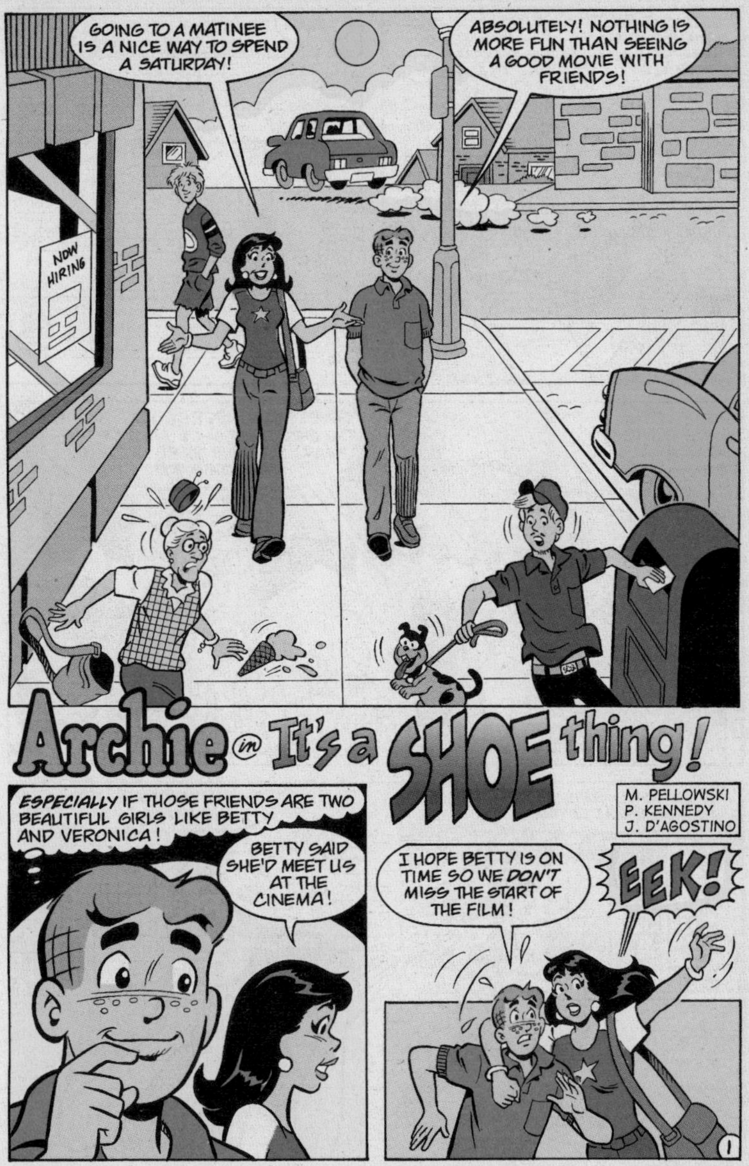
GOING TO A MATINEE IS A NICE WAY TO SPEND A SATURDAY!
ABSOLUTELY! NOTHING IS MORE FUN THAN SEEING A GOOD MOVIE WITH FRIENDS!
NOW HIRING
Archie in It's a SHOE thing!
M. PELLOWSKI
P. KENNEDY
J. D'AGOSTINO
ESPECIALLY IF THOSE FRIENDS ARE TWO BEAUTIFUL GIRLS LIKE BETTY AND VERONICA!
BETTY SAID SHE'D MEET US AT THE CINEMA!
I HOPE BETTY IS ON TIME SO WE DON'T MISS THE START OF THE FILM!
EEK!
1

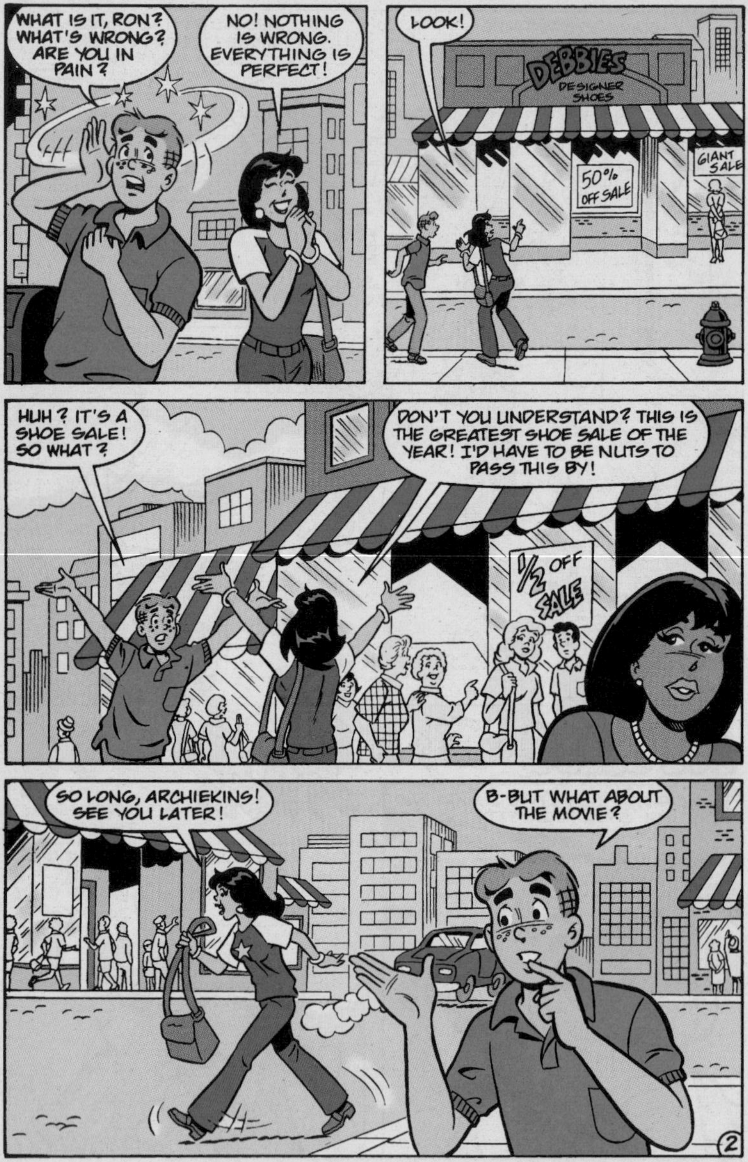
WHAT IS IT, RON? WHAT'S WRONG? ARE YOU IN PAIN?
NO! NOTHING IS WRONG. EVERYTHING IS PERFECT!
LOOK!
DEBBIE'S
DESIGNER SHOES
50% OFF SALE
GIANT SALE
HUH? IT'S A SHOE SALE! SO WHAT?
DON'T YOU UNDERSTAND? THIS IS THE GREATEST SHOE SALE OF THE YEAR! I'D HAVE TO BE NUTS TO PASS THIS BY!
1/2 OFF SALE
SO LONG, ARCHIEKINS! SEE YOU LATER!
B-BUT WHAT ABOUT THE MOVIE?
2

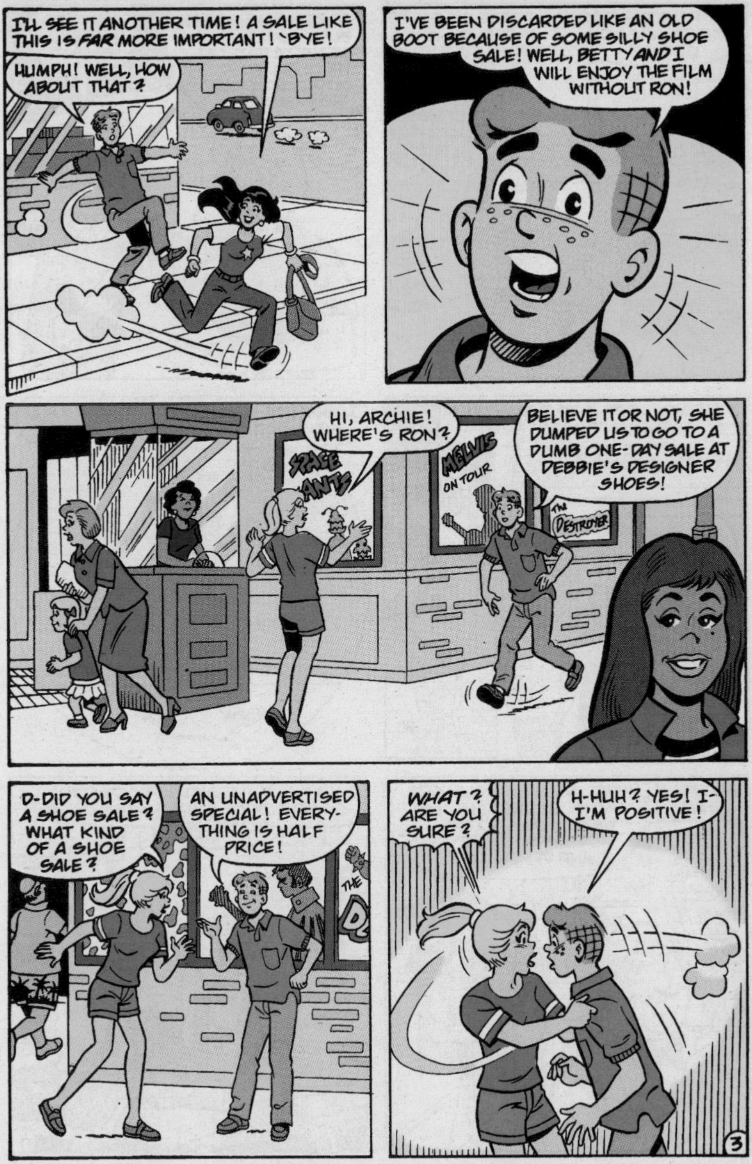
I'LL SEE IT ANOTHER TIME! A SALE LIKE THIS IS FAR MORE IMPORTANT! 'BYE!
HUMPH! WELL, HOW ABOUT THAT?
I'VE BEEN DISCARDED LIKE AN OLD BOOT BECAUSE OF SOME SILLY SHOE SALE! WELL, BETTY AND I WILL ENJOY THE FILM WITHOUT RON!
HI, ARCHIE! WHERE'S RON?
BELIEVE IT OR NOT, SHE DUMPED US TO GO TO A DUMB ONE-DAY SALE AT DEBBIE'S DESIGNER SHOES!
SPACE ANTS
MELVIS ON TOUR
THE DESTROYER
D-DID YOU SAY A SHOE SALE? WHAT KIND OF A SHOE SALE?
AN UNADVERTISED SPECIAL! EVERYTHING IS HALF PRICE!
WHAT? ARE YOU SURE?
H-HUH? YES! I-I'M POSITIVE!
3

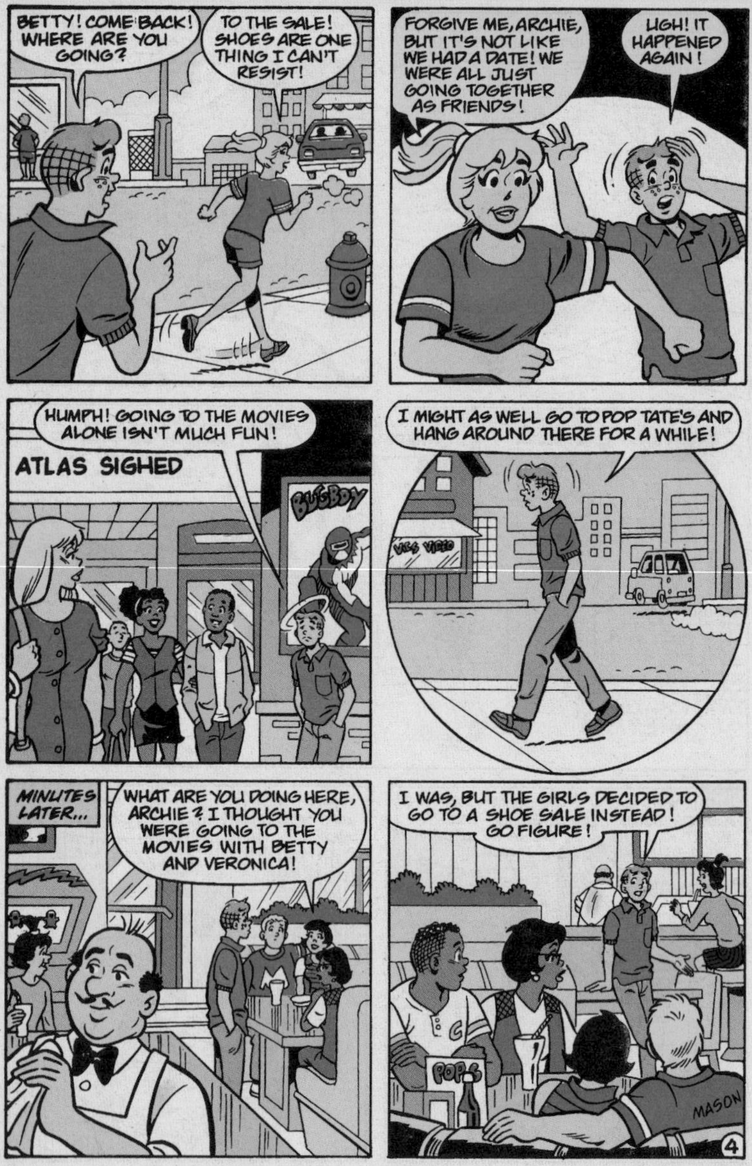
BETTY! COME BACK! WHERE ARE YOU GOING?
TO THE SALE! SHOES ARE ONE THING I CAN'T RESIST!
FORGIVE ME, ARCHIE, BUT IT'S NOT LIKE WE HAD A DATE! WE WERE ALL JUST GOING TOGETHER AS FRIENDS!
UGH! IT HAPPENED AGAIN!
HUMPH! GOING TO THE MOVIES ALONE ISN'T MUCH FUN!
ATLAS SIGHED
BUGBOY
I MIGHT AS WELL GO TO POP TATE'S AND HANG AROUND THERE FOR A WHILE!
VIC'S VIDEO
MINUTES LATER...
WHAT ARE YOU DOING HERE, ARCHIE? I THOUGHT YOU WERE GOING TO THE MOVIES WITH BETTY AND VERONICA!
I WAS, BUT THE GIRLS DECIDED TO GO TO A SHOE SALE INSTEAD! GO FIGURE!
POP'S
MASON
4

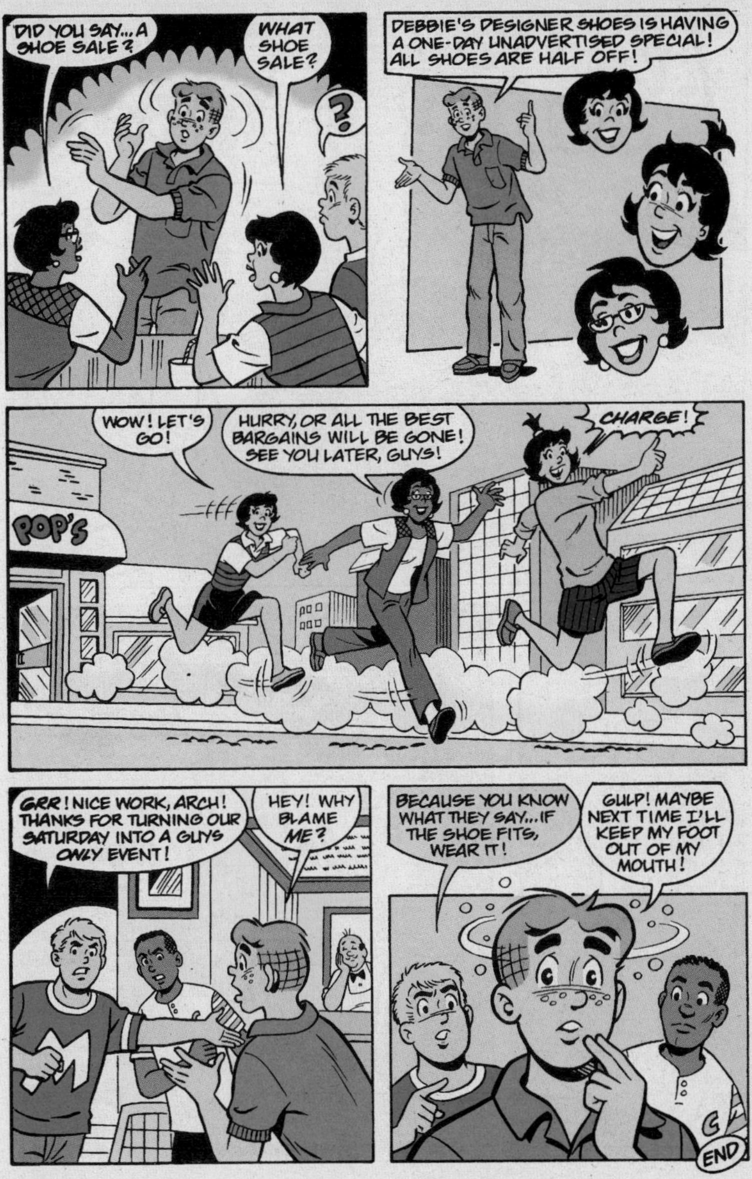
DID YOU SAY... A SHOE SALE?
WHAT SHOE SALE?
?
DEBBIE'S DESIGNER SHOES IS HAVING A ONE-DAY UNADVERTISED SPECIAL! ALL SHOES ARE HALF OFF!
WOW! LET'S GO!
HURRY, OR ALL THE BEST BARGAINS WILL BE GONE! SEE YOU LATER, GUYS!
CHARGE!
POP'S
GRR! NICE WORK, ARCH! THANKS FOR TURNING OUR SATURDAY INTO A GUYS ONLY EVENT!
HEY! WHY BLAME ME?
BECAUSE YOU KNOW WHAT THEY SAY... IF THE SHOE FITS, WEAR IT!
GULP! MAYBE NEXT TIME I'LL KEEP MY FOOT OUT OF MY MOUTH!
END

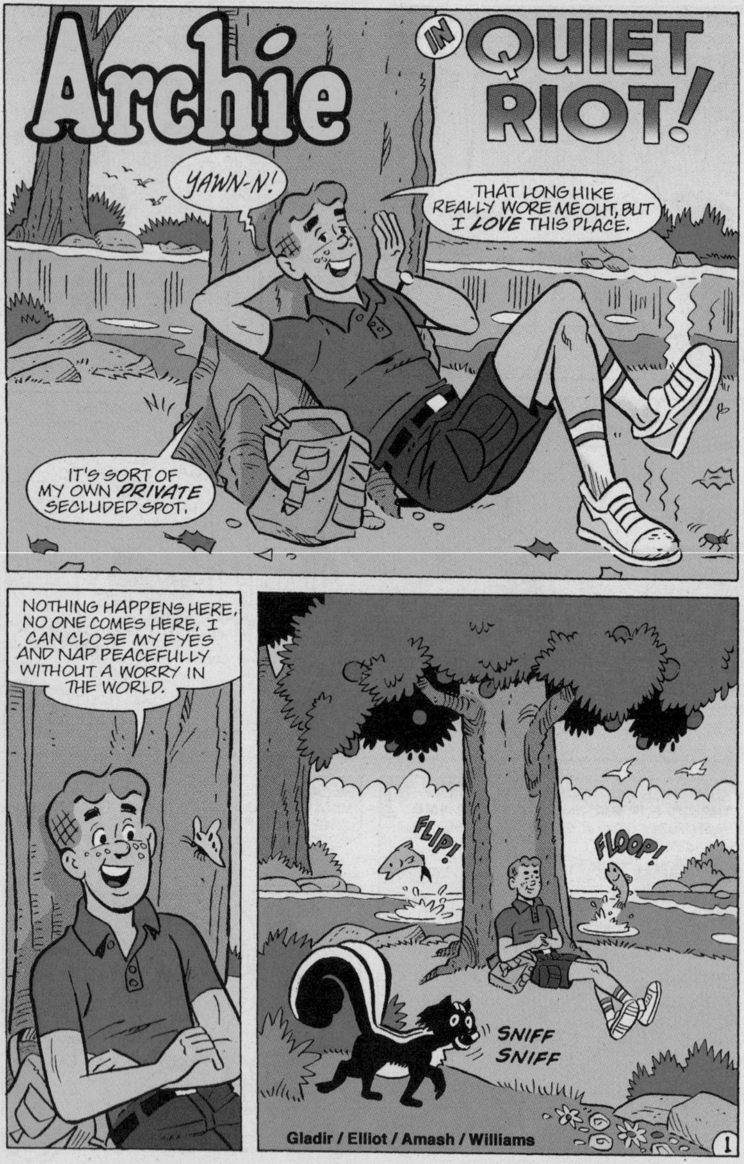
Archie
IN
QUIET RIOT!
YAWN-N!
THAT LONG HIKE REALLY WORE ME OUT, BUT I LOVE THIS PLACE.
IT'S SORT OF MY OWN PRIVATE SECLUDED SPOT.
NOTHING HAPPENS HERE. NO ONE COMES HERE. I CAN CLOSE MY EYES AND NAP PEACEFULLY WITHOUT A WORRY IN THE WORLD.
FLIP!
FLOOP!
SNIFF SNIFF
Gladir / Elliot / Amash / Williams
1

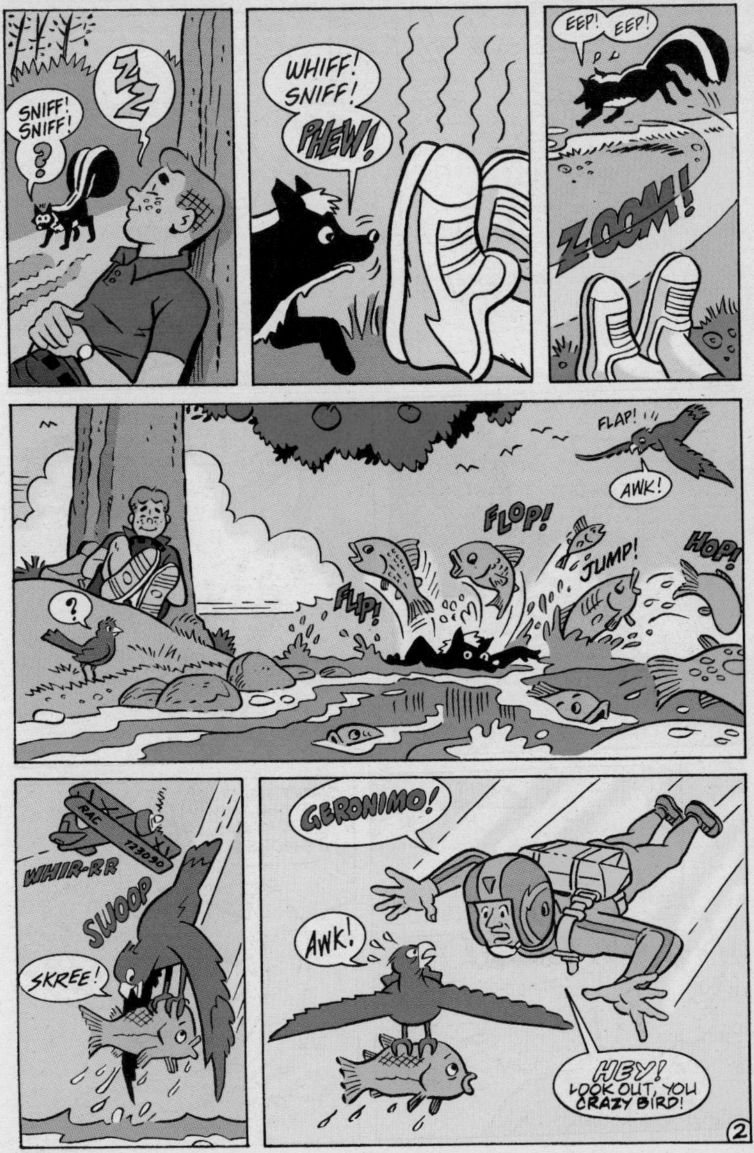

SNIFF! SNIFF!
?
Z Z
WHIFF! SNIFF!
PHEW!
EEP! EEP!
ZOOM!
FLAP!
AWK!
FLOP!
JUMP!
HOP!
FLIP!
?
RAC
T23090
WHIR-RR
SWOOP
SKREE!
GERONIMO!
AWK!
HEY! LOOK OUT, YOU CRAZY BIRD!

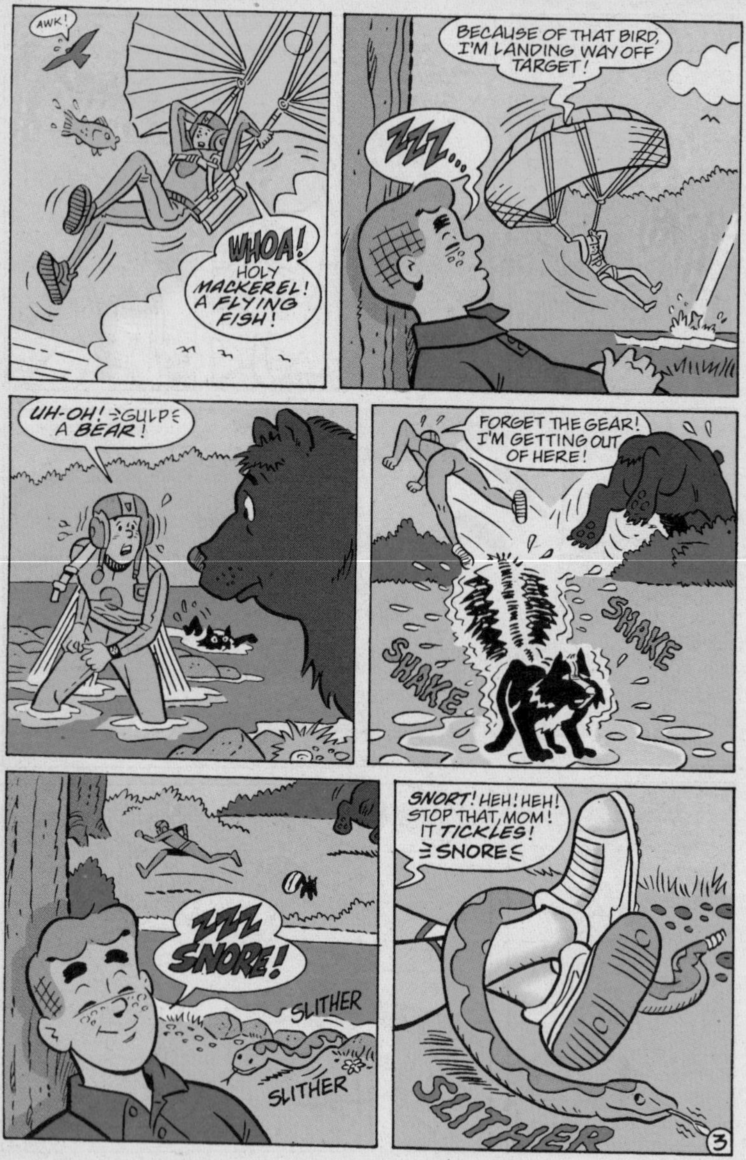
AWK!
WHOA! HOLY MACKEREL! A FLYING FISH!
BECAUSE OF THAT BIRD, I'M LANDING WAY OFF TARGET!
ZZZ...
UH-OH! ≥GULP≤ A BEAR!
FORGET THE GEAR! I'M GETTING OUT OF HERE!
SHAKE
SHAKE
ZZZ SNORE!
SLITHER
SLITHER
SNORT! HEH! HEH! STOP THAT, MOM! IT TICKLES! ≥SNORE≤
SLITHER
3

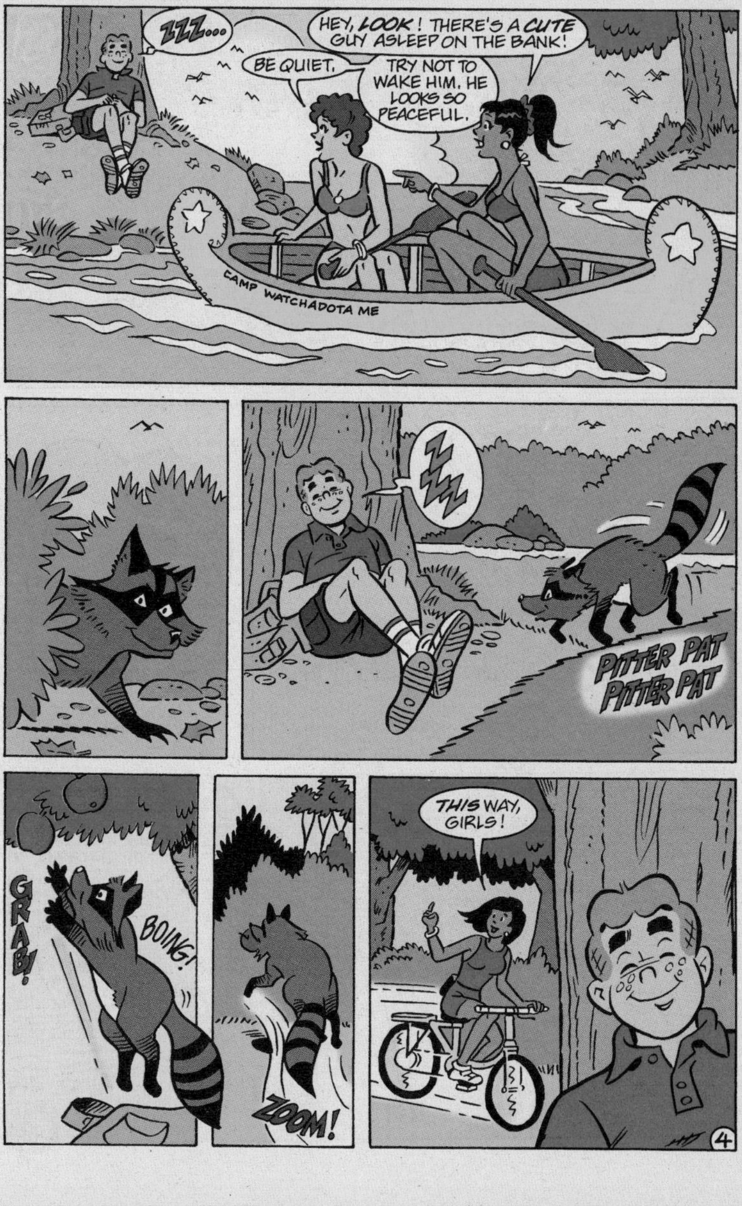
ZZZ...
HEY, LOOK! THERE'S A CUTE GUY ASLEEP ON THE BANK!
BE QUIET.
TRY NOT TO WAKE HIM. HE LOOKS SO PEACEFUL.
CAMP WATCHADOTA ME
Z
PITTER PAT
PITTER PAT
GRAB!
BOING!
ZOOM!
THIS WAY, GIRLS!
4

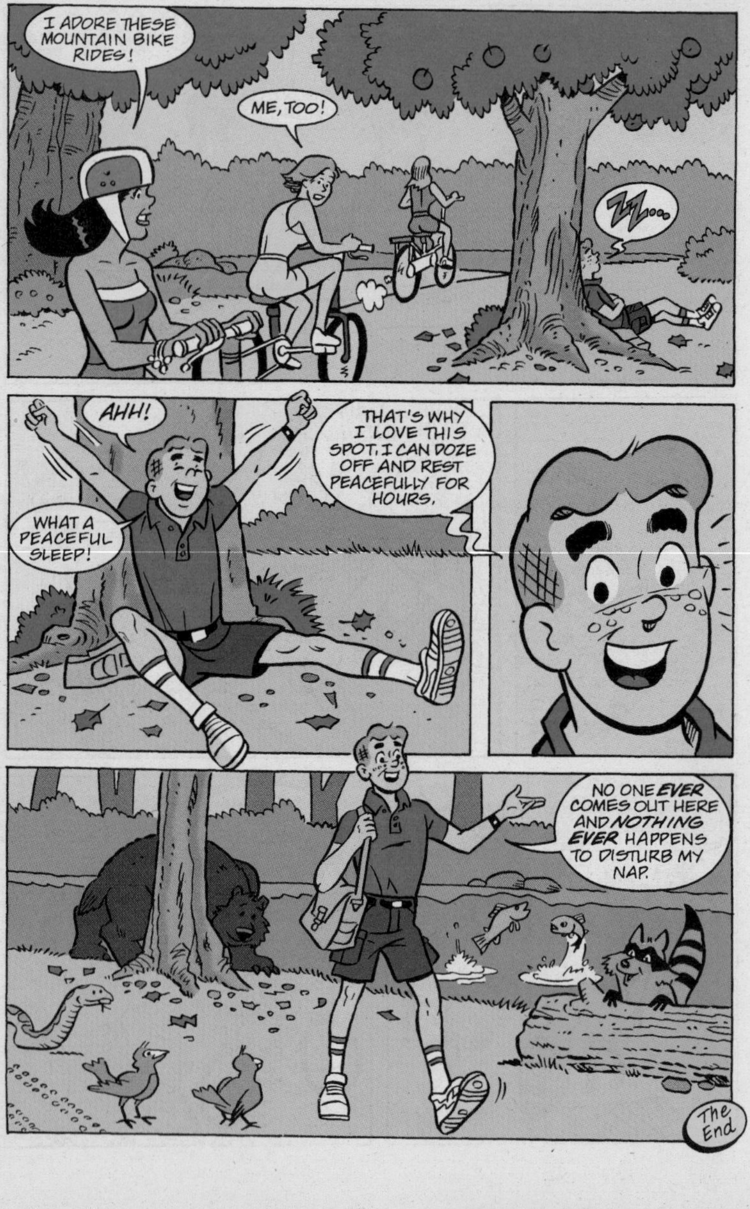
I ADORE THESE MOUNTAIN BIKE RIDES!
ME, TOO!
ZZZ...
AHH!
WHAT A PEACEFUL SLEEP!
THAT'S WHY I LOVE THIS SPOT. I CAN DOZE OFF AND REST PEACEFULLY FOR HOURS.
NO ONE *EVER* COMES OUT HERE AND *NOTHING EVER* HAPPENS TO DISTURB MY NAP.
The End

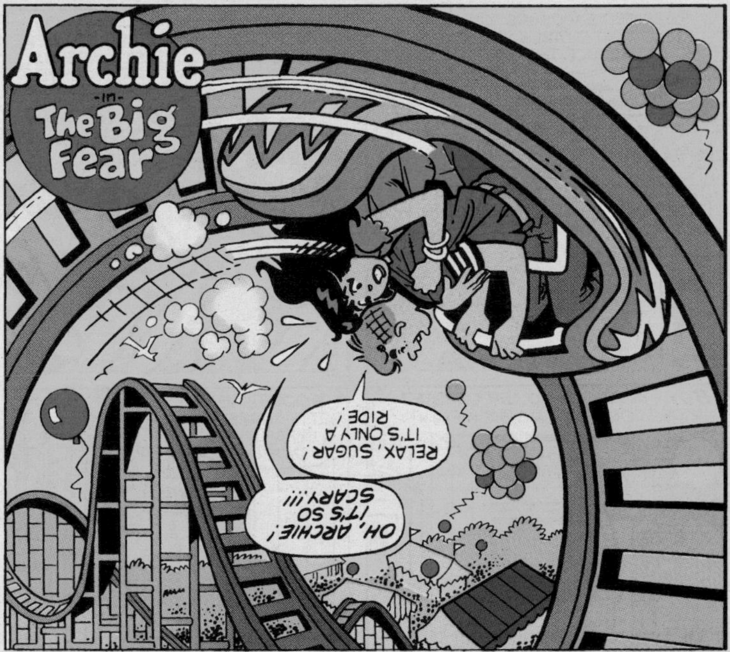
Archie
-in-
The Big Fear
OH, ARCHIE! IT'S SO SCARY!!!
RELAX, SUGAR! IT'S ONLY A RIDE!

Script: Frank Doyle / Pencils: Stan Goldberg / Inks: Henry Scarpelli / Letters: Bill Yoshida

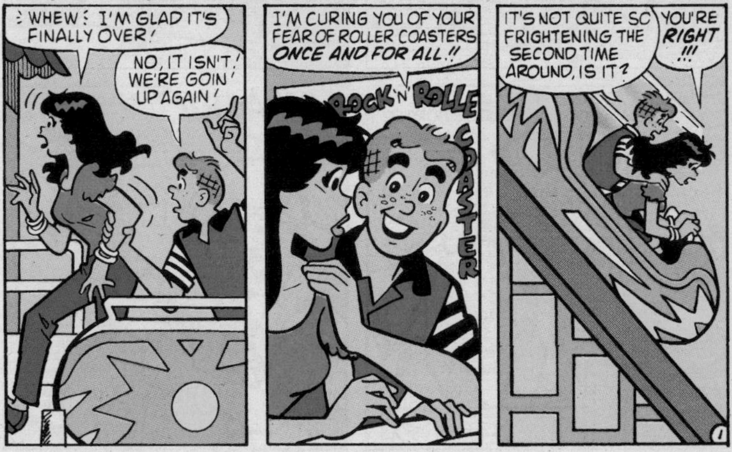
WHEW! I'M GLAD IT'S FINALLY OVER!
NO, IT ISN'T! WE'RE GOIN' UP AGAIN!
I'M CURING YOU OF YOUR FEAR OF ROLLER COASTERS ONCE AND FOR ALL!!
ROCK 'N' ROLLER COASTER
IT'S NOT QUITE SO FRIGHTENING THE SECOND TIME AROUND, IS IT?
YOU'RE RIGHT!!!
1

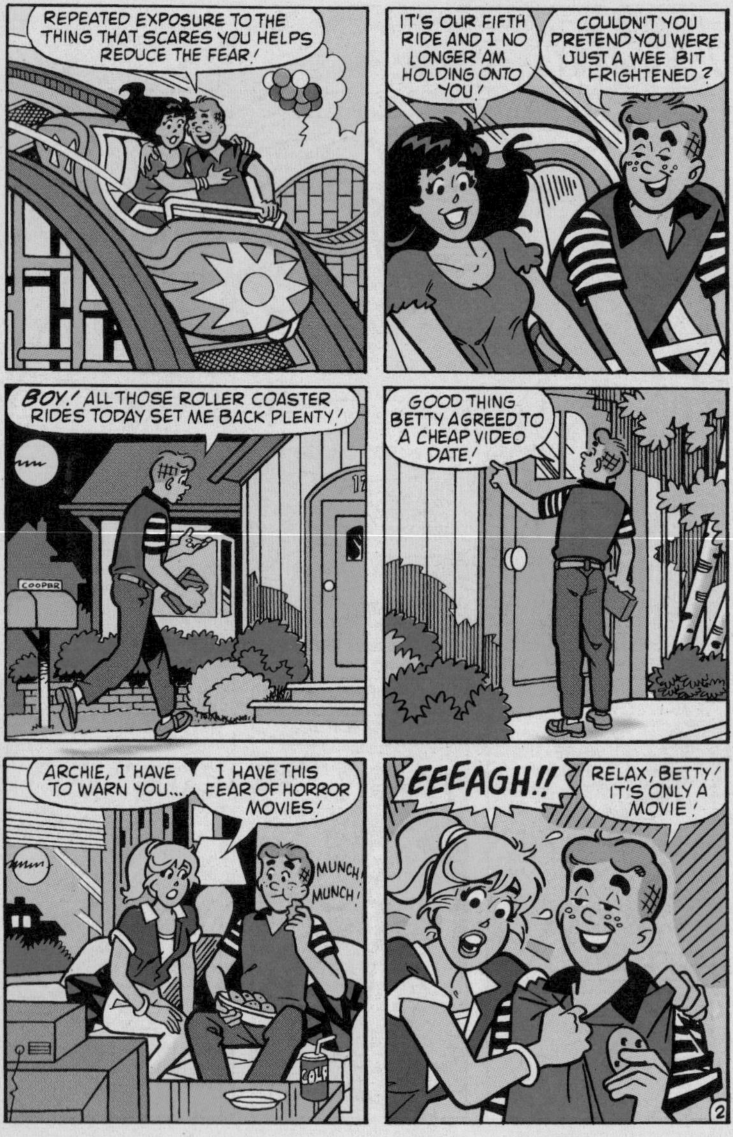
REPEATED EXPOSURE TO THE THING THAT SCARES YOU HELPS REDUCE THE FEAR!
IT'S OUR FIFTH RIDE AND I NO LONGER AM HOLDING ONTO YOU!
COULDN'T YOU PRETEND YOU WERE JUST A WEE BIT FRIGHTENED?
BOY! ALL THOSE ROLLER COASTER RIDES TODAY SET ME BACK PLENTY!
COOPER
GOOD THING BETTY AGREED TO A CHEAP VIDEO DATE!
ARCHIE, I HAVE TO WARN YOU...
I HAVE THIS FEAR OF HORROR MOVIES!
MUNCH!
MUNCH!
EEEAGH!!
RELAX, BETTY! IT'S ONLY A MOVIE!
2

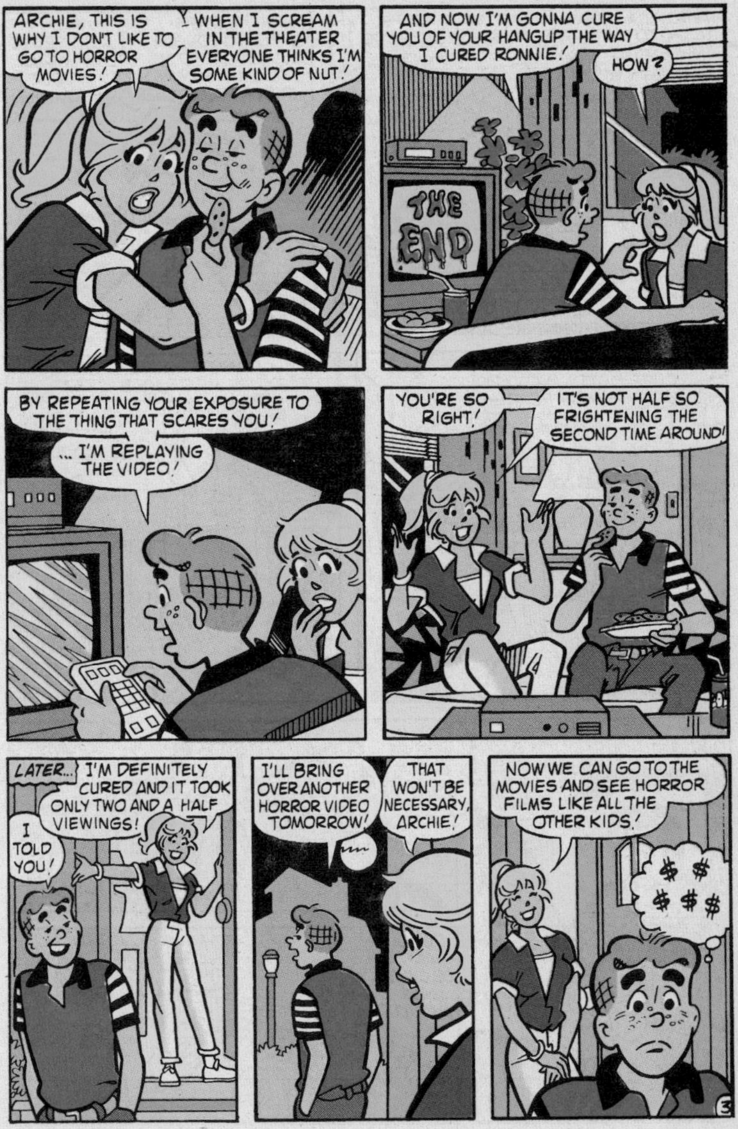
ARCHIE, THIS IS WHY I DON'T LIKE TO GO TO HORROR MOVIES!
WHEN I SCREAM IN THE THEATER EVERYONE THINKS I'M SOME KIND OF NUT!
AND NOW I'M GONNA CURE YOU OF YOUR HANGUP THE WAY I CURED RONNIE!
HOW?
THE END
BY REPEATING YOUR EXPOSURE TO THE THING THAT SCARES YOU!
... I'M REPLAYING THE VIDEO!
YOU'RE SO RIGHT!
IT'S NOT HALF SO FRIGHTENING THE SECOND TIME AROUND!
LATER...
I'M DEFINITELY CURED AND IT TOOK ONLY TWO AND A HALF VIEWINGS!
I TOLD YOU!
I'LL BRING OVER ANOTHER HORROR VIDEO TOMORROW!
THAT WON'T BE NECESSARY, ARCHIE!
NOW WE CAN GO TO THE MOVIES AND SEE HORROR FILMS LIKE ALL THE OTHER KIDS!
$ $ $ $ $
3

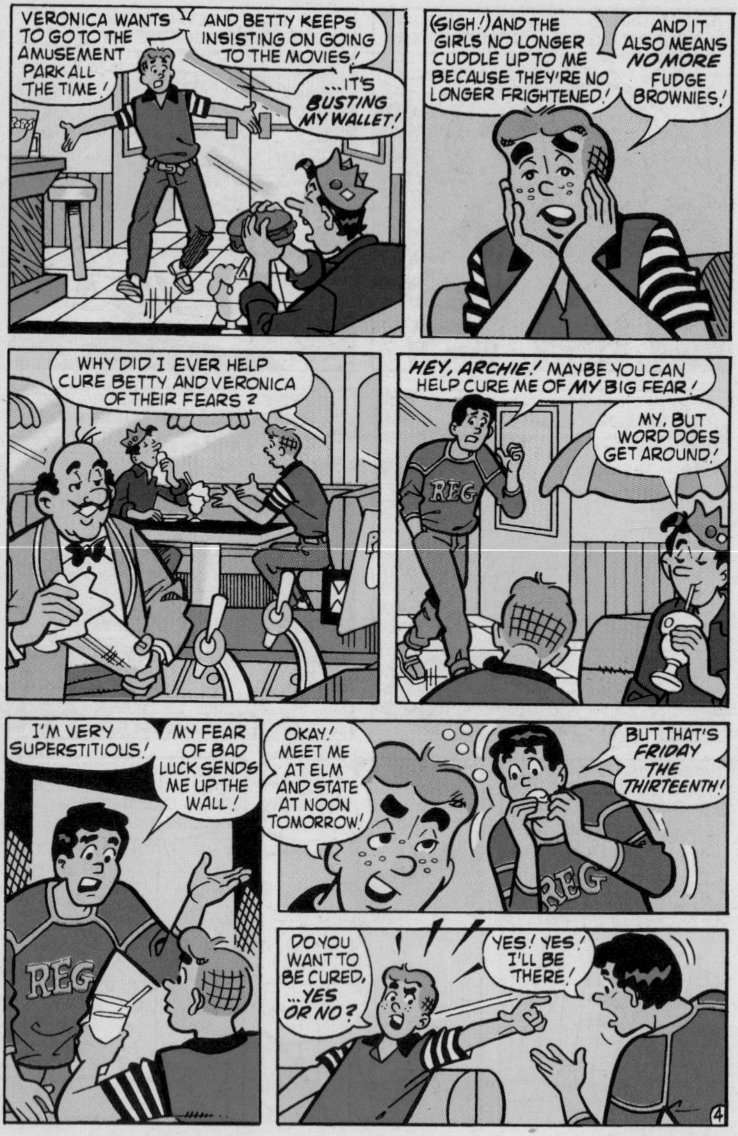

VERONICA WANTS TO GO TO THE AMUSEMENT PARK ALL THE TIME!
AND BETTY KEEPS INSISTING ON GOING TO THE MOVIES!
...IT'S BUSTING MY WALLET!
(SIGH!) AND THE GIRLS NO LONGER CUDDLE UP TO ME BECAUSE THEY'RE NO LONGER FRIGHTENED!
AND IT ALSO MEANS NO MORE FUDGE BROWNIES!
WHY DID I EVER HELP CURE BETTY AND VERONICA OF THEIR FEARS?
HEY, ARCHIE! MAYBE YOU CAN HELP CURE ME OF MY BIG FEAR!
MY, BUT WORD DOES GET AROUND!
REG
I'M VERY SUPERSTITIOUS!
MY FEAR OF BAD LUCK SENDS ME UP THE WALL!
REG
OKAY! MEET ME AT ELM AND STATE AT NOON TOMORROW!
BUT THAT'S FRIDAY THE THIRTEENTH!
REG
DO YOU WANT TO BE CURED, ...YES OR NO?
YES! YES! I'LL BE THERE!
4

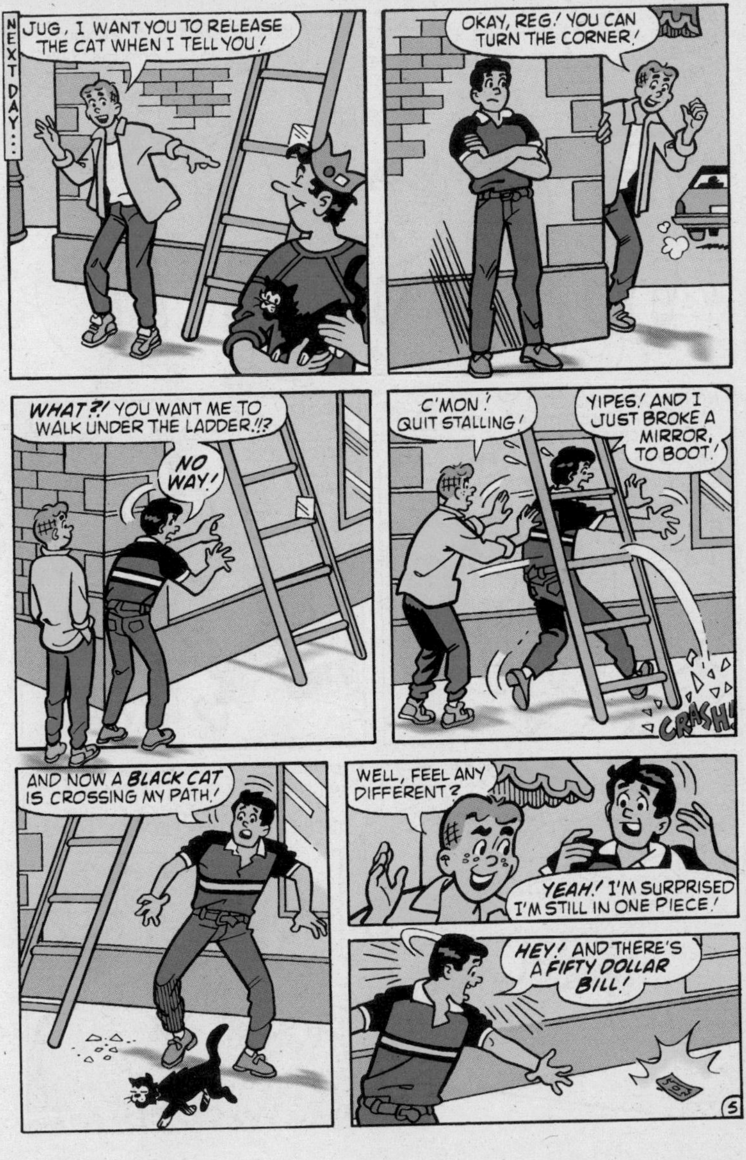
NEXT DAY...
JUG, I WANT YOU TO RELEASE THE CAT WHEN I TELL YOU!
OKAY, REG! YOU CAN TURN THE CORNER!
WHAT?! YOU WANT ME TO WALK UNDER THE LADDER!!?
NO WAY!
C'MON! QUIT STALLING!
YIPES! AND I JUST BROKE A MIRROR, TO BOOT!
CRASH!
AND NOW A BLACK CAT IS CROSSING MY PATH!
WELL, FEEL ANY DIFFERENT?
YEAH! I'M SURPRISED I'M STILL IN ONE PIECE!
HEY! AND THERE'S A FIFTY DOLLAR BILL!
5

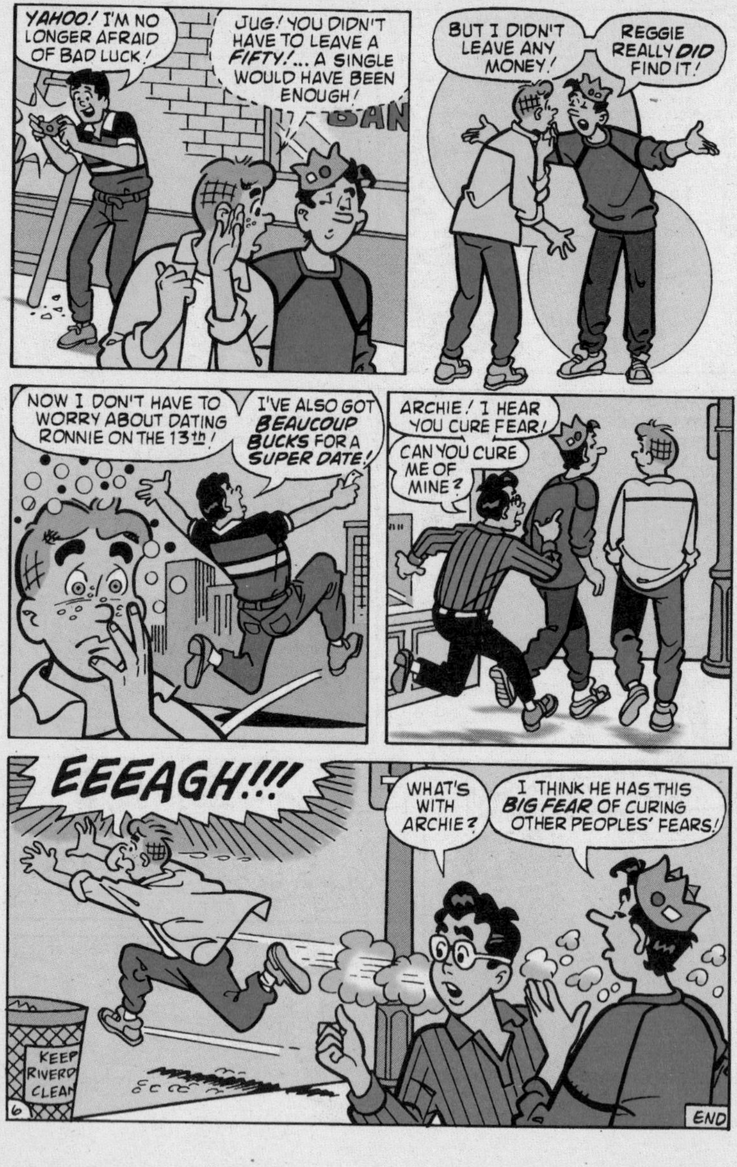
YAHOO! I'M NO LONGER AFRAID OF BAD LUCK!
JUG! YOU DIDN'T HAVE TO LEAVE A FIFTY!... A SINGLE WOULD HAVE BEEN ENOUGH!
BAN
BUT I DIDN'T LEAVE ANY MONEY!
REGGIE REALLY DID FIND IT!
NOW I DON'T HAVE TO WORRY ABOUT DATING RONNIE ON THE 13th!
I'VE ALSO GOT BEAUCOUP BUCKS FOR A SUPER DATE!
ARCHIE! I HEAR YOU CURE FEAR!
CAN YOU CURE ME OF MINE?
EEEAGH!!!!
WHAT'S WITH ARCHIE?
I THINK HE HAS THIS BIG FEAR OF CURING OTHER PEOPLES' FEARS!
KEEP RIVERD CLEAN
6
END

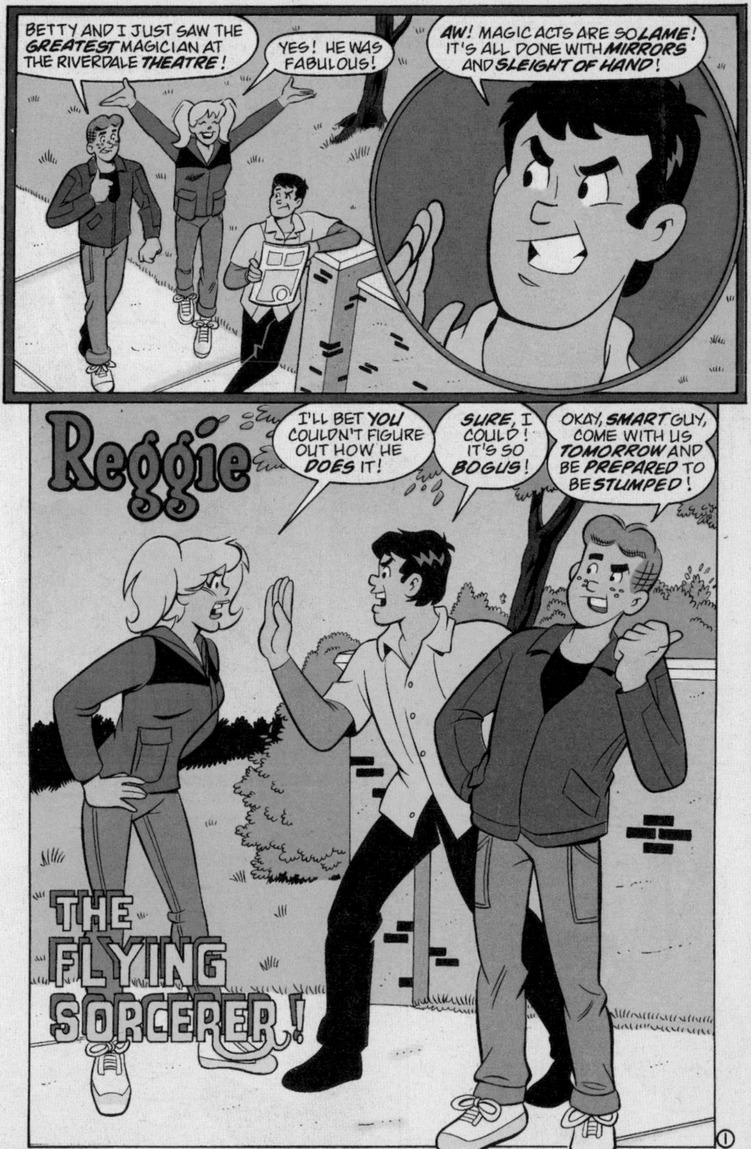

BETTY AND I JUST SAW THE GREATEST MAGICIAN AT THE RIVERDALE THEATRE!
YES! HE WAS FABULOUS!
AW! MAGIC ACTS ARE SO LAME! IT'S ALL DONE WITH MIRRORS AND SLEIGHT OF HAND!
Reggie
I'LL BET YOU COULDN'T FIGURE OUT HOW HE DOES IT!
SURE, I COULD! IT'S SO BOGUS!
OKAY, SMART GUY, COME WITH US TOMORROW AND BE PREPARED TO BE STUMPED!
THE FLYING SORCERER!
1

•SMITH•RUIZ•AMASH•

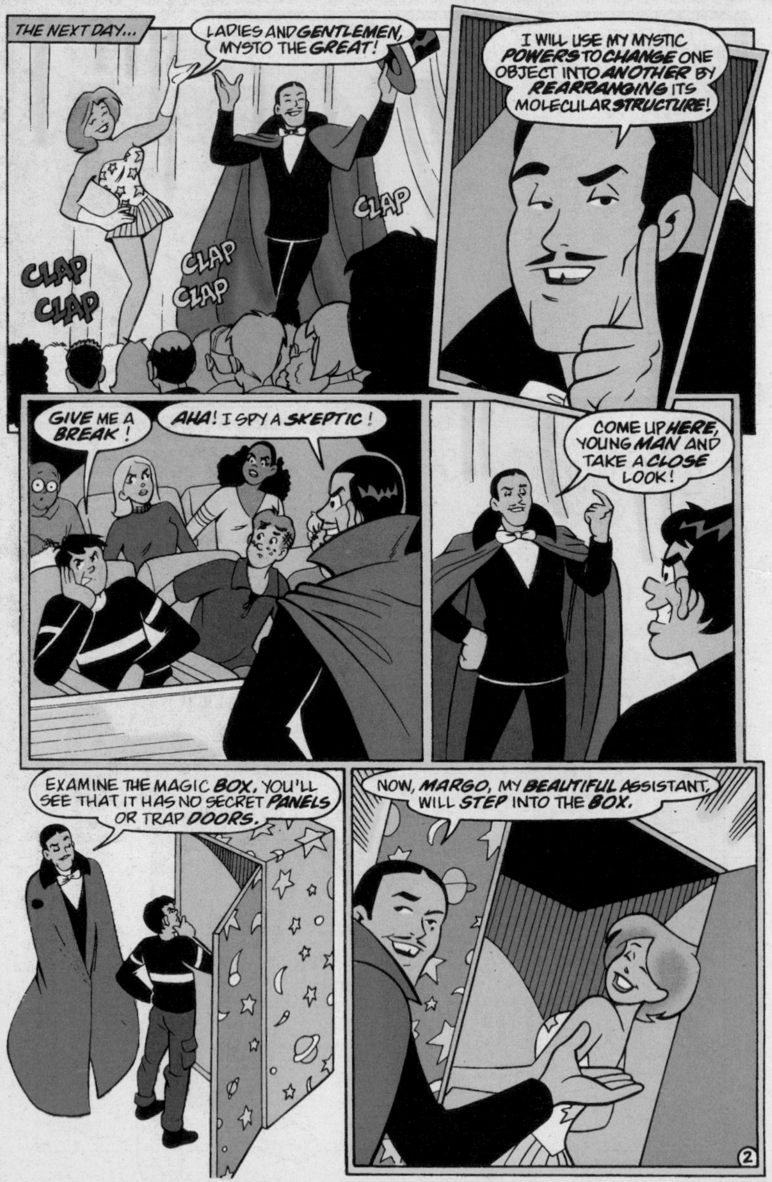
THE NEXT DAY...
LADIES AND GENTLEMEN, MYSTO THE GREAT!
CLAP
CLAP
CLAP
CLAP
CLAP
I WILL USE MY MYSTIC POWERS TO CHANGE ONE OBJECT INTO ANOTHER BY REARRANGING ITS MOLECULAR STRUCTURE!
GIVE ME A BREAK!
AHA! I SPY A SKEPTIC!
COME UP HERE, YOUNG MAN AND TAKE A CLOSE LOOK!
EXAMINE THE MAGIC BOX. YOU'LL SEE THAT IT HAS NO SECRET PANELS OR TRAP DOORS.
NOW, MARGO, MY BEAUTIFUL ASSISTANT, WILL STEP INTO THE BOX.
2

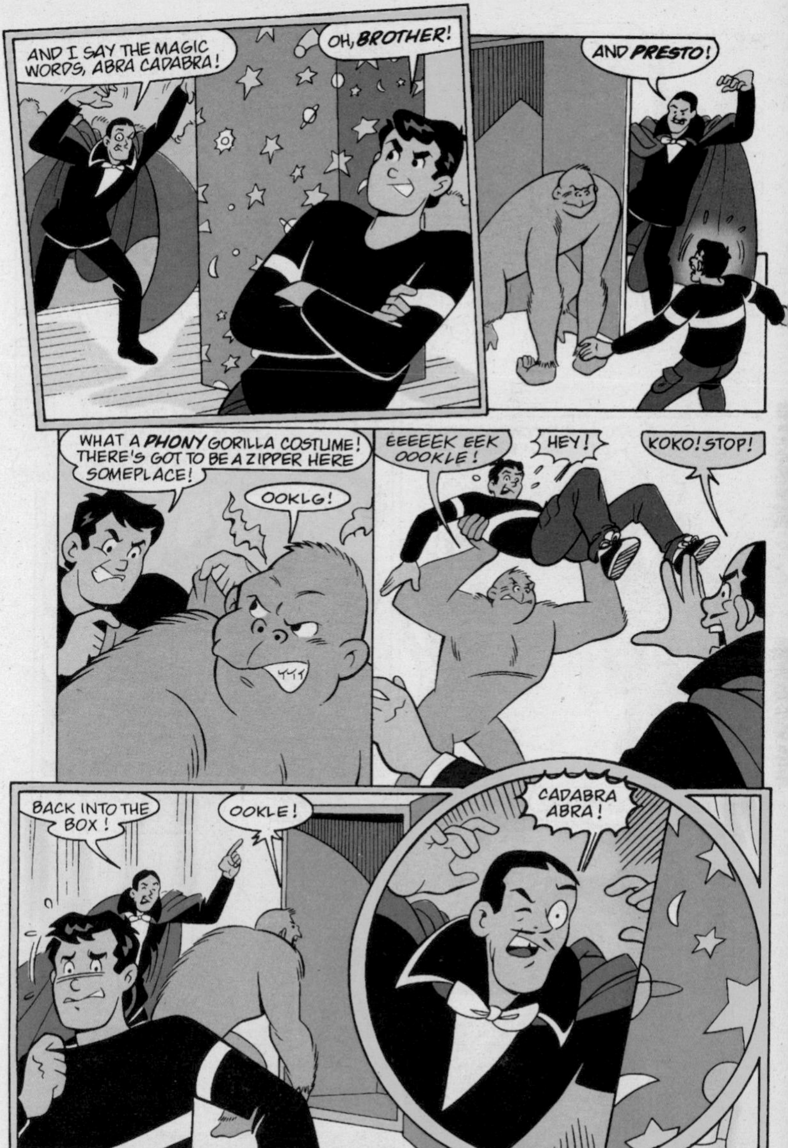
AND I SAY THE MAGIC WORDS, ABRA CADABRA!
OH, BROTHER!
AND PRESTO!
WHAT A PHONY GORILLA COSTUME! THERE'S GOT TO BE A ZIPPER HERE SOMEPLACE!
OOKLG!
EEEEEK EEK OOOKLE!
HEY!
KOKO! STOP!
BACK INTO THE BOX!
OOKLE!
CADABRA ABRA!

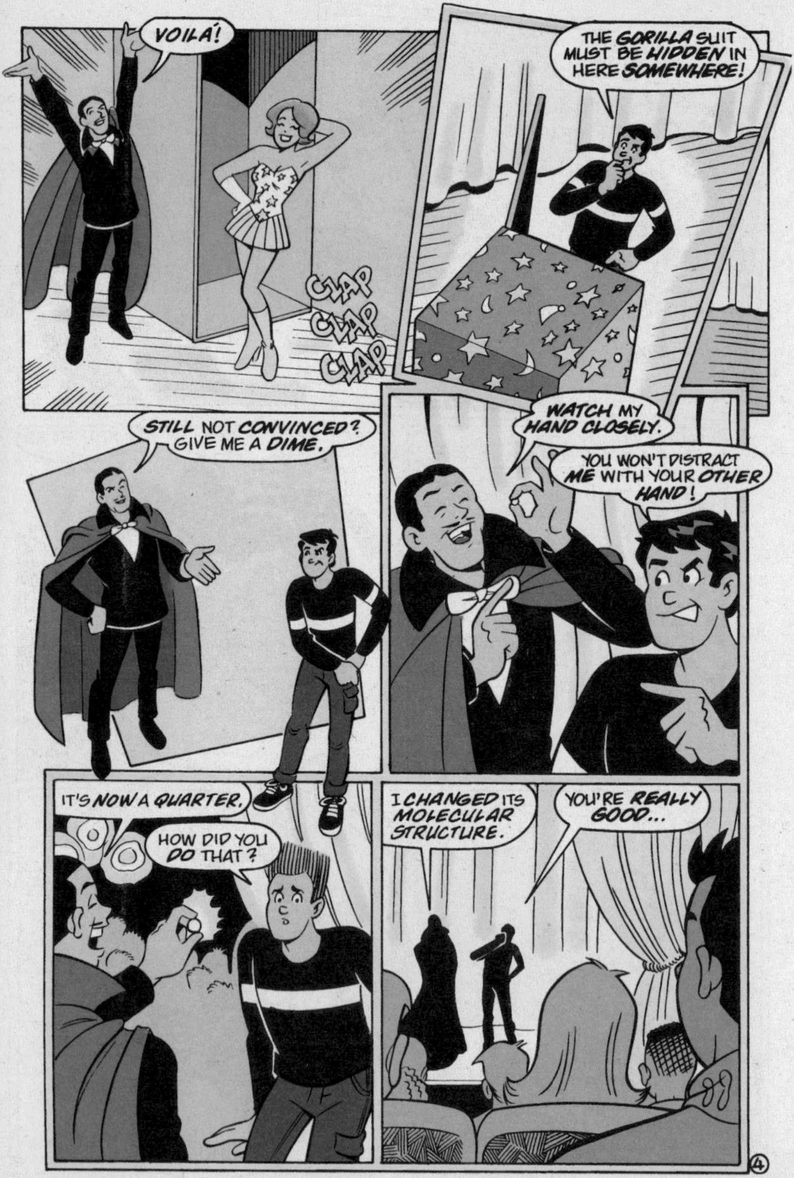
VOILÁ!
CLAP CLAP CLAP
THE GORILLA SUIT MUST BE HIDDEN IN HERE SOMEWHERE!
STILL NOT CONVINCED? GIVE ME A DIME.
WATCH MY HAND CLOSELY.
YOU WON'T DISTRACT ME WITH YOUR OTHER HAND!
IT'S NOW A QUARTER.
HOW DID YOU DO THAT?
I CHANGED ITS MOLECULAR STRUCTURE.
YOU'RE REALLY GOOD...

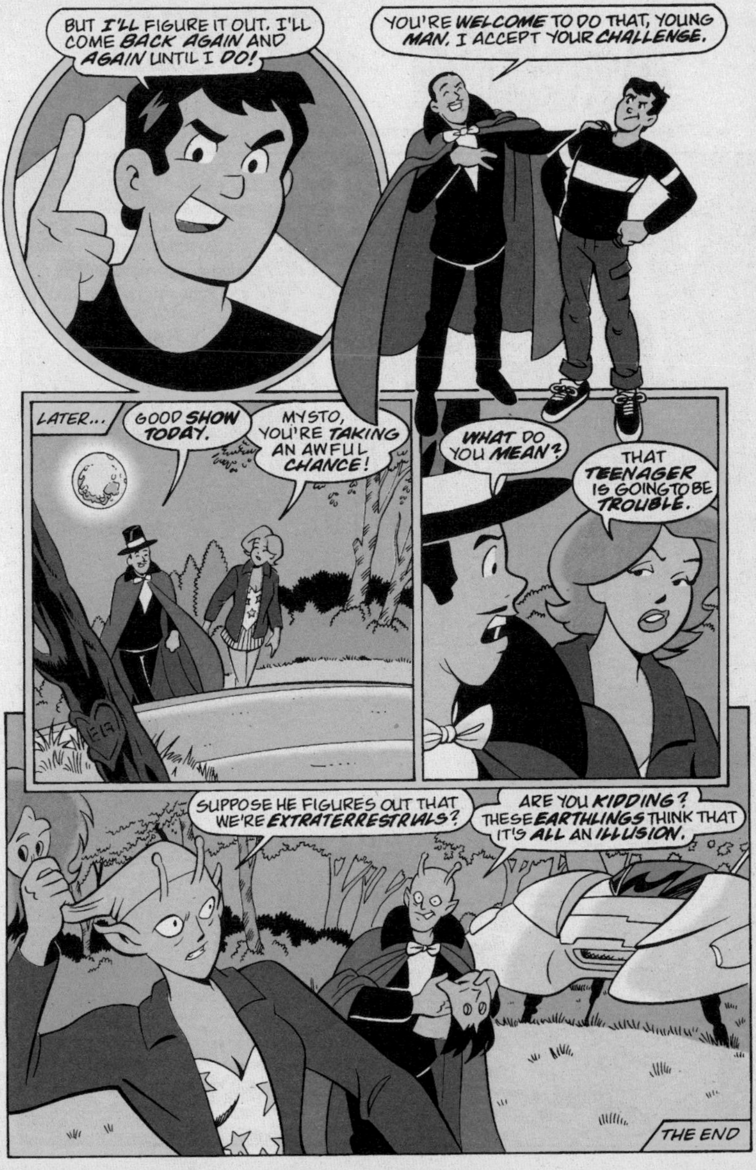
BUT I'LL FIGURE IT OUT. I'LL COME BACK AGAIN AND AGAIN UNTIL I DO!
YOU'RE WELCOME TO DO THAT, YOUNG MAN. I ACCEPT YOUR CHALLENGE.
LATER...
GOOD SHOW TODAY.
MYSTO, YOU'RE TAKING AN AWFUL CHANCE!
WHAT DO YOU MEAN?
THAT TEENAGER IS GOING TO BE TROUBLE.
SUPPOSE HE FIGURES OUT THAT WE'RE EXTRATERRESTRIALS?
ARE YOU KIDDING? THESE EARTHLINGS THINK THAT IT'S ALL AN ILLUSION.
THE END

Archie in "STILL WATER"

Doyle / Goldberg / D'Agostino / Yoshida / Grossman

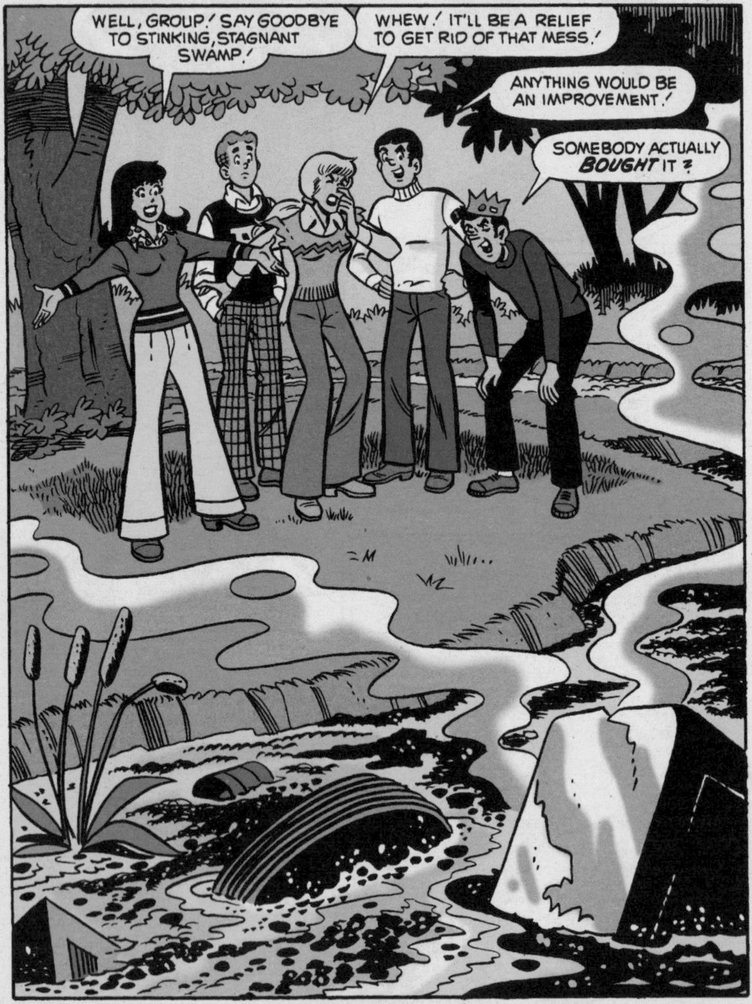
WELL, GROUP! SAY GOODBYE TO STINKING, STAGNANT SWAMP!
WHEW! IT'LL BE A RELIEF TO GET RID OF THAT MESS!
ANYTHING WOULD BE AN IMPROVEMENT!
SOMEBODY ACTUALLY BOUGHT IT?

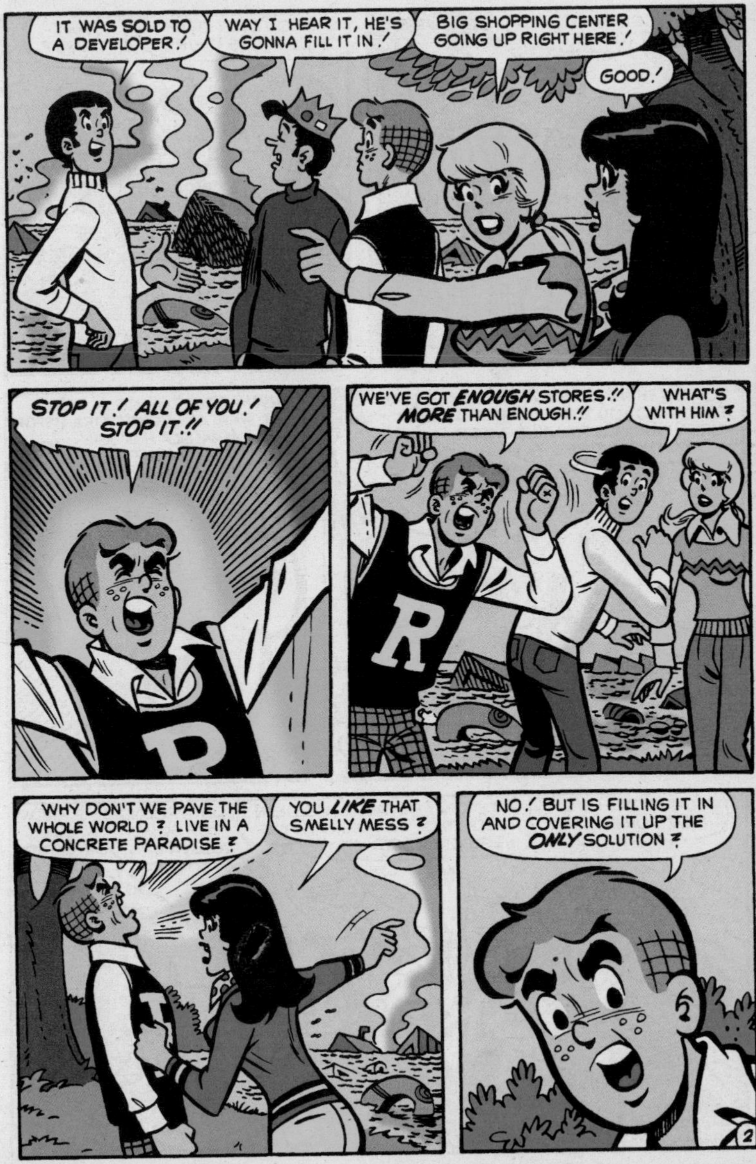
IT WAS SOLD TO A DEVELOPER!
WAY I HEAR IT, HE'S GONNA FILL IT IN!
BIG SHOPPING CENTER GOING UP RIGHT HERE!
GOOD!
STOP IT! ALL OF YOU! STOP IT!!
WE'VE GOT ENOUGH STORES!! MORE THAN ENOUGH!!
WHAT'S WITH HIM?
WHY DON'T WE PAVE THE WHOLE WORLD? LIVE IN A CONCRETE PARADISE?
YOU LIKE THAT SMELLY MESS?
NO! BUT IS FILLING IT IN AND COVERING IT UP THE ONLY SOLUTION?
2

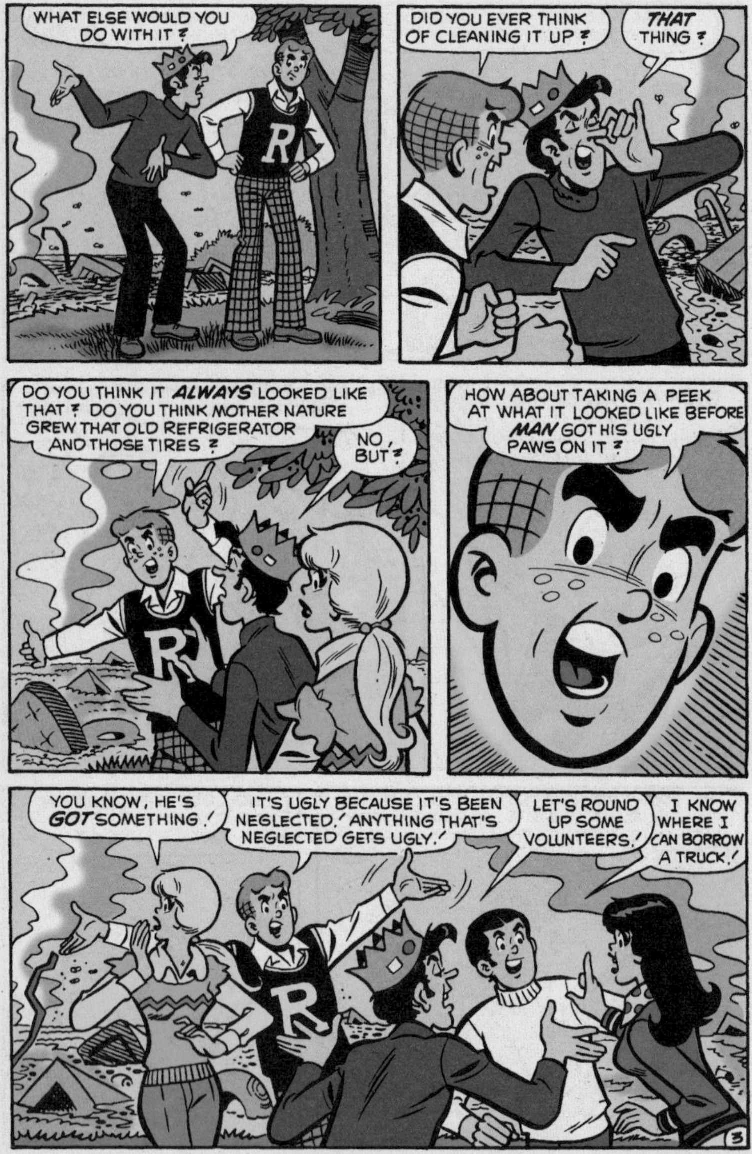
WHAT ELSE WOULD YOU DO WITH IT ?
DID YOU EVER THINK OF CLEANING IT UP ?
THAT THING ?
DO YOU THINK IT ALWAYS LOOKED LIKE THAT ? DO YOU THINK MOTHER NATURE GREW THAT OLD REFRIGERATOR AND THOSE TIRES ?
NO, BUT ?
HOW ABOUT TAKING A PEEK AT WHAT IT LOOKED LIKE BEFORE MAN GOT HIS UGLY PAWS ON IT ?
YOU KNOW, HE'S GOT SOMETHING !
IT'S UGLY BECAUSE IT'S BEEN NEGLECTED ! ANYTHING THAT'S NEGLECTED GETS UGLY !
LET'S ROUND UP SOME VOLUNTEERS !
I KNOW WHERE I CAN BORROW A TRUCK !
3

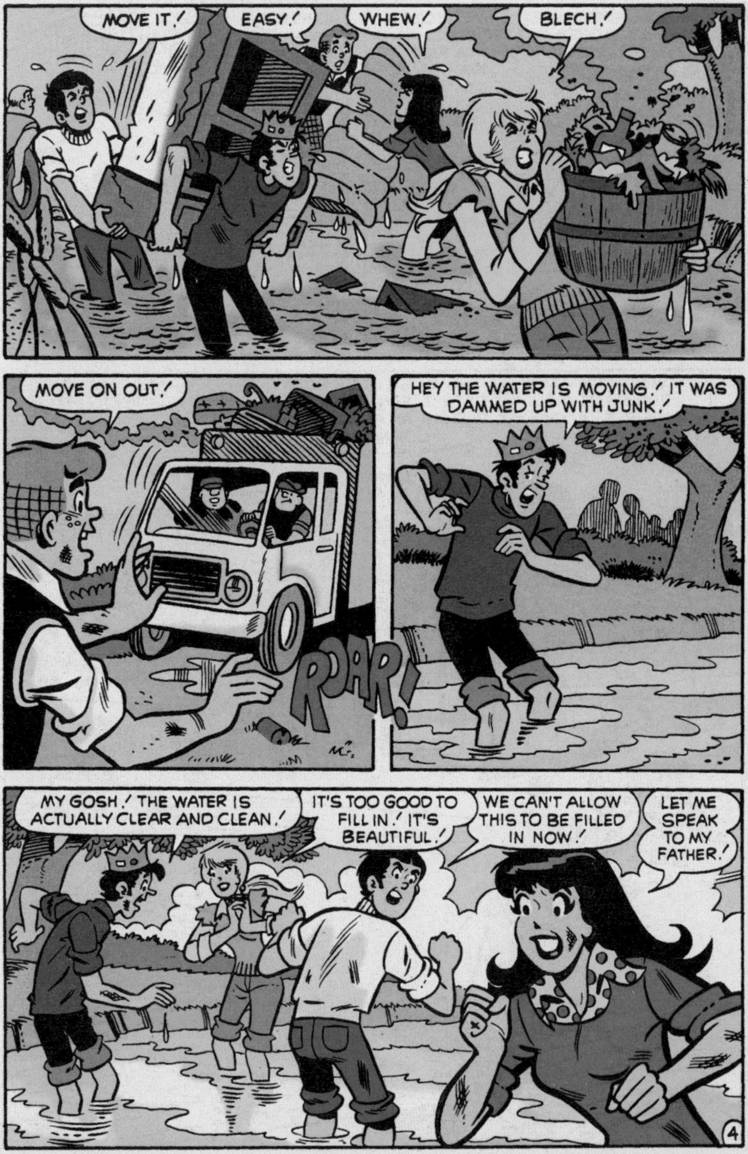
MOVE IT!
EASY!
WHEW!
BLECH!
MOVE ON OUT!
ROAR!
HEY THE WATER IS MOVING! IT WAS DAMMED UP WITH JUNK!
MY GOSH! THE WATER IS ACTUALLY CLEAR AND CLEAN!
IT'S TOO GOOD TO FILL IN! IT'S BEAUTIFUL!
WE CAN'T ALLOW THIS TO BE FILLED IN NOW!
LET ME SPEAK TO MY FATHER!
4

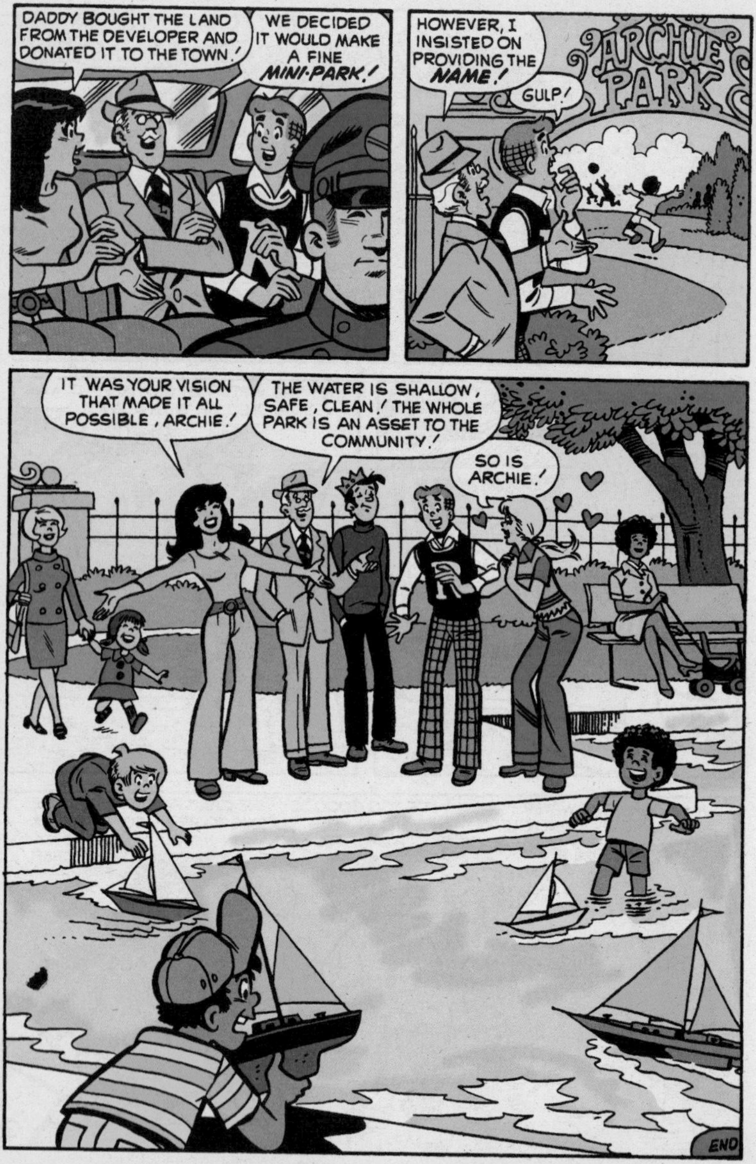
DADDY BOUGHT THE LAND FROM THE DEVELOPER AND DONATED IT TO THE TOWN!
WE DECIDED IT WOULD MAKE A FINE MINI-PARK!
HOWEVER, I INSISTED ON PROVIDING THE NAME!
ARCHIE PARK
GULP!
IT WAS YOUR VISION THAT MADE IT ALL POSSIBLE, ARCHIE!
THE WATER IS SHALLOW, SAFE, CLEAN! THE WHOLE PARK IS AN ASSET TO THE COMMUNITY!
SO IS ARCHIE!
END

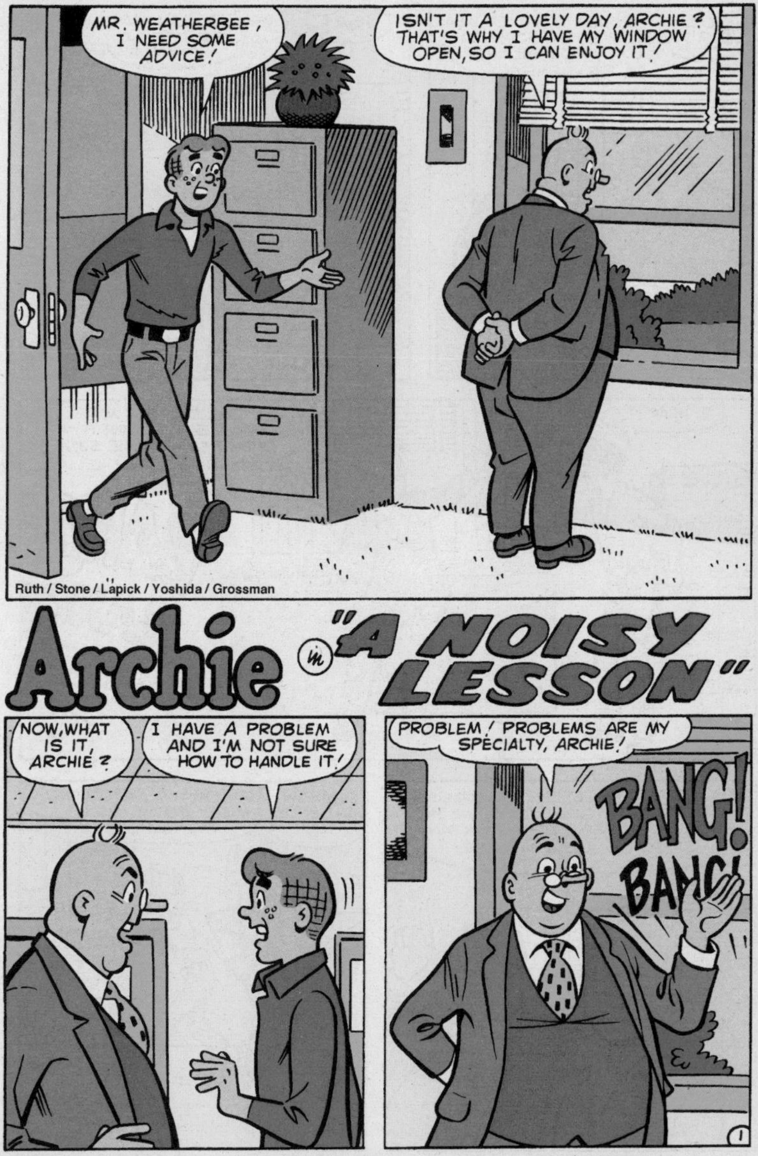
MR. WEATHERBEE, I NEED SOME ADVICE!
ISN'T IT A LOVELY DAY, ARCHIE? THAT'S WHY I HAVE MY WINDOW OPEN, SO I CAN ENJOY IT!
Ruth / Stone / Lapick / Yoshida / Grossman
Archie in "A NOISY LESSON"
NOW, WHAT IS IT, ARCHIE?
I HAVE A PROBLEM AND I'M NOT SURE HOW TO HANDLE IT!
PROBLEM! PROBLEMS ARE MY SPECIALTY, ARCHIE!
BANG!
1

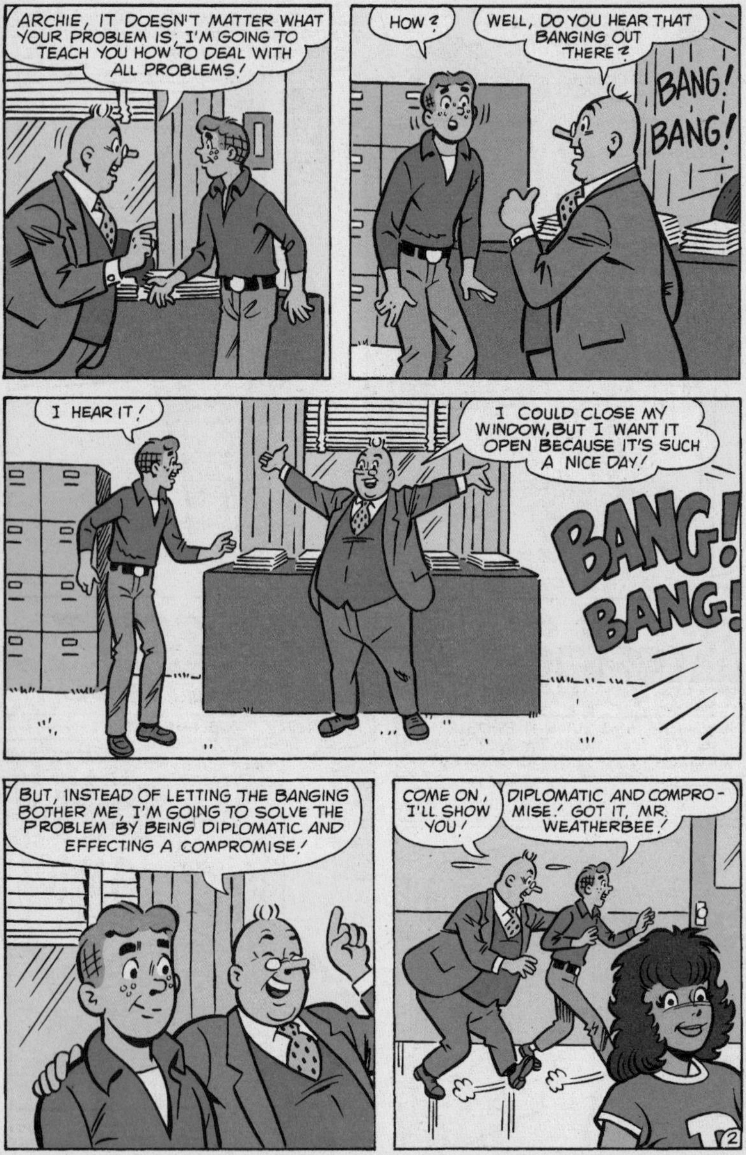
ARCHIE, IT DOESN'T MATTER WHAT YOUR PROBLEM IS; I'M GOING TO TEACH YOU HOW TO DEAL WITH ALL PROBLEMS!
HOW?
WELL, DO YOU HEAR THAT BANGING OUT THERE?
BANG! BANG!
I HEAR IT!
I COULD CLOSE MY WINDOW, BUT I WANT IT OPEN BECAUSE IT'S SUCH A NICE DAY!
BANG! BANG!
BUT, INSTEAD OF LETTING THE BANGING BOTHER ME, I'M GOING TO SOLVE THE PROBLEM BY BEING DIPLOMATIC AND EFFECTING A COMPROMISE!
COME ON, I'LL SHOW YOU!
DIPLOMATIC AND COMPROMISE! GOT IT, MR. WEATHERBEE!
2

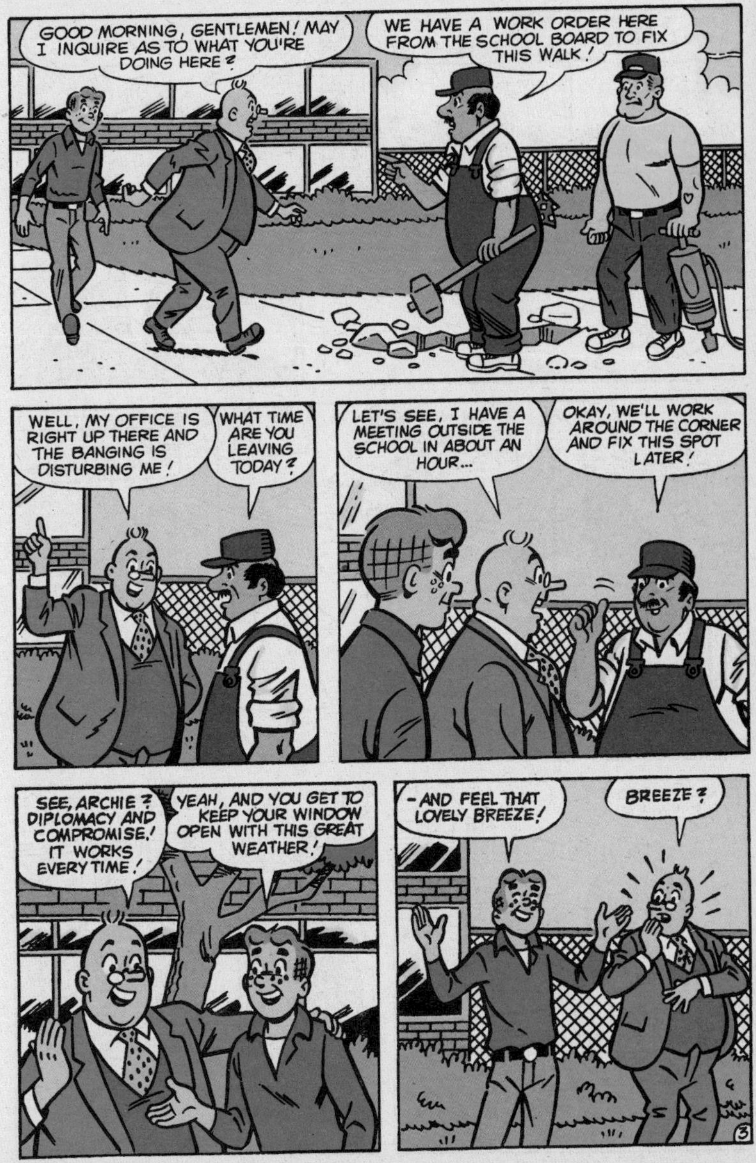
GOOD MORNING, GENTLEMEN! MAY I INQUIRE AS TO WHAT YOU'RE DOING HERE?
WE HAVE A WORK ORDER HERE FROM THE SCHOOL BOARD TO FIX THIS WALK!
WELL, MY OFFICE IS RIGHT UP THERE AND THE BANGING IS DISTURBING ME!
WHAT TIME ARE YOU LEAVING TODAY?
LET'S SEE, I HAVE A MEETING OUTSIDE THE SCHOOL IN ABOUT AN HOUR...
OKAY, WE'LL WORK AROUND THE CORNER AND FIX THIS SPOT LATER!
SEE, ARCHIE? DIPLOMACY AND COMPROMISE! IT WORKS EVERY TIME!
YEAH, AND YOU GET TO KEEP YOUR WINDOW OPEN WITH THIS GREAT WEATHER!
-AND FEEL THAT LOVELY BREEZE!
BREEZE?
3

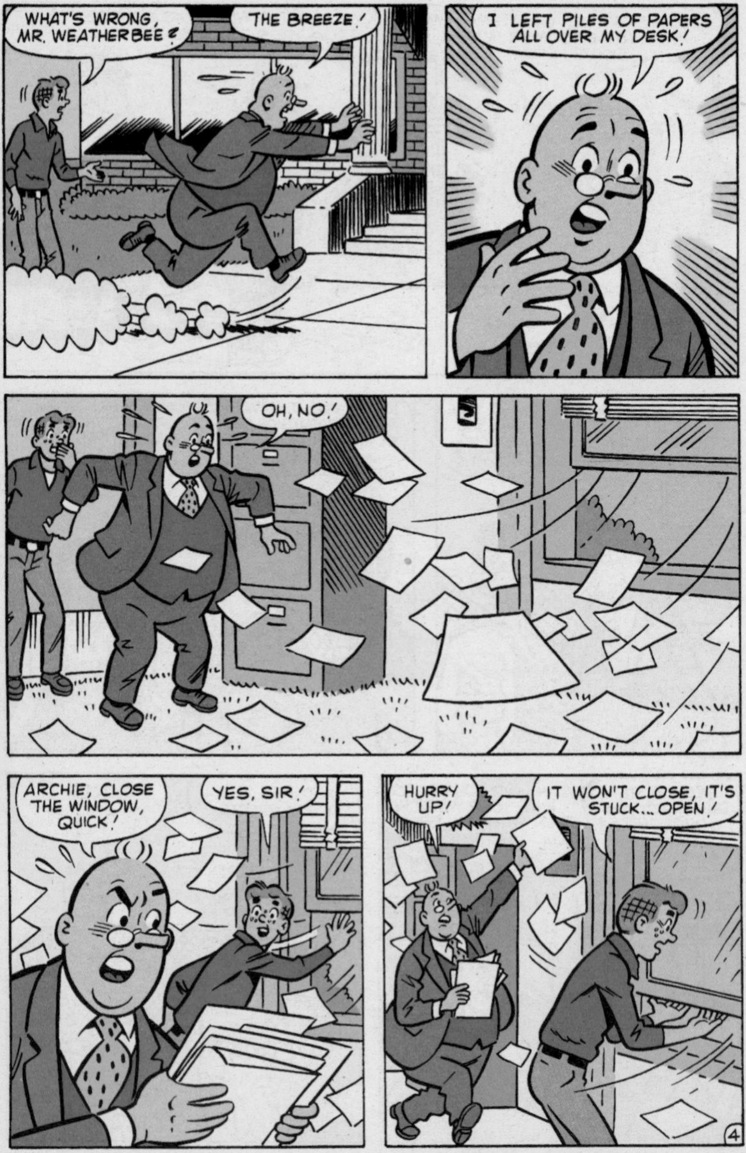
WHAT'S WRONG, MR. WEATHERBEE?
THE BREEZE!
I LEFT PILES OF PAPERS ALL OVER MY DESK!
OH, NO!
ARCHIE, CLOSE THE WINDOW, QUICK!
YES, SIR!
HURRY UP!
IT WON'T CLOSE, IT'S STUCK... OPEN!
4

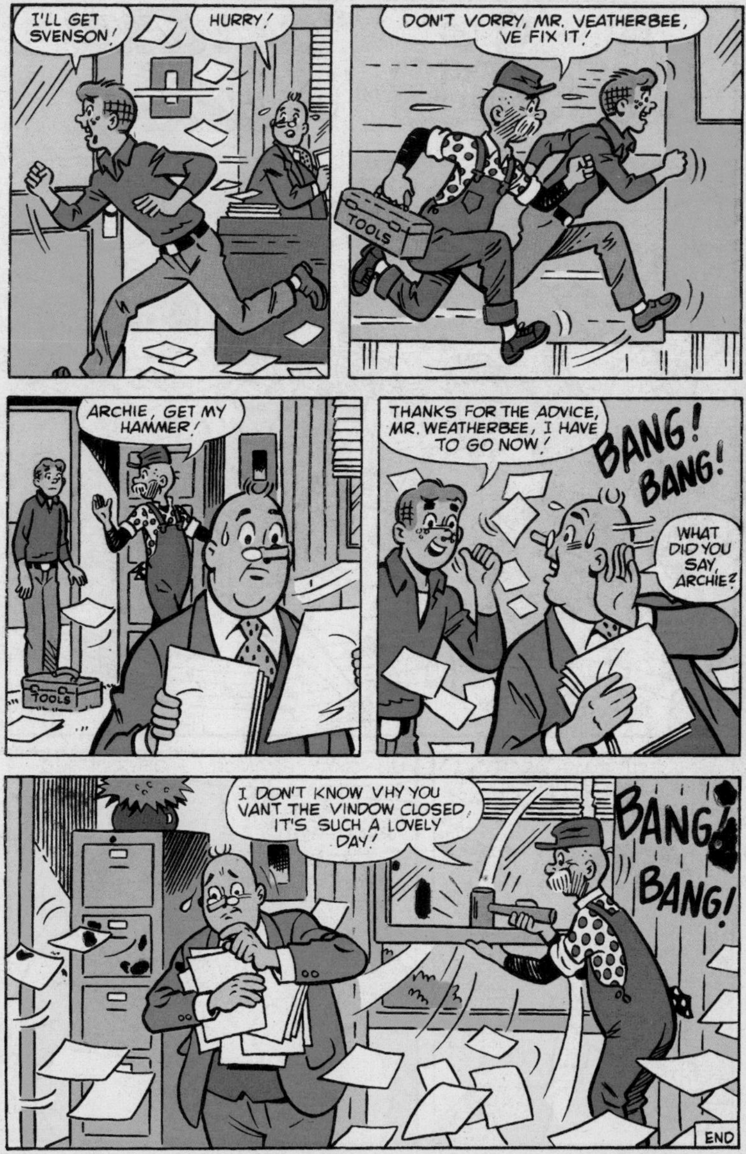
I'LL GET SVENSON!
HURRY!
DON'T VORRY, MR. VEATHERBEE, VE FIX IT!
TOOLS
ARCHIE, GET MY HAMMER!
TOOLS
THANKS FOR THE ADVICE, MR. WEATHERBEE, I HAVE TO GO NOW!
BANG! BANG!
WHAT DID YOU SAY, ARCHIE?
I DON'T KNOW VHY YOU VANT THE VINDOW CLOSED, IT'S SUCH A LOVELY DAY!
BANG! BANG!
END

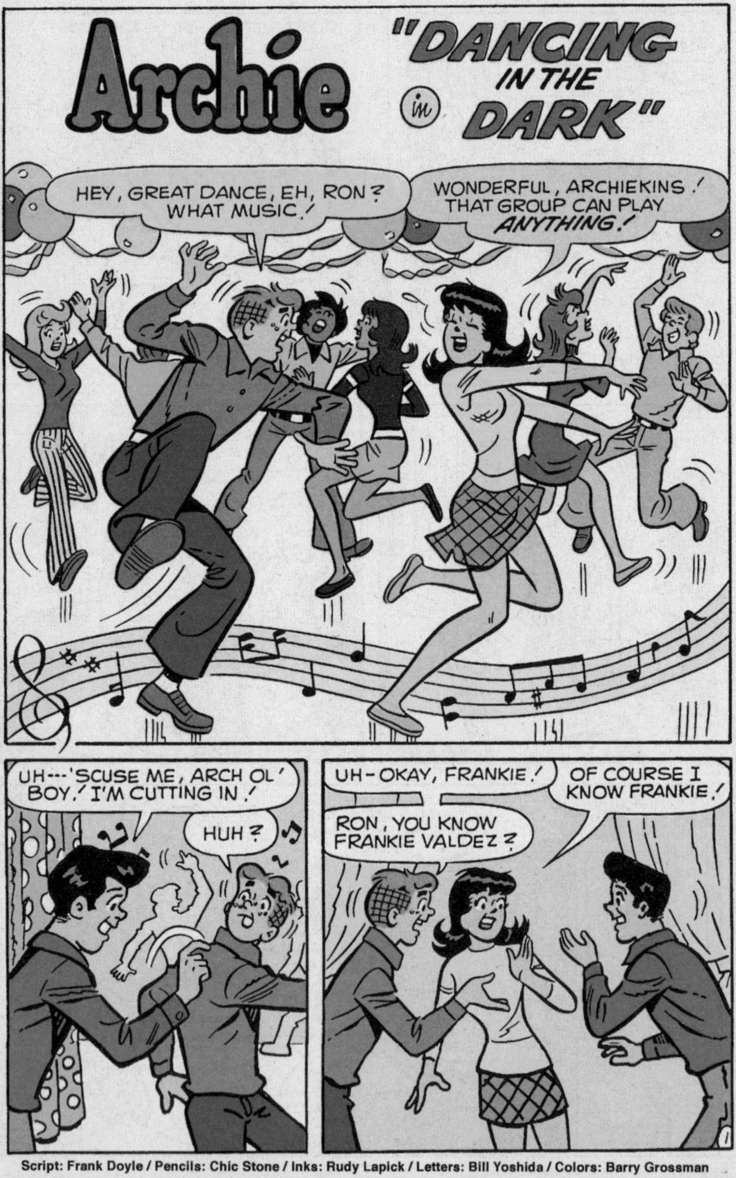
Archie
in
"DANCING IN THE DARK"
HEY, GREAT DANCE, EH, RON? WHAT MUSIC!
WONDERFUL, ARCHIEKINS! THAT GROUP CAN PLAY ANYTHING!
UH---'SCUSE ME, ARCH OL' BOY! I'M CUTTING IN!
HUH?
UH-OKAY, FRANKIE!
RON, YOU KNOW FRANKIE VALDEZ?
OF COURSE I KNOW FRANKIE!
1

Script: Frank Doyle / Pencils: Chic Stone / Inks: Rudy Lapick / Letters: Bill Yoshida / Colors: Barry Grossman

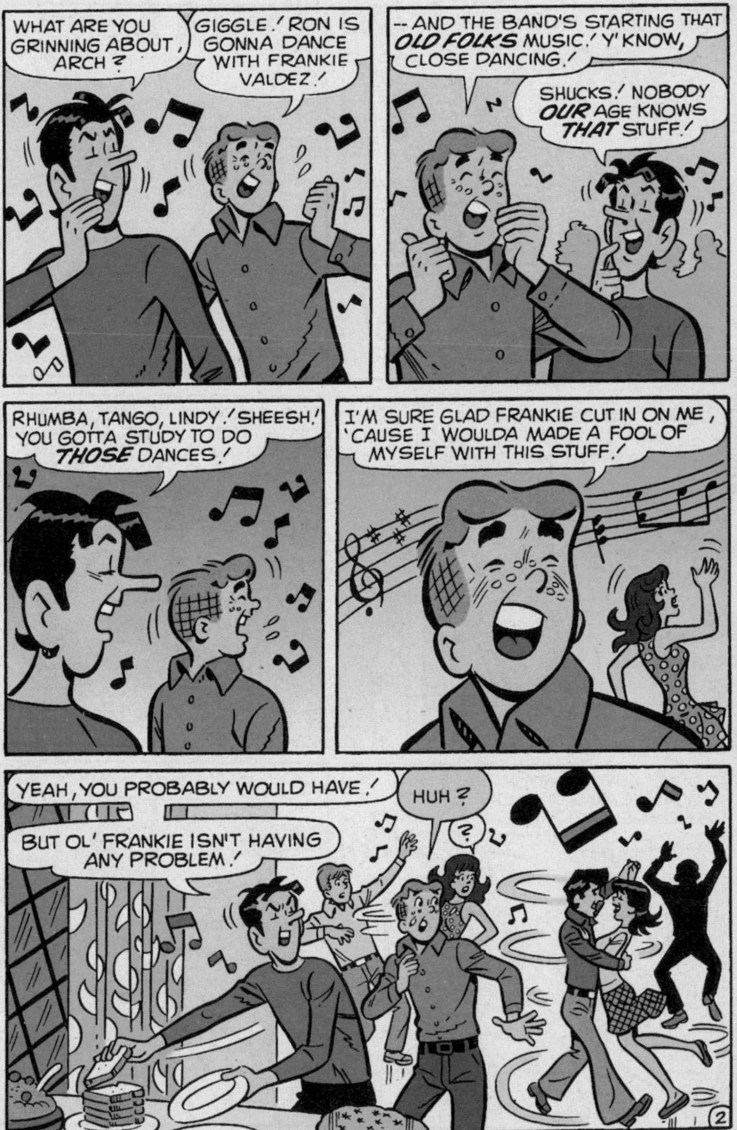
WHAT ARE YOU GRINNING ABOUT, ARCH?
GIGGLE! RON IS GONNA DANCE WITH FRANKIE VALDEZ!
-- AND THE BAND'S STARTING THAT OLD FOLKS MUSIC! Y'KNOW, CLOSE DANCING!
SHUCKS! NOBODY OUR AGE KNOWS THAT STUFF!
RHUMBA, TANGO, LINDY! SHEESH! YOU GOTTA STUDY TO DO THOSE DANCES!
I'M SURE GLAD FRANKIE CUT IN ON ME, 'CAUSE I WOULDA MADE A FOOL OF MYSELF WITH THIS STUFF!
YEAH, YOU PROBABLY WOULD HAVE!
BUT OL' FRANKIE ISN'T HAVING ANY PROBLEM!
HUH?
?
2

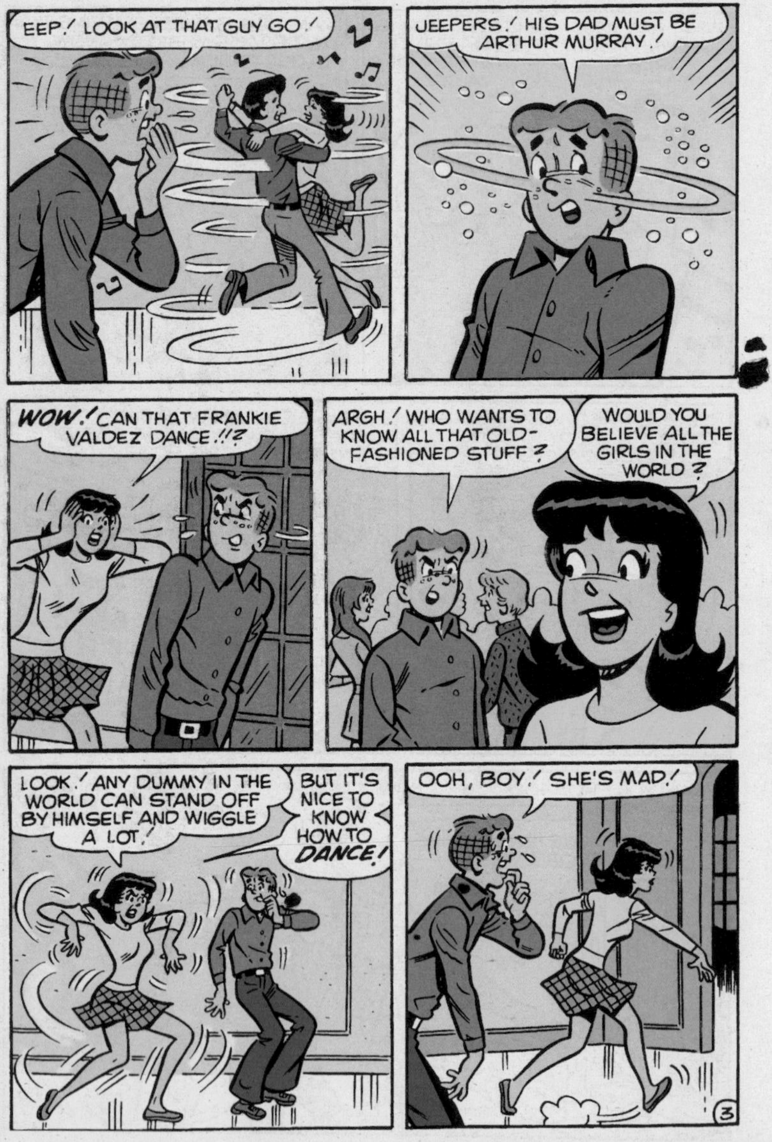
EEP! LOOK AT THAT GUY GO!
JEEPERS! HIS DAD MUST BE ARTHUR MURRAY!
WOW! CAN THAT FRANKIE VALDEZ DANCE!!?
ARGH! WHO WANTS TO KNOW ALL THAT OLD-FASHIONED STUFF?
WOULD YOU BELIEVE ALL THE GIRLS IN THE WORLD?
LOOK! ANY DUMMY IN THE WORLD CAN STAND OFF BY HIMSELF AND WIGGLE A LOT!
BUT IT'S NICE TO KNOW HOW TO DANCE!
OOH, BOY! SHE'S MAD!
3

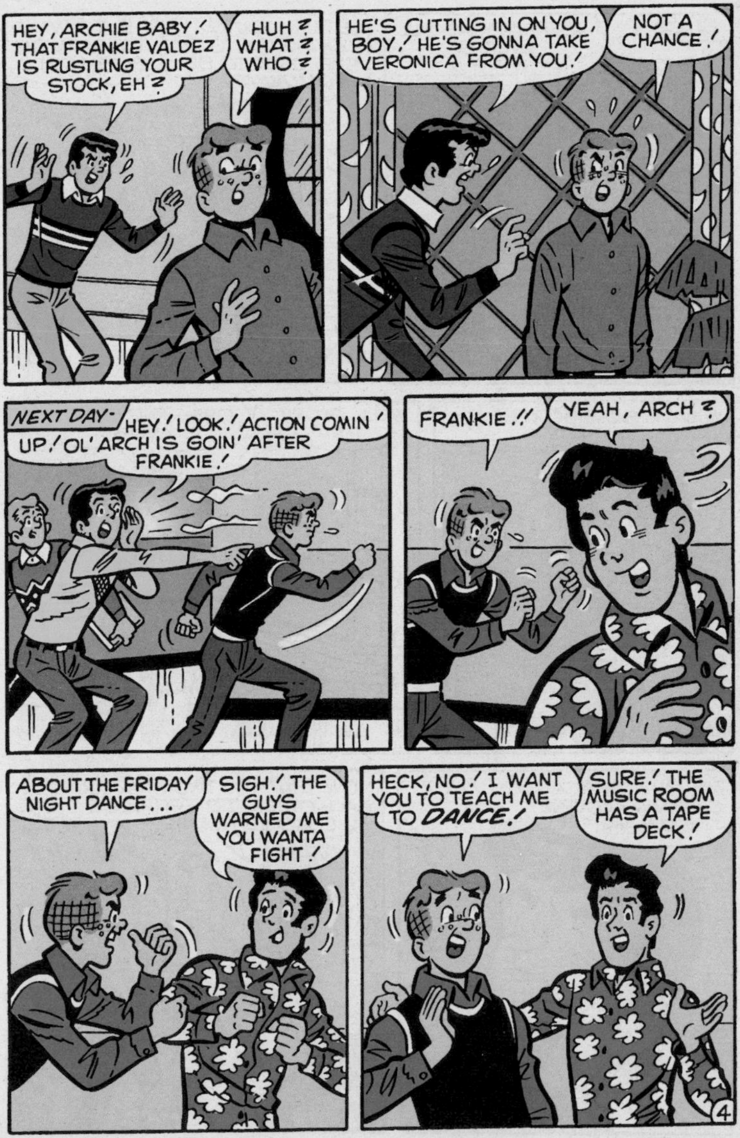
HEY, ARCHIE BABY! THAT FRANKIE VALDEZ IS RUSTLING YOUR STOCK, EH?
HUH? WHAT? WHO?
HE'S CUTTING IN ON YOU, BOY! HE'S GONNA TAKE VERONICA FROM YOU!
NOT A CHANCE!
NEXT DAY-
HEY! LOOK! ACTION COMIN' UP! OL' ARCH IS GOIN' AFTER FRANKIE!
FRANKIE!!
YEAH, ARCH?
ABOUT THE FRIDAY NIGHT DANCE...
SIGH! THE GUYS WARNED ME YOU WANTA FIGHT!
HECK, NO! I WANT YOU TO TEACH ME TO DANCE!
SURE! THE MUSIC ROOM HAS A TAPE DECK!
4

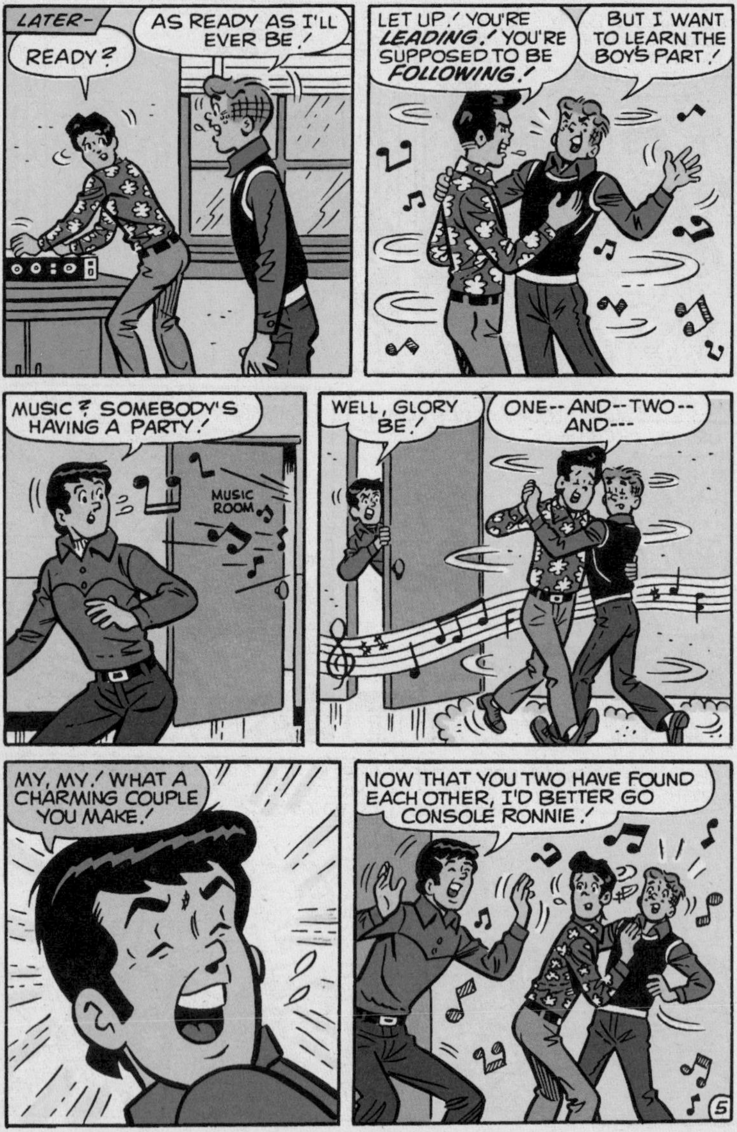
LATER-
READY?
AS READY AS I'LL EVER BE!
LET UP! YOU'RE LEADING! YOU'RE SUPPOSED TO BE FOLLOWING!
BUT I WANT TO LEARN THE BOY'S PART!
MUSIC? SOMEBODY'S HAVING A PARTY!
MUSIC ROOM
WELL, GLORY BE!
ONE--AND--TWO--AND---
MY, MY! WHAT A CHARMING COUPLE YOU MAKE!
NOW THAT YOU TWO HAVE FOUND EACH OTHER, I'D BETTER GO CONSOLE RONNIE!
5

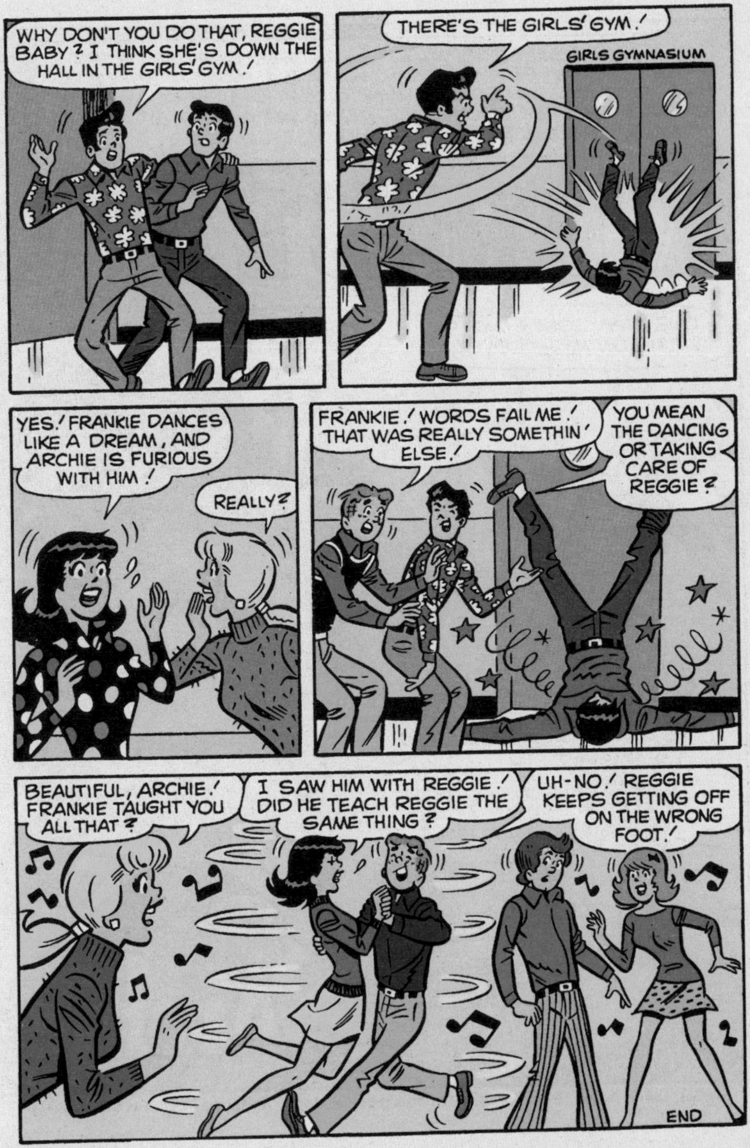
WHY DON'T YOU DO THAT, REGGIE BABY? I THINK SHE'S DOWN THE HALL IN THE GIRLS' GYM!
THERE'S THE GIRLS' GYM!
GIRLS GYMNASIUM
YES! FRANKIE DANCES LIKE A DREAM, AND ARCHIE IS FURIOUS WITH HIM!
REALLY?
FRANKIE! WORDS FAIL ME! THAT WAS REALLY SOMETHIN' ELSE!
YOU MEAN THE DANCING OR TAKING CARE OF REGGIE?
BEAUTIFUL, ARCHIE! FRANKIE TAUGHT YOU ALL THAT?
I SAW HIM WITH REGGIE! DID HE TEACH REGGIE THE SAME THING?
UH-NO! REGGIE KEEPS GETTING OFF ON THE WRONG FOOT!
END

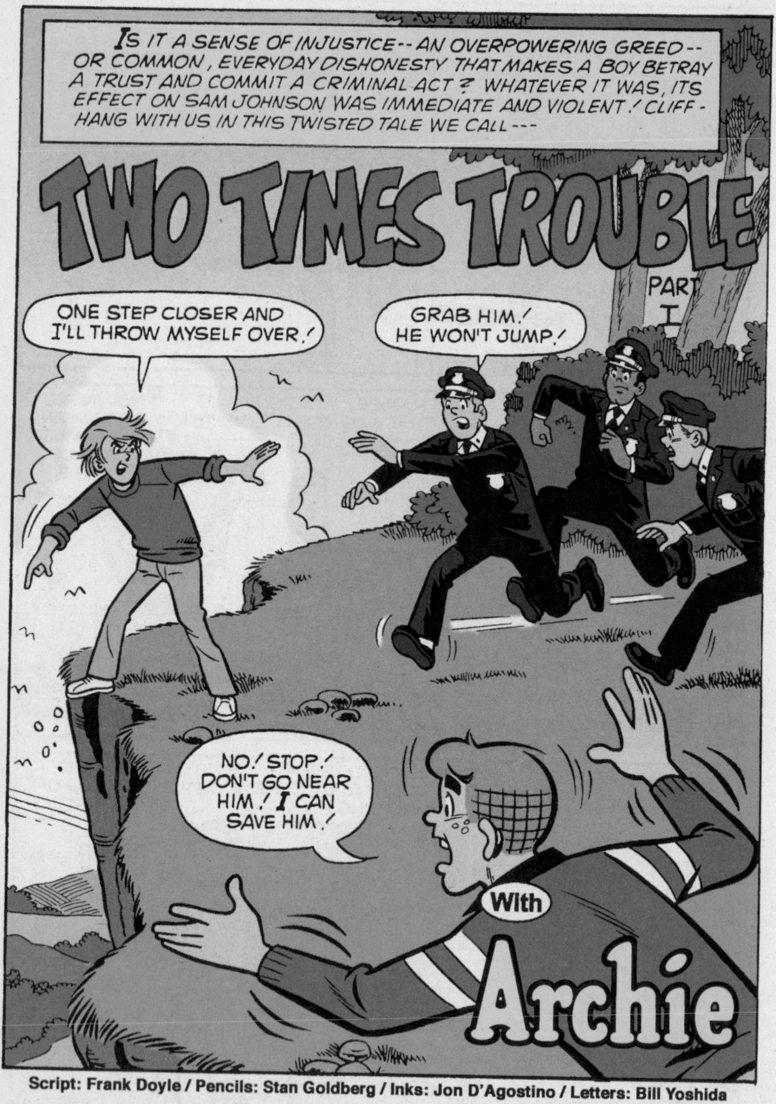

IS IT A SENSE OF INJUSTICE-- AN OVERPOWERING GREED-- OR COMMON, EVERYDAY DISHONESTY THAT MAKES A BOY BETRAY A TRUST AND COMMIT A CRIMINAL ACT? WHATEVER IT WAS, ITS EFFECT ON SAM JOHNSON WAS IMMEDIATE AND VIOLENT! CLIFF-HANG WITH US IN THIS TWISTED TALE WE CALL---
TWO TIMES TROUBLE
PART I
ONE STEP CLOSER AND I'LL THROW MYSELF OVER!
GRAB HIM! HE WON'T JUMP!
NO! STOP! DON'T GO NEAR HIM! I CAN SAVE HIM!
With
Archie

Script: Frank Doyle / Pencils: Stan Goldberg / Inks: Jon D'Agostino / Letters: Bill Yoshida

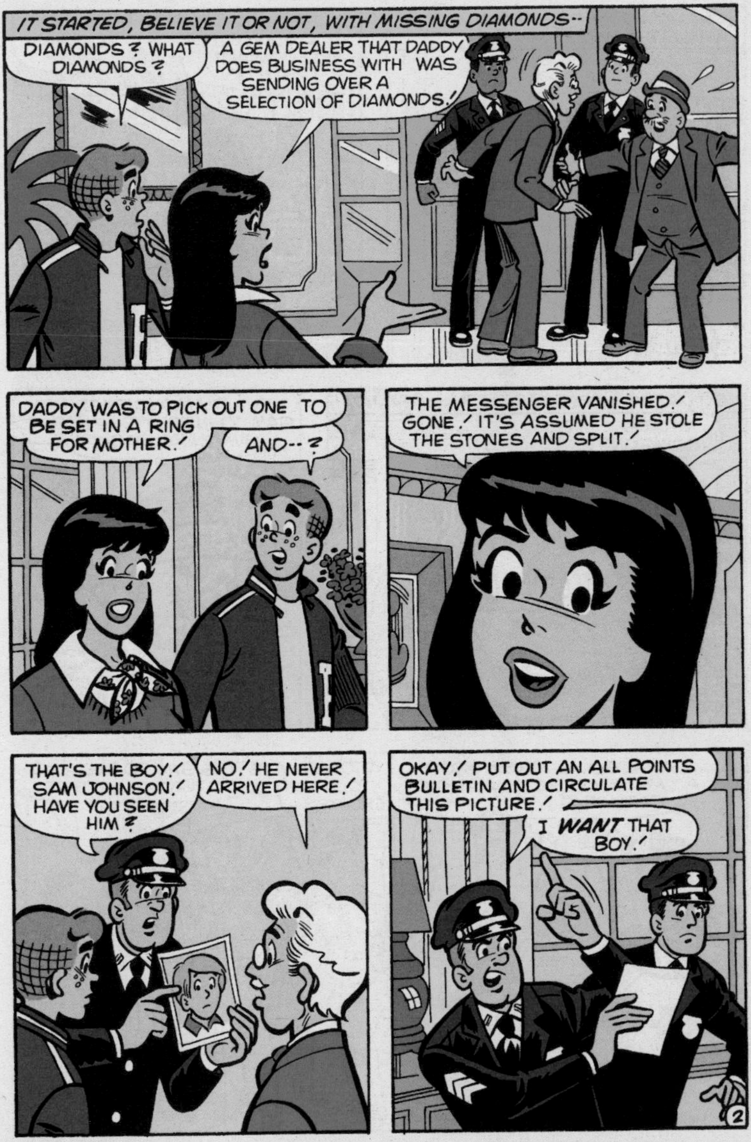
IT STARTED, BELIEVE IT OR NOT, WITH MISSING DIAMONDS--
DIAMONDS? WHAT DIAMONDS?
A GEM DEALER THAT DADDY DOES BUSINESS WITH WAS SENDING OVER A SELECTION OF DIAMONDS!
DADDY WAS TO PICK OUT ONE TO BE SET IN A RING FOR MOTHER!
AND--?
THE MESSENGER VANISHED! GONE! IT'S ASSUMED HE STOLE THE STONES AND SPLIT!
THAT'S THE BOY! SAM JOHNSON! HAVE YOU SEEN HIM?
NO! HE NEVER ARRIVED HERE!
OKAY! PUT OUT AN ALL POINTS BULLETIN AND CIRCULATE THIS PICTURE!
I WANT THAT BOY!
2

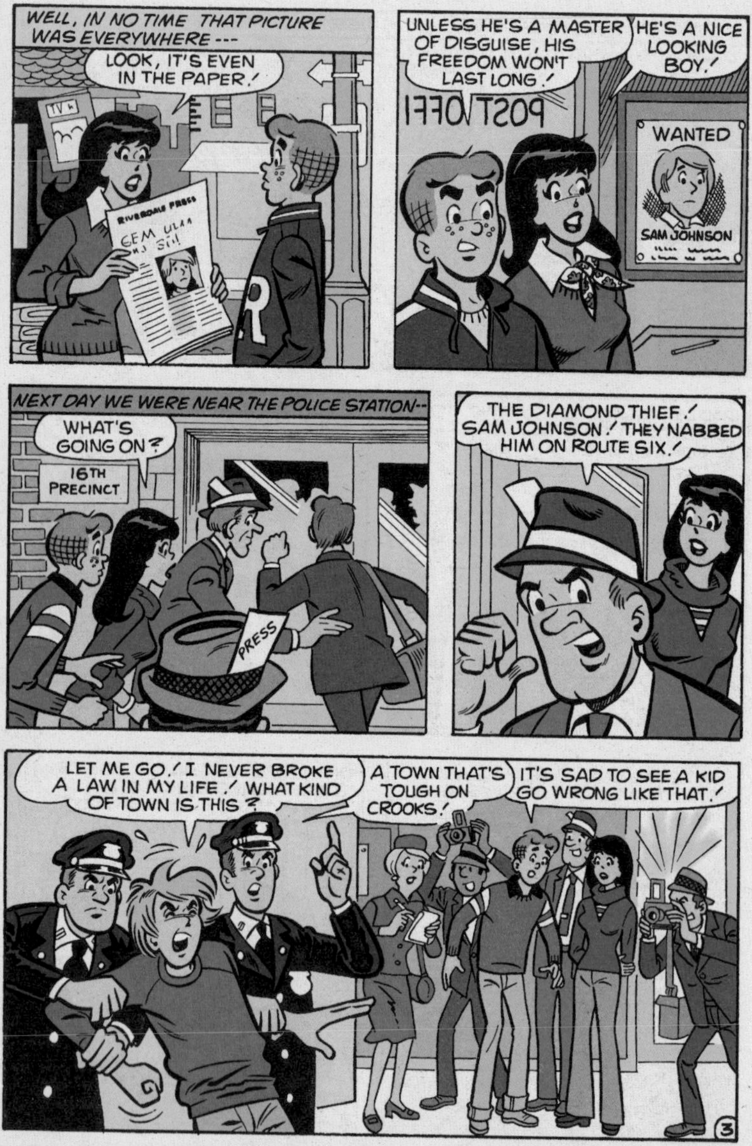
WELL, IN NO TIME THAT PICTURE WAS EVERYWHERE ---
LOOK, IT'S EVEN IN THE PAPER!
RIVERDALE PRESS
UNLESS HE'S A MASTER OF DISGUISE, HIS FREEDOM WON'T LAST LONG!
HE'S A NICE LOOKING BOY!
POST OFFI
WANTED
SAM JOHNSON
NEXT DAY WE WERE NEAR THE POLICE STATION--
WHAT'S GOING ON?
16TH PRECINCT
PRESS
THE DIAMOND THIEF! SAM JOHNSON! THEY NABBED HIM ON ROUTE SIX!
LET ME GO! I NEVER BROKE A LAW IN MY LIFE! WHAT KIND OF TOWN IS THIS?
A TOWN THAT'S TOUGH ON CROOKS!
IT'S SAD TO SEE A KID GO WRONG LIKE THAT!
3

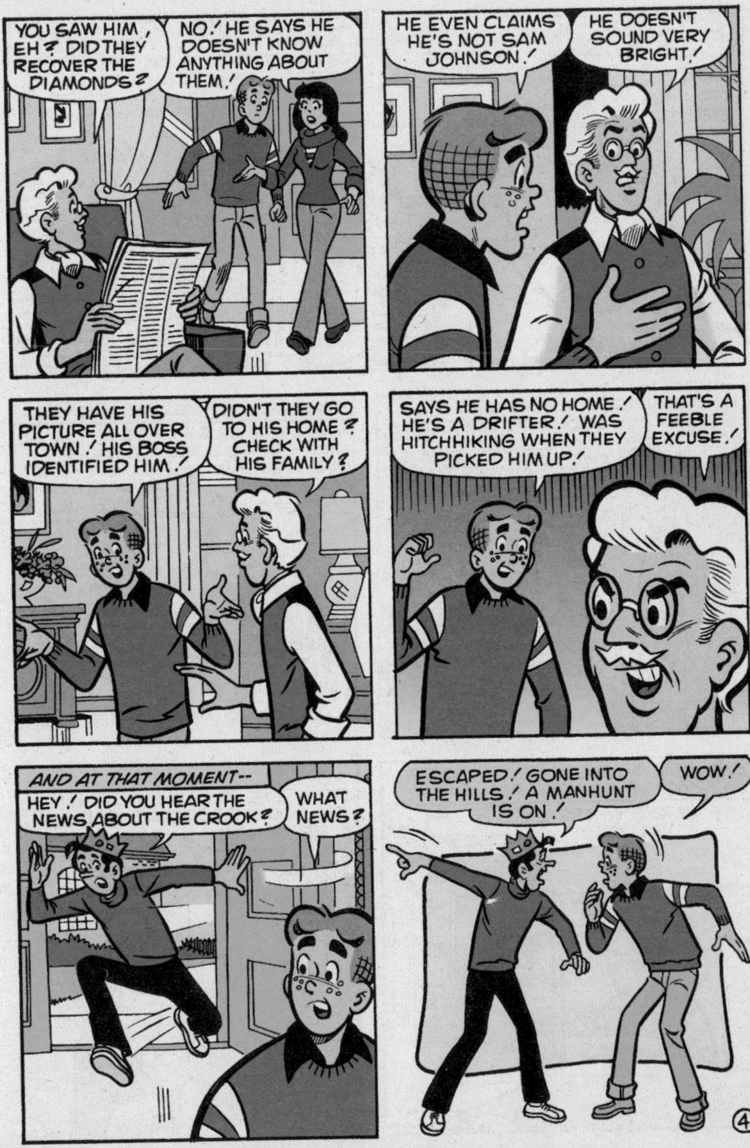
YOU SAW HIM, EH? DID THEY RECOVER THE DIAMONDS?
NO! HE SAYS HE DOESN'T KNOW ANYTHING ABOUT THEM!
HE EVEN CLAIMS HE'S NOT SAM JOHNSON!
HE DOESN'T SOUND VERY BRIGHT!
THEY HAVE HIS PICTURE ALL OVER TOWN! HIS BOSS IDENTIFIED HIM!
DIDN'T THEY GO TO HIS HOME? CHECK WITH HIS FAMILY?
SAYS HE HAS NO HOME! HE'S A DRIFTER! WAS HITCHHIKING WHEN THEY PICKED HIM UP!
THAT'S A FEEBLE EXCUSE!
AND AT THAT MOMENT--
HEY! DID YOU HEAR THE NEWS ABOUT THE CROOK?
WHAT NEWS?
ESCAPED! GONE INTO THE HILLS! A MANHUNT IS ON!
WOW!
4

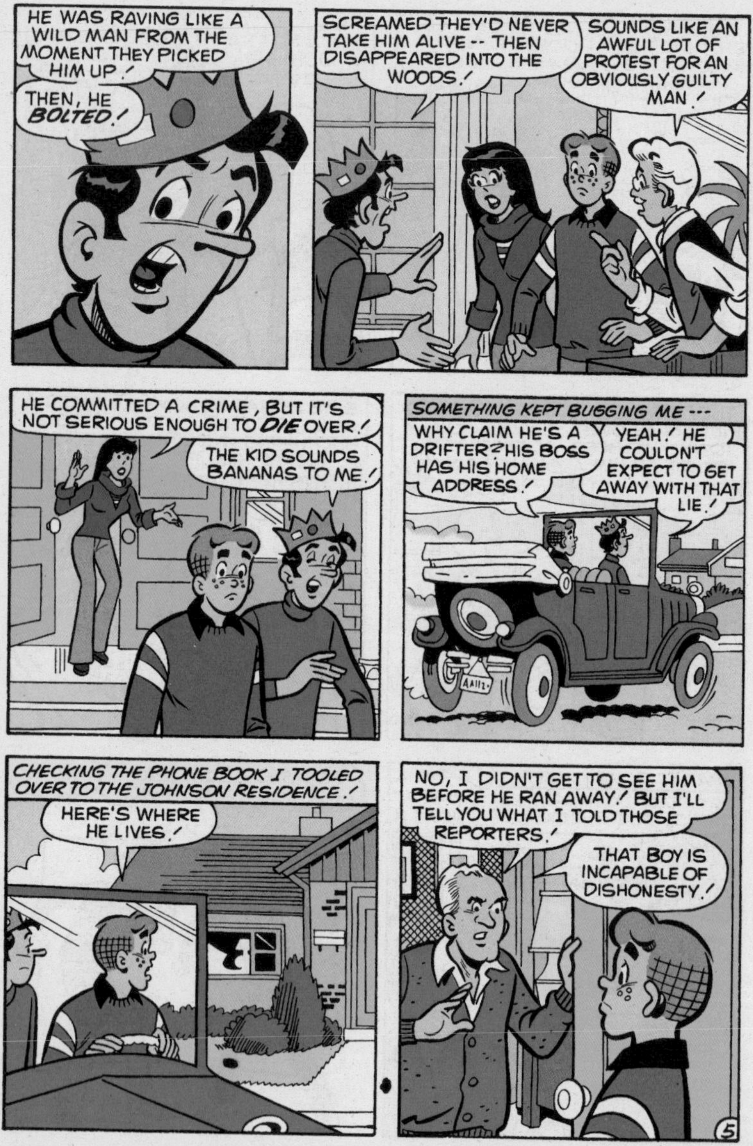
HE WAS RAVING LIKE A WILD MAN FROM THE MOMENT THEY PICKED HIM UP!
THEN, HE BOLTED!
SCREAMED THEY'D NEVER TAKE HIM ALIVE -- THEN DISAPPEARED INTO THE WOODS!
SOUNDS LIKE AN AWFUL LOT OF PROTEST FOR AN OBVIOUSLY GUILTY MAN!
HE COMMITTED A CRIME, BUT IT'S NOT SERIOUS ENOUGH TO DIE OVER!
THE KID SOUNDS BANANAS TO ME!
SOMETHING KEPT BUGGING ME ---
WHY CLAIM HE'S A DRIFTER? HIS BOSS HAS HIS HOME ADDRESS!
YEAH! HE COULDN'T EXPECT TO GET AWAY WITH THAT LIE!
CHECKING THE PHONE BOOK I TOOLED OVER TO THE JOHNSON RESIDENCE!
HERE'S WHERE HE LIVES!
NO, I DIDN'T GET TO SEE HIM BEFORE HE RAN AWAY! BUT I'LL TELL YOU WHAT I TOLD THOSE REPORTERS!
THAT BOY IS INCAPABLE OF DISHONESTY!
5

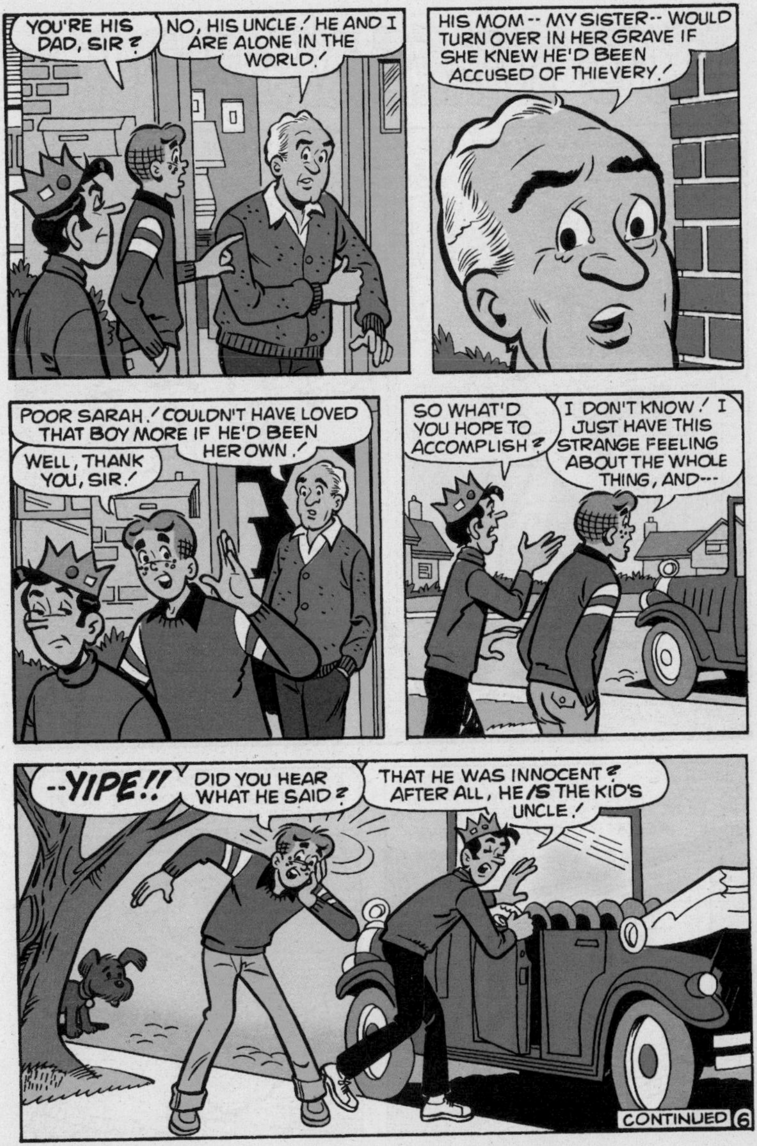
YOU'RE HIS DAD, SIR?
NO, HIS UNCLE! HE AND I ARE ALONE IN THE WORLD!
HIS MOM -- MY SISTER -- WOULD TURN OVER IN HER GRAVE IF SHE KNEW HE'D BEEN ACCUSED OF THIEVERY!
POOR SARAH! COULDN'T HAVE LOVED THAT BOY MORE IF HE'D BEEN HER OWN!
WELL, THANK YOU, SIR!
SO WHAT'D YOU HOPE TO ACCOMPLISH?
I DON'T KNOW! I JUST HAVE THIS STRANGE FEELING ABOUT THE WHOLE THING, AND---
--YIPE!!
DID YOU HEAR WHAT HE SAID?
THAT HE WAS INNOCENT? AFTER ALL, HE IS THE KID'S UNCLE!
CONTINUED 6

TWO TIMES TROUBLE PART II

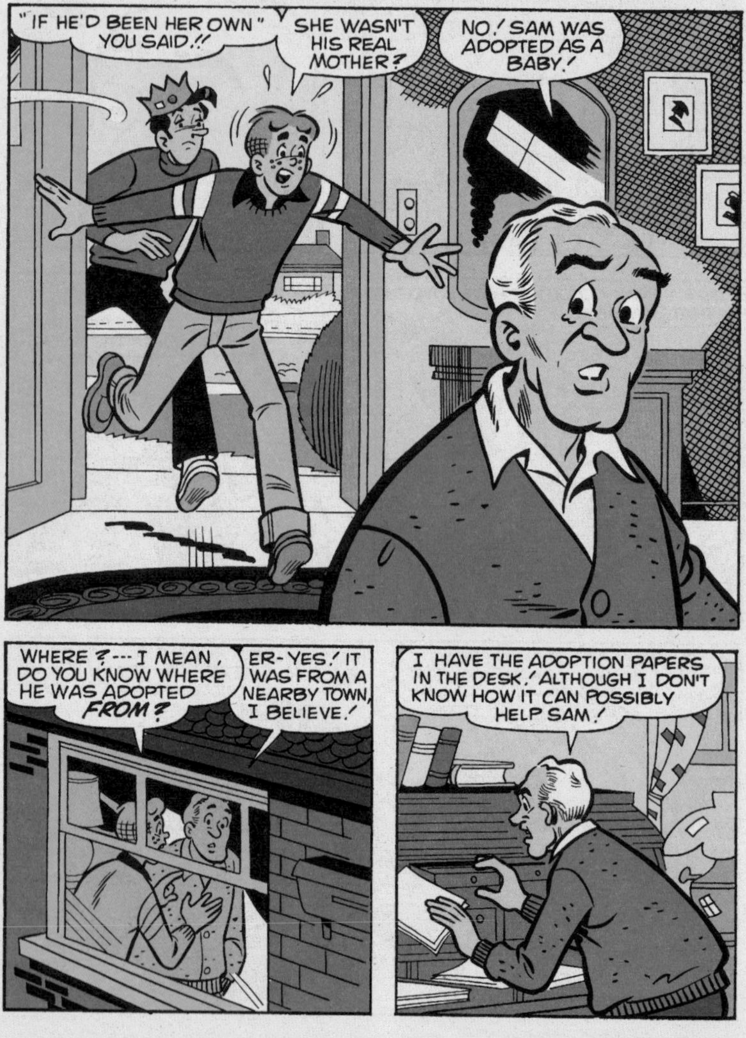

"IF HE'D BEEN HER OWN" YOU SAID!!
SHE WASN'T HIS REAL MOTHER?
NO! SAM WAS ADOPTED AS A BABY!
WHERE? --- I MEAN, DO YOU KNOW WHERE HE WAS ADOPTED *FROM*?
ER-YES! IT WAS FROM A NEARBY TOWN, I BELIEVE!
I HAVE THE ADOPTION PAPERS IN THE DESK! ALTHOUGH I DON'T KNOW HOW IT CAN POSSIBLY HELP SAM!

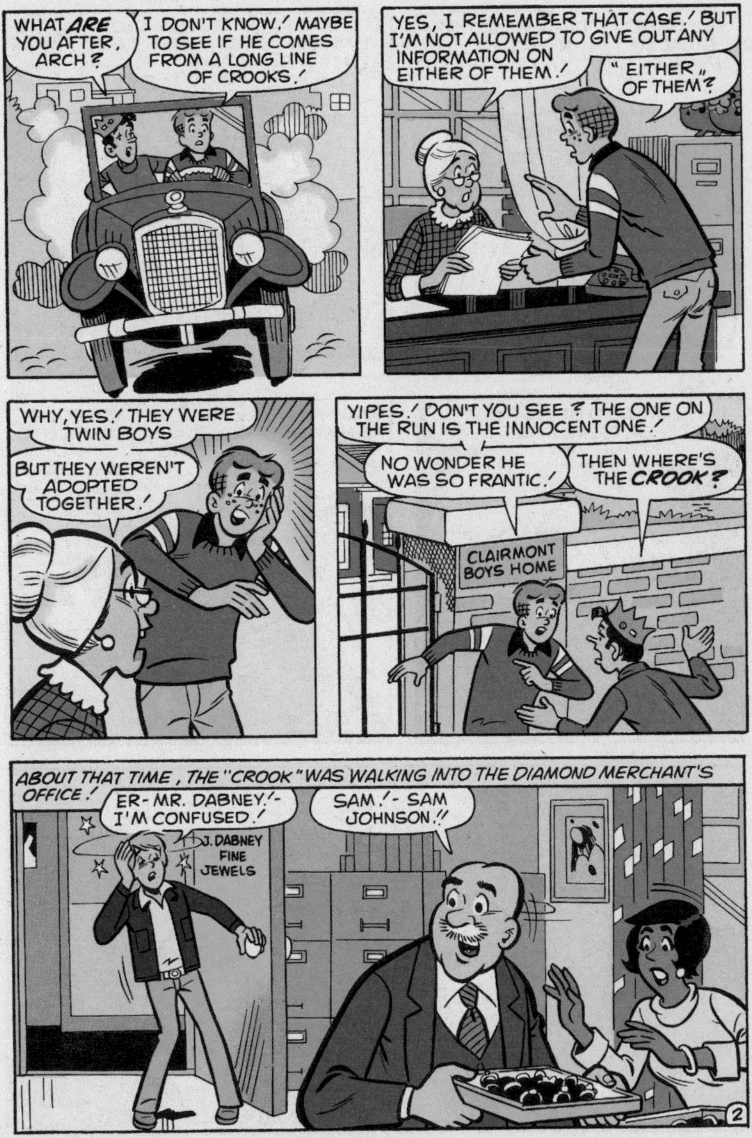
WHAT ARE YOU AFTER, ARCH?
I DON'T KNOW! MAYBE TO SEE IF HE COMES FROM A LONG LINE OF CROOKS!
YES, I REMEMBER THAT CASE! BUT I'M NOT ALLOWED TO GIVE OUT ANY INFORMATION ON EITHER OF THEM!
"EITHER" OF THEM?
WHY, YES! THEY WERE TWIN BOYS
BUT THEY WEREN'T ADOPTED TOGETHER!
YIPES! DON'T YOU SEE? THE ONE ON THE RUN IS THE INNOCENT ONE!
NO WONDER HE WAS SO FRANTIC!
THEN WHERE'S THE CROOK?
CLAIRMONT BOYS HOME
ABOUT THAT TIME, THE "CROOK" WAS WALKING INTO THE DIAMOND MERCHANT'S OFFICE!
ER- MR. DABNEY!- I'M CONFUSED!
J. DABNEY FINE JEWELS
SAM!- SAM JOHNSON!!
2

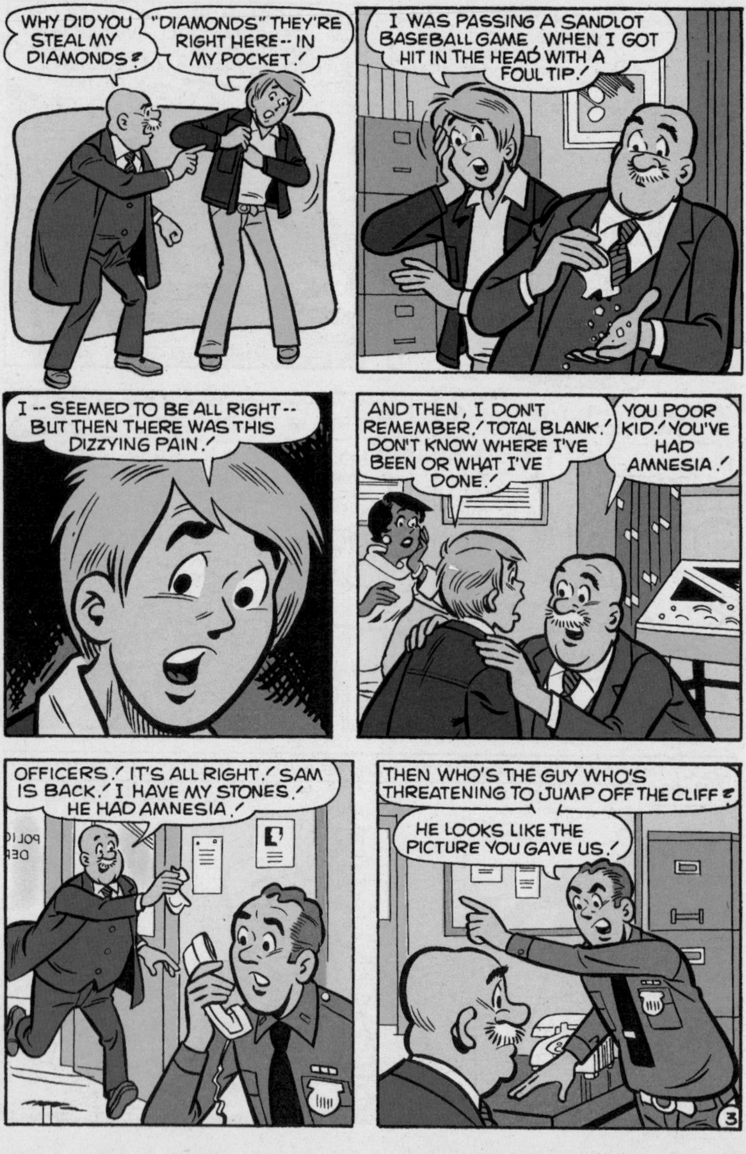
WHY DID YOU STEAL MY DIAMONDS?
"DIAMONDS" THEY'RE RIGHT HERE-- IN MY POCKET!
I WAS PASSING A SANDLOT BASEBALL GAME, WHEN I GOT HIT IN THE HEAD WITH A FOUL TIP!
I -- SEEMED TO BE ALL RIGHT-- BUT THEN THERE WAS THIS DIZZYING PAIN!
AND THEN, I DON'T REMEMBER! TOTAL BLANK! DON'T KNOW WHERE I'VE BEEN OR WHAT I'VE DONE!
YOU POOR KID! YOU'VE HAD AMNESIA!
OFFICERS! IT'S ALL RIGHT! SAM IS BACK! I HAVE MY STONES! HE HAD AMNESIA!
THEN WHO'S THE GUY WHO'S THREATENING TO JUMP OFF THE CLIFF?
HE LOOKS LIKE THE PICTURE YOU GAVE US!
3

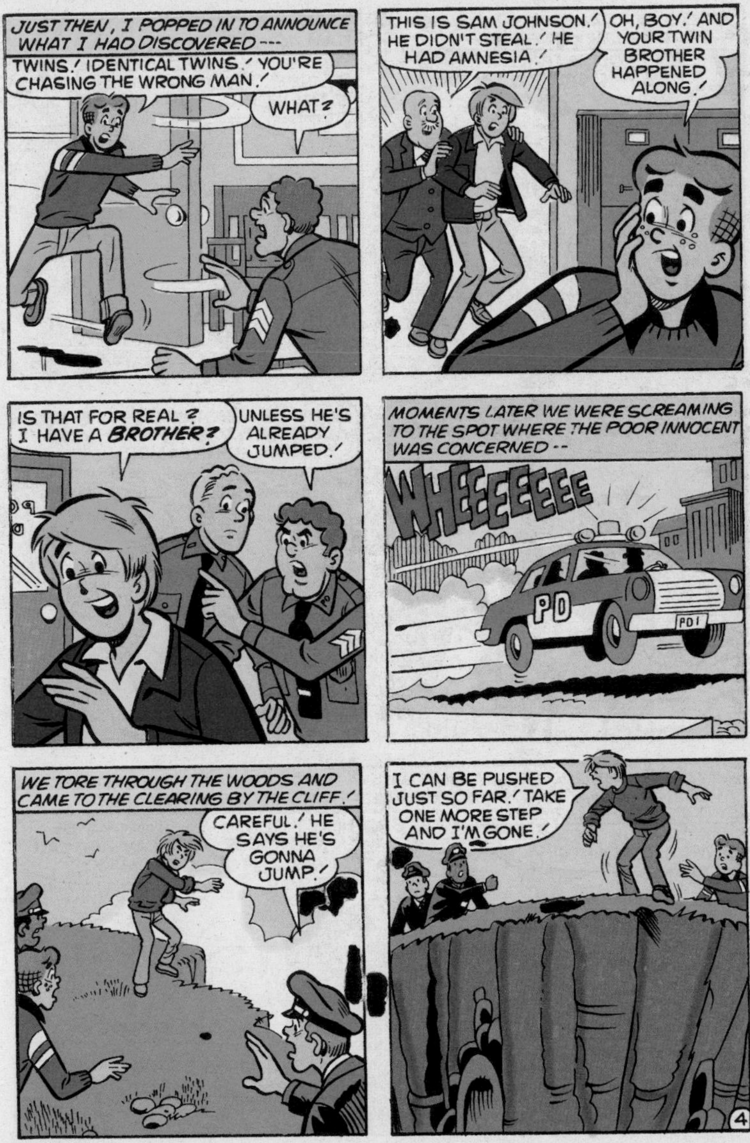
JUST THEN, I POPPED IN TO ANNOUNCE WHAT I HAD DISCOVERED---
TWINS! IDENTICAL TWINS! YOU'RE CHASING THE WRONG MAN!
WHAT?
THIS IS SAM JOHNSON! HE DIDN'T STEAL! HE HAD AMNESIA!
OH, BOY! AND YOUR TWIN BROTHER HAPPENED ALONG!
IS THAT FOR REAL? I HAVE A BROTHER?
UNLESS HE'S ALREADY JUMPED!
MOMENTS LATER WE WERE SCREAMING TO THE SPOT WHERE THE POOR INNOCENT WAS CONCERNED --
WHEEEEEEE
PD
PD 1
WE TORE THROUGH THE WOODS AND CAME TO THE CLEARING BY THE CLIFF!
CAREFUL! HE SAYS HE'S GONNA JUMP!
I CAN BE PUSHED JUST SO FAR! TAKE ONE MORE STEP AND I'M GONE!
4

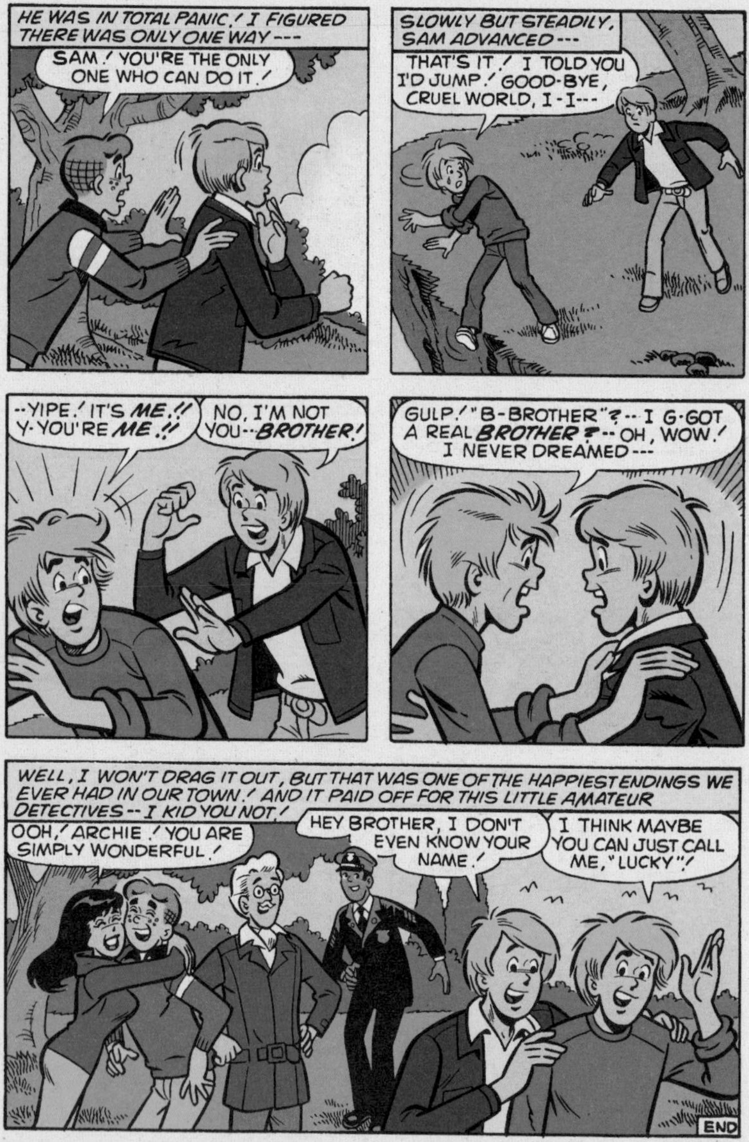
HE WAS IN TOTAL PANIC! I FIGURED THERE WAS ONLY ONE WAY---
SAM! YOU'RE THE ONLY ONE WHO CAN DO IT!
SLOWLY BUT STEADILY, SAM ADVANCED---
THAT'S IT! I TOLD YOU I'D JUMP! GOOD-BYE, CRUEL WORLD, I-I---
--YIPE! IT'S ME!! Y-YOU'RE ME!!
NO, I'M NOT YOU--BROTHER!
GULP! "B-BROTHER"?--I G-GOT A REAL BROTHER?--OH, WOW! I NEVER DREAMED---
WELL, I WON'T DRAG IT OUT, BUT THAT WAS ONE OF THE HAPPIEST ENDINGS WE EVER HAD IN OUR TOWN! AND IT PAID OFF FOR THIS LITTLE AMATEUR DETECTIVES--I KID YOU NOT!
OOH! ARCHIE! YOU ARE SIMPLY WONDERFUL!
HEY BROTHER, I DON'T EVEN KNOW YOUR NAME!
I THINK MAYBE YOU CAN JUST CALL ME, "LUCKY"!
END

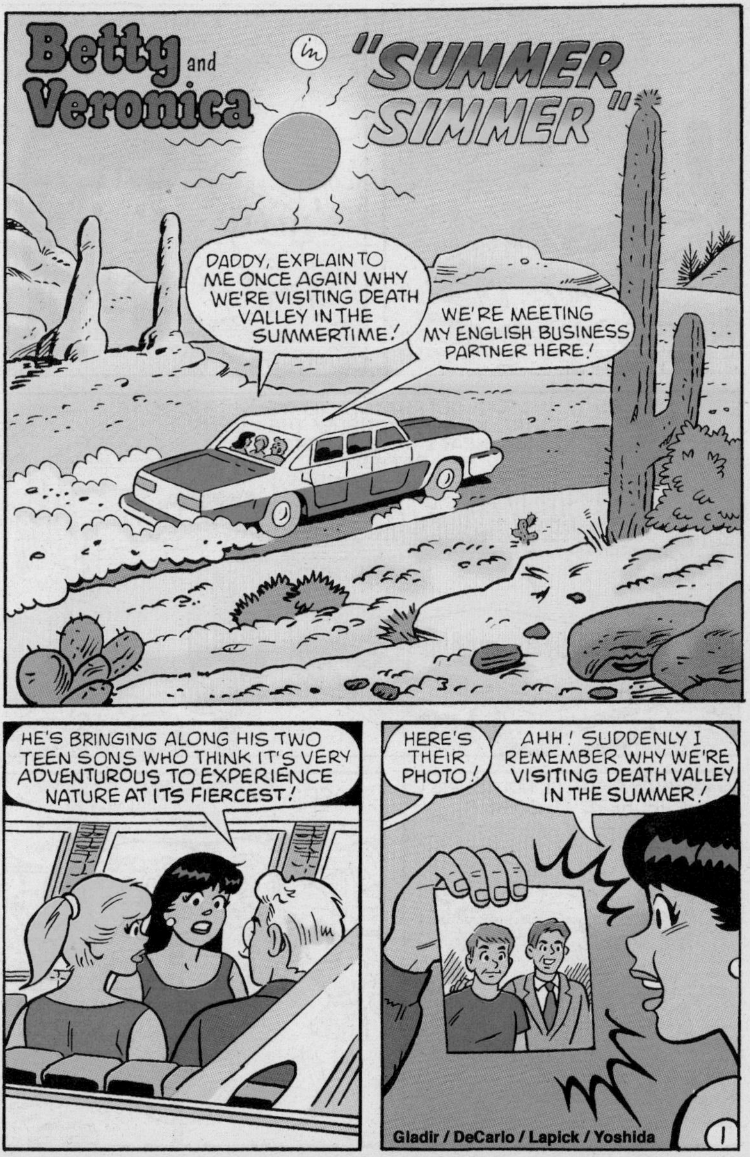
Betty and Veronica in "SUMMER SIMMER"
DADDY, EXPLAIN TO ME ONCE AGAIN WHY WE'RE VISITING DEATH VALLEY IN THE SUMMERTIME!
WE'RE MEETING MY ENGLISH BUSINESS PARTNER HERE!
HE'S BRINGING ALONG HIS TWO TEEN SONS WHO THINK IT'S VERY ADVENTUROUS TO EXPERIENCE NATURE AT ITS FIERCEST!
HERE'S THEIR PHOTO!
AHH! SUDDENLY I REMEMBER WHY WE'RE VISITING DEATH VALLEY IN THE SUMMER!
Gladir / DeCarlo / Lapick / Yoshida
1

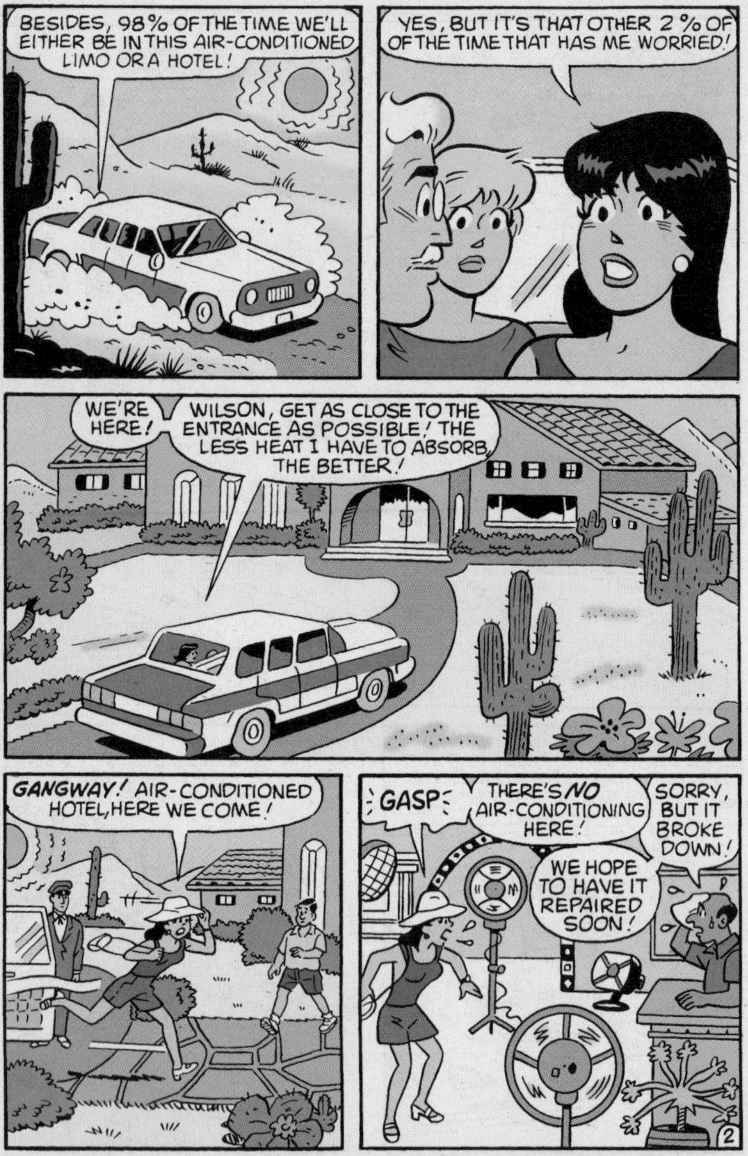
BESIDES, 98% OF THE TIME WE'LL EITHER BE IN THIS AIR-CONDITIONED LIMO OR A HOTEL!
YES, BUT IT'S THAT OTHER 2% OF OF THE TIME THAT HAS ME WORRIED!
WE'RE HERE!
WILSON, GET AS CLOSE TO THE ENTRANCE AS POSSIBLE! THE LESS HEAT I HAVE TO ABSORB, THE BETTER!
GANGWAY! AIR-CONDITIONED HOTEL, HERE WE COME!
GASP
THERE'S NO AIR-CONDITIONING HERE!
SORRY, BUT IT BROKE DOWN!
WE HOPE TO HAVE IT REPAIRED SOON!
2

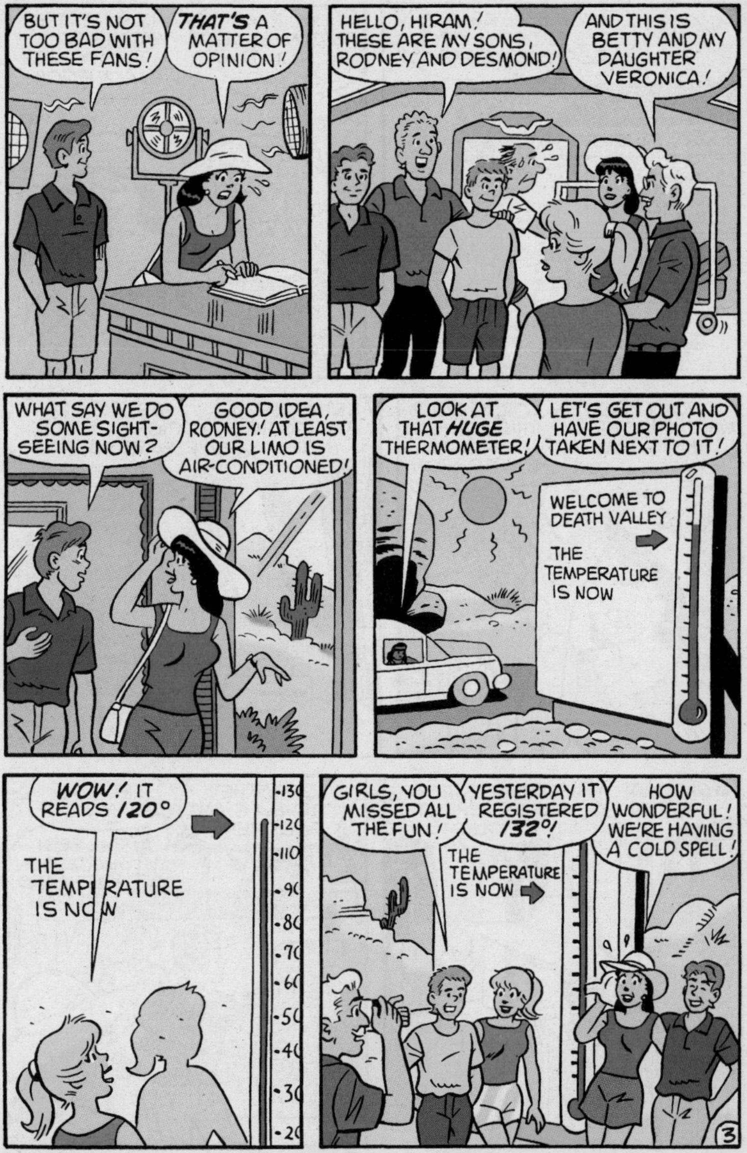
BUT IT'S NOT TOO BAD WITH THESE FANS!
THAT'S A MATTER OF OPINION!
HELLO, HIRAM! THESE ARE MY SONS, RODNEY AND DESMOND!
AND THIS IS BETTY AND MY DAUGHTER VERONICA!
WHAT SAY WE DO SOME SIGHT-SEEING NOW?
GOOD IDEA, RODNEY! AT LEAST OUR LIMO IS AIR-CONDITIONED!
LOOK AT THAT HUGE THERMOMETER!
LET'S GET OUT AND HAVE OUR PHOTO TAKEN NEXT TO IT!
WELCOME TO DEATH VALLEY
THE TEMPERATURE IS NOW
WOW! IT READS 120°
THE TEMPERATURE IS NOW
GIRLS, YOU MISSED ALL THE FUN!
YESTERDAY IT REGISTERED 132°!
HOW WONDERFUL! WE'RE HAVING A COLD SPELL!
THE TEMPERATURE IS NOW
3

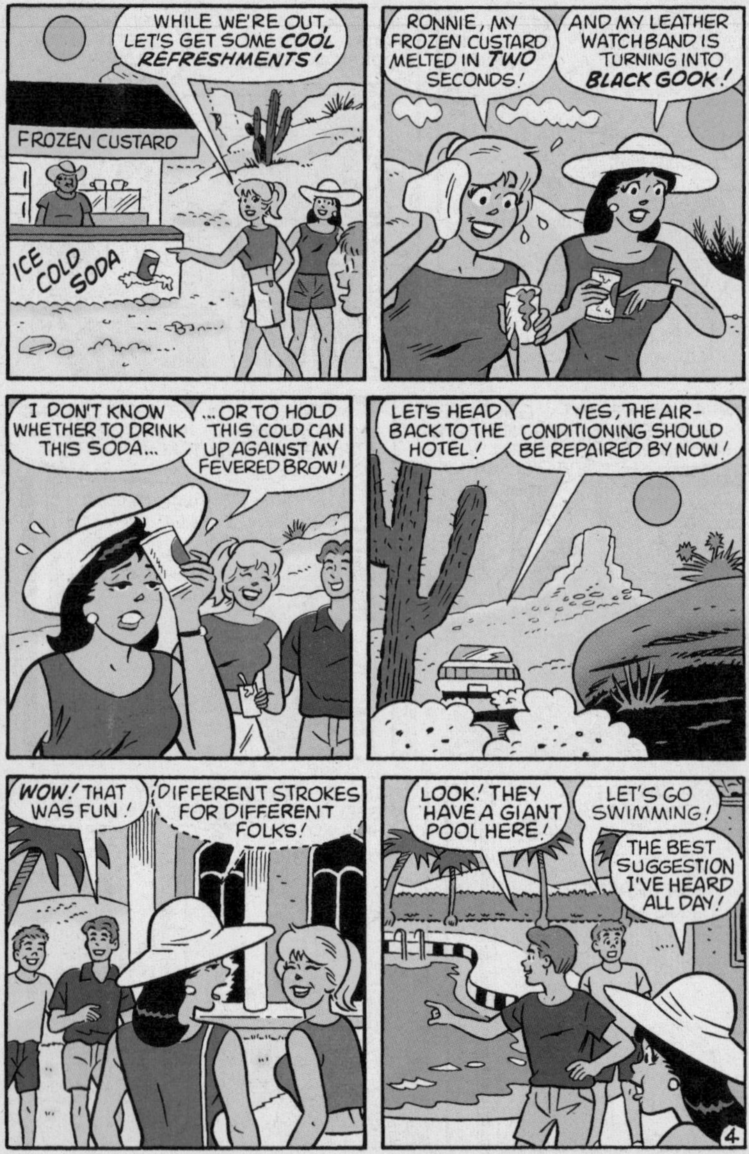
WHILE WE'RE OUT, LET'S GET SOME COOL REFRESHMENTS!
FROZEN CUSTARD
ICE COLD SODA
RONNIE, MY FROZEN CUSTARD MELTED IN TWO SECONDS!
AND MY LEATHER WATCHBAND IS TURNING INTO BLACK GOOK!
I DON'T KNOW WHETHER TO DRINK THIS SODA...
...OR TO HOLD THIS COLD CAN UP AGAINST MY FEVERED BROW!
LET'S HEAD BACK TO THE HOTEL!
YES, THE AIR-CONDITIONING SHOULD BE REPAIRED BY NOW!
WOW! THAT WAS FUN!
DIFFERENT STROKES FOR DIFFERENT FOLKS!
LOOK! THEY HAVE A GIANT POOL HERE!
LET'S GO SWIMMING!
THE BEST SUGGESTION I'VE HEARD ALL DAY!
4

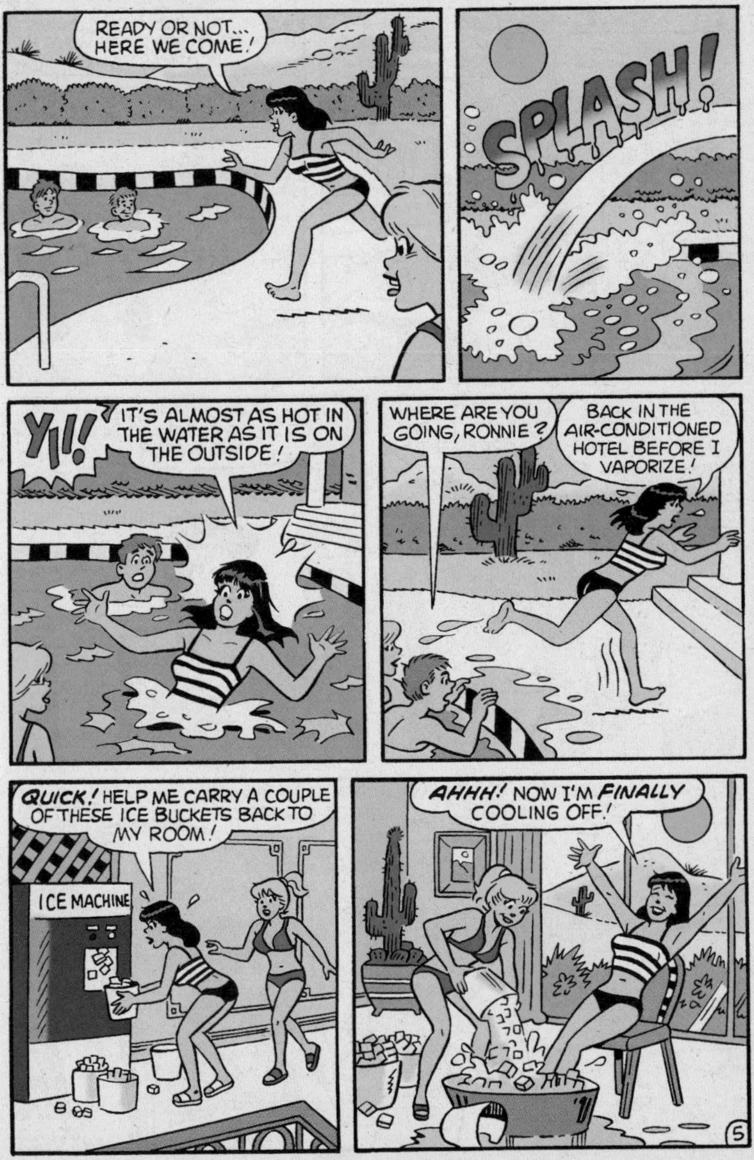

READY OR NOT... HERE WE COME!
SPLASH!
YI!!
IT'S ALMOST AS HOT IN THE WATER AS IT IS ON THE OUTSIDE!
WHERE ARE YOU GOING, RONNIE?
BACK IN THE AIR-CONDITIONED HOTEL BEFORE I VAPORIZE!
QUICK! HELP ME CARRY A COUPLE OF THESE ICE BUCKETS BACK TO MY ROOM!
ICE MACHINE
AHHH! NOW I'M FINALLY COOLING OFF!

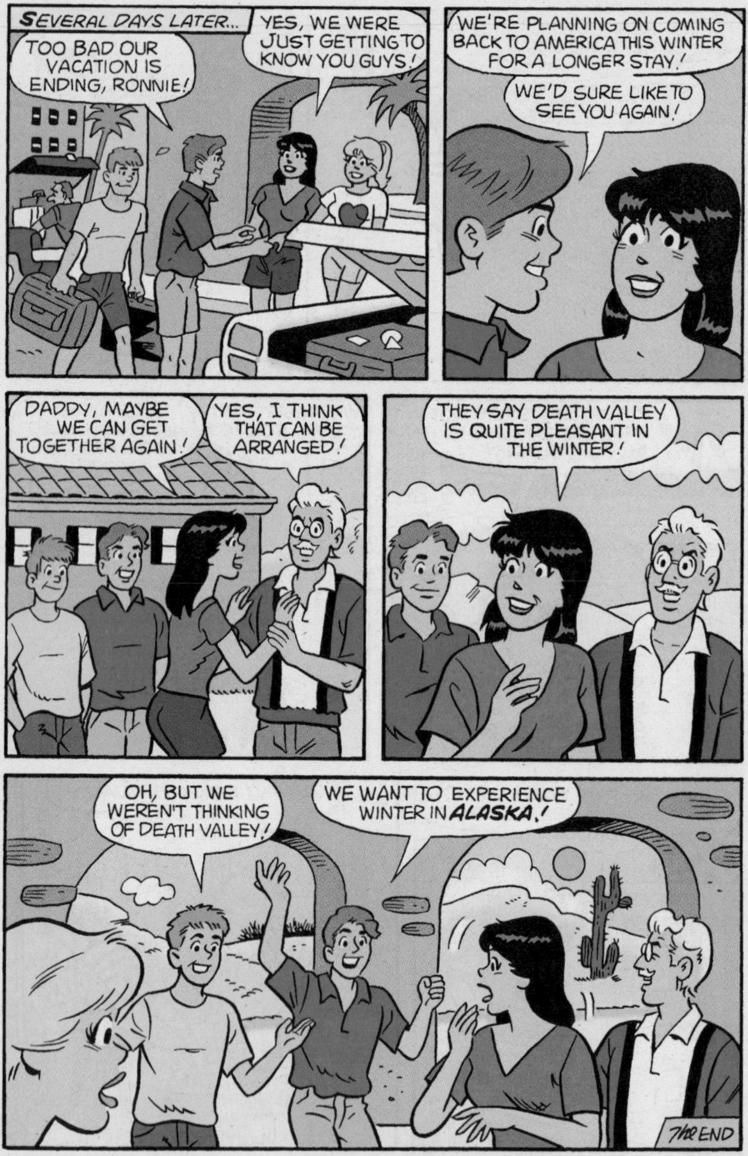
SEVERAL DAYS LATER...
TOO BAD OUR VACATION IS ENDING, RONNIE!
YES, WE WERE JUST GETTING TO KNOW YOU GUYS!
WE'RE PLANNING ON COMING BACK TO AMERICA THIS WINTER FOR A LONGER STAY!
WE'D SURE LIKE TO SEE YOU AGAIN!
DADDY, MAYBE WE CAN GET TOGETHER AGAIN!
YES, I THINK THAT CAN BE ARRANGED!
THEY SAY DEATH VALLEY IS QUITE PLEASANT IN THE WINTER!
OH, BUT WE WEREN'T THINKING OF DEATH VALLEY!
WE WANT TO EXPERIENCE WINTER IN ALASKA!
THE END

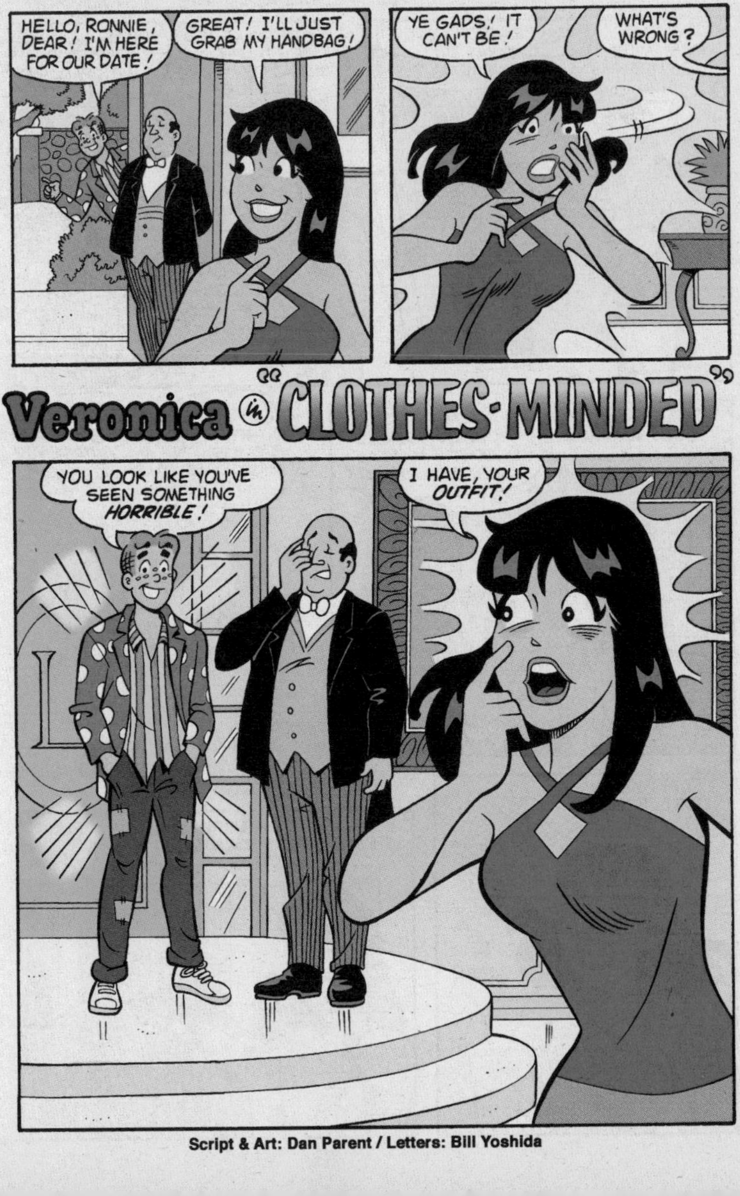
HELLO, RONNIE, DEAR! I'M HERE FOR OUR DATE!
GREAT! I'LL JUST GRAB MY HANDBAG!
YE GADS! IT CAN'T BE!
WHAT'S WRONG?
Veronica in "CLOTHES-MINDED"
YOU LOOK LIKE YOU'VE SEEN SOMETHING HORRIBLE!
I HAVE, YOUR OUTFIT!

Script & Art: Dan Parent / Letters: Bill Yoshida

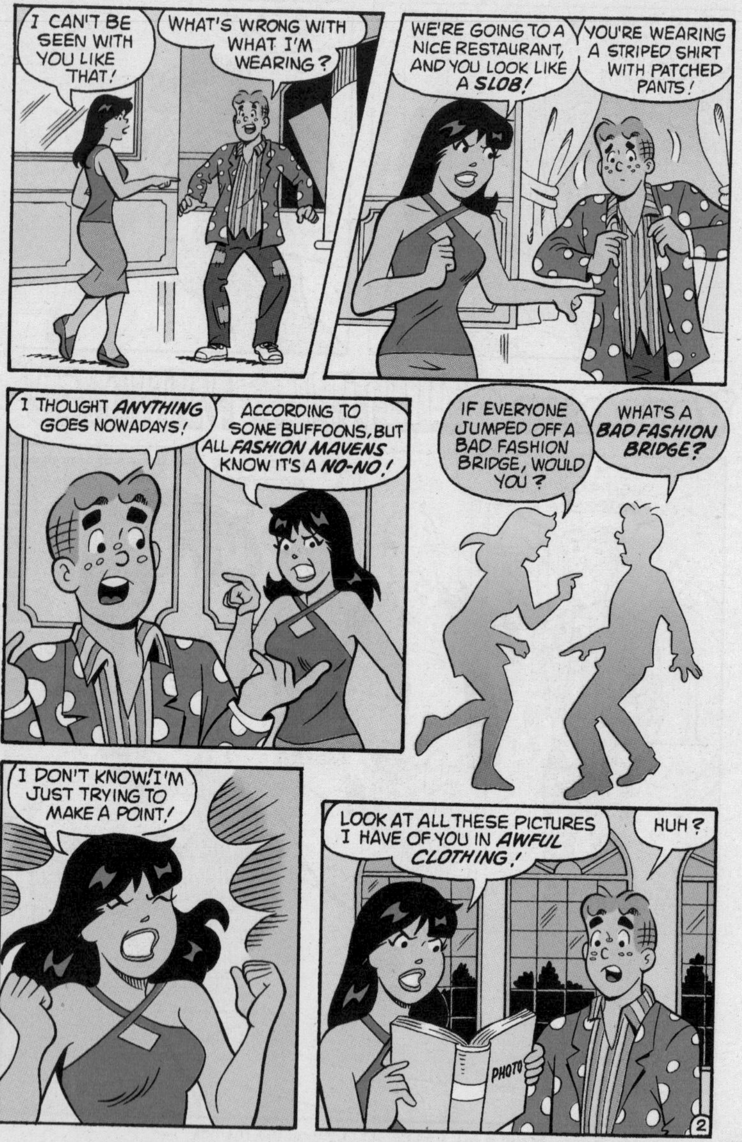

I CAN'T BE SEEN WITH YOU LIKE THAT!
WHAT'S WRONG WITH WHAT I'M WEARING?
WE'RE GOING TO A NICE RESTAURANT, AND YOU LOOK LIKE A SLOB!
YOU'RE WEARING A STRIPED SHIRT WITH PATCHED PANTS!
I THOUGHT ANYTHING GOES NOWADAYS!
ACCORDING TO SOME BUFFOONS, BUT ALL FASHION MAVENS KNOW IT'S A NO-NO!
IF EVERYONE JUMPED OFF A BAD FASHION BRIDGE, WOULD YOU?
WHAT'S A BAD FASHION BRIDGE?
I DON'T KNOW! I'M JUST TRYING TO MAKE A POINT!
LOOK AT ALL THESE PICTURES I HAVE OF YOU IN AWFUL CLOTHING!
HUH?
PHOTO
2

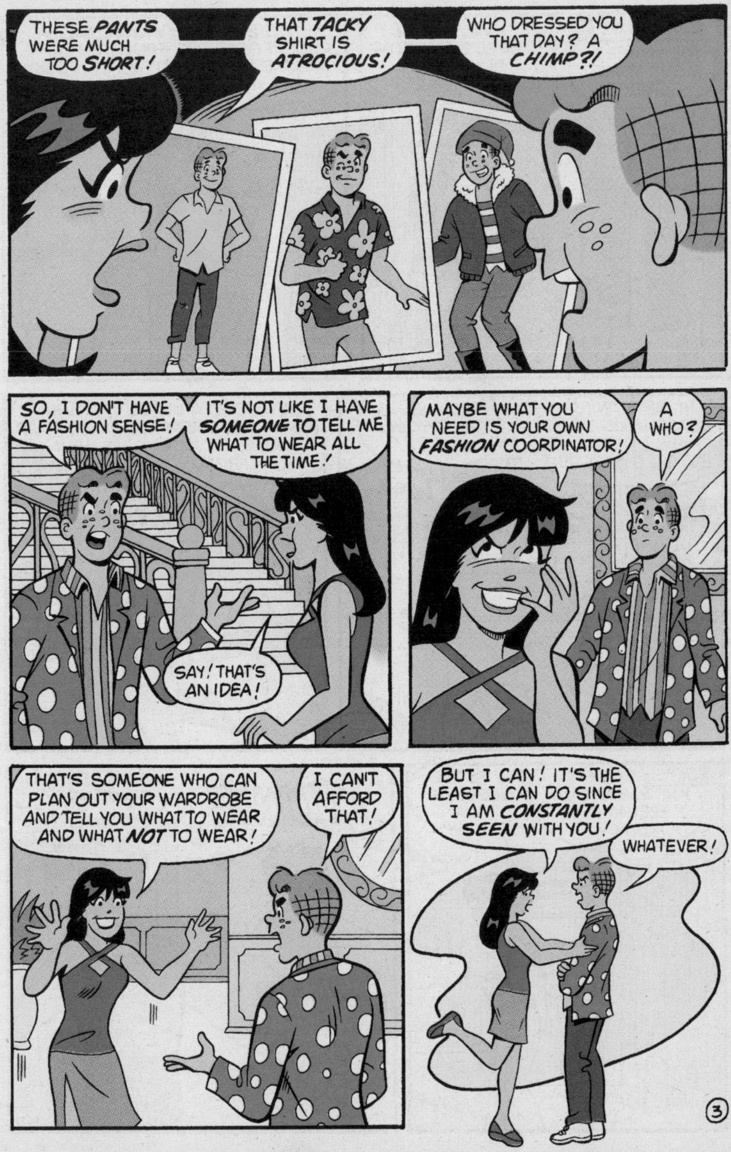
THESE PANTS WERE MUCH TOO SHORT!
THAT TACKY SHIRT IS ATROCIOUS!
WHO DRESSED YOU THAT DAY? A CHIMP?!
SO, I DON'T HAVE A FASHION SENSE!
IT'S NOT LIKE I HAVE SOMEONE TO TELL ME WHAT TO WEAR ALL THE TIME!
SAY! THAT'S AN IDEA!
MAYBE WHAT YOU NEED IS YOUR OWN FASHION COORDINATOR!
A WHO?
THAT'S SOMEONE WHO CAN PLAN OUT YOUR WARDROBE AND TELL YOU WHAT TO WEAR AND WHAT NOT TO WEAR!
I CAN'T AFFORD THAT!
BUT I CAN! IT'S THE LEAST I CAN DO SINCE I AM CONSTANTLY SEEN WITH YOU!
WHATEVER!
3

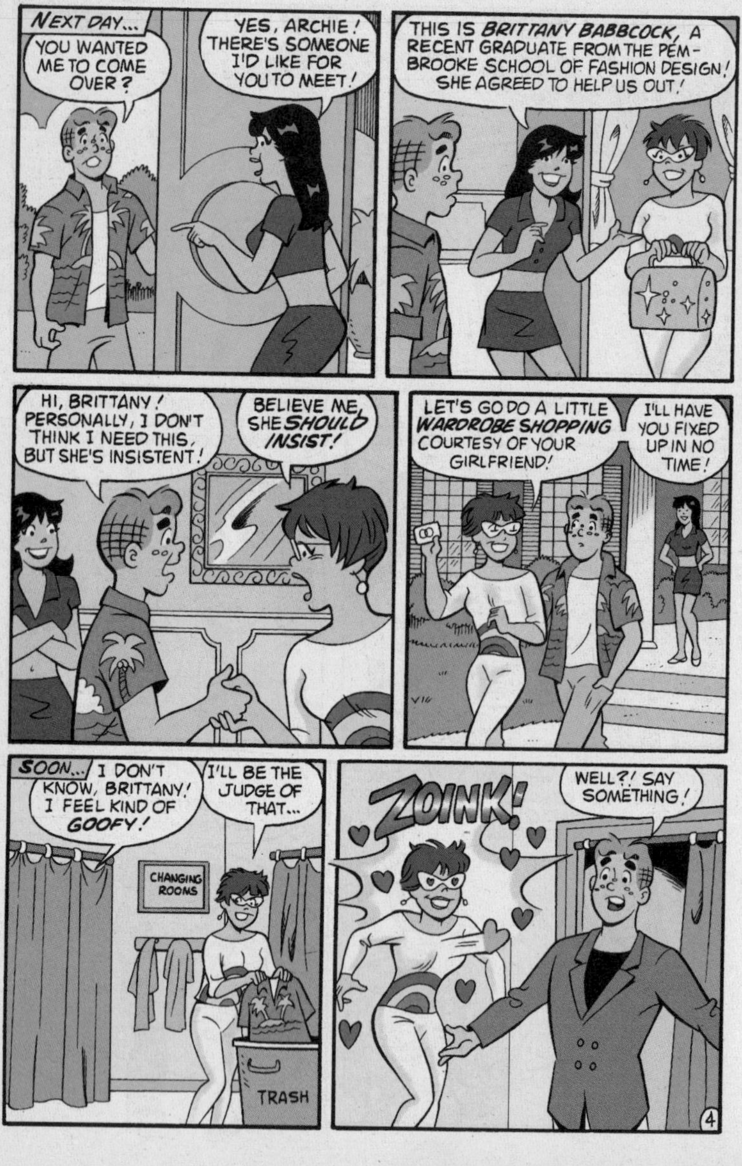
NEXT DAY...
YOU WANTED ME TO COME OVER?
YES, ARCHIE! THERE'S SOMEONE I'D LIKE FOR YOU TO MEET!
THIS IS BRITTANY BABBCOCK, A RECENT GRADUATE FROM THE PEM-BROOKE SCHOOL OF FASHION DESIGN! SHE AGREED TO HELP US OUT!
HI, BRITTANY! PERSONALLY, I DON'T THINK I NEED THIS, BUT SHE'S INSISTENT!
BELIEVE ME, SHE SHOULD INSIST!
LET'S GO DO A LITTLE WARDROBE SHOPPING COURTESY OF YOUR GIRLFRIEND!
I'LL HAVE YOU FIXED UP IN NO TIME!
SOON...
I DON'T KNOW, BRITTANY! I FEEL KIND OF GOOFY!
I'LL BE THE JUDGE OF THAT...
CHANGING ROOMS
TRASH
ZOINK!
WELL?! SAY SOMETHING!
4

Panel 1:
IT'S TRUE! CLOTHES DO *MAKE THE MAN!*

AND *WHAT A MAN* THEY MAKE!

Panel 2:
LATER... WHERE IS ARCHIE? HE WAS SUPPOSED TO MEET ME HERE AN *HOUR AGO* TO SHOW ME HIS *NEW LOOK!*

Panel 3:
HELLO, VERONICA!

ARCHIE, WHERE HAVE YOU...

... YOU LOOK *GREAT!!*

Panel 4:
THANKS! I OWE IT ALL TO BRITTANY!

SHE'S THE REASON I'M LATE, TOO!

HOW'S THAT?

Panel 5:
SHE INSISTS WE'RE GOING TO HAVE TO SPEND *MORE* AND *MORE TIME* TOGETHER SO SHE CAN BETTER PLAN OUT MY WARDROBE!

OH, SHE DOES, *DOES SHE?*

Panel 6:
EXCUSE ME, BUT YOU LOOK *FAMILIAR!*

I DO?!

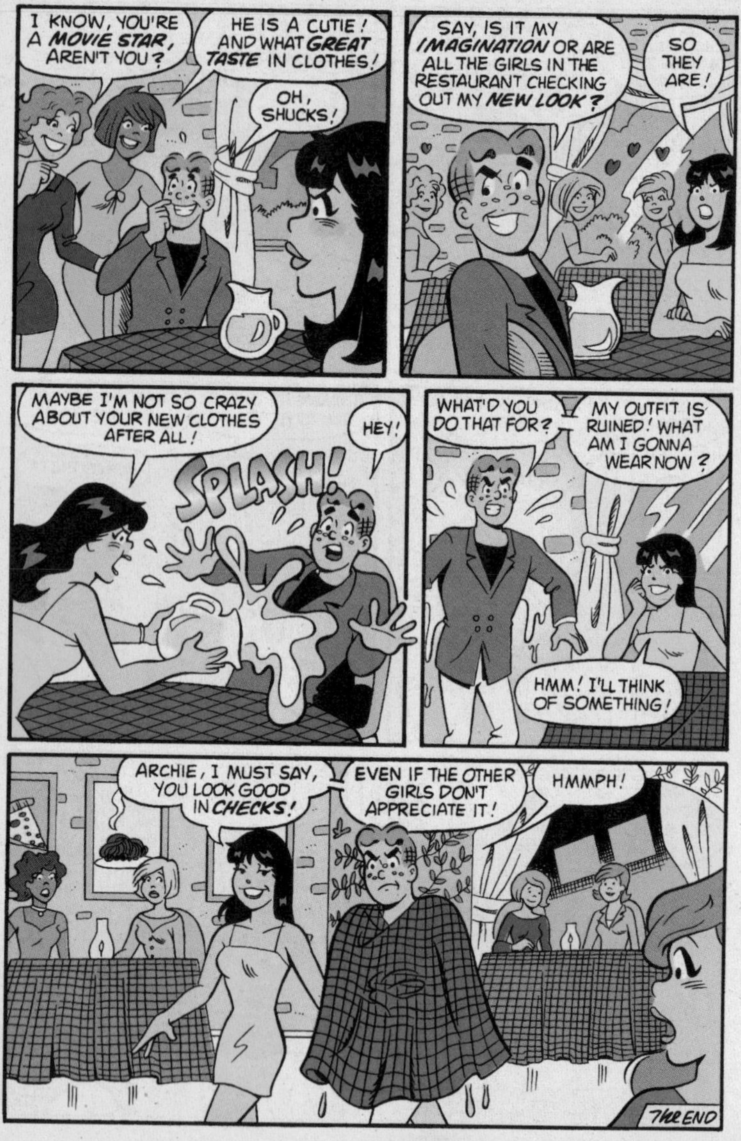
I KNOW, YOU'RE A MOVIE STAR, AREN'T YOU?
HE IS A CUTIE! AND WHAT GREAT TASTE IN CLOTHES!
OH, SHUCKS!
SAY, IS IT MY IMAGINATION OR ARE ALL THE GIRLS IN THE RESTAURANT CHECKING OUT MY NEW LOOK?
SO THEY ARE!
MAYBE I'M NOT SO CRAZY ABOUT YOUR NEW CLOTHES AFTER ALL!
HEY!
SPLASH!
WHAT'D YOU DO THAT FOR?
MY OUTFIT IS RUINED! WHAT AM I GONNA WEAR NOW?
HMM! I'LL THINK OF SOMETHING!
ARCHIE, I MUST SAY, YOU LOOK GOOD IN CHECKS!
EVEN IF THE OTHER GIRLS DON'T APPRECIATE IT!
HMMPH!
THE END

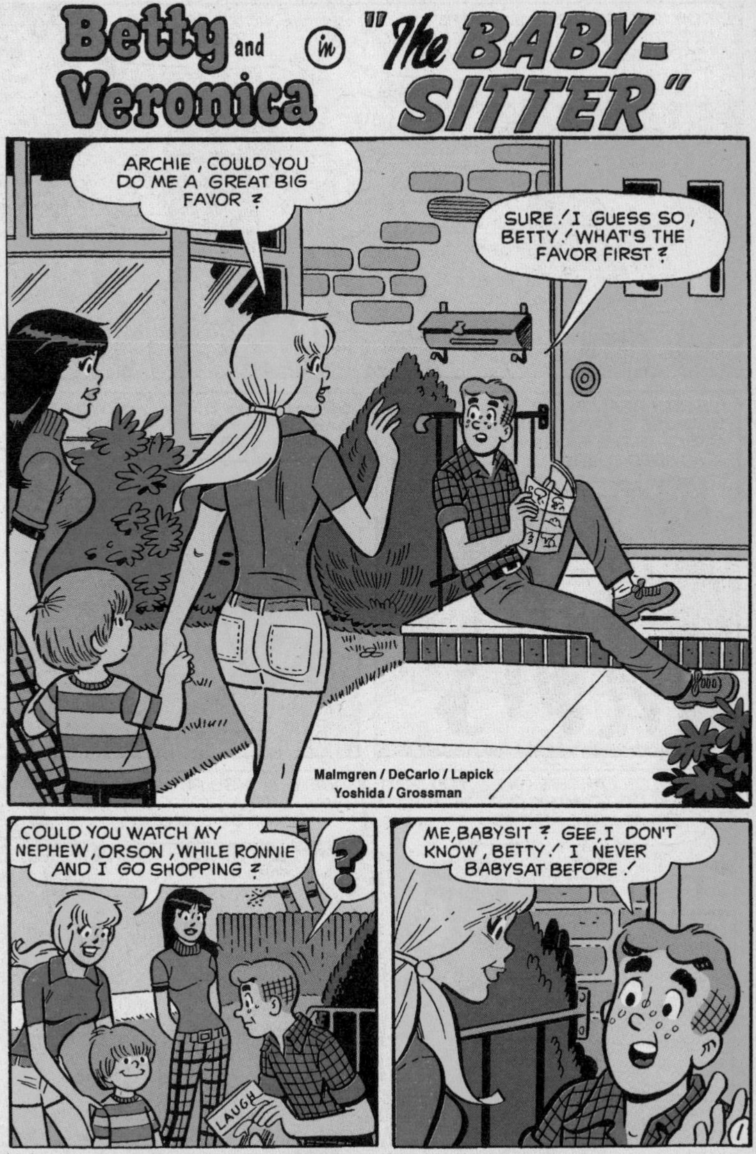
Betty and Veronica in "The BABY-SITTER"
ARCHIE, COULD YOU DO ME A GREAT BIG FAVOR ?
SURE! I GUESS SO, BETTY! WHAT'S THE FAVOR FIRST ?
Malmgren / DeCarlo / Lapick
Yoshida / Grossman
COULD YOU WATCH MY NEPHEW, ORSON, WHILE RONNIE AND I GO SHOPPING ?
?
LAUGH
ME, BABYSIT ? GEE, I DON'T KNOW, BETTY! I NEVER BABYSAT BEFORE!
1

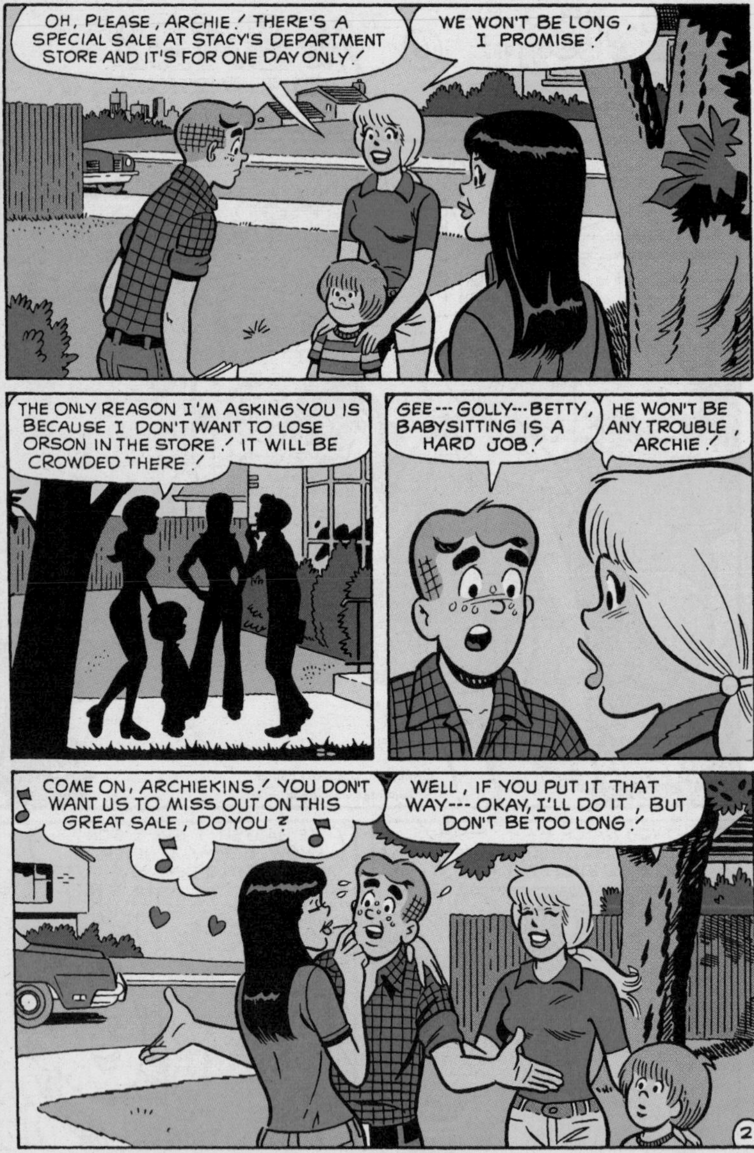
OH, PLEASE, ARCHIE! THERE'S A SPECIAL SALE AT STACY'S DEPARTMENT STORE AND IT'S FOR ONE DAY ONLY!
WE WON'T BE LONG, I PROMISE!
THE ONLY REASON I'M ASKING YOU IS BECAUSE I DON'T WANT TO LOSE ORSON IN THE STORE! IT WILL BE CROWDED THERE!
GEE --- GOLLY --- BETTY, BABYSITTING IS A HARD JOB!
HE WON'T BE ANY TROUBLE, ARCHIE!
COME ON, ARCHIEKINS! YOU DON'T WANT US TO MISS OUT ON THIS GREAT SALE, DO YOU?
WELL, IF YOU PUT IT THAT WAY--- OKAY, I'LL DO IT, BUT DON'T BE TOO LONG!
2

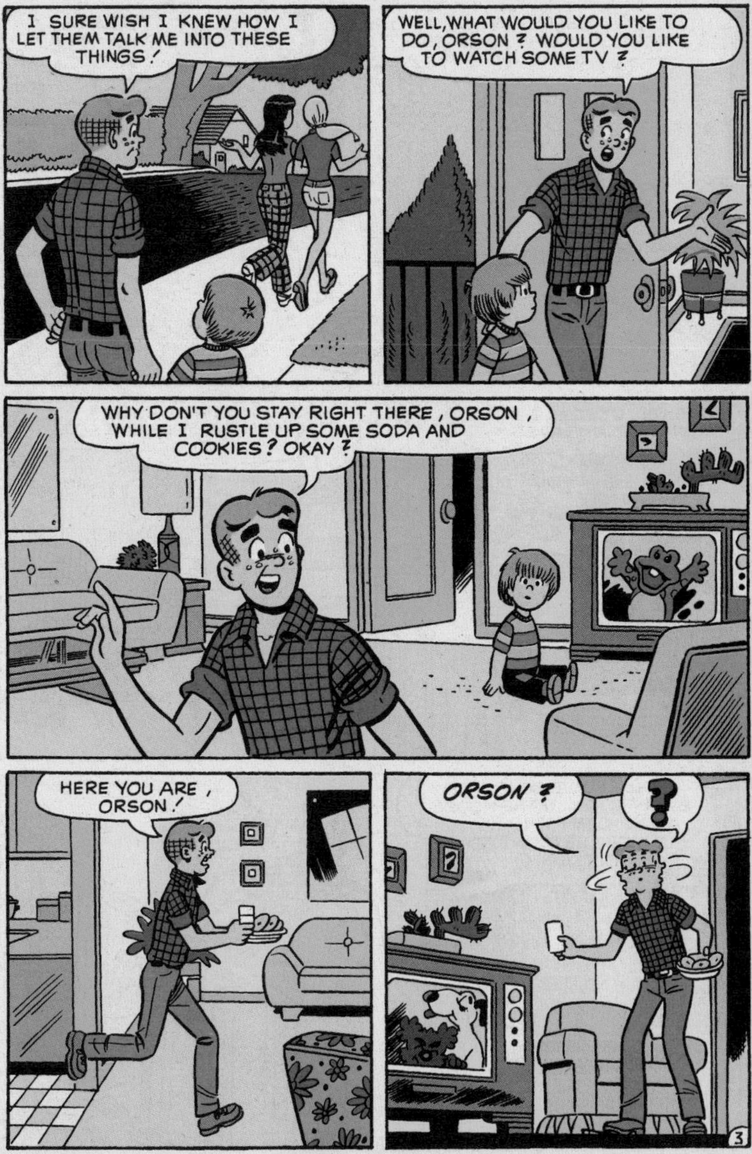
I SURE WISH I KNEW HOW I LET THEM TALK ME INTO THESE THINGS!
WELL, WHAT WOULD YOU LIKE TO DO, ORSON? WOULD YOU LIKE TO WATCH SOME TV?
WHY DON'T YOU STAY RIGHT THERE, ORSON, WHILE I RUSTLE UP SOME SODA AND COOKIES? OKAY?
HERE YOU ARE, ORSON!
ORSON?
?!
3

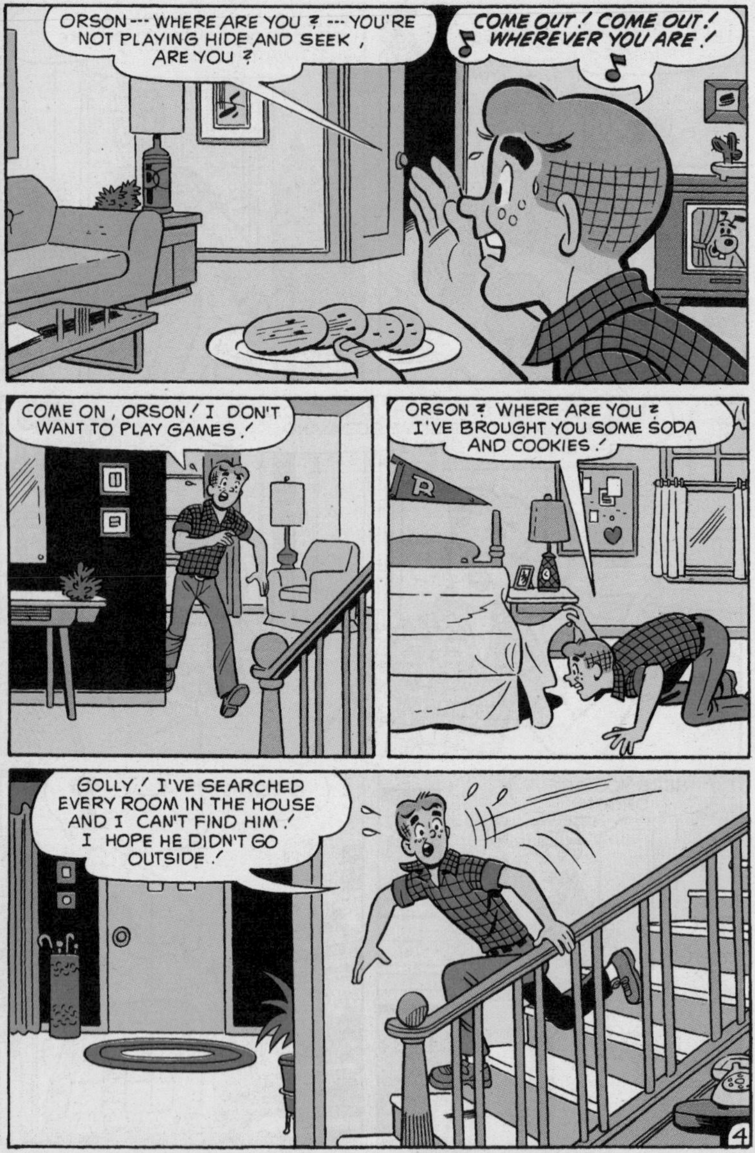
ORSON --- WHERE ARE YOU ? --- YOU'RE NOT PLAYING HIDE AND SEEK , ARE YOU ?
COME OUT ! COME OUT ! WHEREVER YOU ARE !
COME ON , ORSON ! I DON'T WANT TO PLAY GAMES !
ORSON ? WHERE ARE YOU ? I'VE BROUGHT YOU SOME SODA AND COOKIES !
GOLLY ! I'VE SEARCHED EVERY ROOM IN THE HOUSE AND I CAN'T FIND HIM ! I HOPE HE DIDN'T GO OUTSIDE !
4

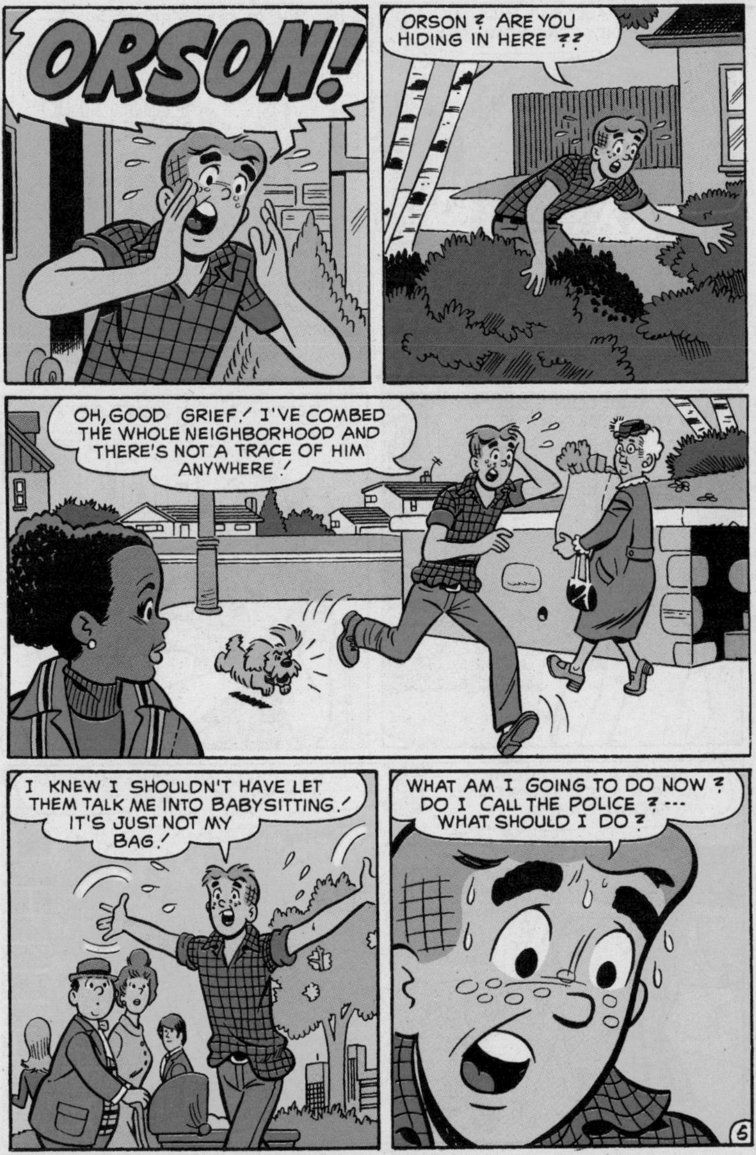
ORSON!
ORSON ? ARE YOU HIDING IN HERE ??
OH, GOOD GRIEF! I'VE COMBED THE WHOLE NEIGHBORHOOD AND THERE'S NOT A TRACE OF HIM ANYWHERE!
I KNEW I SHOULDN'T HAVE LET THEM TALK ME INTO BABYSITTING! IT'S JUST NOT MY BAG!
WHAT AM I GOING TO DO NOW ? DO I CALL THE POLICE ? --- WHAT SHOULD I DO ?
5

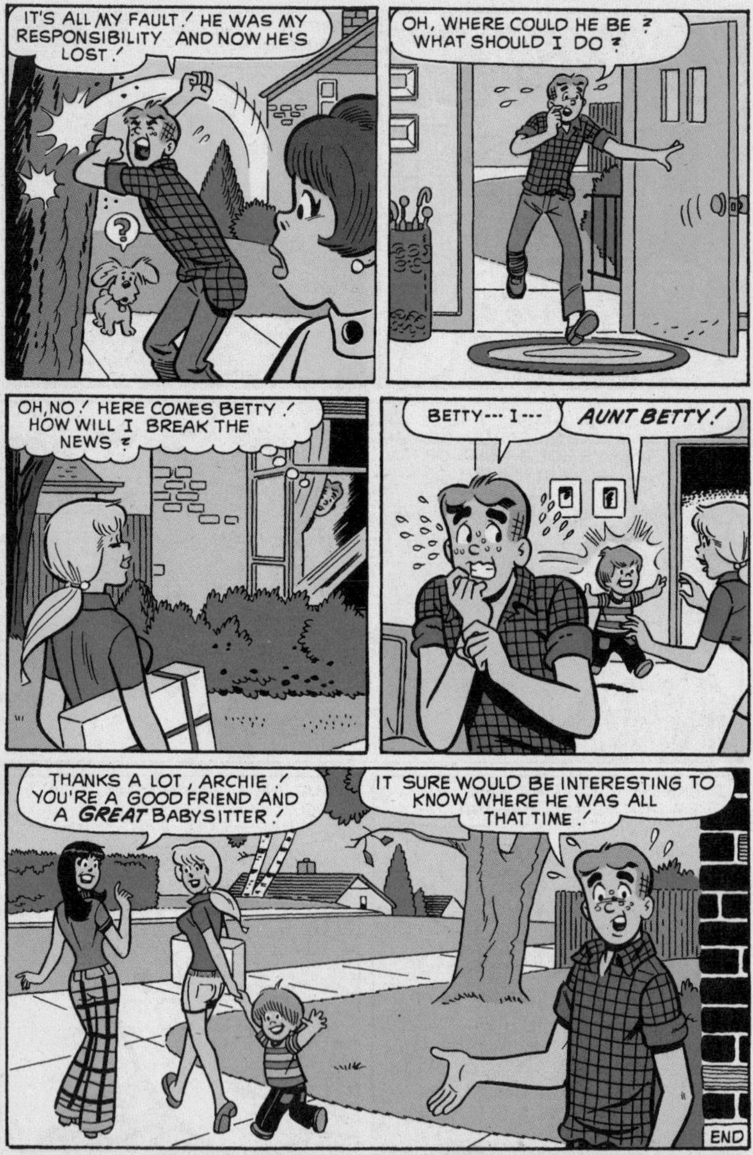
IT'S ALL MY FAULT! HE WAS MY RESPONSIBILITY AND NOW HE'S LOST!
OH, WHERE COULD HE BE? WHAT SHOULD I DO?
OH, NO! HERE COMES BETTY! HOW WILL I BREAK THE NEWS?
BETTY--- I---
AUNT BETTY!
THANKS A LOT, ARCHIE! YOU'RE A GOOD FRIEND AND A GREAT BABYSITTER!
IT SURE WOULD BE INTERESTING TO KNOW WHERE HE WAS ALL THAT TIME!
END

Betty and Veronica in "THE WAY THE BALL BOUNCES.."

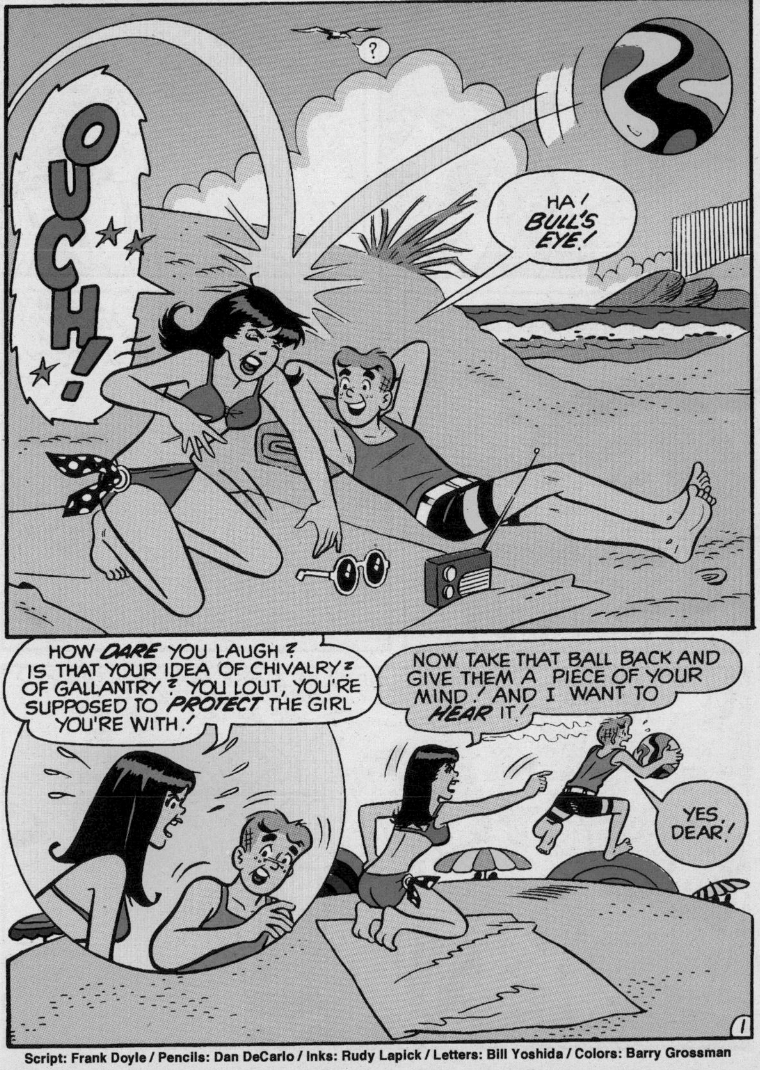
?
OUCH!
HA! BULL'S EYE!
HOW DARE YOU LAUGH? IS THAT YOUR IDEA OF CHIVALRY? OF GALLANTRY? YOU LOUT, YOU'RE SUPPOSED TO PROTECT THE GIRL YOU'RE WITH!
NOW TAKE THAT BALL BACK AND GIVE THEM A PIECE OF YOUR MIND! AND I WANT TO HEAR IT!
YES, DEAR!
1

Script: Frank Doyle / Pencils: Dan DeCarlo / Inks: Rudy Lapick / Letters: Bill Yoshida / Colors: Barry Grossman

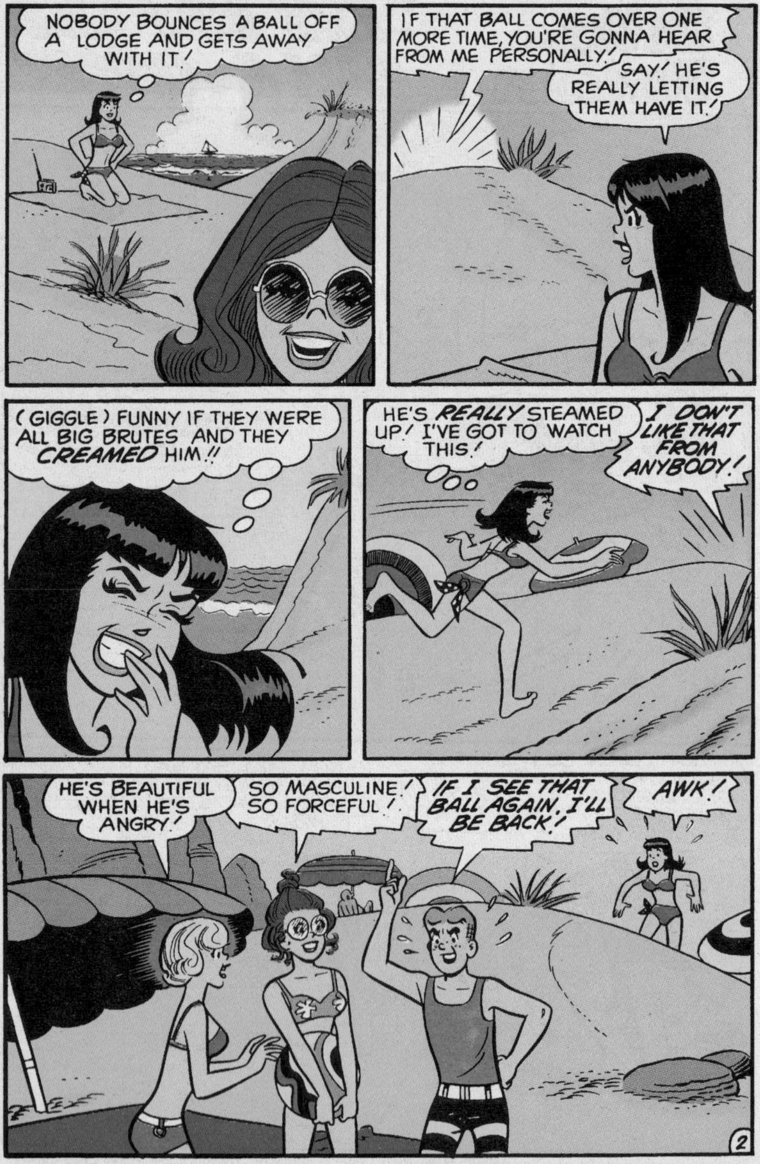
NOBODY BOUNCES A BALL OFF A LODGE AND GETS AWAY WITH IT!
IF THAT BALL COMES OVER ONE MORE TIME, YOU'RE GONNA HEAR FROM ME PERSONALLY!
SAY! HE'S REALLY LETTING THEM HAVE IT!
(GIGGLE) FUNNY IF THEY WERE ALL BIG BRUTES AND THEY CREAMED HIM!!
HE'S REALLY STEAMED UP! I'VE GOT TO WATCH THIS!
I DON'T LIKE THAT FROM ANYBODY!
HE'S BEAUTIFUL WHEN HE'S ANGRY!
SO MASCULINE! SO FORCEFUL!
IF I SEE THAT BALL AGAIN, I'LL BE BACK!
AWK!
2

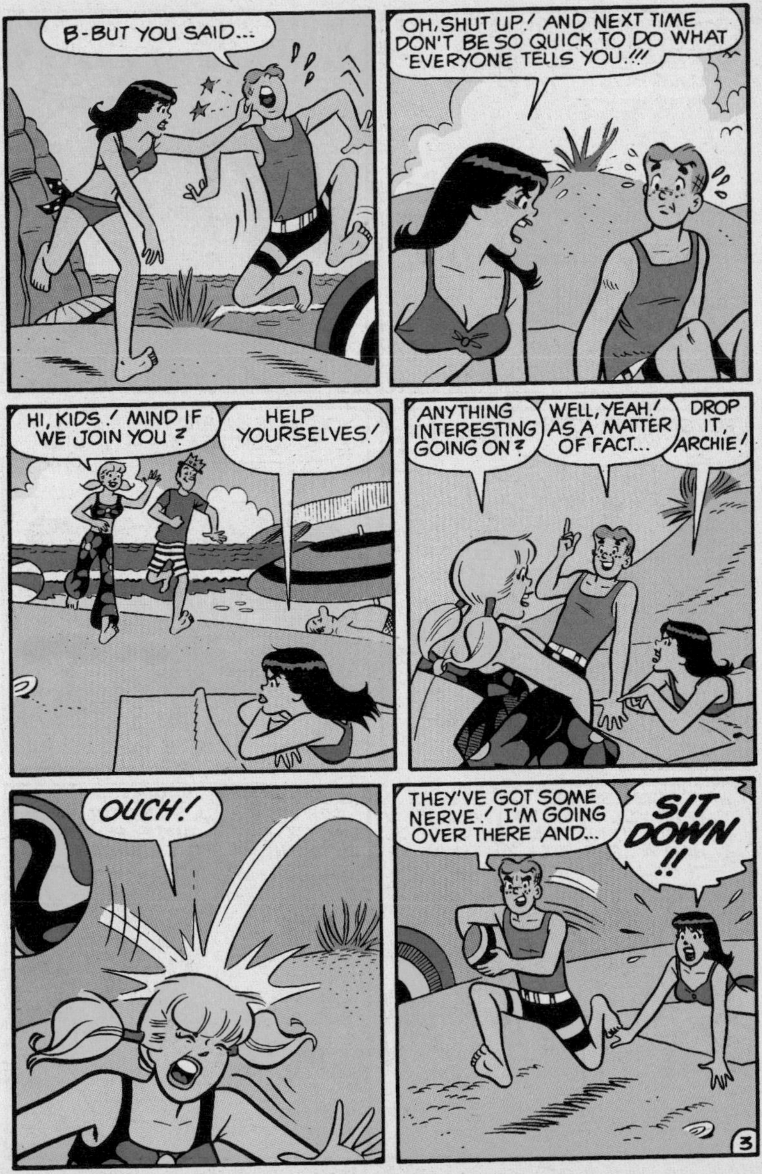
B-BUT YOU SAID...
OH, SHUT UP! AND NEXT TIME DON'T BE SO QUICK TO DO WHAT EVERYONE TELLS YOU!!!
HI, KIDS! MIND IF WE JOIN YOU?
HELP YOURSELVES!
ANYTHING INTERESTING GOING ON?
WELL, YEAH! AS A MATTER OF FACT...
DROP IT, ARCHIE!
OUCH!
THEY'VE GOT SOME NERVE! I'M GOING OVER THERE AND...
SIT DOWN!!
3

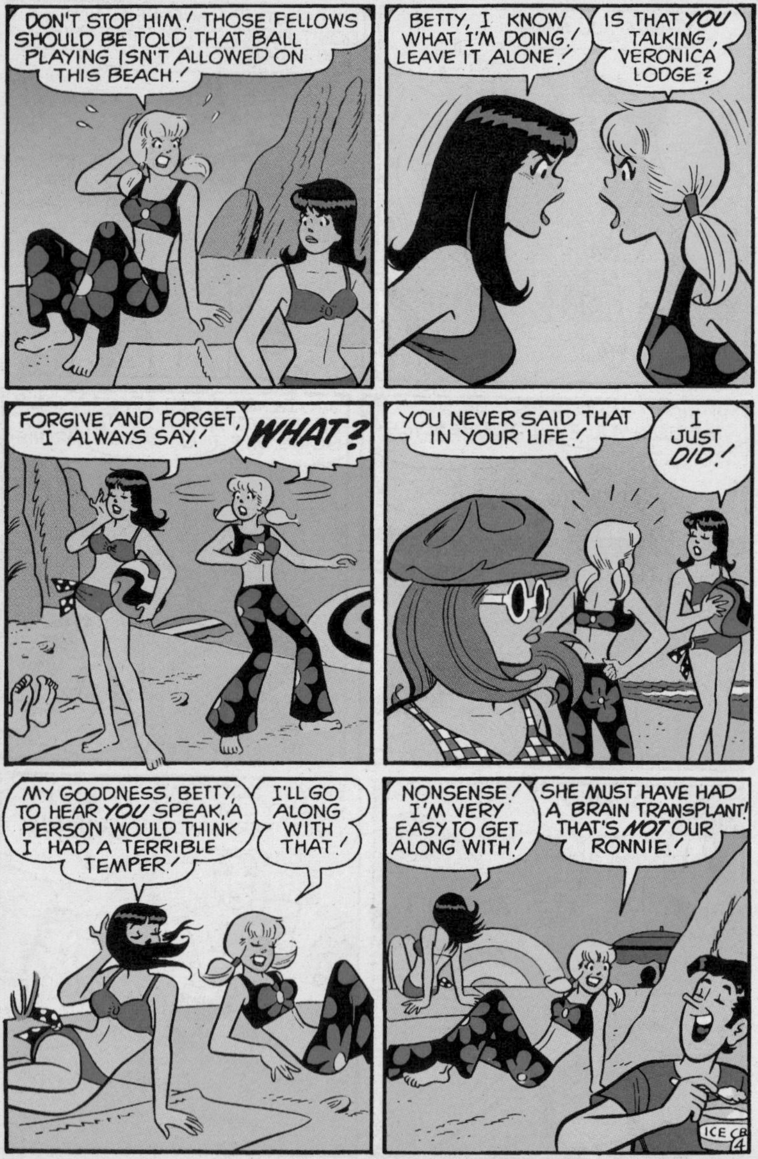
DON'T STOP HIM! THOSE FELLOWS SHOULD BE TOLD THAT BALL PLAYING ISN'T ALLOWED ON THIS BEACH!
BETTY, I KNOW WHAT I'M DOING! LEAVE IT ALONE!
IS THAT YOU TALKING, VERONICA LODGE?
FORGIVE AND FORGET, I ALWAYS SAY!
WHAT?
YOU NEVER SAID THAT IN YOUR LIFE!
I JUST DID!
MY GOODNESS, BETTY, TO HEAR YOU SPEAK, A PERSON WOULD THINK I HAD A TERRIBLE TEMPER!
I'LL GO ALONG WITH THAT!
NONSENSE! I'M VERY EASY TO GET ALONG WITH!
SHE MUST HAVE HAD A BRAIN TRANSPLANT! THAT'S NOT OUR RONNIE!
ICE CR
4

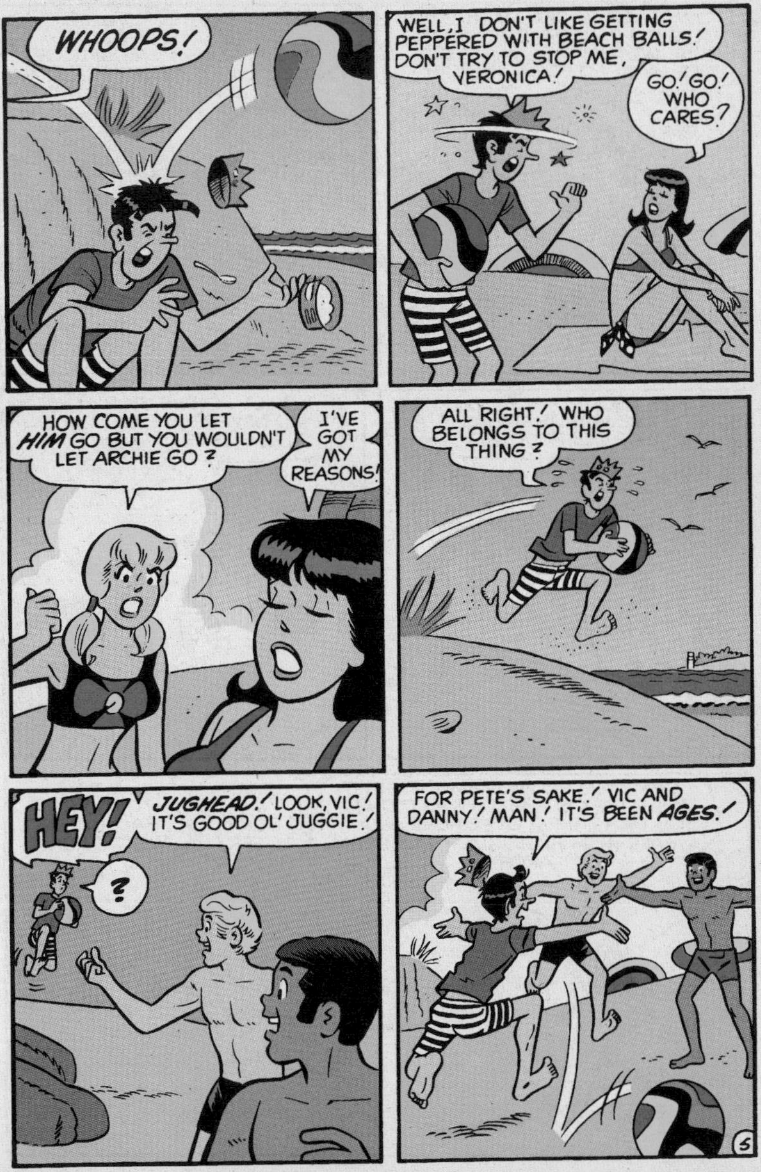
WHOOPS!
WELL, I DON'T LIKE GETTING PEPPERED WITH BEACH BALLS! DON'T TRY TO STOP ME, VERONICA!
GO! GO! WHO CARES?
HOW COME YOU LET HIM GO BUT YOU WOULDN'T LET ARCHIE GO?
I'VE GOT MY REASONS!
ALL RIGHT! WHO BELONGS TO THIS THING?
HEY!
JUGHEAD! LOOK, VIC! IT'S GOOD OL' JUGGIE!
?
FOR PETE'S SAKE! VIC AND DANNY! MAN! IT'S BEEN AGES!
5

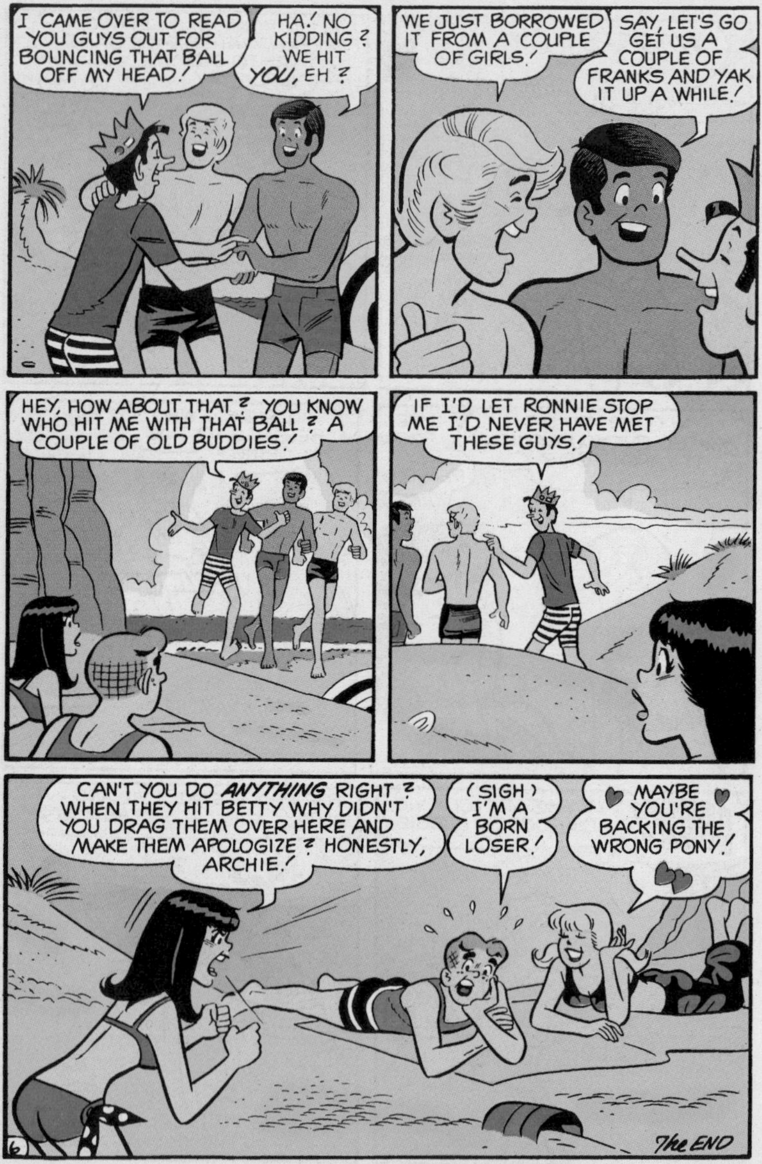
I CAME OVER TO READ YOU GUYS OUT FOR BOUNCING THAT BALL OFF MY HEAD!
HA! NO KIDDING? WE HIT YOU, EH?
WE JUST BORROWED IT FROM A COUPLE OF GIRLS!
SAY, LET'S GO GET US A COUPLE OF FRANKS AND YAK IT UP A WHILE!
HEY, HOW ABOUT THAT? YOU KNOW WHO HIT ME WITH THAT BALL? A COUPLE OF OLD BUDDIES!
IF I'D LET RONNIE STOP ME I'D NEVER HAVE MET THESE GUYS!
CAN'T YOU DO ANYTHING RIGHT? WHEN THEY HIT BETTY WHY DIDN'T YOU DRAG THEM OVER HERE AND MAKE THEM APOLOGIZE? HONESTLY, ARCHIE!
(SIGH) I'M A BORN LOSER!
MAYBE YOU'RE BACKING THE WRONG PONY!
6
The END

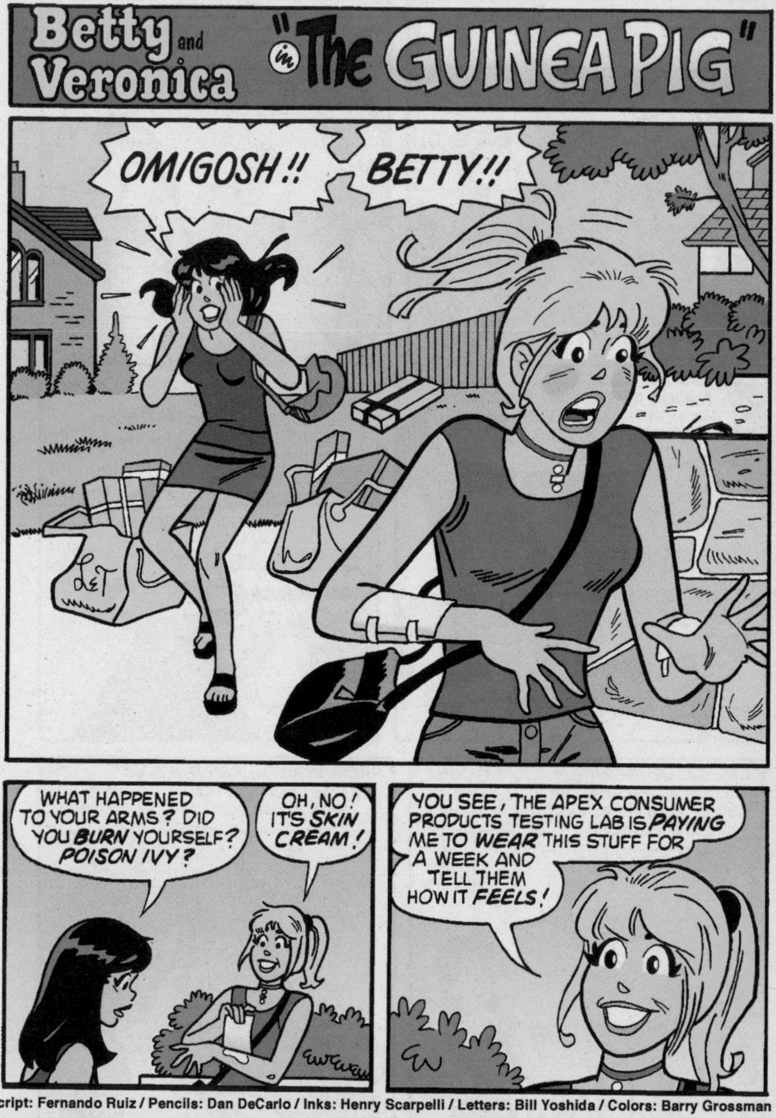
Betty and Veronica in "The GUINEA PIG"
OMIGOSH!! BETTY!!
WHAT HAPPENED TO YOUR ARMS? DID YOU BURN YOURSELF? POISON IVY?
OH, NO! IT'S SKIN CREAM!
YOU SEE, THE APEX CONSUMER PRODUCTS TESTING LAB IS PAYING ME TO WEAR THIS STUFF FOR A WEEK AND TELL THEM HOW IT FEELS!

Script: Fernando Ruiz / Pencils: Dan DeCarlo / Inks: Henry Scarpelli / Letters: Bill Yoshida / Colors: Barry Grossman

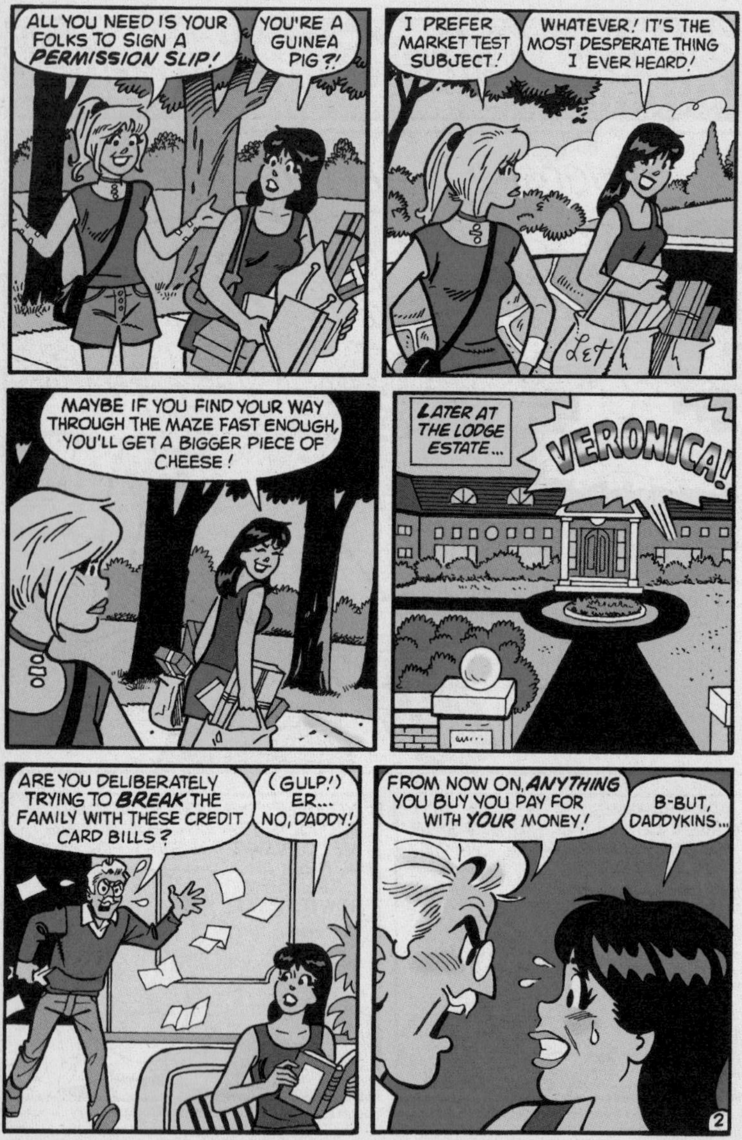
ALL YOU NEED IS YOUR FOLKS TO SIGN A PERMISSION SLIP!
YOU'RE A GUINEA PIG?!
I PREFER MARKET TEST SUBJECT!
WHATEVER! IT'S THE MOST DESPERATE THING I EVER HEARD!
MAYBE IF YOU FIND YOUR WAY THROUGH THE MAZE FAST ENOUGH, YOU'LL GET A BIGGER PIECE OF CHEESE!
LATER AT THE LODGE ESTATE...
VERONICA!
ARE YOU DELIBERATELY TRYING TO BREAK THE FAMILY WITH THESE CREDIT CARD BILLS?
(GULP!) ER... NO, DADDY!
FROM NOW ON, ANYTHING YOU BUY YOU PAY FOR WITH YOUR MONEY!
B-BUT, DADDYKINS...
2

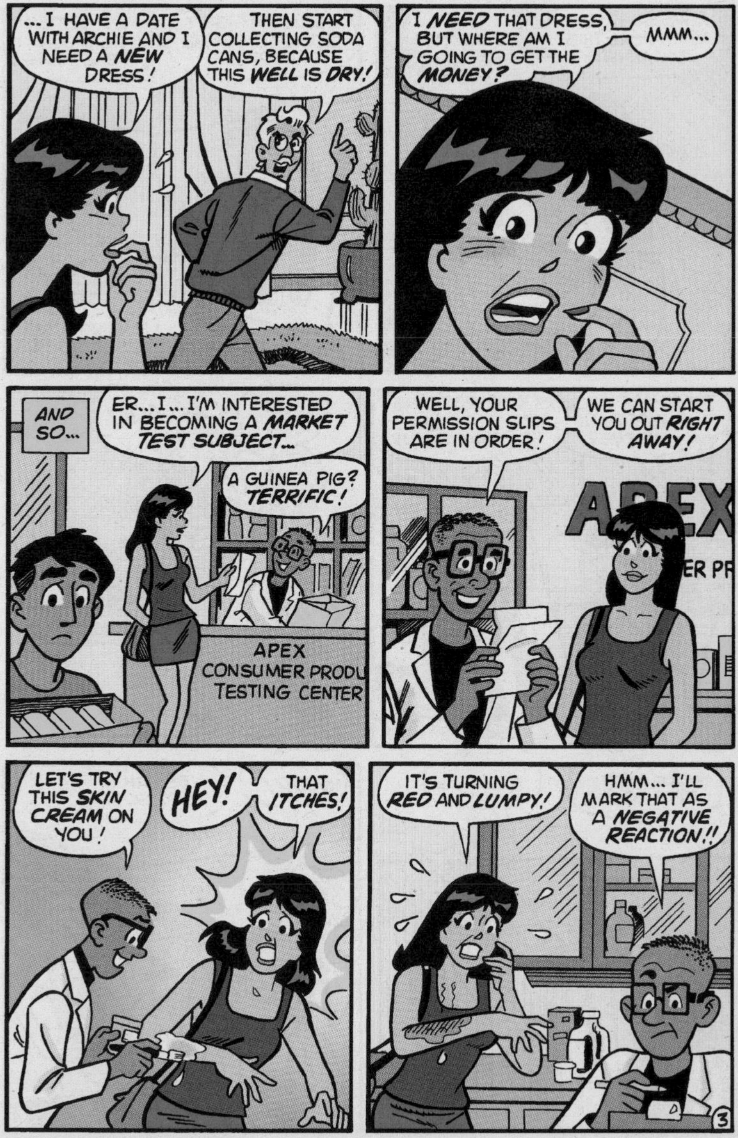

...I HAVE A DATE WITH ARCHIE AND I NEED A NEW DRESS!
THEN START COLLECTING SODA CANS, BECAUSE THIS WELL IS DRY!
I NEED THAT DRESS, BUT WHERE AM I GOING TO GET THE MONEY?
MMM...
AND SO...
ER...I...I'M INTERESTED IN BECOMING A MARKET TEST SUBJECT...
A GUINEA PIG? TERRIFIC!
APEX CONSUMER PRODU TESTING CENTER
WELL, YOUR PERMISSION SLIPS ARE IN ORDER!
WE CAN START YOU OUT RIGHT AWAY!
LET'S TRY THIS SKIN CREAM ON YOU!
HEY!
THAT ITCHES!
IT'S TURNING RED AND LUMPY!
HMM... I'LL MARK THAT AS A NEGATIVE REACTION!!
3

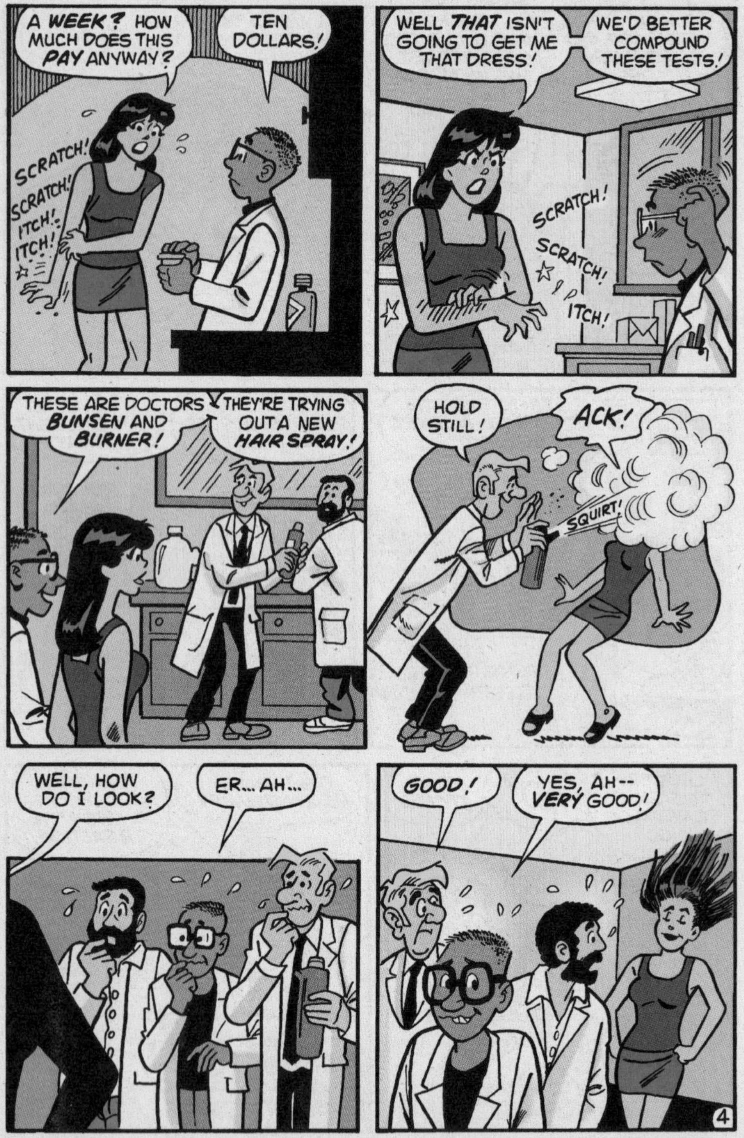
A WEEK? HOW MUCH DOES THIS PAY ANYWAY?
TEN DOLLARS!
SCRATCH!
SCRATCH!
ITCH!
ITCH!
WELL THAT ISN'T GOING TO GET ME THAT DRESS!
WE'D BETTER COMPOUND THESE TESTS!
SCRATCH!
SCRATCH!
ITCH!
THESE ARE DOCTORS BUNSEN AND BURNER!
THEY'RE TRYING OUT A NEW HAIR SPRAY!
HOLD STILL!
ACK!
SQUIRT!
WELL, HOW DO I LOOK?
ER... AH...
GOOD!
YES, AH-- VERY GOOD!
4

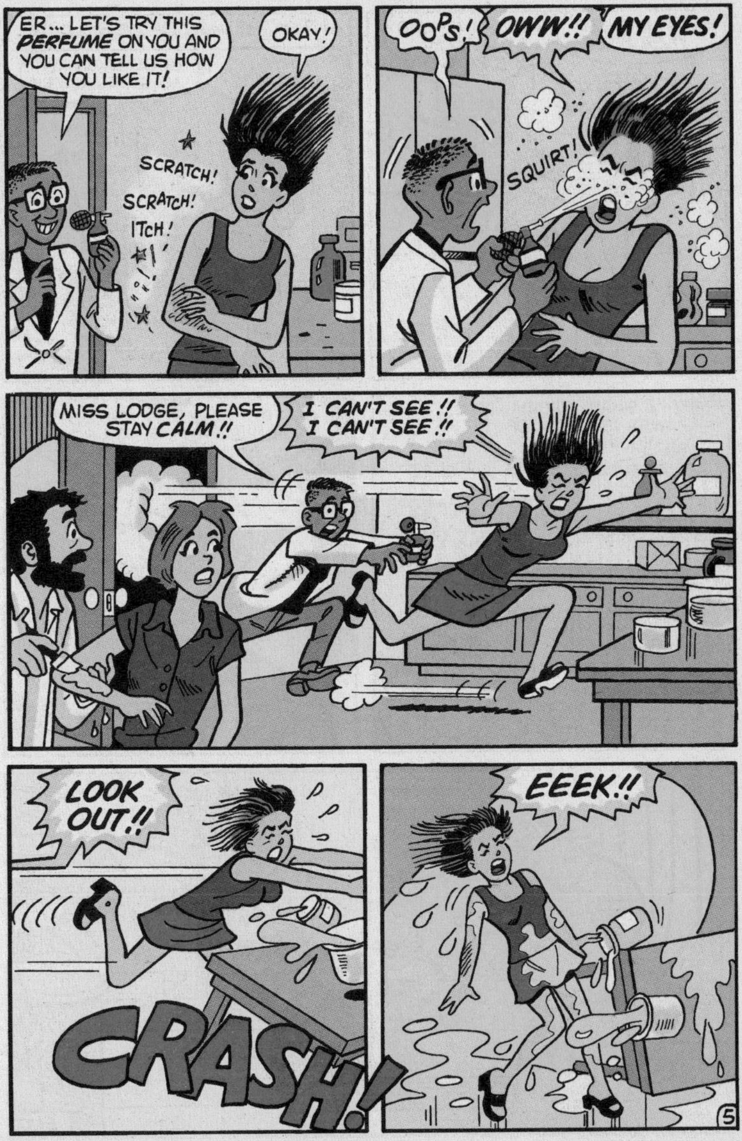
ER... LET'S TRY THIS PERFUME ON YOU AND YOU CAN TELL US HOW YOU LIKE IT!
OKAY!
SCRATCH!
SCRATCH!
ITCH!
OOPS!
OWW!!
MY EYES!
SQUIRT!
MISS LODGE, PLEASE STAY CALM!!
I CAN'T SEE!! I CAN'T SEE!!
LOOK OUT!!
CRASH!
EEEK!!
5

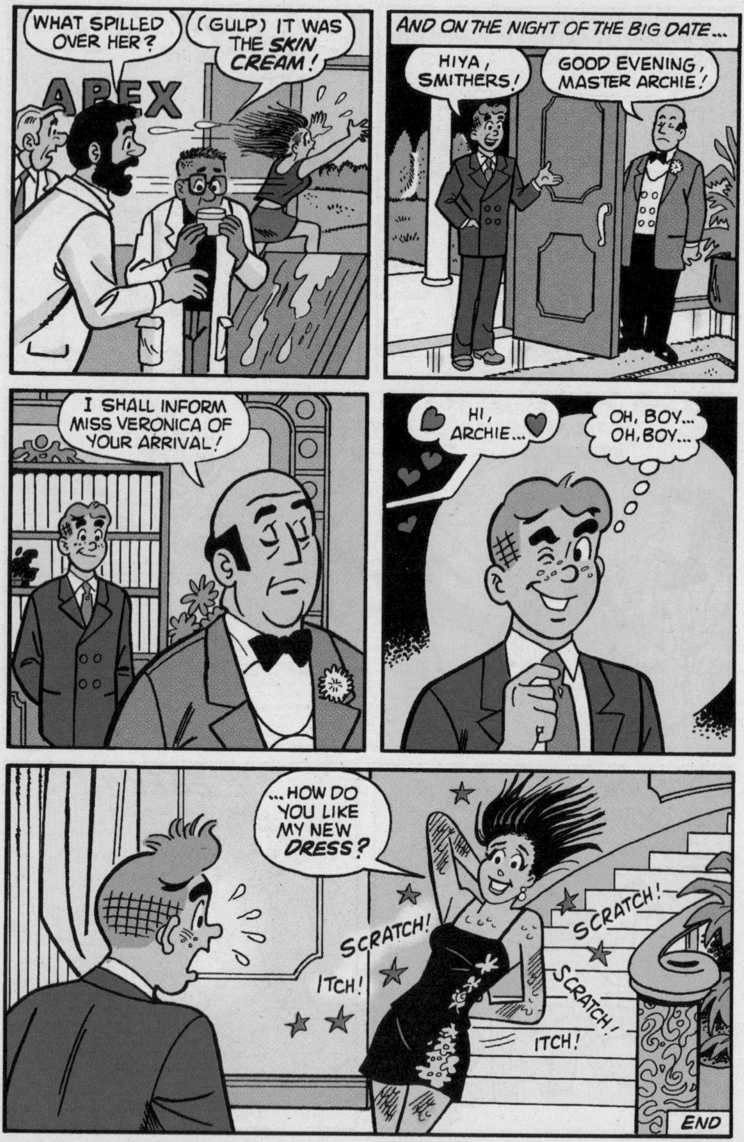
WHAT SPILLED OVER HER?
(GULP) IT WAS THE SKIN CREAM!
APEX
AND ON THE NIGHT OF THE BIG DATE...
HIYA, SMITHERS!
GOOD EVENING, MASTER ARCHIE!
I SHALL INFORM MISS VERONICA OF YOUR ARRIVAL!
HI, ARCHIE...
OH, BOY... OH, BOY...
...HOW DO YOU LIKE MY NEW DRESS?
SCRATCH!
SCRATCH!
SCRATCH!
ITCH!
ITCH!
END

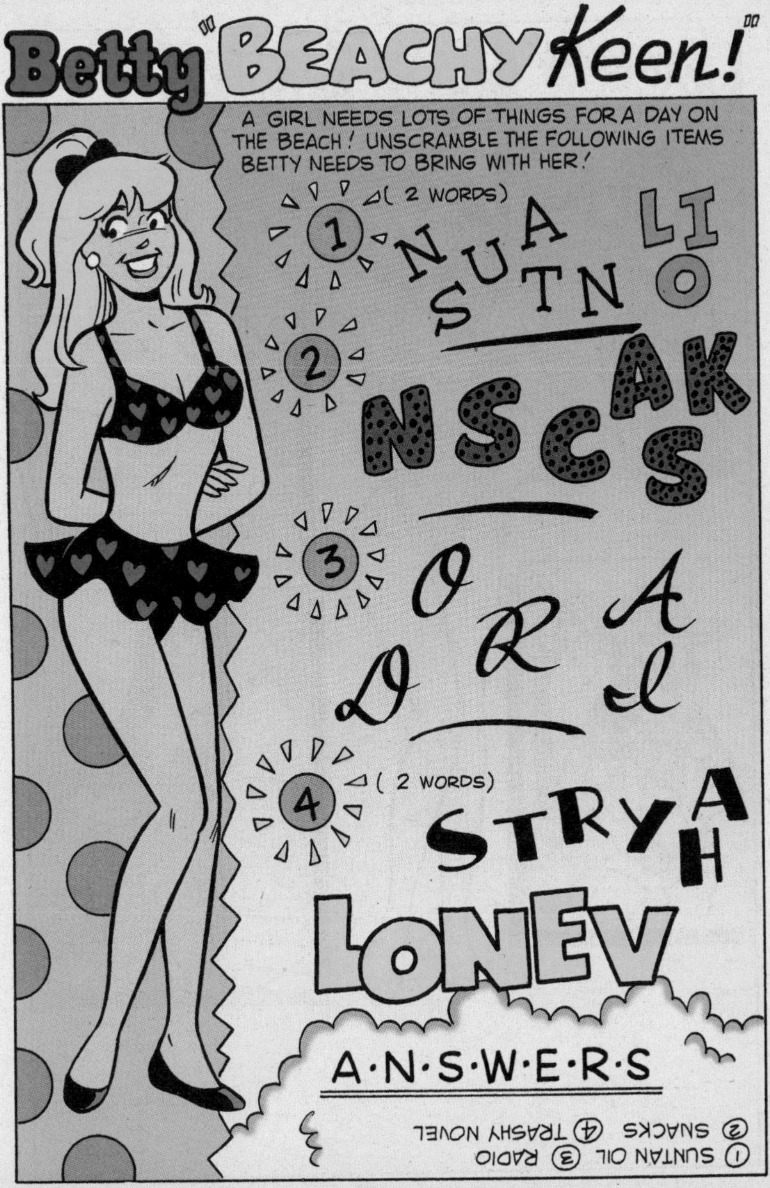
Betty "BEACHY Keen!"
A GIRL NEEDS LOTS OF THINGS FOR A DAY ON THE BEACH! UNSCRAMBLE THE FOLLOWING ITEMS BETTY NEEDS TO BRING WITH HER!
1 (2 WORDS)
NUALI SUTNO
2
NSCAKS
3
ORADI
4 (2 WORDS)
STRYAH
LONEV
A·N·S·W·E·R·S
1 SUNTAN OIL 3 RADIO
2 SNACKS 4 TRASHY NOVEL

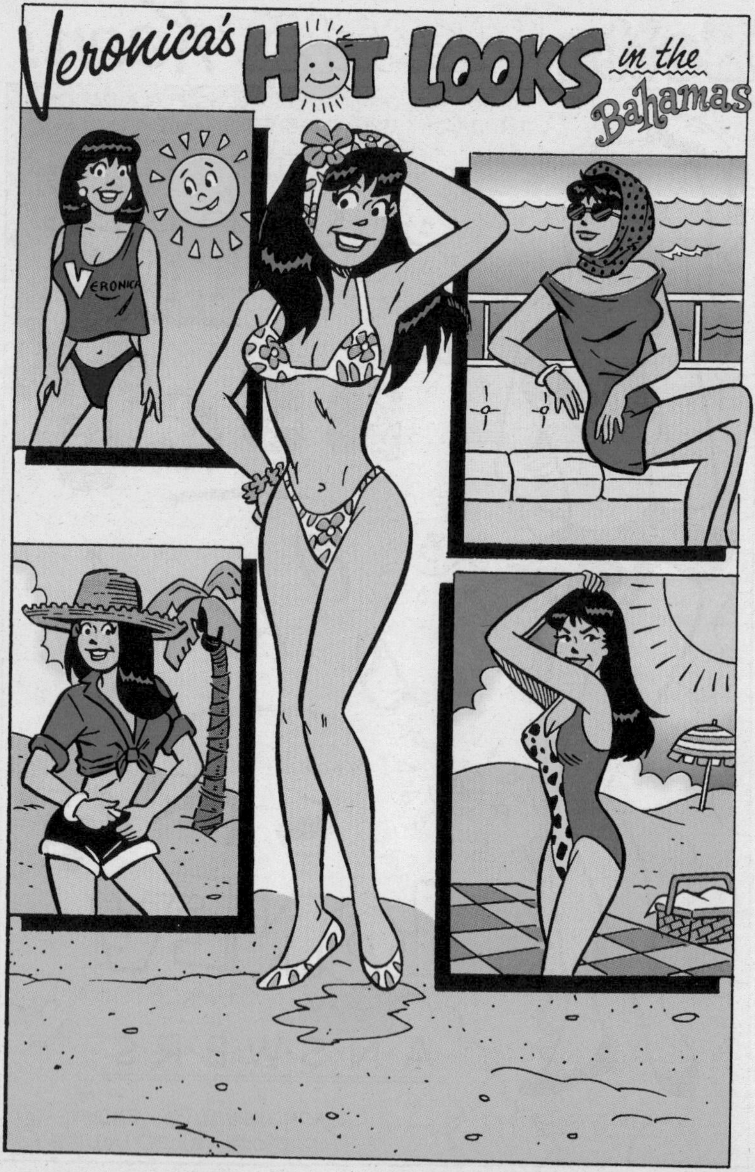
Veronica's HOT LOOKS in the Bahamas
VERONICA

Archie "The INVADERS" PART I

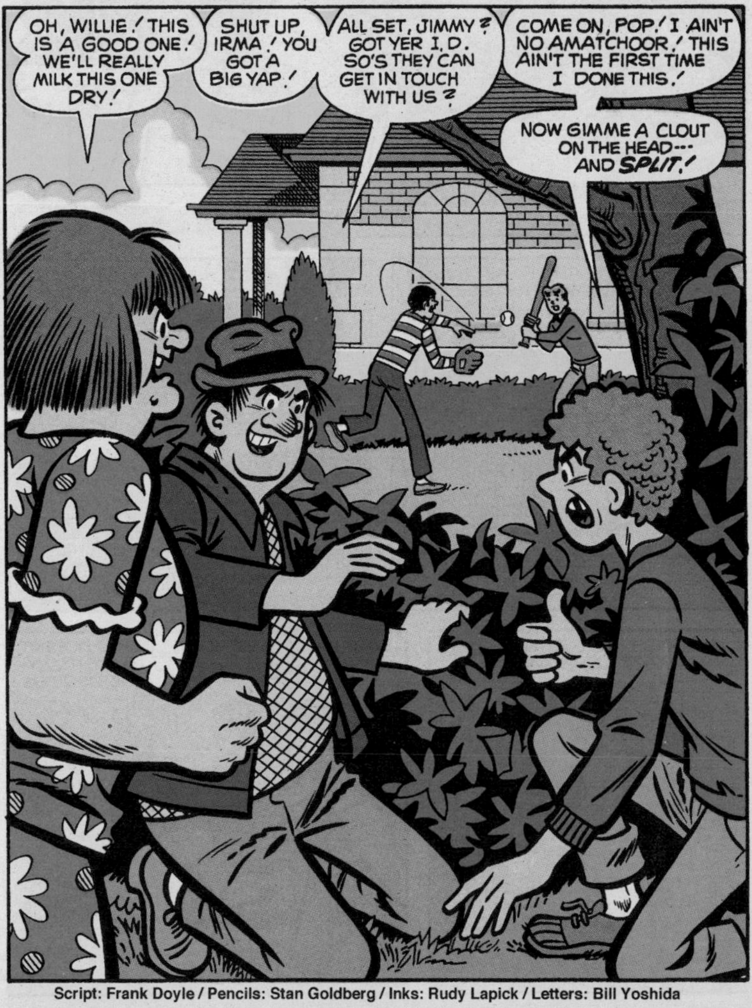
OH, WILLIE! THIS IS A GOOD ONE! WE'LL REALLY MILK THIS ONE DRY!
SHUT UP, IRMA! YOU GOT A BIG YAP!
ALL SET, JIMMY? GOT YER I.D. SO'S THEY CAN GET IN TOUCH WITH US?
COME ON, POP! I AIN'T NO AMATCHOOR! THIS AIN'T THE FIRST TIME I DONE THIS!
NOW GIMME A CLOUT ON THE HEAD--- AND SPLIT!

Script: Frank Doyle / Pencils: Stan Goldberg / Inks: Rudy Lapick / Letters: Bill Yoshida

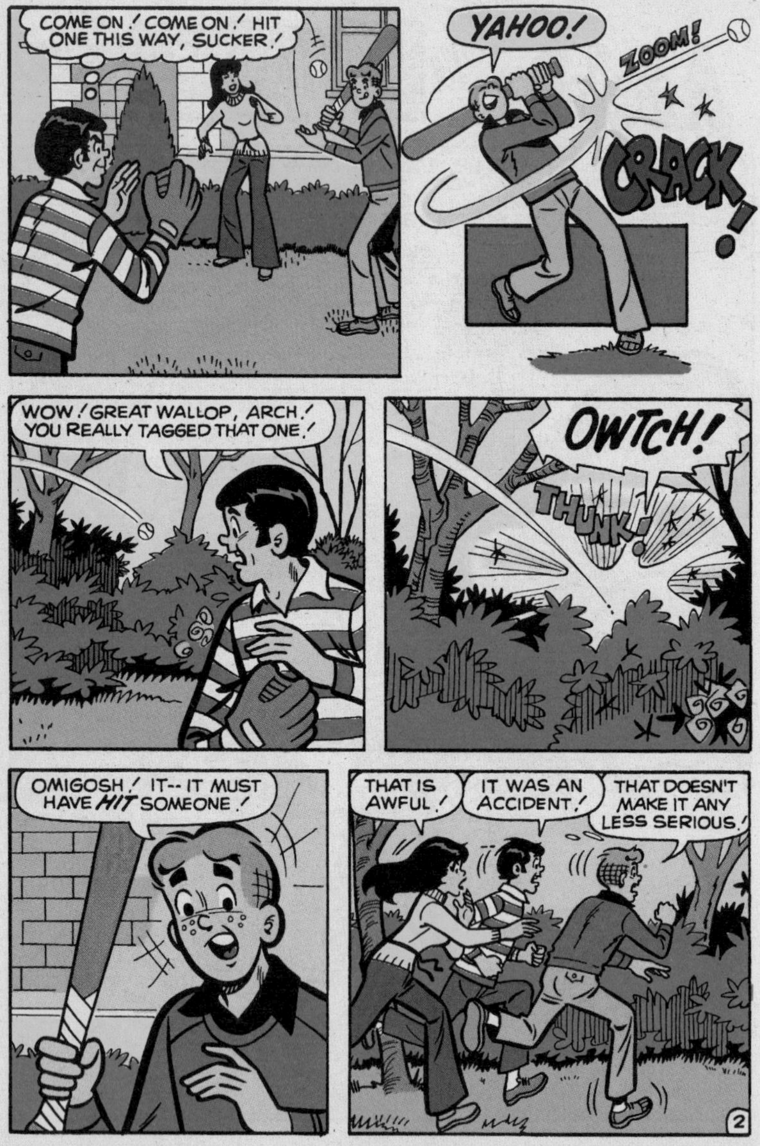

COME ON ! COME ON ! HIT ONE THIS WAY, SUCKER !
YAHOO!
ZOOM!
CRACK!
WOW ! GREAT WALLOP, ARCH ! YOU REALLY TAGGED THAT ONE !
OWTCH!
THUNK!
OMIGOSH ! IT-- IT MUST HAVE HIT SOMEONE !
THAT IS AWFUL !
IT WAS AN ACCIDENT !
THAT DOESN'T MAKE IT ANY LESS SERIOUS !
2

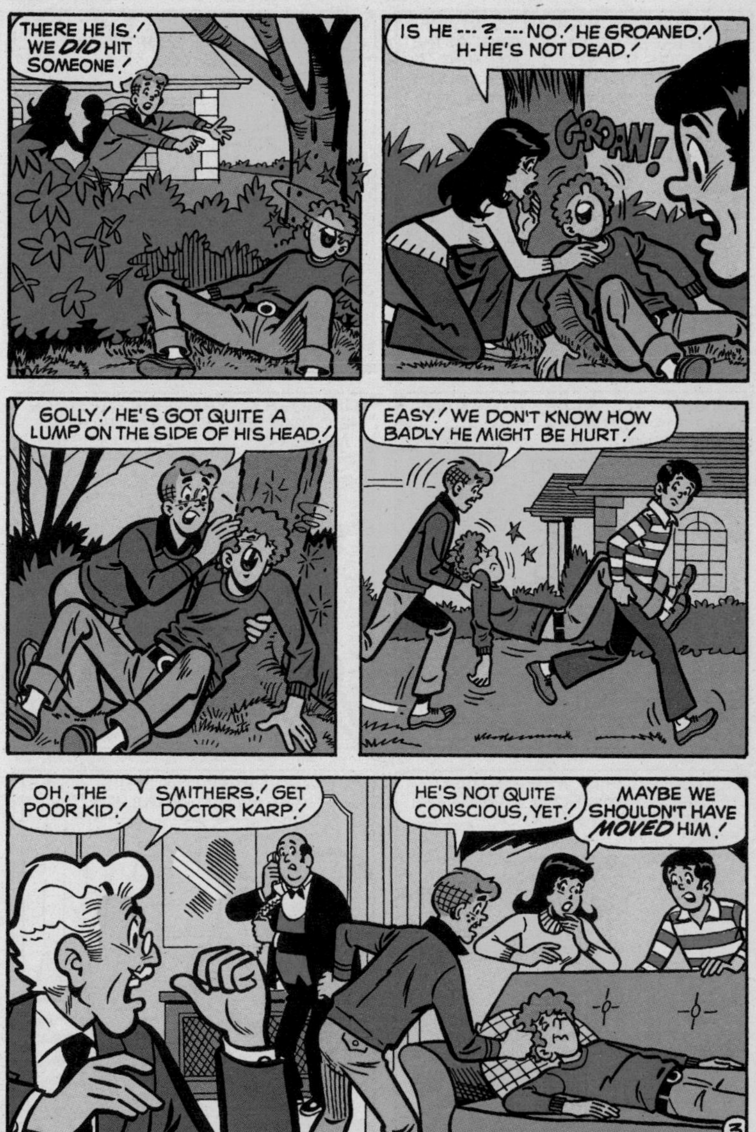
THERE HE IS! WE DID HIT SOMEONE!
IS HE --- ? --- NO! HE GROANED! H-HE'S NOT DEAD!
GROAN!
GOLLY! HE'S GOT QUITE A LUMP ON THE SIDE OF HIS HEAD!
EASY! WE DON'T KNOW HOW BADLY HE MIGHT BE HURT!
OH, THE POOR KID!
SMITHERS! GET DOCTOR KARP!
HE'S NOT QUITE CONSCIOUS, YET!
MAYBE WE SHOULDN'T HAVE MOVED HIM!
3

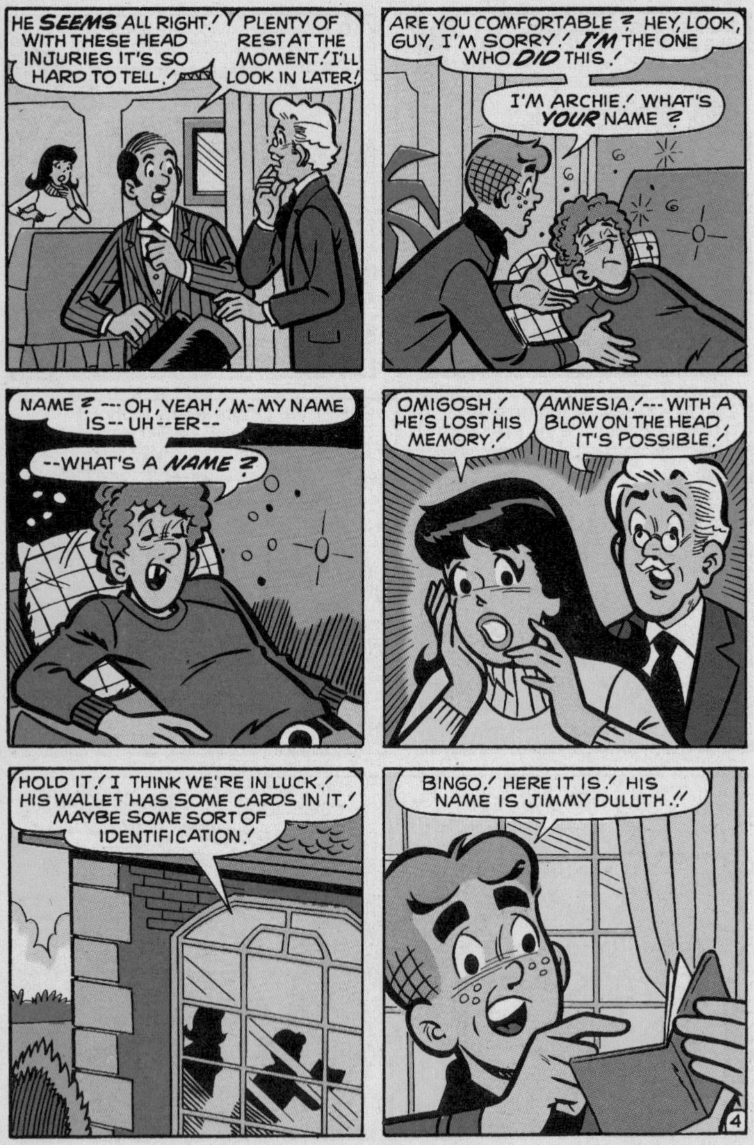
HE SEEMS ALL RIGHT! WITH THESE HEAD INJURIES IT'S SO HARD TO TELL!
PLENTY OF REST AT THE MOMENT! I'LL LOOK IN LATER!
ARE YOU COMFORTABLE ? HEY, LOOK, GUY, I'M SORRY! I'M THE ONE WHO DID THIS!
I'M ARCHIE! WHAT'S YOUR NAME ?
NAME ? --- OH, YEAH! M-MY NAME IS-- UH--ER--
--WHAT'S A NAME ?
OMIGOSH! HE'S LOST HIS MEMORY!
AMNESIA! --- WITH A BLOW ON THE HEAD, IT'S POSSIBLE!
HOLD IT! I THINK WE'RE IN LUCK! HIS WALLET HAS SOME CARDS IN IT! MAYBE SOME SORT OF IDENTIFICATION!
BINGO! HERE IT IS! HIS NAME IS JIMMY DULUTH!!
4

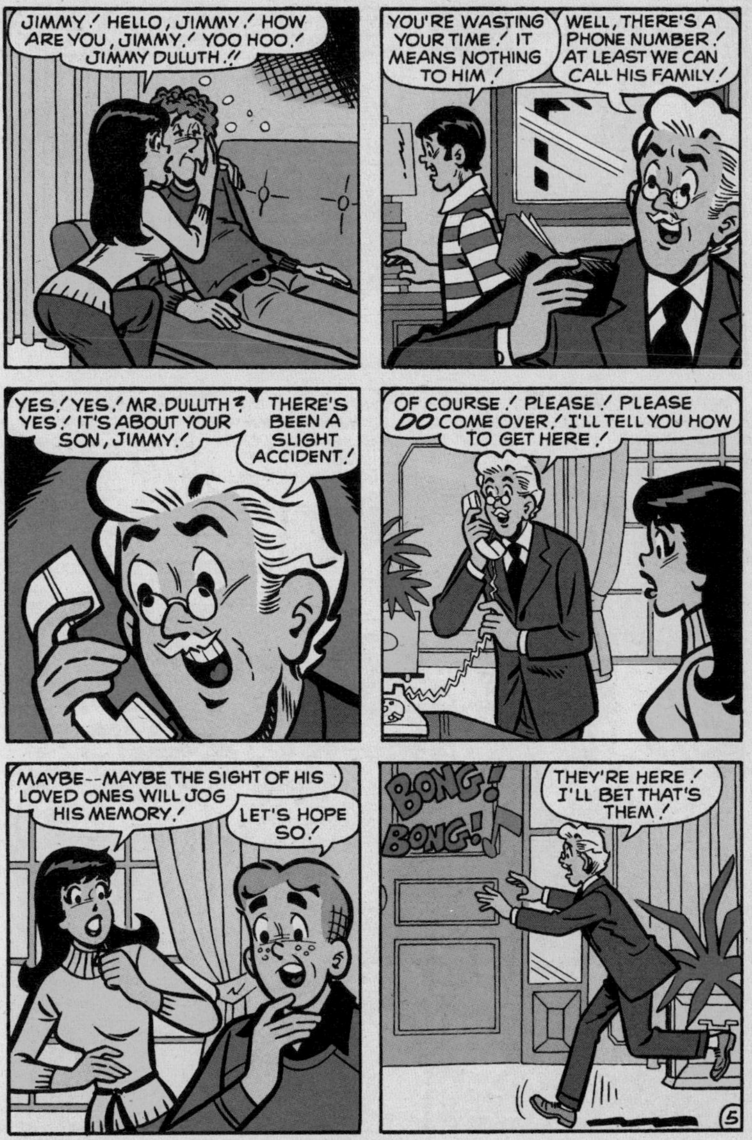
JIMMY! HELLO, JIMMY! HOW ARE YOU, JIMMY! YOO HOO! JIMMY DULUTH!!
YOU'RE WASTING YOUR TIME! IT MEANS NOTHING TO HIM!
WELL, THERE'S A PHONE NUMBER! AT LEAST WE CAN CALL HIS FAMILY!
YES! YES! MR. DULUTH? YES! IT'S ABOUT YOUR SON, JIMMY!
THERE'S BEEN A SLIGHT ACCIDENT!
OF COURSE! PLEASE! PLEASE DO COME OVER! I'LL TELL YOU HOW TO GET HERE!
MAYBE--MAYBE THE SIGHT OF HIS LOVED ONES WILL JOG HIS MEMORY!
LET'S HOPE SO!
BONG! BONG!
THEY'RE HERE! I'LL BET THAT'S THEM!
5

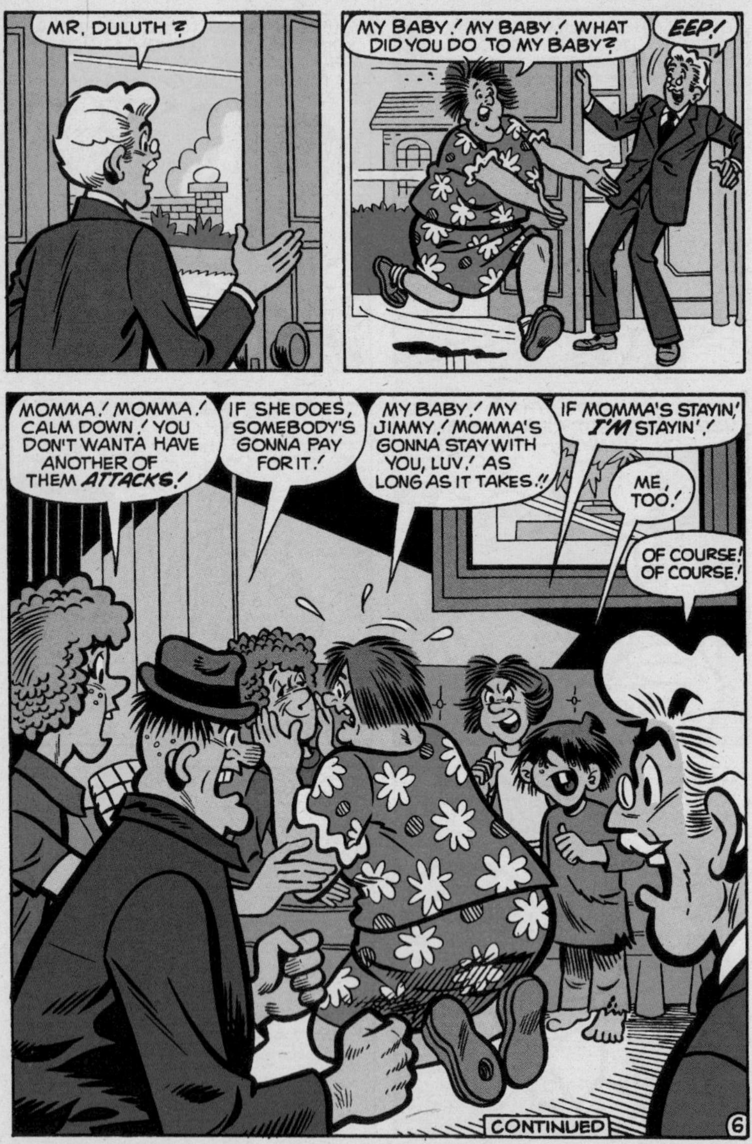

MR. DULUTH ?
MY BABY! MY BABY! WHAT DID YOU DO TO MY BABY?
EEP!
MOMMA! MOMMA! CALM DOWN! YOU DON'T WANTA HAVE ANOTHER OF THEM ATTACKS!
IF SHE DOES, SOMEBODY'S GONNA PAY FOR IT!
MY BABY! MY JIMMY! MOMMA'S GONNA STAY WITH YOU, LUV! AS LONG AS IT TAKES!!
IF MOMMA'S STAYIN', I'M STAYIN'!
ME, TOO!
OF COURSE! OF COURSE!
CONTINUED
6

Archie "The INVADERS" PART II

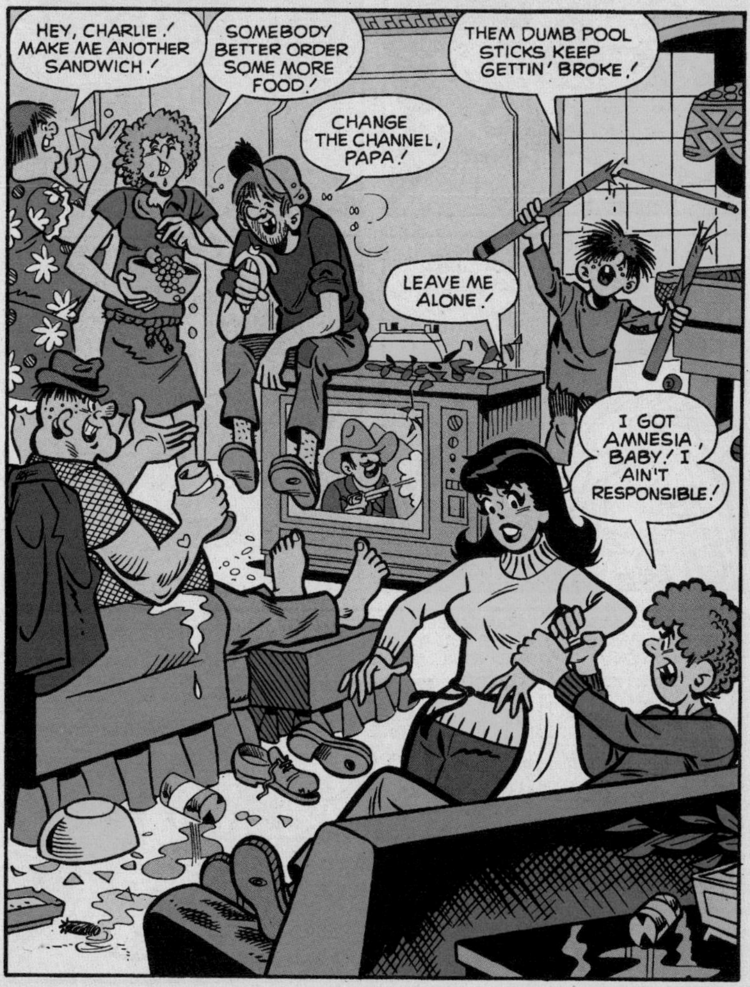
HEY, CHARLIE.! MAKE ME ANOTHER SANDWICH.!
SOMEBODY BETTER ORDER SOME MORE FOOD.!
THEM DUMB POOL STICKS KEEP GETTIN' BROKE.!
CHANGE THE CHANNEL, PAPA.!
LEAVE ME ALONE.!
I GOT AMNESIA, BABY.! I AIN'T RESPONSIBLE.!

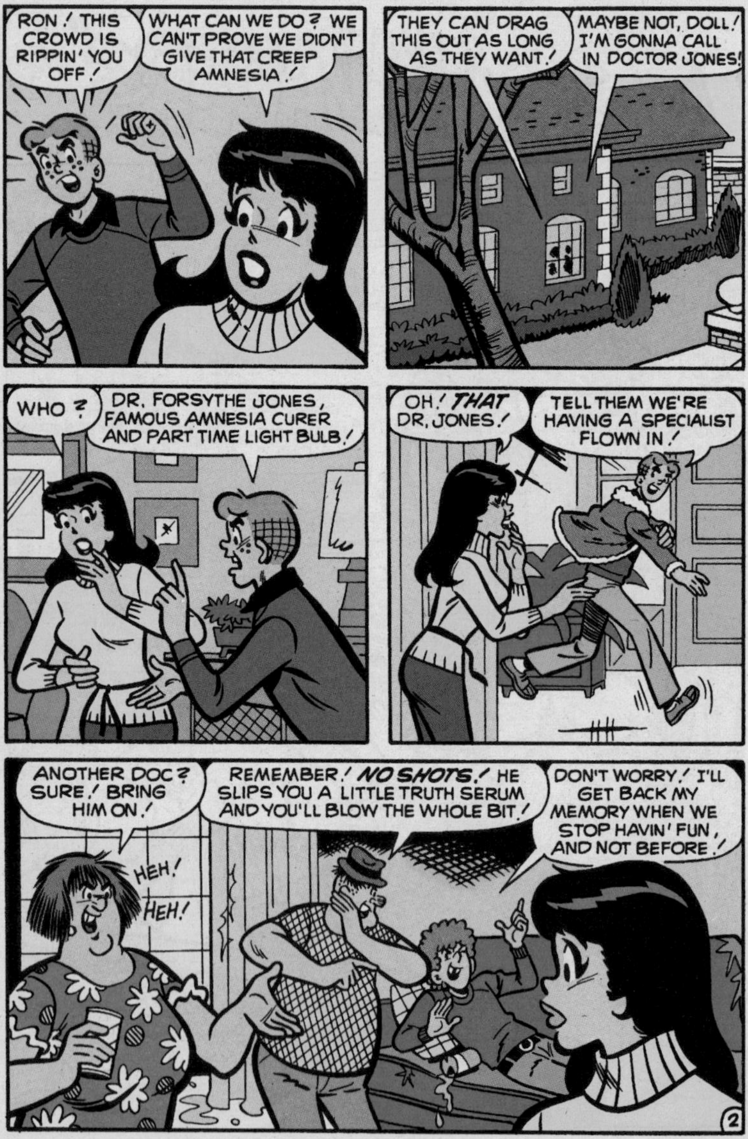

RON! THIS CROWD IS RIPPIN' YOU OFF!
WHAT CAN WE DO? WE CAN'T PROVE WE DIDN'T GIVE THAT CREEP AMNESIA!
THEY CAN DRAG THIS OUT AS LONG AS THEY WANT!
MAYBE NOT, DOLL! I'M GONNA CALL IN DOCTOR JONES!
WHO?
DR. FORSYTHE JONES, FAMOUS AMNESIA CURER AND PART TIME LIGHT BULB!
OH! THAT DR. JONES!
TELL THEM WE'RE HAVING A SPECIALIST FLOWN IN!
ANOTHER DOC? SURE! BRING HIM ON!
HEH! HEH!
REMEMBER! NO SHOTS! HE SLIPS YOU A LITTLE TRUTH SERUM AND YOU'LL BLOW THE WHOLE BIT!
DON'T WORRY! I'LL GET BACK MY MEMORY WHEN WE STOP HAVIN' FUN, AND NOT BEFORE!
2

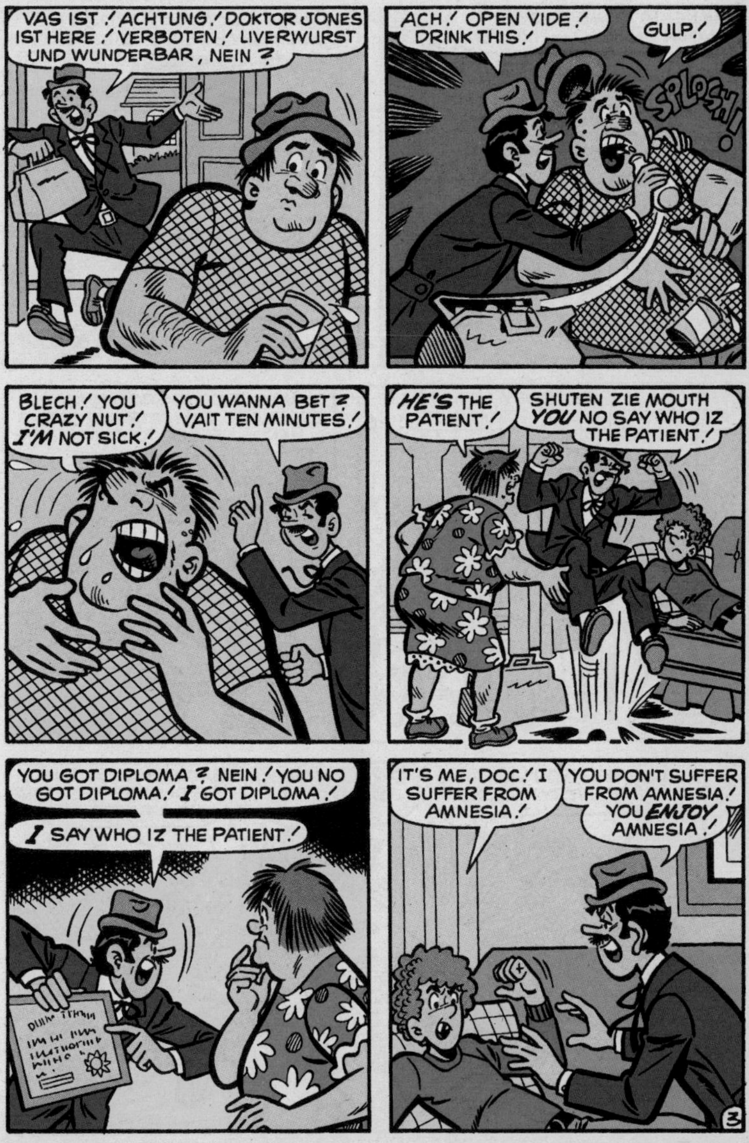
VAS IST! ACHTUNG! DOKTOR JONES IST HERE! VERBOTEN! LIVERWURST UND WUNDERBAR, NEIN?
ACH! OPEN VIDE! DRINK THIS!
GULP!
SPLOSH!
BLECH! YOU CRAZY NUT! I'M NOT SICK!
YOU WANNA BET? VAIT TEN MINUTES!
HE'S THE PATIENT!
SHUTEN ZIE MOUTH YOU NO SAY WHO IZ THE PATIENT!
YOU GOT DIPLOMA? NEIN! YOU NO GOT DIPLOMA! I GOT DIPLOMA!
I SAY WHO IZ THE PATIENT!
IT'S ME, DOC! I SUFFER FROM AMNESIA!
YOU DON'T SUFFER FROM AMNESIA! YOU ENJOY AMNESIA!
3

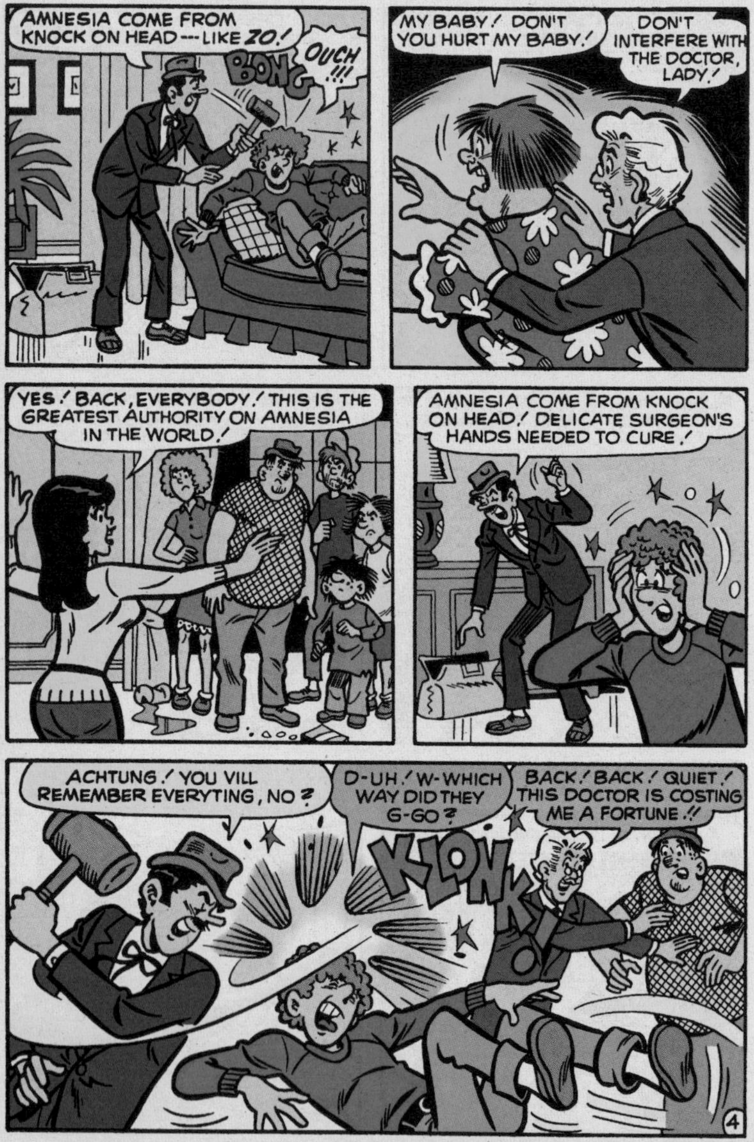
AMNESIA COME FROM KNOCK ON HEAD---LIKE ZO!
BONG
OUCH !!!
MY BABY! DON'T YOU HURT MY BABY!
DON'T INTERFERE WITH THE DOCTOR, LADY!
YES! BACK, EVERYBODY! THIS IS THE GREATEST AUTHORITY ON AMNESIA IN THE WORLD!
AMNESIA COME FROM KNOCK ON HEAD! DELICATE SURGEON'S HANDS NEEDED TO CURE!
ACHTUNG! YOU VILL REMEMBER EVERYTING, NO?
D-UH! W-WHICH WAY DID THEY G-GO?
BACK! BACK! QUIET! THIS DOCTOR IS COSTING ME A FORTUNE!!
KLONK
4

UF COURSE, VEN VE RUN EENTO *STUBBORN* CASE---

EEP!

I REMEMBER! I REMEMBER! I'M JIMMY DULUTH! I WANTA GO HOME!!

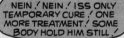

NEIN! NEIN! ISS ONLY TEMPORARY CURE! ONE MORE TREATMENT! SOME BODY HOLD HIM STILL!

RUN!

HEAD FER THE HILLS!

I'LL NEVER *LIVE* THROUGH A PERMANENT CURE!

ARCHIE, THAT WAS A STROKE OF GENIUS!

HOW ABOUT THAT CRAZY DOCTOR?

BEAUTIFUL, JUGHEAD! I WAS GOING BROKE FEEDING THAT CREW!

WAIT'LL YOU GET MY *BILL*!

END

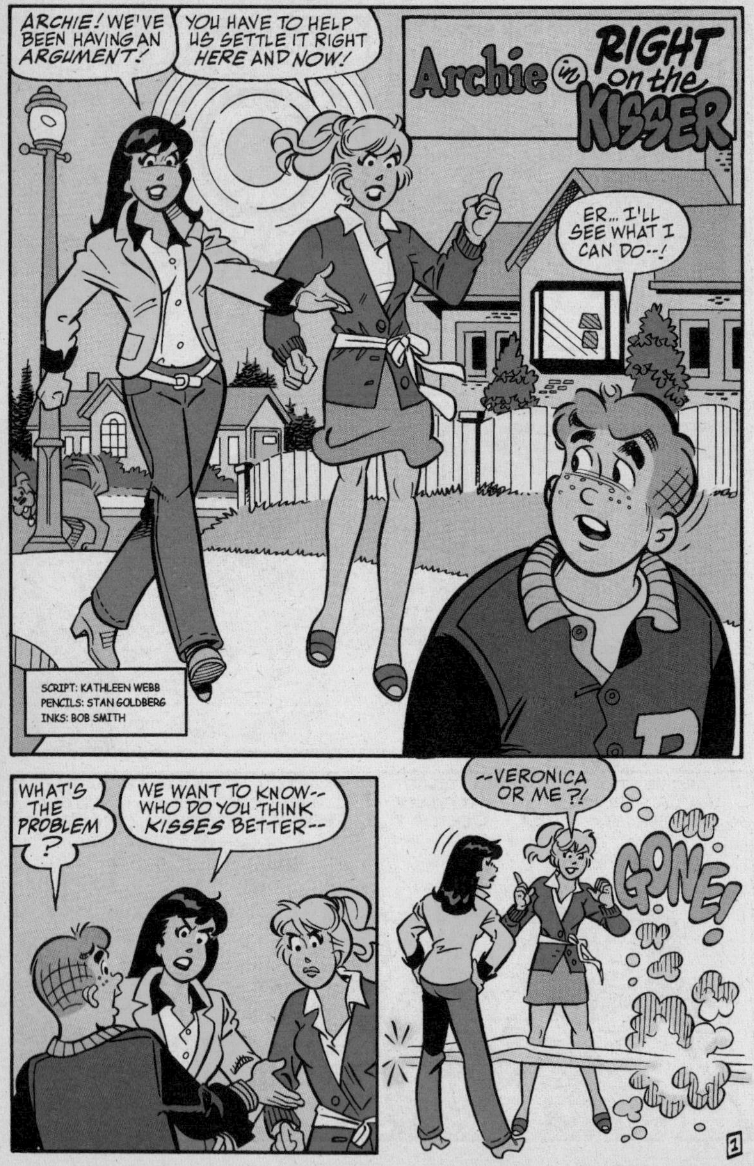
ARCHIE! WE'VE BEEN HAVING AN ARGUMENT!
YOU HAVE TO HELP US SETTLE IT RIGHT HERE AND NOW!
Archie in RIGHT on the KISSER
ER... I'LL SEE WHAT I CAN DO--!
SCRIPT: KATHLEEN WEBB
PENCILS: STAN GOLDBERG
INKS: BOB SMITH
WHAT'S THE PROBLEM?
WE WANT TO KNOW-- WHO DO YOU THINK KISSES BETTER--
--VERONICA OR ME?!
GONE!
1

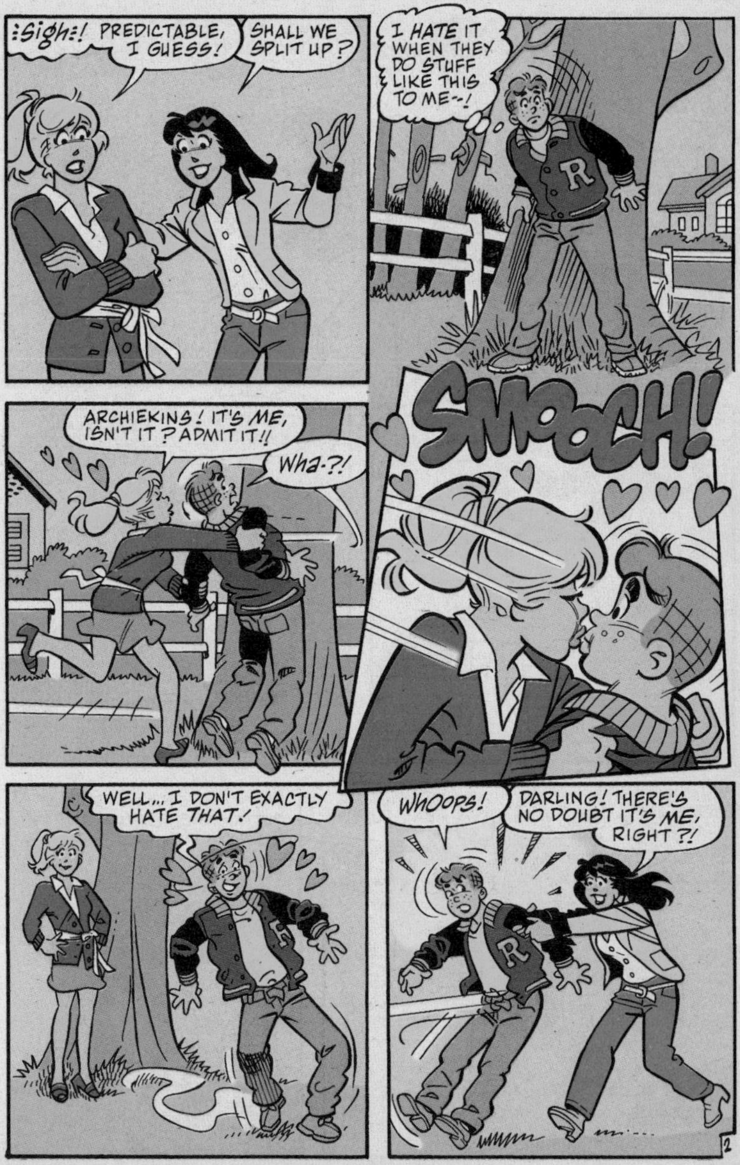
:Sigh:! PREDICTABLE, I GUESS!
SHALL WE SPLIT UP?
I HATE IT WHEN THEY DO STUFF LIKE THIS TO ME--!
ARCHIEKINS! IT'S ME, ISN'T IT? ADMIT IT!!
Wha-?!
SMOOCH!
WELL... I DON'T EXACTLY HATE THAT!
WhOOPS!
DARLING! THERE'S NO DOUBT IT'S ME, RIGHT?!

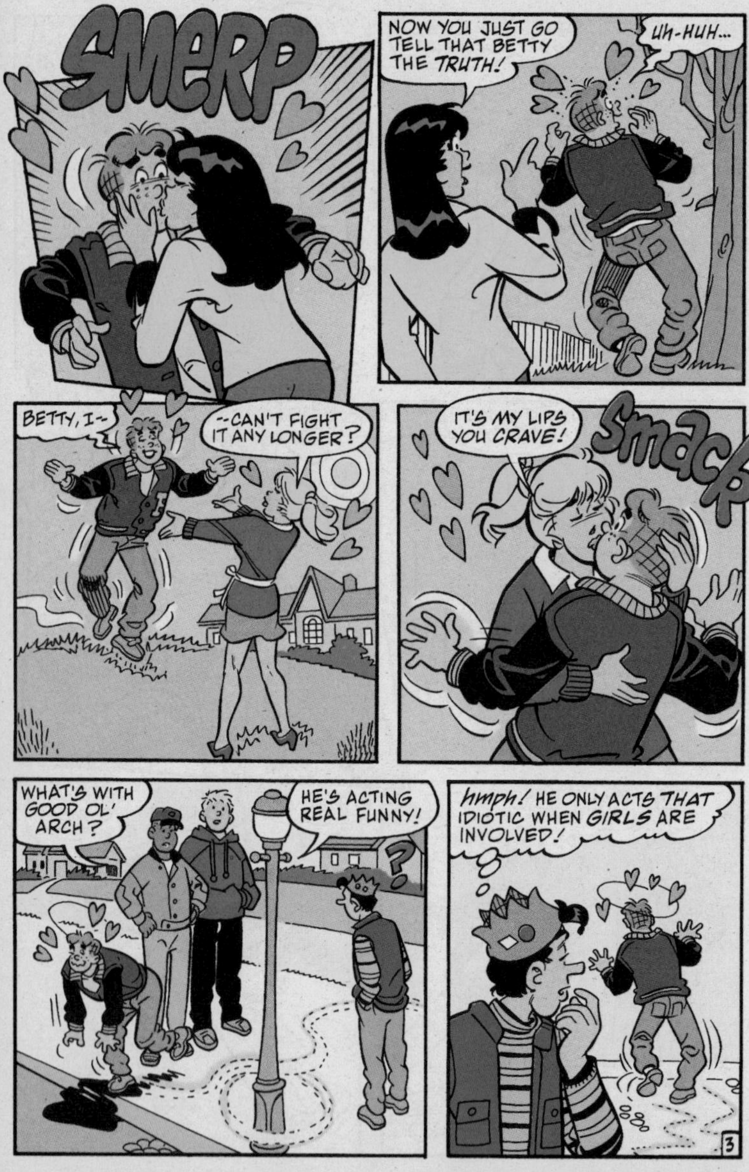
SMERP
NOW YOU JUST GO TELL THAT BETTY THE TRUTH!
UH-HUH...
BETTY, I--
--CAN'T FIGHT IT ANY LONGER?
IT'S MY LIPS YOU CRAVE!
SMACK
WHAT'S WITH GOOD OL' ARCH?
HE'S ACTING REAL FUNNY!
?
hmph! HE ONLY ACTS THAT IDIOTIC WHEN GIRLS ARE INVOLVED!
3

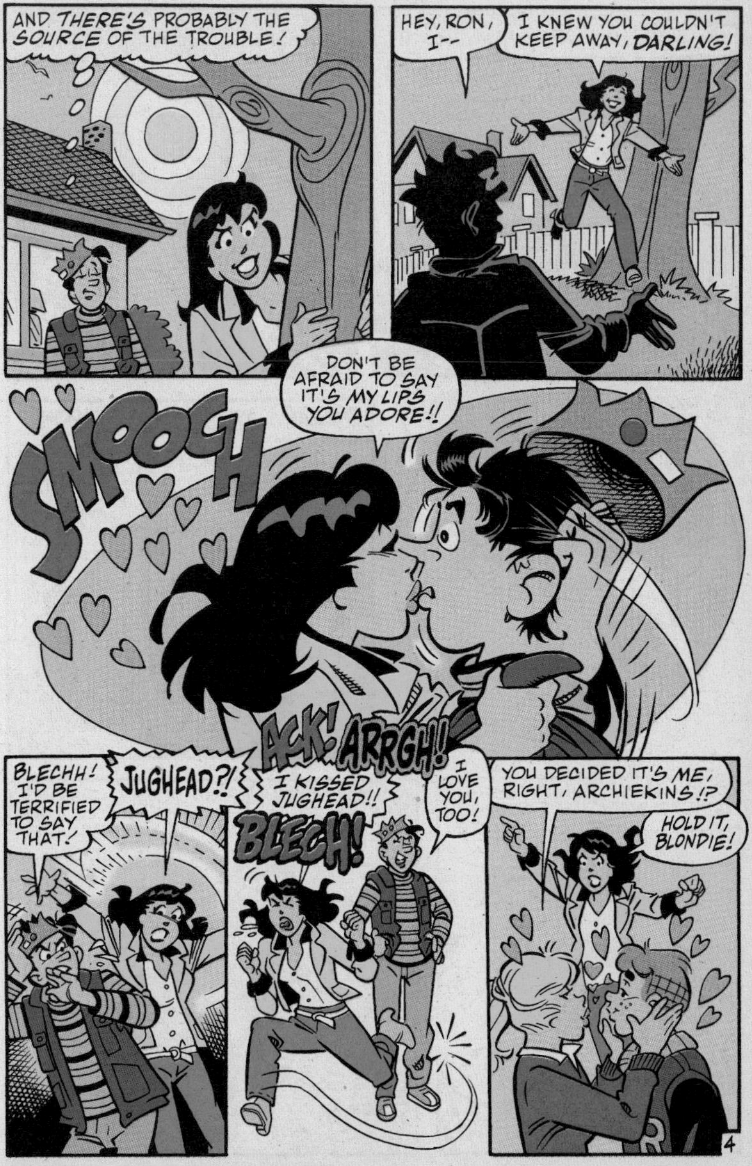

AND THERE'S PROBABLY THE SOURCE OF THE TROUBLE!
HEY, RON, I--
I KNEW YOU COULDN'T KEEP AWAY, DARLING!
DON'T BE AFRAID TO SAY IT'S MY LIPS YOU ADORE!!
SMOOCH
ACK!
ARRGH!
BLECHH! I'D BE TERRIFIED TO SAY THAT!
JUGHEAD?!
I KISSED JUGHEAD!!
BLECH!
I LOVE YOU, TOO!
YOU DECIDED IT'S ME, RIGHT, ARCHIEKINS!?
HOLD IT, BLONDIE!

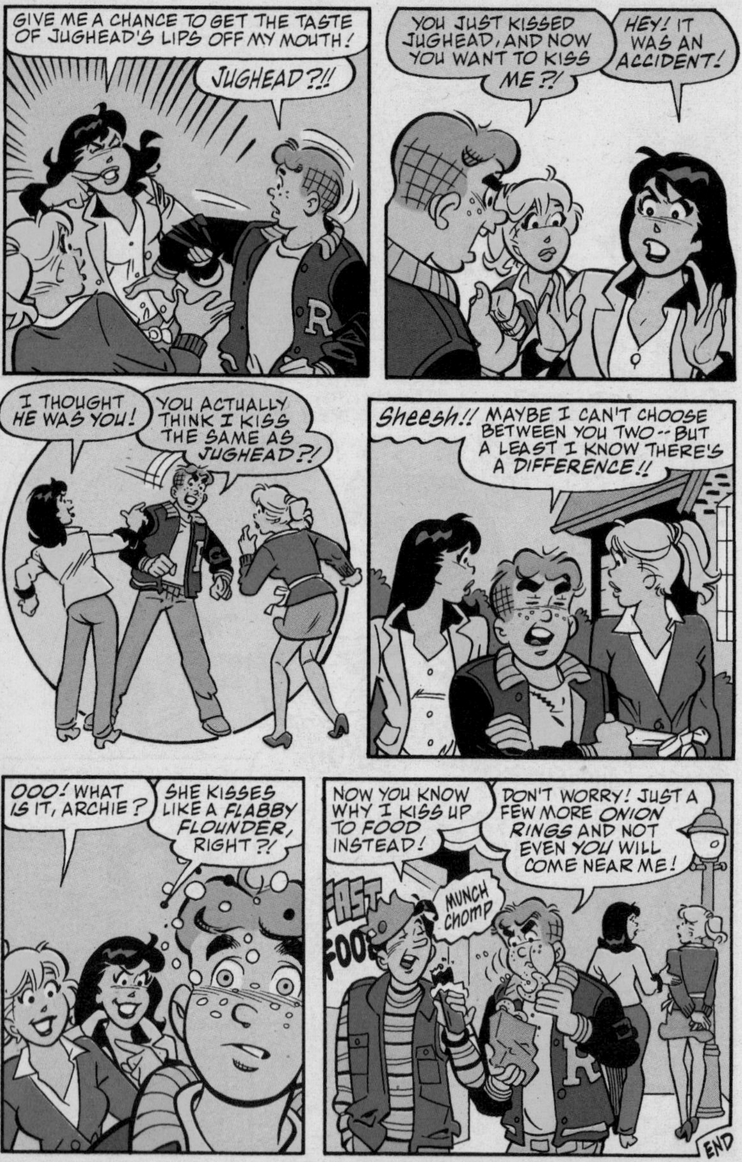
GIVE ME A CHANCE TO GET THE TASTE OF JUGHEAD'S LIPS OFF MY MOUTH!
JUGHEAD?!!
YOU JUST KISSED JUGHEAD, AND NOW YOU WANT TO KISS ME?!
HEY! IT WAS AN ACCIDENT!
I THOUGHT HE WAS YOU!
YOU ACTUALLY THINK I KISS THE SAME AS JUGHEAD?!
Sheesh!! MAYBE I CAN'T CHOOSE BETWEEN YOU TWO -- BUT A LEAST I KNOW THERE'S A DIFFERENCE!!
OOO! WHAT IS IT, ARCHIE?
SHE KISSES LIKE A FLABBY FLOUNDER, RIGHT?!
NOW YOU KNOW WHY I KISS UP TO FOOD INSTEAD!
DON'T WORRY! JUST A FEW MORE ONION RINGS AND NOT EVEN YOU WILL COME NEAR ME!
MUNCH chomp
FAST FOO
END

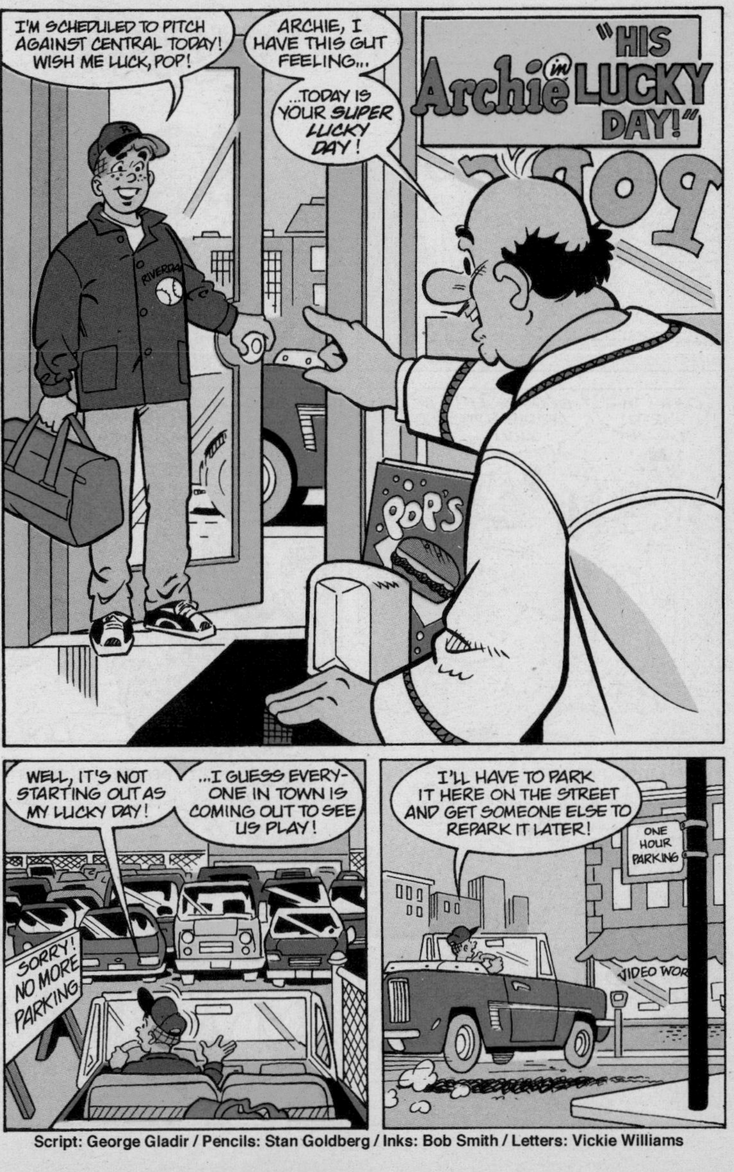
Archie in "HIS LUCKY DAY!"
I'M SCHEDULED TO PITCH AGAINST CENTRAL TODAY! WISH ME LUCK, POP!
ARCHIE, I HAVE THIS GUT FEELING...
...TODAY IS YOUR SUPER LUCKY DAY!
POP'S
RIVERDALE
POP'S
WELL, IT'S NOT STARTING OUT AS MY LUCKY DAY!
...I GUESS EVERY-ONE IN TOWN IS COMING OUT TO SEE US PLAY!
SORRY! NO MORE PARKING
I'LL HAVE TO PARK IT HERE ON THE STREET AND GET SOMEONE ELSE TO REPARK IT LATER!
ONE HOUR PARKING
VIDEO WOR

Script: George Gladir / Pencils: Stan Goldberg / Inks: Bob Smith / Letters: Vickie Williams

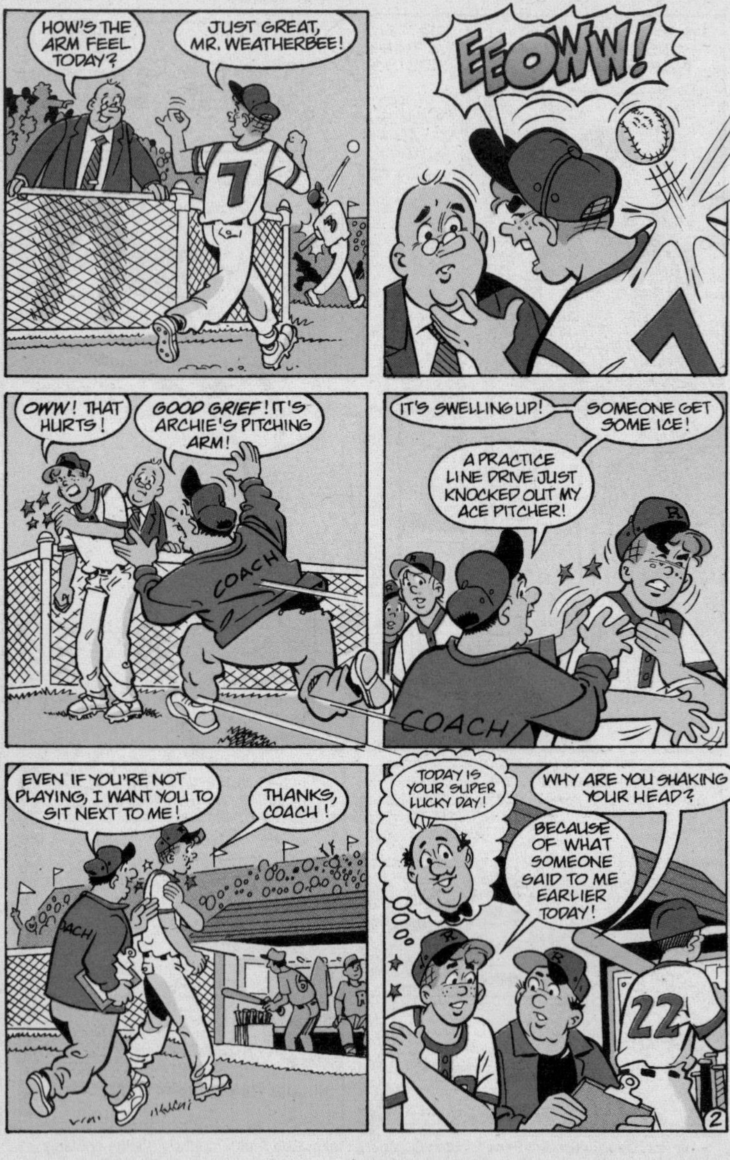
HOW'S THE ARM FEEL TODAY?
JUST GREAT, MR. WEATHERBEE!
EEOWW!
OWW! THAT HURTS!
GOOD GRIEF! IT'S ARCHIE'S PITCHING ARM!
COACH
IT'S SWELLING UP!
SOMEONE GET SOME ICE!
A PRACTICE LINE DRIVE JUST KNOCKED OUT MY ACE PITCHER!
COACH
EVEN IF YOU'RE NOT PLAYING, I WANT YOU TO SIT NEXT TO ME!
THANKS, COACH!
TODAY IS YOUR SUPER LUCKY DAY!
WHY ARE YOU SHAKING YOUR HEAD?
BECAUSE OF WHAT SOMEONE SAID TO ME EARLIER TODAY!
22

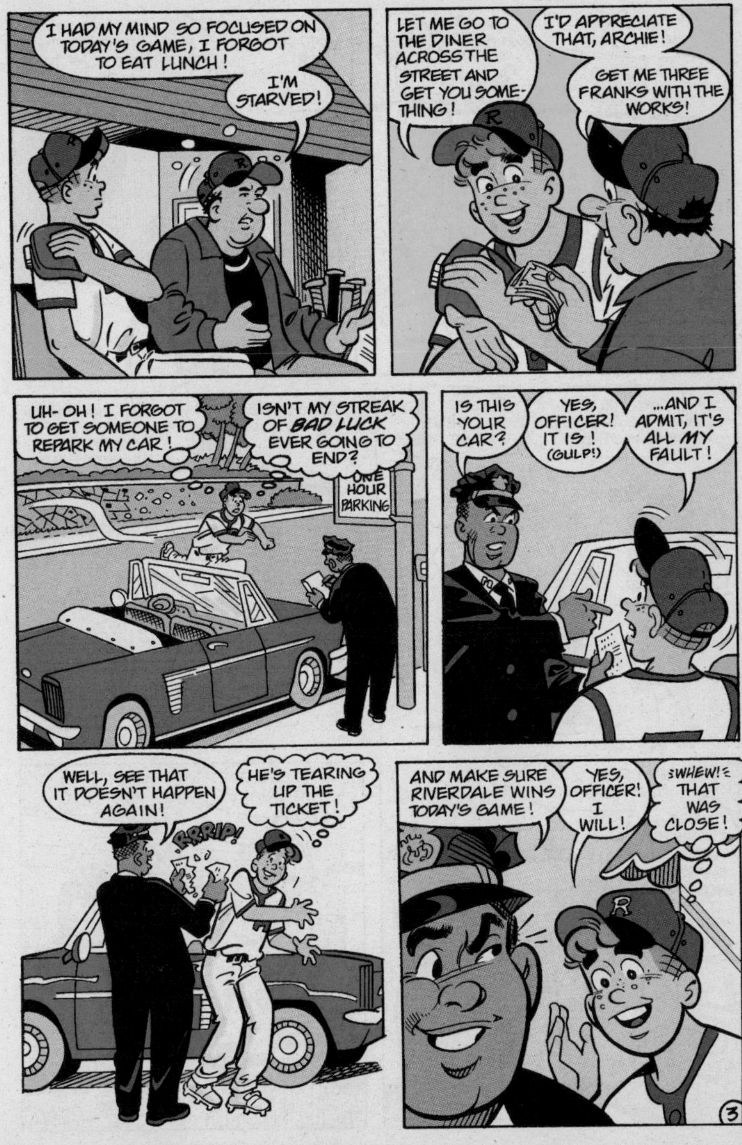

I HAD MY MIND SO FOCUSED ON TODAY'S GAME, I FORGOT TO EAT LUNCH!
I'M STARVED!
LET ME GO TO THE DINER ACROSS THE STREET AND GET YOU SOME-THING!
I'D APPRECIATE THAT, ARCHIE!
GET ME THREE FRANKS WITH THE WORKS!
UH-OH! I FORGOT TO GET SOMEONE TO REPARK MY CAR!
ISN'T MY STREAK OF BAD LUCK EVER GOING TO END?
ONE HOUR PARKING
IS THIS YOUR CAR?
YES, OFFICER! IT IS! (GULP!)
...AND I ADMIT, IT'S ALL MY FAULT!
WELL, SEE THAT IT DOESN'T HAPPEN AGAIN!
RRRIP!
HE'S TEARING UP THE TICKET!
AND MAKE SURE RIVERDALE WINS TODAY'S GAME!
YES, OFFICER! I WILL!
WHEW! THAT WAS CLOSE!
3

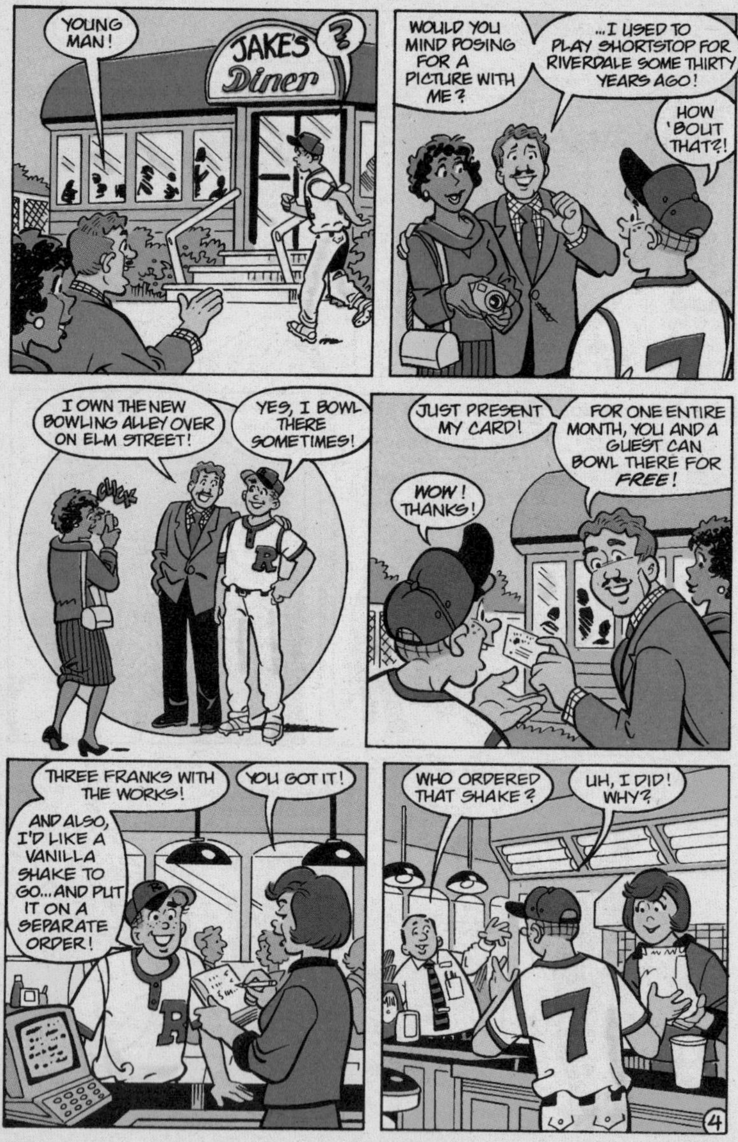
YOUNG MAN!
JAKE'S Diner
?
WOULD YOU MIND POSING FOR A PICTURE WITH ME?
...I USED TO PLAY SHORTSTOP FOR RIVERDALE SOME THIRTY YEARS AGO!
HOW 'BOUT THAT?!
I OWN THE NEW BOWLING ALLEY OVER ON ELM STREET!
YES, I BOWL THERE SOMETIMES!
CLICK
JUST PRESENT MY CARD!
FOR ONE ENTIRE MONTH, YOU AND A GUEST CAN BOWL THERE FOR FREE!
WOW! THANKS!
THREE FRANKS WITH THE WORKS!
YOU GOT IT!
AND ALSO, I'D LIKE A VANILLA SHAKE TO GO...AND PUT IT ON A SEPARATE ORDER!
WHO ORDERED THAT SHAKE?
UH, I DID! WHY?
4

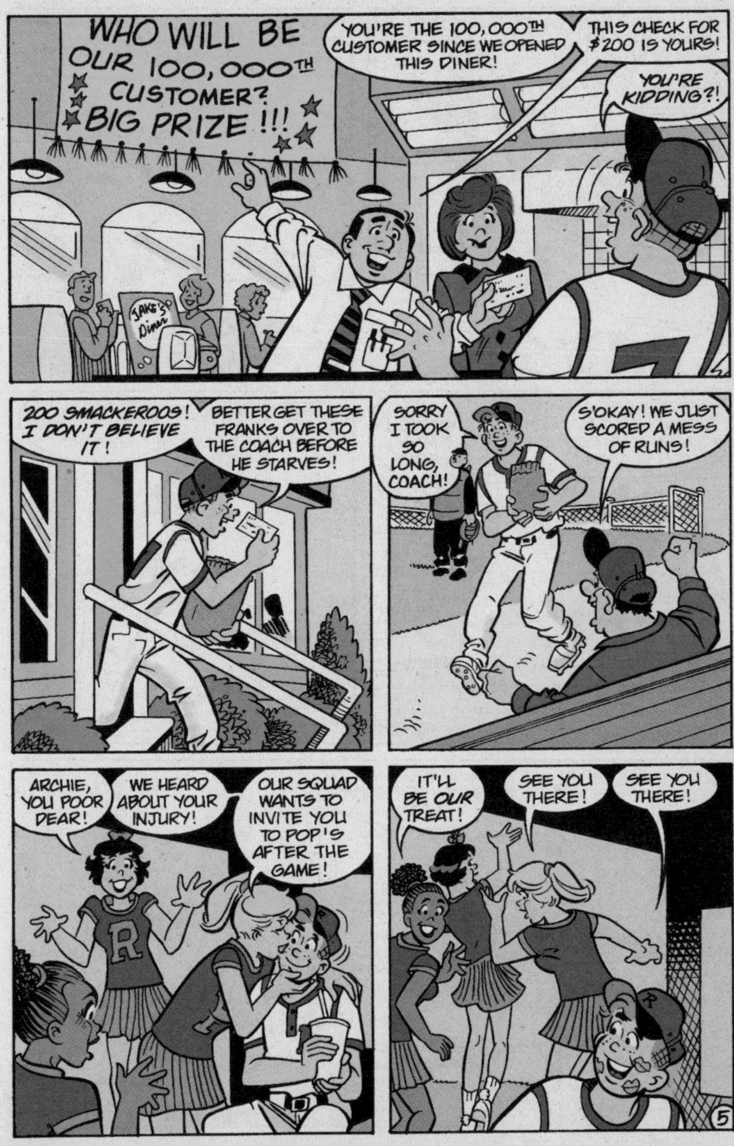
WHO WILL BE OUR 100,000TH CUSTOMER? BIG PRIZE !!!
YOU'RE THE 100,000TH CUSTOMER SINCE WE OPENED THIS DINER!
THIS CHECK FOR $200 IS YOURS!
YOU'RE KIDDING?!
JAKE'S Diner
200 SMACKEROOS! I DON'T BELIEVE IT!
BETTER GET THESE FRANKS OVER TO THE COACH BEFORE HE STARVES!
SORRY I TOOK SO LONG, COACH!
S'OKAY! WE JUST SCORED A MESS OF RUNS!
ARCHIE, YOU POOR DEAR!
WE HEARD ABOUT YOUR INJURY!
OUR SQUAD WANTS TO INVITE YOU TO POP'S AFTER THE GAME!
IT'LL BE OUR TREAT!
SEE YOU THERE!
SEE YOU THERE!
5

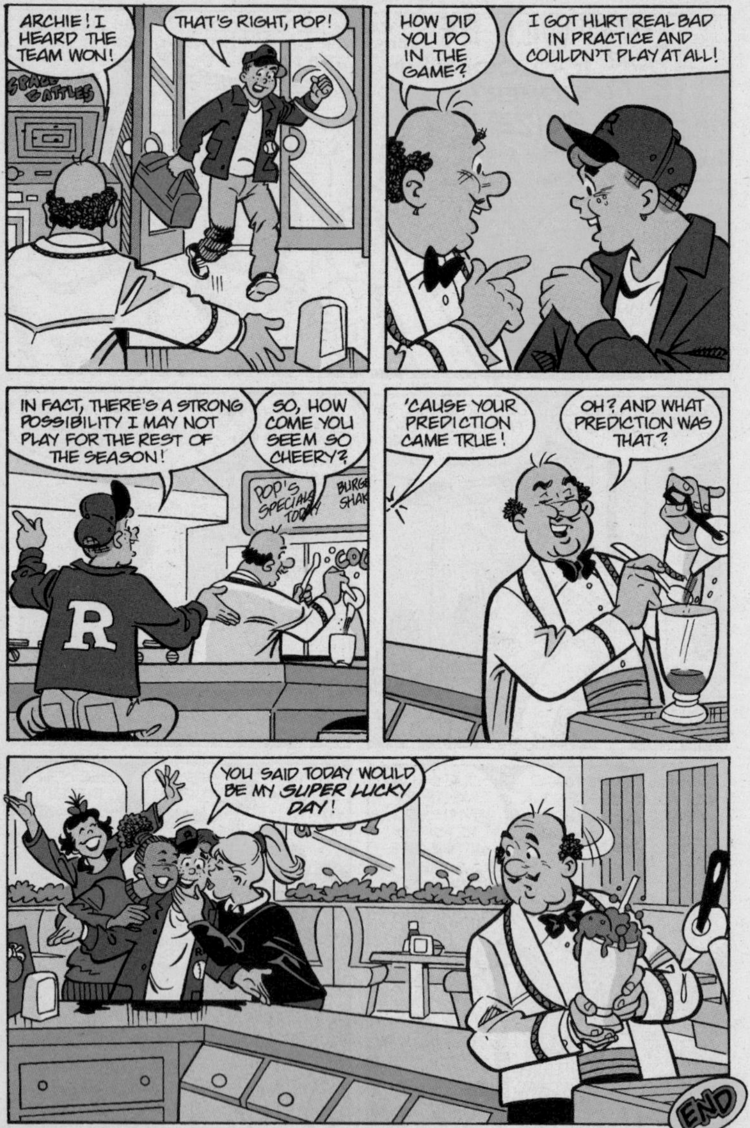
ARCHIE! I HEARD THE TEAM WON!
THAT'S RIGHT, POP!
SPACE BATTLES
HOW DID YOU DO IN THE GAME?
I GOT HURT REAL BAD IN PRACTICE AND COULDN'T PLAY AT ALL!
IN FACT, THERE'S A STRONG POSSIBILITY I MAY NOT PLAY FOR THE REST OF THE SEASON!
SO, HOW COME YOU SEEM SO CHEERY?
POP'S SPECIALS TODAY
'CAUSE YOUR PREDICTION CAME TRUE!
OH? AND WHAT PREDICTION WAS THAT?
YOU SAID TODAY WOULD BE MY *SUPER LUCKY DAY*!
END

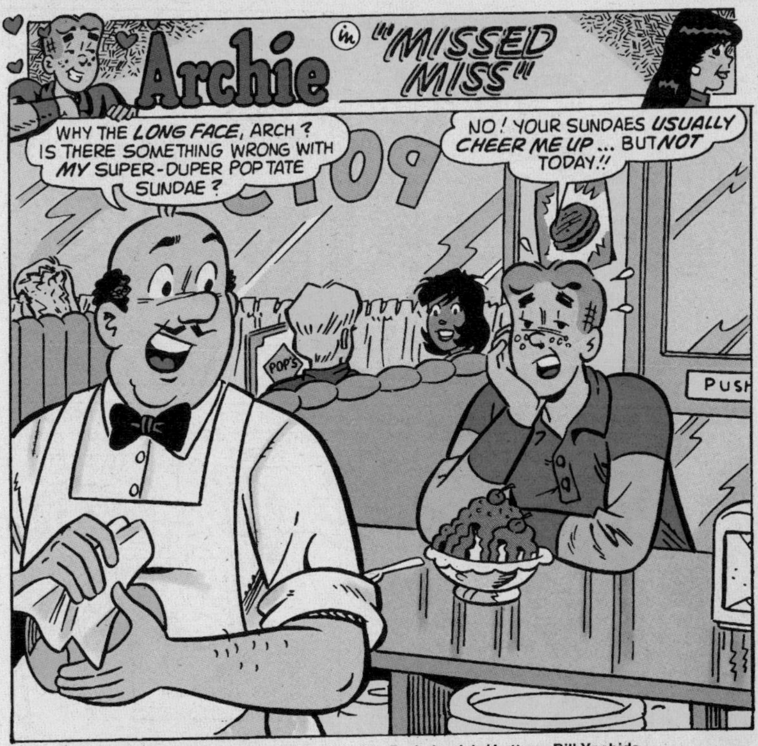
Archie
in
"MISSED MISS"
WHY THE LONG FACE, ARCH ? IS THERE SOMETHING WRONG WITH MY SUPER-DUPER POP TATE SUNDAE ?
NO! YOUR SUNDAES USUALLY CHEER ME UP ... BUT NOT TODAY!!
POP'S
PUSH

Script & Pencils: Fernando Ruiz / Inks: Rudy Lapick / Letters: Bill Yoshida

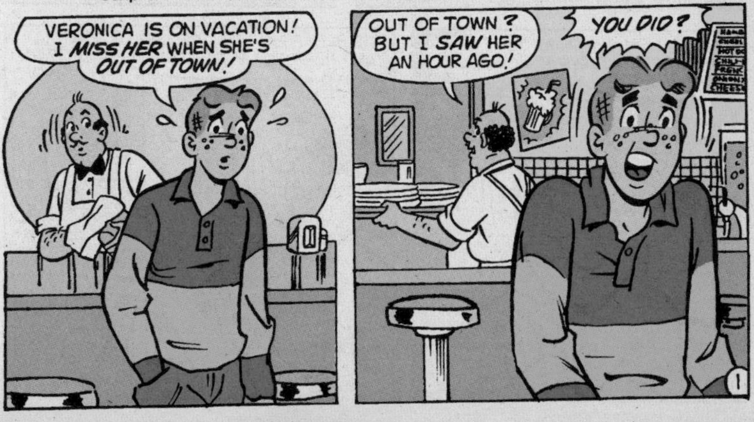
VERONICA IS ON VACATION! I MISS HER WHEN SHE'S OUT OF TOWN!
OUT OF TOWN ? BUT I SAW HER AN HOUR AGO!
YOU DID ?

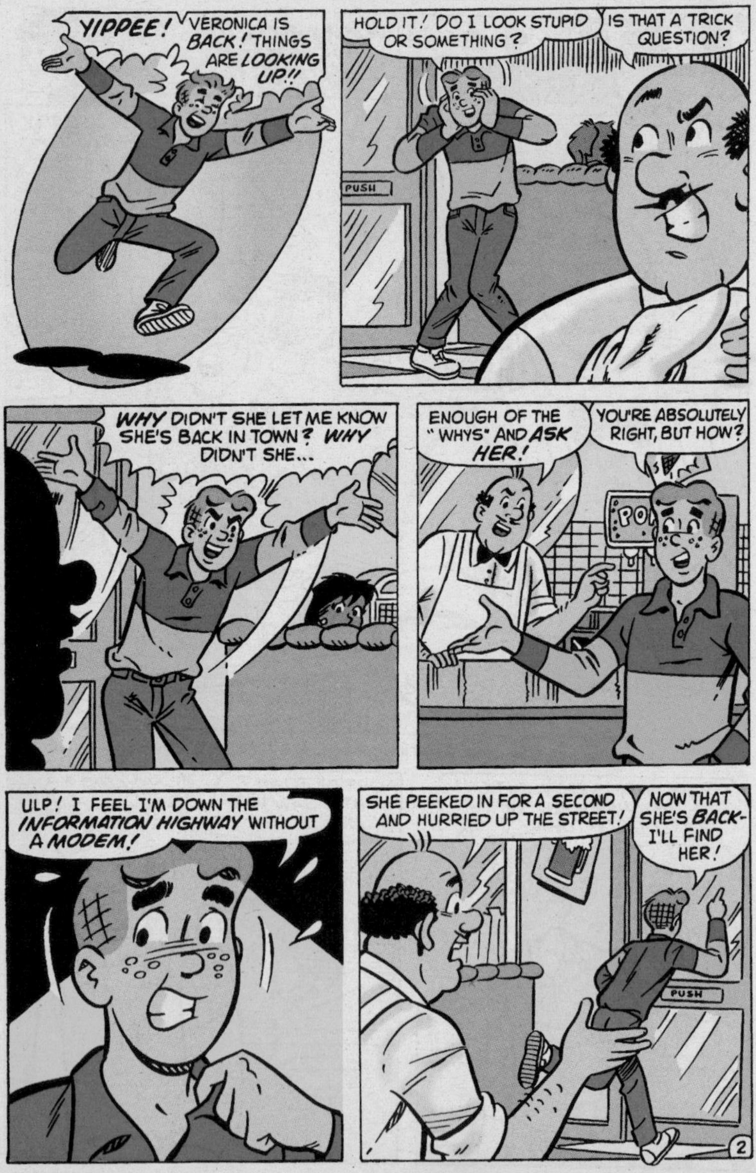

YIPPEE!
VERONICA IS BACK! THINGS ARE LOOKING UP!!
HOLD IT! DO I LOOK STUPID OR SOMETHING?
IS THAT A TRICK QUESTION?
PUSH
WHY DIDN'T SHE LET ME KNOW SHE'S BACK IN TOWN? WHY DIDN'T SHE...
ENOUGH OF THE "WHYS" AND ASK HER!
YOU'RE ABSOLUTELY RIGHT, BUT HOW?
ULP! I FEEL I'M DOWN THE INFORMATION HIGHWAY WITHOUT A MODEM!
SHE PEEKED IN FOR A SECOND AND HURRIED UP THE STREET!
NOW THAT SHE'S BACK-I'LL FIND HER!
PUSH
2

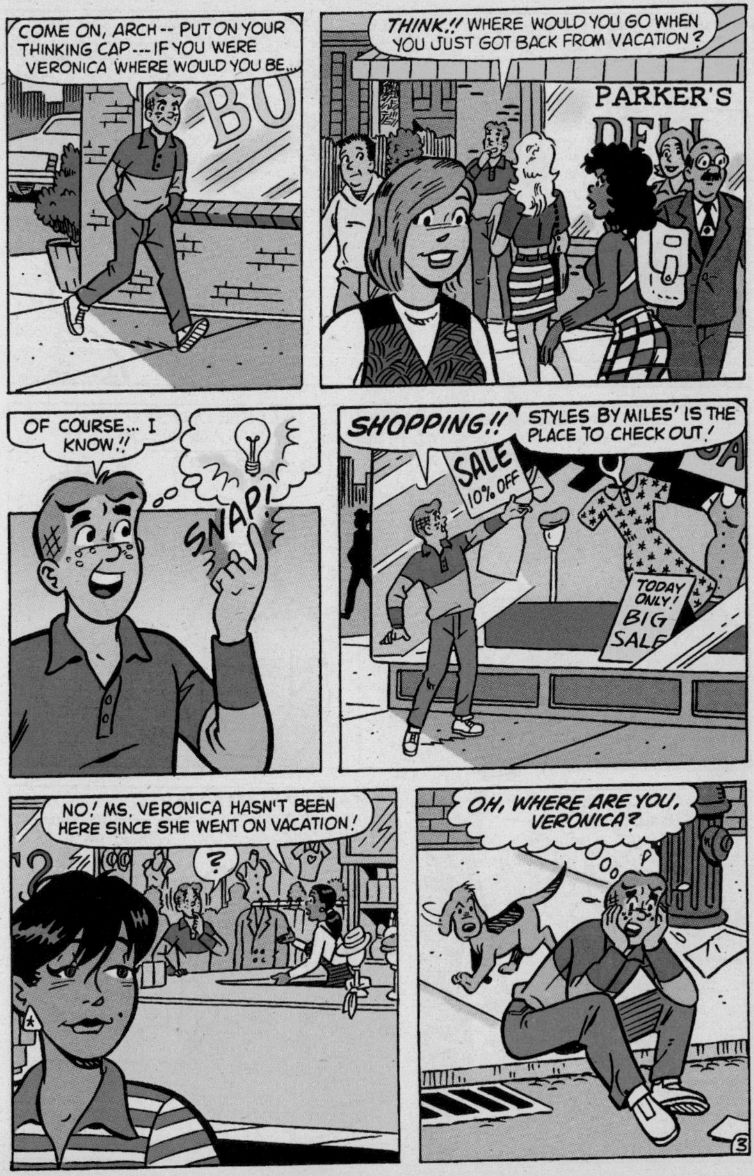

COME ON, ARCH -- PUT ON YOUR THINKING CAP --- IF YOU WERE VERONICA WHERE WOULD YOU BE...
THINK!! WHERE WOULD YOU GO WHEN YOU JUST GOT BACK FROM VACATION?
PARKER'S
OF COURSE... I KNOW!!
SNAP!
SHOPPING!!
STYLES BY MILES' IS THE PLACE TO CHECK OUT!
SALE 10% OFF
TODAY ONLY! BIG SALE
NO! MS. VERONICA HASN'T BEEN HERE SINCE SHE WENT ON VACATION!
?
OH, WHERE ARE YOU, VERONICA?
3

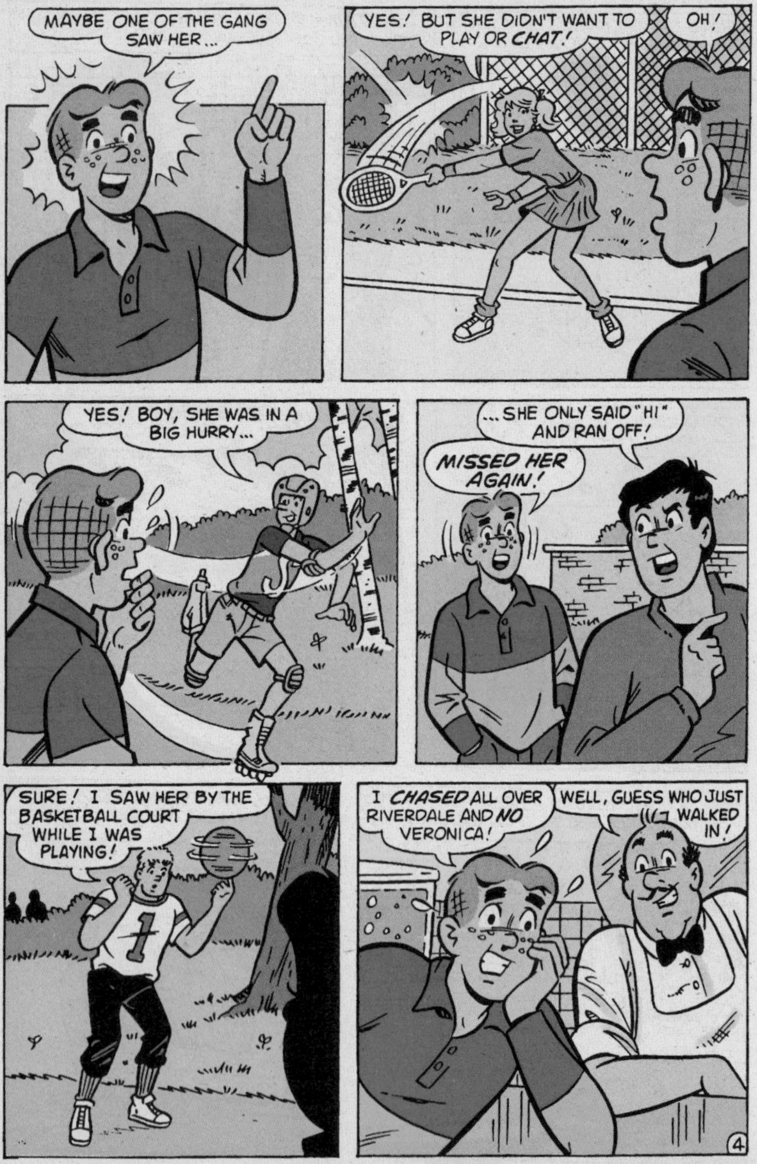
MAYBE ONE OF THE GANG SAW HER...
YES! BUT SHE DIDN'T WANT TO PLAY OR CHAT!
OH!
YES! BOY, SHE WAS IN A BIG HURRY...
...SHE ONLY SAID "HI" AND RAN OFF!
MISSED HER AGAIN!
SURE! I SAW HER BY THE BASKETBALL COURT WHILE I WAS PLAYING!
1
I CHASED ALL OVER RIVERDALE AND NO VERONICA!
WELL, GUESS WHO JUST WALKED IN!
4

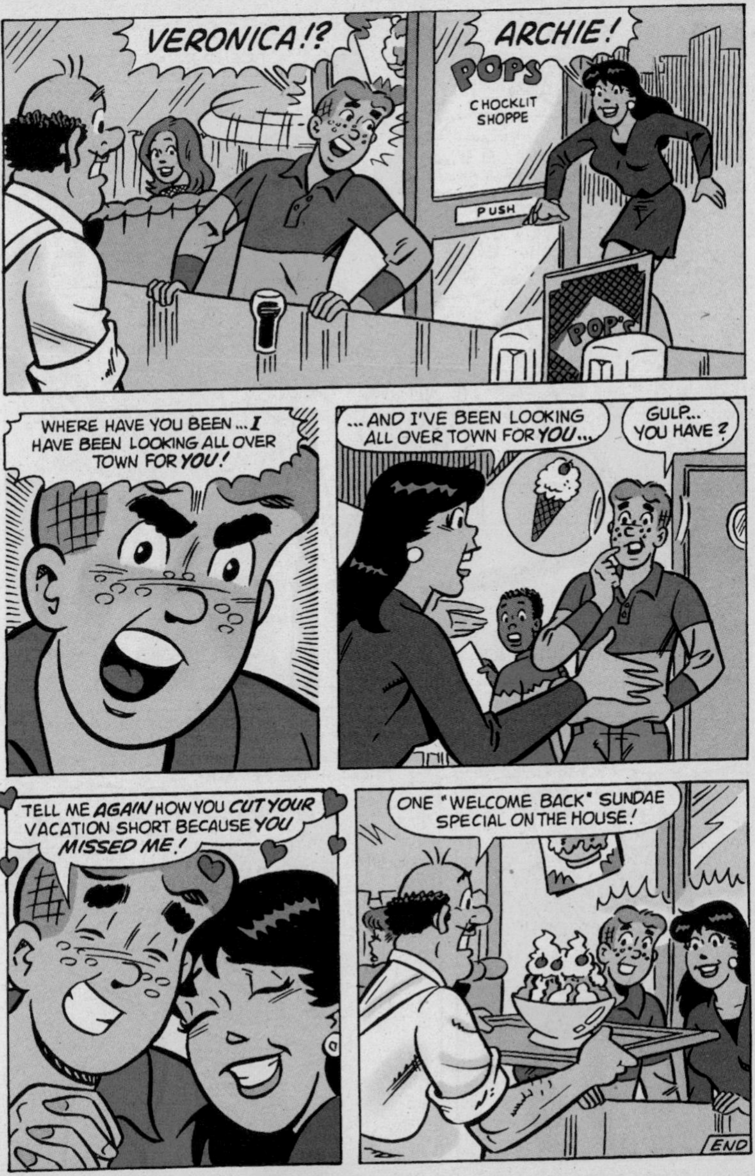
VERONICA!?
ARCHIE!
POPS
CHOCKLIT SHOPPE
PUSH
POP'S
WHERE HAVE YOU BEEN ... I HAVE BEEN LOOKING ALL OVER TOWN FOR YOU!
... AND I'VE BEEN LOOKING ALL OVER TOWN FOR YOU...
GULP... YOU HAVE?
TELL ME AGAIN HOW YOU CUT YOUR VACATION SHORT BECAUSE YOU MISSED ME!
ONE "WELCOME BACK" SUNDAE SPECIAL ON THE HOUSE!
END

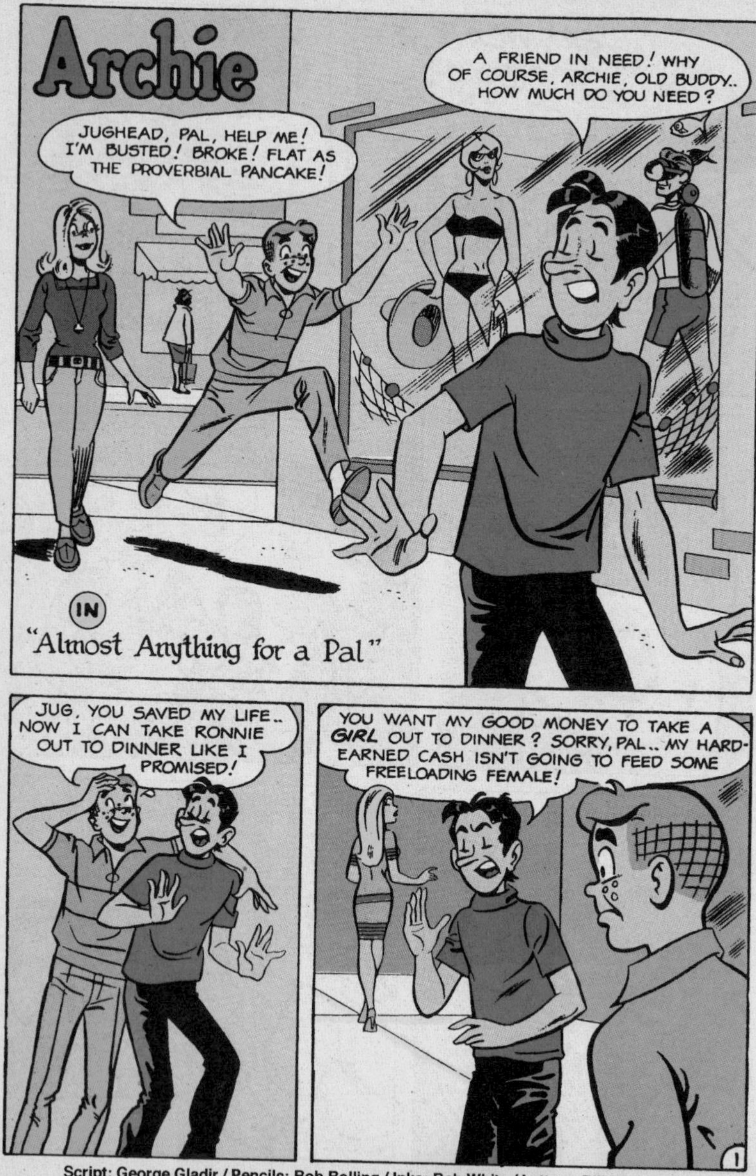
Archie
JUGHEAD, PAL, HELP ME! I'M BUSTED! BROKE! FLAT AS THE PROVERBIAL PANCAKE!
A FRIEND IN NEED! WHY OF COURSE, ARCHIE, OLD BUDDY.. HOW MUCH DO YOU NEED?
IN
"Almost Anything for a Pal"
JUG, YOU SAVED MY LIFE.. NOW I CAN TAKE RONNIE OUT TO DINNER LIKE I PROMISED!
YOU WANT MY GOOD MONEY TO TAKE A GIRL OUT TO DINNER? SORRY, PAL.. MY HARD-EARNED CASH ISN'T GOING TO FEED SOME FREELOADING FEMALE!
1

Script: George Gladir / Pencils: Bob Bolling / Inks: Bob White / Letters: Bill Yoshida

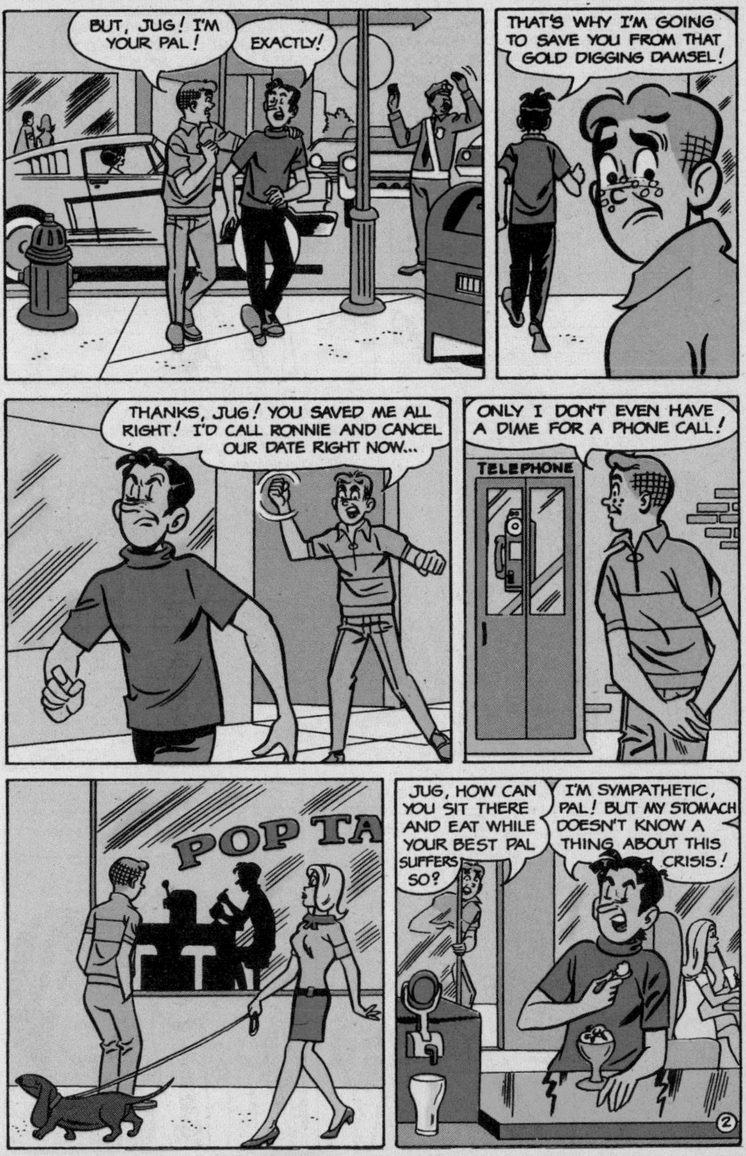
BUT, JUG! I'M YOUR PAL!
EXACTLY!
THAT'S WHY I'M GOING TO SAVE YOU FROM THAT GOLD DIGGING DAMSEL!
THANKS, JUG! YOU SAVED ME ALL RIGHT! I'D CALL RONNIE AND CANCEL OUR DATE RIGHT NOW...
ONLY I DON'T EVEN HAVE A DIME FOR A PHONE CALL!
TELEPHONE
POP TA
JUG, HOW CAN YOU SIT THERE AND EAT WHILE YOUR BEST PAL SUFFERS SO?
I'M SYMPATHETIC, PAL! BUT MY STOMACH DOESN'T KNOW A THING ABOUT THIS CRISIS!
2

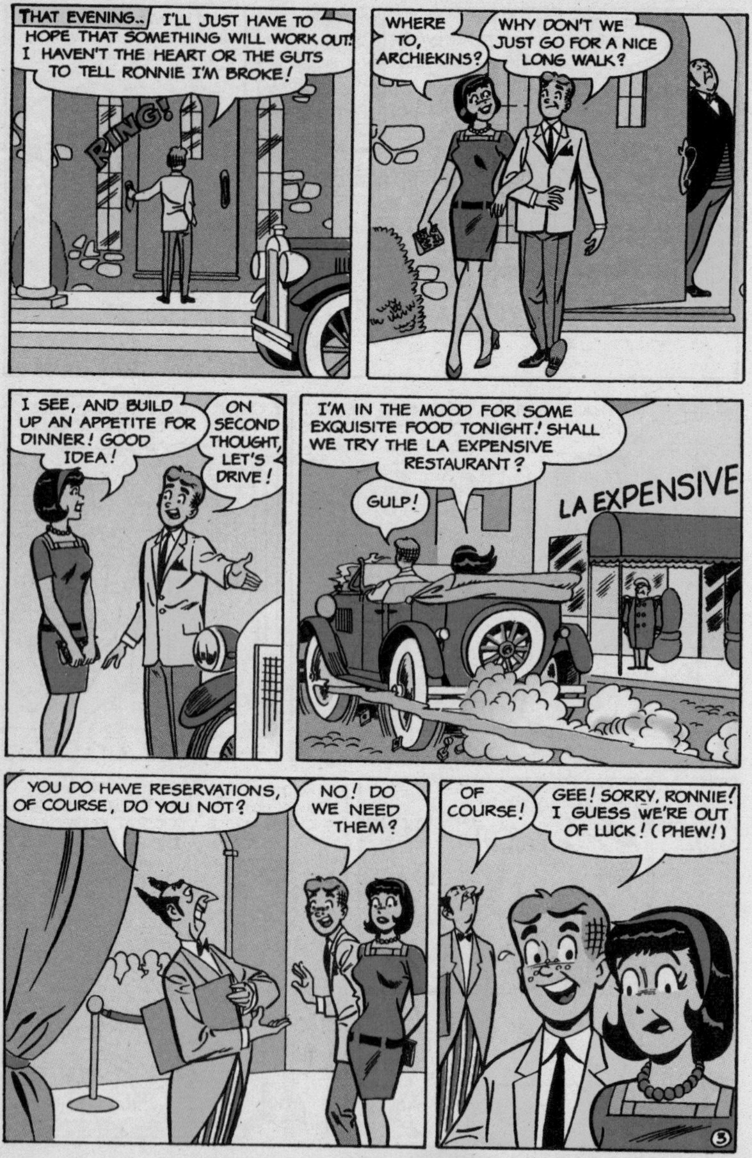
THAT EVENING..
I'LL JUST HAVE TO HOPE THAT SOMETHING WILL WORK OUT! I HAVEN'T THE HEART OR THE GUTS TO TELL RONNIE I'M BROKE!
RING!
WHERE TO, ARCHIEKINS?
WHY DON'T WE JUST GO FOR A NICE LONG WALK?
I SEE, AND BUILD UP AN APPETITE FOR DINNER! GOOD IDEA!
ON SECOND THOUGHT, LET'S DRIVE!
I'M IN THE MOOD FOR SOME EXQUISITE FOOD TONIGHT! SHALL WE TRY THE LA EXPENSIVE RESTAURANT?
GULP!
LA EXPENSIVE
YOU DO HAVE RESERVATIONS, OF COURSE, DO YOU NOT?
NO! DO WE NEED THEM?
OF COURSE!
GEE! SORRY, RONNIE! I GUESS WE'RE OUT OF LUCK! (PHEW!)
5

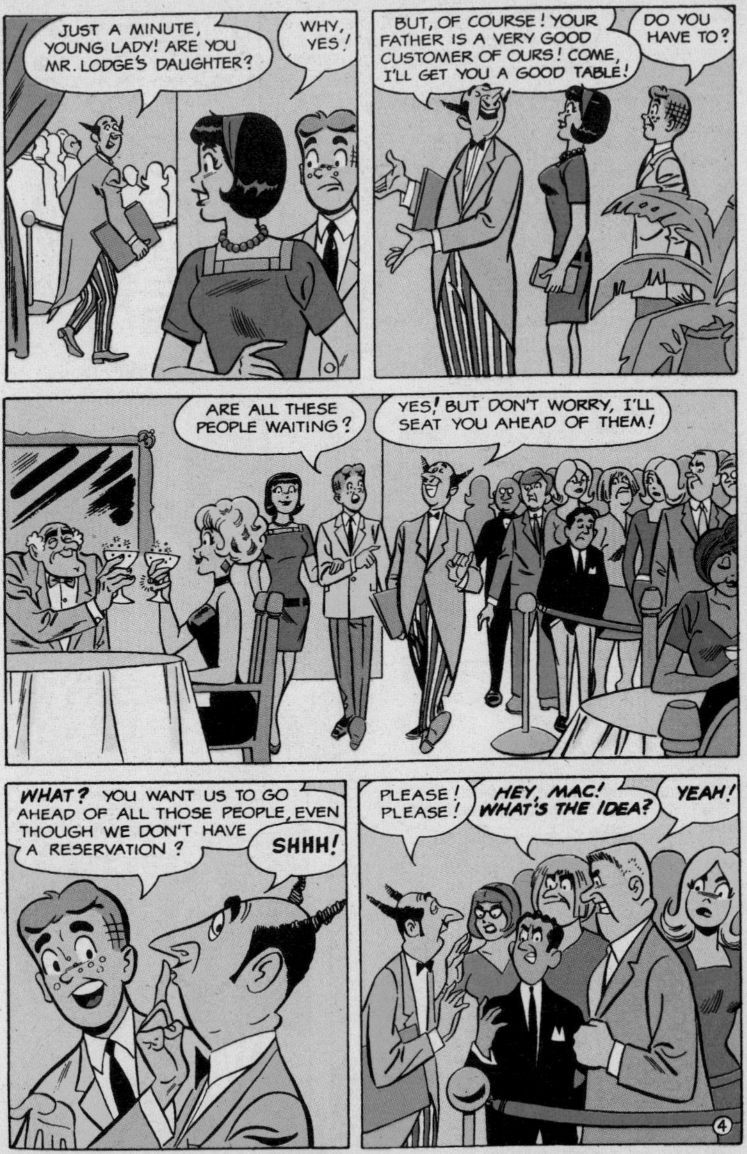
JUST A MINUTE, YOUNG LADY! ARE YOU MR. LODGE'S DAUGHTER?
WHY, YES!
BUT, OF COURSE! YOUR FATHER IS A VERY GOOD CUSTOMER OF OURS! COME, I'LL GET YOU A GOOD TABLE!
DO YOU HAVE TO?
ARE ALL THESE PEOPLE WAITING?
YES! BUT DON'T WORRY, I'LL SEAT YOU AHEAD OF THEM!
WHAT? YOU WANT US TO GO AHEAD OF ALL THOSE PEOPLE, EVEN THOUGH WE DON'T HAVE A RESERVATION?
SHHH!
PLEASE! PLEASE!
HEY, MAC! WHAT'S THE IDEA?
YEAH!
4

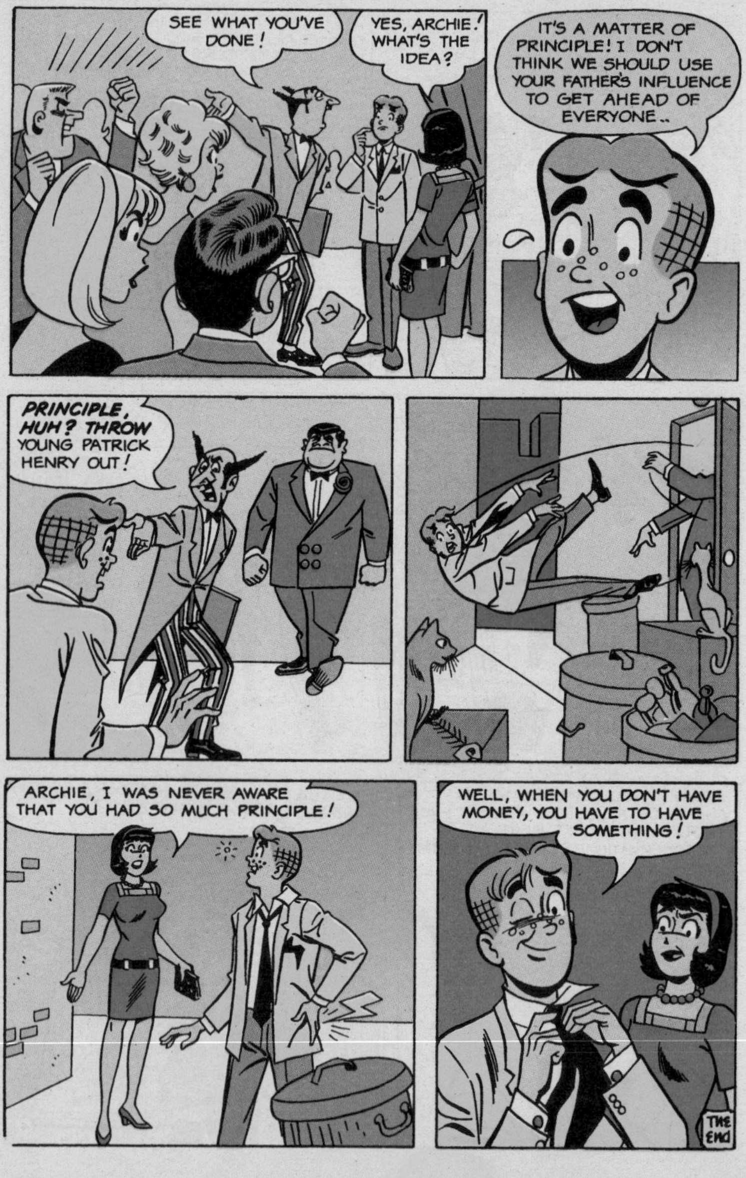
SEE WHAT YOU'VE DONE!
YES, ARCHIE! WHAT'S THE IDEA?
IT'S A MATTER OF PRINCIPLE! I DON'T THINK WE SHOULD USE YOUR FATHER'S INFLUENCE TO GET AHEAD OF EVERYONE..
PRINCIPLE, HUH? THROW YOUNG PATRICK HENRY OUT!
ARCHIE, I WAS NEVER AWARE THAT YOU HAD SO MUCH PRINCIPLE!
WELL, WHEN YOU DON'T HAVE MONEY, YOU HAVE TO HAVE SOMETHING!
THE END

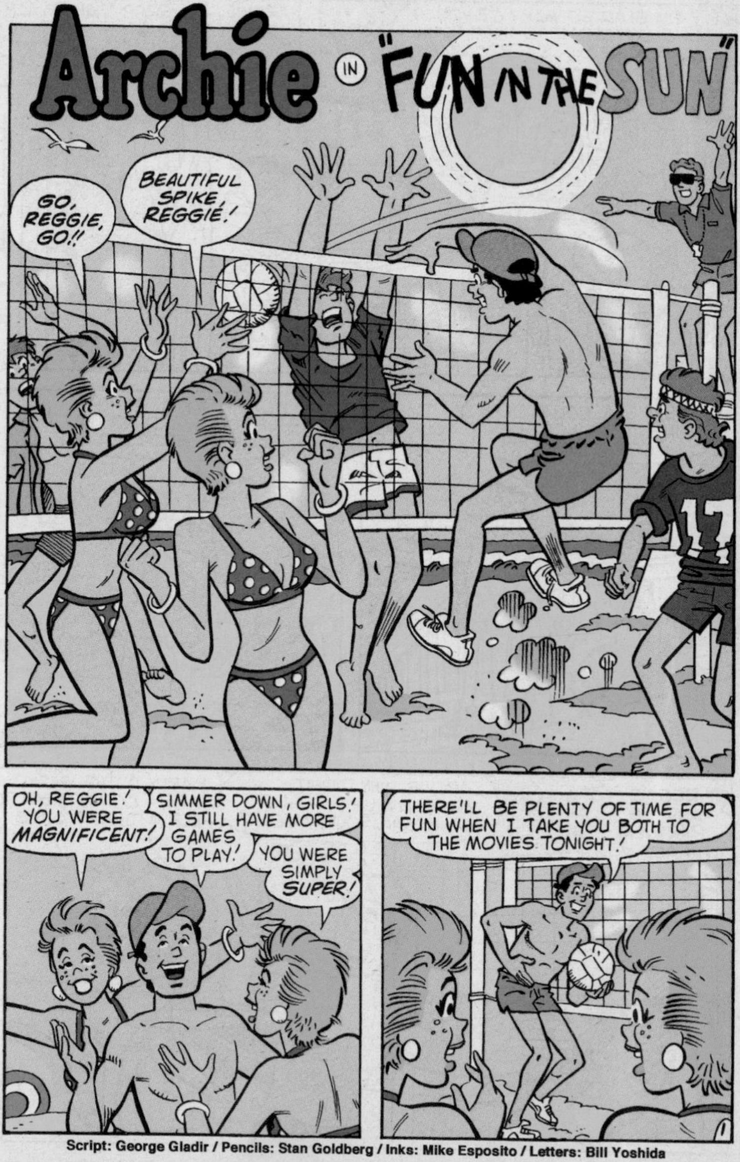
Archie IN "FUN IN THE SUN"
GO, REGGIE, GO!!
BEAUTIFUL SPIKE, REGGIE!
OH, REGGIE! YOU WERE MAGNIFICENT!
SIMMER DOWN, GIRLS! I STILL HAVE MORE GAMES TO PLAY!
YOU WERE SIMPLY SUPER!
THERE'LL BE PLENTY OF TIME FOR FUN WHEN I TAKE YOU BOTH TO THE MOVIES TONIGHT!
1

Script: George Gladir / Pencils: Stan Goldberg / Inks: Mike Esposito / Letters: Bill Yoshida

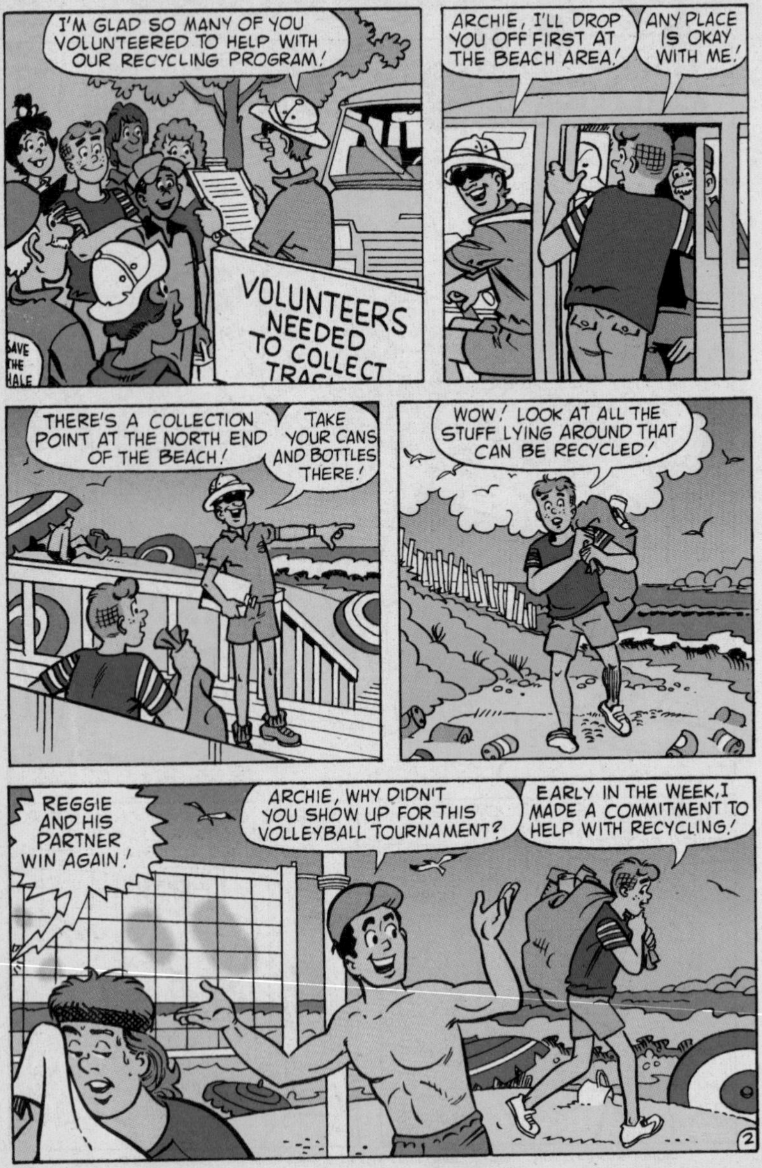

I'M GLAD SO MANY OF YOU VOLUNTEERED TO HELP WITH OUR RECYCLING PROGRAM!
VOLUNTEERS NEEDED TO COLLECT
ARCHIE, I'LL DROP YOU OFF FIRST AT THE BEACH AREA!
ANY PLACE IS OKAY WITH ME!
THERE'S A COLLECTION POINT AT THE NORTH END OF THE BEACH!
TAKE YOUR CANS AND BOTTLES THERE!
WOW! LOOK AT ALL THE STUFF LYING AROUND THAT CAN BE RECYCLED!
REGGIE AND HIS PARTNER WIN AGAIN!
ARCHIE, WHY DIDN'T YOU SHOW UP FOR THIS VOLLEYBALL TOURNAMENT?
EARLY IN THE WEEK, I MADE A COMMITMENT TO HELP WITH RECYCLING!
2

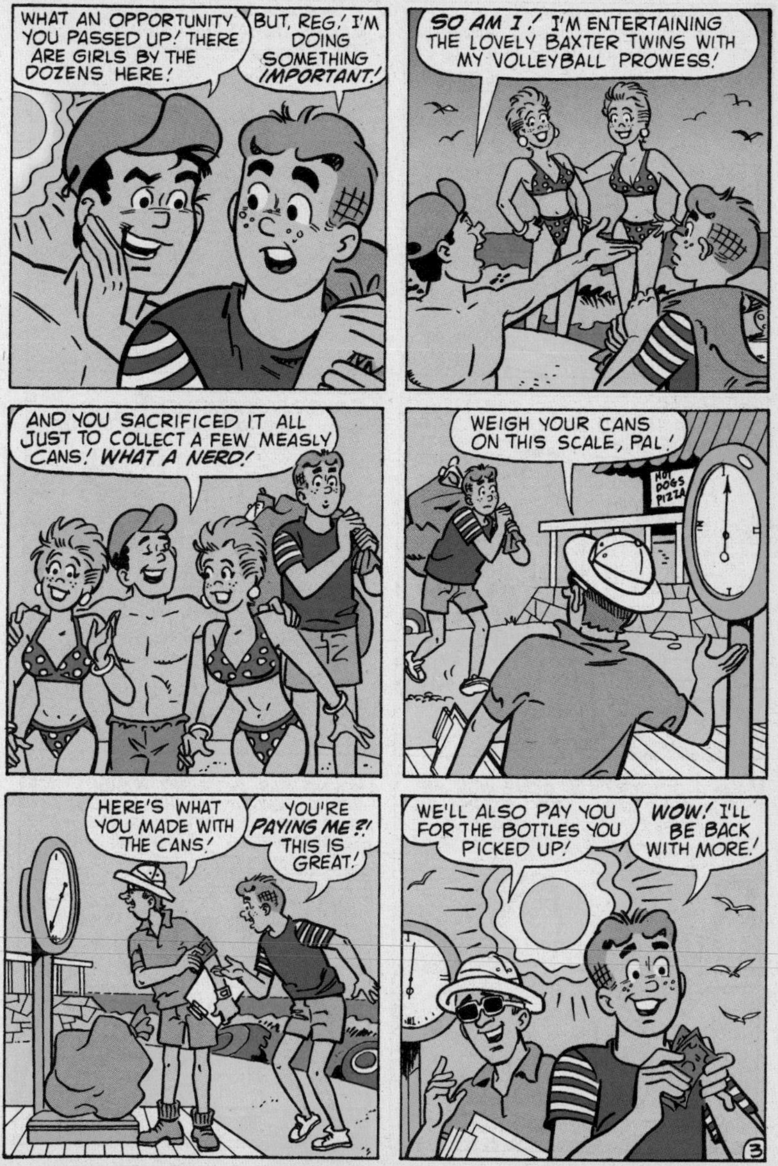
WHAT AN OPPORTUNITY YOU PASSED UP! THERE ARE GIRLS BY THE DOZENS HERE!
BUT, REG! I'M DOING SOMETHING IMPORTANT!
SO AM I! I'M ENTERTAINING THE LOVELY BAXTER TWINS WITH MY VOLLEYBALL PROWESS!
AND YOU SACRIFICED IT ALL JUST TO COLLECT A FEW MEASLY CANS! WHAT A NERD!
WEIGH YOUR CANS ON THIS SCALE, PAL!
HOT DOGS PIZZA
HERE'S WHAT YOU MADE WITH THE CANS!
YOU'RE PAYING ME ?! THIS IS GREAT!
WE'LL ALSO PAY YOU FOR THE BOTTLES YOU PICKED UP!
WOW! I'LL BE BACK WITH MORE!
3

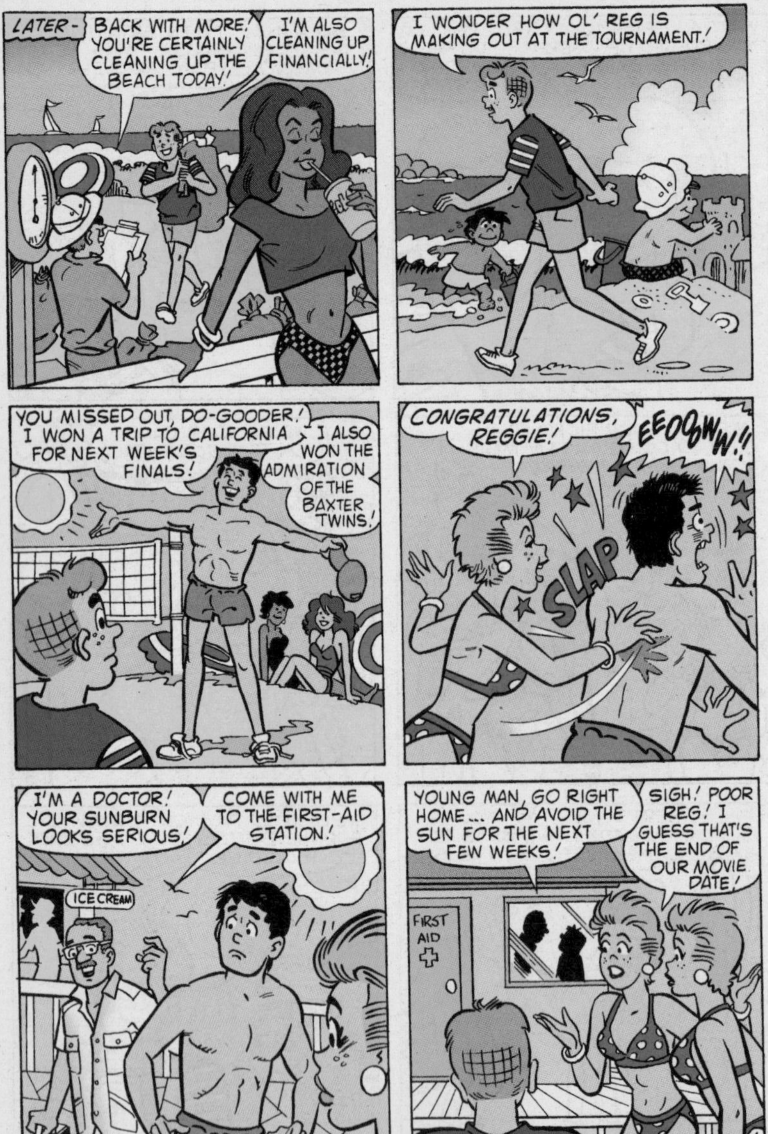
LATER -
BACK WITH MORE! YOU'RE CERTAINLY CLEANING UP THE BEACH TODAY!
I'M ALSO CLEANING UP FINANCIALLY!
I WONDER HOW OL' REG IS MAKING OUT AT THE TOURNAMENT!
YOU MISSED OUT, DO-GOODER! I WON A TRIP TO CALIFORNIA FOR NEXT WEEK'S FINALS!
I ALSO WON THE ADMIRATION OF THE BAXTER TWINS!
CONGRATULATIONS, REGGIE!
EEOOOWW!!
SLAP
I'M A DOCTOR! YOUR SUNBURN LOOKS SERIOUS!
COME WITH ME TO THE FIRST-AID STATION!
ICE CREAM
YOUNG MAN, GO RIGHT HOME ... AND AVOID THE SUN FOR THE NEXT FEW WEEKS!
SIGH! POOR REG! I GUESS THAT'S THE END OF OUR MOVIE DATE!
FIRST AID
4

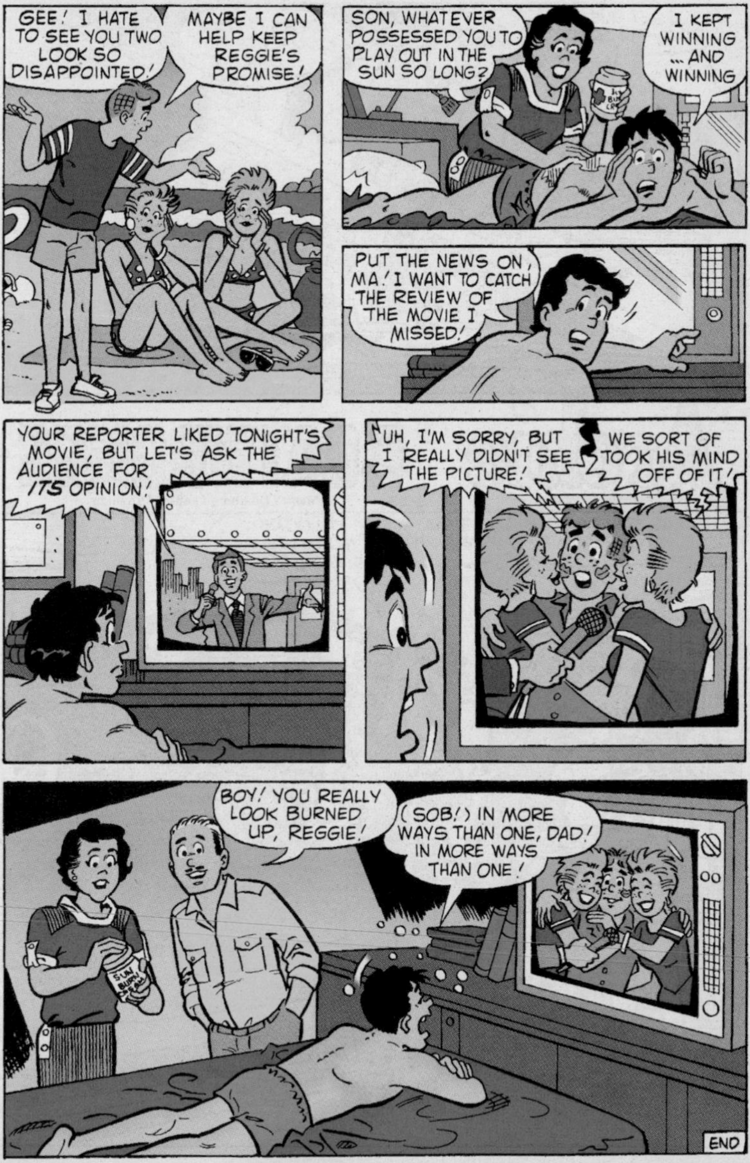
GEE! I HATE TO SEE YOU TWO LOOK SO DISAPPOINTED!
MAYBE I CAN HELP KEEP REGGIE'S PROMISE!
SON, WHATEVER POSSESSED YOU TO PLAY OUT IN THE SUN SO LONG?
I KEPT WINNING ...AND WINNING
PUT THE NEWS ON, MA! I WANT TO CATCH THE REVIEW OF THE MOVIE I MISSED!
YOUR REPORTER LIKED TONIGHT'S MOVIE, BUT LET'S ASK THE AUDIENCE FOR *ITS* OPINION!
UH, I'M SORRY, BUT I REALLY DIDN'T SEE THE PICTURE!
WE SORT OF TOOK HIS MIND OFF OF IT!
BOY! YOU REALLY LOOK BURNED UP, REGGIE!
(SOB!) IN MORE WAYS THAN ONE, DAD! IN MORE WAYS THAN ONE!
SUN BURN CREAM
END

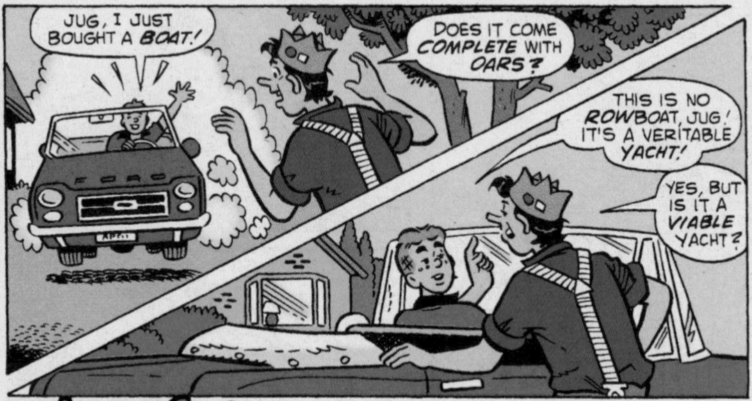
JUG, I JUST BOUGHT A BOAT!
DOES IT COME COMPLETE WITH OARS?
THIS IS NO ROWBOAT, JUG! IT'S A VERITABLE YACHT!
YES, BUT IS IT A VIABLE YACHT?

Archie (IN) BOATWRONGS

Gladir / Goldberg / Lapick / Yoshida

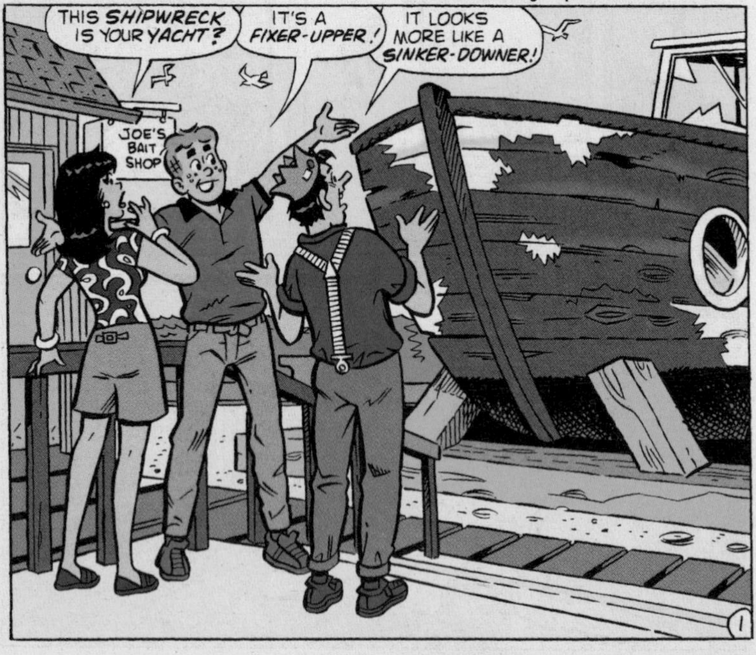
THIS SHIPWRECK IS YOUR YACHT?
IT'S A FIXER-UPPER!
IT LOOKS MORE LIKE A SINKER-DOWNER!
JOE'S BAIT SHOP

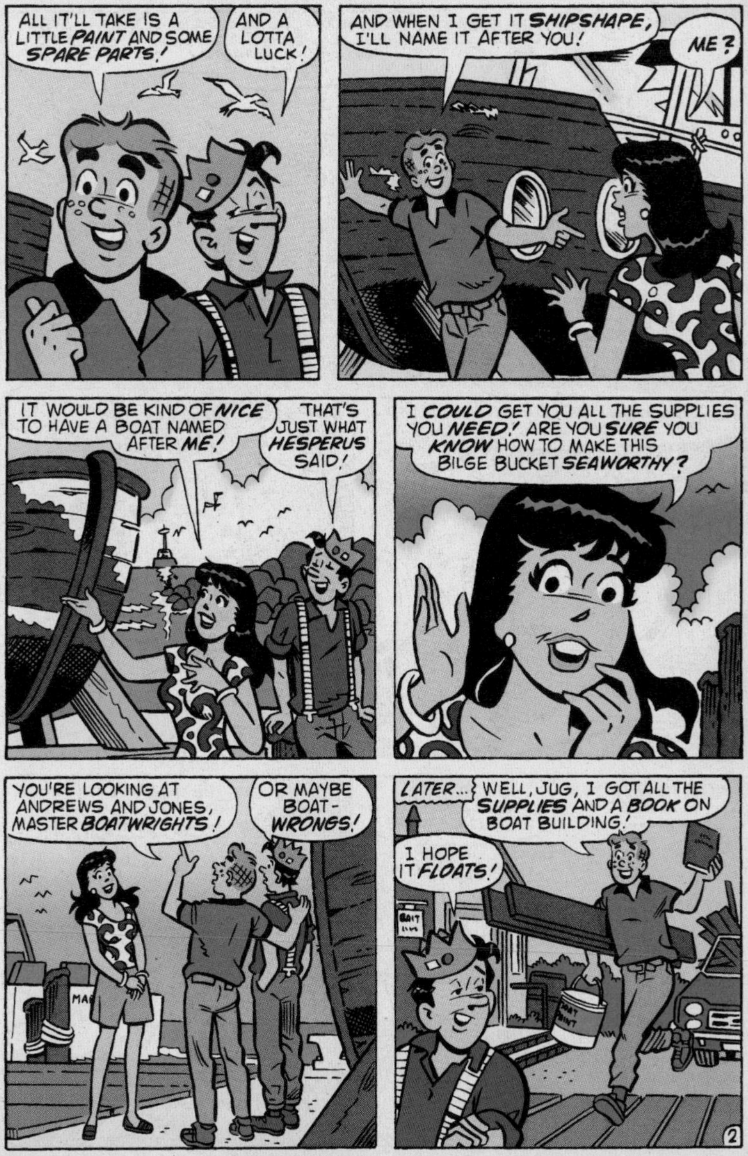
ALL IT'LL TAKE IS A LITTLE PAINT AND SOME SPARE PARTS!
AND A LOTTA LUCK!
AND WHEN I GET IT SHIPSHAPE, I'LL NAME IT AFTER YOU!
ME?
IT WOULD BE KIND OF NICE TO HAVE A BOAT NAMED AFTER ME!
THAT'S JUST WHAT HESPERUS SAID!
I COULD GET YOU ALL THE SUPPLIES YOU NEED! ARE YOU SURE YOU KNOW HOW TO MAKE THIS BILGE BUCKET SEAWORTHY?
YOU'RE LOOKING AT ANDREWS AND JONES, MASTER BOATWRIGHTS!
OR MAYBE BOAT-WRONGS!
LATER...
WELL, JUG, I GOT ALL THE SUPPLIES AND A BOOK ON BOAT BUILDING!
I HOPE IT FLOATS!
BAIT
2

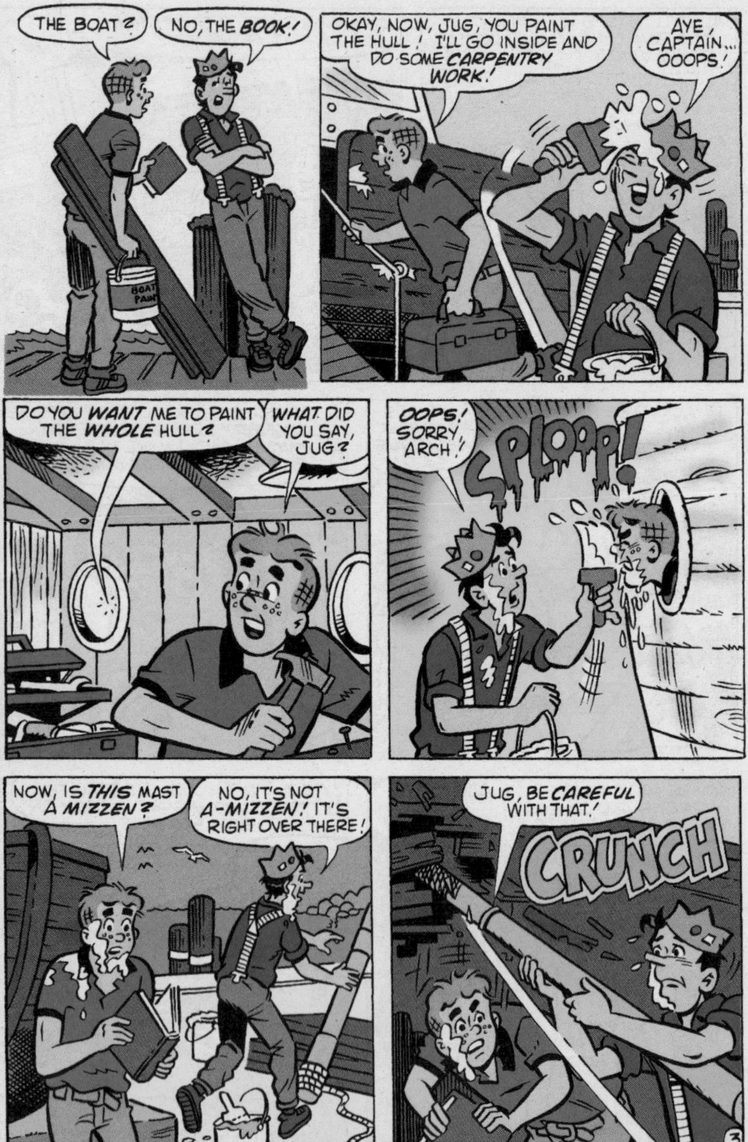
THE BOAT?
NO, THE BOOK!
BOAT PAINT
OKAY, NOW, JUG, YOU PAINT THE HULL! I'LL GO INSIDE AND DO SOME CARPENTRY WORK!
AYE, CAPTAIN... OOOPS!
DO YOU WANT ME TO PAINT THE WHOLE HULL?
WHAT DID YOU SAY, JUG?
OOPS! SORRY, ARCH!
SPLOOP!
NOW, IS THIS MAST A MIZZEN?
NO, IT'S NOT A-MIZZEN! IT'S RIGHT OVER THERE!
JUG, BE CAREFUL WITH THAT!
CRUNCH
3

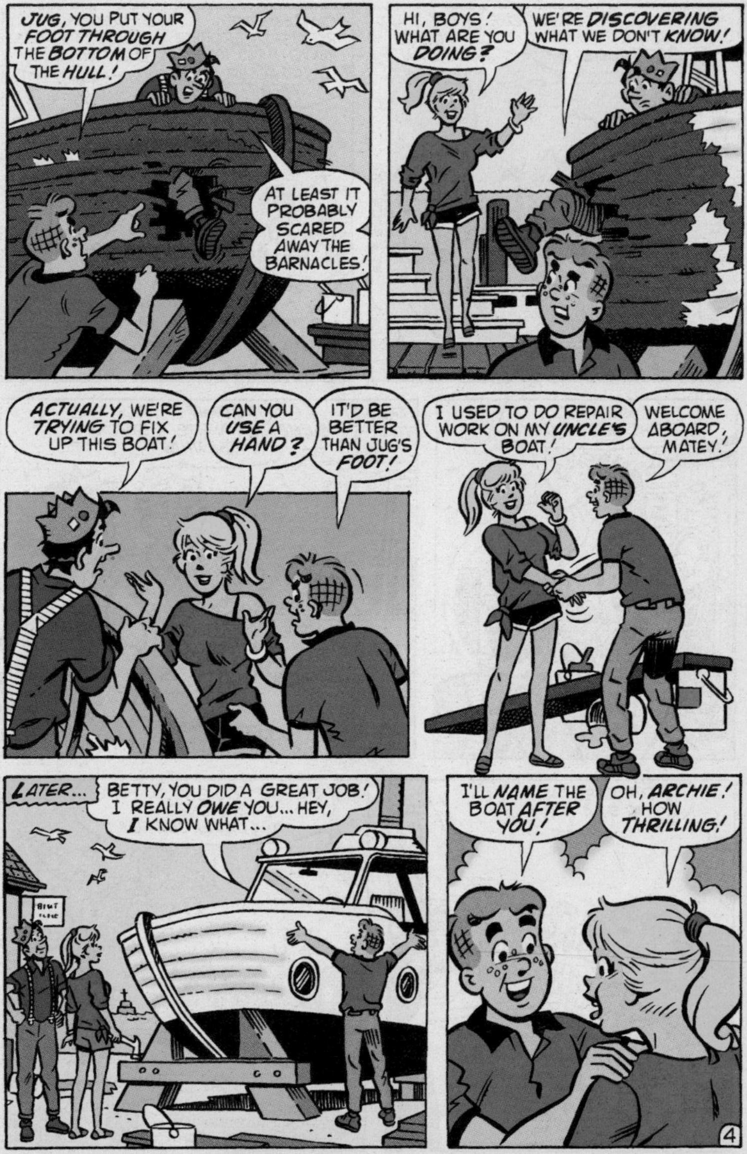
JUG, YOU PUT YOUR FOOT THROUGH THE BOTTOM OF THE HULL!
AT LEAST IT PROBABLY SCARED AWAY THE BARNACLES!
HI, BOYS! WHAT ARE YOU DOING?
WE'RE DISCOVERING WHAT WE DON'T KNOW!
ACTUALLY, WE'RE TRYING TO FIX UP THIS BOAT!
CAN YOU USE A HAND?
IT'D BE BETTER THAN JUG'S FOOT!
I USED TO DO REPAIR WORK ON MY UNCLE'S BOAT!
WELCOME ABOARD, MATEY!
LATER...
BETTY, YOU DID A GREAT JOB! I REALLY OWE YOU... HEY, I KNOW WHAT...
I'LL NAME THE BOAT AFTER YOU!
OH, ARCHIE! HOW THRILLING!
4

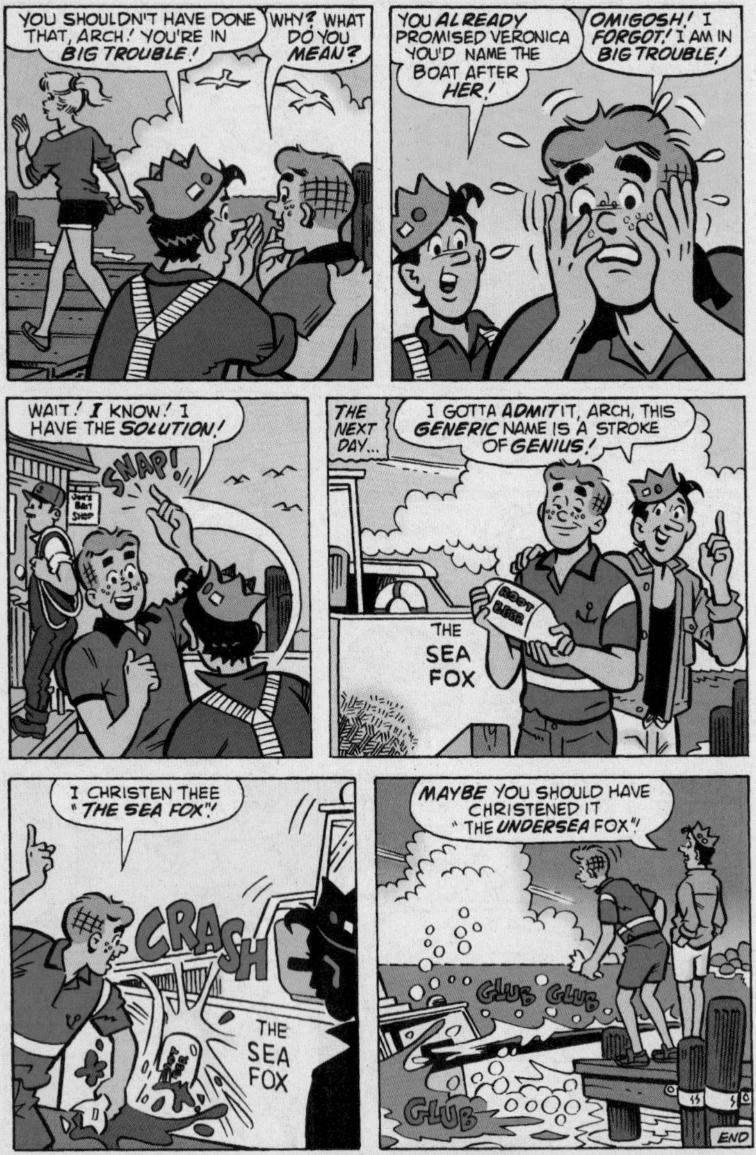

YOU SHOULDN'T HAVE DONE THAT, ARCH! YOU'RE IN BIG TROUBLE!
WHY? WHAT DO YOU MEAN?
YOU ALREADY PROMISED VERONICA YOU'D NAME THE BOAT AFTER HER!
OMIGOSH! I FORGOT! I AM IN BIG TROUBLE!
WAIT! I KNOW! I HAVE THE SOLUTION!
SNAP!
JOE'S BAIT SHOP
THE NEXT DAY...
I GOTTA ADMIT IT, ARCH, THIS GENERIC NAME IS A STROKE OF GENIUS!
ROOT BEER
THE SEA FOX
I CHRISTEN THEE "THE SEA FOX"!
CRASH
THE SEA FOX
MAYBE YOU SHOULD HAVE CHRISTENED IT "THE UNDERSEA FOX"!
GLUB GLUB
GLUB
END

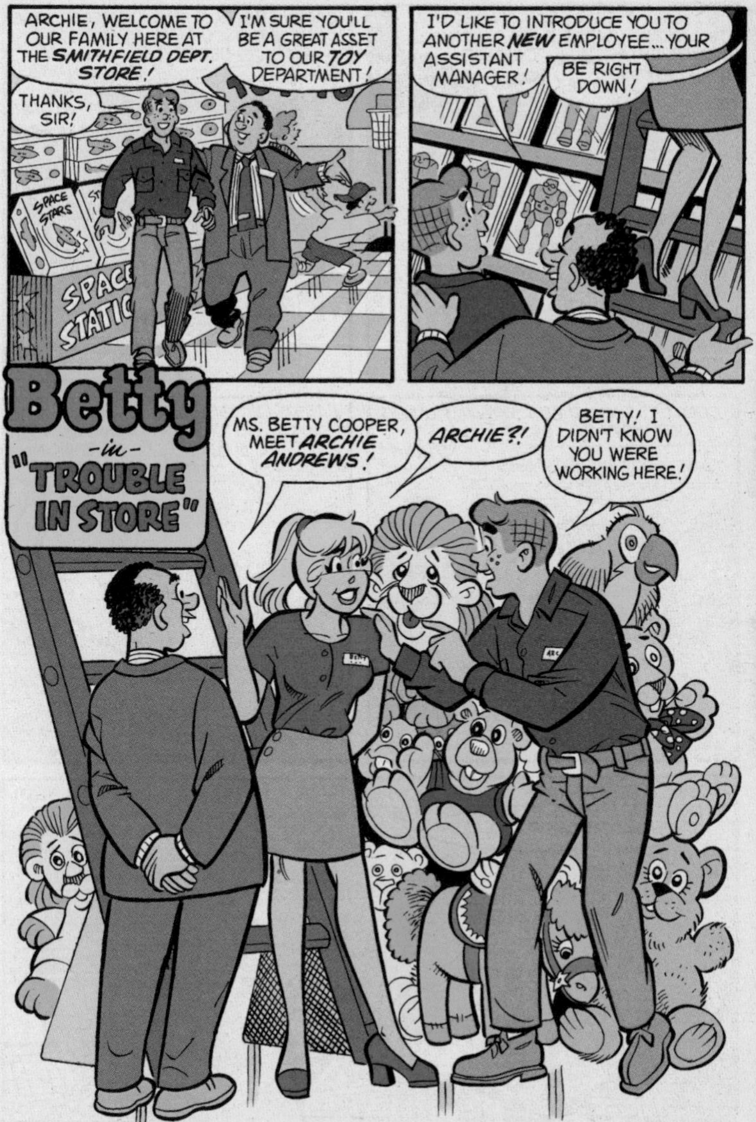
ARCHIE, WELCOME TO OUR FAMILY HERE AT THE SMITHFIELD DEPT. STORE!
I'M SURE YOU'LL BE A GREAT ASSET TO OUR TOY DEPARTMENT!
THANKS, SIR!
SPACE STARS
SPACE STATIO
I'D LIKE TO INTRODUCE YOU TO ANOTHER NEW EMPLOYEE... YOUR ASSISTANT MANAGER!
BE RIGHT DOWN!
Betty -in- "TROUBLE IN STORE"
MS. BETTY COOPER, MEET ARCHIE ANDREWS!
ARCHIE?!
BETTY! I DIDN'T KNOW YOU WERE WORKING HERE!

Script: Bill Golliher / Pencils: Stan Goldberg / Inks: John Lowe / Letters: Bill Yoshida

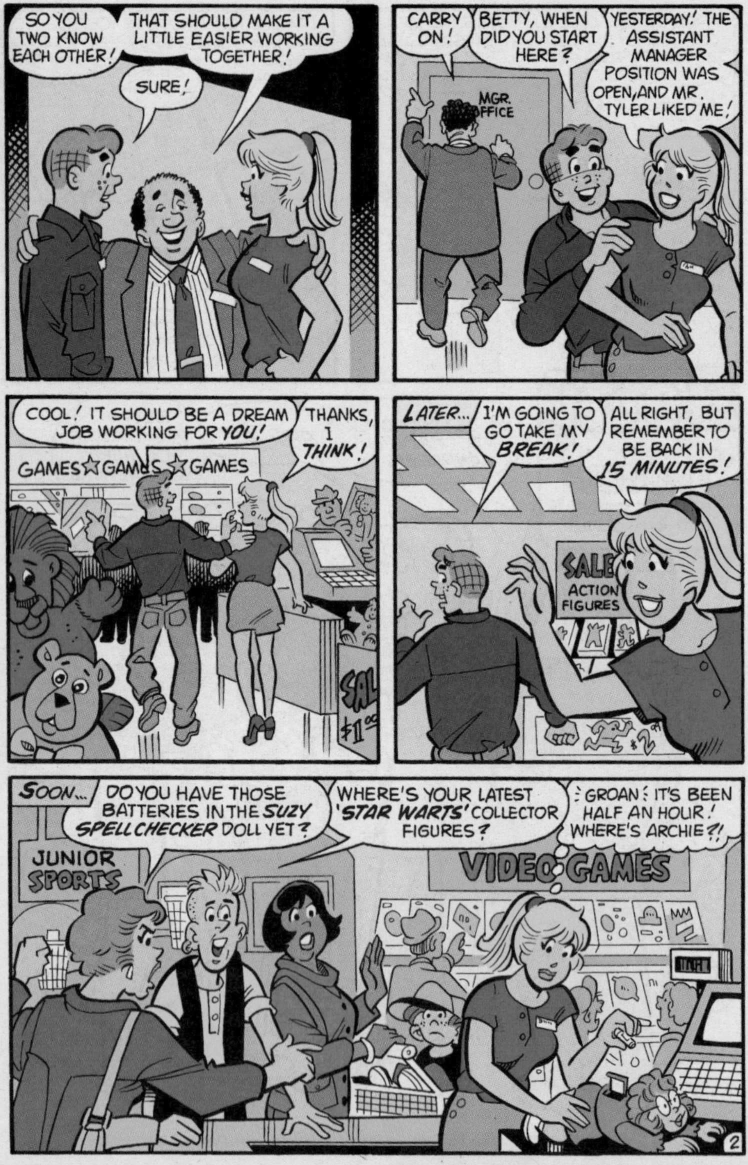

SO YOU TWO KNOW EACH OTHER!
THAT SHOULD MAKE IT A LITTLE EASIER WORKING TOGETHER!
SURE!
CARRY ON!
MGR. OFFICE
BETTY, WHEN DID YOU START HERE?
YESTERDAY! THE ASSISTANT MANAGER POSITION WAS OPEN, AND MR. TYLER LIKED ME!
COOL! IT SHOULD BE A DREAM JOB WORKING FOR YOU!
THANKS, I THINK!
GAMES☆GAMES☆GAMES
LATER...
I'M GOING TO GO TAKE MY BREAK!
ALL RIGHT, BUT REMEMBER TO BE BACK IN 15 MINUTES!
SALE ACTION FIGURES
SOON...
DO YOU HAVE THOSE BATTERIES IN THE SUZY SPELLCHECKER DOLL YET?
WHERE'S YOUR LATEST 'STAR WARTS' COLLECTOR FIGURES?
GROAN! IT'S BEEN HALF AN HOUR! WHERE'S ARCHIE?!
JUNIOR SPORTS
VIDEO GAMES
2

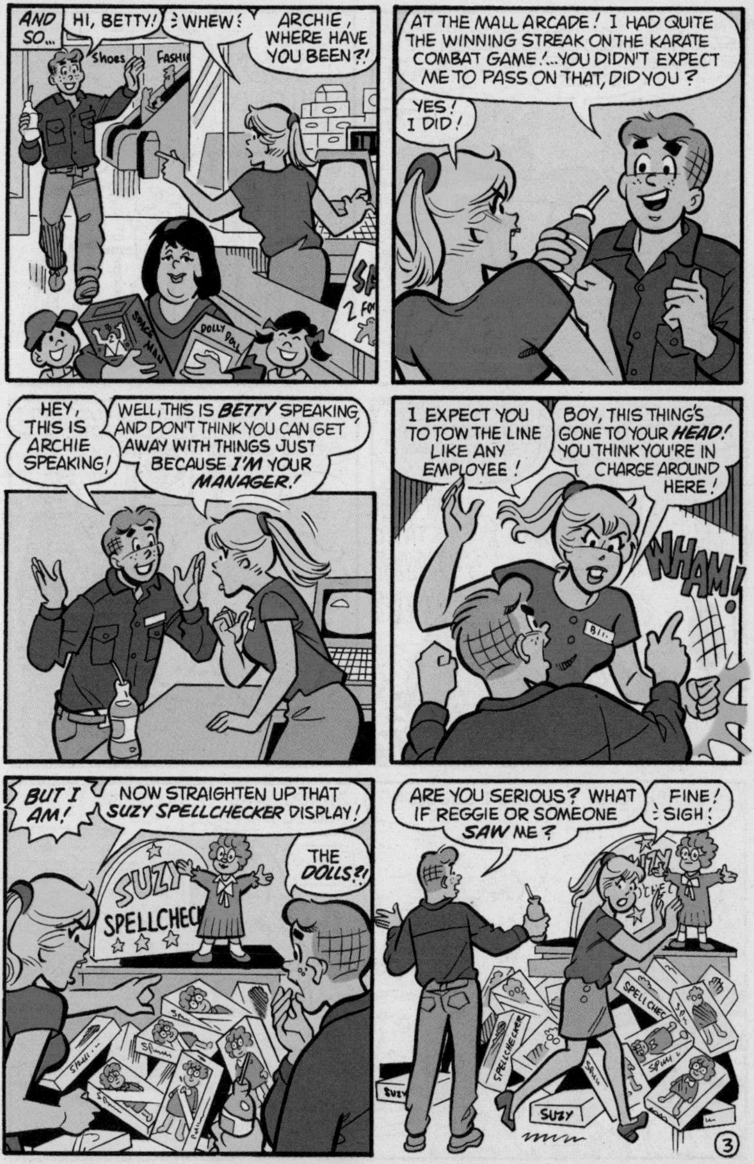
AND SO...
HI, BETTY!
WHEW!
ARCHIE, WHERE HAVE YOU BEEN?!
SHOES
AT THE MALL ARCADE! I HAD QUITE THE WINNING STREAK ON THE KARATE COMBAT GAME!...YOU DIDN'T EXPECT ME TO PASS ON THAT, DID YOU?
YES! I DID!
HEY, THIS IS ARCHIE SPEAKING!
WELL, THIS IS BETTY SPEAKING, AND DON'T THINK YOU CAN GET AWAY WITH THINGS JUST BECAUSE I'M YOUR MANAGER!
I EXPECT YOU TO TOW THE LINE LIKE ANY EMPLOYEE!
BOY, THIS THING'S GONE TO YOUR HEAD! YOU THINK YOU'RE IN CHARGE AROUND HERE!
WHAM!
BUT I AM!
NOW STRAIGHTEN UP THAT SUZY SPELLCHECKER DISPLAY!
THE DOLLS?!
ARE YOU SERIOUS? WHAT IF REGGIE OR SOMEONE SAW ME?
FINE! SIGH!
SUZY
SPELLCHECKER
SUZY

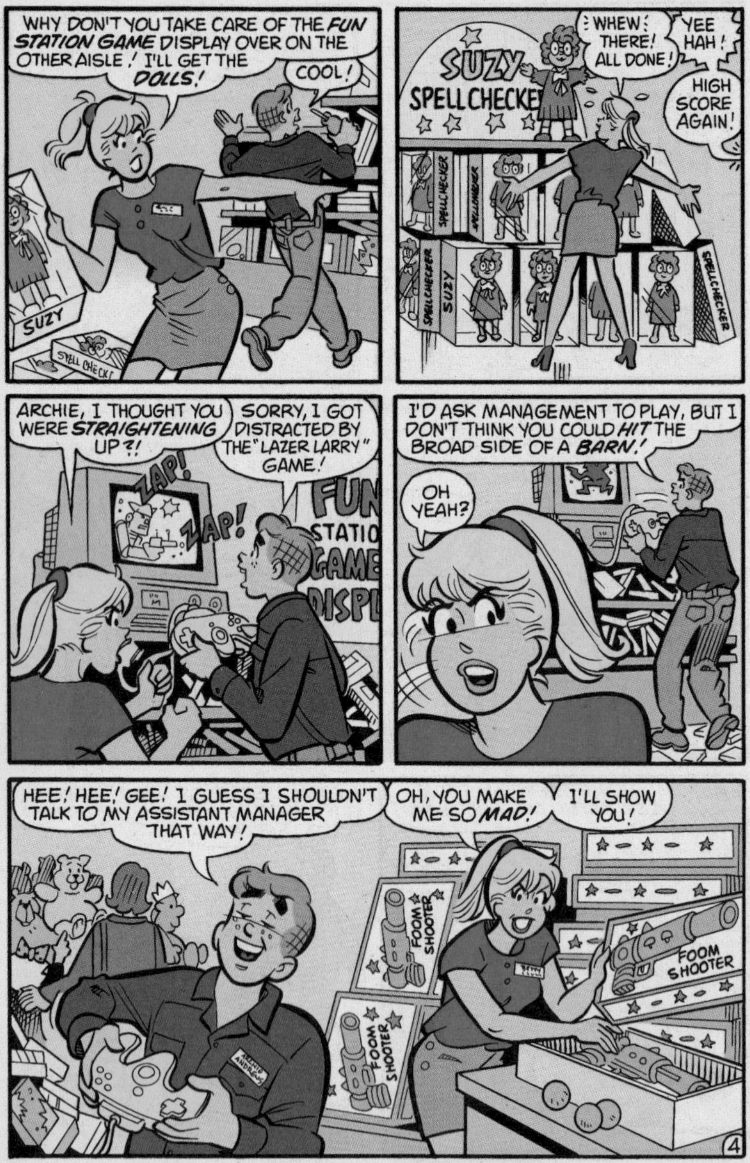

WHY DON'T YOU TAKE CARE OF THE FUN STATION GAME DISPLAY OVER ON THE OTHER AISLE! I'LL GET THE DOLLS!
COOL!
SUZY
SPELL CHECK
WHEW! THERE! ALL DONE!
YEE HAH!
HIGH SCORE AGAIN!
SUZY
SPELLCHECKER
ARCHIE, I THOUGHT YOU WERE STRAIGHTENING UP ?!
SORRY, I GOT DISTRACTED BY THE "LAZER LARRY" GAME!
ZAP!
ZAP!
I'D ASK MANAGEMENT TO PLAY, BUT I DON'T THINK YOU COULD HIT THE BROAD SIDE OF A BARN!
OH YEAH?
HEE! HEE! GEE! I GUESS I SHOULDN'T TALK TO MY ASSISTANT MANAGER THAT WAY!
OH, YOU MAKE ME SO MAD!
I'LL SHOW YOU!
FOOM SHOOTER
FOOM SHOOTER
FOOM SHOOTER

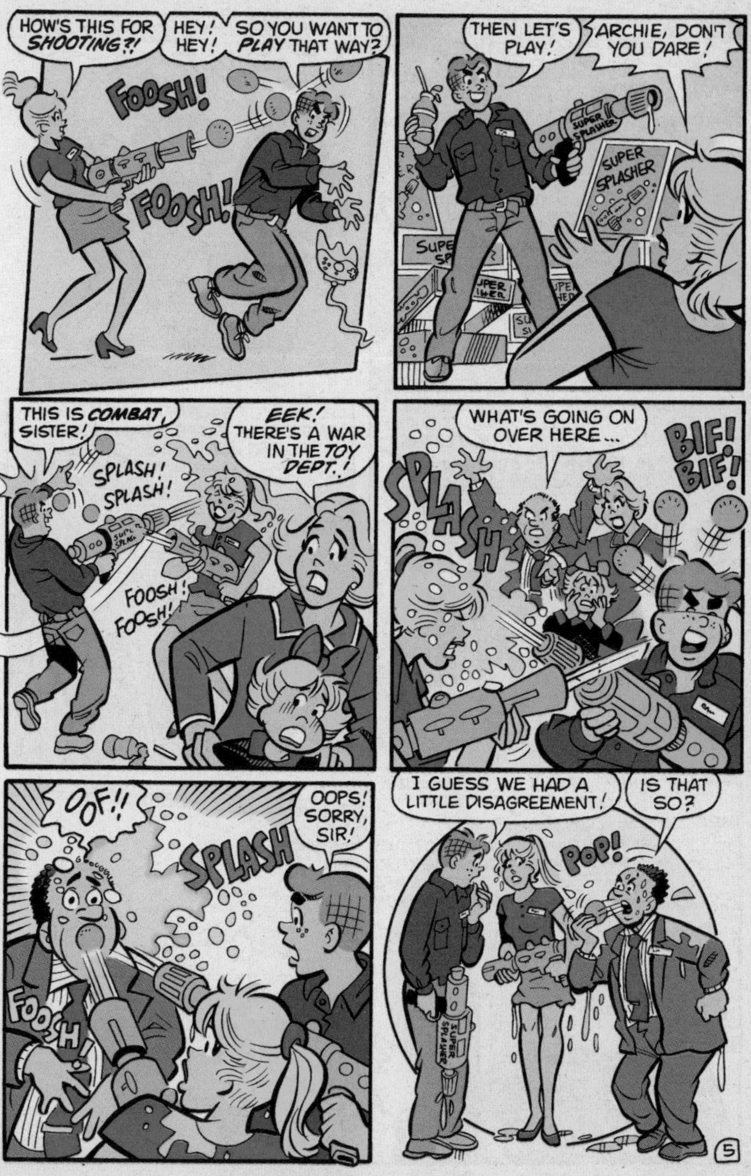
HOW'S THIS FOR SHOOTING?!
HEY! HEY!
SO YOU WANT TO PLAY THAT WAY?
FOOSH!
FOOSH!
THEN LET'S PLAY!
ARCHIE, DON'T YOU DARE!
SUPER SPLASHER
SUPER SPLASHER
THIS IS COMBAT, SISTER!
SPLASH! SPLASH!
EEK! THERE'S A WAR IN THE TOY DEPT.!
FOOSH! FOOSH!
WHAT'S GOING ON OVER HERE...
SPLASH
BIF! BIF!
OOF!!
SPLASH
OOPS! SORRY, SIR!
FOOSH!
I GUESS WE HAD A LITTLE DISAGREEMENT!
IS THAT SO?
POP!
SUPER SPLASHER
5

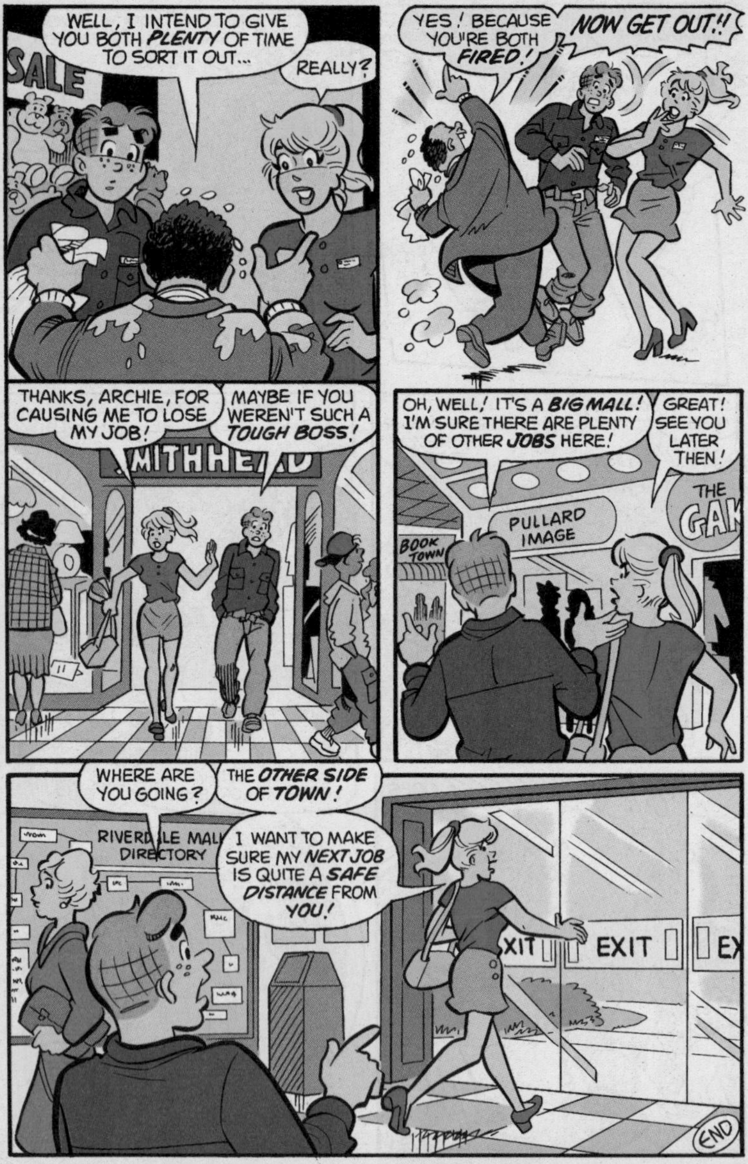
WELL, I INTEND TO GIVE YOU BOTH PLENTY OF TIME TO SORT IT OUT...
SALE
REALLY?
YES! BECAUSE YOU'RE BOTH FIRED!
NOW GET OUT!!
THANKS, ARCHIE, FOR CAUSING ME TO LOSE MY JOB!
MAYBE IF YOU WEREN'T SUCH A TOUGH BOSS!
MITHHEAD
OH, WELL! IT'S A BIG MALL! I'M SURE THERE ARE PLENTY OF OTHER JOBS HERE!
GREAT! SEE YOU LATER THEN!
PULLARD IMAGE
BOOK TOWN
WHERE ARE YOU GOING?
THE OTHER SIDE OF TOWN!
I WANT TO MAKE SURE MY NEXT JOB IS QUITE A SAFE DISTANCE FROM YOU!
RIVERDALE MALL DIRECTORY
EXIT
END

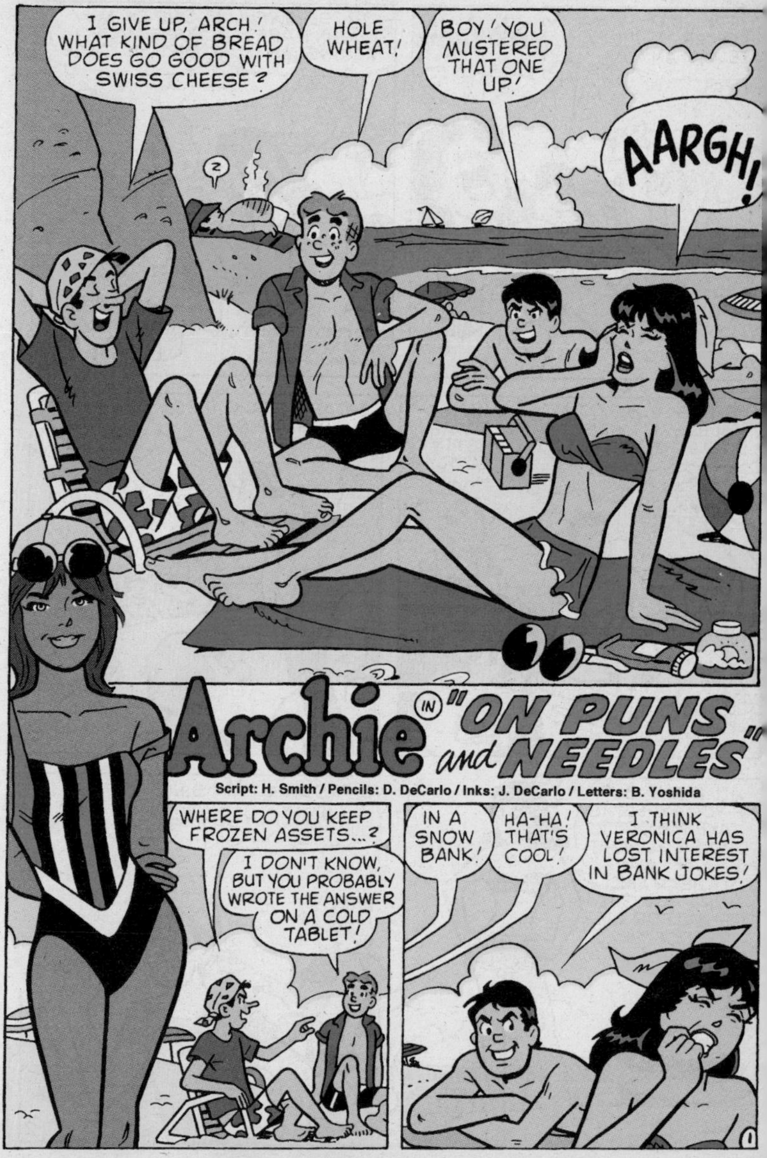

I GIVE UP, ARCH! WHAT KIND OF BREAD DOES GO GOOD WITH SWISS CHEESE?
HOLE WHEAT!
BOY! YOU MUSTERED THAT ONE UP!
AARGH!
Archie IN "ON PUNS and NEEDLES"
Script: H. Smith / Pencils: D. DeCarlo / Inks: J. DeCarlo / Letters: B. Yoshida
WHERE DO YOU KEEP FROZEN ASSETS...?
I DON'T KNOW, BUT YOU PROBABLY WROTE THE ANSWER ON A COLD TABLET!
IN A SNOW BANK!
HA-HA! THAT'S COOL!
I THINK VERONICA HAS LOST INTEREST IN BANK JOKES!
1

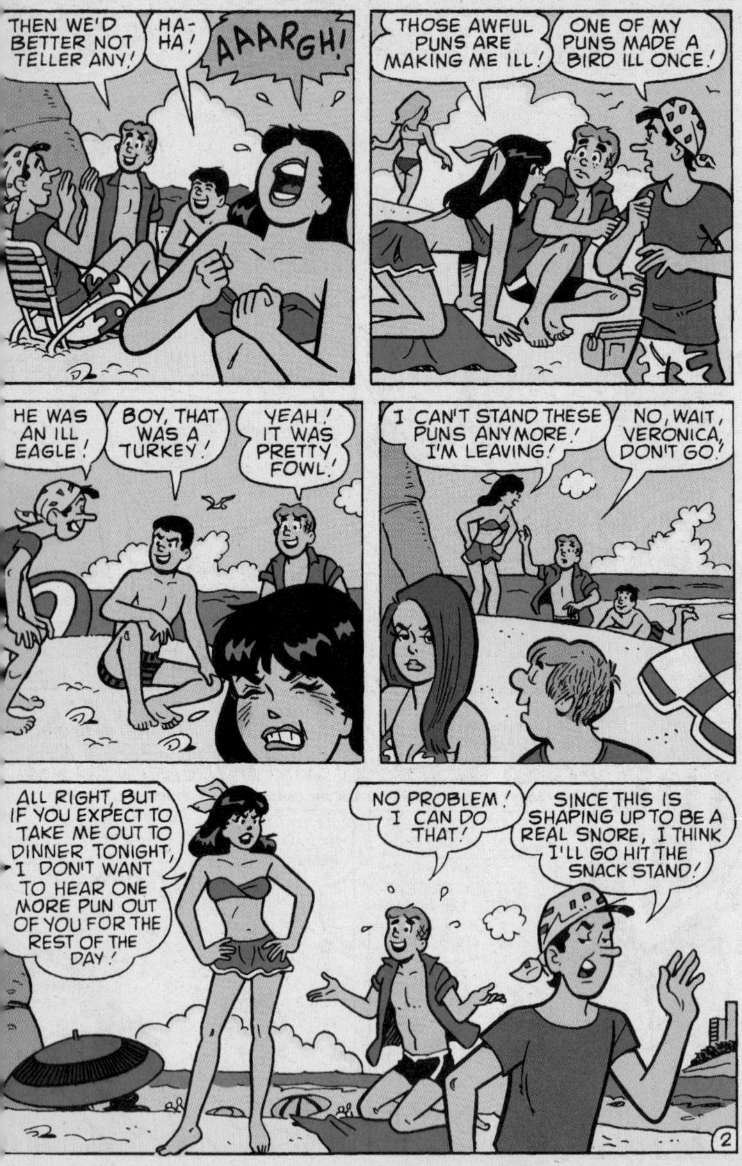
THEN WE'D BETTER NOT TELLER ANY!
HA-HA!
AAARGH!
THOSE AWFUL PUNS ARE MAKING ME ILL!
ONE OF MY PUNS MADE A BIRD ILL ONCE!
HE WAS AN ILL EAGLE!
BOY, THAT WAS A TURKEY!
YEAH! IT WAS PRETTY FOWL!
I CAN'T STAND THESE PUNS ANYMORE! I'M LEAVING!
NO, WAIT, VERONICA, DON'T GO!
ALL RIGHT, BUT IF YOU EXPECT TO TAKE ME OUT TO DINNER TONIGHT, I DON'T WANT TO HEAR ONE MORE PUN OUT OF YOU FOR THE REST OF THE DAY!
NO PROBLEM! I CAN DO THAT!
SINCE THIS IS SHAPING UP TO BE A REAL SNORE, I THINK I'LL GO HIT THE SNACK STAND!
2

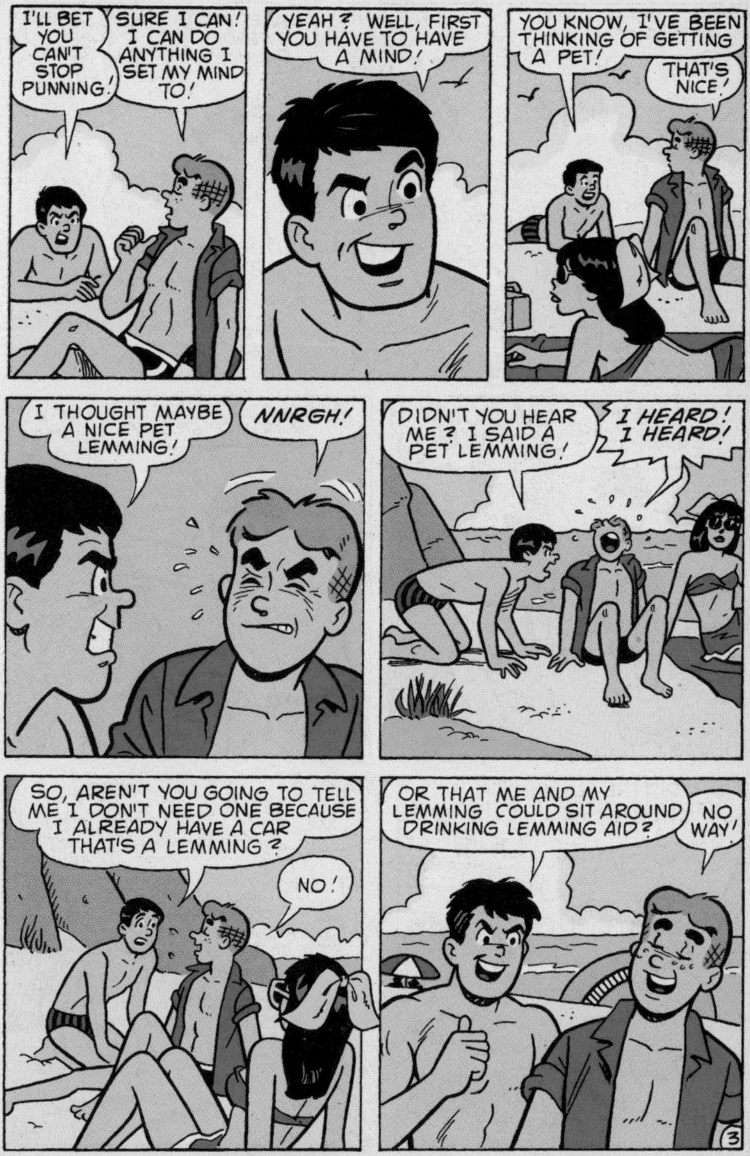
I'LL BET YOU CAN'T STOP PUNNING!
SURE I CAN! I CAN DO ANYTHING I SET MY MIND TO!
YEAH? WELL, FIRST YOU HAVE TO HAVE A MIND!
YOU KNOW, I'VE BEEN THINKING OF GETTING A PET!
THAT'S NICE!
I THOUGHT MAYBE A NICE PET LEMMING!
NNRGH!
DIDN'T YOU HEAR ME? I SAID A PET LEMMING!
I HEARD! I HEARD!
SO, AREN'T YOU GOING TO TELL ME I DON'T NEED ONE BECAUSE I ALREADY HAVE A CAR THAT'S A LEMMING?
NO!
OR THAT ME AND MY LEMMING COULD SIT AROUND DRINKING LEMMING AID?
NO WAY!
3

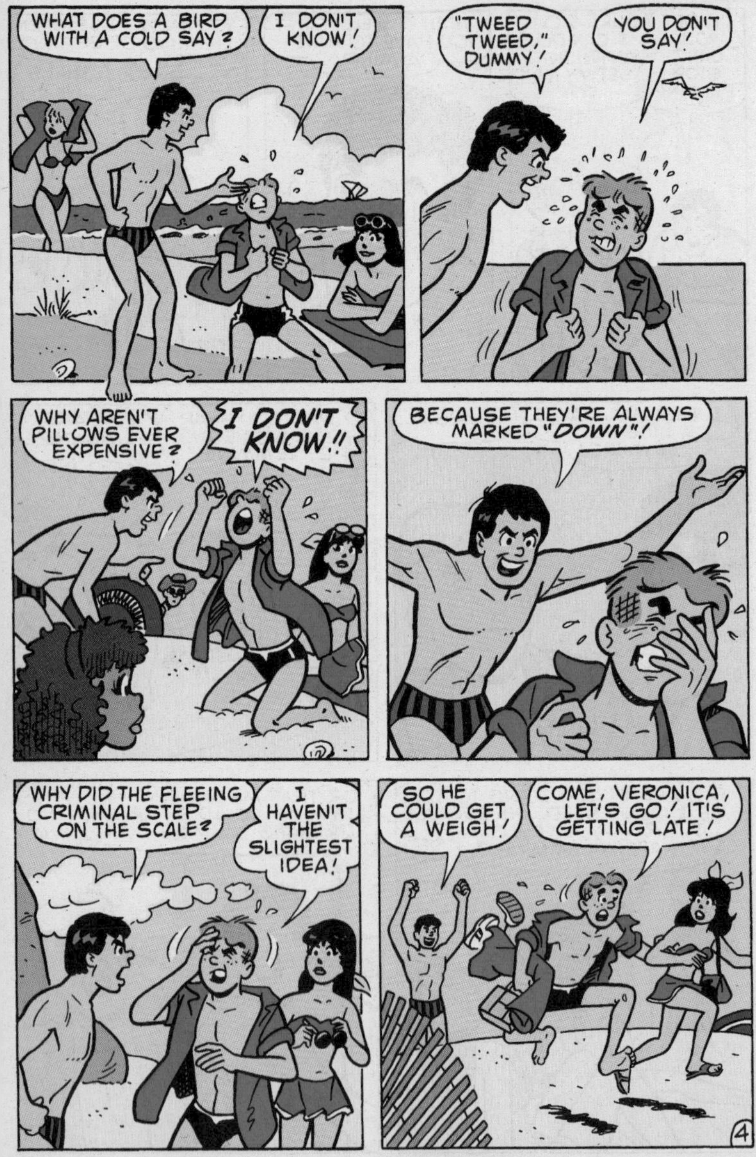

WHAT DOES A BIRD WITH A COLD SAY?
I DON'T KNOW!
"TWEED TWEED," DUMMY!
YOU DON'T SAY!
WHY AREN'T PILLOWS EVER EXPENSIVE?
I DON'T KNOW!!
BECAUSE THEY'RE ALWAYS MARKED "DOWN"!
WHY DID THE FLEEING CRIMINAL STEP ON THE SCALE?
I HAVEN'T THE SLIGHTEST IDEA!
SO HE COULD GET A WEIGH!
COME, VERONICA, LET'S GO! IT'S GETTING LATE!
4

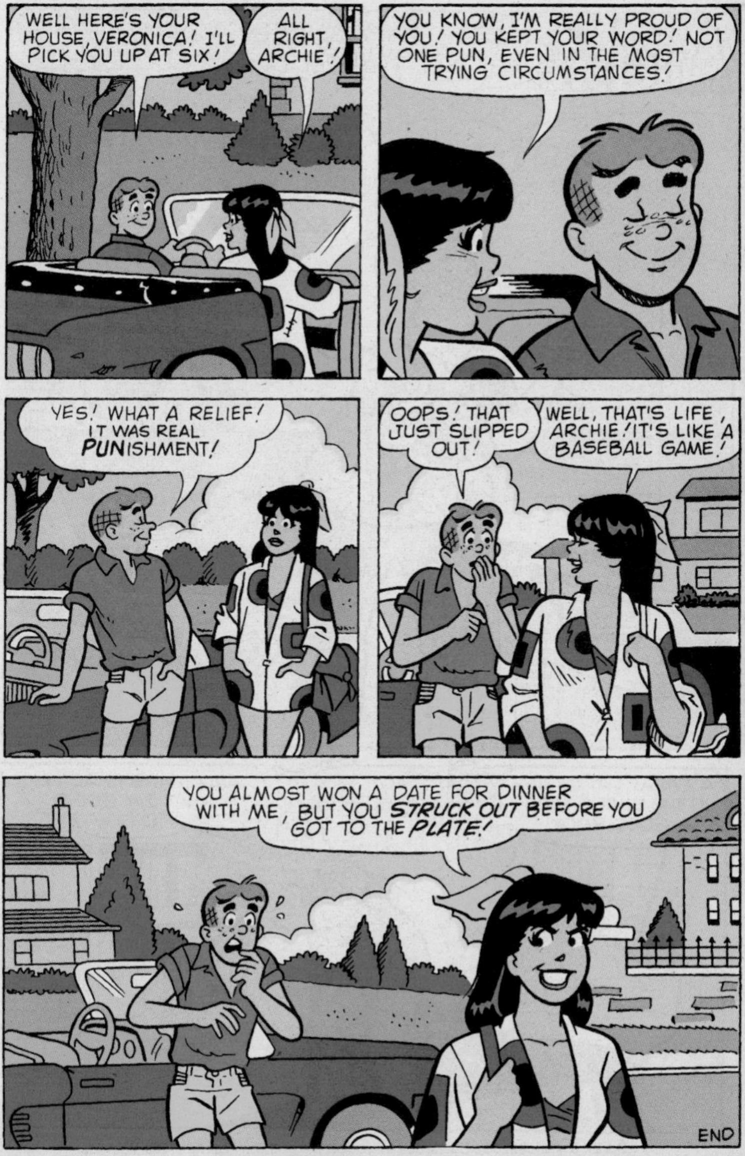
WELL HERE'S YOUR HOUSE, VERONICA! I'LL PICK YOU UP AT SIX!
ALL RIGHT, ARCHIE!
YOU KNOW, I'M REALLY PROUD OF YOU! YOU KEPT YOUR WORD! NOT ONE PUN, EVEN IN THE MOST TRYING CIRCUMSTANCES!
YES! WHAT A RELIEF! IT WAS REAL PUNISHMENT!
OOPS! THAT JUST SLIPPED OUT!
WELL, THAT'S LIFE, ARCHIE! IT'S LIKE A BASEBALL GAME!
YOU ALMOST WON A DATE FOR DINNER WITH ME, BUT YOU STRUCK OUT BEFORE YOU GOT TO THE PLATE!
END

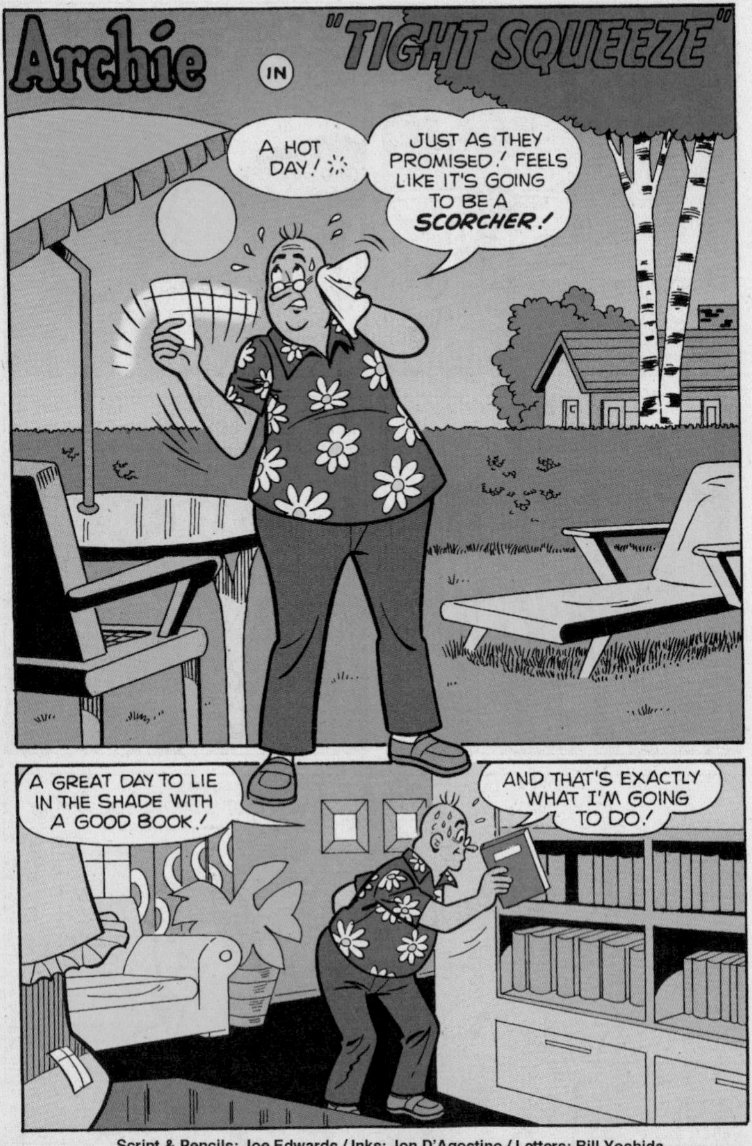
Archie IN "TIGHT SQUEEEZE"
A HOT DAY!
JUST AS THEY PROMISED! FEELS LIKE IT'S GOING TO BE A SCORCHER!
A GREAT DAY TO LIE IN THE SHADE WITH A GOOD BOOK!
AND THAT'S EXACTLY WHAT I'M GOING TO DO!

Script & Pencils: Joe Edwards / Inks: Jon D'Agostino / Letters: Bill Yoshida

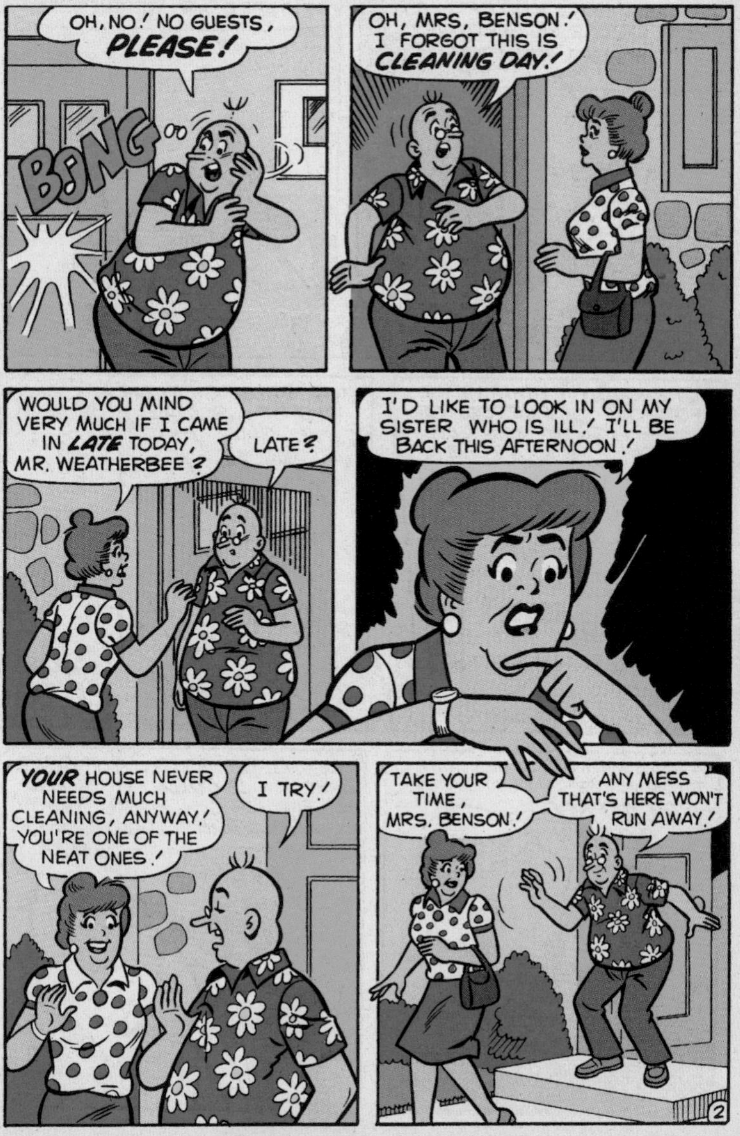
OH, NO! NO GUESTS, PLEASE!
BONG
OH, MRS, BENSON! I FORGOT THIS IS CLEANING DAY!
WOULD YOU MIND VERY MUCH IF I CAME IN LATE TODAY, MR. WEATHERBEE?
LATE?
I'D LIKE TO LOOK IN ON MY SISTER WHO IS ILL! I'LL BE BACK THIS AFTERNOON!
YOUR HOUSE NEVER NEEDS MUCH CLEANING, ANYWAY! YOU'RE ONE OF THE NEAT ONES!
I TRY!
TAKE YOUR TIME, MRS. BENSON!
ANY MESS THAT'S HERE WON'T RUN AWAY!
2

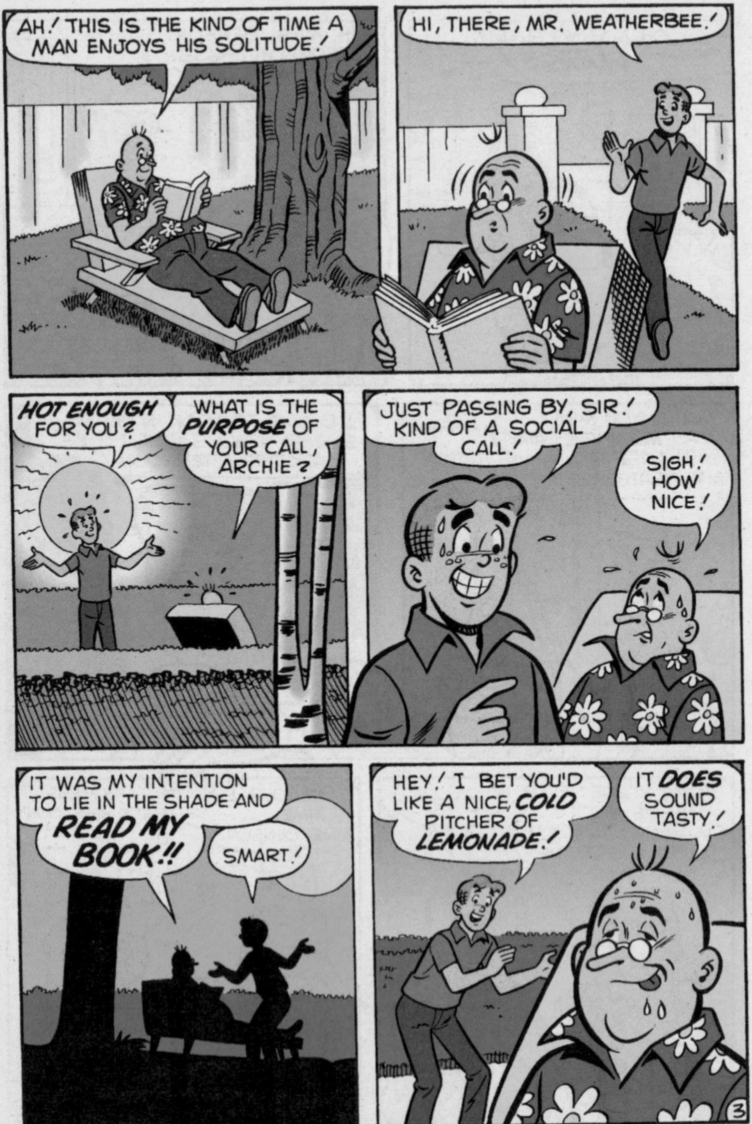
AH! THIS IS THE KIND OF TIME A MAN ENJOYS HIS SOLITUDE!
HI, THERE, MR. WEATHERBEE!
HOT ENOUGH FOR YOU?
WHAT IS THE PURPOSE OF YOUR CALL, ARCHIE?
JUST PASSING BY, SIR! KIND OF A SOCIAL CALL!
SIGH! HOW NICE!
IT WAS MY INTENTION TO LIE IN THE SHADE AND READ MY BOOK!!
SMART!
HEY! I BET YOU'D LIKE A NICE, COLD PITCHER OF LEMONADE!
IT DOES SOUND TASTY!
3

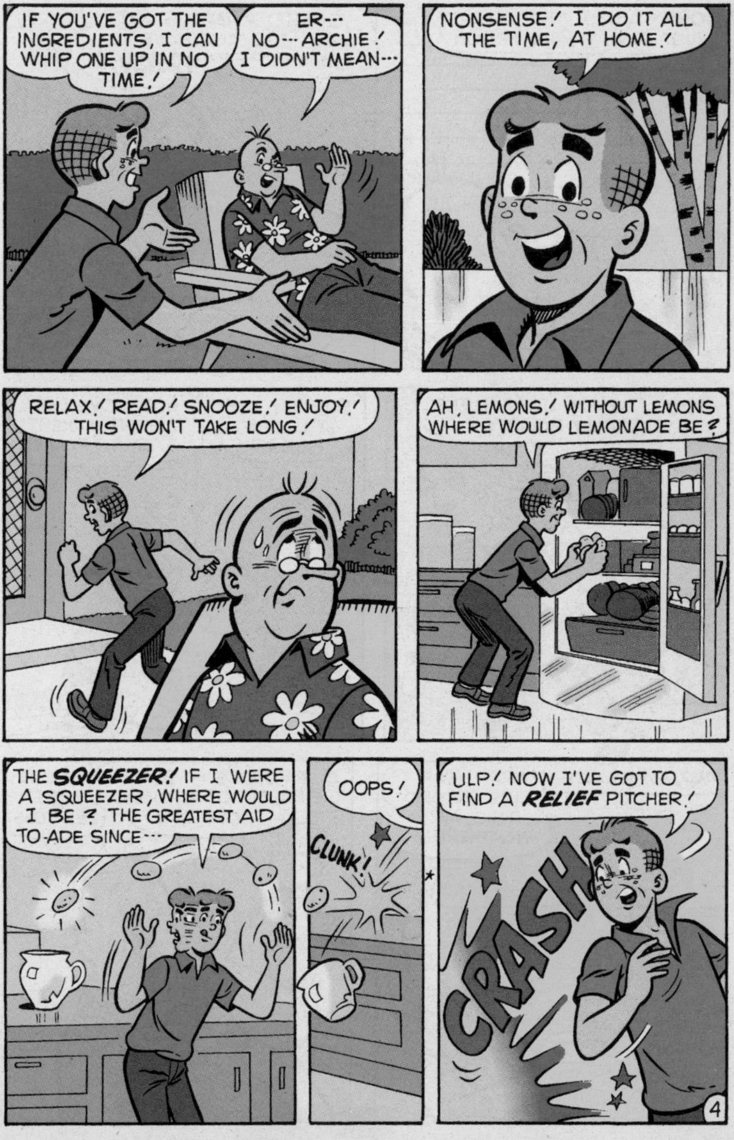

IF YOU'VE GOT THE INGREDIENTS, I CAN WHIP ONE UP IN NO TIME!
ER--- NO--- ARCHIE! I DIDN'T MEAN---
NONSENSE! I DO IT ALL THE TIME, AT HOME!
RELAX! READ! SNOOZE! ENJOY! THIS WON'T TAKE LONG!
AH, LEMONS! WITHOUT LEMONS WHERE WOULD LEMONADE BE?
THE **SQUEEZER!** IF I WERE A SQUEEZER, WHERE WOULD I BE? THE GREATEST AID TO-ADE SINCE---
OOPS!
CLUNK!
ULP! NOW I'VE GOT TO FIND A **RELIEF** PITCHER!
CRASH
4

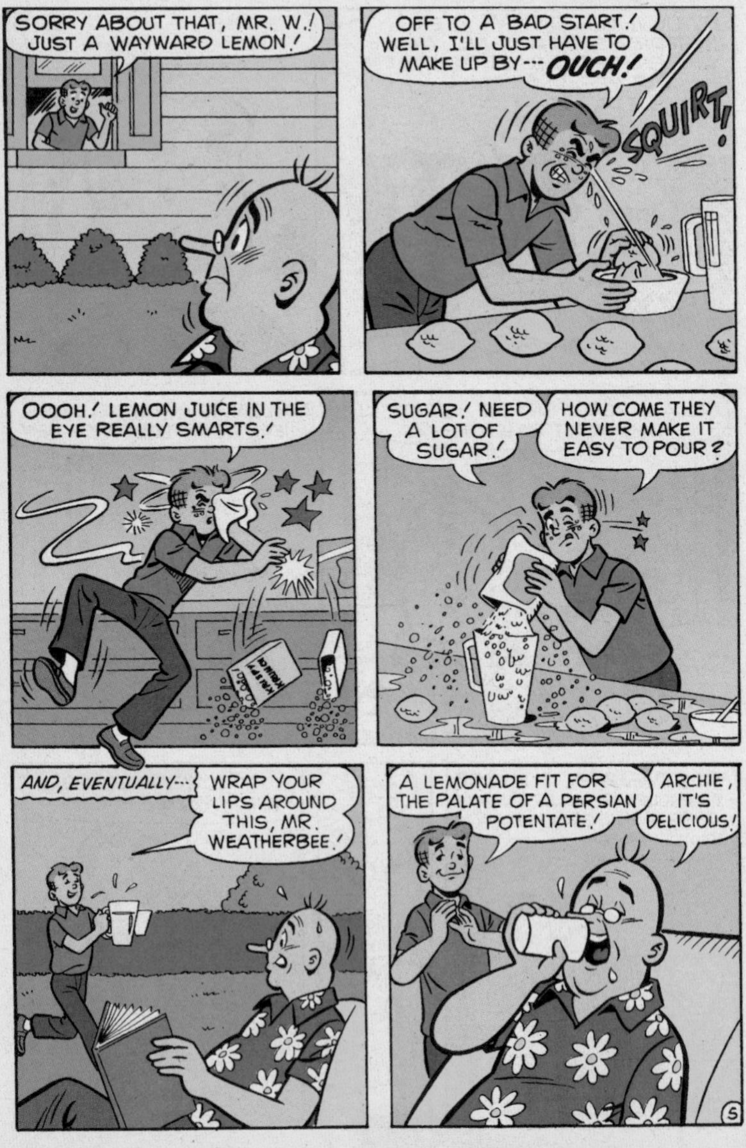
SORRY ABOUT THAT, MR. W.! JUST A WAYWARD LEMON!
OFF TO A BAD START! WELL, I'LL JUST HAVE TO MAKE UP BY--- OUCH!
SQUIRT!
OOOH! LEMON JUICE IN THE EYE REALLY SMARTS!
SUGAR! NEED A LOT OF SUGAR!
HOW COME THEY NEVER MAKE IT EASY TO POUR?
AND, EVENTUALLY...
WRAP YOUR LIPS AROUND THIS, MR. WEATHERBEE!
A LEMONADE FIT FOR THE PALATE OF A PERSIAN POTENTATE!
ARCHIE, IT'S DELICIOUS!

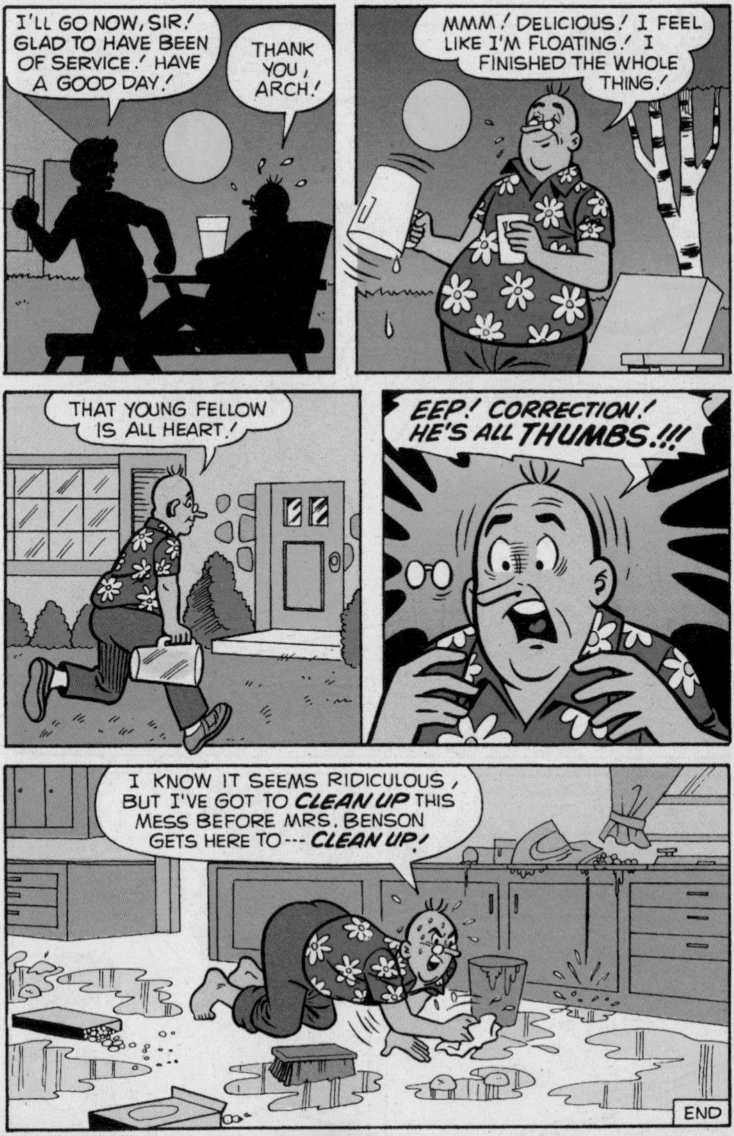
I'LL GO NOW, SIR! GLAD TO HAVE BEEN OF SERVICE! HAVE A GOOD DAY!
THANK YOU, ARCH!
MMM! DELICIOUS! I FEEL LIKE I'M FLOATING! I FINISHED THE WHOLE THING!
THAT YOUNG FELLOW IS ALL HEART!
EEP! CORRECTION! HE'S ALL THUMBS!!!
I KNOW IT SEEMS RIDICULOUS, BUT I'VE GOT TO CLEAN UP THIS MESS BEFORE MRS. BENSON GETS HERE TO--- CLEAN UP!
END

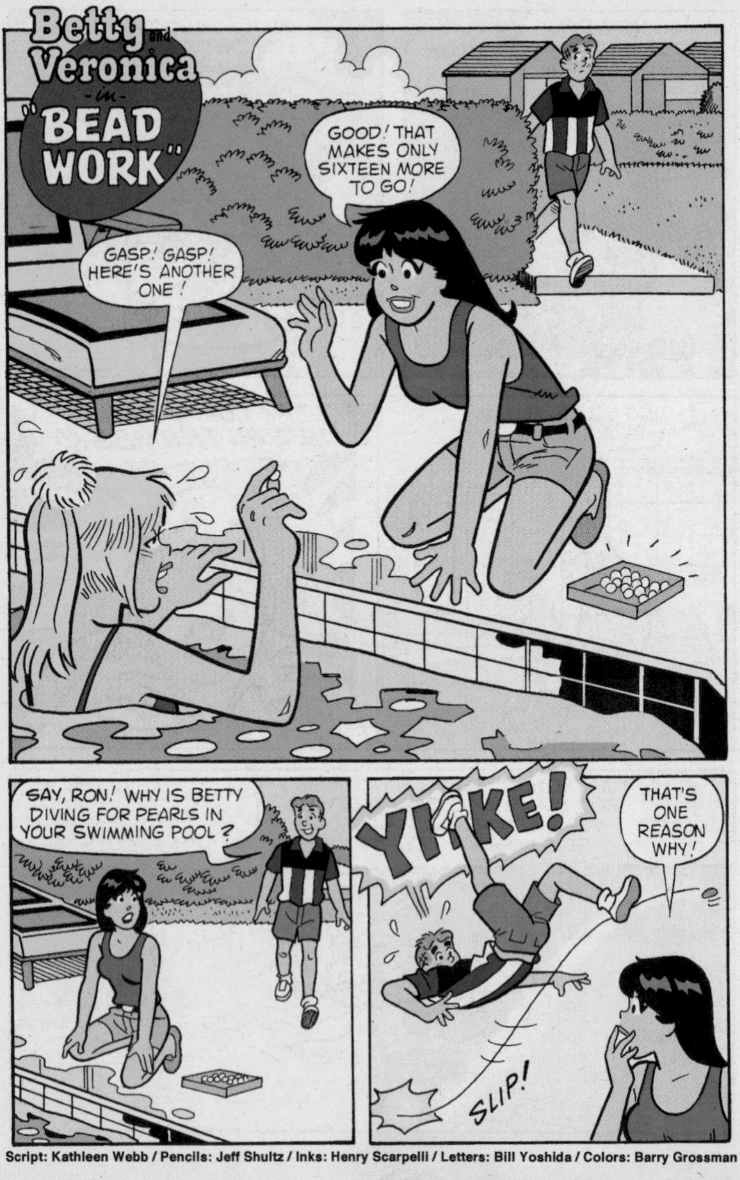
Betty and Veronica
-in-
"BEAD WORK"
GOOD! THAT MAKES ONLY SIXTEEN MORE TO GO!
GASP! GASP! HERE'S ANOTHER ONE!
SAY, RON! WHY IS BETTY DIVING FOR PEARLS IN YOUR SWIMMING POOL?
YIKE!
THAT'S ONE REASON WHY!
SLIP!

Script: Kathleen Webb / Pencils: Jeff Shultz / Inks: Henry Scarpelli / Letters: Bill Yoshida / Colors: Barry Grossman

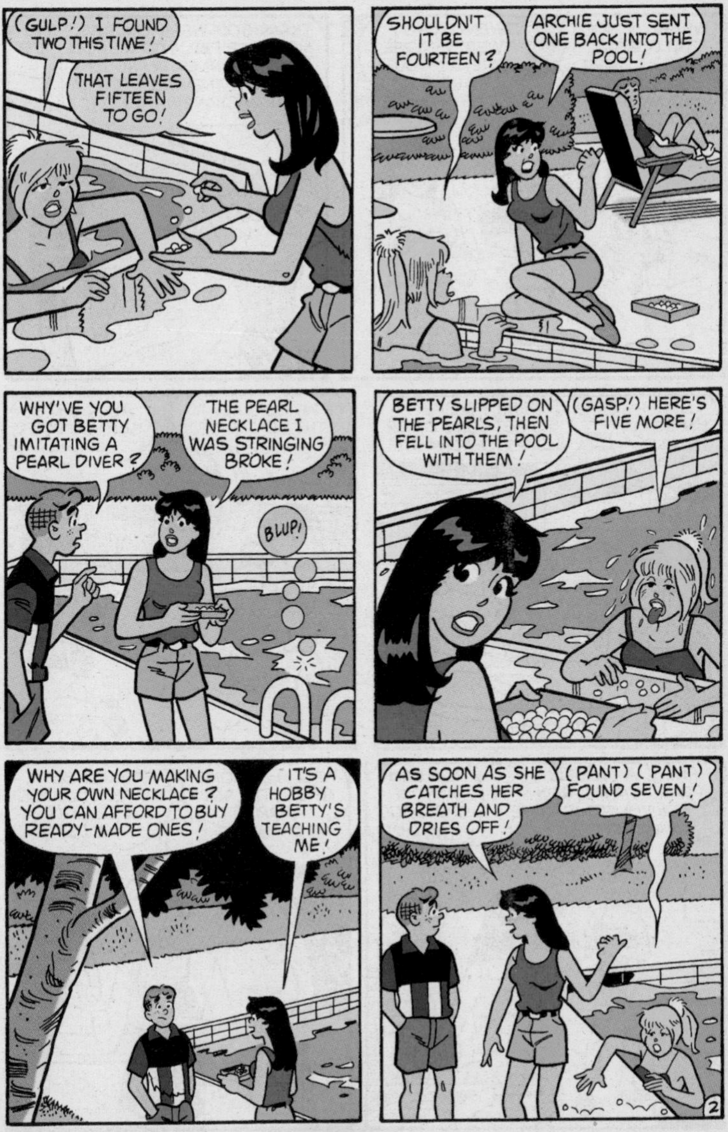
(GULP!) I FOUND TWO THIS TIME!
THAT LEAVES FIFTEEN TO GO!
SHOULDN'T IT BE FOURTEEN?
ARCHIE JUST SENT ONE BACK INTO THE POOL!
WHY'VE YOU GOT BETTY IMITATING A PEARL DIVER?
THE PEARL NECKLACE I WAS STRINGING BROKE!
BLUP!
BETTY SLIPPED ON THE PEARLS, THEN FELL INTO THE POOL WITH THEM!
(GASP!) HERE'S FIVE MORE!
WHY ARE YOU MAKING YOUR OWN NECKLACE? YOU CAN AFFORD TO BUY READY-MADE ONES!
IT'S A HOBBY BETTY'S TEACHING ME!
AS SOON AS SHE CATCHES HER BREATH AND DRIES OFF!
(PANT) (PANT) FOUND SEVEN!
2

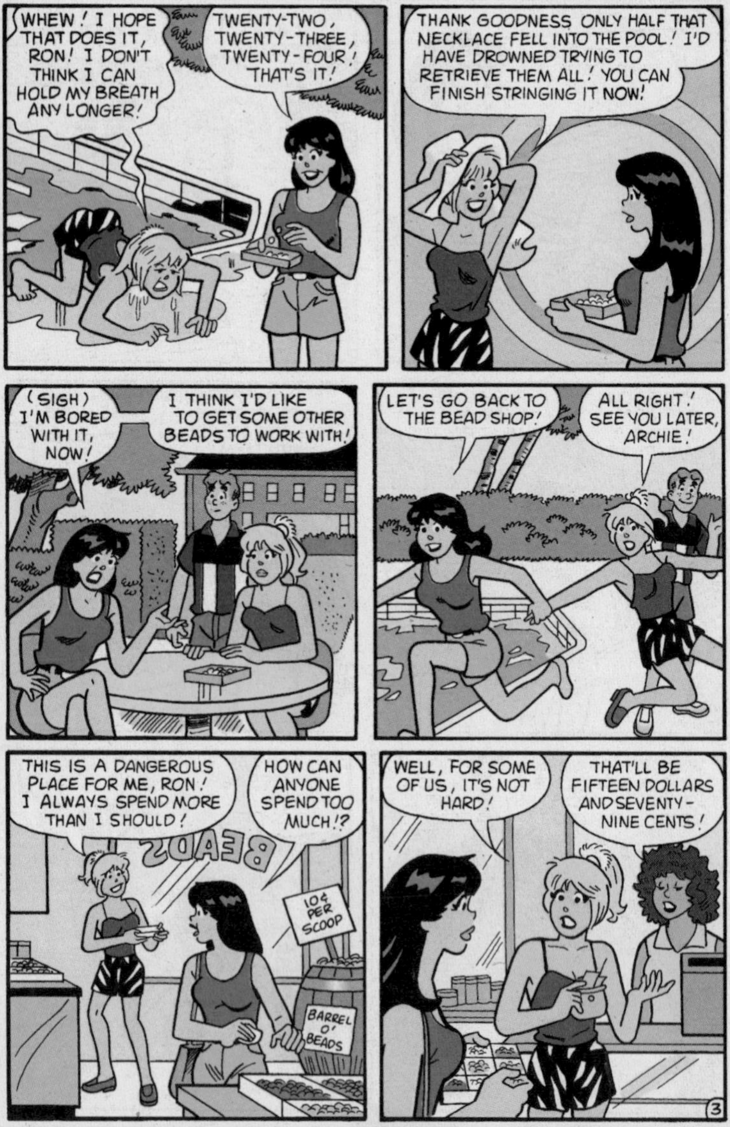
WHEW! I HOPE THAT DOES IT, RON! I DON'T THINK I CAN HOLD MY BREATH ANY LONGER!
TWENTY-TWO, TWENTY-THREE, TWENTY-FOUR! THAT'S IT!
THANK GOODNESS ONLY HALF THAT NECKLACE FELL INTO THE POOL! I'D HAVE DROWNED TRYING TO RETRIEVE THEM ALL! YOU CAN FINISH STRINGING IT NOW!
(SIGH) I'M BORED WITH IT, NOW!
I THINK I'D LIKE TO GET SOME OTHER BEADS TO WORK WITH!
LET'S GO BACK TO THE BEAD SHOP!
ALL RIGHT! SEE YOU LATER, ARCHIE!
THIS IS A DANGEROUS PLACE FOR ME, RON! I ALWAYS SPEND MORE THAN I SHOULD!
HOW CAN ANYONE SPEND TOO MUCH!?
BEADS
10¢ PER SCOOP
BARREL O' BEADS
WELL, FOR SOME OF US, IT'S NOT HARD!
THAT'LL BE FIFTEEN DOLLARS AND SEVENTY-NINE CENTS!
3

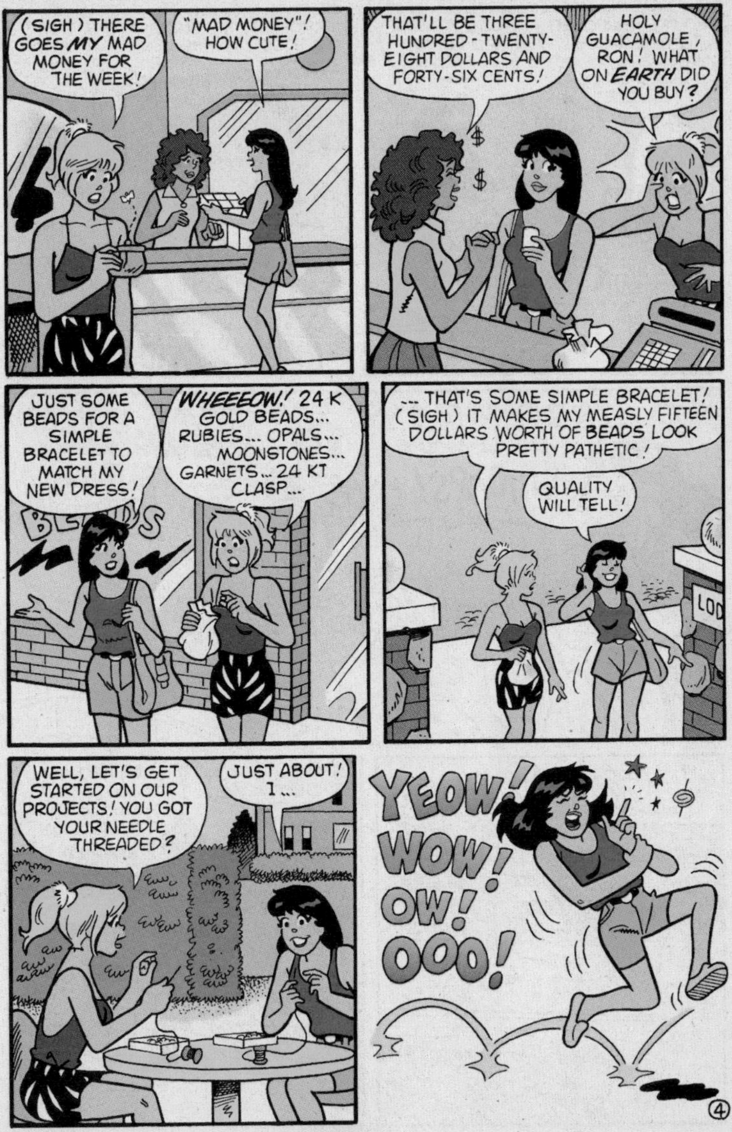
(SIGH) THERE GOES MY MAD MONEY FOR THE WEEK!
"MAD MONEY"! HOW CUTE!
THAT'LL BE THREE HUNDRED-TWENTY-EIGHT DOLLARS AND FORTY-SIX CENTS!
$
$
HOLY GUACAMOLE, RON! WHAT ON EARTH DID YOU BUY?
JUST SOME BEADS FOR A SIMPLE BRACELET TO MATCH MY NEW DRESS!
WHEEEOW! 24 K GOLD BEADS... RUBIES... OPALS... MOONSTONES... GARNETS... 24 KT CLASP...
BEADS
... THAT'S SOME SIMPLE BRACELET! (SIGH) IT MAKES MY MEASLY FIFTEEN DOLLARS WORTH OF BEADS LOOK PRETTY PATHETIC!
QUALITY WILL TELL!
LOD
WELL, LET'S GET STARTED ON OUR PROJECTS! YOU GOT YOUR NEEDLE THREADED?
JUST ABOUT! I...
YEOW! WOW! OW! OOO!
4

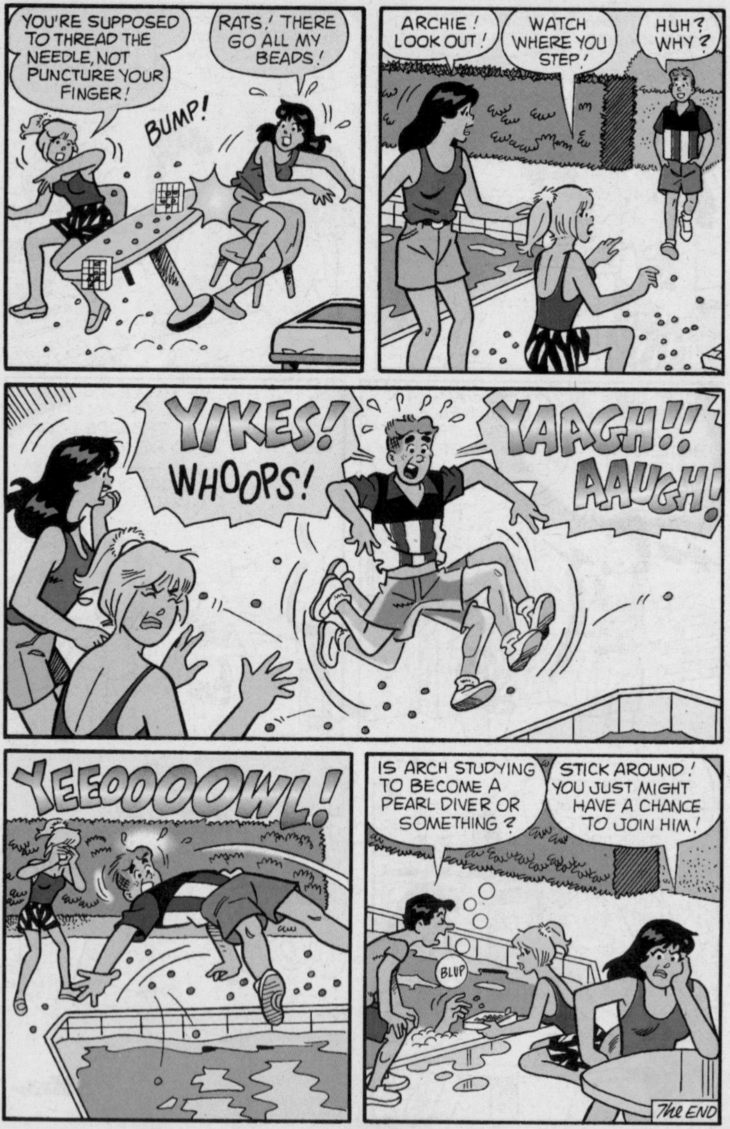
YOU'RE SUPPOSED TO THREAD THE NEEDLE, NOT PUNCTURE YOUR FINGER!
RATS! THERE GO ALL MY BEADS!
BUMP!
ARCHIE! LOOK OUT!
WATCH WHERE YOU STEP!
HUH? WHY?
YIKES!
WHOOPS!
YAAGH!!
AAUGH!
YEEOOOOOWL!
IS ARCH STUDYING TO BECOME A PEARL DIVER OR SOMETHING?
STICK AROUND! YOU JUST MIGHT HAVE A CHANCE TO JOIN HIM!
BLUP
The END

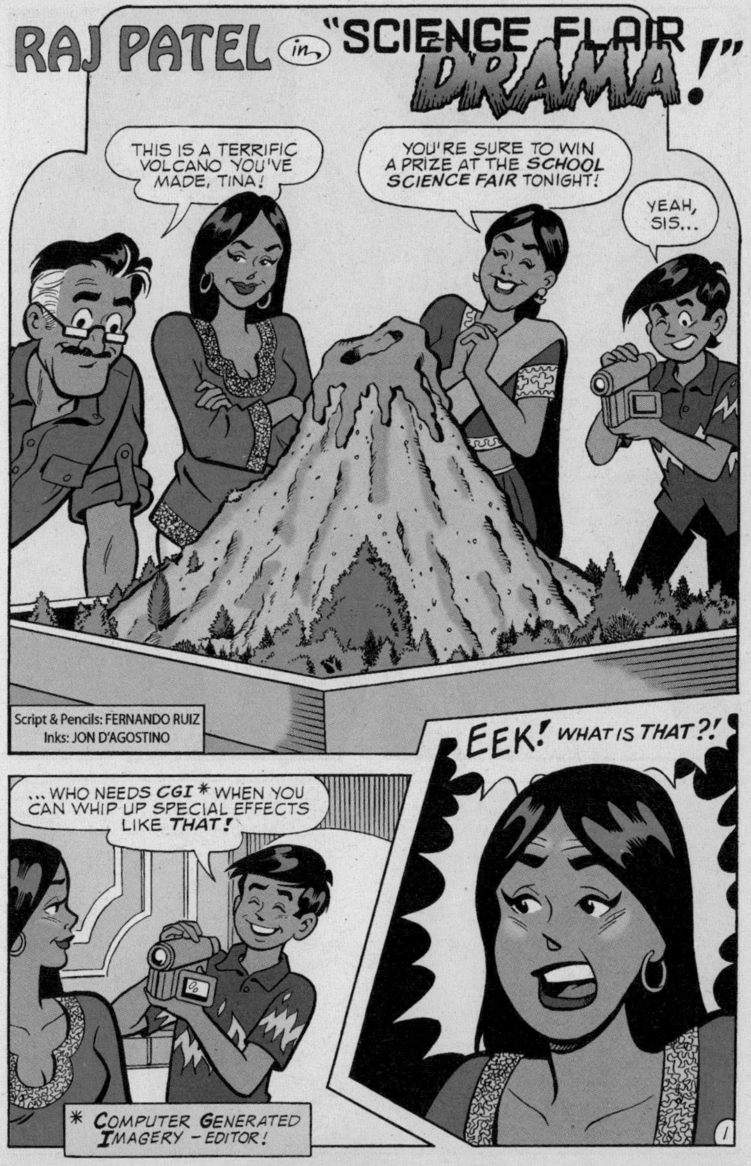
RAJ PATEL in "SCIENCE FLAIR DRAMA!"
THIS IS A TERRIFIC VOLCANO YOU'VE MADE, TINA!
YOU'RE SURE TO WIN A PRIZE AT THE SCHOOL SCIENCE FAIR TONIGHT!
YEAH, SIS...
Script & Pencils: FERNANDO RUIZ
Inks: JON D'AGOSTINO
...WHO NEEDS CGI* WHEN YOU CAN WHIP UP SPECIAL EFFECTS LIKE THAT!
* COMPUTER GENERATED IMAGERY - EDITOR!
EEK! WHAT IS THAT?!
1

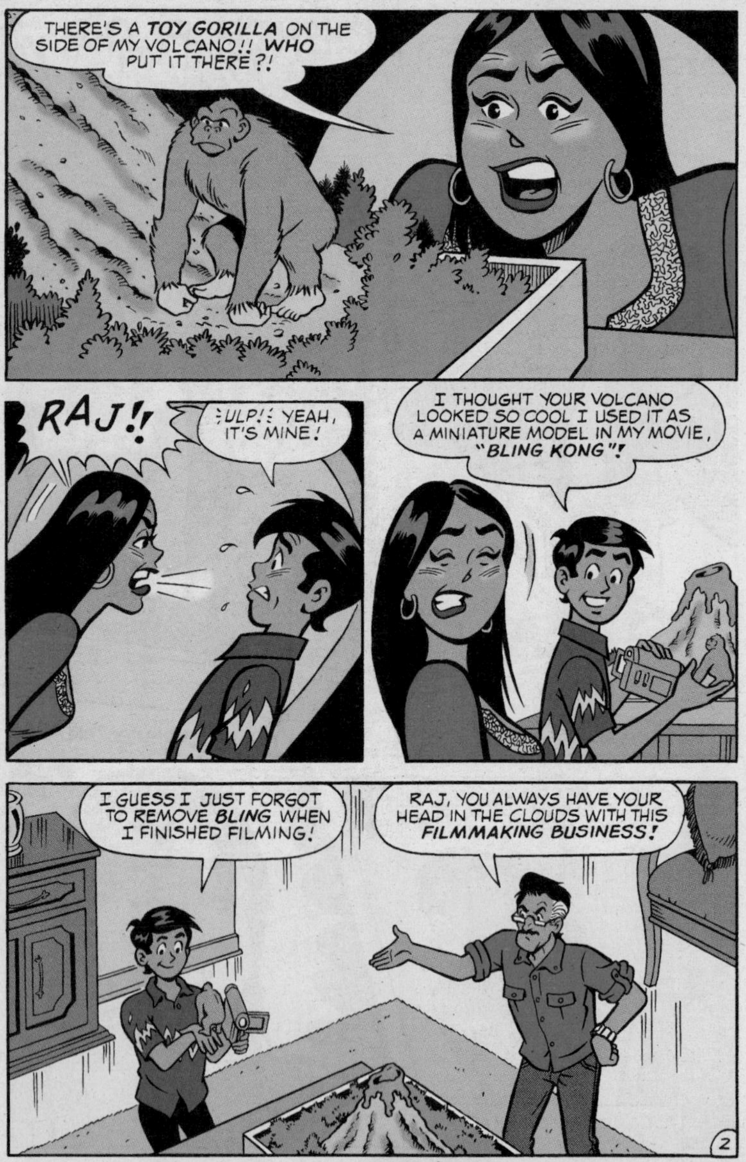
THERE'S A TOY GORILLA ON THE SIDE OF MY VOLCANO!! WHO PUT IT THERE?!
RAJ!!
ULP!! YEAH, IT'S MINE!
I THOUGHT YOUR VOLCANO LOOKED SO COOL I USED IT AS A MINIATURE MODEL IN MY MOVIE, "BLING KONG"!
I GUESS I JUST FORGOT TO REMOVE BLING WHEN I FINISHED FILMING!
RAJ, YOU ALWAYS HAVE YOUR HEAD IN THE CLOUDS WITH THIS FILMMAKING BUSINESS!
2

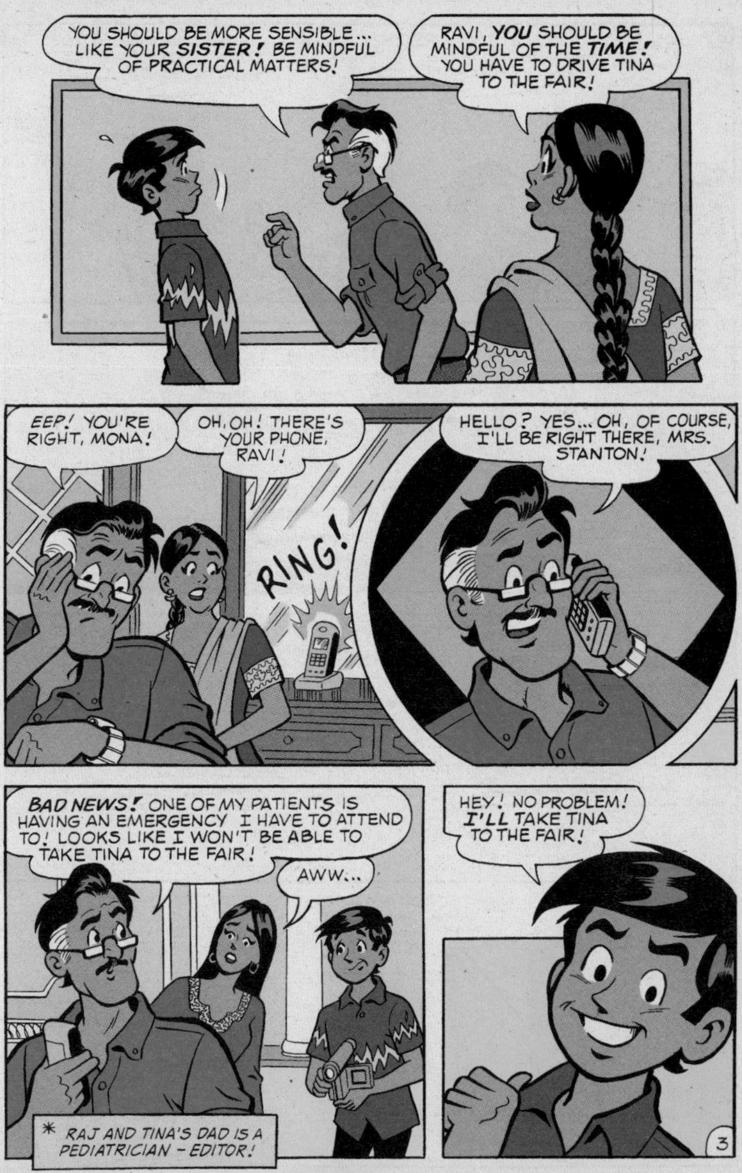
YOU SHOULD BE MORE SENSIBLE... LIKE YOUR SISTER! BE MINDFUL OF PRACTICAL MATTERS!
RAVI, YOU SHOULD BE MINDFUL OF THE TIME! YOU HAVE TO DRIVE TINA TO THE FAIR!
EEP! YOU'RE RIGHT, MONA!
OH, OH! THERE'S YOUR PHONE, RAVI!
RING!
HELLO? YES... OH, OF COURSE, I'LL BE RIGHT THERE, MRS. STANTON!
BAD NEWS!* ONE OF MY PATIENTS IS HAVING AN EMERGENCY I HAVE TO ATTEND TO! LOOKS LIKE I WON'T BE ABLE TO TAKE TINA TO THE FAIR!
AWW...
* RAJ AND TINA'S DAD IS A PEDIATRICIAN – EDITOR!
HEY! NO PROBLEM! I'LL TAKE TINA TO THE FAIR!
3

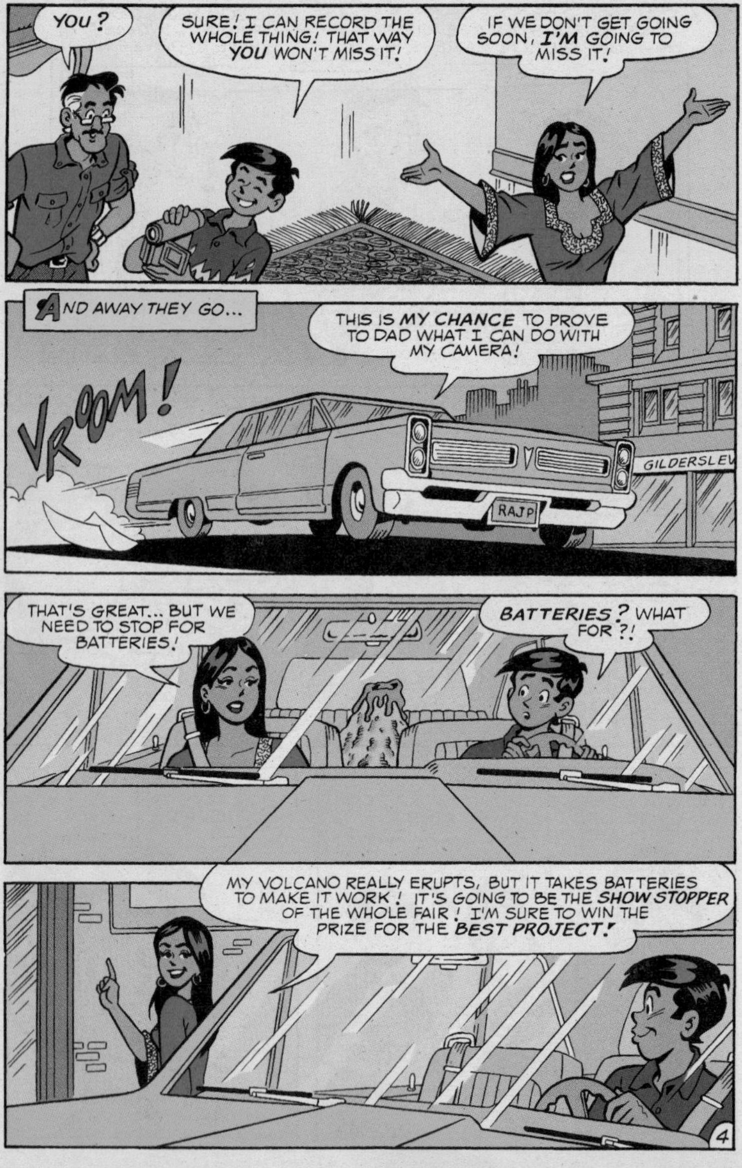
YOU?
SURE! I CAN RECORD THE WHOLE THING! THAT WAY YOU WON'T MISS IT!
IF WE DON'T GET GOING SOON, I'M GOING TO MISS IT!
AND AWAY THEY GO...
THIS IS MY CHANCE TO PROVE TO DAD WHAT I CAN DO WITH MY CAMERA!
VROOM!
GILDERSLEV
RAJP
THAT'S GREAT... BUT WE NEED TO STOP FOR BATTERIES!
BATTERIES? WHAT FOR?!
MY VOLCANO REALLY ERUPTS, BUT IT TAKES BATTERIES TO MAKE IT WORK! IT'S GOING TO BE THE SHOW STOPPER OF THE WHOLE FAIR! I'M SURE TO WIN THE PRIZE FOR THE BEST PROJECT!

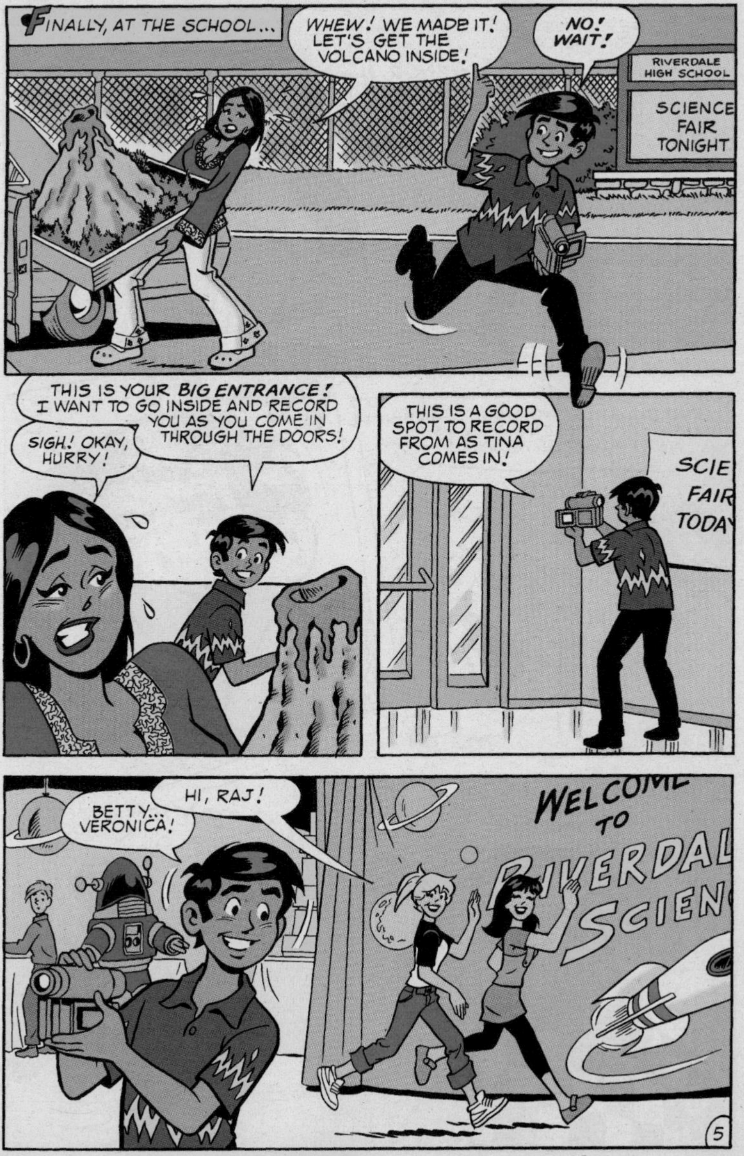
FINALLY, AT THE SCHOOL...
WHEW! WE MADE IT! LET'S GET THE VOLCANO INSIDE!
NO! WAIT!
RIVERDALE HIGH SCHOOL
SCIENCE FAIR TONIGHT
THIS IS YOUR BIG ENTRANCE! I WANT TO GO INSIDE AND RECORD YOU AS YOU COME IN THROUGH THE DOORS!
SIGH! OKAY, HURRY!
THIS IS A GOOD SPOT TO RECORD FROM AS TINA COMES IN!
SCIE FAIR TODAY
BETTY... VERONICA!
HI, RAJ!
WELCOME TO RIVERDAL SCIEN

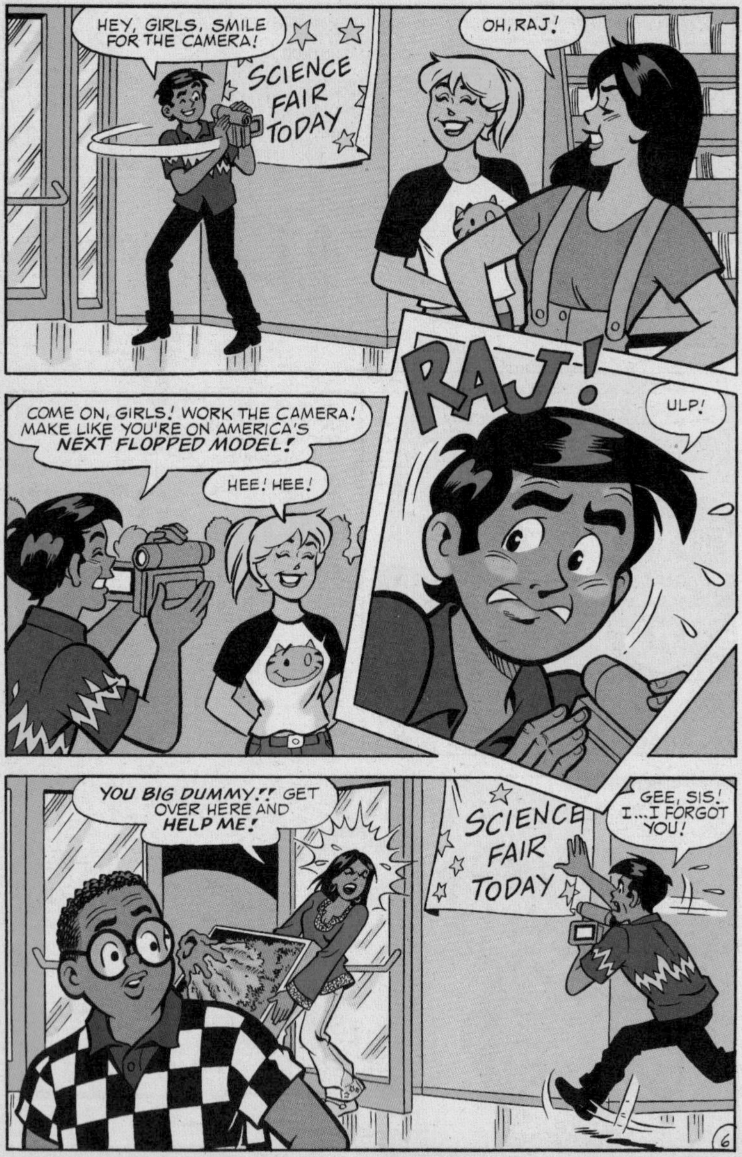
HEY, GIRLS, SMILE FOR THE CAMERA!
SCIENCE FAIR TODAY
OH, RAJ!
RAJ!
COME ON, GIRLS! WORK THE CAMERA! MAKE LIKE YOU'RE ON AMERICA'S NEXT FLOPPED MODEL!
HEE! HEE!
ULP!
YOU BIG DUMMY!?! GET OVER HERE AND HELP ME!
SCIENCE FAIR TODAY
GEE, SIS! I...I FORGOT YOU!

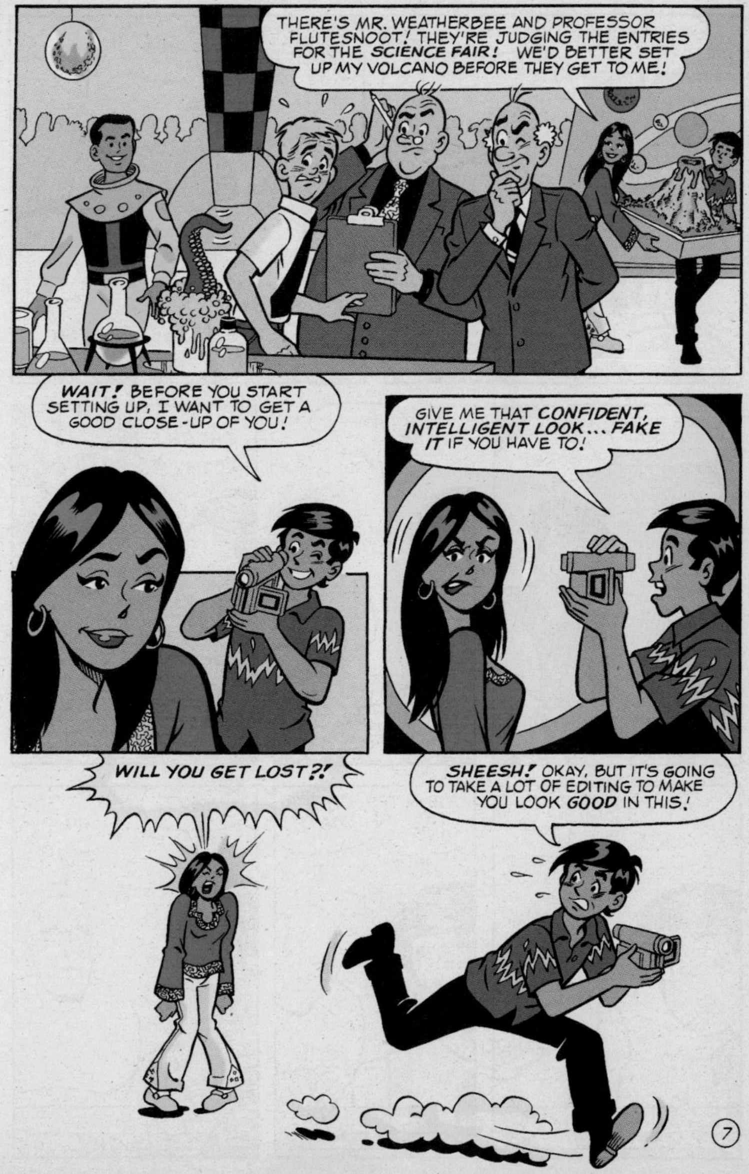
THERE'S MR. WEATHERBEE AND PROFESSOR FLUTESNOOT! THEY'RE JUDGING THE ENTRIES FOR THE SCIENCE FAIR! WE'D BETTER SET UP MY VOLCANO BEFORE THEY GET TO ME!
WAIT! BEFORE YOU START SETTING UP, I WANT TO GET A GOOD CLOSE-UP OF YOU!
GIVE ME THAT CONFIDENT, INTELLIGENT LOOK... FAKE IT IF YOU HAVE TO!
WILL YOU GET LOST?!
SHEESH! OKAY, BUT IT'S GOING TO TAKE A LOT OF EDITING TO MAKE YOU LOOK GOOD IN THIS!

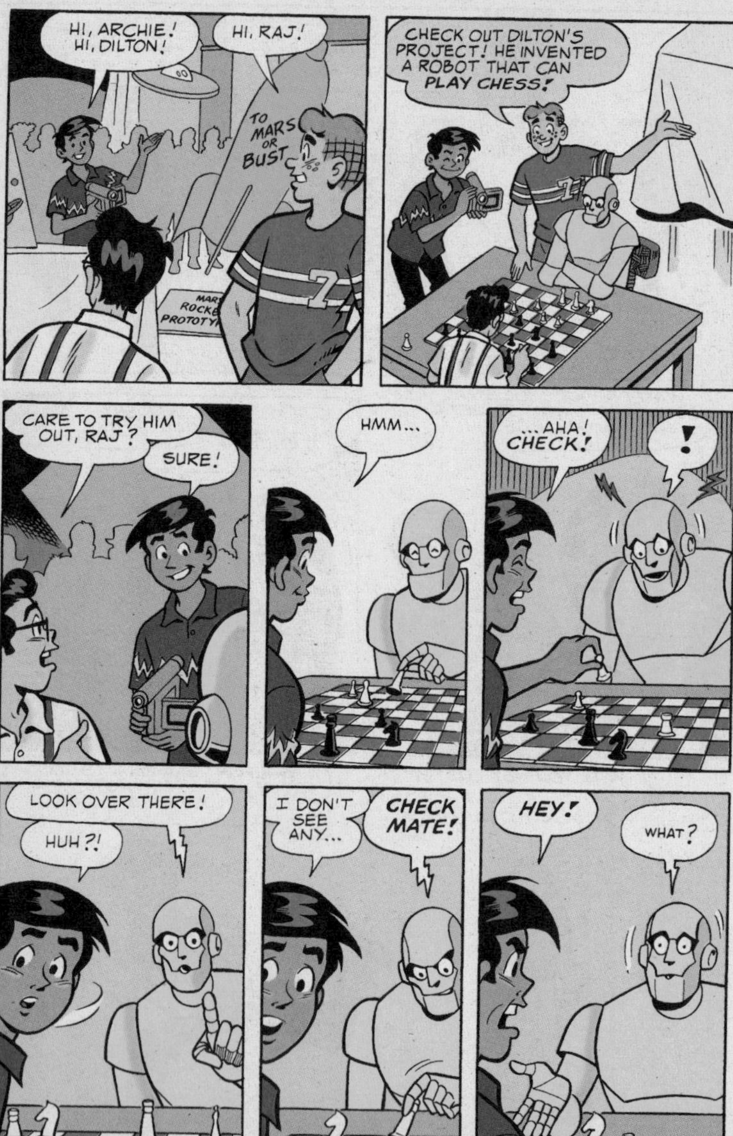
HI, ARCHIE! HI, DILTON!
HI, RAJ!
TO MARS OR BUST
CHECK OUT DILTON'S PROJECT! HE INVENTED A ROBOT THAT CAN PLAY CHESS!
CARE TO TRY HIM OUT, RAJ?
SURE!
HMM...
...AHA! CHECK!
!
LOOK OVER THERE!
HUH?!
I DON'T SEE ANY...
CHECK MATE!
HEY!
WHAT?
8

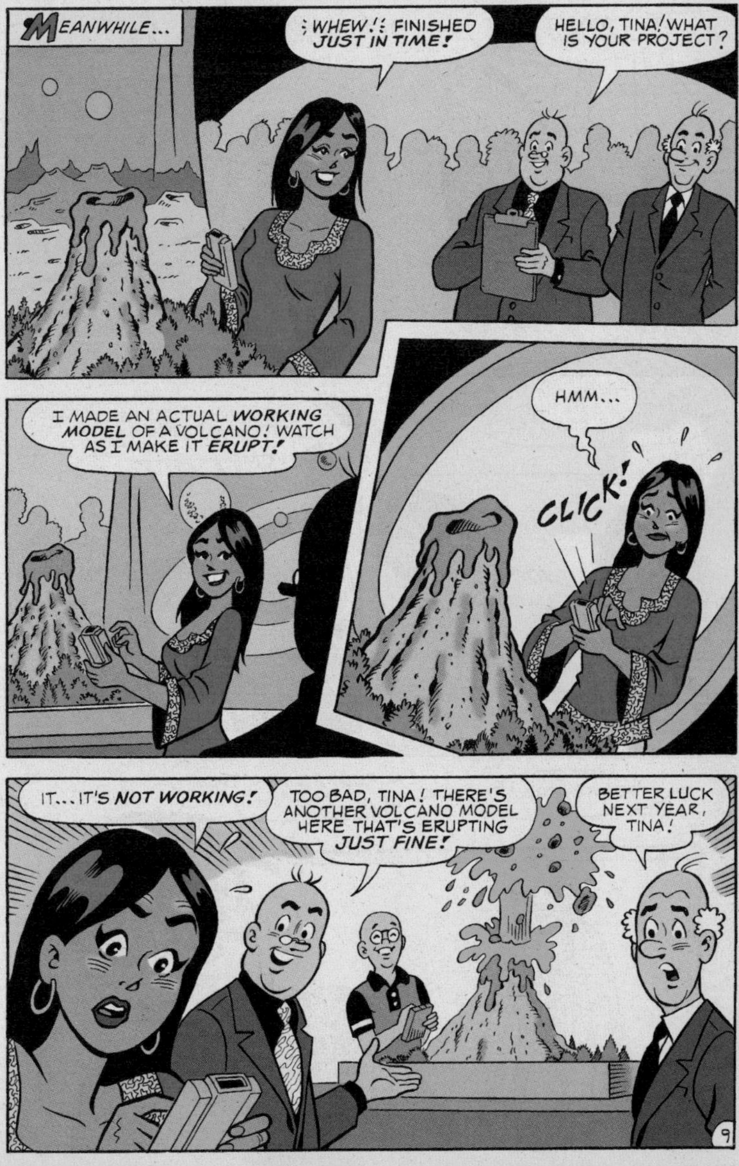
MEANWHILE...
WHEW! FINISHED JUST IN TIME!
HELLO, TINA! WHAT IS YOUR PROJECT?
I MADE AN ACTUAL WORKING MODEL OF A VOLCANO! WATCH AS I MAKE IT ERUPT!
HMM...
CLICK!
IT... IT'S NOT WORKING!
TOO BAD, TINA! THERE'S ANOTHER VOLCANO MODEL HERE THAT'S ERUPTING JUST FINE!
BETTER LUCK NEXT YEAR, TINA!
9

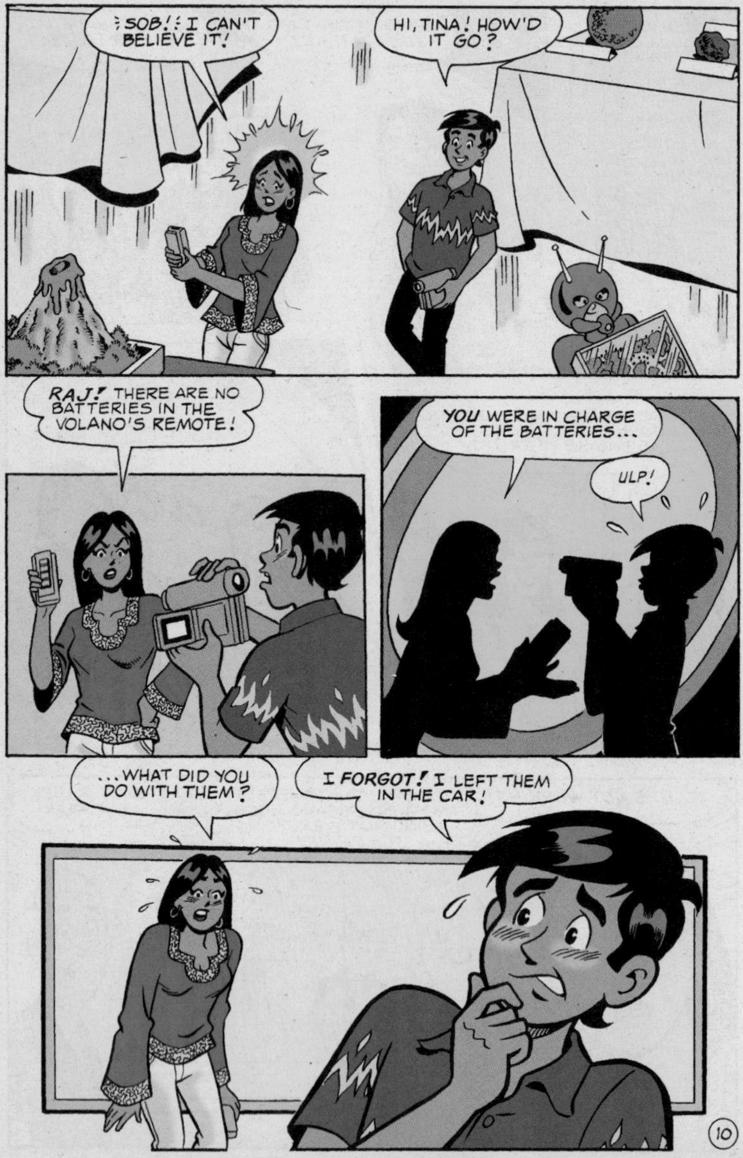

SOB! I CAN'T BELIEVE IT!
HI, TINA! HOW'D IT GO?
RAJ! THERE ARE NO BATTERIES IN THE VOLANO'S REMOTE!
YOU WERE IN CHARGE OF THE BATTERIES...
ULP!
...WHAT DID YOU DO WITH THEM?
I FORGOT! I LEFT THEM IN THE CAR!

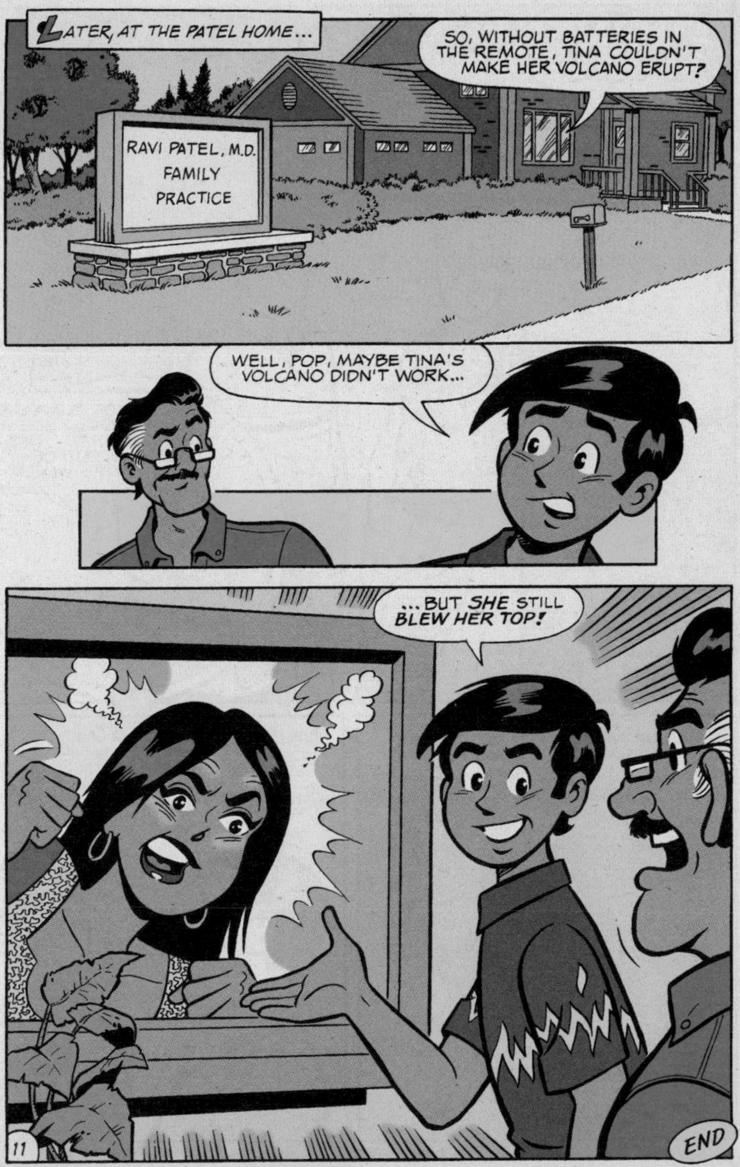
LATER, AT THE PATEL HOME...
SO, WITHOUT BATTERIES IN THE REMOTE, TINA COULDN'T MAKE HER VOLCANO ERUPT?
RAVI PATEL, M.D. FAMILY PRACTICE
WELL, POP, MAYBE TINA'S VOLCANO DIDN'T WORK...
...BUT SHE STILL BLEW HER TOP!
11
END

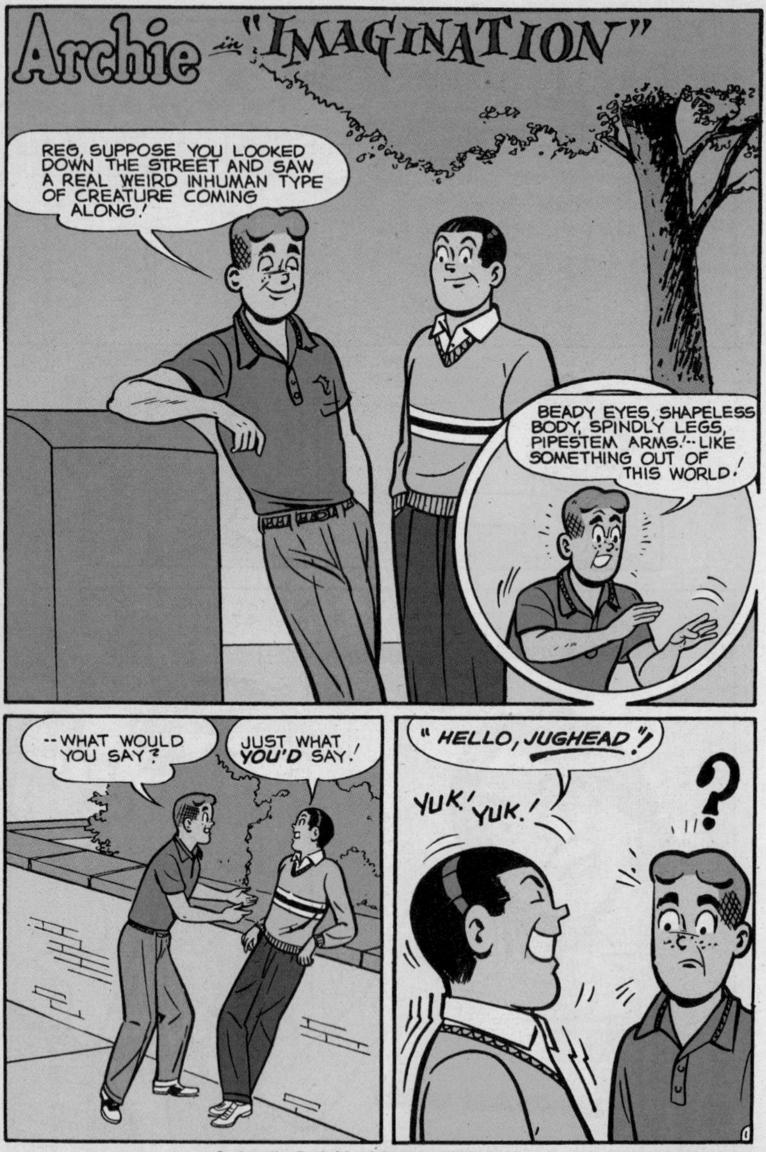
Archie in "IMAGINATION"
REG, SUPPOSE YOU LOOKED DOWN THE STREET AND SAW A REAL WEIRD INHUMAN TYPE OF CREATURE COMING ALONG!
BEADY EYES, SHAPELESS BODY, SPINDLY LEGS, PIPESTEM ARMS!-- LIKE SOMETHING OUT OF THIS WORLD!
--WHAT WOULD YOU SAY?
JUST WHAT YOU'D SAY!
" HELLO, JUGHEAD "!
YUK! YUK!
?
1

Script: Jim Ruth / Art & Letters: Bill Vigoda

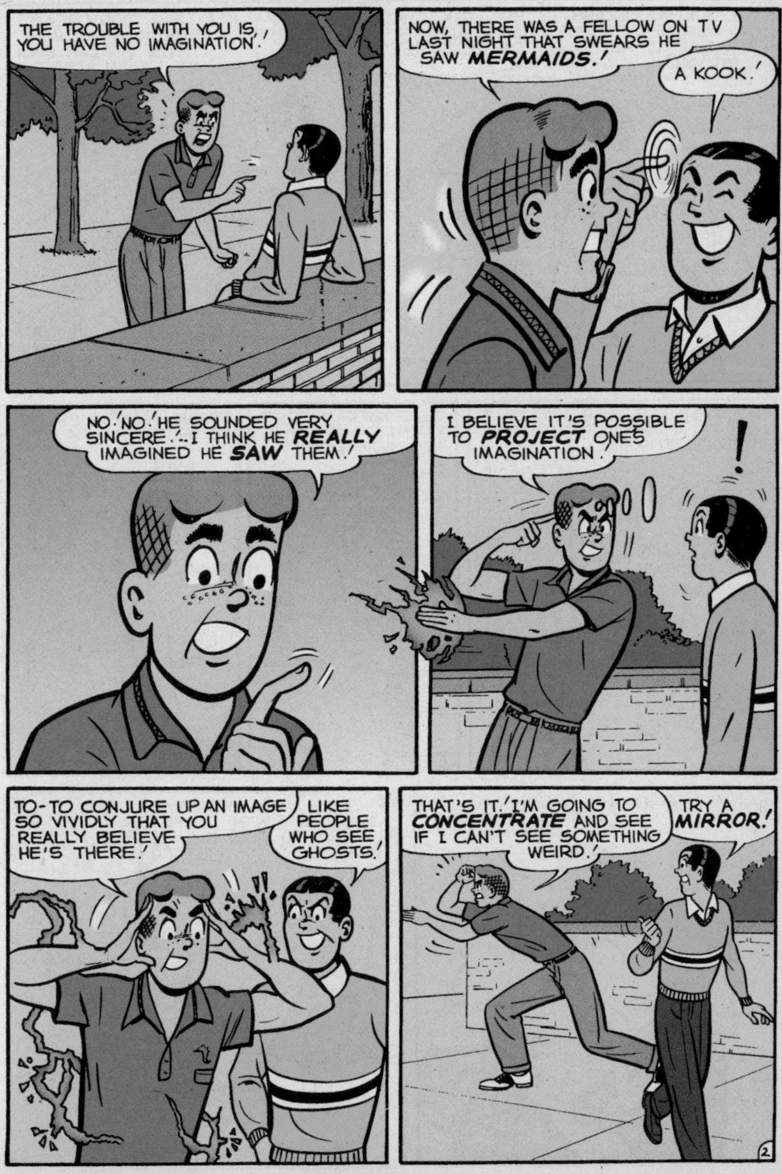
THE TROUBLE WITH YOU IS, YOU HAVE NO IMAGINATION!
NOW, THERE WAS A FELLOW ON TV LAST NIGHT THAT SWEARS HE SAW MERMAIDS!
A KOOK!
NO! NO! HE SOUNDED VERY SINCERE!..I THINK HE REALLY IMAGINED HE SAW THEM!
I BELIEVE IT'S POSSIBLE TO PROJECT ONE'S IMAGINATION!
!
TO-TO CONJURE UP AN IMAGE SO VIVIDLY THAT YOU REALLY BELIEVE HE'S THERE!
LIKE PEOPLE WHO SEE GHOSTS!
THAT'S IT! I'M GOING TO CONCENTRATE AND SEE IF I CAN'T SEE SOMETHING WEIRD!
TRY A MIRROR!
2

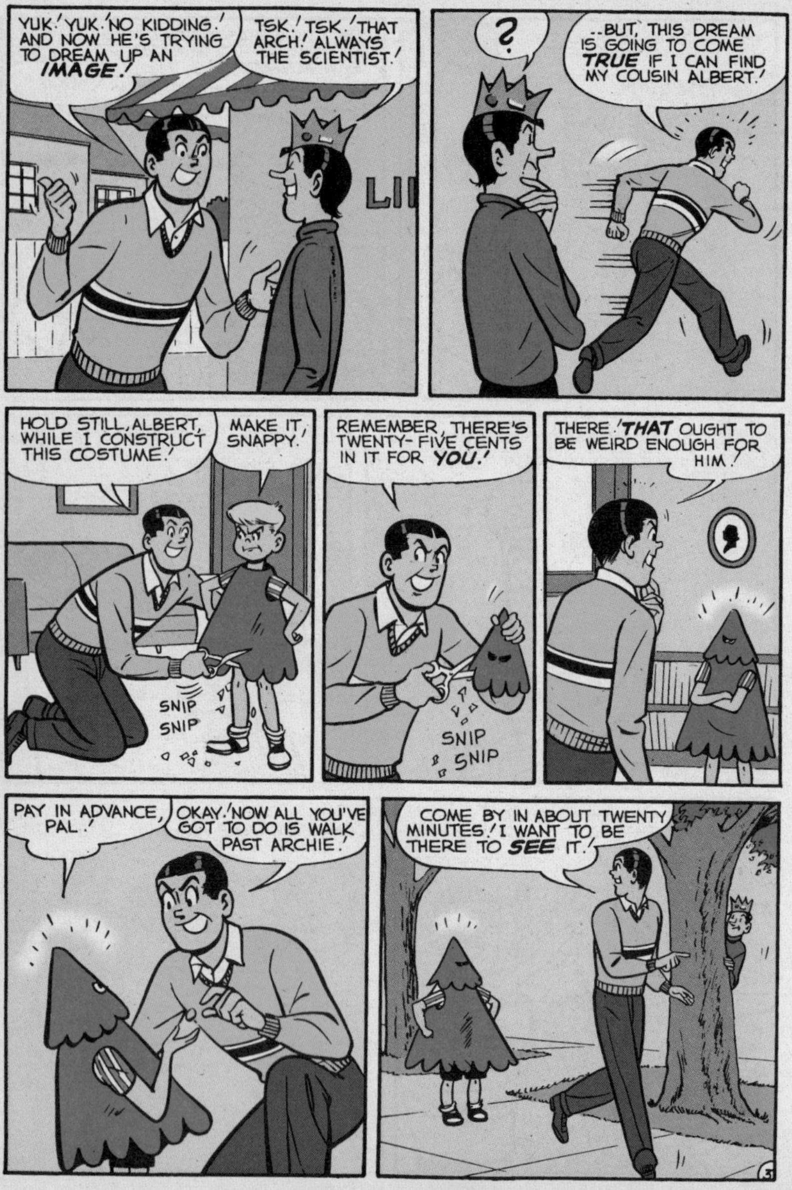
YUK! YUK! NO KIDDING! AND NOW HE'S TRYING TO DREAM UP AN IMAGE!
TSK! TSK! THAT ARCH! ALWAYS THE SCIENTIST!
?
..BUT, THIS DREAM IS GOING TO COME TRUE IF I CAN FIND MY COUSIN ALBERT!
HOLD STILL, ALBERT, WHILE I CONSTRUCT THIS COSTUME!
MAKE IT SNAPPY!
SNIP
SNIP
REMEMBER, THERE'S TWENTY-FIVE CENTS IN IT FOR YOU!
SNIP
SNIP
THERE! THAT OUGHT TO BE WEIRD ENOUGH FOR HIM!
PAY IN ADVANCE, PAL!
OKAY! NOW ALL YOU'VE GOT TO DO IS WALK PAST ARCHIE!
COME BY IN ABOUT TWENTY MINUTES! I WANT TO BE THERE TO SEE IT!
3

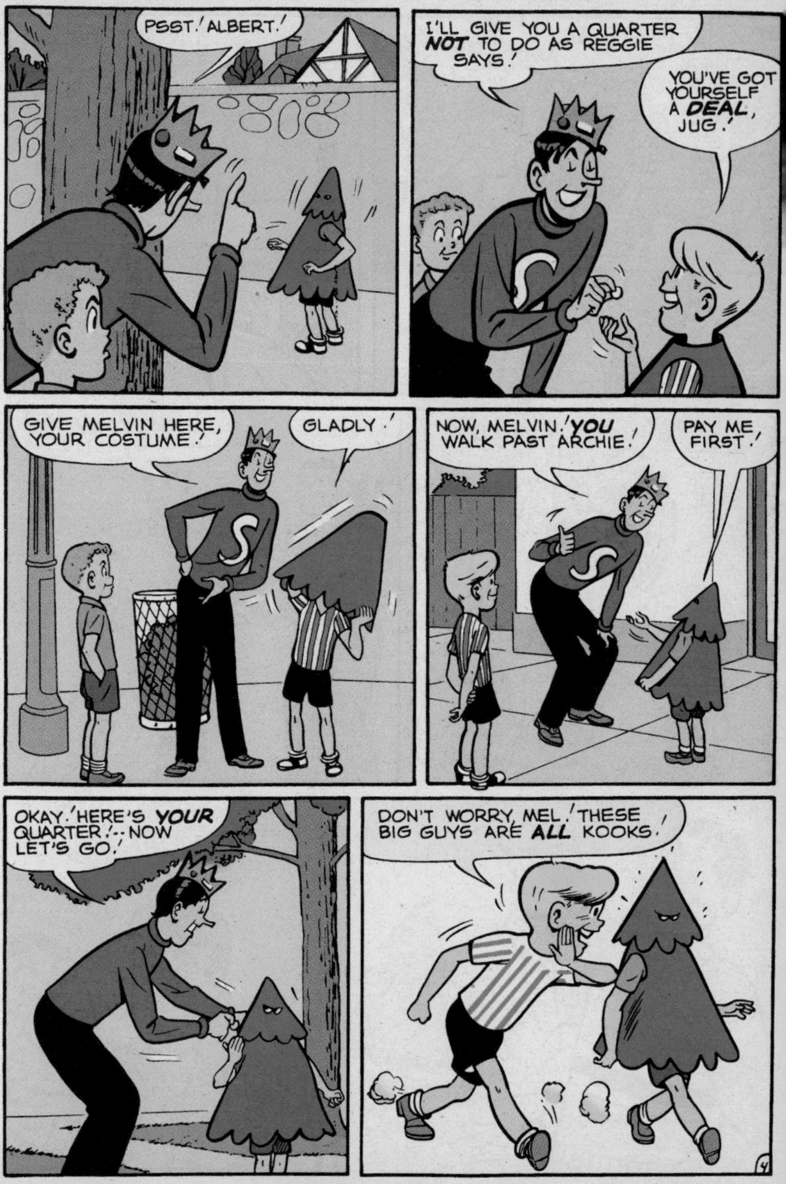
PSST.! ALBERT.!
I'LL GIVE YOU A QUARTER **NOT** TO DO AS REGGIE SAYS.!
YOU'VE GOT YOURSELF A **DEAL**, JUG.!
GIVE MELVIN HERE, YOUR COSTUME.!
GLADLY.!
NOW, MELVIN.! **YOU** WALK PAST ARCHIE.!
PAY ME FIRST.!
OKAY.! HERE'S **YOUR** QUARTER!-- NOW LET'S GO.!
DON'T WORRY, MEL.! THESE BIG GUYS ARE **ALL** KOOKS.
4

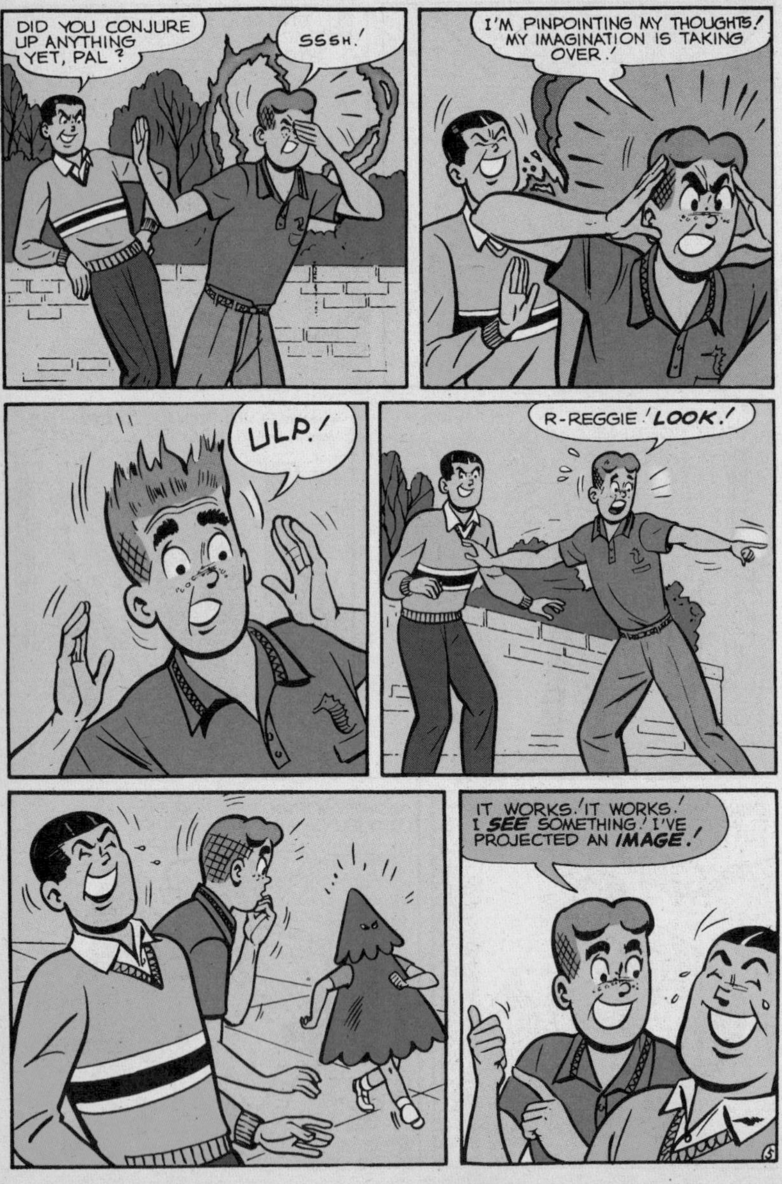
DID YOU CONJURE UP ANYTHING YET, PAL?
SSSH!
I'M PINPOINTING MY THOUGHTS! MY IMAGINATION IS TAKING OVER!
ULP!
R-REGGIE! LOOK!
IT WORKS! IT WORKS! I SEE SOMETHING! I'VE PROJECTED AN IMAGE!
5

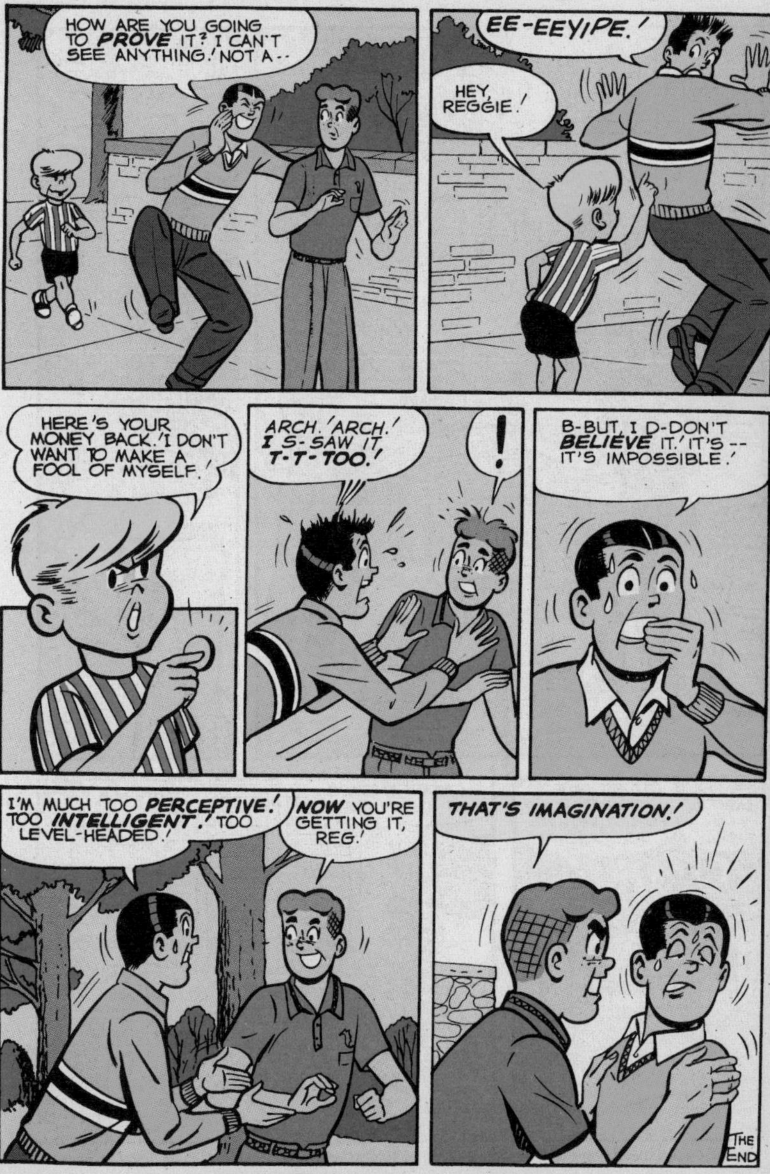
HOW ARE YOU GOING TO PROVE IT? I CAN'T SEE ANYTHING! NOT A--
EE-EEYIPE!
HEY, REGGIE!
HERE'S YOUR MONEY BACK! I DON'T WANT TO MAKE A FOOL OF MYSELF!
ARCH! ARCH! I S-SAW IT T-T-TOO!
!
B-BUT, I D-DON'T BELIEVE IT! IT'S -- IT'S IMPOSSIBLE!
I'M MUCH TOO PERCEPTIVE! TOO INTELLIGENT! TOO LEVEL-HEADED!
NOW YOU'RE GETTING IT, REG!
THAT'S IMAGINATION!
THE END

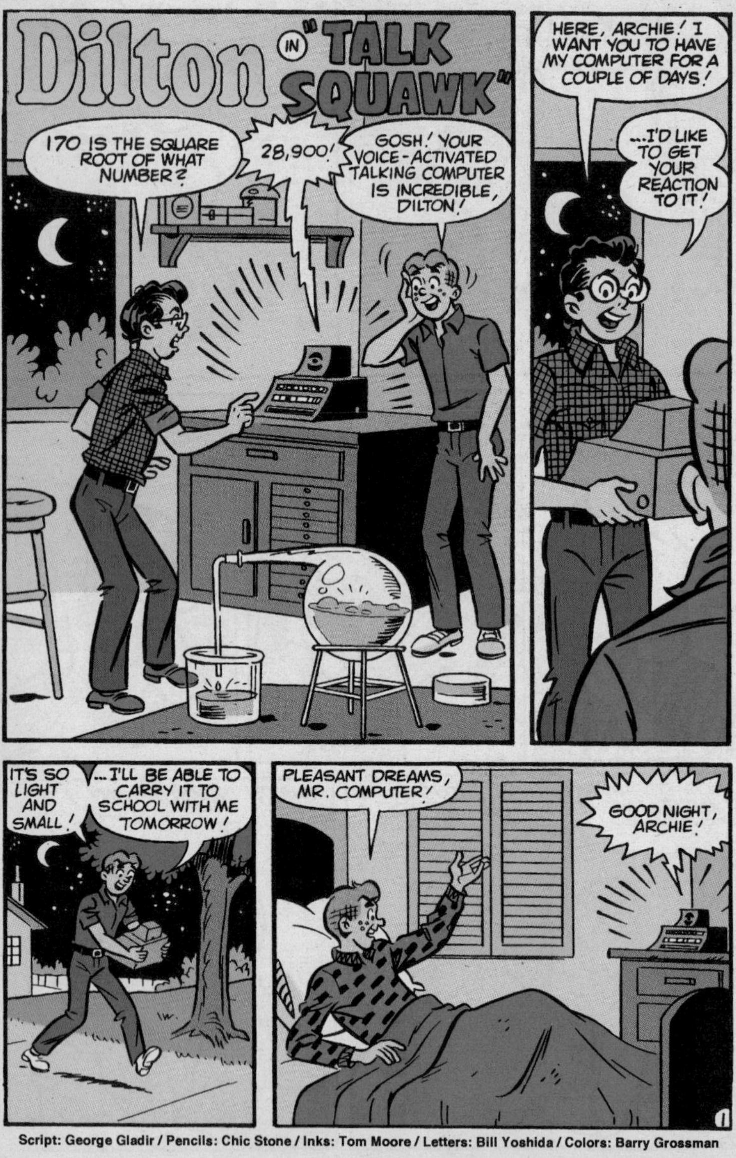
Dilton in "TALK SQUAWK"
170 IS THE SQUARE ROOT OF WHAT NUMBER?
28,900!
GOSH! YOUR VOICE-ACTIVATED TALKING COMPUTER IS INCREDIBLE, DILTON!
HERE, ARCHIE! I WANT YOU TO HAVE MY COMPUTER FOR A COUPLE OF DAYS!
...I'D LIKE TO GET YOUR REACTION TO IT!
IT'S SO LIGHT AND SMALL!
...I'LL BE ABLE TO CARRY IT TO SCHOOL WITH ME TOMORROW!
PLEASANT DREAMS, MR. COMPUTER!
GOOD NIGHT, ARCHIE!
1

Script: George Gladir / Pencils: Chic Stone / Inks: Tom Moore / Letters: Bill Yoshida / Colors: Barry Grossman

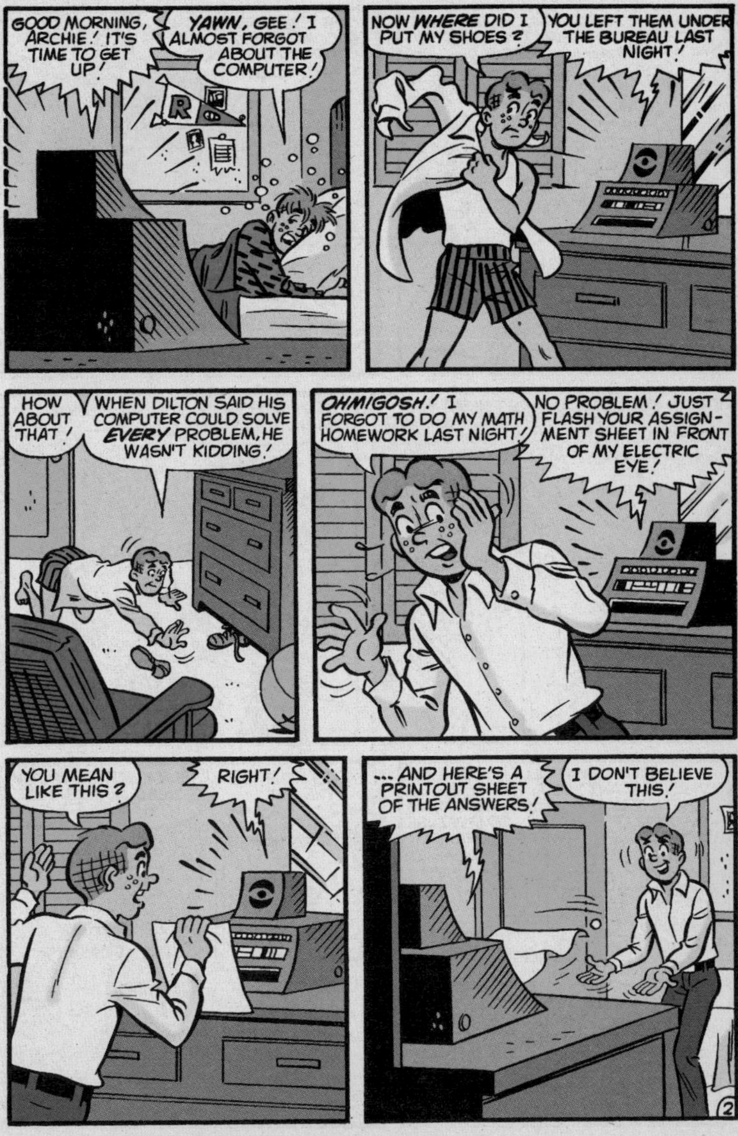
GOOD MORNING, ARCHIE! IT'S TIME TO GET UP!
YAWN. GEE! I ALMOST FORGOT ABOUT THE COMPUTER!
NOW WHERE DID I PUT MY SHOES?
YOU LEFT THEM UNDER THE BUREAU LAST NIGHT!
HOW ABOUT THAT!
WHEN DILTON SAID HIS COMPUTER COULD SOLVE EVERY PROBLEM, HE WASN'T KIDDING!
OHMIGOSH! I FORGOT TO DO MY MATH HOMEWORK LAST NIGHT!
NO PROBLEM! JUST FLASH YOUR ASSIGNMENT SHEET IN FRONT OF MY ELECTRIC EYE!
YOU MEAN LIKE THIS?
RIGHT!
... AND HERE'S A PRINTOUT SHEET OF THE ANSWERS!
I DON'T BELIEVE THIS!
2

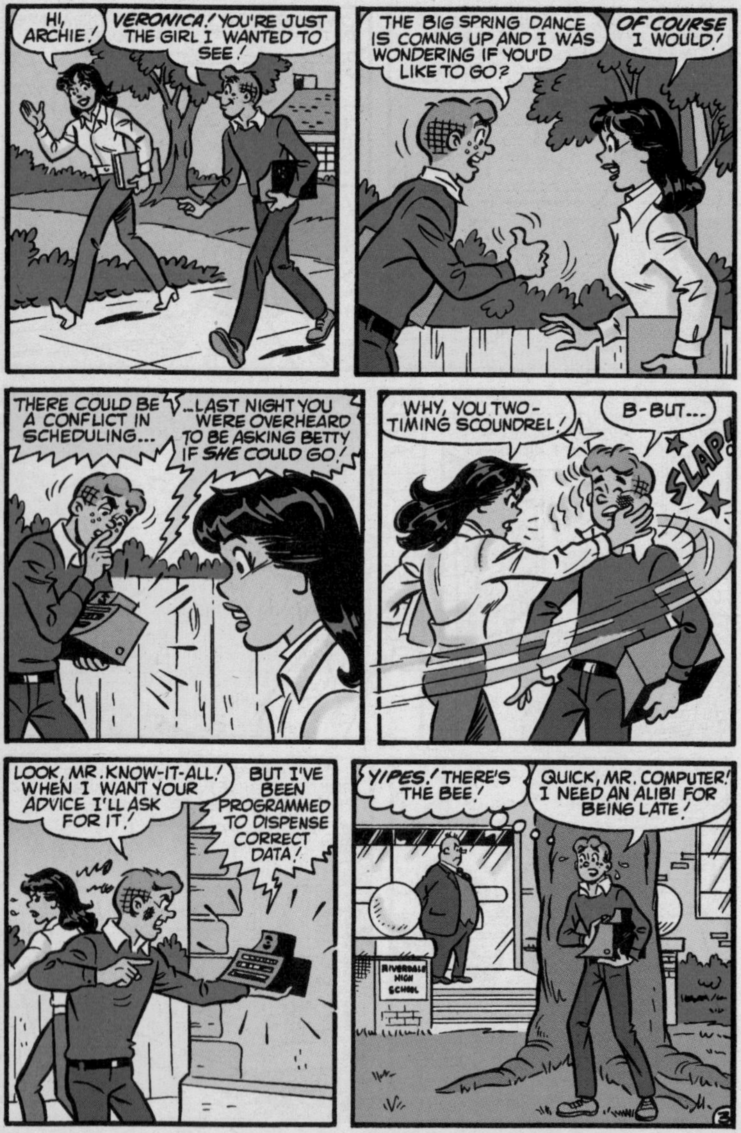
HI, ARCHIE!
VERONICA! YOU'RE JUST THE GIRL I WANTED TO SEE!
THE BIG SPRING DANCE IS COMING UP AND I WAS WONDERING IF YOU'D LIKE TO GO?
OF COURSE I WOULD!
THERE COULD BE A CONFLICT IN SCHEDULING...
...LAST NIGHT YOU WERE OVERHEARD TO BE ASKING BETTY IF SHE COULD GO!
WHY, YOU TWO-TIMING SCOUNDREL!
B-BUT...
SLAP!
LOOK, MR. KNOW-IT-ALL! WHEN I WANT YOUR ADVICE I'LL ASK FOR IT!
BUT I'VE BEEN PROGRAMMED TO DISPENSE CORRECT DATA!
YIPES! THERE'S THE BEE!
QUICK, MR. COMPUTER! I NEED AN ALIBI FOR BEING LATE!
RIVERDALE HIGH SCHOOL
3

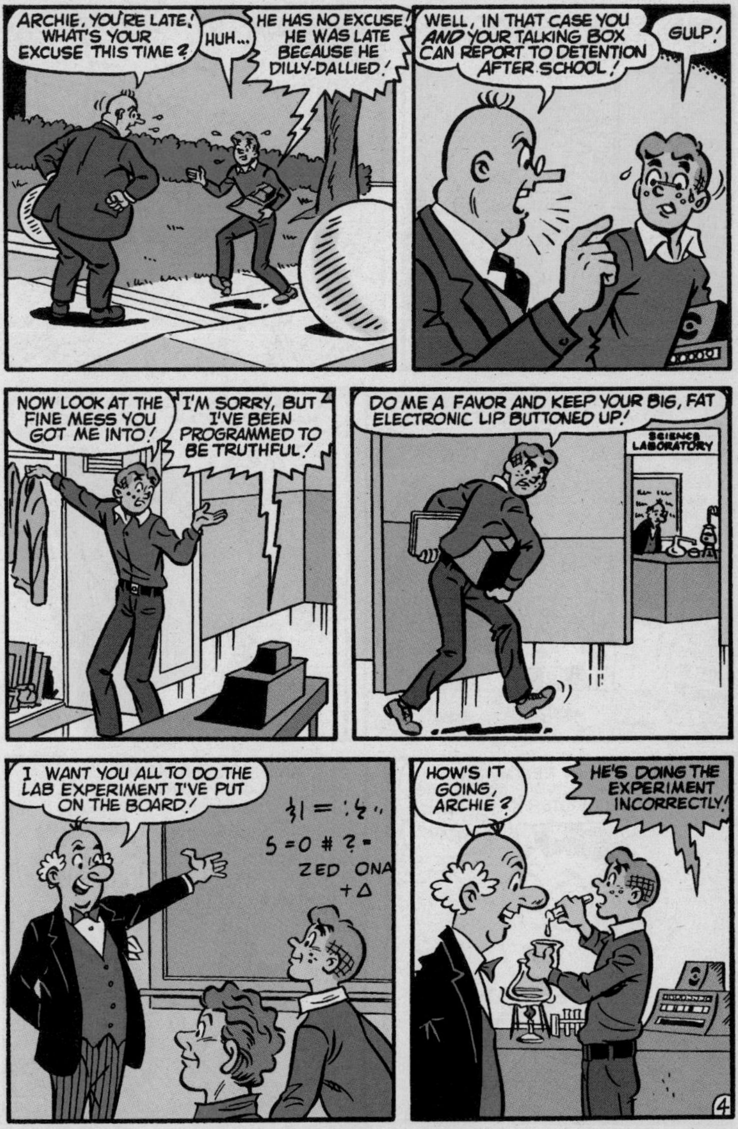
ARCHIE, YOU'RE LATE! WHAT'S YOUR EXCUSE THIS TIME?
HUH...
HE HAS NO EXCUSE! HE WAS LATE BECAUSE HE DILLY-DALLIED!
WELL, IN THAT CASE YOU AND YOUR TALKING BOX CAN REPORT TO DETENTION AFTER SCHOOL!
GULP!
NOW LOOK AT THE FINE MESS YOU GOT ME INTO!
I'M SORRY, BUT I'VE BEEN PROGRAMMED TO BE TRUTHFUL!
DO ME A FAVOR AND KEEP YOUR BIG, FAT ELECTRONIC LIP BUTTONED UP!
SCIENCE LABORATORY
I WANT YOU ALL TO DO THE LAB EXPERIMENT I'VE PUT ON THE BOARD!
ZED ONA
HOW'S IT GOING, ARCHIE?
HE'S DOING THE EXPERIMENT INCORRECTLY!
4

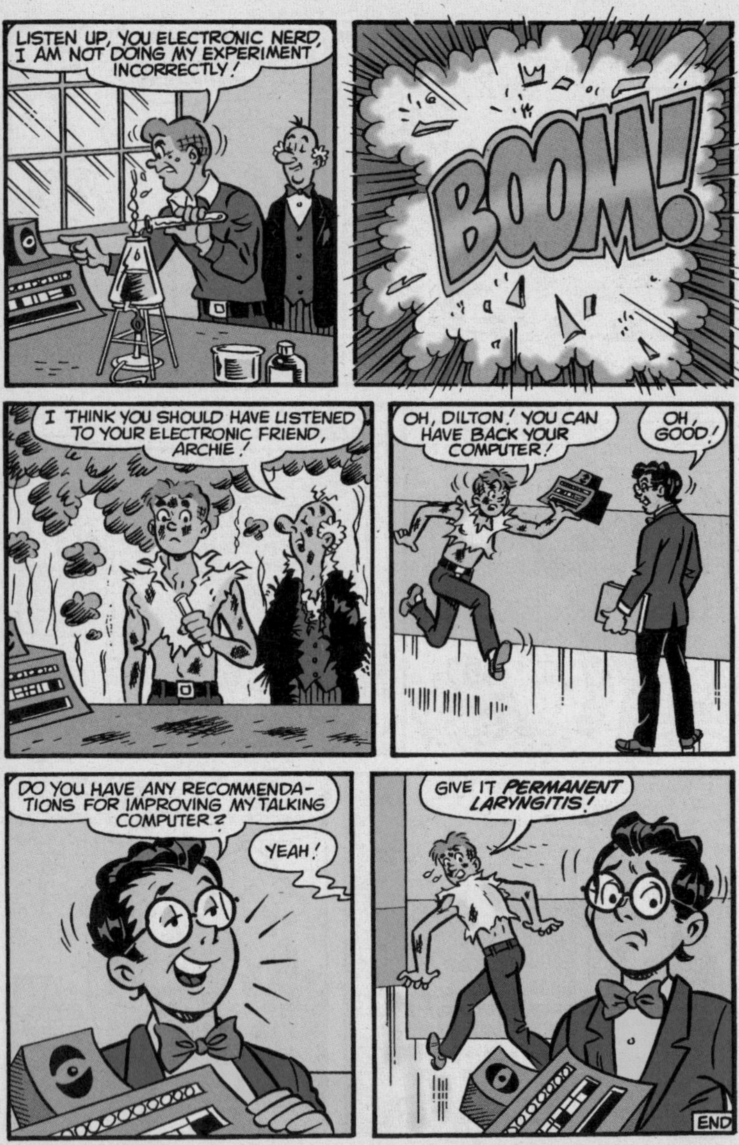
LISTEN UP, YOU ELECTRONIC NERD, I AM NOT DOING MY EXPERIMENT INCORRECTLY!
BOOM!
I THINK YOU SHOULD HAVE LISTENED TO YOUR ELECTRONIC FRIEND, ARCHIE!
OH, DILTON! YOU CAN HAVE BACK YOUR COMPUTER!
OH, GOOD!
DO YOU HAVE ANY RECOMMENDA-TIONS FOR IMPROVING MY TALKING COMPUTER?
YEAH!
GIVE IT *PERMANENT LARYNGITIS*!
END

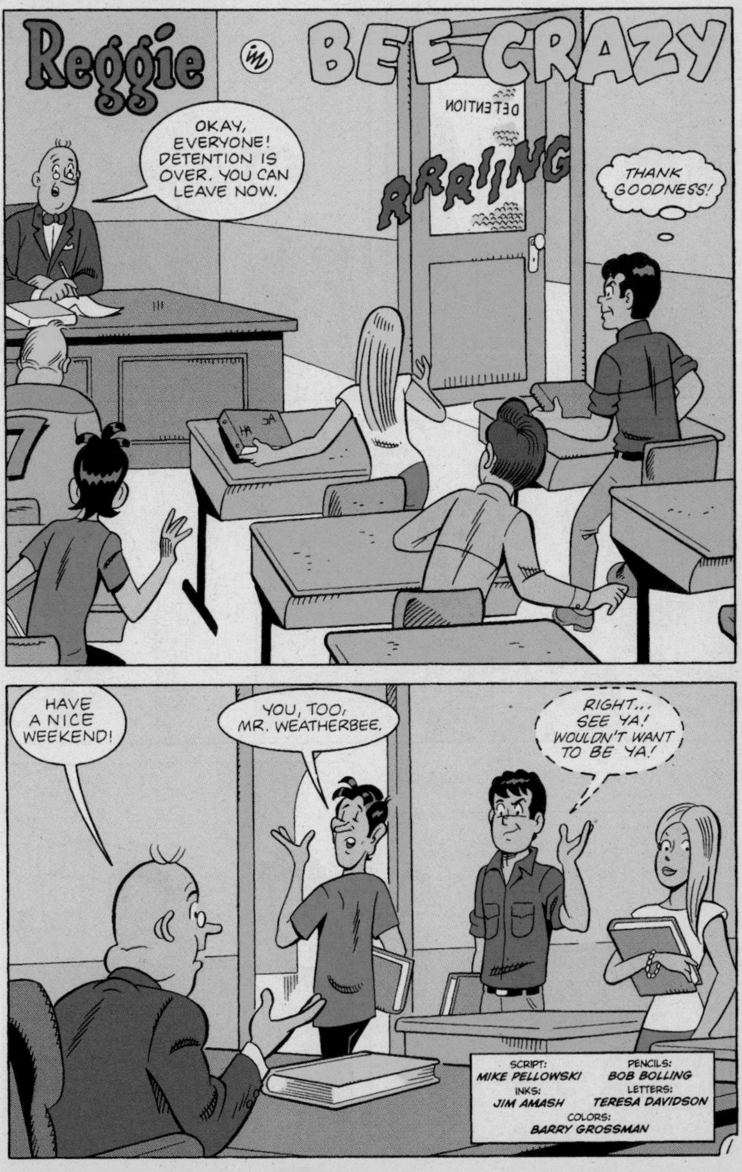
Reggie in BEE CRAZY
OKAY, EVERYONE! DETENTION IS OVER. YOU CAN LEAVE NOW.
DETENTION
RRRIIING
THANK GOODNESS!
HA HA
HAVE A NICE WEEKEND!
YOU, TOO, MR. WEATHERBEE.
RIGHT... SEE YA! WOULDN'T WANT TO BE YA!
SCRIPT: MIKE PELLOWSKI
PENCILS: BOB BOLLING
INKS: JIM AMASH
LETTERS: TERESA DAVIDSON
COLORS: BARRY GROSSMAN

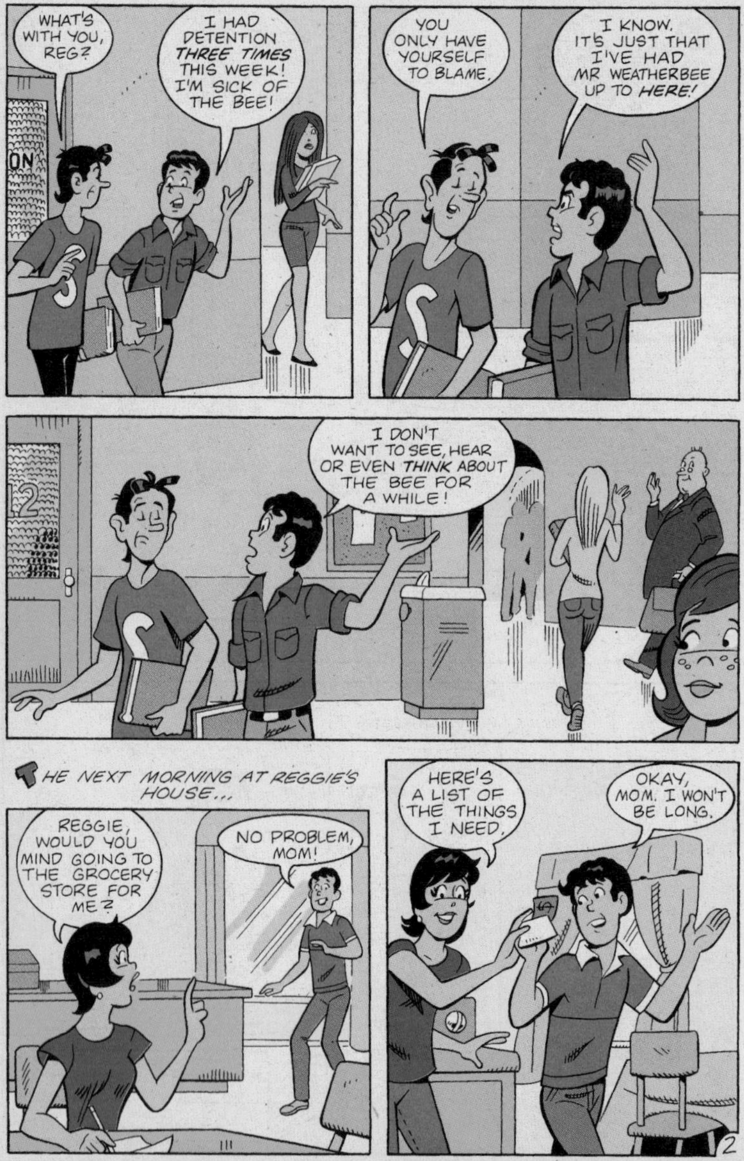
WHAT'S WITH YOU, REG?
I HAD DETENTION THREE TIMES THIS WEEK! I'M SICK OF THE BEE!
YOU ONLY HAVE YOURSELF TO BLAME.
I KNOW. IT'S JUST THAT I'VE HAD MR WEATHERBEE UP TO HERE!
I DON'T WANT TO SEE, HEAR OR EVEN THINK ABOUT THE BEE FOR A WHILE!
THE NEXT MORNING AT REGGIE'S HOUSE...
REGGIE, WOULD YOU MIND GOING TO THE GROCERY STORE FOR ME?
NO PROBLEM, MOM!
HERE'S A LIST OF THE THINGS I NEED.
OKAY, MOM. I WON'T BE LONG.
2

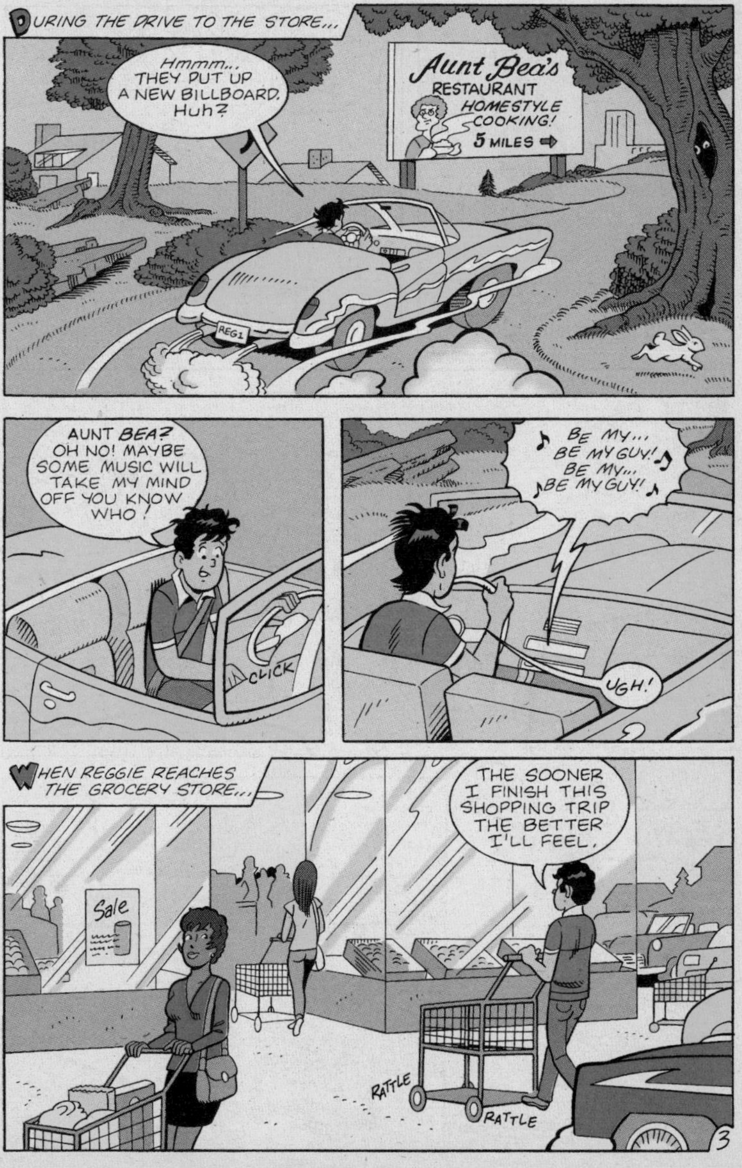
DURING THE DRIVE TO THE STORE...
Hmmm... THEY PUT UP A NEW BILLBOARD. Huh?
Aunt Bea's RESTAURANT HOMESTYLE COOKING! 5 MILES
REG1
AUNT BEA? OH NO! MAYBE SOME MUSIC WILL TAKE MY MIND OFF YOU KNOW WHO!
CLICK
BE MY... BE MY GUY! BE MY... BE MY GUY!
UGH!
WHEN REGGIE REACHES THE GROCERY STORE...
THE SOONER I FINISH THIS SHOPPING TRIP THE BETTER I'LL FEEL.
Sale
RATTLE
RATTLE

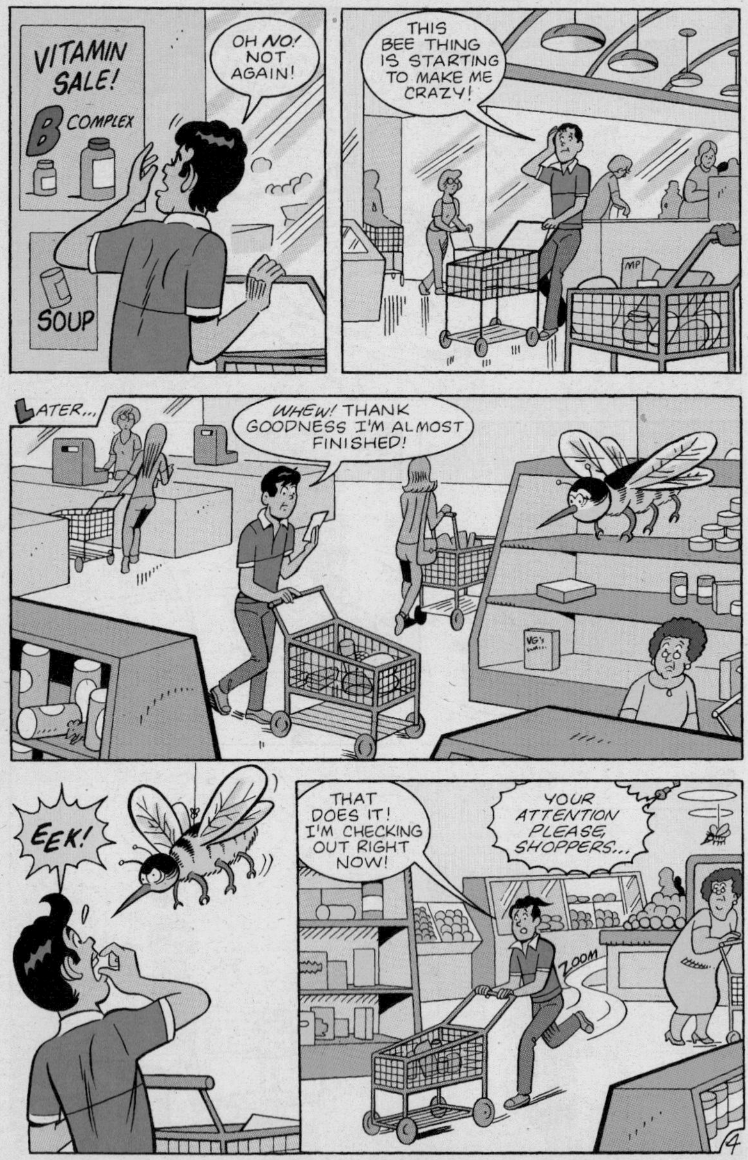
VITAMIN SALE!
B COMPLEX
SOUP
OH NO! NOT AGAIN!
THIS BEE THING IS STARTING TO MAKE ME CRAZY!
MP
LATER...
WHEW! THANK GOODNESS I'M ALMOST FINISHED!
EEK!
THAT DOES IT! I'M CHECKING OUT RIGHT NOW!
YOUR ATTENTION PLEASE, SHOPPERS...
ZOOM
4

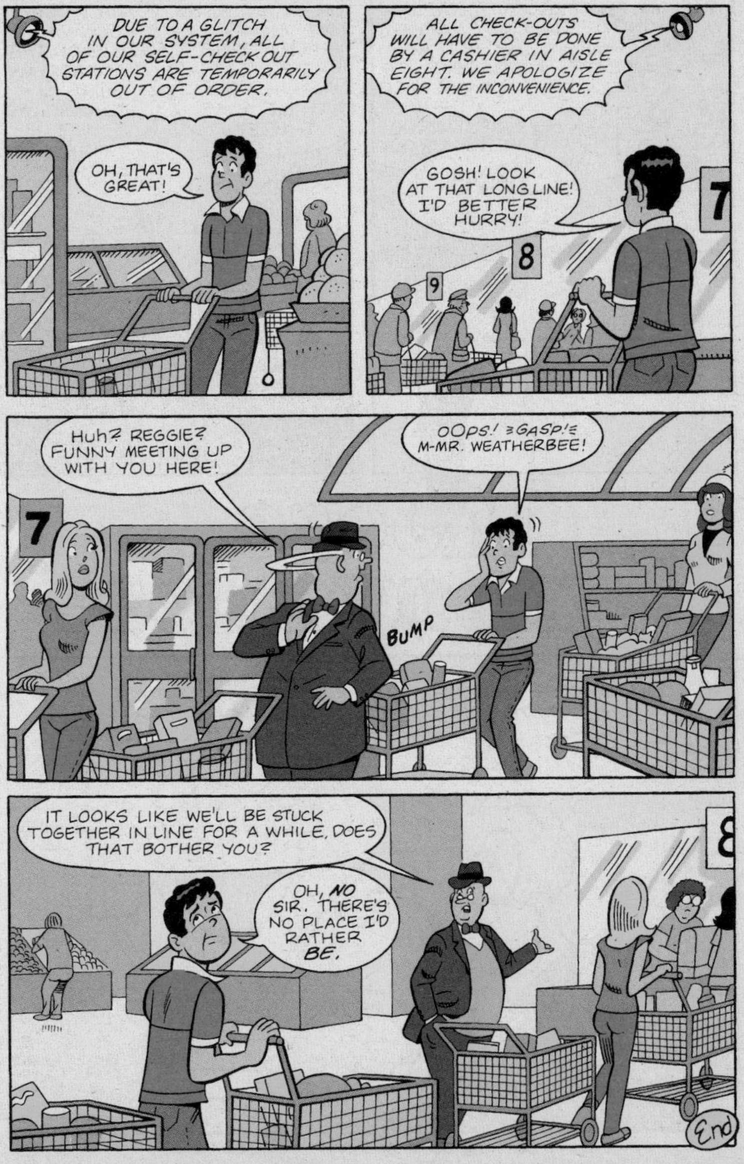
DUE TO A GLITCH IN OUR SYSTEM, ALL OF OUR SELF-CHECK OUT STATIONS ARE TEMPORARILY OUT OF ORDER.
OH, THAT'S GREAT!
ALL CHECK-OUTS WILL HAVE TO BE DONE BY A CASHIER IN AISLE EIGHT. WE APOLOGIZE FOR THE INCONVENIENCE.
GOSH! LOOK AT THAT LONG LINE! I'D BETTER HURRY!
7
8
9
Huh? REGGIE? FUNNY MEETING UP WITH YOU HERE!
OOPS! GASP! M-MR. WEATHERBEE!
7
BUMP
IT LOOKS LIKE WE'LL BE STUCK TOGETHER IN LINE FOR A WHILE, DOES THAT BOTHER YOU?
OH, NO SIR. THERE'S NO PLACE I'D RATHER BE.
8
End

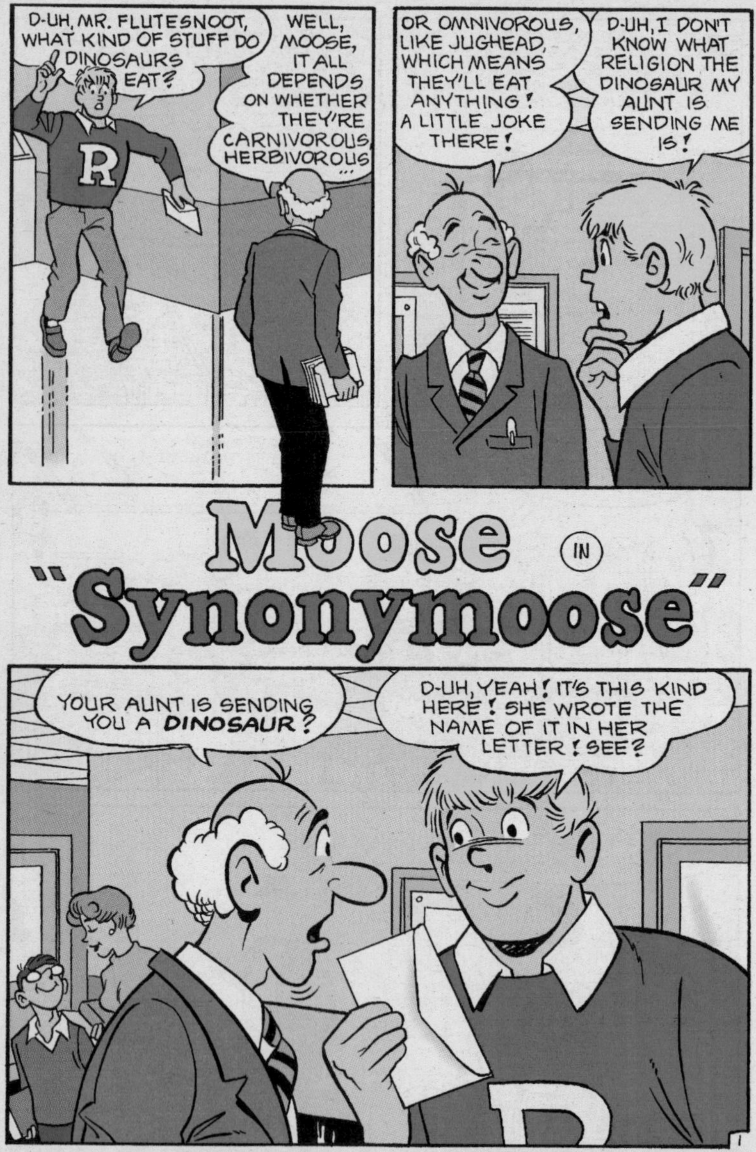
D-UH, MR. FLUTESNOOT, WHAT KIND OF STUFF DO DINOSAURS EAT?
WELL, MOOSE, IT ALL DEPENDS ON WHETHER THEY'RE CARNIVOROUS, HERBIVOROUS...
OR OMNIVOROUS, LIKE JUGHEAD, WHICH MEANS THEY'LL EAT ANYTHING! A LITTLE JOKE THERE!
D-UH, I DON'T KNOW WHAT RELIGION THE DINOSAUR MY AUNT IS SENDING ME IS!
Moose IN
"Synonymoose"
YOUR AUNT IS SENDING YOU A **DINOSAUR**?
D-UH, YEAH! IT'S THIS KIND HERE! SHE WROTE THE NAME OF IT IN HER LETTER! SEE?
1

Script: George Gladir / Art & Letters: Samm Schwartz

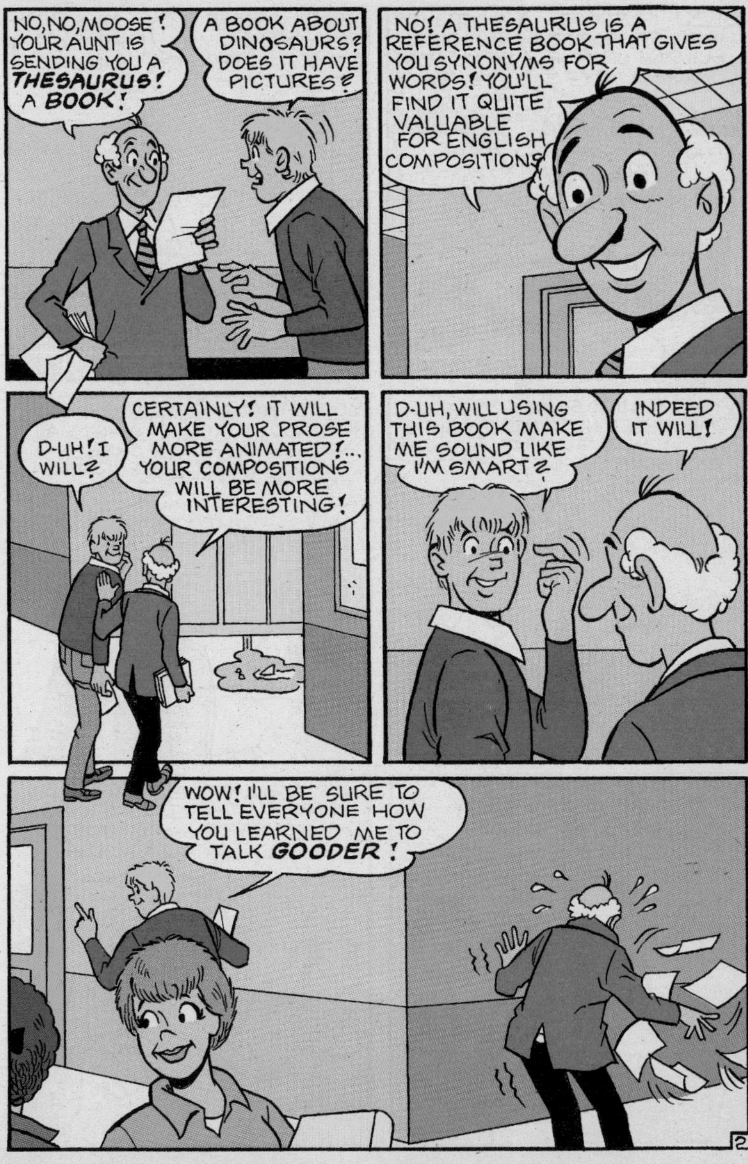
NO, NO, MOOSE! YOUR AUNT IS SENDING YOU A THESAURUS! A BOOK!
A BOOK ABOUT DINOSAURS? DOES IT HAVE PICTURES?
NO! A THESAURUS IS A REFERENCE BOOK THAT GIVES YOU SYNONYMS FOR WORDS! YOU'LL FIND IT QUITE VALUABLE FOR ENGLISH COMPOSITIONS!
D-UH! I WILL?
CERTAINLY! IT WILL MAKE YOUR PROSE MORE ANIMATED!... YOUR COMPOSITIONS WILL BE MORE INTERESTING!
D-UH, WILL USING THIS BOOK MAKE ME SOUND LIKE I'M SMART?
INDEED IT WILL!
WOW! I'LL BE SURE TO TELL EVERYONE HOW YOU LEARNED ME TO TALK GOODER!
2

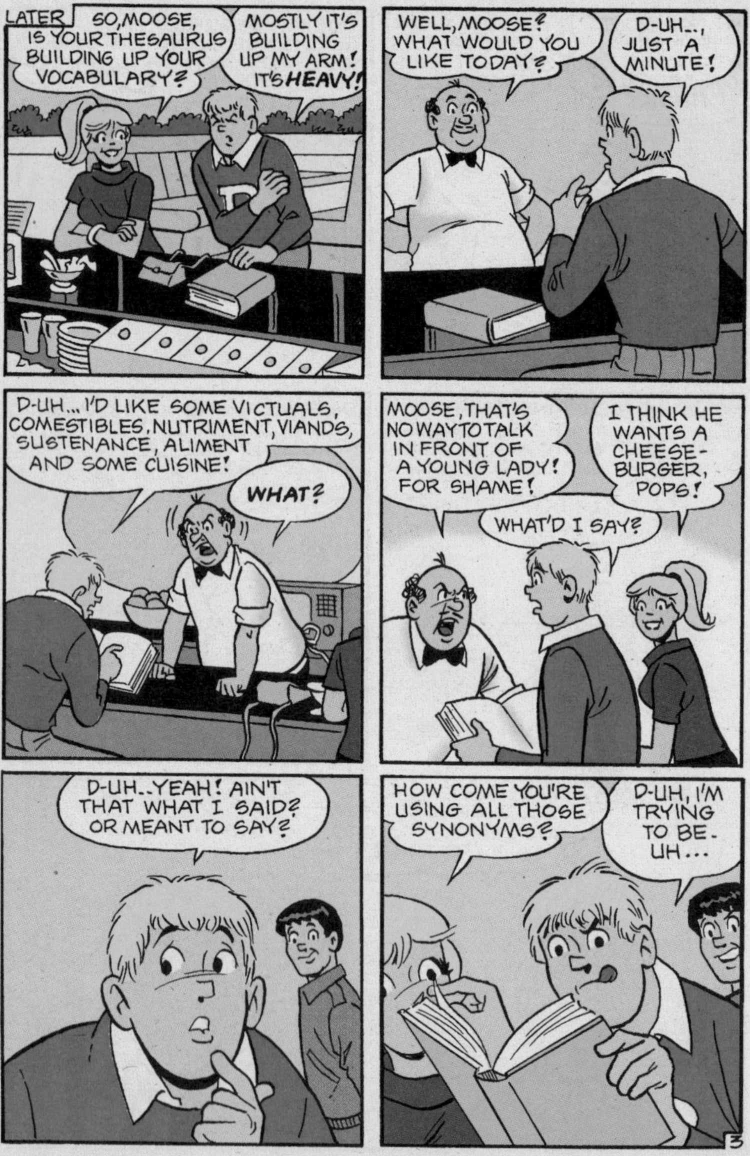
LATER
SO, MOOSE, IS YOUR THESAURUS BUILDING UP YOUR VOCABULARY?
MOSTLY IT'S BUILDING UP MY ARM! IT'S HEAVY!
WELL, MOOSE? WHAT WOULD YOU LIKE TODAY?
D-UH.., JUST A MINUTE!
D-UH... I'D LIKE SOME VICTUALS, COMESTIBLES, NUTRIMENT, VIANDS, SUSTENANCE, ALIMENT AND SOME CUISINE!
WHAT?
MOOSE, THAT'S NO WAY TO TALK IN FRONT OF A YOUNG LADY! FOR SHAME!
I THINK HE WANTS A CHEESE-BURGER, POPS!
WHAT'D I SAY?
D-UH..YEAH! AIN'T THAT WHAT I SAID? OR MEANT TO SAY?
HOW COME YOU'RE USING ALL THOSE SYNONYMS?
D-UH, I'M TRYING TO BE-UH...
3

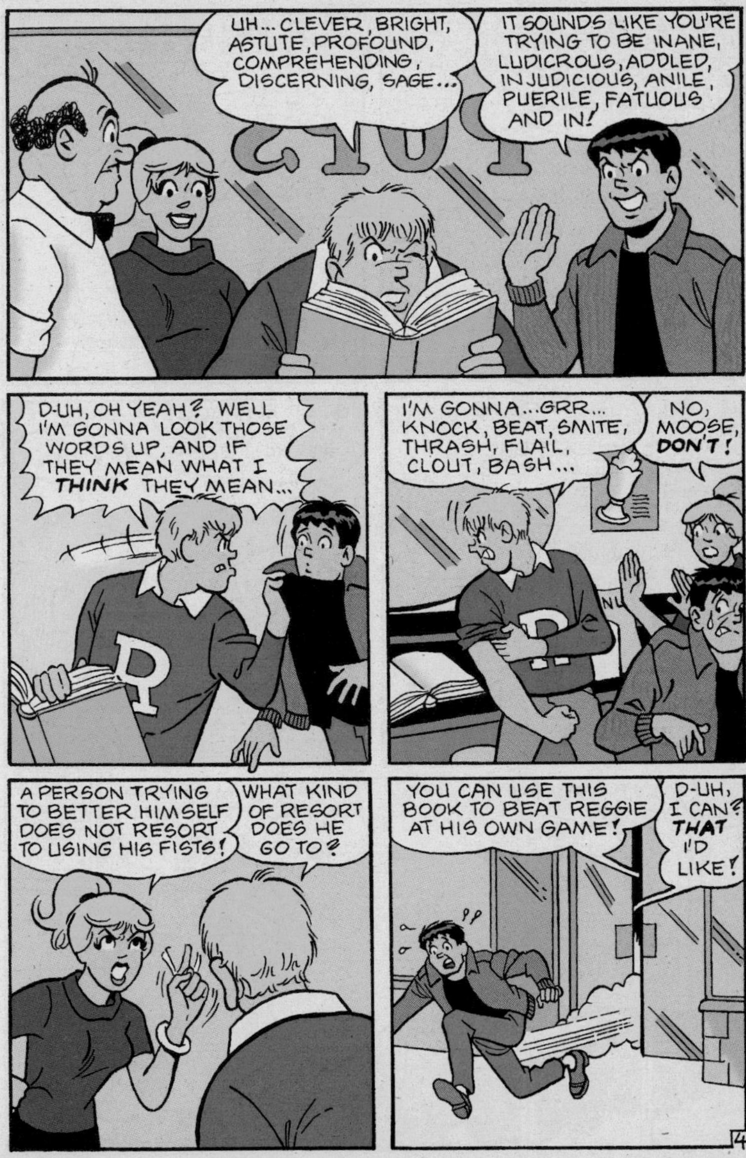
UH... CLEVER, BRIGHT, ASTUTE, PROFOUND, COMPREHENDING, DISCERNING, SAGE...
IT SOUNDS LIKE YOU'RE TRYING TO BE INANE, LUDICROUS, ADDLED, INJUDICIOUS, ANILE, PUERILE, FATUOUS AND IN!
D-UH, OH YEAH? WELL I'M GONNA LOOK THOSE WORDS UP, AND IF THEY MEAN WHAT I THINK THEY MEAN...
I'M GONNA...GRR... KNOCK, BEAT, SMITE, THRASH, FLAIL, CLOUT, BASH...
NO, MOOSE, DON'T!
A PERSON TRYING TO BETTER HIMSELF DOES NOT RESORT TO USING HIS FISTS!
WHAT KIND OF RESORT DOES HE GO TO?
YOU CAN USE THIS BOOK TO BEAT REGGIE AT HIS OWN GAME!
D-UH, I CAN? THAT I'D LIKE!

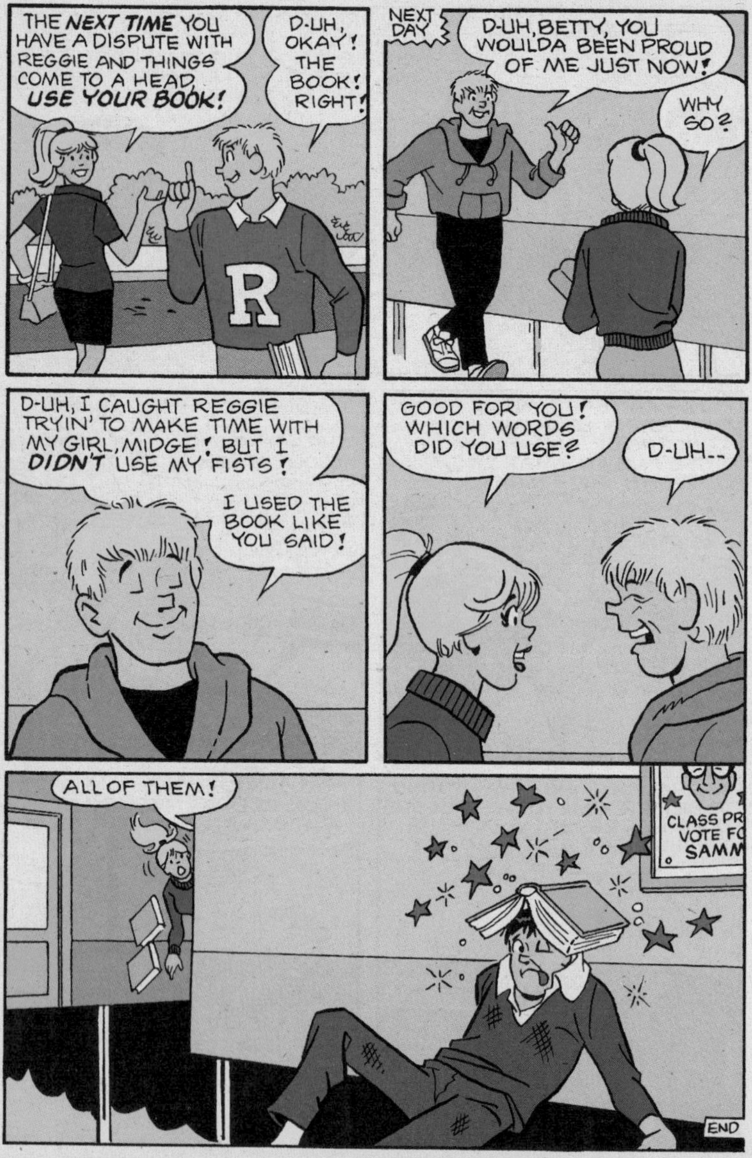
THE NEXT TIME YOU HAVE A DISPUTE WITH REGGIE AND THINGS COME TO A HEAD, USE YOUR BOOK!
D-UH, OKAY! THE BOOK! RIGHT!
NEXT DAY
D-UH, BETTY, YOU WOULDA BEEN PROUD OF ME JUST NOW!
WHY SO?
D-UH, I CAUGHT REGGIE TRYIN' TO MAKE TIME WITH MY GIRL, MIDGE! BUT I DIDN'T USE MY FISTS!
I USED THE BOOK LIKE YOU SAID!
GOOD FOR YOU! WHICH WORDS DID YOU USE?
D-UH..
ALL OF THEM!
CLASS PR
VOTE FO
SAMM
END

Veronica in "Little Ron on the Prairie" PART I

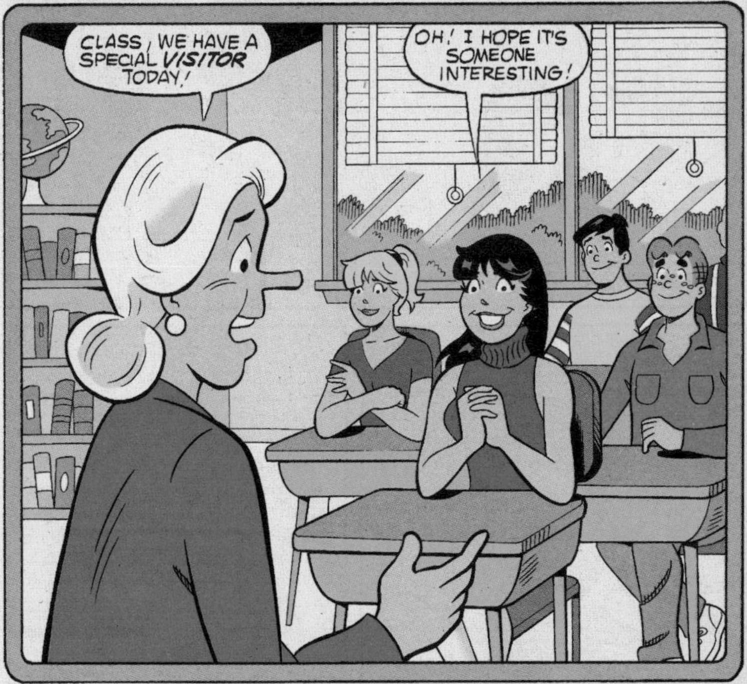
CLASS, WE HAVE A SPECIAL VISITOR TODAY!
OH! I HOPE IT'S SOMEONE INTERESTING!

Script & Pencils: Dan Parent / Inks: Jim Amash / Letters: Bill Yoshida / Colors: Barry Grossman

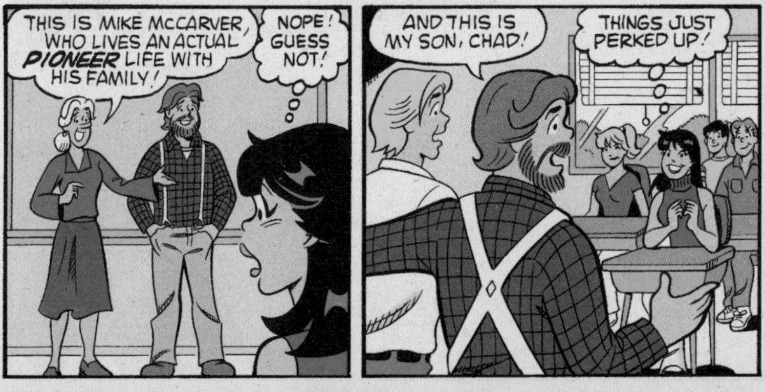
THIS IS MIKE McCARVER, WHO LIVES AN ACTUAL PIONEER LIFE WITH HIS FAMILY!
NOPE! GUESS NOT!
AND THIS IS MY SON, CHAD!
THINGS JUST PERKED UP!

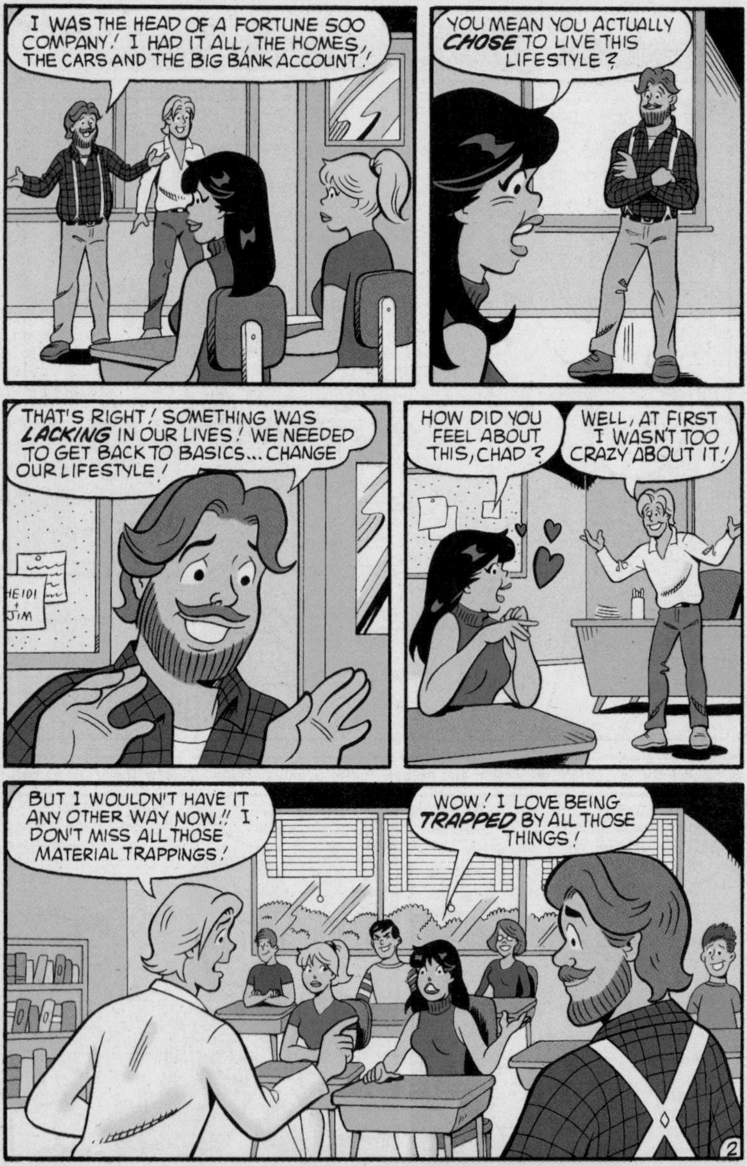
I WAS THE HEAD OF A FORTUNE 500 COMPANY! I HAD IT ALL, THE HOMES, THE CARS AND THE BIG BANK ACCOUNT!
YOU MEAN YOU ACTUALLY **CHOSE** TO LIVE THIS LIFESTYLE?
THAT'S RIGHT! SOMETHING WAS **LACKING** IN OUR LIVES! WE NEEDED TO GET BACK TO BASICS... CHANGE OUR LIFESTYLE!
HEIDI + JIM
HOW DID YOU FEEL ABOUT THIS, CHAD?
WELL, AT FIRST I WASN'T TOO CRAZY ABOUT IT!
BUT I WOULDN'T HAVE IT ANY OTHER WAY NOW!! I DON'T MISS ALL THOSE MATERIAL TRAPPINGS!
WOW! I LOVE BEING **TRAPPED** BY ALL THOSE THINGS!
2

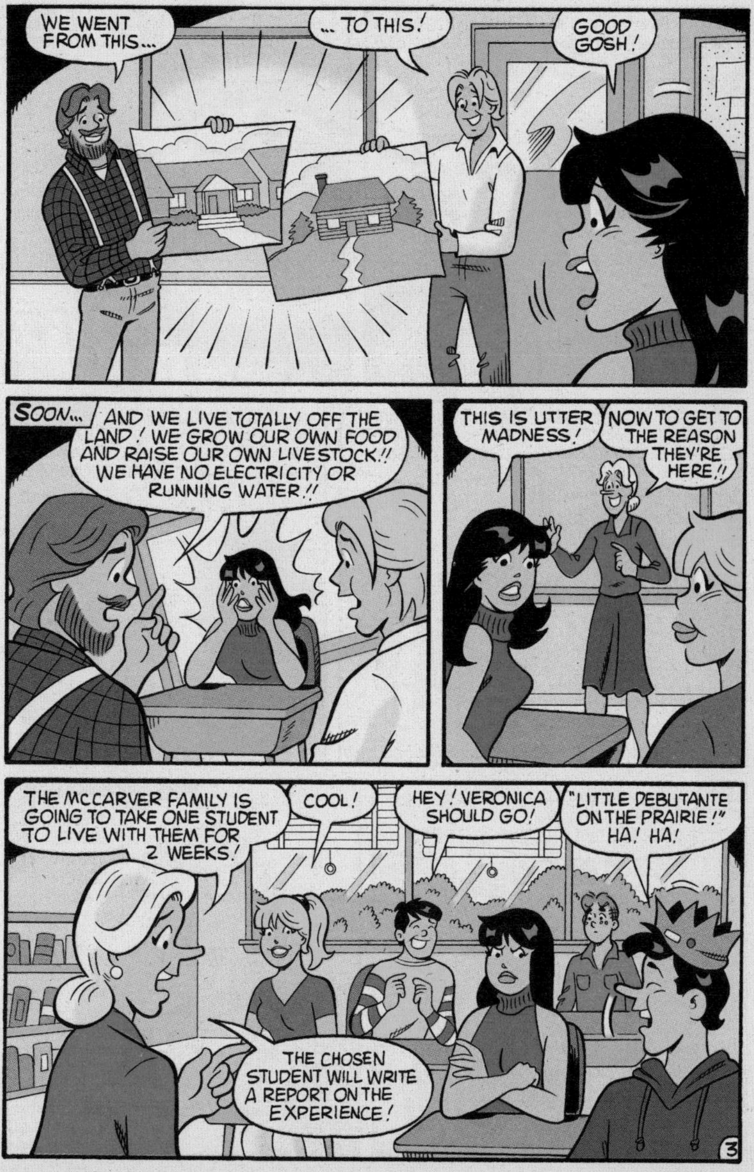
WE WENT FROM THIS...
... TO THIS!
GOOD GOSH!
SOON...
AND WE LIVE TOTALLY OFF THE LAND! WE GROW OUR OWN FOOD AND RAISE OUR OWN LIVESTOCK!! WE HAVE NO ELECTRICITY OR RUNNING WATER!!
THIS IS UTTER MADNESS!
NOW TO GET TO THE REASON THEY'RE HERE!!
THE McCARVER FAMILY IS GOING TO TAKE ONE STUDENT TO LIVE WITH THEM FOR 2 WEEKS!
COOL!
HEY! VERONICA SHOULD GO!
"LITTLE DEBUTANTE ON THE PRAIRIE!" HA! HA!
THE CHOSEN STUDENT WILL WRITE A REPORT ON THE EXPERIENCE!
3

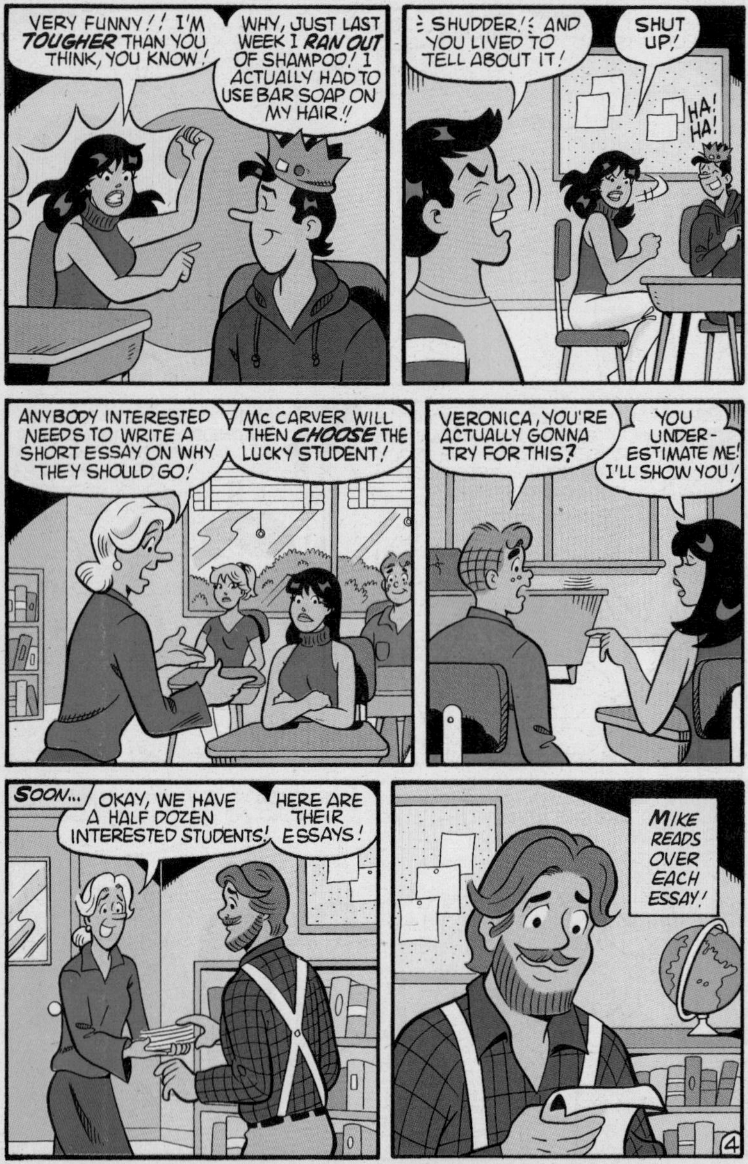
VERY FUNNY!! I'M TOUGHER THAN YOU THINK, YOU KNOW!
WHY, JUST LAST WEEK I RAN OUT OF SHAMPOO! I ACTUALLY HAD TO USE BAR SOAP ON MY HAIR!!
SHUDDER! AND YOU LIVED TO TELL ABOUT IT!
SHUT UP!
HA! HA!
ANYBODY INTERESTED NEEDS TO WRITE A SHORT ESSAY ON WHY THEY SHOULD GO!
Mc CARVER WILL THEN CHOOSE THE LUCKY STUDENT!
VERONICA, YOU'RE ACTUALLY GONNA TRY FOR THIS?
YOU UNDER-ESTIMATE ME! I'LL SHOW YOU!
SOON...
OKAY, WE HAVE A HALF DOZEN INTERESTED STUDENTS!
HERE ARE THEIR ESSAYS!
MIKE READS OVER EACH ESSAY!
4

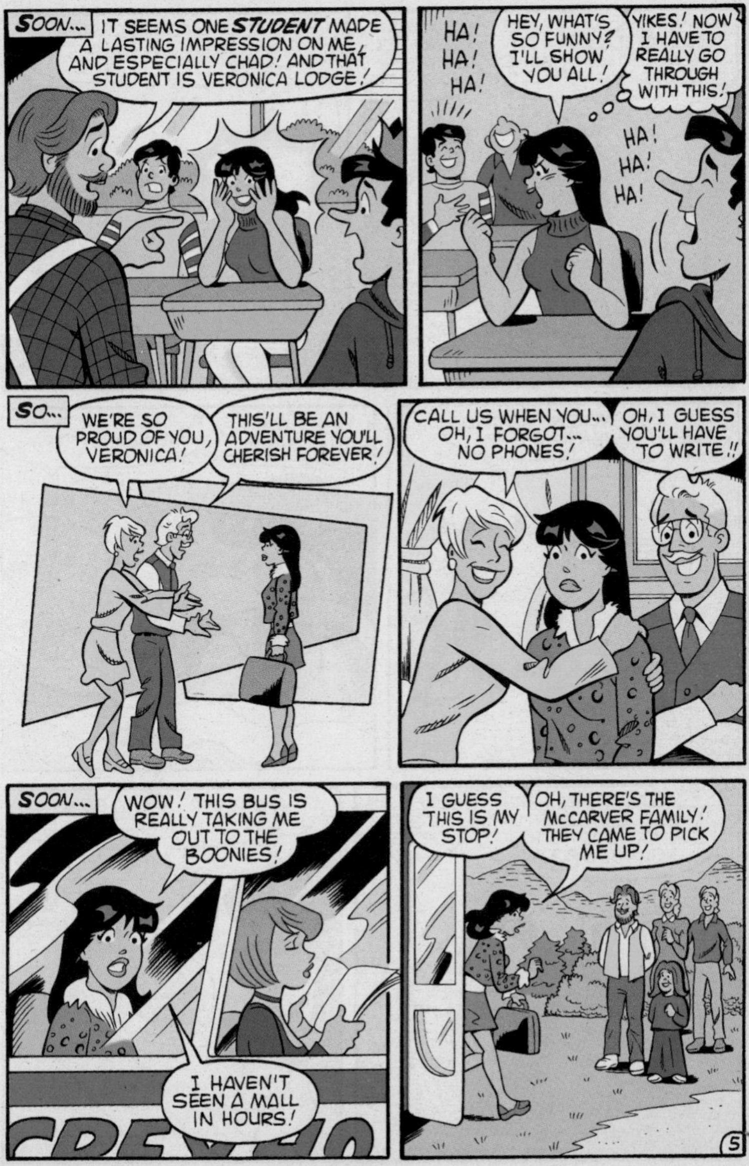
SOON...
IT SEEMS ONE STUDENT MADE A LASTING IMPRESSION ON ME, AND ESPECIALLY CHAD! AND THAT STUDENT IS VERONICA LODGE!
HA! HA! HA!
HEY, WHAT'S SO FUNNY? I'LL SHOW YOU ALL!
YIKES! NOW I HAVE TO REALLY GO THROUGH WITH THIS!
HA! HA! HA!
SO...
WE'RE SO PROUD OF YOU, VERONICA!
THIS'LL BE AN ADVENTURE YOU'LL CHERISH FOREVER!
CALL US WHEN YOU... OH, I FORGOT... NO PHONES!
OH, I GUESS YOU'LL HAVE TO WRITE!!
SOON...
WOW! THIS BUS IS REALLY TAKING ME OUT TO THE BOONIES!
I HAVEN'T SEEN A MALL IN HOURS!
I GUESS THIS IS MY STOP!
OH, THERE'S THE McCARVER FAMILY! THEY CAME TO PICK ME UP!

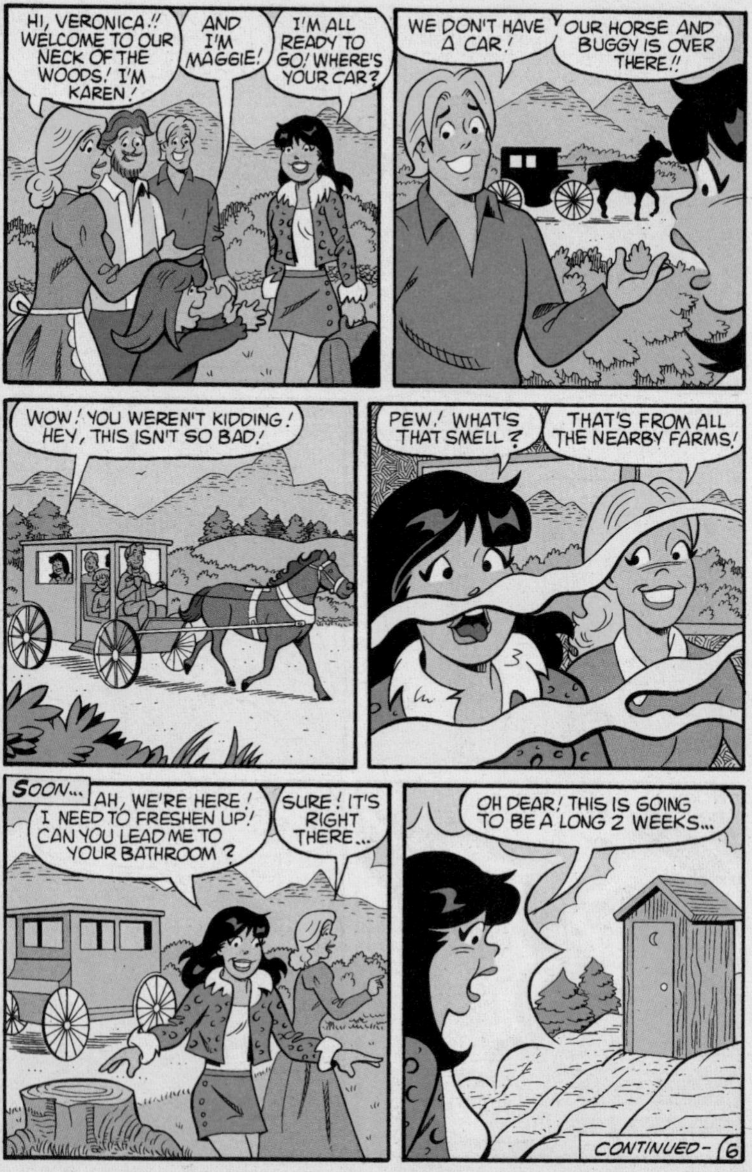
HI, VERONICA.!! WELCOME TO OUR NECK OF THE WOODS! I'M KAREN!
AND I'M MAGGIE!
I'M ALL READY TO GO! WHERE'S YOUR CAR?
WE DON'T HAVE A CAR!
OUR HORSE AND BUGGY IS OVER THERE!!
WOW! YOU WEREN'T KIDDING! HEY, THIS ISN'T SO BAD!
PEW! WHAT'S THAT SMELL?
THAT'S FROM ALL THE NEARBY FARMS!
SOON...
AH, WE'RE HERE! I NEED TO FRESHEN UP! CAN YOU LEAD ME TO YOUR BATHROOM?
SURE! IT'S RIGHT THERE...
OH DEAR! THIS IS GOING TO BE A LONG 2 WEEKS...
CONTINUED-
6

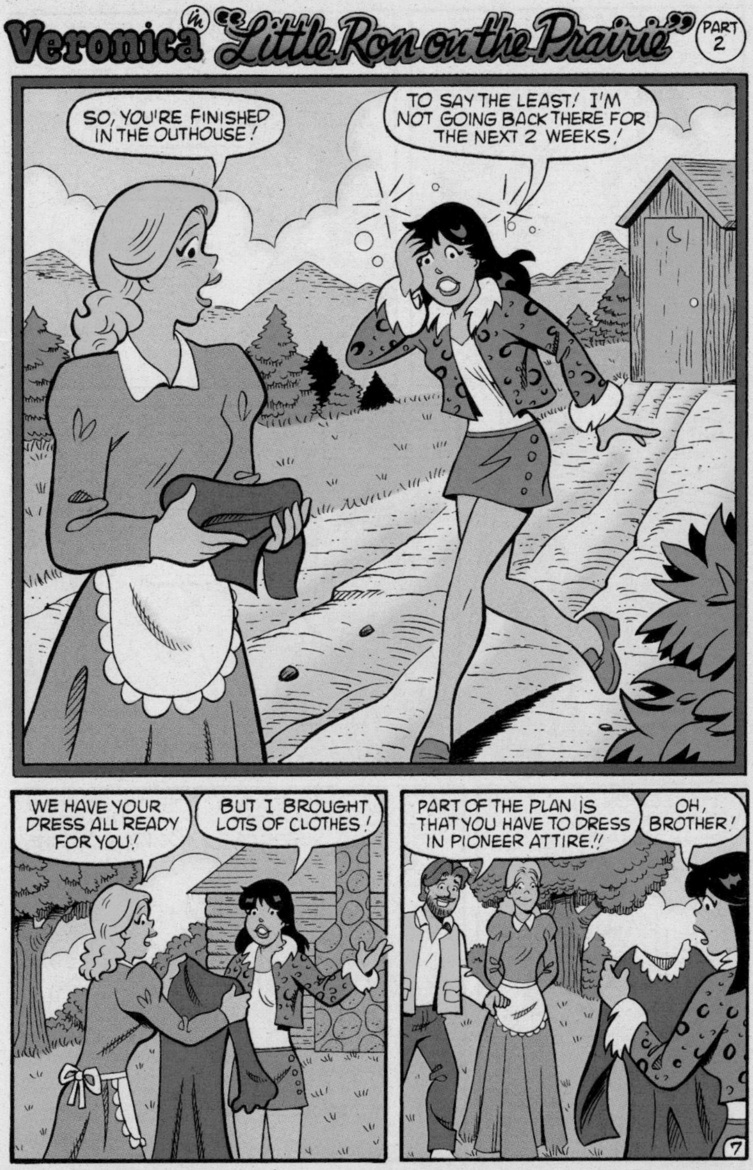
Veronica in "Little Ron on the Prairie" PART 2
SO, YOU'RE FINISHED IN THE OUTHOUSE!
TO SAY THE LEAST! I'M NOT GOING BACK THERE FOR THE NEXT 2 WEEKS!
WE HAVE YOUR DRESS ALL READY FOR YOU!
BUT I BROUGHT LOTS OF CLOTHES!
PART OF THE PLAN IS THAT YOU HAVE TO DRESS IN PIONEER ATTIRE!!
OH, BROTHER!
7

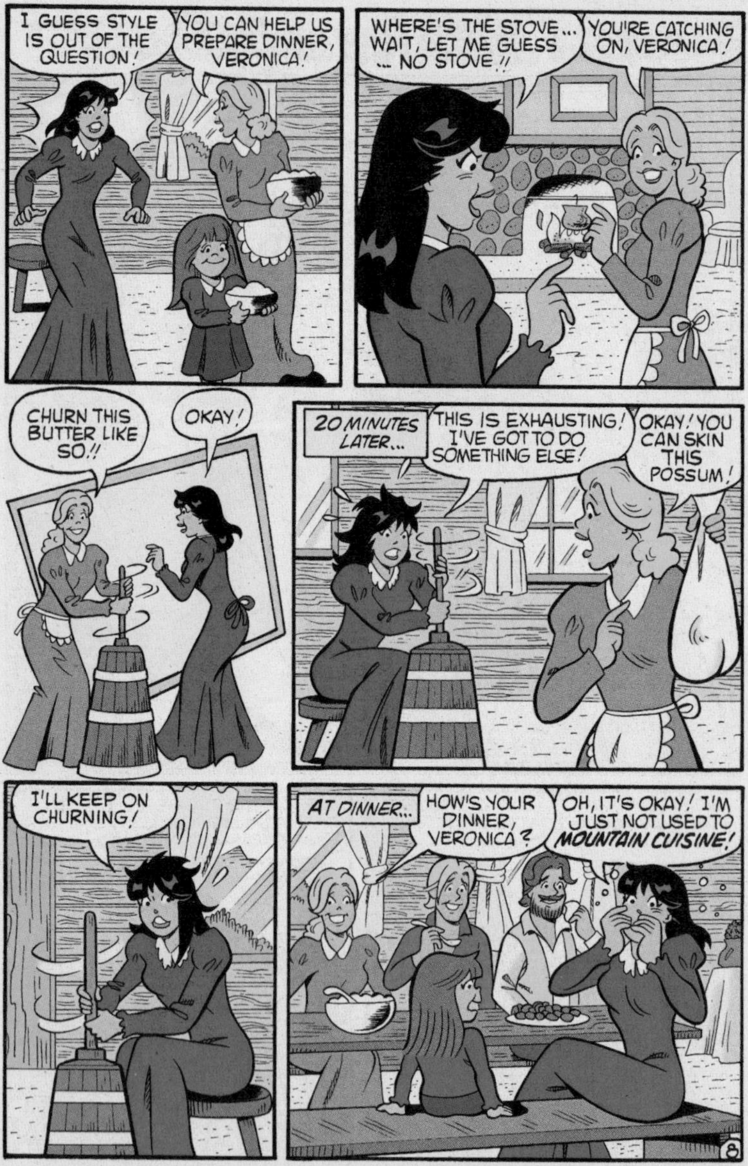

I GUESS STYLE IS OUT OF THE QUESTION!
YOU CAN HELP US PREPARE DINNER, VERONICA!
WHERE'S THE STOVE... WAIT, LET ME GUESS ... NO STOVE!!
YOU'RE CATCHING ON, VERONICA!
CHURN THIS BUTTER LIKE SO!!
OKAY!
20 MINUTES LATER...
THIS IS EXHAUSTING! I'VE GOT TO DO SOMETHING ELSE!
OKAY! YOU CAN SKIN THIS POSSUM!
I'LL KEEP ON CHURNING!
AT DINNER...
HOW'S YOUR DINNER, VERONICA?
OH, IT'S OKAY! I'M JUST NOT USED TO MOUNTAIN CUISINE!

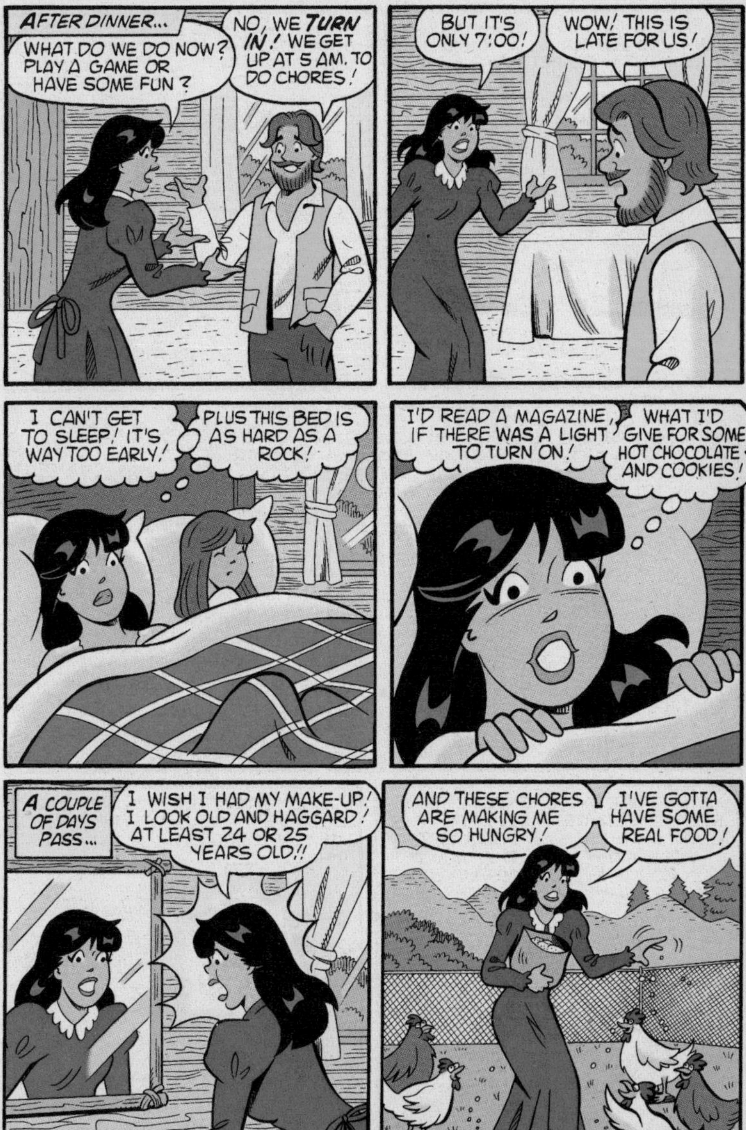
AFTER DINNER...
WHAT DO WE DO NOW? PLAY A GAME OR HAVE SOME FUN?
NO, WE TURN IN! WE GET UP AT 5 AM. TO DO CHORES!
BUT IT'S ONLY 7:00!
WOW! THIS IS LATE FOR US!
I CAN'T GET TO SLEEP! IT'S WAY TOO EARLY!
PLUS THIS BED IS AS HARD AS A ROCK!
I'D READ A MAGAZINE, IF THERE WAS A LIGHT TO TURN ON!
WHAT I'D GIVE FOR SOME HOT CHOCOLATE AND COOKIES!
A COUPLE OF DAYS PASS...
I WISH I HAD MY MAKE-UP! I LOOK OLD AND HAGGARD! AT LEAST 24 OR 25 YEARS OLD!!
AND THESE CHORES ARE MAKING ME SO HUNGRY!
I'VE GOTTA HAVE SOME REAL FOOD!
9

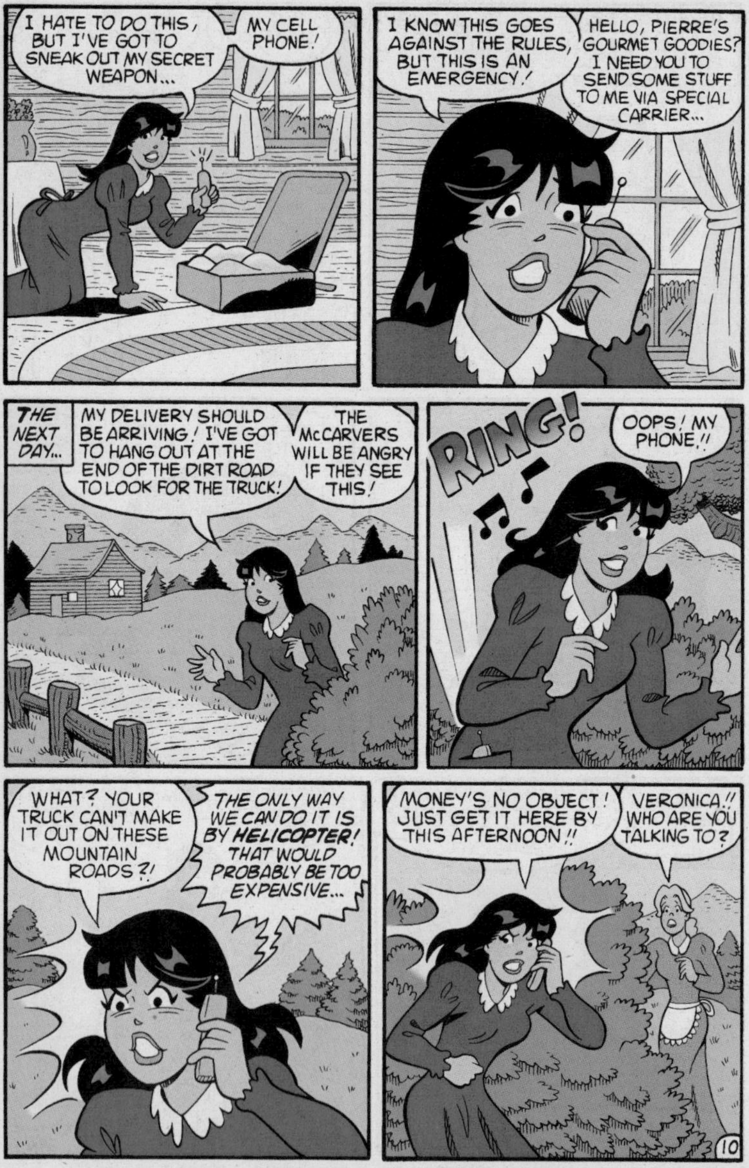
I HATE TO DO THIS, BUT I'VE GOT TO SNEAK OUT MY SECRET WEAPON...
MY CELL PHONE!
I KNOW THIS GOES AGAINST THE RULES, BUT THIS IS AN EMERGENCY!
HELLO, PIERRE'S GOURMET GOODIES? I NEED YOU TO SEND SOME STUFF TO ME VIA SPECIAL CARRIER...
THE NEXT DAY...
MY DELIVERY SHOULD BE ARRIVING! I'VE GOT TO HANG OUT AT THE END OF THE DIRT ROAD TO LOOK FOR THE TRUCK!
THE McCARVERS WILL BE ANGRY IF THEY SEE THIS!
RING!
OOPS! MY PHONE!!
WHAT? YOUR TRUCK CAN'T MAKE IT OUT ON THESE MOUNTAIN ROADS?!
THE ONLY WAY WE CAN DO IT IS BY HELICOPTER! THAT WOULD PROBABLY BE TOO EXPENSIVE...
MONEY'S NO OBJECT! JUST GET IT HERE BY THIS AFTERNOON!!
VERONICA!! WHO ARE YOU TALKING TO?
10

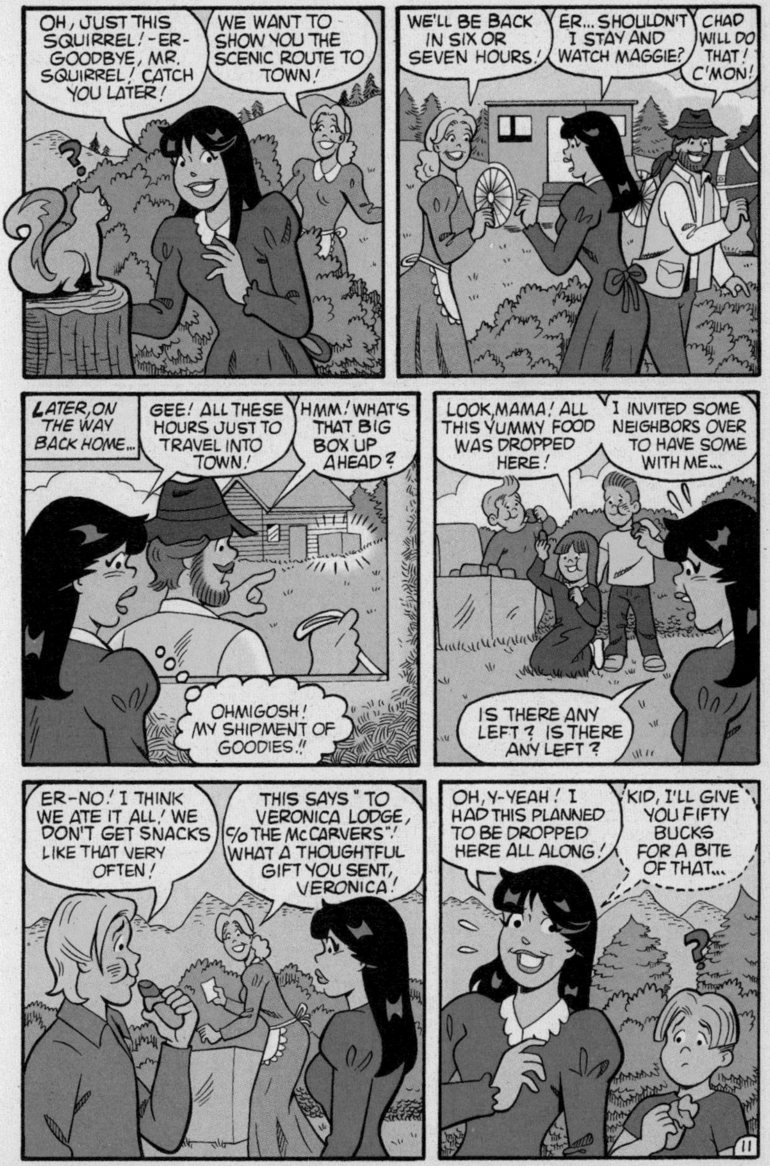
OH, JUST THIS SQUIRREL! -ER- GOODBYE, MR. SQUIRREL! CATCH YOU LATER!
WE WANT TO SHOW YOU THE SCENIC ROUTE TO TOWN!
WE'LL BE BACK IN SIX OR SEVEN HOURS!
ER... SHOULDN'T I STAY AND WATCH MAGGIE?
CHAD WILL DO THAT! C'MON!
LATER, ON THE WAY BACK HOME...
GEE! ALL THESE HOURS JUST TO TRAVEL INTO TOWN!
HMM! WHAT'S THAT BIG BOX UP AHEAD?
OHMIGOSH! MY SHIPMENT OF GOODIES!!
LOOK, MAMA! ALL THIS YUMMY FOOD WAS DROPPED HERE!
I INVITED SOME NEIGHBORS OVER TO HAVE SOME WITH ME...
IS THERE ANY LEFT? IS THERE ANY LEFT?
ER-NO! I THINK WE ATE IT ALL! WE DON'T GET SNACKS LIKE THAT VERY OFTEN!
THIS SAYS "TO VERONICA LODGE, C/O THE McCARVERS"! WHAT A THOUGHTFUL GIFT YOU SENT, VERONICA!
OH, Y-YEAH! I HAD THIS PLANNED TO BE DROPPED HERE ALL ALONG!
KID, I'LL GIVE YOU FIFTY BUCKS FOR A BITE OF THAT...

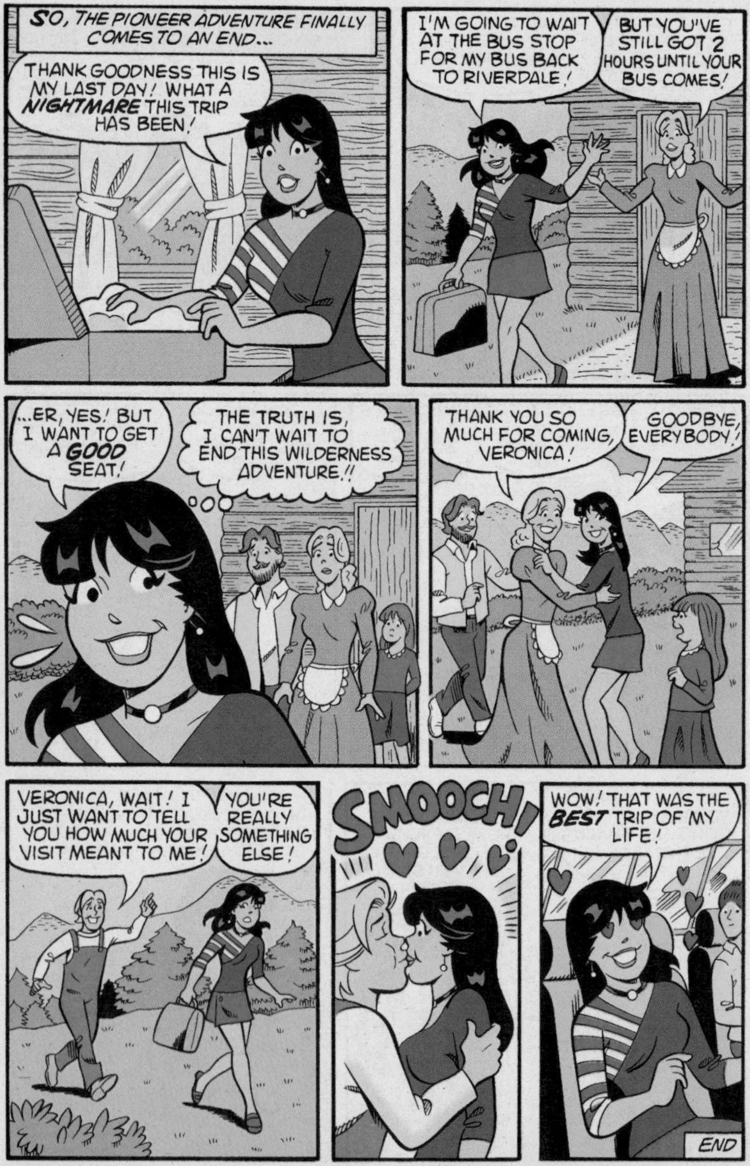
SO, THE PIONEER ADVENTURE FINALLY COMES TO AN END...
THANK GOODNESS THIS IS MY LAST DAY! WHAT A NIGHTMARE THIS TRIP HAS BEEN!
I'M GOING TO WAIT AT THE BUS STOP FOR MY BUS BACK TO RIVERDALE!
BUT YOU'VE STILL GOT 2 HOURS UNTIL YOUR BUS COMES!
...ER, YES! BUT I WANT TO GET A GOOD SEAT!
THE TRUTH IS, I CAN'T WAIT TO END THIS WILDERNESS ADVENTURE!!
THANK YOU SO MUCH FOR COMING, VERONICA!
GOODBYE, EVERYBODY!
VERONICA, WAIT! I JUST WANT TO TELL YOU HOW MUCH YOUR VISIT MEANT TO ME!
YOU'RE REALLY SOMETHING ELSE!
SMOOCH!
WOW! THAT WAS THE BEST TRIP OF MY LIFE!
END

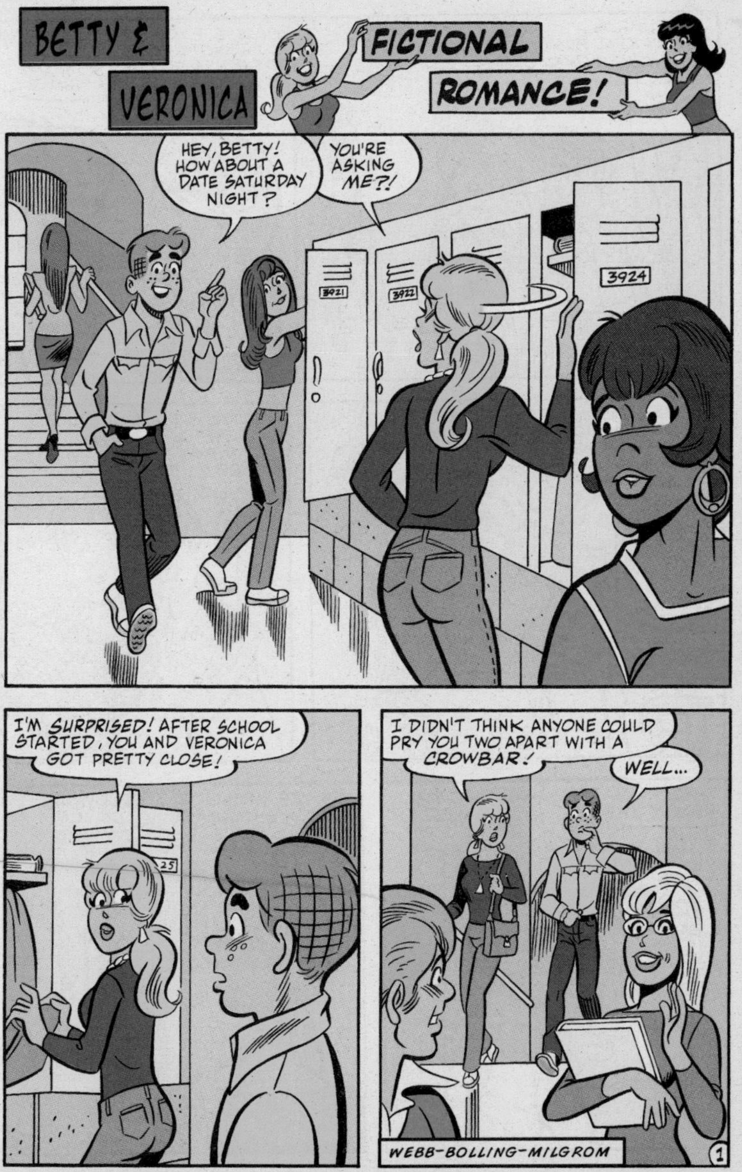
BETTY &
VERONICA
FICTIONAL
ROMANCE!
HEY, BETTY! HOW ABOUT A DATE SATURDAY NIGHT?
YOU'RE ASKING ME?!
3921
3922
3924
I'M SURPRISED! AFTER SCHOOL STARTED, YOU AND VERONICA GOT PRETTY CLOSE!
I DIDN'T THINK ANYONE COULD PRY YOU TWO APART WITH A CROWBAR!
WELL...
WEBB-BOLLING-MILGROM
1

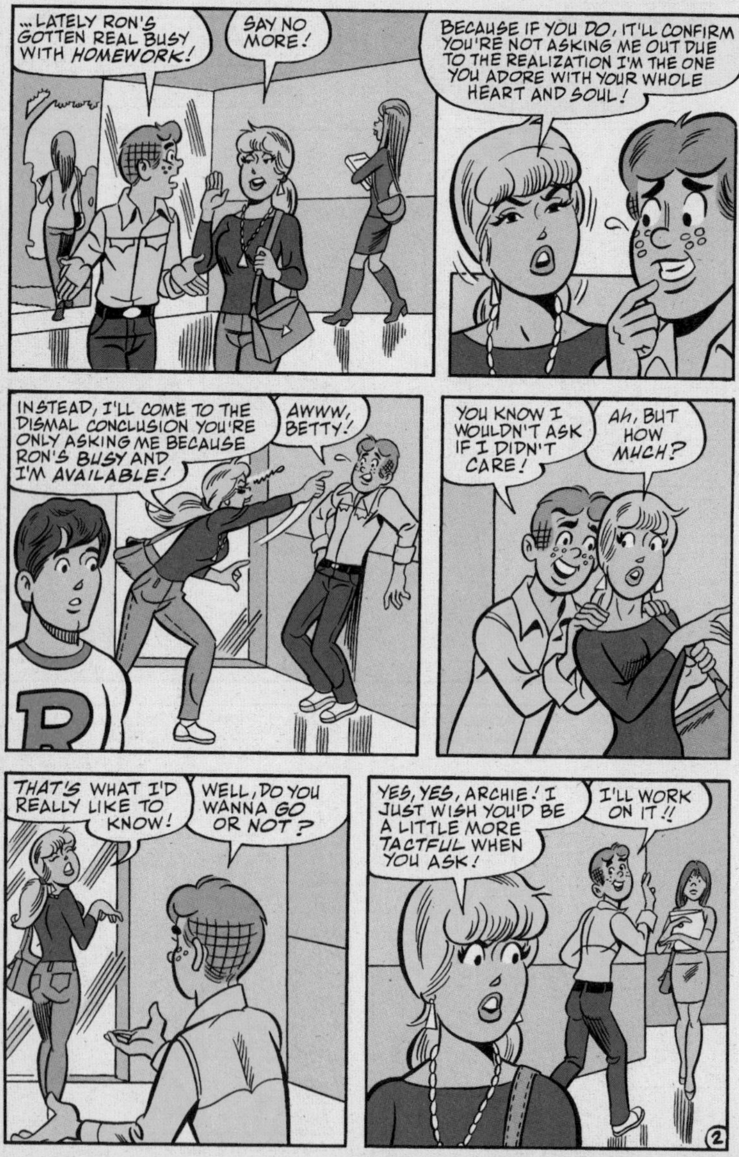
...LATELY RON'S GOTTEN REAL BUSY WITH HOMEWORK!
SAY NO MORE!
BECAUSE IF YOU DO, IT'LL CONFIRM YOU'RE NOT ASKING ME OUT DUE TO THE REALIZATION I'M THE ONE YOU ADORE WITH YOUR WHOLE HEART AND SOUL!
INSTEAD, I'LL COME TO THE DISMAL CONCLUSION YOU'RE ONLY ASKING ME BECAUSE RON'S BUSY AND I'M AVAILABLE!
AWWW, BETTY!
YOU KNOW I WOULDN'T ASK IF I DIDN'T CARE!
Ah, BUT HOW MUCH?
THAT'S WHAT I'D REALLY LIKE TO KNOW!
WELL, DO YOU WANNA GO OR NOT?
YES, YES, ARCHIE! I JUST WISH YOU'D BE A LITTLE MORE TACTFUL WHEN YOU ASK!
I'LL WORK ON IT!!
2

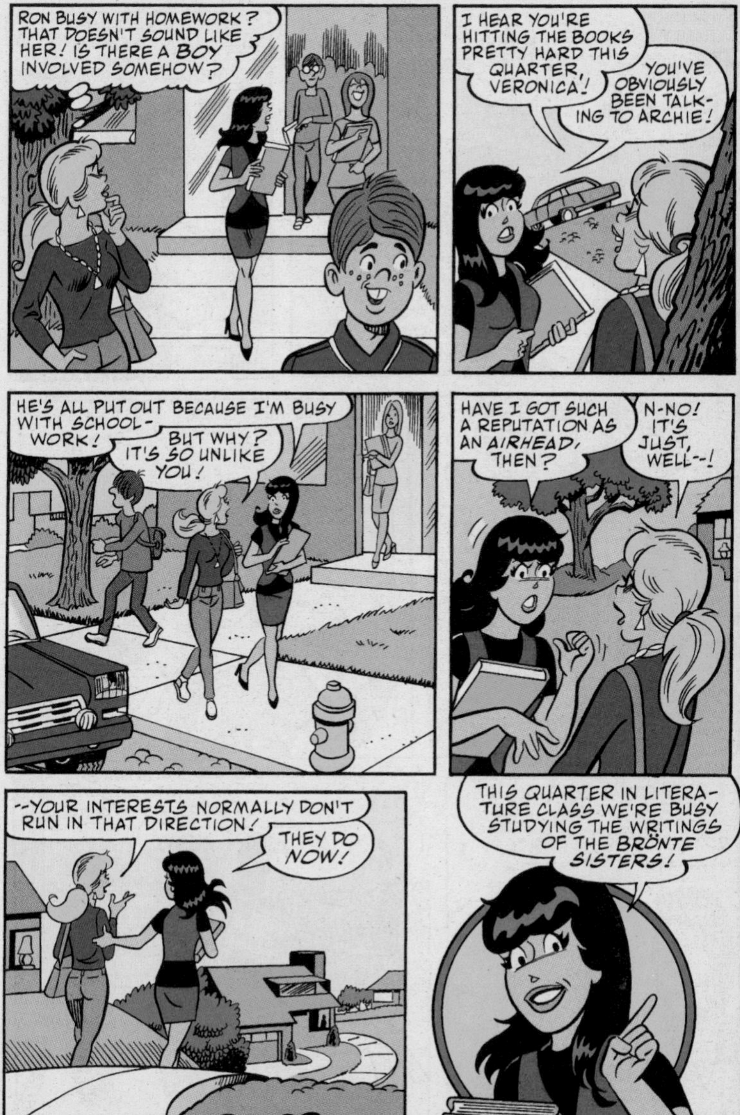
RON BUSY WITH HOMEWORK? THAT DOESN'T SOUND LIKE HER! IS THERE A BOY INVOLVED SOMEHOW?
I HEAR YOU'RE HITTING THE BOOKS PRETTY HARD THIS QUARTER, VERONICA!
YOU'VE OBVIOUSLY BEEN TALKING TO ARCHIE!
HE'S ALL PUT OUT BECAUSE I'M BUSY WITH SCHOOL-WORK!
BUT WHY? IT'S SO UNLIKE YOU!
HAVE I GOT SUCH A REPUTATION AS AN AIRHEAD, THEN?
N-NO! IT'S JUST, WELL--!
--YOUR INTERESTS NORMALLY DON'T RUN IN THAT DIRECTION!
THEY DO NOW!
THIS QUARTER IN LITERATURE CLASS WE'RE BUSY STUDYING THE WRITINGS OF THE BRÖNTE SISTERS!
3

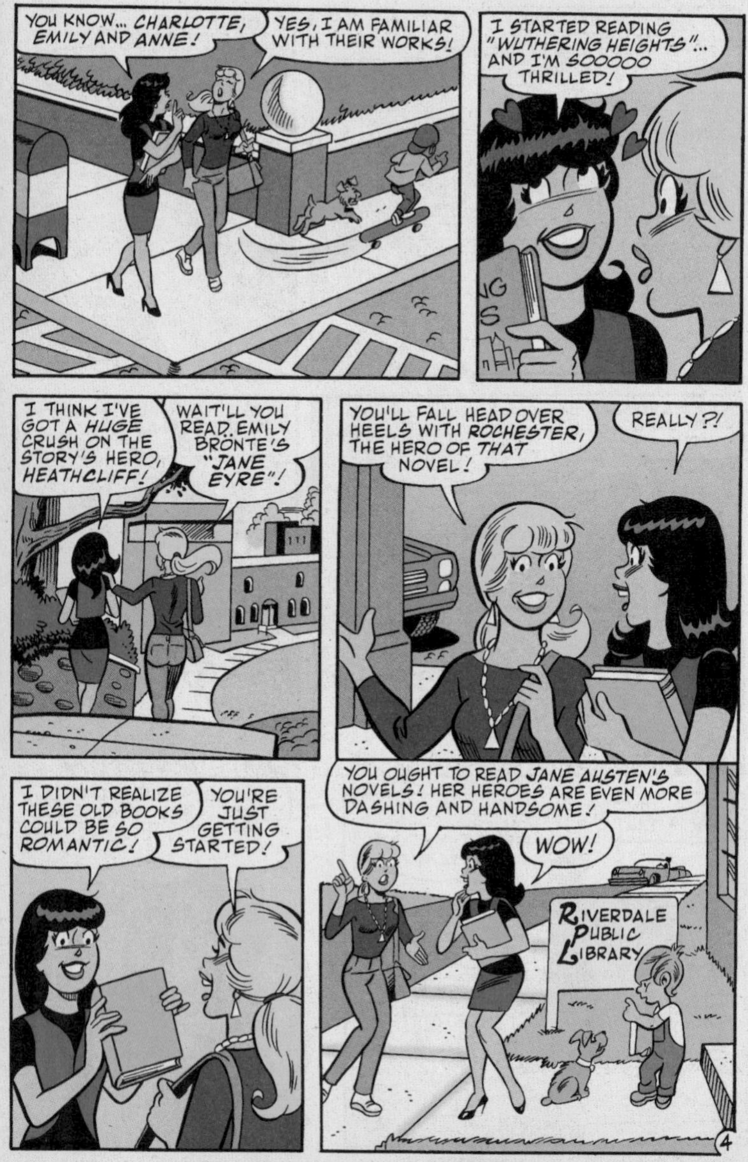

YOU KNOW... CHARLOTTE, EMILY AND ANNE!
YES, I AM FAMILIAR WITH THEIR WORKS!
I STARTED READING "WUTHERING HEIGHTS"... AND I'M SOOOOO THRILLED!
I THINK I'VE GOT A HUGE CRUSH ON THE STORY'S HERO, HEATHCLIFF!
WAIT'LL YOU READ EMILY BRÖNTE'S "JANE EYRE"!
YOU'LL FALL HEAD OVER HEELS WITH ROCHESTER, THE HERO OF THAT NOVEL!
REALLY ?!
I DIDN'T REALIZE THESE OLD BOOKS COULD BE SO ROMANTIC!
YOU'RE JUST GETTING STARTED!
YOU OUGHT TO READ JANE AUSTEN'S NOVELS! HER HEROES ARE EVEN MORE DASHING AND HANDSOME!
WOW!
RIVERDALE PUBLIC LIBRARY
4

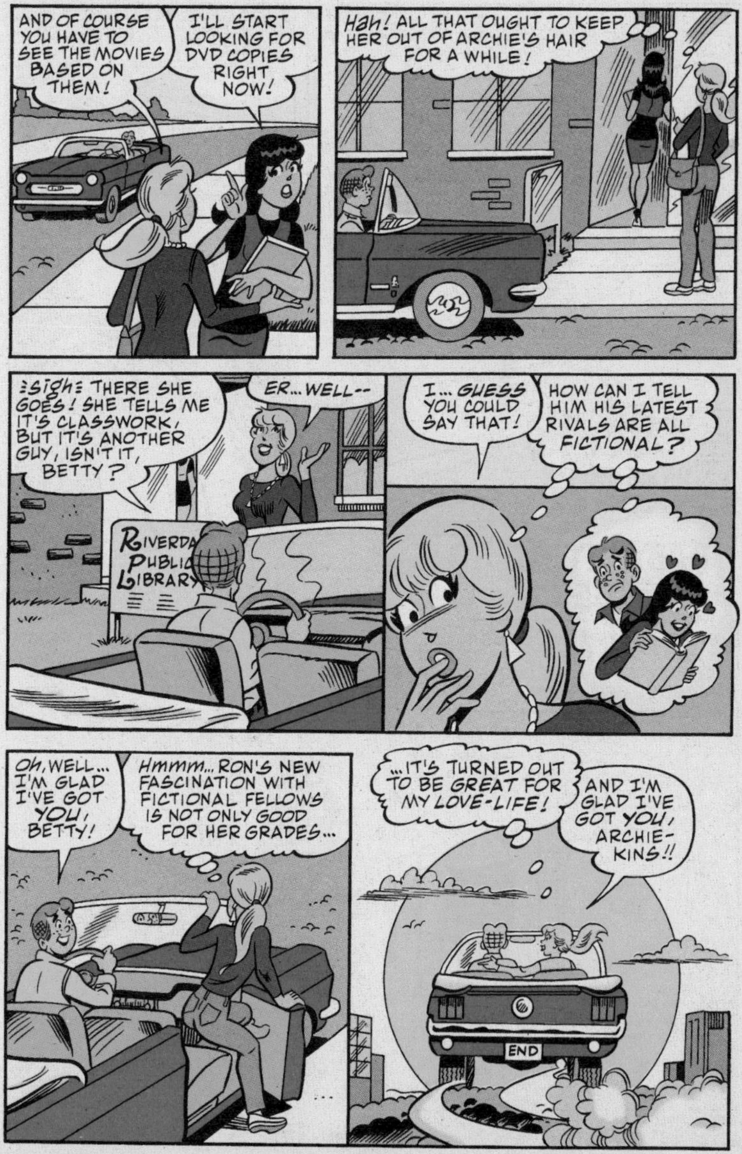
AND OF COURSE YOU HAVE TO SEE THE MOVIES BASED ON THEM!
I'LL START LOOKING FOR DVD COPIES RIGHT NOW!
Hah! ALL THAT OUGHT TO KEEP HER OUT OF ARCHIE'S HAIR FOR A WHILE!
:sigh: THERE SHE GOES! SHE TELLS ME IT'S CLASSWORK, BUT IT'S ANOTHER GUY, ISN'T IT, BETTY?
ER... WELL--
RIVERDA
PUBLI
LIBRARY
I... GUESS YOU COULD SAY THAT!
HOW CAN I TELL HIM HIS LATEST RIVALS ARE ALL FICTIONAL?
Oh, WELL... I'M GLAD I'VE GOT YOU, BETTY!
Hmmm... RON'S NEW FASCINATION WITH FICTIONAL FELLOWS IS NOT ONLY GOOD FOR HER GRADES...
...IT'S TURNED OUT TO BE GREAT FOR MY LOVE-LIFE!
AND I'M GLAD I'VE GOT YOU, ARCHIE-KINS!!
END

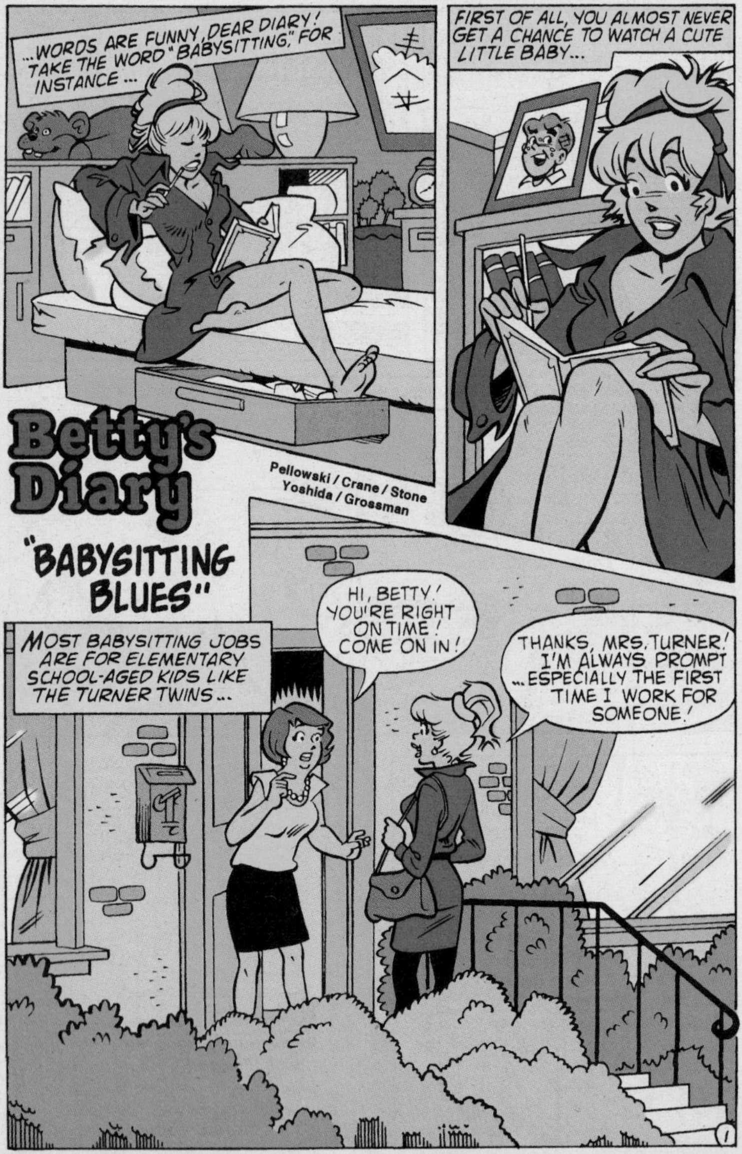

...WORDS ARE FUNNY, DEAR DIARY! TAKE THE WORD "BABYSITTING," FOR INSTANCE ...
FIRST OF ALL, YOU ALMOST NEVER GET A CHANCE TO WATCH A CUTE LITTLE BABY...
Betty's Diary
Pellowski / Crane / Stone
Yoshida / Grossman
"BABYSITTING BLUES"
MOST BABYSITTING JOBS ARE FOR ELEMENTARY SCHOOL-AGED KIDS LIKE THE TURNER TWINS...
HI, BETTY! YOU'RE RIGHT ON TIME! COME ON IN!
THANKS, MRS. TURNER! I'M ALWAYS PROMPT ...ESPECIALLY THE FIRST TIME I WORK FOR SOMEONE!
1

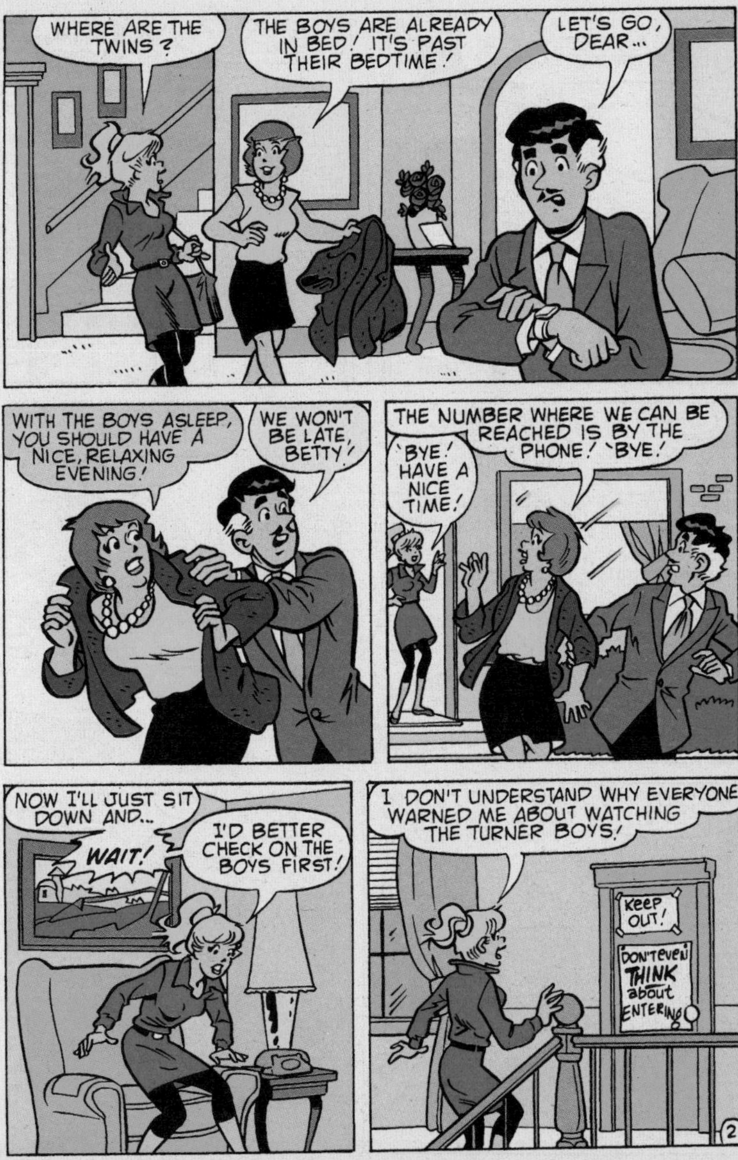
WHERE ARE THE TWINS?
THE BOYS ARE ALREADY IN BED! IT'S PAST THEIR BEDTIME!
LET'S GO, DEAR...
WITH THE BOYS ASLEEP, YOU SHOULD HAVE A NICE, RELAXING EVENING!
WE WON'T BE LATE, BETTY!
THE NUMBER WHERE WE CAN BE REACHED IS BY THE PHONE! 'BYE!
'BYE! HAVE A NICE TIME!
NOW I'LL JUST SIT DOWN AND...
WAIT!
I'D BETTER CHECK ON THE BOYS FIRST!
I DON'T UNDERSTAND WHY EVERYONE WARNED ME ABOUT WATCHING THE TURNER BOYS!
KEEP OUT!
DON'T EVEN THINK about ENTERING
2

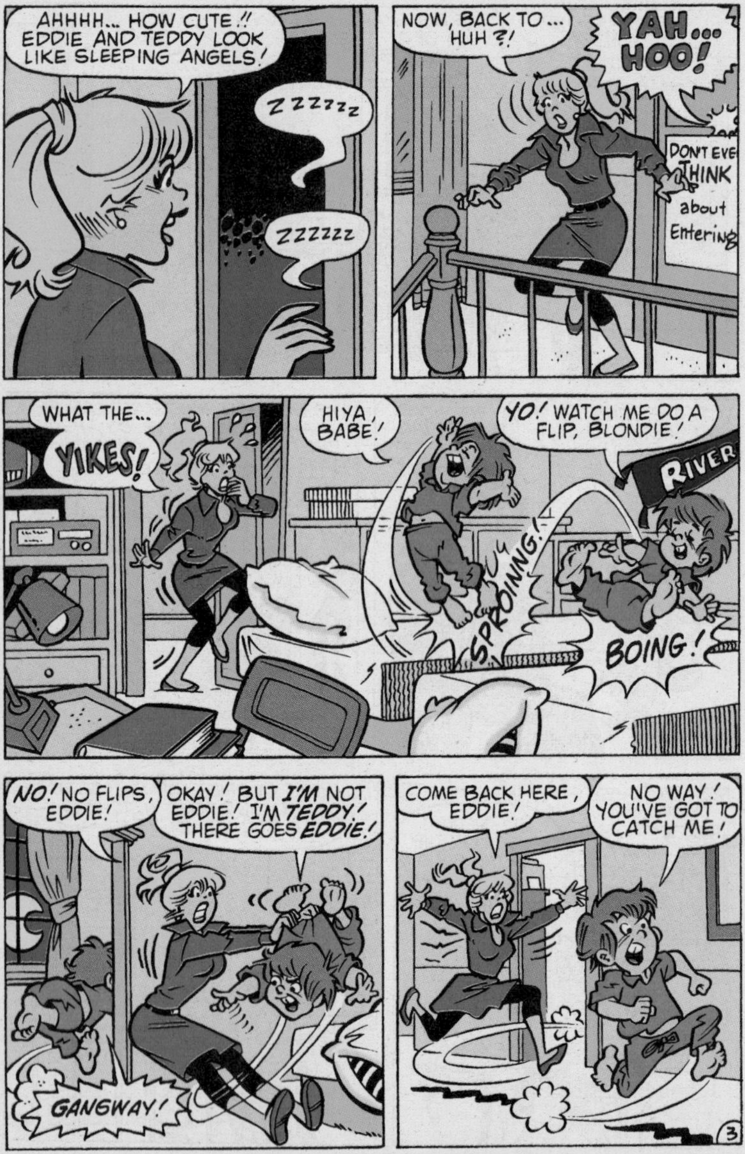
AHHHH... HOW CUTE!! EDDIE AND TEDDY LOOK LIKE SLEEPING ANGELS!
ZZZZZZ
ZZZZZZ
NOW, BACK TO... HUH ?!
YAH... HOO!
DON'T EVE
THINK
about
Entering
WHAT THE...
YIKES!
HIYA, BABE!
YO! WATCH ME DO A FLIP, BLONDIE!
RIVER
SPROING!
BOING!
NO! NO FLIPS, EDDIE!
OKAY! BUT I'M NOT EDDIE! I'M TEDDY! THERE GOES EDDIE!
GANGWAY!
COME BACK HERE, EDDIE!
NO WAY! YOU'VE GOT TO CATCH ME!
3

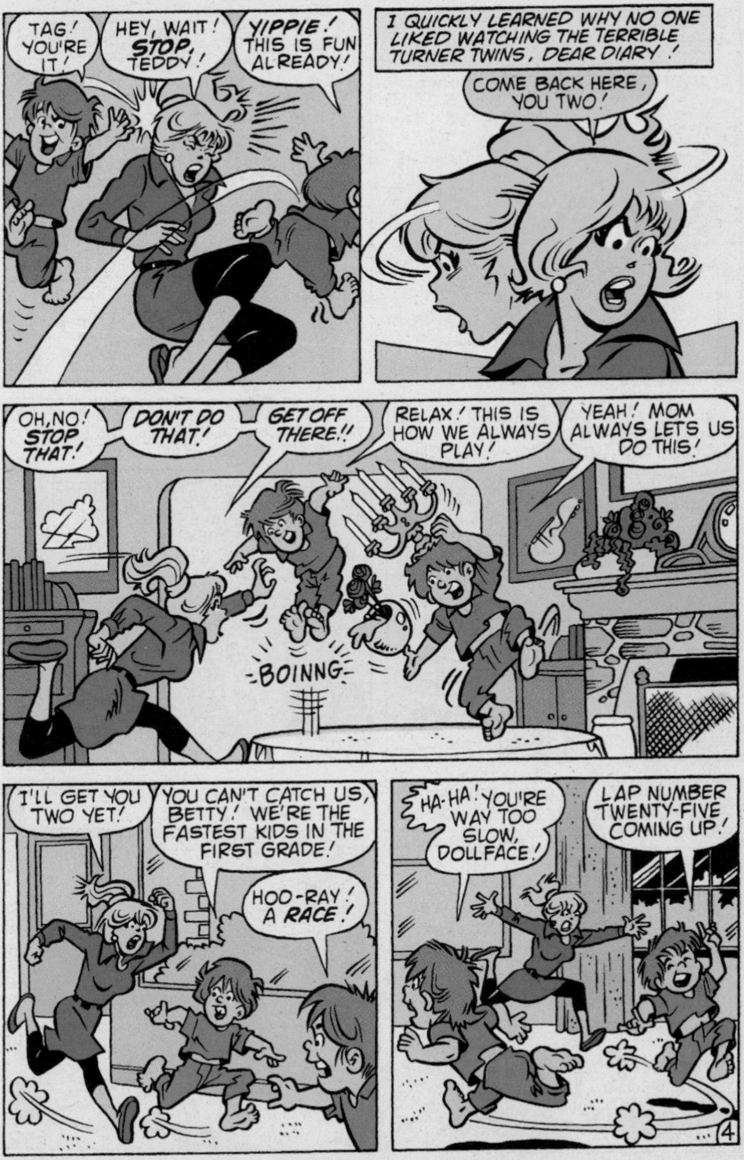
TAG! YOU'RE IT!
HEY, WAIT! STOP, TEDDY!
YIPPIE! THIS IS FUN ALREADY!
I QUICKLY LEARNED WHY NO ONE LIKED WATCHING THE TERRIBLE TURNER TWINS, DEAR DIARY!
COME BACK HERE, YOU TWO!
OH, NO! STOP THAT!
DON'T DO THAT!
GET OFF THERE!!
RELAX! THIS IS HOW WE ALWAYS PLAY!
YEAH! MOM ALWAYS LETS US DO THIS!
BOINNG
I'LL GET YOU TWO YET!
YOU CAN'T CATCH US, BETTY! WE'RE THE FASTEST KIDS IN THE FIRST GRADE!
HOO-RAY! A RACE!
HA-HA! YOU'RE WAY TOO SLOW, DOLLFACE!
LAP NUMBER TWENTY-FIVE COMING UP!
4

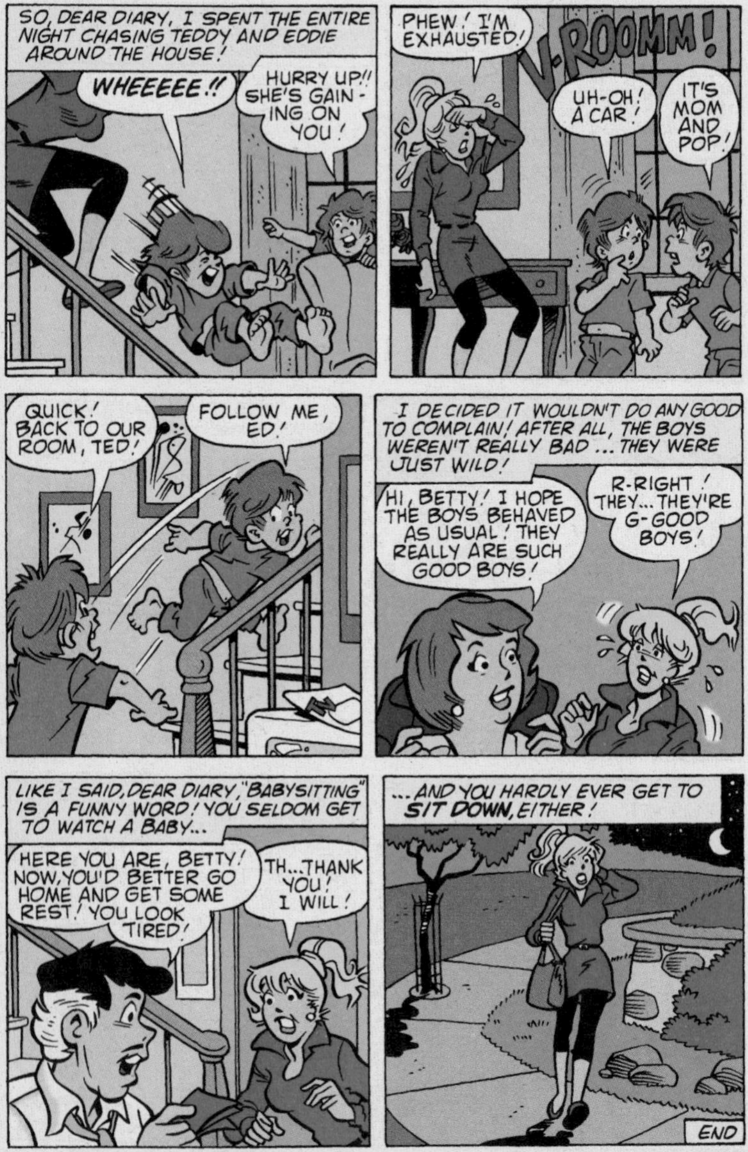
SO, DEAR DIARY, I SPENT THE ENTIRE NIGHT CHASING TEDDY AND EDDIE AROUND THE HOUSE!
WHEEEEEE!!
HURRY UP!! SHE'S GAIN-ING ON YOU!
PHEW! I'M EXHAUSTED!
V-ROOMM!
UH-OH! A CAR!
IT'S MOM AND POP!
QUICK! BACK TO OUR ROOM, TED!
FOLLOW ME, ED!
I DECIDED IT WOULDN'T DO ANY GOOD TO COMPLAIN! AFTER ALL, THE BOYS WEREN'T REALLY BAD ... THEY WERE JUST WILD!
HI, BETTY! I HOPE THE BOYS BEHAVED AS USUAL! THEY REALLY ARE SUCH GOOD BOYS!
R-RIGHT! THEY... THEY'RE G-GOOD BOYS!
LIKE I SAID, DEAR DIARY, "BABYSITTING" IS A FUNNY WORD! YOU SELDOM GET TO WATCH A BABY...
HERE YOU ARE, BETTY! NOW, YOU'D BETTER GO HOME AND GET SOME REST! YOU LOOK TIRED!
TH...THANK YOU! I WILL!
... AND YOU HARDLY EVER GET TO SIT DOWN, EITHER!
END

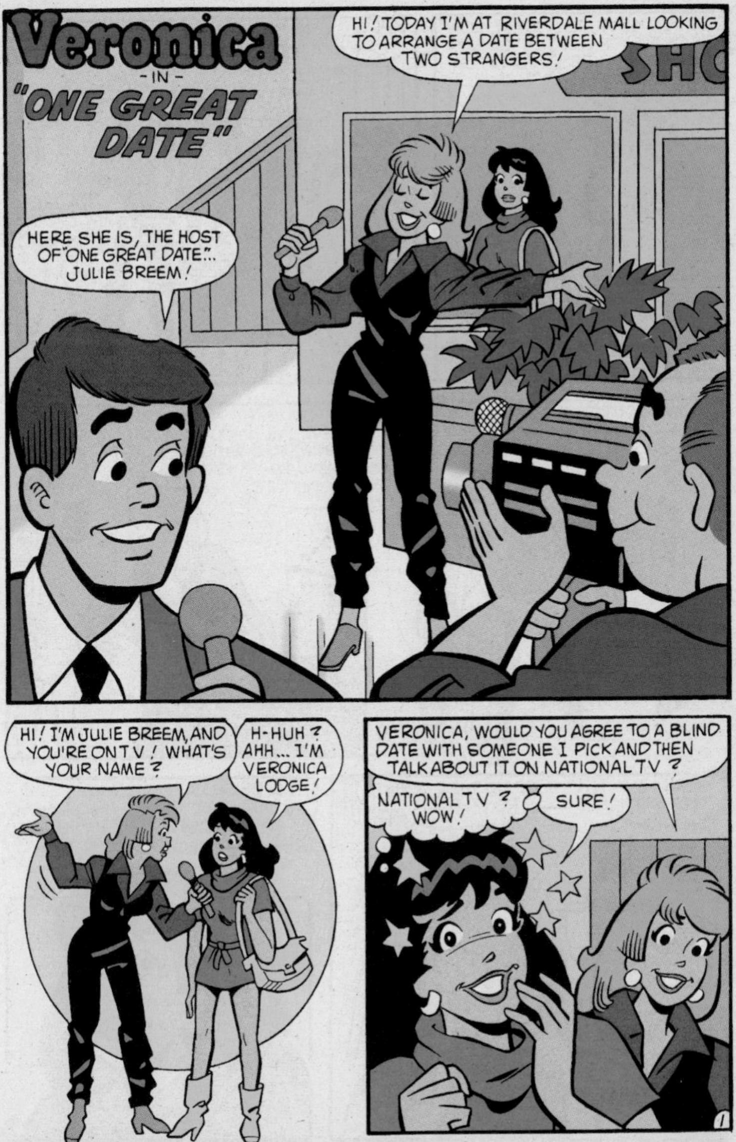

Veronica
-IN-
"ONE GREAT DATE"
HERE SHE IS, THE HOST OF "ONE GREAT DATE"... JULIE BREEM!
HI! TODAY I'M AT RIVERDALE MALL LOOKING TO ARRANGE A DATE BETWEEN TWO STRANGERS!
SHO
HI! I'M JULIE BREEM, AND YOU'RE ON TV! WHAT'S YOUR NAME?
H-HUH? AHH... I'M VERONICA LODGE!
VERONICA, WOULD YOU AGREE TO A BLIND DATE WITH SOMEONE I PICK AND THEN TALK ABOUT IT ON NATIONAL TV?
NATIONAL TV? WOW!
SURE!
1

Script: Mike Pellowski / Pencils: Tim Kennedy / Inks: Pat Kennedy / Inks: Bill Yoshida / Colors: Barry Grossman

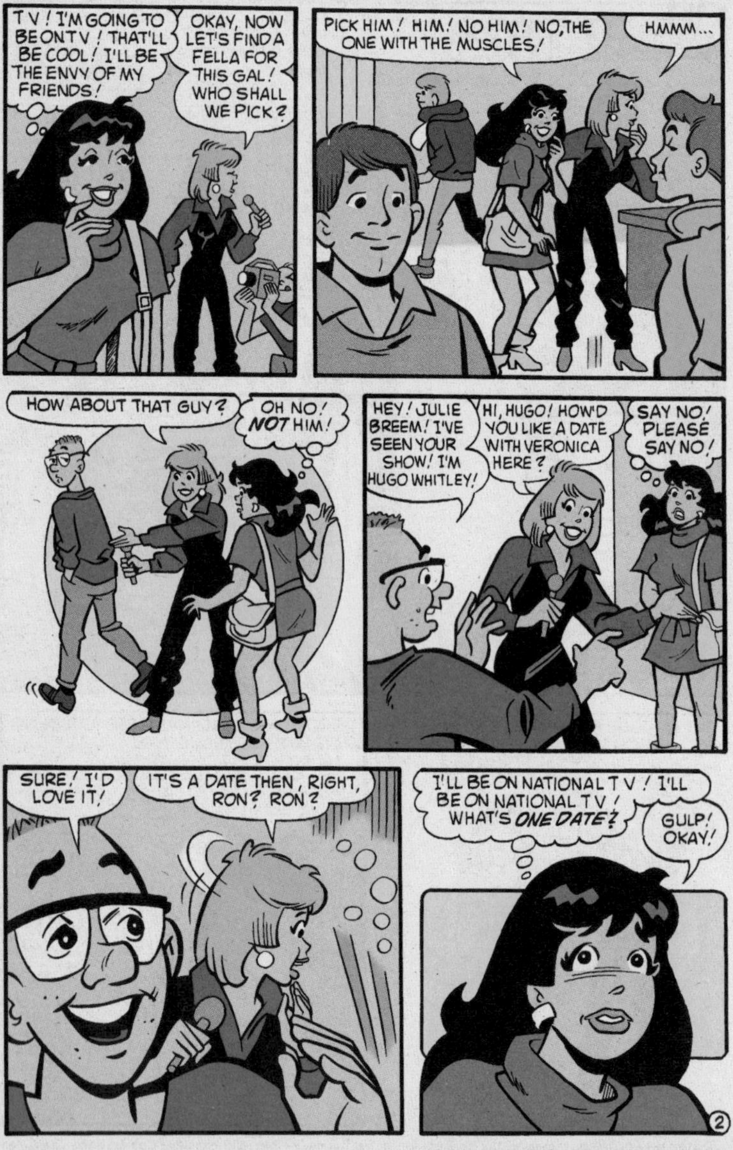
T V! I'M GOING TO BE ON T V! THAT'LL BE COOL! I'LL BE THE ENVY OF MY FRIENDS!
OKAY, NOW LET'S FIND A FELLA FOR THIS GAL! WHO SHALL WE PICK?
PICK HIM! HIM! NO HIM! NO, THE ONE WITH THE MUSCLES!
HMMM...
HOW ABOUT THAT GUY?
OH NO! NOT HIM!
HEY! JULIE BREEM! I'VE SEEN YOUR SHOW! I'M HUGO WHITLEY!
HI, HUGO! HOW'D YOU LIKE A DATE WITH VERONICA HERE?
SAY NO! PLEASE SAY NO!
SURE! I'D LOVE IT!
IT'S A DATE THEN, RIGHT, RON? RON?
I'LL BE ON NATIONAL T V! I'LL BE ON NATIONAL T V! WHAT'S ONE DATE?
GULP! OKAY!
2

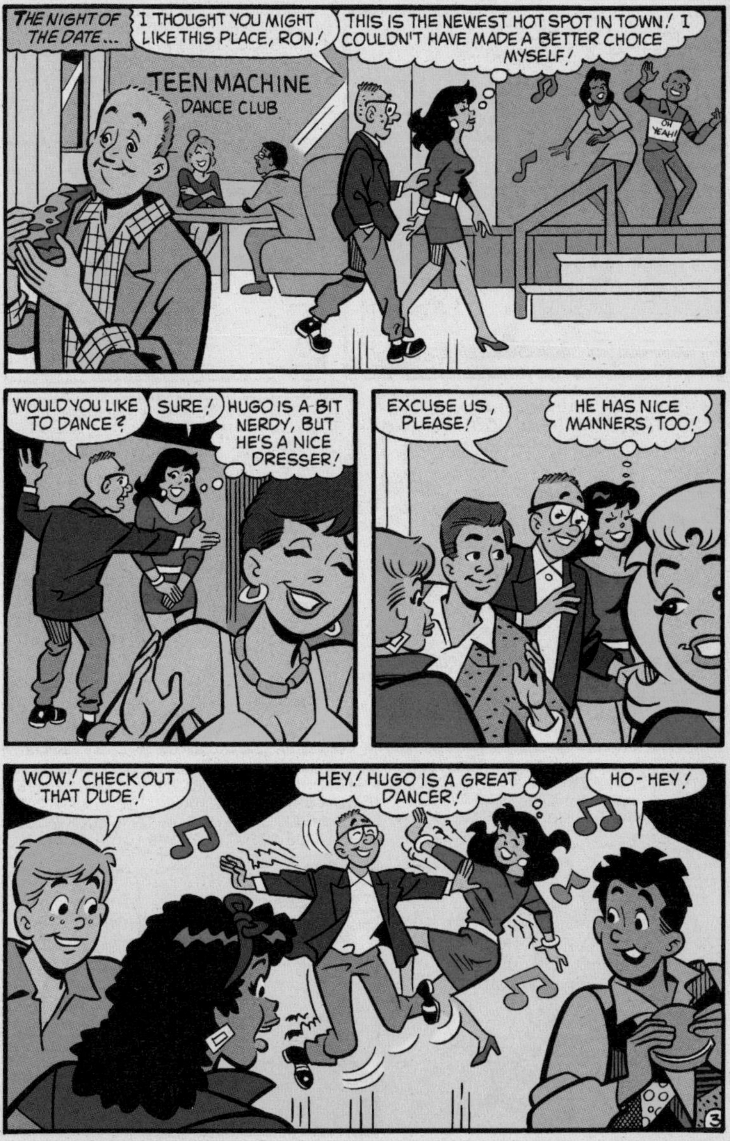
THE NIGHT OF THE DATE...
I THOUGHT YOU MIGHT LIKE THIS PLACE, RON!
THIS IS THE NEWEST HOT SPOT IN TOWN! I COULDN'T HAVE MADE A BETTER CHOICE MYSELF!
TEEN MACHINE DANCE CLUB
OH YEAH!
WOULD YOU LIKE TO DANCE?
SURE!
HUGO IS A BIT NERDY, BUT HE'S A NICE DRESSER!
EXCUSE US, PLEASE!
HE HAS NICE MANNERS, TOO!
WOW! CHECK OUT THAT DUDE!
HEY! HUGO IS A GREAT DANCER!
HO-HEY!
3

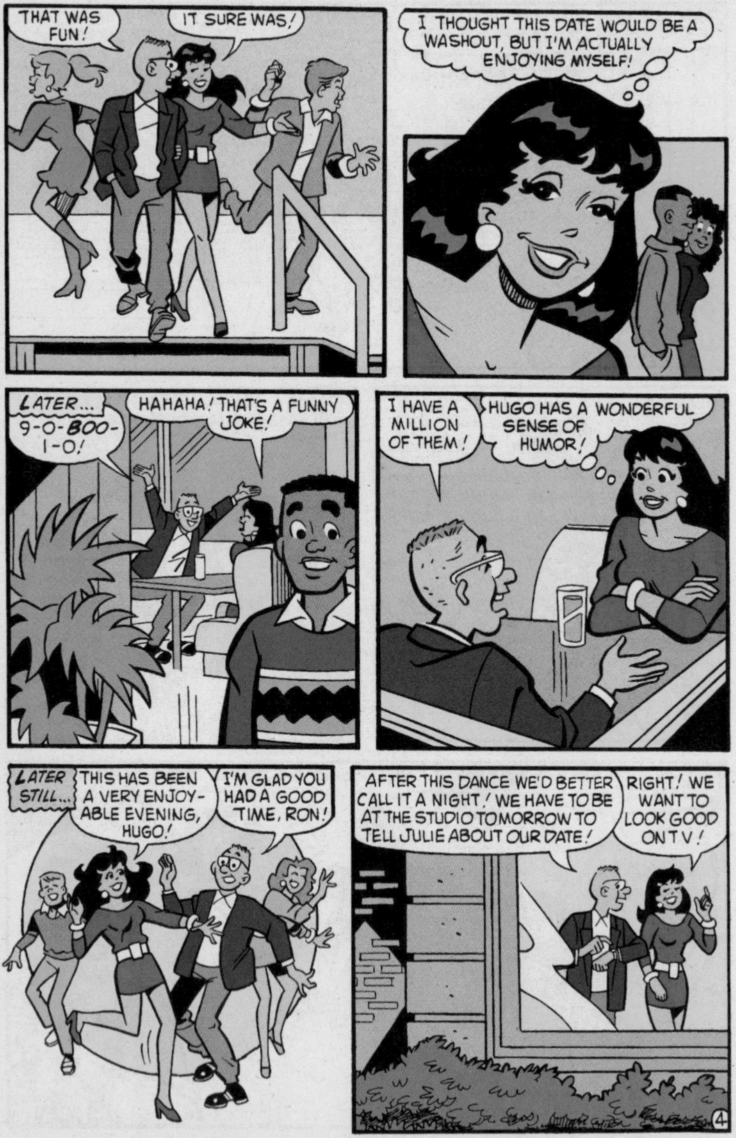

THAT WAS FUN!
IT SURE WAS!
I THOUGHT THIS DATE WOULD BE A WASHOUT, BUT I'M ACTUALLY ENJOYING MYSELF!
LATER...
9-0-BOO-1-0!
HAHAHA! THAT'S A FUNNY JOKE!
I HAVE A MILLION OF THEM!
HUGO HAS A WONDERFUL SENSE OF HUMOR!
LATER STILL...
THIS HAS BEEN A VERY ENJOYABLE EVENING, HUGO!
I'M GLAD YOU HAD A GOOD TIME, RON!
AFTER THIS DANCE WE'D BETTER CALL IT A NIGHT! WE HAVE TO BE AT THE STUDIO TOMORROW TO TELL JULIE ABOUT OUR DATE!
RIGHT! WE WANT TO LOOK GOOD ON TV!
4

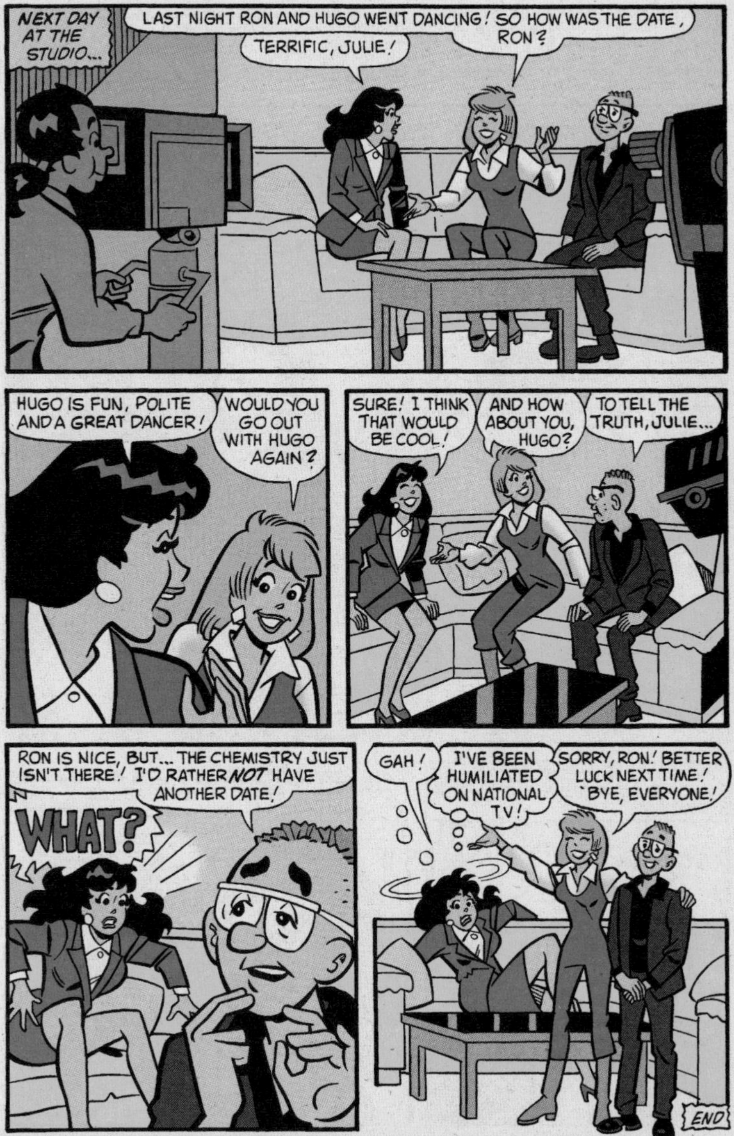
NEXT DAY AT THE STUDIO...
LAST NIGHT RON AND HUGO WENT DANCING! SO HOW WAS THE DATE, RON?
TERRIFIC, JULIE!
HUGO IS FUN, POLITE AND A GREAT DANCER!
WOULD YOU GO OUT WITH HUGO AGAIN?
SURE! I THINK THAT WOULD BE COOL!
AND HOW ABOUT YOU, HUGO?
TO TELL THE TRUTH, JULIE...
RON IS NICE, BUT... THE CHEMISTRY JUST ISN'T THERE! I'D RATHER NOT HAVE ANOTHER DATE!
WHAT?
GAH!
I'VE BEEN HUMILIATED ON NATIONAL TV!
SORRY, RON! BETTER LUCK NEXT TIME! 'BYE, EVERYONE!
END

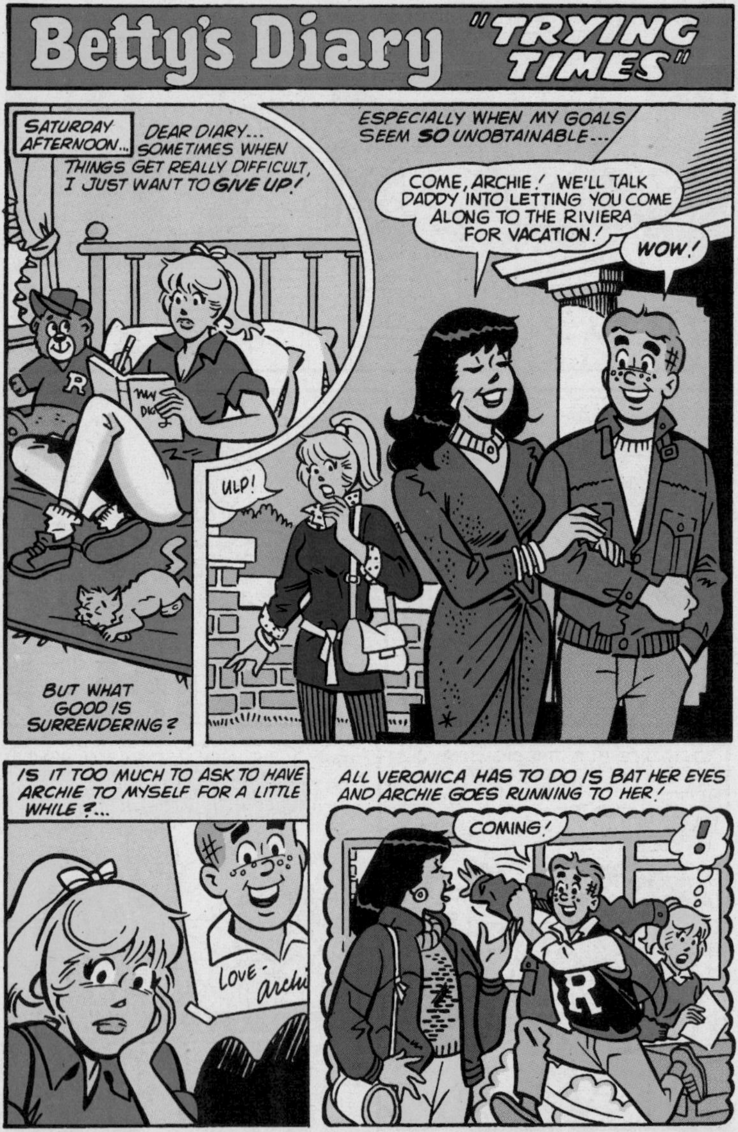
Betty's Diary
"TRYING TIMES"
SATURDAY AFTERNOON...
DEAR DIARY... SOMETIMES WHEN THINGS GET REALLY DIFFICULT, I JUST WANT TO GIVE UP!
MY DIARY
BUT WHAT GOOD IS SURRENDERING?
ESPECIALLY WHEN MY GOALS SEEM SO UNOBTAINABLE...
COME, ARCHIE! WE'LL TALK DADDY INTO LETTING YOU COME ALONG TO THE RIVIERA FOR VACATION!
WOW!
ULP!
IS IT TOO MUCH TO ASK TO HAVE ARCHIE TO MYSELF FOR A LITTLE WHILE?...
LOVE - archie
ALL VERONICA HAS TO DO IS BAT HER EYES AND ARCHIE GOES RUNNING TO HER!
COMING!
!

Script: Rod Ollerenshaw / Pencils: Stan Goldberg / Inks: Rudy Lapick / Letters: Bill Yoshida

HOW ABOUT LAST WEEK, WHEN I HAD THAT PHYSICS EXAM? ...

MY WORST SUBJECT!

PHYSICS TEST TODAY!

I HAD TO STUDY EVERY NIGHT TO GET A DECENT GRADE!

MASS = X R Y 3207 + INERTIA!

...BUT DILTON GETS A PERFECT TEST SCORE WITHOUT EVEN TRYING...

DILTON!

A+

AND THERE WAS PITCHING IN THE GIRLS' SOFTBALL LEAGUE LAST FALL...

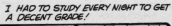

UH, OH!

ANOTHER HOME RUN!

WHACK!

ETHEL HAD TO COACH ME ALMOST EVERY DAY AFTER SCHOOL...

WHIP YOUR WRIST TO THE SIDE...

SHE MADE IT LOOK SO EASY... WITHOUT TRYING!

LIKE THIS!

PERFECT!

SMACK!

2

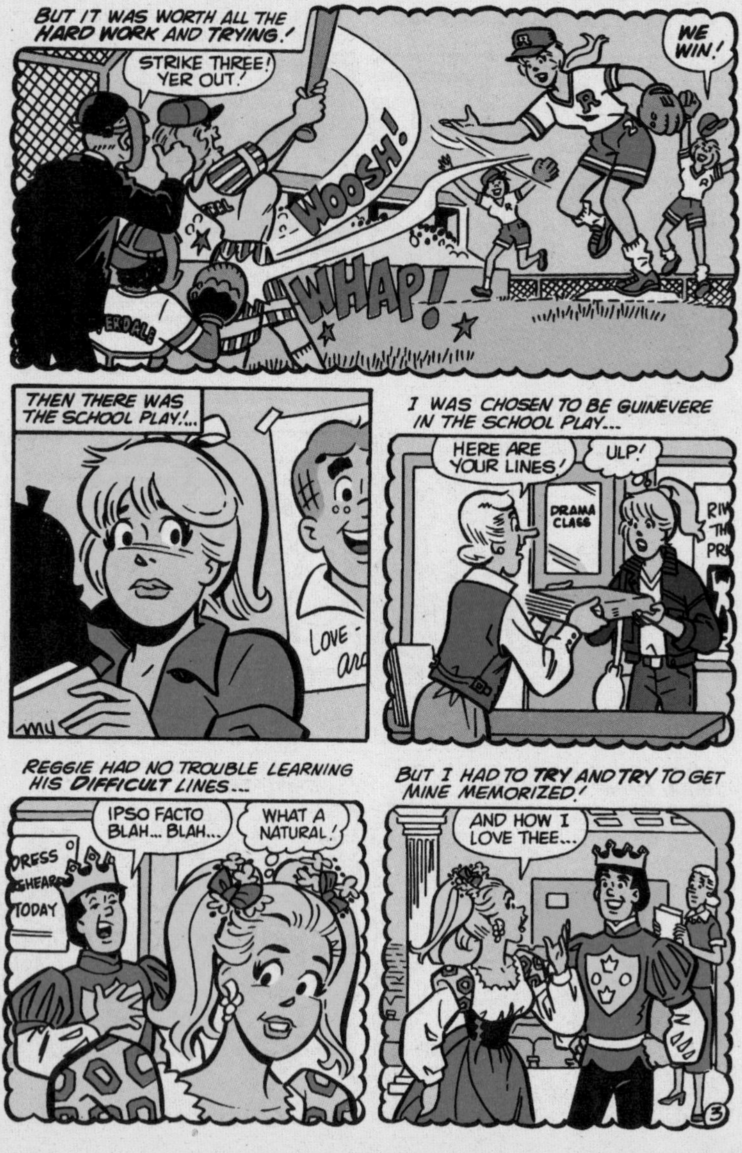

BUT IT WAS WORTH ALL THE HARD WORK AND TRYING!
STRIKE THREE! YER OUT!
WOOSH!
WE WIN!
WHAP!
THEN THERE WAS THE SCHOOL PLAY!...
LOVE -
I WAS CHOSEN TO BE GUINEVERE IN THE SCHOOL PLAY...
HERE ARE YOUR LINES!
ULP!
DRAMA CLASS
REGGIE HAD NO TROUBLE LEARNING HIS DIFFICULT LINES...
IPSO FACTO BLAH... BLAH...
WHAT A NATURAL!
TODAY
BUT I HAD TO TRY AND TRY TO GET MINE MEMORIZED!
AND HOW I LOVE THEE...

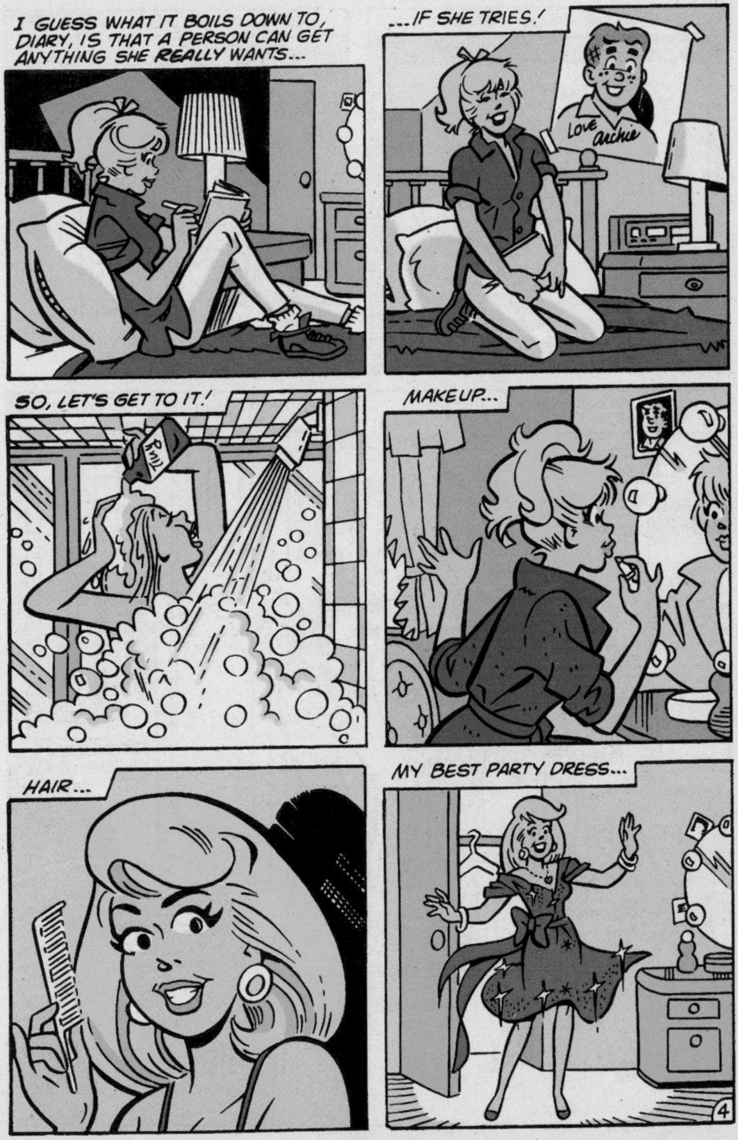
I GUESS WHAT IT BOILS DOWN TO, DIARY, IS THAT A PERSON CAN GET ANYTHING SHE REALLY WANTS...
...IF SHE TRIES!
Love Archie
SO, LET'S GET TO IT!
MAKEUP...
HAIR...
MY BEST PARTY DRESS...

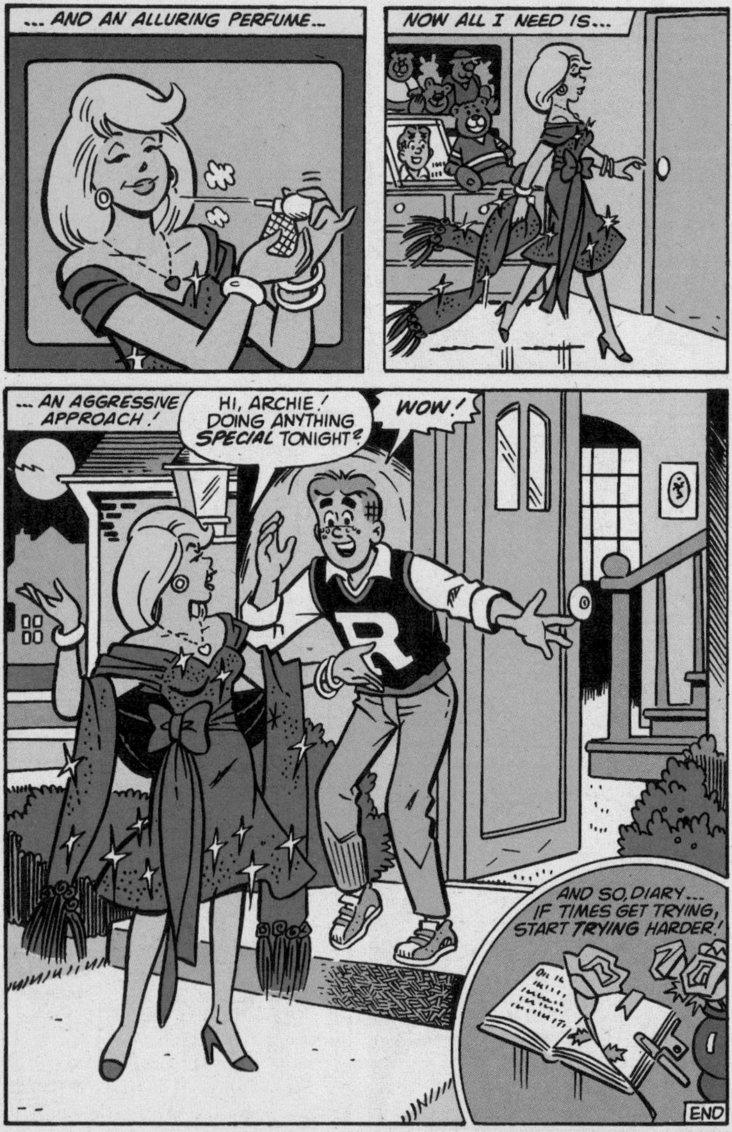
... AND AN ALLURING PERFUME...
NOW ALL I NEED IS...
... AN AGGRESSIVE APPROACH!
HI, ARCHIE! DOING ANYTHING SPECIAL TONIGHT?
WOW!
AND SO, DIARY... IF TIMES GET TRYING, START TRYING HARDER!
END

Archie & Friends in The Emperor's Used Clothes

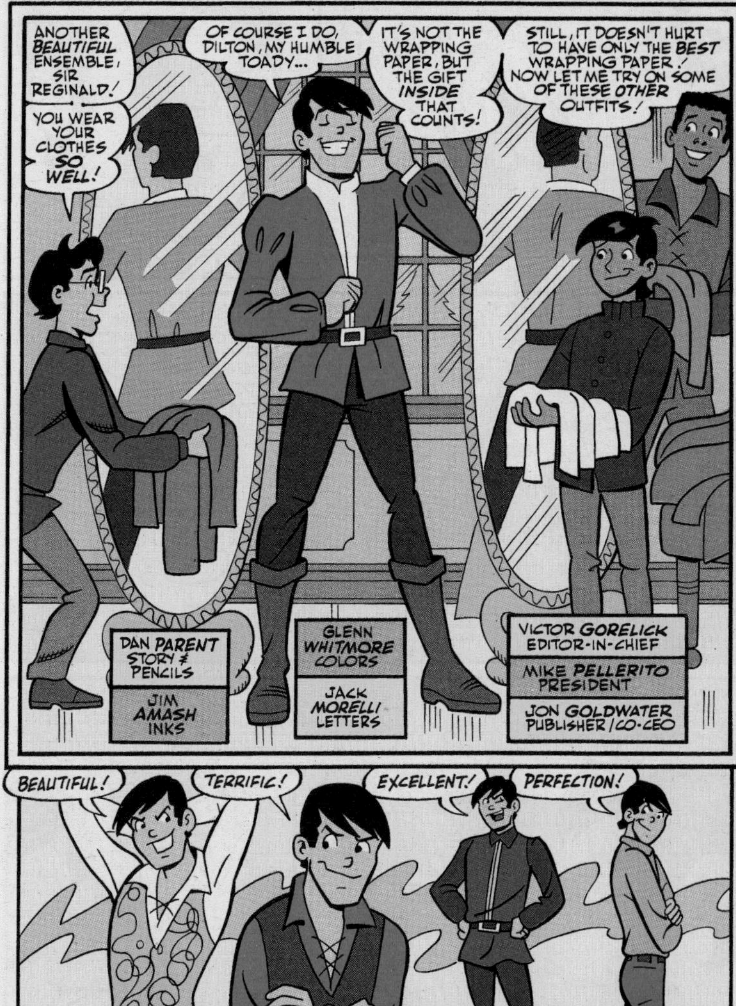
ANOTHER BEAUTIFUL ENSEMBLE, SIR REGINALD!
YOU WEAR YOUR CLOTHES SO WELL!
OF COURSE I DO, DILTON, MY HUMBLE TOADY...
IT'S NOT THE WRAPPING PAPER, BUT THE GIFT INSIDE THAT COUNTS!
STILL, IT DOESN'T HURT TO HAVE ONLY THE BEST WRAPPING PAPER! NOW LET ME TRY ON SOME OF THESE OTHER OUTFITS!
DAN PARENT STORY & PENCILS
JIM AMASH INKS
GLENN WHITMORE COLORS
JACK MORELLI LETTERS
VICTOR GORELICK EDITOR-IN-CHIEF
MIKE PELLERITO PRESIDENT
JON GOLDWATER PUBLISHER/CO-CEO
BEAUTIFUL!
TERRIFIC!
EXCELLENT!
PERFECTION!

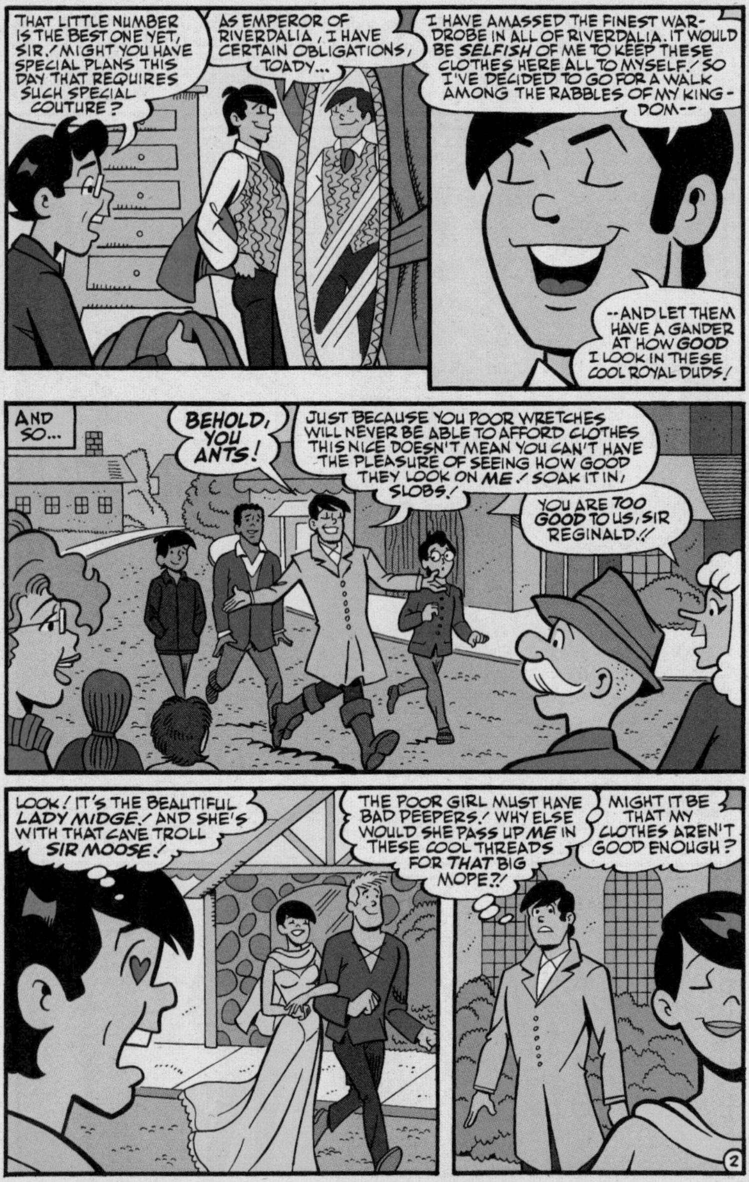
THAT LITTLE NUMBER IS THE BEST ONE YET, SIR! MIGHT YOU HAVE SPECIAL PLANS THIS DAY THAT REQUIRES SUCH SPECIAL COUTURE?
AS EMPEROR OF RIVERDALIA, I HAVE CERTAIN OBLIGATIONS, TOADY...
I HAVE AMASSED THE FINEST WARDROBE IN ALL OF RIVERDALIA. IT WOULD BE SELFISH OF ME TO KEEP THESE CLOTHES HERE ALL TO MYSELF! SO I'VE DECIDED TO GO FOR A WALK AMONG THE RABBLES OF MY KINGDOM--
--AND LET THEM HAVE A GANDER AT HOW GOOD I LOOK IN THESE COOL ROYAL DUDS!
AND SO...
BEHOLD, YOU ANTS!
JUST BECAUSE YOU POOR WRETCHES WILL NEVER BE ABLE TO AFFORD CLOTHES THIS NICE DOESN'T MEAN YOU CAN'T HAVE THE PLEASURE OF SEEING HOW GOOD THEY LOOK ON ME! SOAK IT IN, SLOBS!
YOU ARE TOO GOOD TO US, SIR REGINALD!!
LOOK! IT'S THE BEAUTIFUL LADY MIDGE! AND SHE'S WITH THAT CAVE TROLL SIR MOOSE!
THE POOR GIRL MUST HAVE BAD PEEPERS! WHY ELSE WOULD SHE PASS UP ME IN THESE COOL THREADS FOR THAT BIG MOPE?!
MIGHT IT BE THAT MY CLOTHES AREN'T GOOD ENOUGH?
2

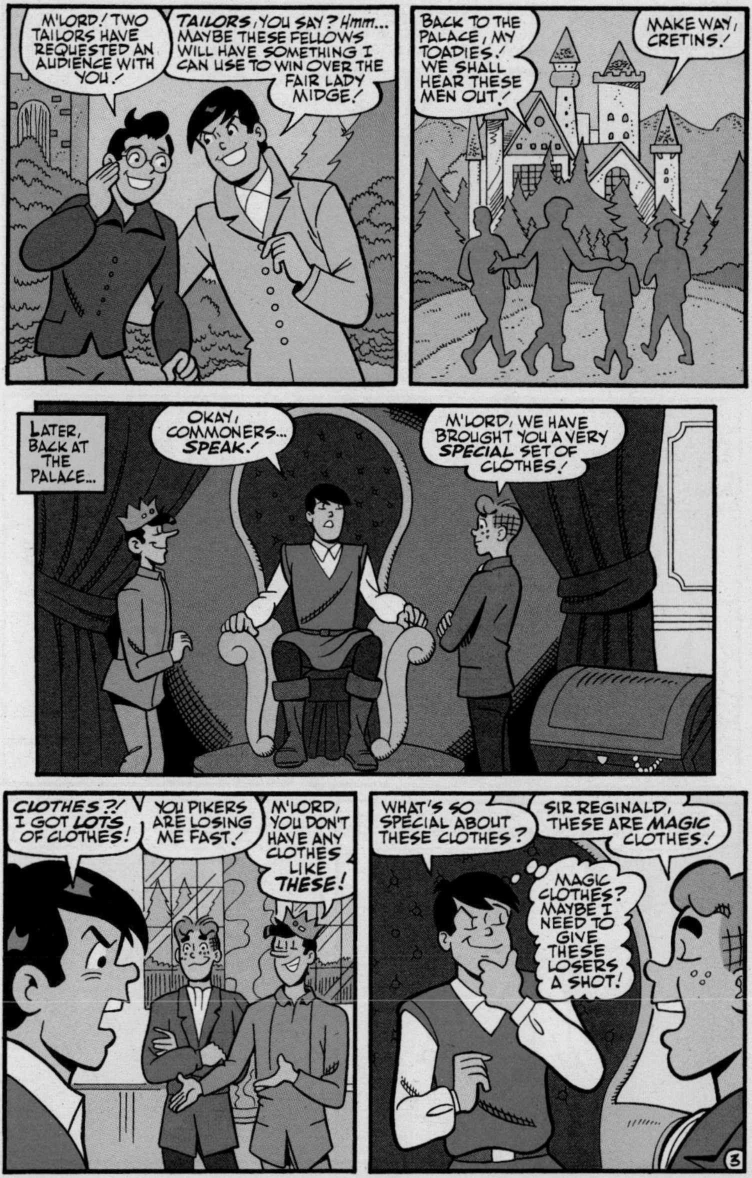

M'LORD! TWO TAILORS HAVE REQUESTED AN AUDIENCE WITH YOU!
TAILORS, YOU SAY? Hmm... MAYBE THESE FELLOWS WILL HAVE SOMETHING I CAN USE TO WIN OVER THE FAIR LADY MIDGE!
BACK TO THE PALACE, MY TOADIES! WE SHALL HEAR THESE MEN OUT!
MAKE WAY, CRETINS!
LATER, BACK AT THE PALACE...
OKAY, COMMONERS... SPEAK!
M'LORD, WE HAVE BROUGHT YOU A VERY SPECIAL SET OF CLOTHES!
CLOTHES?! I GOT LOTS OF CLOTHES!
YOU PIKERS ARE LOSING ME FAST!
M'LORD, YOU DON'T HAVE ANY CLOTHES LIKE THESE!
WHAT'S SO SPECIAL ABOUT THESE CLOTHES?
SIR REGINALD, THESE ARE MAGIC CLOTHES!
MAGIC CLOTHES? MAYBE I NEED TO GIVE THESE LOSERS A SHOT!
3

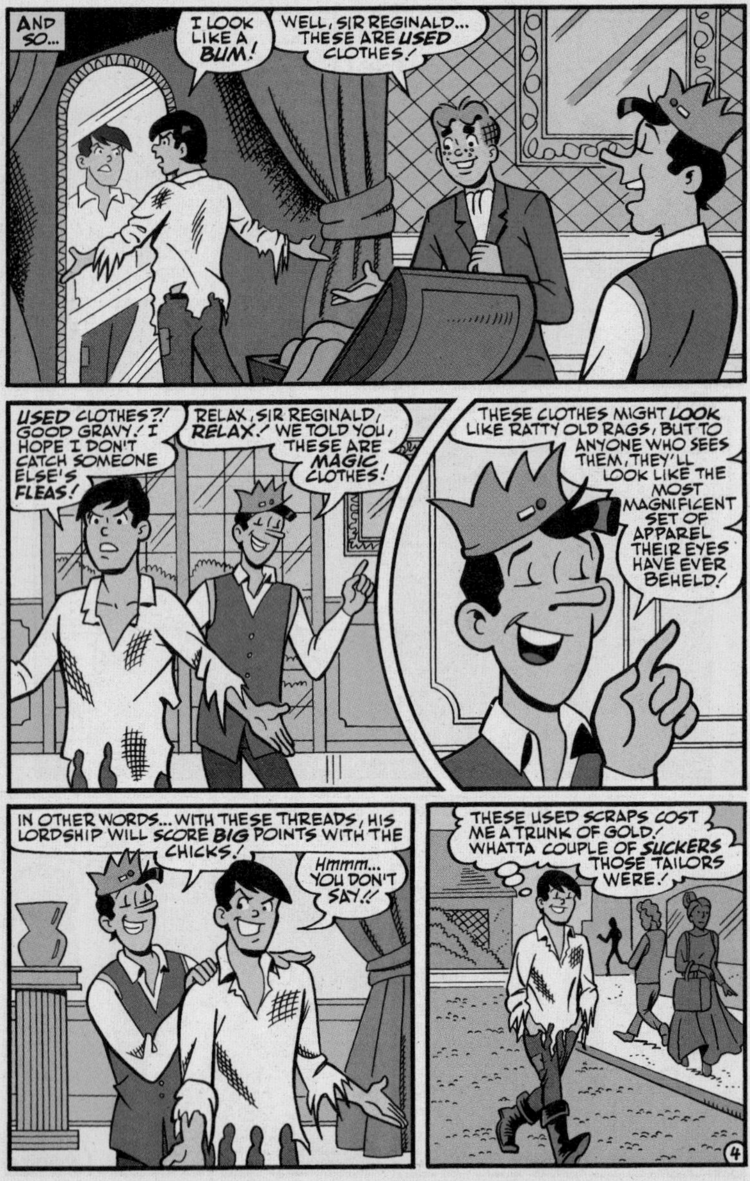
AND SO...
I LOOK LIKE A BUM!
WELL, SIR REGINALD... THESE ARE USED CLOTHES!
USED CLOTHES?! GOOD GRAVY! I HOPE I DON'T CATCH SOMEONE ELSE'S FLEAS!
RELAX, SIR REGINALD, RELAX! WE TOLD YOU, THESE ARE MAGIC CLOTHES!
THESE CLOTHES MIGHT LOOK LIKE RATTY OLD RAGS, BUT TO ANYONE WHO SEES THEM, THEY'LL LOOK LIKE THE MOST MAGNIFICENT SET OF APPAREL THEIR EYES HAVE EVER BEHELD!
IN OTHER WORDS... WITH THESE THREADS, HIS LORDSHIP WILL SCORE BIG POINTS WITH THE CHICKS!
Hmmm... YOU DON'T SAY!!
THESE USED SCRAPS COST ME A TRUNK OF GOLD! WHATTA COUPLE OF SUCKERS THOSE TAILORS WERE!
4

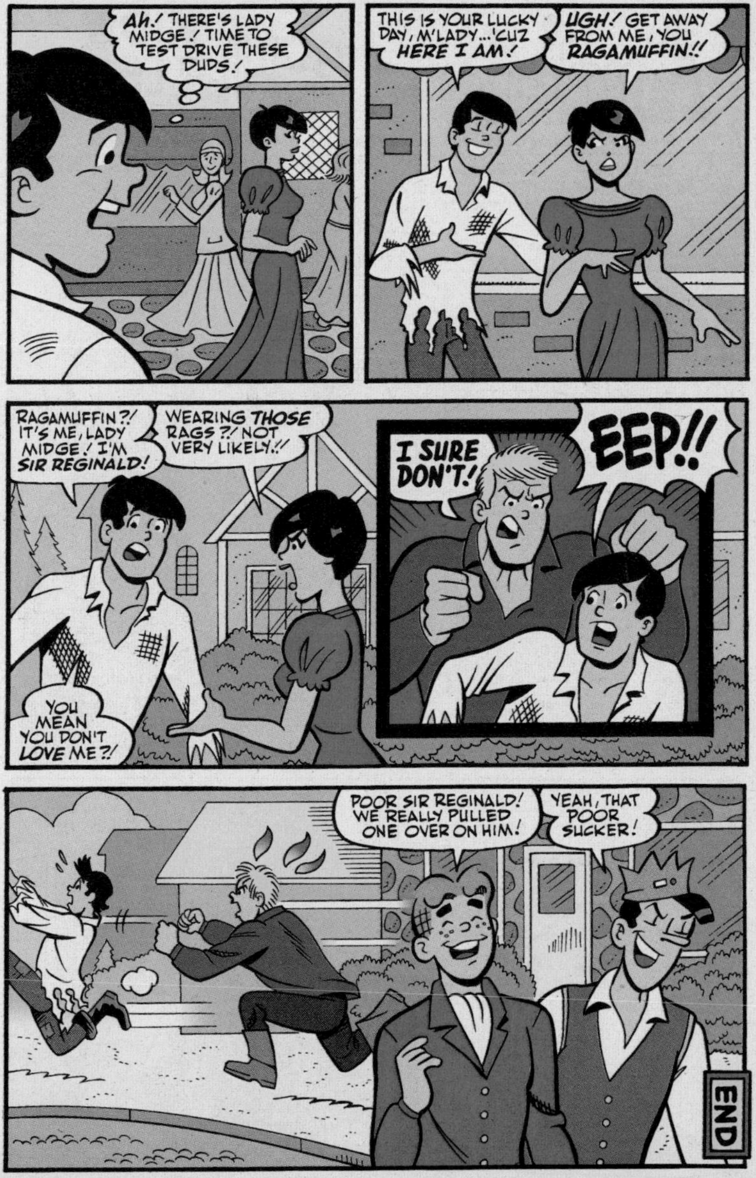
AH! THERE'S LADY MIDGE! TIME TO TEST DRIVE THESE DUDS!
THIS IS YOUR LUCKY DAY, M'LADY...'CUZ HERE I AM!
UGH! GET AWAY FROM ME, YOU RAGAMUFFIN!!
RAGAMUFFIN?! IT'S ME, LADY MIDGE! I'M SIR REGINALD!
WEARING THOSE RAGS?! NOT VERY LIKELY!!
YOU MEAN YOU DON'T LOVE ME?!
I SURE DON'T!
EEP!!
POOR SIR REGINALD! WE REALLY PULLED ONE OVER ON HIM!
YEAH, THAT POOR SUCKER!
END

Archie in SOME KIDS NEVER LEARN

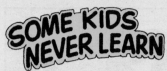

Script: George Gladir / Pencils: Stan Goldberg / Inks: Rich Koslowski / Letters: Bill Yoshida

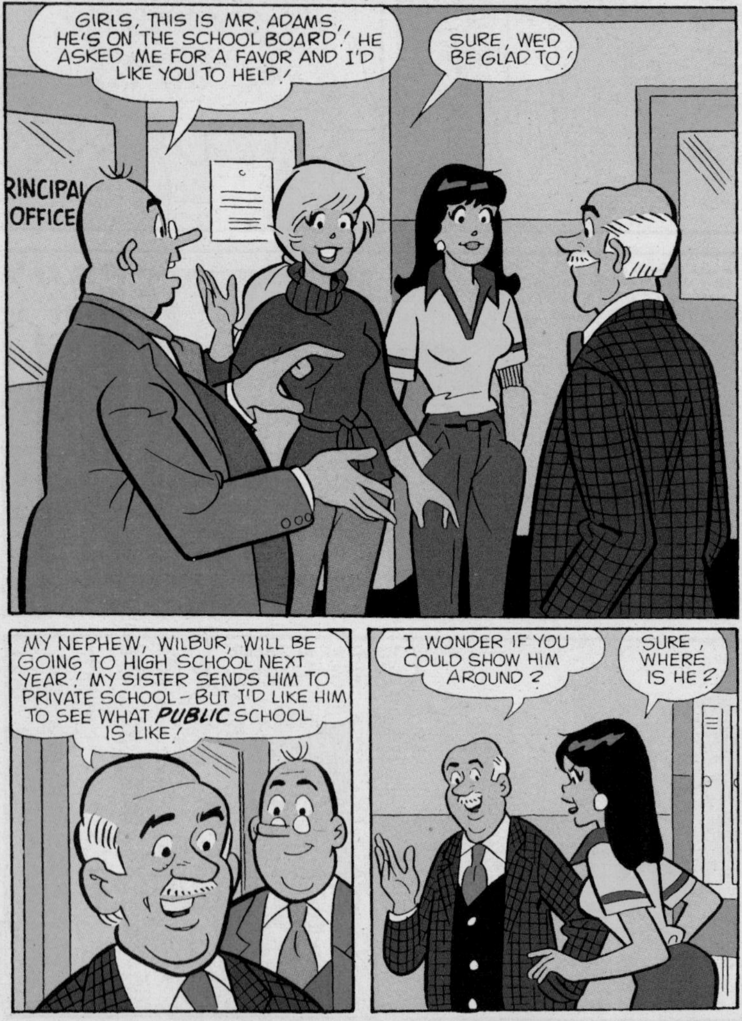
GIRLS, THIS IS MR. ADAMS, HE'S ON THE SCHOOL BOARD! HE ASKED ME FOR A FAVOR AND I'D LIKE YOU TO HELP!
SURE, WE'D BE GLAD TO!
RINCIPAL OFFICE
MY NEPHEW, WILBUR, WILL BE GOING TO HIGH SCHOOL NEXT YEAR! MY SISTER SENDS HIM TO PRIVATE SCHOOL - BUT I'D LIKE HIM TO SEE WHAT PUBLIC SCHOOL IS LIKE!
I WONDER IF YOU COULD SHOW HIM AROUND?
SURE, WHERE IS HE?

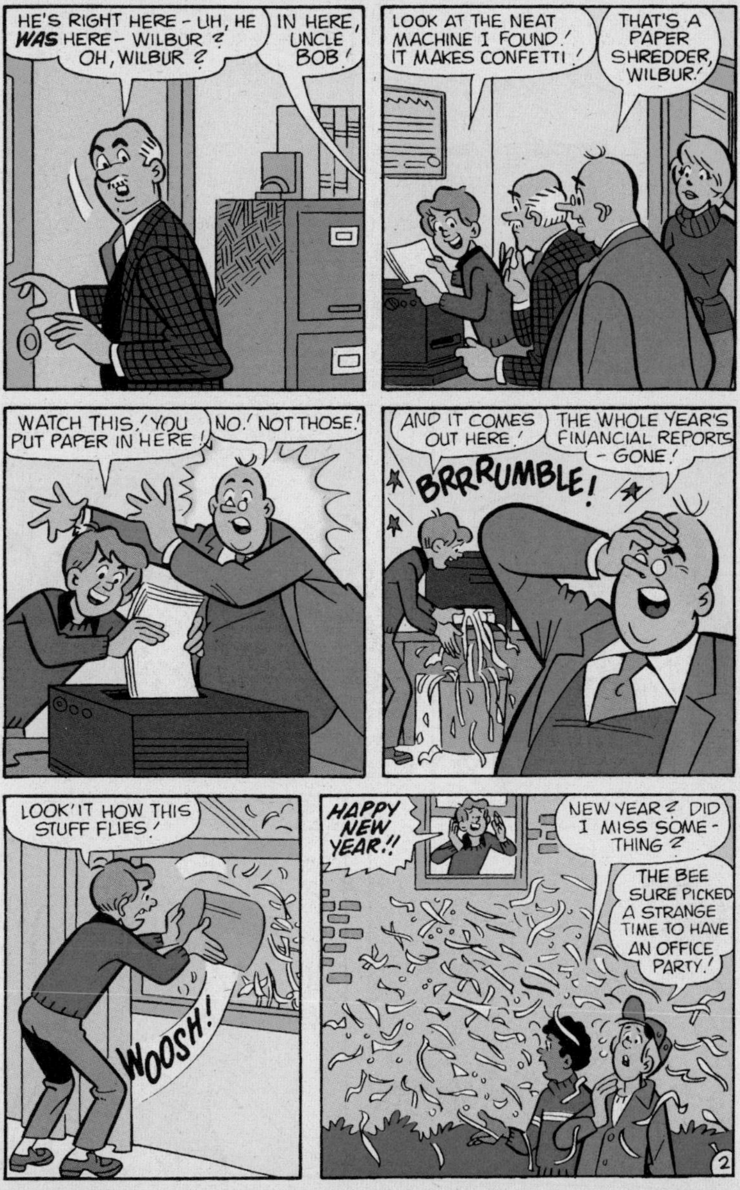
HE'S RIGHT HERE - UH, HE WAS HERE - WILBUR ? OH, WILBUR ?
IN HERE, UNCLE BOB!
LOOK AT THE NEAT MACHINE I FOUND! IT MAKES CONFETTI!
THAT'S A PAPER SHREDDER, WILBUR!
WATCH THIS! YOU PUT PAPER IN HERE!
NO! NOT THOSE!
AND IT COMES OUT HERE!
THE WHOLE YEAR'S FINANCIAL REPORTS - GONE!
BRRRUMBLE!
LOOK'IT HOW THIS STUFF FLIES!
WOOSH!
HAPPY NEW YEAR!!
NEW YEAR? DID I MISS SOME-THING?
THE BEE SURE PICKED A STRANGE TIME TO HAVE AN OFFICE PARTY!
2

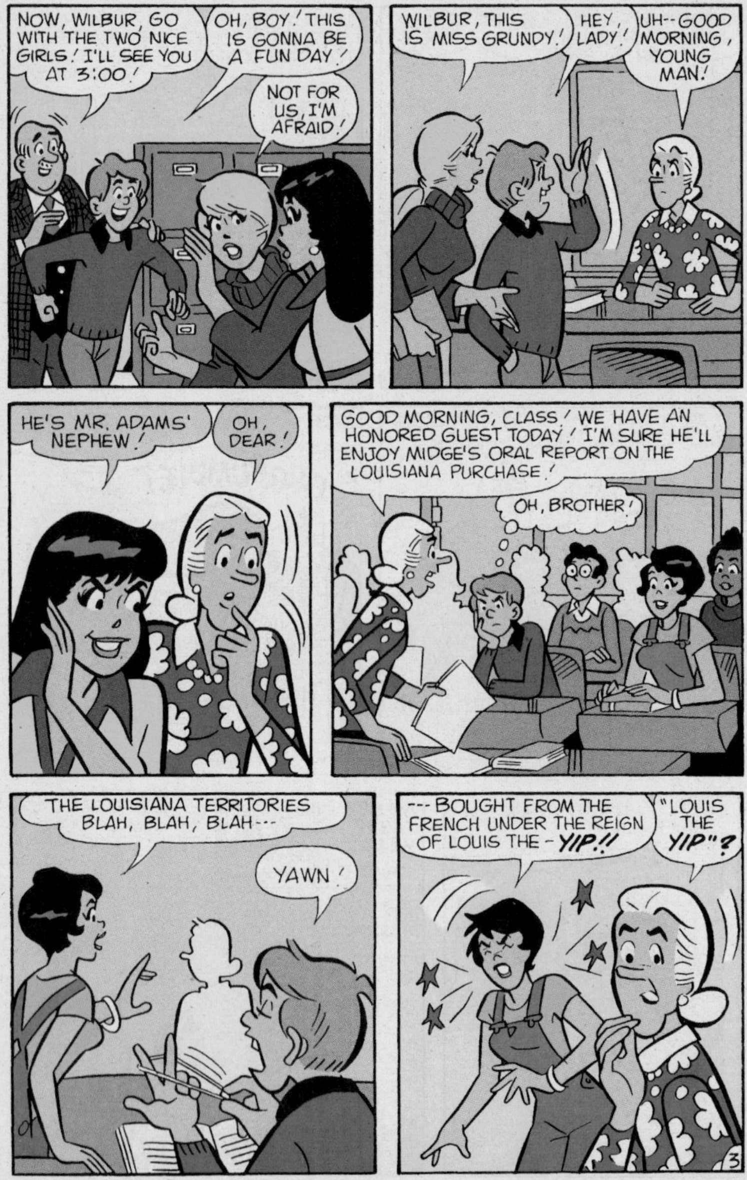
NOW, WILBUR, GO WITH THE TWO NICE GIRLS! I'LL SEE YOU AT 3:00!
OH, BOY! THIS IS GONNA BE A FUN DAY!
NOT FOR US, I'M AFRAID!
WILBUR, THIS IS MISS GRUNDY!
HEY, LADY!
UH--GOOD MORNING, YOUNG MAN!
HE'S MR. ADAMS' NEPHEW!
OH, DEAR!
GOOD MORNING, CLASS! WE HAVE AN HONORED GUEST TODAY! I'M SURE HE'LL ENJOY MIDGE'S ORAL REPORT ON THE LOUISIANA PURCHASE!
OH, BROTHER!
THE LOUISIANA TERRITORIES BLAH, BLAH, BLAH---
YAWN!
---BOUGHT FROM THE FRENCH UNDER THE REIGN OF LOUIS THE - YIP!!
"LOUIS THE YIP"?
3

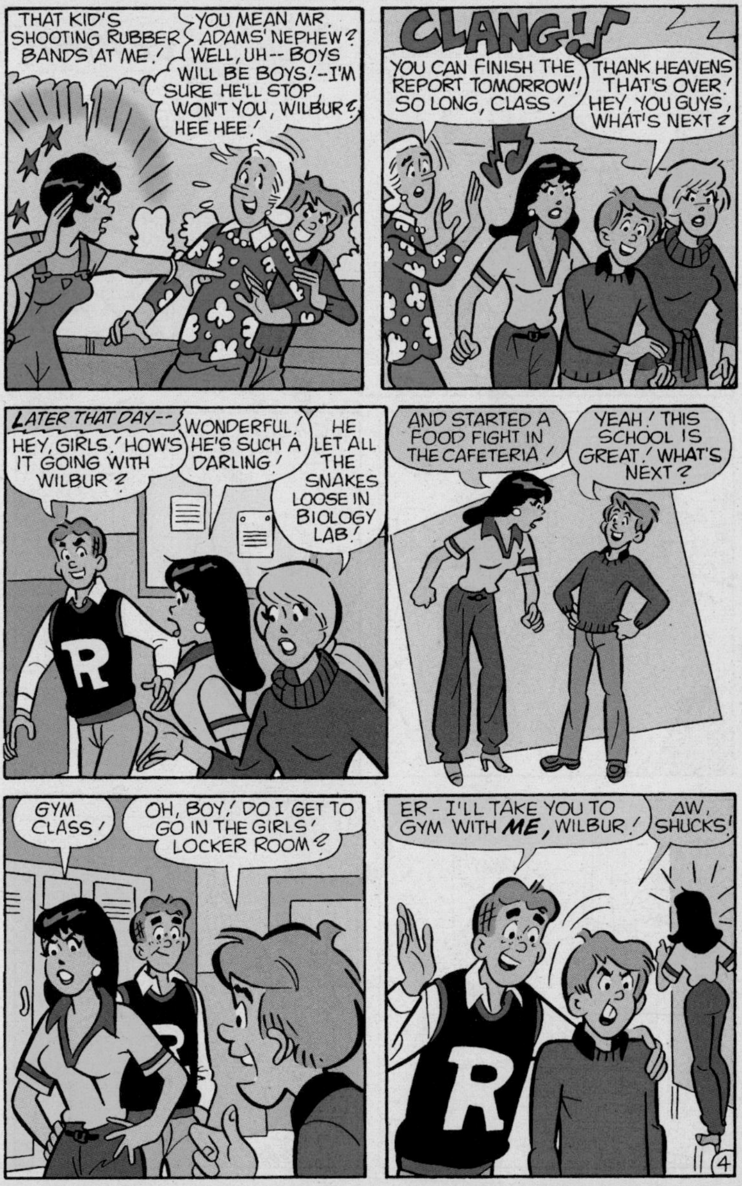
THAT KID'S SHOOTING RUBBER BANDS AT ME!
YOU MEAN MR. ADAMS' NEPHEW? WELL, UH -- BOYS WILL BE BOYS!--I'M SURE HE'LL STOP, WON'T YOU, WILBUR? HEE HEE!
CLANG!
YOU CAN FINISH THE REPORT TOMORROW! SO LONG, CLASS!
THANK HEAVENS THAT'S OVER! HEY, YOU GUYS, WHAT'S NEXT?
LATER THAT DAY--
HEY, GIRLS! HOW'S IT GOING WITH WILBUR?
WONDERFUL! HE'S SUCH A DARLING!
HE LET ALL THE SNAKES LOOSE IN BIOLOGY LAB!
AND STARTED A FOOD FIGHT IN THE CAFETERIA!
YEAH! THIS SCHOOL IS GREAT! WHAT'S NEXT?
GYM CLASS!
OH, BOY! DO I GET TO GO IN THE GIRLS' LOCKER ROOM?
ER - I'LL TAKE YOU TO GYM WITH ME, WILBUR!
AW, SHUCKS!
4

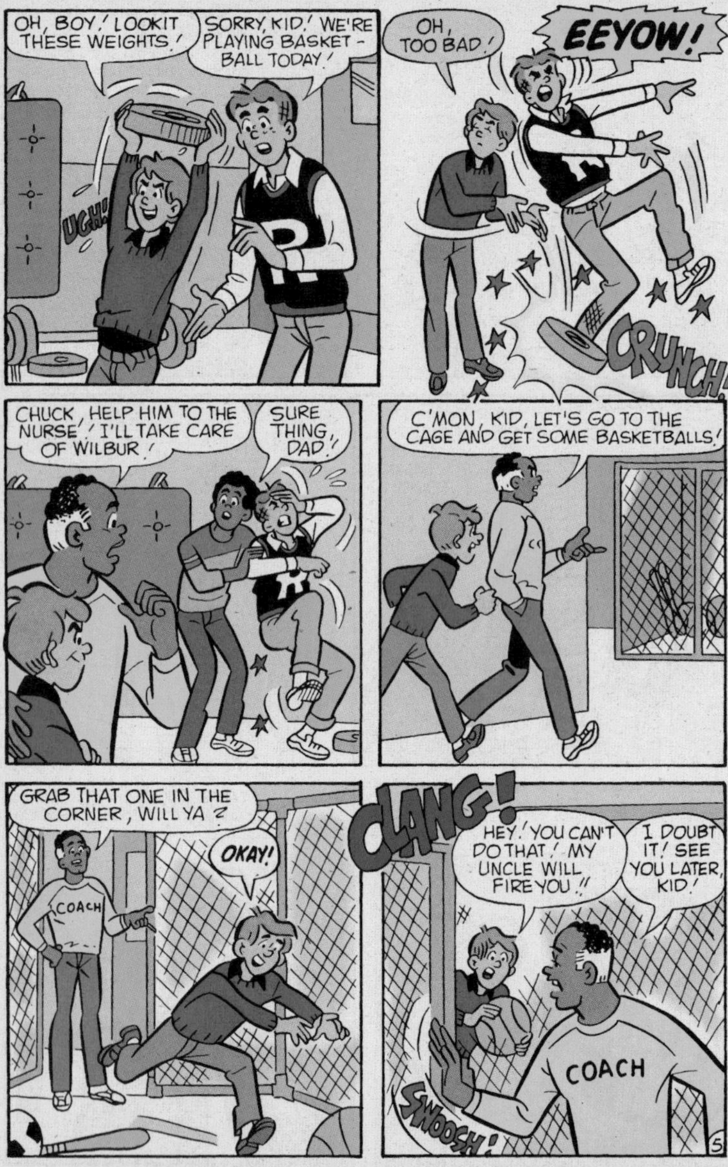
OH, BOY! LOOKIT THESE WEIGHTS!
UGH!
SORRY, KID! WE'RE PLAYING BASKET-BALL TODAY!
OH, TOO BAD!
EEYOW!
CRUNCH!
CHUCK, HELP HIM TO THE NURSE! I'LL TAKE CARE OF WILBUR!
SURE THING, DAD!
C'MON, KID, LET'S GO TO THE CAGE AND GET SOME BASKETBALLS!
GRAB THAT ONE IN THE CORNER, WILL YA?
OKAY!
COACH
CLANG!
HEY! YOU CAN'T DO THAT! MY UNCLE WILL FIRE YOU!!
I DOUBT IT! SEE YOU LATER, KID!
COACH
SWOOSH!
5

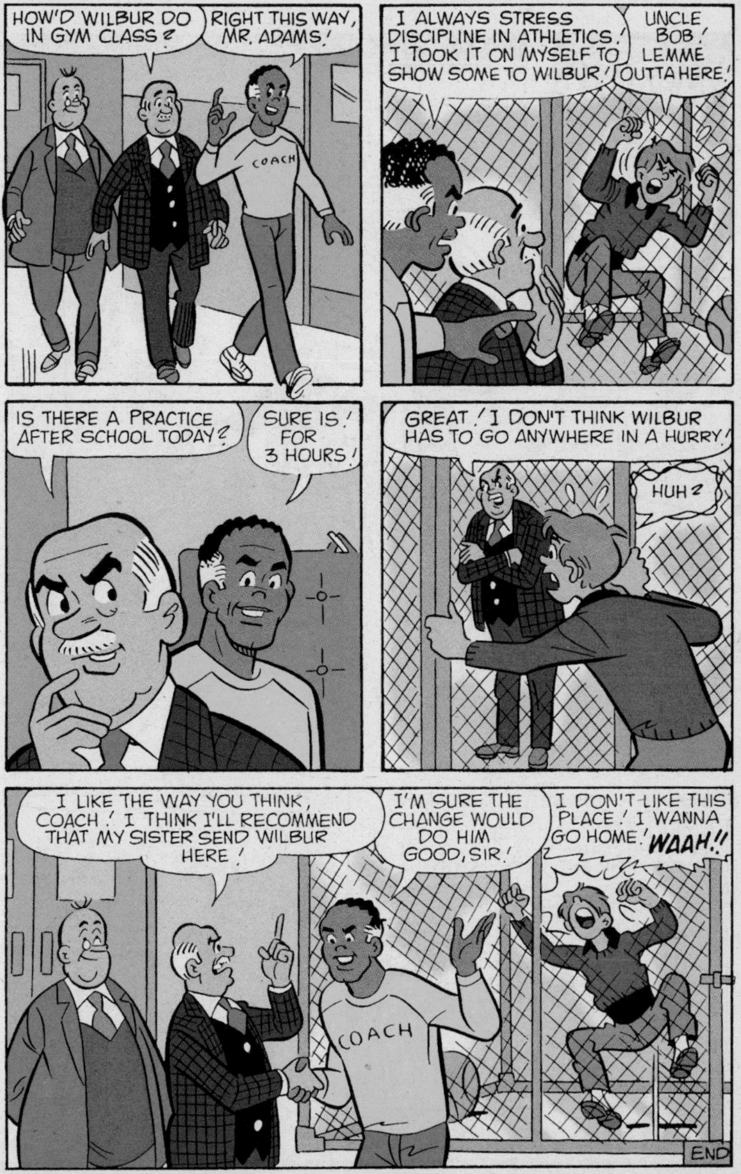
HOW'D WILBUR DO IN GYM CLASS?
RIGHT THIS WAY, MR. ADAMS!
I ALWAYS STRESS DISCIPLINE IN ATHLETICS! I TOOK IT ON MYSELF TO SHOW SOME TO WILBUR!
UNCLE BOB! LEMME OUTTA HERE!
COACH
IS THERE A PRACTICE AFTER SCHOOL TODAY?
SURE IS! FOR 3 HOURS!
GREAT! I DON'T THINK WILBUR HAS TO GO ANYWHERE IN A HURRY!
HUH?
I LIKE THE WAY YOU THINK, COACH! I THINK I'LL RECOMMEND THAT MY SISTER SEND WILBUR HERE!
I'M SURE THE CHANGE WOULD DO HIM GOOD, SIR!
I DON'T LIKE THIS PLACE! I WANNA GO HOME! WAAH!!
COACH
END

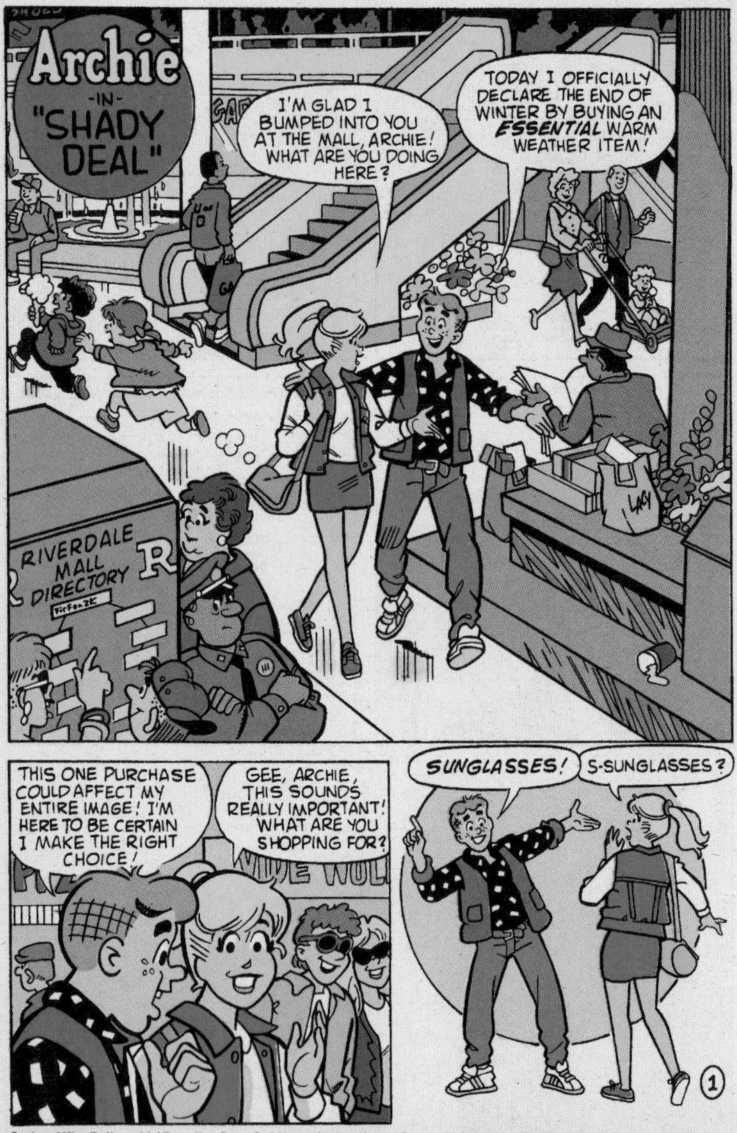
Archie
-IN-
"SHADY DEAL"
I'M GLAD I BUMPED INTO YOU AT THE MALL, ARCHIE! WHAT ARE YOU DOING HERE?
TODAY I OFFICIALLY DECLARE THE END OF WINTER BY BUYING AN ESSENTIAL WARM WEATHER ITEM!
RIVERDALE MALL DIRECTORY
THIS ONE PURCHASE COULD AFFECT MY ENTIRE IMAGE! I'M HERE TO BE CERTAIN I MAKE THE RIGHT CHOICE!
GEE, ARCHIE, THIS SOUNDS REALLY IMPORTANT! WHAT ARE YOU SHOPPING FOR?
SUNGLASSES!
S-SUNGLASSES?
1

Script: Mike Pellowski / Pencils: Stan Goldberg / Inks: Henry Scarpelli / Letters: Bill Yoshida / Colors: Barry Grossman

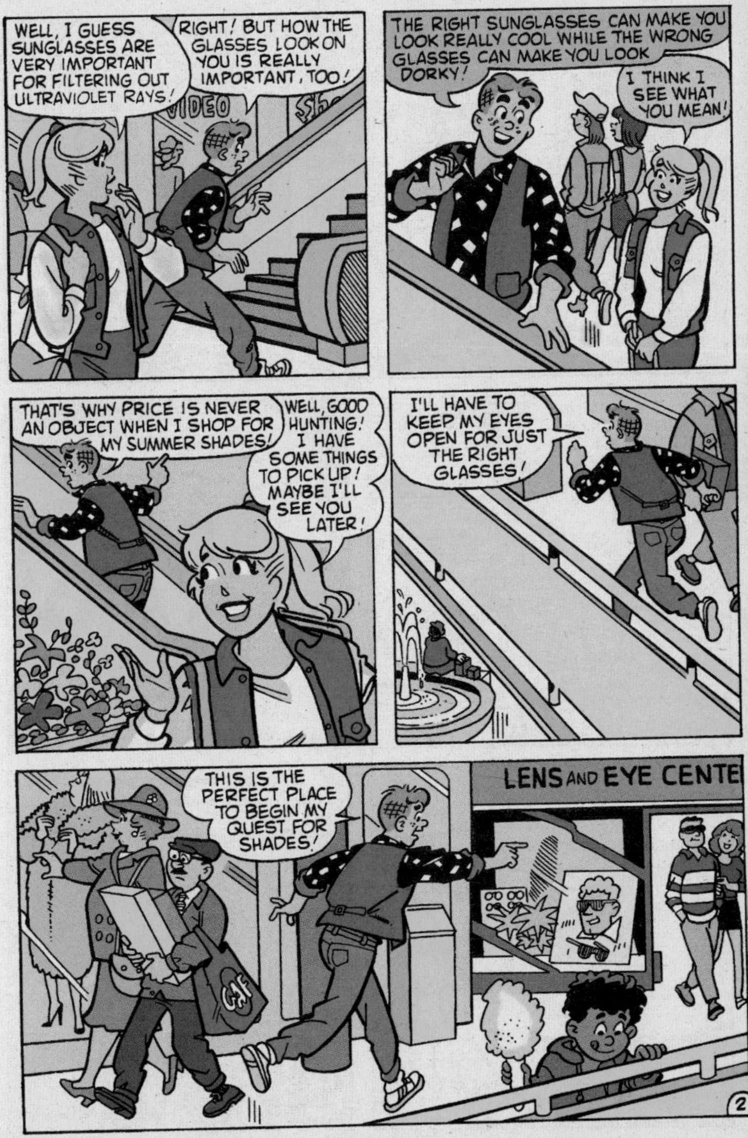
WELL, I GUESS SUNGLASSES ARE VERY IMPORTANT FOR FILTERING OUT ULTRAVIOLET RAYS!
RIGHT! BUT HOW THE GLASSES LOOK ON YOU IS REALLY IMPORTANT, TOO!
VIDEO
THE RIGHT SUNGLASSES CAN MAKE YOU LOOK REALLY COOL WHILE THE WRONG GLASSES CAN MAKE YOU LOOK DORKY!
I THINK I SEE WHAT YOU MEAN!
THAT'S WHY PRICE IS NEVER AN OBJECT WHEN I SHOP FOR MY SUMMER SHADES!
WELL, GOOD HUNTING! I HAVE SOME THINGS TO PICK UP! MAYBE I'LL SEE YOU LATER!
I'LL HAVE TO KEEP MY EYES OPEN FOR JUST THE RIGHT GLASSES!
THIS IS THE PERFECT PLACE TO BEGIN MY QUEST FOR SHADES!
LENS AND EYE CENTE
2

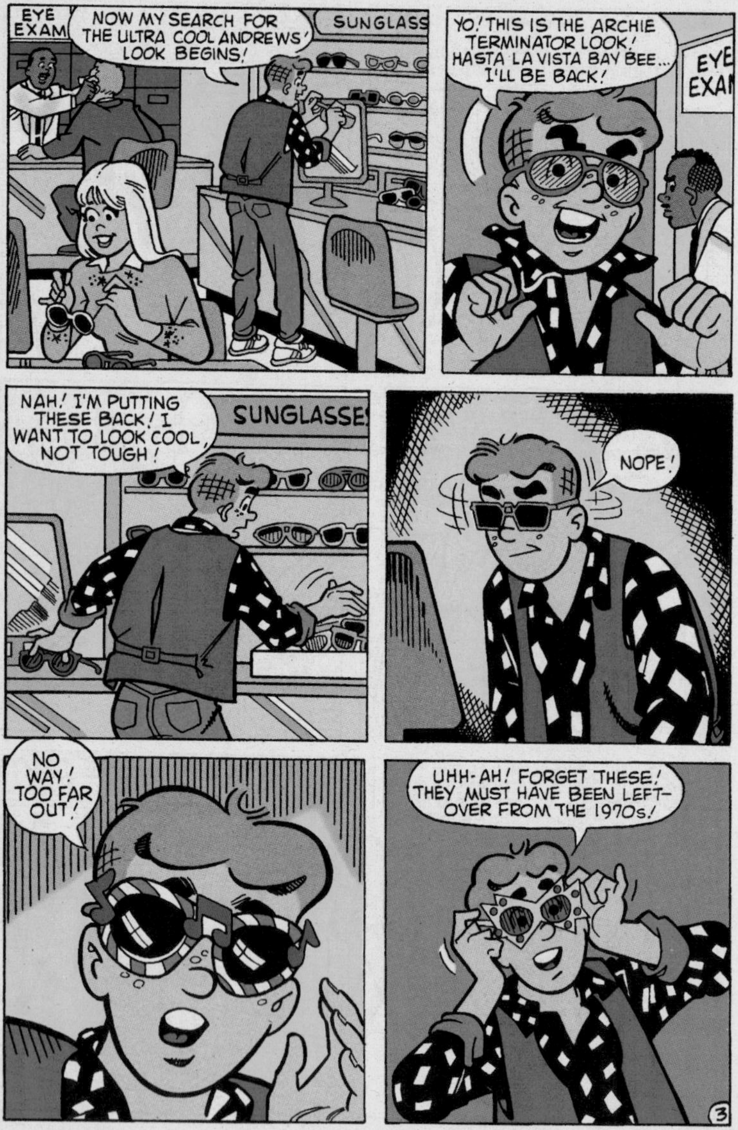
EYE EXAM
NOW MY SEARCH FOR THE ULTRA COOL ANDREWS' LOOK BEGINS!
SUNGLASS
YO! THIS IS THE ARCHIE TERMINATOR LOOK! HASTA LA VISTA BAY BEE... I'LL BE BACK!
EYE EXAM
NAH! I'M PUTTING THESE BACK! I WANT TO LOOK COOL, NOT TOUGH!
SUNGLASSES
NOPE!
NO WAY! TOO FAR OUT!
UHH-AH! FORGET THESE! THEY MUST HAVE BEEN LEFT-OVER FROM THE 1970s!
3

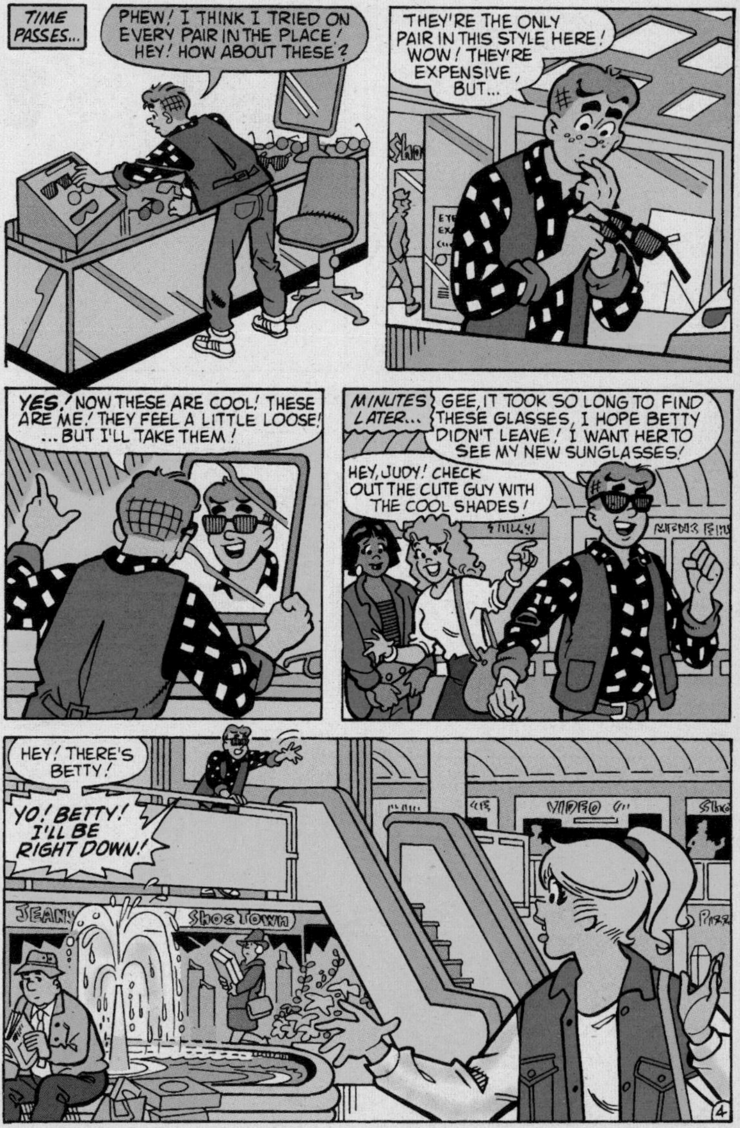
TIME PASSES...
PHEW! I THINK I TRIED ON EVERY PAIR IN THE PLACE! HEY! HOW ABOUT THESE?
THEY'RE THE ONLY PAIR IN THIS STYLE HERE! WOW! THEY'RE EXPENSIVE, BUT...
YES! NOW THESE ARE COOL! THESE ARE ME! THEY FEEL A LITTLE LOOSE! ...BUT I'LL TAKE THEM!
MINUTES LATER...
GEE, IT TOOK SO LONG TO FIND THESE GLASSES, I HOPE BETTY DIDN'T LEAVE! I WANT HER TO SEE MY NEW SUNGLASSES!
HEY, JUDY! CHECK OUT THE CUTE GUY WITH THE COOL SHADES!
HEY! THERE'S BETTY!
YO! BETTY! I'LL BE RIGHT DOWN!
VIDEO
JEANS
SHOE TOWN
4

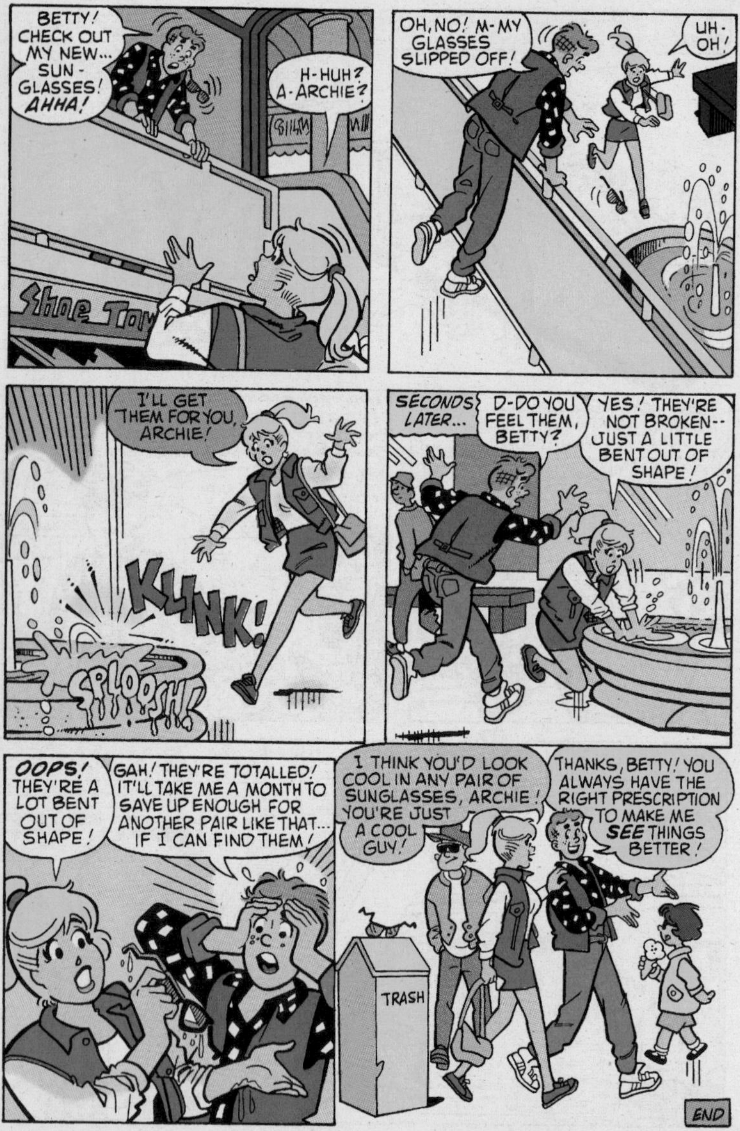
BETTY! CHECK OUT MY NEW... SUN-GLASSES! AHHA!
H-HUH? A-ARCHIE?
Shoe Tow
OH, NO! M-MY GLASSES SLIPPED OFF!
UH-OH!
I'LL GET THEM FOR YOU, ARCHIE!
KLUNK!
SPLOOSH!
SECONDS LATER...
D-DO YOU FEEL THEM, BETTY?
YES! THEY'RE NOT BROKEN-- JUST A LITTLE BENT OUT OF SHAPE!
OOPS! THEY'RE A LOT BENT OUT OF SHAPE!
GAH! THEY'RE TOTALLED! IT'LL TAKE ME A MONTH TO SAVE UP ENOUGH FOR ANOTHER PAIR LIKE THAT... IF I CAN FIND THEM!
I THINK YOU'D LOOK COOL IN ANY PAIR OF SUNGLASSES, ARCHIE! YOU'RE JUST A COOL GUY!
THANKS, BETTY! YOU ALWAYS HAVE THE RIGHT PRESCRIPTION TO MAKE ME SEE THINGS BETTER!
TRASH
END

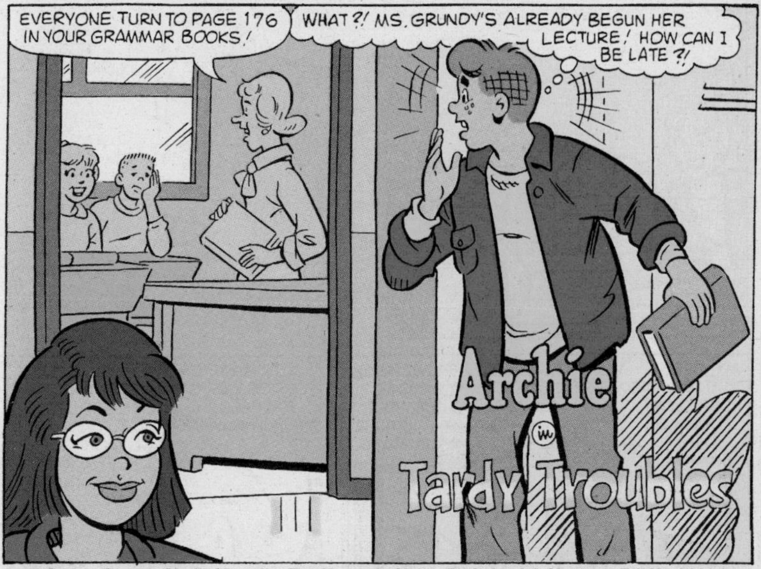
EVERYONE TURN TO PAGE 176 IN YOUR GRAMMAR BOOKS!
WHAT?! MS. GRUNDY'S ALREADY BEGUN HER LECTURE! HOW CAN I BE LATE?!
Archie
in
Tardy Troubles

Script: George Gladir / Pencils: Tim Kennedy / Inks: Rudy Lapick / Letters: Bill Yoshida

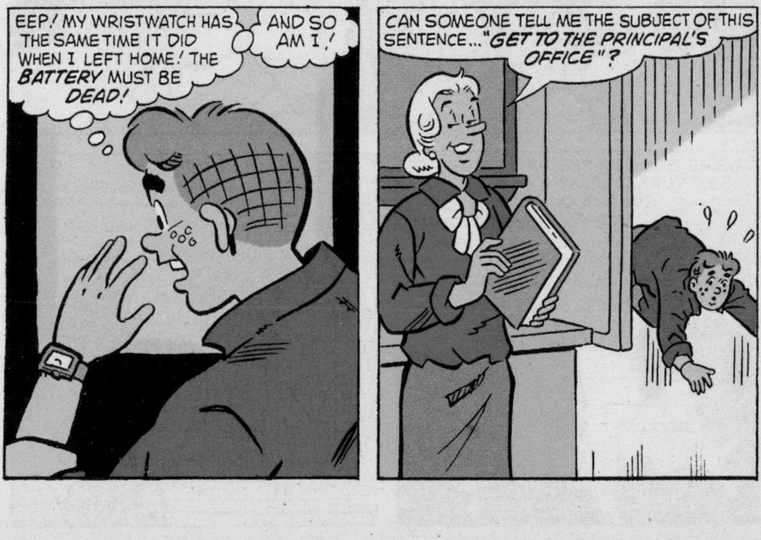
EEP! MY WRISTWATCH HAS THE SAME TIME IT DID WHEN I LEFT HOME! THE *BATTERY* MUST BE *DEAD!*
AND SO AM I!
CAN SOMEONE TELL ME THE SUBJECT OF THIS SENTENCE..."*GET TO THE PRINCIPAL'S OFFICE*"?

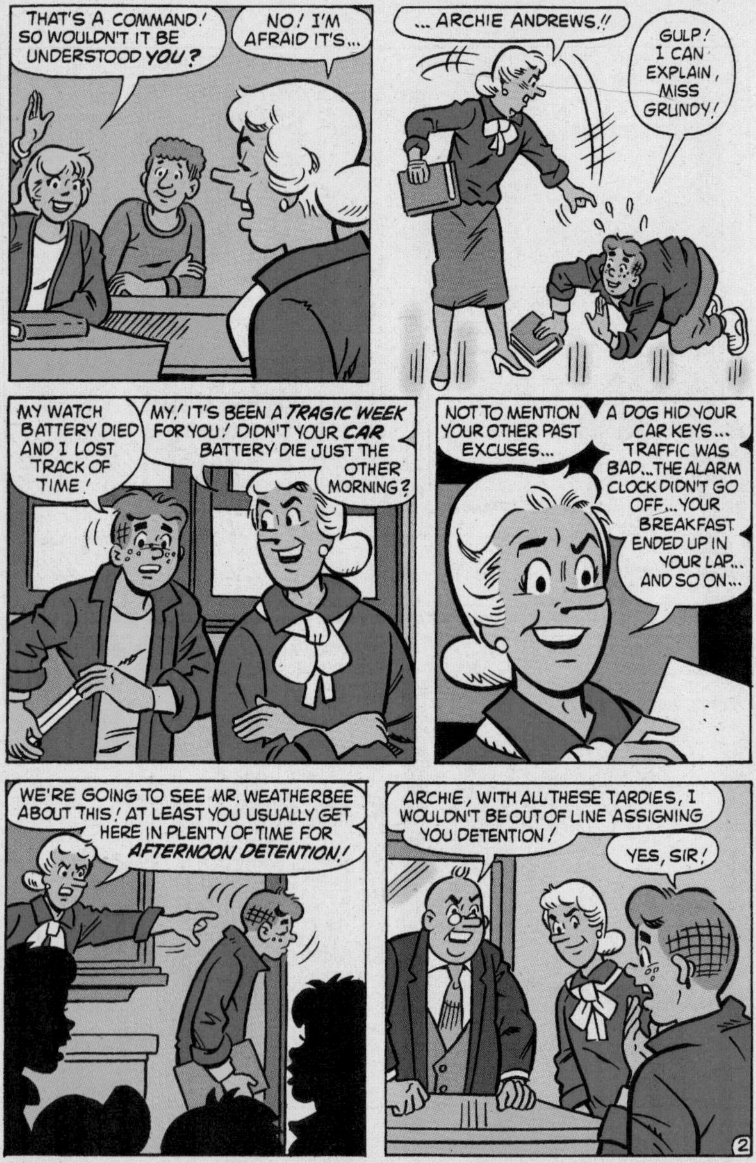
THAT'S A COMMAND! SO WOULDN'T IT BE UNDERSTOOD YOU?
NO! I'M AFRAID IT'S...
... ARCHIE ANDREWS.!!
GULP! I CAN EXPLAIN, MISS GRUNDY!
MY WATCH BATTERY DIED AND I LOST TRACK OF TIME!
MY! IT'S BEEN A TRAGIC WEEK FOR YOU! DIDN'T YOUR CAR BATTERY DIE JUST THE OTHER MORNING?
NOT TO MENTION YOUR OTHER PAST EXCUSES...
A DOG HID YOUR CAR KEYS... TRAFFIC WAS BAD... THE ALARM CLOCK DIDN'T GO OFF... YOUR BREAKFAST ENDED UP IN YOUR LAP... AND SO ON...
WE'RE GOING TO SEE MR. WEATHERBEE ABOUT THIS! AT LEAST YOU USUALLY GET HERE IN PLENTY OF TIME FOR AFTERNOON DETENTION!
ARCHIE, WITH ALL THESE TARDIES, I WOULDN'T BE OUT OF LINE ASSIGNING YOU DETENTION!
YES, SIR!
2

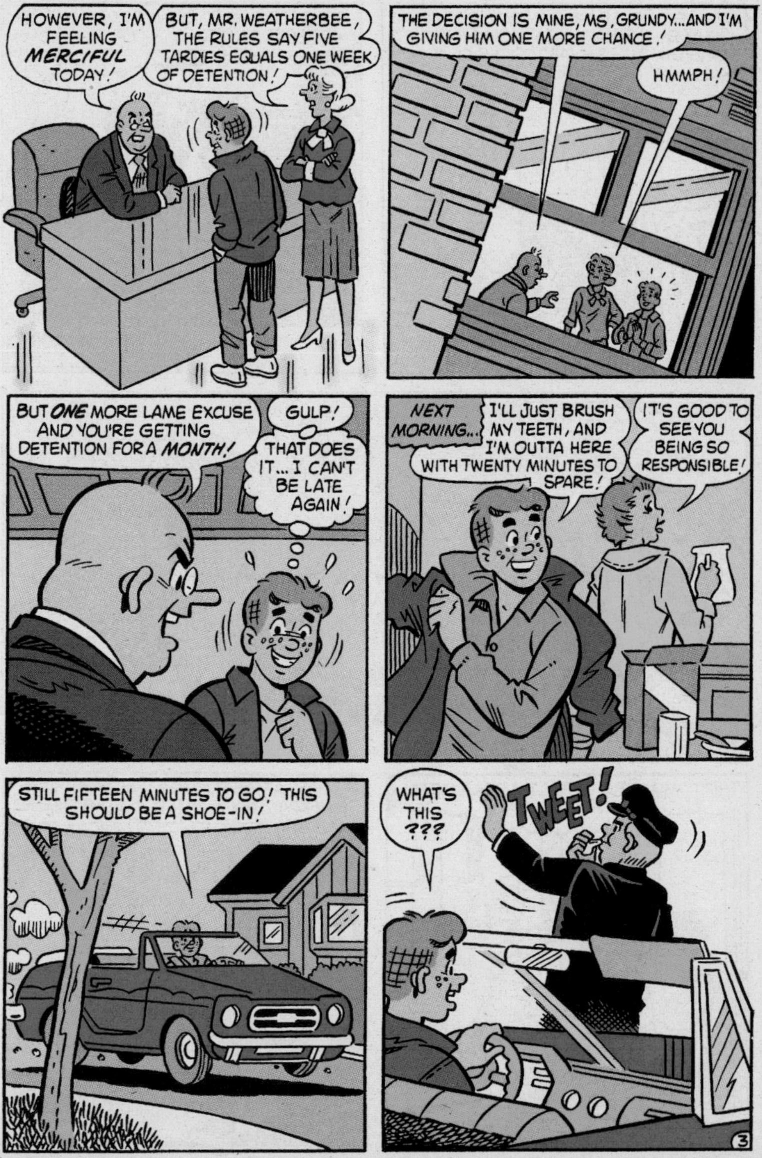
HOWEVER, I'M FEELING *MERCIFUL* TODAY!
BUT, MR. WEATHERBEE, THE RULES SAY FIVE TARDIES EQUALS ONE WEEK OF DETENTION!
THE DECISION IS MINE, MS. GRUNDY...AND I'M GIVING HIM ONE MORE CHANCE!
HMMPH!
BUT *ONE* MORE LAME EXCUSE AND YOU'RE GETTING DETENTION FOR A *MONTH!*
GULP!
THAT DOES IT... I CAN'T BE LATE AGAIN!
NEXT MORNING...
I'LL JUST BRUSH MY TEETH, AND I'M OUTTA HERE WITH TWENTY MINUTES TO SPARE!
IT'S GOOD TO SEE YOU BEING SO RESPONSIBLE!
STILL FIFTEEN MINUTES TO GO! THIS SHOULD BE A SHOE-IN!
WHAT'S THIS ???
TWEET!
3

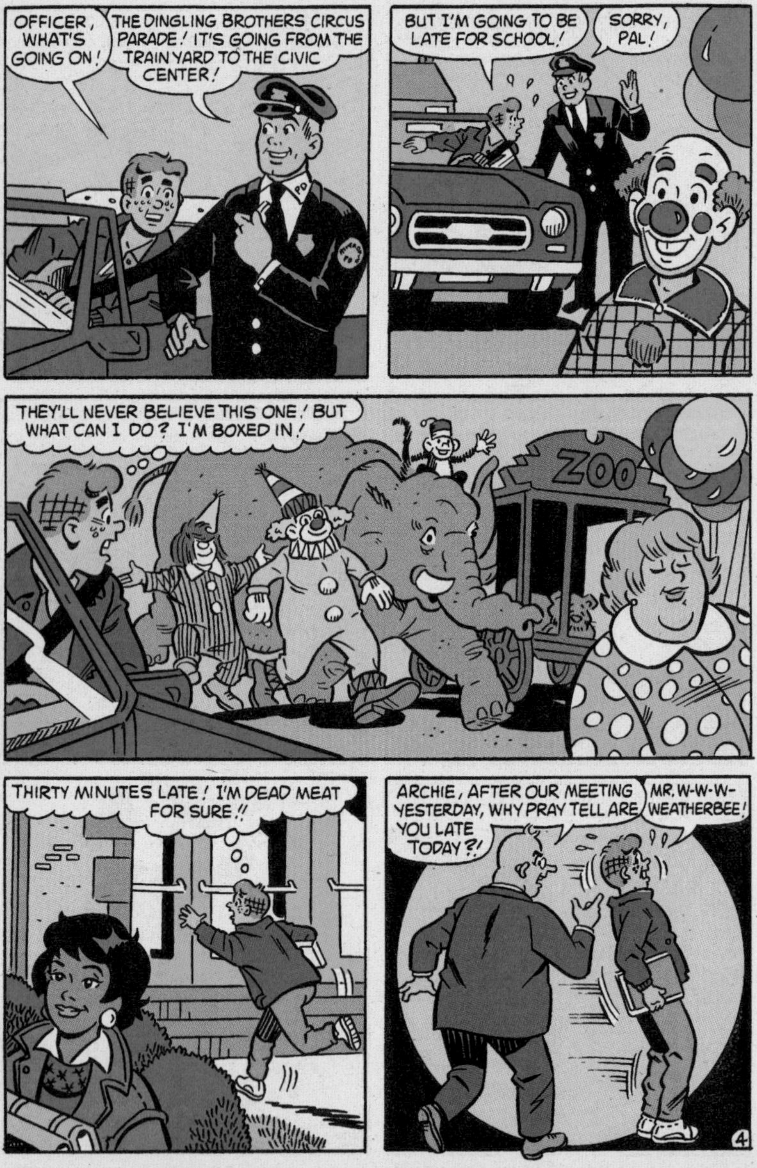
OFFICER, WHAT'S GOING ON!
THE DINGLING BROTHERS CIRCUS PARADE! IT'S GOING FROM THE TRAIN YARD TO THE CIVIC CENTER!
BUT I'M GOING TO BE LATE FOR SCHOOL!
SORRY, PAL!
THEY'LL NEVER BELIEVE THIS ONE! BUT WHAT CAN I DO? I'M BOXED IN!
ZOO
THIRTY MINUTES LATE! I'M DEAD MEAT FOR SURE!!
ARCHIE, AFTER OUR MEETING YESTERDAY, WHY PRAY TELL ARE YOU LATE TODAY?!
MR. W-W-W-WEATHERBEE!
4

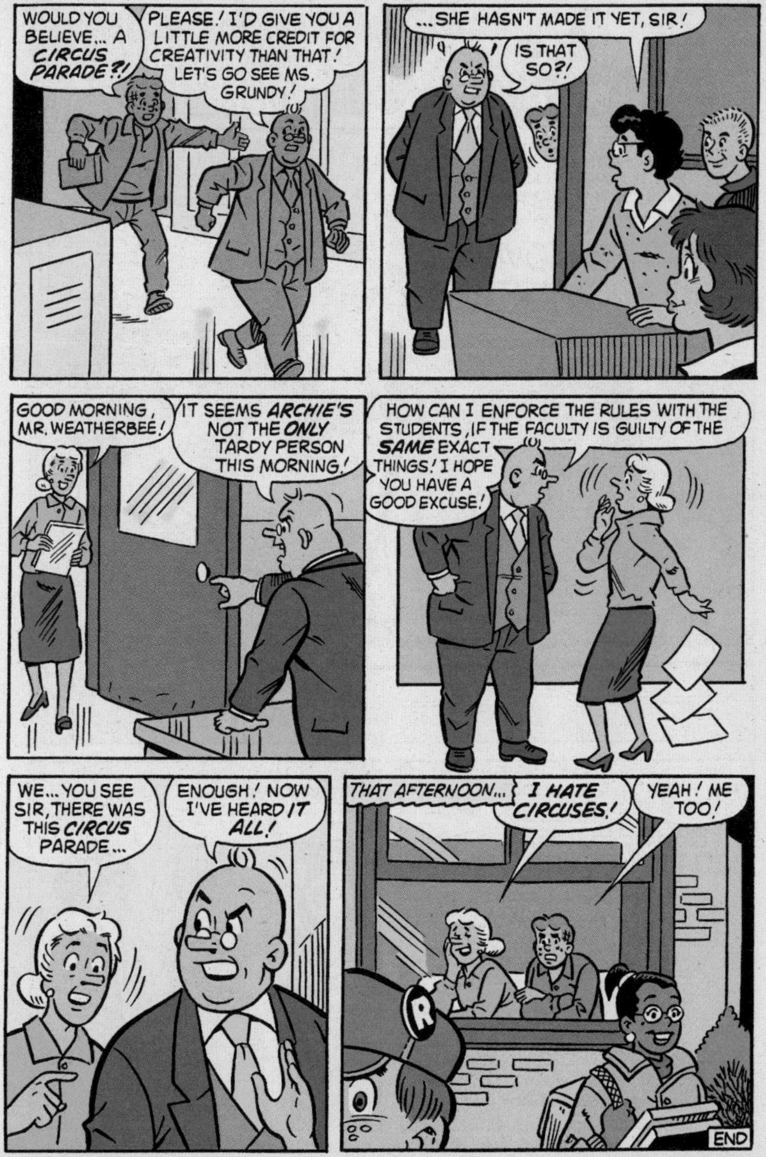

WOULD YOU BELIEVE... A CIRCUS PARADE?!
PLEASE! I'D GIVE YOU A LITTLE MORE CREDIT FOR CREATIVITY THAN THAT! LET'S GO SEE MS. GRUNDY!
...SHE HASN'T MADE IT YET, SIR!
IS THAT SO?!
GOOD MORNING, MR. WEATHERBEE!
IT SEEMS ARCHIE'S NOT THE ONLY TARDY PERSON THIS MORNING!
HOW CAN I ENFORCE THE RULES WITH THE STUDENTS, IF THE FACULTY IS GUILTY OF THE SAME EXACT THINGS! I HOPE YOU HAVE A GOOD EXCUSE!
WE... YOU SEE SIR, THERE WAS THIS CIRCUS PARADE...
ENOUGH! NOW I'VE HEARD IT ALL!
THAT AFTERNOON...
I HATE CIRCUSES!
YEAH! ME TOO!
R
END

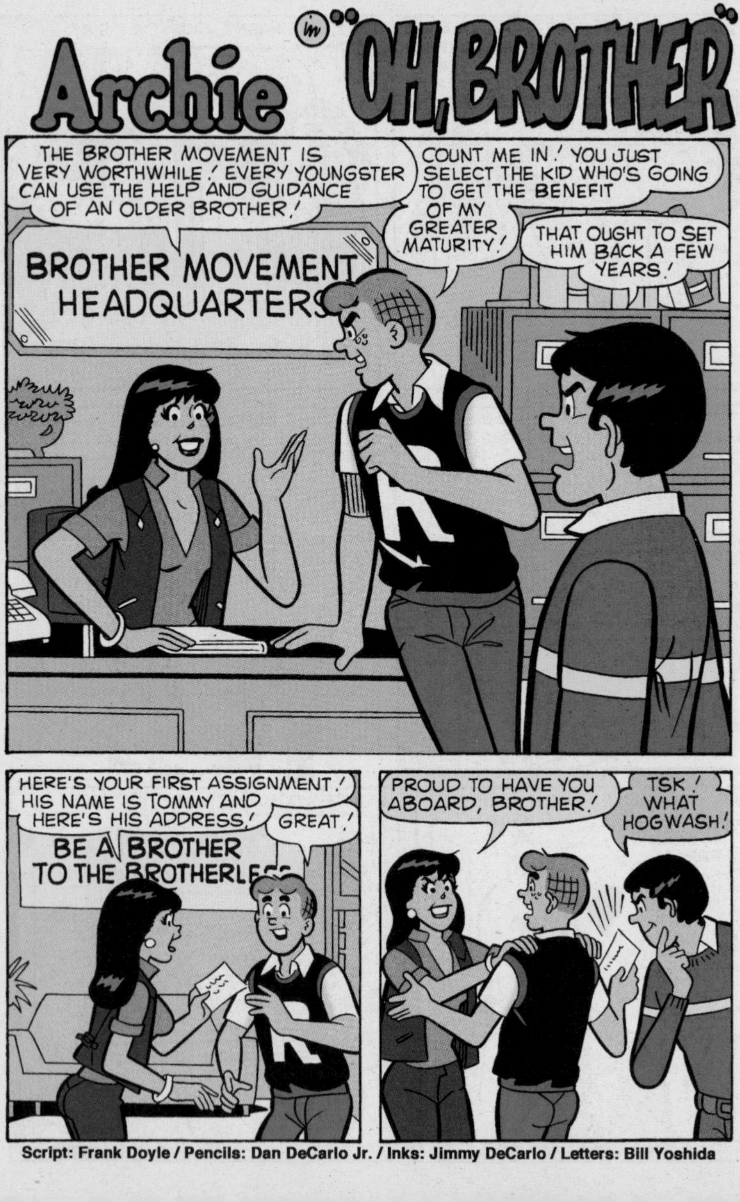
Archie in "OH, BROTHER"
THE BROTHER MOVEMENT IS VERY WORTHWHILE! EVERY YOUNGSTER CAN USE THE HELP AND GUIDANCE OF AN OLDER BROTHER!
COUNT ME IN! YOU JUST SELECT THE KID WHO'S GOING TO GET THE BENEFIT OF MY GREATER MATURITY!
THAT OUGHT TO SET HIM BACK A FEW YEARS!
BROTHER MOVEMENT HEADQUARTERS
HERE'S YOUR FIRST ASSIGNMENT! HIS NAME IS TOMMY AND HERE'S HIS ADDRESS!
GREAT!
BE A BROTHER TO THE BROTHERLESS
PROUD TO HAVE YOU ABOARD, BROTHER!
TSK! WHAT HOGWASH!

Script: Frank Doyle / Pencils: Dan DeCarlo Jr. / Inks: Jimmy DeCarlo / Letters: Bill Yoshida

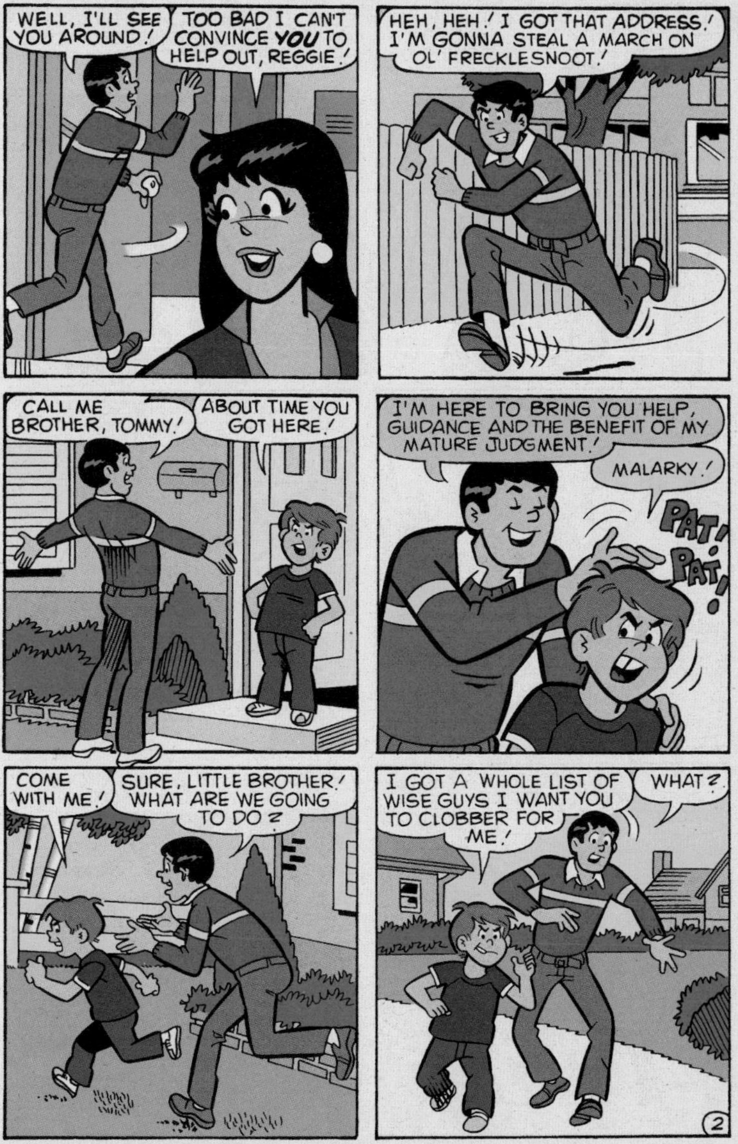
WELL, I'LL SEE YOU AROUND!
TOO BAD I CAN'T CONVINCE YOU TO HELP OUT, REGGIE!
HEH, HEH! I GOT THAT ADDRESS! I'M GONNA STEAL A MARCH ON OL' FRECKLESNOOT!
CALL ME BROTHER, TOMMY!
ABOUT TIME YOU GOT HERE!
I'M HERE TO BRING YOU HELP, GUIDANCE AND THE BENEFIT OF MY MATURE JUDGMENT!
MALARKY!
PAT! PAT!
COME WITH ME!
SURE, LITTLE BROTHER! WHAT ARE WE GOING TO DO?
I GOT A WHOLE LIST OF WISE GUYS I WANT YOU TO CLOBBER FOR ME!
WHAT?
2

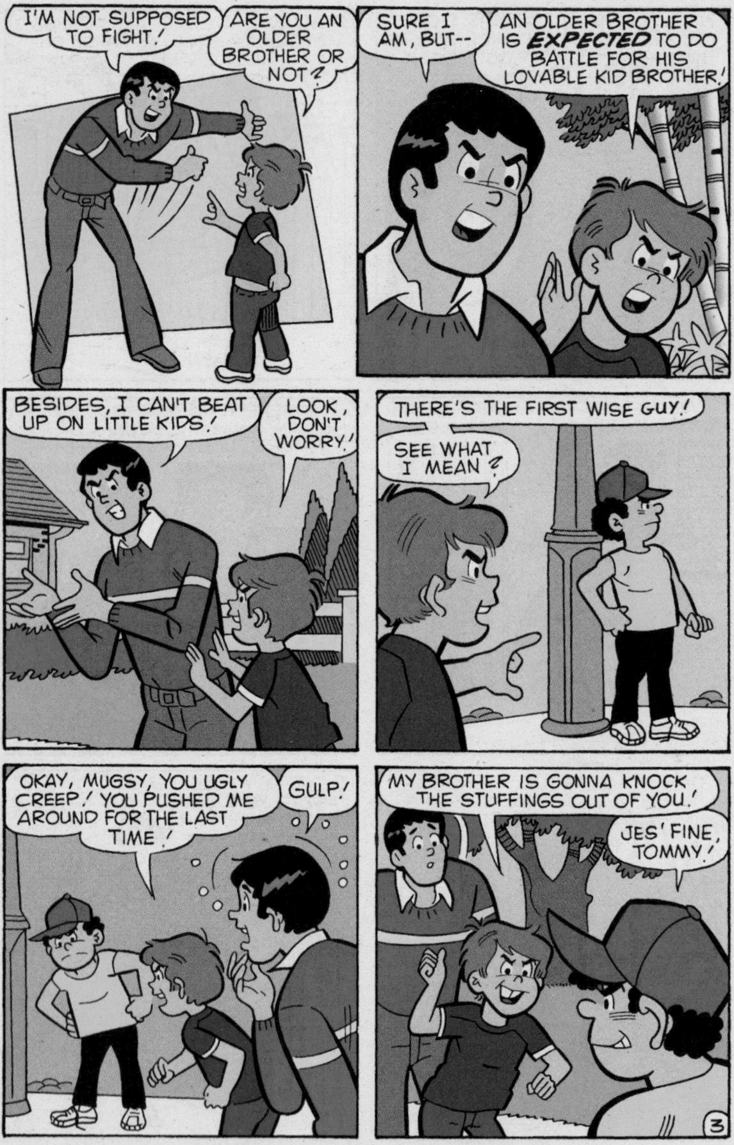
I'M NOT SUPPOSED TO FIGHT!
ARE YOU AN OLDER BROTHER OR NOT?
SURE I AM, BUT--
AN OLDER BROTHER IS EXPECTED TO DO BATTLE FOR HIS LOVABLE KID BROTHER!
BESIDES, I CAN'T BEAT UP ON LITTLE KIDS!
LOOK, DON'T WORRY!
THERE'S THE FIRST WISE GUY!
SEE WHAT I MEAN?
OKAY, MUGSY, YOU UGLY CREEP! YOU PUSHED ME AROUND FOR THE LAST TIME!
GULP!
MY BROTHER IS GONNA KNOCK THE STUFFINGS OUT OF YOU!
JES' FINE, TOMMY!
3

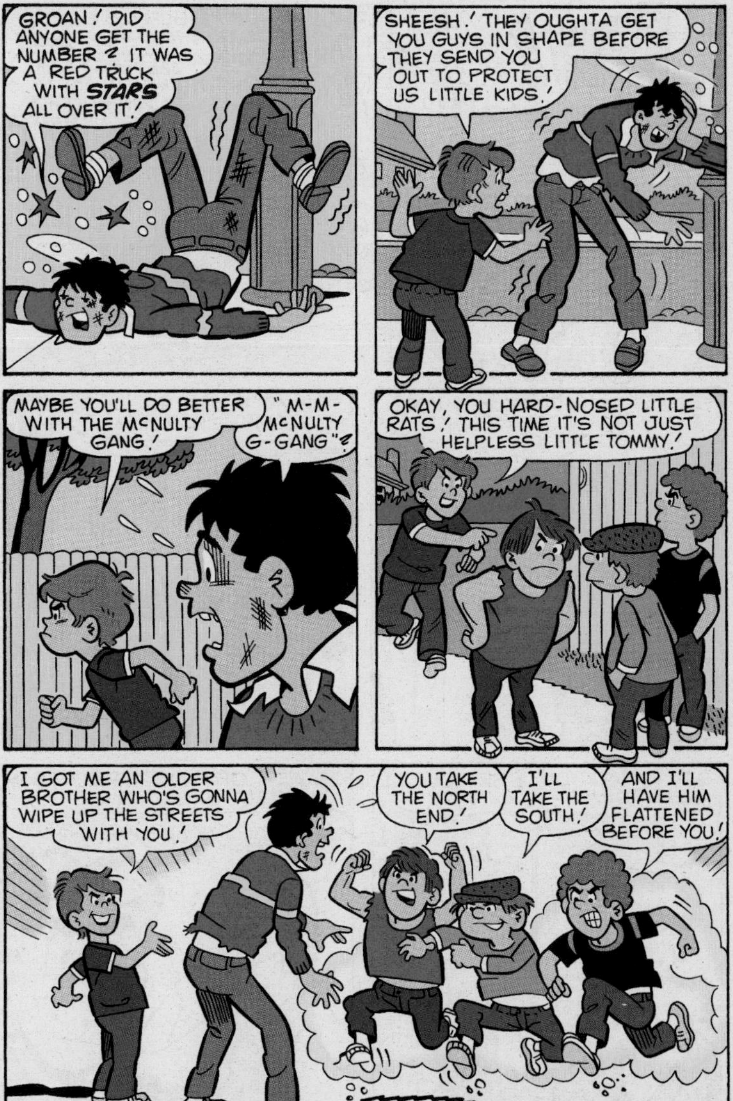
GROAN! DID ANYONE GET THE NUMBER? IT WAS A RED TRUCK WITH STARS ALL OVER IT!
SHEESH! THEY OUGHTA GET YOU GUYS IN SHAPE BEFORE THEY SEND YOU OUT TO PROTECT US LITTLE KIDS!
MAYBE YOU'LL DO BETTER WITH THE McNULTY GANG!
"M-M-McNULTY G-GANG"?
OKAY, YOU HARD-NOSED LITTLE RATS! THIS TIME IT'S NOT JUST HELPLESS LITTLE TOMMY!
I GOT ME AN OLDER BROTHER WHO'S GONNA WIPE UP THE STREETS WITH YOU!
YOU TAKE THE NORTH END!
I'LL TAKE THE SOUTH!
AND I'LL HAVE HIM FLATTENED BEFORE YOU!
4

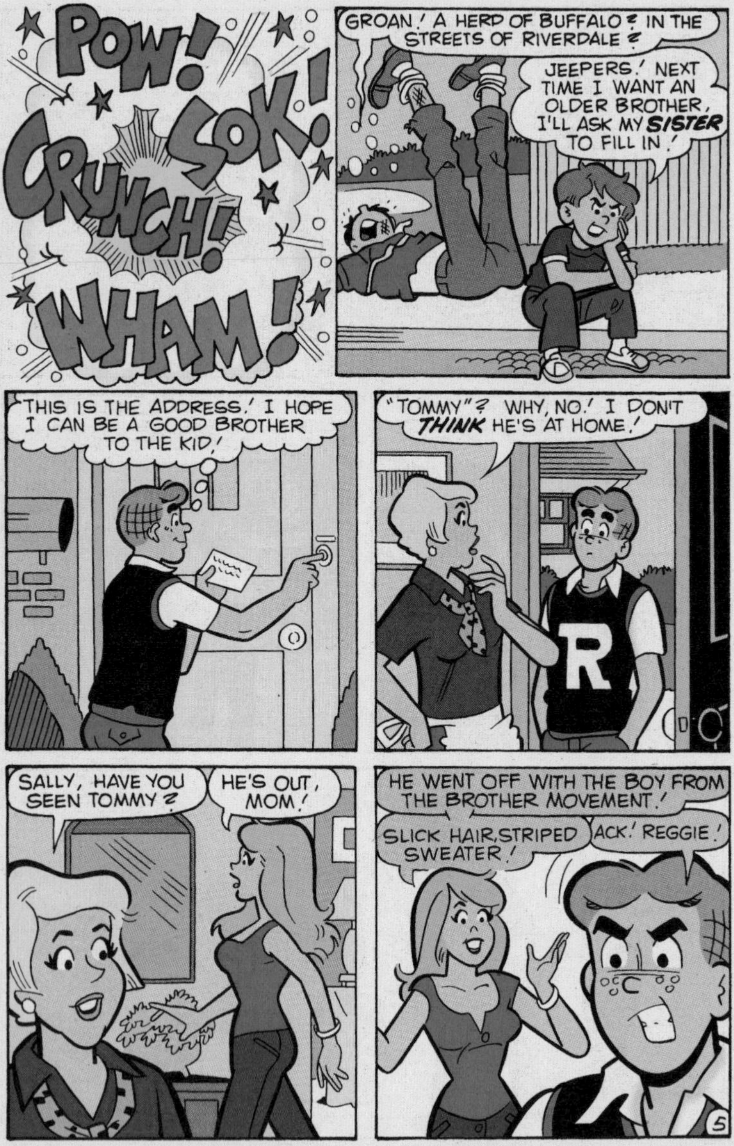
POW!
CRUNCH!
SOK!
WHAM!
GROAN! A HERD OF BUFFALO? IN THE STREETS OF RIVERDALE?
JEEPERS! NEXT TIME I WANT AN OLDER BROTHER, I'LL ASK MY SISTER TO FILL IN!
THIS IS THE ADDRESS! I HOPE I CAN BE A GOOD BROTHER TO THE KID!
"TOMMY"? WHY, NO! I DON'T THINK HE'S AT HOME!
SALLY, HAVE YOU SEEN TOMMY?
HE'S OUT, MOM!
HE WENT OFF WITH THE BOY FROM THE BROTHER MOVEMENT!
SLICK HAIR, STRIPED SWEATER!
ACK! REGGIE!

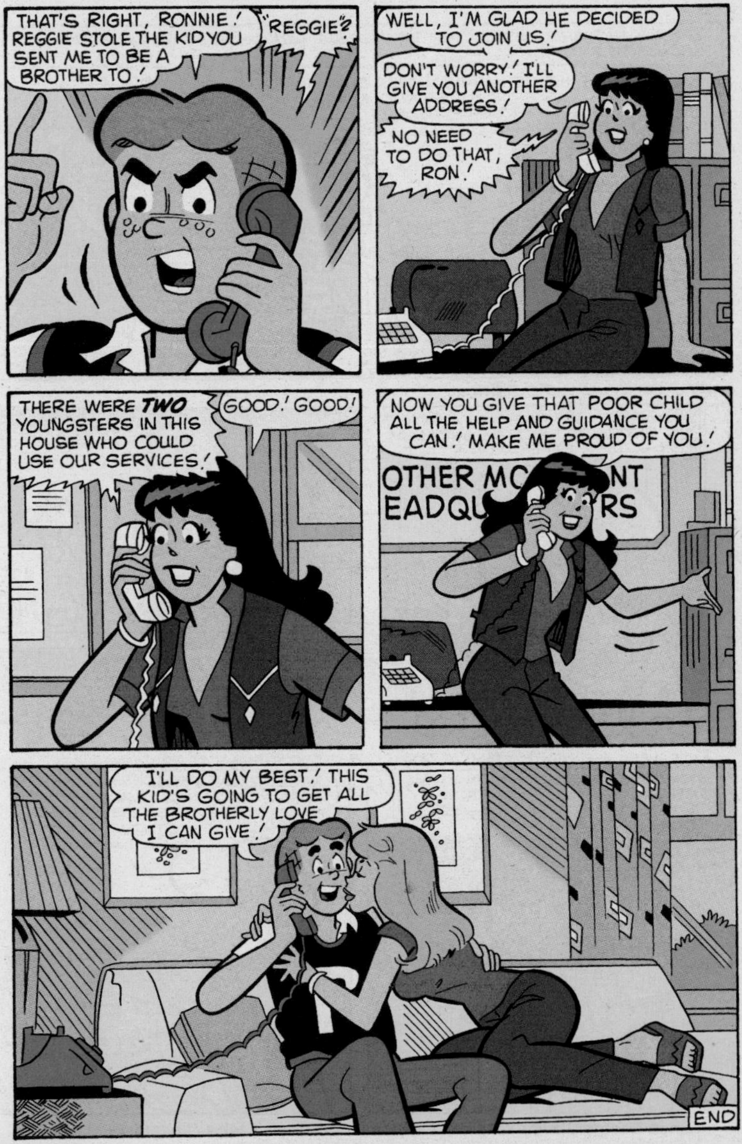
THAT'S RIGHT, RONNIE! REGGIE STOLE THE KID YOU SENT ME TO BE A BROTHER TO!
"REGGIE"?
WELL, I'M GLAD HE DECIDED TO JOIN US!
DON'T WORRY! I'LL GIVE YOU ANOTHER ADDRESS!
NO NEED TO DO THAT, RON!
THERE WERE TWO YOUNGSTERS IN THIS HOUSE WHO COULD USE OUR SERVICES!
GOOD! GOOD!
NOW YOU GIVE THAT POOR CHILD ALL THE HELP AND GUIDANCE YOU CAN! MAKE ME PROUD OF YOU!
I'LL DO MY BEST! THIS KID'S GOING TO GET ALL THE BROTHERLY LOVE I CAN GIVE!
END

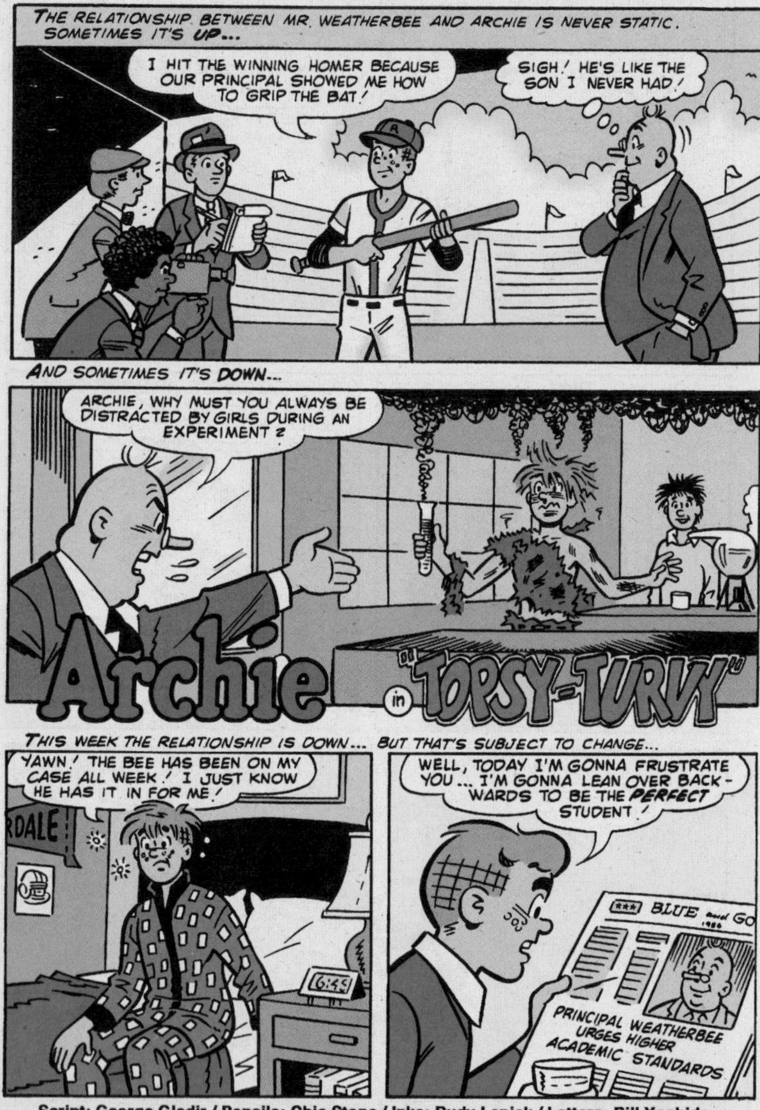
THE RELATIONSHIP BETWEEN MR. WEATHERBEE AND ARCHIE IS NEVER STATIC. SOMETIMES IT'S UP...
I HIT THE WINNING HOMER BECAUSE OUR PRINCIPAL SHOWED ME HOW TO GRIP THE BAT!
SIGH! HE'S LIKE THE SON I NEVER HAD!
AND SOMETIMES IT'S DOWN...
ARCHIE, WHY MUST YOU ALWAYS BE DISTRACTED BY GIRLS DURING AN EXPERIMENT?
Archie in "TOPSY-TURVY"
THIS WEEK THE RELATIONSHIP IS DOWN... BUT THAT'S SUBJECT TO CHANGE...
YAWN! THE BEE HAS BEEN ON MY CASE ALL WEEK! I JUST KNOW HE HAS IT IN FOR ME!
RDALE
6:45
WELL, TODAY I'M GONNA FRUSTRATE YOU... I'M GONNA LEAN OVER BACK-WARDS TO BE THE PERFECT STUDENT!
BLUE AND GO
PRINCIPAL WEATHERBEE URGES HIGHER ACADEMIC STANDARDS

Script: George Gladir / Pencils: Chic Stone / Inks: Rudy Lapick / Letters: Bill Yoshida

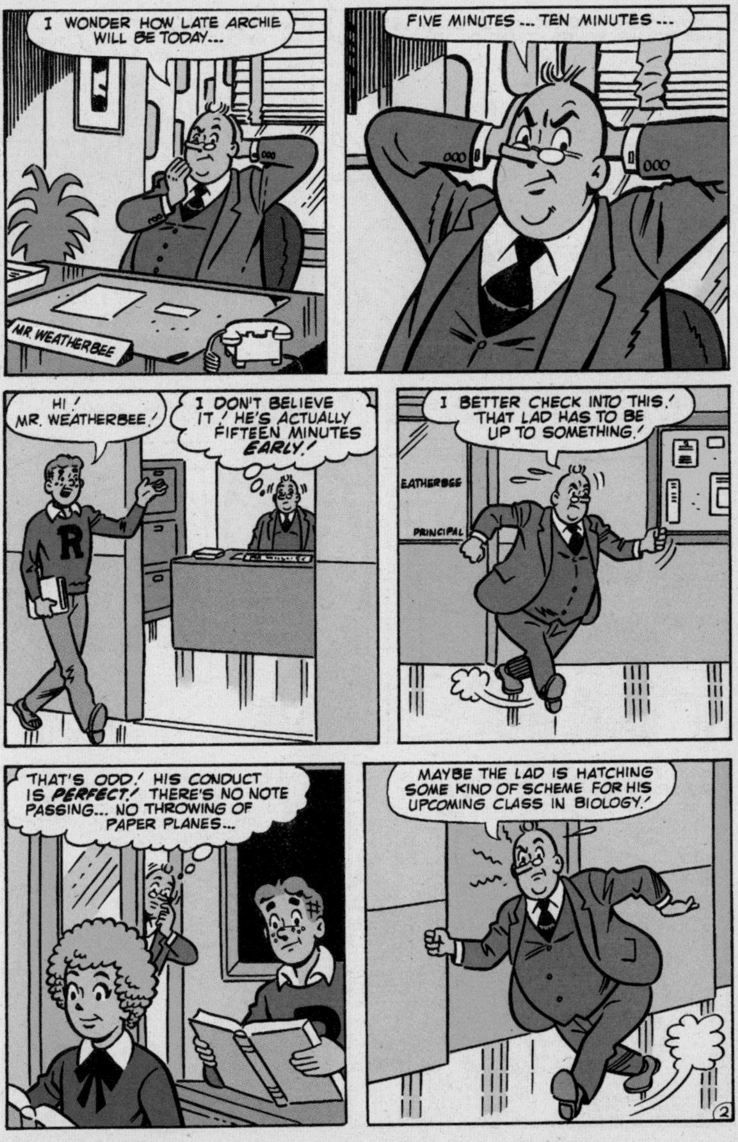
I WONDER HOW LATE ARCHIE WILL BE TODAY...
MR. WEATHERBEE
FIVE MINUTES ... TEN MINUTES ...
HI! MR. WEATHERBEE!
I DON'T BELIEVE IT! HE'S ACTUALLY FIFTEEN MINUTES EARLY!
I BETTER CHECK INTO THIS! THAT LAD HAS TO BE UP TO SOMETHING!
EATHERBEE
PRINCIPAL
THAT'S ODD! HIS CONDUCT IS PERFECT! THERE'S NO NOTE PASSING... NO THROWING OF PAPER PLANES...
MAYBE THE LAD IS HATCHING SOME KIND OF SCHEME FOR HIS UPCOMING CLASS IN BIOLOGY!
2

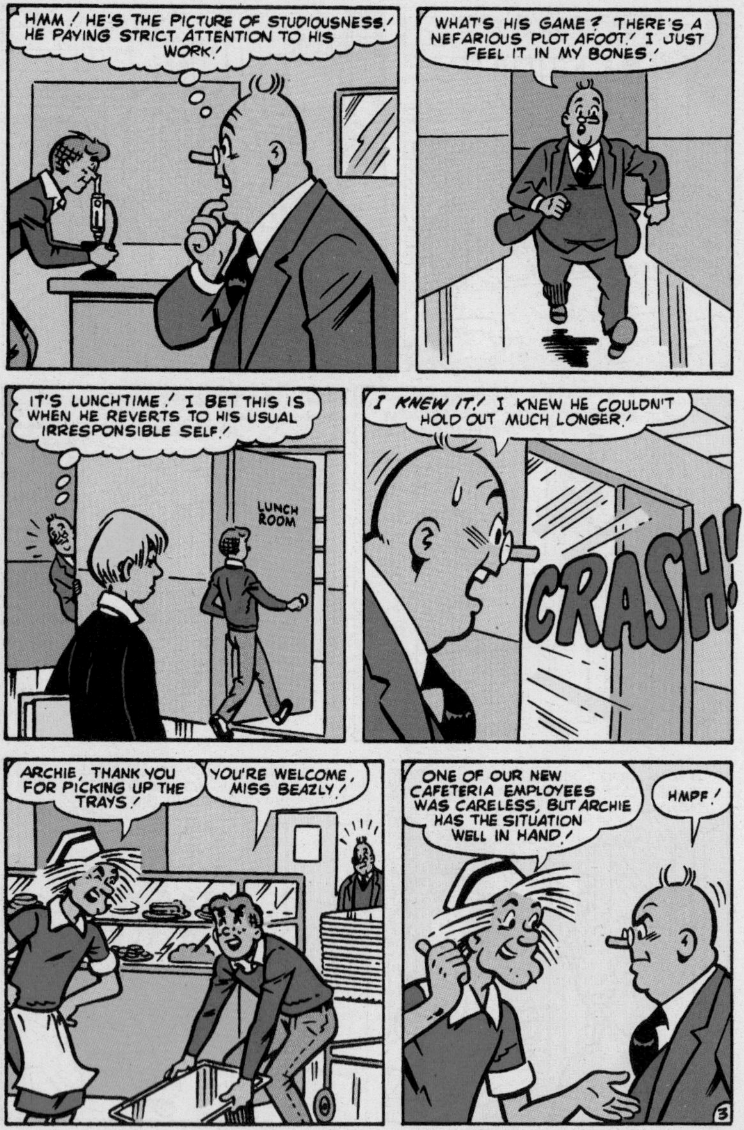
HMM! HE'S THE PICTURE OF STUDIOUSNESS! HE PAYING STRICT ATTENTION TO HIS WORK!
WHAT'S HIS GAME? THERE'S A NEFARIOUS PLOT AFOOT! I JUST FEEL IT IN MY BONES!
IT'S LUNCHTIME! I BET THIS IS WHEN HE REVERTS TO HIS USUAL IRRESPONSIBLE SELF!
LUNCH ROOM
I KNEW IT! I KNEW HE COULDN'T HOLD OUT MUCH LONGER!
CRASH!
ARCHIE, THANK YOU FOR PICKING UP THE TRAYS!
YOU'RE WELCOME, MISS BEAZLY!
ONE OF OUR NEW CAFETERIA EMPLOYEES WAS CARELESS, BUT ARCHIE HAS THE SITUATION WELL IN HAND!
HMPF!
3

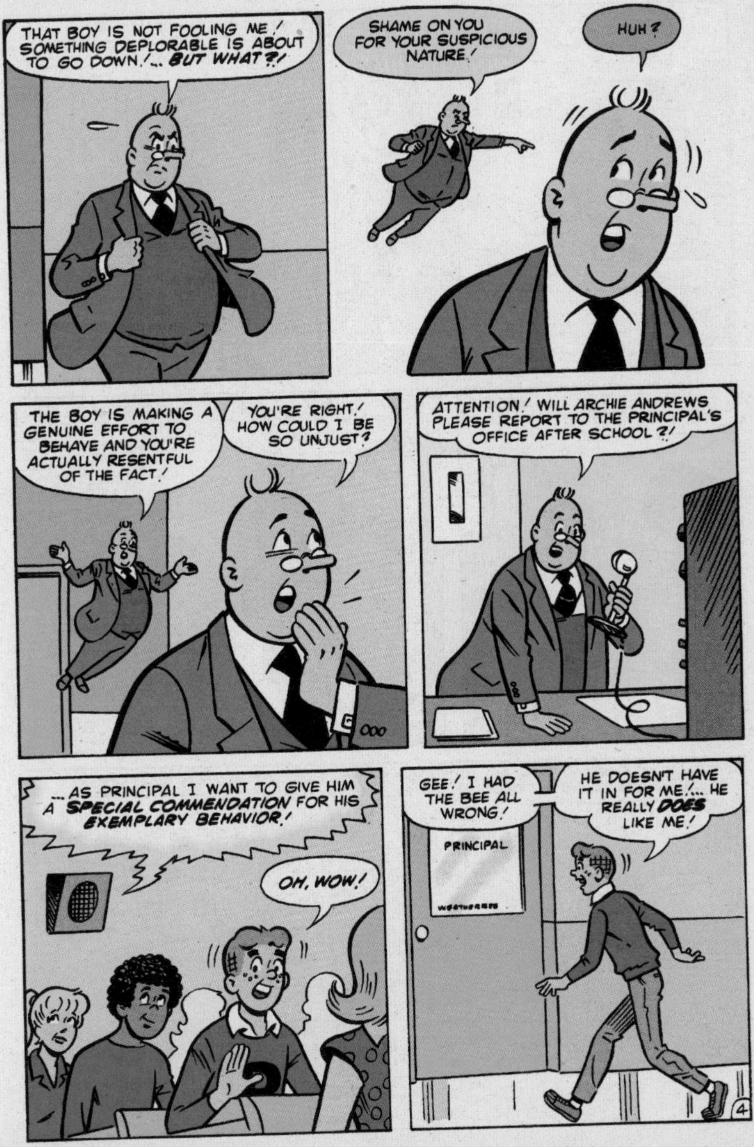
THAT BOY IS NOT FOOLING ME! SOMETHING DEPLORABLE IS ABOUT TO GO DOWN!... BUT WHAT?!
SHAME ON YOU FOR YOUR SUSPICIOUS NATURE!
HUH?
THE BOY IS MAKING A GENUINE EFFORT TO BEHAVE AND YOU'RE ACTUALLY RESENTFUL OF THE FACT!
YOU'RE RIGHT! HOW COULD I BE SO UNJUST?
ATTENTION! WILL ARCHIE ANDREWS PLEASE REPORT TO THE PRINCIPAL'S OFFICE AFTER SCHOOL?!
...AS PRINCIPAL I WANT TO GIVE HIM A SPECIAL COMMENDATION FOR HIS EXEMPLARY BEHAVIOR!
OH, WOW!
GEE! I HAD THE BEE ALL WRONG!
HE DOESN'T HAVE IT IN FOR ME!... HE REALLY DOES LIKE ME!
PRINCIPAL
4

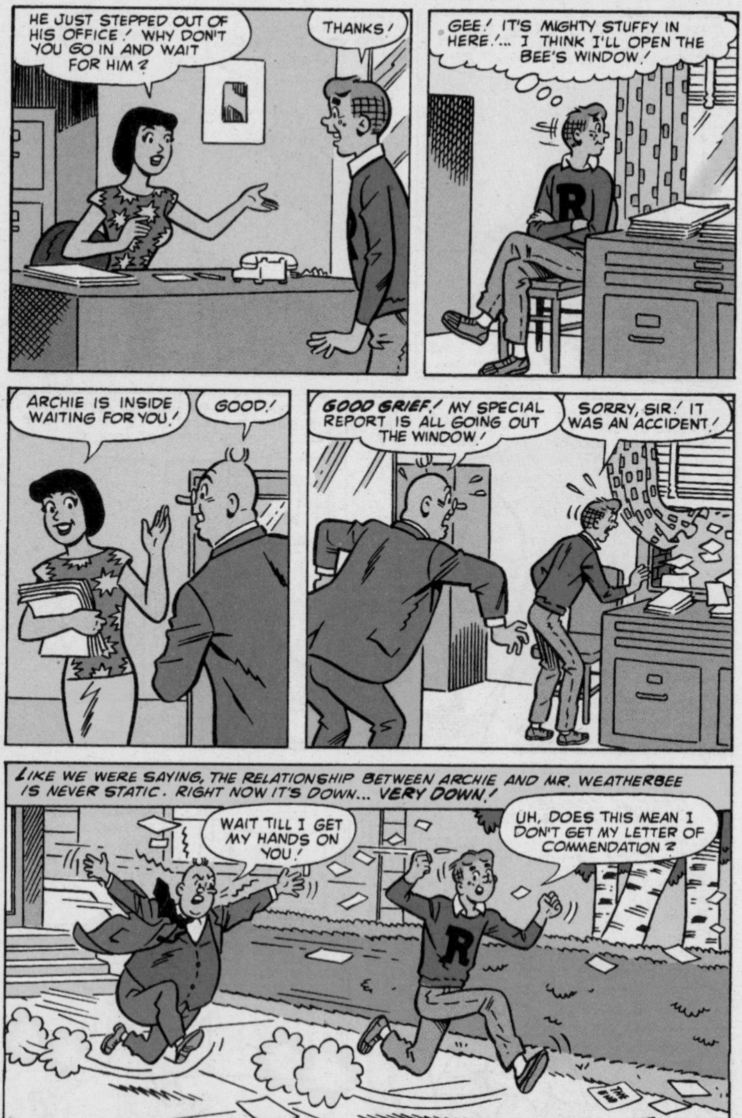
HE JUST STEPPED OUT OF HIS OFFICE! WHY DON'T YOU GO IN AND WAIT FOR HIM?
THANKS!
GEE! IT'S MIGHTY STUFFY IN HERE!... I THINK I'LL OPEN THE BEE'S WINDOW!
ARCHIE IS INSIDE WAITING FOR YOU!
GOOD!
GOOD GRIEF! MY SPECIAL REPORT IS ALL GOING OUT THE WINDOW!
SORRY, SIR! IT WAS AN ACCIDENT!
LIKE WE WERE SAYING, THE RELATIONSHIP BETWEEN ARCHIE AND MR. WEATHERBEE IS NEVER STATIC. RIGHT NOW IT'S DOWN... VERY DOWN!
WAIT TILL I GET MY HANDS ON YOU!
UH, DOES THIS MEAN I DON'T GET MY LETTER OF COMMENDATION?

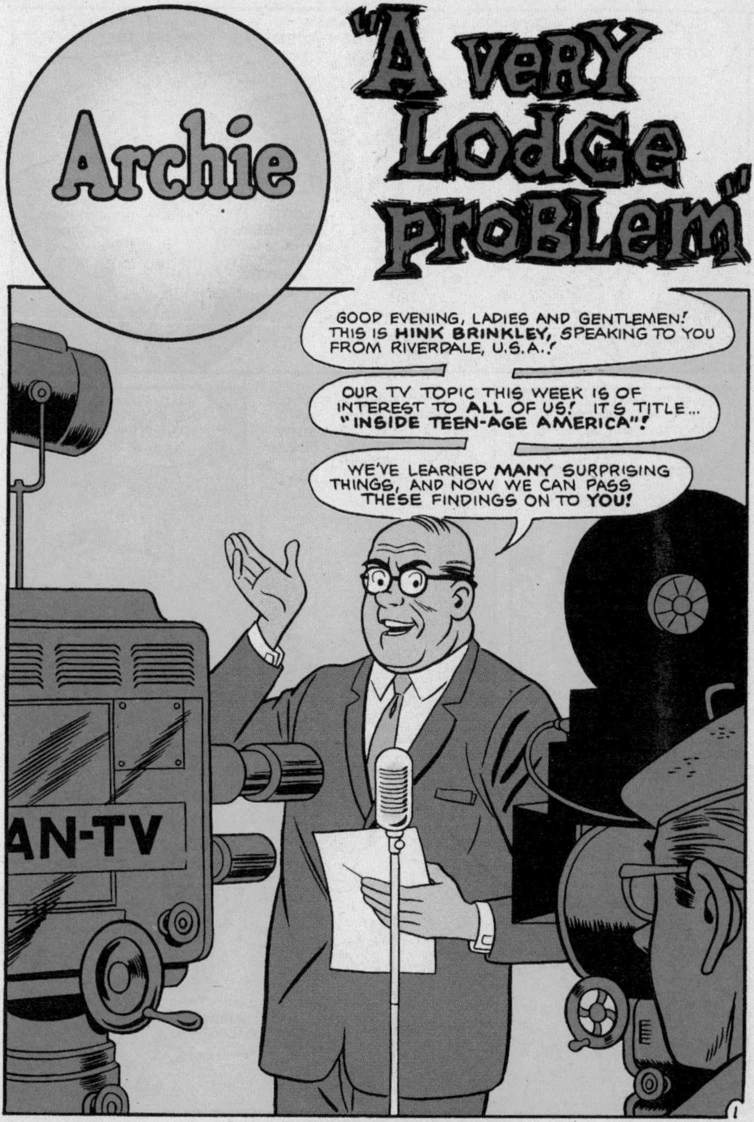
Archie
"A Very Lodge Problem"
GOOD EVENING, LADIES AND GENTLEMEN! THIS IS HINK BRINKLEY, SPEAKING TO YOU FROM RIVERDALE, U.S.A.!
OUR TV TOPIC THIS WEEK IS OF INTEREST TO ALL OF US! ITS TITLE... "INSIDE TEEN-AGE AMERICA"!
WE'VE LEARNED MANY SURPRISING THINGS, AND NOW WE CAN PASS THESE FINDINGS ON TO YOU!
AN-TV

Script: Sy Reit / Art & Letters: Bob White

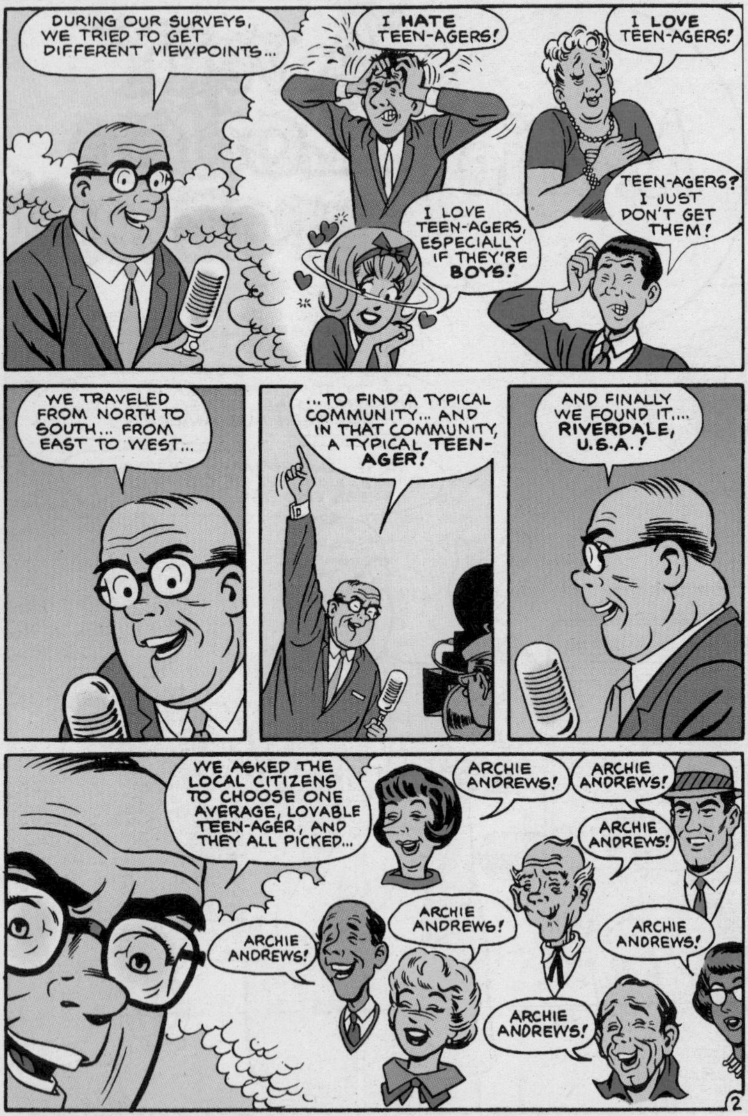
DURING OUR SURVEYS, WE TRIED TO GET DIFFERENT VIEWPOINTS...
I HATE TEEN-AGERS!
I LOVE TEEN-AGERS!
I LOVE TEEN-AGERS, ESPECIALLY IF THEY'RE BOYS!
TEEN-AGERS? I JUST DON'T GET THEM!
WE TRAVELED FROM NORTH TO SOUTH... FROM EAST TO WEST...
...TO FIND A TYPICAL COMMUNITY... AND IN THAT COMMUNITY, A TYPICAL TEEN-AGER!
AND FINALLY WE FOUND IT.... RIVERDALE, U.S.A.!
WE ASKED THE LOCAL CITIZENS TO CHOOSE ONE AVERAGE, LOVABLE TEEN-AGER, AND THEY ALL PICKED...
ARCHIE ANDREWS!
ARCHIE ANDREWS!
ARCHIE ANDREWS!
ARCHIE ANDREWS!
ARCHIE ANDREWS!
ARCHIE ANDREWS!
ARCHIE ANDREWS!

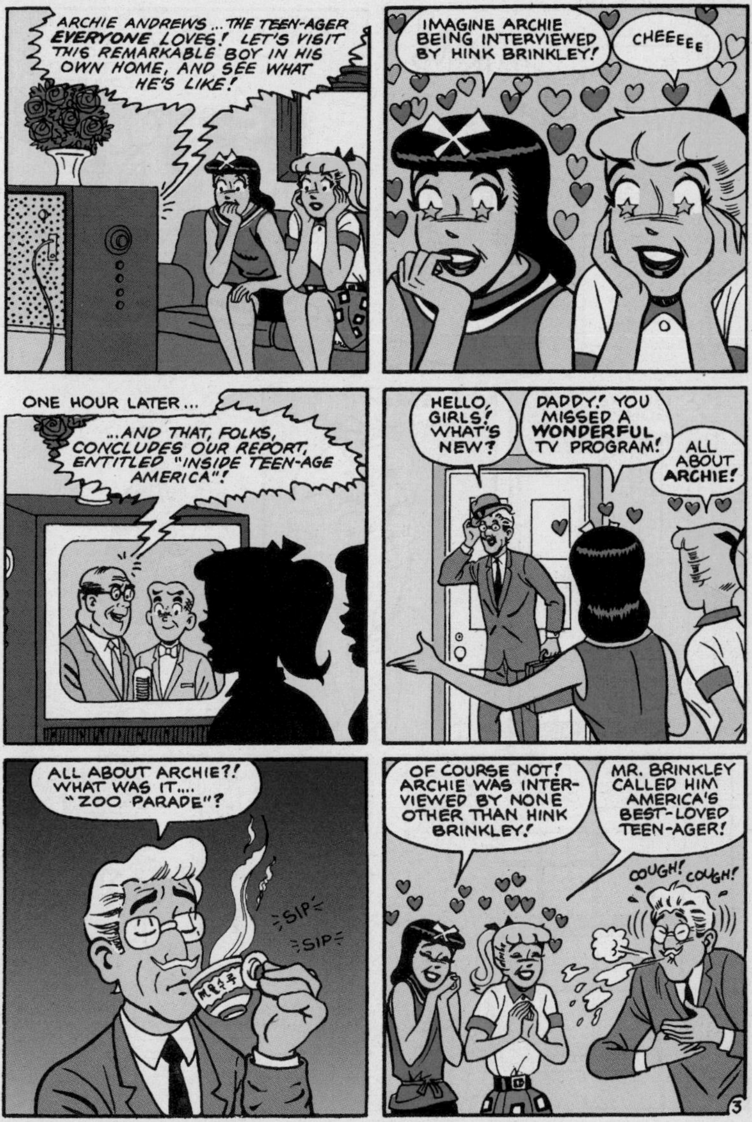

ARCHIE ANDREWS ... THE TEEN-AGER EVERYONE LOVES! LET'S VISIT THIS REMARKABLE BOY IN HIS OWN HOME, AND SEE WHAT HE'S LIKE!
IMAGINE ARCHIE BEING INTERVIEWED BY HINK BRINKLEY!
CHEEEEEE
ONE HOUR LATER...
...AND THAT, FOLKS, CONCLUDES OUR REPORT, ENTITLED "INSIDE TEEN-AGE AMERICA"!
HELLO, GIRLS! WHAT'S NEW?
DADDY! YOU MISSED A WONDERFUL TV PROGRAM!
ALL ABOUT ARCHIE!
ALL ABOUT ARCHIE?! WHAT WAS IT.... "ZOO PARADE"?
SIP
SIP
OF COURSE NOT! ARCHIE WAS INTER-VIEWED BY NONE OTHER THAN HINK BRINKLEY!
MR. BRINKLEY CALLED HIM AMERICA'S BEST-LOVED TEEN-AGER!
COUGH! COUGH!
3

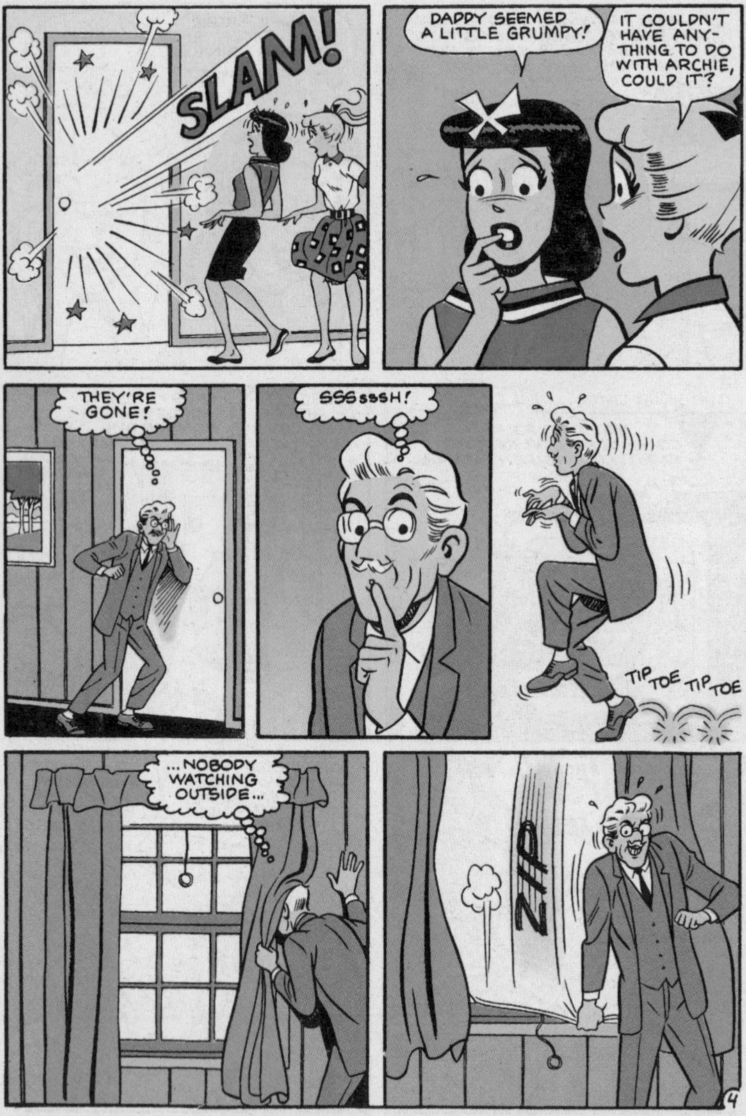
SLAM!
DADDY SEEMED A LITTLE GRUMPY!
IT COULDN'T HAVE ANY-THING TO DO WITH ARCHIE, COULD IT?
THEY'RE GONE!
SSSsssH!
TIP TOE TIP TOE
...NOBODY WATCHING OUTSIDE...
ZIP

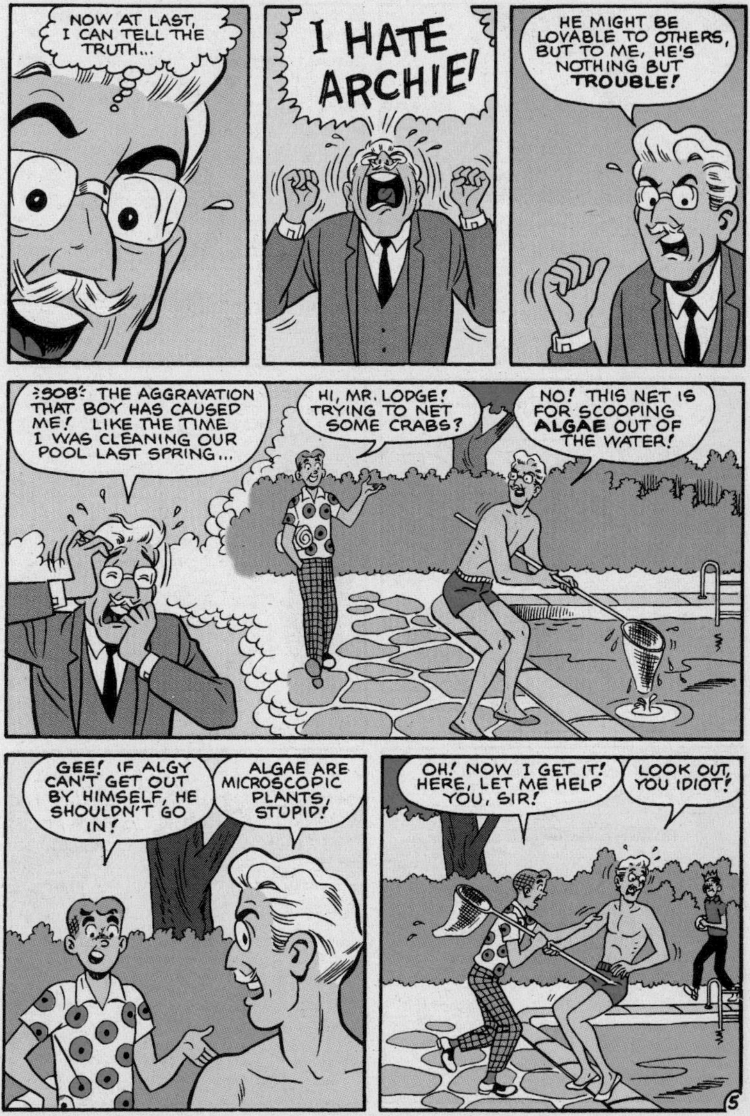
NOW AT LAST, I CAN TELL THE TRUTH...
I HATE ARCHIE!
HE MIGHT BE LOVABLE TO OTHERS, BUT TO ME, HE'S NOTHING BUT TROUBLE!
SOB THE AGGRAVATION THAT BOY HAS CAUSED ME! LIKE THE TIME I WAS CLEANING OUR POOL LAST SPRING...
HI, MR. LODGE! TRYING TO NET SOME CRABS?
NO! THIS NET IS FOR SCOOPING ALGAE OUT OF THE WATER!
GEE! IF ALGY CAN'T GET OUT BY HIMSELF, HE SHOULDN'T GO IN!
ALGAE ARE MICROSCOPIC PLANTS, STUPID!
OH! NOW I GET IT! HERE, LET ME HELP YOU, SIR!
LOOK OUT, YOU IDIOT!
5

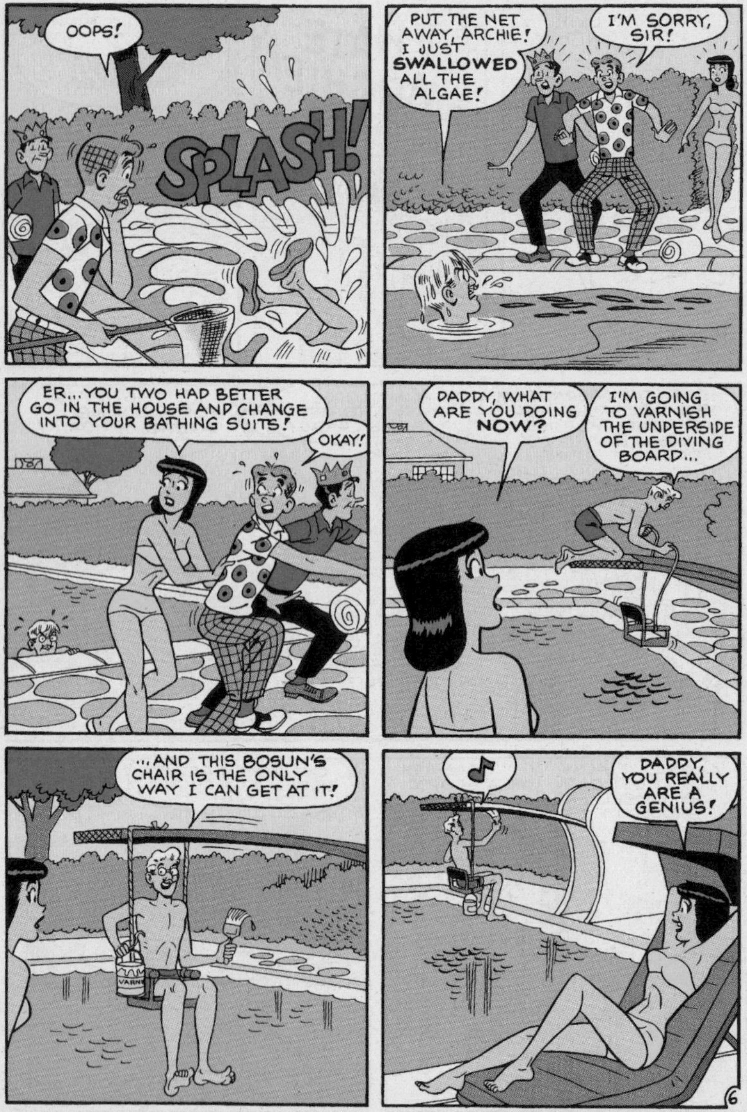
OOPS!
SPLASH!
PUT THE NET AWAY, ARCHIE! I JUST SWALLOWED ALL THE ALGAE!
I'M SORRY, SIR!
ER... YOU TWO HAD BETTER GO IN THE HOUSE AND CHANGE INTO YOUR BATHING SUITS!
OKAY!
DADDY, WHAT ARE YOU DOING NOW?
I'M GOING TO VARNISH THE UNDERSIDE OF THE DIVING BOARD...
...AND THIS BOSUN'S CHAIR IS THE ONLY WAY I CAN GET AT IT!
DADDY, YOU REALLY ARE A GENIUS!

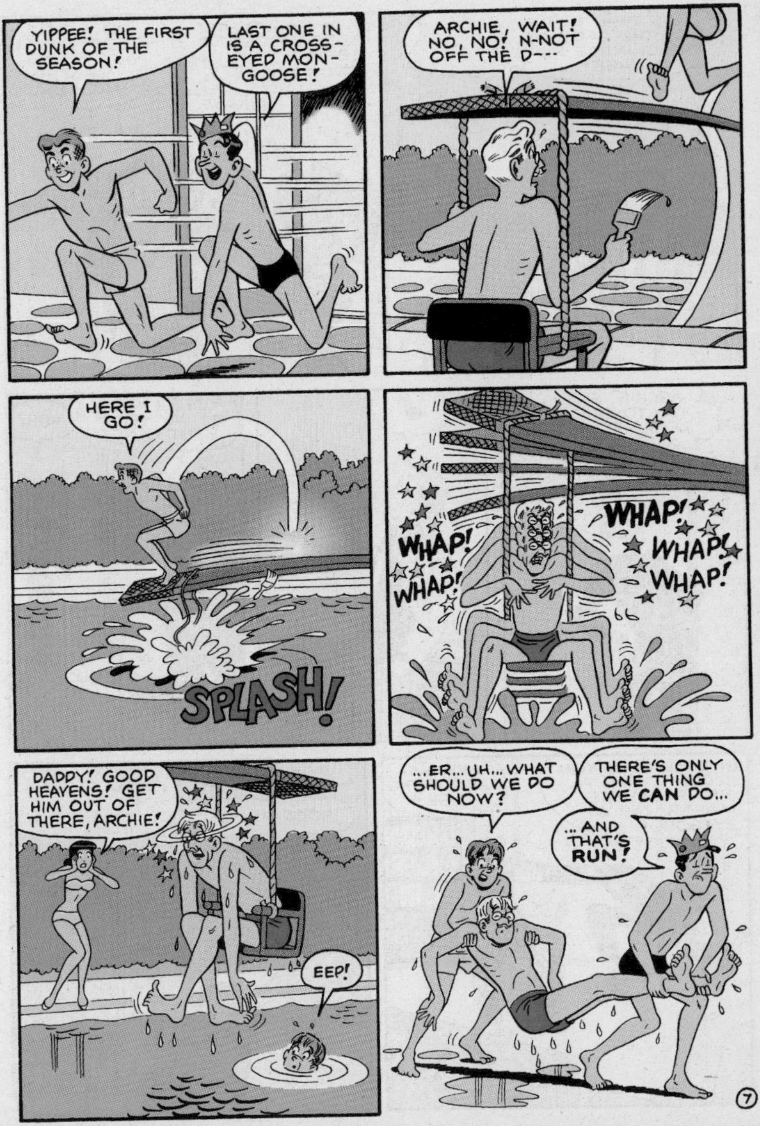
YIPPEE! THE FIRST DUNK OF THE SEASON!
LAST ONE IN IS A CROSS-EYED MON-GOOSE!
ARCHIE, WAIT! NO, NO! N-NOT OFF THE D---
HERE I GO!
SPLASH!
WHAP!
WHAP!
WHAP!
WHAP!
WHAP!
DADDY! GOOD HEAVENS! GET HIM OUT OF THERE, ARCHIE!
EEP!
...ER...UH...WHAT SHOULD WE DO NOW?
THERE'S ONLY ONE THING WE CAN DO...
...AND THAT'S RUN!
7

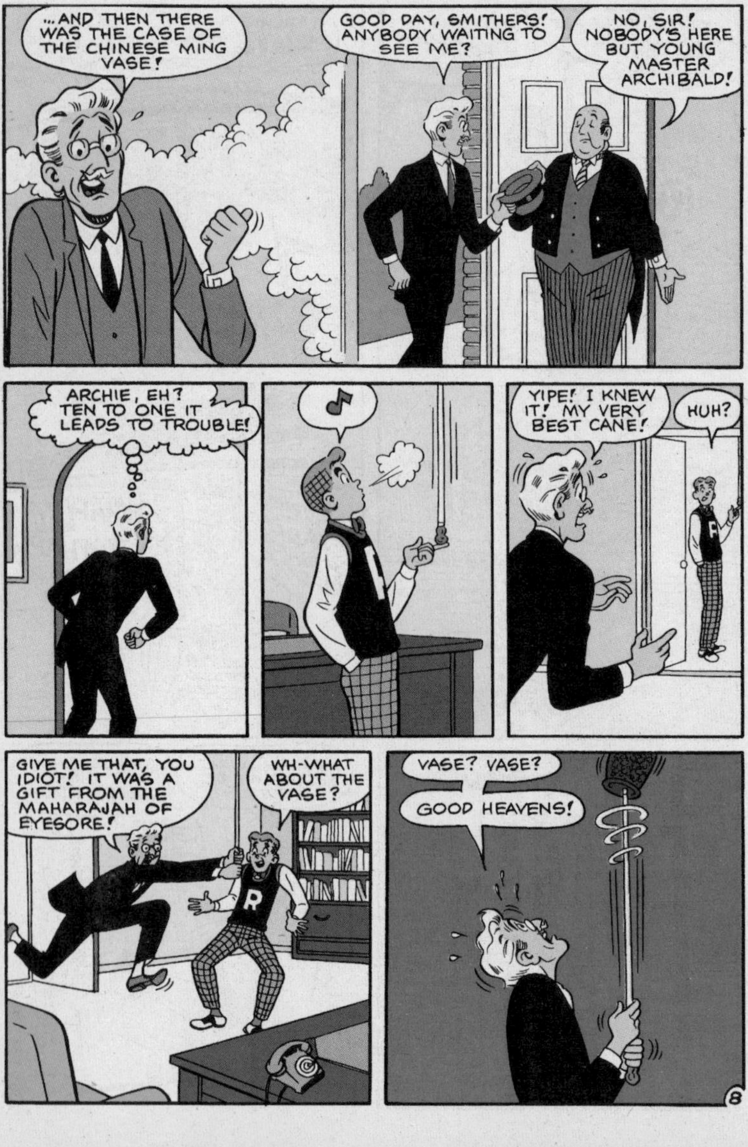
...AND THEN THERE WAS THE CASE OF THE CHINESE MING VASE!
GOOD DAY, SMITHERS! ANYBODY WAITING TO SEE ME?
NO, SIR! NOBODY'S HERE BUT YOUNG MASTER ARCHIBALD!
ARCHIE, EH? TEN TO ONE IT LEADS TO TROUBLE!
YIPE! I KNEW IT! MY VERY BEST CANE!
HUH?
GIVE ME THAT, YOU IDIOT! IT WAS A GIFT FROM THE MAHARAJAH OF EYESORE!
WH-WHAT ABOUT THE VASE?
VASE? VASE?
GOOD HEAVENS!
8

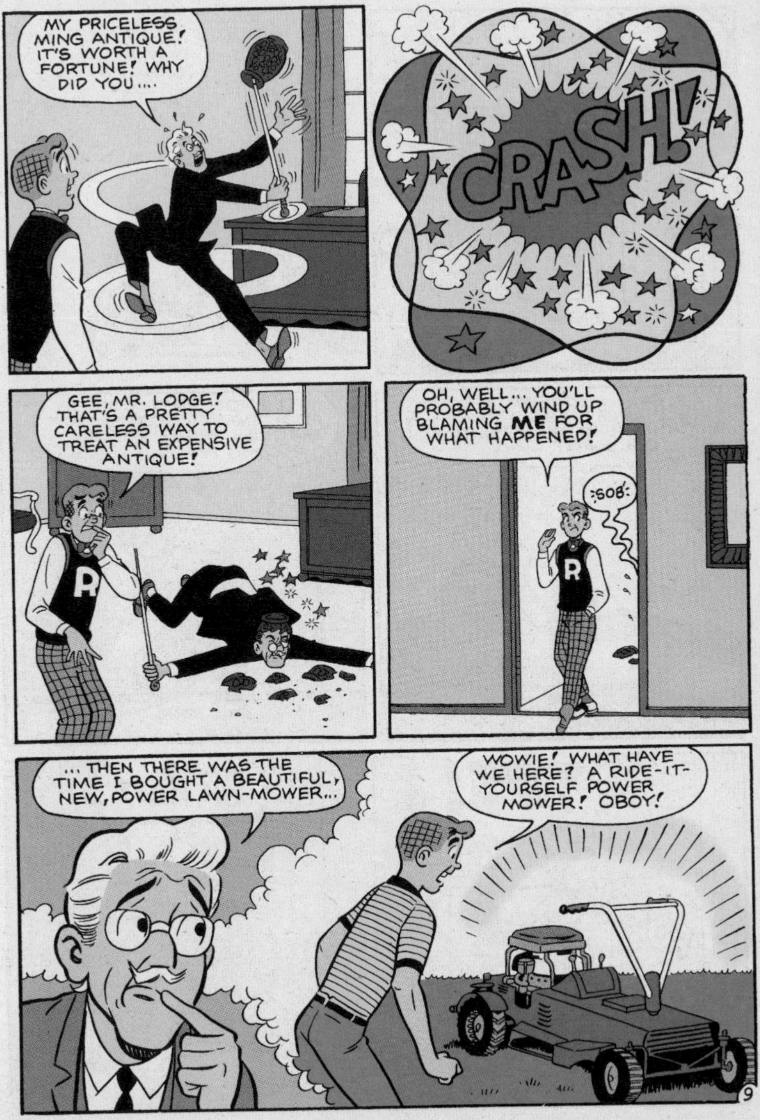

MY PRICELESS MING ANTIQUE! IT'S WORTH A FORTUNE! WHY DID YOU....
CRASH!
GEE, MR. LODGE! THAT'S A PRETTY CARELESS WAY TO TREAT AN EXPENSIVE ANTIQUE!
OH, WELL... YOU'LL PROBABLY WIND UP BLAMING ME FOR WHAT HAPPENED!
SOB
...THEN THERE WAS THE TIME I BOUGHT A BEAUTIFUL, NEW, POWER LAWN-MOWER...
WOWIE! WHAT HAVE WE HERE? A RIDE-IT-YOURSELF POWER MOWER! OBOY!

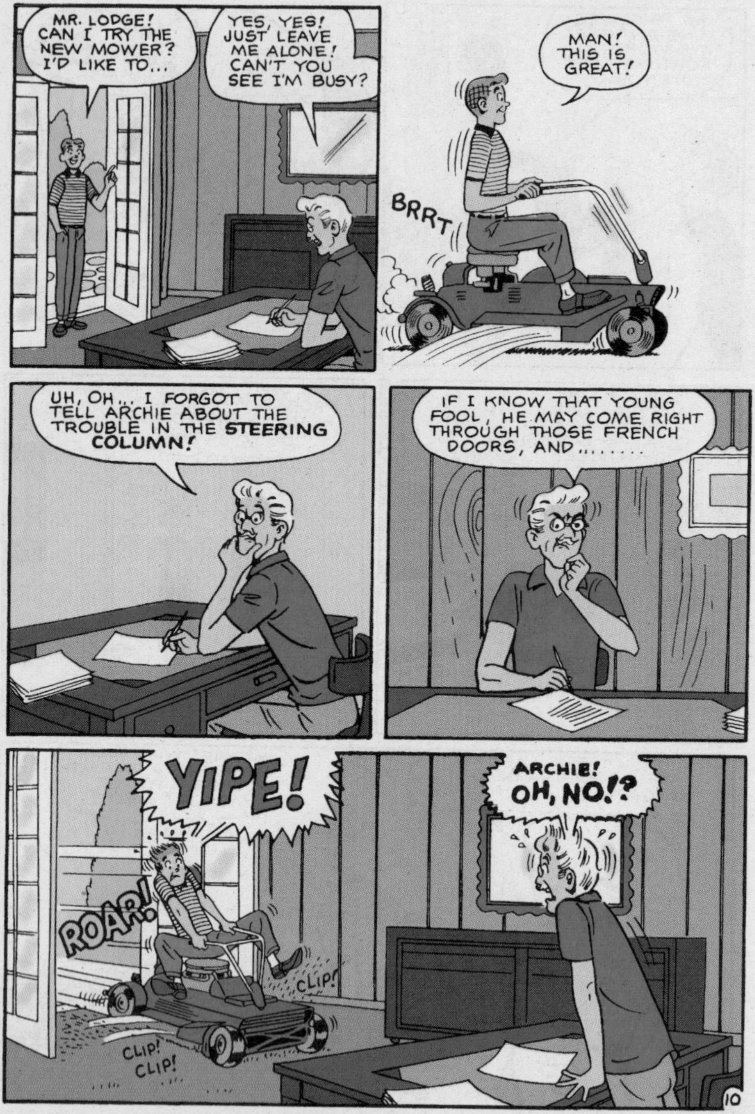
MR. LODGE! CAN I TRY THE NEW MOWER? I'D LIKE TO...
YES, YES! JUST LEAVE ME ALONE! CAN'T YOU SEE I'M BUSY?
MAN! THIS IS GREAT!
BRRRT
UH, OH... I FORGOT TO TELL ARCHIE ABOUT THE TROUBLE IN THE **STEERING COLUMN!**
IF I KNOW THAT YOUNG FOOL, HE MAY COME RIGHT THROUGH THOSE FRENCH DOORS, AND.......
YIPE!
ARCHIE! OH, NO!?
ROAR!
CLIP!
CLIP! CLIP!

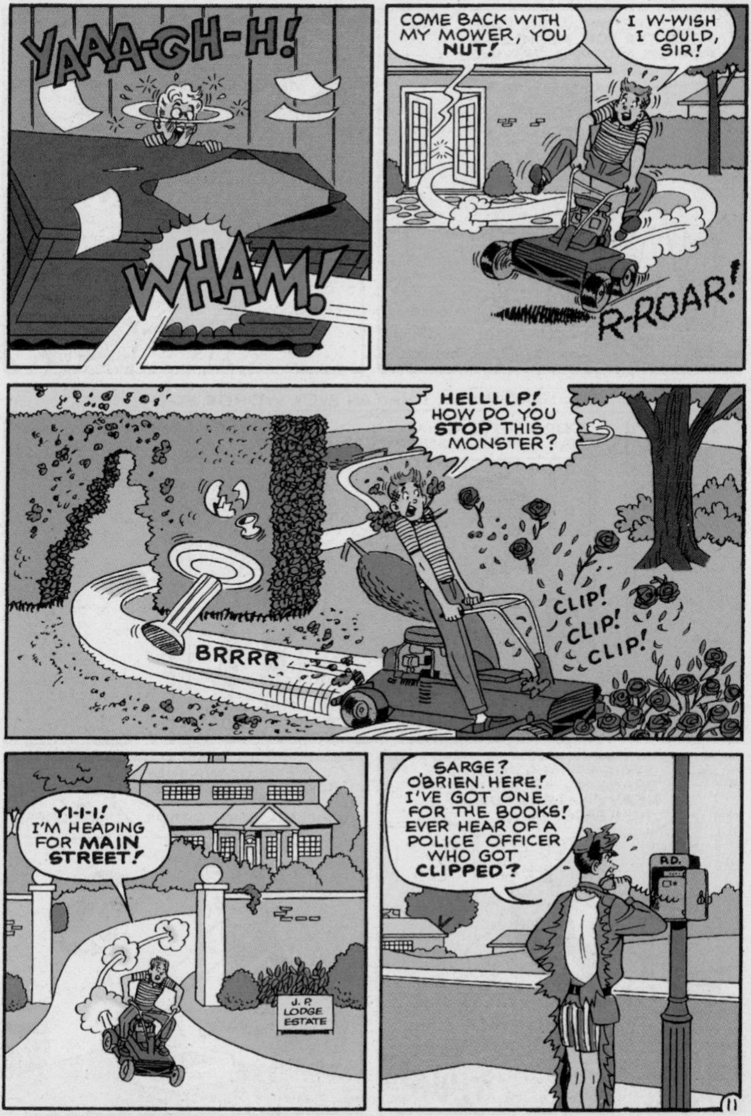
YAAA-GH-H!
WHAM!
COME BACK WITH MY MOWER, YOU NUT!
I W-WISH I COULD, SIR!
R-ROAR!
HELLLLP! HOW DO YOU STOP THIS MONSTER?
BRRRR
CLIP! CLIP! CLIP!
YI-I-I! I'M HEADING FOR MAIN STREET!
J. P. LODGE ESTATE
SARGE? O'BRIEN HERE! I'VE GOT ONE FOR THE BOOKS! EVER HEAR OF A POLICE OFFICER WHO GOT CLIPPED?
P.D.

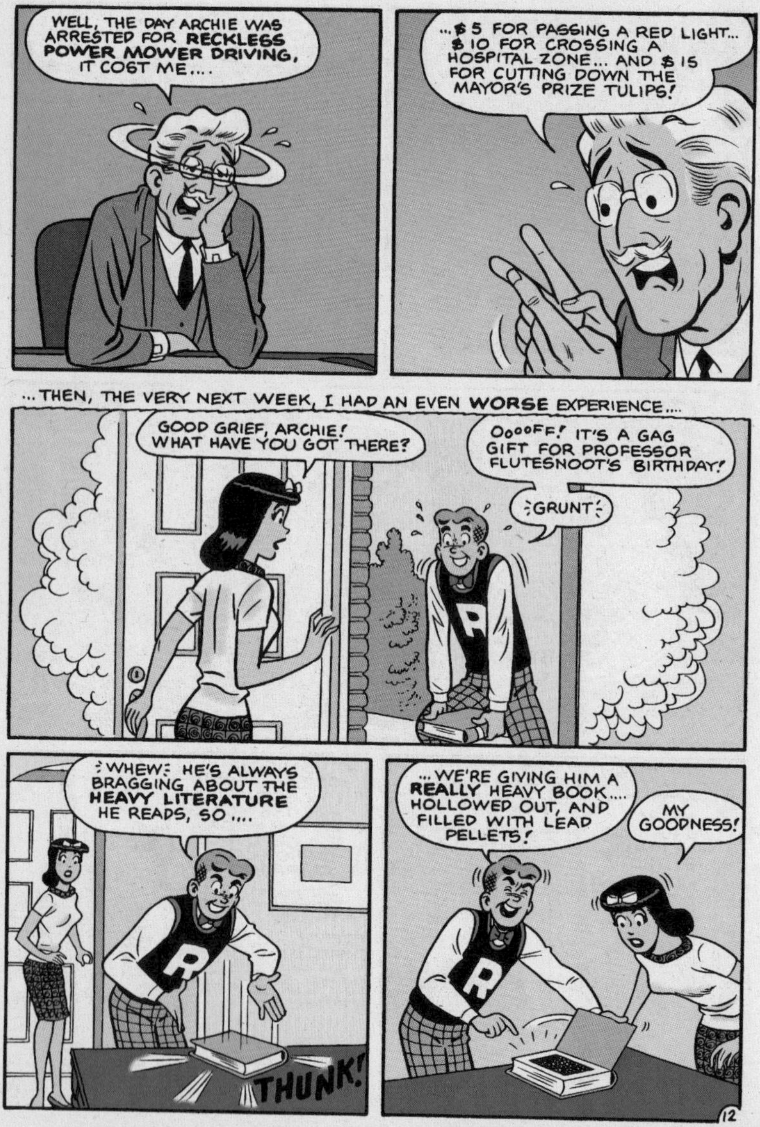
WELL, THE DAY ARCHIE WAS ARRESTED FOR **RECKLESS POWER MOWER DRIVING,** IT COST ME....
...$ 5 FOR PASSING A RED LIGHT... $ 10 FOR CROSSING A HOSPITAL ZONE... AND $ 15 FOR CUTTING DOWN THE MAYOR'S PRIZE TULIPS!
...THEN, THE VERY NEXT WEEK, I HAD AN EVEN **WORSE** EXPERIENCE....
GOOD GRIEF, ARCHIE! WHAT HAVE YOU GOT THERE?
OoooFF! IT'S A GAG GIFT FOR PROFESSOR FLUTESNOOT'S BIRTHDAY!
GRUNT
WHEW! HE'S ALWAYS BRAGGING ABOUT THE **HEAVY LITERATURE** HE READS, SO....
THUNK!
...WE'RE GIVING HIM A **REALLY** HEAVY BOOK.... HOLLOWED OUT, AND FILLED WITH LEAD PELLETS!
MY GOODNESS!

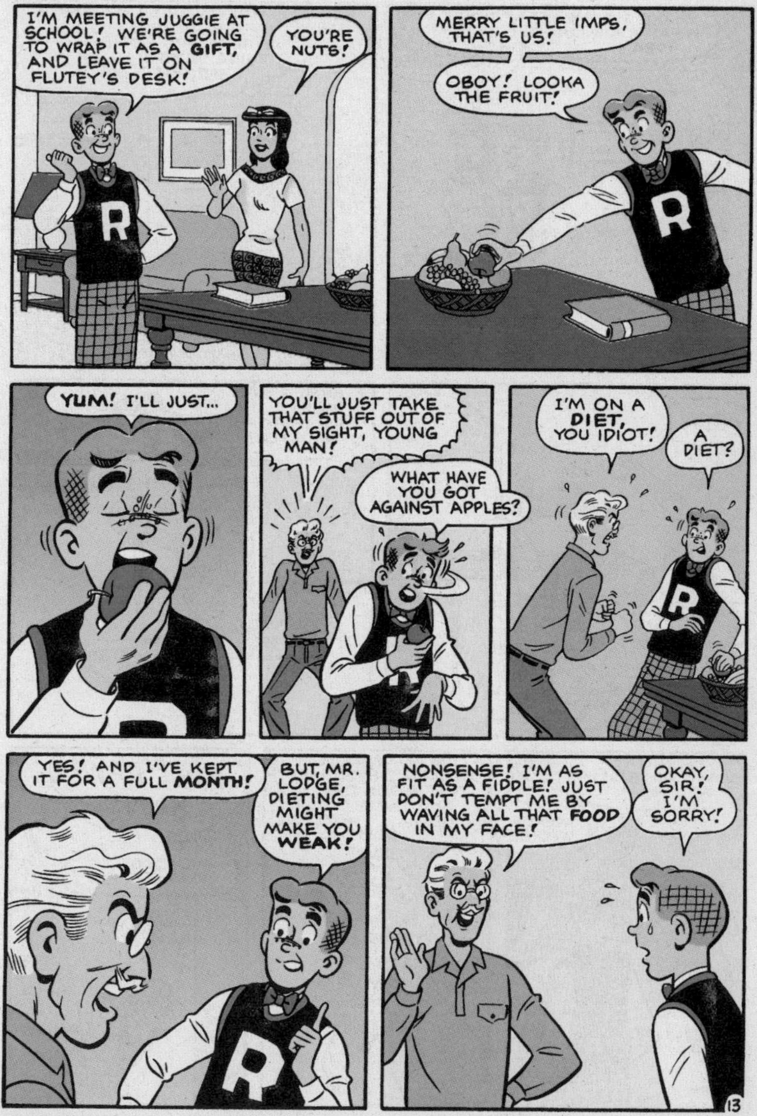
I'M MEETING JUGGIE AT SCHOOL! WE'RE GOING TO WRAP IT AS A GIFT, AND LEAVE IT ON FLUTEY'S DESK!
YOU'RE NUTS!
MERRY LITTLE IMPS, THAT'S US!
OBOY! LOOKA THE FRUIT!
YUM! I'LL JUST...
YOU'LL JUST TAKE THAT STUFF OUT OF MY SIGHT, YOUNG MAN!
WHAT HAVE YOU GOT AGAINST APPLES?
I'M ON A DIET, YOU IDIOT!
A DIET?
YES! AND I'VE KEPT IT FOR A FULL MONTH!
BUT, MR. LODGE, DIETING MIGHT MAKE YOU WEAK!
NONSENSE! I'M AS FIT AS A FIDDLE! JUST DON'T TEMPT ME BY WAVING ALL THAT FOOD IN MY FACE!
OKAY, SIR! I'M SORRY!
13

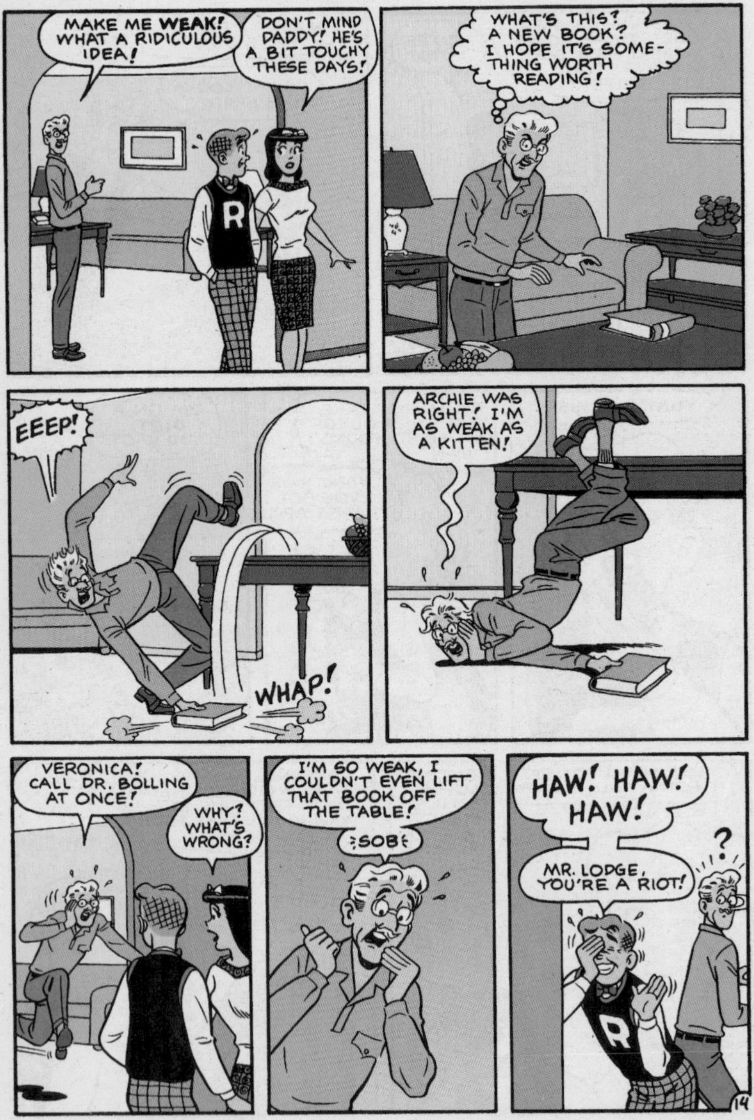
MAKE ME WEAK! WHAT A RIDICULOUS IDEA!
DON'T MIND DADDY! HE'S A BIT TOUCHY THESE DAYS!
WHAT'S THIS? A NEW BOOK? I HOPE IT'S SOMETHING WORTH READING!
EEEP!
WHAP!
ARCHIE WAS RIGHT! I'M AS WEAK AS A KITTEN!
VERONICA! CALL DR. BOLLING AT ONCE!
WHY? WHAT'S WRONG?
I'M SO WEAK, I COULDN'T EVEN LIFT THAT BOOK OFF THE TABLE!
SOB
HAW! HAW! HAW!
MR. LODGE, YOU'RE A RIOT!
?
14

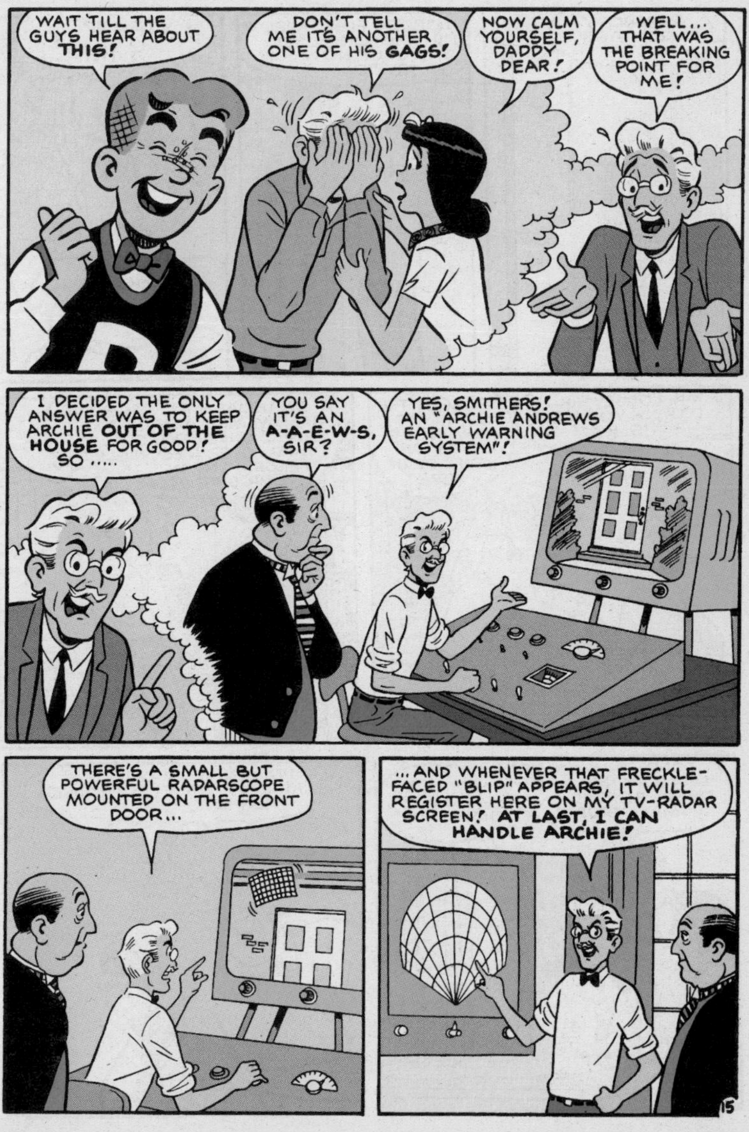
WAIT 'TILL THE GUYS HEAR ABOUT THIS!
DON'T TELL ME IT'S ANOTHER ONE OF HIS GAGS!
NOW CALM YOURSELF, DADDY DEAR!
WELL... THAT WAS THE BREAKING POINT FOR ME!
I DECIDED THE ONLY ANSWER WAS TO KEEP ARCHIE OUT OF THE HOUSE FOR GOOD! SO .....
YOU SAY IT'S AN A-A-E-W-S, SIR?
YES, SMITHERS! AN "ARCHIE ANDREWS EARLY WARNING SYSTEM"!
THERE'S A SMALL BUT POWERFUL RADARSCOPE MOUNTED ON THE FRONT DOOR...
...AND WHENEVER THAT FRECKLE-FACED "BLIP" APPEARS, IT WILL REGISTER HERE ON MY TV-RADAR SCREEN! AT LAST, I CAN HANDLE ARCHIE!

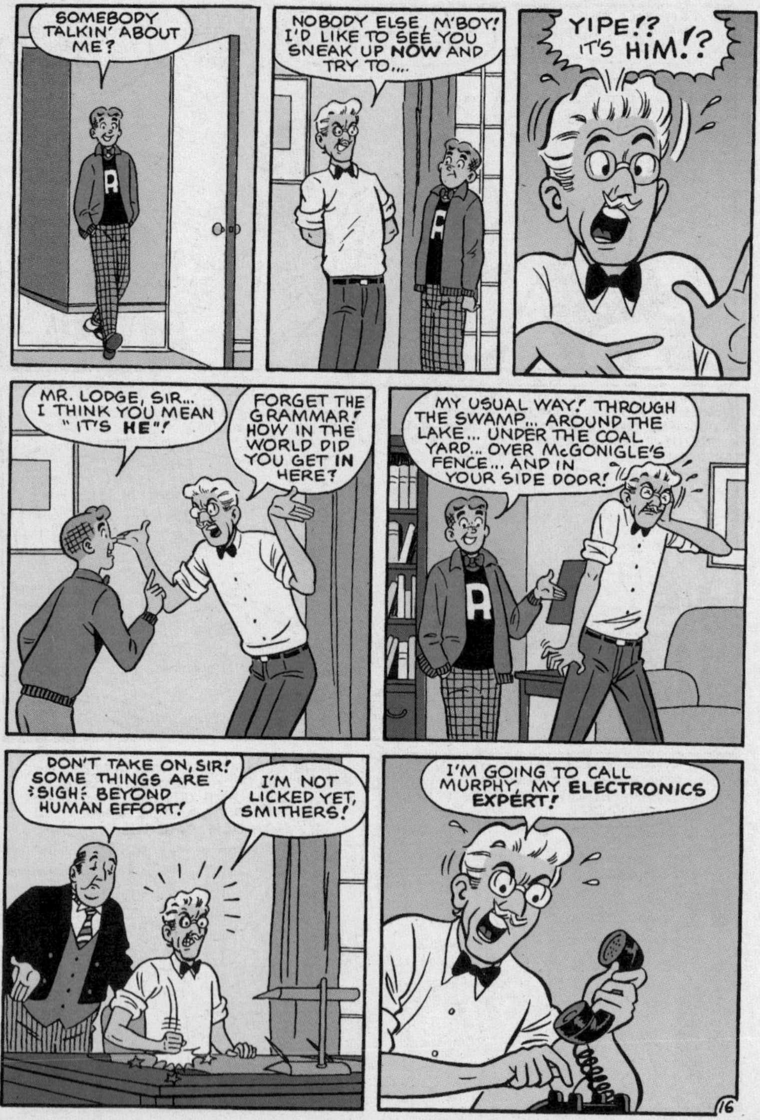
SOMEBODY TALKIN' ABOUT ME?
NOBODY ELSE, M'BOY! I'D LIKE TO SEE YOU SNEAK UP NOW AND TRY TO....
YIPE!? IT'S HIM!?
MR. LODGE, SIR... I THINK YOU MEAN "IT'S HE"!
FORGET THE GRAMMAR! HOW IN THE WORLD DID YOU GET IN HERE?
MY USUAL WAY! THROUGH THE SWAMP... AROUND THE LAKE... UNDER THE COAL YARD... OVER McGONIGLE'S FENCE... AND IN YOUR SIDE DOOR!
DON'T TAKE ON, SIR! SOME THINGS ARE =SIGH= BEYOND HUMAN EFFORT!
I'M NOT LICKED YET, SMITHERS!
I'M GOING TO CALL MURPHY, MY ELECTRONICS EXPERT!
16

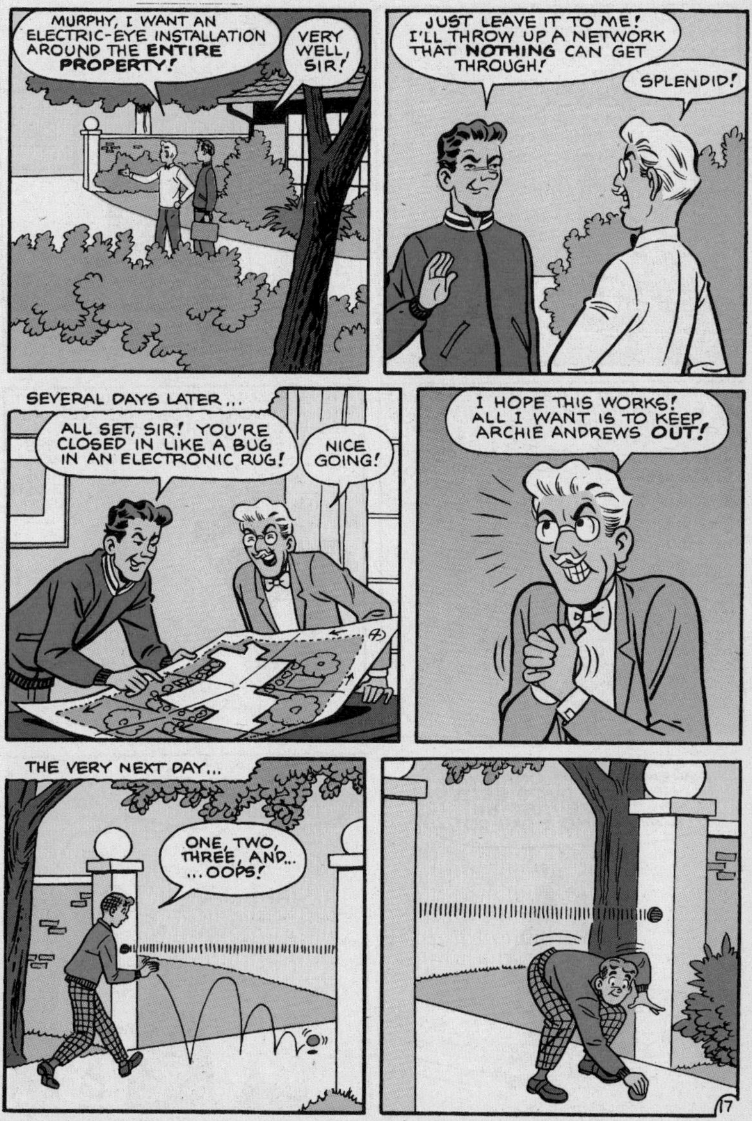
MURPHY, I WANT AN ELECTRIC-EYE INSTALLATION AROUND THE **ENTIRE PROPERTY**!
VERY WELL, SIR!
JUST LEAVE IT TO ME! I'LL THROW UP A NETWORK THAT **NOTHING** CAN GET THROUGH!
SPLENDID!
SEVERAL DAYS LATER...
ALL SET, SIR! YOU'RE CLOSED IN LIKE A BUG IN AN ELECTRONIC RUG!
NICE GOING!
I HOPE THIS WORKS! ALL I WANT IS TO KEEP ARCHIE ANDREWS **OUT**!
THE VERY NEXT DAY...
ONE, TWO, THREE, AND... ...OOPS!

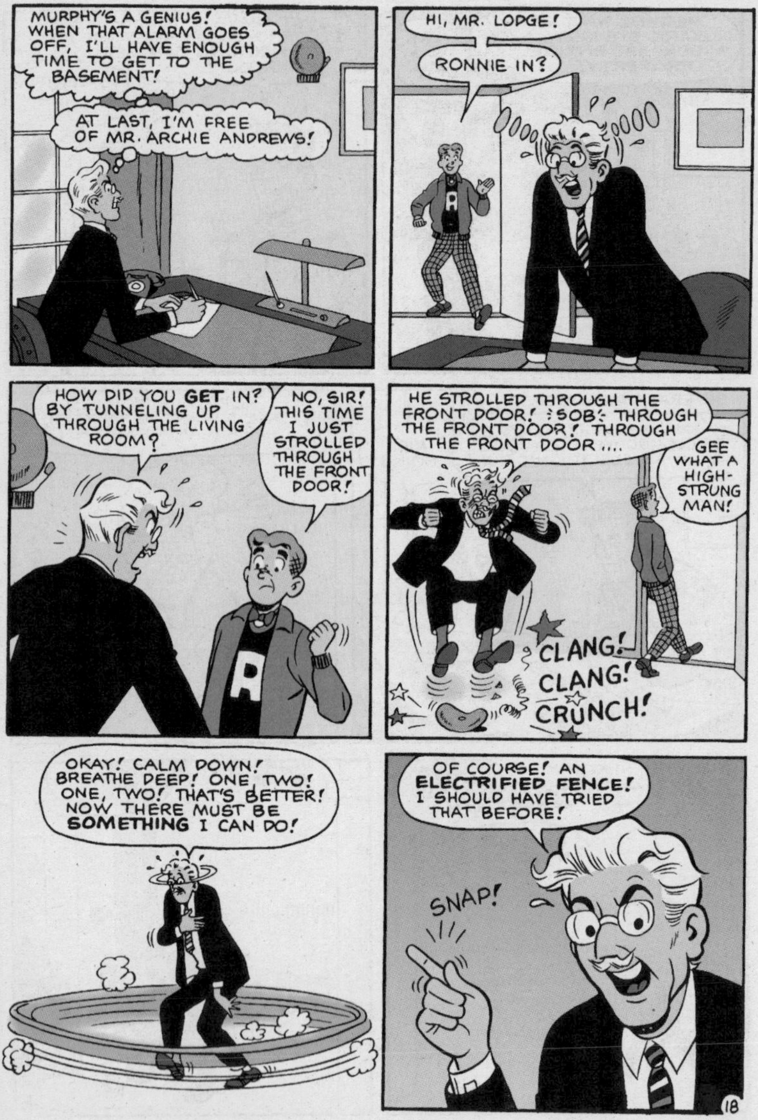

MURPHY'S A GENIUS! WHEN THAT ALARM GOES OFF, I'LL HAVE ENOUGH TIME TO GET TO THE BASEMENT!
AT LAST, I'M FREE OF MR. ARCHIE ANDREWS!
HI, MR. LODGE!
RONNIE IN?
HOW DID YOU GET IN? BY TUNNELING UP THROUGH THE LIVING ROOM?
NO, SIR! THIS TIME I JUST STROLLED THROUGH THE FRONT DOOR!
HE STROLLED THROUGH THE FRONT DOOR! SOB - THROUGH THE FRONT DOOR! THROUGH THE FRONT DOOR ....
GEE WHAT A HIGH-STRUNG MAN!
CLANG!
CLANG!
CRUNCH!
OKAY! CALM DOWN! BREATHE DEEP! ONE, TWO! ONE, TWO! THAT'S BETTER! NOW THERE MUST BE SOMETHING I CAN DO!
OF COURSE! AN ELECTRIFIED FENCE! I SHOULD HAVE TRIED THAT BEFORE!
SNAP!

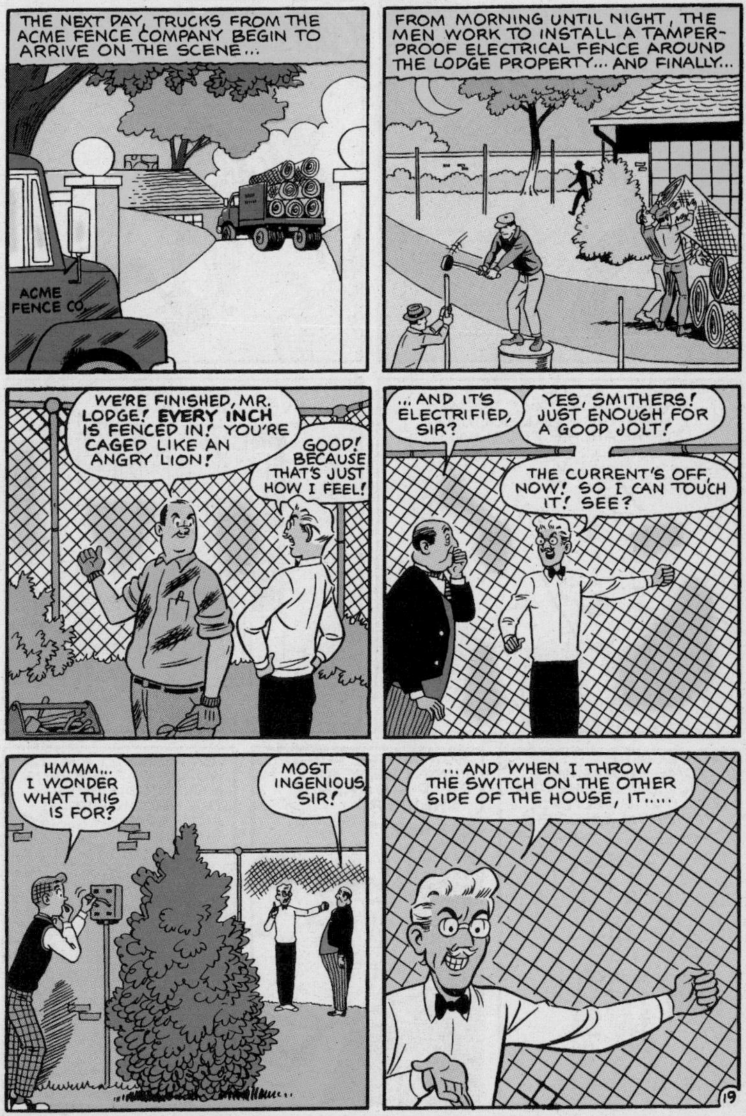

THE NEXT DAY, TRUCKS FROM THE ACME FENCE COMPANY BEGIN TO ARRIVE ON THE SCENE...
ACME FENCE CO.
FROM MORNING UNTIL NIGHT, THE MEN WORK TO INSTALL A TAMPER-PROOF ELECTRICAL FENCE AROUND THE LODGE PROPERTY... AND FINALLY...
WE'RE FINISHED, MR. LODGE! EVERY INCH IS FENCED IN! YOU'RE CAGED LIKE AN ANGRY LION!
GOOD! BECAUSE THAT'S JUST HOW I FEEL!
... AND IT'S ELECTRIFIED, SIR?
YES, SMITHERS! JUST ENOUGH FOR A GOOD JOLT!
THE CURRENT'S OFF, NOW! SO I CAN TOUCH IT! SEE?
HMMM... I WONDER WHAT THIS IS FOR?
MOST INGENIOUS, SIR!
... AND WHEN I THROW THE SWITCH ON THE OTHER SIDE OF THE HOUSE, IT.....

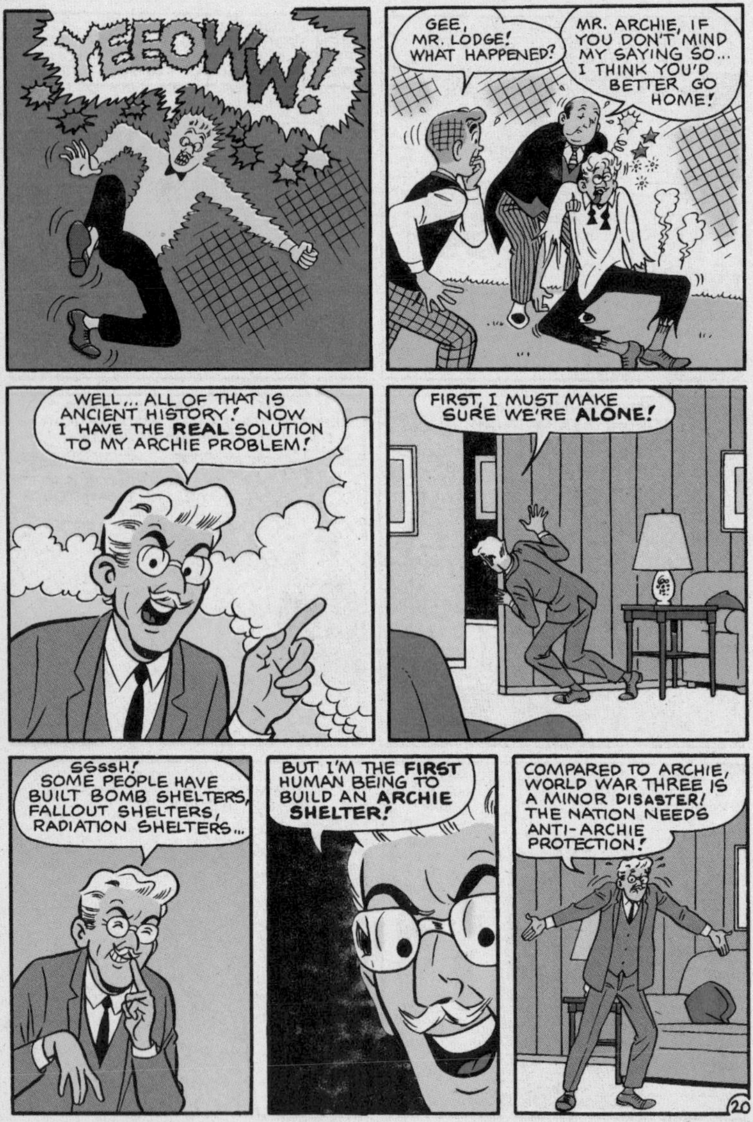

YEEOWW!
GEE, MR. LODGE! WHAT HAPPENED?
MR. ARCHIE, IF YOU DON'T MIND MY SAYING SO... I THINK YOU'D BETTER GO HOME!
WELL... ALL OF THAT IS ANCIENT HISTORY! NOW I HAVE THE REAL SOLUTION TO MY ARCHIE PROBLEM!
FIRST, I MUST MAKE SURE WE'RE ALONE!
SSssH! SOME PEOPLE HAVE BUILT BOMB SHELTERS, FALLOUT SHELTERS, RADIATION SHELTERS...
BUT I'M THE FIRST HUMAN BEING TO BUILD AN ARCHIE SHELTER!
COMPARED TO ARCHIE, WORLD WAR THREE IS A MINOR DISASTER! THE NATION NEEDS ANTI-ARCHIE PROTECTION!
20

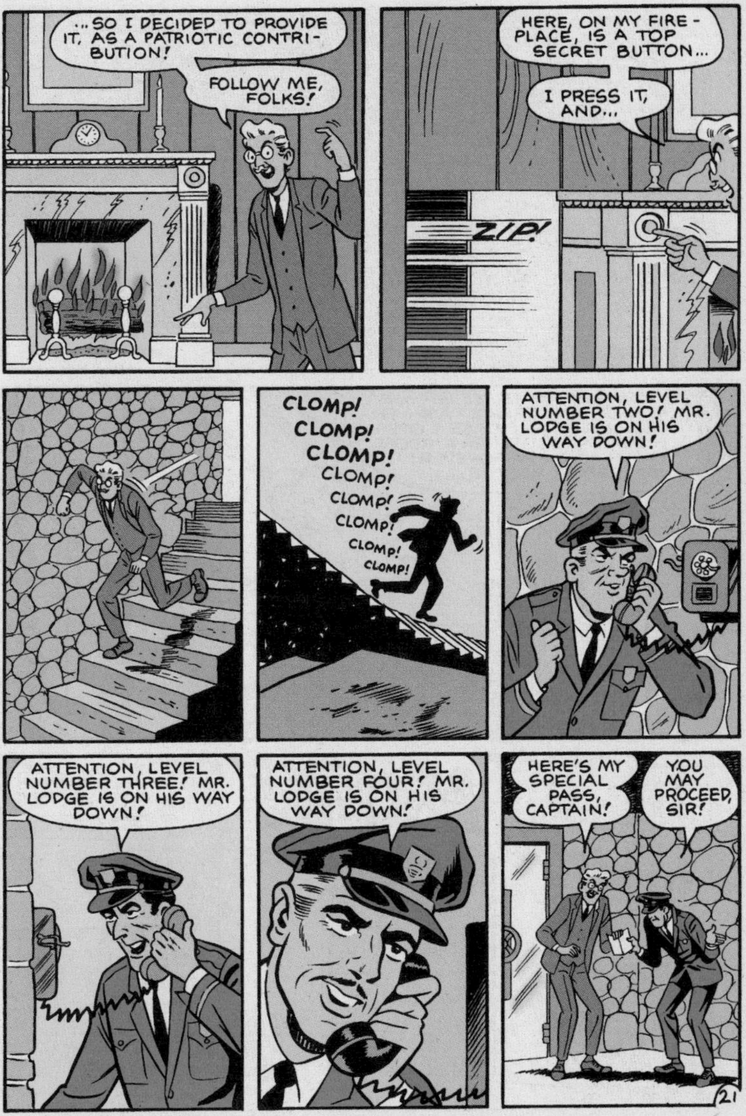
...SO I DECIDED TO PROVIDE IT, AS A PATRIOTIC CONTRIBUTION!
FOLLOW ME, FOLKS!
HERE, ON MY FIRE-PLACE, IS A TOP SECRET BUTTON...
I PRESS IT, AND...
ZIP!
CLOMP! CLOMP! CLOMP! CLOMP! CLOMP! CLOMP! CLOMP! CLOMP!
ATTENTION, LEVEL NUMBER TWO! MR. LODGE IS ON HIS WAY DOWN!
ATTENTION, LEVEL NUMBER THREE! MR. LODGE IS ON HIS WAY DOWN!
ATTENTION, LEVEL NUMBER FOUR! MR. LODGE IS ON HIS WAY DOWN!
HERE'S MY SPECIAL PASS, CAPTAIN!
YOU MAY PROCEED, SIR!

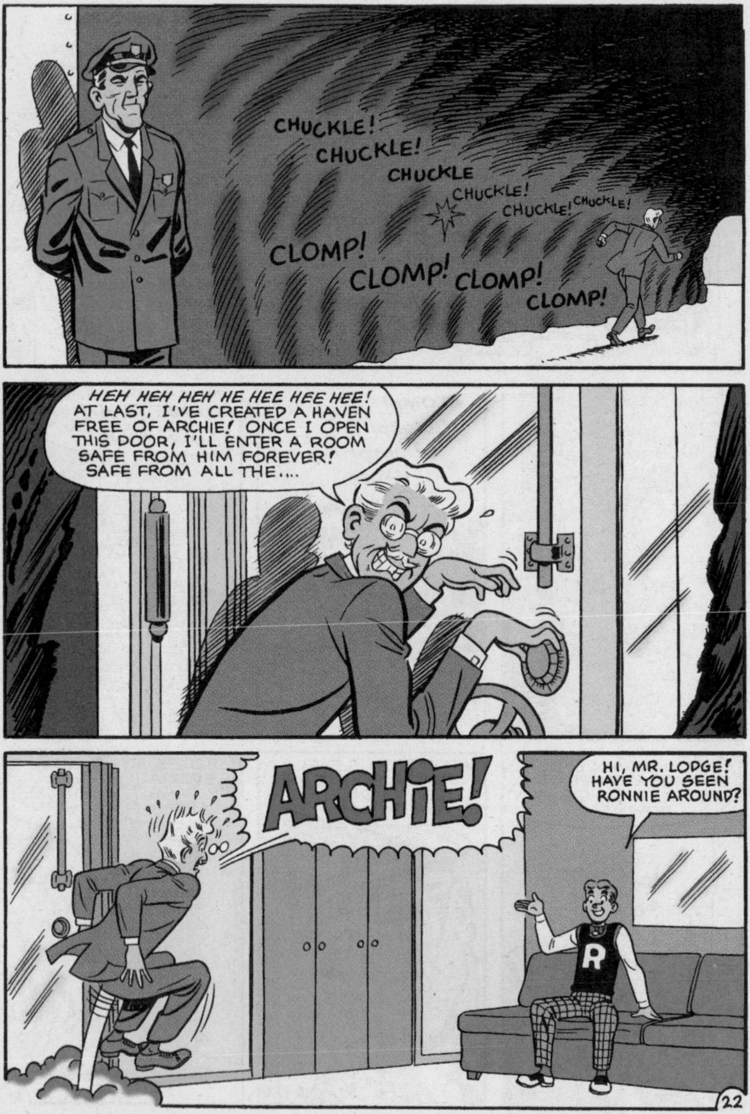
CHUCKLE!
CHUCKLE!
CHUCKLE
CHUCKLE!
CHUCKLE!
CHUCKLE!
CLOMP!
CLOMP!
CLOMP!
CLOMP!
HEH HEH HEH HE HEE HEE HEE! AT LAST, I'VE CREATED A HAVEN FREE OF ARCHIE! ONCE I OPEN THIS DOOR, I'LL ENTER A ROOM SAFE FROM HIM FOREVER! SAFE FROM ALL THE....
ARCHIE!
HI, MR. LODGE! HAVE YOU SEEN RONNIE AROUND?

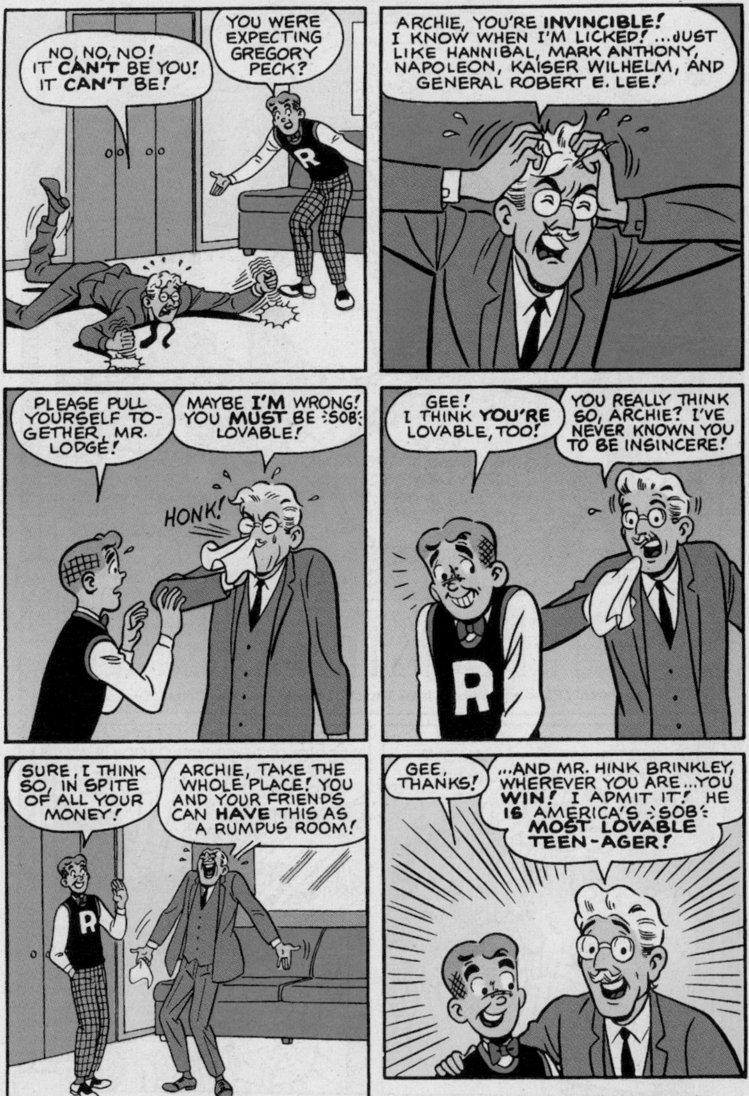
NO, NO, NO! IT CAN'T BE YOU! IT CAN'T BE!
YOU WERE EXPECTING GREGORY PECK?
ARCHIE, YOU'RE INVINCIBLE! I KNOW WHEN I'M LICKED! ...JUST LIKE HANNIBAL, MARK ANTHONY, NAPOLEON, KAISER WILHELM, AND GENERAL ROBERT E. LEE!
PLEASE PULL YOURSELF TOGETHER, MR. LODGE!
MAYBE I'M WRONG! YOU MUST BE -SOB- LOVABLE!
HONK!
GEE! I THINK YOU'RE LOVABLE, TOO!
YOU REALLY THINK SO, ARCHIE? I'VE NEVER KNOWN YOU TO BE INSINCERE!
SURE, I THINK SO, IN SPITE OF ALL YOUR MONEY!
ARCHIE, TAKE THE WHOLE PLACE! YOU AND YOUR FRIENDS CAN HAVE THIS AS A RUMPUS ROOM!
GEE, THANKS!
...AND MR. HINK BRINKLEY, WHEREVER YOU ARE...YOU WIN! I ADMIT IT! HE IS AMERICA'S -SOB- MOST LOVABLE TEEN-AGER!

THE END.

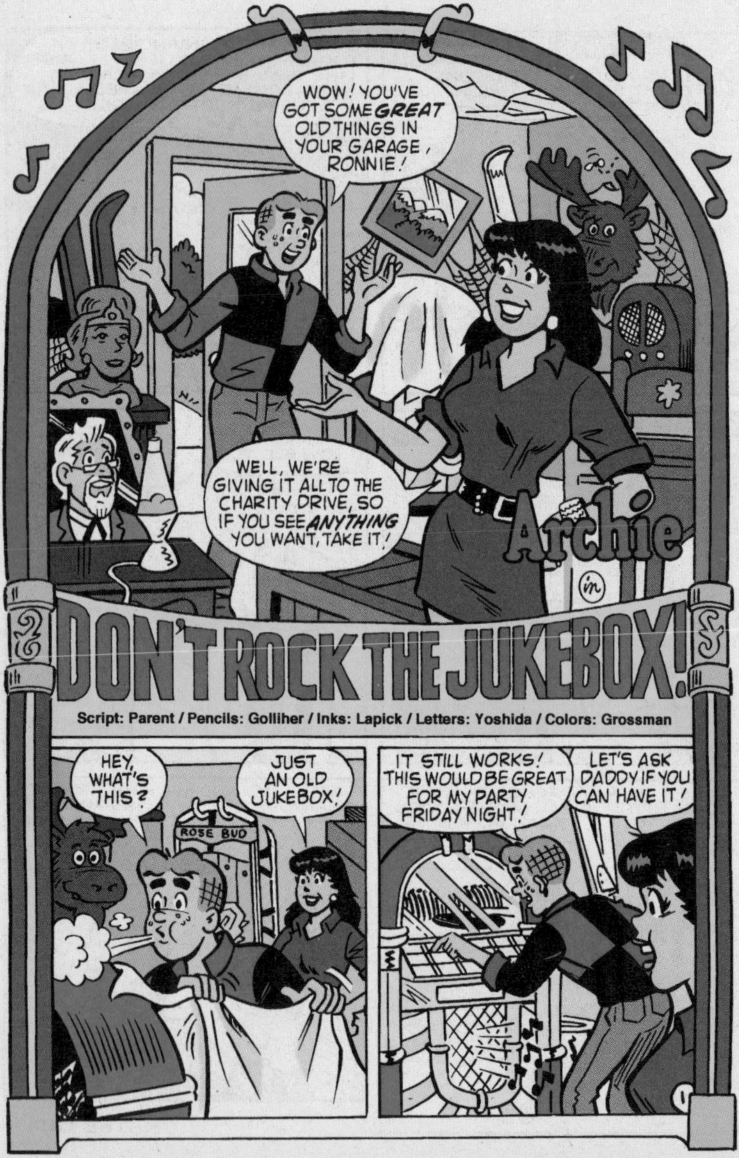
WOW! YOU'VE GOT SOME GREAT OLD THINGS IN YOUR GARAGE, RONNIE!
WELL, WE'RE GIVING IT ALL TO THE CHARITY DRIVE, SO IF YOU SEE ANYTHING YOU WANT, TAKE IT!
Archie
in
DON'T ROCK THE JUKEBOX!
Script: Parent / Pencils: Golliher / Inks: Lapick / Letters: Yoshida / Colors: Grossman
HEY, WHAT'S THIS?
JUST AN OLD JUKEBOX!
ROSE BUD
IT STILL WORKS! THIS WOULD BE GREAT FOR MY PARTY FRIDAY NIGHT!
LET'S ASK DADDY IF YOU CAN HAVE IT!

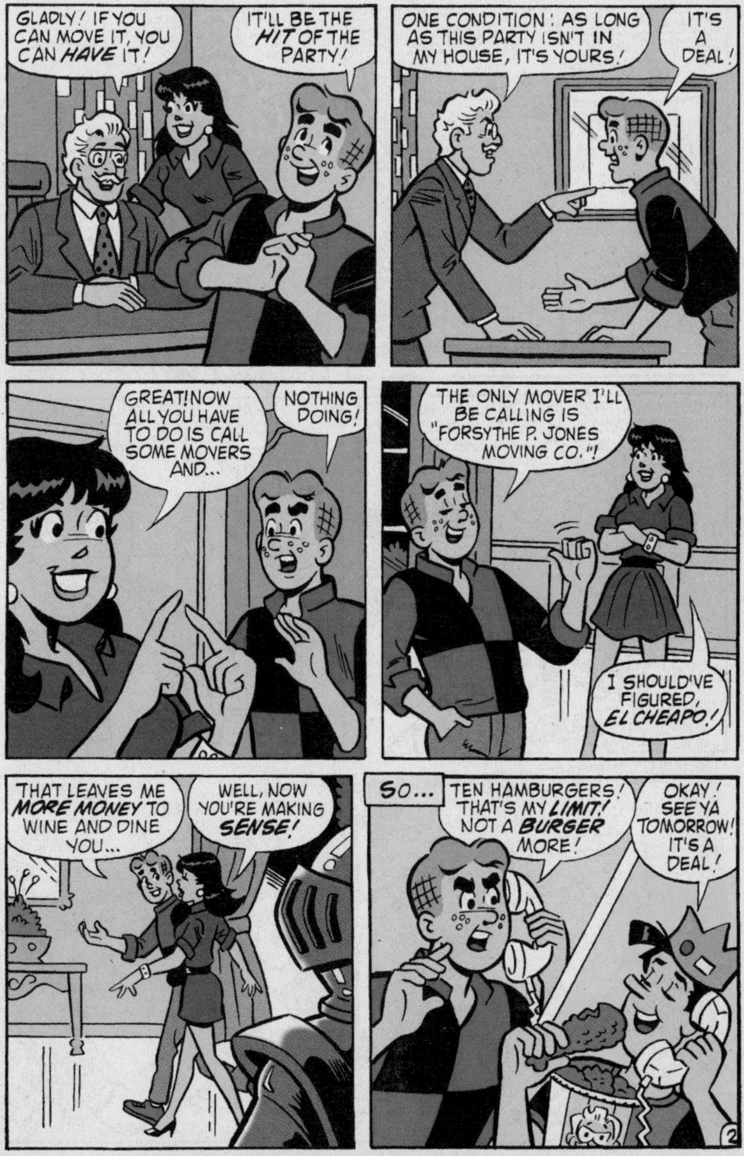
GLADLY! IF YOU CAN MOVE IT, YOU CAN HAVE IT!
IT'LL BE THE HIT OF THE PARTY!
ONE CONDITION: AS LONG AS THIS PARTY ISN'T IN MY HOUSE, IT'S YOURS!
IT'S A DEAL!
GREAT! NOW ALL YOU HAVE TO DO IS CALL SOME MOVERS AND...
NOTHING DOING!
THE ONLY MOVER I'LL BE CALLING IS "FORSYTHE P. JONES MOVING CO."!
I SHOULD'VE FIGURED, EL CHEAPO!
THAT LEAVES ME MORE MONEY TO WINE AND DINE YOU...
WELL, NOW YOU'RE MAKING SENSE!
SO...
TEN HAMBURGERS! THAT'S MY LIMIT! NOT A BURGER MORE!
OKAY! SEE YA TOMORROW! IT'S A DEAL!
2

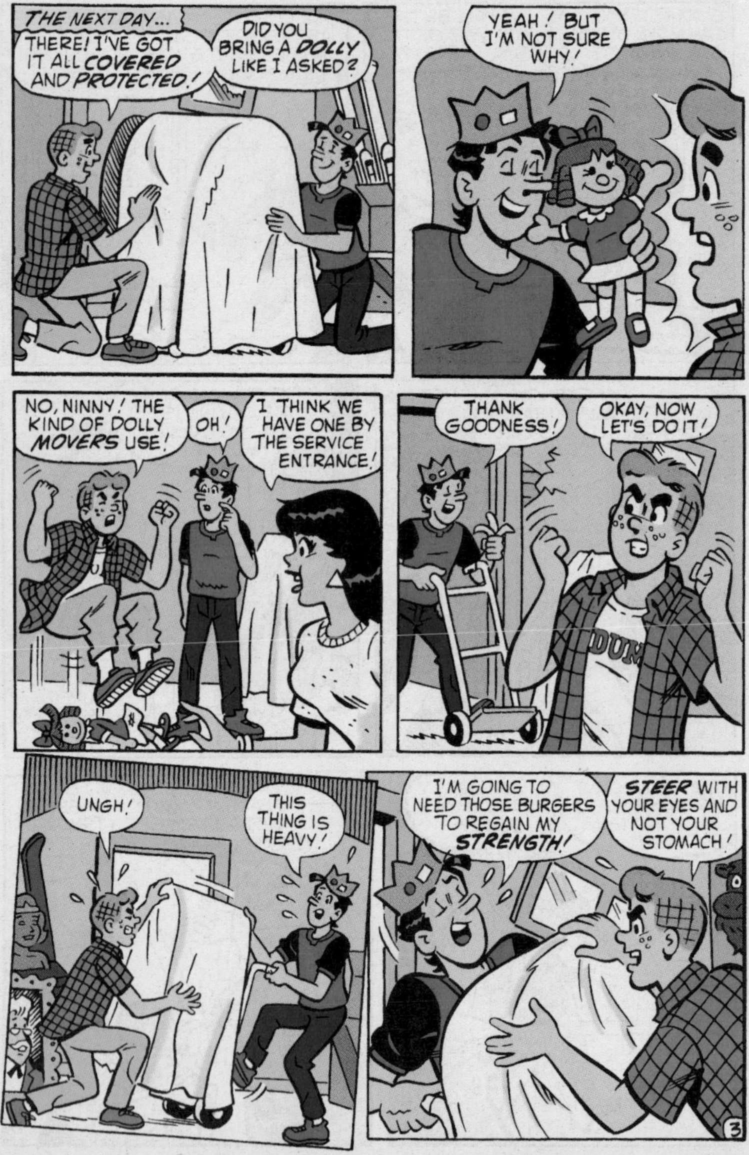
THE NEXT DAY...
THERE! I'VE GOT IT ALL COVERED AND PROTECTED!
DID YOU BRING A DOLLY LIKE I ASKED?
YEAH! BUT I'M NOT SURE WHY!
NO, NINNY! THE KIND OF DOLLY MOVERS USE!
OH!
I THINK WE HAVE ONE BY THE SERVICE ENTRANCE!
THANK GOODNESS!
OKAY, NOW LET'S DO IT!
UNGH!
THIS THING IS HEAVY!
I'M GOING TO NEED THOSE BURGERS TO REGAIN MY STRENGTH!
STEER WITH YOUR EYES AND NOT YOUR STOMACH!
3

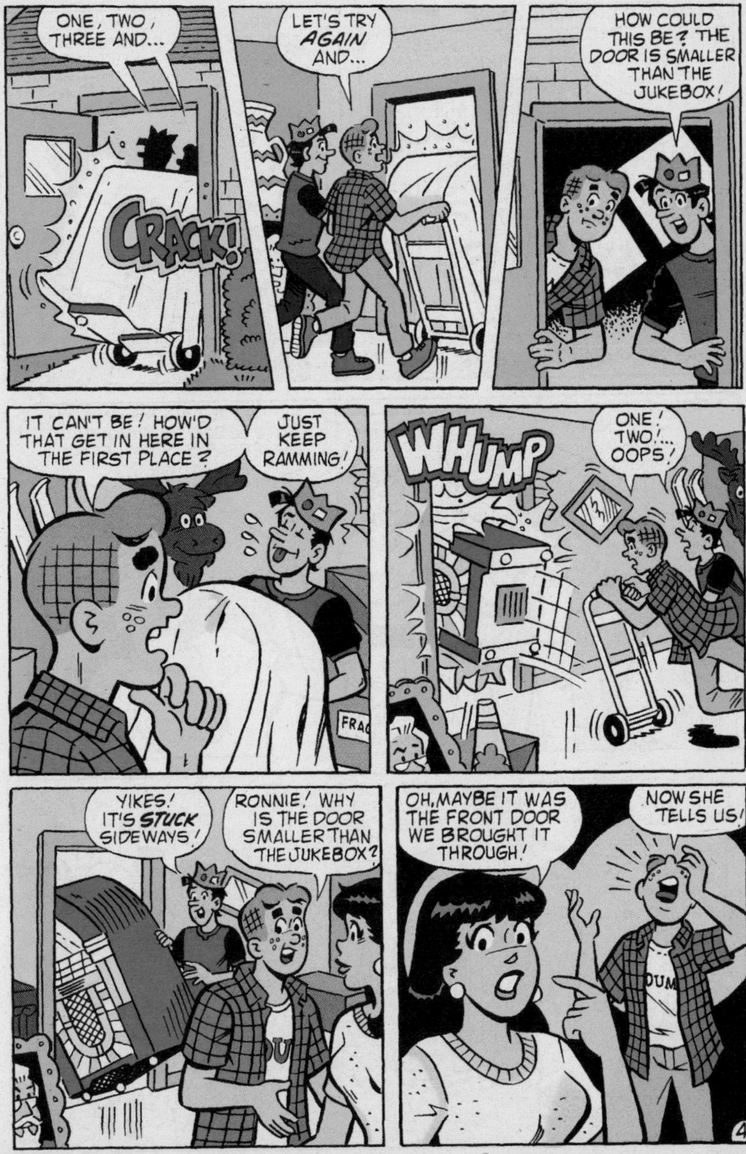

ONE, TWO, THREE AND...
CRACK!
LET'S TRY AGAIN AND...
HOW COULD THIS BE? THE DOOR IS SMALLER THAN THE JUKEBOX!
IT CAN'T BE! HOW'D THAT GET IN HERE IN THE FIRST PLACE?
JUST KEEP RAMMING!
FRAG
WHUMP
ONE! TWO!... OOPS!
YIKES! IT'S STUCK SIDEWAYS!
RONNIE! WHY IS THE DOOR SMALLER THAN THE JUKEBOX?
OH, MAYBE IT WAS THE FRONT DOOR WE BROUGHT IT THROUGH!
NOW SHE TELLS US!
4

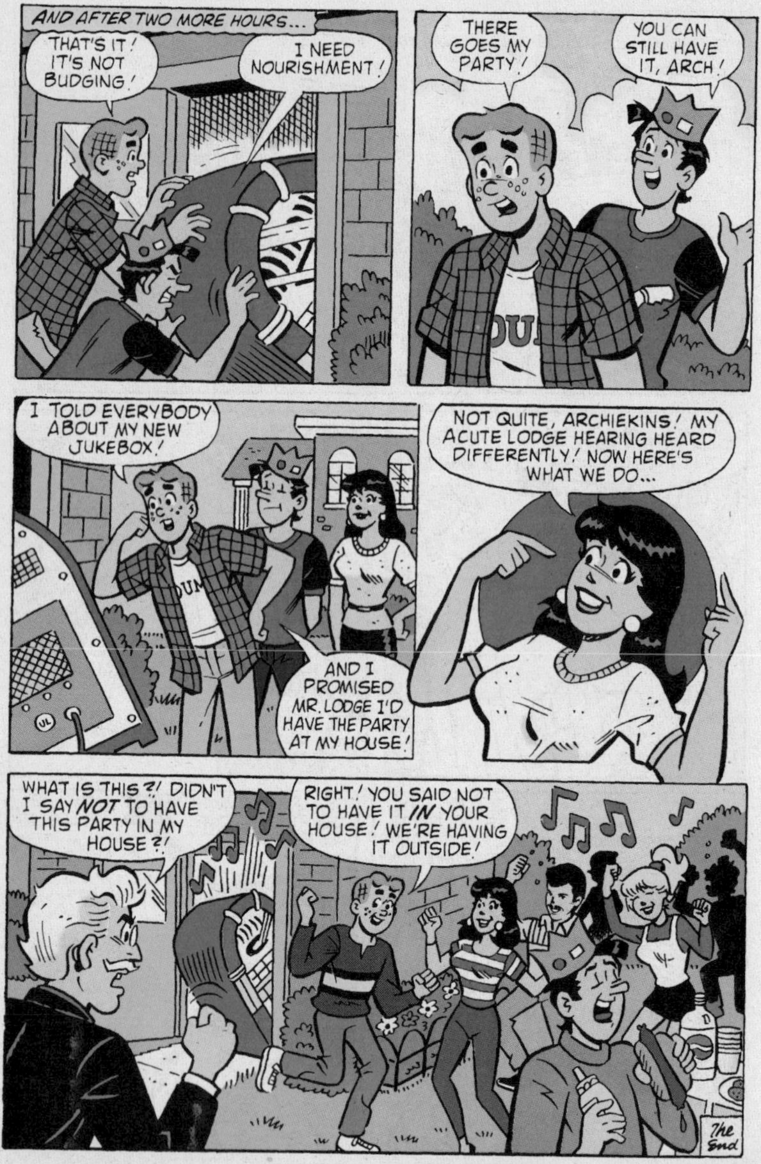
AND AFTER TWO MORE HOURS...
THAT'S IT! IT'S NOT BUDGING!
I NEED NOURISHMENT!
THERE GOES MY PARTY!
YOU CAN STILL HAVE IT, ARCH!
I TOLD EVERYBODY ABOUT MY NEW JUKEBOX!
AND I PROMISED MR. LODGE I'D HAVE THE PARTY AT MY HOUSE!
NOT QUITE, ARCHIEKINS! MY ACUTE LODGE HEARING HEARD DIFFERENTLY! NOW HERE'S WHAT WE DO...
WHAT IS THIS?! DIDN'T I SAY *NOT* TO HAVE THIS PARTY IN MY HOUSE?!
RIGHT! YOU SAID NOT TO HAVE IT *IN* YOUR HOUSE! WE'RE HAVING IT OUTSIDE!
The End

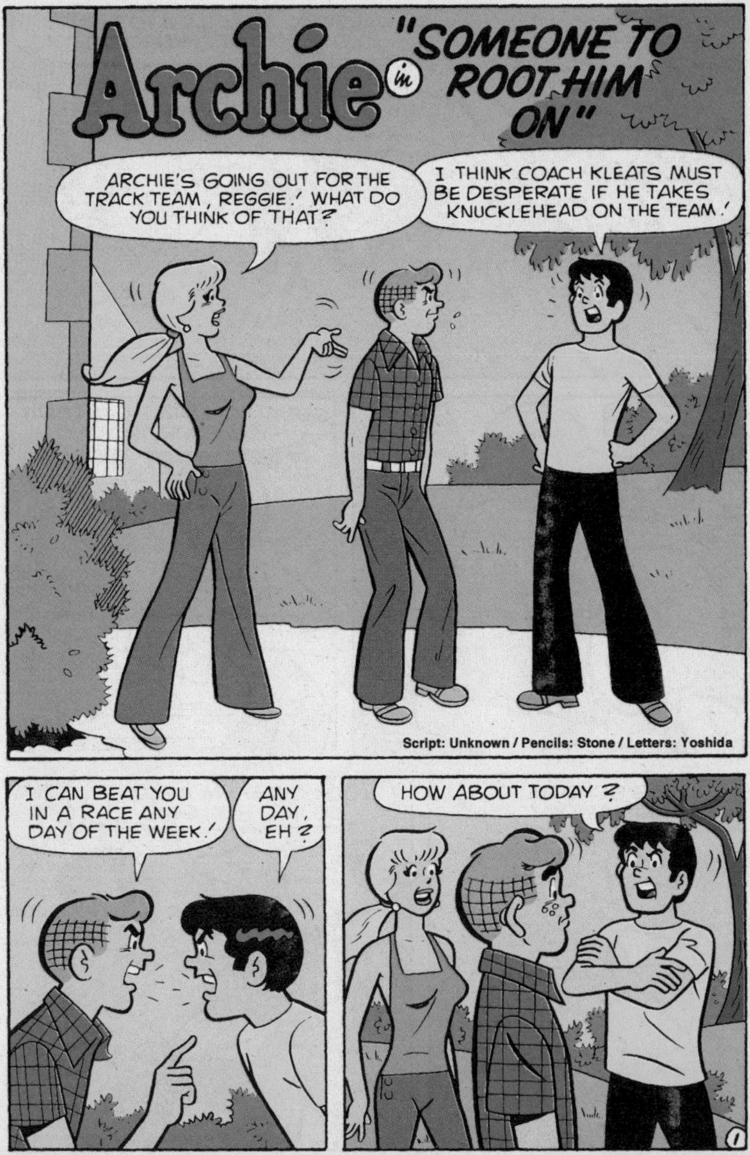
Archie in
"SOMEONE TO ROOT HIM ON"
ARCHIE'S GOING OUT FOR THE TRACK TEAM, REGGIE! WHAT DO YOU THINK OF THAT?
I THINK COACH KLEATS MUST BE DESPERATE IF HE TAKES KNUCKLEHEAD ON THE TEAM!
Script: Unknown / Pencils: Stone / Letters: Yoshida
I CAN BEAT YOU IN A RACE ANY DAY OF THE WEEK!
ANY DAY, EH?
HOW ABOUT TODAY?
1

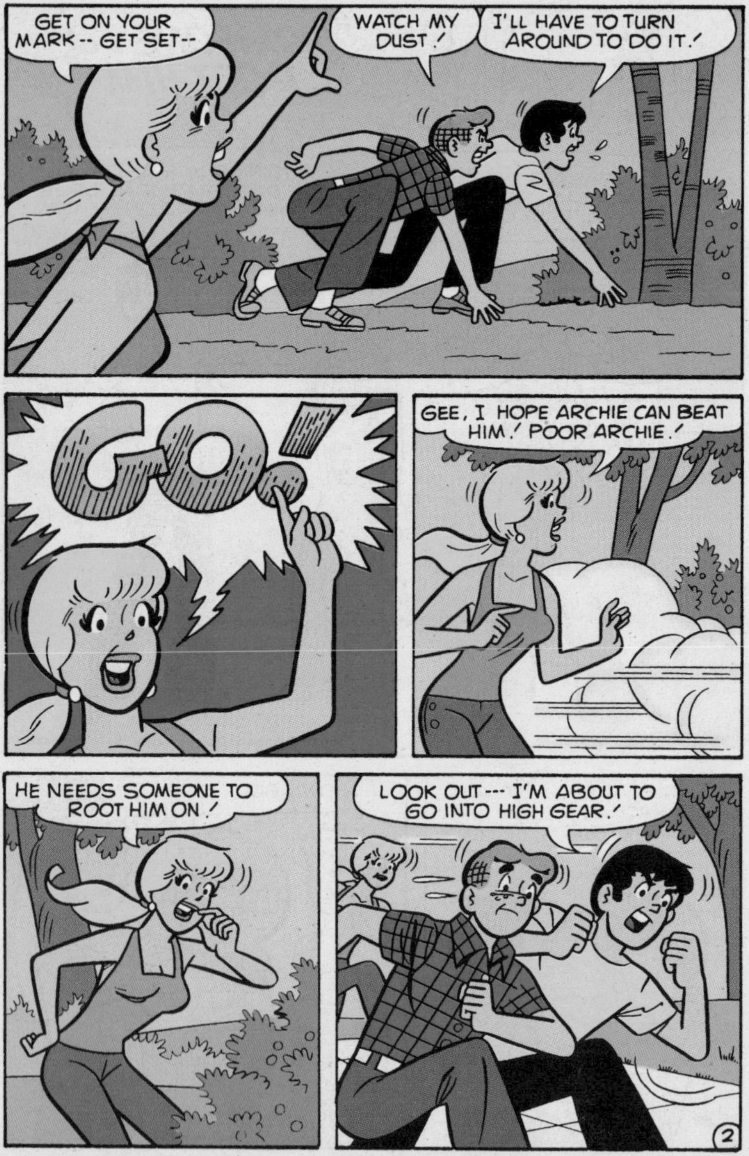
GET ON YOUR MARK -- GET SET --
WATCH MY DUST!
I'LL HAVE TO TURN AROUND TO DO IT!
GO!
GEE, I HOPE ARCHIE CAN BEAT HIM! POOR ARCHIE!
HE NEEDS SOMEONE TO ROOT HIM ON!
LOOK OUT --- I'M ABOUT TO GO INTO HIGH GEAR!
2

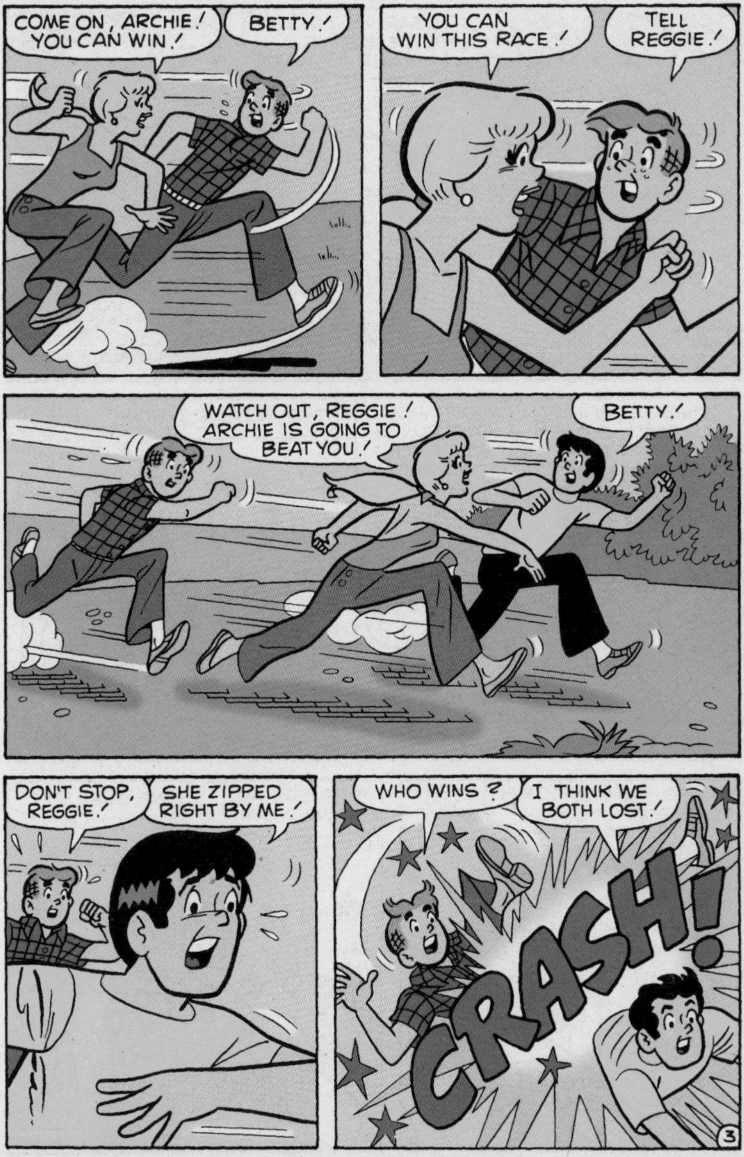
COME ON, ARCHIE! YOU CAN WIN!
BETTY!
YOU CAN WIN THIS RACE!
TELL REGGIE!
WATCH OUT, REGGIE! ARCHIE IS GOING TO BEAT YOU!
BETTY!
DON'T STOP, REGGIE!
SHE ZIPPED RIGHT BY ME!
WHO WINS?
I THINK WE BOTH LOST!
CRASH!
3

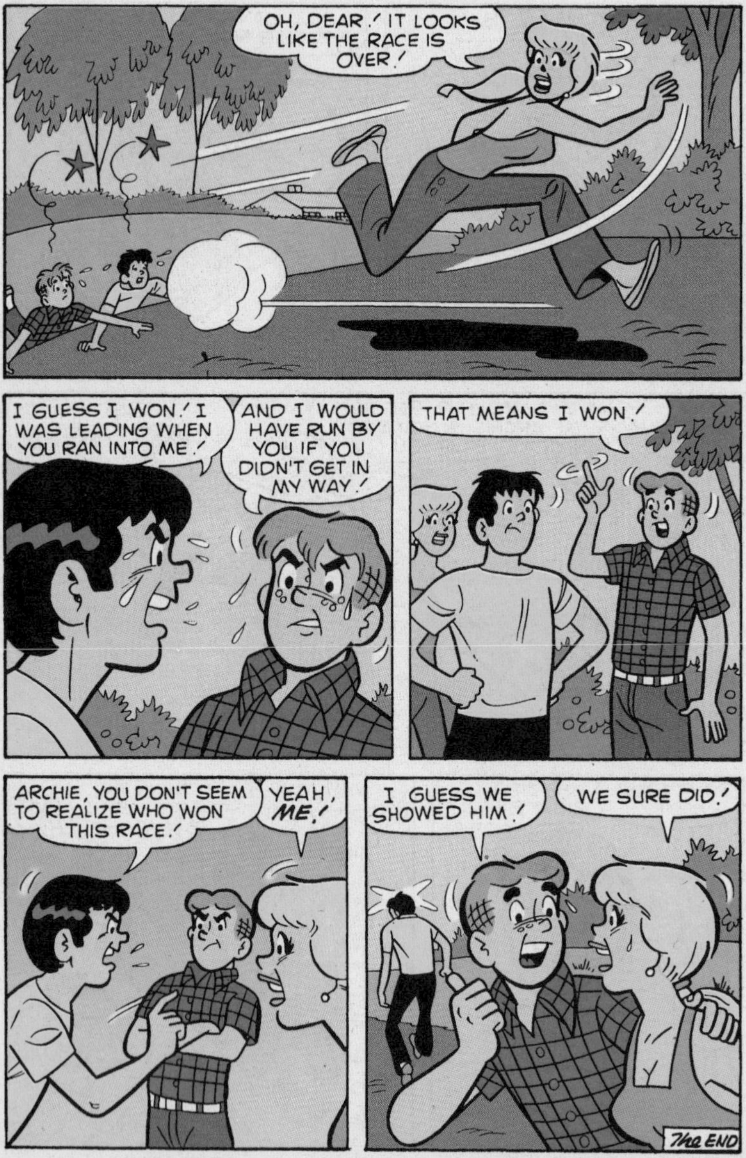
OH, DEAR! IT LOOKS LIKE THE RACE IS OVER!
I GUESS I WON! I WAS LEADING WHEN YOU RAN INTO ME!
AND I WOULD HAVE RUN BY YOU IF YOU DIDN'T GET IN MY WAY!
THAT MEANS I WON!
ARCHIE, YOU DON'T SEEM TO REALIZE WHO WON THIS RACE!
YEAH, ME!
I GUESS WE SHOWED HIM!
WE SURE DID!
The END

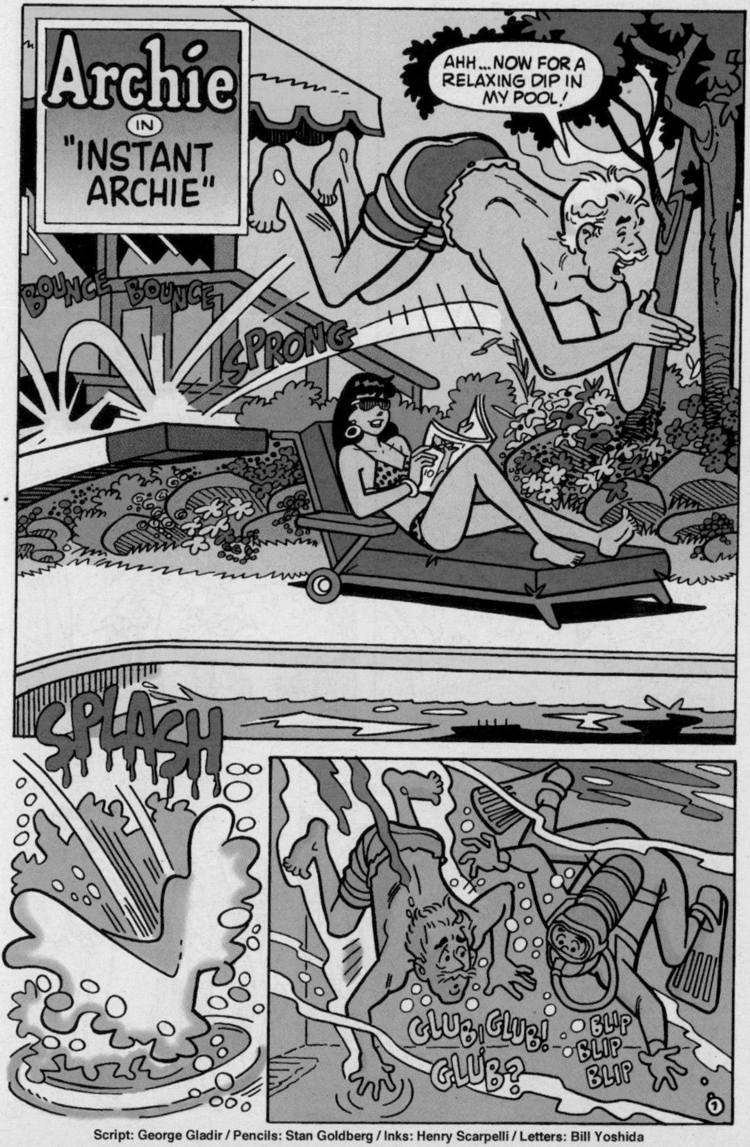
Archie
IN
"INSTANT ARCHIE"
AHH...NOW FOR A RELAXING DIP IN MY POOL!
BOUNCE BOUNCE
SPRONG
SPLASH
GLUB! GLUB!
GLUB?
BLIP
BLIP
BLIP
1

Script: George Gladir / Pencils: Stan Goldberg / Inks: Henry Scarpelli / Letters: Bill Yoshida

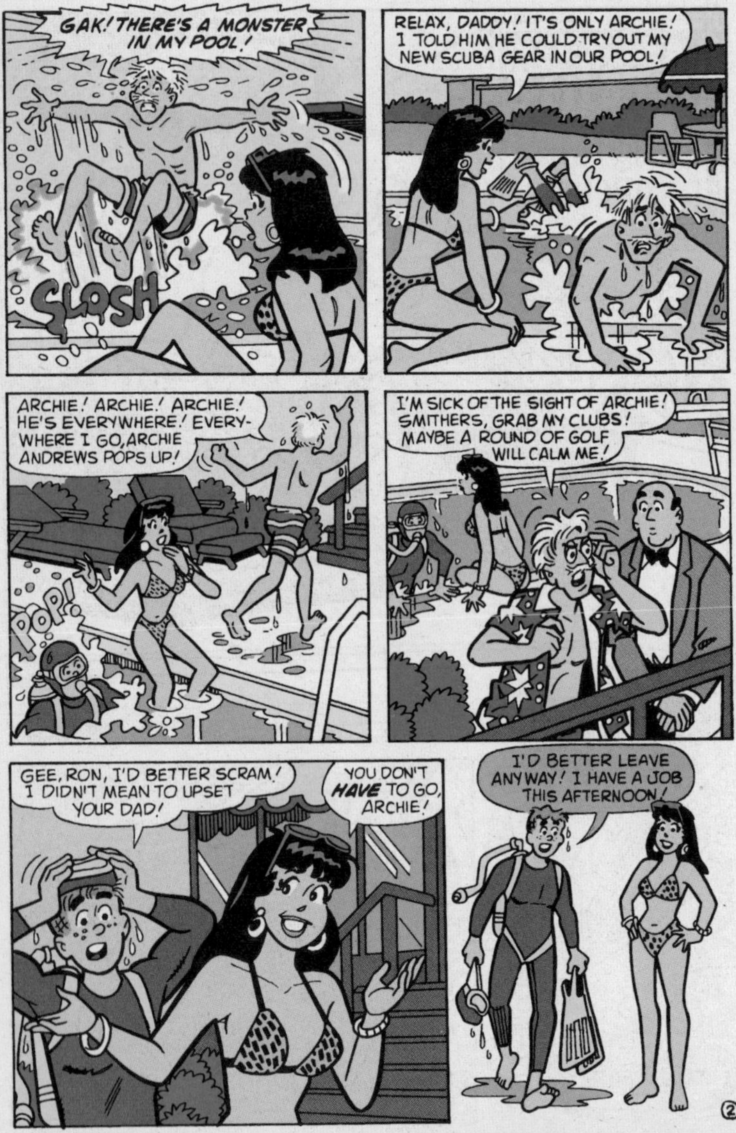
GAK! THERE'S A MONSTER IN MY POOL!
SLOSH
RELAX, DADDY! IT'S ONLY ARCHIE! I TOLD HIM HE COULD TRY OUT MY NEW SCUBA GEAR IN OUR POOL!
ARCHIE! ARCHIE! ARCHIE! HE'S EVERYWHERE! EVERY-WHERE I GO, ARCHIE ANDREWS POPS UP!
POP!
I'M SICK OF THE SIGHT OF ARCHIE! SMITHERS, GRAB MY CLUBS! MAYBE A ROUND OF GOLF WILL CALM ME!
GEE, RON, I'D BETTER SCRAM! I DIDN'T MEAN TO UPSET YOUR DAD!
YOU DON'T HAVE TO GO, ARCHIE!
I'D BETTER LEAVE ANYWAY! I HAVE A JOB THIS AFTERNOON!

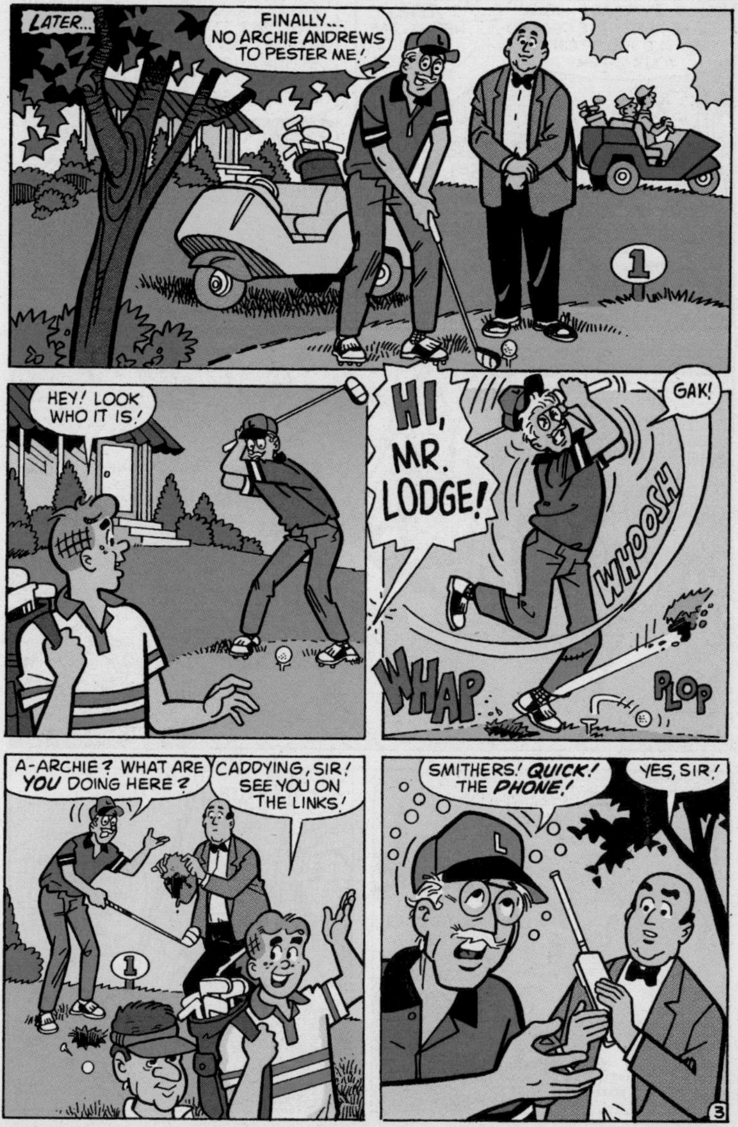
LATER...
FINALLY... NO ARCHIE ANDREWS TO PESTER ME!
1
HEY! LOOK WHO IT IS!
HI, MR. LODGE!
GAK!
WHOOSH
WHAP
PLOP
A-ARCHIE? WHAT ARE YOU DOING HERE?
CADDYING, SIR! SEE YOU ON THE LINKS!
1
SMITHERS! QUICK! THE PHONE!
YES, SIR!
3

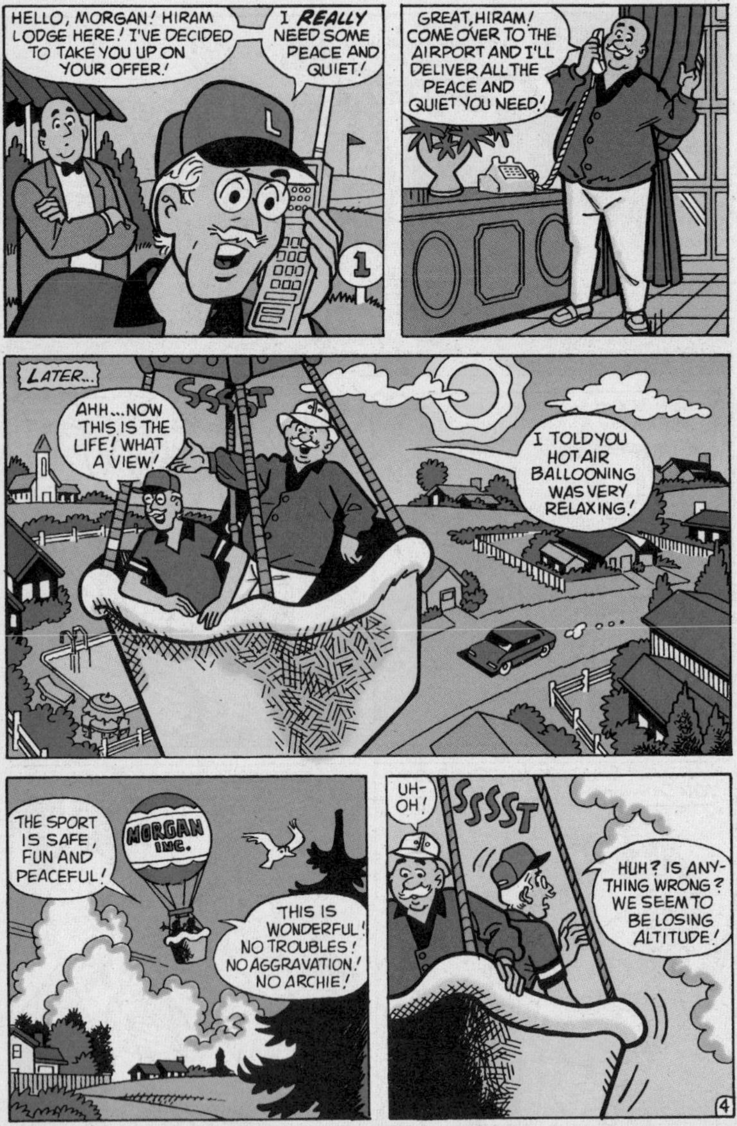
HELLO, MORGAN! HIRAM LODGE HERE! I'VE DECIDED TO TAKE YOU UP ON YOUR OFFER!
I REALLY NEED SOME PEACE AND QUIET!
1
GREAT, HIRAM! COME OVER TO THE AIRPORT AND I'LL DELIVER ALL THE PEACE AND QUIET YOU NEED!
LATER...
SSSST
AHH...NOW THIS IS THE LIFE! WHAT A VIEW!
I TOLD YOU HOT AIR BALLOONING WAS VERY RELAXING!
THE SPORT IS SAFE, FUN AND PEACEFUL!
MORGAN INC.
THIS IS WONDERFUL! NO TROUBLES! NO AGGRAVATION! NO ARCHIE!
UH-OH!
SSSST
HUH? IS ANYTHING WRONG? WE SEEM TO BE LOSING ALTITUDE!
4

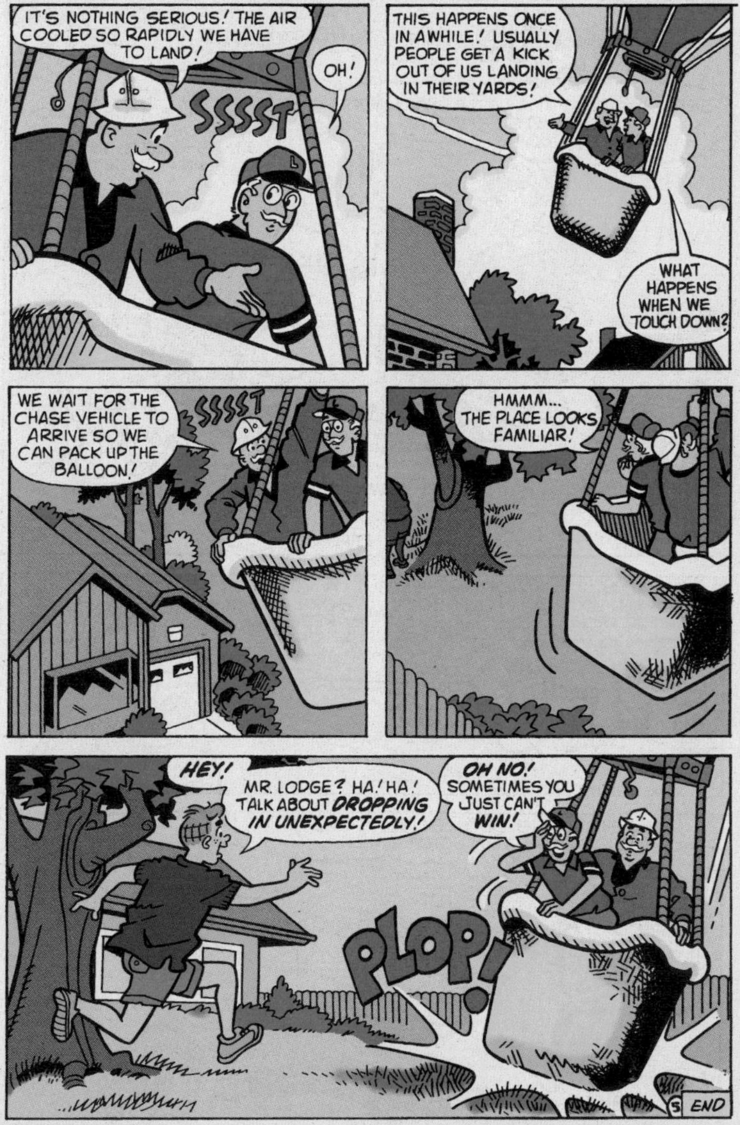
IT'S NOTHING SERIOUS! THE AIR COOLED SO RAPIDLY WE HAVE TO LAND!
SSSST
OH!
THIS HAPPENS ONCE IN A WHILE! USUALLY PEOPLE GET A KICK OUT OF US LANDING IN THEIR YARDS!
WHAT HAPPENS WHEN WE TOUCH DOWN?
WE WAIT FOR THE CHASE VEHICLE TO ARRIVE SO WE CAN PACK UP THE BALLOON!
SSSST
HMMM... THE PLACE LOOKS FAMILIAR!
HEY!
MR. LODGE? HA! HA! TALK ABOUT DROPPING IN UNEXPECTEDLY!
OH NO! SOMETIMES YOU JUST CAN'T WIN!
PLOP!
5
END

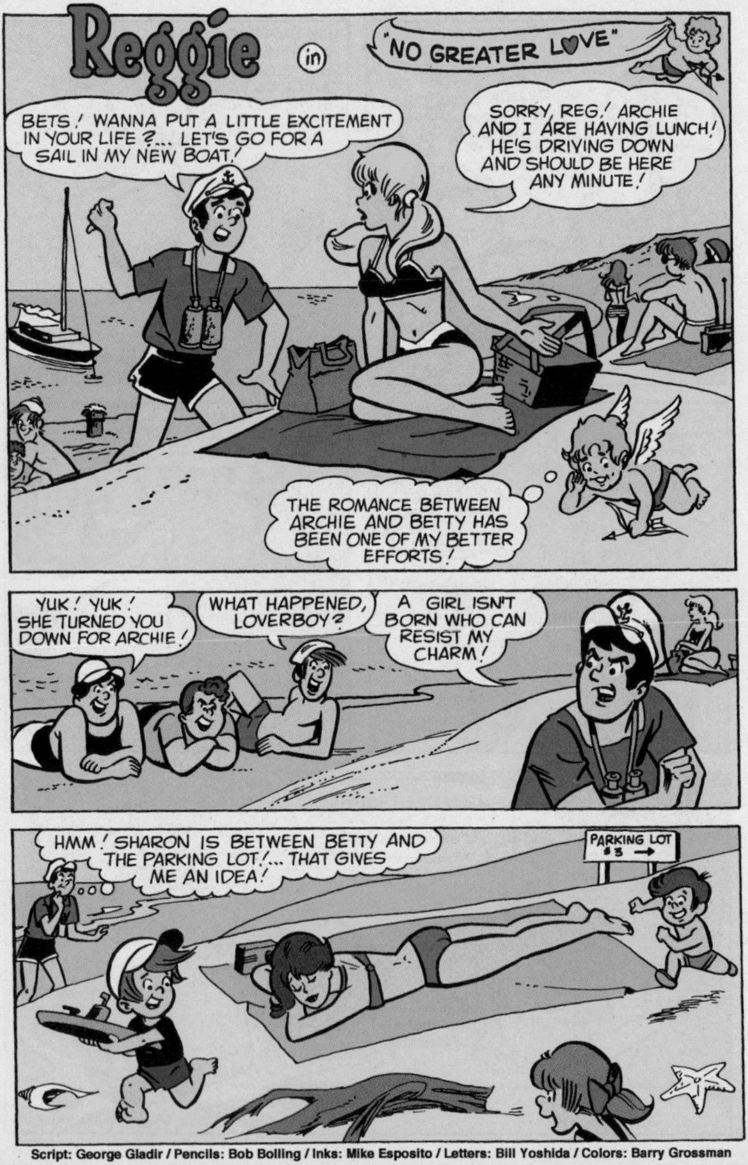
Reggie in
"NO GREATER LOVE"
BETS! WANNA PUT A LITTLE EXCITEMENT IN YOUR LIFE?... LET'S GO FOR A SAIL IN MY NEW BOAT!
SORRY, REG! ARCHIE AND I ARE HAVING LUNCH! HE'S DRIVING DOWN AND SHOULD BE HERE ANY MINUTE!
THE ROMANCE BETWEEN ARCHIE AND BETTY HAS BEEN ONE OF MY BETTER EFFORTS!
YUK! YUK! SHE TURNED YOU DOWN FOR ARCHIE!
WHAT HAPPENED, LOVERBOY?
A GIRL ISN'T BORN WHO CAN RESIST MY CHARM!
HMM! SHARON IS BETWEEN BETTY AND THE PARKING LOT!... THAT GIVES ME AN IDEA!
PARKING LOT $3 →

Script: George Gladir / Pencils: Bob Bolling / Inks: Mike Esposito / Letters: Bill Yoshida / Colors: Barry Grossman

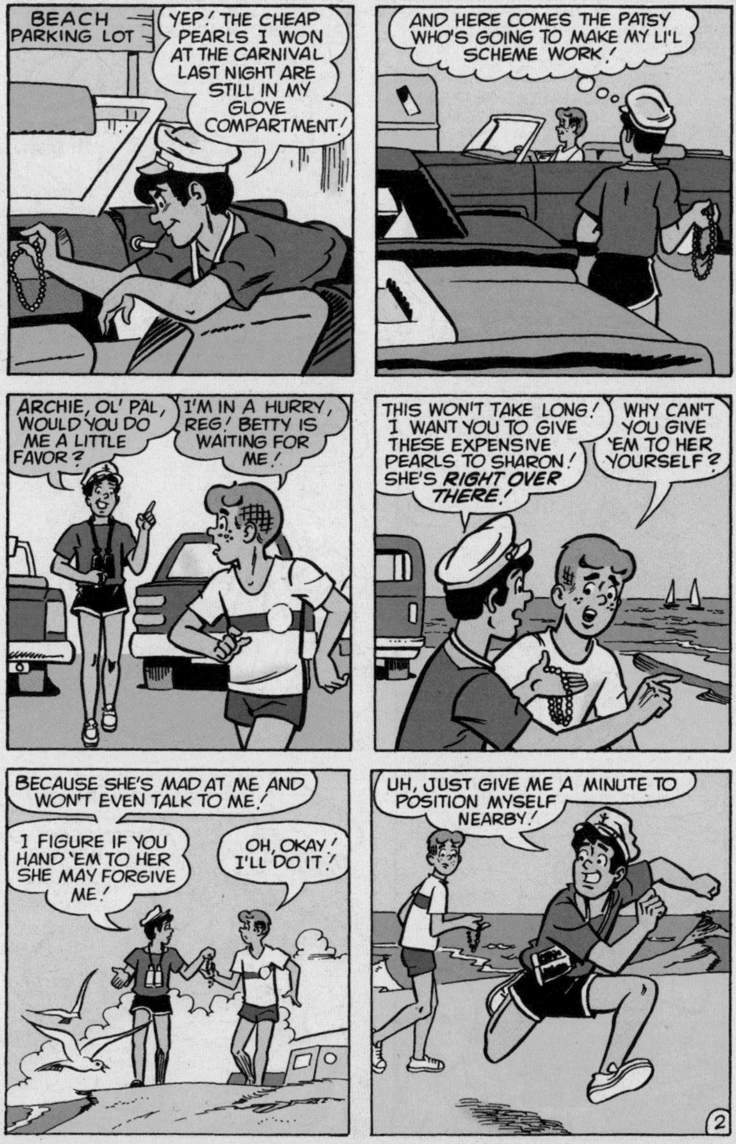
BEACH
PARKING LOT
YEP! THE CHEAP PEARLS I WON AT THE CARNIVAL LAST NIGHT ARE STILL IN MY GLOVE COMPARTMENT!
AND HERE COMES THE PATSY WHO'S GOING TO MAKE MY LI'L SCHEME WORK!
ARCHIE, OL' PAL, WOULD YOU DO ME A LITTLE FAVOR?
I'M IN A HURRY, REG! BETTY IS WAITING FOR ME!
THIS WON'T TAKE LONG! I WANT YOU TO GIVE THESE EXPENSIVE PEARLS TO SHARON! SHE'S ***RIGHT OVER THERE!***
WHY CAN'T YOU GIVE 'EM TO HER YOURSELF?
BECAUSE SHE'S *MAD* AT ME AND WON'T EVEN TALK TO ME!
I FIGURE IF YOU HAND 'EM TO HER SHE MAY FORGIVE ME!
OH, OKAY! I'LL DO IT!
UH, JUST GIVE ME A MINUTE TO POSITION MYSELF NEARBY!
2

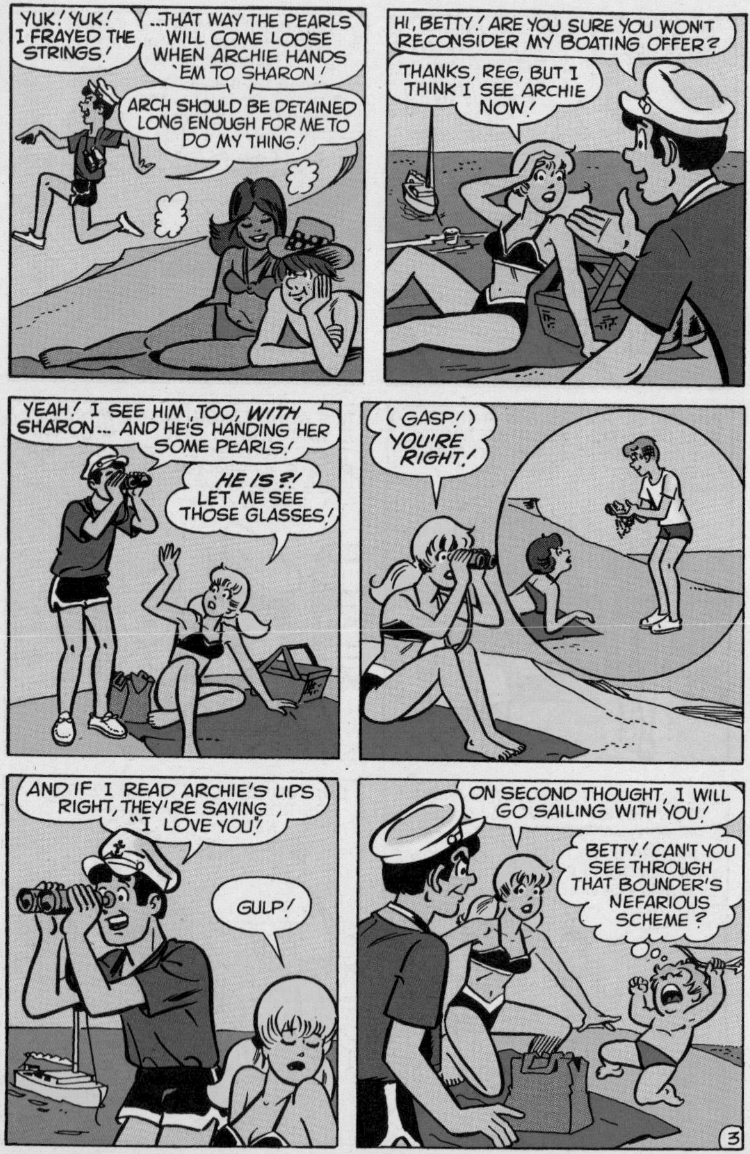
YUK! YUK! I FRAYED THE STRINGS!
...THAT WAY THE PEARLS WILL COME LOOSE WHEN ARCHIE HANDS 'EM TO SHARON!
ARCH SHOULD BE DETAINED LONG ENOUGH FOR ME TO DO MY THING!
HI, BETTY! ARE YOU SURE YOU WON'T RECONSIDER MY BOATING OFFER?
THANKS, REG, BUT I THINK I SEE ARCHIE NOW!
YEAH! I SEE HIM, TOO, WITH SHARON... AND HE'S HANDING HER SOME PEARLS!
HE IS?! LET ME SEE THOSE GLASSES!
(GASP!) YOU'RE RIGHT!
AND IF I READ ARCHIE'S LIPS RIGHT, THEY'RE SAYING, "I LOVE YOU"!
GULP!
ON SECOND THOUGHT, I WILL GO SAILING WITH YOU!
BETTY! CAN'T YOU SEE THROUGH THAT BOUNDER'S NEFARIOUS SCHEME?
3

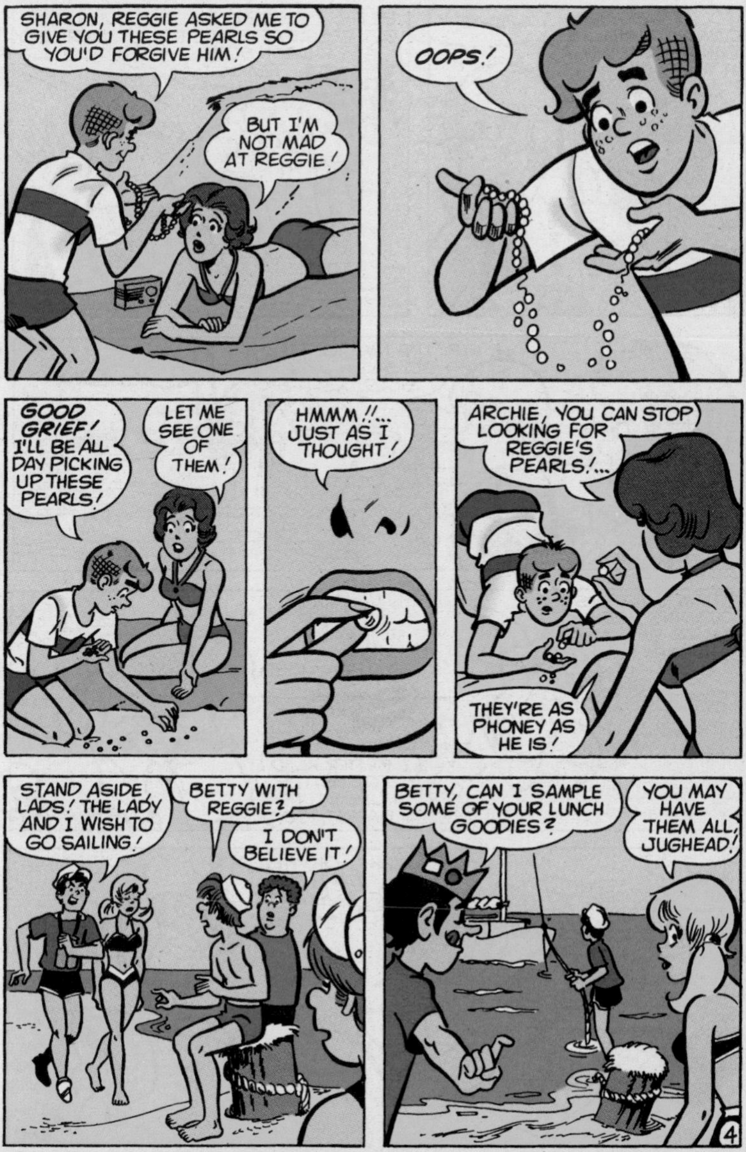
SHARON, REGGIE ASKED ME TO GIVE YOU THESE PEARLS SO YOU'D FORGIVE HIM!
BUT I'M NOT MAD AT REGGIE!
OOPS!
GOOD GRIEF! I'LL BE ALL DAY PICKING UP THESE PEARLS!
LET ME SEE ONE OF THEM!
HMMM!!... JUST AS I THOUGHT!
ARCHIE, YOU CAN STOP LOOKING FOR REGGIE'S PEARLS!...
THEY'RE AS PHONEY AS HE IS!
STAND ASIDE, LADS! THE LADY AND I WISH TO GO SAILING!
BETTY WITH REGGIE?
I DON'T BELIEVE IT!
BETTY, CAN I SAMPLE SOME OF YOUR LUNCH GOODIES?
YOU MAY HAVE THEM ALL, JUGHEAD!
4

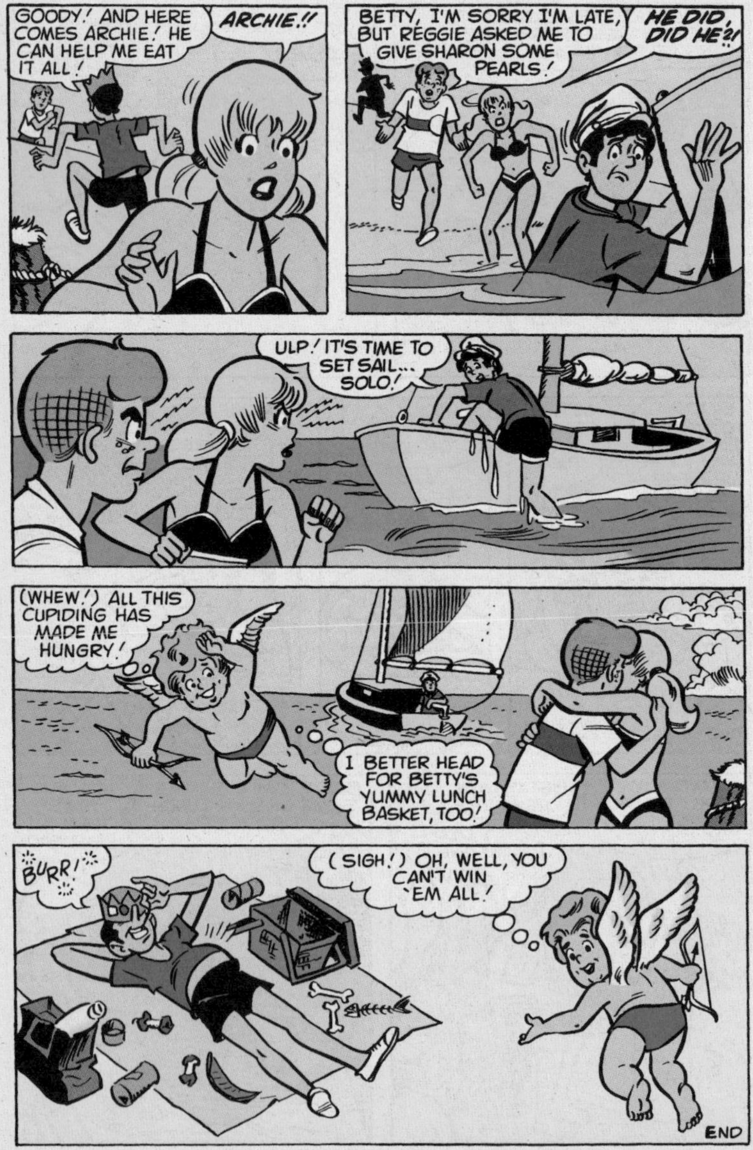
GOODY! AND HERE COMES ARCHIE! HE CAN HELP ME EAT IT ALL!
ARCHIE!!
BETTY, I'M SORRY I'M LATE, BUT REGGIE ASKED ME TO GIVE SHARON SOME PEARLS!
HE DID, DID HE?!
ULP! IT'S TIME TO SET SAIL... SOLO!
(WHEW!) ALL THIS CUPIDING HAS MADE ME HUNGRY!
I BETTER HEAD FOR BETTY'S YUMMY LUNCH BASKET, TOO!
BURR!
(SIGH!) OH, WELL, YOU CAN'T WIN 'EM ALL!
END

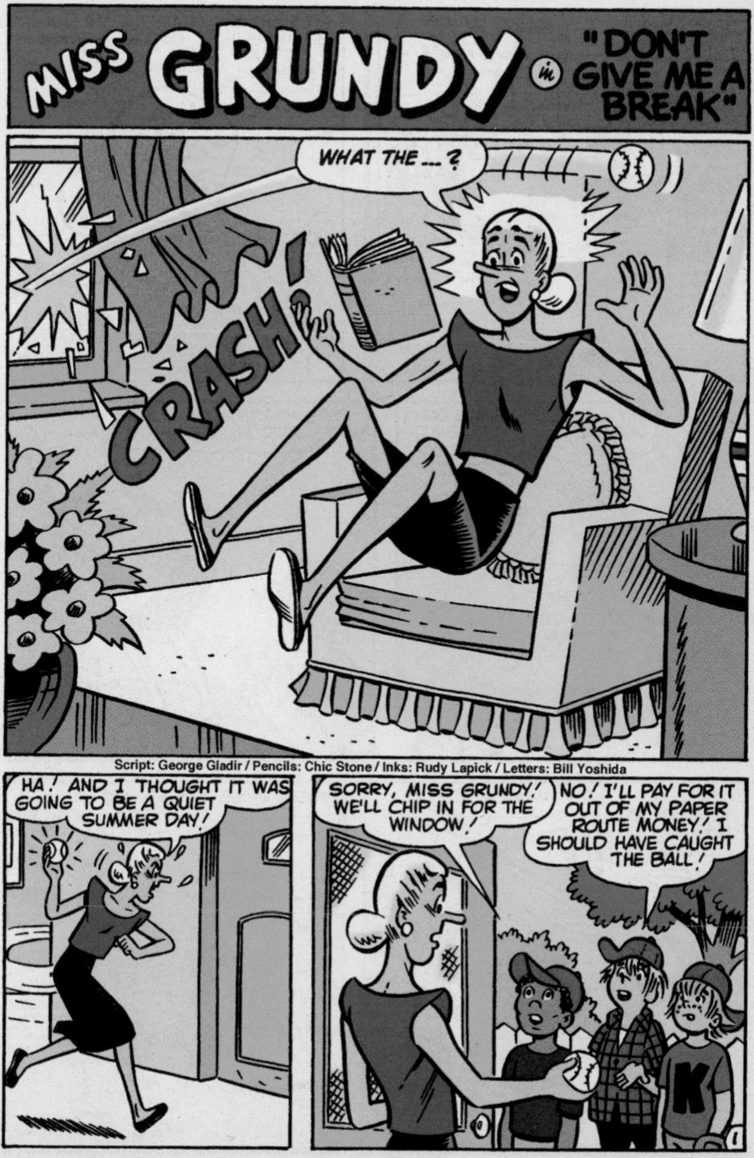
MISS GRUNDY in "DON'T GIVE ME A BREAK"
WHAT THE ...?
CRASH!
Script: George Gladir / Pencils: Chic Stone / Inks: Rudy Lapick / Letters: Bill Yoshida
HA! AND I THOUGHT IT WAS GOING TO BE A QUIET SUMMER DAY!
SORRY, MISS GRUNDY! WE'LL CHIP IN FOR THE WINDOW!
NO! I'LL PAY FOR IT OUT OF MY PAPER ROUTE MONEY! I SHOULD HAVE CAUGHT THE BALL!
K
1

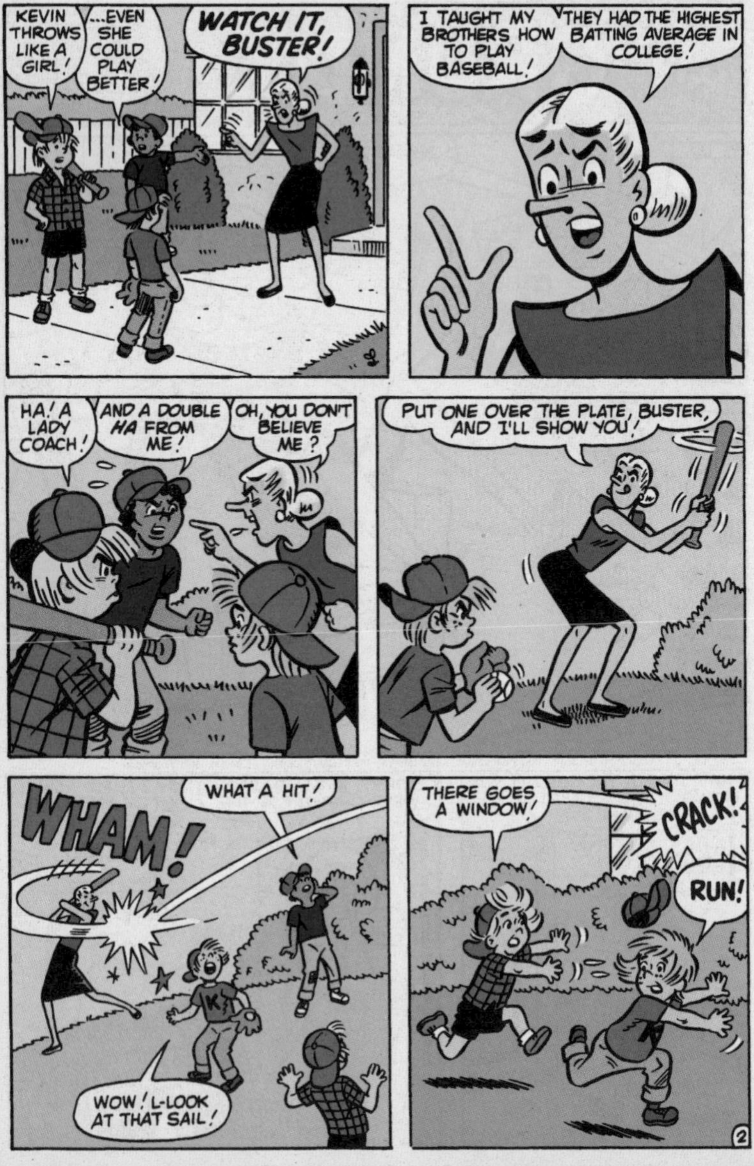
KEVIN THROWS LIKE A GIRL!
...EVEN SHE COULD PLAY BETTER!
WATCH IT, BUSTER!
I TAUGHT MY BROTHERS HOW TO PLAY BASEBALL!
THEY HAD THE HIGHEST BATTING AVERAGE IN COLLEGE!
HA! A LADY COACH!
AND A DOUBLE HA FROM ME!
OH, YOU DON'T BELIEVE ME?
PUT ONE OVER THE PLATE, BUSTER, AND I'LL SHOW YOU!
WHAM!
WHAT A HIT!
WOW! L-LOOK AT THAT SAIL!
THERE GOES A WINDOW!
CRACK!
RUN!
2

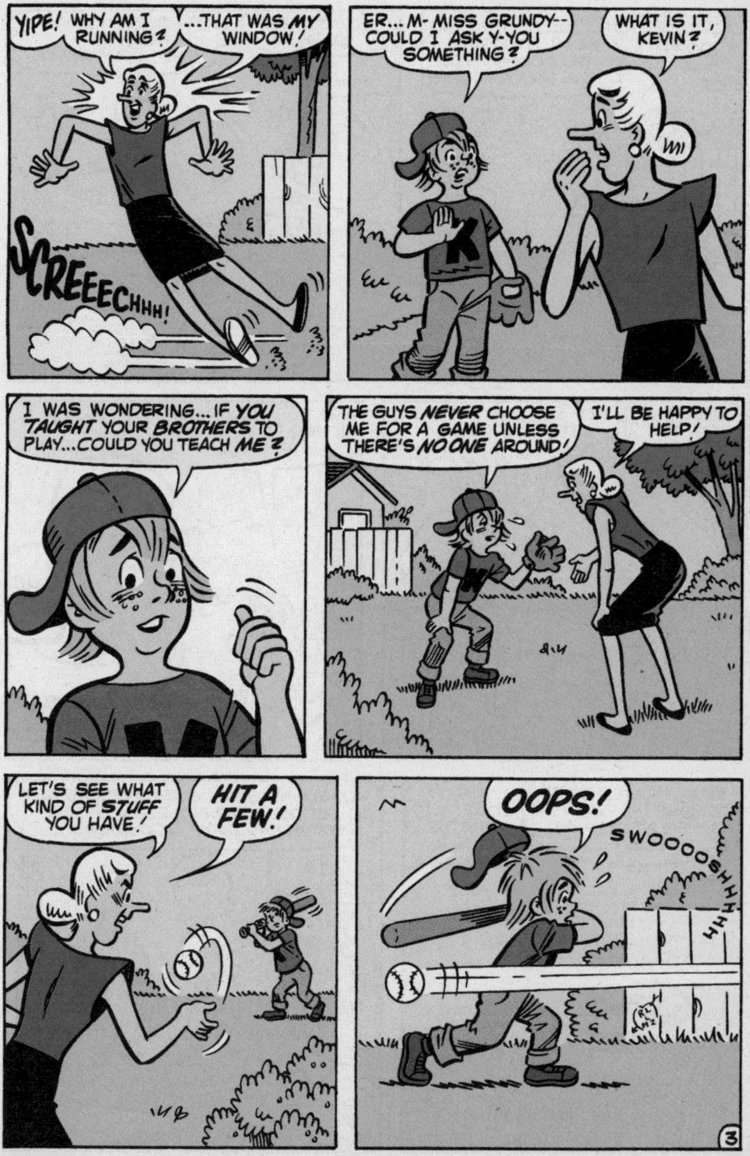
YIPE! WHY AM I RUNNING?
...THAT WAS MY WINDOW!
SCREEECHHH!
ER... M- MISS GRUNDY-- COULD I ASK Y-YOU SOMETHING?
WHAT IS IT, KEVIN?
I WAS WONDERING... IF YOU TAUGHT YOUR BROTHERS TO PLAY...COULD YOU TEACH ME?
THE GUYS NEVER CHOOSE ME FOR A GAME UNLESS THERE'S NO ONE AROUND!
I'LL BE HAPPY TO HELP!
LET'S SEE WHAT KIND OF STUFF YOU HAVE!
HIT A FEW!
OOPS!
SWOOOOSHHHH
3

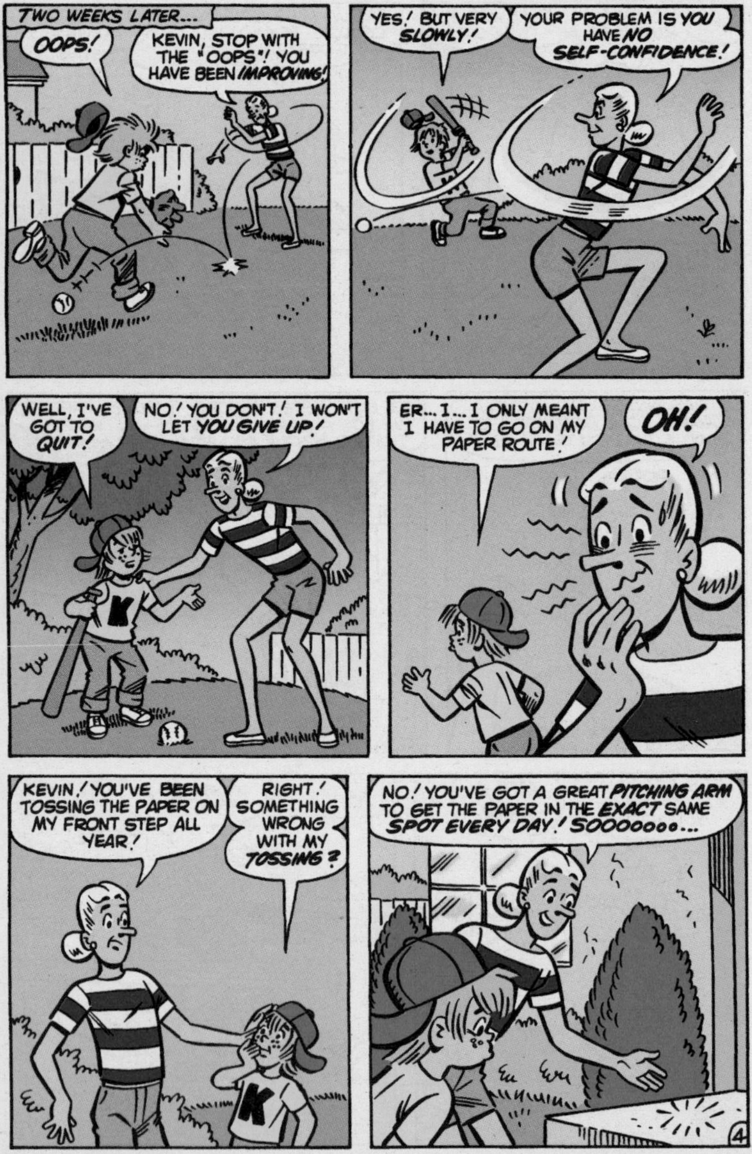
TWO WEEKS LATER...
OOPS!
KEVIN, STOP WITH THE "OOPS"! YOU HAVE BEEN IMPROVING!
YES! BUT VERY SLOWLY!
YOUR PROBLEM IS YOU HAVE NO SELF-CONFIDENCE!
WELL, I'VE GOT TO QUIT!
NO! YOU DON'T! I WON'T LET YOU GIVE UP!
ER... I... I ONLY MEANT I HAVE TO GO ON MY PAPER ROUTE!
OH!
KEVIN! YOU'VE BEEN TOSSING THE PAPER ON MY FRONT STEP ALL YEAR!
RIGHT! SOMETHING WRONG WITH MY TOSSING?
NO! YOU'VE GOT A GREAT PITCHING ARM TO GET THE PAPER IN THE EXACT SAME SPOT EVERY DAY! SOOOOOOO...
4

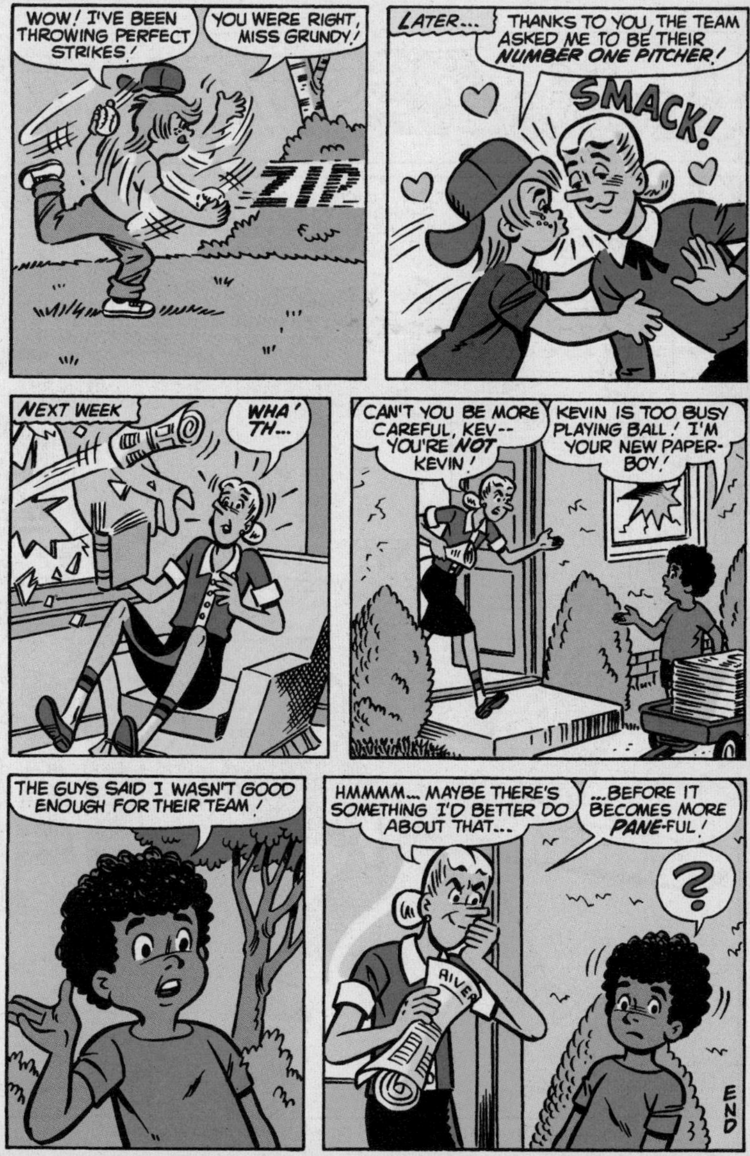

WOW! I'VE BEEN THROWING PERFECT STRIKES!
YOU WERE RIGHT, MISS GRUNDY!
ZIP
LATER...
THANKS TO YOU, THE TEAM ASKED ME TO BE THEIR NUMBER ONE PITCHER!
SMACK!
NEXT WEEK
WHA' TH...
CAN'T YOU BE MORE CAREFUL, KEV-- YOU'RE NOT KEVIN!
KEVIN IS TOO BUSY PLAYING BALL! I'M YOUR NEW PAPER-BOY!
THE GUYS SAID I WASN'T GOOD ENOUGH FOR THEIR TEAM!
HMMMM... MAYBE THERE'S SOMETHING I'D BETTER DO ABOUT THAT...
...BEFORE IT BECOMES MORE PANE-FUL!
?
RIVER
END

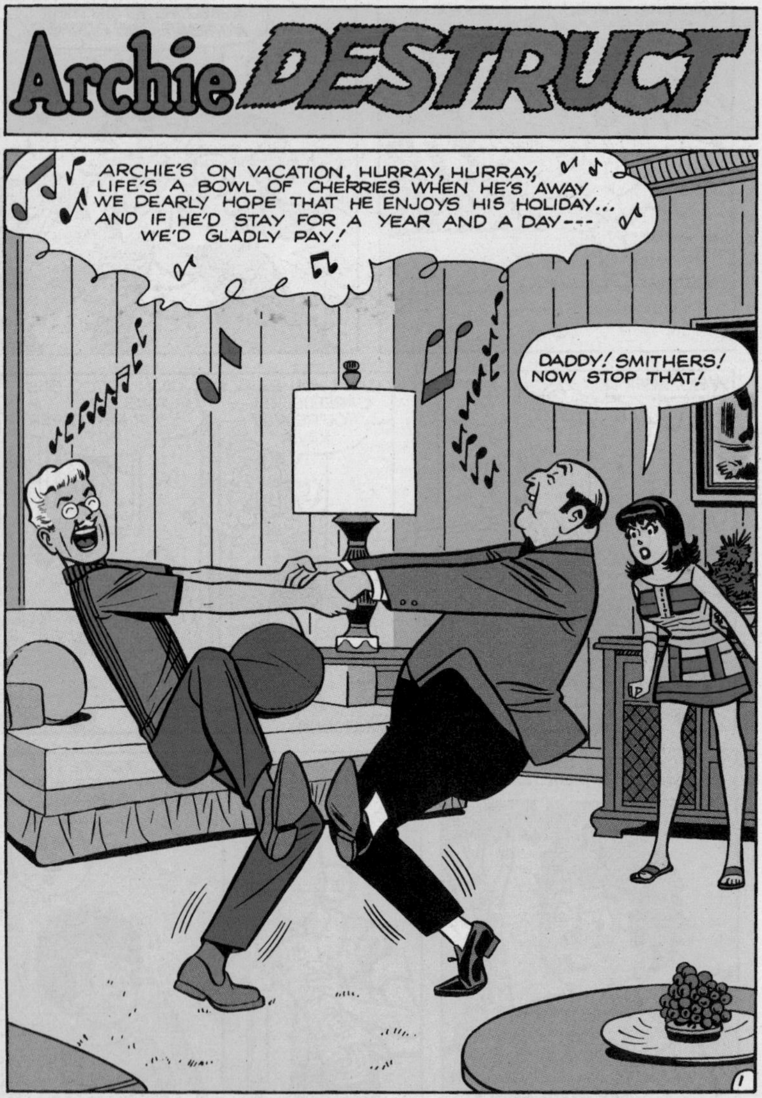
Archie DESTRUCT
ARCHIE'S ON VACATION, HURRAY, HURRAY, LIFE'S A BOWL OF CHERRIES WHEN HE'S AWAY WE DEARLY HOPE THAT HE ENJOYS HIS HOLIDAY... AND IF HE'D STAY FOR A YEAR AND A DAY--- WE'D GLADLY PAY!
DADDY! SMITHERS! NOW STOP THAT!
1

Script: Frank Doyle / Art: Harry Lucey / Inks & Letters: Mario Acquaviva

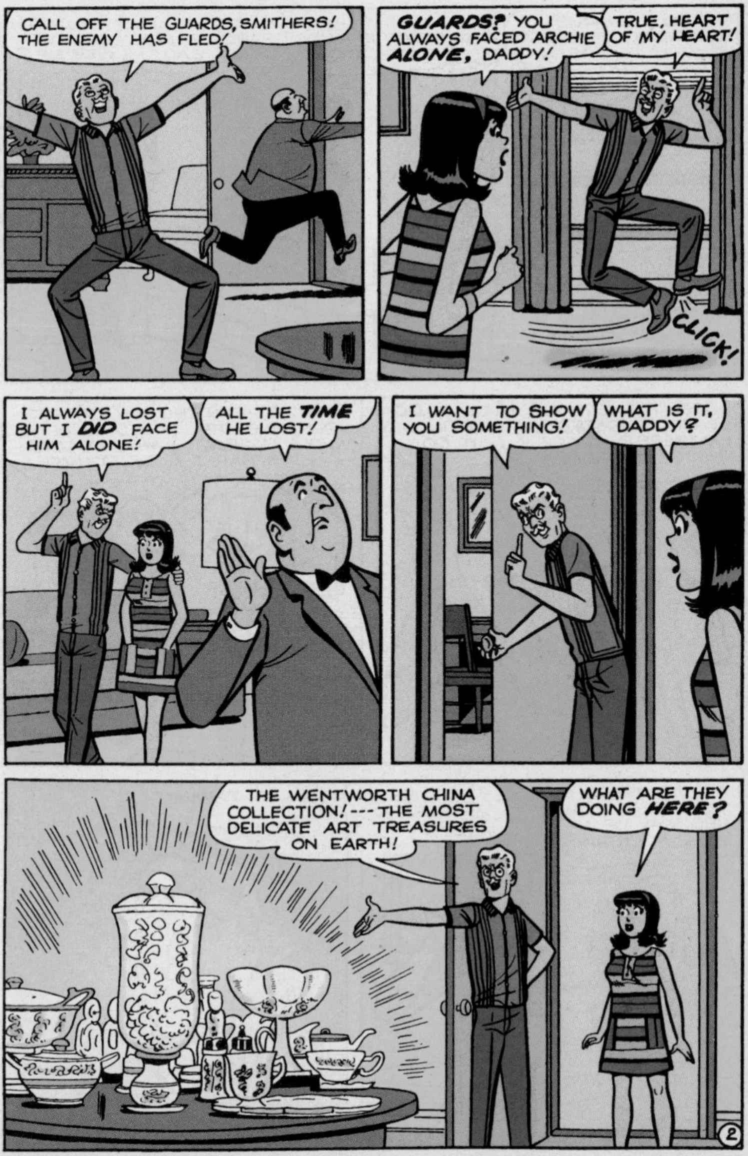
CALL OFF THE GUARDS, SMITHERS! THE ENEMY HAS FLED!
GUARDS? YOU ALWAYS FACED ARCHIE ALONE, DADDY!
TRUE, HEART OF MY HEART!
CLICK!
I ALWAYS LOST BUT I DID FACE HIM ALONE!
ALL THE TIME HE LOST!
I WANT TO SHOW YOU SOMETHING!
WHAT IS IT, DADDY?
THE WENTWORTH CHINA COLLECTION! --- THE MOST DELICATE ART TREASURES ON EARTH!
WHAT ARE THEY DOING HERE?
2

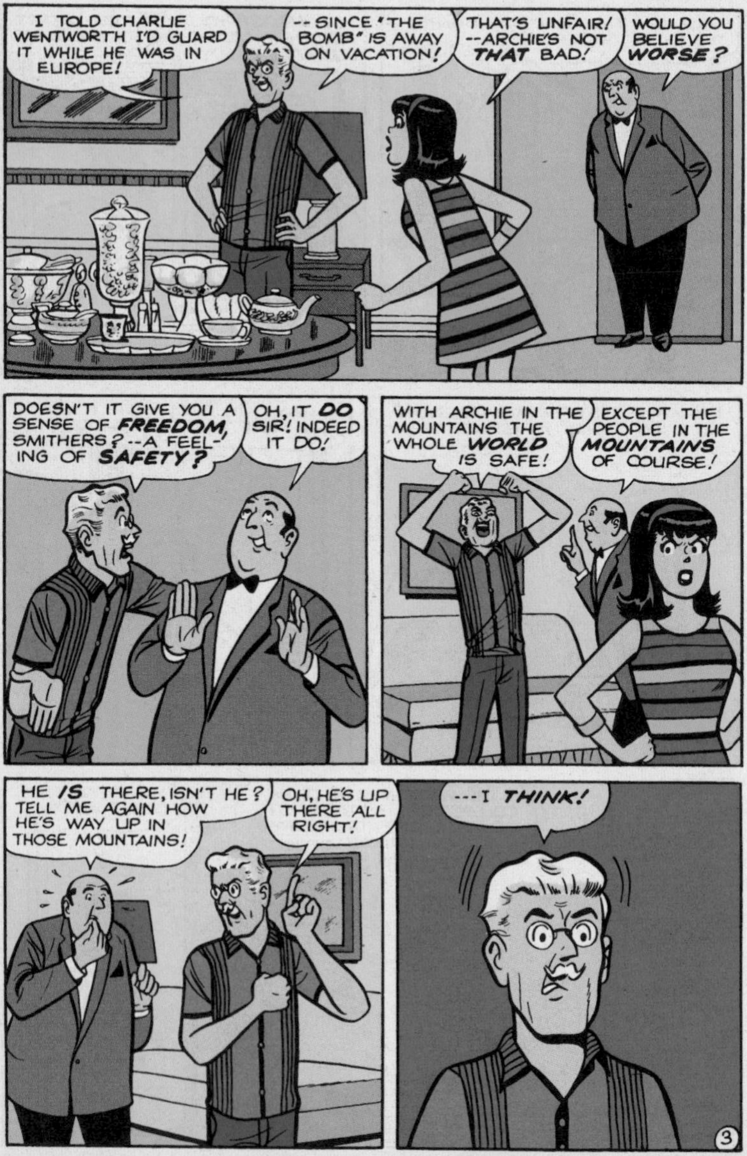
I TOLD CHARLIE WENTWORTH I'D GUARD IT WHILE HE WAS IN EUROPE!
-- SINCE "THE BOMB" IS AWAY ON VACATION!
THAT'S UNFAIR! --ARCHIE'S NOT THAT BAD!
WOULD YOU BELIEVE WORSE?
DOESN'T IT GIVE YOU A SENSE OF FREEDOM, SMITHERS? --A FEEL-ING OF SAFETY?
OH, IT DO SIR! INDEED IT DO!
WITH ARCHIE IN THE MOUNTAINS THE WHOLE WORLD IS SAFE!
EXCEPT THE PEOPLE IN THE MOUNTAINS OF COURSE!
HE IS THERE, ISN'T HE? TELL ME AGAIN HOW HE'S WAY UP IN THOSE MOUNTAINS!
OH, HE'S UP THERE ALL RIGHT!
---I THINK!
3

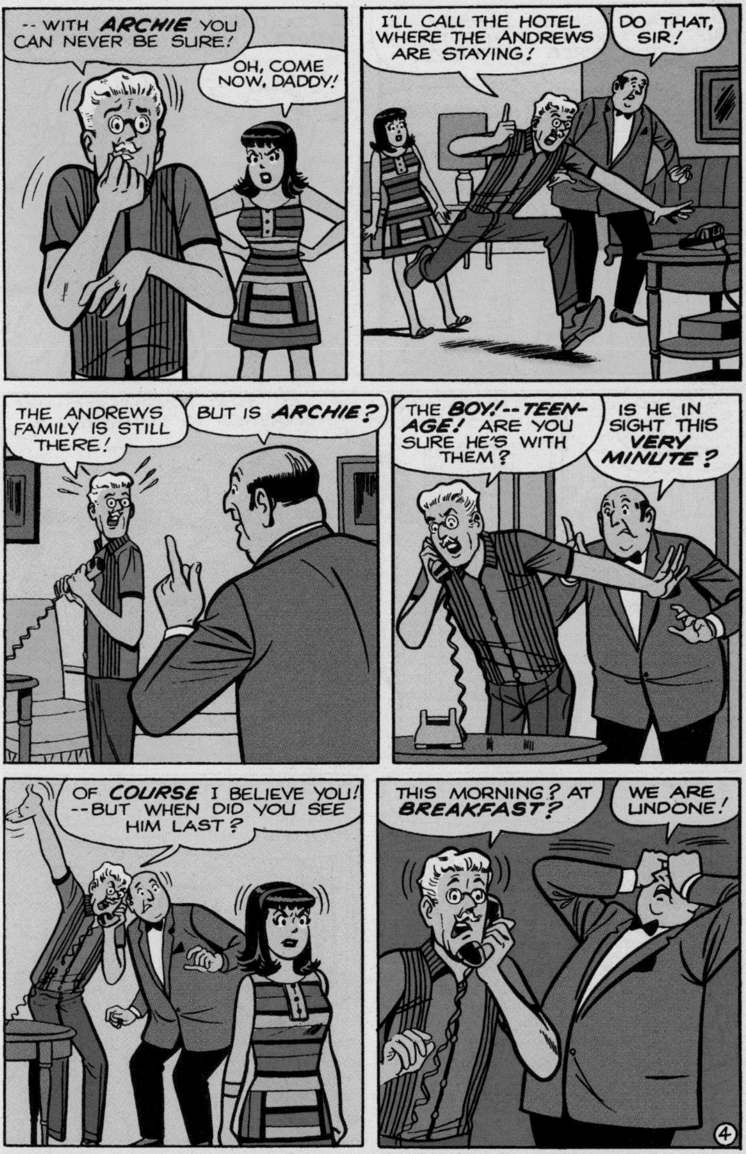
-- WITH ARCHIE YOU CAN NEVER BE SURE!
OH, COME NOW, DADDY!
I'LL CALL THE HOTEL WHERE THE ANDREWS ARE STAYING!
DO THAT, SIR!
THE ANDREWS FAMILY IS STILL THERE!
BUT IS ARCHIE?
THE BOY!--TEEN-AGE! ARE YOU SURE HE'S WITH THEM?
IS HE IN SIGHT THIS VERY MINUTE?
OF COURSE I BELIEVE YOU! --BUT WHEN DID YOU SEE HIM LAST?
THIS MORNING? AT BREAKFAST?
WE ARE UNDONE!
4

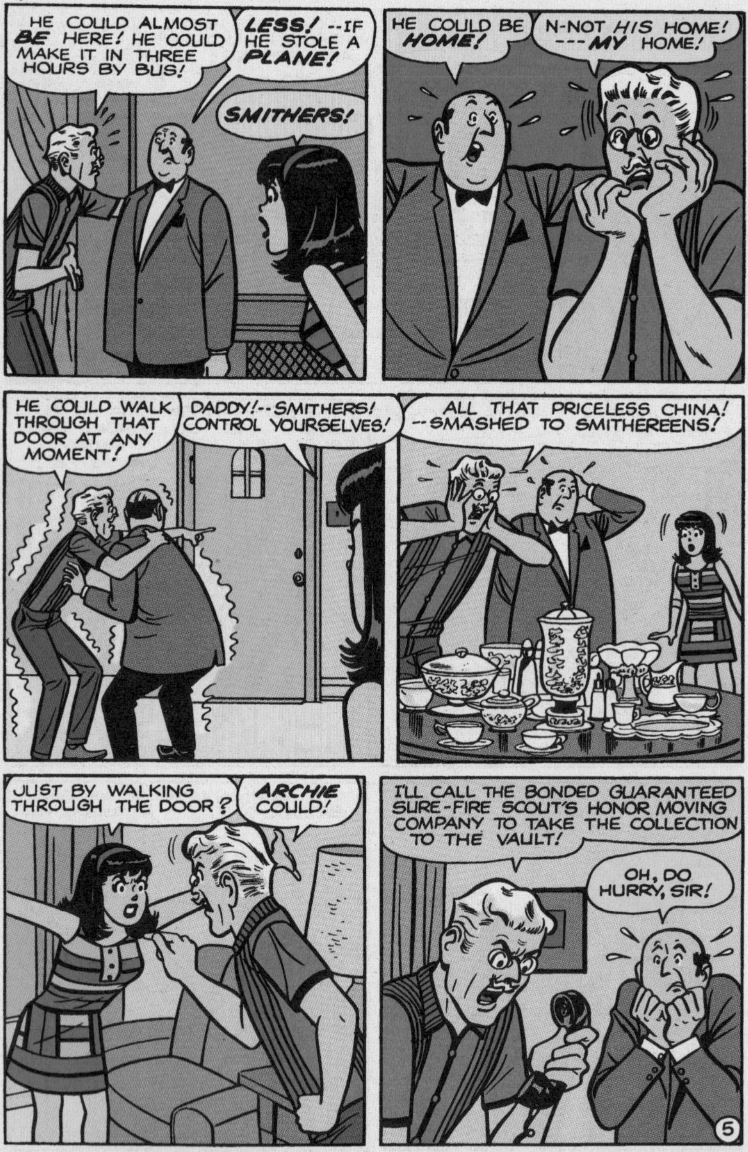
HE COULD ALMOST BE HERE! HE COULD MAKE IT IN THREE HOURS BY BUS!
LESS! --IF HE STOLE A PLANE!
SMITHERS!
HE COULD BE HOME!
N-NOT HIS HOME! ---MY HOME!
HE COULD WALK THROUGH THAT DOOR AT ANY MOMENT!
DADDY!--SMITHERS! CONTROL YOURSELVES!
ALL THAT PRICELESS CHINA! --SMASHED TO SMITHEREENS!
JUST BY WALKING THROUGH THE DOOR?
ARCHIE COULD!
I'LL CALL THE BONDED GUARANTEED SURE-FIRE SCOUT'S HONOR MOVING COMPANY TO TAKE THE COLLECTION TO THE VAULT!
OH, DO HURRY, SIR!
5

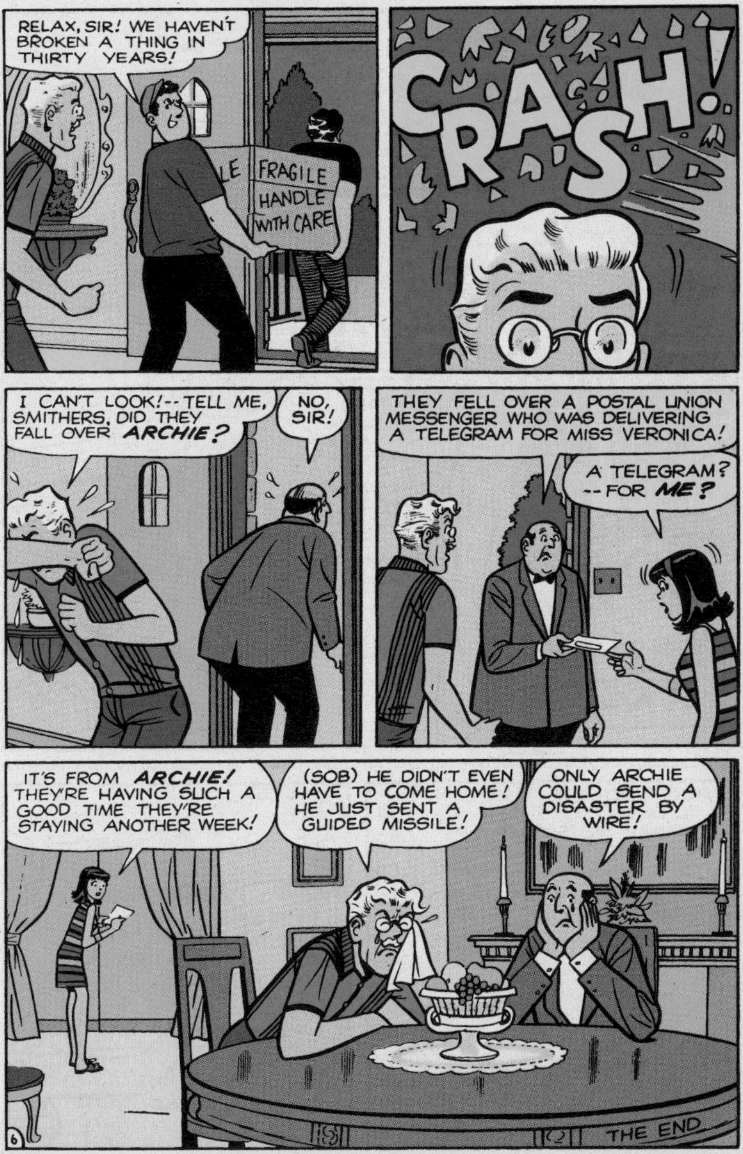
RELAX, SIR! WE HAVEN'T BROKEN A THING IN THIRTY YEARS!
LE FRAGILE HANDLE WITH CARE
CRASH!
I CAN'T LOOK!--TELL ME, SMITHERS, DID THEY FALL OVER ARCHIE?
NO, SIR!
THEY FELL OVER A POSTAL UNION MESSENGER WHO WAS DELIVERING A TELEGRAM FOR MISS VERONICA!
A TELEGRAM? --FOR ME?
IT'S FROM ARCHIE! THEY'RE HAVING SUCH A GOOD TIME THEY'RE STAYING ANOTHER WEEK!
(SOB) HE DIDN'T EVEN HAVE TO COME HOME! HE JUST SENT A GUIDED MISSILE!
ONLY ARCHIE COULD SEND A DISASTER BY WIRE!
THE END

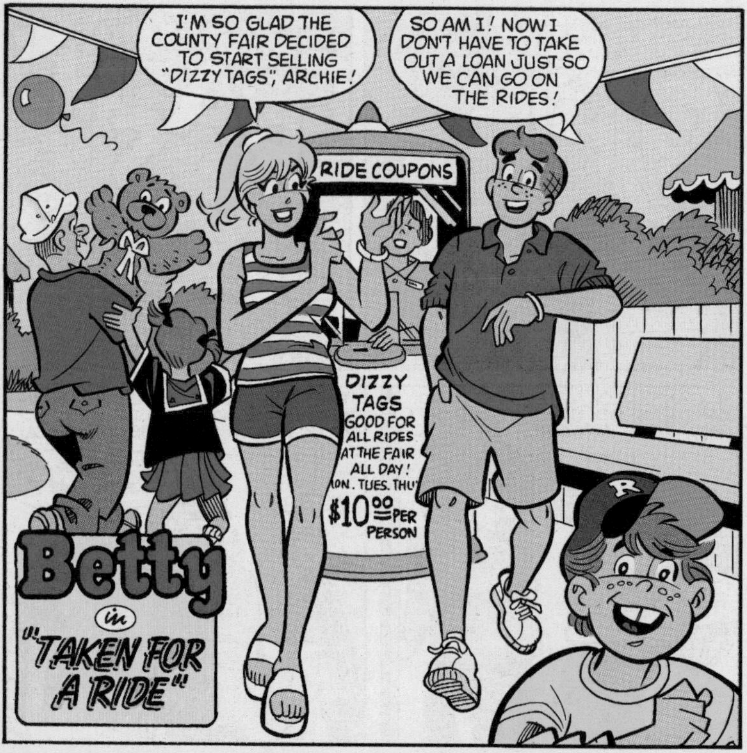
I'M SO GLAD THE COUNTY FAIR DECIDED TO START SELLING "DIZZY TAGS", ARCHIE!
SO AM I! NOW I DON'T HAVE TO TAKE OUT A LOAN JUST SO WE CAN GO ON THE RIDES!
RIDE COUPONS
DIZZY TAGS GOOD FOR ALL RIDES AT THE FAIR ALL DAY!
ON. TUES. THU
$10.00 PER PERSON
Betty
in
"TAKEN FOR A RIDE"

Script: Kathleen Webb / Pencils: Stan Goldberg / Inks: John Lowe / Letters: Bill Yoshida / Colors: Barry Grossman

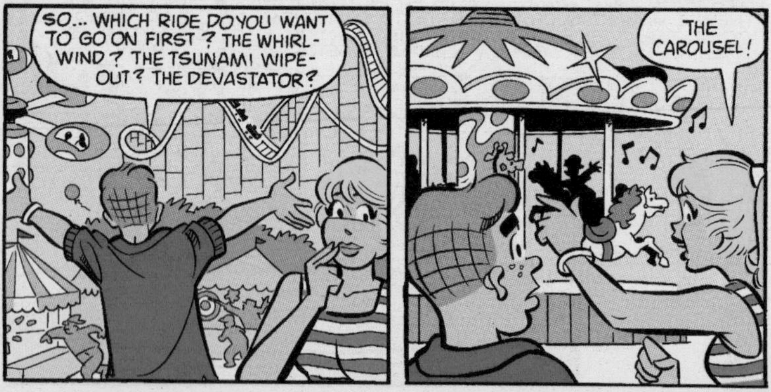
SO... WHICH RIDE DO YOU WANT TO GO ON FIRST? THE WHIRLWIND? THE TSUNAMI WIPE-OUT? THE DEVASTATOR?
THE CAROUSEL!

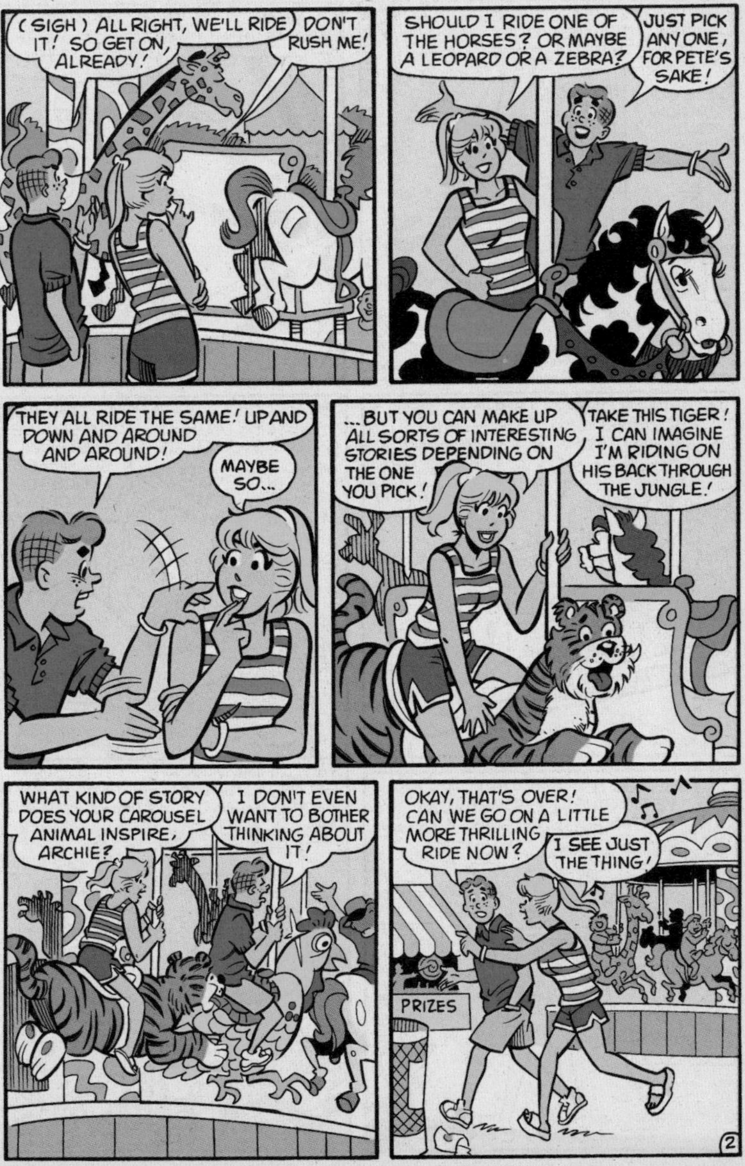

(SIGH) ALL RIGHT, WE'LL RIDE IT! SO GET ON, ALREADY!
DON'T RUSH ME!
SHOULD I RIDE ONE OF THE HORSES? OR MAYBE A LEOPARD OR A ZEBRA?
JUST PICK ANY ONE, FOR PETE'S SAKE!
THEY ALL RIDE THE SAME! UP AND DOWN AND AROUND AND AROUND!
MAYBE SO...
...BUT YOU CAN MAKE UP ALL SORTS OF INTERESTING STORIES DEPENDING ON THE ONE YOU PICK!
TAKE THIS TIGER! I CAN IMAGINE I'M RIDING ON HIS BACK THROUGH THE JUNGLE!
WHAT KIND OF STORY DOES YOUR CAROUSEL ANIMAL INSPIRE, ARCHIE?
I DON'T EVEN WANT TO BOTHER THINKING ABOUT IT!
OKAY, THAT'S OVER! CAN WE GO ON A LITTLE MORE THRILLING RIDE NOW?
I SEE JUST THE THING!
PRIZES

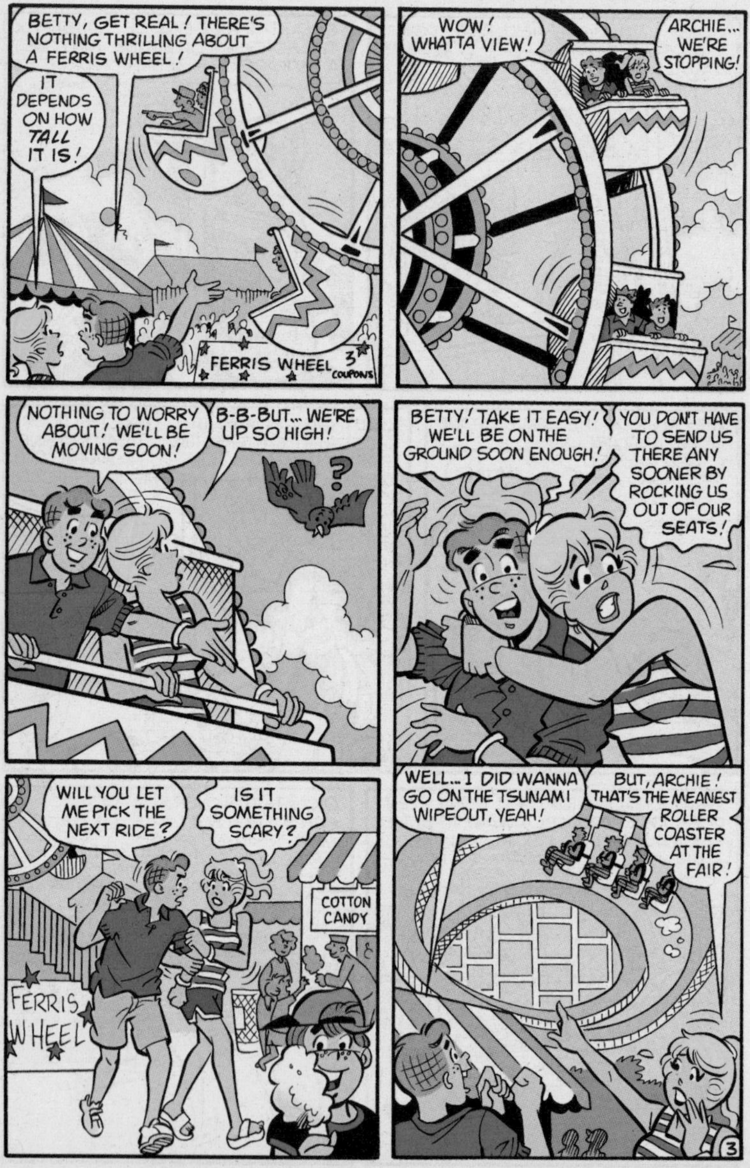
BETTY, GET REAL! THERE'S NOTHING THRILLING ABOUT A FERRIS WHEEL!
IT DEPENDS ON HOW TALL IT IS!
FERRIS WHEEL 3 COUPONS
WOW! WHATTA VIEW!
ARCHIE... WE'RE STOPPING!
NOTHING TO WORRY ABOUT! WE'LL BE MOVING SOON!
B-B-BUT... WE'RE UP SO HIGH!
?
BETTY! TAKE IT EASY! WE'LL BE ON THE GROUND SOON ENOUGH!
YOU DON'T HAVE TO SEND US THERE ANY SOONER BY ROCKING US OUT OF OUR SEATS!
WILL YOU LET ME PICK THE NEXT RIDE?
IS IT SOMETHING SCARY?
COTTON CANDY
FERRIS WHEEL
WELL... I DID WANNA GO ON THE TSUNAMI WIPEOUT, YEAH!
BUT, ARCHIE! THAT'S THE MEANEST ROLLER COASTER AT THE FAIR!
3

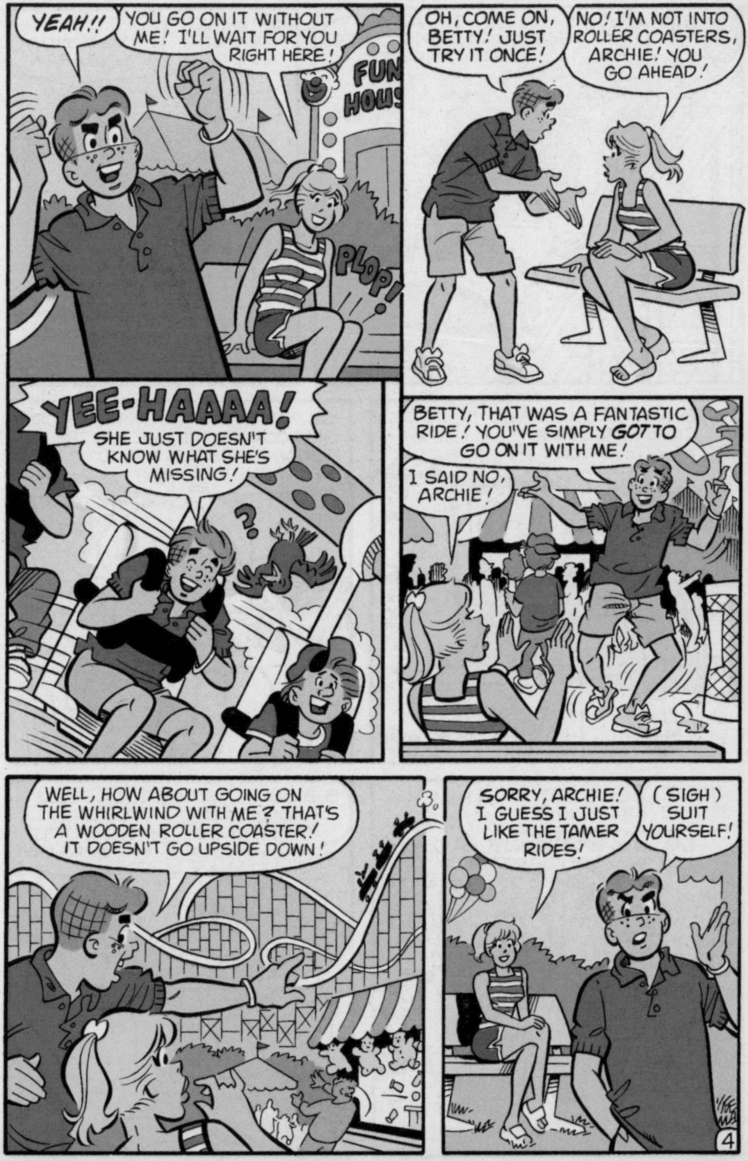
YEAH!!
YOU GO ON IT WITHOUT ME! I'LL WAIT FOR YOU RIGHT HERE!
FUN HOUS
PLOP!
OH, COME ON, BETTY! JUST TRY IT ONCE!
NO! I'M NOT INTO ROLLER COASTERS, ARCHIE! YOU GO AHEAD!
YEE-HAAAA!
SHE JUST DOESN'T KNOW WHAT SHE'S MISSING!
?
BETTY, THAT WAS A FANTASTIC RIDE! YOU'VE SIMPLY GOT TO GO ON IT WITH ME!
I SAID NO, ARCHIE!
WELL, HOW ABOUT GOING ON THE WHIRLWIND WITH ME? THAT'S A WOODEN ROLLER COASTER! IT DOESN'T GO UPSIDE DOWN!
SORRY, ARCHIE! I GUESS I JUST LIKE THE TAMER RIDES!
(SIGH) SUIT YOURSELF!
4

WAHOOO!

I'M GLAD I'M NOT A SCAREDYCAT WHEN IT COMES TO COASTERS!

WHIRLWIND

HAD ENOUGH OF YOUR THRILL RIDES YET?

NOPE! I'M GOING ON THE TSUNAMI WIPEOUT AGAIN!

HI, BETTY! I THOUGHT YOU CAME TO THE PARK WITH ARCHIE!

I DID, MARIA!

POP CORN

POP CORN

OH! WHEN I SAW HIM WITH GLORIA GUDLOOKS IN THE LINE FOR THE TSUNAMI WIPEOUT, I THOUGHT HE'D COME WITH HER!

WITH GLORIA?!

ARCHIE! I CHANGED MY MIND! I'LL RIDE WITH YOU!

HUH? RATS!

★ TSUNAMI WIPEOUT ★

B-B-BUT-- I THOUGHT YOU ONLY LIKED THE TAMER RIDES?

SO I DECIDED I'D LIKE TO LIVE A LITTLE DANGEROUSLY!

5

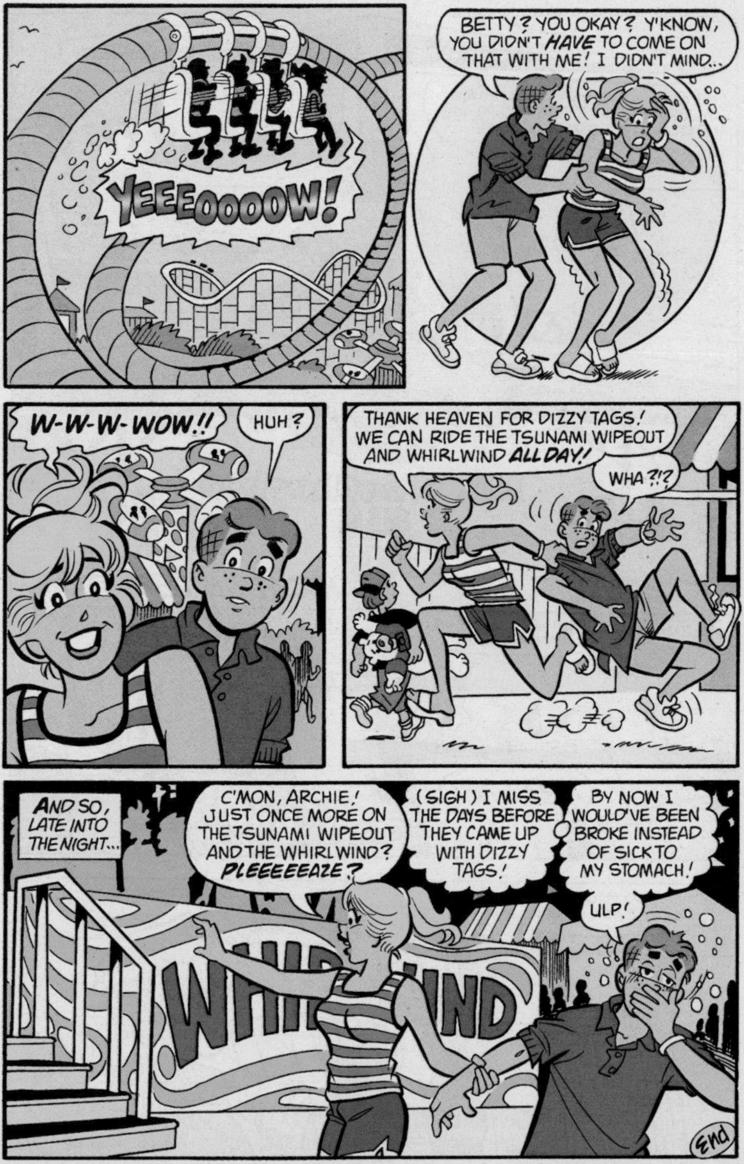

YEEEOOOOOW!
BETTY? YOU OKAY? Y'KNOW, YOU DIDN'T HAVE TO COME ON THAT WITH ME! I DIDN'T MIND...
W-W-W-WOW!!
HUH?
THANK HEAVEN FOR DIZZY TAGS! WE CAN RIDE THE TSUNAMI WIPEOUT AND WHIRLWIND ALL DAY!
WHA?!?
AND SO, LATE INTO THE NIGHT...
C'MON, ARCHIE! JUST ONCE MORE ON THE TSUNAMI WIPEOUT AND THE WHIRLWIND? PLEEEEEAZE?
(SIGH) I MISS THE DAYS BEFORE THEY CAME UP WITH DIZZY TAGS!
BY NOW I WOULD'VE BEEN BROKE INSTEAD OF SICK TO MY STOMACH!
ULP!
End

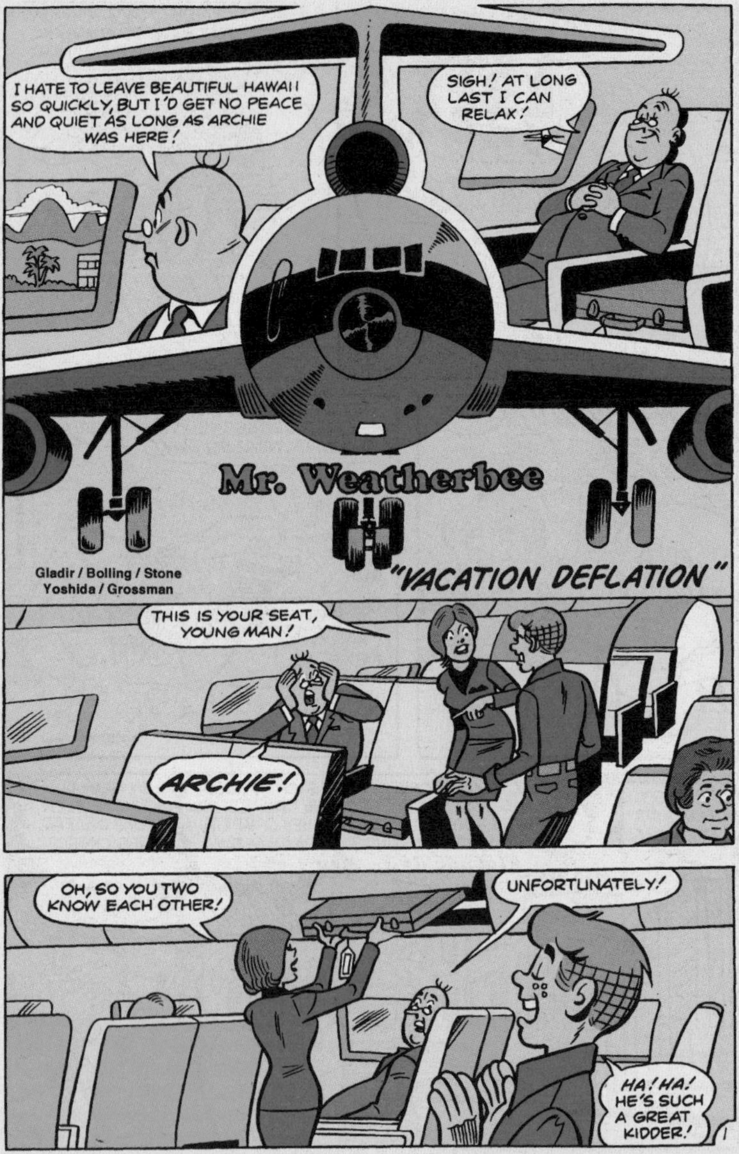
I HATE TO LEAVE BEAUTIFUL HAWAII SO QUICKLY, BUT I'D GET NO PEACE AND QUIET AS LONG AS ARCHIE WAS HERE!
SIGH! AT LONG LAST I CAN RELAX!
Mr. Weatherbee
Gladir / Bolling / Stone
Yoshida / Grossman
"VACATION DEFLATION"
THIS IS YOUR SEAT, YOUNG MAN!
ARCHIE!
OH, SO YOU TWO KNOW EACH OTHER!
UNFORTUNATELY!
HA! HA! HE'S SUCH A GREAT KIDDER!
1

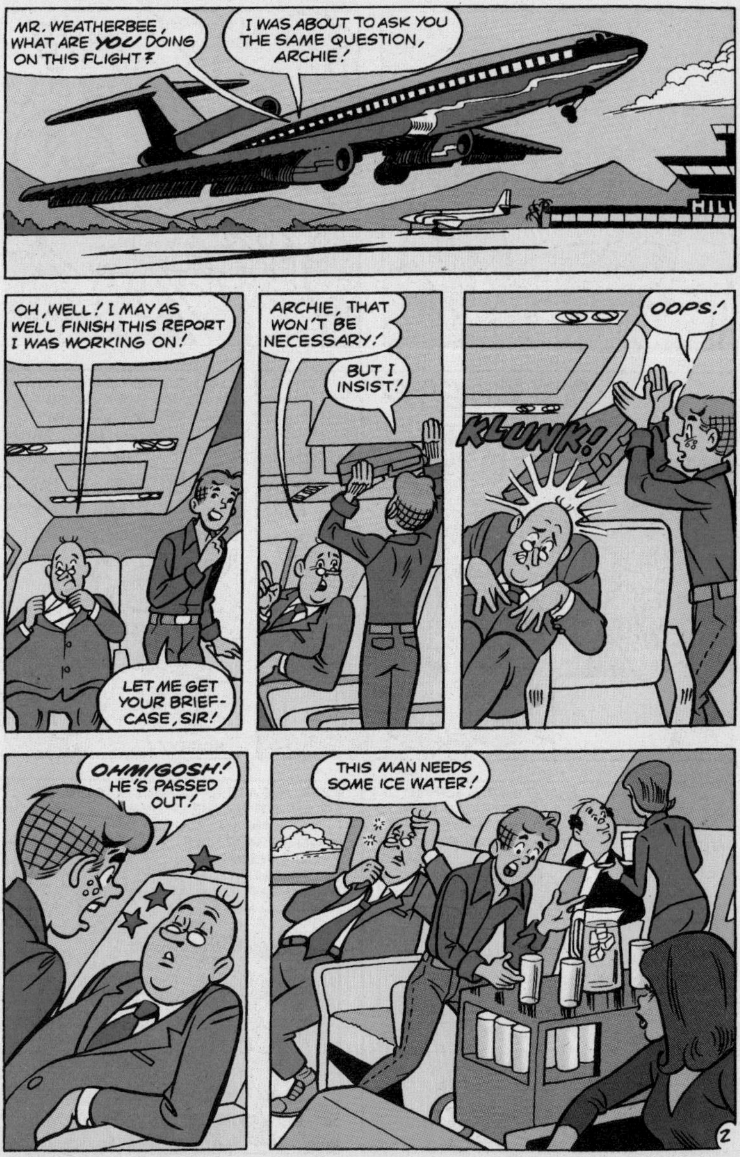
MR. WEATHERBEE, WHAT ARE YOU DOING ON THIS FLIGHT?
I WAS ABOUT TO ASK YOU THE SAME QUESTION, ARCHIE!
OH, WELL! I MAY AS WELL FINISH THIS REPORT I WAS WORKING ON!
LET ME GET YOUR BRIEF-CASE, SIR!
ARCHIE, THAT WON'T BE NECESSARY!
BUT I INSIST!
OOPS!
KLUNK!
OHMIGOSH! HE'S PASSED OUT!
THIS MAN NEEDS SOME ICE WATER!
2

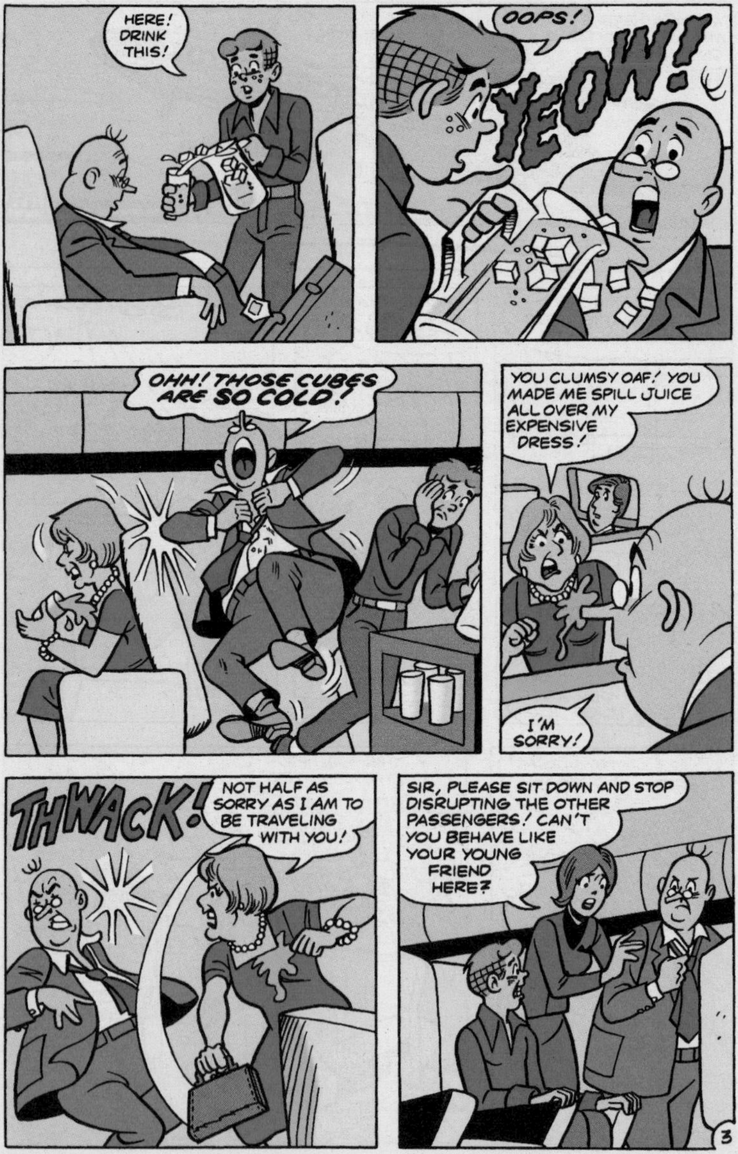
HERE! DRINK THIS!
OOPS!
YEOW!
OHH! THOSE CUBES ARE SO COLD!
YOU CLUMSY OAF! YOU MADE ME SPILL JUICE ALL OVER MY EXPENSIVE DRESS!
I'M SORRY!
THWACK!
NOT HALF AS SORRY AS I AM TO BE TRAVELING WITH YOU!
SIR, PLEASE SIT DOWN AND STOP DISRUPTING THE OTHER PASSENGERS! CAN'T YOU BEHAVE LIKE YOUR YOUNG FRIEND HERE?

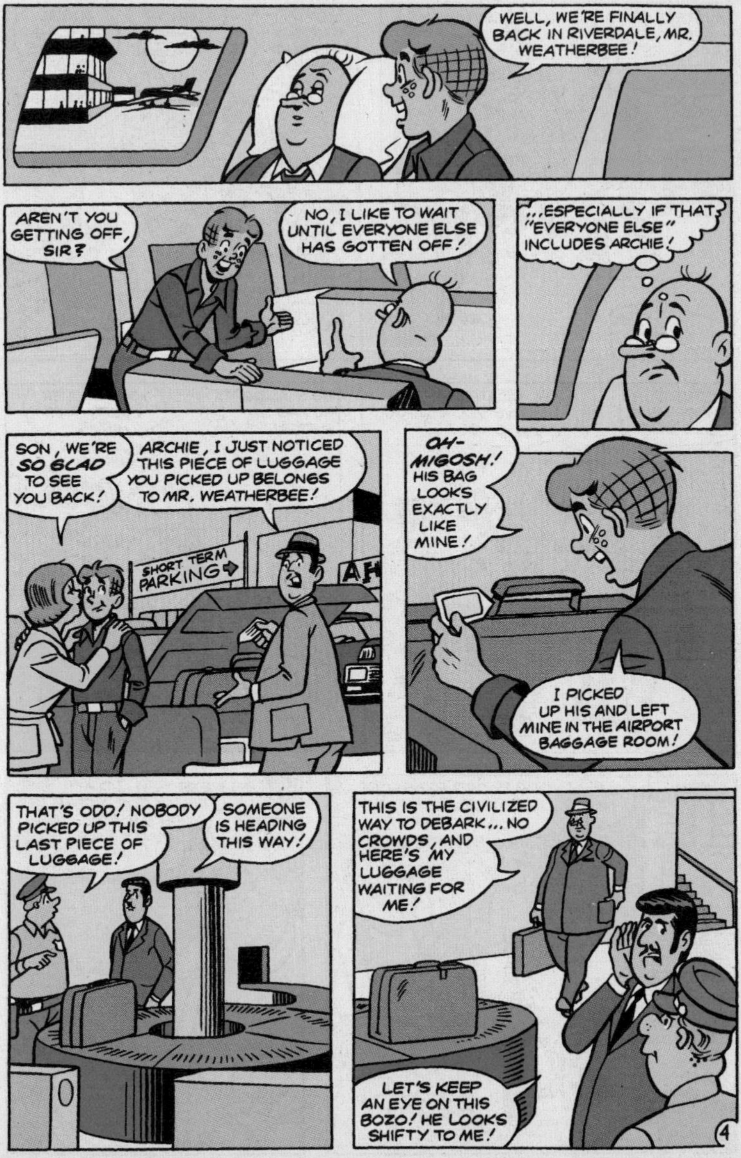

WELL, WE'RE FINALLY BACK IN RIVERDALE, MR. WEATHERBEE!
AREN'T YOU GETTING OFF, SIR?
NO, I LIKE TO WAIT UNTIL EVERYONE ELSE HAS GOTTEN OFF!
...ESPECIALLY IF THAT "EVERYONE ELSE" INCLUDES ARCHIE!
SON, WE'RE SO GLAD TO SEE YOU BACK!
ARCHIE, I JUST NOTICED THIS PIECE OF LUGGAGE YOU PICKED UP BELONGS TO MR. WEATHERBEE!
SHORT TERM PARKING
OH-MIGOSH! HIS BAG LOOKS EXACTLY LIKE MINE!
I PICKED UP HIS AND LEFT MINE IN THE AIRPORT BAGGAGE ROOM!
THAT'S ODD! NOBODY PICKED UP THIS LAST PIECE OF LUGGAGE!
SOMEONE IS HEADING THIS WAY!
THIS IS THE CIVILIZED WAY TO DEBARK... NO CROWDS, AND HERE'S MY LUGGAGE WAITING FOR ME!
LET'S KEEP AN EYE ON THIS BOZO! HE LOOKS SHIFTY TO ME!
4

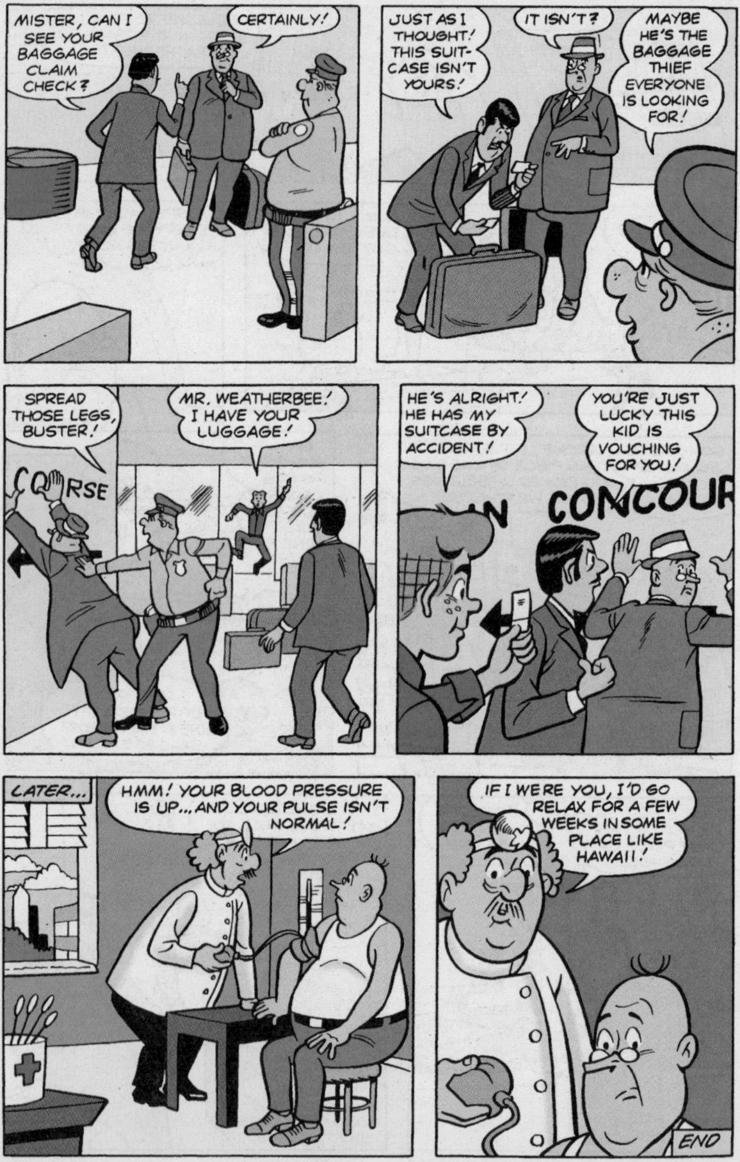

MISTER, CAN I SEE YOUR BAGGAGE CLAIM CHECK?
CERTAINLY!
JUST AS I THOUGHT! THIS SUIT-CASE ISN'T YOURS!
IT ISN'T?
MAYBE HE'S THE BAGGAGE THIEF EVERYONE IS LOOKING FOR!
SPREAD THOSE LEGS, BUSTER!
MR. WEATHERBEE! I HAVE YOUR LUGGAGE!
HE'S ALRIGHT! HE HAS MY SUITCASE BY ACCIDENT!
YOU'RE JUST LUCKY THIS KID IS VOUCHING FOR YOU!
CONCOUR
LATER...
HMM! YOUR BLOOD PRESSURE IS UP... AND YOUR PULSE ISN'T NORMAL!
IF I WERE YOU, I'D GO RELAX FOR A FEW WEEKS IN SOME PLACE LIKE HAWAII!
END

Veronica in Music To Her Ears — PART ONE

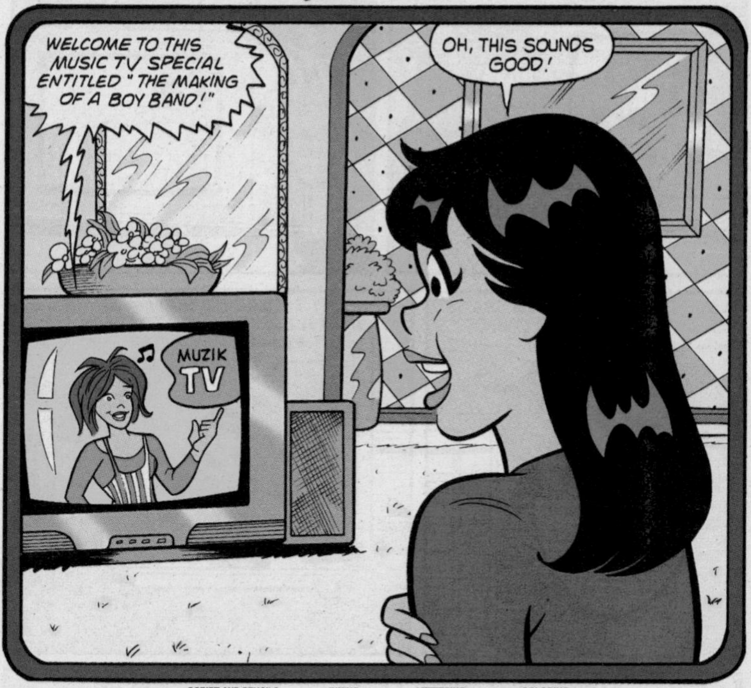
WELCOME TO THIS MUSIC TV SPECIAL ENTITLED "THE MAKING OF A BOY BAND!"
OH, THIS SOUNDS GOOD!
MUZIK TV

SCRIPT AND PENCILS: DAN PARENT INKING: RICH KOSLOWSKI LETTERING: BILL YOSHIDA COLORING: BARRY GROSSMAN

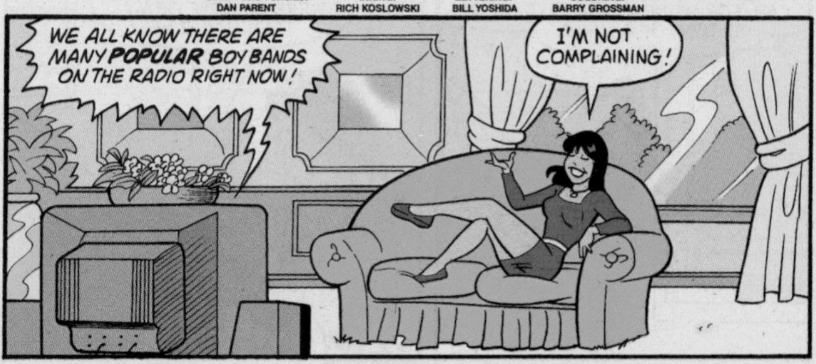
WE ALL KNOW THERE ARE MANY POPULAR BOY BANDS ON THE RADIO RIGHT NOW!
I'M NOT COMPLAINING!

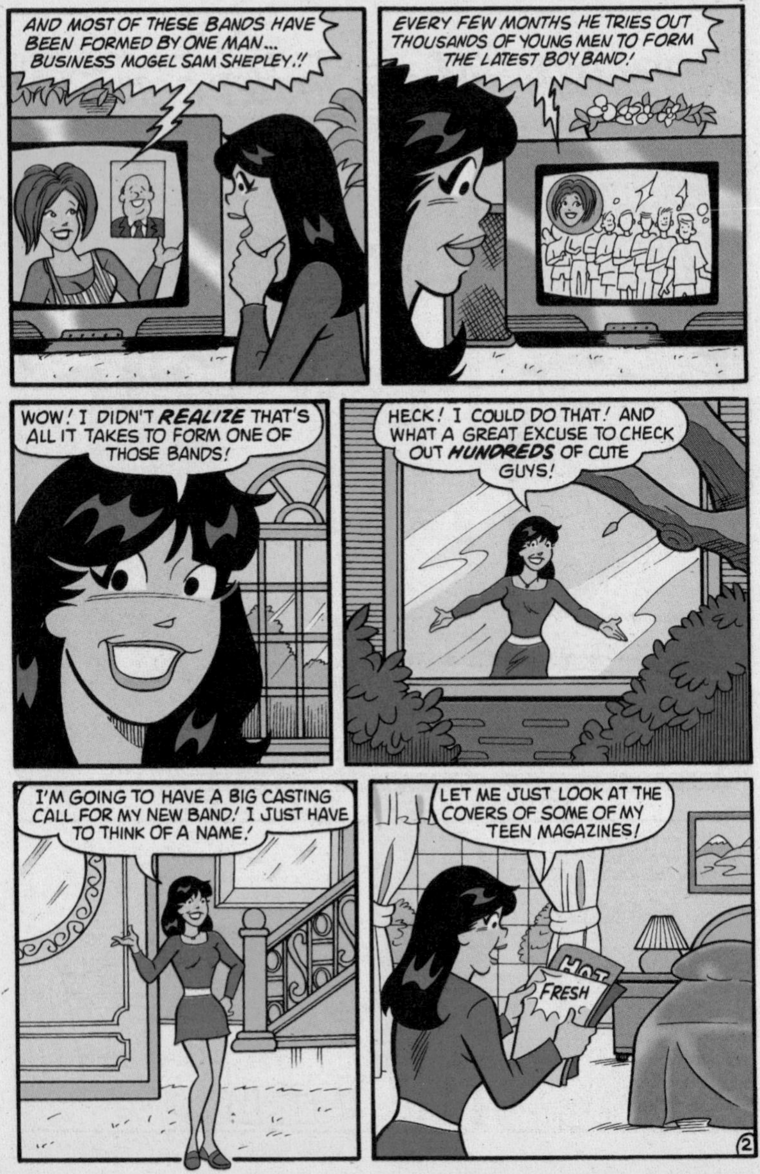
AND MOST OF THESE BANDS HAVE BEEN FORMED BY ONE MAN... BUSINESS MOGEL SAM SHEPLEY.!!
EVERY FEW MONTHS HE TRIES OUT THOUSANDS OF YOUNG MEN TO FORM THE LATEST BOY BAND!
WOW! I DIDN'T REALIZE THAT'S ALL IT TAKES TO FORM ONE OF THOSE BANDS!
HECK! I COULD DO THAT! AND WHAT A GREAT EXCUSE TO CHECK OUT HUNDREDS OF CUTE GUYS!
I'M GOING TO HAVE A BIG CASTING CALL FOR MY NEW BAND! I JUST HAVE TO THINK OF A NAME!
LET ME JUST LOOK AT THE COVERS OF SOME OF MY TEEN MAGAZINES!
HOT
FRESH
2

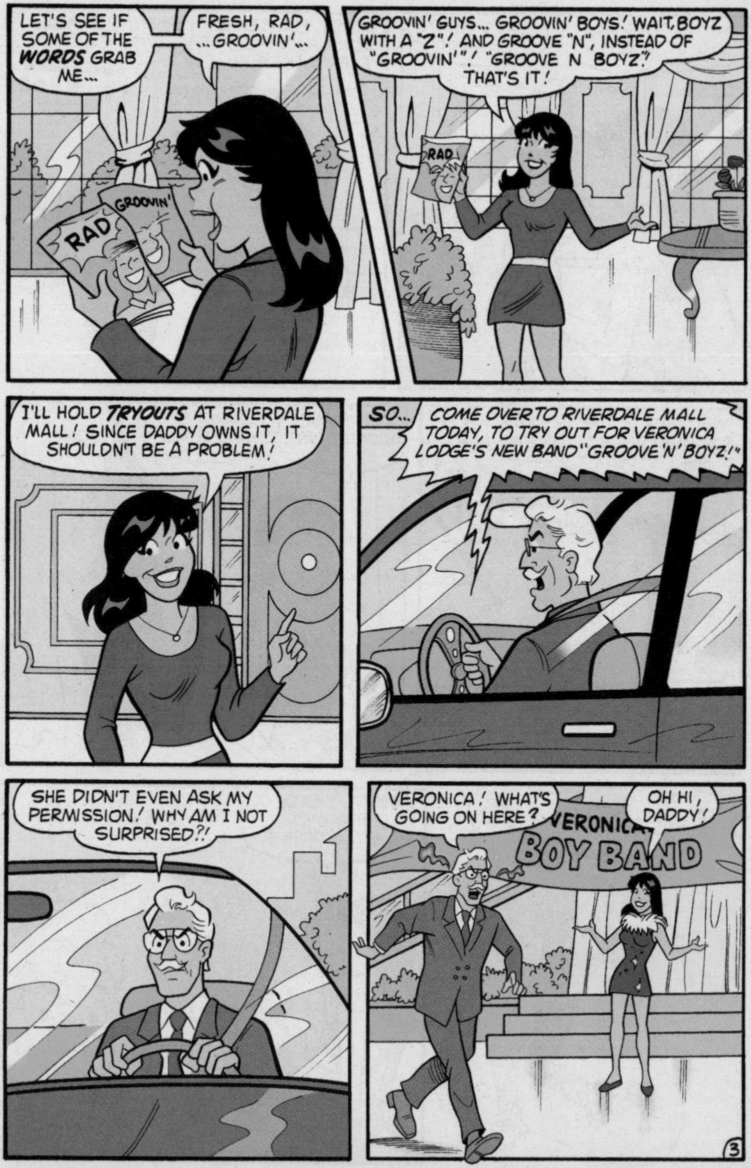
LET'S SEE IF SOME OF THE WORDS GRAB ME...
FRESH, RAD, ...GROOVIN'...
RAD
GROOVIN'
GROOVIN' GUYS... GROOVIN' BOYS! WAIT, BOYZ WITH A "Z"! AND GROOVE "N", INSTEAD OF "GROOVIN'"! "GROOVE N BOYZ"! THAT'S IT!
RAD
I'LL HOLD TRYOUTS AT RIVERDALE MALL! SINCE DADDY OWNS IT, IT SHOULDN'T BE A PROBLEM!
SO... COME OVER TO RIVERDALE MALL TODAY, TO TRY OUT FOR VERONICA LODGE'S NEW BAND "GROOVE 'N' BOYZ!"
SHE DIDN'T EVEN ASK MY PERMISSION! WHY AM I NOT SURPRISED?!
VERONICA! WHAT'S GOING ON HERE?
OH HI, DADDY!
BOY BAND
3

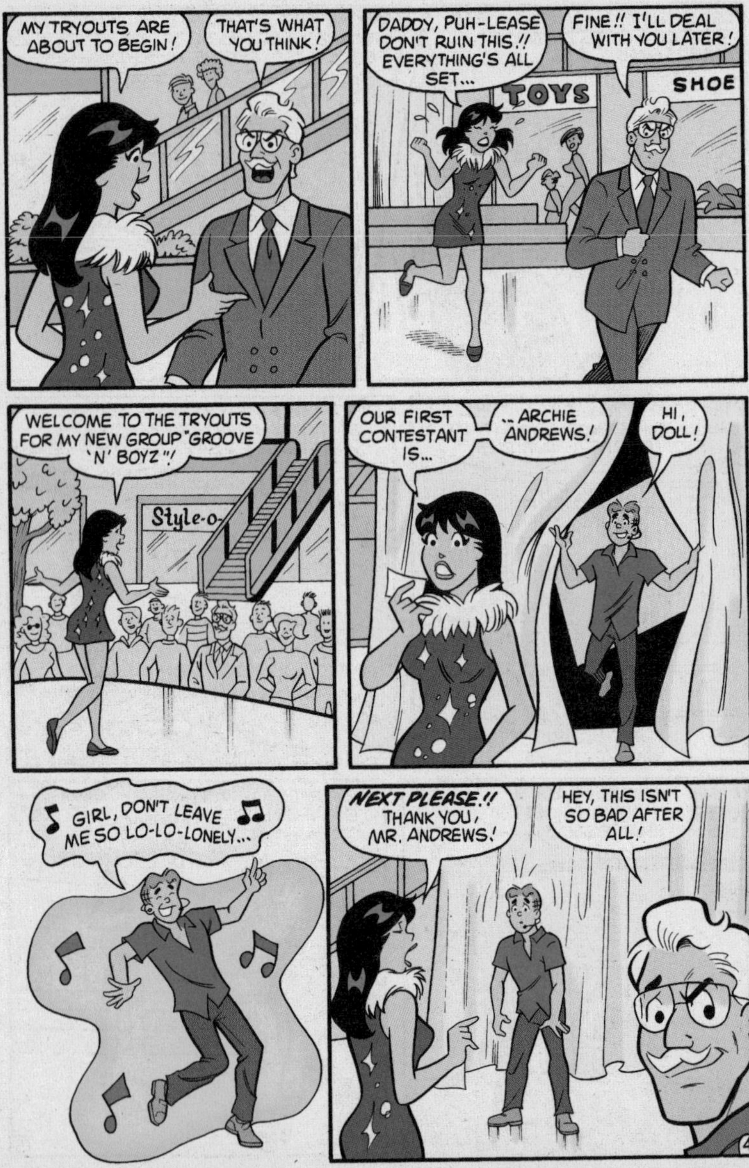
MY TRYOUTS ARE ABOUT TO BEGIN!
THAT'S WHAT YOU THINK!
DADDY, PUH-LEASE DON'T RUIN THIS.!! EVERYTHING'S ALL SET...
FINE.!! I'LL DEAL WITH YOU LATER!
TOYS
SHOE
WELCOME TO THE TRYOUTS FOR MY NEW GROUP "GROOVE 'N' BOYZ"!
Style-o-
OUR FIRST CONTESTANT IS...
...ARCHIE ANDREWS!
HI, DOLL!
GIRL, DON'T LEAVE ME SO LO-LO-LONELY...
NEXT PLEASE.!! THANK YOU, MR. ANDREWS!
HEY, THIS ISN'T SO BAD AFTER ALL!
4

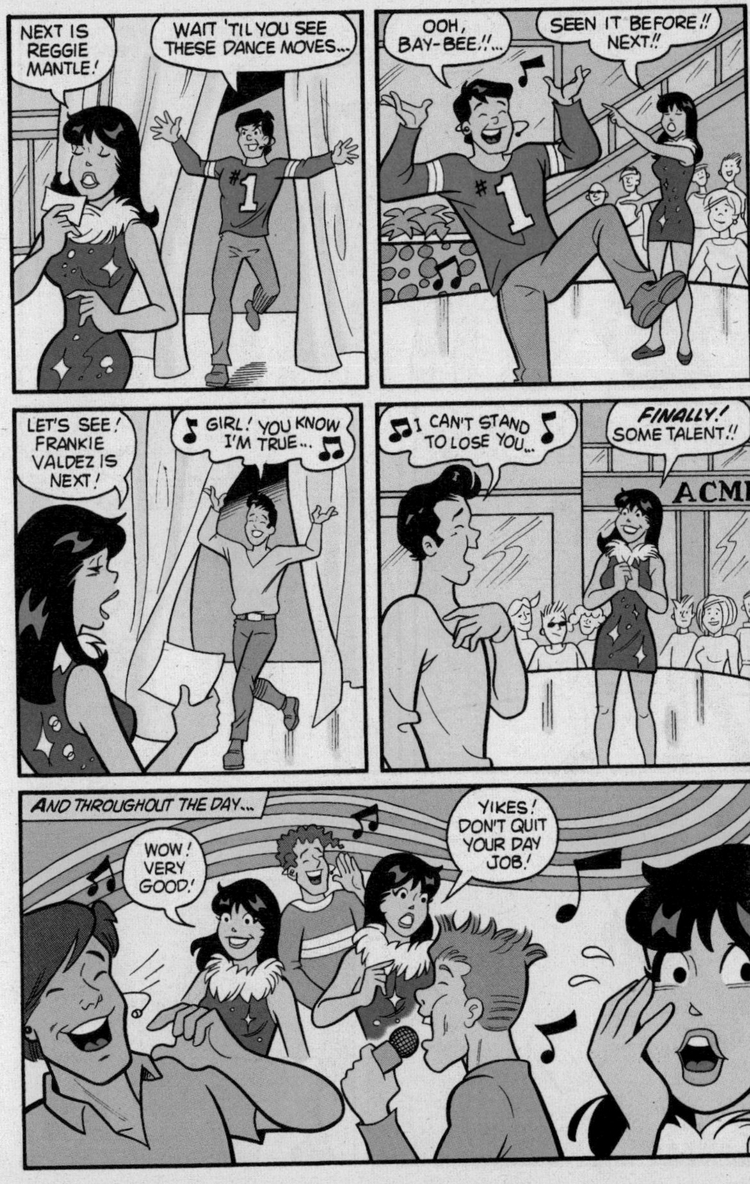
NEXT IS REGGIE MANTLE!
WAIT 'TIL YOU SEE THESE DANCE MOVES...
OOH, BAY-BEE!!...
SEEN IT BEFORE!! NEXT!!
LET'S SEE! FRANKIE VALDEZ IS NEXT!
GIRL! YOU KNOW I'M TRUE...
I CAN'T STAND TO LOSE YOU...
FINALLY! SOME TALENT!!
ACM
AND THROUGHOUT THE DAY...
WOW! VERY GOOD!
YIKES! DON'T QUIT YOUR DAY JOB!
5

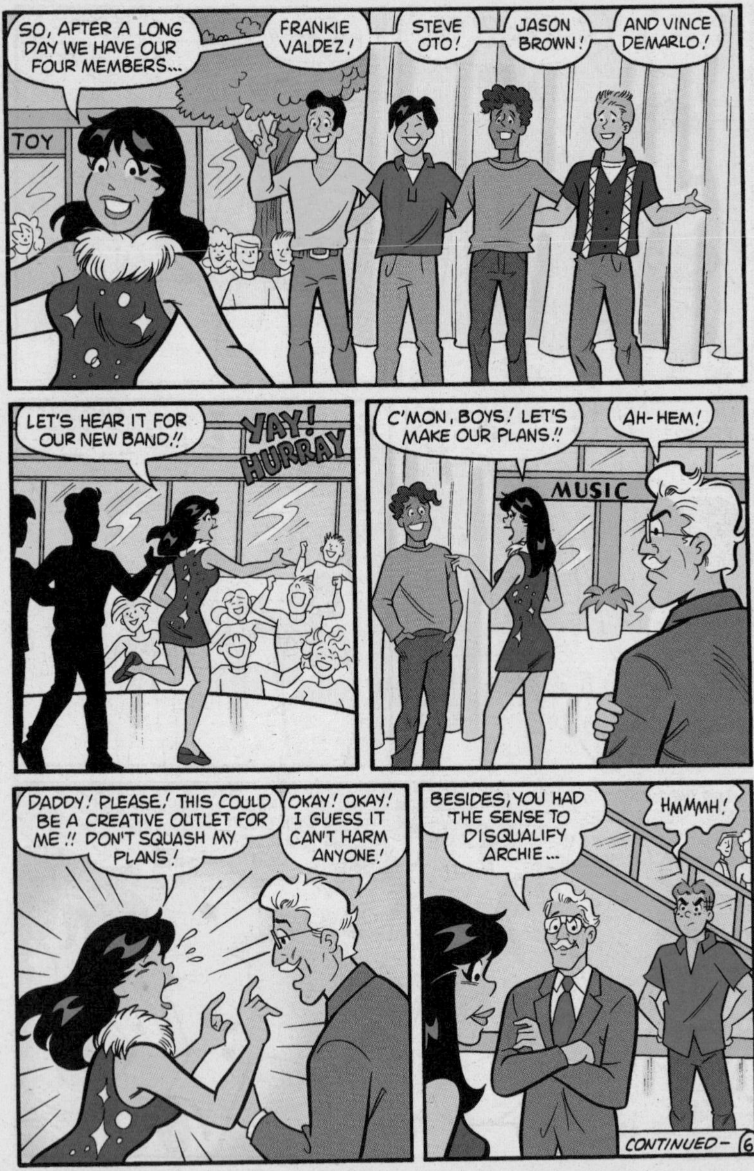
SO, AFTER A LONG DAY WE HAVE OUR FOUR MEMBERS...
FRANKIE VALDEZ!
STEVE OTO!
JASON BROWN!
AND VINCE DEMARLO!
TOY
LET'S HEAR IT FOR OUR NEW BAND!!
YAY! HURRAY
C'MON, BOYS! LET'S MAKE OUR PLANS!!
AH-HEM!
MUSIC
DADDY! PLEASE! THIS COULD BE A CREATIVE OUTLET FOR ME!! DON'T SQUASH MY PLANS!
OKAY! OKAY! I GUESS IT CAN'T HARM ANYONE!
BESIDES, YOU HAD THE SENSE TO DISQUALIFY ARCHIE...
HMMMH!
CONTINUED- 6

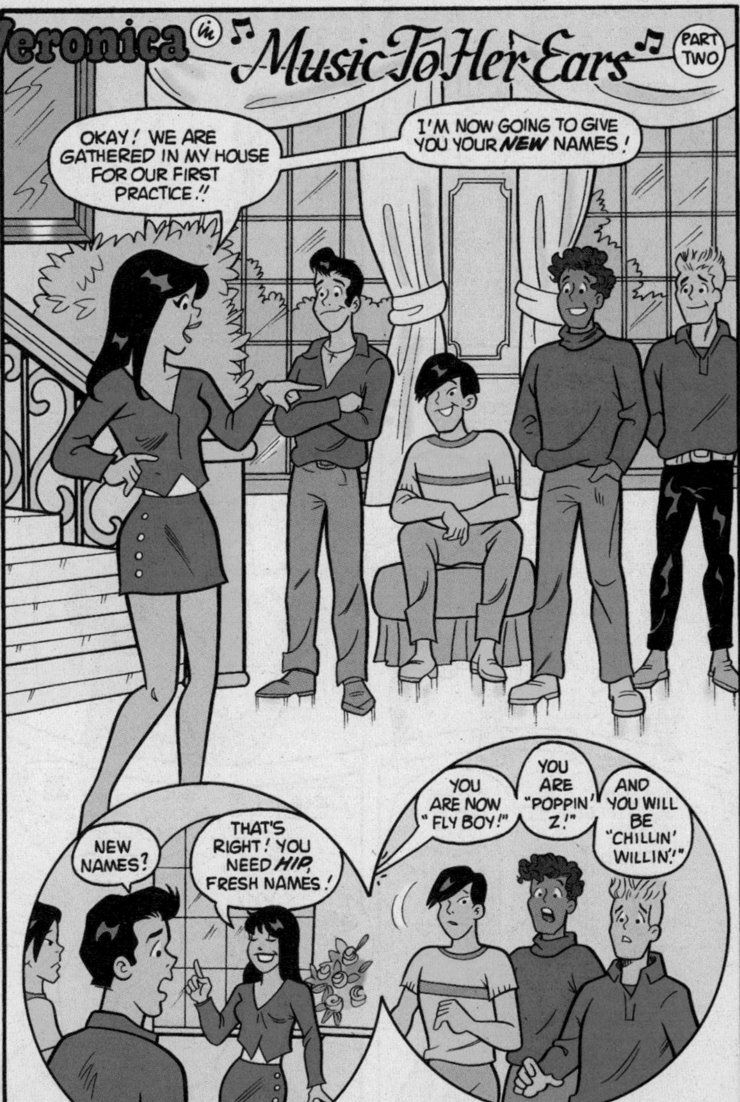
Veronica in
Music To Her Ears
PART TWO
OKAY! WE ARE GATHERED IN MY HOUSE FOR OUR FIRST PRACTICE!!
I'M NOW GOING TO GIVE YOU YOUR NEW NAMES!
NEW NAMES?
THAT'S RIGHT! YOU NEED HIP, FRESH NAMES!
YOU ARE NOW "FLY BOY!"
YOU ARE "POPPIN' Z!"
AND YOU WILL BE "CHILLIN' WILLIN'!"

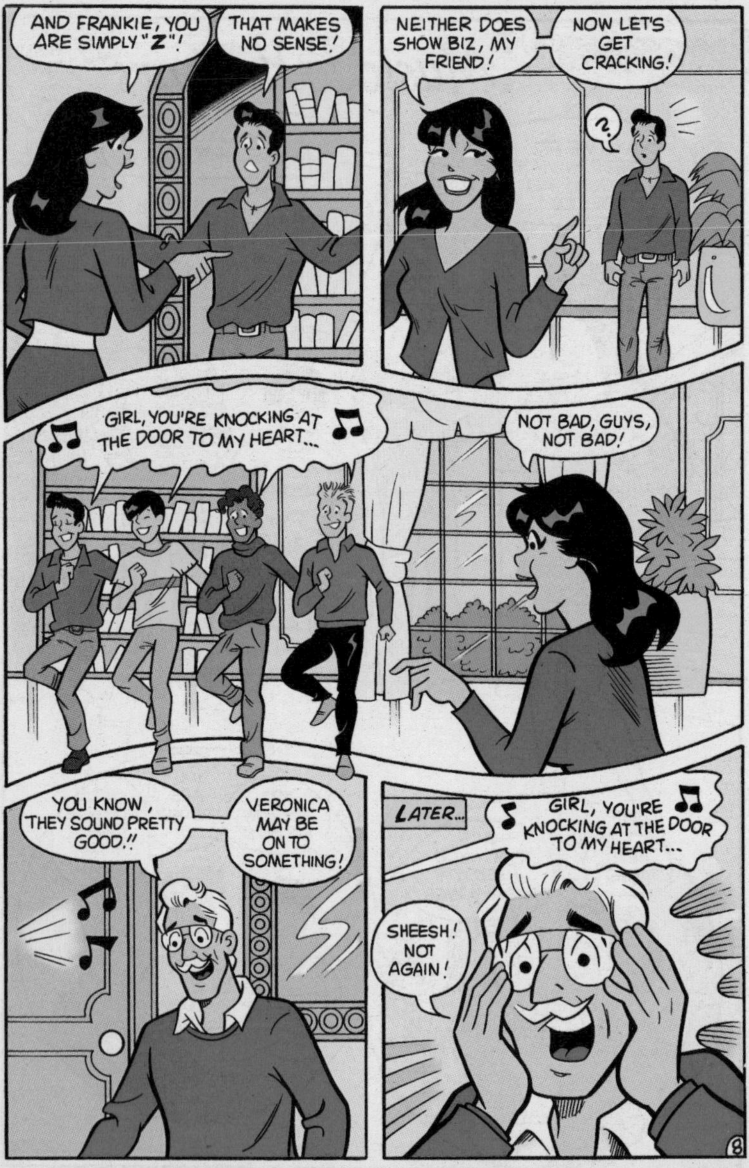
AND FRANKIE, YOU ARE SIMPLY "Z"!
THAT MAKES NO SENSE!
NEITHER DOES SHOW BIZ, MY FRIEND!
NOW LET'S GET CRACKING!
?
GIRL, YOU'RE KNOCKING AT THE DOOR TO MY HEART...
NOT BAD, GUYS, NOT BAD!
YOU KNOW, THEY SOUND PRETTY GOOD!!
VERONICA MAY BE ON TO SOMETHING!
LATER...
GIRL, YOU'RE KNOCKING AT THE DOOR TO MY HEART...
SHEESH! NOT AGAIN!
8

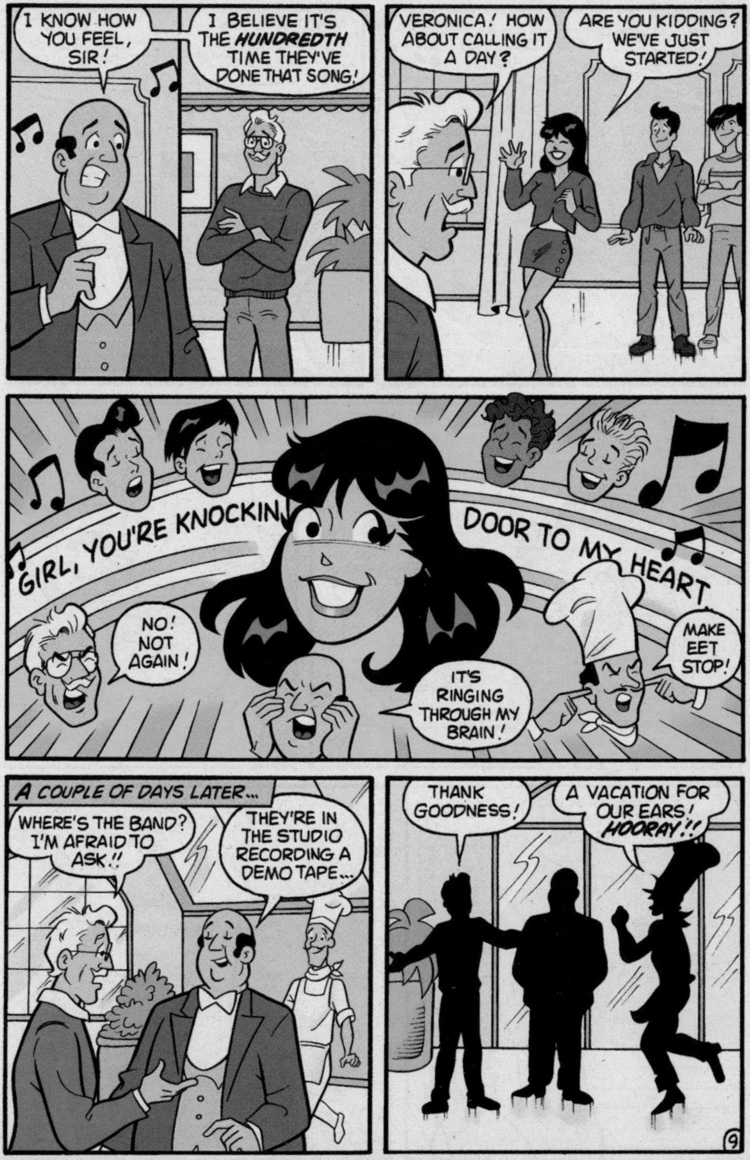

I KNOW HOW YOU FEEL, SIR!
I BELIEVE IT'S THE HUNDREDTH TIME THEY'VE DONE THAT SONG!
VERONICA! HOW ABOUT CALLING IT A DAY?
ARE YOU KIDDING? WE'VE JUST STARTED!
GIRL, YOU'RE KNOCKIN
DOOR TO MY HEART
NO! NOT AGAIN!
IT'S RINGING THROUGH MY BRAIN!
MAKE EET STOP!
A COUPLE OF DAYS LATER...
WHERE'S THE BAND? I'M AFRAID TO ASK!!
THEY'RE IN THE STUDIO RECORDING A DEMO TAPE...
THANK GOODNESS!
A VACATION FOR OUR EARS! HOORAY!!

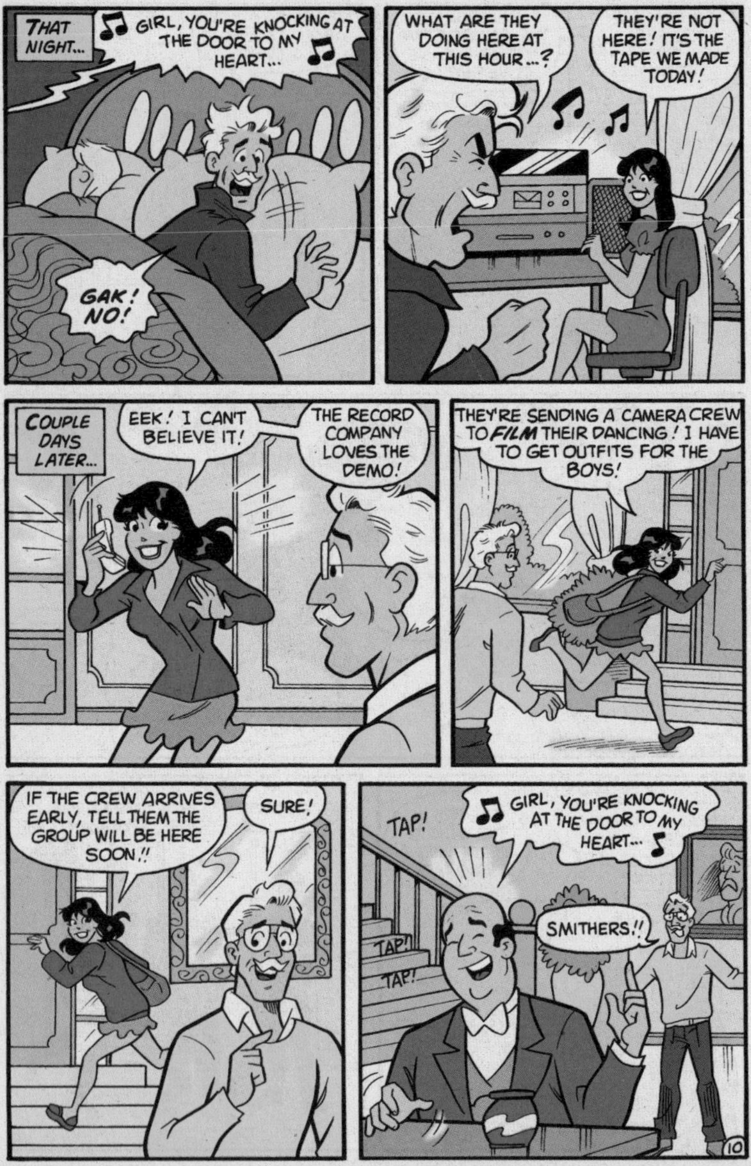
THAT NIGHT...
GIRL, YOU'RE KNOCKING AT THE DOOR TO MY HEART...
GAK! NO!
WHAT ARE THEY DOING HERE AT THIS HOUR...?
THEY'RE NOT HERE! IT'S THE TAPE WE MADE TODAY!
COUPLE DAYS LATER...
EEK! I CAN'T BELIEVE IT!
THE RECORD COMPANY LOVES THE DEMO!
THEY'RE SENDING A CAMERA CREW TO FILM THEIR DANCING! I HAVE TO GET OUTFITS FOR THE BOYS!
IF THE CREW ARRIVES EARLY, TELL THEM THE GROUP WILL BE HERE SOON.!!
SURE!
TAP!
TAP!
TAP!
GIRL, YOU'RE KNOCKING AT THE DOOR TO MY HEART...
SMITHERS!!

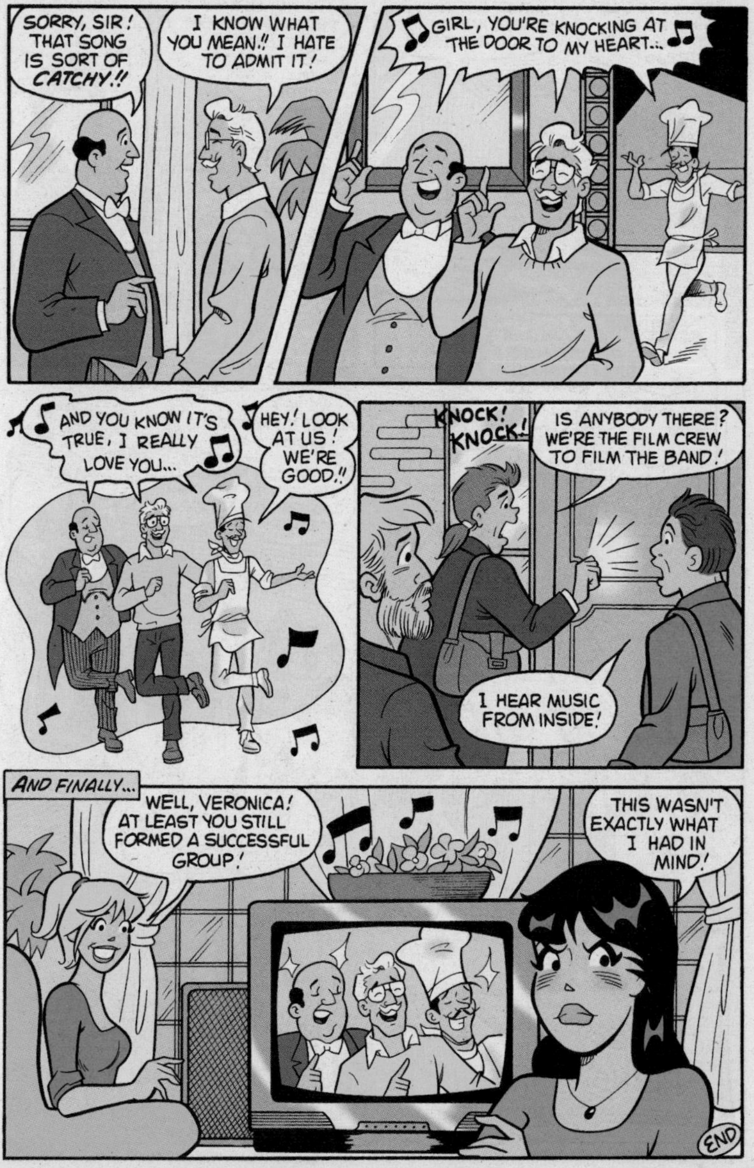
SORRY, SIR! THAT SONG IS SORT OF CATCHY!!
I KNOW WHAT YOU MEAN!! I HATE TO ADMIT IT!
GIRL, YOU'RE KNOCKING AT THE DOOR TO MY HEART...
AND YOU KNOW IT'S TRUE, I REALLY LOVE YOU...
HEY! LOOK AT US! WE'RE GOOD!!
KNOCK! KNOCK!
IS ANYBODY THERE? WE'RE THE FILM CREW TO FILM THE BAND!
I HEAR MUSIC FROM INSIDE!
AND FINALLY...
WELL, VERONICA! AT LEAST YOU STILL FORMED A SUCCESSFUL GROUP!
THIS WASN'T EXACTLY WHAT I HAD IN MIND!
END

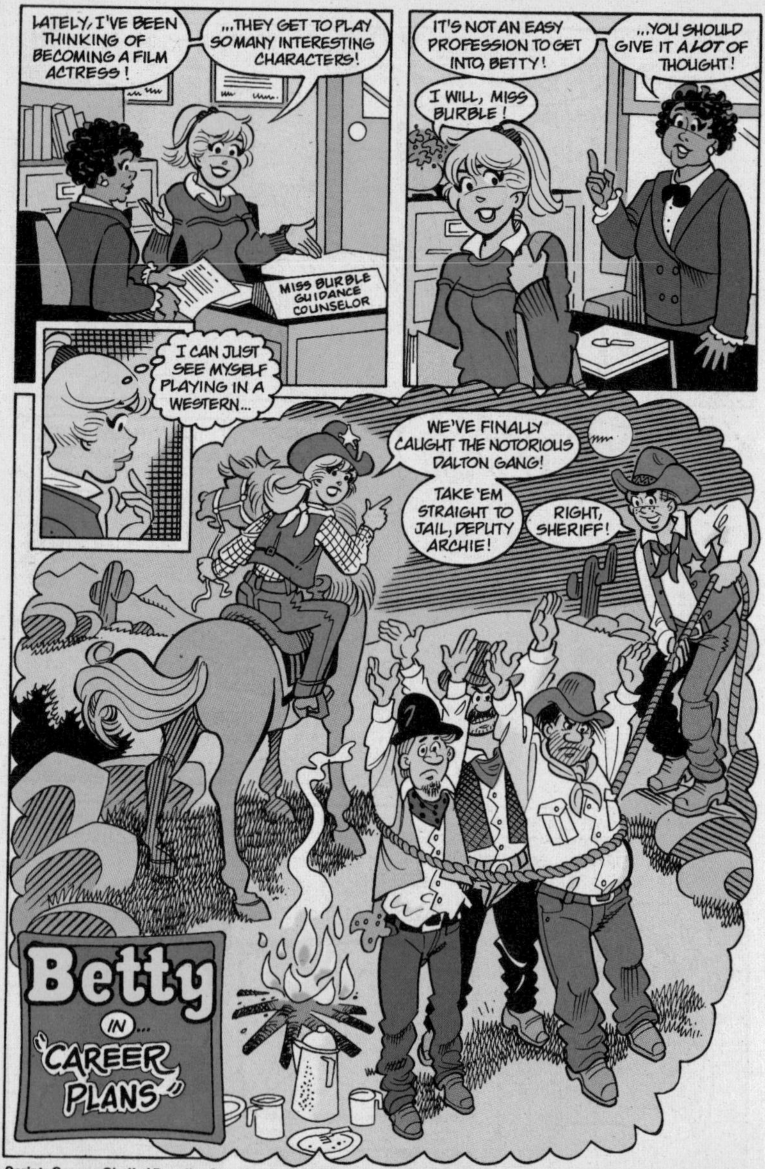
LATELY, I'VE BEEN THINKING OF BECOMING A FILM ACTRESS!
...THEY GET TO PLAY SO MANY INTERESTING CHARACTERS!
MISS BURBLE GUIDANCE COUNSELOR
IT'S NOT AN EASY PROFESSION TO GET INTO, BETTY!
...YOU SHOULD GIVE IT A LOT OF THOUGHT!
I WILL, MISS BURBLE!
I CAN JUST SEE MYSELF PLAYING IN A WESTERN...
WE'VE FINALLY CAUGHT THE NOTORIOUS DALTON GANG!
TAKE 'EM STRAIGHT TO JAIL, DEPUTY ARCHIE!
RIGHT, SHERIFF!
Betty
IN...
CAREER PLANS

Script: George Gladir / Pencils: Stan Goldberg / Inks: John Lowe / Letters: Vickie Williams / Colors: Barry Grossman

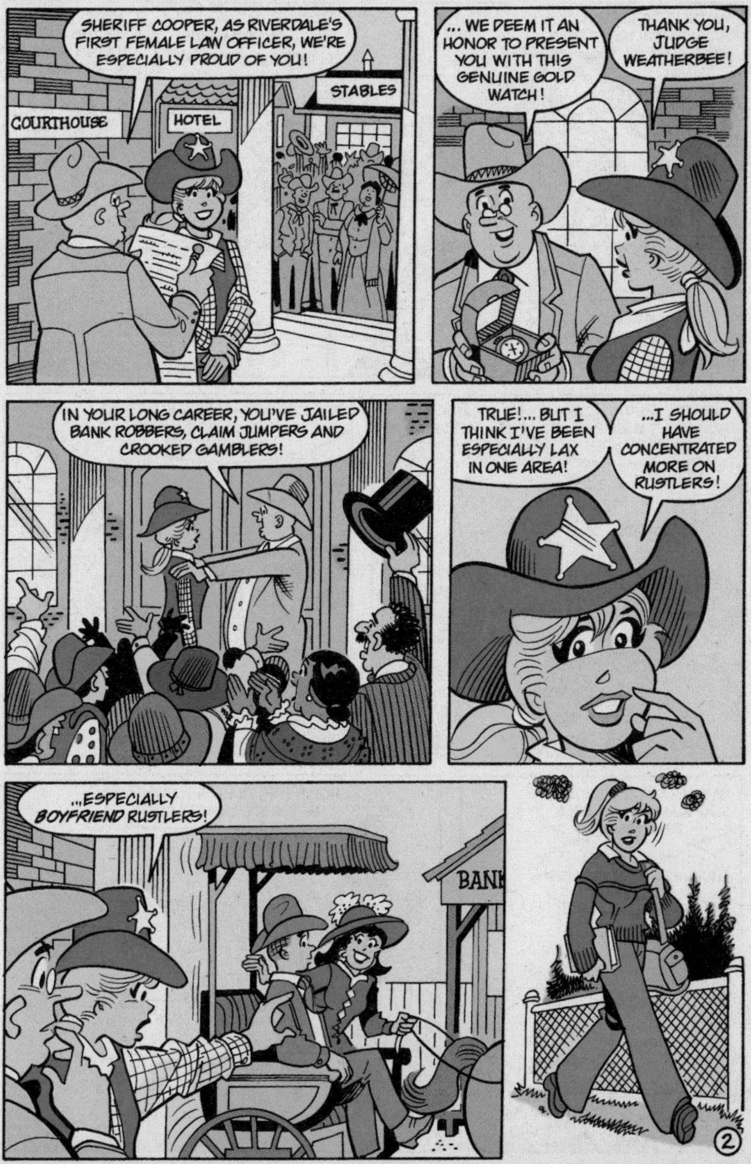
SHERIFF COOPER, AS RIVERDALE'S FIRST FEMALE LAW OFFICER, WE'RE ESPECIALLY PROUD OF YOU!
COURTHOUSE
HOTEL
STABLES
... WE DEEM IT AN HONOR TO PRESENT YOU WITH THIS GENUINE GOLD WATCH!
THANK YOU, JUDGE WEATHERBEE!
IN YOUR LONG CAREER, YOU'VE JAILED BANK ROBBERS, CLAIM JUMPERS AND CROOKED GAMBLERS!
TRUE!... BUT I THINK I'VE BEEN ESPECIALLY LAX IN ONE AREA!
...I SHOULD HAVE CONCENTRATED MORE ON RUSTLERS!
...ESPECIALLY BOYFRIEND RUSTLERS!
BANK
2

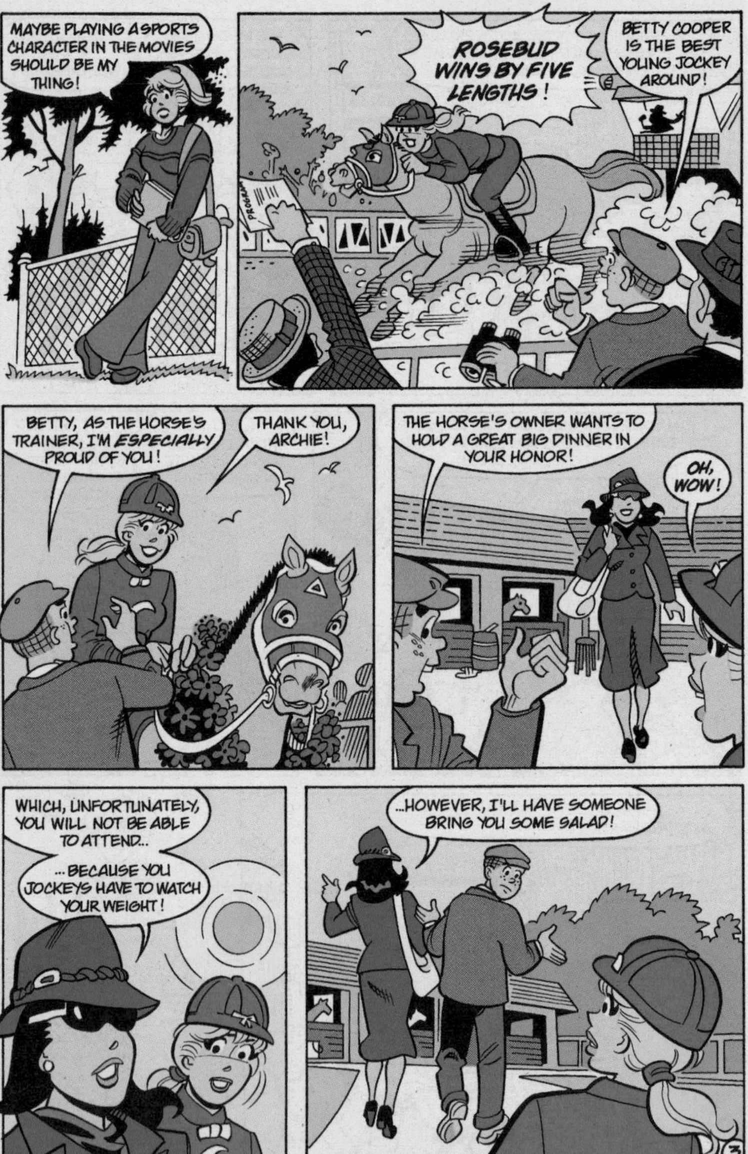
MAYBE PLAYING A SPORTS CHARACTER IN THE MOVIES SHOULD BE MY THING!
ROSEBUD WINS BY FIVE LENGTHS!
BETTY COOPER IS THE BEST YOUNG JOCKEY AROUND!
PROGRAM
BETTY, AS THE HORSE'S TRAINER, I'M ESPECIALLY PROUD OF YOU!
THANK YOU, ARCHIE!
THE HORSE'S OWNER WANTS TO HOLD A GREAT BIG DINNER IN YOUR HONOR!
OH, WOW!
WHICH, UNFORTUNATELY, YOU WILL NOT BE ABLE TO ATTEND...
...BECAUSE YOU JOCKEYS HAVE TO WATCH YOUR WEIGHT!
...HOWEVER, I'LL HAVE SOMEONE BRING YOU SOME SALAD!
3

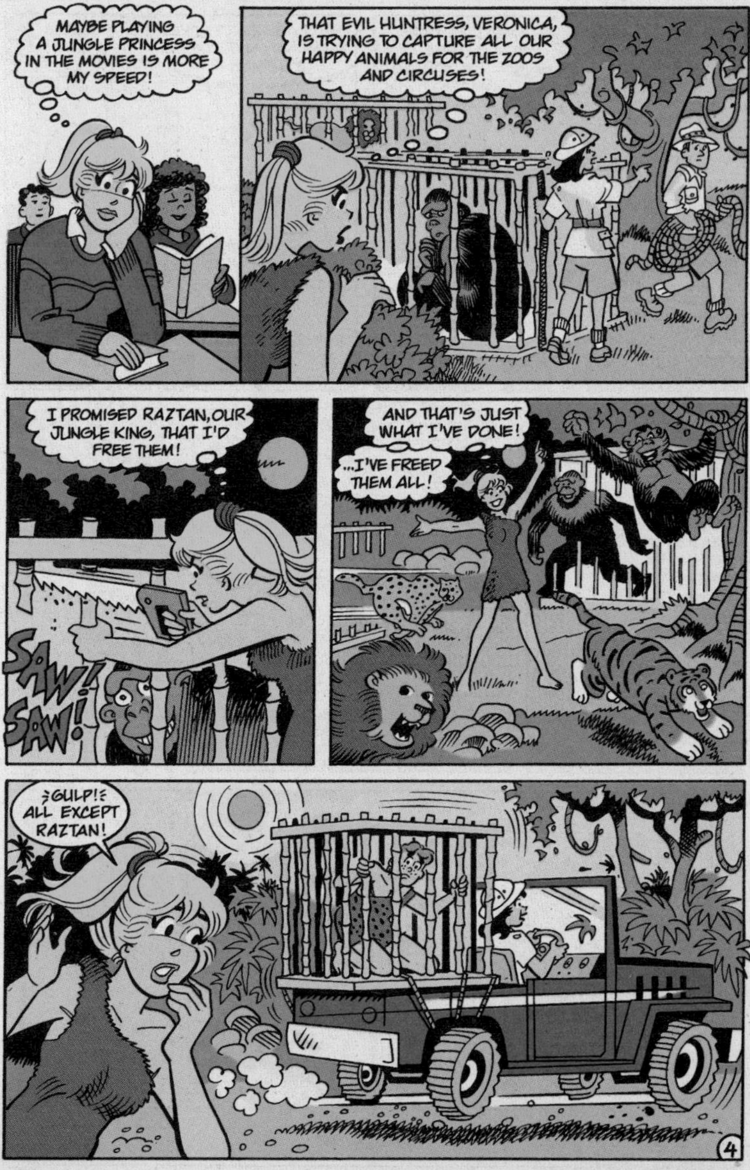

MAYBE PLAYING A JUNGLE PRINCESS IN THE MOVIES IS MORE MY SPEED!
THAT EVIL HUNTRESS, VERONICA, IS TRYING TO CAPTURE ALL OUR HAPPY ANIMALS FOR THE ZOOS AND CIRCUSES!
I PROMISED RAZTAN, OUR JUNGLE KING, THAT I'D FREE THEM!
SAW! SAW!
AND THAT'S JUST WHAT I'VE DONE!
...I'VE FREED THEM ALL!
GULP! ALL EXCEPT RAZTAN!

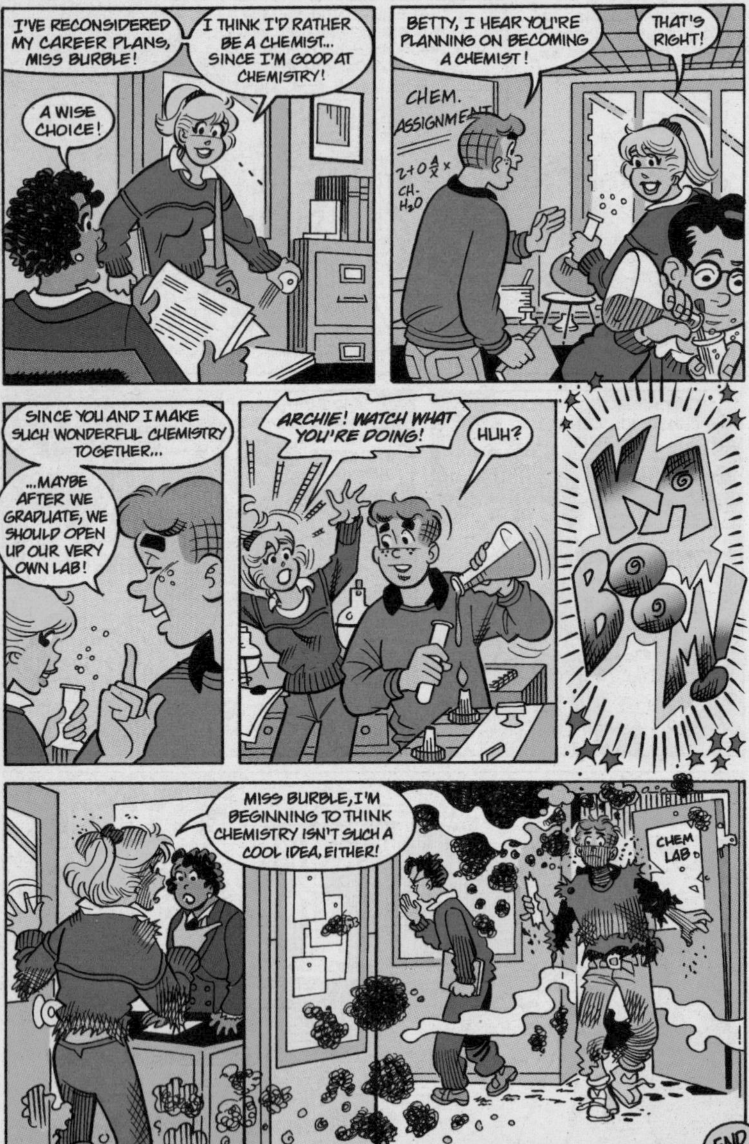
I'VE RECONSIDERED MY CAREER PLANS, MISS BURBLE!
I THINK I'D RATHER BE A CHEMIST... SINCE I'M GOOD AT CHEMISTRY!
A WISE CHOICE!
BETTY, I HEAR YOU'RE PLANNING ON BECOMING A CHEMIST!
THAT'S RIGHT!
CHEM. ASSIGNMENT
SINCE YOU AND I MAKE SUCH WONDERFUL CHEMISTRY TOGETHER...
...MAYBE AFTER WE GRADUATE, WE SHOULD OPEN UP OUR VERY OWN LAB!
ARCHIE! WATCH WHAT YOU'RE DOING!
HUH?
KA BOOM!
MISS BURBLE, I'M BEGINNING TO THINK CHEMISTRY ISN'T SUCH A COOL IDEA, EITHER!
CHEM LAB
END

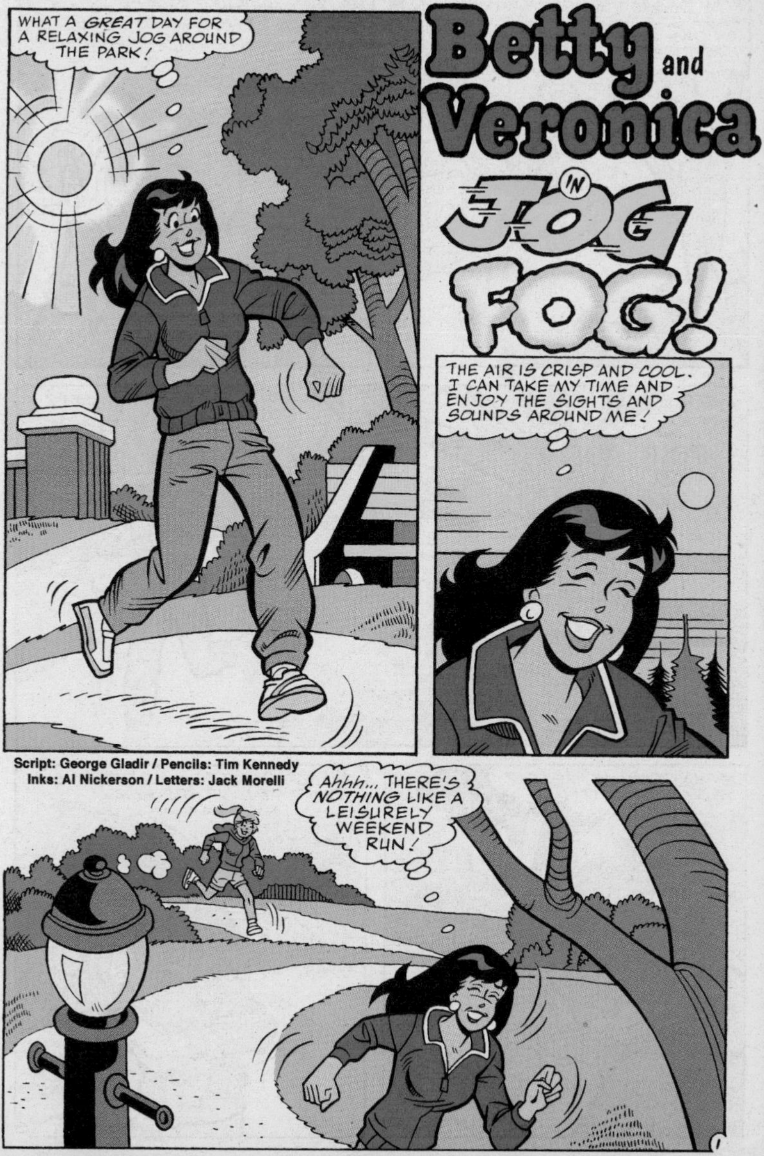
WHAT A GREAT DAY FOR A RELAXING JOG AROUND THE PARK!
Betty and Veronica
IN
JOG FOG!
THE AIR IS CRISP AND COOL. I CAN TAKE MY TIME AND ENJOY THE SIGHTS AND SOUNDS AROUND ME!
Script: George Gladir / Pencils: Tim Kennedy
Inks: Al Nickerson / Letters: Jack Morelli
Ahhh... THERE'S NOTHING LIKE A LEISURELY WEEKEND RUN!

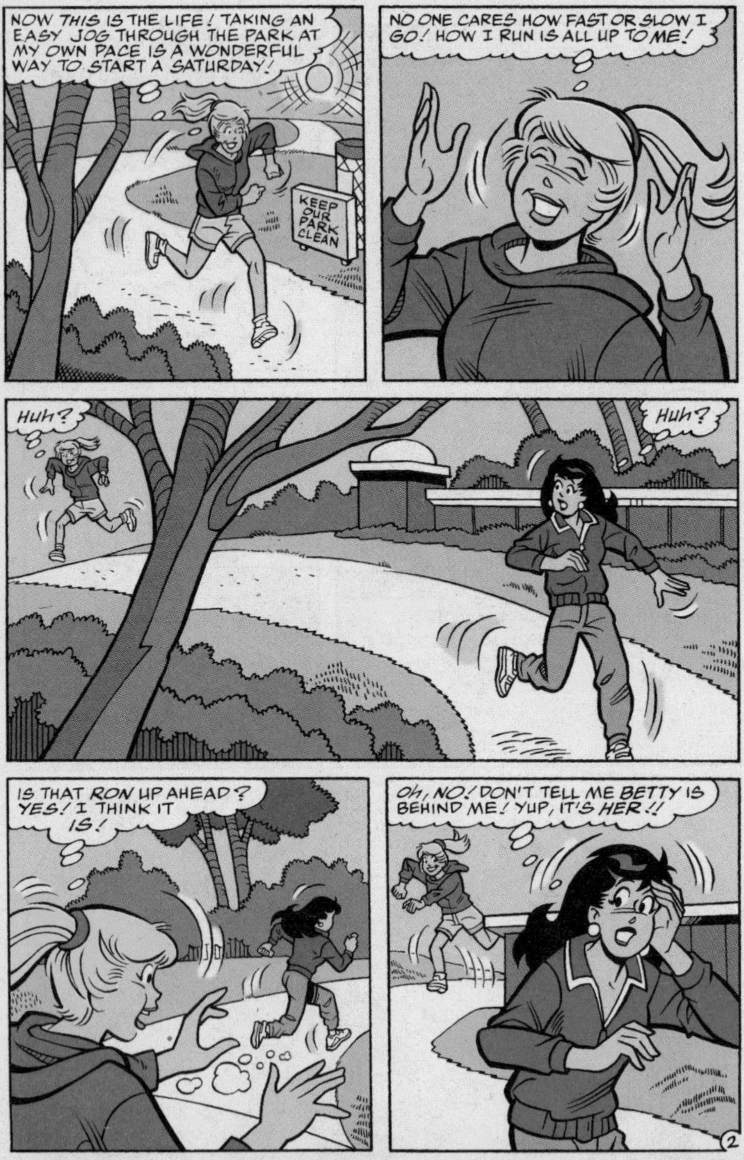

NOW THIS IS THE LIFE! TAKING AN EASY JOG THROUGH THE PARK AT MY OWN PACE IS A WONDERFUL WAY TO START A SATURDAY!
KEEP OUR PARK CLEAN
NO ONE CARES HOW FAST OR SLOW I GO! HOW I RUN IS ALL UP TO ME!
Huh?
Huh?
IS THAT RON UP AHEAD? YES! I THINK IT IS!
Oh, NO! DON'T TELL ME BETTY IS BEHIND ME! YUP, IT'S HER!!
2

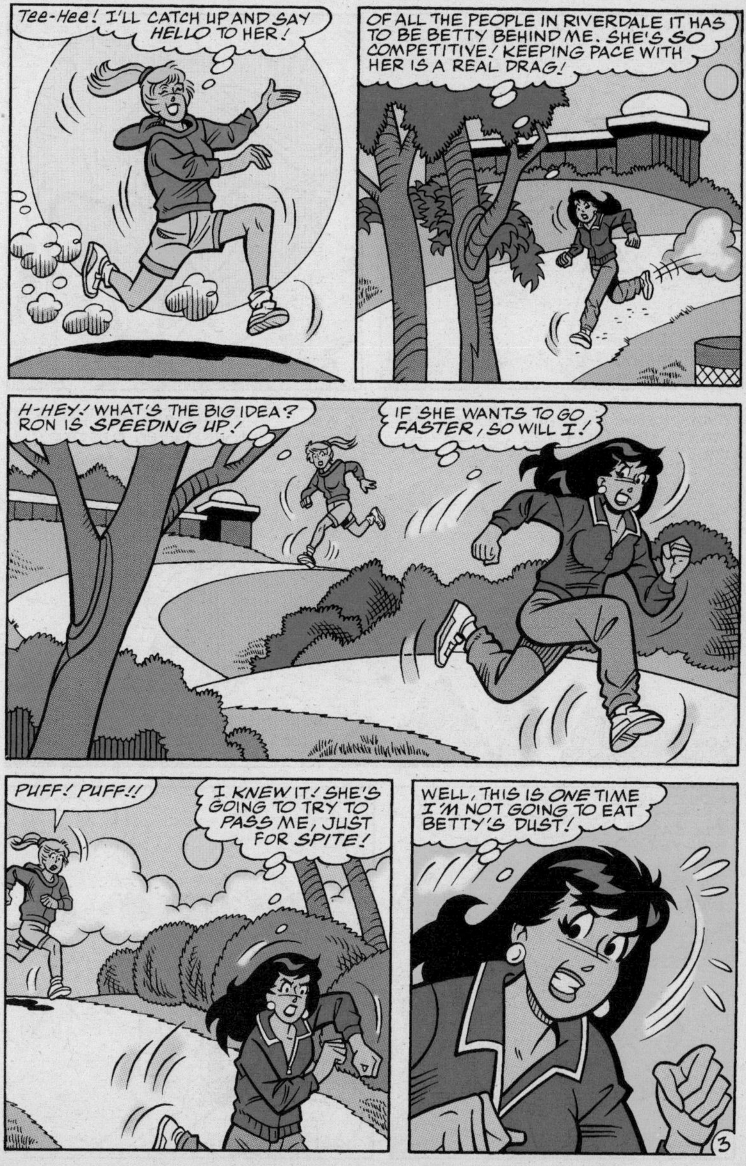
Tee-Hee! I'LL CATCH UP AND SAY HELLO TO HER!
OF ALL THE PEOPLE IN RIVERDALE IT HAS TO BE BETTY BEHIND ME. SHE'S SO COMPETITIVE! KEEPING PACE WITH HER IS A REAL DRAG!
H-HEY! WHAT'S THE BIG IDEA? RON IS SPEEDING UP!
IF SHE WANTS TO GO FASTER, SO WILL I!
PUFF! PUFF!!
I KNEW IT! SHE'S GOING TO TRY TO PASS ME, JUST FOR SPITE!
WELL, THIS IS ONE TIME I'M NOT GOING TO EAT BETTY'S DUST!

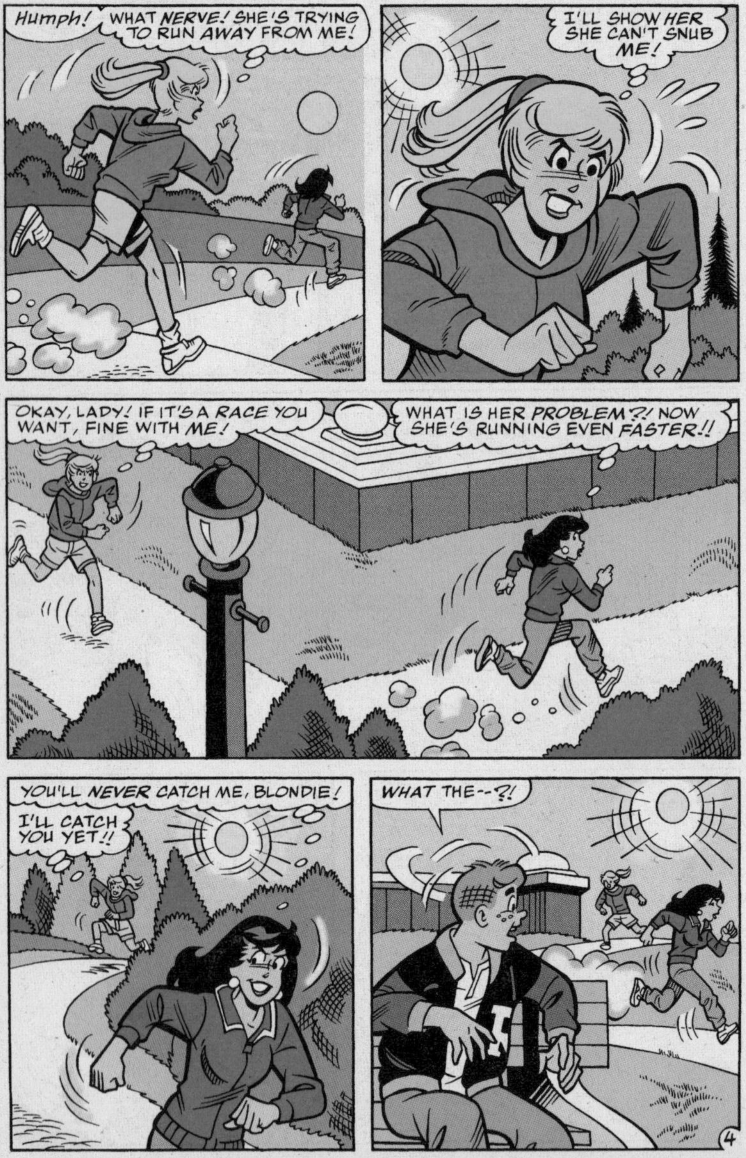

Humph!
WHAT NERVE! SHE'S TRYING TO RUN AWAY FROM ME!
I'LL SHOW HER SHE CAN'T SNUB ME!
OKAY, LADY! IF IT'S A RACE YOU WANT, FINE WITH ME!
WHAT IS HER PROBLEM?! NOW SHE'S RUNNING EVEN FASTER!!
YOU'LL NEVER CATCH ME, BLONDIE!
I'LL CATCH YOU YET!!
WHAT THE--?!
4

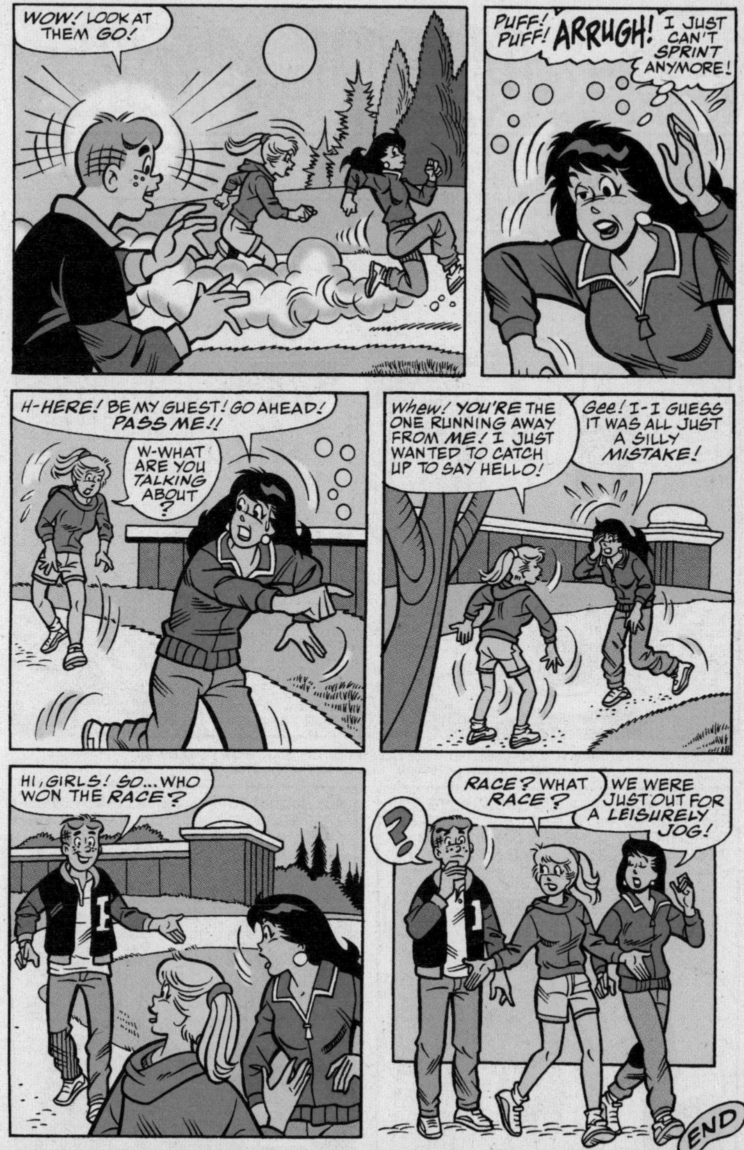
WOW! LOOK AT THEM GO!
PUFF! PUFF! ARRUGH! I JUST CAN'T SPRINT ANYMORE!
H-HERE! BE MY GUEST! GO AHEAD! PASS ME!!
W-WHAT ARE YOU TALKING ABOUT?
Whew! YOU'RE THE ONE RUNNING AWAY FROM ME! I JUST WANTED TO CATCH UP TO SAY HELLO!
Gee! I-I GUESS IT WAS ALL JUST A SILLY MISTAKE!
HI, GIRLS! SO... WHO WON THE RACE?
?
RACE? WHAT RACE?
WE WERE JUST OUT FOR A LEISURELY JOG!
END

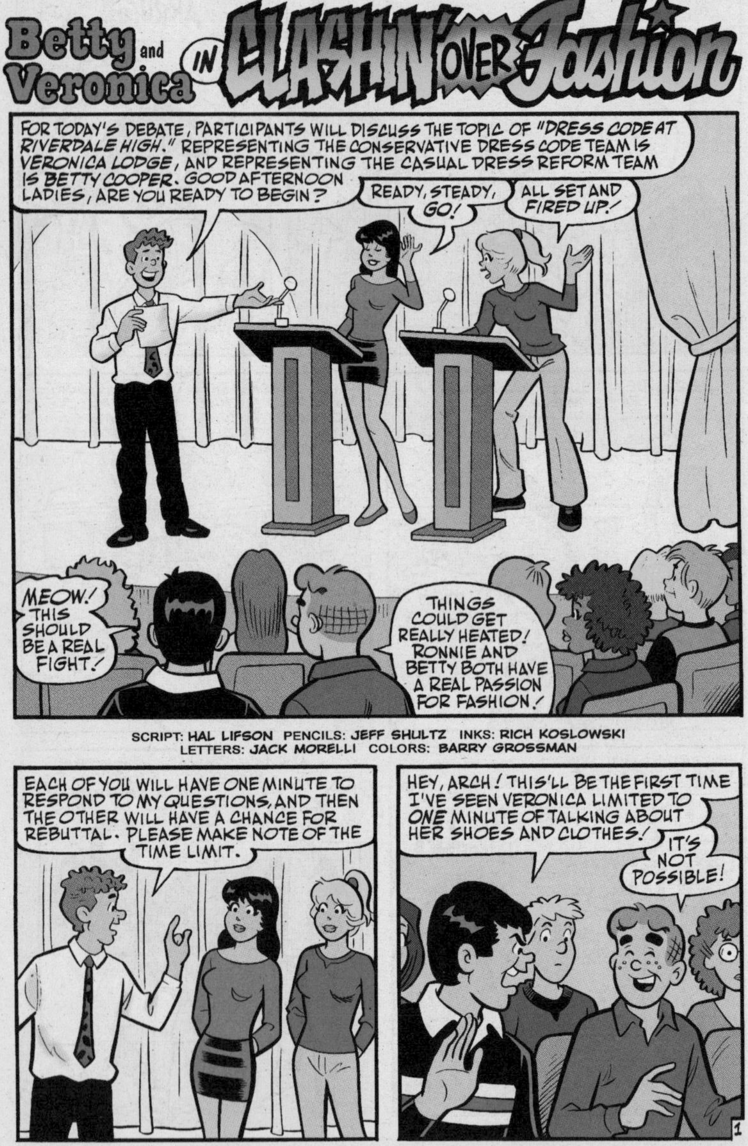
Betty and Veronica IN CLASHIN' OVER Fashion
FOR TODAY'S DEBATE, PARTICIPANTS WILL DISCUSS THE TOPIC OF "DRESS CODE AT RIVERDALE HIGH." REPRESENTING THE CONSERVATIVE DRESS CODE TEAM IS VERONICA LODGE, AND REPRESENTING THE CASUAL DRESS REFORM TEAM IS BETTY COOPER. GOOD AFTERNOON LADIES, ARE YOU READY TO BEGIN?
READY, STEADY, GO!
ALL SET AND FIRED UP!
MEOW! THIS SHOULD BE A REAL FIGHT!
THINGS COULD GET REALLY HEATED! RONNIE AND BETTY BOTH HAVE A REAL PASSION FOR FASHION!
SCRIPT: HAL LIFSON PENCILS: JEFF SHULTZ INKS: RICH KOSLOWSKI
LETTERS: JACK MORELLI COLORS: BARRY GROSSMAN
EACH OF YOU WILL HAVE ONE MINUTE TO RESPOND TO MY QUESTIONS, AND THEN THE OTHER WILL HAVE A CHANCE FOR REBUTTAL. PLEASE MAKE NOTE OF THE TIME LIMIT.
HEY, ARCH! THIS'LL BE THE FIRST TIME I'VE SEEN VERONICA LIMITED TO ONE MINUTE OF TALKING ABOUT HER SHOES AND CLOTHES!
IT'S NOT POSSIBLE!
1

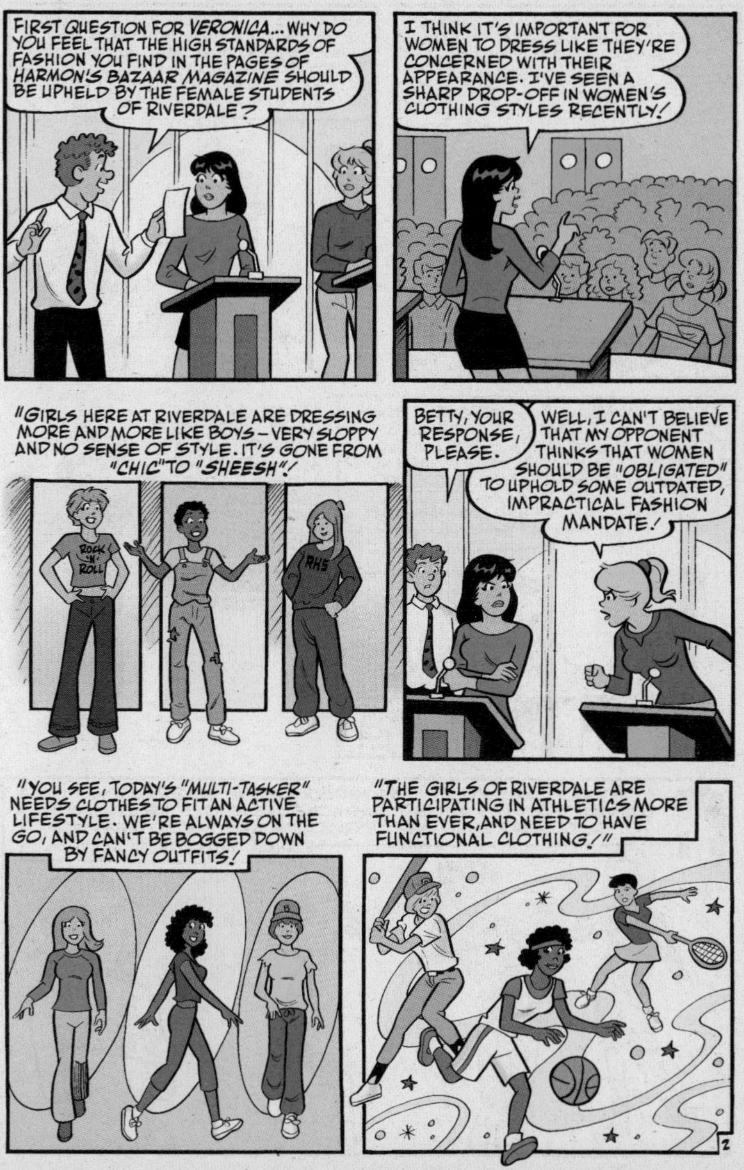
FIRST QUESTION FOR VERONICA... WHY DO YOU FEEL THAT THE HIGH STANDARDS OF FASHION YOU FIND IN THE PAGES OF HARMON'S BAZAAR MAGAZINE SHOULD BE UPHELD BY THE FEMALE STUDENTS OF RIVERDALE?
I THINK IT'S IMPORTANT FOR WOMEN TO DRESS LIKE THEY'RE CONCERNED WITH THEIR APPEARANCE. I'VE SEEN A SHARP DROP-OFF IN WOMEN'S CLOTHING STYLES RECENTLY!
"GIRLS HERE AT RIVERDALE ARE DRESSING MORE AND MORE LIKE BOYS – VERY SLOPPY AND NO SENSE OF STYLE. IT'S GONE FROM "CHIC" TO "SHEESH"!
ROCK 'N' ROLL
RHS
BETTY, YOUR RESPONSE, PLEASE.
WELL, I CAN'T BELIEVE THAT MY OPPONENT THINKS THAT WOMEN SHOULD BE "OBLIGATED" TO UPHOLD SOME OUTDATED, IMPRACTICAL FASHION MANDATE!
"YOU SEE, TODAY'S "MULTI-TASKER" NEEDS CLOTHES TO FIT AN ACTIVE LIFESTYLE. WE'RE ALWAYS ON THE GO, AND CAN'T BE BOGGED DOWN BY FANCY OUTFITS!
"THE GIRLS OF RIVERDALE ARE PARTICIPATING IN ATHLETICS MORE THAN EVER, AND NEED TO HAVE FUNCTIONAL CLOTHING!"
2

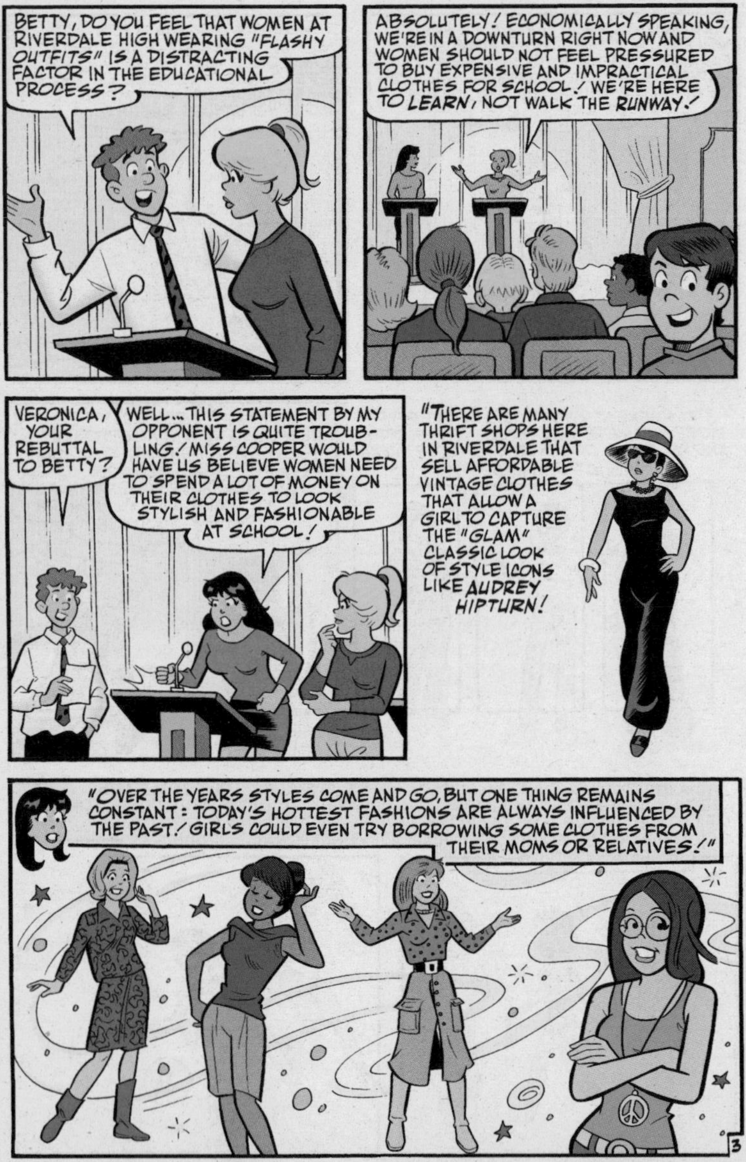
BETTY, DO YOU FEEL THAT WOMEN AT RIVERDALE HIGH WEARING "FLASHY OUTFITS" IS A DISTRACTING FACTOR IN THE EDUCATIONAL PROCESS?
ABSOLUTELY! ECONOMICALLY SPEAKING, WE'RE IN A DOWNTURN RIGHT NOW AND WOMEN SHOULD NOT FEEL PRESSURED TO BUY EXPENSIVE AND IMPRACTICAL CLOTHES FOR SCHOOL! WE'RE HERE TO LEARN, NOT WALK THE RUNWAY!
VERONICA, YOUR REBUTTAL TO BETTY?
WELL... THIS STATEMENT BY MY OPPONENT IS QUITE TROUBLING! MISS COOPER WOULD HAVE US BELIEVE WOMEN NEED TO SPEND A LOT OF MONEY ON THEIR CLOTHES TO LOOK STYLISH AND FASHIONABLE AT SCHOOL!
"THERE ARE MANY THRIFT SHOPS HERE IN RIVERDALE THAT SELL AFFORDABLE VINTAGE CLOTHES THAT ALLOW A GIRL TO CAPTURE THE "GLAM" CLASSIC LOOK OF STYLE ICONS LIKE AUDREY HIPTURN!
"OVER THE YEARS STYLES COME AND GO, BUT ONE THING REMAINS CONSTANT: TODAY'S HOTTEST FASHIONS ARE ALWAYS INFLUENCED BY THE PAST! GIRLS COULD EVEN TRY BORROWING SOME CLOTHES FROM THEIR MOMS OR RELATIVES!"
3

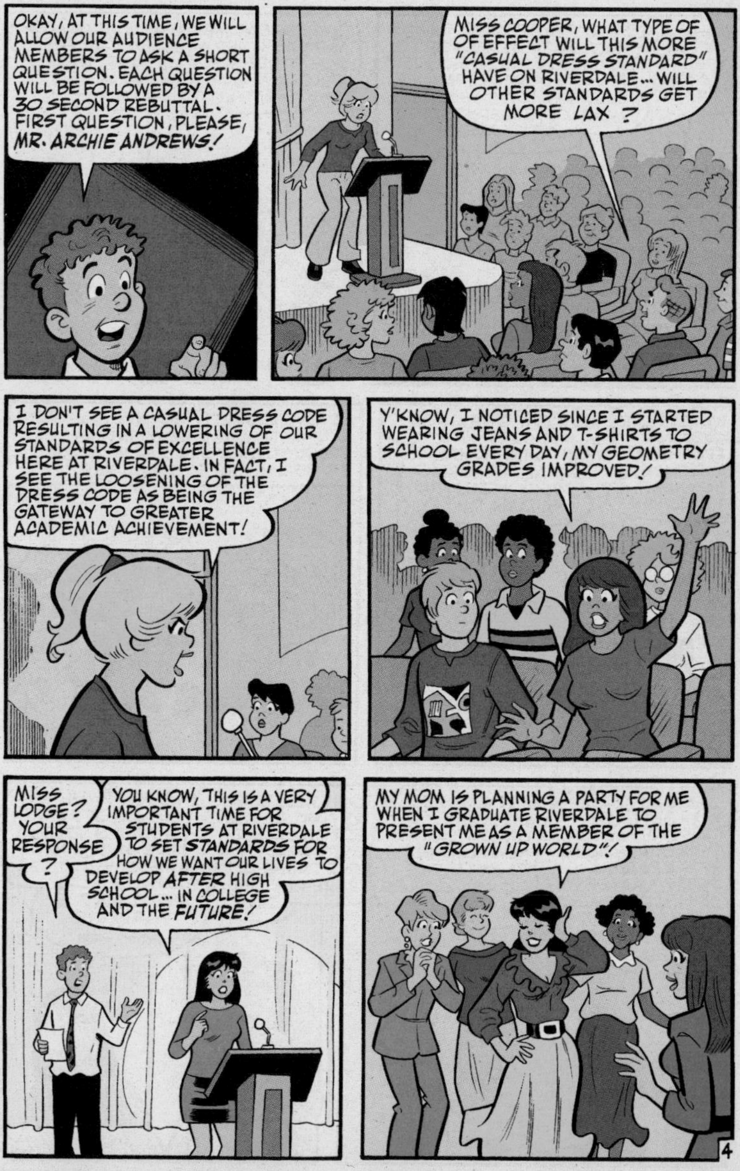
OKAY, AT THIS TIME, WE WILL ALLOW OUR AUDIENCE MEMBERS TO ASK A SHORT QUESTION. EACH QUESTION WILL BE FOLLOWED BY A 30 SECOND REBUTTAL. FIRST QUESTION, PLEASE, MR. ARCHIE ANDREWS!
MISS COOPER, WHAT TYPE OF OF EFFECT WILL THIS MORE "CASUAL DRESS STANDARD" HAVE ON RIVERDALE... WILL OTHER STANDARDS GET MORE LAX ?
I DON'T SEE A CASUAL DRESS CODE RESULTING IN A LOWERING OF OUR STANDARDS OF EXCELLENCE HERE AT RIVERDALE. IN FACT, I SEE THE LOOSENING OF THE DRESS CODE AS BEING THE GATEWAY TO GREATER ACADEMIC ACHIEVEMENT!
Y'KNOW, I NOTICED SINCE I STARTED WEARING JEANS AND T-SHIRTS TO SCHOOL EVERY DAY, MY GEOMETRY GRADES IMPROVED!
MISS LODGE? YOUR RESPONSE ?
YOU KNOW, THIS IS A VERY IMPORTANT TIME FOR STUDENTS AT RIVERDALE TO SET STANDARDS FOR HOW WE WANT OUR LIVES TO DEVELOP AFTER HIGH SCHOOL... IN COLLEGE AND THE FUTURE!
MY MOM IS PLANNING A PARTY FOR ME WHEN I GRADUATE RIVERDALE TO PRESENT ME AS A MEMBER OF THE "GROWN UP WORLD"!
4

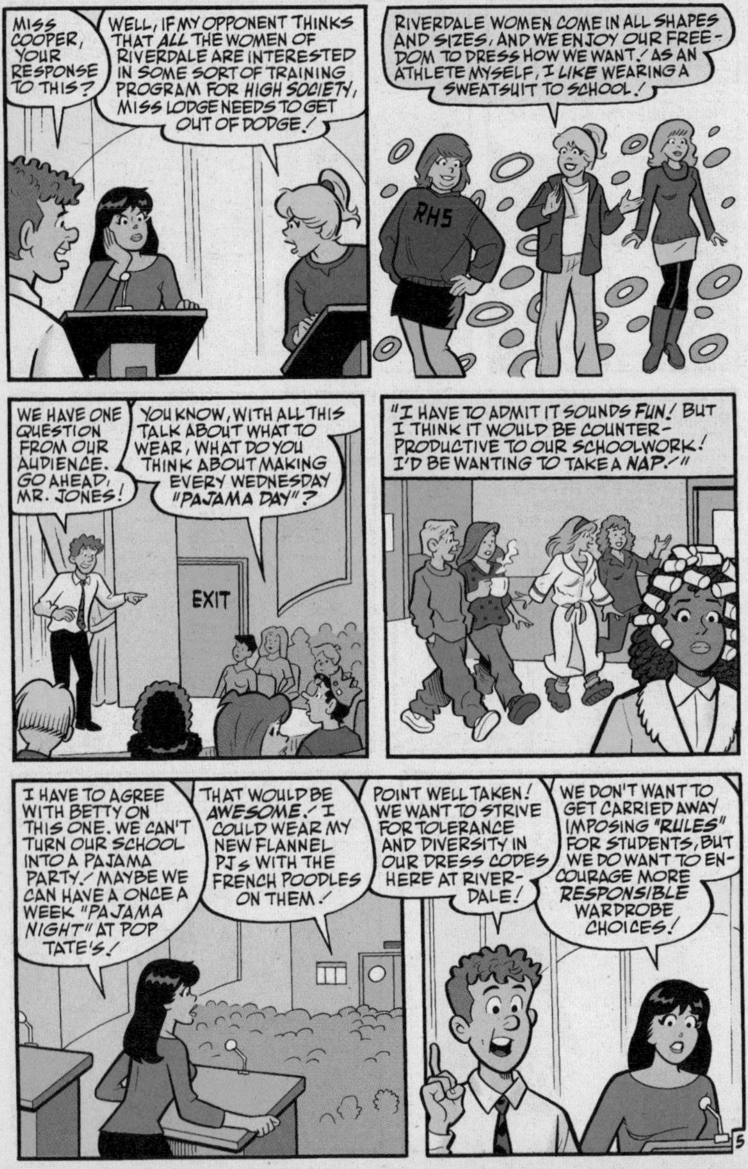
MISS COOPER, YOUR RESPONSE TO THIS?
WELL, IF MY OPPONENT THINKS THAT ALL THE WOMEN OF RIVERDALE ARE INTERESTED IN SOME SORT OF TRAINING PROGRAM FOR HIGH SOCIETY, MISS LODGE NEEDS TO GET OUT OF DODGE!
RIVERDALE WOMEN COME IN ALL SHAPES AND SIZES, AND WE ENJOY OUR FREE-DOM TO DRESS HOW WE WANT! AS AN ATHLETE MYSELF, I LIKE WEARING A SWEATSUIT TO SCHOOL!
RHS
WE HAVE ONE QUESTION FROM OUR AUDIENCE. GO AHEAD, MR. JONES!
YOU KNOW, WITH ALL THIS TALK ABOUT WHAT TO WEAR, WHAT DO YOU THINK ABOUT MAKING EVERY WEDNESDAY "PAJAMA DAY"?
EXIT
"I HAVE TO ADMIT IT SOUNDS FUN! BUT I THINK IT WOULD BE COUNTER-PRODUCTIVE TO OUR SCHOOLWORK! I'D BE WANTING TO TAKE A NAP!"
I HAVE TO AGREE WITH BETTY ON THIS ONE. WE CAN'T TURN OUR SCHOOL INTO A PAJAMA PARTY! MAYBE WE CAN HAVE A ONCE A WEEK "PAJAMA NIGHT" AT POP TATE'S!
THAT WOULD BE AWESOME! I COULD WEAR MY NEW FLANNEL PJs WITH THE FRENCH POODLES ON THEM!
POINT WELL TAKEN! WE WANT TO STRIVE FOR TOLERANCE AND DIVERSITY IN OUR DRESS CODES HERE AT RIVER-DALE!
WE DON'T WANT TO GET CARRIED AWAY IMPOSING "RULES" FOR STUDENTS, BUT WE DO WANT TO EN-COURAGE MORE RESPONSIBLE WARDROBE CHOICES!

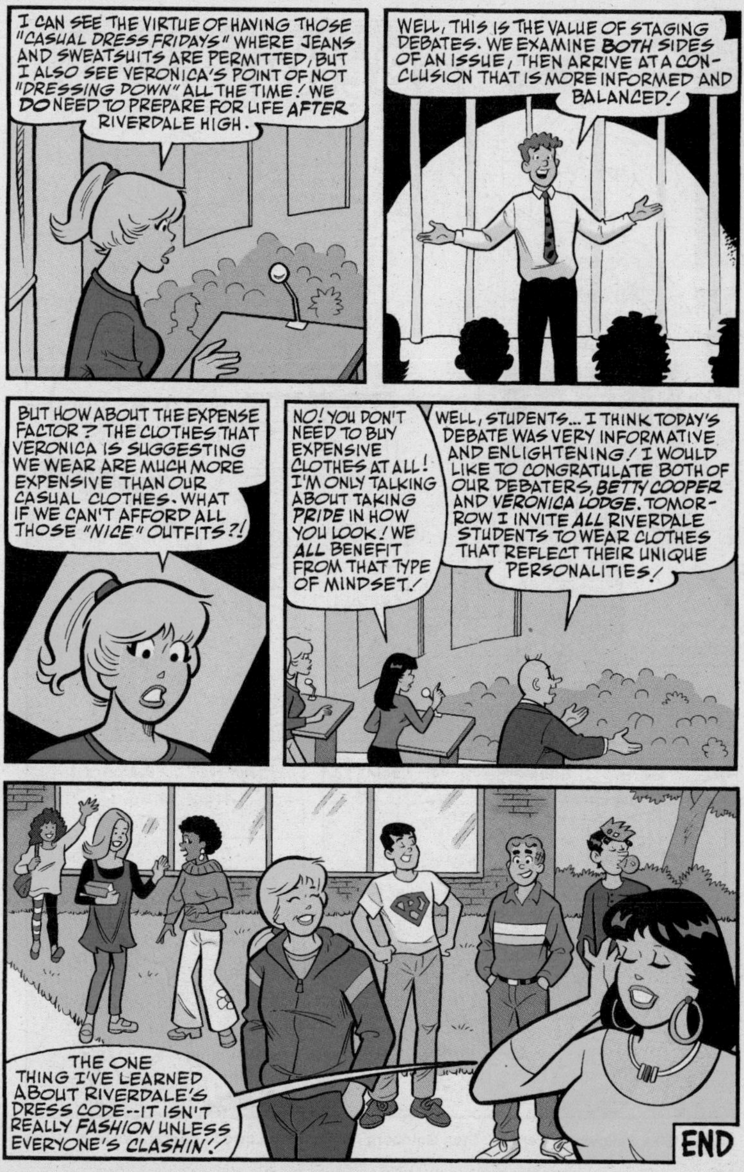
I CAN SEE THE VIRTUE OF HAVING THOSE "CASUAL DRESS FRIDAYS" WHERE JEANS AND SWEATSUITS ARE PERMITTED, BUT I ALSO SEE VERONICA'S POINT OF NOT "DRESSING DOWN" ALL THE TIME! WE DO NEED TO PREPARE FOR LIFE AFTER RIVERDALE HIGH.
WELL, THIS IS THE VALUE OF STAGING DEBATES. WE EXAMINE BOTH SIDES OF AN ISSUE, THEN ARRIVE AT A CONCLUSION THAT IS MORE INFORMED AND BALANCED!
BUT HOW ABOUT THE EXPENSE FACTOR? THE CLOTHES THAT VERONICA IS SUGGESTING WE WEAR ARE MUCH MORE EXPENSIVE THAN OUR CASUAL CLOTHES. WHAT IF WE CAN'T AFFORD ALL THOSE "NICE" OUTFITS?!
NO! YOU DON'T NEED TO BUY EXPENSIVE CLOTHES AT ALL! I'M ONLY TALKING ABOUT TAKING PRIDE IN HOW YOU LOOK! WE ALL BENEFIT FROM THAT TYPE OF MINDSET!
WELL, STUDENTS... I THINK TODAY'S DEBATE WAS VERY INFORMATIVE AND ENLIGHTENING! I WOULD LIKE TO CONGRATULATE BOTH OF OUR DEBATERS, BETTY COOPER AND VERONICA LODGE. TOMORROW I INVITE ALL RIVERDALE STUDENTS TO WEAR CLOTHES THAT REFLECT THEIR UNIQUE PERSONALITIES!
THE ONE THING I'VE LEARNED ABOUT RIVERDALE'S DRESS CODE--IT ISN'T REALLY FASHION UNLESS EVERYONE'S CLASHIN'!
END

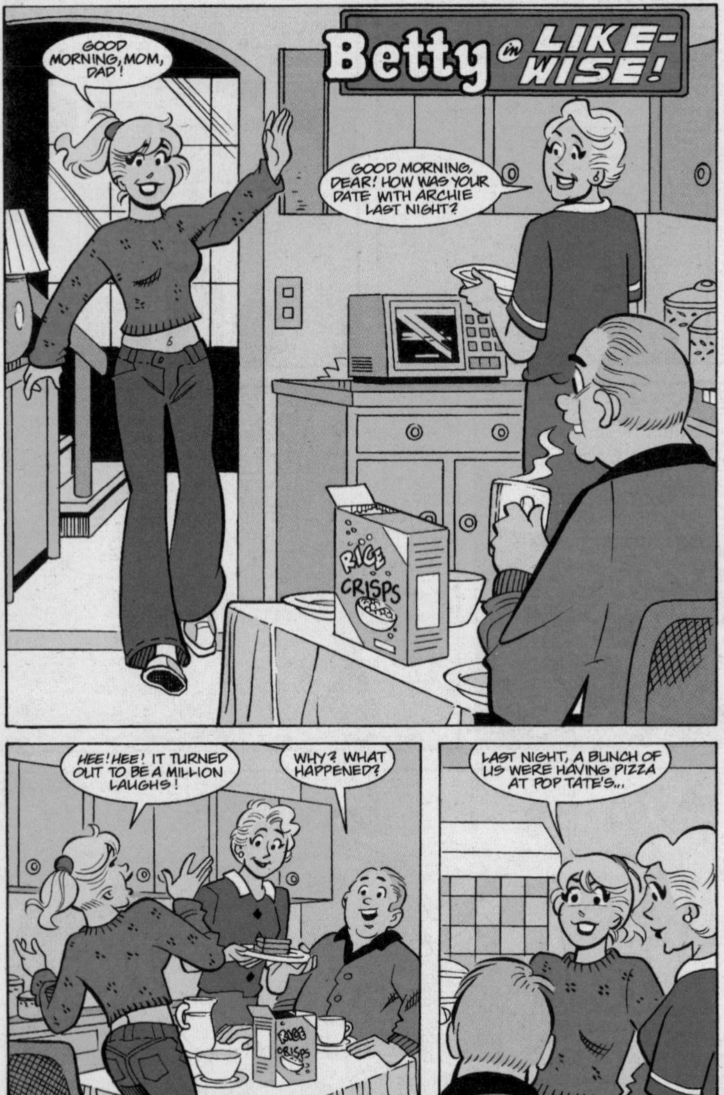
Betty in LIKE-WISE!
GOOD MORNING, MOM, DAD!
GOOD MORNING, DEAR! HOW WAS YOUR DATE WITH ARCHIE LAST NIGHT?
RICE CRISPS
HEE! HEE! IT TURNED OUT TO BE A MILLION LAUGHS!
WHY? WHAT HAPPENED?
LAST NIGHT, A BUNCH OF US WERE HAVING PIZZA AT POP TATE'S...

Script: Mike Pellowski / Pencils: Stan Goldberg / Inks: John Lowe / Letters: Vickie Williams

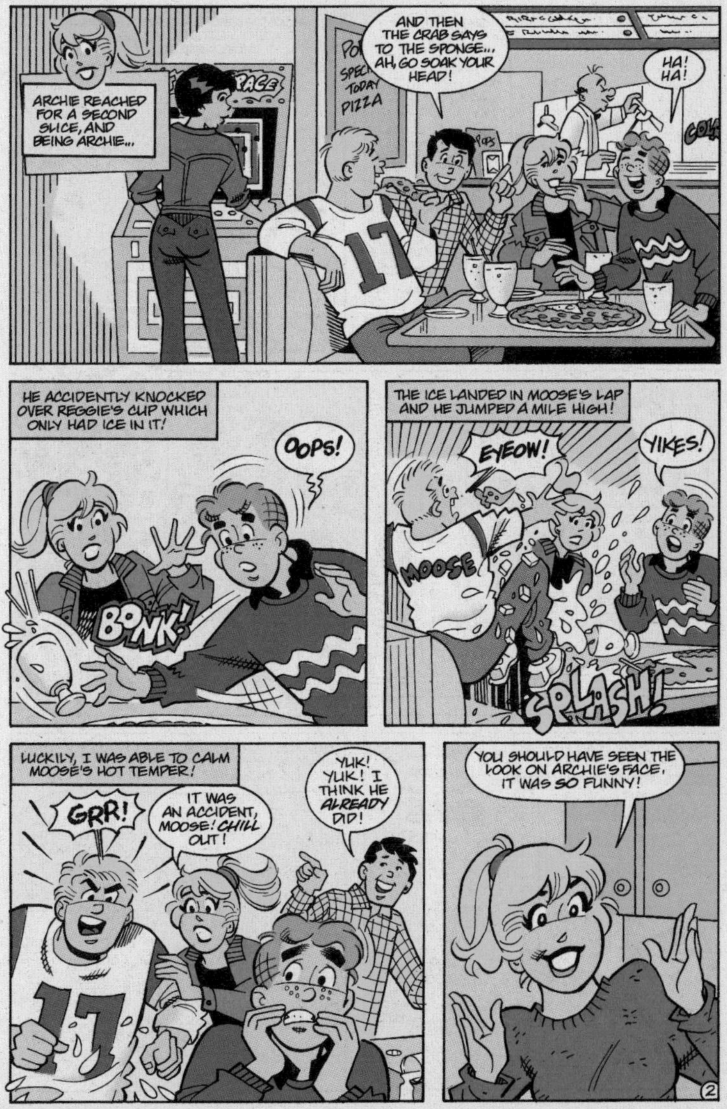
ARCHIE REACHED FOR A SECOND SLICE, AND BEING ARCHIE...
AND THEN THE CRAB SAYS TO THE SPONGE... AH, GO SOAK YOUR HEAD!
HA! HA!
POP'S SPECIAL TODAY PIZZA
HE ACCIDENTLY KNOCKED OVER REGGIE'S CUP WHICH ONLY HAD ICE IN IT!
OOPS!
BONK!
THE ICE LANDED IN MOOSE'S LAP AND HE JUMPED A MILE HIGH!
EYEOW!
YIKES!
MOOSE
SPLASH!
LUCKILY, I WAS ABLE TO CALM MOOSE'S HOT TEMPER!
GRR!
IT WAS AN ACCIDENT, MOOSE! CHILL OUT!
YUK! YUK! I THINK HE ALREADY DID!
YOU SHOULD HAVE SEEN THE LOOK ON ARCHIE'S FACE, IT WAS SO FUNNY!
2

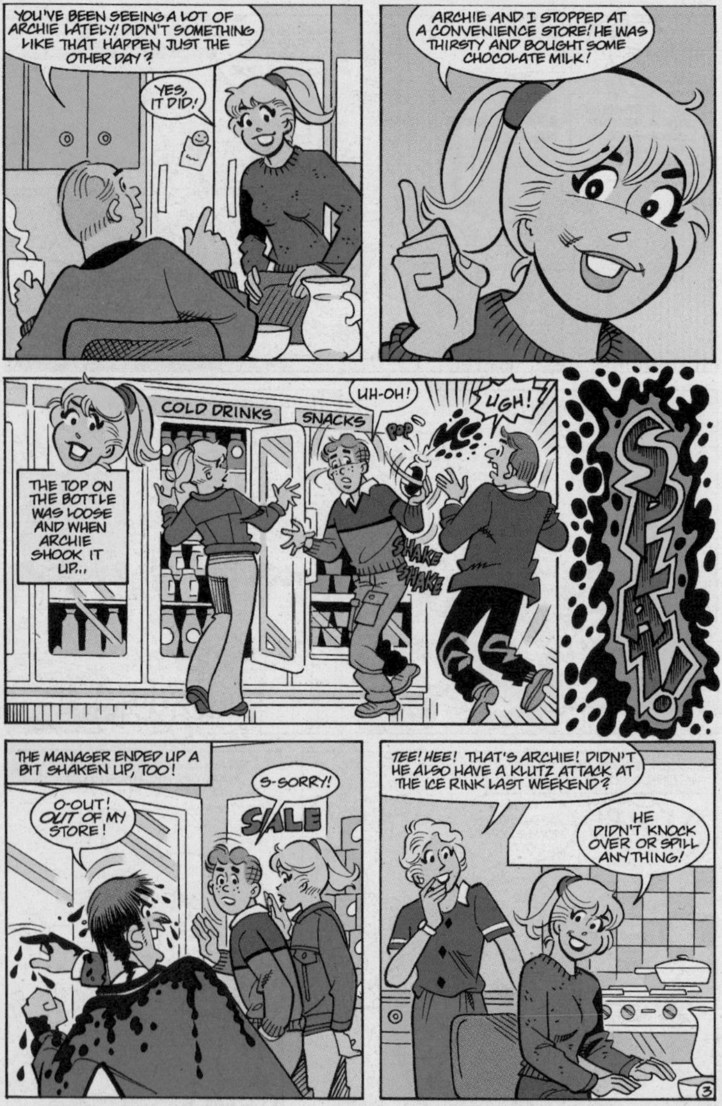
YOU'VE BEEN SEEING A LOT OF ARCHIE LATELY! DIDN'T SOMETHING LIKE THAT HAPPEN JUST THE OTHER DAY?
YES, IT DID!
ARCHIE AND I STOPPED AT A CONVENIENCE STORE! HE WAS THIRSTY AND BOUGHT SOME CHOCOLATE MILK!
THE TOP ON THE BOTTLE WAS LOOSE AND WHEN ARCHIE SHOOK IT UP...
COLD DRINKS
SNACKS
UH-OH!
POP
UGH!
SHAKE
SHAKE
THE MANAGER ENDED UP A BIT SHAKEN UP, TOO!
S-SORRY!
O-OUT! OUT OF MY STORE!
SALE
TEE! HEE! THAT'S ARCHIE! DIDN'T HE ALSO HAVE A KLUTZ ATTACK AT THE ICE RINK LAST WEEKEND?
HE DIDN'T KNOCK OVER OR SPILL ANYTHING!
3

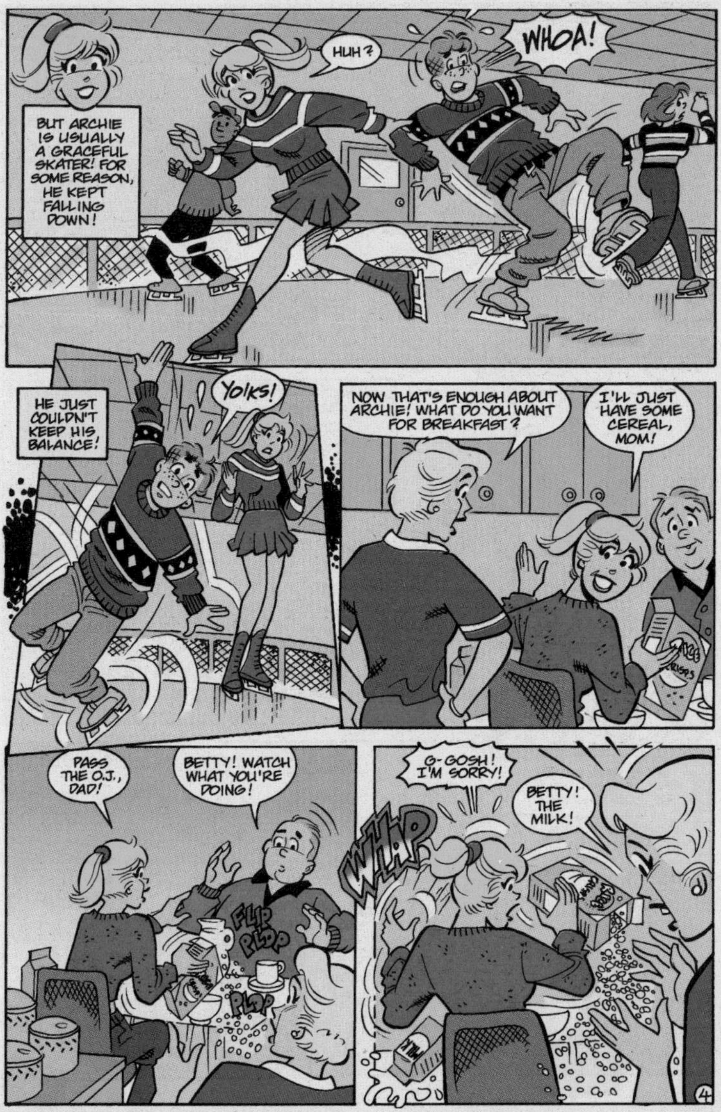
BUT ARCHIE IS USUALLY A GRACEFUL SKATER! FOR SOME REASON, HE KEPT FALLING DOWN!
HUH?
WHOA!
HE JUST COULDN'T KEEP HIS BALANCE!
YOIKS!
NOW THAT'S ENOUGH ABOUT ARCHIE! WHAT DO YOU WANT FOR BREAKFAST?
I'LL JUST HAVE SOME CEREAL, MOM!
PASS THE O.J., DAD!
BETTY! WATCH WHAT YOU'RE DOING!
FLIP
PLOP
PLOP
G-GOSH! I'M SORRY!
BETTY! THE MILK!
WHAP
MILK
4

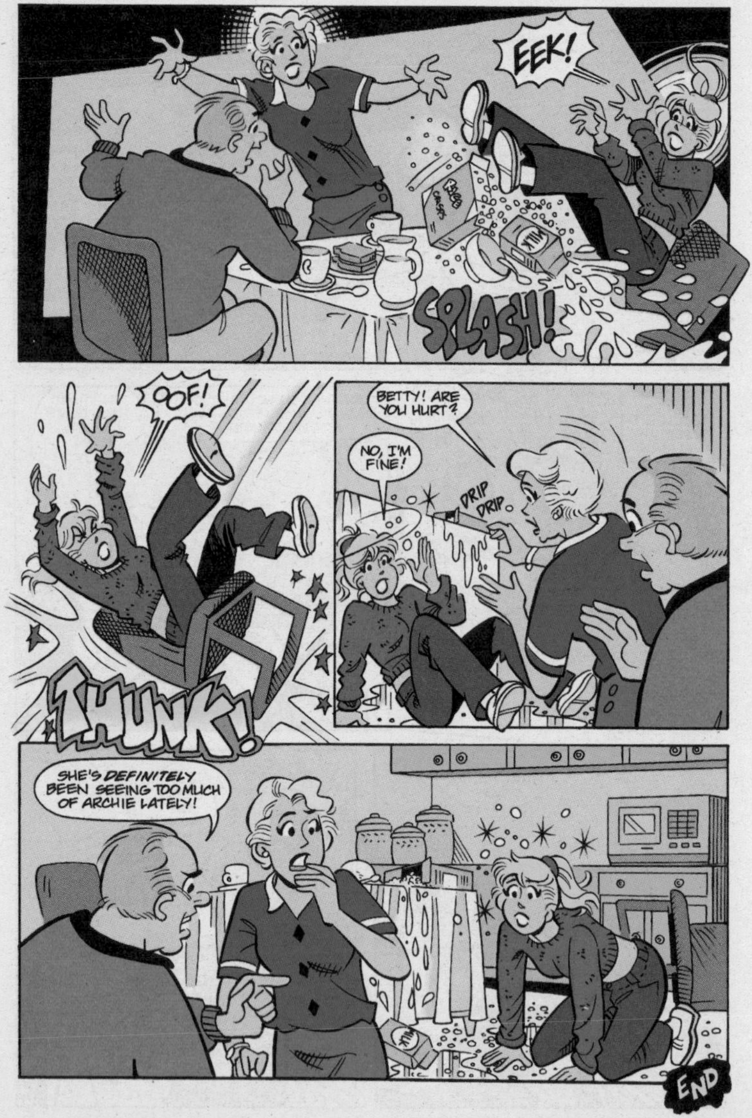
EEK!
SPLASH!
OOF!
THUNK!
BETTY! ARE YOU HURT?
NO, I'M FINE!
DRIP DRIP
SHE'S *DEFINITELY* BEEN SEEING TOO MUCH OF ARCHIE LATELY!
END

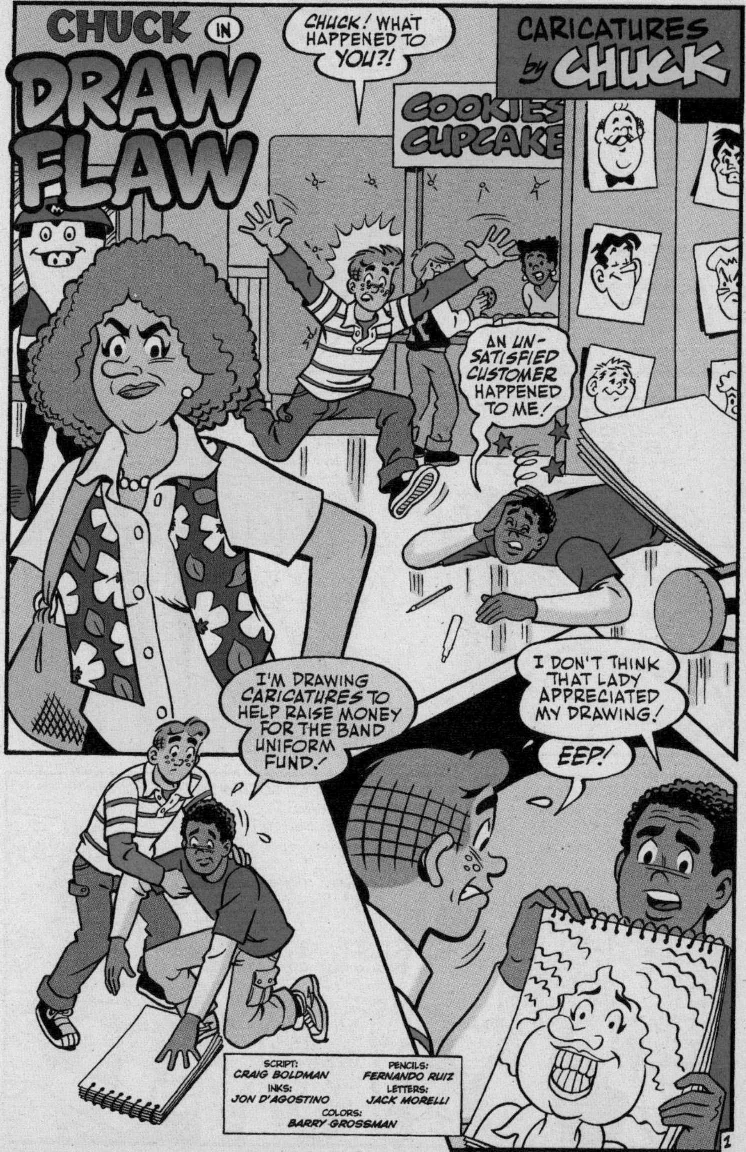
CHUCK IN
DRAW FLAW
CARICATURES by CHUCK
COOKIES CUPCAKE
CHUCK! WHAT HAPPENED TO YOU?!
AN UN-SATISFIED CUSTOMER HAPPENED TO ME!
I'M DRAWING CARICATURES TO HELP RAISE MONEY FOR THE BAND UNIFORM FUND!
I DON'T THINK THAT LADY APPRECIATED MY DRAWING!
EEP!
SCRIPT: CRAIG BOLDMAN
PENCILS: FERNANDO RUIZ
INKS: JON D'AGOSTINO
LETTERS: JACK MORELLI
COLORS: BARRY GROSSMAN
1

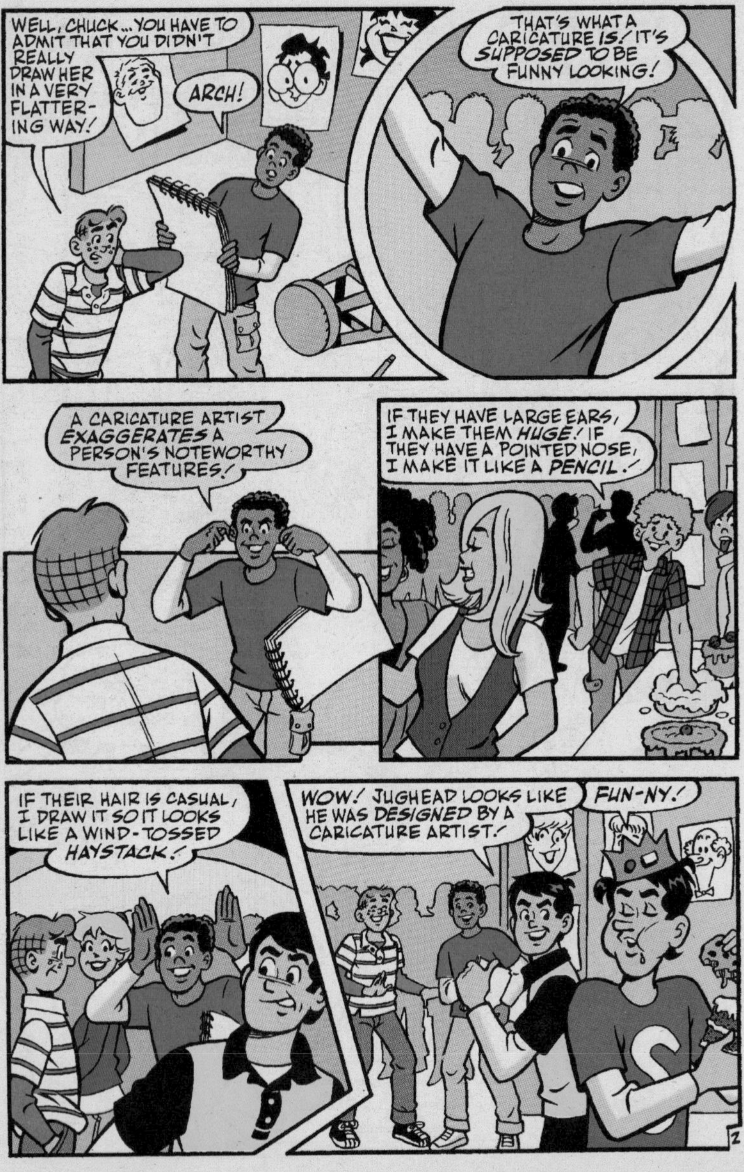
WELL, CHUCK... YOU HAVE TO ADMIT THAT YOU DIDN'T REALLY DRAW HER IN A VERY FLATTERING WAY!
ARCH!
THAT'S WHAT A CARICATURE IS! IT'S SUPPOSED TO BE FUNNY LOOKING!
A CARICATURE ARTIST EXAGGERATES A PERSON'S NOTEWORTHY FEATURES!
IF THEY HAVE LARGE EARS, I MAKE THEM HUGE! IF THEY HAVE A POINTED NOSE, I MAKE IT LIKE A PENCIL!
IF THEIR HAIR IS CASUAL, I DRAW IT SO IT LOOKS LIKE A WIND-TOSSED HAYSTACK!
WOW! JUGHEAD LOOKS LIKE HE WAS DESIGNED BY A CARICATURE ARTIST!
FUN-NY!
2

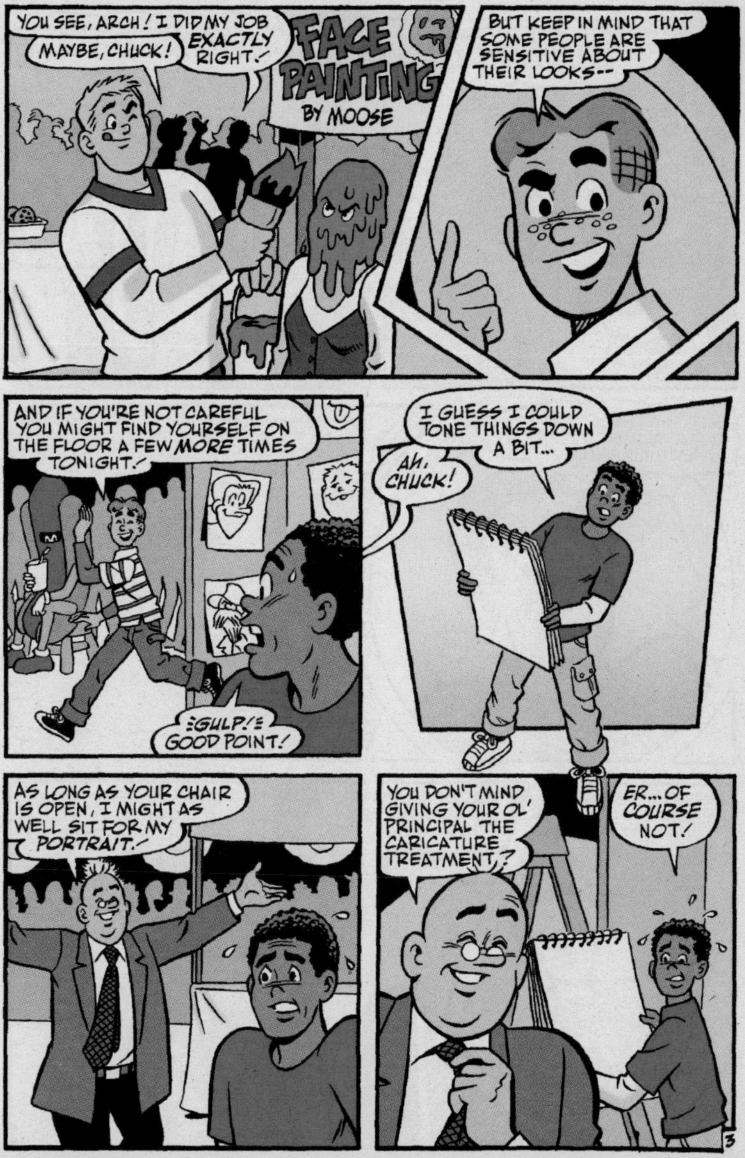
YOU SEE, ARCH! I DID MY JOB EXACTLY RIGHT!
MAYBE, CHUCK!
FACE PAINTING BY MOOSE
BUT KEEP IN MIND THAT SOME PEOPLE ARE SENSITIVE ABOUT THEIR LOOKS--
AND IF YOU'RE NOT CAREFUL YOU MIGHT FIND YOURSELF ON THE FLOOR A FEW MORE TIMES TONIGHT!
GULP! GOOD POINT!
I GUESS I COULD TONE THINGS DOWN A BIT...
AH, CHUCK!
AS LONG AS YOUR CHAIR IS OPEN, I MIGHT AS WELL SIT FOR MY PORTRAIT!
YOU DON'T MIND GIVING YOUR OL' PRINCIPAL THE CARICATURE TREATMENT?
ER...OF COURSE NOT!
3

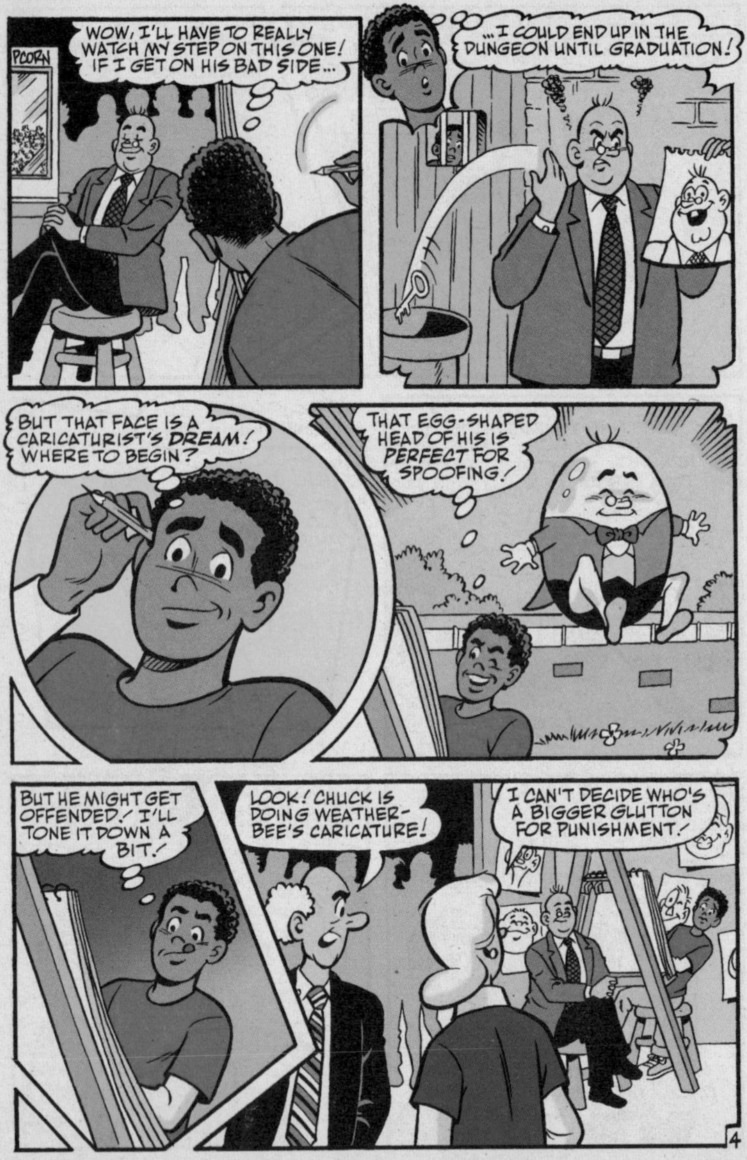
PCORN
WOW, I'LL HAVE TO REALLY WATCH MY STEP ON THIS ONE! IF I GET ON HIS BAD SIDE...
...I COULD END UP IN THE DUNGEON UNTIL GRADUATION!
BUT THAT FACE IS A CARICATURIST'S DREAM! WHERE TO BEGIN?
THAT EGG-SHAPED HEAD OF HIS IS PERFECT FOR SPOOFING!
BUT HE MIGHT GET OFFENDED! I'LL TONE IT DOWN A BIT!
LOOK! CHUCK IS DOING WEATHER-BEE'S CARICATURE!
I CAN'T DECIDE WHO'S A BIGGER GLUTTON FOR PUNISHMENT!
4

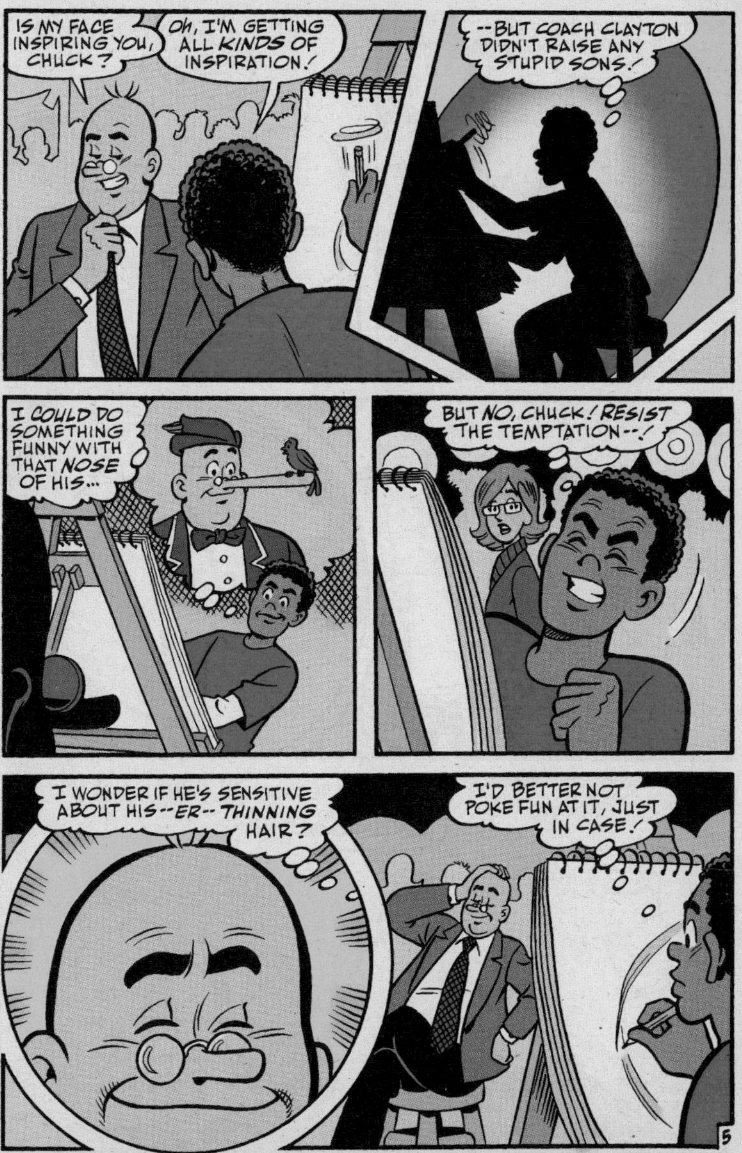
IS MY FACE INSPIRING YOU, CHUCK?
Oh, I'M GETTING ALL KINDS OF INSPIRATION!
--BUT COACH CLAYTON DIDN'T RAISE ANY STUPID SONS!
I COULD DO SOMETHING FUNNY WITH THAT NOSE OF HIS...
BUT NO, CHUCK! RESIST THE TEMPTATION--!
I WONDER IF HE'S SENSITIVE ABOUT HIS--ER--THINNING HAIR?
I'D BETTER NOT POKE FUN AT IT, JUST IN CASE!
5

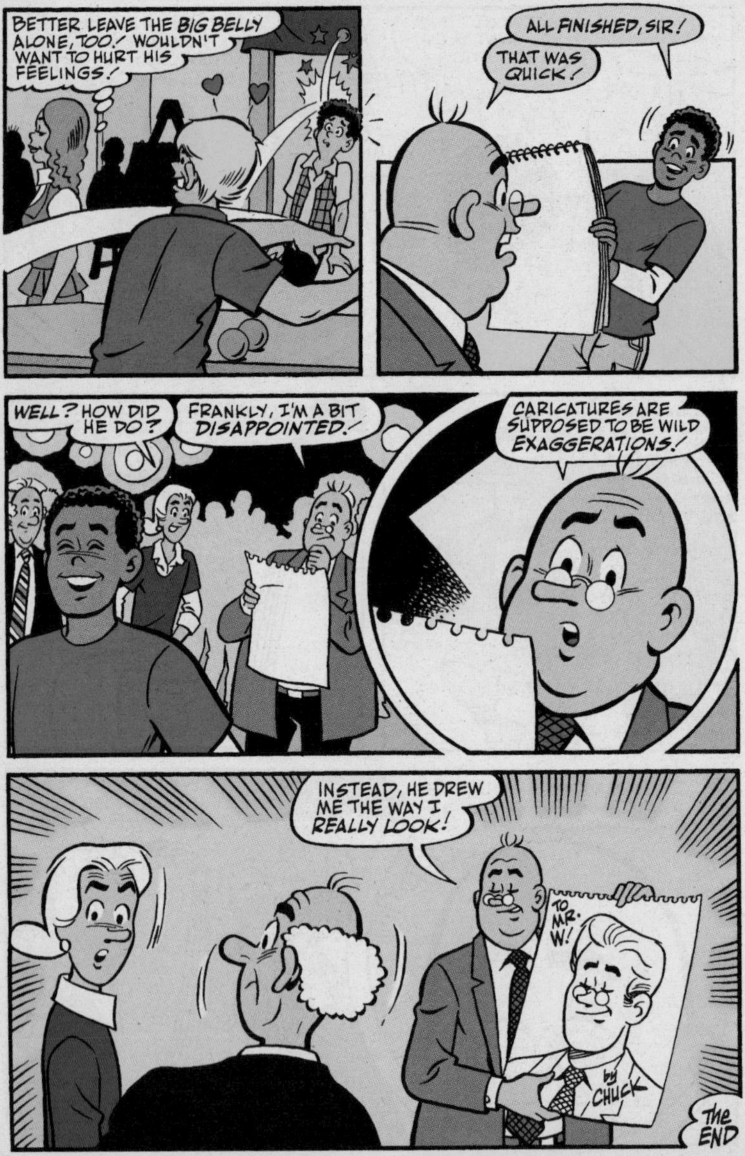
BETTER LEAVE THE BIG BELLY ALONE, TOO! WOULDN'T WANT TO HURT HIS FEELINGS!
ALL FINISHED, SIR!
THAT WAS QUICK!
WELL? HOW DID HE DO?
FRANKLY, I'M A BIT DISAPPOINTED!
CARICATURES ARE SUPPOSED TO BE WILD EXAGGERATIONS!
INSTEAD, HE DREW ME THE WAY I REALLY LOOK!
TO MR. W!
by CHUCK
The END

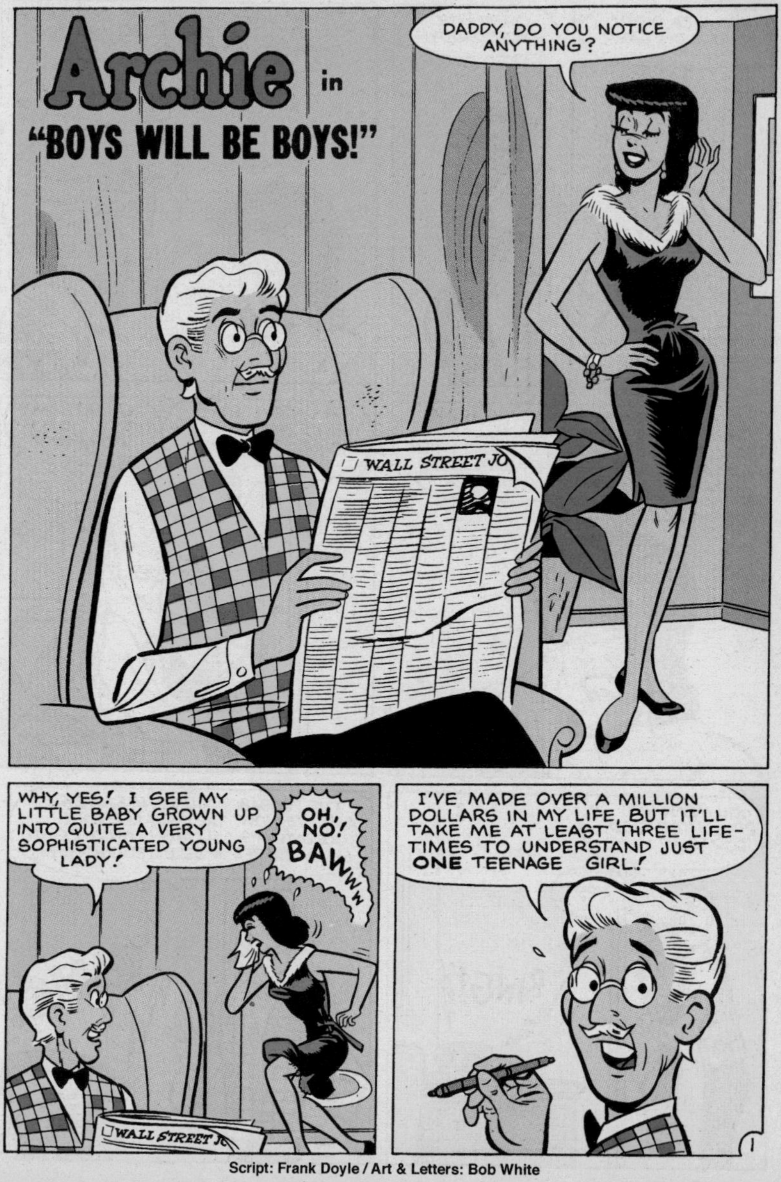
Archie in
"BOYS WILL BE BOYS!"
DADDY, DO YOU NOTICE ANYTHING?
WALL STREET JO
WHY, YES! I SEE MY LITTLE BABY GROWN UP INTO QUITE A VERY SOPHISTICATED YOUNG LADY!
OH, NO! BAWWWW
WALL STREET JO
I'VE MADE OVER A MILLION DOLLARS IN MY LIFE, BUT IT'LL TAKE ME AT LEAST THREE LIFE-TIMES TO UNDERSTAND JUST ONE TEENAGE GIRL!
1

Script: Frank Doyle / Art & Letters: Bob White

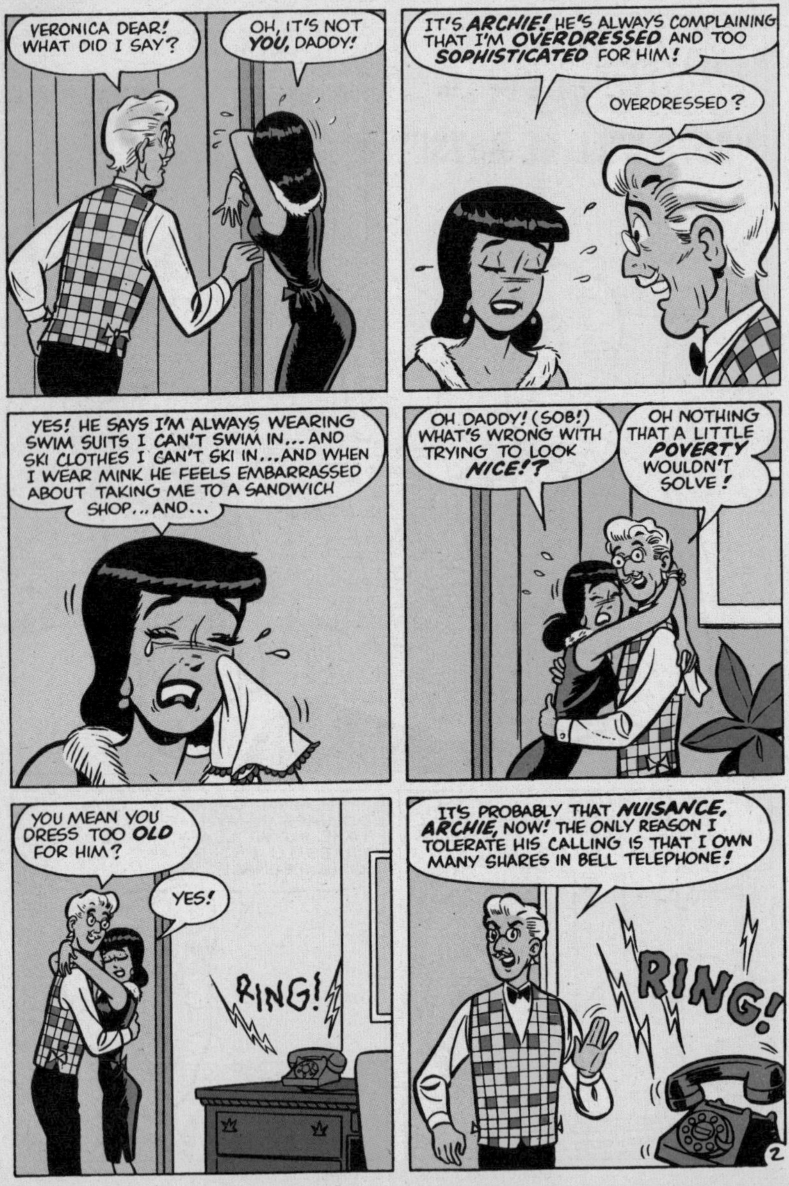
VERONICA DEAR! WHAT DID I SAY?
OH, IT'S NOT YOU, DADDY!
IT'S ARCHIE! HE'S ALWAYS COMPLAINING THAT I'M OVERDRESSED AND TOO SOPHISTICATED FOR HIM!
OVERDRESSED?
YES! HE SAYS I'M ALWAYS WEARING SWIM SUITS I CAN'T SWIM IN... AND SKI CLOTHES I CAN'T SKI IN... AND WHEN I WEAR MINK HE FEELS EMBARRASSED ABOUT TAKING ME TO A SANDWICH SHOP... AND...
OH DADDY! (SOB!) WHAT'S WRONG WITH TRYING TO LOOK NICE!?
OH NOTHING THAT A LITTLE POVERTY WOULDN'T SOLVE!
YOU MEAN YOU DRESS TOO OLD FOR HIM?
YES!
RING!
IT'S PROBABLY THAT NUISANCE, ARCHIE, NOW! THE ONLY REASON I TOLERATE HIS CALLING IS THAT I OWN MANY SHARES IN BELL TELEPHONE!
RING!
2

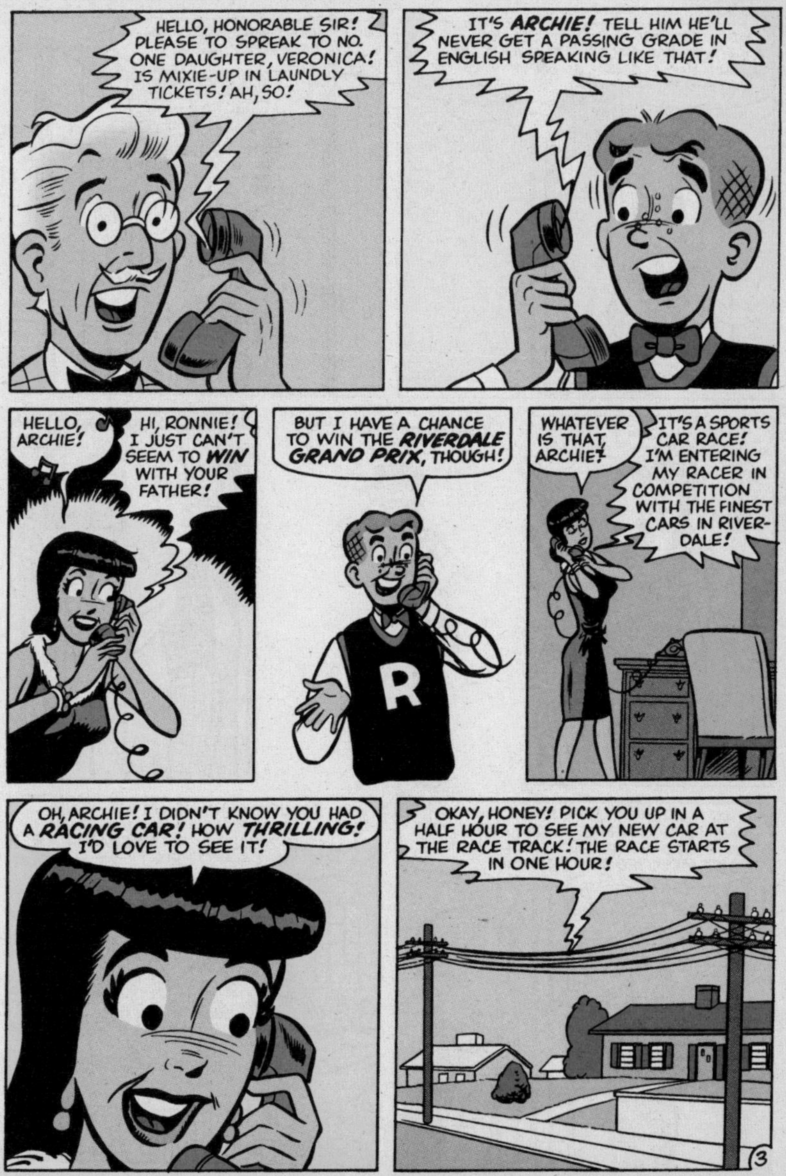
HELLO, HONORABLE SIR! PLEASE TO SPREAK TO NO. ONE DAUGHTER, VERONICA! IS MIXIE-UP IN LAUNDLY TICKETS! AH, SO!
IT'S ARCHIE! TELL HIM HE'LL NEVER GET A PASSING GRADE IN ENGLISH SPEAKING LIKE THAT!
HELLO, ARCHIE!
HI, RONNIE! I JUST CAN'T SEEM TO WIN WITH YOUR FATHER!
BUT I HAVE A CHANCE TO WIN THE RIVERDALE GRAND PRIX, THOUGH!
WHATEVER IS THAT, ARCHIE?
IT'S A SPORTS CAR RACE! I'M ENTERING MY RACER IN COMPETITION WITH THE FINEST CARS IN RIVER-DALE!
OH, ARCHIE! I DIDN'T KNOW YOU HAD A RACING CAR! HOW THRILLING! I'D LOVE TO SEE IT!
OKAY, HONEY! PICK YOU UP IN A HALF HOUR TO SEE MY NEW CAR AT THE RACE TRACK! THE RACE STARTS IN ONE HOUR!

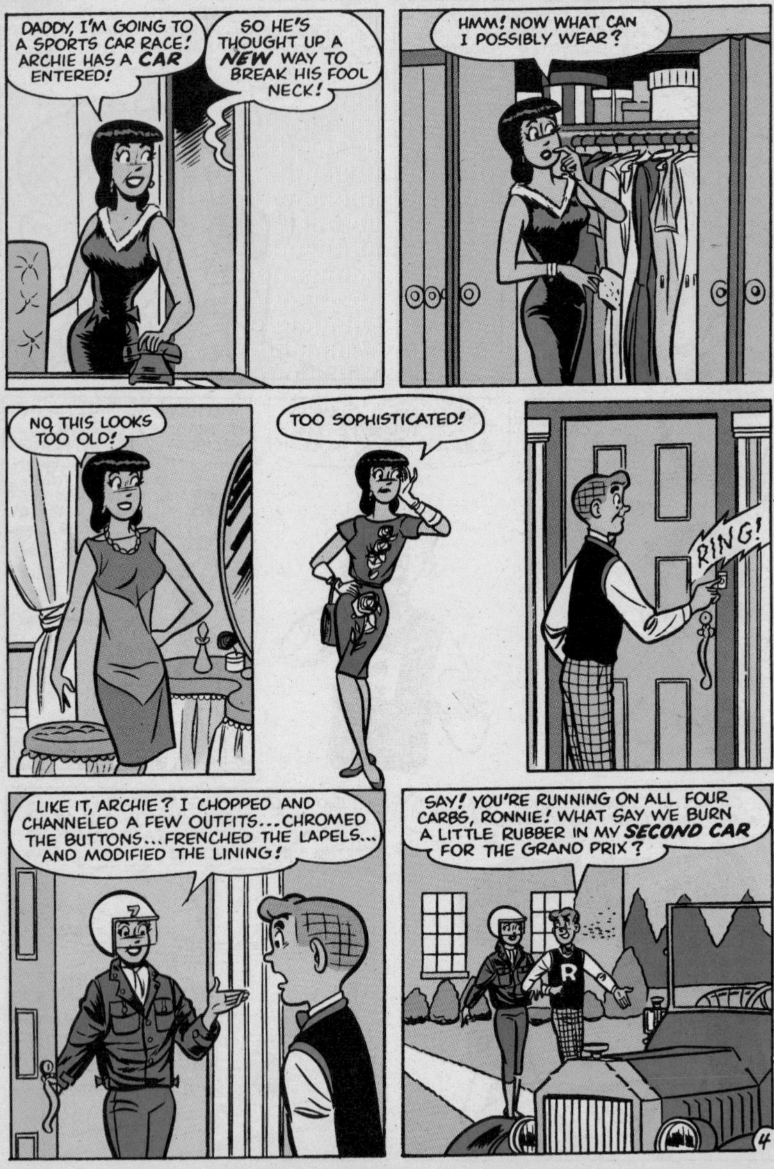
DADDY, I'M GOING TO A SPORTS CAR RACE! ARCHIE HAS A CAR ENTERED!
SO HE'S THOUGHT UP A NEW WAY TO BREAK HIS FOOL NECK!
HMM! NOW WHAT CAN I POSSIBLY WEAR?
NO, THIS LOOKS TOO OLD!
TOO SOPHISTICATED!
RING!
LIKE IT, ARCHIE? I CHOPPED AND CHANNELED A FEW OUTFITS... CHROMED THE BUTTONS... FRENCHED THE LAPELS... AND MODIFIED THE LINING!
SAY! YOU'RE RUNNING ON ALL FOUR CARBS, RONNIE! WHAT SAY WE BURN A LITTLE RUBBER IN MY SECOND CAR FOR THE GRAND PRIX?
4

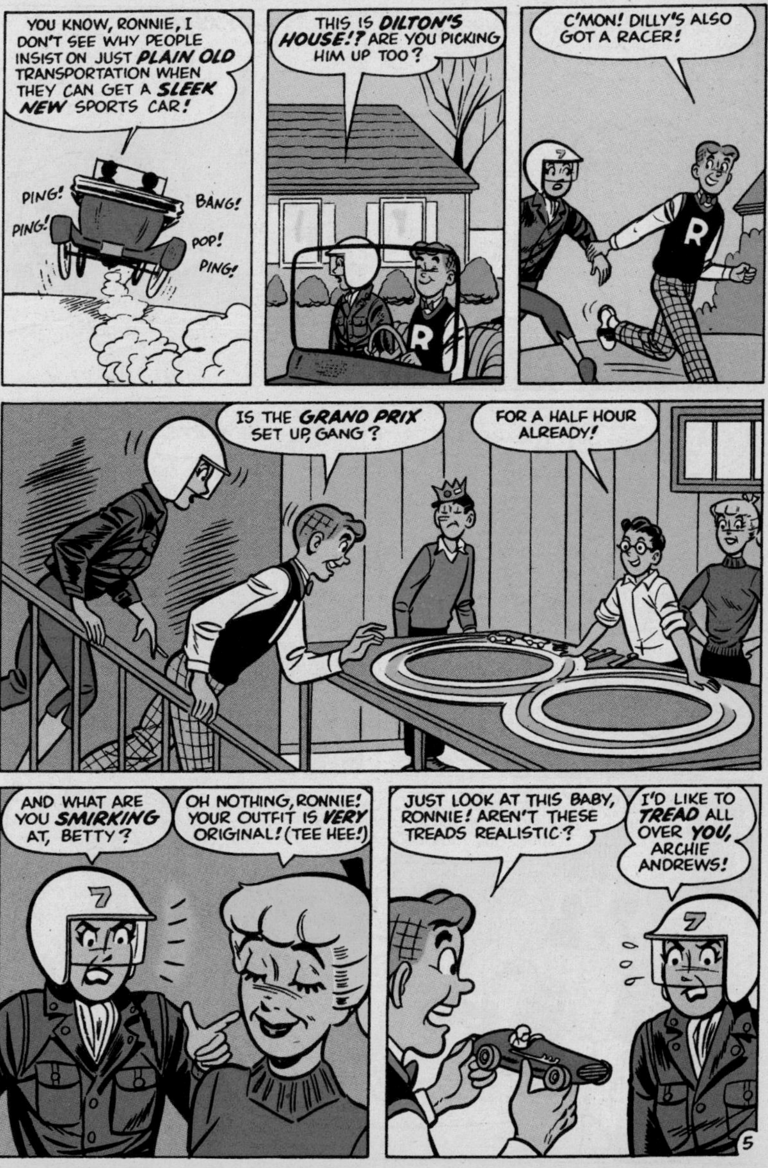
YOU KNOW, RONNIE, I DON'T SEE WHY PEOPLE INSIST ON JUST PLAIN OLD TRANSPORTATION WHEN THEY CAN GET A SLEEK NEW SPORTS CAR!
PING!
PING!
BANG!
POP!
PING!
THIS IS DILTON'S HOUSE!? ARE YOU PICKING HIM UP TOO?
C'MON! DILLY'S ALSO GOT A RACER!
IS THE GRAND PRIX SET UP, GANG?
FOR A HALF HOUR ALREADY!
AND WHAT ARE YOU SMIRKING AT, BETTY?
OH NOTHING, RONNIE! YOUR OUTFIT IS VERY ORIGINAL! (TEE HEE!)
JUST LOOK AT THIS BABY, RONNIE! AREN'T THESE TREADS REALISTIC?
I'D LIKE TO TREAD ALL OVER YOU, ARCHIE ANDREWS!

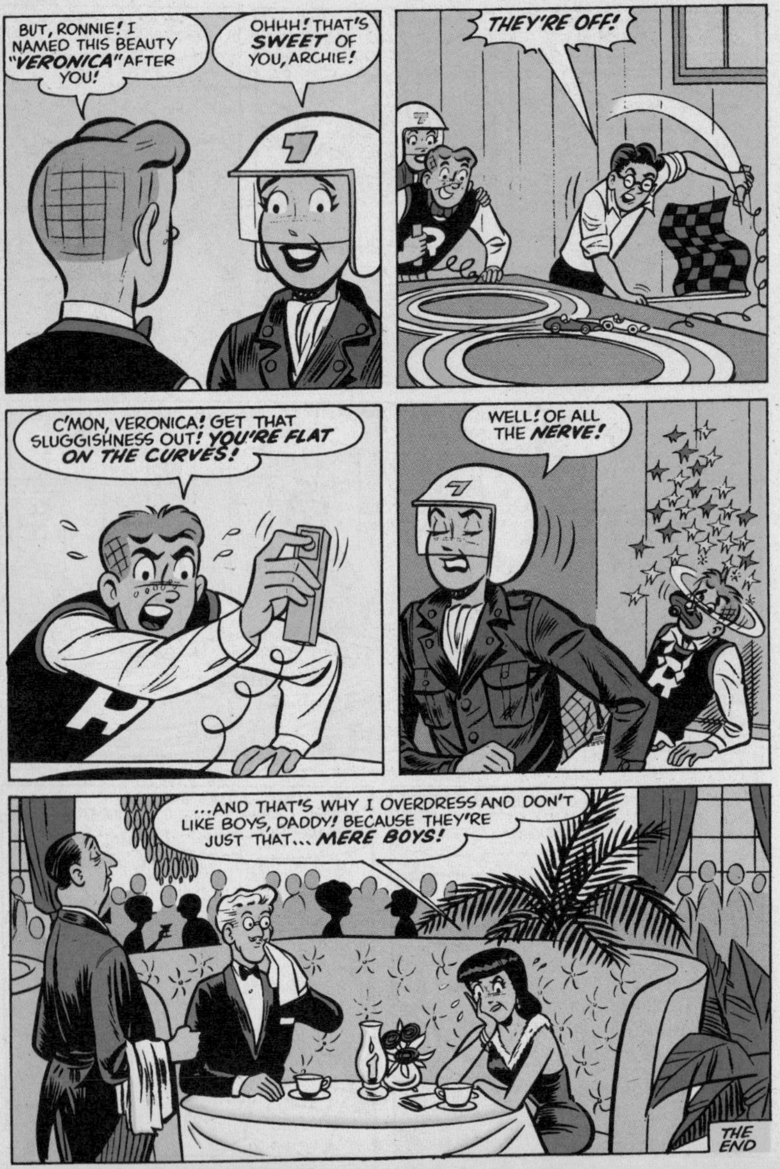
BUT, RONNIE! I NAMED THIS BEAUTY "VERONICA" AFTER YOU!
OHHH! THAT'S SWEET OF YOU, ARCHIE!
THEY'RE OFF!
C'MON, VERONICA! GET THAT SLUGGISHNESS OUT! YOU'RE FLAT ON THE CURVES!
WELL! OF ALL THE NERVE!
...AND THAT'S WHY I OVERDRESS AND DON'T LIKE BOYS, DADDY! BECAUSE THEY'RE JUST THAT... MERE BOYS!
THE END

Reggie in ON THE BALL!

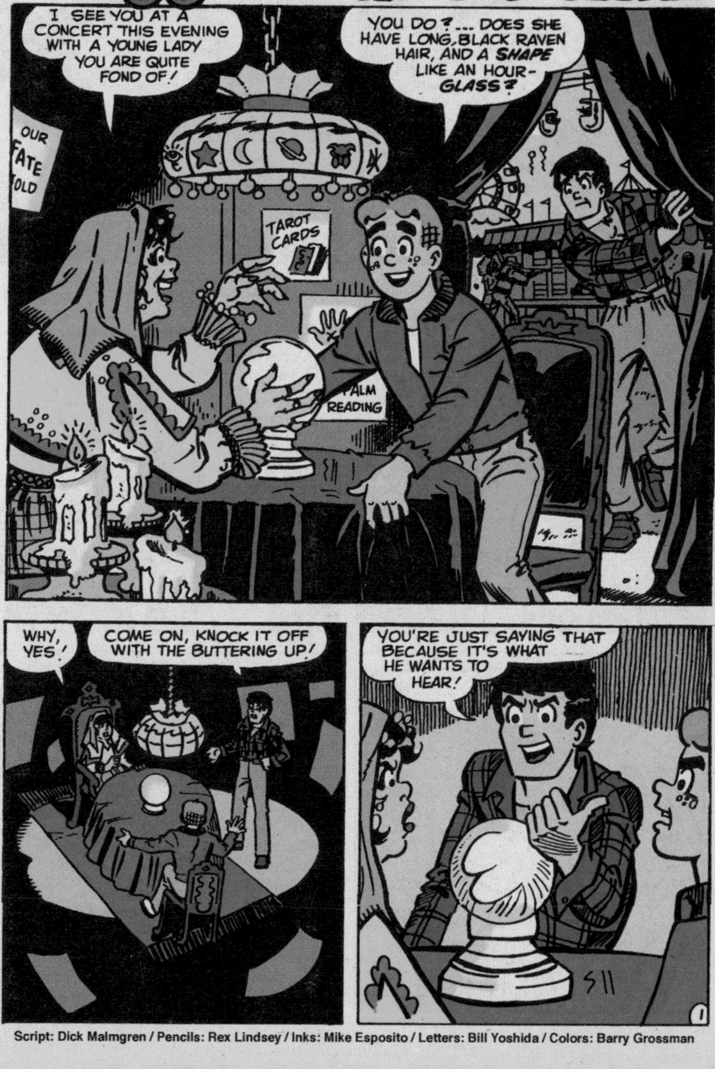
I SEE YOU AT A CONCERT THIS EVENING WITH A YOUNG LADY YOU ARE QUITE FOND OF!
YOU DO?... DOES SHE HAVE LONG, BLACK RAVEN HAIR, AND A SHAPE LIKE AN HOUR-GLASS?
TAROT CARDS
PALM READING
WHY, YES!
COME ON, KNOCK IT OFF WITH THE BUTTERING UP!
YOU'RE JUST SAYING THAT BECAUSE IT'S WHAT HE WANTS TO HEAR!
1

Script: Dick Malmgren / Pencils: Rex Lindsey / Inks: Mike Esposito / Letters: Bill Yoshida / Colors: Barry Grossman

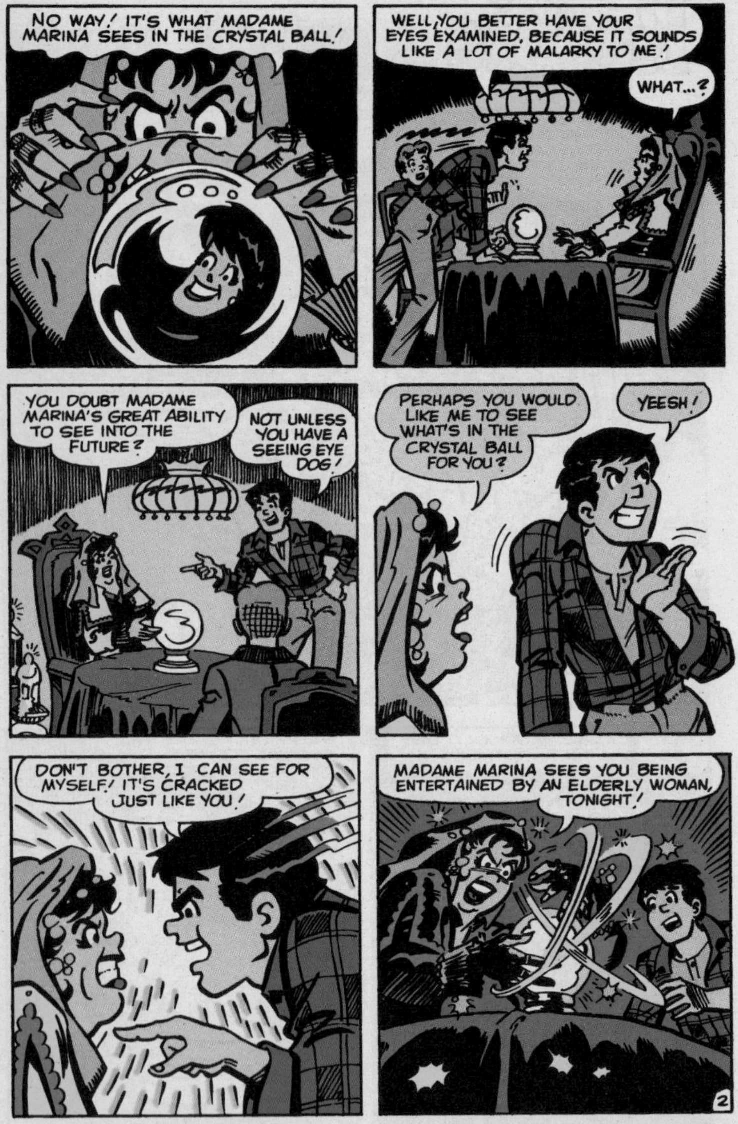

NO WAY! IT'S WHAT MADAME MARINA SEES IN THE CRYSTAL BALL!
WELL, YOU BETTER HAVE YOUR EYES EXAMINED, BECAUSE IT SOUNDS LIKE A LOT OF MALARKY TO ME!
WHAT...?
YOU DOUBT MADAME MARINA'S GREAT ABILITY TO SEE INTO THE FUTURE?
NOT UNLESS YOU HAVE A SEEING EYE DOG!
PERHAPS YOU WOULD LIKE ME TO SEE WHAT'S IN THE CRYSTAL BALL FOR YOU?
YEESH!
DON'T BOTHER, I CAN SEE FOR MYSELF! IT'S CRACKED JUST LIKE YOU!
MADAME MARINA SEES YOU BEING ENTERTAINED BY AN ELDERLY WOMAN, TONIGHT!
2

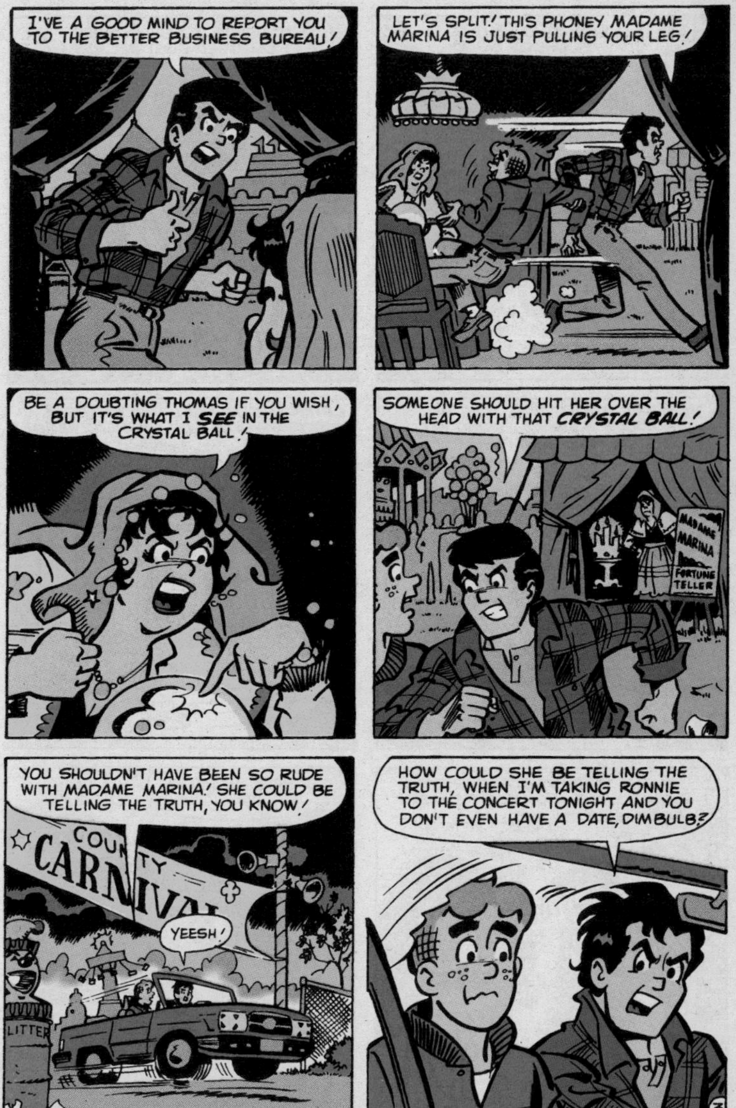
I'VE A GOOD MIND TO REPORT YOU TO THE BETTER BUSINESS BUREAU!
LET'S SPLIT! THIS PHONEY MADAME MARINA IS JUST PULLING YOUR LEG!
BE A DOUBTING THOMAS IF YOU WISH, BUT IT'S WHAT I SEE IN THE CRYSTAL BALL!
SOMEONE SHOULD HIT HER OVER THE HEAD WITH THAT CRYSTAL BALL!
MADAME MARINA FORTUNE TELLER
YOU SHOULDN'T HAVE BEEN SO RUDE WITH MADAME MARINA! SHE COULD BE TELLING THE TRUTH, YOU KNOW!
COUNTY CARNIVAL
YEESH!
LITTER
HOW COULD SHE BE TELLING THE TRUTH, WHEN I'M TAKING RONNIE TO THE CONCERT TONIGHT AND YOU DON'T EVEN HAVE A DATE, DIMBULB?
3

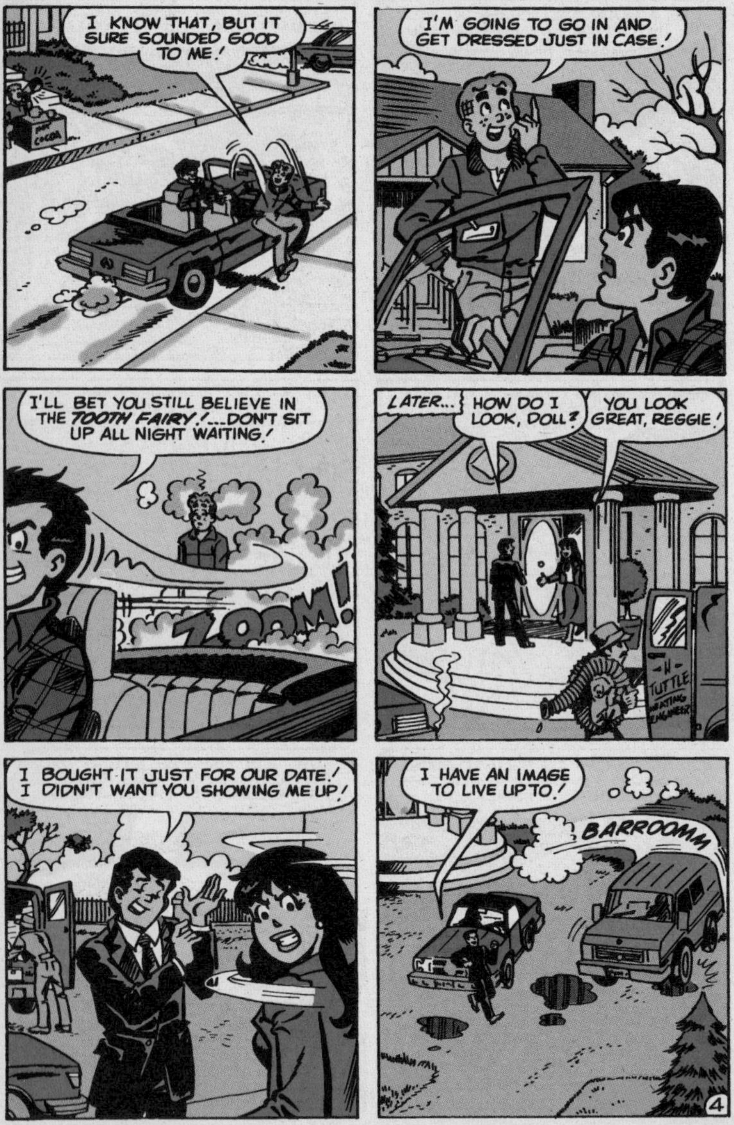
I KNOW THAT, BUT IT SURE SOUNDED GOOD TO ME!
I'M GOING TO GO IN AND GET DRESSED JUST IN CASE!
I'LL BET YOU STILL BELIEVE IN THE TOOTH FAIRY!...DON'T SIT UP ALL NIGHT WAITING!
ZOOM!
LATER...
HOW DO I LOOK, DOLL?
YOU LOOK GREAT, REGGIE!
H TUTTLE
I BOUGHT IT JUST FOR OUR DATE! I DIDN'T WANT YOU SHOWING ME UP!
I HAVE AN IMAGE TO LIVE UP TO!
BARROOMM
4

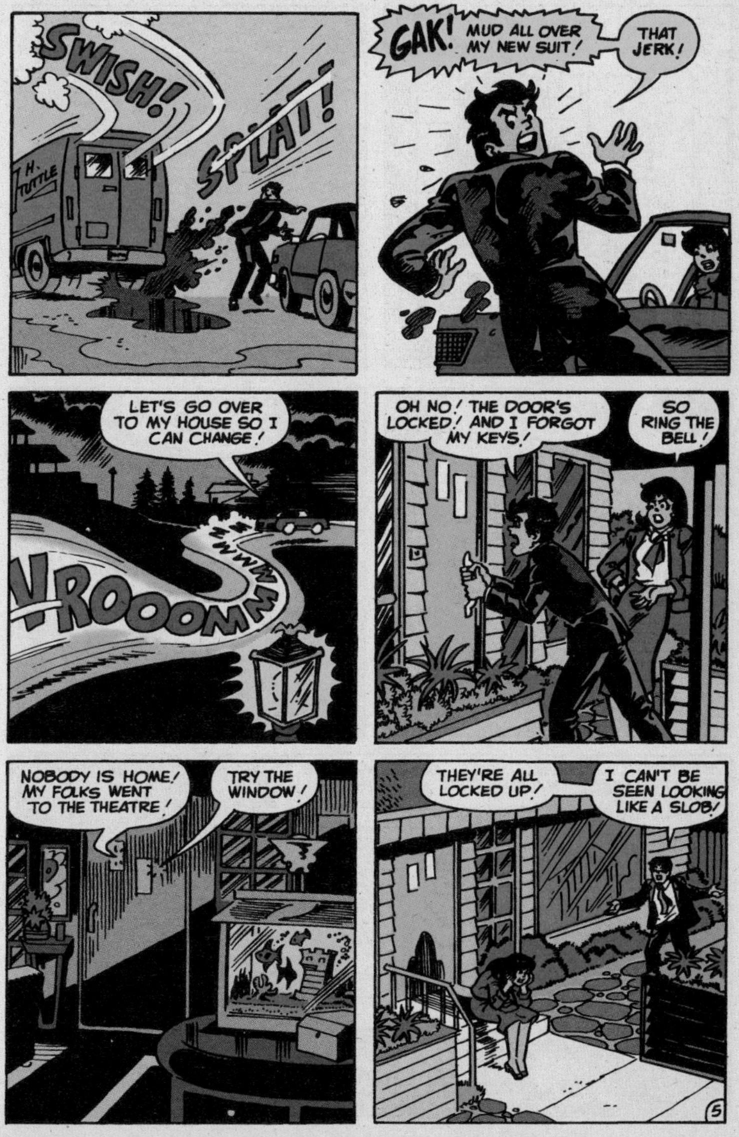
SWISH!
SPLAT!
H. TUTTLE
GAK! MUD ALL OVER MY NEW SUIT!
THAT JERK!
LET'S GO OVER TO MY HOUSE SO I CAN CHANGE!
VROOOMMMMMMM
OH NO! THE DOOR'S LOCKED! AND I FORGOT MY KEYS!
SO RING THE BELL!
NOBODY IS HOME! MY FOLKS WENT TO THE THEATRE!
TRY THE WINDOW!
THEY'RE ALL LOCKED UP!
I CAN'T BE SEEN LOOKING LIKE A SLOB!
5

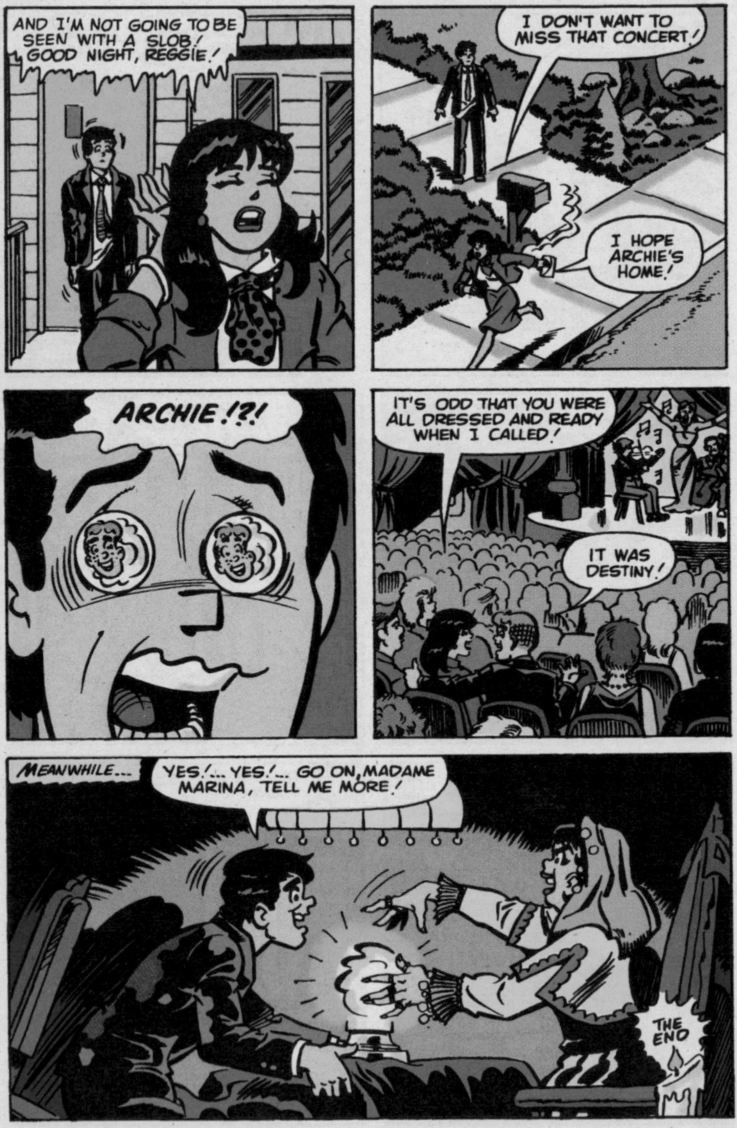
AND I'M NOT GOING TO BE SEEN WITH A SLOB! GOOD NIGHT, REGGIE!
I DON'T WANT TO MISS THAT CONCERT!
I HOPE ARCHIE'S HOME!
ARCHIE!?!
IT'S ODD THAT YOU WERE ALL DRESSED AND READY WHEN I CALLED!
IT WAS DESTINY!
MEANWHILE...
YES!... YES!... GO ON, MADAME MARINA, TELL ME MORE!
THE END

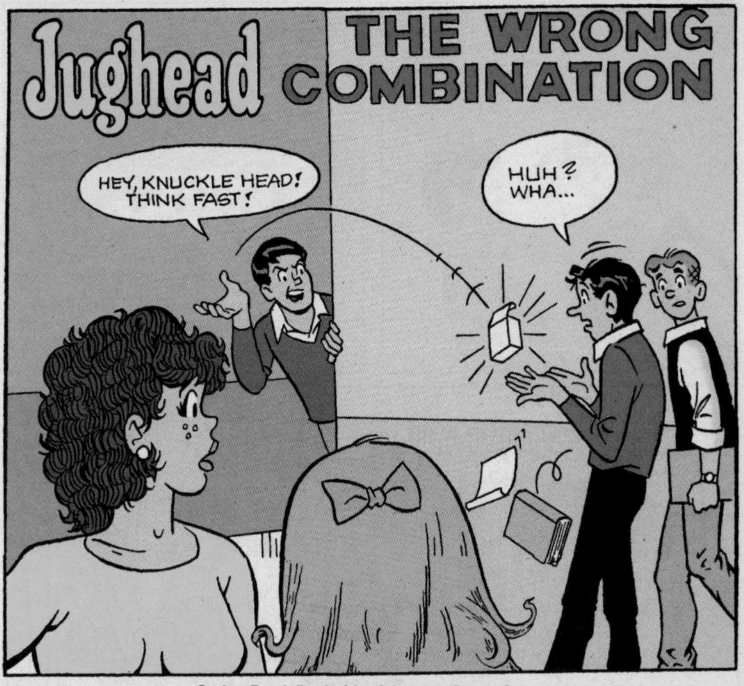
Jughead
THE WRONG COMBINATION
HEY, KNUCKLE HEAD! THINK FAST!
HUH? WHA...

Script: Frank Doyle / Art & Letters: Samm Schwartz

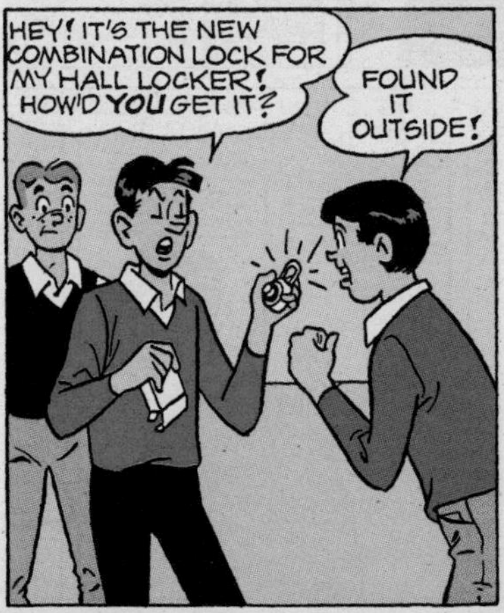
HEY! IT'S THE NEW COMBINATION LOCK FOR MY HALL LOCKER! HOW'D YOU GET IT?
FOUND IT OUTSIDE!

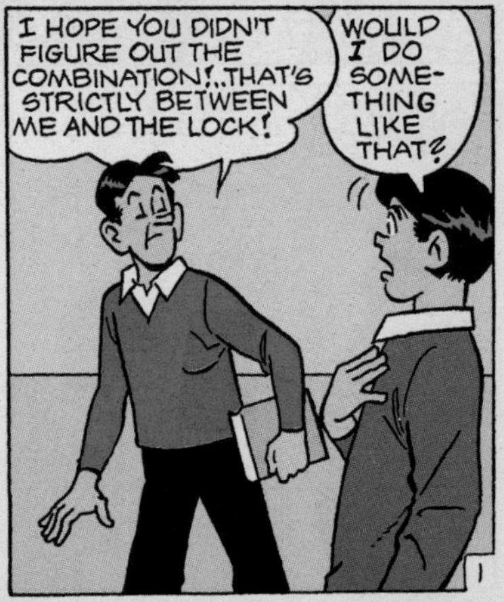
I HOPE YOU DIDN'T FIGURE OUT THE COMBINATION!..THAT'S STRICTLY BETWEEN ME AND THE LOCK!
WOULD I DO SOME-THING LIKE THAT?

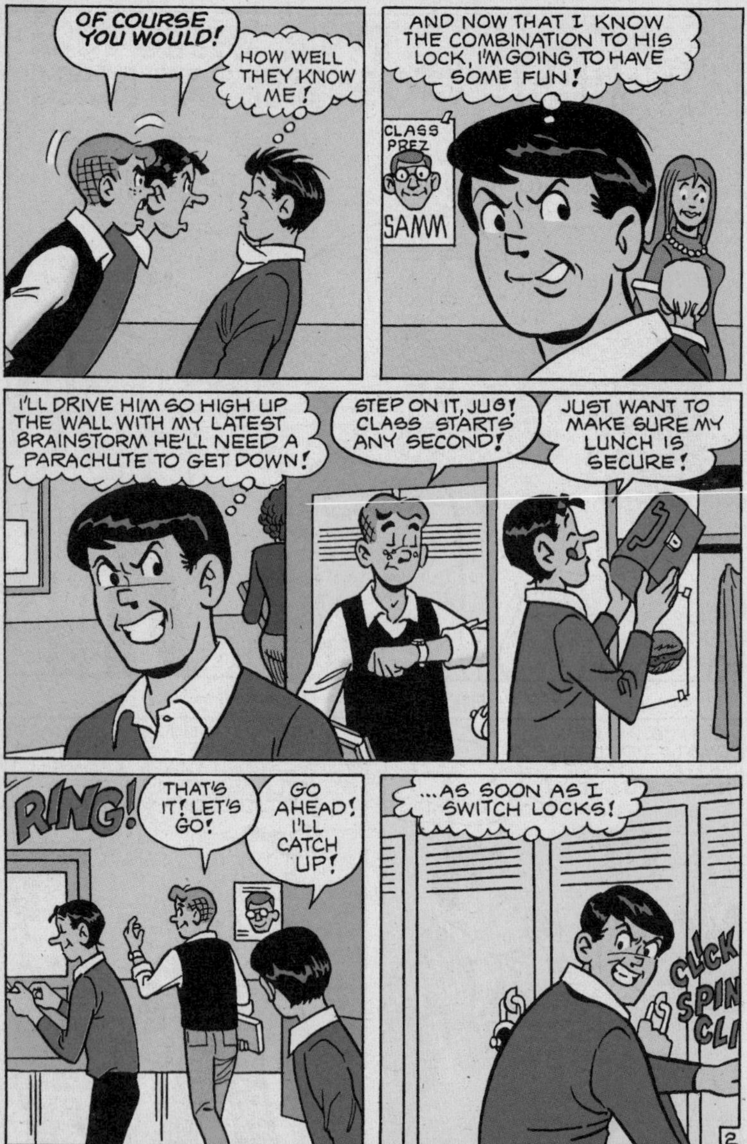
OF COURSE YOU WOULD!
HOW WELL THEY KNOW ME!
AND NOW THAT I KNOW THE COMBINATION TO HIS LOCK, I'M GOING TO HAVE SOME FUN!
CLASS PREZ
SAMM
I'LL DRIVE HIM SO HIGH UP THE WALL WITH MY LATEST BRAINSTORM HE'LL NEED A PARACHUTE TO GET DOWN!
STEP ON IT, JUG! CLASS STARTS ANY SECOND!
JUST WANT TO MAKE SURE MY LUNCH IS SECURE!
RING!
THAT'S IT! LET'S GO!
GO AHEAD! I'LL CATCH UP!
...AS SOON AS I SWITCH LOCKS!
CLICK
SPIN
CLI
2

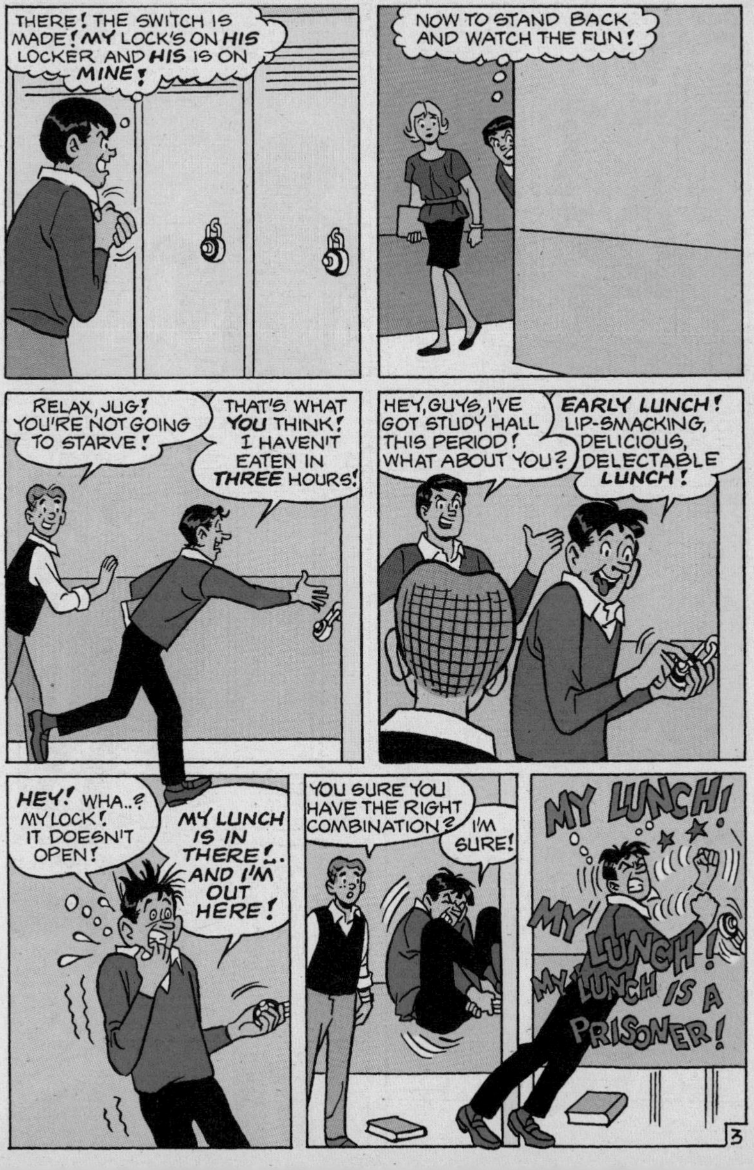
THERE! THE SWITCH IS MADE! MY LOCK'S ON HIS LOCKER AND HIS IS ON MINE!
NOW TO STAND BACK AND WATCH THE FUN!
RELAX, JUG! YOU'RE NOT GOING TO STARVE!
THAT'S WHAT YOU THINK! I HAVEN'T EATEN IN THREE HOURS!
HEY, GUYS, I'VE GOT STUDY HALL THIS PERIOD! WHAT ABOUT YOU?
EARLY LUNCH! LIP-SMACKING, DELICIOUS, DELECTABLE LUNCH!
HEY! WHA..? MY LOCK! IT DOESN'T OPEN!
MY LUNCH IS IN THERE!.. AND I'M OUT HERE!
YOU SURE YOU HAVE THE RIGHT COMBINATION?
I'M SURE!
MY LUNCH!
MY LUNCH!
MY LUNCH IS A PRISONER!

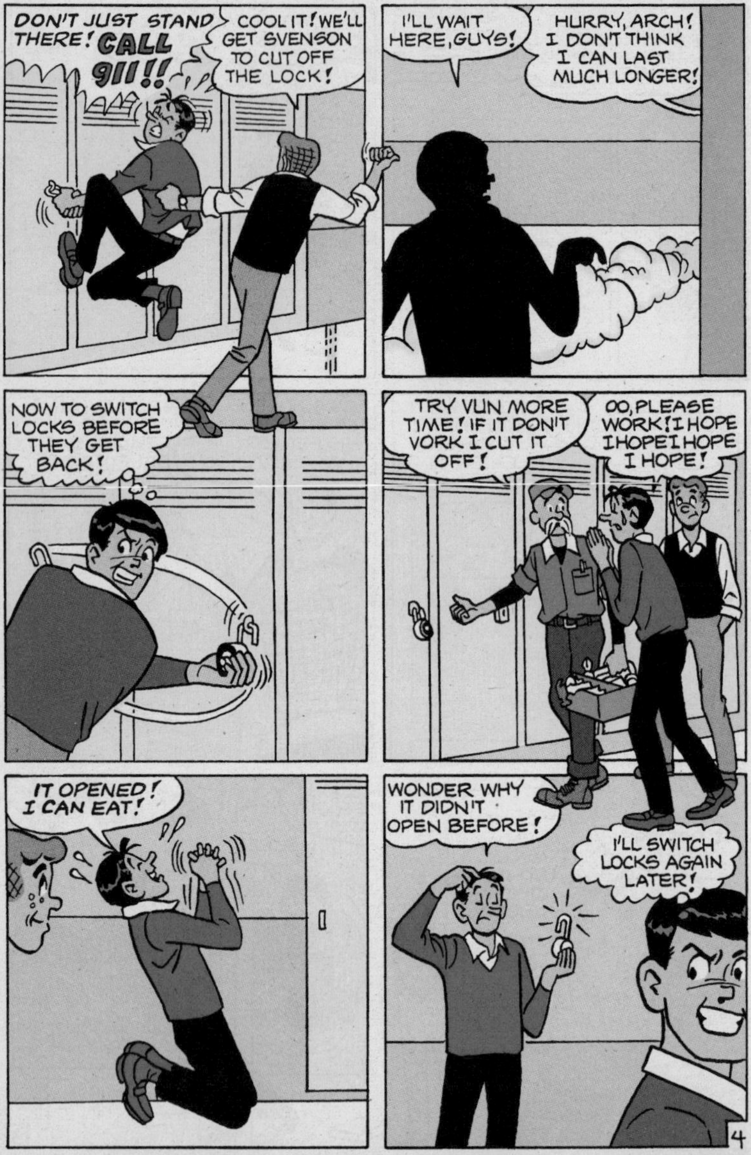
DON'T JUST STAND THERE! CALL 911!!
COOL IT! WE'LL GET SVENSON TO CUT OFF THE LOCK!
I'LL WAIT HERE, GUYS!
HURRY, ARCH! I DON'T THINK I CAN LAST MUCH LONGER!
NOW TO SWITCH LOCKS BEFORE THEY GET BACK!
TRY VUN MORE TIME! IF IT DON'T VORK I CUT IT OFF!
OO, PLEASE WORK! I HOPE I HOPE I HOPE I HOPE!
IT OPENED! I CAN EAT!
WONDER WHY IT DIDN'T OPEN BEFORE!
I'LL SWITCH LOCKS AGAIN LATER!
4

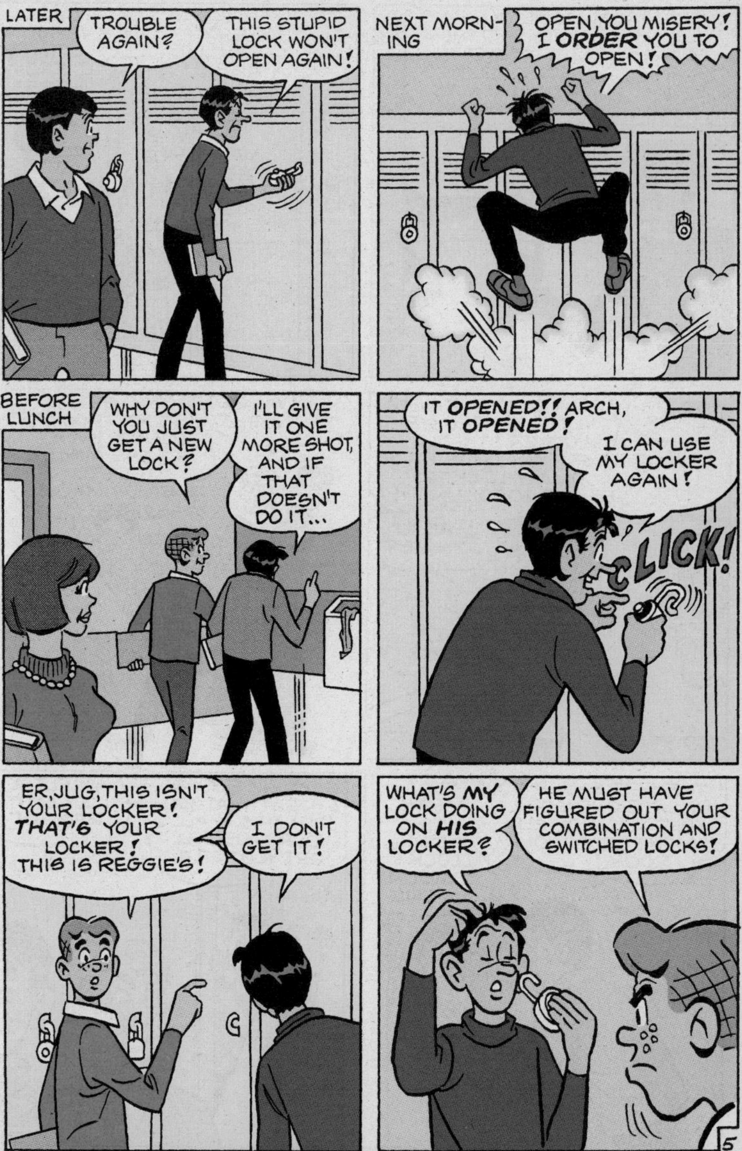
LATER
TROUBLE AGAIN?
THIS STUPID LOCK WON'T OPEN AGAIN!
NEXT MORNING
OPEN, YOU MISERY! I ORDER YOU TO OPEN!
BEFORE LUNCH
WHY DON'T YOU JUST GET A NEW LOCK?
I'LL GIVE IT ONE MORE SHOT, AND IF THAT DOESN'T DO IT...
IT OPENED!! ARCH, IT OPENED!
I CAN USE MY LOCKER AGAIN!
CLICK!
ER, JUG, THIS ISN'T YOUR LOCKER! THAT'S YOUR LOCKER! THIS IS REGGIE'S!
I DON'T GET IT!
WHAT'S MY LOCK DOING ON HIS LOCKER?
HE MUST HAVE FIGURED OUT YOUR COMBINATION AND SWITCHED LOCKS!
5

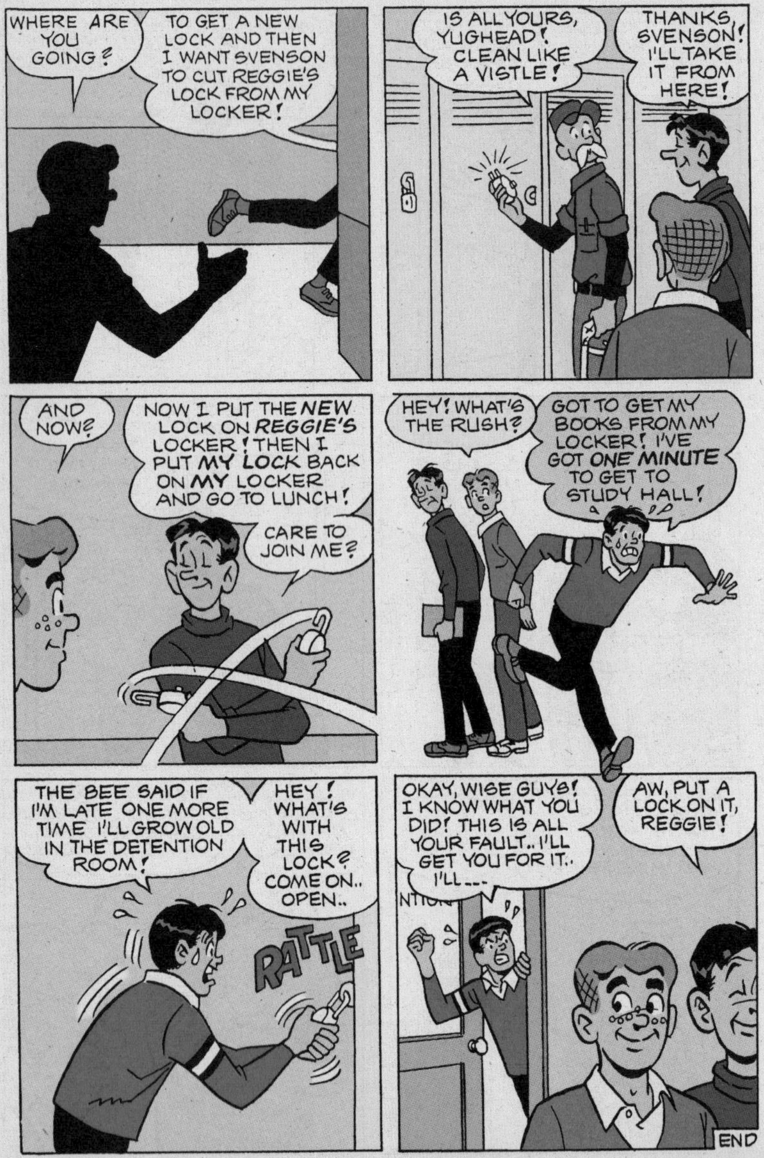
WHERE ARE YOU GOING?
TO GET A NEW LOCK AND THEN I WANT SVENSON TO CUT REGGIE'S LOCK FROM MY LOCKER!
IS ALL YOURS, YUGHEAD! CLEAN LIKE A VISTLE!
THANKS, SVENSON! I'LL TAKE IT FROM HERE!
AND NOW?
NOW I PUT THE NEW LOCK ON REGGIE'S LOCKER! THEN I PUT MY LOCK BACK ON MY LOCKER AND GO TO LUNCH!
CARE TO JOIN ME?
HEY! WHAT'S THE RUSH?
GOT TO GET MY BOOKS FROM MY LOCKER! I'VE GOT ONE MINUTE TO GET TO STUDY HALL!
THE BEE SAID IF I'M LATE ONE MORE TIME I'LL GROW OLD IN THE DETENTION ROOM!
HEY! WHAT'S WITH THIS LOCK? COME ON.. OPEN..
RATTLE
OKAY, WISE GUYS! I KNOW WHAT YOU DID! THIS IS ALL YOUR FAULT.. I'LL GET YOU FOR IT.. I'LL ---
AW, PUT A LOCK ON IT, REGGIE!
END

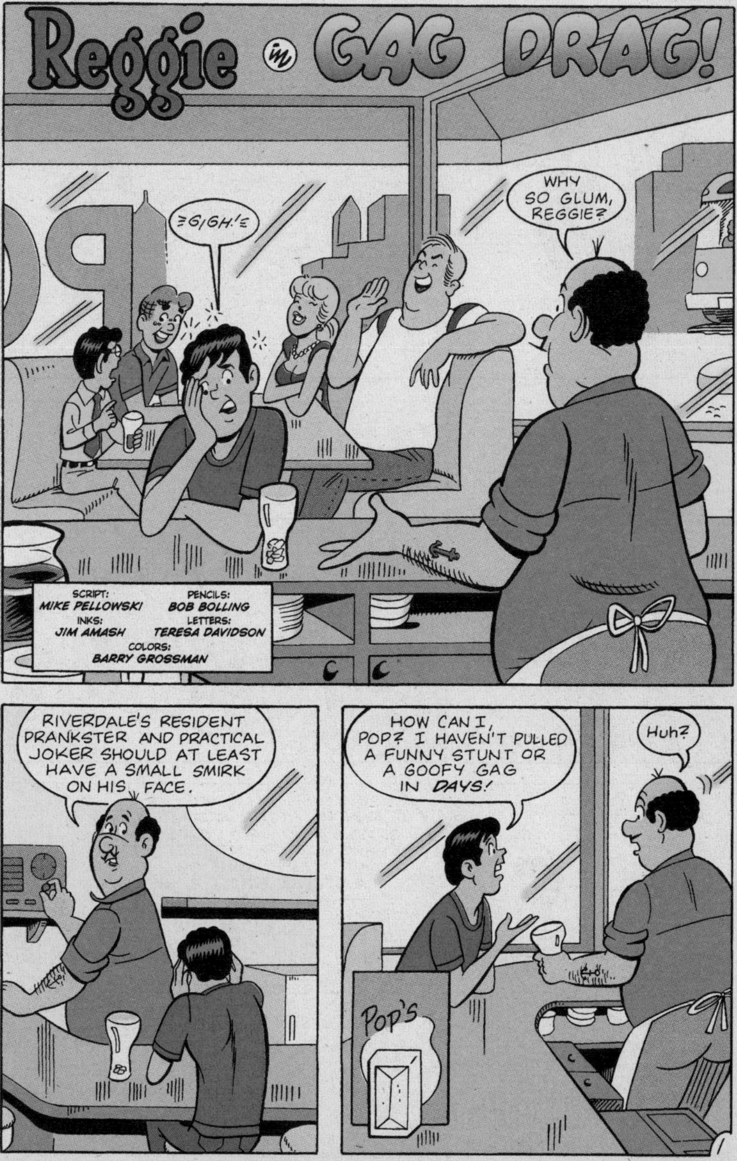
Reggie in GAG DRAG!
WHY SO GLUM, REGGIE?
SIGH!
SCRIPT: MIKE PELLOWSKI
PENCILS: BOB BOLLING
INKS: JIM AMASH
LETTERS: TERESA DAVIDSON
COLORS: BARRY GROSSMAN
RIVERDALE'S RESIDENT PRANKSTER AND PRACTICAL JOKER SHOULD AT LEAST HAVE A SMALL SMIRK ON HIS FACE.
HOW CAN I, POP? I HAVEN'T PULLED A FUNNY STUNT OR A GOOFY GAG IN DAYS!
Huh?
Pop's

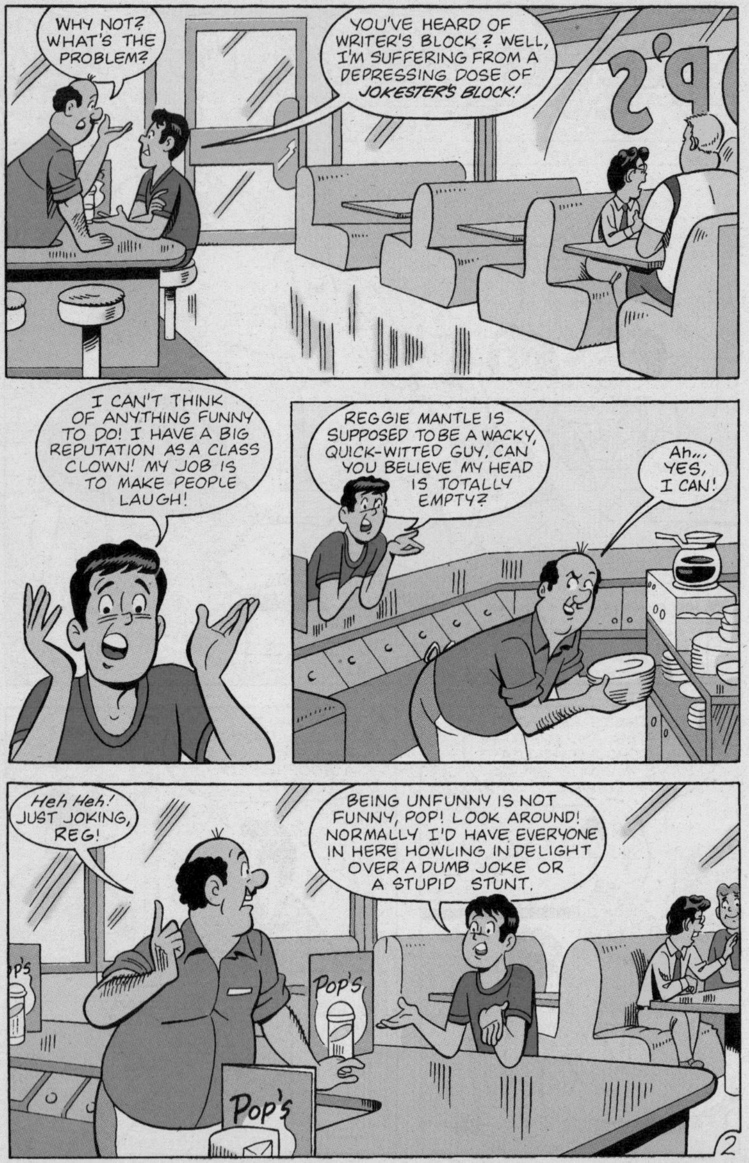
WHY NOT? WHAT'S THE PROBLEM?
YOU'VE HEARD OF WRITER'S BLOCK? WELL, I'M SUFFERING FROM A DEPRESSING DOSE OF JOKESTER'S BLOCK!
POP'S
I CAN'T THINK OF ANYTHING FUNNY TO DO! I HAVE A BIG REPUTATION AS A CLASS CLOWN! MY JOB IS TO MAKE PEOPLE LAUGH!
REGGIE MANTLE IS SUPPOSED TO BE A WACKY, QUICK-WITTED GUY, CAN YOU BELIEVE MY HEAD IS TOTALLY EMPTY?
Ah... YES, I CAN!
Heh Heh! JUST JOKING, REG!
BEING UNFUNNY IS NOT FUNNY, POP! LOOK AROUND! NORMALLY I'D HAVE EVERYONE IN HERE HOWLING IN DELIGHT OVER A DUMB JOKE OR A STUPID STUNT.
Pop's
Pop's

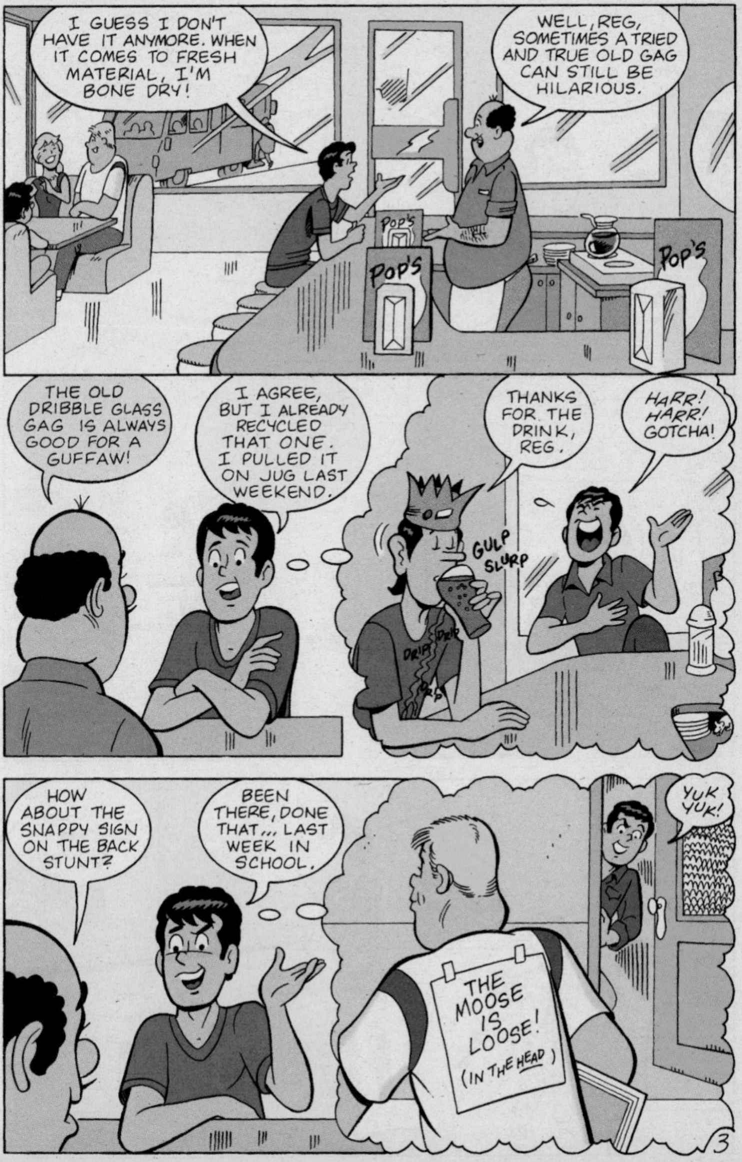
I GUESS I DON'T HAVE IT ANYMORE. WHEN IT COMES TO FRESH MATERIAL, I'M BONE DRY!
WELL, REG, SOMETIMES A TRIED AND TRUE OLD GAG CAN STILL BE HILARIOUS.
POP'S
POP'S
POP'S
THE OLD DRIBBLE GLASS GAG IS ALWAYS GOOD FOR A GUFFAW!
I AGREE, BUT I ALREADY RECYCLED THAT ONE. I PULLED IT ON JUG LAST WEEKEND.
THANKS FOR THE DRINK, REG.
HARR! HARR! GOTCHA!
GULP SLURP
DRIP DRIP DRIP
HOW ABOUT THE SNAPPY SIGN ON THE BACK STUNT?
BEEN THERE, DONE THAT... LAST WEEK IN SCHOOL.
YUK YUK!
THE MOOSE IS LOOSE! (IN THE HEAD)

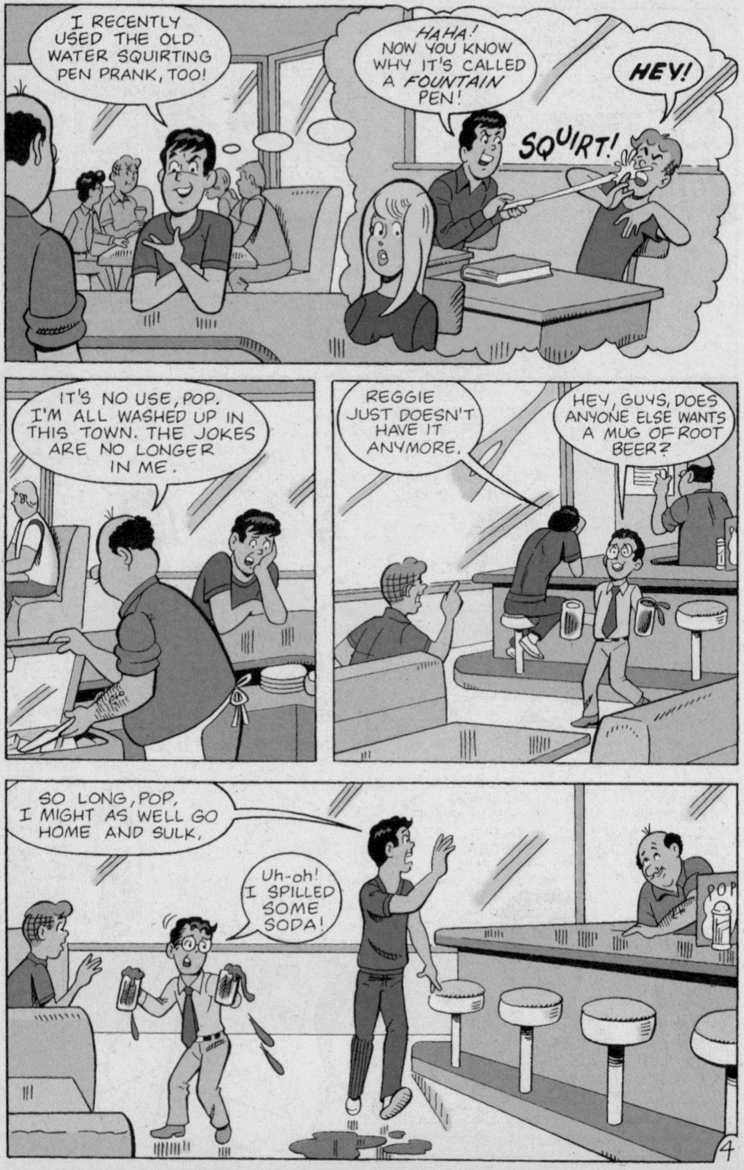
I RECENTLY USED THE OLD WATER SQUIRTING PEN PRANK, TOO!
HAHA! NOW YOU KNOW WHY IT'S CALLED A FOUNTAIN PEN!
HEY!
SQUIRT!
IT'S NO USE, POP. I'M ALL WASHED UP IN THIS TOWN. THE JOKES ARE NO LONGER IN ME.
REGGIE JUST DOESN'T HAVE IT ANYMORE.
HEY, GUYS, DOES ANYONE ELSE WANTS A MUG OF ROOT BEER?
SO LONG, POP, I MIGHT AS WELL GO HOME AND SULK.
Uh-oh! I SPILLED SOME SODA!

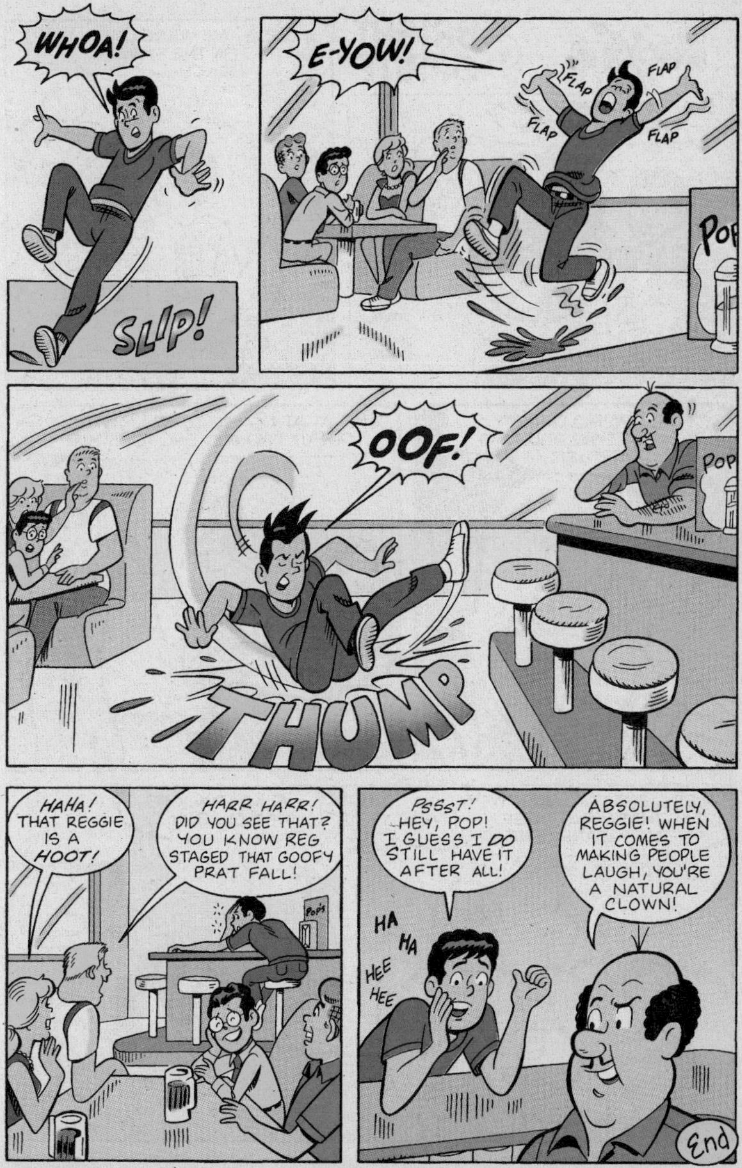
WHOA!
SLIP!
E-YOW!
FLAP
FLAP
FLAP
FLAP
POP
OOF!
POP
THUMP
HAHA! THAT REGGIE IS A HOOT!
HARR HARR! DID YOU SEE THAT? YOU KNOW REG STAGED THAT GOOFY PRAT FALL!
POP'S
PSSST! HEY, POP! I GUESS I DO STILL HAVE IT AFTER ALL!
ABSOLUTELY, REGGIE! WHEN IT COMES TO MAKING PEOPLE LAUGH, YOU'RE A NATURAL CLOWN!
HA
HA
HEE
HEE
End

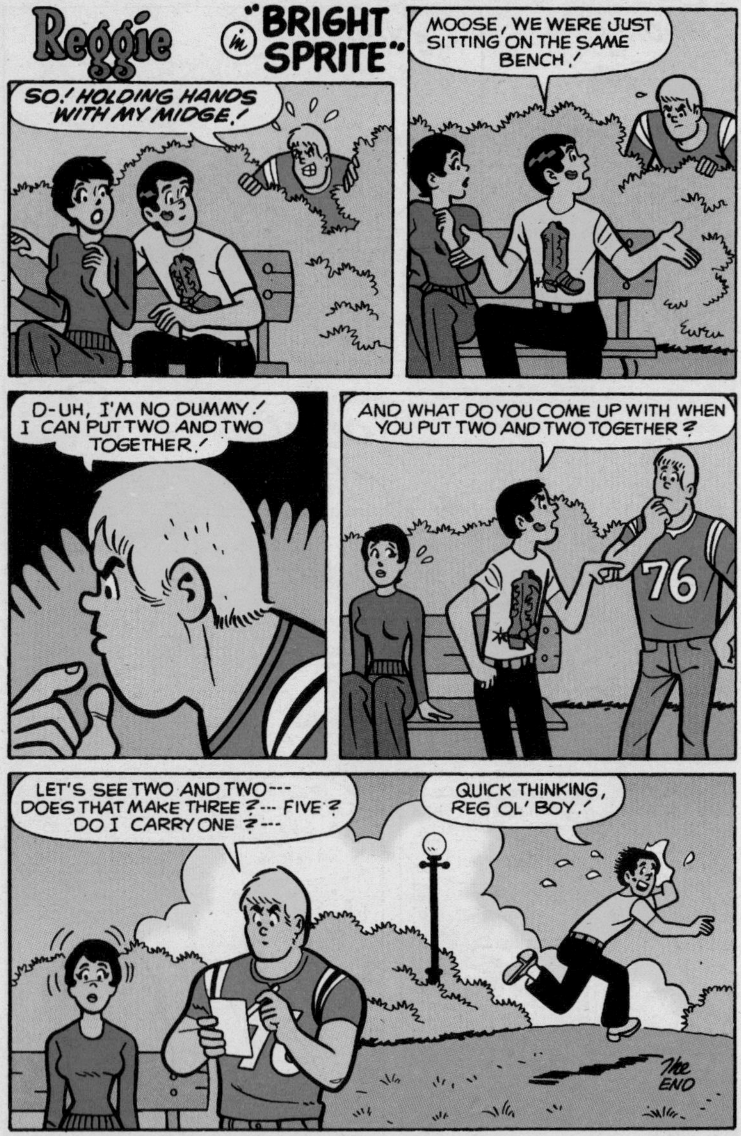
Reggie
in "BRIGHT SPRITE"
SO! HOLDING HANDS WITH MY MIDGE!
MOOSE, WE WERE JUST SITTING ON THE SAME BENCH!
D-UH, I'M NO DUMMY! I CAN PUT TWO AND TWO TOGETHER!
AND WHAT DO YOU COME UP WITH WHEN YOU PUT TWO AND TWO TOGETHER?
76
LET'S SEE TWO AND TWO--- DOES THAT MAKE THREE?--- FIVE? DO I CARRY ONE?---
QUICK THINKING, REG OL' BOY!
THE END

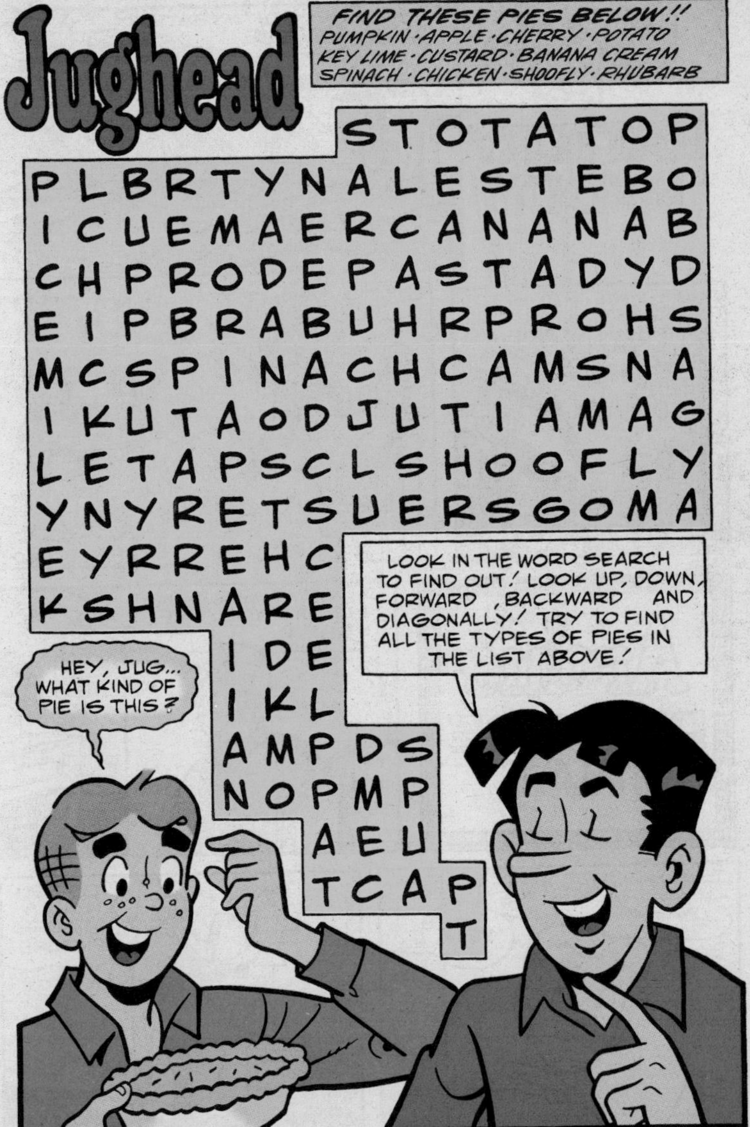
Jughead
FIND THESE PIES BELOW!!
PUMPKIN · APPLE · CHERRY · POTATO
KEY LIME · CUSTARD · BANANA CREAM
SPINACH · CHICKEN · SHOOFLY · RHUBARB
STOTATOP
PLBRTYNALESTEBO
ICUEMAERCANANAB
CHPRODEPASTADYD
EIPBRABUHRPROHS
MCSPINACHCAMSNA
IKUTAODJUTIAMAG
LETAPSCLSHOOFLY
YNYRETSUERSGOMA
EYRREHC
KSHNARE
IDE
IKL
AMPDS
NOPMP
AEU
TCAP
T
LOOK IN THE WORD SEARCH TO FIND OUT! LOOK UP, DOWN, FORWARD, BACKWARD AND DIAGONALLY! TRY TO FIND ALL THE TYPES OF PIES IN THE LIST ABOVE!
HEY, JUG... WHAT KIND OF PIE IS THIS?

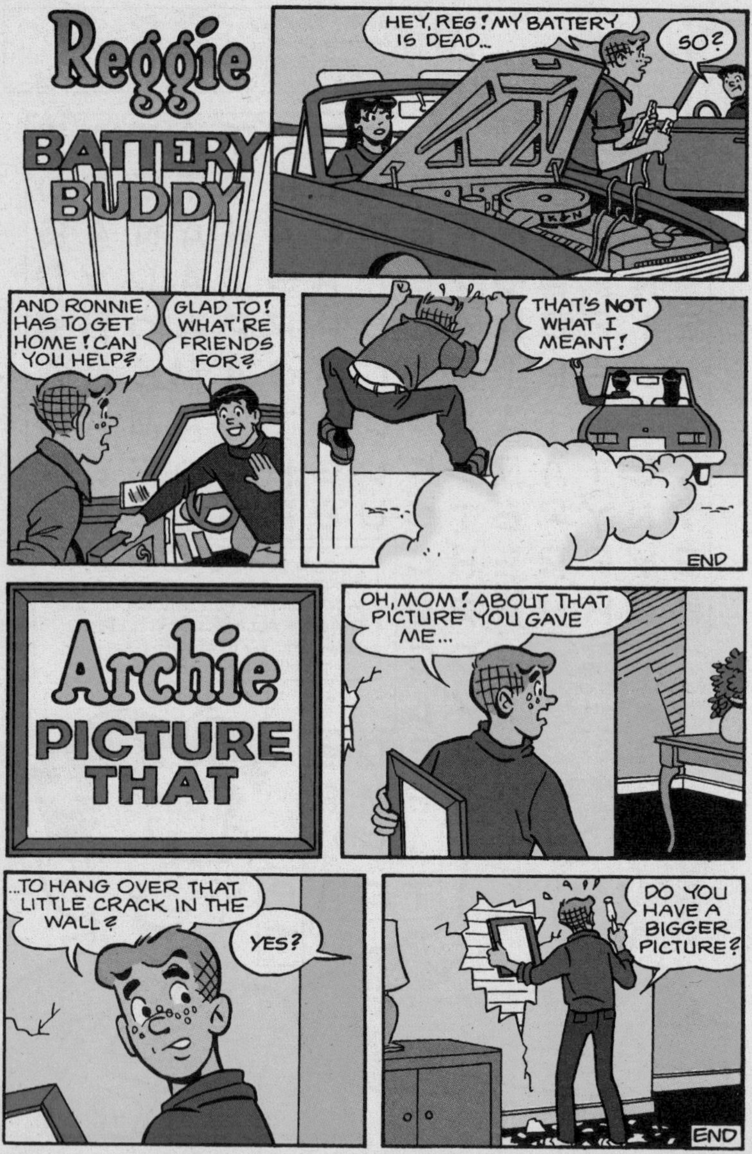
Reggie
BATTERY BUDDY
HEY, REG! MY BATTERY IS DEAD...
SO?
AND RONNIE HAS TO GET HOME! CAN YOU HELP?
GLAD TO! WHAT'RE FRIENDS FOR?
THAT'S NOT WHAT I MEANT!
END
Archie
PICTURE THAT
OH, MOM! ABOUT THAT PICTURE YOU GAVE ME...
...TO HANG OVER THAT LITTLE CRACK IN THE WALL?
YES?
DO YOU HAVE A BIGGER PICTURE?
END

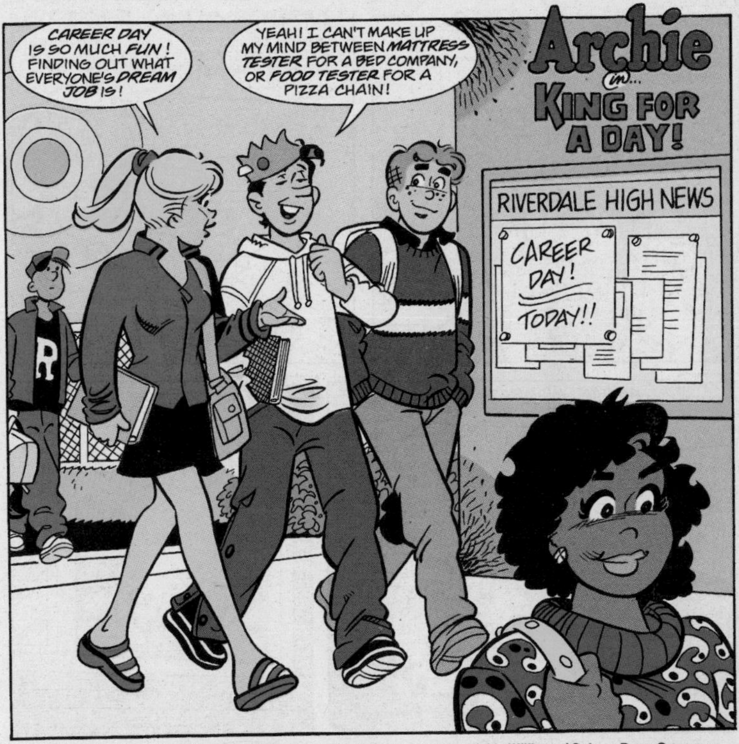
Archie
in...
KING FOR A DAY!
CAREER DAY IS SO MUCH FUN! FINDING OUT WHAT EVERYONE'S DREAM JOB IS!
YEAH! I CAN'T MAKE UP MY MIND BETWEEN MATTRESS TESTER FOR A BED COMPANY, OR FOOD TESTER FOR A PIZZA CHAIN!
RIVERDALE HIGH NEWS
CAREER DAY! TODAY!!
R

Script: Bill Golliher / Pencils: Stan Goldberg / Inks: Bob Smith / Letters: Vickie Williams / Colors: Barry Grossman

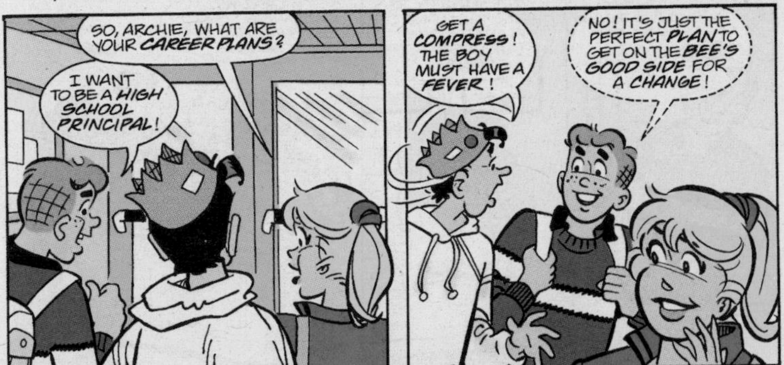
SO, ARCHIE, WHAT ARE YOUR CAREER PLANS?
I WANT TO BE A HIGH SCHOOL PRINCIPAL!
GET A COMPRESS! THE BOY MUST HAVE A FEVER!
NO! IT'S JUST THE PERFECT PLAN TO GET ON THE BEE'S GOOD SIDE FOR A CHANGE!

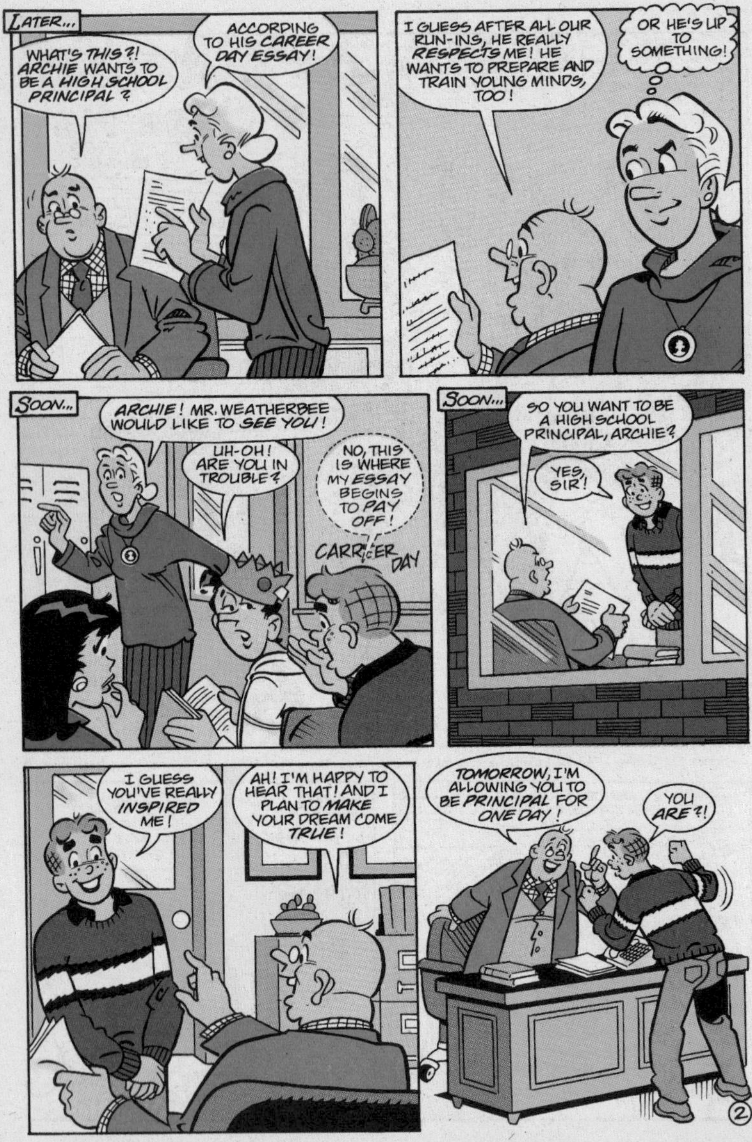
LATER...
WHAT'S THIS?! ARCHIE WANTS TO BE A HIGH SCHOOL PRINCIPAL?
ACCORDING TO HIS CAREER DAY ESSAY!
I GUESS AFTER ALL OUR RUN-INS, HE REALLY RESPECTS ME! HE WANTS TO PREPARE AND TRAIN YOUNG MINDS, TOO!
OR HE'S UP TO SOMETHING!
SOON...
ARCHIE! MR. WEATHERBEE WOULD LIKE TO SEE YOU!
UH-OH! ARE YOU IN TROUBLE?
NO, THIS IS WHERE MY ESSAY BEGINS TO PAY OFF!
CARREER DAY
SOON...
SO YOU WANT TO BE A HIGH SCHOOL PRINCIPAL, ARCHIE?
YES, SIR!
I GUESS YOU'VE REALLY INSPIRED ME!
AH! I'M HAPPY TO HEAR THAT! AND I PLAN TO MAKE YOUR DREAM COME TRUE!
TOMORROW, I'M ALLOWING YOU TO BE PRINCIPAL FOR ONE DAY!
YOU ARE?!
2

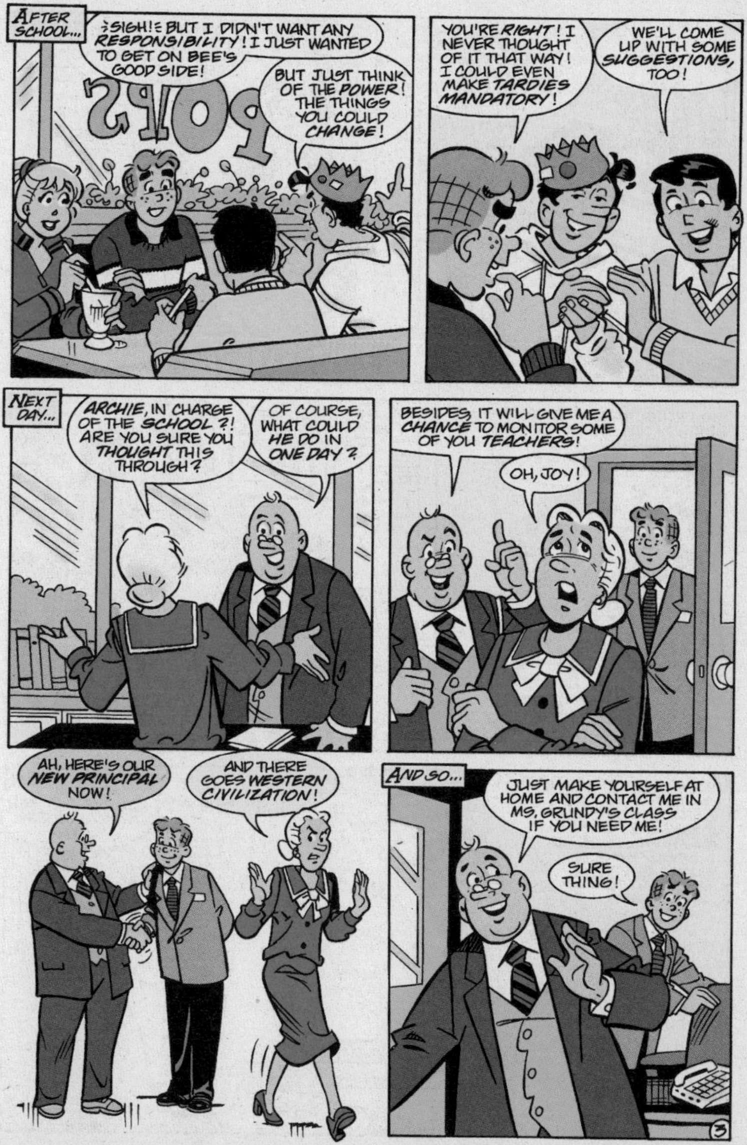
AFTER SCHOOL...
SIGH! BUT I DIDN'T WANT ANY RESPONSIBILITY! I JUST WANTED TO GET ON BEE'S GOOD SIDE!
BUT JUST THINK OF THE POWER! THE THINGS YOU COULD CHANGE!
POP'S
YOU'RE RIGHT! I NEVER THOUGHT OF IT THAT WAY! I COULD EVEN MAKE TARDIES MANDATORY!
WE'LL COME UP WITH SOME SUGGESTIONS, TOO!
NEXT DAY...
ARCHIE, IN CHARGE OF THE SCHOOL?! ARE YOU SURE YOU THOUGHT THIS THROUGH?
OF COURSE, WHAT COULD HE DO IN ONE DAY?
BESIDES, IT WILL GIVE ME A CHANCE TO MONITOR SOME OF YOU TEACHERS!
OH, JOY!
AH, HERE'S OUR NEW PRINCIPAL NOW!
AND THERE GOES WESTERN CIVILIZATION!
AND SO...
JUST MAKE YOURSELF AT HOME AND CONTACT ME IN MS. GRUNDY'S CLASS IF YOU NEED ME!
SURE THING!

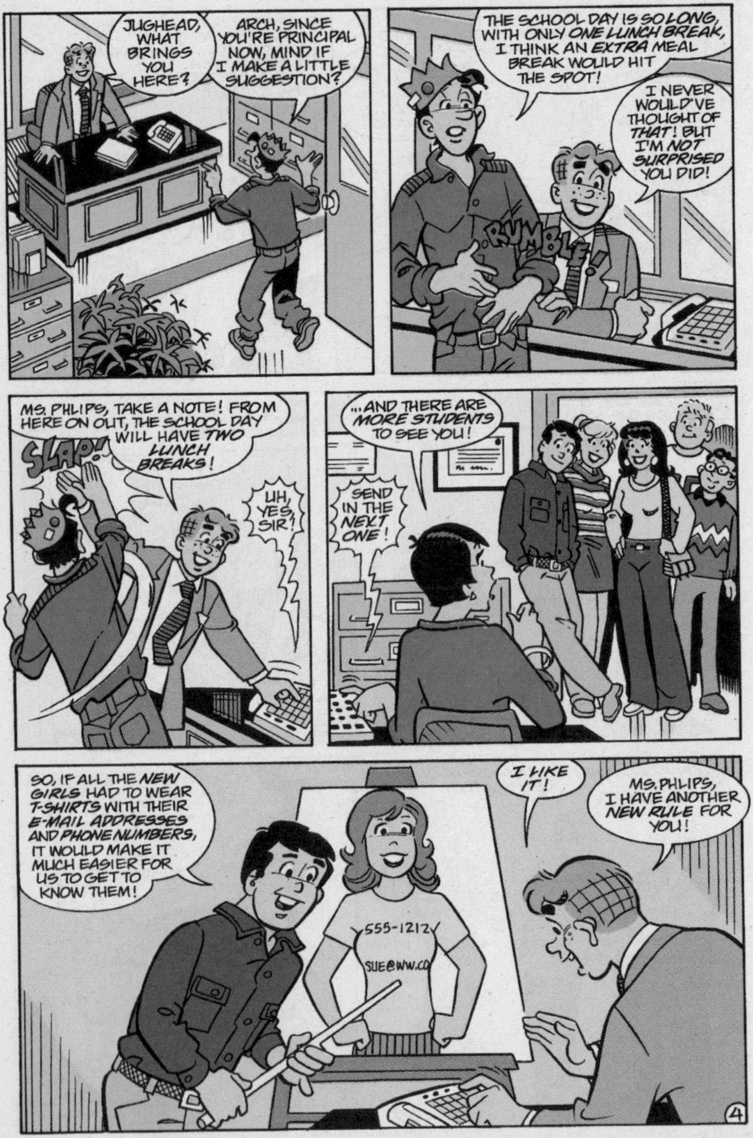
JUGHEAD, WHAT BRINGS YOU HERE?
ARCH, SINCE YOU'RE PRINCIPAL NOW, MIND IF I MAKE A LITTLE SUGGESTION?
THE SCHOOL DAY IS SO LONG, WITH ONLY ONE LUNCH BREAK, I THINK AN EXTRA MEAL BREAK WOULD HIT THE SPOT!
RUMBLE!
I NEVER WOULD'VE THOUGHT OF THAT! BUT I'M NOT SURPRISED YOU DID!
MS. PHLIPS, TAKE A NOTE! FROM HERE ON OUT, THE SCHOOL DAY WILL HAVE TWO LUNCH BREAKS!
SLAP!
UH, YES, SIR!
...AND THERE ARE MORE STUDENTS TO SEE YOU!
SEND IN THE NEXT ONE!
SO, IF ALL THE NEW GIRLS HAD TO WEAR T-SHIRTS WITH THEIR E-MAIL ADDRESSES AND PHONE NUMBERS, IT WOULD MAKE IT MUCH EASIER FOR US TO GET TO KNOW THEM!
I LIKE IT!
MS. PHLIPS, I HAVE ANOTHER NEW RULE FOR YOU!
555-1212
SUE@WW.CO
4

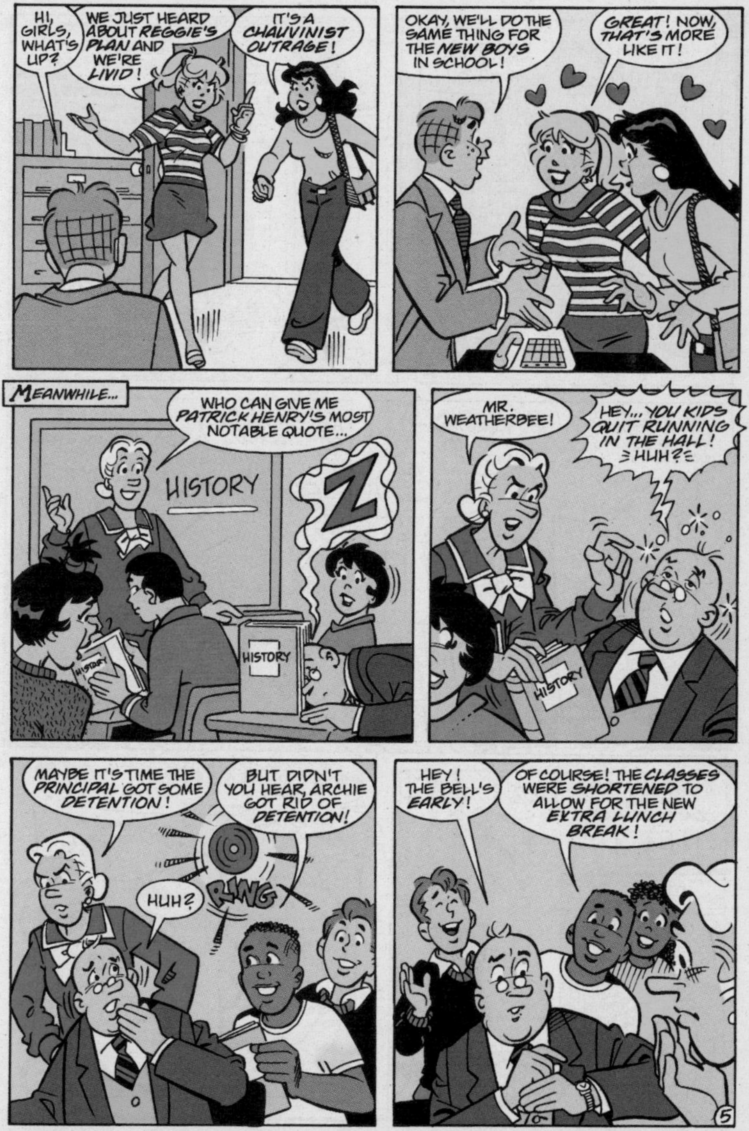
HI, GIRLS, WHAT'S UP?
WE JUST HEARD ABOUT REGGIE'S PLAN AND WE'RE LIVID!
IT'S A CHAUVINIST OUTRAGE!
OKAY, WE'LL DO THE SAME THING FOR THE NEW BOYS IN SCHOOL!
GREAT! NOW, THAT'S MORE LIKE IT!
MEANWHILE...
WHO CAN GIVE ME PATRICK HENRY'S MOST NOTABLE QUOTE...
HISTORY
Z
HISTORY
HISTORY
MR. WEATHERBEE!
HEY... YOU KIDS QUIT RUNNING IN THE HALL! HUH?
HISTORY
MAYBE IT'S TIME THE PRINCIPAL GOT SOME DETENTION!
BUT DIDN'T YOU HEAR, ARCHIE GOT RID OF DETENTION!
HUH?
RING
HEY! THE BELL'S EARLY!
OF COURSE! THE CLASSES WERE SHORTENED TO ALLOW FOR THE NEW EXTRA LUNCH BREAK!

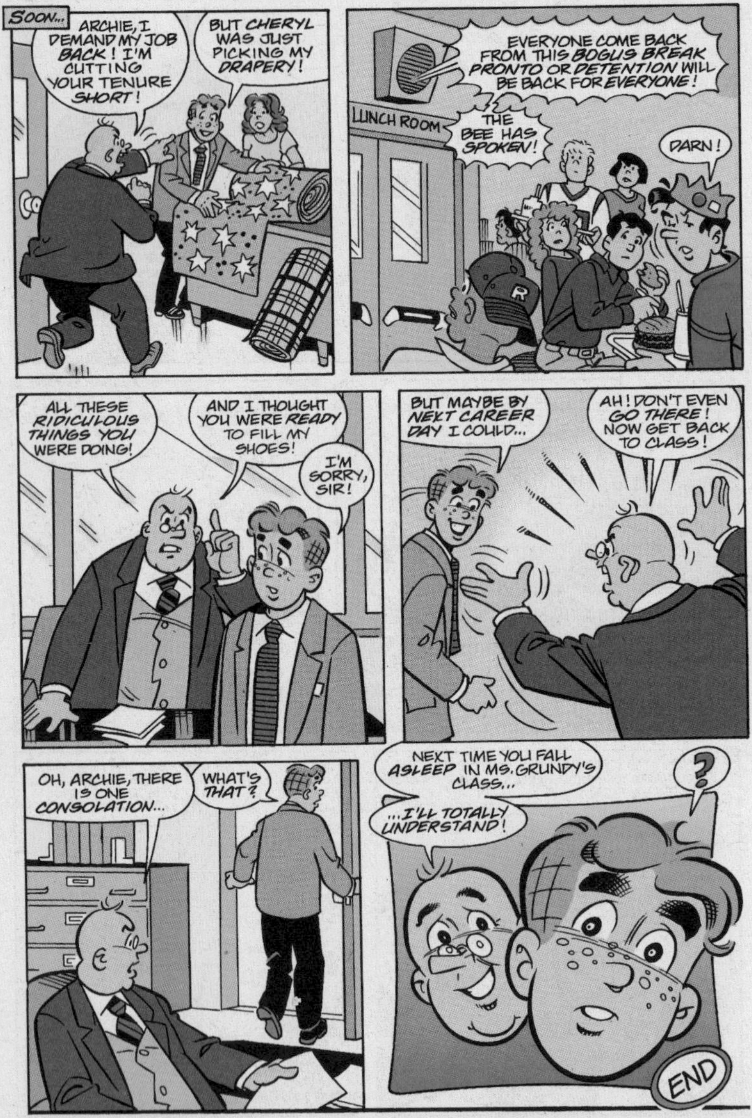
SOON...
ARCHIE, I DEMAND MY JOB BACK! I'M CUTTING YOUR TENURE SHORT!
BUT CHERYL WAS JUST PICKING MY DRAPERY!
EVERYONE COME BACK FROM THIS BOGUS BREAK PRONTO OR DETENTION WILL BE BACK FOR EVERYONE!
LUNCH ROOM
THE BEE HAS SPOKEN!
DARN!
ALL THESE RIDICULOUS THINGS YOU WERE DOING!
AND I THOUGHT YOU WERE READY TO FILL MY SHOES!
I'M SORRY, SIR!
BUT MAYBE BY NEXT CAREER DAY I COULD...
AH! DON'T EVEN GO THERE! NOW GET BACK TO CLASS!
OH, ARCHIE, THERE IS ONE CONSOLATION...
WHAT'S THAT?
NEXT TIME YOU FALL ASLEEP IN MS. GRUNDY'S CLASS...
...I'LL TOTALLY UNDERSTAND!
?
END

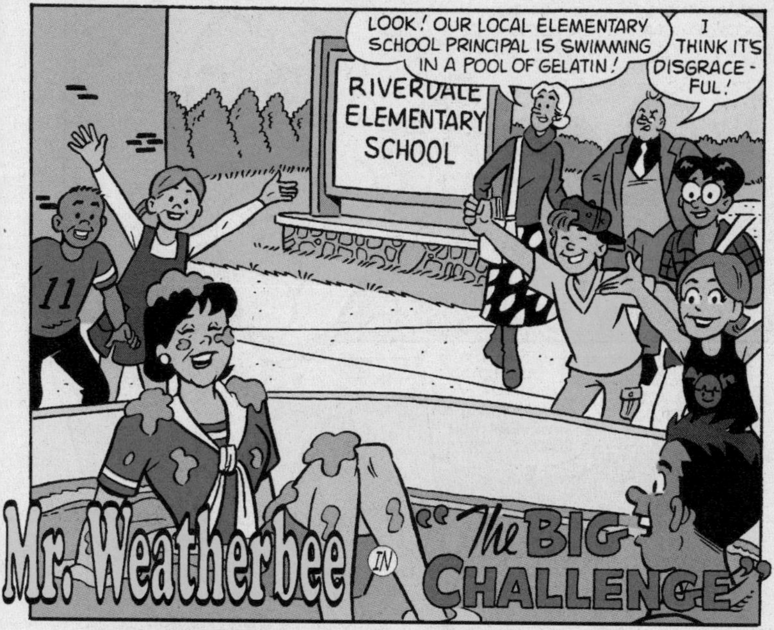
LOOK! OUR LOCAL ELEMENTARY SCHOOL PRINCIPAL IS SWIMMING IN A POOL OF GELATIN!
I THINK IT'S DISGRACE-FUL!
RIVERDALE ELEMENTARY SCHOOL
11
Mr. Weatherbee IN "The BIG CHALLENGE"

SCRIPT: GEORGE GLADIR PENCILS: FERNANDO RUIZ INKS: RUDY LAPICK
COLORS: BARRY GROSSMAN LETTERS: BILL YOSHIDA

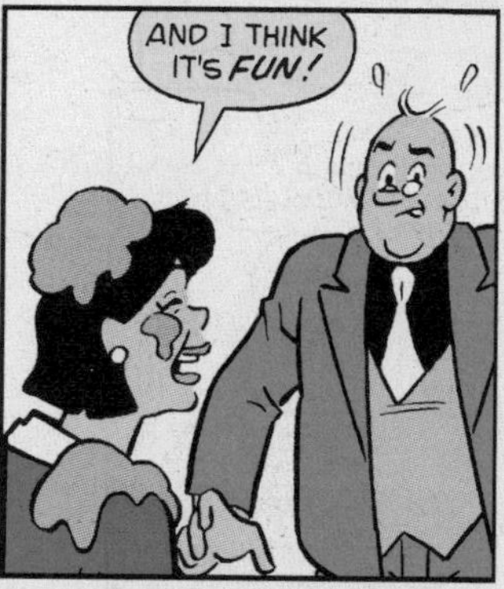
AND I THINK IT'S *FUN*!

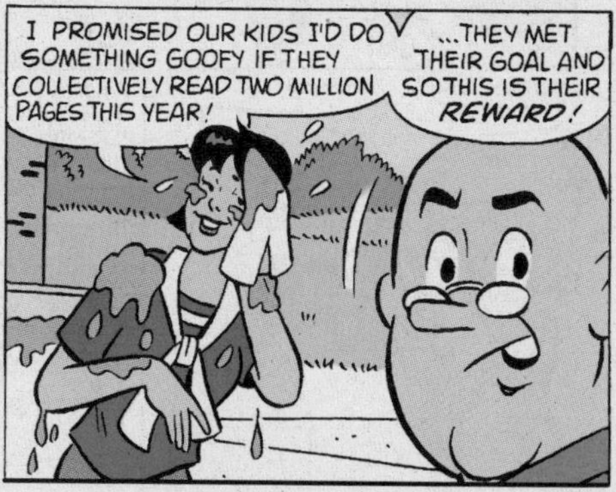
I PROMISED OUR KIDS I'D DO SOMETHING GOOFY IF THEY COLLECTIVELY READ TWO MILLION PAGES THIS YEAR!
...THEY MET THEIR GOAL AND SO THIS IS THEIR *REWARD*!

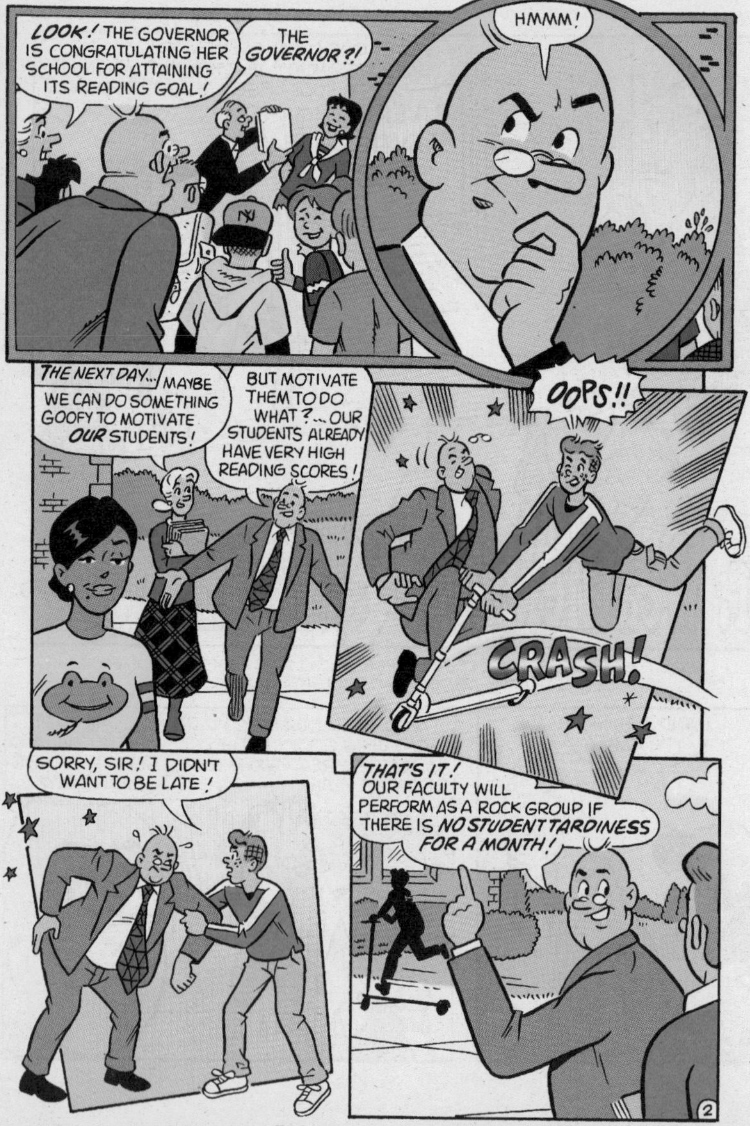
LOOK! THE GOVERNOR IS CONGRATULATING HER SCHOOL FOR ATTAINING ITS READING GOAL!
THE GOVERNOR?!
HMMM!
THE NEXT DAY...
MAYBE WE CAN DO SOMETHING GOOFY TO MOTIVATE OUR STUDENTS!
BUT MOTIVATE THEM TO DO WHAT?... OUR STUDENTS ALREADY HAVE VERY HIGH READING SCORES!
OOPS!!
CRASH!
SORRY, SIR! I DIDN'T WANT TO BE LATE!
THAT'S IT! OUR FACULTY WILL PERFORM AS A ROCK GROUP IF THERE IS NO STUDENT TARDINESS FOR A MONTH!

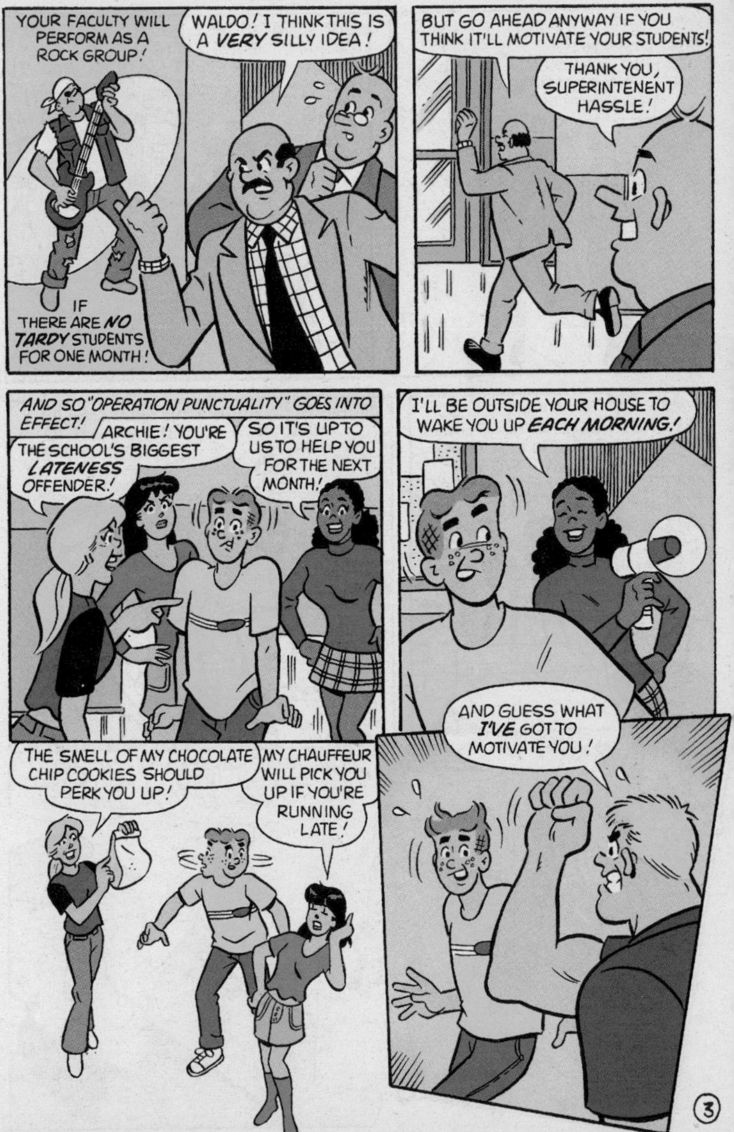

YOUR FACULTY WILL PERFORM AS A ROCK GROUP!
IF THERE ARE NO TARDY STUDENTS FOR ONE MONTH!
WALDO! I THINK THIS IS A VERY SILLY IDEA!
BUT GO AHEAD ANYWAY IF YOU THINK IT'LL MOTIVATE YOUR STUDENTS!
THANK YOU, SUPERINTENENT HASSLE!
AND SO "OPERATION PUNCTUALITY" GOES INTO EFFECT!
ARCHIE! YOU'RE THE SCHOOL'S BIGGEST LATENESS OFFENDER!
SO IT'S UP TO US TO HELP YOU FOR THE NEXT MONTH!
I'LL BE OUTSIDE YOUR HOUSE TO WAKE YOU UP EACH MORNING!
THE SMELL OF MY CHOCOLATE CHIP COOKIES SHOULD PERK YOU UP!
MY CHAUFFEUR WILL PICK YOU UP IF YOU'RE RUNNING LATE!
AND GUESS WHAT I'VE GOT TO MOTIVATE YOU!

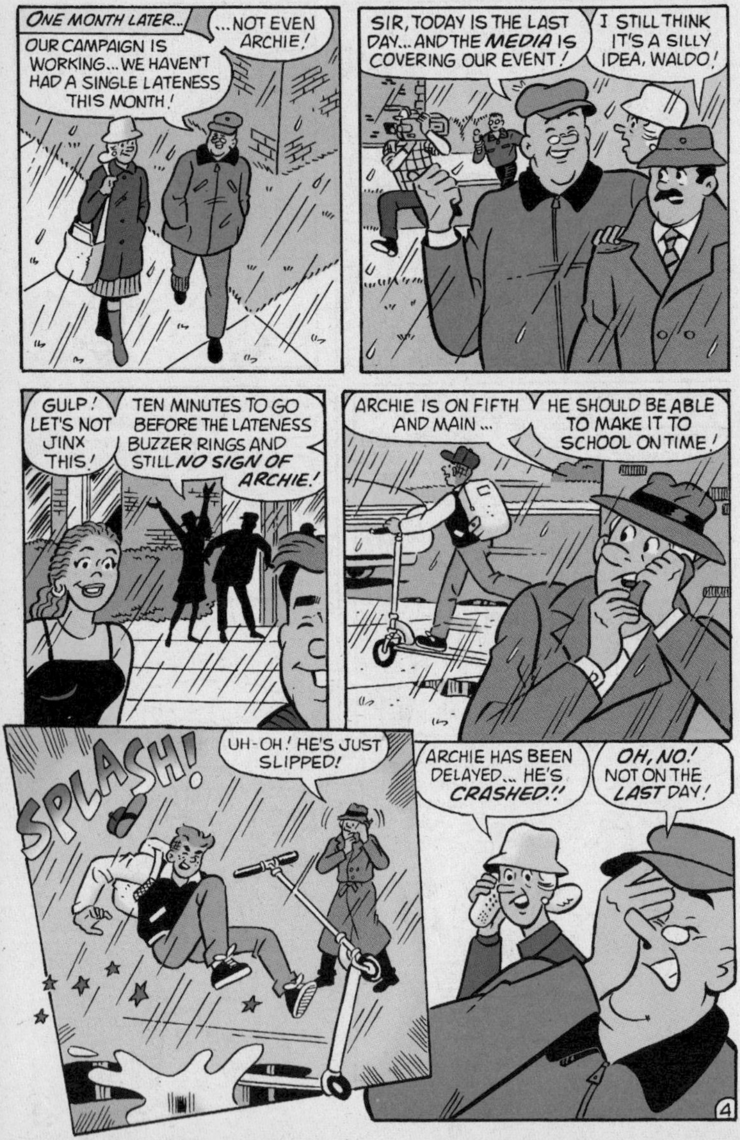
ONE MONTH LATER...
OUR CAMPAIGN IS WORKING... WE HAVEN'T HAD A SINGLE LATENESS THIS MONTH!
...NOT EVEN ARCHIE!
SIR, TODAY IS THE LAST DAY... AND THE MEDIA IS COVERING OUR EVENT!
I STILL THINK IT'S A SILLY IDEA, WALDO!
GULP! LET'S NOT JINX THIS!
TEN MINUTES TO GO BEFORE THE LATENESS BUZZER RINGS AND STILL NO SIGN OF ARCHIE!
ARCHIE IS ON FIFTH AND MAIN...
HE SHOULD BE ABLE TO MAKE IT TO SCHOOL ON TIME!
SPLASH!
UH-OH! HE'S JUST SLIPPED!
ARCHIE HAS BEEN DELAYED... HE'S CRASHED!!
OH, NO! NOT ON THE LAST DAY!
4

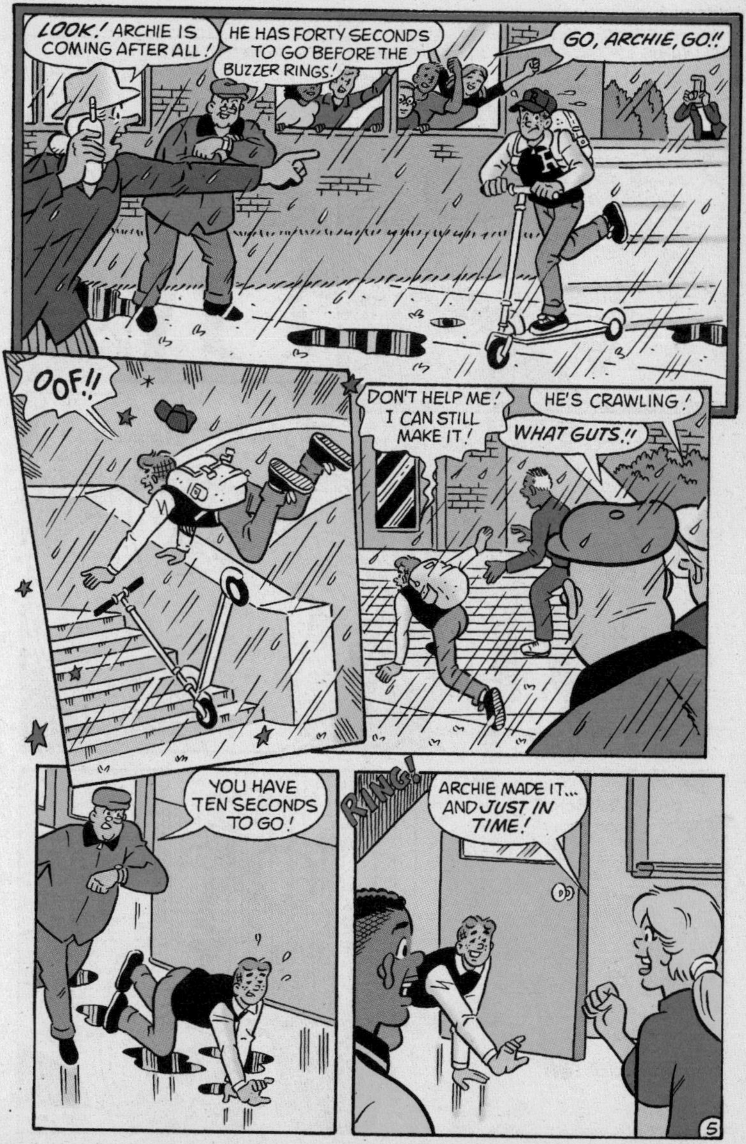
LOOK! ARCHIE IS COMING AFTER ALL!
HE HAS FORTY SECONDS TO GO BEFORE THE BUZZER RINGS!
GO, ARCHIE, GO!!
OOF!!
DON'T HELP ME! I CAN STILL MAKE IT!
HE'S CRAWLING!
WHAT GUTS!!
YOU HAVE TEN SECONDS TO GO!
RING!
ARCHIE MADE IT... AND JUST IN TIME!

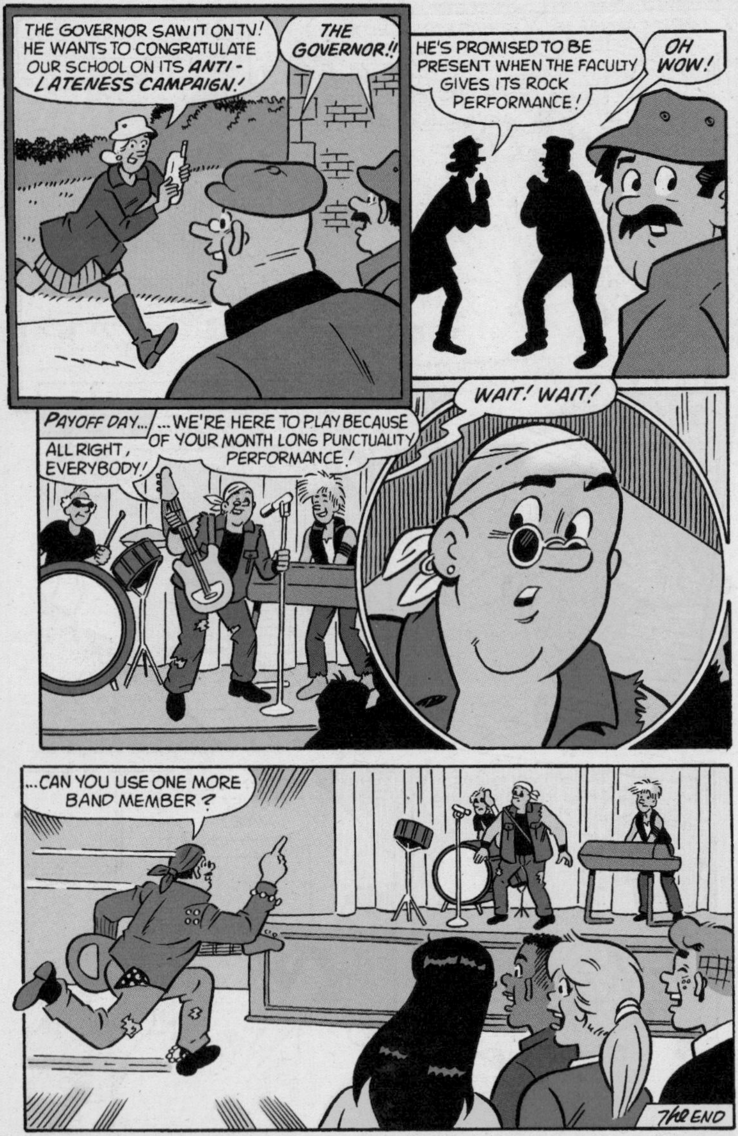
THE GOVERNOR SAW IT ON TV! HE WANTS TO CONGRATULATE OUR SCHOOL ON ITS ANTI-LATENESS CAMPAIGN!
THE GOVERNOR!!
HE'S PROMISED TO BE PRESENT WHEN THE FACULTY GIVES ITS ROCK PERFORMANCE!
OH WOW!
PAYOFF DAY...
ALL RIGHT, EVERYBODY!
...WE'RE HERE TO PLAY BECAUSE OF YOUR MONTH LONG PUNCTUALITY PERFORMANCE!
WAIT! WAIT!
...CAN YOU USE ONE MORE BAND MEMBER?
THE END

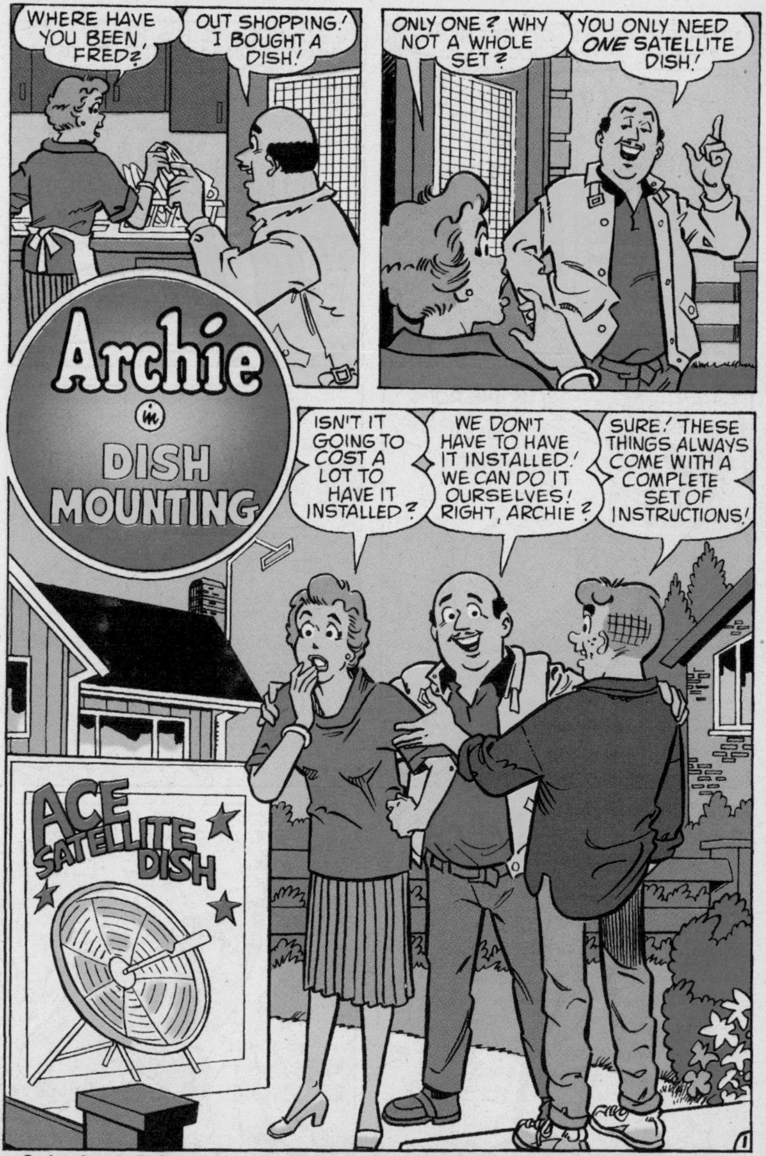
WHERE HAVE YOU BEEN, FRED?
OUT SHOPPING! I BOUGHT A DISH!
ONLY ONE? WHY NOT A WHOLE SET?
YOU ONLY NEED ONE SATELLITE DISH!
Archie in DISH MOUNTING
ISN'T IT GOING TO COST A LOT TO HAVE IT INSTALLED?
WE DON'T HAVE TO HAVE IT INSTALLED! WE CAN DO IT OURSELVES! RIGHT, ARCHIE?
SURE! THESE THINGS ALWAYS COME WITH A COMPLETE SET OF INSTRUCTIONS!
ACE SATELLITE DISH
1

Script: Angelo DeCesare / Pencils: Stan Goldberg / Inks: Mike Esposito / Letters: Bill Yoshida

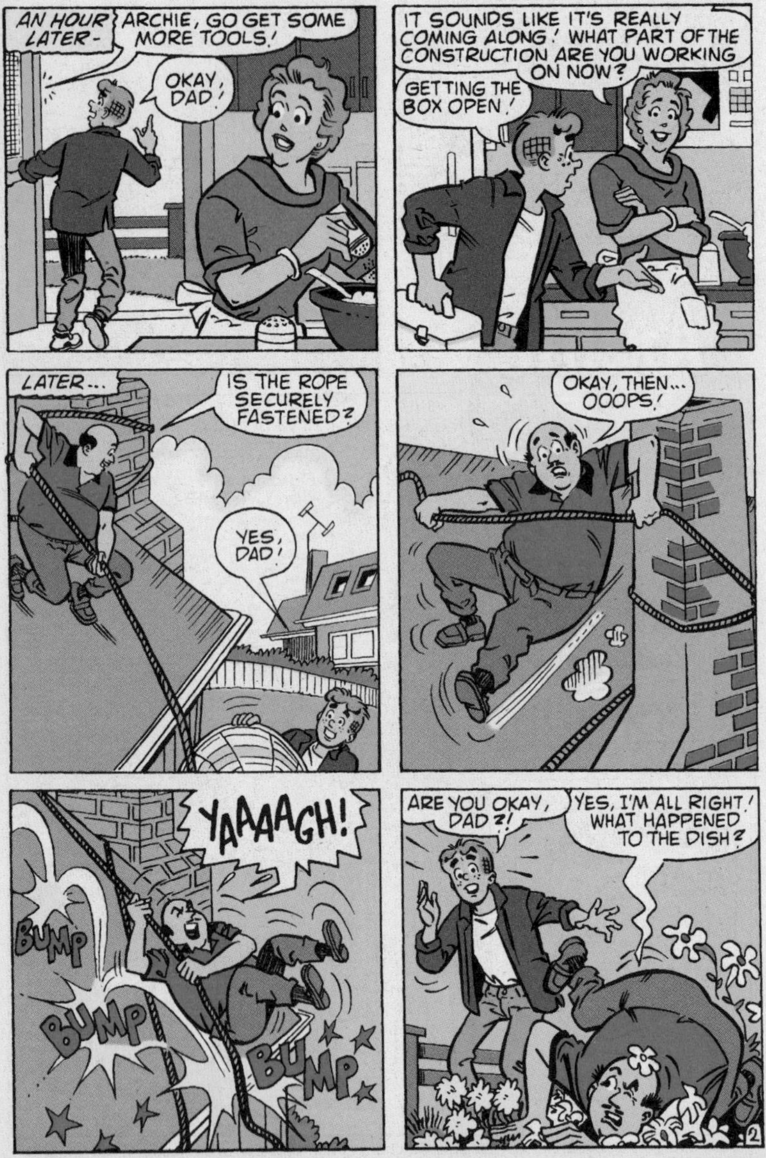
AN HOUR LATER -
ARCHIE, GO GET SOME MORE TOOLS!
OKAY, DAD!
IT SOUNDS LIKE IT'S REALLY COMING ALONG! WHAT PART OF THE CONSTRUCTION ARE YOU WORKING ON NOW?
GETTING THE BOX OPEN!
LATER...
IS THE ROPE SECURELY FASTENED?
YES, DAD!
OKAY, THEN... OOOPS!
YAAAAGH!
BUMP
BUMP
BUMP
ARE YOU OKAY, DAD?!
YES, I'M ALL RIGHT! WHAT HAPPENED TO THE DISH?
2

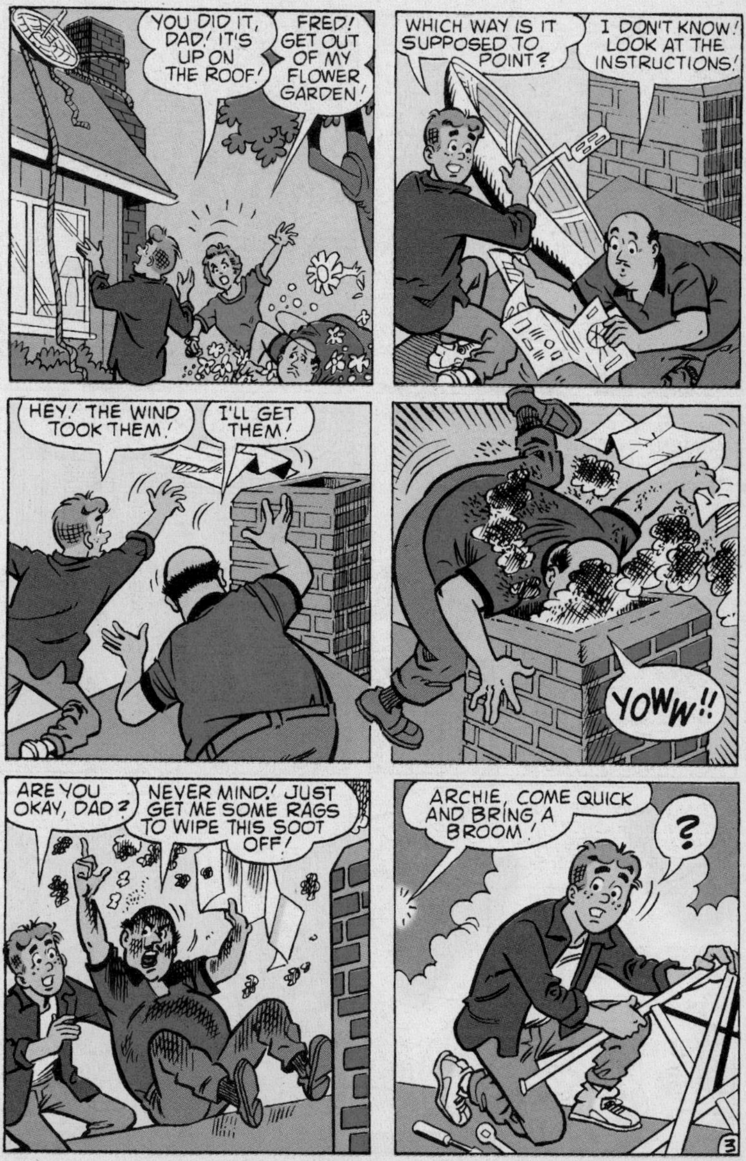

YOU DID IT, DAD! IT'S UP ON THE ROOF!
FRED! GET OUT OF MY FLOWER GARDEN!
WHICH WAY IS IT SUPPOSED TO POINT?
I DON'T KNOW! LOOK AT THE INSTRUCTIONS!
HEY! THE WIND TOOK THEM!
I'LL GET THEM!
YOWW!!
ARE YOU OKAY, DAD?
NEVER MIND! JUST GET ME SOME RAGS TO WIPE THIS SOOT OFF!
ARCHIE, COME QUICK AND BRING A BROOM!
?
3

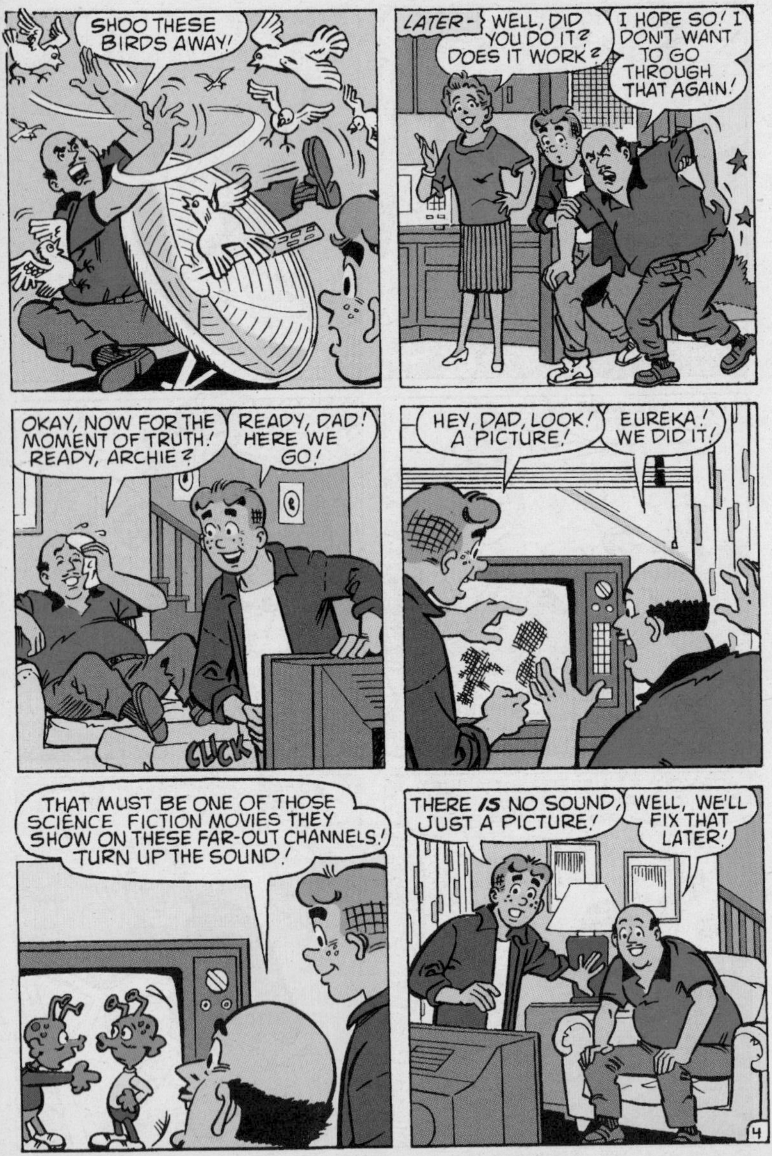
SHOO THESE BIRDS AWAY!
LATER-
WELL, DID YOU DO IT? DOES IT WORK?
I HOPE SO! I DON'T WANT TO GO THROUGH THAT AGAIN!
OKAY, NOW FOR THE MOMENT OF TRUTH! READY, ARCHIE?
READY, DAD! HERE WE GO!
CLICK
HEY, DAD, LOOK! A PICTURE!
EUREKA! WE DID IT!
THAT MUST BE ONE OF THOSE SCIENCE FICTION MOVIES THEY SHOW ON THESE FAR-OUT CHANNELS! TURN UP THE SOUND!
THERE IS NO SOUND, JUST A PICTURE!
WELL, WE'LL FIX THAT LATER!
4

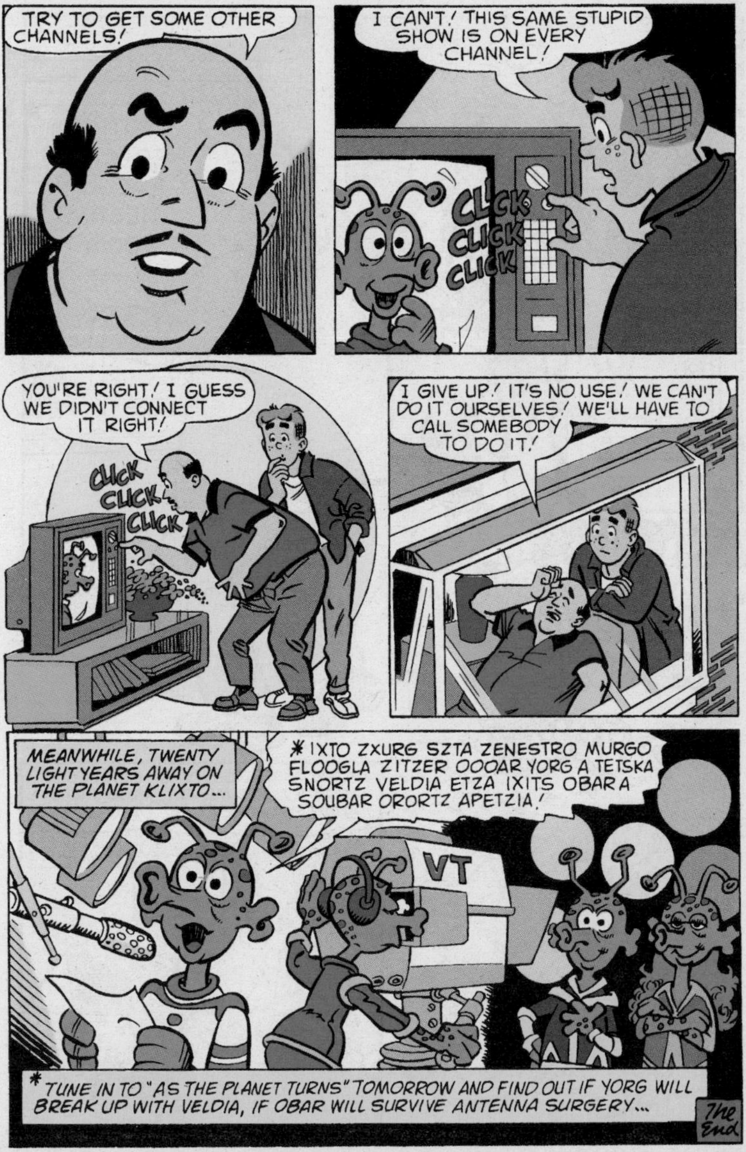

TRY TO GET SOME OTHER CHANNELS!
I CAN'T! THIS SAME STUPID SHOW IS ON EVERY CHANNEL!
CLICK CLICK CLICK
YOU'RE RIGHT! I GUESS WE DIDN'T CONNECT IT RIGHT!
CLICK CLICK CLICK
I GIVE UP! IT'S NO USE! WE CAN'T DO IT OURSELVES! WE'LL HAVE TO CALL SOMEBODY TO DO IT!
MEANWHILE, TWENTY LIGHT YEARS AWAY ON THE PLANET KLIXTO...
* IXTO ZXURG SZTA ZENESTRO MURGO FLOOGLA ZITZER OOOAR YORG A TETSKA SNORTZ VELDIA ETZA IXITS OBAR A SOUBAR ORORTZ APETZIA!
VT
* TUNE IN TO "AS THE PLANET TURNS" TOMORROW AND FIND OUT IF YORG WILL BREAK UP WITH VELDIA, IF OBAR WILL SURVIVE ANTENNA SURGERY...
The End

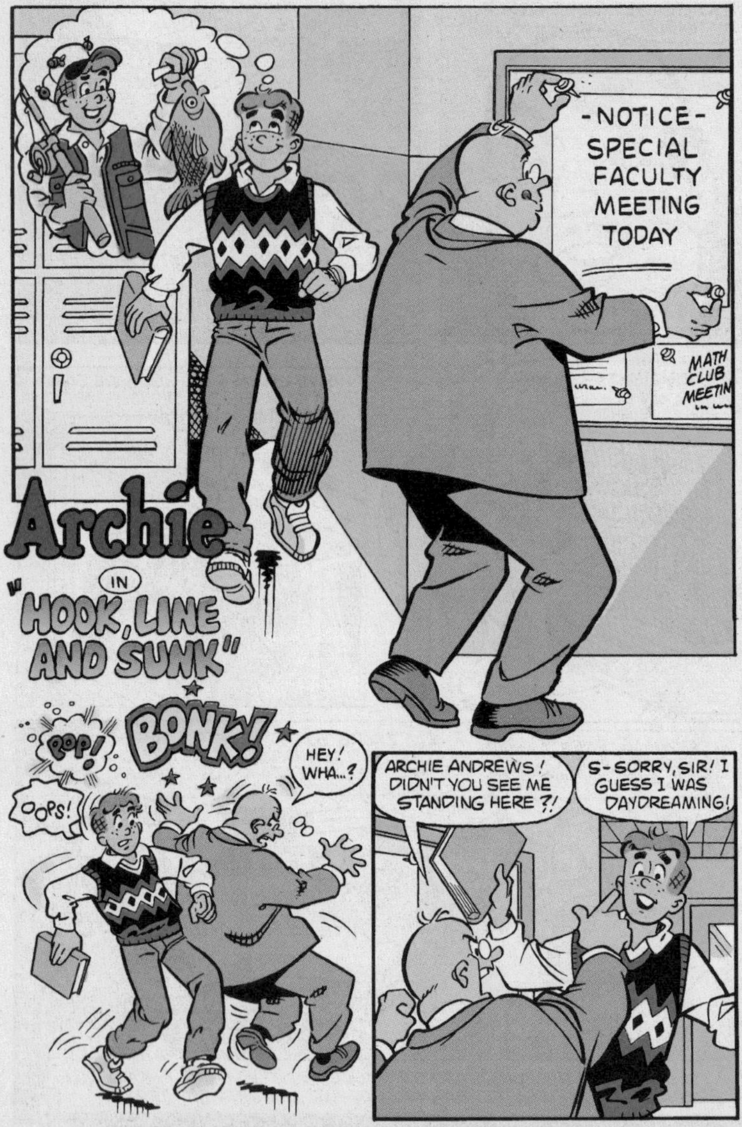
-NOTICE-
SPECIAL FACULTY MEETING TODAY
MATH CLUB MEETIN
Archie
IN
"HOOK, LINE AND SUNK"
POP!
BONK!
OOPS!
HEY! WHA...?
ARCHIE ANDREWS! DIDN'T YOU SEE ME STANDING HERE?!
S-SORRY, SIR! I GUESS I WAS DAYDREAMING!

Script: Mike Pellowski / Pencils: Stan Goldberg / Inks: Bob Smith / Letters: Bill Yoshida

DAYDREAMING... ABOUT WHAT?

FISHING, SIR!

SPECIAL FACULTY MEETING TODAY

COACH CLAYTON

FISHING?

POP! YIKES! BUMP! NOT AGAIN?

GEE... SORRY, MR. WEATHERBEE! MY MIND WAS ELSEWHERE!

DON'T TELL ME!

RIGHT, SIR! JUG AND I ARE GOING FISHING SATURDAY MORNING!

WHY DOES THAT *NOT* SURPRISE ME?

- NOTICE SPECIAL FACULTY MEETING DAY

AREN'T YOU BOYS JUMPING THE GUN A BIT?

NO, SIR! A LOT OF EXPERT ANGLERS CLAIM FISHING IS GREAT *ALL* YEAR 'ROUND!

PRINCIP

2

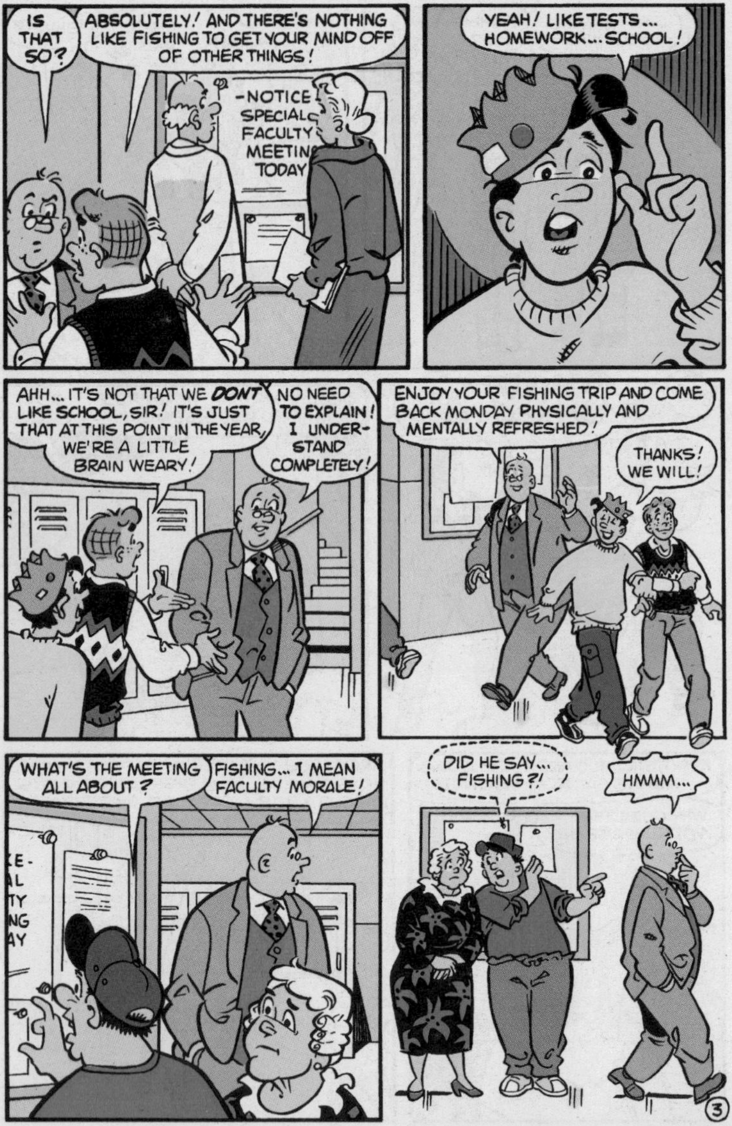
IS THAT SO?
ABSOLUTELY! AND THERE'S NOTHING LIKE FISHING TO GET YOUR MIND OFF OF OTHER THINGS!
-NOTICE SPECIAL FACULTY MEETIN TODAY
YEAH! LIKE TESTS... HOMEWORK... SCHOOL!
AHH... IT'S NOT THAT WE DONT LIKE SCHOOL, SIR! IT'S JUST THAT AT THIS POINT IN THE YEAR, WE'RE A LITTLE BRAIN WEARY!
NO NEED TO EXPLAIN! I UNDER-STAND COMPLETELY!
ENJOY YOUR FISHING TRIP AND COME BACK MONDAY PHYSICALLY AND MENTALLY REFRESHED!
THANKS! WE WILL!
WHAT'S THE MEETING ALL ABOUT?
FISHING... I MEAN FACULTY MORALE!
DID HE SAY... FISHING?!
HMMM...

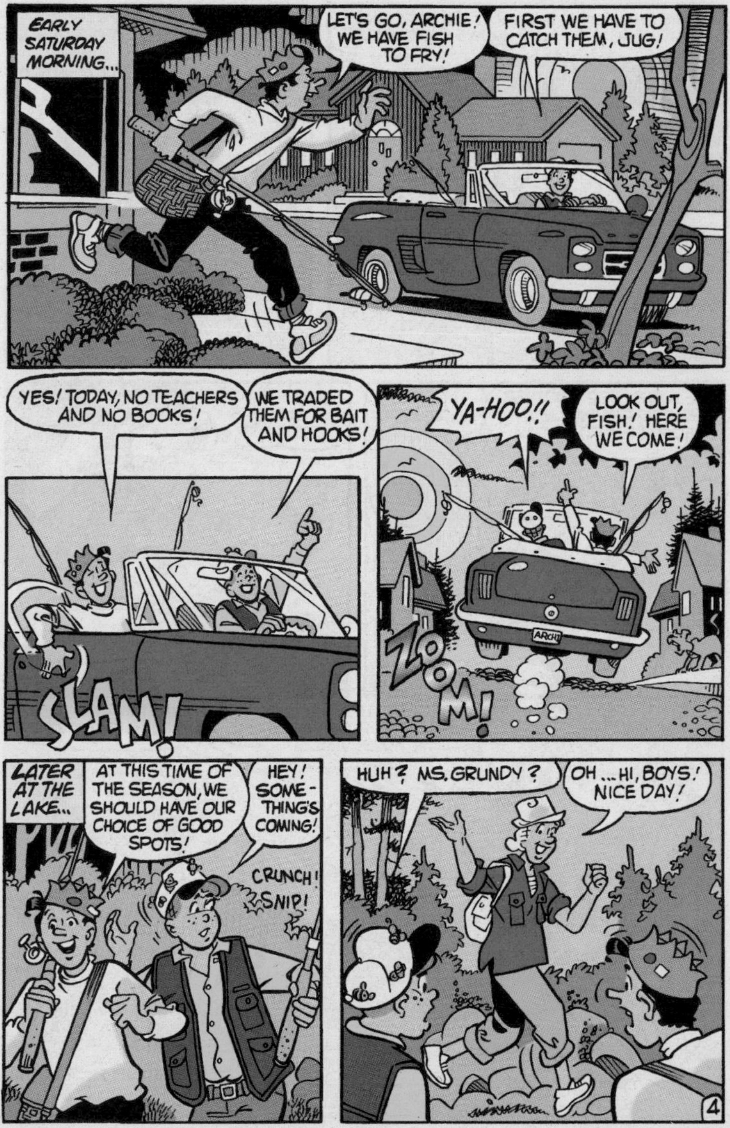
EARLY SATURDAY MORNING...
LET'S GO, ARCHIE! WE HAVE FISH TO FRY!
FIRST WE HAVE TO CATCH THEM, JUG!
YES! TODAY, NO TEACHERS AND NO BOOKS!
WE TRADED THEM FOR BAIT AND HOOKS!
SLAM!
YA-HOO!!
LOOK OUT, FISH! HERE WE COME!
ZOOM!
LATER AT THE LAKE...
AT THIS TIME OF THE SEASON, WE SHOULD HAVE OUR CHOICE OF GOOD SPOTS!
HEY! SOME-THING'S COMING!
CRUNCH!
SNIP!
HUH? MS. GRUNDY?
OH ... HI, BOYS! NICE DAY!
4

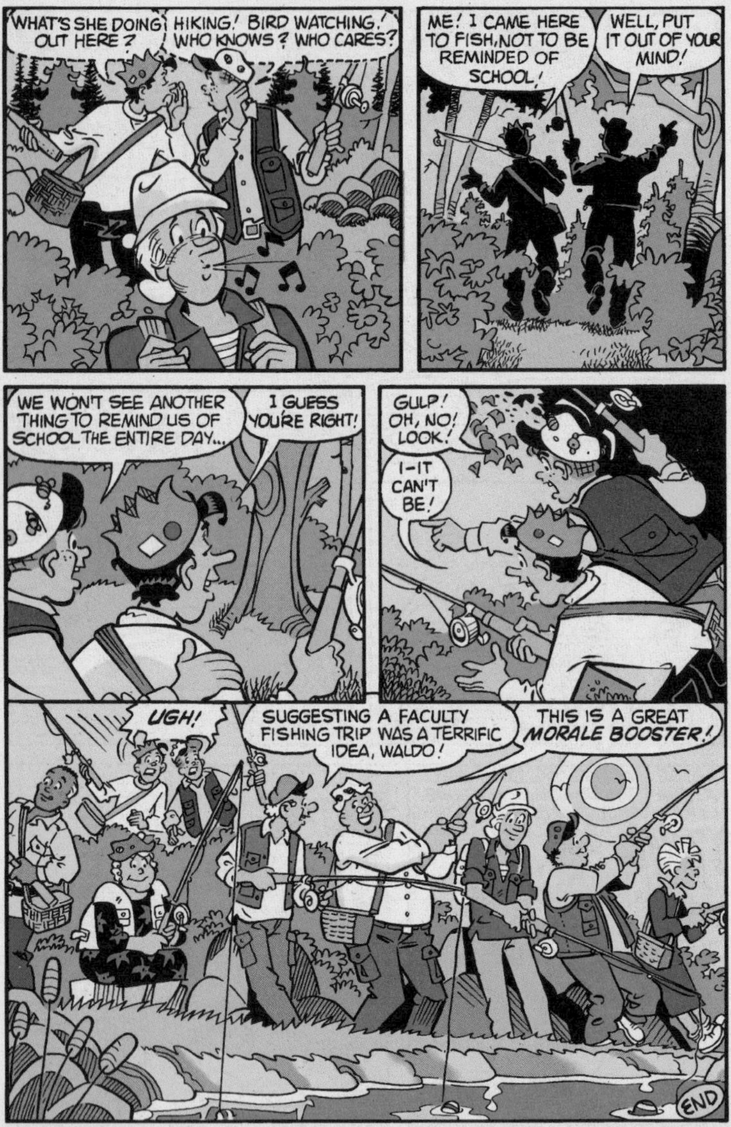
WHAT'S SHE DOING OUT HERE?
HIKING! BIRD WATCHING! WHO KNOWS? WHO CARES?
ME! I CAME HERE TO FISH, NOT TO BE REMINDED OF SCHOOL!
WELL, PUT IT OUT OF YOUR MIND!
WE WON'T SEE ANOTHER THING TO REMIND US OF SCHOOL THE ENTIRE DAY...
I GUESS YOU'RE RIGHT!
GULP! OH, NO! LOOK!
I-IT CAN'T BE!
UGH!
SUGGESTING A FACULTY FISHING TRIP WAS A TERRIFIC IDEA, WALDO!
THIS IS A GREAT MORALE BOOSTER!
END

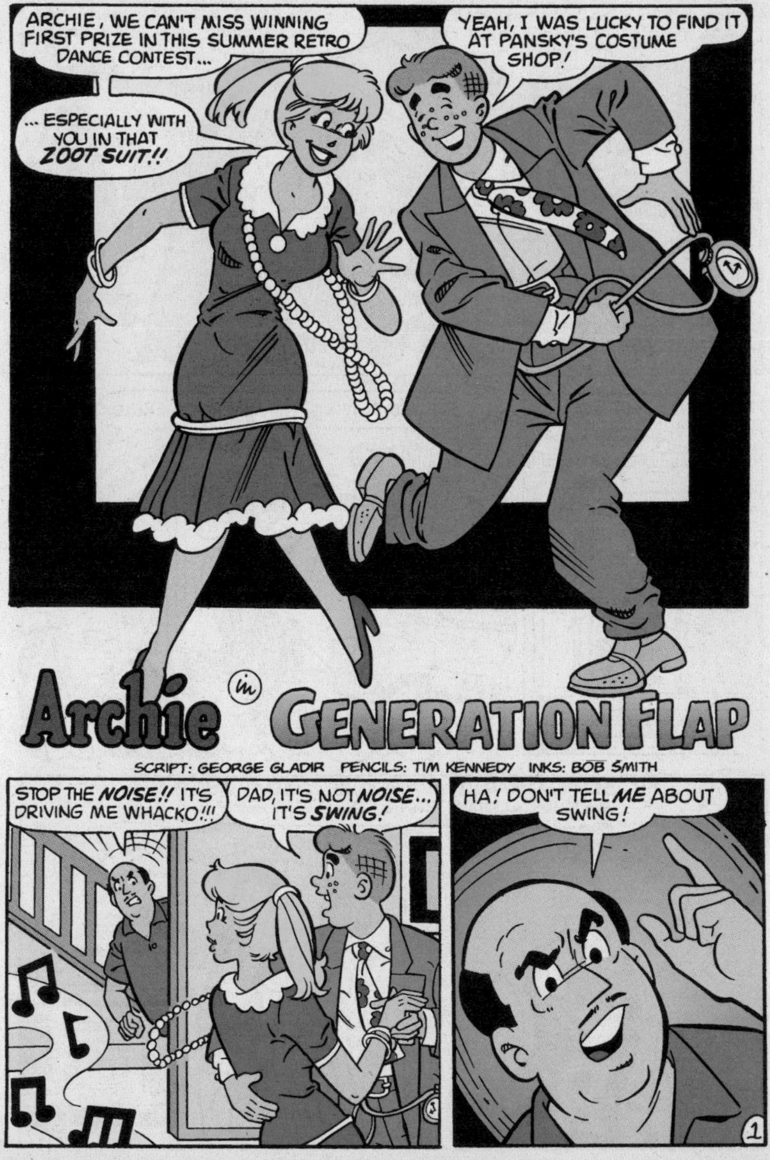
ARCHIE, WE CAN'T MISS WINNING FIRST PRIZE IN THIS SUMMER RETRO DANCE CONTEST...
... ESPECIALLY WITH YOU IN THAT ZOOT SUIT!!
YEAH, I WAS LUCKY TO FIND IT AT PANSKY'S COSTUME SHOP!
Archie in GENERATION FLAP
SCRIPT: GEORGE GLADIR PENCILS: TIM KENNEDY INKS: BOB SMITH
STOP THE NOISE!! IT'S DRIVING ME WHACKO!!!
DAD, IT'S NOT NOISE... IT'S SWING!
HA! DON'T TELL ME ABOUT SWING!
1

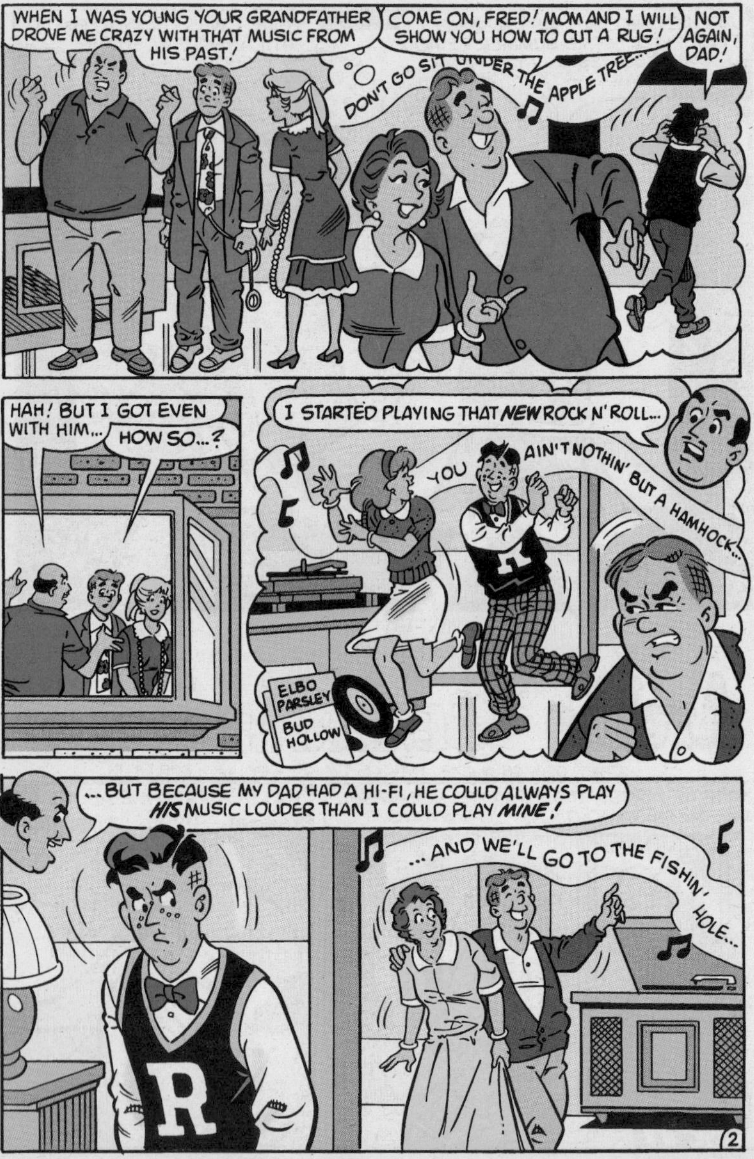
WHEN I WAS YOUNG YOUR GRANDFATHER DROVE ME CRAZY WITH THAT MUSIC FROM HIS PAST!
COME ON, FRED! MOM AND I WILL SHOW YOU HOW TO CUT A RUG!
NOT AGAIN, DAD!
DON'T GO SIT UNDER THE APPLE TREE...
HAH! BUT I GOT EVEN WITH HIM...
HOW SO...?
I STARTED PLAYING THAT NEW ROCK N' ROLL...
YOU AIN'T NOTHIN' BUT A HAMHOCK...
ELBO PARSLEY
BUD HOLLOW
...BUT BECAUSE MY DAD HAD A HI-FI, HE COULD ALWAYS PLAY HIS MUSIC LOUDER THAN I COULD PLAY MINE!
...AND WE'LL GO TO THE FISHIN' HOLE...
2

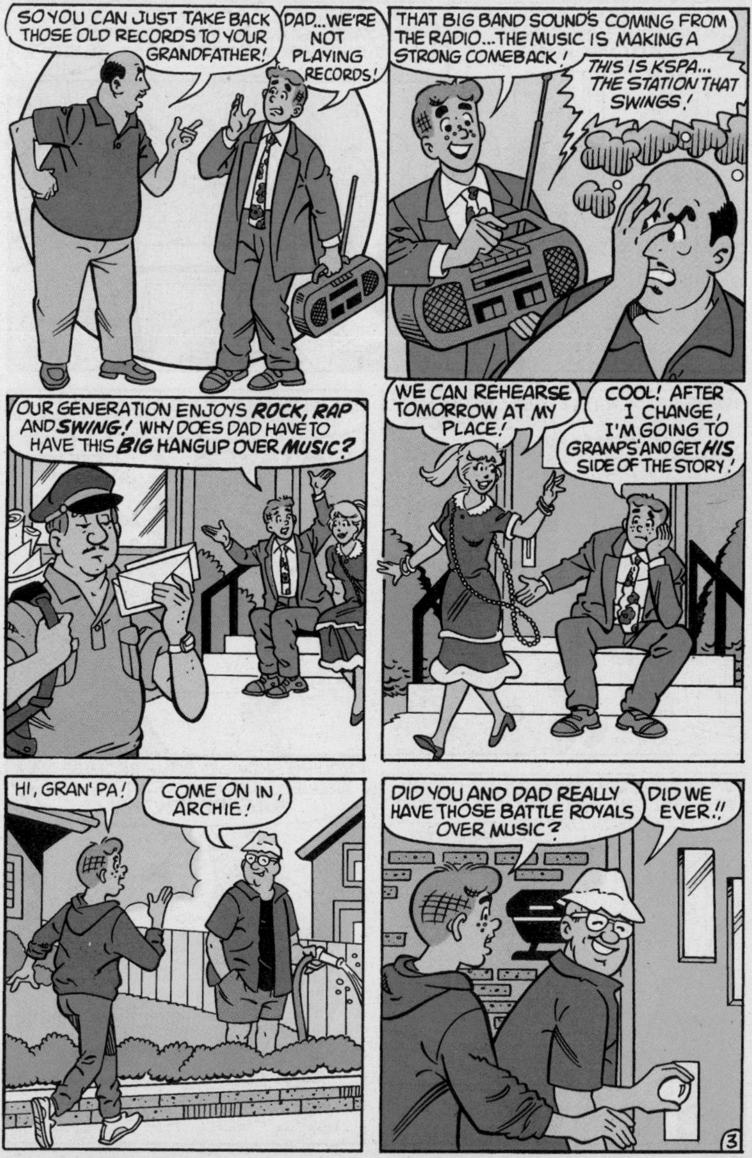
SO YOU CAN JUST TAKE BACK THOSE OLD RECORDS TO YOUR GRANDFATHER!
DAD...WE'RE NOT PLAYING RECORDS!
THAT BIG BAND SOUND'S COMING FROM THE RADIO...THE MUSIC IS MAKING A STRONG COMEBACK!
THIS IS KSPA... THE STATION THAT SWINGS!
OUR GENERATION ENJOYS ROCK, RAP AND SWING! WHY DOES DAD HAVE TO HAVE THIS BIG HANGUP OVER MUSIC?
WE CAN REHEARSE TOMORROW AT MY PLACE!
COOL! AFTER I CHANGE, I'M GOING TO GRAMPS' AND GET HIS SIDE OF THE STORY!
HI, GRAN' PA!
COME ON IN, ARCHIE!
DID YOU AND DAD REALLY HAVE THOSE BATTLE ROYALS OVER MUSIC?
DID WE EVER.!!
3

...BUT I GUESS DIFFERENT GENERATIONS HAVE ALWAYS ARGUED OVER MUSIC!

MY DAD'S IDEA OF GOOD MUSIC WAS *THIS* INSTRUMENT! HE BROUGHT IT OVER FROM *SCOTLAND!*

WOW! A GENUINE BAGPIPE!

WE'VE HELD ONTO IT AS A FAMILY *HEIRLOOM!*

GEE! SUDDENLY I FEEL MY ROOTS...

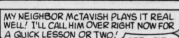

...I WONDER IF I COULD LEARN TO PLAY IT OVER TIME!

I DON'T SEE WHY NOT!

GRONK

MY NEIGHBOR McTAVISH PLAYS IT REAL WELL! I'LL CALL HIM OVER RIGHT NOW FOR A QUICK LESSON OR TWO!

GEE, I'D APPRECIATE THAT!

YOU'RE SHOWING SOME PROMISE, ARCHIE!... THE IMPORTANT THING IS *BREATH CONTROL!*

④

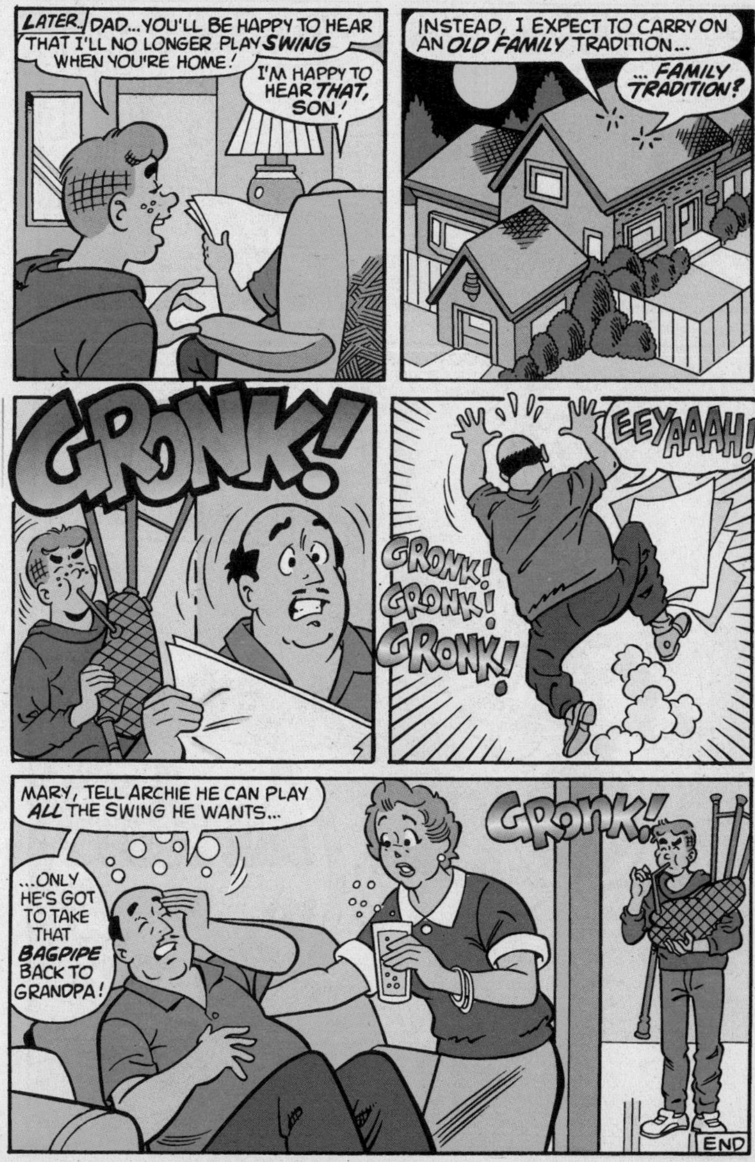
LATER.
DAD... YOU'LL BE HAPPY TO HEAR THAT I'LL NO LONGER PLAY SWING WHEN YOU'RE HOME!
I'M HAPPY TO HEAR THAT, SON!
INSTEAD, I EXPECT TO CARRY ON AN OLD FAMILY TRADITION...
... FAMILY TRADITION?
GRONK!
EEYAAAH!
GRONK! GRONK! GRONK!
MARY, TELL ARCHIE HE CAN PLAY ALL THE SWING HE WANTS...
...ONLY HE'S GOT TO TAKE THAT BAGPIPE BACK TO GRANDPA!
GRONK!
END

THE SUPERINTENDENT CALLED TO SAY HE'D DROP BY SHORTLY TO CONGRATULATE THE SCHOOL ON ITS SAFETY RECORD!

HOW NICE!

PRINCIPAL WEATHERBEE

YES, I CAN JUST SEE THE DISTRICT'S SAFETY TROPHY IN OUR TROPHY ROOM!

Script: George Gladir / Pencils: Stan Goldberg / Inks: Mike Esposito / Letters: Bill Yoshida / Colors: Barry Grossman

GOOD HEAVENS! WHY DID ARCHIE PICK *THIS* MOMENT TO MAKE LIKE A *DAREDEVIL*?

Archie in RAD DAD

1

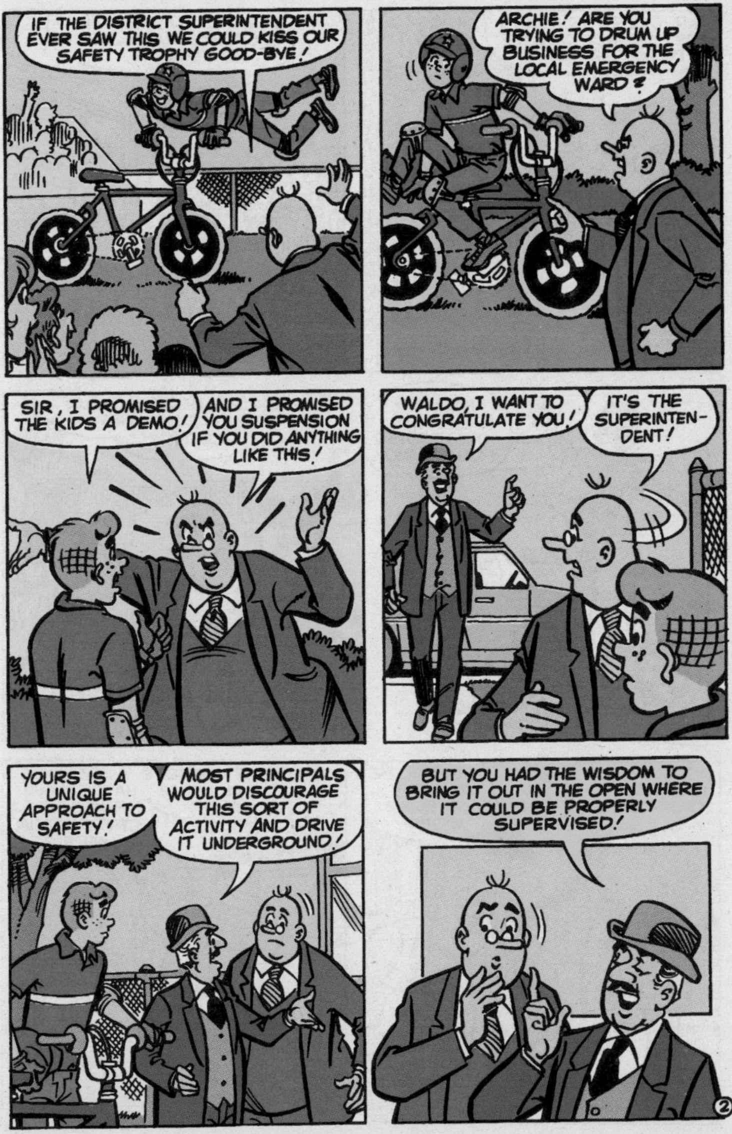
IF THE DISTRICT SUPERINTENDENT EVER SAW THIS WE COULD KISS OUR SAFETY TROPHY GOOD-BYE!
ARCHIE! ARE YOU TRYING TO DRUM UP BUSINESS FOR THE LOCAL EMERGENCY WARD?
SIR, I PROMISED THE KIDS A DEMO!
AND I PROMISED YOU SUSPENSION IF YOU DID ANYTHING LIKE THIS!
WALDO, I WANT TO CONGRATULATE YOU!
IT'S THE SUPERINTEN-DENT!
YOURS IS A UNIQUE APPROACH TO SAFETY!
MOST PRINCIPALS WOULD DISCOURAGE THIS SORT OF ACTIVITY AND DRIVE IT UNDERGROUND!
BUT YOU HAD THE WISDOM TO BRING IT OUT IN THE OPEN WHERE IT COULD BE PROPERLY SUPERVISED!
2

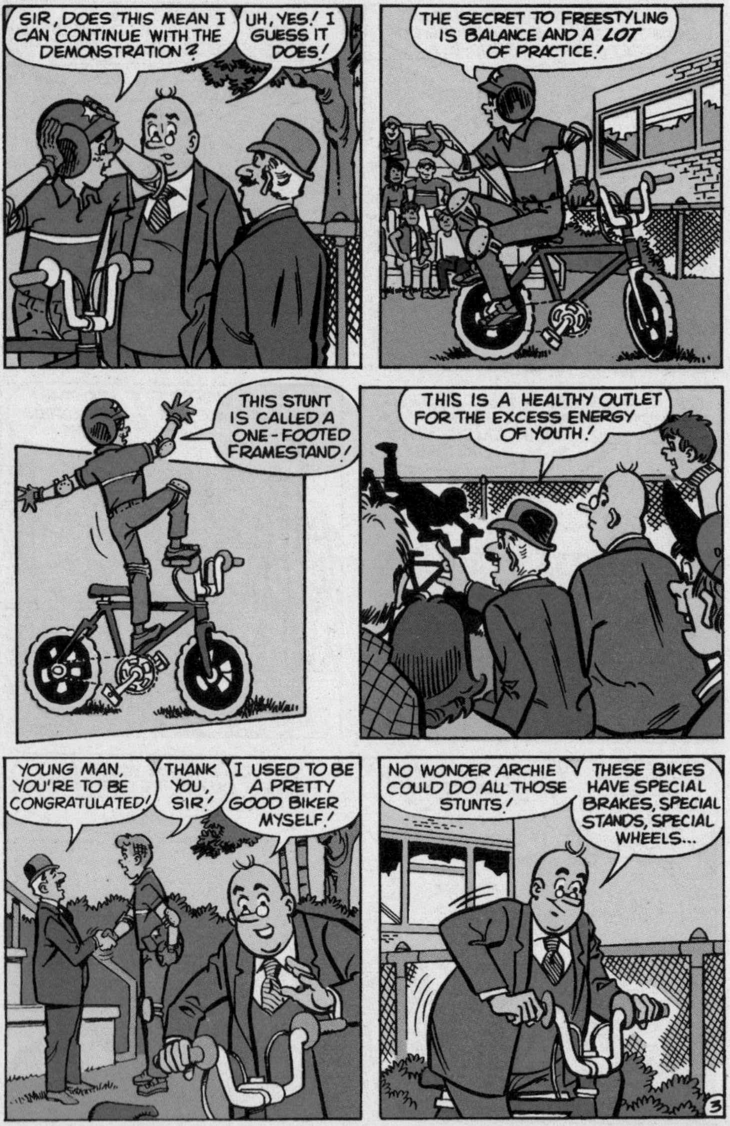
SIR, DOES THIS MEAN I CAN CONTINUE WITH THE DEMONSTRATION?
UH, YES! I GUESS IT DOES!
THE SECRET TO FREESTYLING IS BALANCE AND A LOT OF PRACTICE!
THIS STUNT IS CALLED A ONE-FOOTED FRAMESTAND!
THIS IS A HEALTHY OUTLET FOR THE EXCESS ENERGY OF YOUTH!
YOUNG MAN, YOU'RE TO BE CONGRATULATED!
THANK YOU, SIR!
I USED TO BE A PRETTY GOOD BIKER MYSELF!
NO WONDER ARCHIE COULD DO ALL THOSE STUNTS!
THESE BIKES HAVE SPECIAL BRAKES, SPECIAL STANDS, SPECIAL WHEELS...
3

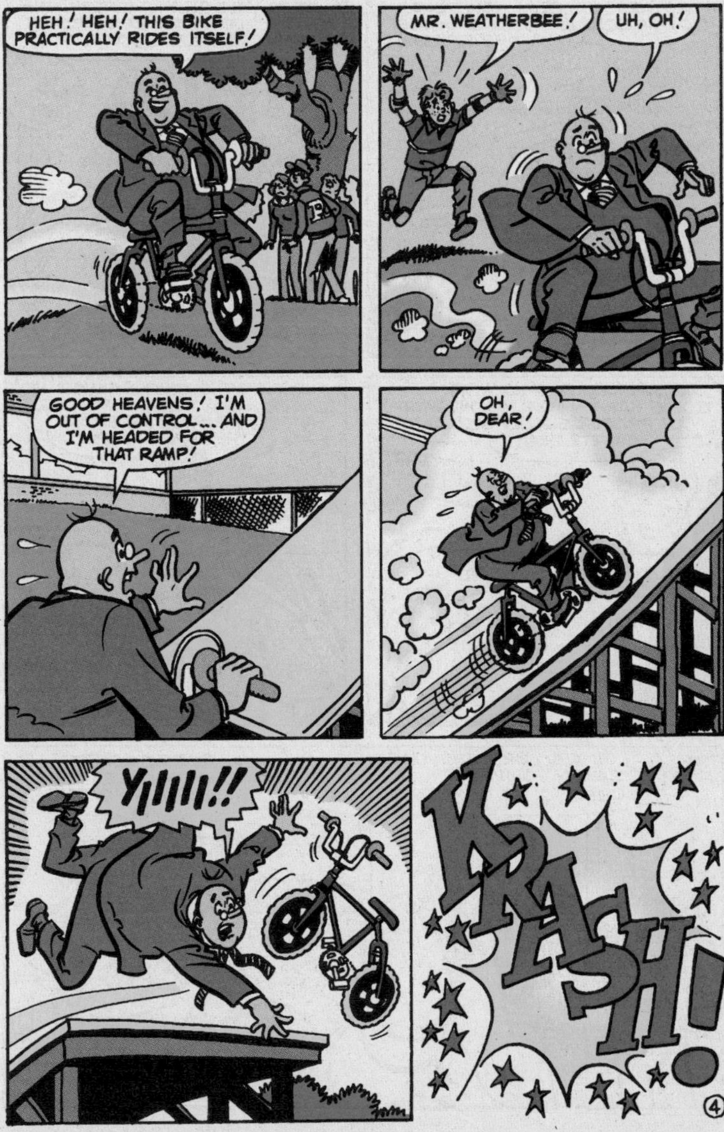
HEH! HEH! THIS BIKE PRACTICALLY RIDES ITSELF!
MR. WEATHERBEE!
UH, OH!
GOOD HEAVENS! I'M OUT OF CONTROL... AND I'M HEADED FOR THAT RAMP!
OH, DEAR!
YIIIII!!
KRASH!

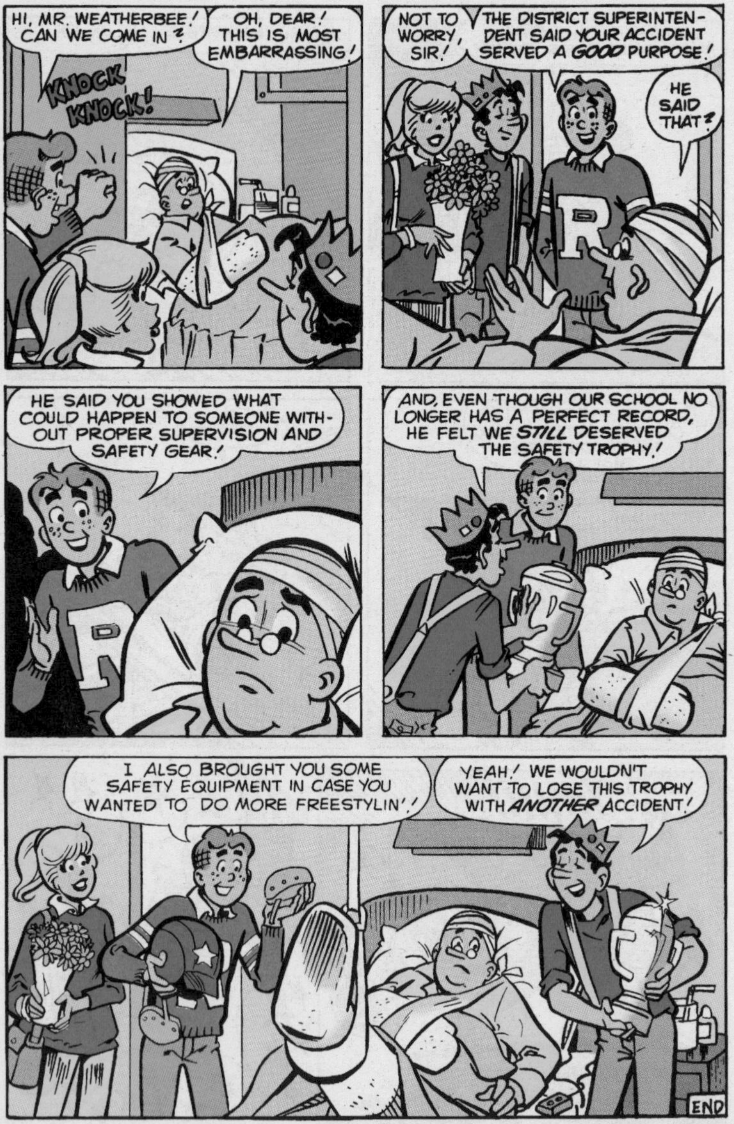
HI, MR. WEATHERBEE! CAN WE COME IN?
KNOCK KNOCK!
OH, DEAR! THIS IS MOST EMBARRASSING!
NOT TO WORRY, SIR!
THE DISTRICT SUPERINTEN-DENT SAID YOUR ACCIDENT SERVED A GOOD PURPOSE!
HE SAID THAT?
HE SAID YOU SHOWED WHAT COULD HAPPEN TO SOMEONE WITH-OUT PROPER SUPERVISION AND SAFETY GEAR!
AND, EVEN THOUGH OUR SCHOOL NO LONGER HAS A PERFECT RECORD, HE FELT WE STILL DESERVED THE SAFETY TROPHY!
I ALSO BROUGHT YOU SOME SAFETY EQUIPMENT IN CASE YOU WANTED TO DO MORE FREESTYLIN'!
YEAH! WE WOULDN'T WANT TO LOSE THIS TROPHY WITH ANOTHER ACCIDENT!
END

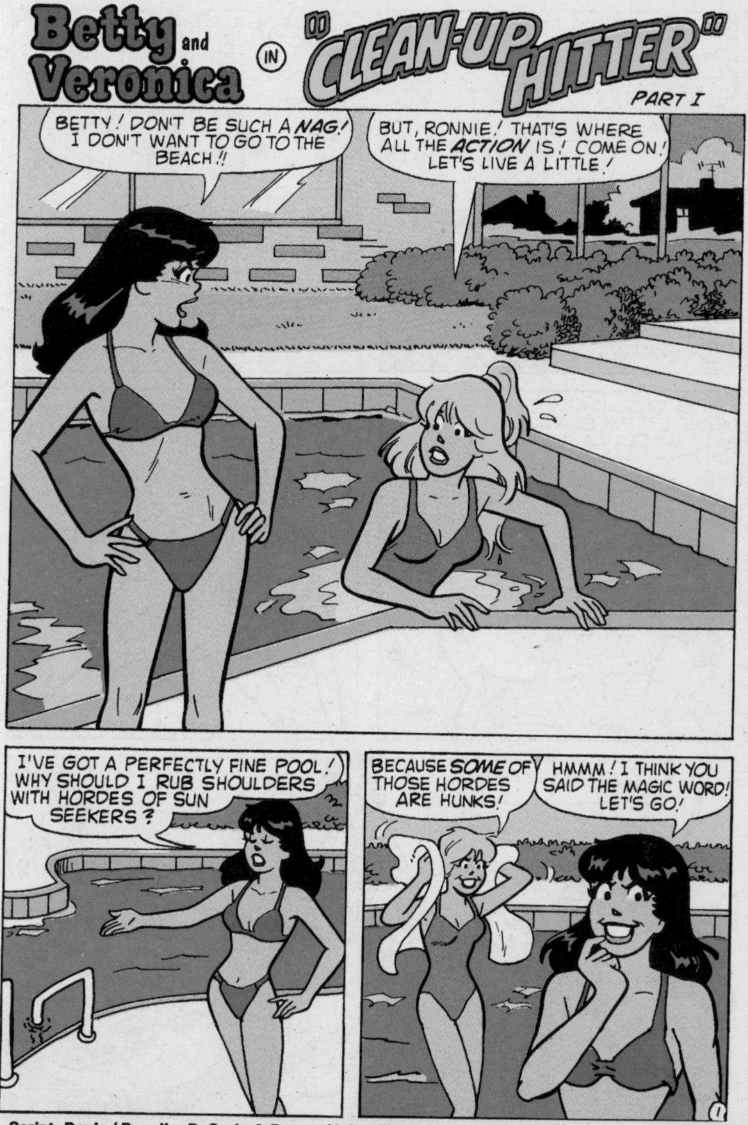
Betty and Veronica IN "CLEAN-UP HITTER" PART I
BETTY! DON'T BE SUCH A NAG! I DON'T WANT TO GO TO THE BEACH!!
BUT, RONNIE! THAT'S WHERE ALL THE ACTION IS! COME ON! LET'S LIVE A LITTLE!
I'VE GOT A PERFECTLY FINE POOL! WHY SHOULD I RUB SHOULDERS WITH HORDES OF SUN SEEKERS?
BECAUSE SOME OF THOSE HORDES ARE HUNKS!
HMMM! I THINK YOU SAID THE MAGIC WORD! LET'S GO!
1

Script: Doyle / Pencils: DeCarlo & Parent / Inks: Flood / Letters: Yoshida / Colors: Grossman

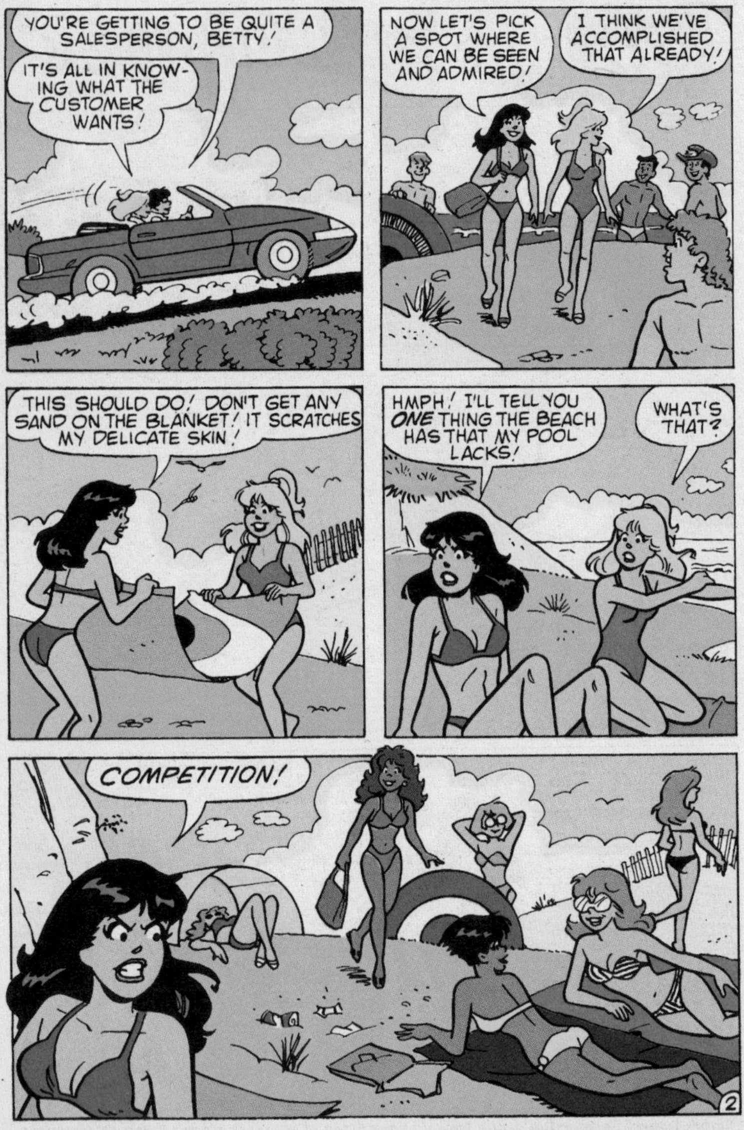
YOU'RE GETTING TO BE QUITE A SALESPERSON, BETTY!
IT'S ALL IN KNOWING WHAT THE CUSTOMER WANTS!
NOW LET'S PICK A SPOT WHERE WE CAN BE SEEN AND ADMIRED!
I THINK WE'VE ACCOMPLISHED THAT ALREADY!
THIS SHOULD DO! DON'T GET ANY SAND ON THE BLANKET! IT SCRATCHES MY DELICATE SKIN!
HMPH! I'LL TELL YOU *ONE* THING THE BEACH HAS THAT MY POOL LACKS!
WHAT'S THAT?
COMPETITION!
2

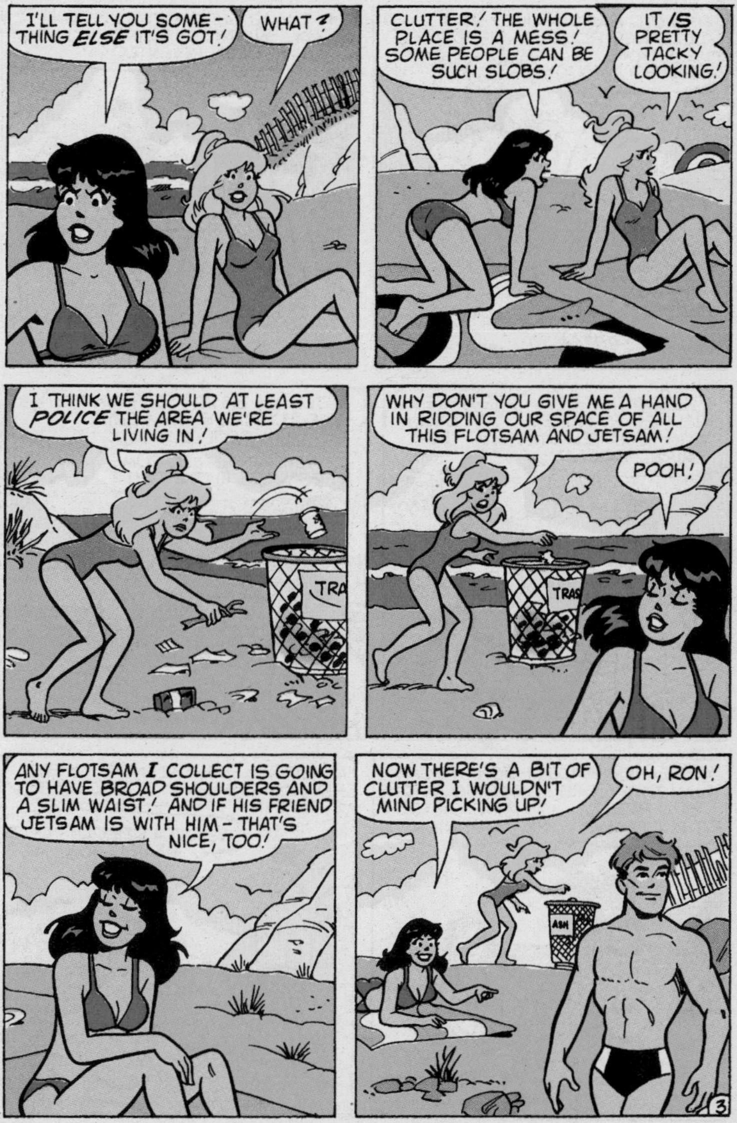
I'LL TELL YOU SOME-THING ELSE IT'S GOT!
WHAT?
CLUTTER! THE WHOLE PLACE IS A MESS! SOME PEOPLE CAN BE SUCH SLOBS!
IT IS PRETTY TACKY LOOKING!
I THINK WE SHOULD AT LEAST POLICE THE AREA WE'RE LIVING IN!
TRAS
WHY DON'T YOU GIVE ME A HAND IN RIDDING OUR SPACE OF ALL THIS FLOTSAM AND JETSAM!
POOH!
TRAS
ANY FLOTSAM I COLLECT IS GOING TO HAVE BROAD SHOULDERS AND A SLIM WAIST! AND IF HIS FRIEND JETSAM IS WITH HIM - THAT'S NICE, TOO!
NOW THERE'S A BIT OF CLUTTER I WOULDN'T MIND PICKING UP!
OH, RON!
ASH
3

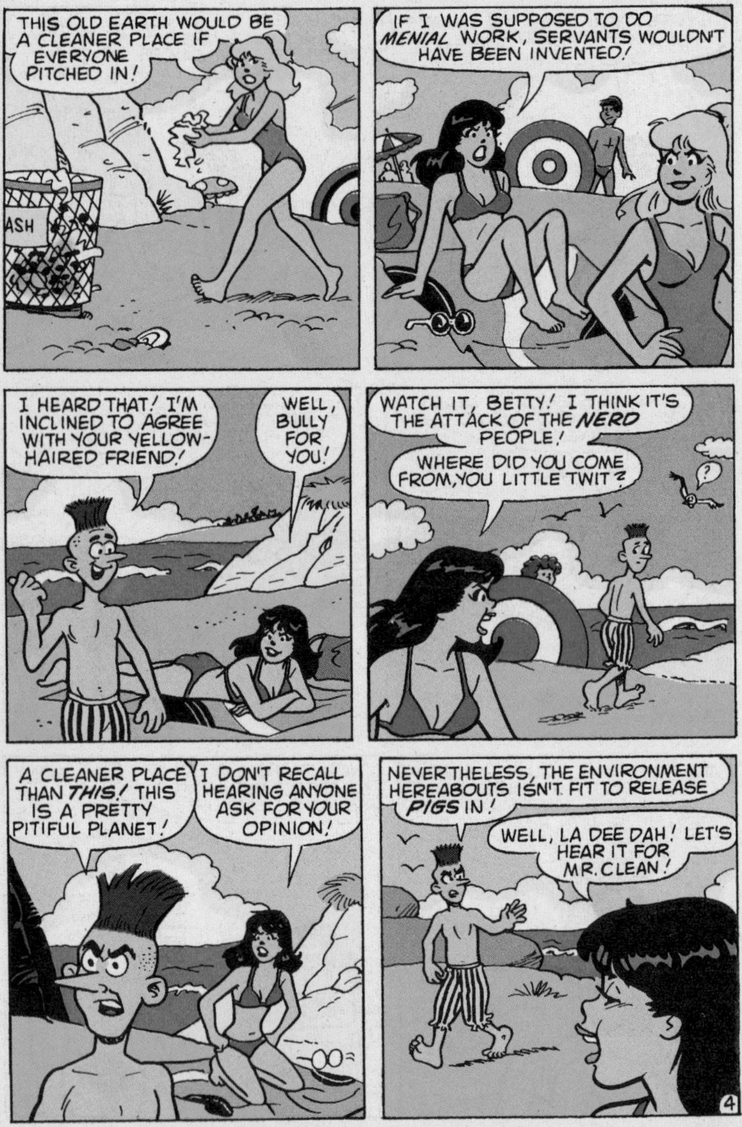
THIS OLD EARTH WOULD BE A CLEANER PLACE IF EVERYONE PITCHED IN!
ASH
IF I WAS SUPPOSED TO DO MENIAL WORK, SERVANTS WOULDN'T HAVE BEEN INVENTED!
I HEARD THAT! I'M INCLINED TO AGREE WITH YOUR YELLOW-HAIRED FRIEND!
WELL, BULLY FOR YOU!
WATCH IT, BETTY! I THINK IT'S THE ATTACK OF THE NERD PEOPLE!
WHERE DID YOU COME FROM, YOU LITTLE TWIT?
?
A CLEANER PLACE THAN THIS! THIS IS A PRETTY PITIFUL PLANET!
I DON'T RECALL HEARING ANYONE ASK FOR YOUR OPINION!
NEVERTHELESS, THE ENVIRONMENT HEREABOUTS ISN'T FIT TO RELEASE PIGS IN!
WELL, LA DEE DAH! LET'S HEAR IT FOR MR. CLEAN!
4

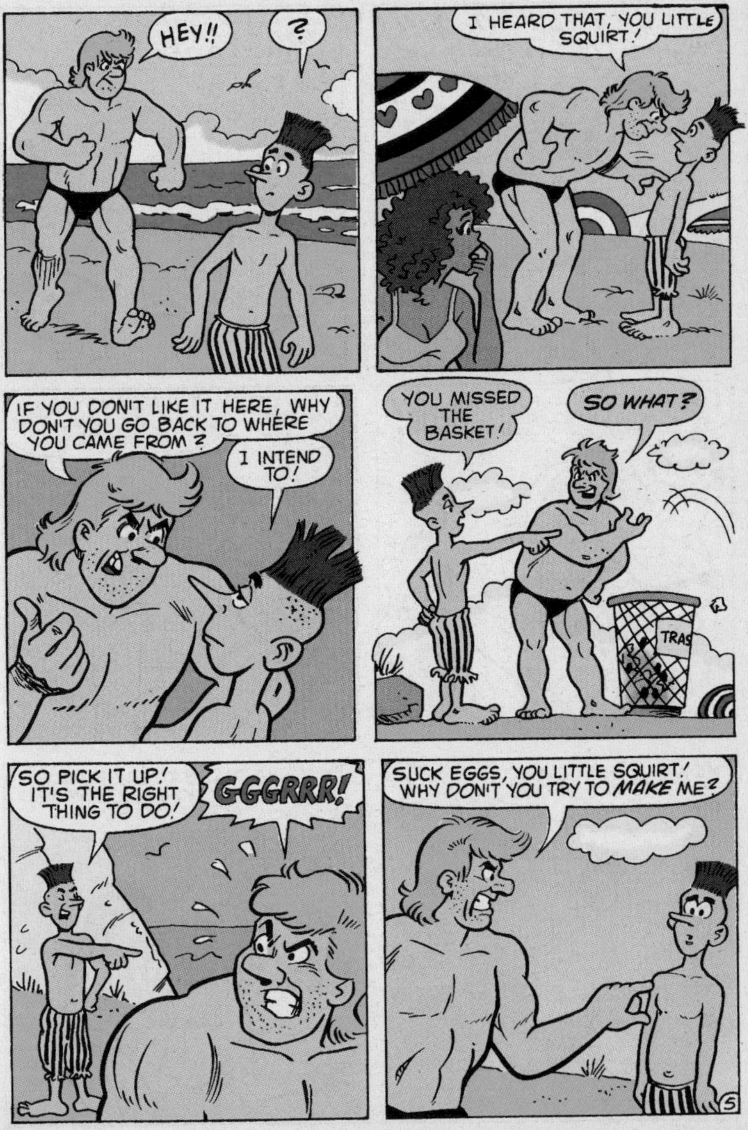
HEY!!
?
I HEARD THAT, YOU LITTLE SQUIRT!
IF YOU DON'T LIKE IT HERE, WHY DON'T YOU GO BACK TO WHERE YOU CAME FROM?
I INTEND TO!
YOU MISSED THE BASKET!
SO WHAT?
TRAS
SO PICK IT UP! IT'S THE RIGHT THING TO DO!
GGGRRR!
SUCK EGGS, YOU LITTLE SQUIRT! WHY DON'T YOU TRY TO MAKE ME?
5

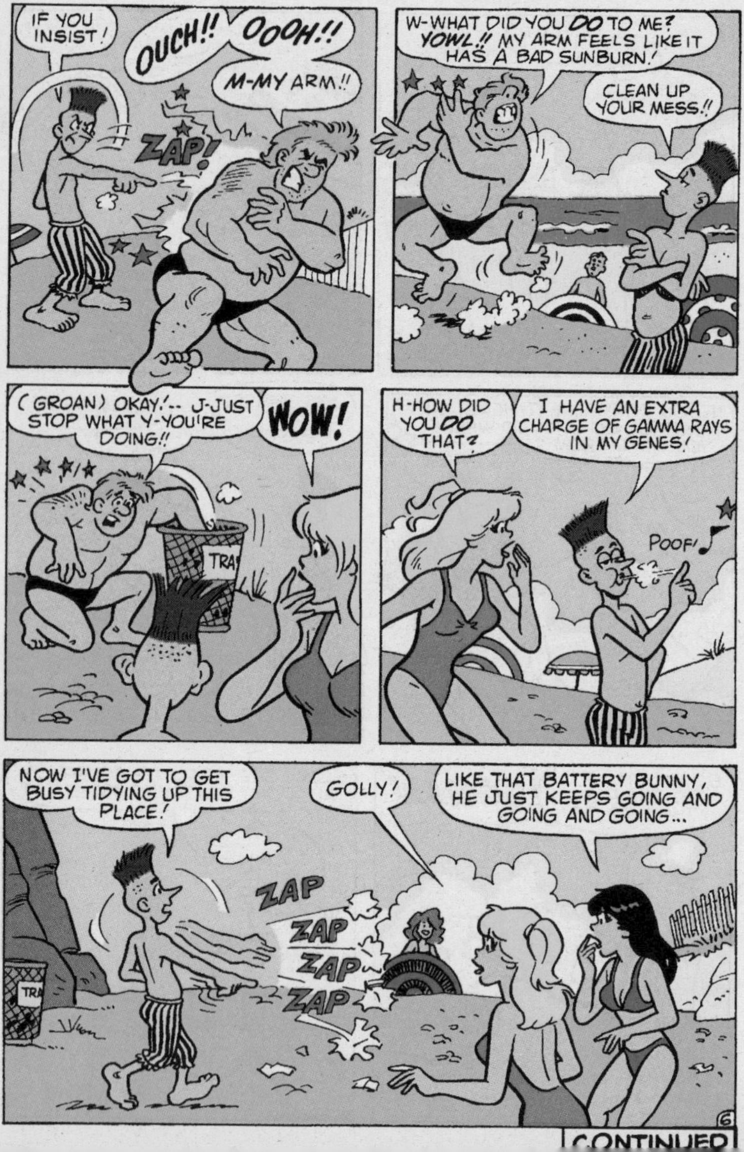
IF YOU INSIST!
OUCH!!
OOOOH!!
M-MY ARM!!
ZAP!
W-WHAT DID YOU DO TO ME? YOWL!! MY ARM FEELS LIKE IT HAS A BAD SUNBURN!
CLEAN UP YOUR MESS!!
(GROAN) OKAY!-- J-JUST STOP WHAT Y-YOU'RE DOING!!
WOW!
TRA
H-HOW DID YOU DO THAT?
I HAVE AN EXTRA CHARGE OF GAMMA RAYS IN MY GENES!
POOF!
NOW I'VE GOT TO GET BUSY TIDYING UP THIS PLACE!
GOLLY!
LIKE THAT BATTERY BUNNY, HE JUST KEEPS GOING AND GOING AND GOING...
ZAP
ZAP
ZAP
ZAP
TRA
6
CONTINUED

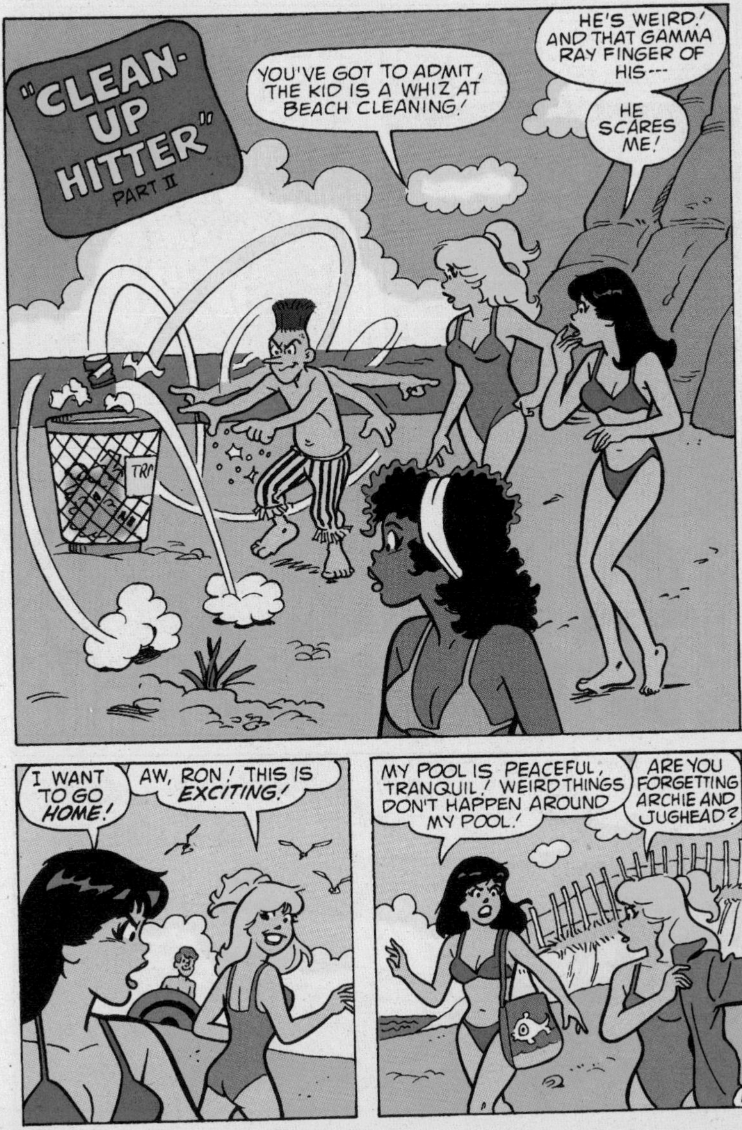
"CLEAN-UP HITTER"
PART II
YOU'VE GOT TO ADMIT, THE KID IS A WHIZ AT BEACH CLEANING!
HE'S WEIRD! AND THAT GAMMA RAY FINGER OF HIS---
HE SCARES ME!
I WANT TO GO HOME!
AW, RON! THIS IS EXCITING!
MY POOL IS PEACEFUL, TRANQUIL! WEIRD THINGS DON'T HAPPEN AROUND MY POOL!
ARE YOU FORGETTING ARCHIE AND JUGHEAD?
1

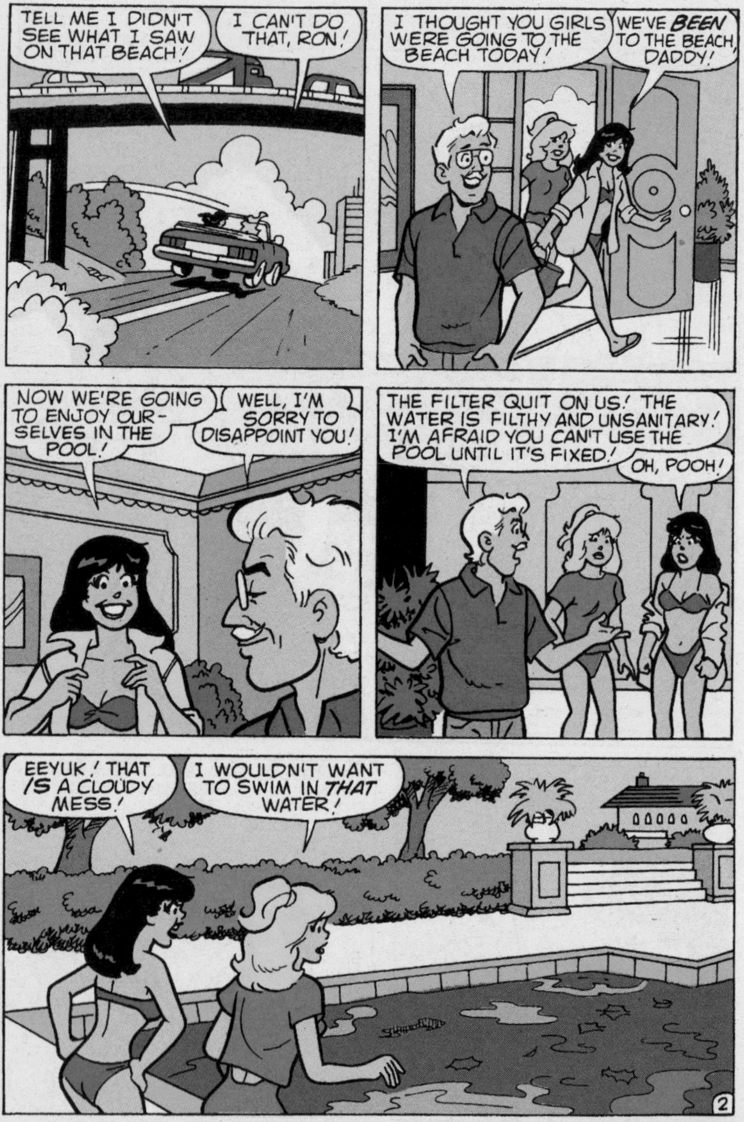
TELL ME I DIDN'T SEE WHAT I SAW ON THAT BEACH!
I CAN'T DO THAT, RON!
I THOUGHT YOU GIRLS WERE GOING TO THE BEACH TODAY!
WE'VE *BEEN* TO THE BEACH, DADDY!
NOW WE'RE GOING TO ENJOY OUR-SELVES IN THE POOL!
WELL, I'M SORRY TO DISAPPOINT YOU!
THE FILTER QUIT ON US! THE WATER IS FILTHY AND UNSANITARY! I'M AFRAID YOU CAN'T USE THE POOL UNTIL IT'S FIXED!
OH, POOH!
EEYUK! THAT *IS* A CLOUDY MESS!
I WOULDN'T WANT TO SWIM IN *THAT* WATER!

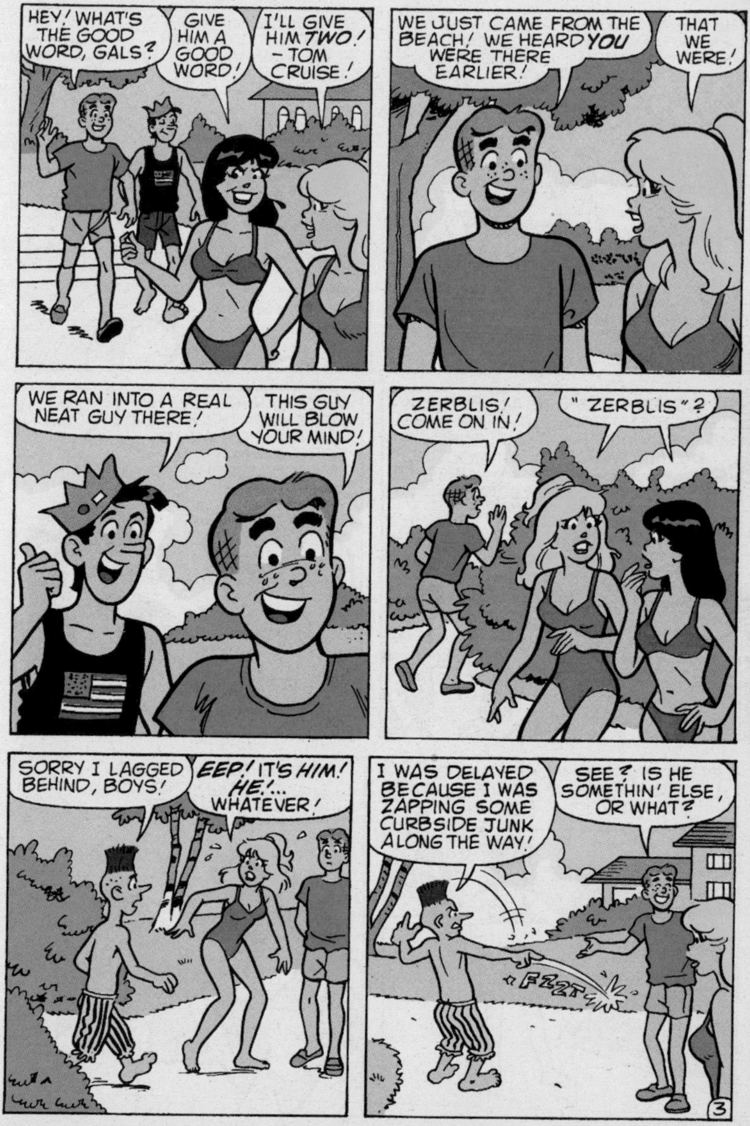

HEY! WHAT'S THE GOOD WORD, GALS?
GIVE HIM A GOOD WORD!
I'LL GIVE HIM TWO! - TOM CRUISE!
WE JUST CAME FROM THE BEACH! WE HEARD YOU WERE THERE EARLIER!
THAT WE WERE!
WE RAN INTO A REAL NEAT GUY THERE!
THIS GUY WILL BLOW YOUR MIND!
ZERBLIS! COME ON IN!
"ZERBLIS"?
SORRY I LAGGED BEHIND, BOYS!
EEP! IT'S HIM! HE!... WHATEVER!
I WAS DELAYED BECAUSE I WAS ZAPPING SOME CURBSIDE JUNK ALONG THE WAY!
SEE? IS HE SOMETHIN' ELSE, OR WHAT?
FZZT
3

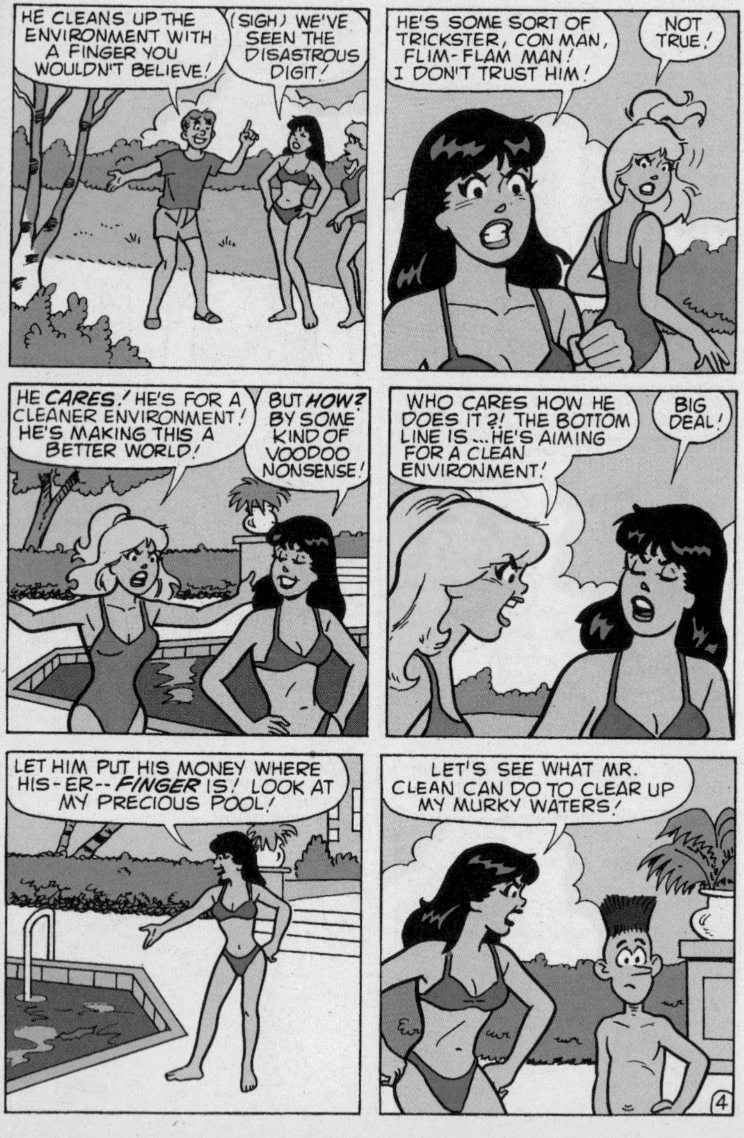
HE CLEANS UP THE ENVIRONMENT WITH A FINGER YOU WOULDN'T BELIEVE!
(SIGH) WE'VE SEEN THE DISASTROUS DIGIT!
HE'S SOME SORT OF TRICKSTER, CON MAN, FLIM-FLAM MAN! I DON'T TRUST HIM!
NOT TRUE!
HE CARES! HE'S FOR A CLEANER ENVIRONMENT! HE'S MAKING THIS A BETTER WORLD!
BUT HOW? BY SOME KIND OF VOODOO NONSENSE!
WHO CARES HOW HE DOES IT?! THE BOTTOM LINE IS... HE'S AIMING FOR A CLEAN ENVIRONMENT!
BIG DEAL!
LET HIM PUT HIS MONEY WHERE HIS-ER--FINGER IS! LOOK AT MY PRECIOUS POOL!
LET'S SEE WHAT MR. CLEAN CAN DO TO CLEAR UP MY MURKY WATERS!
4

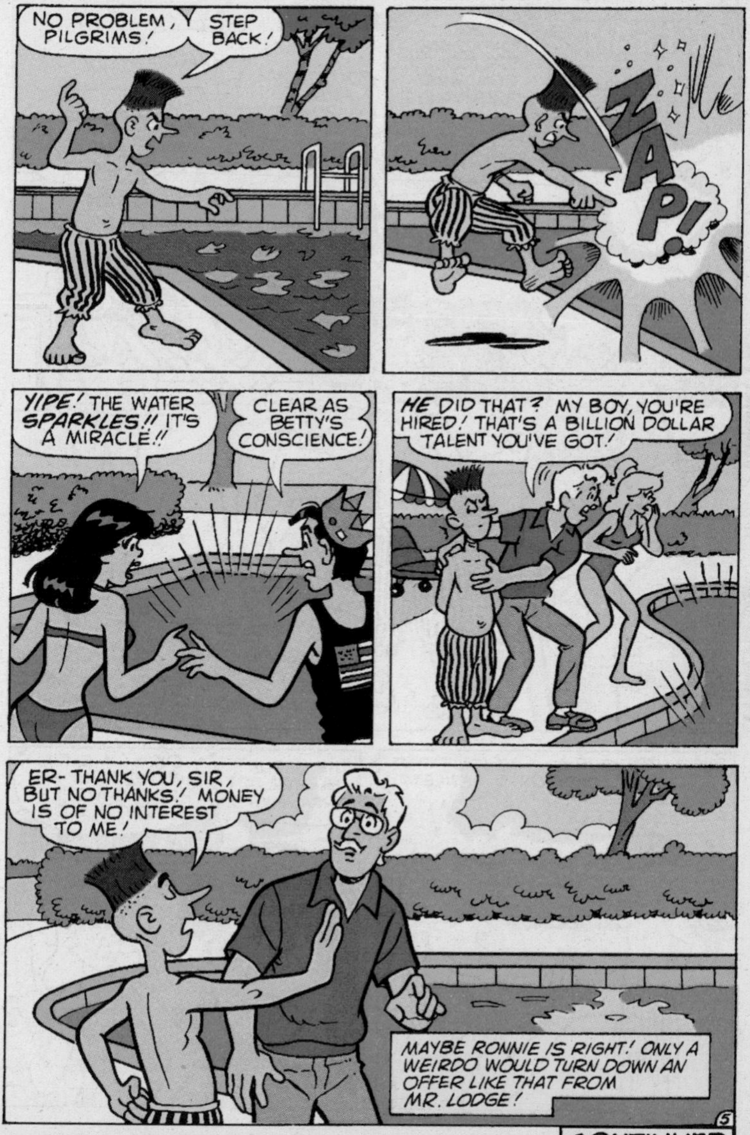
NO PROBLEM, PILGRIMS!
STEP BACK!
ZAP!
YIPE! THE WATER SPARKLES!! IT'S A MIRACLE!!
CLEAR AS BETTY'S CONSCIENCE!
HE DID THAT? MY BOY, YOU'RE HIRED! THAT'S A BILLION DOLLAR TALENT YOU'VE GOT!
ER- THANK YOU, SIR, BUT NO THANKS! MONEY IS OF NO INTEREST TO ME!
MAYBE RONNIE IS RIGHT! ONLY A WEIRDO WOULD TURN DOWN AN OFFER LIKE THAT FROM MR. LODGE!

CONTINUED

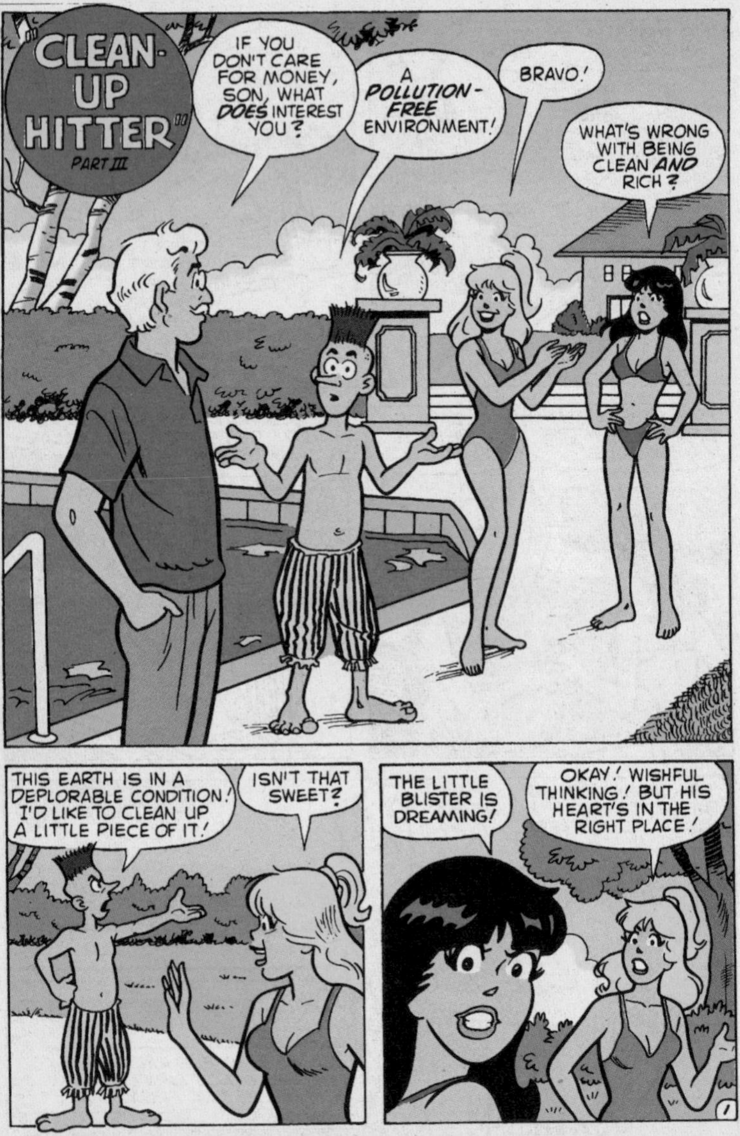
"CLEAN-UP HITTER"
PART III
IF YOU DON'T CARE FOR MONEY, SON, WHAT DOES INTEREST YOU?
A POLLUTION-FREE ENVIRONMENT!
BRAVO!
WHAT'S WRONG WITH BEING CLEAN AND RICH?
THIS EARTH IS IN A DEPLORABLE CONDITION! I'D LIKE TO CLEAN UP A LITTLE PIECE OF IT!
ISN'T THAT SWEET?
THE LITTLE BLISTER IS DREAMING!
OKAY! WISHFUL THINKING! BUT HIS HEART'S IN THE RIGHT PLACE!
1

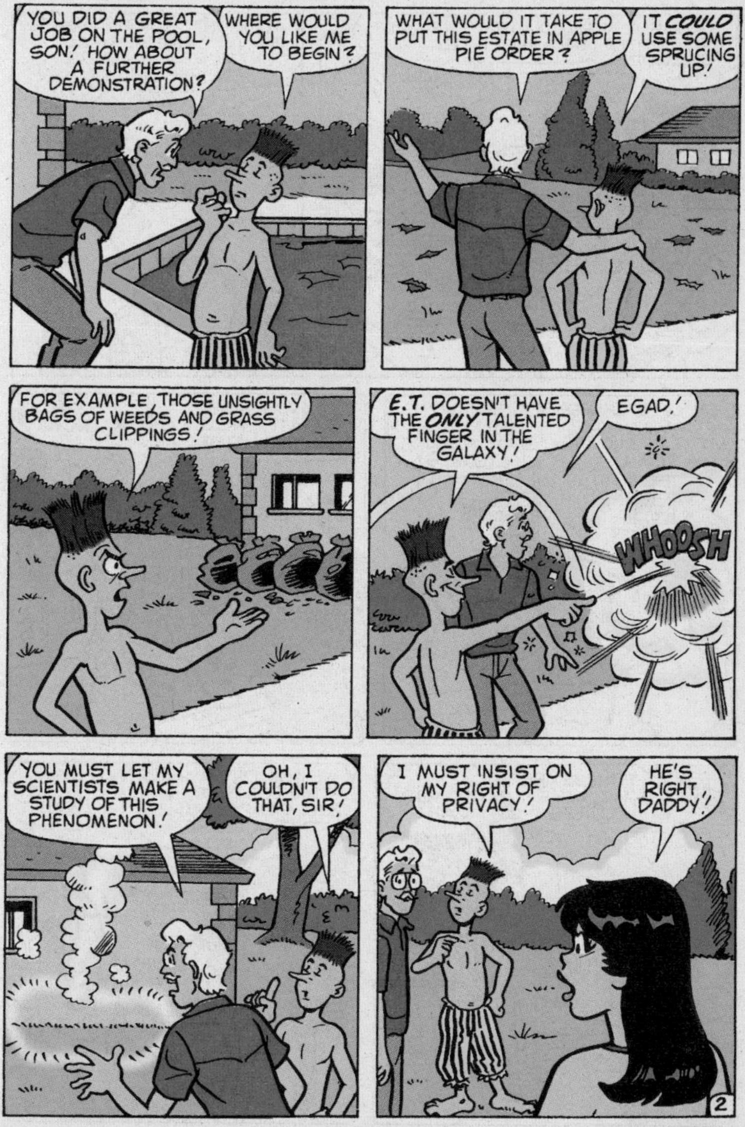

YOU DID A GREAT JOB ON THE POOL, SON! HOW ABOUT A FURTHER DEMONSTRATION?
WHERE WOULD YOU LIKE ME TO BEGIN?
WHAT WOULD IT TAKE TO PUT THIS ESTATE IN APPLE PIE ORDER?
IT COULD USE SOME SPRUCING UP!
FOR EXAMPLE, THOSE UNSIGHTLY BAGS OF WEEDS AND GRASS CLIPPINGS!
E.T. DOESN'T HAVE THE ONLY TALENTED FINGER IN THE GALAXY!
EGAD!
WHOOSH
YOU MUST LET MY SCIENTISTS MAKE A STUDY OF THIS PHENOMENON!
OH, I COULDN'T DO THAT, SIR!
I MUST INSIST ON MY RIGHT OF PRIVACY!
HE'S RIGHT, DADDY!
2

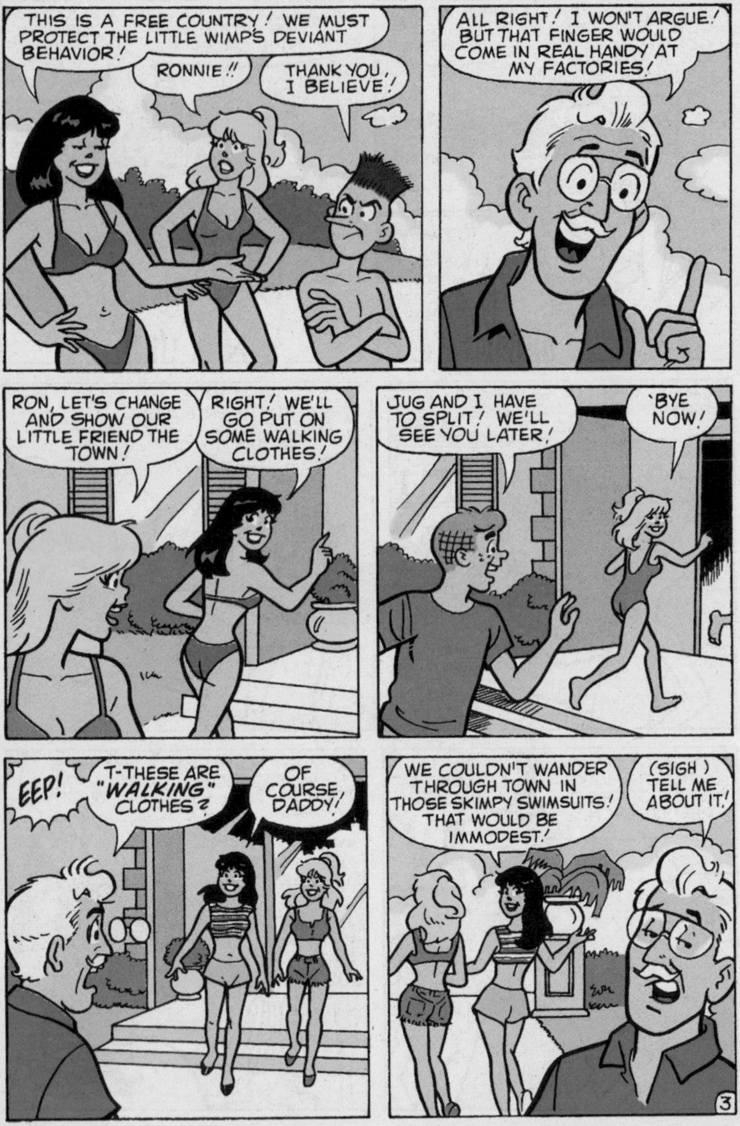

THIS IS A FREE COUNTRY! WE MUST PROTECT THE LITTLE WIMP'S DEVIANT BEHAVIOR!
RONNIE!!
THANK YOU, I BELIEVE!
ALL RIGHT! I WON'T ARGUE! BUT THAT FINGER WOULD COME IN REAL HANDY AT MY FACTORIES!
RON, LET'S CHANGE AND SHOW OUR LITTLE FRIEND THE TOWN!
RIGHT! WE'LL GO PUT ON SOME WALKING CLOTHES!
JUG AND I HAVE TO SPLIT! WE'LL SEE YOU LATER!
'BYE NOW!
EEP!
T-THESE ARE "WALKING" CLOTHES?
OF COURSE, DADDY!
WE COULDN'T WANDER THROUGH TOWN IN THOSE SKIMPY SWIMSUITS! THAT WOULD BE IMMODEST!
(SIGH) TELL ME ABOUT IT!
3

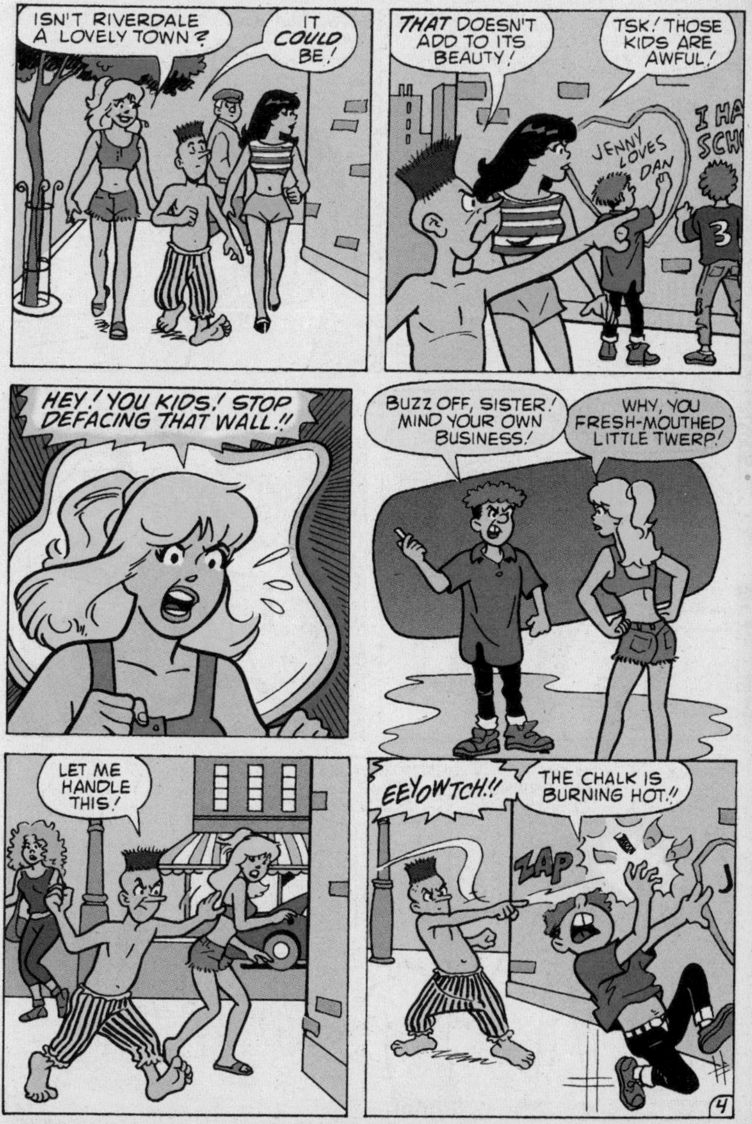

ISN'T RIVERDALE A LOVELY TOWN?
IT COULD BE!
THAT DOESN'T ADD TO ITS BEAUTY!
TSK! THOSE KIDS ARE AWFUL!
JENNY LOVES DAN
HEY! YOU KIDS! STOP DEFACING THAT WALL!!
BUZZ OFF, SISTER! MIND YOUR OWN BUSINESS!
WHY, YOU FRESH-MOUTHED LITTLE TWERP!
LET ME HANDLE THIS!
EEYOWTCH!!
THE CHALK IS BURNING HOT!!
ZAP

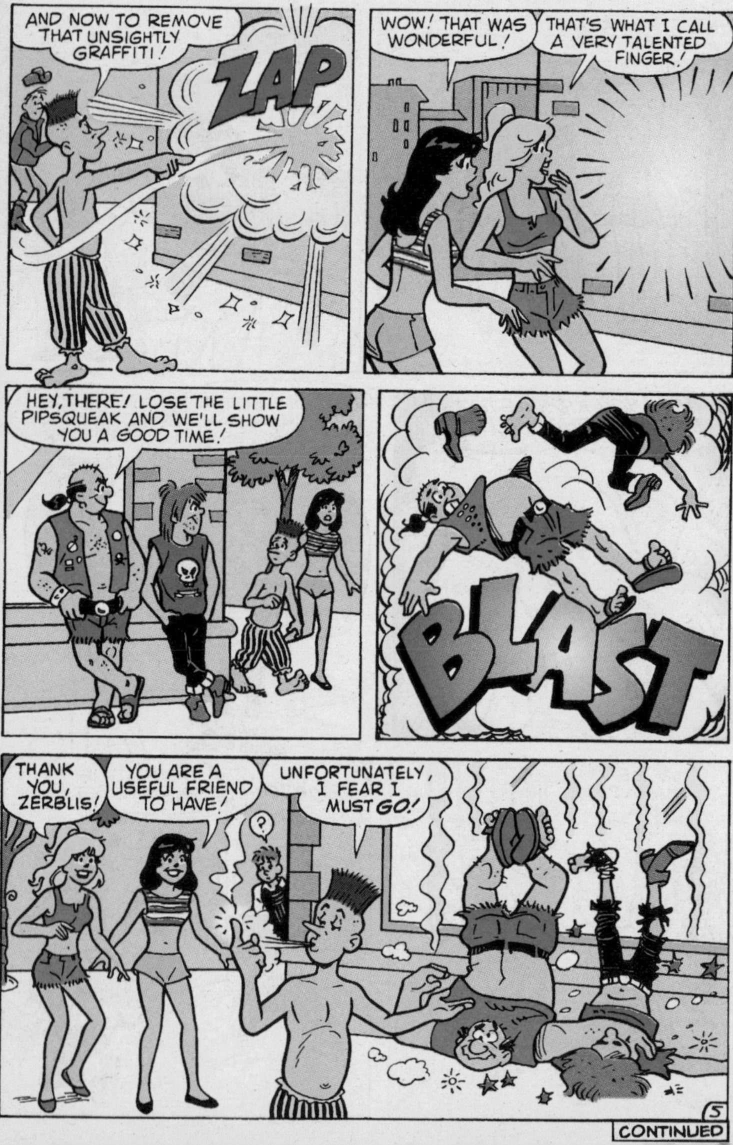
AND NOW TO REMOVE THAT UNSIGHTLY GRAFFITI!
ZAP
WOW! THAT WAS WONDERFUL!
THAT'S WHAT I CALL A VERY TALENTED FINGER!
HEY, THERE! LOSE THE LITTLE PIPSQUEAK AND WE'LL SHOW YOU A GOOD TIME!
BLAST
THANK YOU, ZERBLIS!
YOU ARE A USEFUL FRIEND TO HAVE!
?
UNFORTUNATELY, I FEAR I MUST GO!
5
CONTINUED

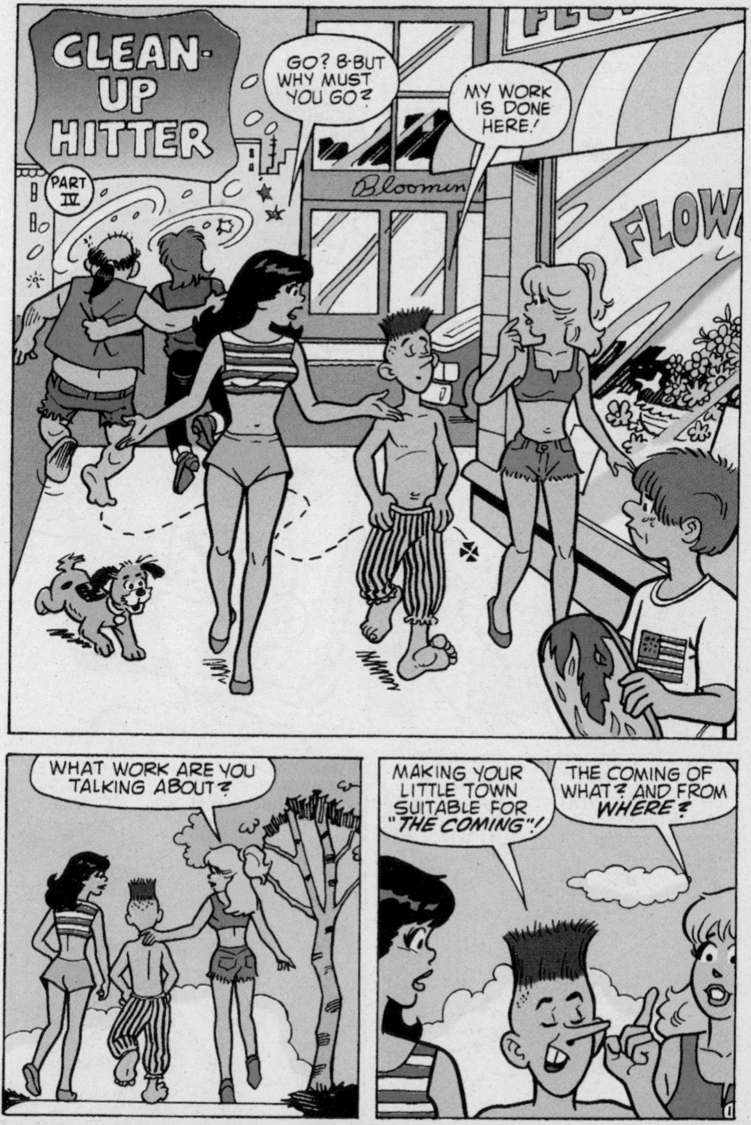
CLEAN-UP HITTER
PART IV
GO? B-BUT WHY MUST YOU GO?
MY WORK IS DONE HERE!
Bloomin
FLOW
WHAT WORK ARE YOU TALKING ABOUT?
MAKING YOUR LITTLE TOWN SUITABLE FOR "THE COMING"!
THE COMING OF WHAT? AND FROM WHERE?
1

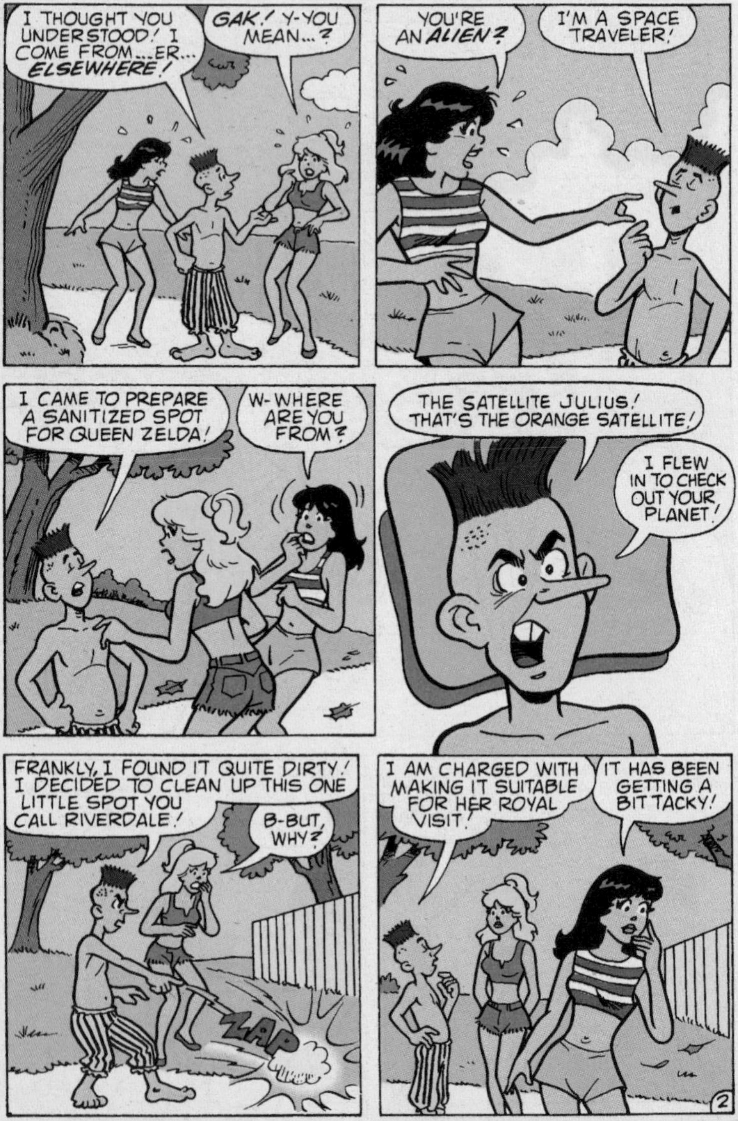
I THOUGHT YOU UNDERSTOOD! I COME FROM...ER... ELSEWHERE!
GAK! Y-YOU MEAN...?
YOU'RE AN ALIEN?
I'M A SPACE TRAVELER!
I CAME TO PREPARE A SANITIZED SPOT FOR QUEEN ZELDA!
W-WHERE ARE YOU FROM?
THE SATELLITE JULIUS! THAT'S THE ORANGE SATELLITE!
I FLEW IN TO CHECK OUT YOUR PLANET!
FRANKLY, I FOUND IT QUITE DIRTY! I DECIDED TO CLEAN UP THIS ONE LITTLE SPOT YOU CALL RIVERDALE!
B-BUT, WHY?
ZAP
I AM CHARGED WITH MAKING IT SUITABLE FOR HER ROYAL VISIT!
IT HAS BEEN GETTING A BIT TACKY!
2

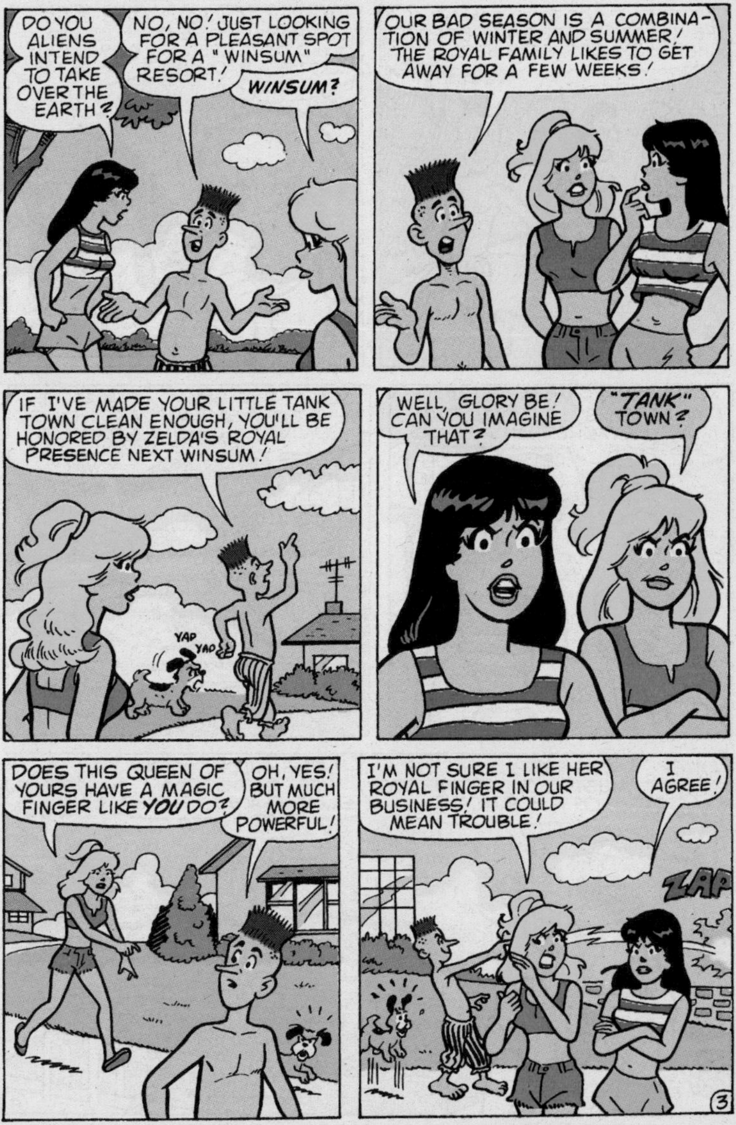
DO YOU ALIENS INTEND TO TAKE OVER THE EARTH?
NO, NO! JUST LOOKING FOR A PLEASANT SPOT FOR A "WINSUM" RESORT!
WINSUM?
OUR BAD SEASON IS A COMBINATION OF WINTER AND SUMMER! THE ROYAL FAMILY LIKES TO GET AWAY FOR A FEW WEEKS!
IF I'VE MADE YOUR LITTLE TANK TOWN CLEAN ENOUGH, YOU'LL BE HONORED BY ZELDA'S ROYAL PRESENCE NEXT WINSUM!
YAP
YAP
WELL, GLORY BE! CAN YOU IMAGINE THAT?
"TANK" TOWN?
DOES THIS QUEEN OF YOURS HAVE A MAGIC FINGER LIKE YOU DO?
OH, YES! BUT MUCH MORE POWERFUL!
I'M NOT SURE I LIKE HER ROYAL FINGER IN OUR BUSINESS! IT COULD MEAN TROUBLE!
I AGREE!
ZAP
3

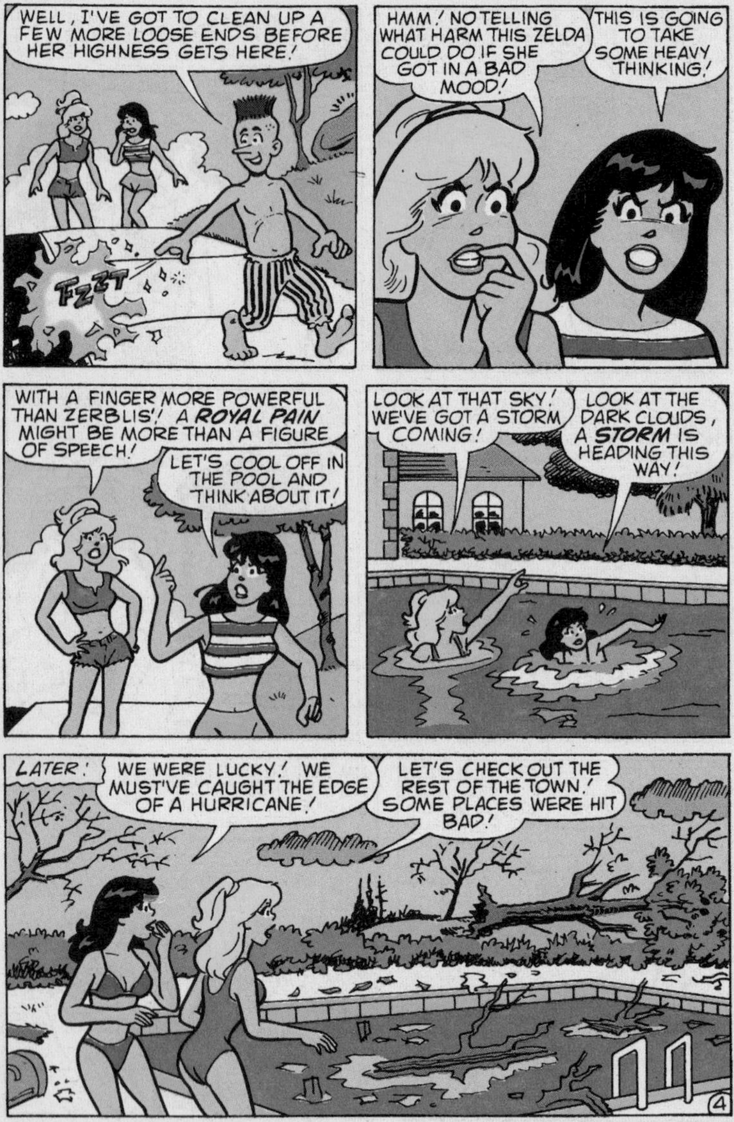
WELL, I'VE GOT TO CLEAN UP A FEW MORE LOOSE ENDS BEFORE HER HIGHNESS GETS HERE!
FZZT
HMM! NO TELLING WHAT HARM THIS ZELDA COULD DO IF SHE GOT IN A BAD MOOD!
THIS IS GOING TO TAKE SOME HEAVY THINKING!
WITH A FINGER MORE POWERFUL THAN ZERBLIS'! A ROYAL PAIN MIGHT BE MORE THAN A FIGURE OF SPEECH!
LET'S COOL OFF IN THE POOL AND THINK ABOUT IT!
LOOK AT THAT SKY! WE'VE GOT A STORM COMING!
LOOK AT THE DARK CLOUDS, A STORM IS HEADING THIS WAY!
LATER!
WE WERE LUCKY! WE MUST'VE CAUGHT THE EDGE OF A HURRICANE!
LET'S CHECK OUT THE REST OF THE TOWN! SOME PLACES WERE HIT BAD!
4

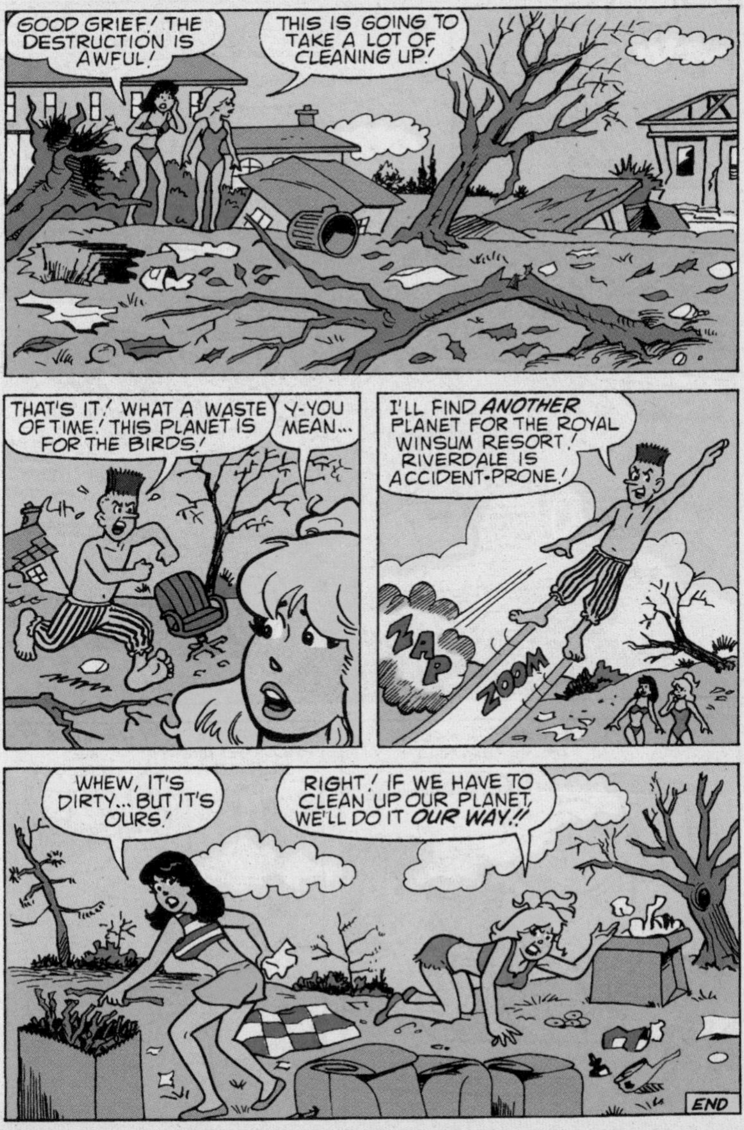
GOOD GRIEF! THE DESTRUCTION IS AWFUL!
THIS IS GOING TO TAKE A LOT OF CLEANING UP!
THAT'S IT! WHAT A WASTE OF TIME! THIS PLANET IS FOR THE BIRDS!
Y-YOU MEAN...
I'LL FIND ANOTHER PLANET FOR THE ROYAL WINSUM RESORT! RIVERDALE IS ACCIDENT-PRONE!
ZAP
ZOOM
WHEW, IT'S DIRTY... BUT IT'S OURS!
RIGHT! IF WE HAVE TO CLEAN UP OUR PLANET, WE'LL DO IT OUR WAY!!
END

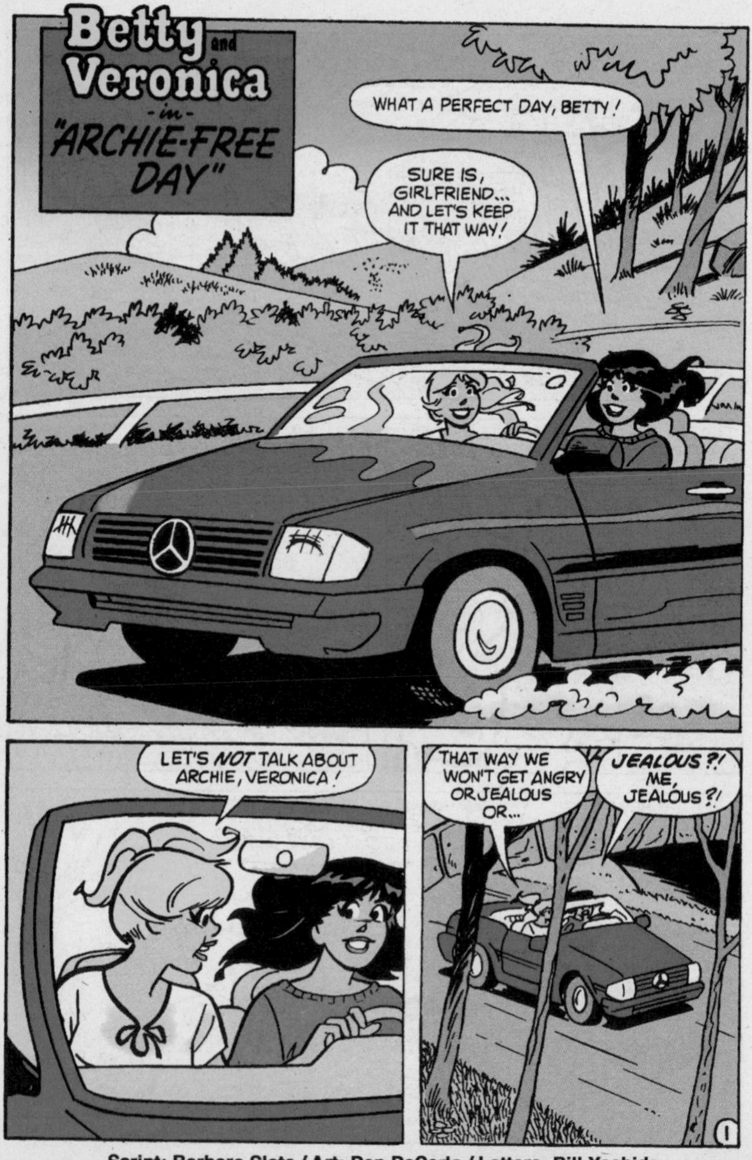
Betty and Veronica
-in-
"ARCHIE-FREE DAY"
WHAT A PERFECT DAY, BETTY!
SURE IS, GIRLFRIEND... AND LET'S KEEP IT THAT WAY!
LET'S NOT TALK ABOUT ARCHIE, VERONICA!
THAT WAY WE WON'T GET ANGRY OR JEALOUS OR...
JEALOUS?! ME, JEALOUS?!
1

Script: Barbara Slate / Art: Dan DeCarlo / Letters: Bill Yoshida

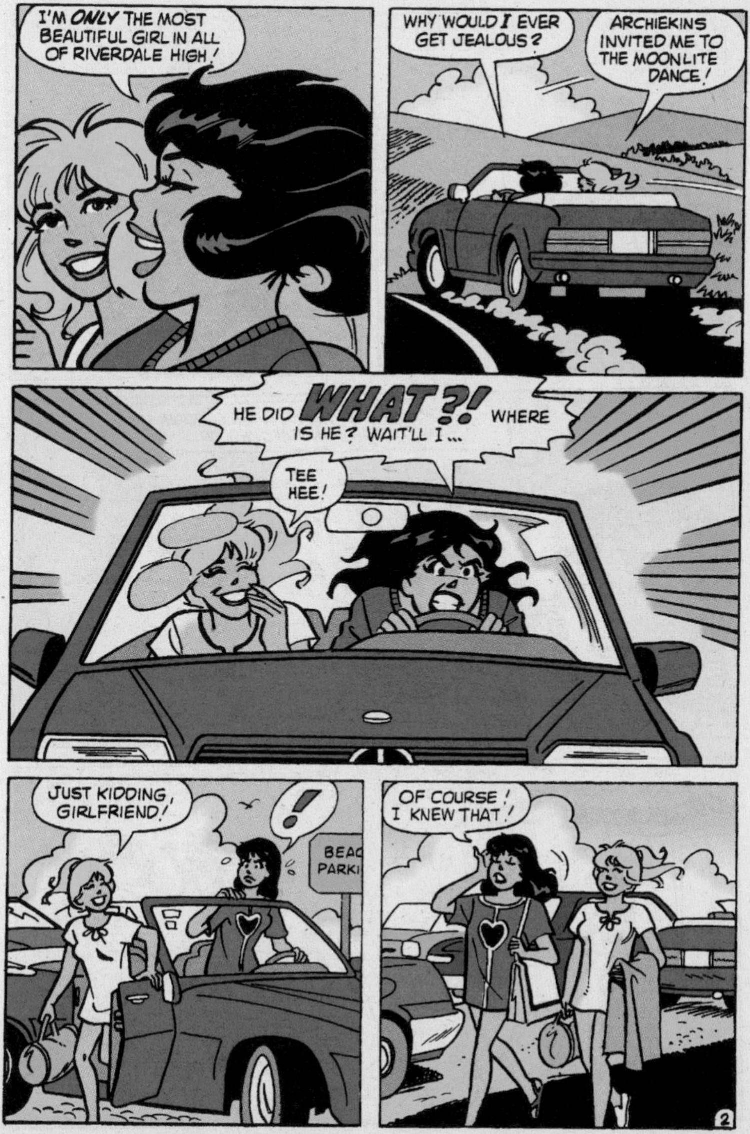
I'M ONLY THE MOST BEAUTIFUL GIRL IN ALL OF RIVERDALE HIGH!
WHY WOULD I EVER GET JEALOUS?
ARCHIEKINS INVITED ME TO THE MOONLITE DANCE!
HE DID WHAT?! WHERE IS HE? WAIT'LL I...
TEE HEE!
JUST KIDDING, GIRLFRIEND!
!
BEAC PARKI
OF COURSE! I KNEW THAT!
2

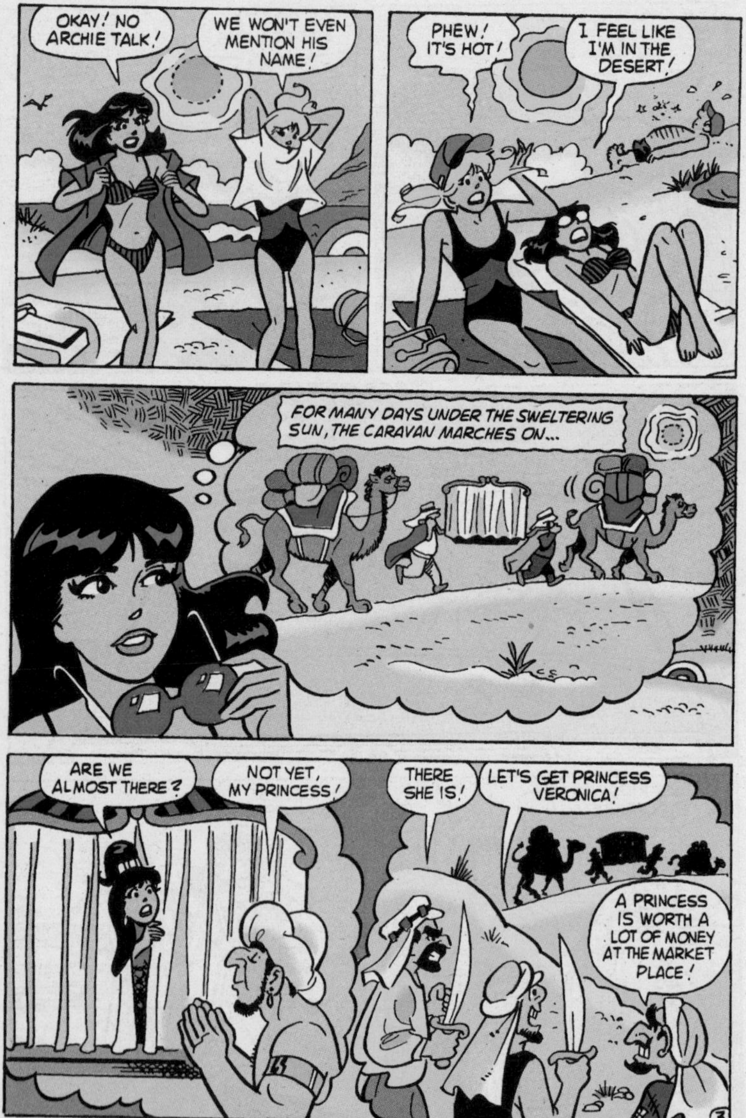

OKAY! NO ARCHIE TALK!
WE WON'T EVEN MENTION HIS NAME!
PHEW! IT'S HOT!
I FEEL LIKE I'M IN THE DESERT!
FOR MANY DAYS UNDER THE SWELTERING SUN, THE CARAVAN MARCHES ON...
ARE WE ALMOST THERE?
NOT YET, MY PRINCESS!
THERE SHE IS!
LET'S GET PRINCESS VERONICA!
A PRINCESS IS WORTH A LOT OF MONEY AT THE MARKET PLACE!

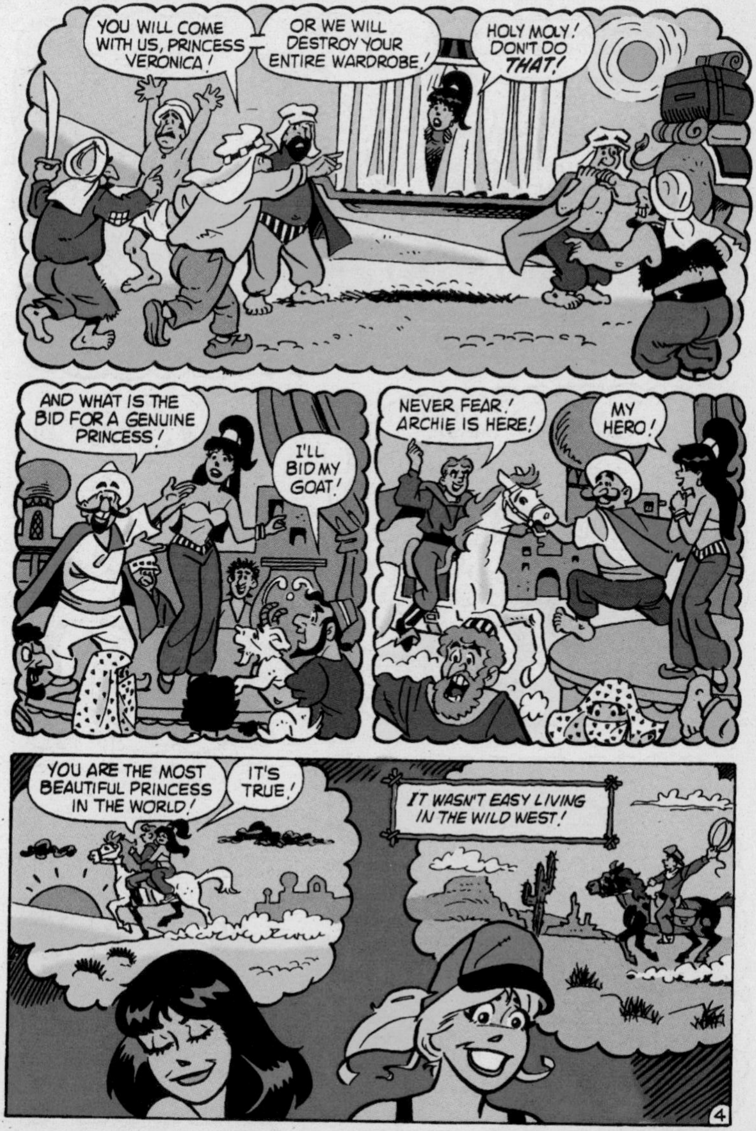
YOU WILL COME WITH US, PRINCESS VERONICA!
OR WE WILL DESTROY YOUR ENTIRE WARDROBE!
HOLY MOLY! DON'T DO THAT!
AND WHAT IS THE BID FOR A GENUINE PRINCESS!
I'LL BID MY GOAT!
NEVER FEAR! ARCHIE IS HERE!
MY HERO!
YOU ARE THE MOST BEAUTIFUL PRINCESS IN THE WORLD!
IT'S TRUE!
IT WASN'T EASY LIVING IN THE WILD WEST!
4

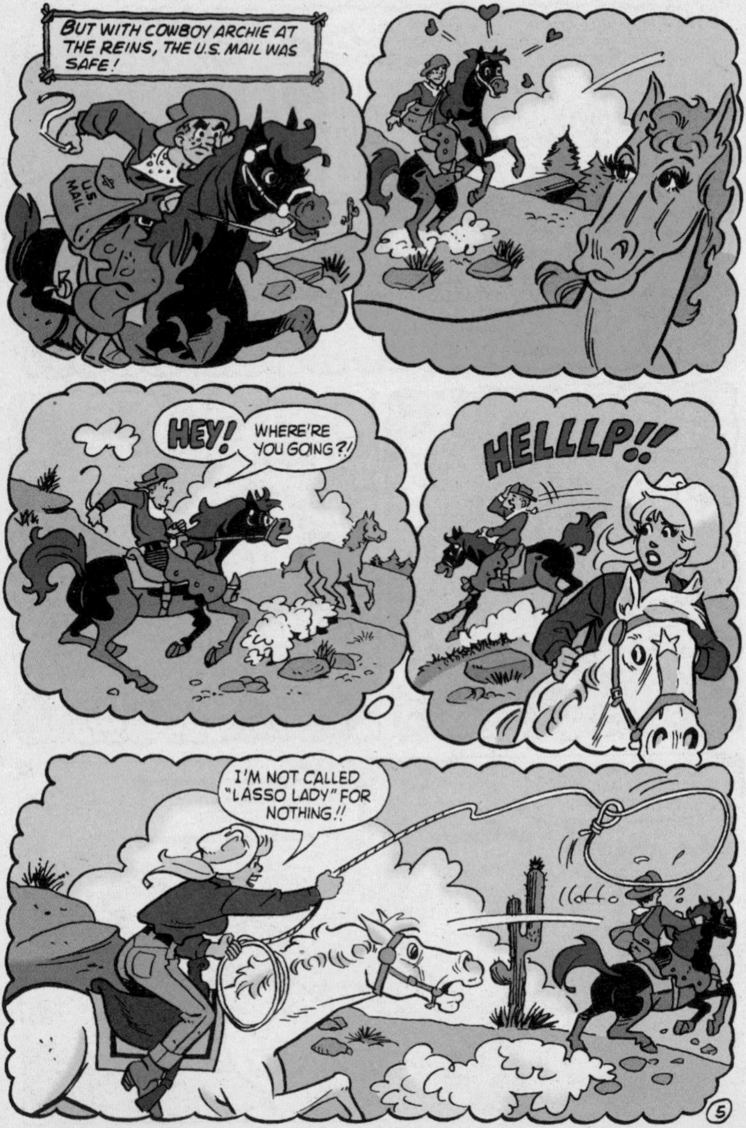

BUT WITH COWBOY ARCHIE AT THE REINS, THE U.S. MAIL WAS SAFE!
U.S. MAIL
HEY!
WHERE'RE YOU GOING?!
HELLLP!!
I'M NOT CALLED "LASSO LADY" FOR NOTHING!!
5

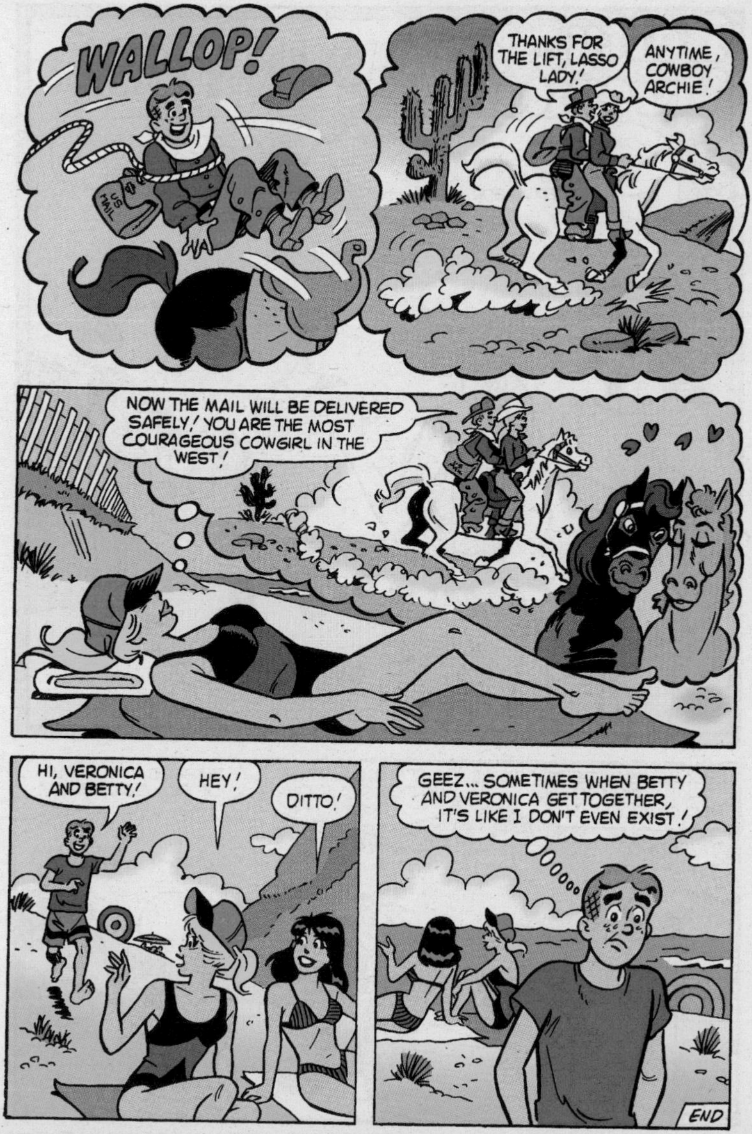
WALLOP!
US MAIL
THANKS FOR THE LIFT, LASSO LADY!
ANYTIME, COWBOY ARCHIE!
NOW THE MAIL WILL BE DELIVERED SAFELY! YOU ARE THE MOST COURAGEOUS COWGIRL IN THE WEST!
HI, VERONICA AND BETTY!
HEY!
DITTO!
GEEZ... SOMETIMES WHEN BETTY AND VERONICA GET TOGETHER, IT'S LIKE I DON'T EVEN EXIST!
END

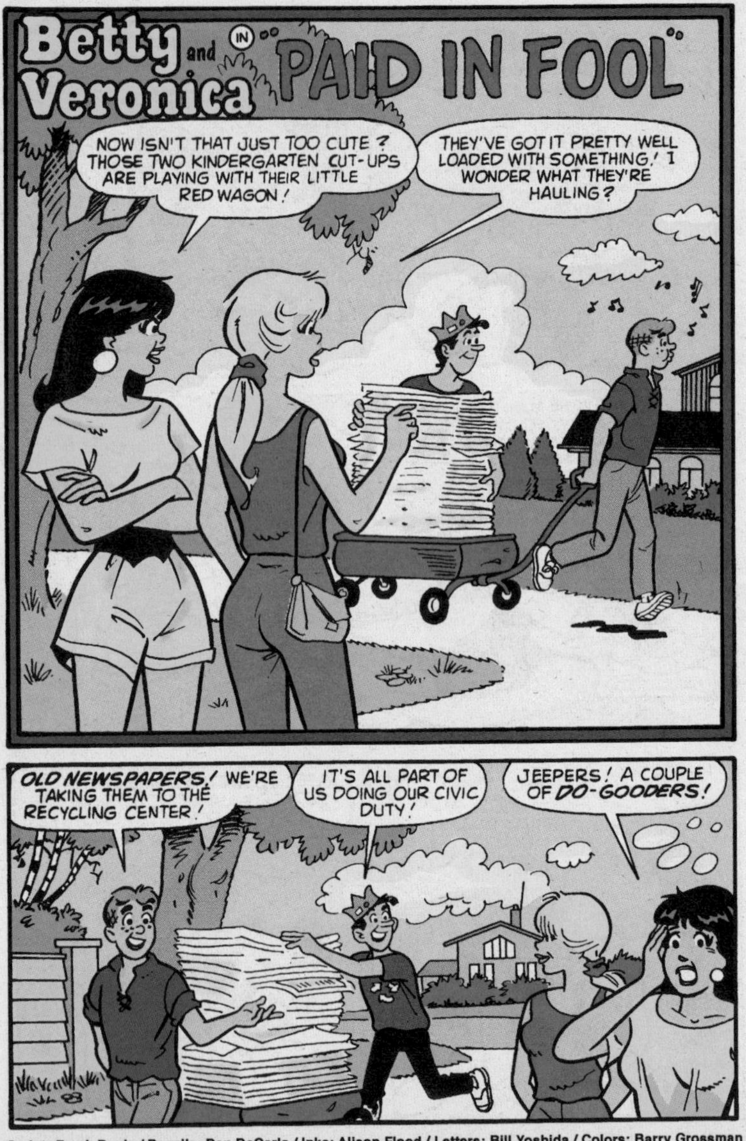
Betty and Veronica
IN
PAID IN FOOL
NOW ISN'T THAT JUST TOO CUTE? THOSE TWO KINDERGARTEN CUT-UPS ARE PLAYING WITH THEIR LITTLE RED WAGON!
THEY'VE GOT IT PRETTY WELL LOADED WITH SOMETHING! I WONDER WHAT THEY'RE HAULING?
OLD NEWSPAPERS! WE'RE TAKING THEM TO THE RECYCLING CENTER!
IT'S ALL PART OF US DOING OUR CIVIC DUTY!
JEEPERS! A COUPLE OF DO-GOODERS!

Script: Frank Doyle / Pencils: Dan DeCarlo / Inks: Alison Flood / Letters: Bill Yoshida / Colors: Barry Grossman

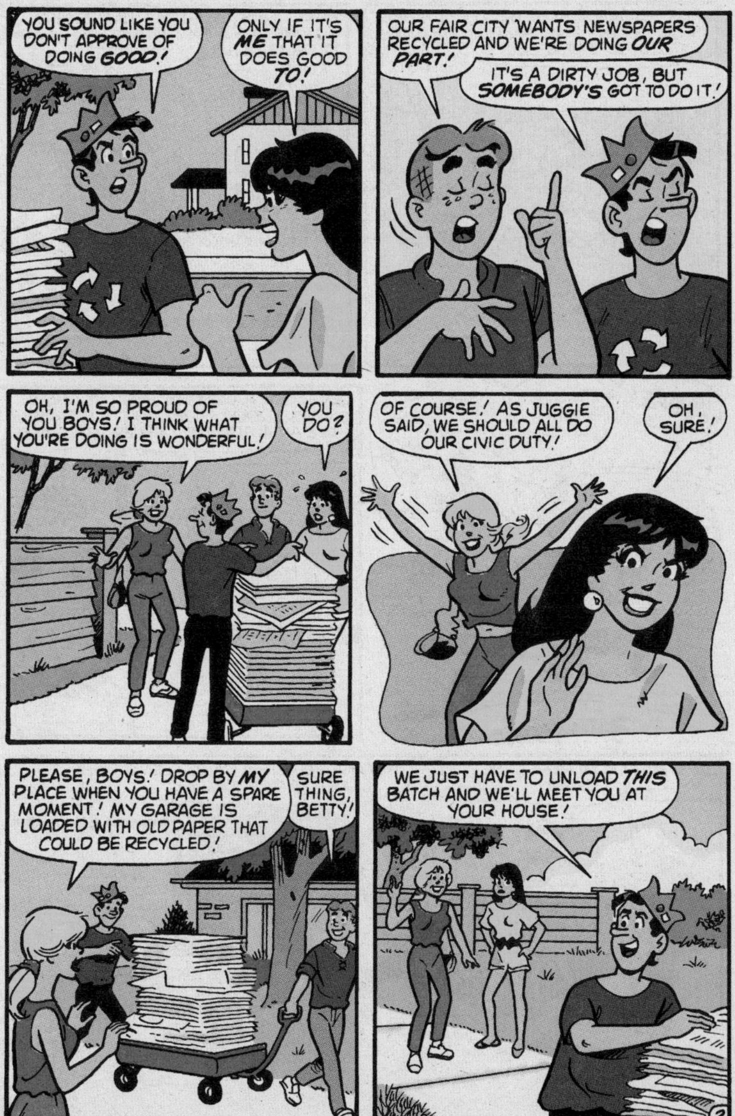
YOU SOUND LIKE YOU DON'T APPROVE OF DOING GOOD!
ONLY IF IT'S ME THAT IT DOES GOOD TO!
OUR FAIR CITY WANTS NEWSPAPERS RECYCLED AND WE'RE DOING OUR PART!
IT'S A DIRTY JOB, BUT SOMEBODY'S GOT TO DO IT!
OH, I'M SO PROUD OF YOU BOYS! I THINK WHAT YOU'RE DOING IS WONDERFUL!
YOU DO?
OF COURSE! AS JUGGIE SAID, WE SHOULD ALL DO OUR CIVIC DUTY!
OH, SURE!
PLEASE, BOYS! DROP BY MY PLACE WHEN YOU HAVE A SPARE MOMENT! MY GARAGE IS LOADED WITH OLD PAPER THAT COULD BE RECYCLED!
SURE THING, BETTY!
WE JUST HAVE TO UNLOAD THIS BATCH AND WE'LL MEET YOU AT YOUR HOUSE!
2

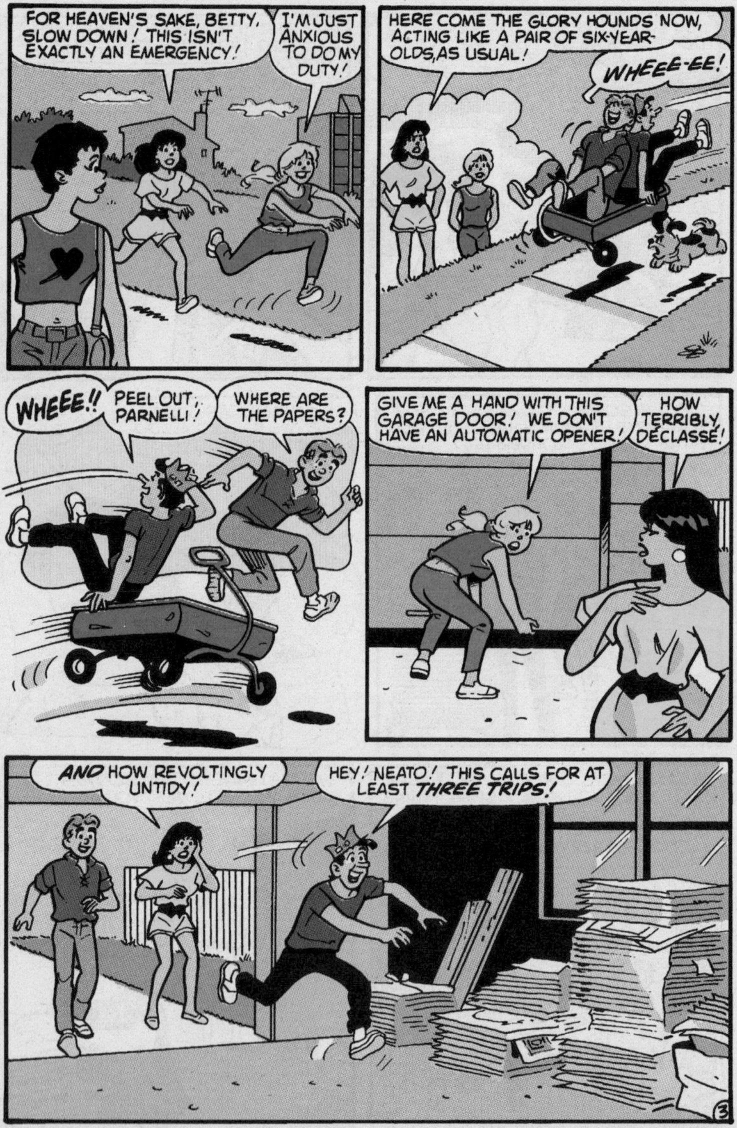
FOR HEAVEN'S SAKE, BETTY, SLOW DOWN! THIS ISN'T EXACTLY AN EMERGENCY!
I'M JUST ANXIOUS TO DO MY DUTY!
HERE COME THE GLORY HOUNDS NOW, ACTING LIKE A PAIR OF SIX-YEAR-OLDS, AS USUAL!
WHEEE-EE!
WHEEE!!
PEEL OUT, PARNELLI!
WHERE ARE THE PAPERS?
GIVE ME A HAND WITH THIS GARAGE DOOR! WE DON'T HAVE AN AUTOMATIC OPENER!
HOW TERRIBLY DÉCLASSÉ!
AND HOW REVOLTINGLY UNTIDY!
HEY! NEATO! THIS CALLS FOR AT LEAST THREE TRIPS!
3

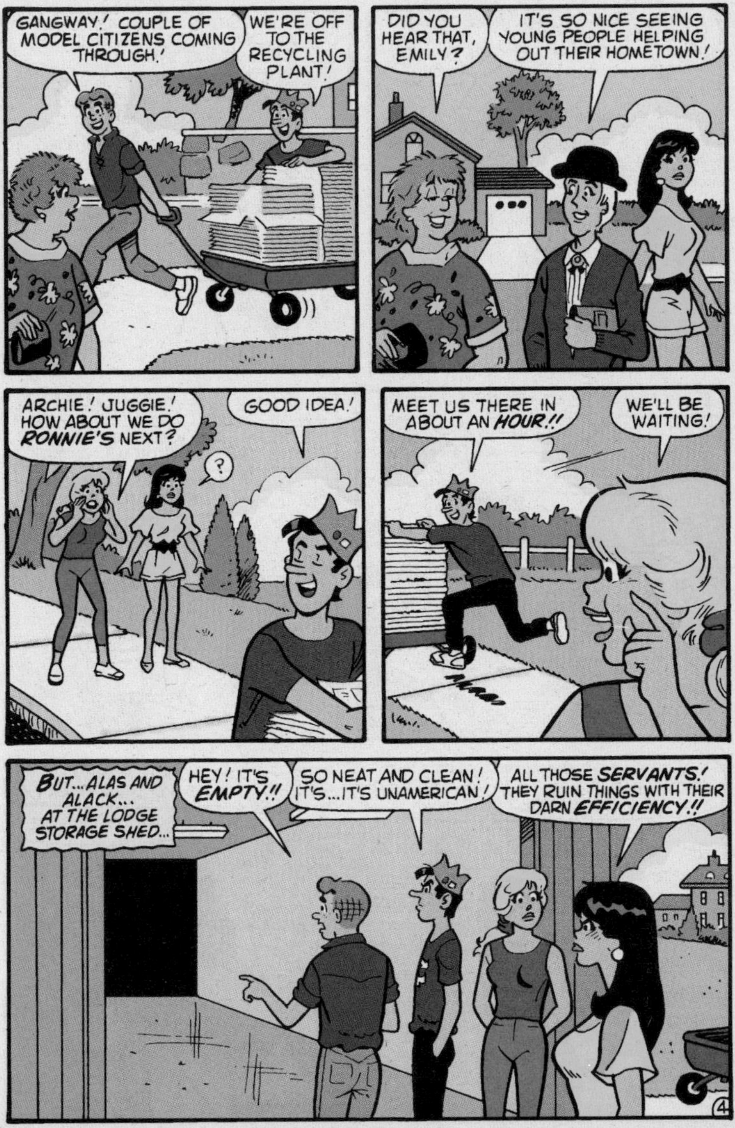
GANGWAY! COUPLE OF MODEL CITIZENS COMING THROUGH!
WE'RE OFF TO THE RECYCLING PLANT!
DID YOU HEAR THAT, EMILY?
IT'S SO NICE SEEING YOUNG PEOPLE HELPING OUT THEIR HOMETOWN!
ARCHIE! JUGGIE! HOW ABOUT WE DO RONNIE'S NEXT?
?
GOOD IDEA!
MEET US THERE IN ABOUT AN HOUR!!
WE'LL BE WAITING!
BUT... ALAS AND ALACK... AT THE LODGE STORAGE SHED...
HEY! IT'S EMPTY!!
SO NEAT AND CLEAN! IT'S... IT'S UNAMERICAN!
ALL THOSE SERVANTS! THEY RUIN THINGS WITH THEIR DARN EFFICIENCY!!
4

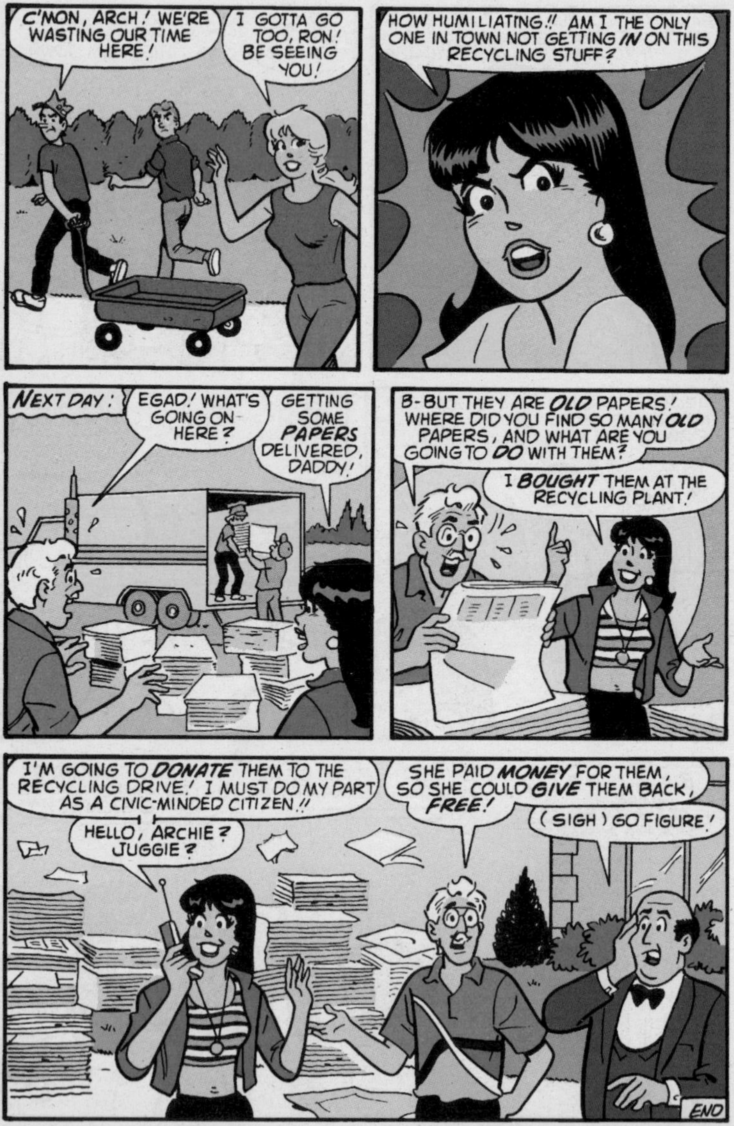
C'MON, ARCH! WE'RE WASTING OUR TIME HERE!
I GOTTA GO TOO, RON! BE SEEING YOU!
HOW HUMILIATING!! AM I THE ONLY ONE IN TOWN NOT GETTING IN ON THIS RECYCLING STUFF?
NEXT DAY:
EGAD! WHAT'S GOING ON HERE?
GETTING SOME PAPERS DELIVERED, DADDY!
B-BUT THEY ARE OLD PAPERS! WHERE DID YOU FIND SO MANY OLD PAPERS, AND WHAT ARE YOU GOING TO DO WITH THEM?
I BOUGHT THEM AT THE RECYCLING PLANT!
I'M GOING TO DONATE THEM TO THE RECYCLING DRIVE! I MUST DO MY PART AS A CIVIC-MINDED CITIZEN!!
HELLO, ARCHIE? JUGGIE?
SHE PAID MONEY FOR THEM, SO SHE COULD GIVE THEM BACK, FREE!
(SIGH) GO FIGURE!
END

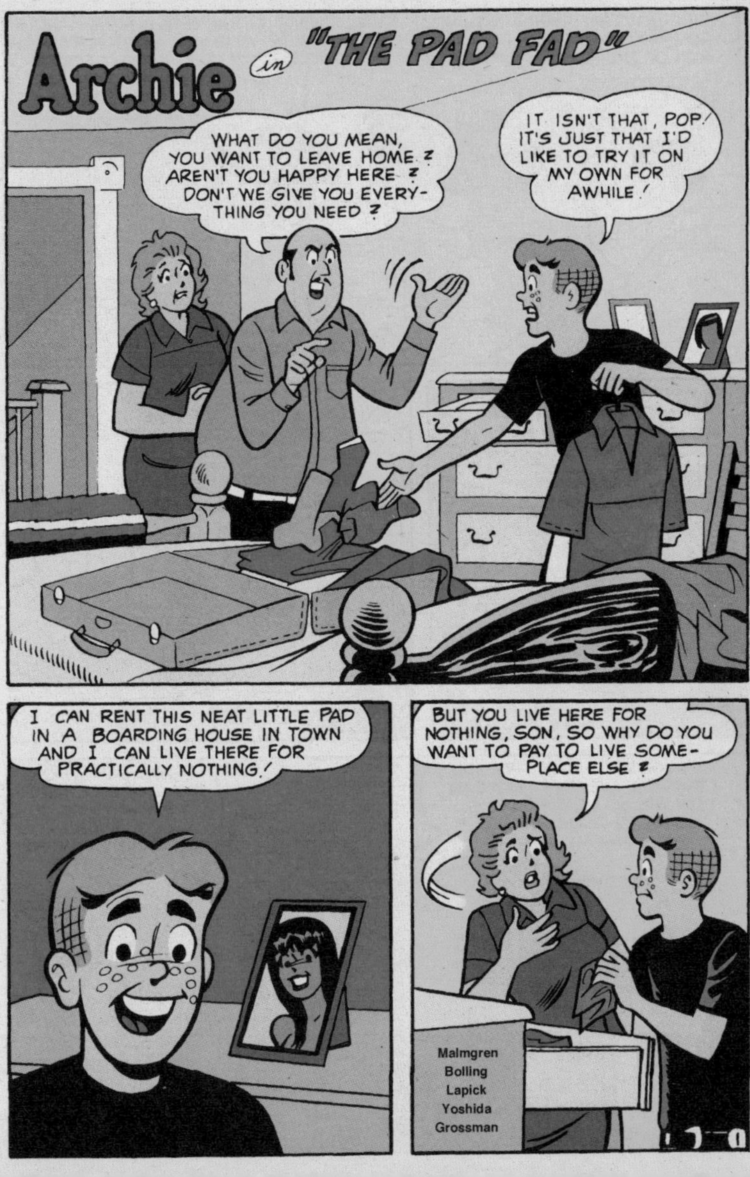
Archie in "THE PAD FAD"
WHAT DO YOU MEAN, YOU WANT TO LEAVE HOME? AREN'T YOU HAPPY HERE? DON'T WE GIVE YOU EVERYTHING YOU NEED?
IT ISN'T THAT, POP! IT'S JUST THAT I'D LIKE TO TRY IT ON MY OWN FOR AWHILE!
I CAN RENT THIS NEAT LITTLE PAD IN A BOARDING HOUSE IN TOWN AND I CAN LIVE THERE FOR PRACTICALLY NOTHING!
BUT YOU LIVE HERE FOR NOTHING, SON, SO WHY DO YOU WANT TO PAY TO LIVE SOMEPLACE ELSE?
Malmgren
Bolling
Lapick
Yoshida
Grossman

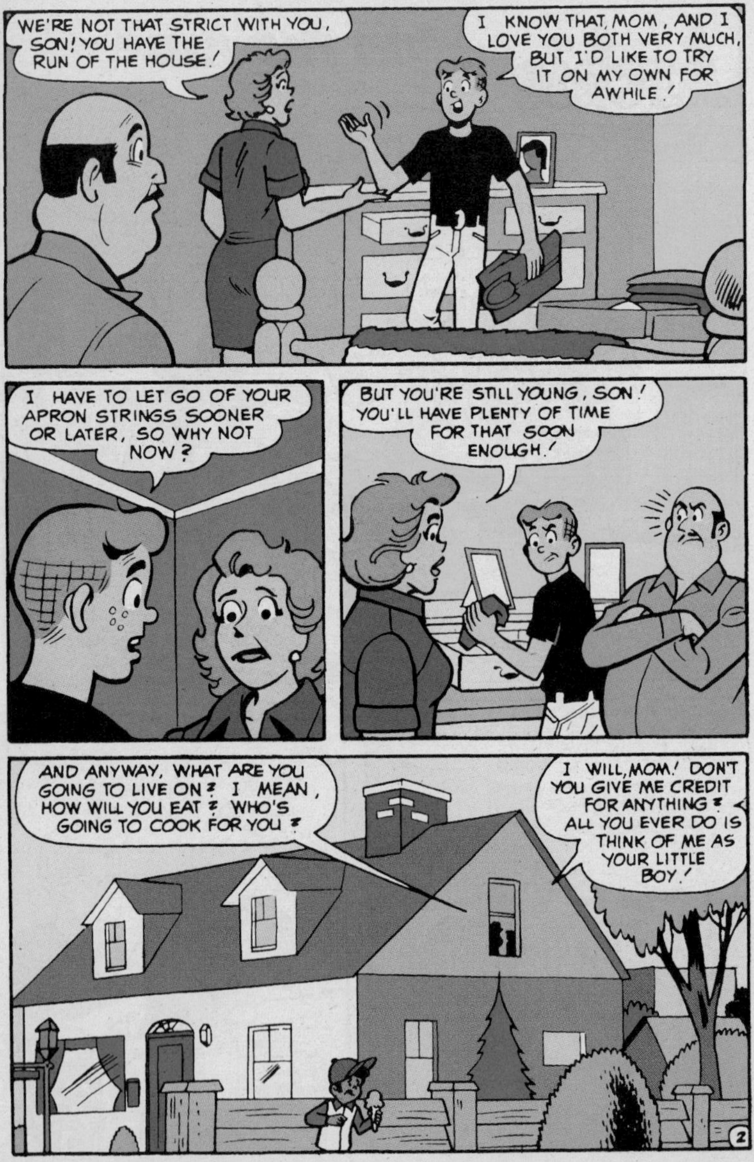
WE'RE NOT THAT STRICT WITH YOU, SON! YOU HAVE THE RUN OF THE HOUSE!
I KNOW THAT, MOM, AND I LOVE YOU BOTH VERY MUCH, BUT I'D LIKE TO TRY IT ON MY OWN FOR AWHILE!
I HAVE TO LET GO OF YOUR APRON STRINGS SOONER OR LATER, SO WHY NOT NOW?
BUT YOU'RE STILL YOUNG, SON! YOU'LL HAVE PLENTY OF TIME FOR THAT SOON ENOUGH!
AND ANYWAY, WHAT ARE YOU GOING TO LIVE ON? I MEAN, HOW WILL YOU EAT? WHO'S GOING TO COOK FOR YOU?
I WILL, MOM! DON'T YOU GIVE ME CREDIT FOR ANYTHING? ALL YOU EVER DO IS THINK OF ME AS YOUR LITTLE BOY!
2

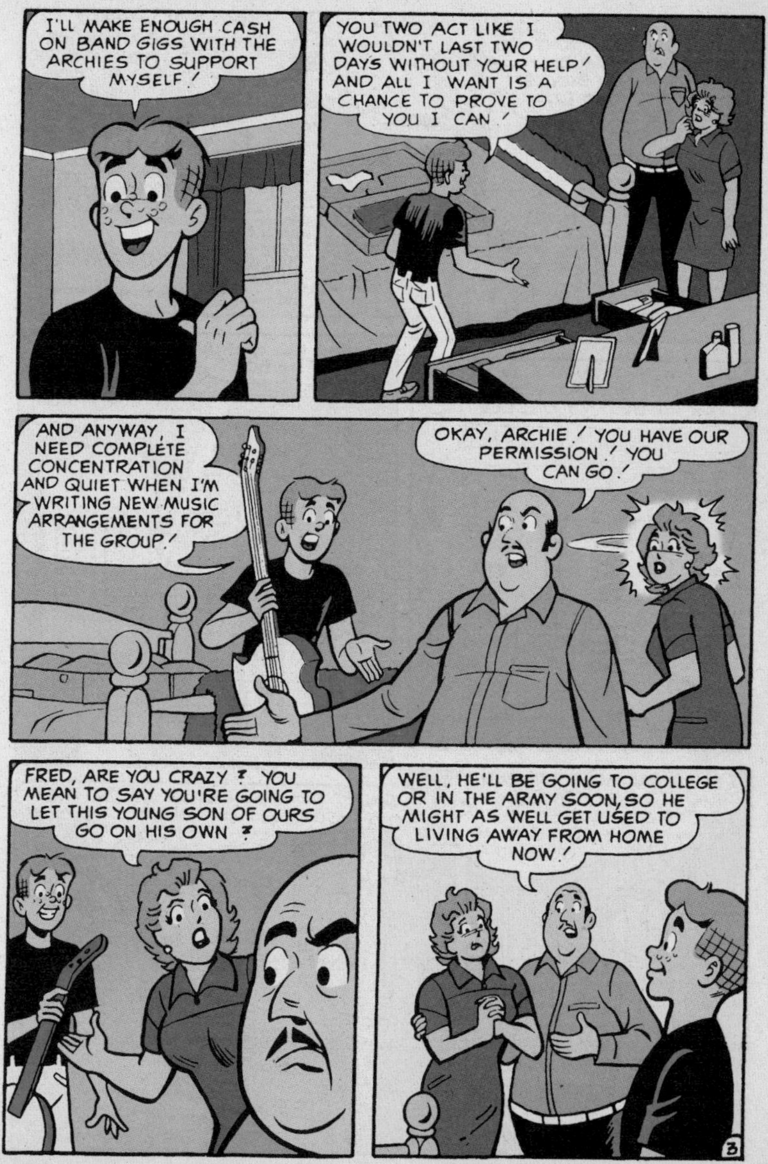
I'LL MAKE ENOUGH CASH ON BAND GIGS WITH THE ARCHIES TO SUPPORT MYSELF!
YOU TWO ACT LIKE I WOULDN'T LAST TWO DAYS WITHOUT YOUR HELP! AND ALL I WANT IS A CHANCE TO PROVE TO YOU I CAN!
AND ANYWAY, I NEED COMPLETE CONCENTRATION AND QUIET WHEN I'M WRITING NEW MUSIC ARRANGEMENTS FOR THE GROUP!
OKAY, ARCHIE! YOU HAVE OUR PERMISSION! YOU CAN GO!
FRED, ARE YOU CRAZY? YOU MEAN TO SAY YOU'RE GOING TO LET THIS YOUNG SON OF OURS GO ON HIS OWN?
WELL, HE'LL BE GOING TO COLLEGE OR IN THE ARMY SOON, SO HE MIGHT AS WELL GET USED TO LIVING AWAY FROM HOME NOW!
3

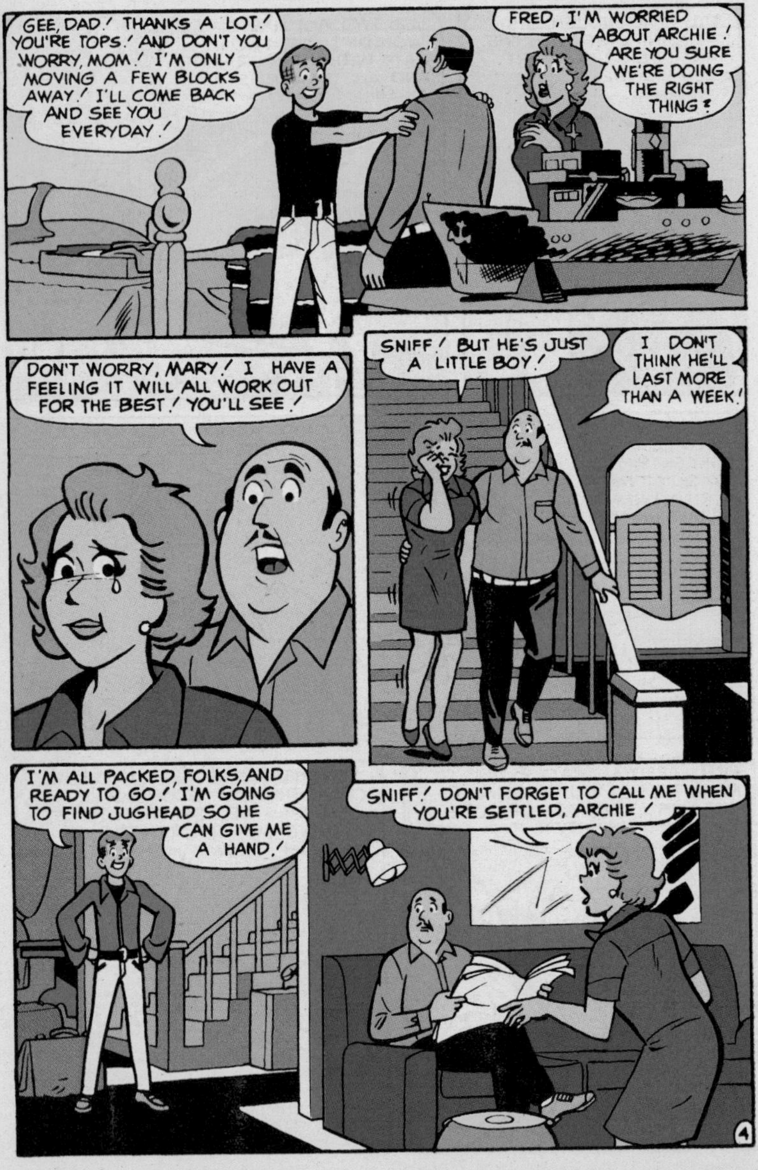
GEE, DAD! THANKS A LOT! YOU'RE TOPS! AND DON'T YOU WORRY, MOM! I'M ONLY MOVING A FEW BLOCKS AWAY! I'LL COME BACK AND SEE YOU EVERYDAY!
FRED, I'M WORRIED ABOUT ARCHIE! ARE YOU SURE WE'RE DOING THE RIGHT THING?
DON'T WORRY, MARY! I HAVE A FEELING IT WILL ALL WORK OUT FOR THE BEST! YOU'LL SEE!
SNIFF! BUT HE'S JUST A LITTLE BOY!
I DON'T THINK HE'LL LAST MORE THAN A WEEK!
I'M ALL PACKED, FOLKS, AND READY TO GO! I'M GOING TO FIND JUGHEAD SO HE CAN GIVE ME A HAND!
SNIFF! DON'T FORGET TO CALL ME WHEN YOU'RE SETTLED, ARCHIE!
4

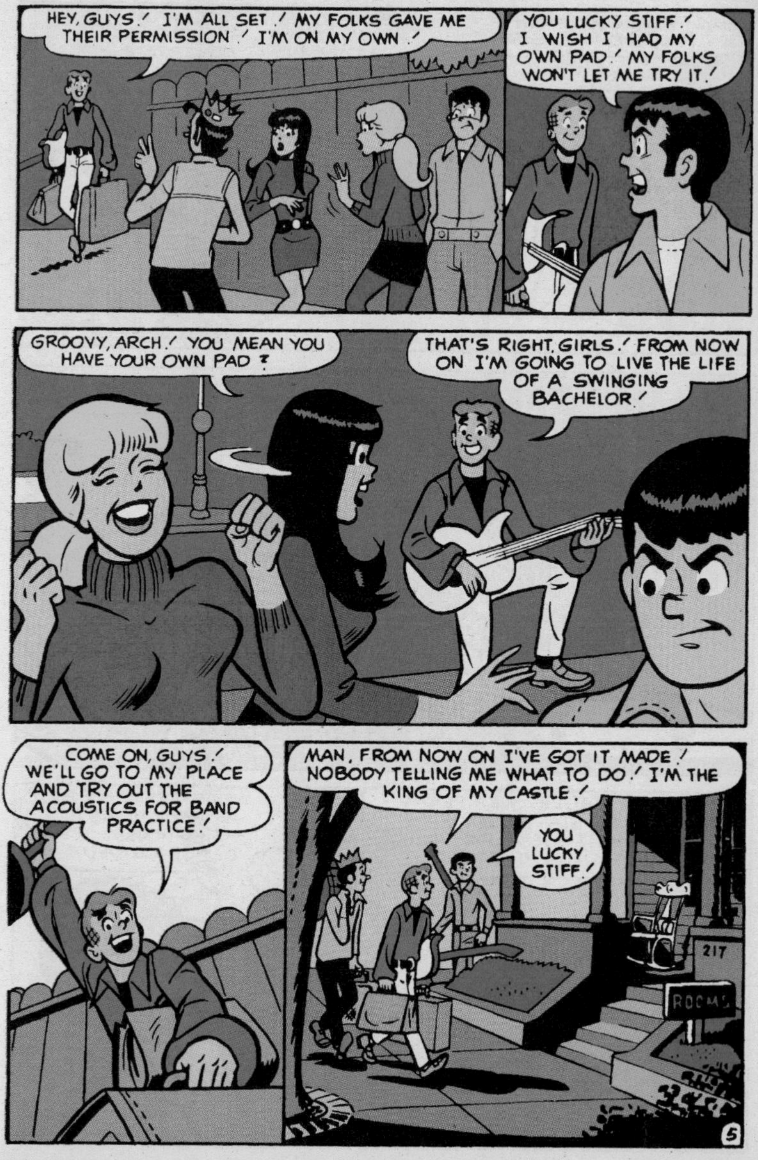
HEY, GUYS! I'M ALL SET! MY FOLKS GAVE ME THEIR PERMISSION! I'M ON MY OWN!
YOU LUCKY STIFF! I WISH I HAD MY OWN PAD! MY FOLKS WON'T LET ME TRY IT!
GROOVY, ARCH! YOU MEAN YOU HAVE YOUR OWN PAD?
THAT'S RIGHT, GIRLS! FROM NOW ON I'M GOING TO LIVE THE LIFE OF A SWINGING BACHELOR!
COME ON, GUYS! WE'LL GO TO MY PLACE AND TRY OUT THE ACOUSTICS FOR BAND PRACTICE!
MAN, FROM NOW ON I'VE GOT IT MADE! NOBODY TELLING ME WHAT TO DO! I'M THE KING OF MY CASTLE!
YOU LUCKY STIFF!
217
ROOMS
5

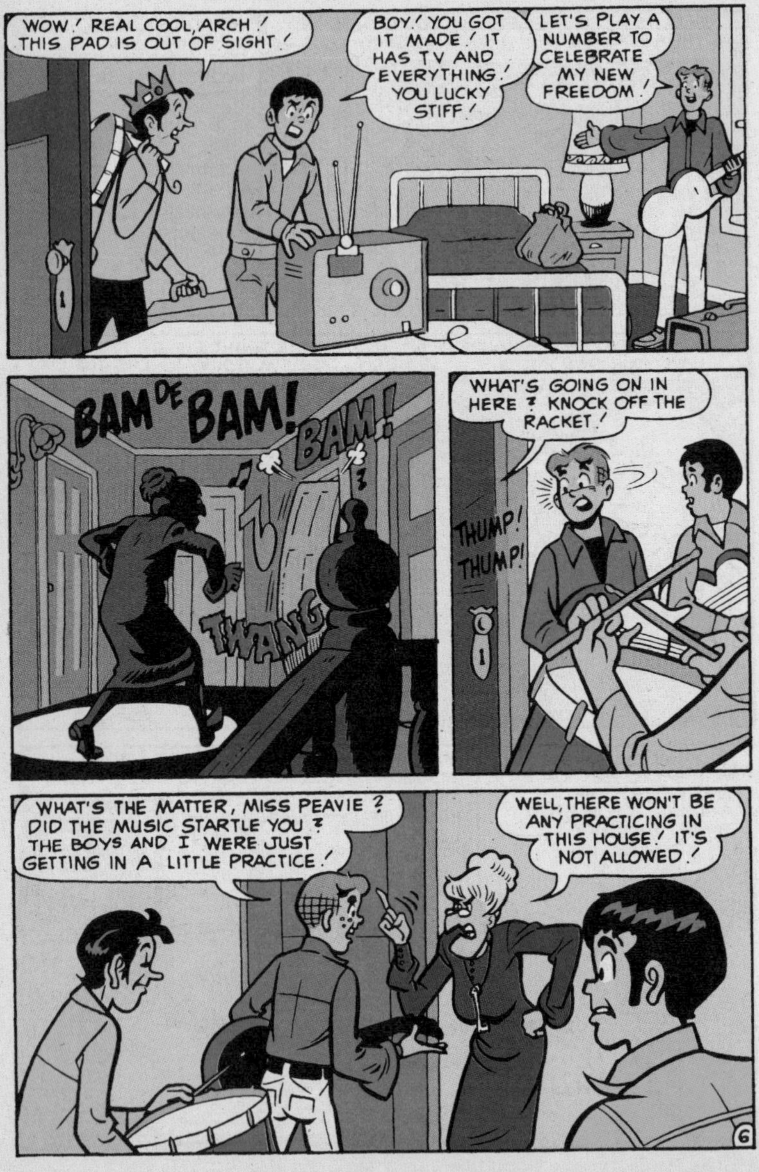

WOW! REAL COOL, ARCH! THIS PAD IS OUT OF SIGHT!
BOY! YOU GOT IT MADE! IT HAS TV AND EVERYTHING! YOU LUCKY STIFF!
LET'S PLAY A NUMBER TO CELEBRATE MY NEW FREEDOM!
BAM DE BAM! BAM!
TWANG
WHAT'S GOING ON IN HERE? KNOCK OFF THE RACKET!
THUMP! THUMP!
WHAT'S THE MATTER, MISS PEAVIE? DID THE MUSIC STARTLE YOU? THE BOYS AND I WERE JUST GETTING IN A LITTLE PRACTICE!
WELL, THERE WON'T BE ANY PRACTICING IN THIS HOUSE! IT'S NOT ALLOWED!
6

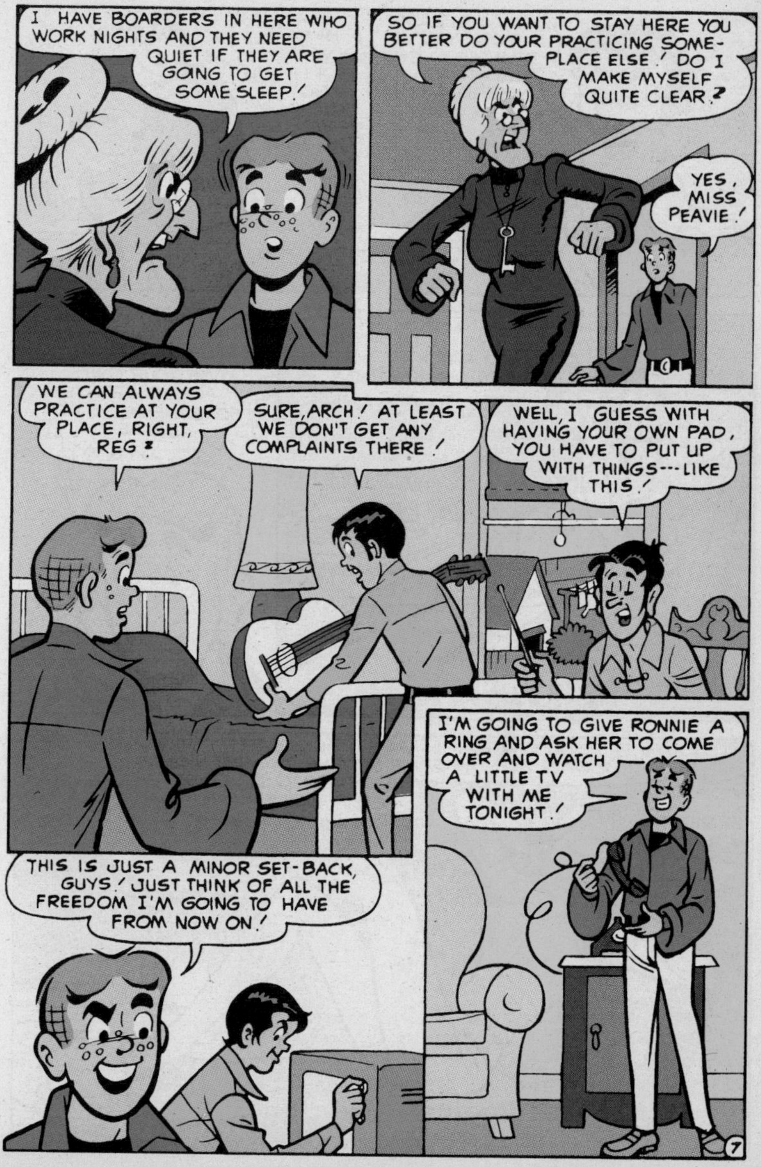
I HAVE BOARDERS IN HERE WHO WORK NIGHTS AND THEY NEED QUIET IF THEY ARE GOING TO GET SOME SLEEP!
SO IF YOU WANT TO STAY HERE YOU BETTER DO YOUR PRACTICING SOME-PLACE ELSE! DO I MAKE MYSELF QUITE CLEAR?
YES, MISS PEAVIE!
WE CAN ALWAYS PRACTICE AT YOUR PLACE, RIGHT, REG?
SURE, ARCH! AT LEAST WE DON'T GET ANY COMPLAINTS THERE!
WELL, I GUESS WITH HAVING YOUR OWN PAD, YOU HAVE TO PUT UP WITH THINGS---LIKE THIS!
THIS IS JUST A MINOR SET-BACK, GUYS! JUST THINK OF ALL THE FREEDOM I'M GOING TO HAVE FROM NOW ON!
I'M GOING TO GIVE RONNIE A RING AND ASK HER TO COME OVER AND WATCH A LITTLE TV WITH ME TONIGHT!
7

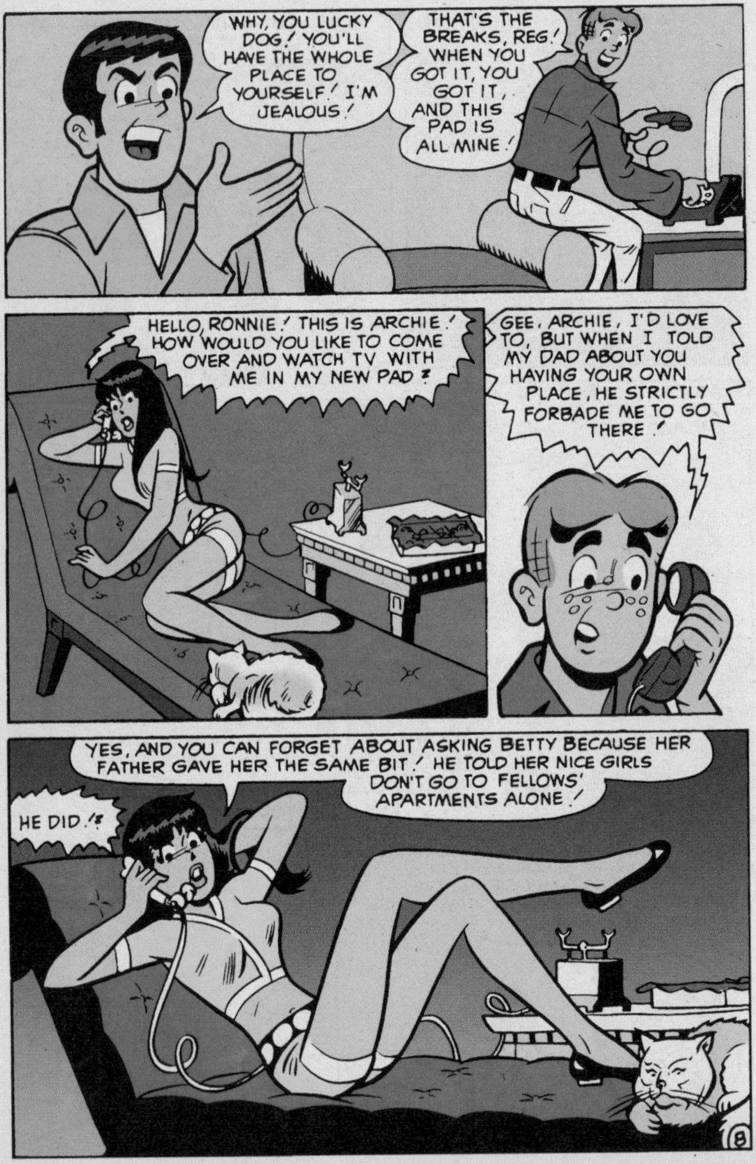
WHY, YOU LUCKY DOG! YOU'LL HAVE THE WHOLE PLACE TO YOURSELF! I'M JEALOUS!
THAT'S THE BREAKS, REG! WHEN YOU GOT IT, YOU GOT IT, AND THIS PAD IS ALL MINE!
HELLO, RONNIE! THIS IS ARCHIE! HOW WOULD YOU LIKE TO COME OVER AND WATCH TV WITH ME IN MY NEW PAD?
GEE, ARCHIE, I'D LOVE TO, BUT WHEN I TOLD MY DAD ABOUT YOU HAVING YOUR OWN PLACE, HE STRICTLY FORBADE ME TO GO THERE!
YES, AND YOU CAN FORGET ABOUT ASKING BETTY BECAUSE HER FATHER GAVE HER THE SAME BIT! HE TOLD HER NICE GIRLS DON'T GO TO FELLOWS' APARTMENTS ALONE!
HE DID!?
8

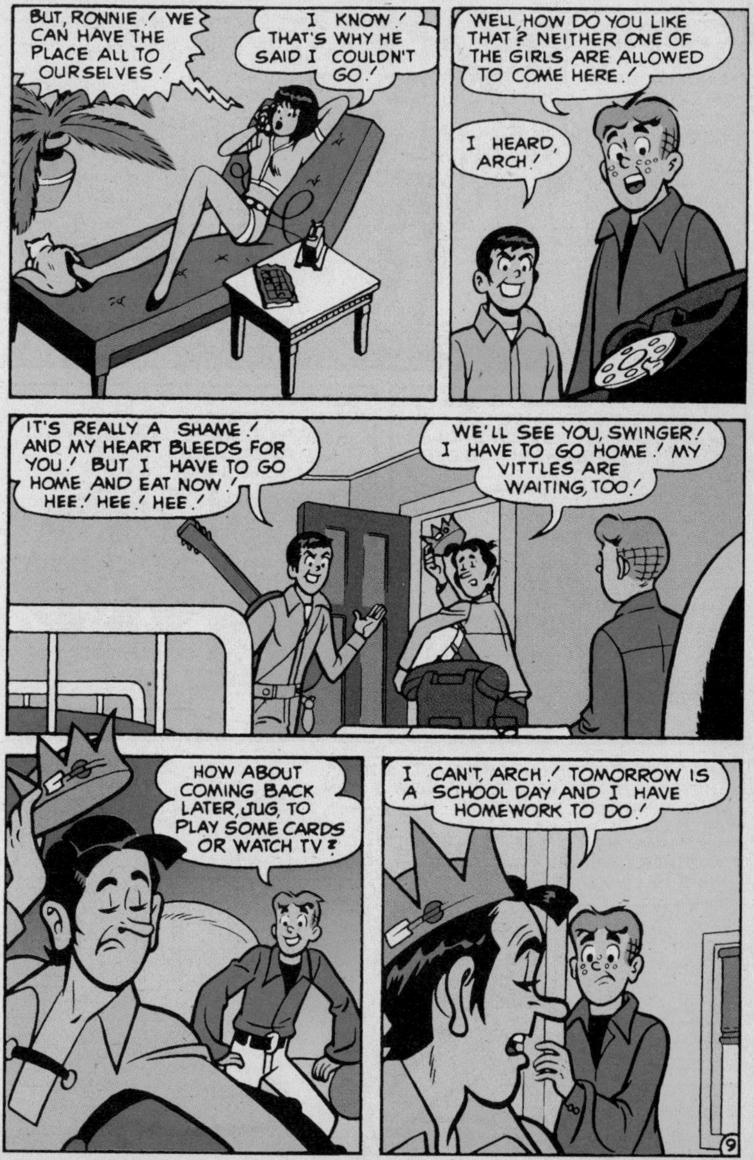
BUT, RONNIE! WE CAN HAVE THE PLACE ALL TO OURSELVES!
I KNOW! THAT'S WHY HE SAID I COULDN'T GO!
WELL, HOW DO YOU LIKE THAT? NEITHER ONE OF THE GIRLS ARE ALLOWED TO COME HERE!
I HEARD, ARCH!
IT'S REALLY A SHAME! AND MY HEART BLEEDS FOR YOU! BUT I HAVE TO GO HOME AND EAT NOW! HEE! HEE! HEE!
WE'LL SEE YOU, SWINGER! I HAVE TO GO HOME! MY VITTLES ARE WAITING, TOO!
HOW ABOUT COMING BACK LATER, JUG, TO PLAY SOME CARDS OR WATCH TV?
I CAN'T, ARCH! TOMORROW IS A SCHOOL DAY AND I HAVE HOMEWORK TO DO!
9

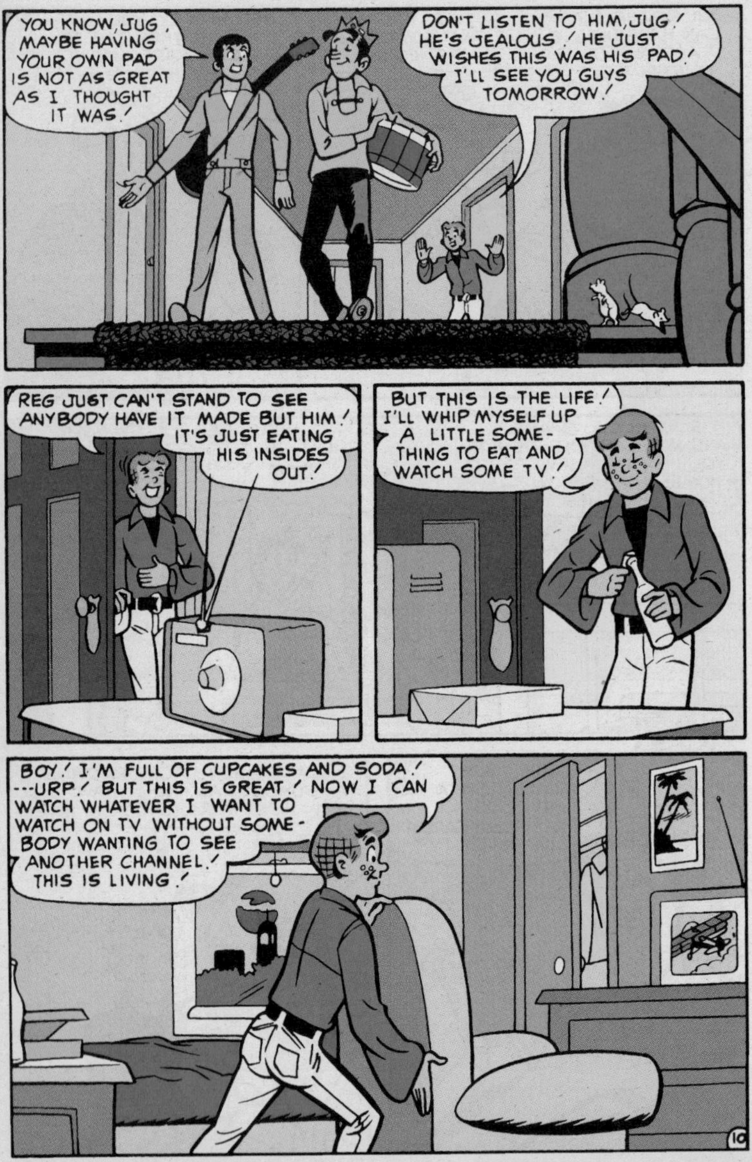
YOU KNOW, JUG, MAYBE HAVING YOUR OWN PAD IS NOT AS GREAT AS I THOUGHT IT WAS!
DON'T LISTEN TO HIM, JUG! HE'S JEALOUS! HE JUST WISHES THIS WAS HIS PAD! I'LL SEE YOU GUYS TOMORROW!
REG JUST CAN'T STAND TO SEE ANYBODY HAVE IT MADE BUT HIM! IT'S JUST EATING HIS INSIDES OUT!
BUT THIS IS THE LIFE! I'LL WHIP MYSELF UP A LITTLE SOMETHING TO EAT AND WATCH SOME TV!
BOY! I'M FULL OF CUPCAKES AND SODA! ---URP! BUT THIS IS GREAT! NOW I CAN WATCH WHATEVER I WANT TO WATCH ON TV WITHOUT SOMEBODY WANTING TO SEE ANOTHER CHANNEL! THIS IS LIVING!
10

IT DOES SEEM FUNNY BEING ALONE! I'M ALWAYS USED TO A CROWDED LIVING ROOM!

BUT I'LL GET USED TO IT! IT JUST TAKES A MATTER OF TIME TO ADJUST TO THE SILENCE! I'LL JUST TURN UP THE TV FOR COMPANY!

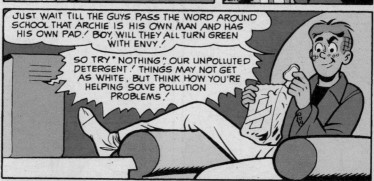

JUST WAIT TILL THE GUYS PASS THE WORD AROUND SCHOOL THAT ARCHIE IS HIS OWN MAN AND HAS HIS OWN PAD! BOY, WILL THEY ALL TURN GREEN WITH ENVY!

SO TRY "NOTHING", OUR UNPOLLUTED DETERGENT! THINGS MAY NOT GET AS WHITE, BUT THINK HOW YOU'RE HELPING SOLVE POLLUTION PROBLEMS!

DO YOU FEEL TIRED, LISTLESS, AND RUN DOWN---

ZZZ ZZZ

OPEN UP IN THERE! OPEN UP!

HUH?

BANG! BANG!

LET'S CUT 'EM OFF AT THE PASS, BUCKEYE!

11

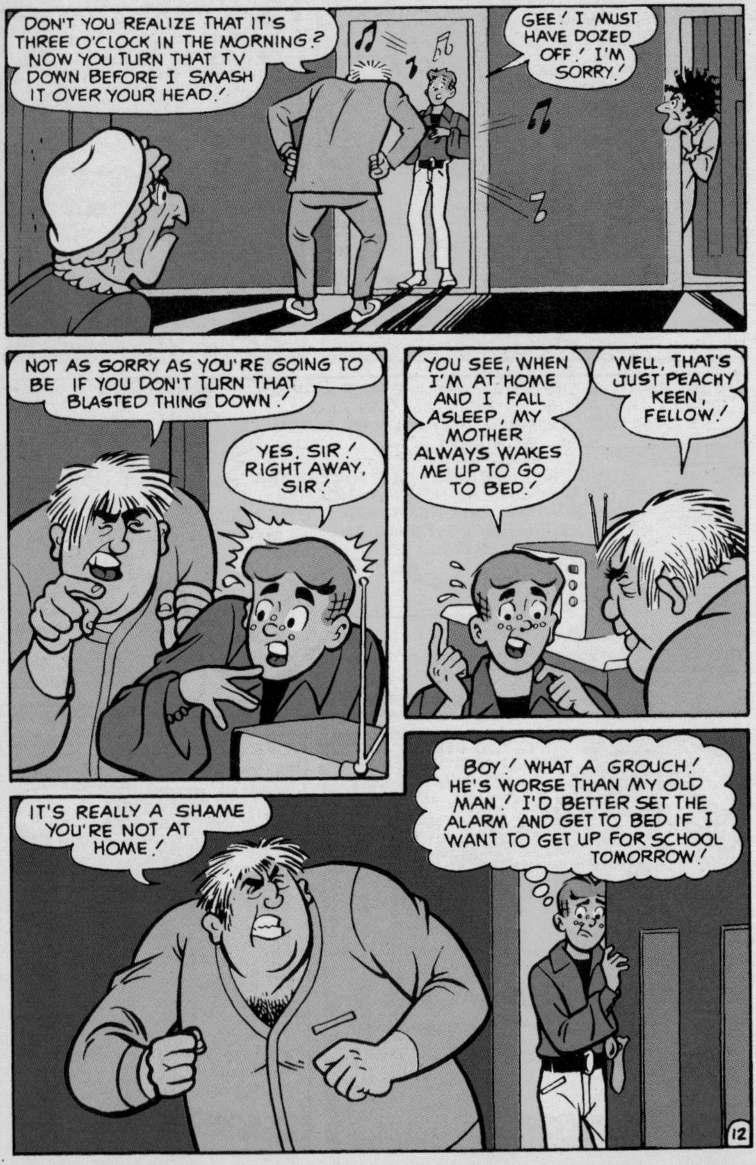
DON'T YOU REALIZE THAT IT'S THREE O'CLOCK IN THE MORNING? NOW YOU TURN THAT TV DOWN BEFORE I SMASH IT OVER YOUR HEAD!
GEE! I MUST HAVE DOZED OFF! I'M SORRY!
NOT AS SORRY AS YOU'RE GOING TO BE IF YOU DON'T TURN THAT BLASTED THING DOWN!
YES, SIR! RIGHT AWAY, SIR!
YOU SEE, WHEN I'M AT HOME AND I FALL ASLEEP, MY MOTHER ALWAYS WAKES ME UP TO GO TO BED!
WELL, THAT'S JUST PEACHY KEEN, FELLOW!
IT'S REALLY A SHAME YOU'RE NOT AT HOME!
BOY! WHAT A GROUCH! HE'S WORSE THAN MY OLD MAN! I'D BETTER SET THE ALARM AND GET TO BED IF I WANT TO GET UP FOR SCHOOL TOMORROW!
12

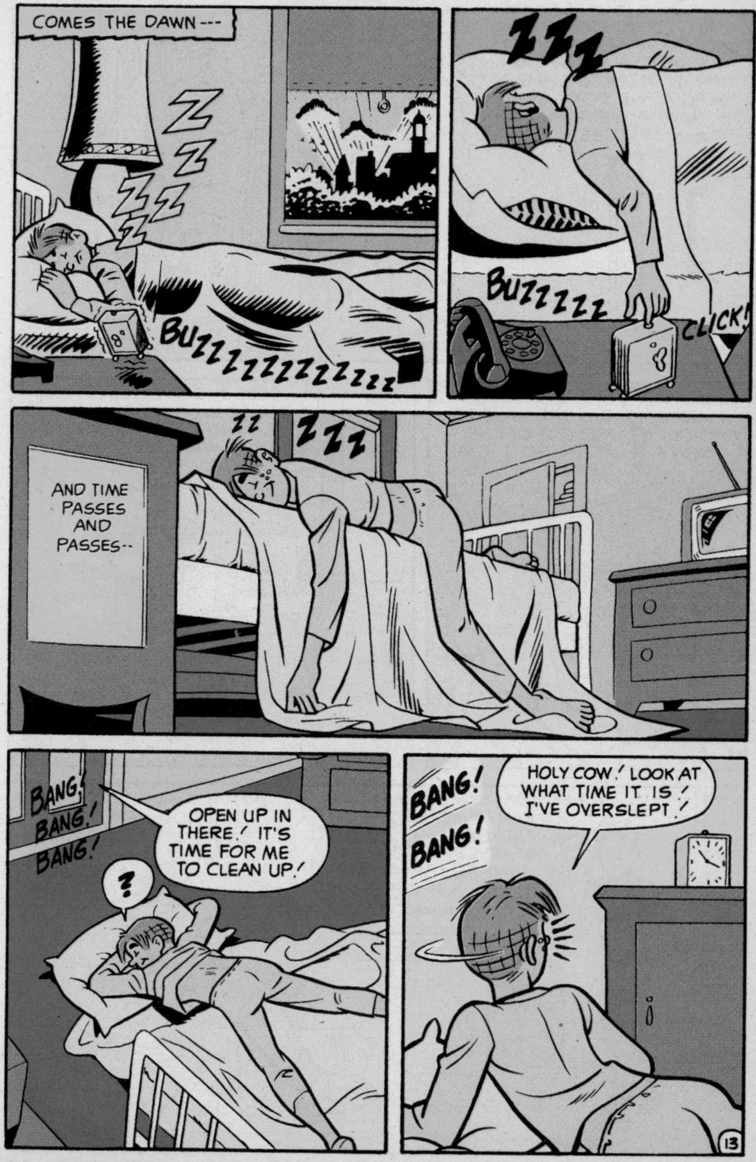
COMES THE DAWN---
ZZZZZ
BUZZZZZZZZZZZZZ
ZZZ
BUZZZZZZ
CLICK!
AND TIME PASSES AND PASSES--
ZZ
ZZZ
BANG! BANG! BANG!
OPEN UP IN THERE! IT'S TIME FOR ME TO CLEAN UP!
?
BANG!
BANG!
HOLY COW! LOOK AT WHAT TIME IT IS! I'VE OVERSLEPT!
13

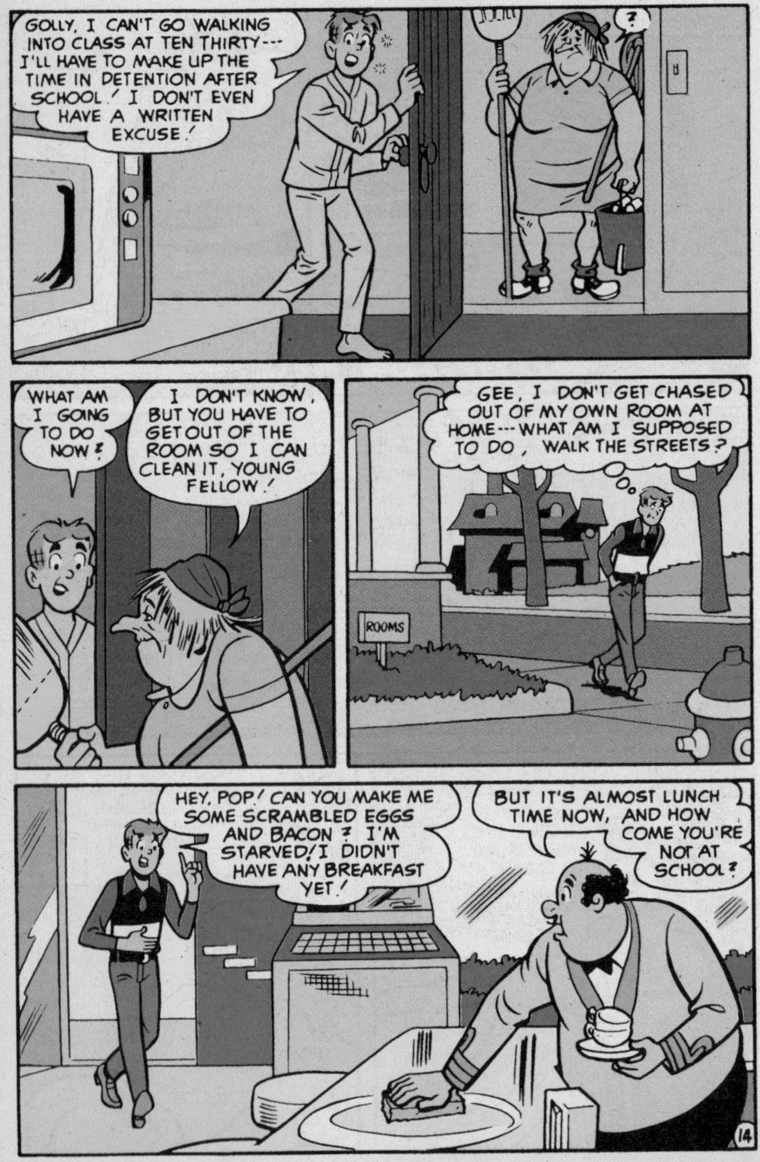
GOLLY, I CAN'T GO WALKING INTO CLASS AT TEN THIRTY--- I'LL HAVE TO MAKE UP THE TIME IN DETENTION AFTER SCHOOL! I DON'T EVEN HAVE A WRITTEN EXCUSE!
?
WHAT AM I GOING TO DO NOW?
I DON'T KNOW, BUT YOU HAVE TO GET OUT OF THE ROOM SO I CAN CLEAN IT, YOUNG FELLOW!
GEE, I DON'T GET CHASED OUT OF MY OWN ROOM AT HOME---WHAT AM I SUPPOSED TO DO, WALK THE STREETS?
ROOMS
HEY, POP! CAN YOU MAKE ME SOME SCRAMBLED EGGS AND BACON? I'M STARVED! I DIDN'T HAVE ANY BREAKFAST YET!
BUT IT'S ALMOST LUNCH TIME NOW, AND HOW COME YOU'RE NOT AT SCHOOL?
14

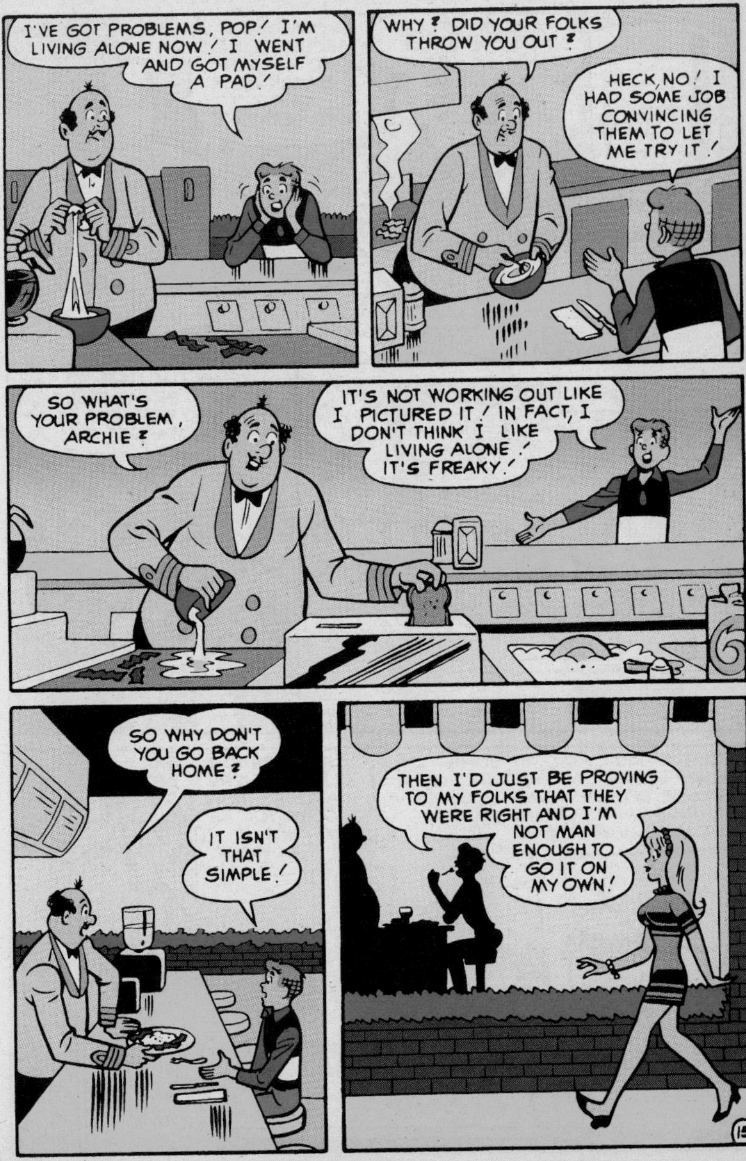
I'VE GOT PROBLEMS, POP! I'M LIVING ALONE NOW! I WENT AND GOT MYSELF A PAD!
WHY? DID YOUR FOLKS THROW YOU OUT?
HECK, NO! I HAD SOME JOB CONVINCING THEM TO LET ME TRY IT!
SO WHAT'S YOUR PROBLEM, ARCHIE?
IT'S NOT WORKING OUT LIKE I PICTURED IT! IN FACT, I DON'T THINK I LIKE LIVING ALONE! IT'S FREAKY!
SO WHY DON'T YOU GO BACK HOME?
IT ISN'T THAT SIMPLE!
THEN I'D JUST BE PROVING TO MY FOLKS THAT THEY WERE RIGHT AND I'M NOT MAN ENOUGH TO GO IT ON MY OWN!

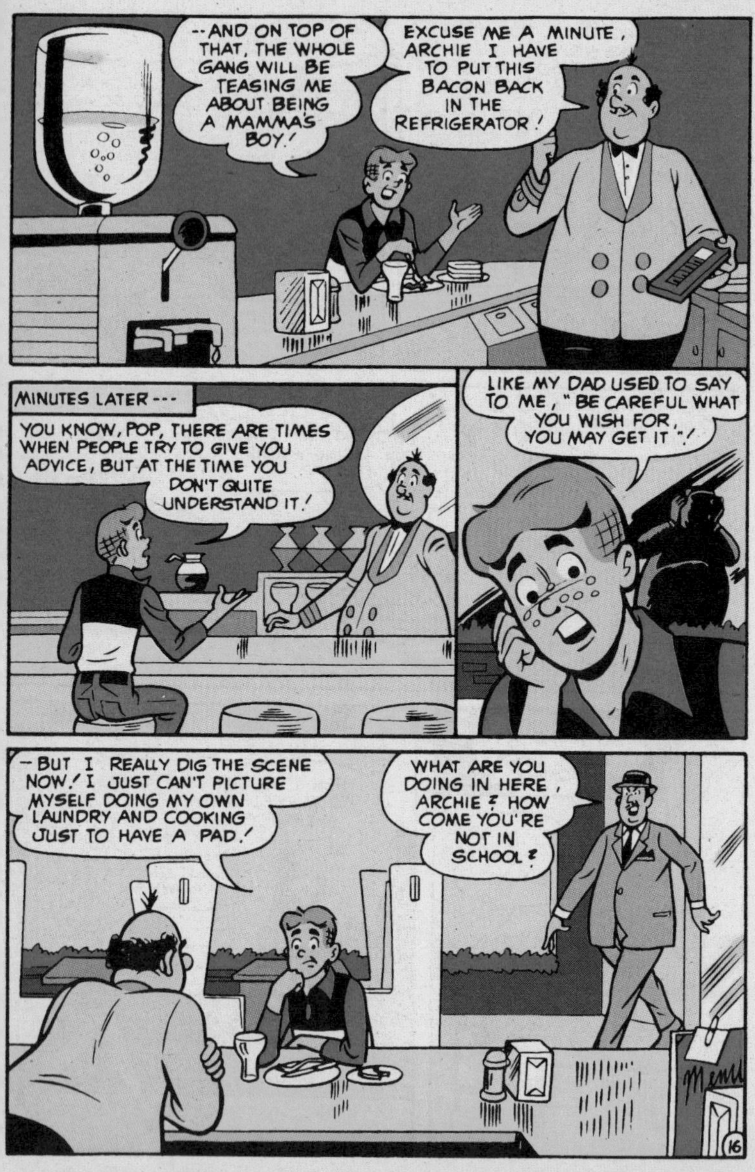
--AND ON TOP OF THAT, THE WHOLE GANG WILL BE TEASING ME ABOUT BEING A MAMMA'S BOY!
EXCUSE ME A MINUTE, ARCHIE I HAVE TO PUT THIS BACON BACK IN THE REFRIGERATOR!
MINUTES LATER---
YOU KNOW, POP, THERE ARE TIMES WHEN PEOPLE TRY TO GIVE YOU ADVICE, BUT AT THE TIME YOU DON'T QUITE UNDERSTAND IT!
LIKE MY DAD USED TO SAY TO ME, "BE CAREFUL WHAT YOU WISH FOR, YOU MAY GET IT"!
-BUT I REALLY DIG THE SCENE NOW! I JUST CAN'T PICTURE MYSELF DOING MY OWN LAUNDRY AND COOKING JUST TO HAVE A PAD!
WHAT ARE YOU DOING IN HERE, ARCHIE? HOW COME YOU'RE NOT IN SCHOOL?
16

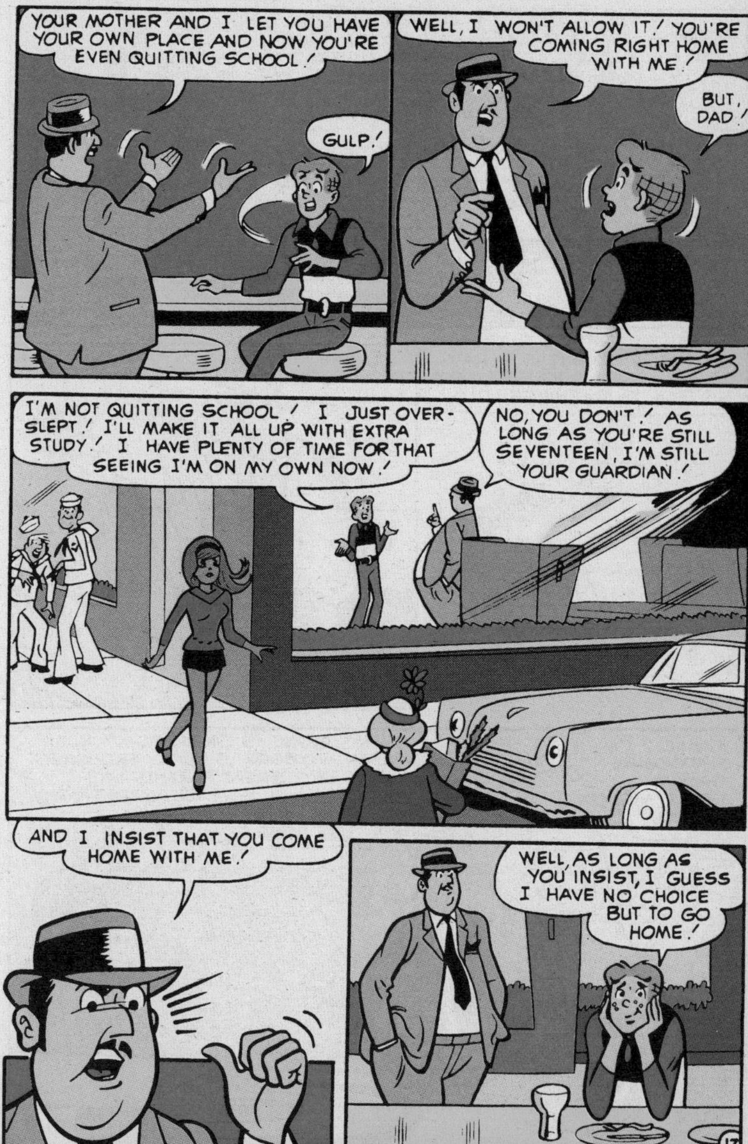
YOUR MOTHER AND I LET YOU HAVE YOUR OWN PLACE AND NOW YOU'RE EVEN QUITTING SCHOOL!
GULP!
WELL, I WON'T ALLOW IT! YOU'RE COMING RIGHT HOME WITH ME!
BUT, DAD!
I'M NOT QUITTING SCHOOL! I JUST OVER-SLEPT! I'LL MAKE IT ALL UP WITH EXTRA STUDY! I HAVE PLENTY OF TIME FOR THAT SEEING I'M ON MY OWN NOW!
NO, YOU DON'T! AS LONG AS YOU'RE STILL SEVENTEEN, I'M STILL YOUR GUARDIAN!
AND I INSIST THAT YOU COME HOME WITH ME!
WELL, AS LONG AS YOU INSIST, I GUESS I HAVE NO CHOICE BUT TO GO HOME!
17

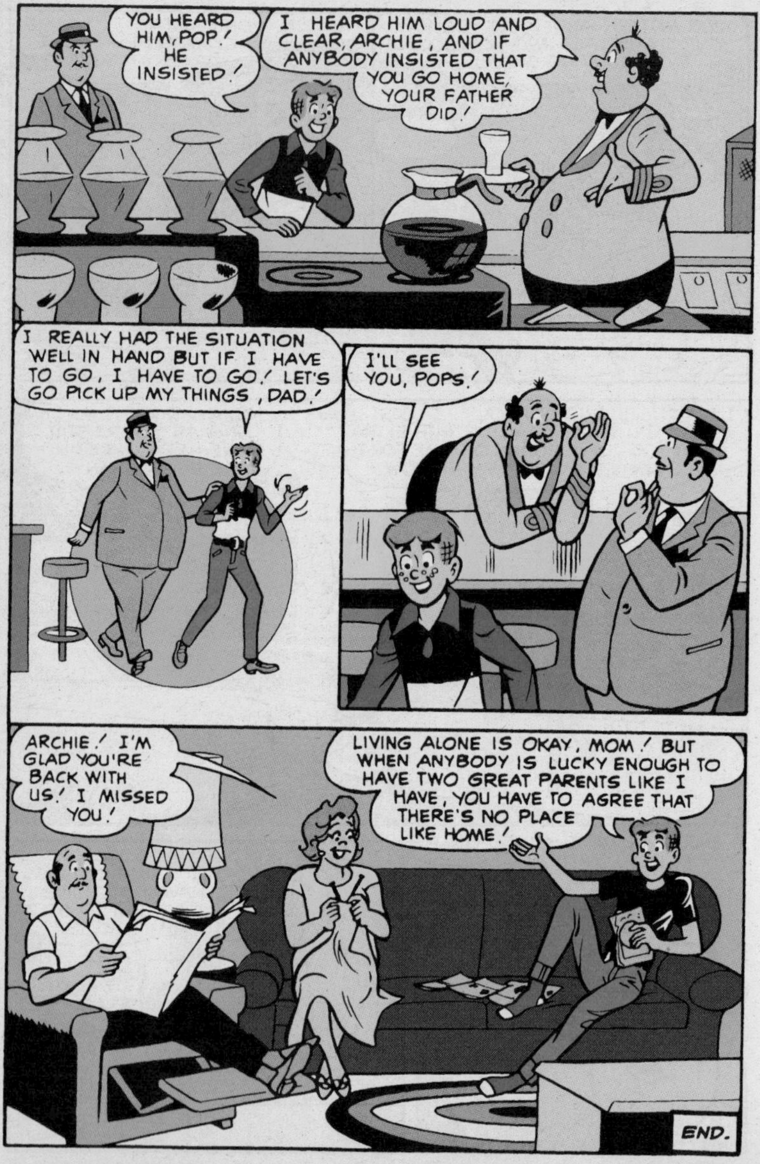
YOU HEARD HIM, POP! HE INSISTED!
I HEARD HIM LOUD AND CLEAR, ARCHIE, AND IF ANYBODY INSISTED THAT YOU GO HOME, YOUR FATHER DID!
I REALLY HAD THE SITUATION WELL IN HAND BUT IF I HAVE TO GO, I HAVE TO GO! LET'S GO PICK UP MY THINGS, DAD!
I'LL SEE YOU, POPS!
ARCHIE! I'M GLAD YOU'RE BACK WITH US! I MISSED YOU!
LIVING ALONE IS OKAY, MOM! BUT WHEN ANYBODY IS LUCKY ENOUGH TO HAVE TWO GREAT PARENTS LIKE I HAVE, YOU HAVE TO AGREE THAT THERE'S NO PLACE LIKE HOME!
END.

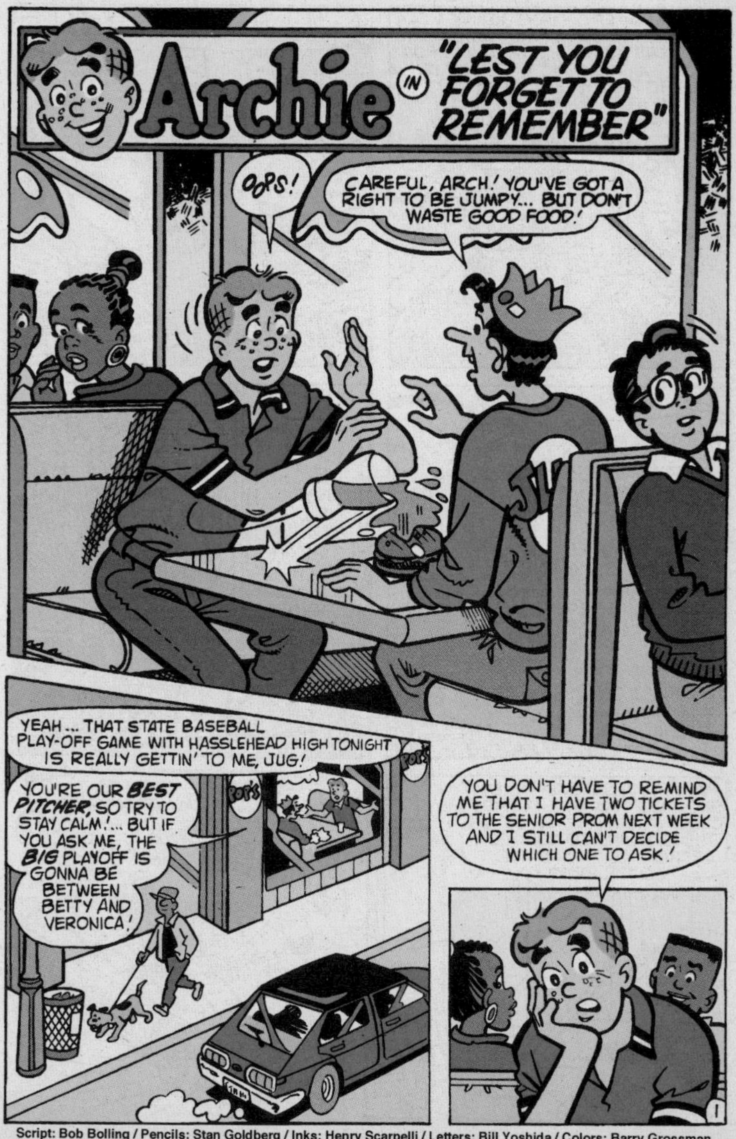
Archie in "LEST YOU FORGET TO REMEMBER"
OOPS!
CAREFUL, ARCH! YOU'VE GOT A RIGHT TO BE JUMPY... BUT DON'T WASTE GOOD FOOD!
YEAH ... THAT STATE BASEBALL PLAY-OFF GAME WITH HASSLEHEAD HIGH TONIGHT IS REALLY GETTIN' TO ME, JUG!
YOU'RE OUR BEST PITCHER, SO TRY TO STAY CALM!... BUT IF YOU ASK ME, THE BIG PLAYOFF IS GONNA BE BETWEEN BETTY AND VERONICA!
POP'S
YOU DON'T HAVE TO REMIND ME THAT I HAVE TWO TICKETS TO THE SENIOR PROM NEXT WEEK AND I STILL CAN'T DECIDE WHICH ONE TO ASK!
1

Script: Bob Bolling / Pencils: Stan Goldberg / Inks: Henry Scarpelli / Letters: Bill Yoshida / Colors: Barry Grossman

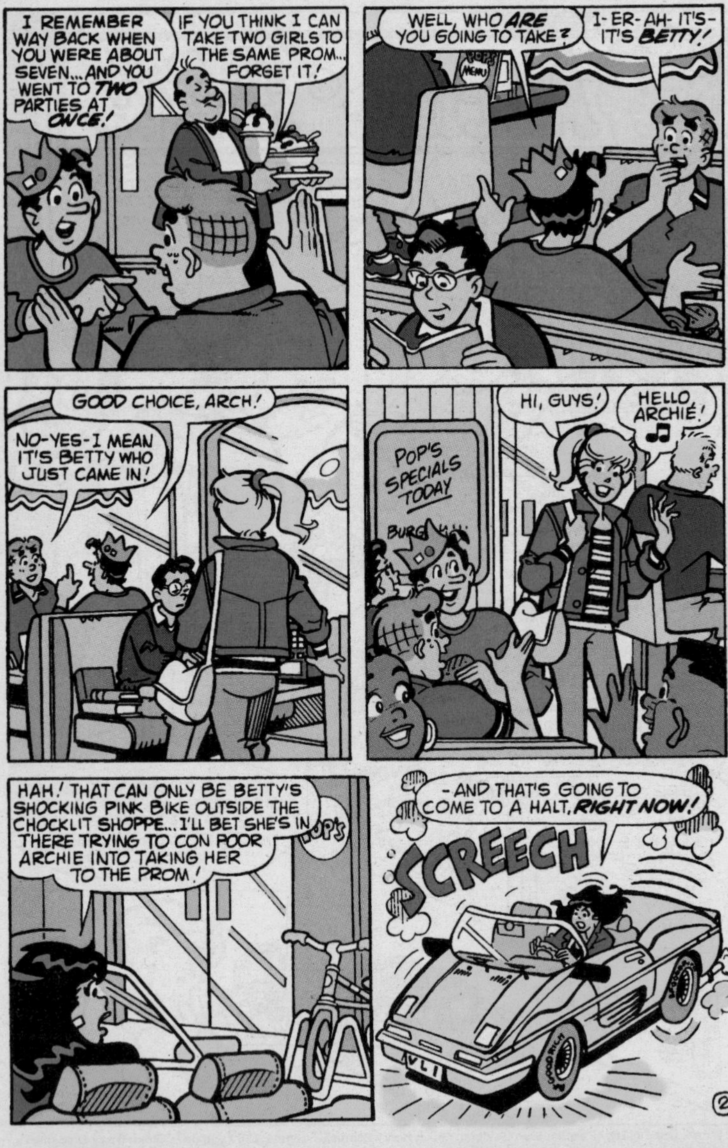
I REMEMBER WAY BACK WHEN YOU WERE ABOUT SEVEN... AND YOU WENT TO TWO PARTIES AT ONCE!
IF YOU THINK I CAN TAKE TWO GIRLS TO THE SAME PROM... FORGET IT!
WELL, WHO ARE YOU GOING TO TAKE?
I-ER-AH- IT'S- IT'S BETTY!
GOOD CHOICE, ARCH!
NO-YES-I MEAN IT'S BETTY WHO JUST CAME IN!
HI, GUYS!
HELLO, ARCHIE!
POP'S SPECIALS TODAY
HAH! THAT CAN ONLY BE BETTY'S SHOCKING PINK BIKE OUTSIDE THE CHOCKLIT SHOPPE... I'LL BET SHE'S IN THERE TRYING TO CON POOR ARCHIE INTO TAKING HER TO THE PROM!
-AND THAT'S GOING TO COME TO A HALT, RIGHT NOW!
SCREECH
VL 1

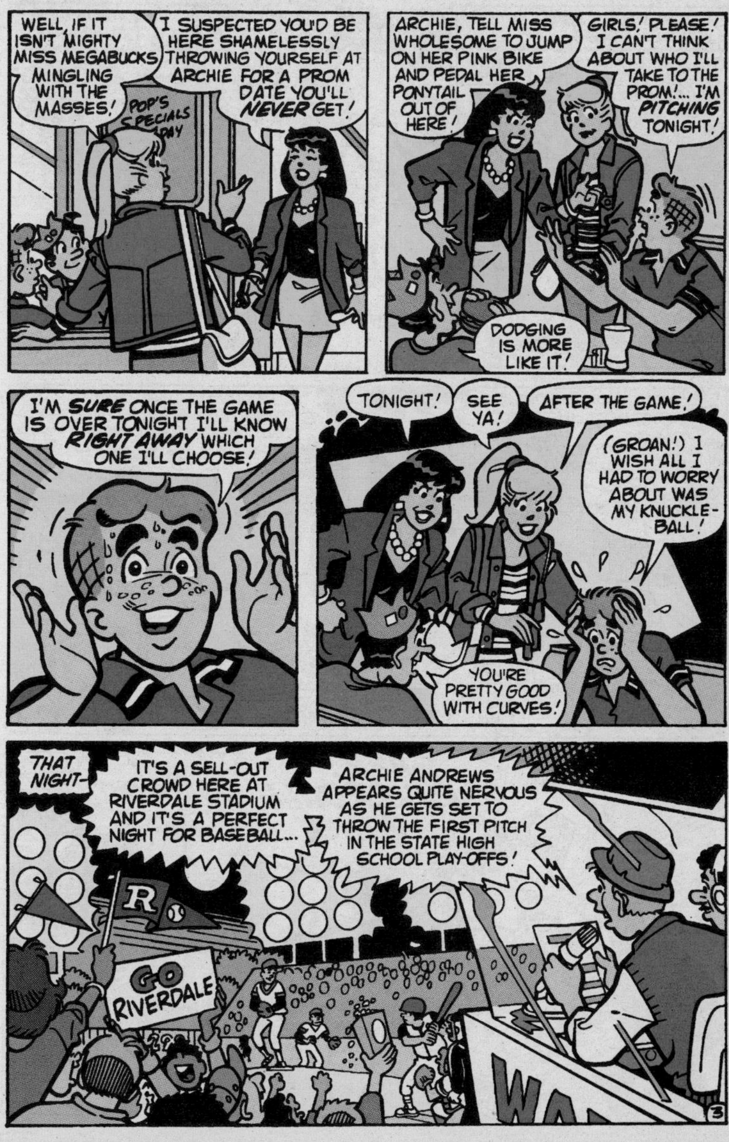
WELL, IF IT ISN'T MIGHTY MISS MEGABUCKS MINGLING WITH THE MASSES!
I SUSPECTED YOU'D BE HERE SHAMELESSLY THROWING YOURSELF AT ARCHIE FOR A PROM DATE YOU'LL NEVER GET!
POP'S SPECIALS
ARCHIE, TELL MISS WHOLESOME TO JUMP ON HER PINK BIKE AND PEDAL HER PONYTAIL OUT OF HERE!
GIRLS! PLEASE! I CAN'T THINK ABOUT WHO I'LL TAKE TO THE PROM!... I'M PITCHING TONIGHT!
DODGING IS MORE LIKE IT!
I'M SURE ONCE THE GAME IS OVER TONIGHT I'LL KNOW RIGHT AWAY WHICH ONE I'LL CHOOSE!
TONIGHT!
SEE YA!
AFTER THE GAME!
(GROAN!) I WISH ALL I HAD TO WORRY ABOUT WAS MY KNUCKLE-BALL!
YOU'RE PRETTY GOOD WITH CURVES!
THAT NIGHT-
IT'S A SELL-OUT CROWD HERE AT RIVERDALE STADIUM AND IT'S A PERFECT NIGHT FOR BASEBALL...
ARCHIE ANDREWS APPEARS QUITE NERVOUS AS HE GETS SET TO THROW THE FIRST PITCH IN THE STATE HIGH SCHOOL PLAY-OFFS!
R
GO RIVERDALE
3

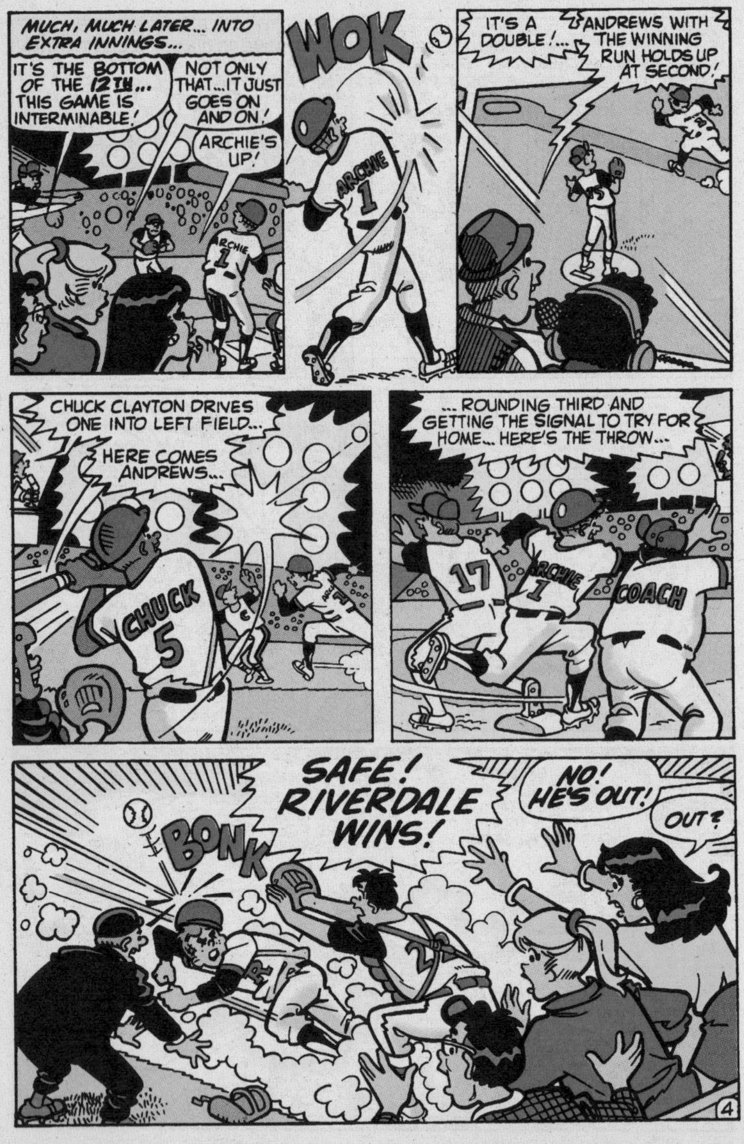
MUCH, MUCH LATER... INTO EXTRA INNINGS...
IT'S THE BOTTOM OF THE 12TH... THIS GAME IS INTERMINABLE!
NOT ONLY THAT...IT JUST GOES ON AND ON!
ARCHIE'S UP!
WOK
IT'S A DOUBLE!...
ANDREWS WITH THE WINNING RUN HOLDS UP AT SECOND!
CHUCK CLAYTON DRIVES ONE INTO LEFT FIELD...
HERE COMES ANDREWS...
... ROUNDING THIRD AND GETTING THE SIGNAL TO TRY FOR HOME... HERE'S THE THROW...
BONK
SAFE! RIVERDALE WINS!
NO! HE'S OUT!
OUT?
4

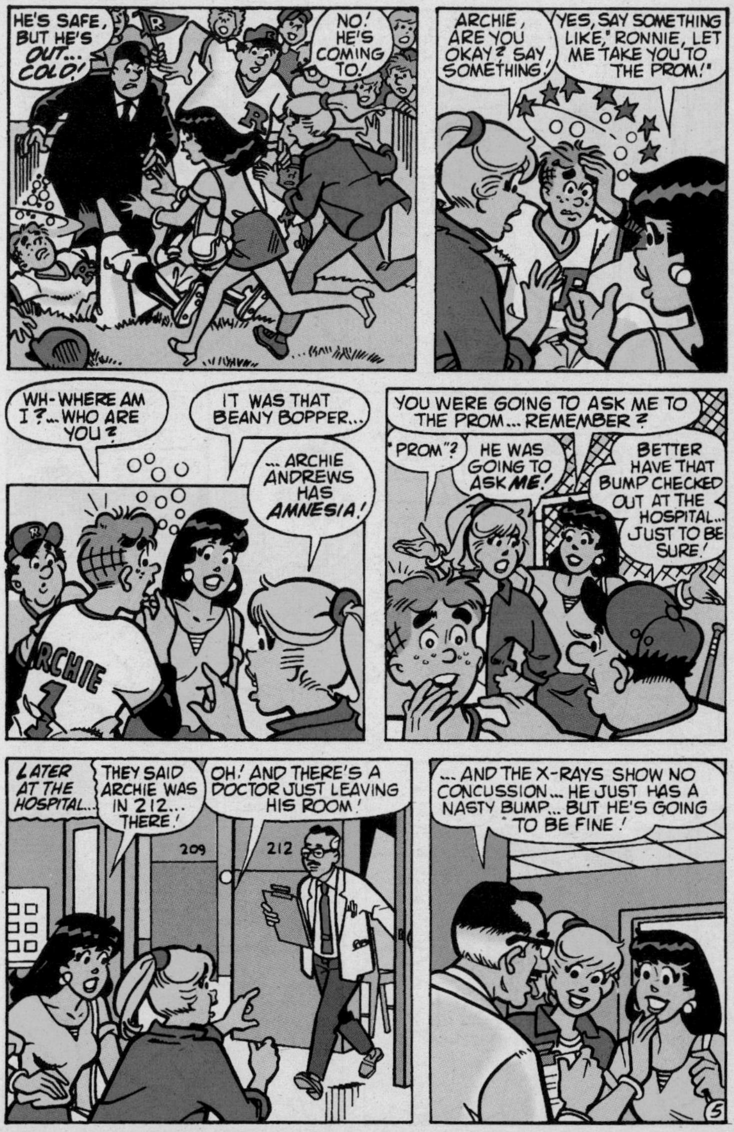
HE'S SAFE, BUT HE'S OUT... COLD!
NO! HE'S COMING TO!
ARCHIE, ARE YOU OKAY? SAY SOMETHING!
YES, SAY SOMETHING LIKE, "RONNIE, LET ME TAKE YOU TO THE PROM!"
WH-WHERE AM I?... WHO ARE YOU?
IT WAS THAT BEANY BOPPER...
... ARCHIE ANDREWS HAS AMNESIA!
YOU WERE GOING TO ASK ME TO THE PROM... REMEMBER?
"PROM"?
HE WAS GOING TO ASK ME!
BETTER HAVE THAT BUMP CHECKED OUT AT THE HOSPITAL... JUST TO BE SURE!
LATER AT THE HOSPITAL...
THEY SAID ARCHIE WAS IN 212... THERE!
OH! AND THERE'S A DOCTOR JUST LEAVING HIS ROOM!
209
212
... AND THE X-RAYS SHOW NO CONCUSSION... HE JUST HAS A NASTY BUMP... BUT HE'S GOING TO BE FINE!
ARCHIE
5

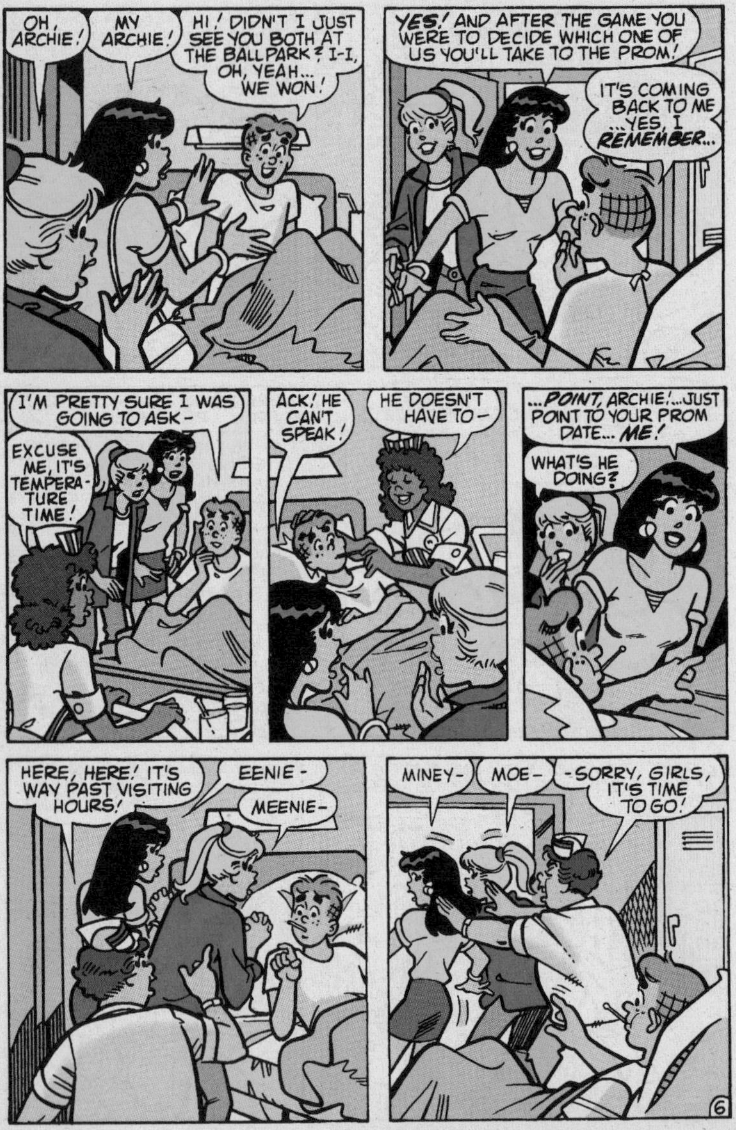

OH, ARCHIE!
MY ARCHIE!
HI! DIDN'T I JUST SEE YOU BOTH AT THE BALLPARK? I-I, OH, YEAH... WE WON!
YES! AND AFTER THE GAME YOU WERE TO DECIDE WHICH ONE OF US YOU'LL TAKE TO THE PROM!
IT'S COMING BACK TO ME ...YES, I REMEMBER...
I'M PRETTY SURE I WAS GOING TO ASK -
EXCUSE ME, IT'S TEMPERATURE TIME!
ACK! HE CAN'T SPEAK!
HE DOESN'T HAVE TO -
...POINT, ARCHIE!...JUST POINT TO YOUR PROM DATE... ME!
WHAT'S HE DOING?
HERE, HERE! IT'S WAY PAST VISITING HOURS!
EENIE -
MEENIE -
MINEY -
MOE -
-SORRY, GIRLS, IT'S TIME TO GO!

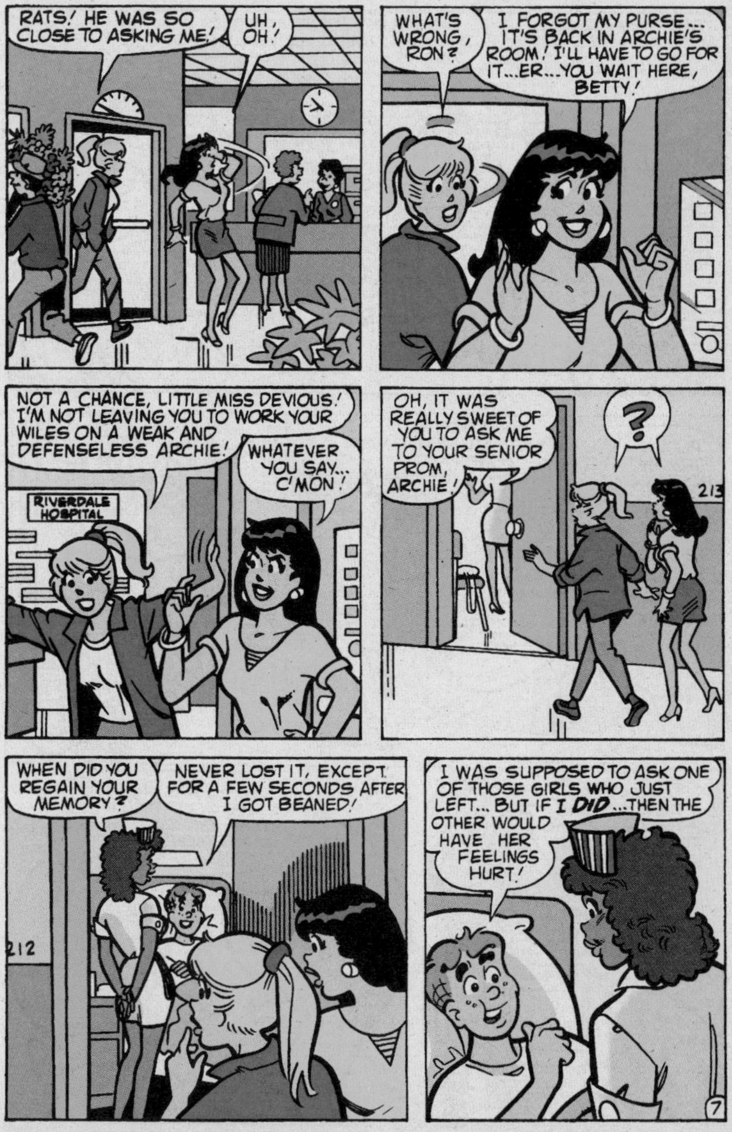
RATS! HE WAS SO CLOSE TO ASKING ME!
UH, OH!
WHAT'S WRONG, RON?
I FORGOT MY PURSE... IT'S BACK IN ARCHIE'S ROOM! I'LL HAVE TO GO FOR IT...ER...YOU WAIT HERE, BETTY!
NOT A CHANCE, LITTLE MISS DEVIOUS! I'M NOT LEAVING YOU TO WORK YOUR WILES ON A WEAK AND DEFENSELESS ARCHIE!
WHATEVER YOU SAY... C'MON!
RIVERDALE HOSPITAL
OH, IT WAS REALLY SWEET OF YOU TO ASK ME TO YOUR SENIOR PROM, ARCHIE!
?
213
WHEN DID YOU REGAIN YOUR MEMORY?
NEVER LOST IT, EXCEPT FOR A FEW SECONDS AFTER I GOT BEANED!
212
I WAS SUPPOSED TO ASK ONE OF THOSE GIRLS WHO JUST LEFT... BUT IF I DID...THEN THE OTHER WOULD HAVE HER FEELINGS HURT!
7

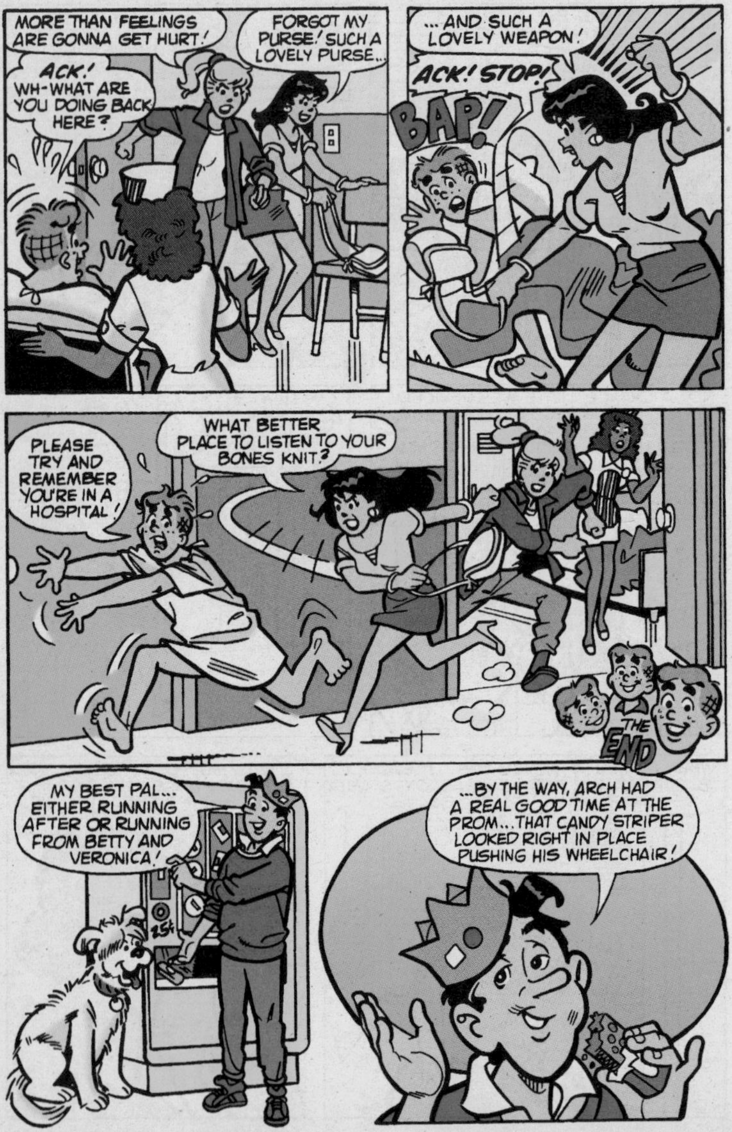
MORE THAN FEELINGS ARE GONNA GET HURT!
ACK! WH-WHAT ARE YOU DOING BACK HERE?
FORGOT MY PURSE! SUCH A LOVELY PURSE...
...AND SUCH A LOVELY WEAPON!
ACK! STOP!
BAP!
PLEASE TRY AND REMEMBER YOU'RE IN A HOSPITAL!
WHAT BETTER PLACE TO LISTEN TO YOUR BONES KNIT?
THE END
MY BEST PAL... EITHER RUNNING AFTER OR RUNNING FROM BETTY AND VERONICA!
25¢
...BY THE WAY, ARCH HAD A REAL GOOD TIME AT THE PROM...THAT CANDY STRIPER LOOKED RIGHT IN PLACE PUSHING HIS WHEELCHAIR!

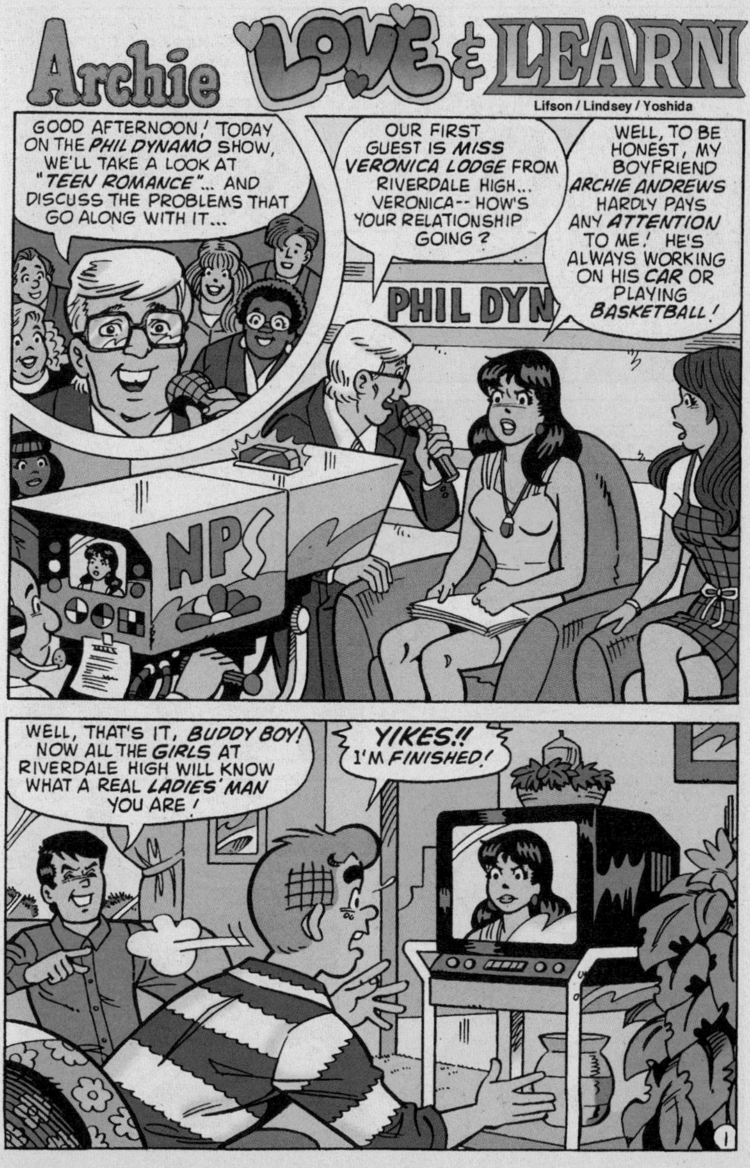
Archie LOVE & LEARN
Lifson / Lindsey / Yoshida
GOOD AFTERNOON! TODAY ON THE PHIL DYNAMO SHOW, WE'LL TAKE A LOOK AT "TEEN ROMANCE"... AND DISCUSS THE PROBLEMS THAT GO ALONG WITH IT...
OUR FIRST GUEST IS MISS VERONICA LODGE FROM RIVERDALE HIGH... VERONICA-- HOW'S YOUR RELATIONSHIP GOING?
WELL, TO BE HONEST, MY BOYFRIEND ARCHIE ANDREWS HARDLY PAYS ANY ATTENTION TO ME! HE'S ALWAYS WORKING ON HIS CAR OR PLAYING BASKETBALL!
PHIL DYN
NPS
WELL, THAT'S IT, BUDDY BOY! NOW ALL THE GIRLS AT RIVERDALE HIGH WILL KNOW WHAT A REAL LADIES' MAN YOU ARE!
YIKES!! I'M FINISHED!
1

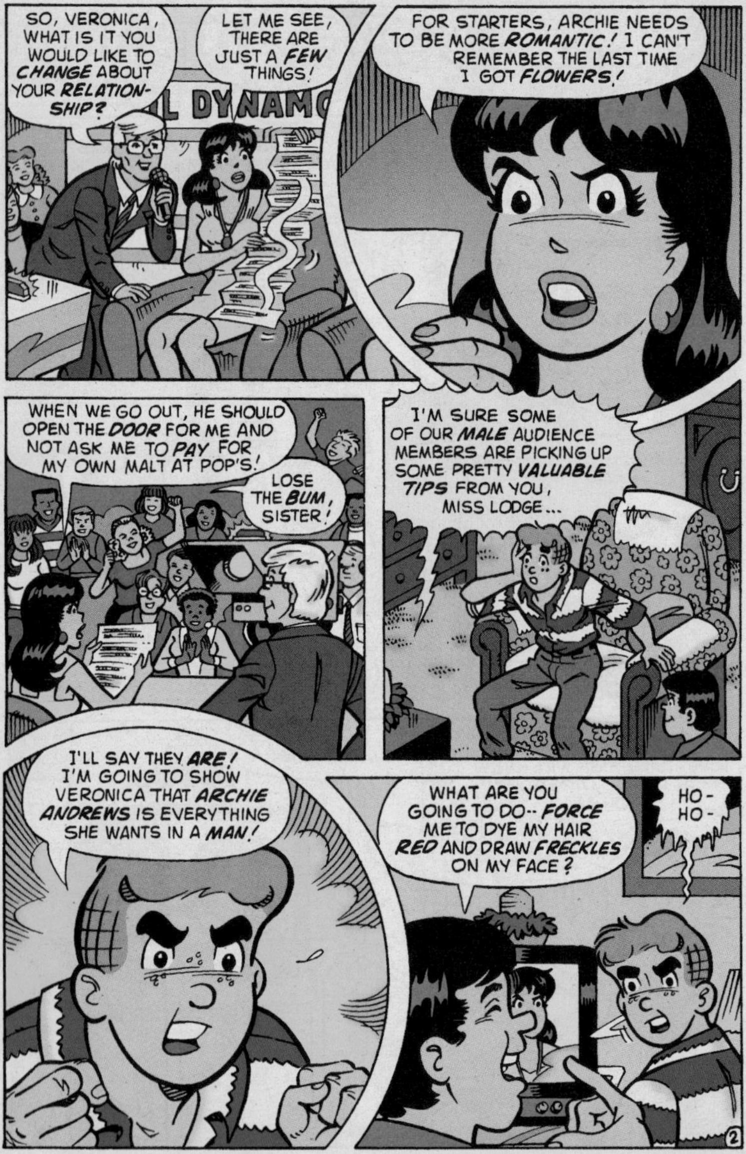
SO, VERONICA, WHAT IS IT YOU WOULD LIKE TO CHANGE ABOUT YOUR RELATION-SHIP?
LET ME SEE, THERE ARE JUST A FEW THINGS!
FOR STARTERS, ARCHIE NEEDS TO BE MORE ROMANTIC! I CAN'T REMEMBER THE LAST TIME I GOT FLOWERS!
WHEN WE GO OUT, HE SHOULD OPEN THE DOOR FOR ME AND NOT ASK ME TO PAY FOR MY OWN MALT AT POP'S!
LOSE THE BUM, SISTER!
I'M SURE SOME OF OUR MALE AUDIENCE MEMBERS ARE PICKING UP SOME PRETTY VALUABLE TIPS FROM YOU, MISS LODGE...
I'LL SAY THEY ARE! I'M GOING TO SHOW VERONICA THAT ARCHIE ANDREWS IS EVERYTHING SHE WANTS IN A MAN!
WHAT ARE YOU GOING TO DO-- FORCE ME TO DYE MY HAIR RED AND DRAW FRECKLES ON MY FACE?
HO-HO-
2

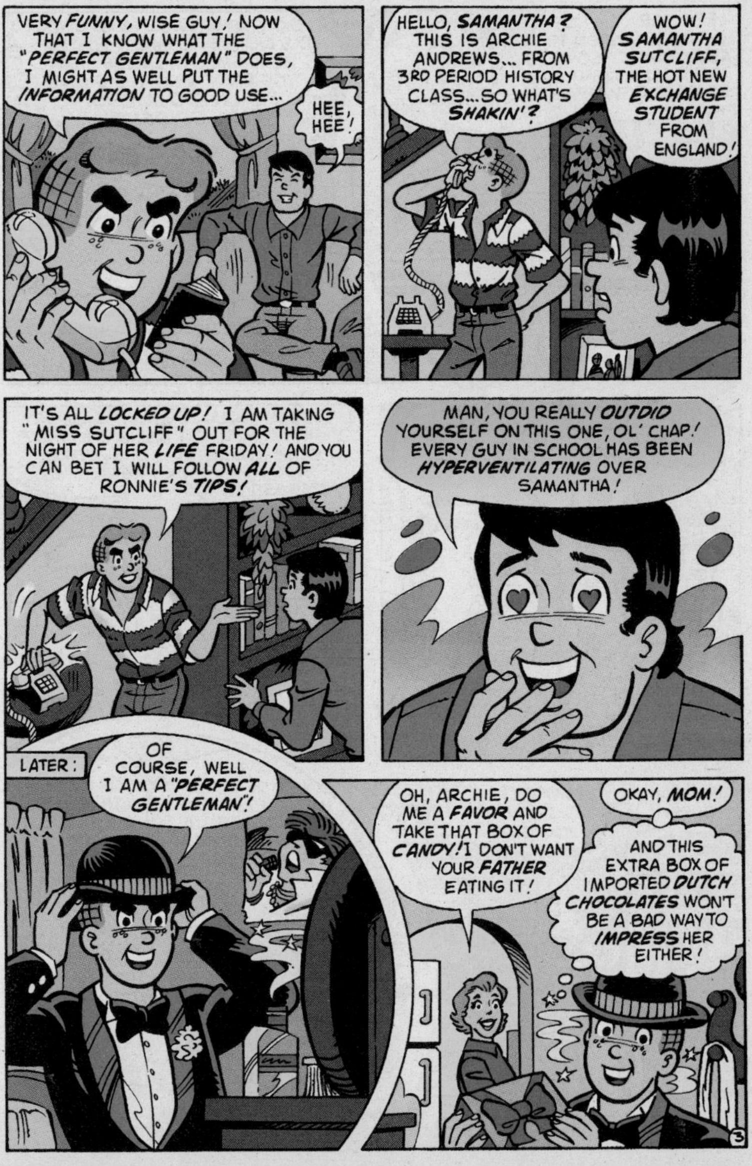
VERY FUNNY, WISE GUY! NOW THAT I KNOW WHAT THE "PERFECT GENTLEMAN" DOES, I MIGHT AS WELL PUT THE INFORMATION TO GOOD USE...
HEE, HEE!
HELLO, SAMANTHA? THIS IS ARCHIE ANDREWS... FROM 3RD PERIOD HISTORY CLASS...SO WHAT'S SHAKIN'?
WOW! SAMANTHA SUTCLIFF, THE HOT NEW EXCHANGE STUDENT FROM ENGLAND!
IT'S ALL LOCKED UP! I AM TAKING "MISS SUTCLIFF" OUT FOR THE NIGHT OF HER LIFE FRIDAY! AND YOU CAN BET I WILL FOLLOW ALL OF RONNIE'S TIPS!
MAN, YOU REALLY OUTDID YOURSELF ON THIS ONE, OL' CHAP! EVERY GUY IN SCHOOL HAS BEEN HYPERVENTILATING OVER SAMANTHA!
LATER:
OF COURSE, WELL I AM A "PERFECT GENTLEMAN"!
OH, ARCHIE, DO ME A FAVOR AND TAKE THAT BOX OF CANDY! I DON'T WANT YOUR FATHER EATING IT!
OKAY, MOM!
AND THIS EXTRA BOX OF IMPORTED DUTCH CHOCOLATES WON'T BE A BAD WAY TO IMPRESS HER EITHER!
3

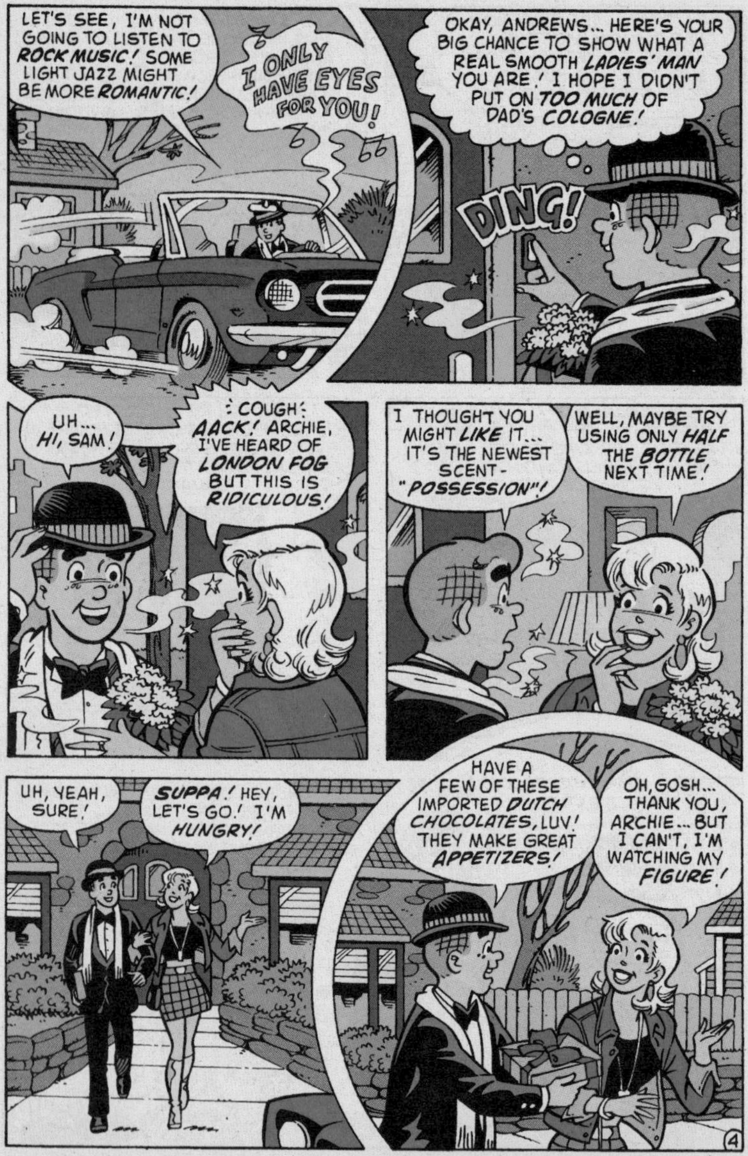
LET'S SEE, I'M NOT GOING TO LISTEN TO ROCK MUSIC! SOME LIGHT JAZZ MIGHT BE MORE ROMANTIC!
I ONLY HAVE EYES FOR YOU!
OKAY, ANDREWS... HERE'S YOUR BIG CHANCE TO SHOW WHAT A REAL SMOOTH LADIES' MAN YOU ARE! I HOPE I DIDN'T PUT ON TOO MUCH OF DAD'S COLOGNE!
DING!
UH... HI, SAM!
COUGH AACK! ARCHIE, I'VE HEARD OF LONDON FOG BUT THIS IS RIDICULOUS!
I THOUGHT YOU MIGHT LIKE IT... IT'S THE NEWEST SCENT- "POSSESSION"!
WELL, MAYBE TRY USING ONLY HALF THE BOTTLE NEXT TIME!
UH, YEAH, SURE!
SUPPA! HEY, LET'S GO! I'M HUNGRY!
HAVE A FEW OF THESE IMPORTED DUTCH CHOCOLATES, LUV! THEY MAKE GREAT APPETIZERS!
OH, GOSH... THANK YOU, ARCHIE... BUT I CAN'T, I'M WATCHING MY FIGURE!
4

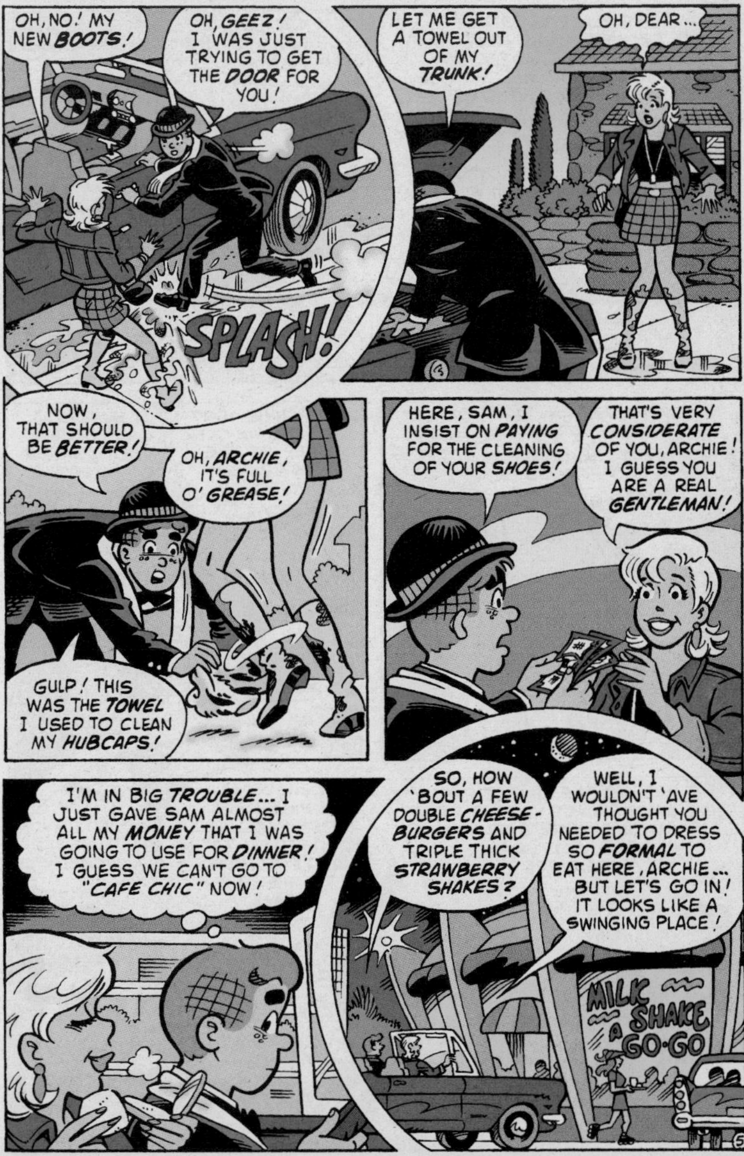

OH, NO! MY NEW BOOTS!
OH, GEEZ! I WAS JUST TRYING TO GET THE DOOR FOR YOU!
SPLASH!
LET ME GET A TOWEL OUT OF MY TRUNK!
OH, DEAR...
NOW, THAT SHOULD BE BETTER!
OH, ARCHIE, IT'S FULL O' GREASE!
GULP! THIS WAS THE TOWEL I USED TO CLEAN MY HUBCAPS!
HERE, SAM, I INSIST ON PAYING FOR THE CLEANING OF YOUR SHOES!
THAT'S VERY CONSIDERATE OF YOU, ARCHIE! I GUESS YOU ARE A REAL GENTLEMAN!
I'M IN BIG TROUBLE... I JUST GAVE SAM ALMOST ALL MY MONEY THAT I WAS GOING TO USE FOR DINNER! I GUESS WE CAN'T GO TO "CAFE CHIC" NOW!
SO, HOW 'BOUT A FEW DOUBLE CHEESE-BURGERS AND TRIPLE THICK STRAWBERRY SHAKES?
WELL, I WOULDN'T 'AVE THOUGHT YOU NEEDED TO DRESS SO FORMAL TO EAT HERE, ARCHIE... BUT LET'S GO IN! IT LOOKS LIKE A SWINGING PLACE!
MILK SHAKE A GO-GO

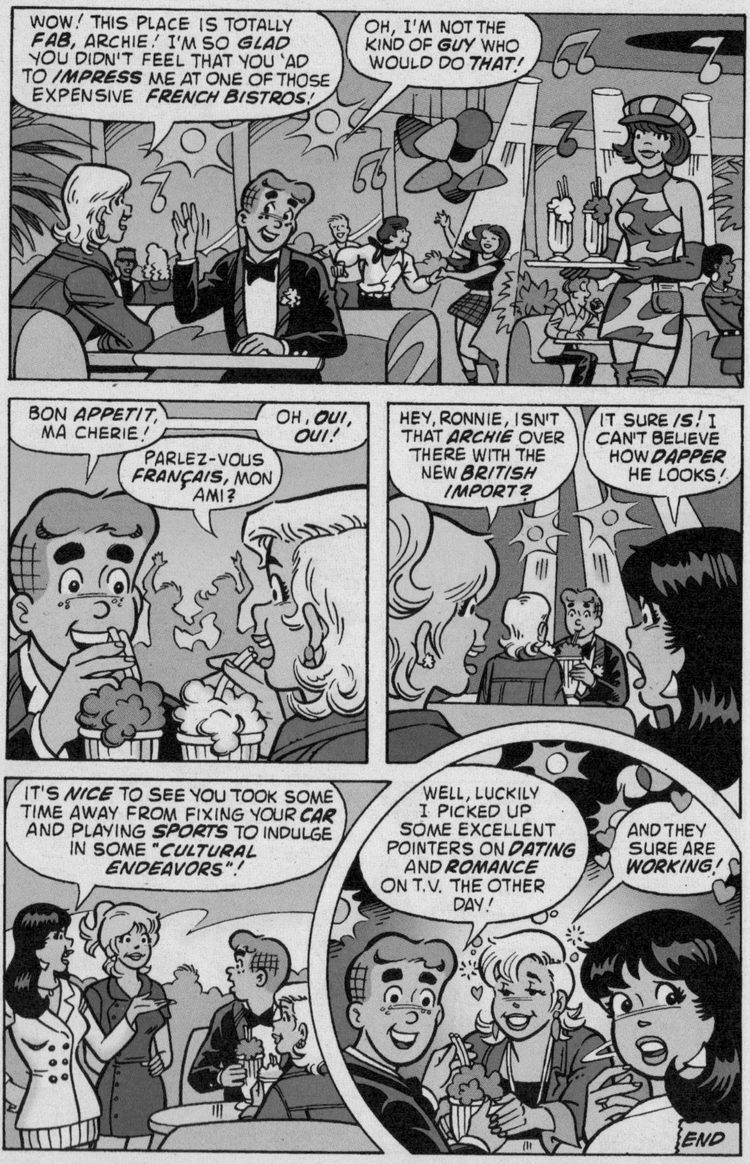
WOW! THIS PLACE IS TOTALLY FAB, ARCHIE! I'M SO GLAD YOU DIDN'T FEEL THAT YOU 'AD TO IMPRESS ME AT ONE OF THOSE EXPENSIVE FRENCH BISTROS!
OH, I'M NOT THE KIND OF GUY WHO WOULD DO THAT!
BON APPETIT, MA CHERIE!
OH, OUI, OUI!
PARLEZ-VOUS FRANÇAIS, MON AMI?
HEY, RONNIE, ISN'T THAT ARCHIE OVER THERE WITH THE NEW BRITISH IMPORT?
IT SURE IS! I CAN'T BELIEVE HOW DAPPER HE LOOKS!
IT'S NICE TO SEE YOU TOOK SOME TIME AWAY FROM FIXING YOUR CAR AND PLAYING SPORTS TO INDULGE IN SOME "CULTURAL ENDEAVORS"!
WELL, LUCKILY I PICKED UP SOME EXCELLENT POINTERS ON DATING AND ROMANCE ON T.V. THE OTHER DAY!
AND THEY SURE ARE WORKING!
END

Archie and his Pals "THE RIVALS" PART I

DO WE NEED TO REMIND YOU THAT RIVALRY RUNS RAMPANT BETWEEN RIVERDALE AND CENTRAL HIGH ? WELL, AS IN MOST SCHOOLS, THERE ARE TREASURED REMINDERS OF PAST GLORIES AND HEROES OF BYGONE DAYS !

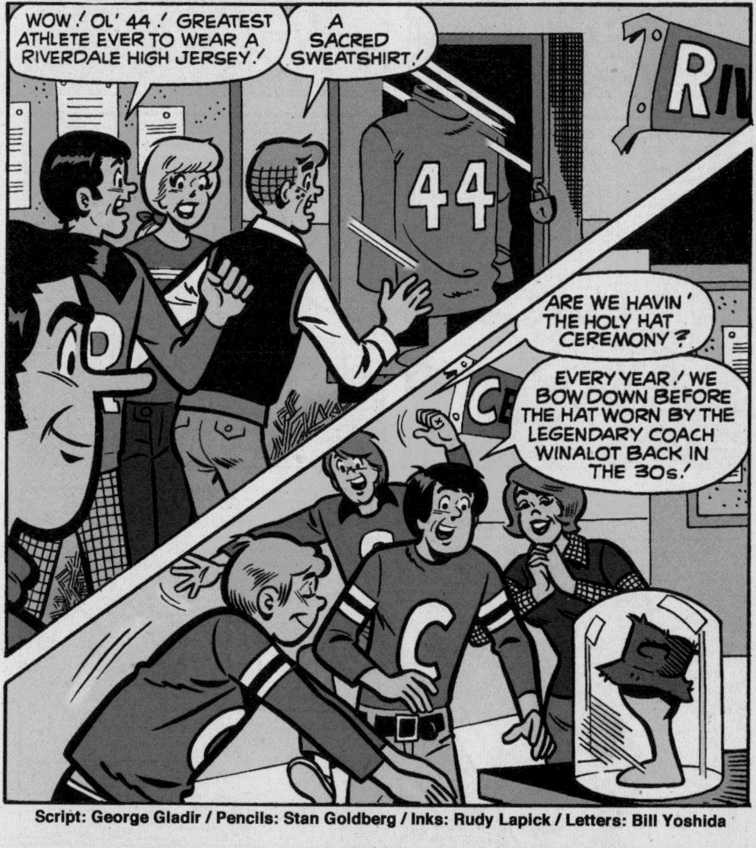
WOW ! OL' 44 ! GREATEST ATHLETE EVER TO WEAR A RIVERDALE HIGH JERSEY !
A SACRED SWEATSHIRT !
44
ARE WE HAVIN' THE HOLY HAT CEREMONY ?
EVERY YEAR ! WE BOW DOWN BEFORE THE HAT WORN BY THE LEGENDARY COACH WINALOT BACK IN THE 30s !

Script: George Gladir / Pencils: Stan Goldberg / Inks: Rudy Lapick / Letters: Bill Yoshida

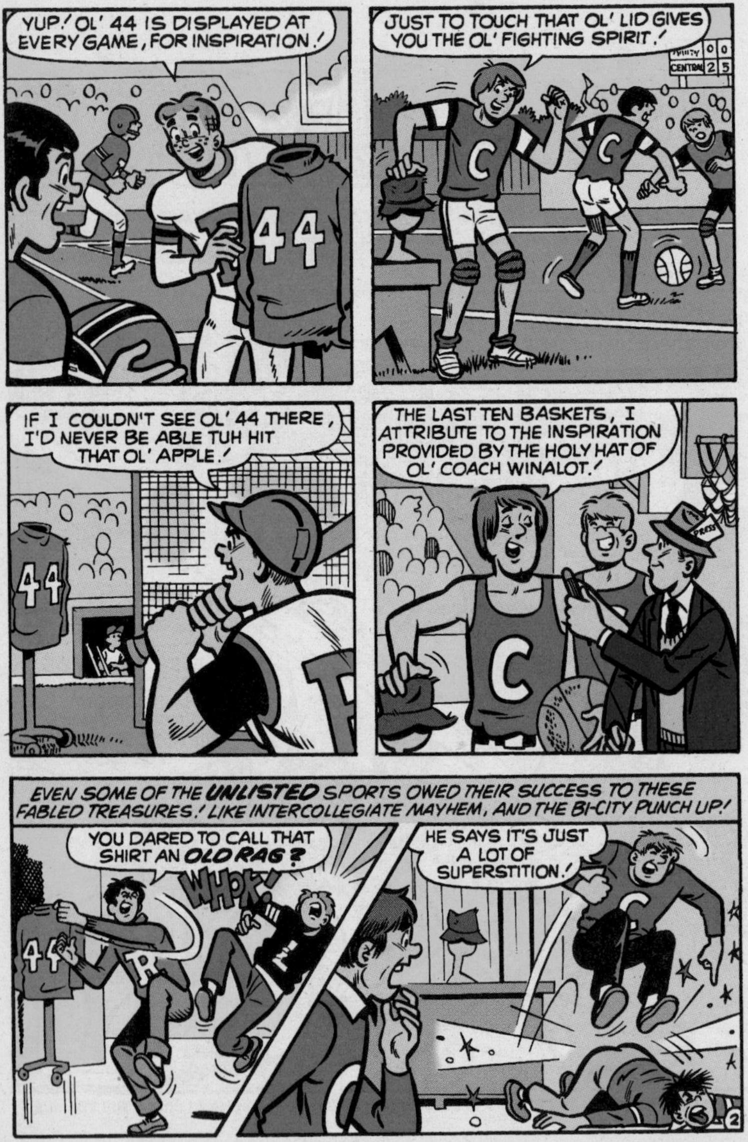
YUP! OL' 44 IS DISPLAYED AT EVERY GAME, FOR INSPIRATION!
44
JUST TO TOUCH THAT OL' LID GIVES YOU THE OL' FIGHTING SPIRIT!
CENTRAL 2 5
IF I COULDN'T SEE OL' 44 THERE, I'D NEVER BE ABLE TUH HIT THAT OL' APPLE!
44
THE LAST TEN BASKETS, I ATTRIBUTE TO THE INSPIRATION PROVIDED BY THE HOLY HAT OF OL' COACH WINALOT!
PRESS
EVEN SOME OF THE UNLISTED SPORTS OWED THEIR SUCCESS TO THESE FABLED TREASURES! LIKE INTERCOLLEGIATE MAYHEM, AND THE BI-CITY PUNCH UP!
YOU DARED TO CALL THAT SHIRT AN OLD RAG?
WHOK!
HE SAYS IT'S JUST A LOT OF SUPERSTITION!
2

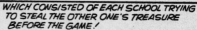

ALL OF WHICH RESULTED IN THE SIDELINE SPORT OF ONEUPMANSHIP!

WHICH CONSISTED OF EACH SCHOOL TRYING TO STEAL THE OTHER ONE'S TREASURE BEFORE THE GAME!

GRAB HIM!

THAT'S A CENTRAL-HIGHER!

GO BACK AND TELL YOUR CRONIES THAT NO CENTRAL HIGH HAND WILL EVER TOUCH OL' 44!

WE WOULDN'T PUT A HAND ON THE OLD RAG!

WE WANTED TO WIPE OUR *FEET* ON IT!

HYUK!

WE'LL GET YOU GUYS AT THE NEXT GAME!

YOU'LL PAY FOR THOSE REMARKS!

3

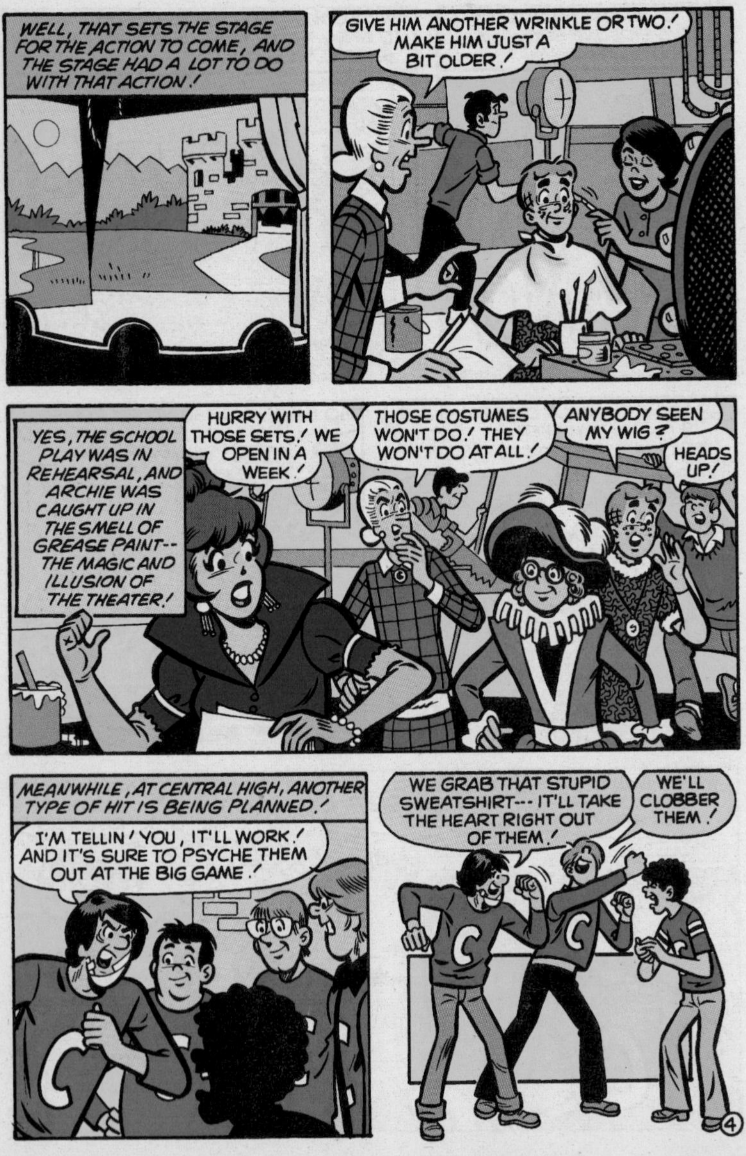

WELL, THAT SETS THE STAGE FOR THE ACTION TO COME, AND THE STAGE HAD A LOT TO DO WITH THAT ACTION!
GIVE HIM ANOTHER WRINKLE OR TWO! MAKE HIM JUST A BIT OLDER!
YES, THE SCHOOL PLAY WAS IN REHEARSAL, AND ARCHIE WAS CAUGHT UP IN THE SMELL OF GREASE PAINT-- THE MAGIC AND ILLUSION OF THE THEATER!
HURRY WITH THOSE SETS! WE OPEN IN A WEEK!
THOSE COSTUMES WON'T DO! THEY WON'T DO AT ALL!
ANYBODY SEEN MY WIG?
HEADS UP!
MEANWHILE, AT CENTRAL HIGH, ANOTHER TYPE OF HIT IS BEING PLANNED!
I'M TELLIN' YOU, IT'LL WORK! AND IT'S SURE TO PSYCHE THEM OUT AT THE BIG GAME!
WE GRAB THAT STUPID SWEATSHIRT--- IT'LL TAKE THE HEART RIGHT OUT OF THEM!
WE'LL CLOBBER THEM!
4

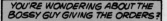

Panel 1:
YOU'RE WONDERING ABOUT THE BOSSY GUY GIVING THE ORDERS?

DON'T ARGUE WITH ME! I SAY IT'LL WORK!

Panel 2:
CLYDE CRUMB! STAR ATHLETE AND MASTER OF MALEVOLENCE!

THEY GUARD THAT SHIRT PRETTY GOOD, YOU KNOW!

ESPECIALLY BEFORE A BIG GAME!

Panel 3:

HIS INJURY OCCURRED WHEN HE VICIOUSLY HURLED HIS FACE INTO THE ELBOW OF A RIVERDALE FORWARD!

THEY EXPECT US TO BE SNEAKY AND TRICKY!

WE'RE NOTED FOR THAT!

Panel 4:

BUT WE'RE GONNA LAUNCH A DIRECT FRONTAL ATTACK THIS TIME!

WE'RE USING *KONG*, HERE!

WOW!

Panel 5:

HE'S GONNA STOMP IN THERE, GRAB THE DUMB SHIRT AND HAUL OUTTA THERE!

AND TOUGH LUCK TO ANYONE THAT GETS IN HIS WAY!

HAH! NOTHIN' SNEAKY ABOUT *THAT!*

LIKE ROLLIN' OVER 'EM WITH A *TANK!*

CENTRAL HIGH SCHOOL

5

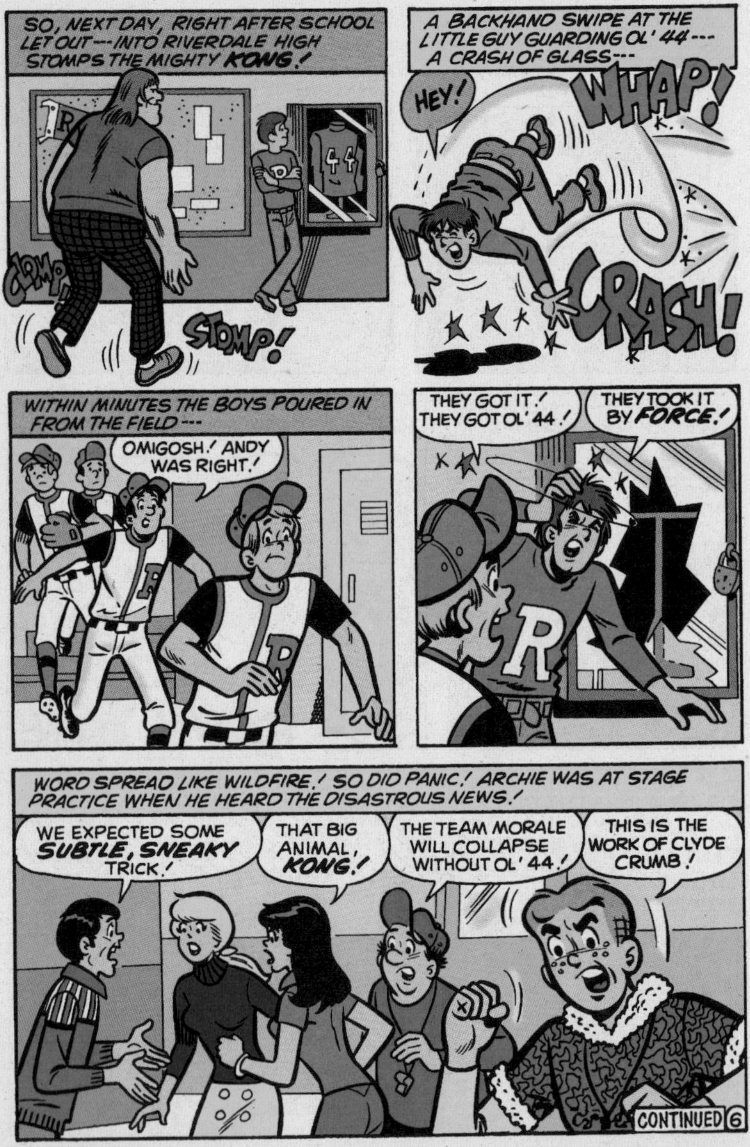
SO, NEXT DAY, RIGHT AFTER SCHOOL LET OUT---INTO RIVERDALE HIGH STOMPS THE MIGHTY KONG!
CLOMP!
STOMP!
A BACKHAND SWIPE AT THE LITTLE GUY GUARDING OL' 44--- A CRASH OF GLASS---
HEY!
WHAP!
CRASH!
WITHIN MINUTES THE BOYS POURED IN FROM THE FIELD---
OMIGOSH! ANDY WAS RIGHT!
THEY GOT IT! THEY GOT OL' 44!
THEY TOOK IT BY FORCE!
WORD SPREAD LIKE WILDFIRE! SO DID PANIC! ARCHIE WAS AT STAGE PRACTICE WHEN HE HEARD THE DISASTROUS NEWS!
WE EXPECTED SOME SUBTLE, SNEAKY TRICK!
THAT BIG ANIMAL, KONG!
THE TEAM MORALE WILL COLLAPSE WITHOUT OL' 44!
THIS IS THE WORK OF CLYDE CRUMB!
CONTINUED 6

Archie and his Pals "THE RIVALS" PART 2

Panel 1: IF WE DON'T GET THAT SWEATSHIRT BACK BEFORE THE GAME --- WE'RE LICKED!

Panel 2: CAN'T WE CATCH THEM BEFORE THEY GET OUT OF RIVERDALE?

Panel 3: I MADE SOME QUICK PHONE CALLS! THE WORD IS OUT!

Panel 4: WE'VE GOT GUYS BLOCKING ALL THE ROADS OUT OF TOWN!

Panel 5: IT WON'T DO ANY GOOD! CLYDE CRUMB IS TOO SLICK TO BE CAUGHT THAT WAY!

Panel 6: THEN WE CONCEDE DEFEAT, EH?

IF WE COULD GET HOLD OF THAT PRECIOUS *HAT* OF THEIRS, WE COULD EVEN THINGS UP!

NO CHANCE!

THEY'LL TRIPLE THE GUARD ON THAT HAT, NOW!

THEIR EVIL GENIUS, CRUMB, IS PROBABLY TAKING CARE OF IT PERSONALLY!

BY GOLLY, YOU'RE RIGHT! AND THAT MIGHT BE THE ANSWER TO OUR PROBLEM!

YOU'D BETTER GO OVER THAT SLOWLY!

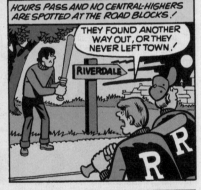

HOURS PASS AND NO CENTRAL-HIGHERS ARE SPOTTED AT THE ROAD BLOCKS!

THEY FOUND ANOTHER WAY OUT, OR THEY NEVER LEFT TOWN!

RIVERDALE

WELL PAST MIDNIGHT, DEEP IN CENTRAL HIGH TERRITORY, A CREAK OF OARLOCKS IS HEARD ON THE RIVER!

CREAK! SQUEAL!

AND A ROWBOAT SOFTLY BUMPS AGAINST A DOCK!

HYUK! HOME FREE!

WE *DID* IT!

2

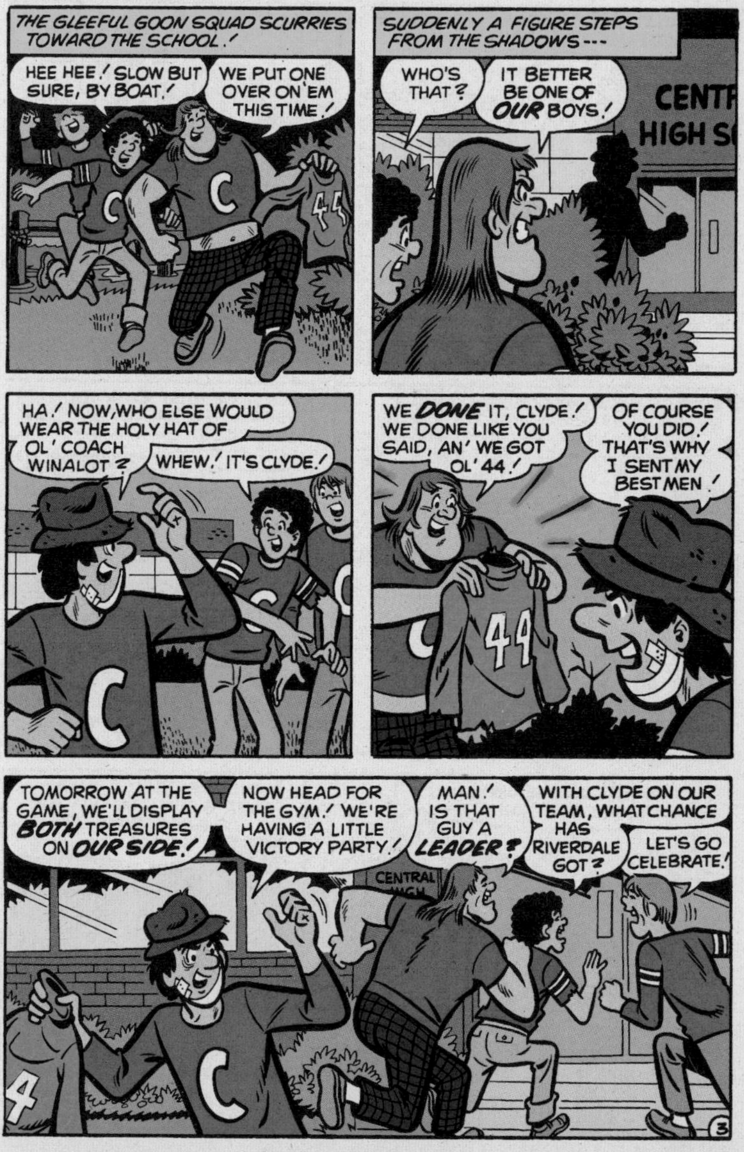
THE GLEEFUL GOON SQUAD SCURRIES TOWARD THE SCHOOL.!
HEE HEE! SLOW BUT SURE, BY BOAT.!
WE PUT ONE OVER ON 'EM THIS TIME!
SUDDENLY A FIGURE STEPS FROM THE SHADOWS---
WHO'S THAT?
IT BETTER BE ONE OF OUR BOYS!
CENTR
HIGH S
HA! NOW, WHO ELSE WOULD WEAR THE HOLY HAT OF OL' COACH WINALOT?
WHEW! IT'S CLYDE!
WE DONE IT, CLYDE! WE DONE LIKE YOU SAID, AN' WE GOT OL' 44!
OF COURSE YOU DID! THAT'S WHY I SENT MY BEST MEN!
TOMORROW AT THE GAME, WE'LL DISPLAY BOTH TREASURES ON OUR SIDE!
NOW HEAD FOR THE GYM! WE'RE HAVING A LITTLE VICTORY PARTY!
MAN! IS THAT GUY A LEADER?
WITH CLYDE ON OUR TEAM, WHAT CHANCE HAS RIVERDALE GOT?
LET'S GO CELEBRATE!
CENTRAL

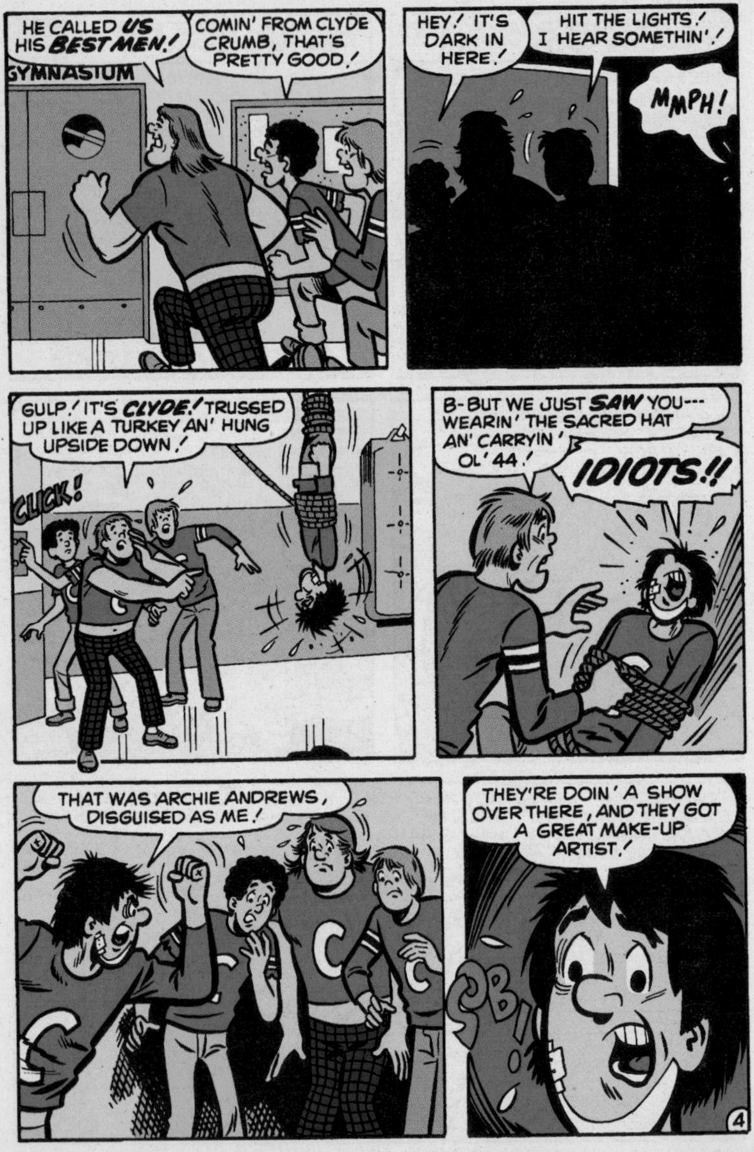
HE CALLED US HIS BEST MEN.!
COMIN' FROM CLYDE CRUMB, THAT'S PRETTY GOOD.!
GYMNASIUM
HEY.! IT'S DARK IN HERE.!
HIT THE LIGHTS.! I HEAR SOMETHIN'.!
MMPH!
GULP.! IT'S CLYDE.! TRUSSED UP LIKE A TURKEY AN' HUNG UPSIDE DOWN.!
CLICK!
B-BUT WE JUST SAW YOU--- WEARIN' THE SACRED HAT AN' CARRYIN' OL' 44.!
IDIOTS!!
THAT WAS ARCHIE ANDREWS, DISGUISED AS ME.!
THEY'RE DOIN' A SHOW OVER THERE, AND THEY GOT A GREAT MAKE-UP ARTIST.!
SOB!
4

WALKED RIGHT IN HERE AND JUMPED ME! PAST THE GUARDS OUTSIDE AND EVERYTHING!

NOW THEY NOT ONLY HAVE THEIR SHIRT BACK, BUT *OUR* TREASURE AS WELL!

EEP!

WELL, SIR, THAT EPISODE TOPPLED OL' CLYDE FROM HIS "BAD GUY" THRONE!

GET LOST, BUM!

WHO NEEDS HIM? WE NEED ONE OF THEM *ARCHIES!*

AFTER WHIPPING CENTRAL EASILY IN THE GAME NEXT DAY, ARCHIE RETURNED THEIR TREASURED HAT!

YOU'RE SENDING IT BACK?

WITH A SMALL *BONUS!*

CENTRAL	0	0		0	0	0
ERDALE	7	9	5		3	6

---ALONG WITH *49 EXACT DUPLICATES,* MADE BY A RIVERDALE COSTUME COMPANY! SOME-HOW THE OLD LID NEVER ACHIEVED ITS FORMER STATUS! I WONDER WHY?

GULP! WHICH IS THE ORIGINAL?

WHO KNOWS? THEY'RE EXACT IN EVERY DETAIL! EVEN THE DIRT AND THE GRIME!

WE CAN'T WORSHIP *50 HATS!*

WE'LL GET YOU FOR THIS, ARCHIE ANDREWS!

EMO

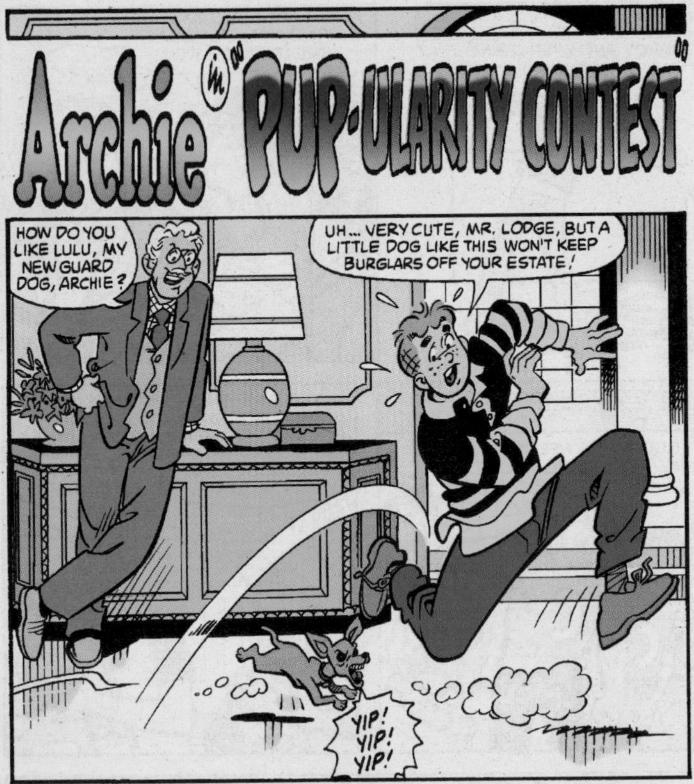
Archie in "PUP-ULARITY CONTEST"
HOW DO YOU LIKE LULU, MY NEW GUARD DOG, ARCHIE?
UH... VERY CUTE, MR. LODGE, BUT A LITTLE DOG LIKE THIS WON'T KEEP BURGLARS OFF YOUR ESTATE!
YIP! YIP! YIP!

Script: Angelo DeCesare / Pencils: Stan Goldberg / Inks: Bob Smith / Letters: Bill Yoshida

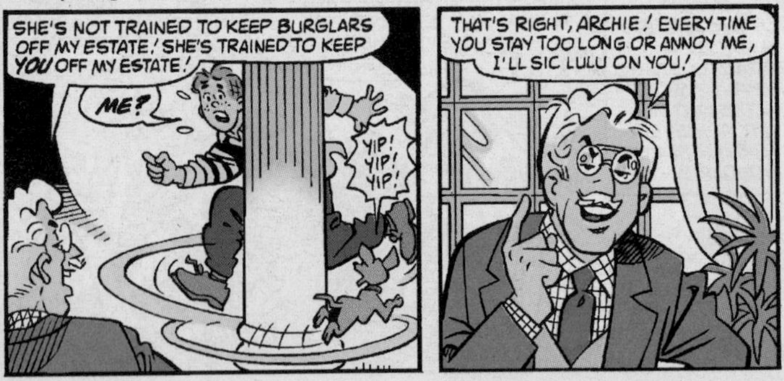
SHE'S NOT TRAINED TO KEEP BURGLARS OFF MY ESTATE! SHE'S TRAINED TO KEEP YOU OFF MY ESTATE!
ME?
YIP! YIP! YIP!
THAT'S RIGHT, ARCHIE! EVERY TIME YOU STAY TOO LONG OR ANNOY ME, I'LL SIC LULU ON YOU!

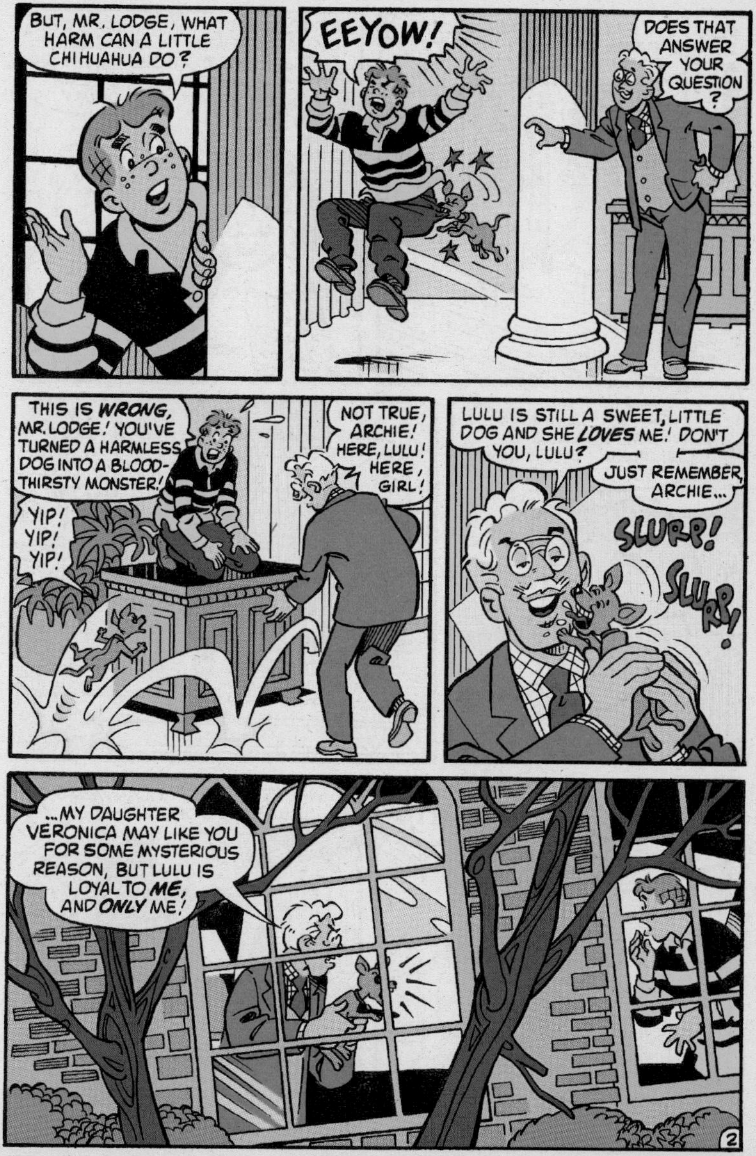
BUT, MR. LODGE, WHAT HARM CAN A LITTLE CHIHUAHUA DO?
EEYOW!
DOES THAT ANSWER YOUR QUESTION?
THIS IS WRONG, MR. LODGE! YOU'VE TURNED A HARMLESS DOG INTO A BLOOD-THIRSTY MONSTER!
YIP! YIP! YIP!
NOT TRUE, ARCHIE! HERE, LULU! HERE, GIRL!
LULU IS STILL A SWEET, LITTLE DOG AND SHE LOVES ME! DON'T YOU, LULU?
JUST REMEMBER, ARCHIE...
SLURP!
SLURP!
...MY DAUGHTER VERONICA MAY LIKE YOU FOR SOME MYSTERIOUS REASON, BUT LULU IS LOYAL TO ME, AND ONLY ME!
2

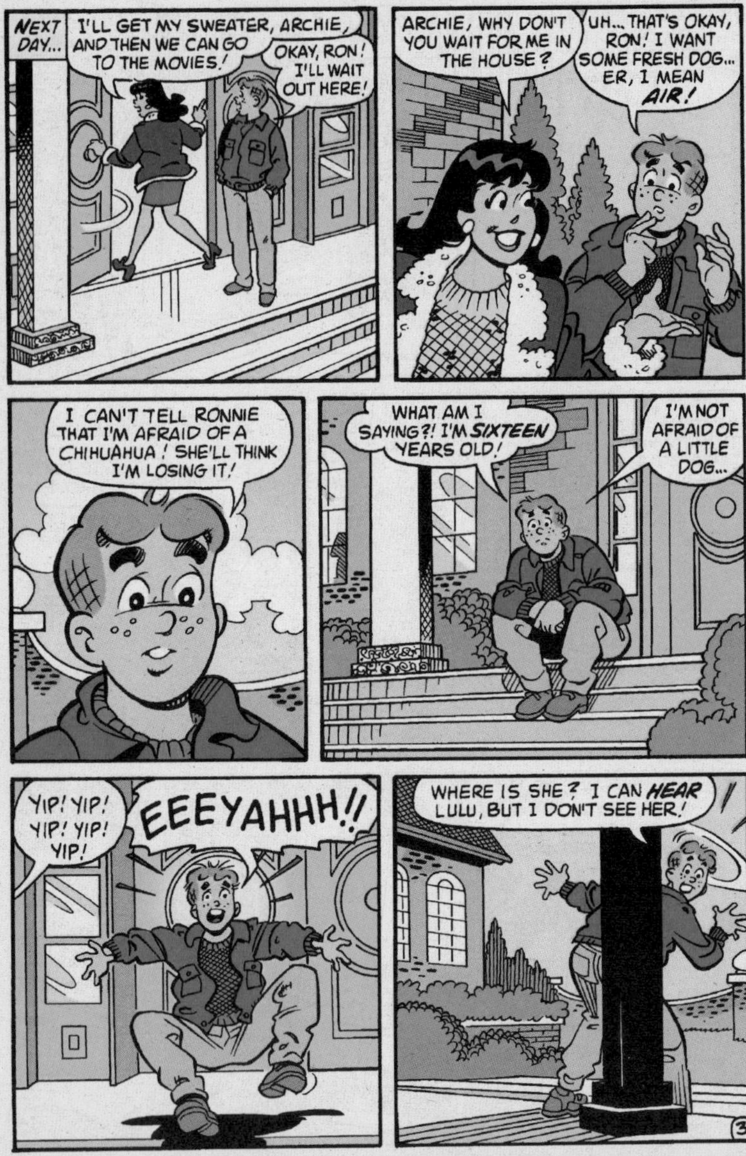
NEXT DAY...
I'LL GET MY SWEATER, ARCHIE, AND THEN WE CAN GO TO THE MOVIES!
OKAY, RON! I'LL WAIT OUT HERE!
ARCHIE, WHY DON'T YOU WAIT FOR ME IN THE HOUSE?
UH... THAT'S OKAY, RON! I WANT SOME FRESH DOG... ER, I MEAN AIR!
I CAN'T TELL RONNIE THAT I'M AFRAID OF A CHIHUAHUA! SHE'LL THINK I'M LOSING IT!
WHAT AM I SAYING?! I'M SIXTEEN YEARS OLD!
I'M NOT AFRAID OF A LITTLE DOG...
YIP! YIP! YIP! YIP! YIP!
EEEYAHHH!!
WHERE IS SHE? I CAN HEAR LULU, BUT I DON'T SEE HER!
3

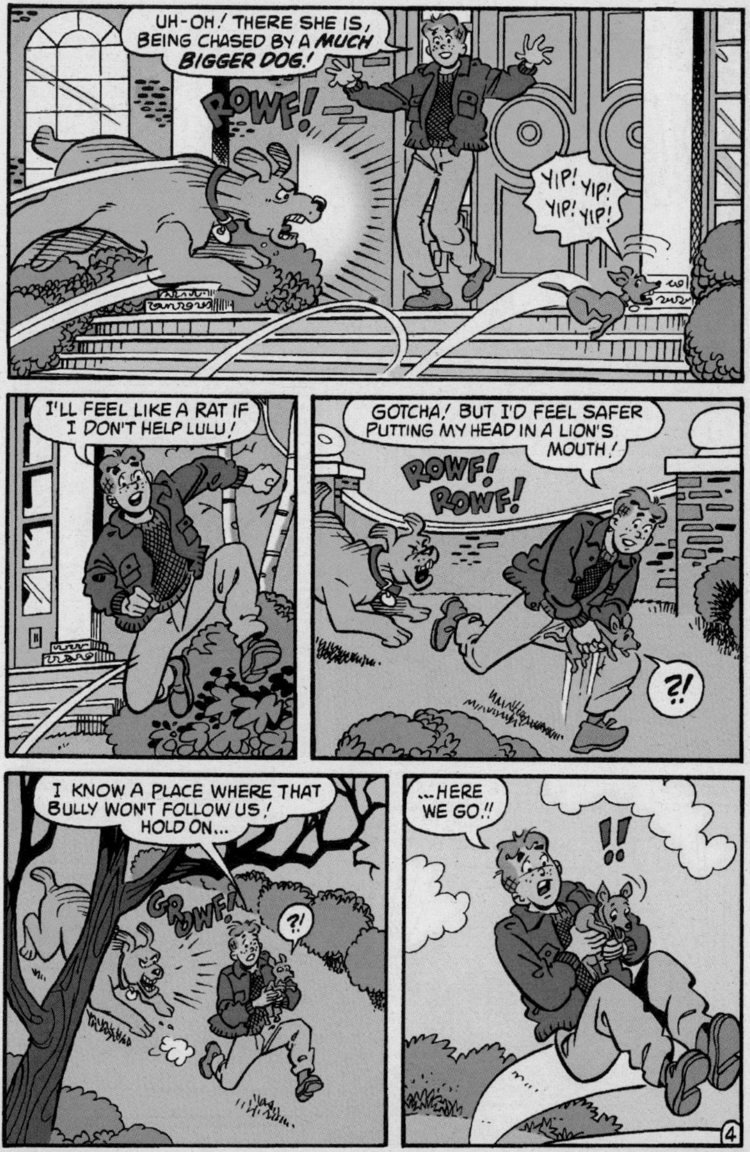
UH-OH! THERE SHE IS, BEING CHASED BY A MUCH BIGGER DOG!
ROWF!
YIP! YIP! YIP! YIP!
I'LL FEEL LIKE A RAT IF I DON'T HELP LULU!
GOTCHA! BUT I'D FEEL SAFER PUTTING MY HEAD IN A LION'S MOUTH!
ROWF! ROWF!
?!
I KNOW A PLACE WHERE THAT BULLY WON'T FOLLOW US! HOLD ON...
GROWF!
?!
...HERE WE GO!!
!!
4

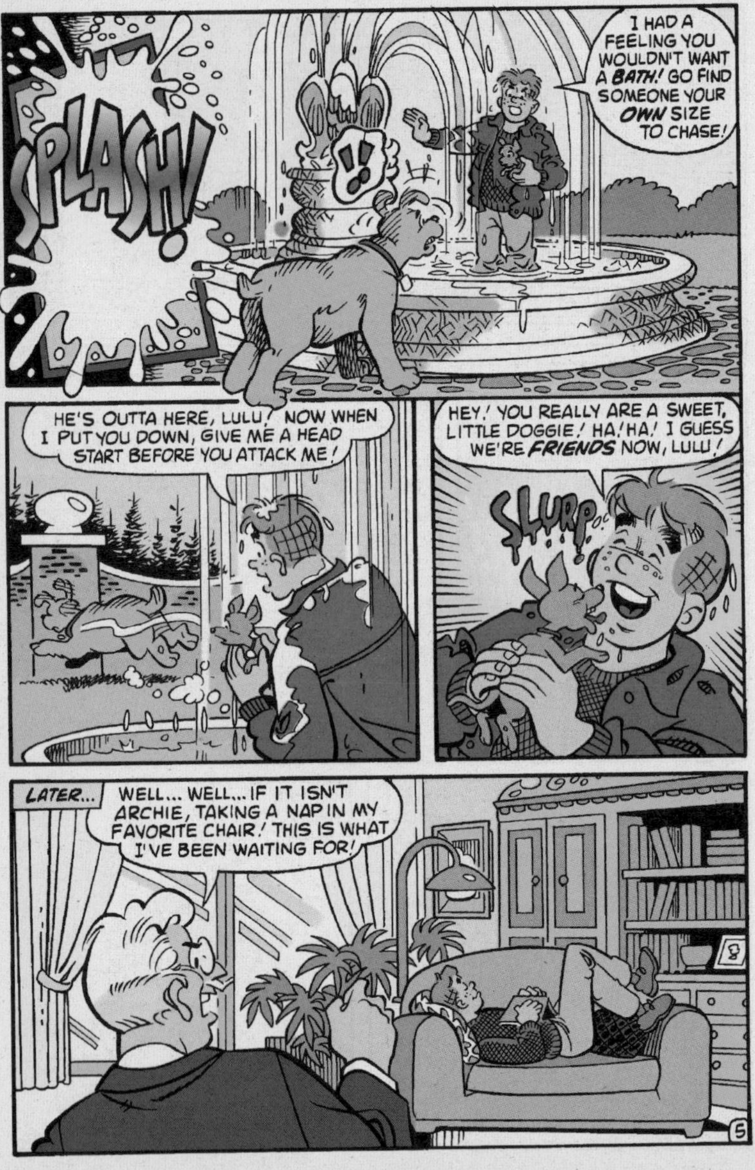
SPLASH!
I HAD A FEELING YOU WOULDN'T WANT A BATH! GO FIND SOMEONE YOUR OWN SIZE TO CHASE!
HE'S OUTTA HERE, LULU! NOW WHEN I PUT YOU DOWN, GIVE ME A HEAD START BEFORE YOU ATTACK ME!
HEY! YOU REALLY ARE A SWEET, LITTLE DOGGIE! HA! HA! I GUESS WE'RE FRIENDS NOW, LULU!
SLURP
LATER...
WELL... WELL... IF IT ISN'T ARCHIE, TAKING A NAP IN MY FAVORITE CHAIR! THIS IS WHAT I'VE BEEN WAITING FOR!
5

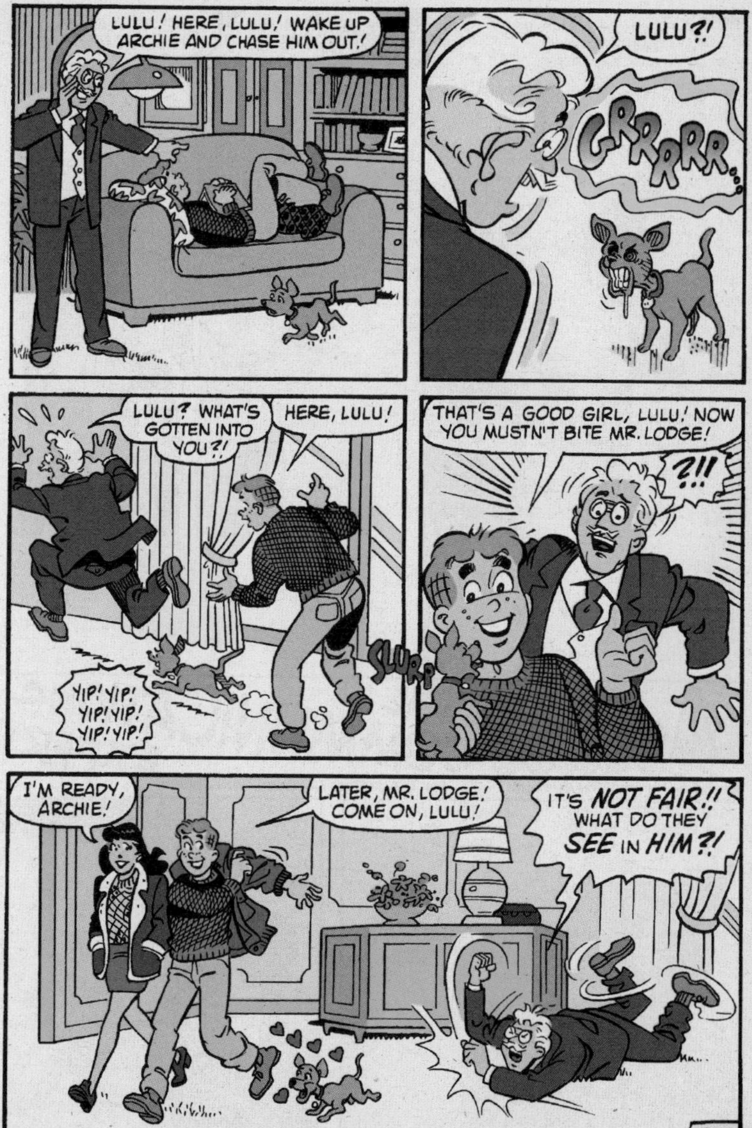
LULU! HERE, LULU! WAKE UP ARCHIE AND CHASE HIM OUT!
LULU?!
GRRRRR...
LULU? WHAT'S GOTTEN INTO YOU?!
HERE, LULU!
YIP! YIP! YIP! YIP! YIP! YIP!
THAT'S A GOOD GIRL, LULU! NOW YOU MUSTN'T BITE MR. LODGE!
?!!
SLURP
I'M READY, ARCHIE!
LATER, MR. LODGE! COME ON, LULU!
IT'S NOT FAIR!! WHAT DO THEY SEE IN HIM?!
END

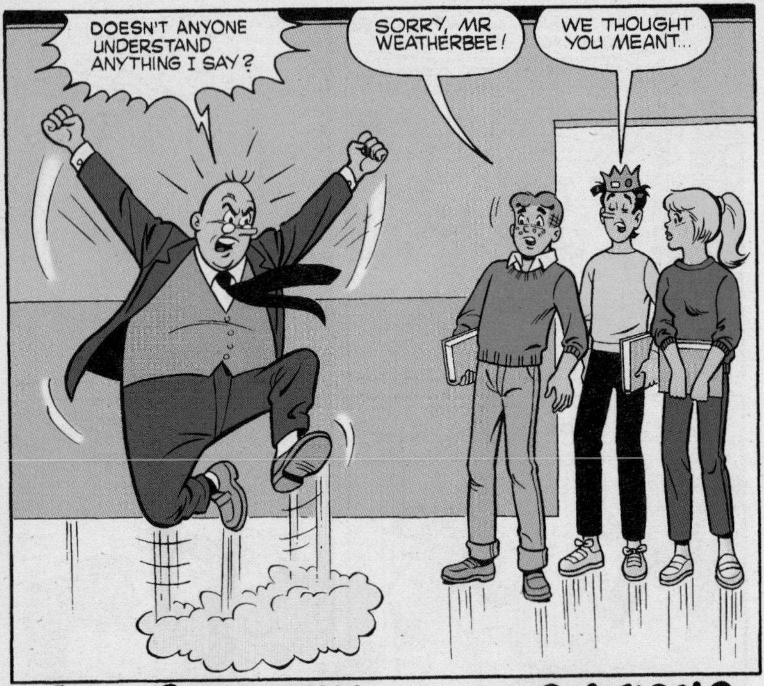
DOESN'T ANYONE UNDERSTAND ANYTHING I SAY?
SORRY, MR WEATHERBEE!
WE THOUGHT YOU MEANT...

Archie THE COMMUNICATIONS EXPERT

Script & Pencils: Joe Edwards / Inks: Jon D'Agostino / Letters: Bill Yoshida

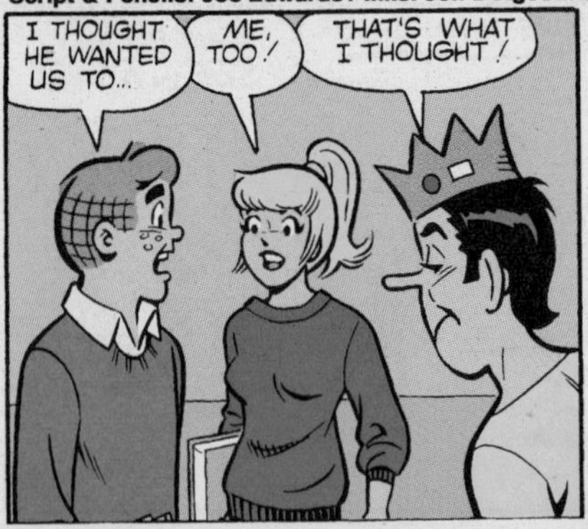
I THOUGHT HE WANTED US TO...
ME, TOO!
THAT'S WHAT I THOUGHT!

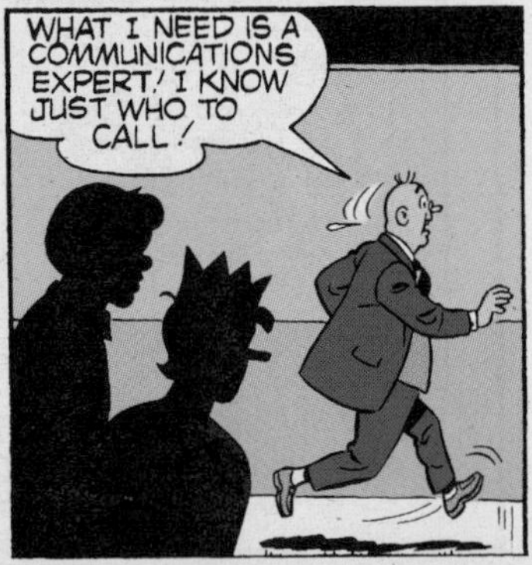
WHAT I NEED IS A COMMUNICATIONS EXPERT! I KNOW JUST WHO TO CALL!

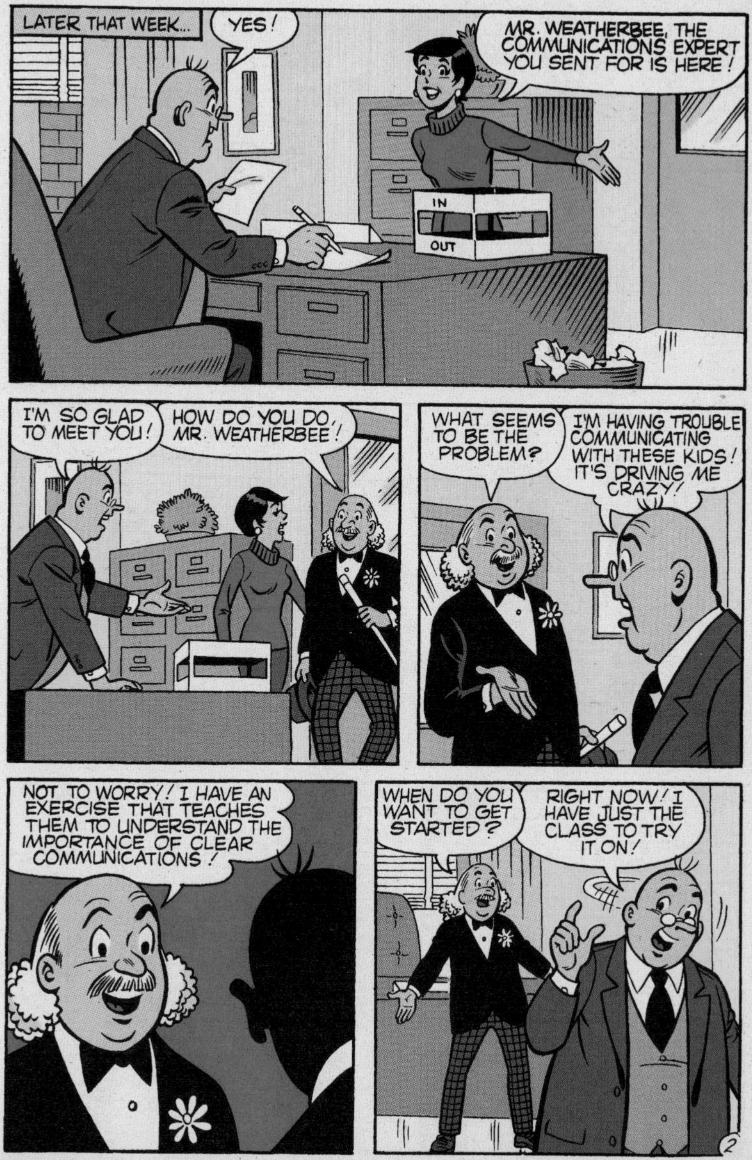
LATER THAT WEEK...
YES!
MR. WEATHERBEE, THE COMMUNICATIONS EXPERT YOU SENT FOR IS HERE!
I'M SO GLAD TO MEET YOU!
HOW DO YOU DO, MR. WEATHERBEE!
WHAT SEEMS TO BE THE PROBLEM?
I'M HAVING TROUBLE COMMUNICATING WITH THESE KIDS! IT'S DRIVING ME CRAZY!
NOT TO WORRY! I HAVE AN EXERCISE THAT TEACHES THEM TO UNDERSTAND THE IMPORTANCE OF CLEAR COMMUNICATIONS!
WHEN DO YOU WANT TO GET STARTED?
RIGHT NOW! I HAVE JUST THE CLASS TO TRY IT ON!
IN
OUT
2

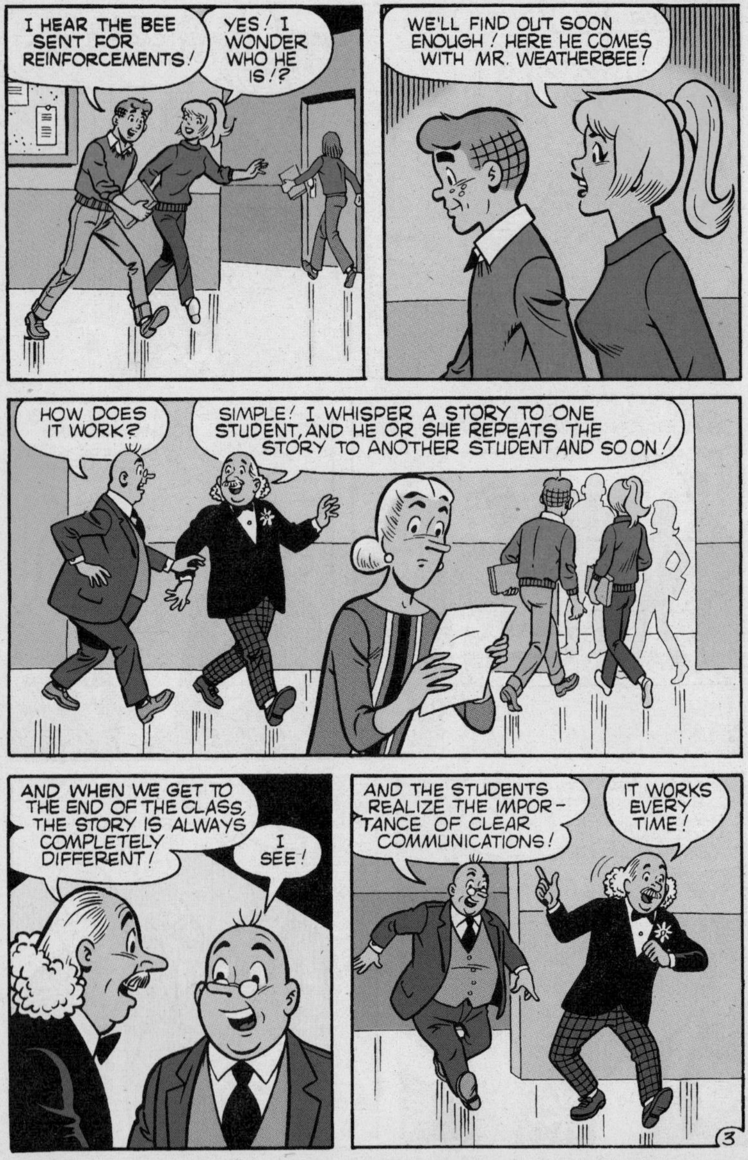
I HEAR THE BEE SENT FOR REINFORCEMENTS!
YES! I WONDER WHO HE IS!?
WE'LL FIND OUT SOON ENOUGH! HERE HE COMES WITH MR. WEATHERBEE!
HOW DOES IT WORK?
SIMPLE! I WHISPER A STORY TO ONE STUDENT, AND HE OR SHE REPEATS THE STORY TO ANOTHER STUDENT AND SO ON!
AND WHEN WE GET TO THE END OF THE CLASS, THE STORY IS ALWAYS COMPLETELY DIFFERENT!
I SEE!
AND THE STUDENTS REALIZE THE IMPORTANCE OF CLEAR COMMUNICATIONS!
IT WORKS EVERY TIME!
3

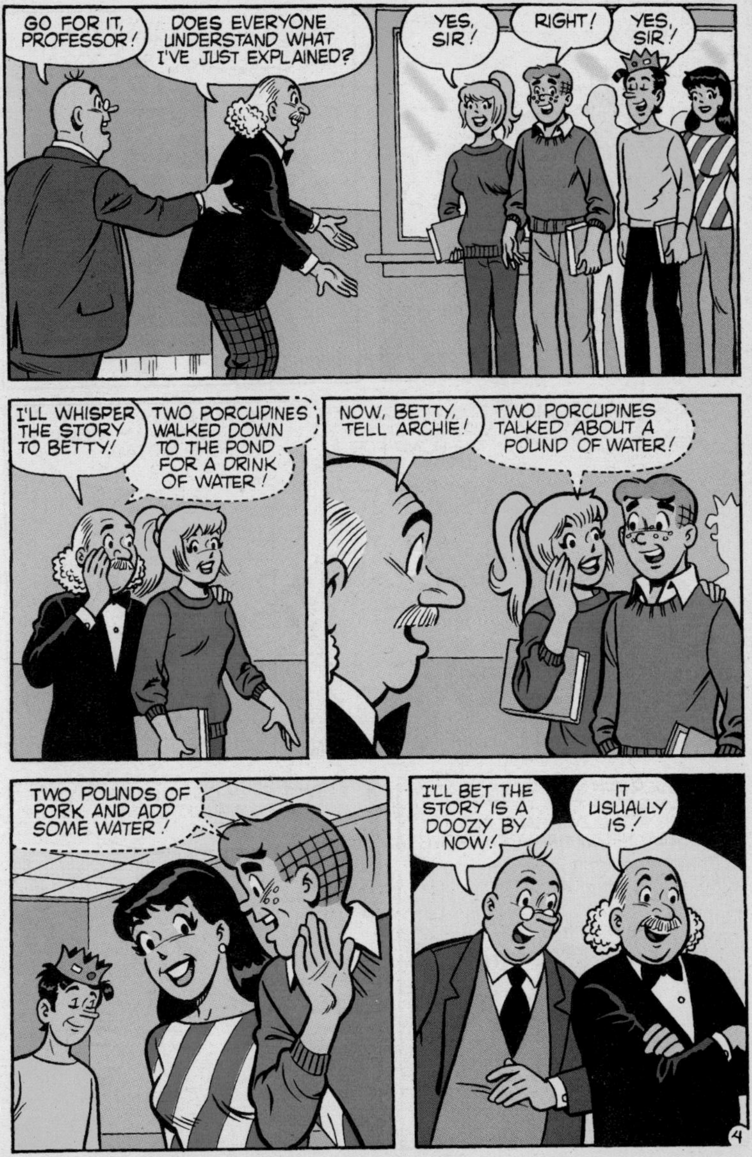
GO FOR IT, PROFESSOR!
DOES EVERYONE UNDERSTAND WHAT I'VE JUST EXPLAINED?
YES, SIR!
RIGHT!
YES, SIR!
I'LL WHISPER THE STORY TO BETTY!
TWO PORCUPINES WALKED DOWN TO THE POND FOR A DRINK OF WATER!
NOW, BETTY, TELL ARCHIE!
TWO PORCUPINES TALKED ABOUT A POUND OF WATER!
TWO POUNDS OF PORK AND ADD SOME WATER!
I'LL BET THE STORY IS A DOOZY BY NOW!
IT USUALLY IS!
4

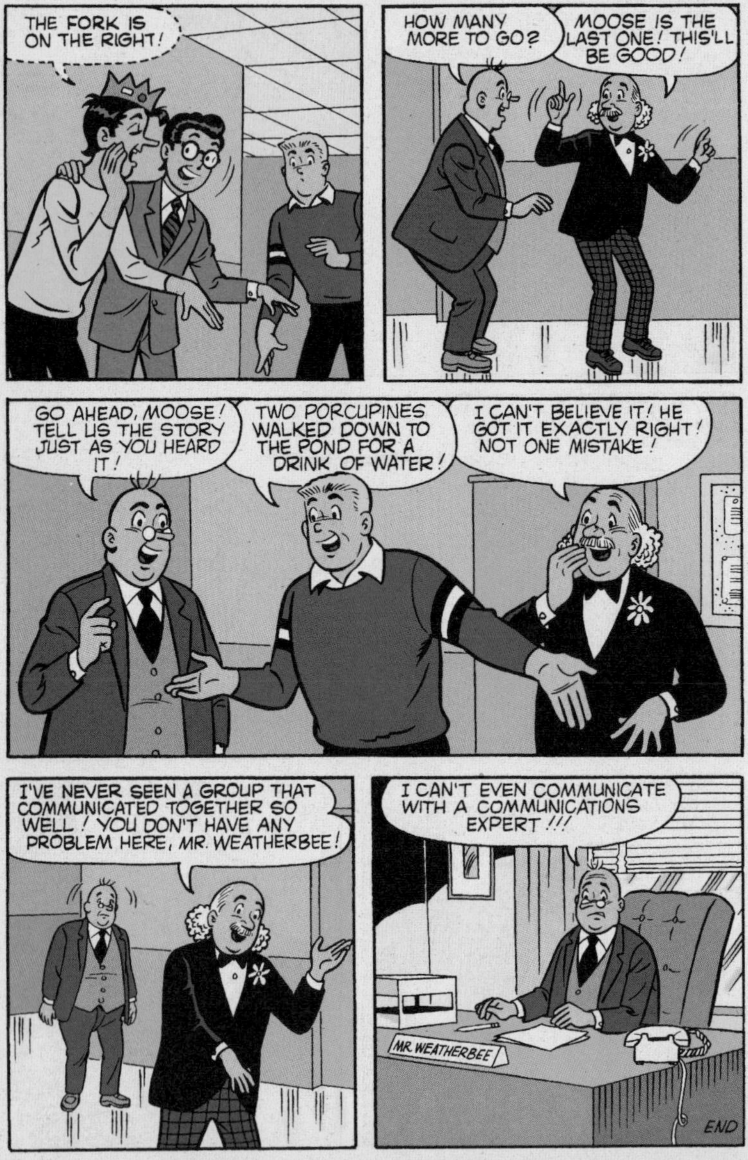
THE FORK IS ON THE RIGHT!
HOW MANY MORE TO GO?
MOOSE IS THE LAST ONE! THIS'LL BE GOOD!
GO AHEAD, MOOSE! TELL US THE STORY JUST AS YOU HEARD IT!
TWO PORCUPINES WALKED DOWN TO THE POND FOR A DRINK OF WATER!
I CAN'T BELIEVE IT! HE GOT IT EXACTLY RIGHT! NOT ONE MISTAKE!
I'VE NEVER SEEN A GROUP THAT COMMUNICATED TOGETHER SO WELL! YOU DON'T HAVE ANY PROBLEM HERE, MR. WEATHERBEE!
I CAN'T EVEN COMMUNICATE WITH A COMMUNICATIONS EXPERT!!!
MR. WEATHERBEE
END

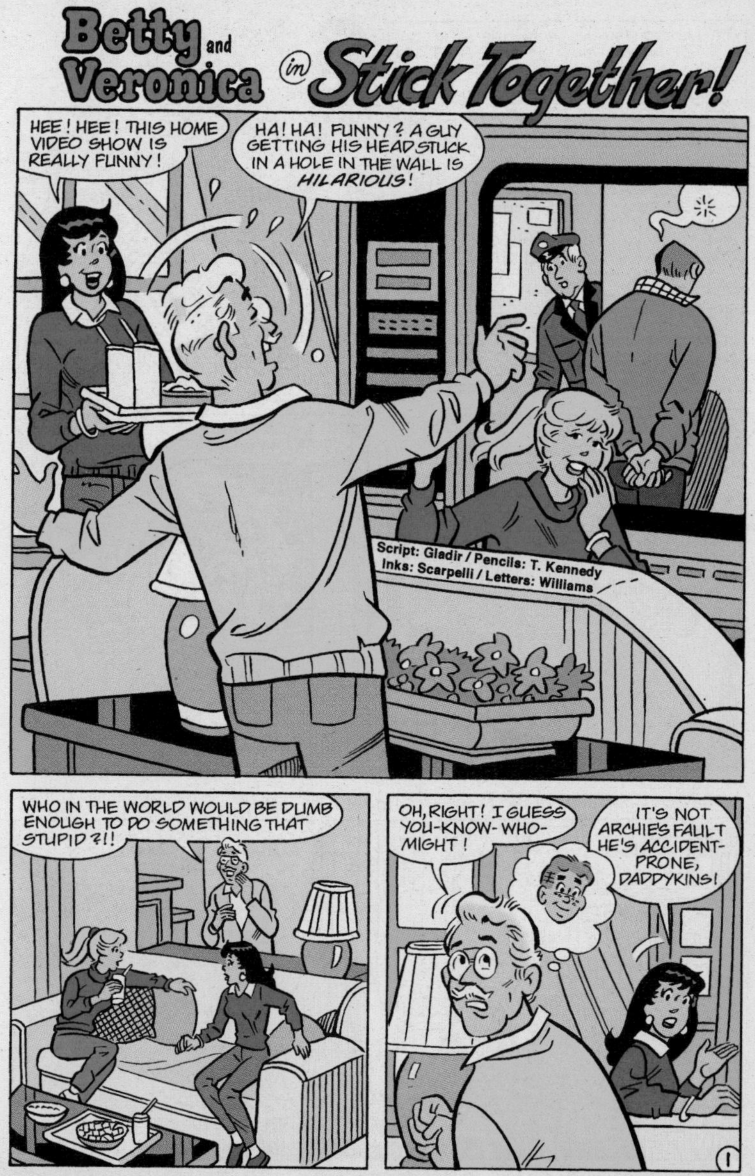
Betty and Veronica in Stick Together!
HEE! HEE! THIS HOME VIDEO SHOW IS REALLY FUNNY!
HA! HA! FUNNY? A GUY GETTING HIS HEAD STUCK IN A HOLE IN THE WALL IS HILARIOUS!
Script: Gladir / Pencils: T. Kennedy
Inks: Scarpelli / Letters: Williams
WHO IN THE WORLD WOULD BE DUMB ENOUGH TO DO SOMETHING THAT STUPID ?!!
OH, RIGHT! I GUESS YOU-KNOW-WHO-MIGHT!
IT'S NOT ARCHIE'S FAULT HE'S ACCIDENT-PRONE, DADDYKINS!
1

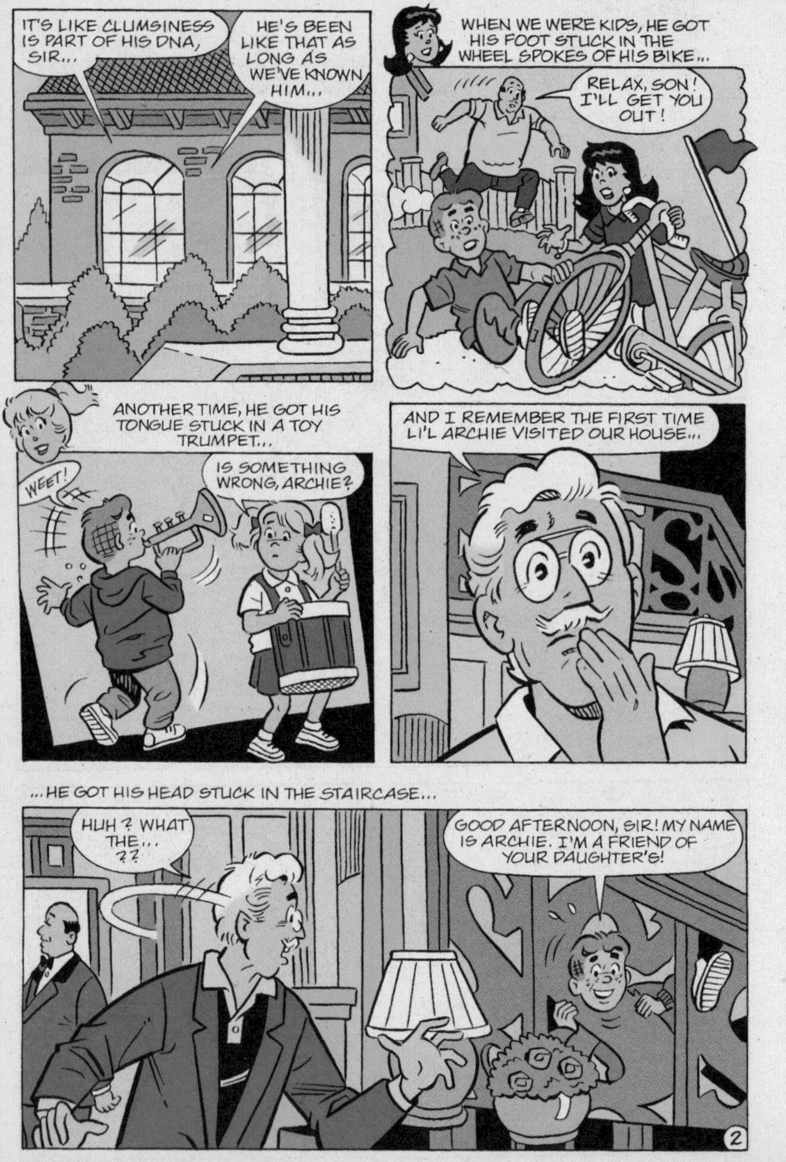
IT'S LIKE CLUMSINESS IS PART OF HIS DNA, SIR...
HE'S BEEN LIKE THAT AS LONG AS WE'VE KNOWN HIM...
WHEN WE WERE KIDS, HE GOT HIS FOOT STUCK IN THE WHEEL SPOKES OF HIS BIKE...
RELAX, SON! I'LL GET YOU OUT!
ANOTHER TIME, HE GOT HIS TONGUE STUCK IN A TOY TRUMPET...
WEET!
IS SOMETHING WRONG, ARCHIE?
AND I REMEMBER THE FIRST TIME LI'L ARCHIE VISITED OUR HOUSE...
...HE GOT HIS HEAD STUCK IN THE STAIRCASE...
HUH? WHAT THE... ??
GOOD AFTERNOON, SIR! MY NAME IS ARCHIE. I'M A FRIEND OF YOUR DAUGHTER'S!
2

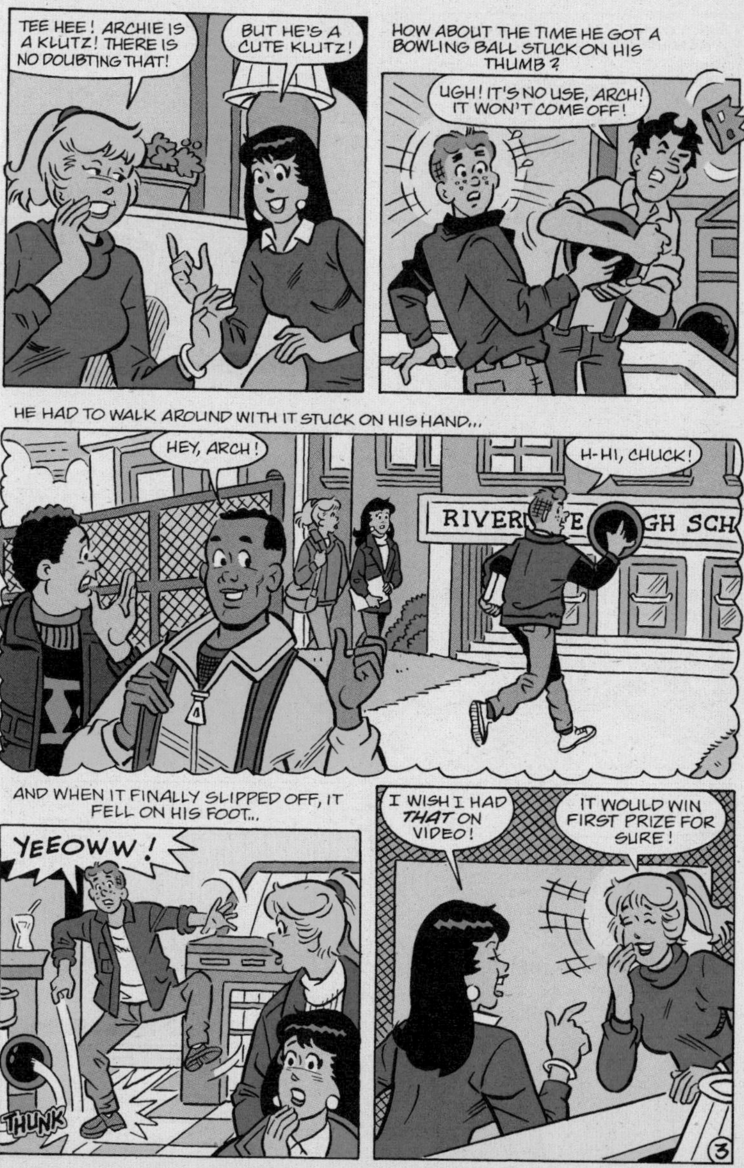
TEE HEE! ARCHIE IS A KLUTZ! THERE IS NO DOUBTING THAT!
BUT HE'S A CUTE KLUTZ!
HOW ABOUT THE TIME HE GOT A BOWLING BALL STUCK ON HIS THUMB?
UGH! IT'S NO USE, ARCH! IT WON'T COME OFF!
HE HAD TO WALK AROUND WITH IT STUCK ON HIS HAND...
HEY, ARCH!
H-HI, CHUCK!
AND WHEN IT FINALLY SLIPPED OFF, IT FELL ON HIS FOOT...
YEEOWW!
THUNK
I WISH I HAD *THAT* ON VIDEO!
IT WOULD WIN FIRST PRIZE FOR SURE!
3

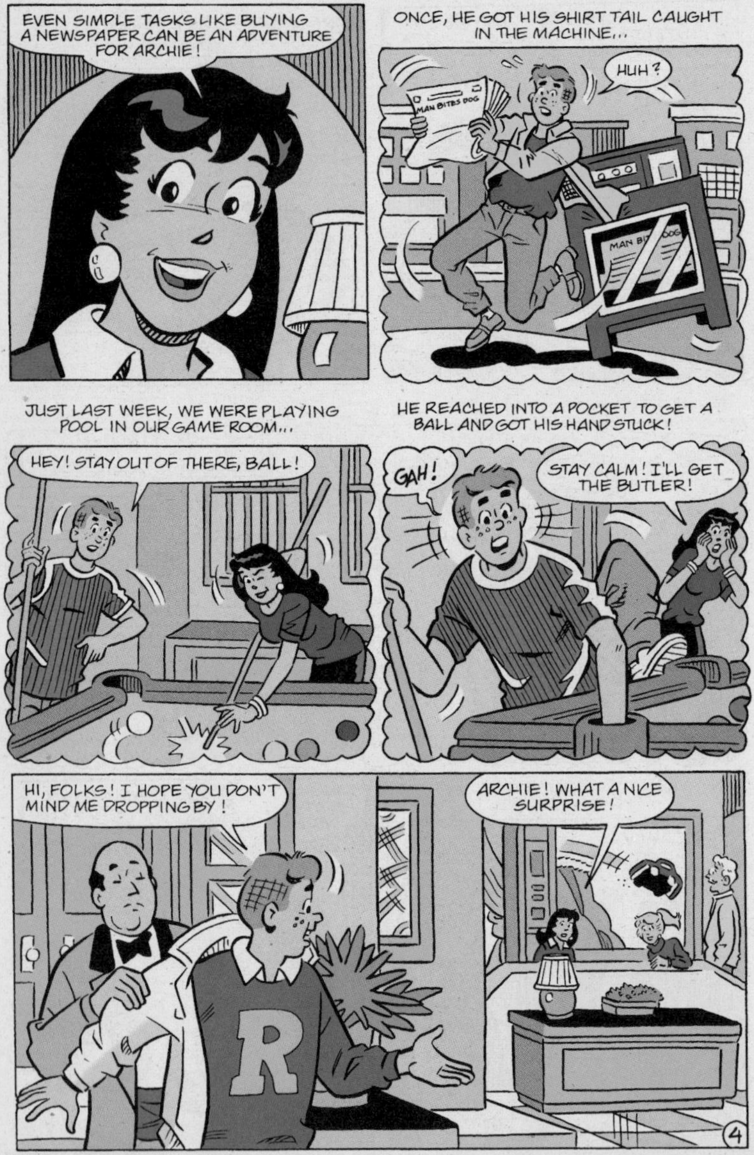
EVEN SIMPLE TASKS LIKE BUYING A NEWSPAPER CAN BE AN ADVENTURE FOR ARCHIE!
ONCE, HE GOT HIS SHIRT TAIL CAUGHT IN THE MACHINE...
MAN BITES DOG
HUH?
JUST LAST WEEK, WE WERE PLAYING POOL IN OUR GAME ROOM...
HEY! STAY OUT OF THERE, BALL!
HE REACHED INTO A POCKET TO GET A BALL AND GOT HIS HAND STUCK!
GAH!
STAY CALM! I'LL GET THE BUTLER!
HI, FOLKS! I HOPE YOU DON'T MIND ME DROPPING BY!
ARCHIE! WHAT A NICE SURPRISE!
R

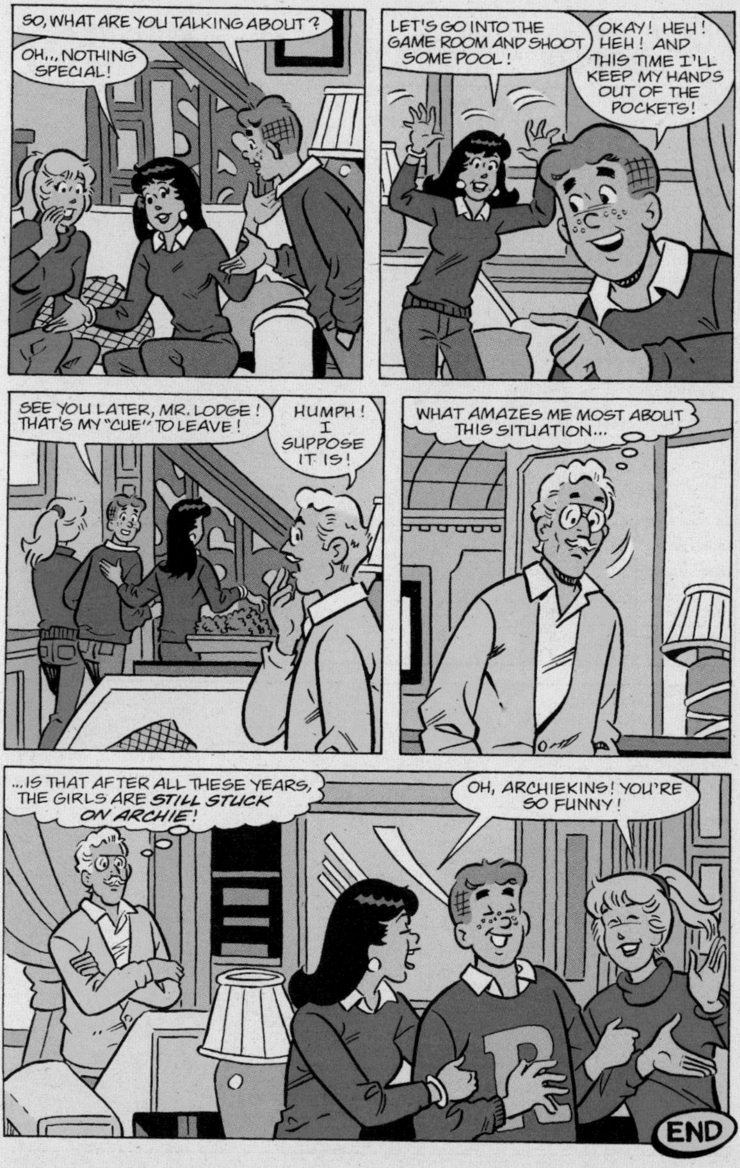
SO, WHAT ARE YOU TALKING ABOUT ?
OH... NOTHING SPECIAL!
LET'S GO INTO THE GAME ROOM AND SHOOT SOME POOL !
OKAY! HEH! HEH! AND THIS TIME I'LL KEEP MY HANDS OUT OF THE POCKETS!
SEE YOU LATER, MR. LODGE! THAT'S MY "CUE" TO LEAVE!
HUMPH! I SUPPOSE IT IS!
WHAT AMAZES ME MOST ABOUT THIS SITUATION...
...IS THAT AFTER ALL THESE YEARS, THE GIRLS ARE STILL STUCK ON ARCHIE!
OH, ARCHIEKINS! YOU'RE SO FUNNY!
END

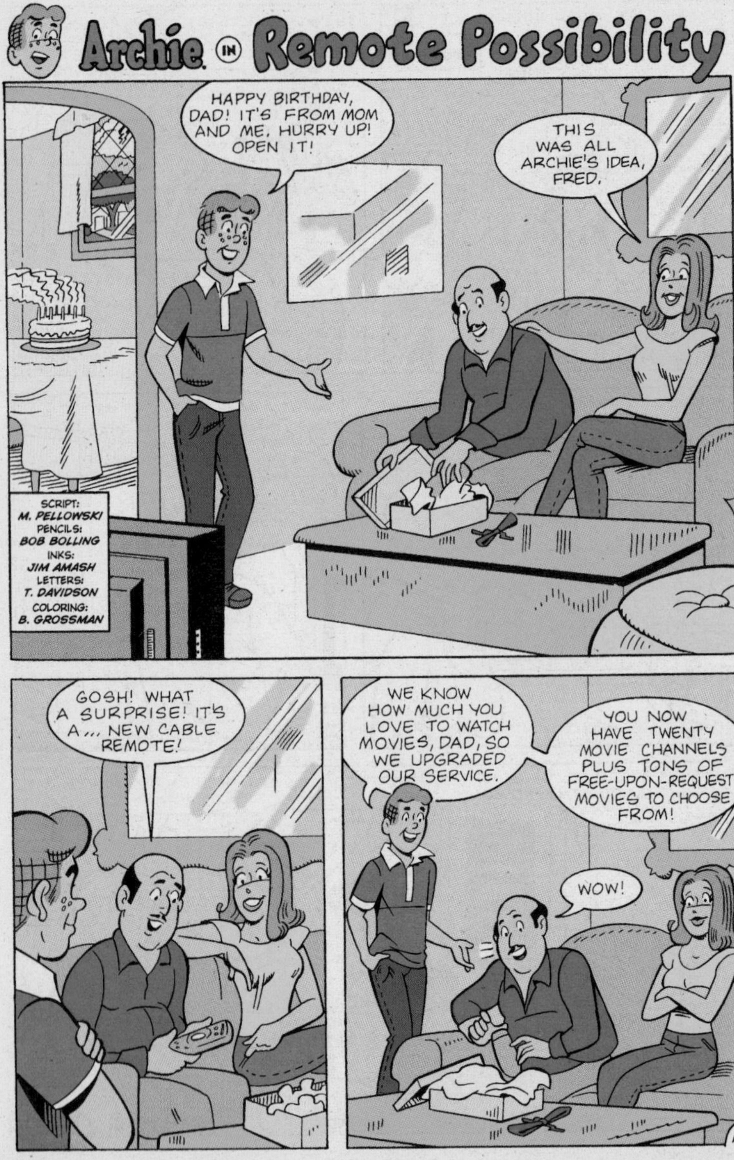
Archie IN Remote Possibility
HAPPY BIRTHDAY, DAD! IT'S FROM MOM AND ME. HURRY UP! OPEN IT!
THIS WAS ALL ARCHIE'S IDEA, FRED.
SCRIPT: M. PELLOWSKI PENCILS: BOB BOLLING INKS: JIM AMASH LETTERS: T. DAVIDSON COLORING: B. GROSSMAN
GOSH! WHAT A SURPRISE! IT'S A... NEW CABLE REMOTE!
WE KNOW HOW MUCH YOU LOVE TO WATCH MOVIES, DAD, SO WE UPGRADED OUR SERVICE.
YOU NOW HAVE TWENTY MOVIE CHANNELS PLUS TONS OF FREE-UPON-REQUEST MOVIES TO CHOOSE FROM!
WOW!

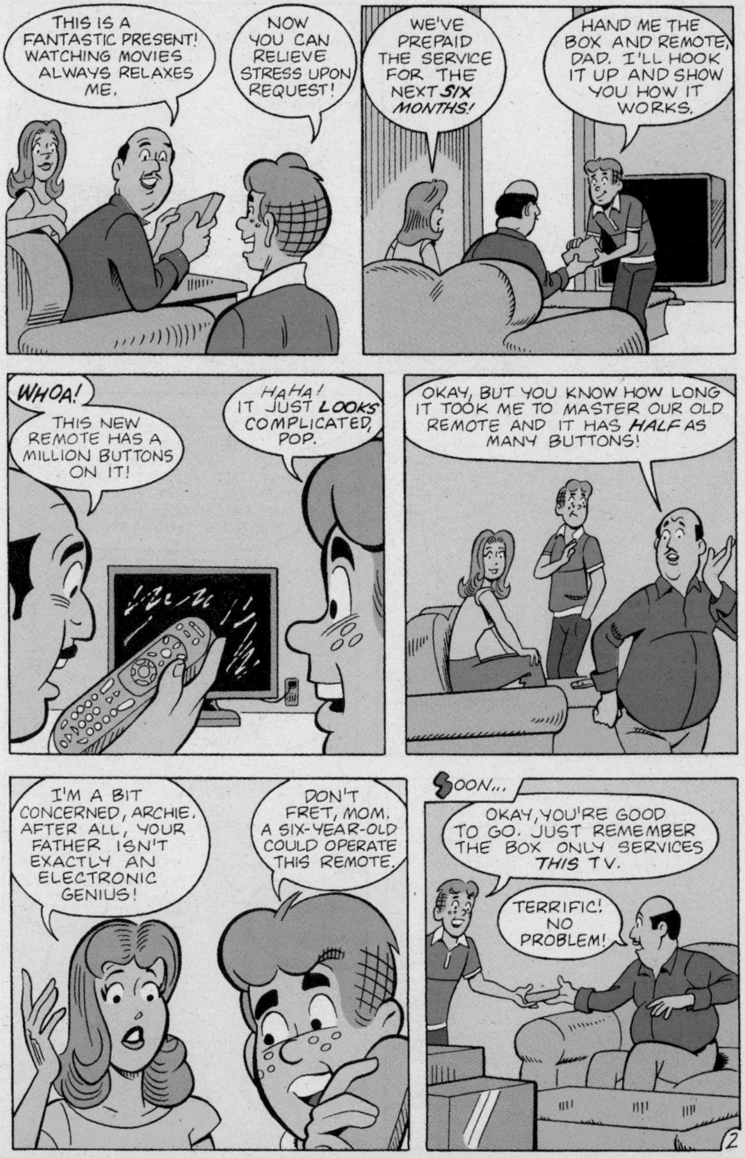
THIS IS A FANTASTIC PRESENT! WATCHING MOVIES ALWAYS RELAXES ME.
NOW YOU CAN RELIEVE STRESS UPON REQUEST!
WE'VE PREPAID THE SERVICE FOR THE NEXT SIX MONTHS!
HAND ME THE BOX AND REMOTE, DAD. I'LL HOOK IT UP AND SHOW YOU HOW IT WORKS.
WHOA!
THIS NEW REMOTE HAS A MILLION BUTTONS ON IT!
HAHA! IT JUST LOOKS COMPLICATED, POP.
OKAY, BUT YOU KNOW HOW LONG IT TOOK ME TO MASTER OUR OLD REMOTE AND IT HAS HALF AS MANY BUTTONS!
I'M A BIT CONCERNED, ARCHIE. AFTER ALL, YOUR FATHER ISN'T EXACTLY AN ELECTRONIC GENIUS!
DON'T FRET, MOM. A SIX-YEAR-OLD COULD OPERATE THIS REMOTE.
SOON...
OKAY, YOU'RE GOOD TO GO. JUST REMEMBER THE BOX ONLY SERVICES THIS TV.
TERRIFIC! NO PROBLEM!
2

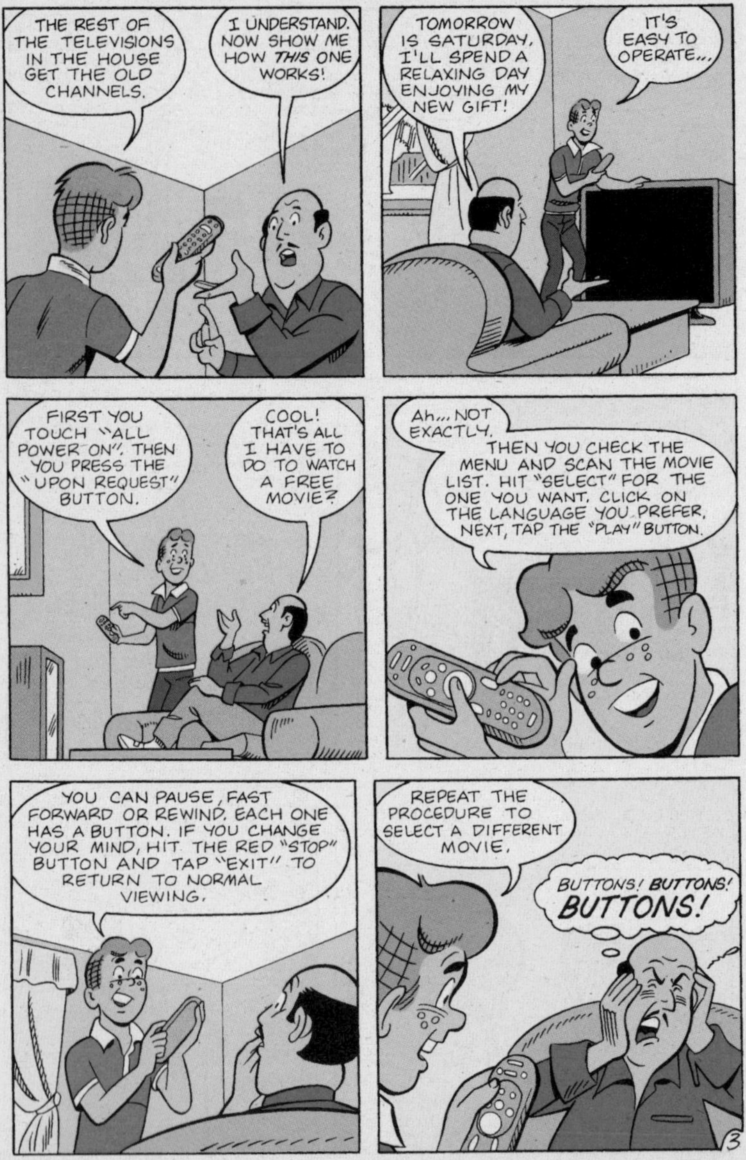
THE REST OF THE TELEVISIONS IN THE HOUSE GET THE OLD CHANNELS.
I UNDERSTAND. NOW SHOW ME HOW *THIS* ONE WORKS!
TOMORROW IS SATURDAY. I'LL SPEND A RELAXING DAY ENJOYING MY NEW GIFT!
IT'S EASY TO OPERATE...
FIRST YOU TOUCH "ALL POWER ON". THEN YOU PRESS THE "UPON REQUEST" BUTTON.
COOL! THAT'S ALL I HAVE TO DO TO WATCH A FREE MOVIE?
Ah... NOT EXACTLY.
THEN YOU CHECK THE MENU AND SCAN THE MOVIE LIST. HIT "SELECT" FOR THE ONE YOU WANT. CLICK ON THE LANGUAGE YOU PREFER. NEXT, TAP THE "PLAY" BUTTON.
YOU CAN PAUSE, FAST FORWARD OR REWIND. EACH ONE HAS A BUTTON. IF YOU CHANGE YOUR MIND, HIT THE RED "STOP" BUTTON AND TAP "EXIT" TO RETURN TO NORMAL VIEWING.
REPEAT THE PROCEDURE TO SELECT A DIFFERENT MOVIE.
BUTTONS! **BUTTONS!** **BUTTONS!**
3

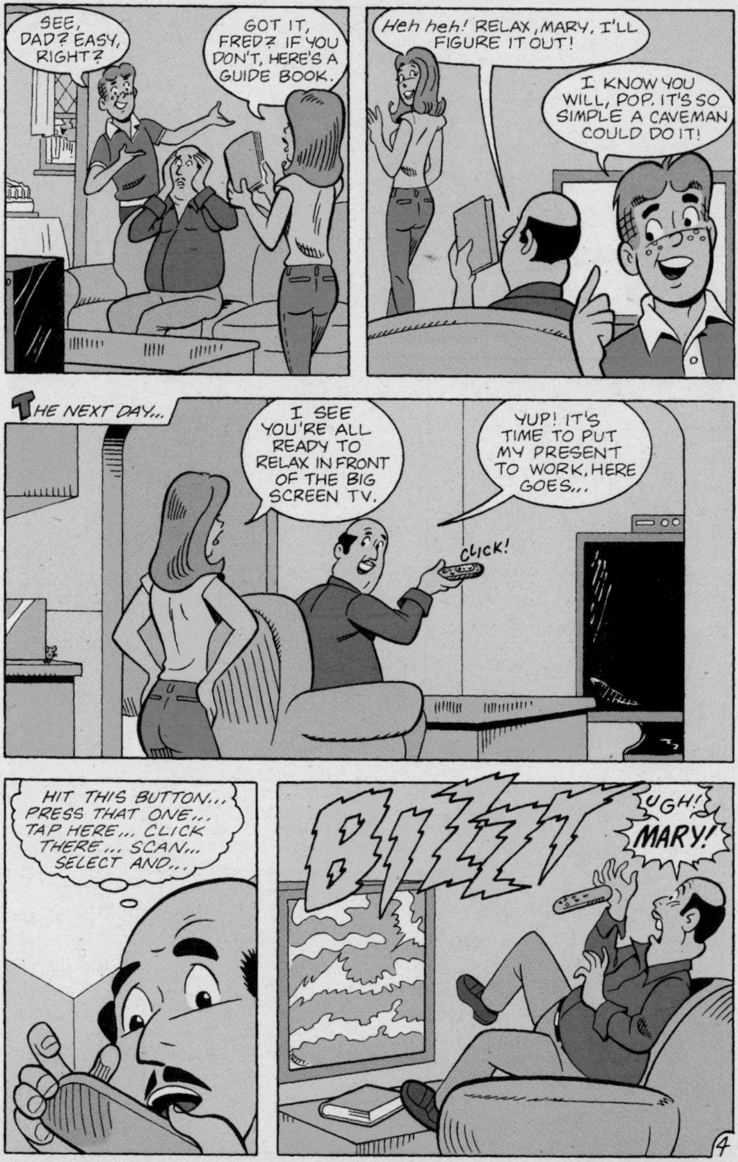
SEE, DAD? EASY, RIGHT?
GOT IT, FRED? IF YOU DON'T, HERE'S A GUIDE BOOK.
Heh heh! RELAX, MARY, I'LL FIGURE IT OUT!
I KNOW YOU WILL, POP. IT'S SO SIMPLE A CAVEMAN COULD DO IT!
THE NEXT DAY...
I SEE YOU'RE ALL READY TO RELAX IN FRONT OF THE BIG SCREEN TV.
YUP! IT'S TIME TO PUT MY PRESENT TO WORK. HERE GOES...
CLICK!
HIT THIS BUTTON... PRESS THAT ONE... TAP HERE... CLICK THERE... SCAN... SELECT AND...
BIZZT
UGH!
MARY!

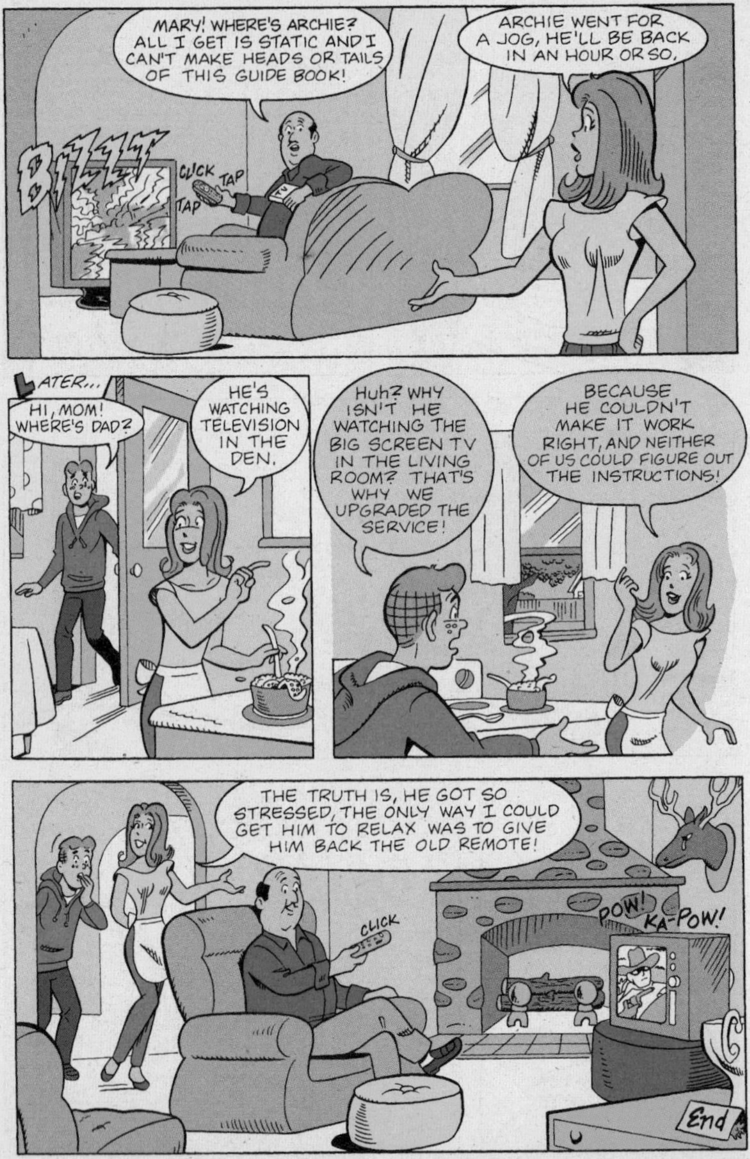
MARY! WHERE'S ARCHIE? ALL I GET IS STATIC AND I CAN'T MAKE HEADS OR TAILS OF THIS GUIDE BOOK!
ARCHIE WENT FOR A JOG, HE'LL BE BACK IN AN HOUR OR SO.
BIZZT
CLICK
TAP
TAP
LATER...
HI, MOM! WHERE'S DAD?
HE'S WATCHING TELEVISION IN THE DEN.
Huh? WHY ISN'T HE WATCHING THE BIG SCREEN TV IN THE LIVING ROOM? THAT'S WHY WE UPGRADED THE SERVICE!
BECAUSE HE COULDN'T MAKE IT WORK RIGHT, AND NEITHER OF US COULD FIGURE OUT THE INSTRUCTIONS!
THE TRUTH IS, HE GOT SO STRESSED, THE ONLY WAY I COULD GET HIM TO RELAX WAS TO GIVE HIM BACK THE OLD REMOTE!
CLICK
POW!
KA-POW!
End

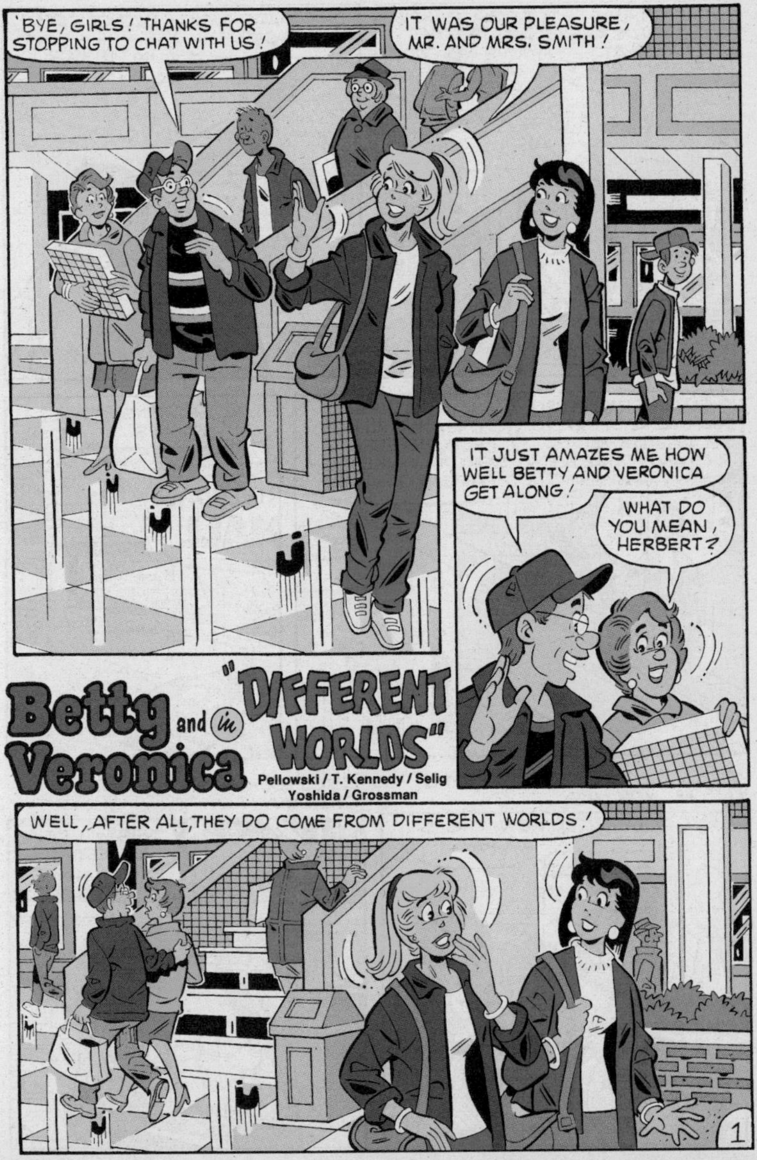
'BYE, GIRLS! THANKS FOR STOPPING TO CHAT WITH US!
IT WAS OUR PLEASURE, MR. AND MRS. SMITH!
Betty and Veronica in "DIFFERENT WORLDS"
Pellowski / T. Kennedy / Selig
Yoshida / Grossman
IT JUST AMAZES ME HOW WELL BETTY AND VERONICA GET ALONG!
WHAT DO YOU MEAN, HERBERT?
WELL, AFTER ALL, THEY DO COME FROM DIFFERENT WORLDS!
1

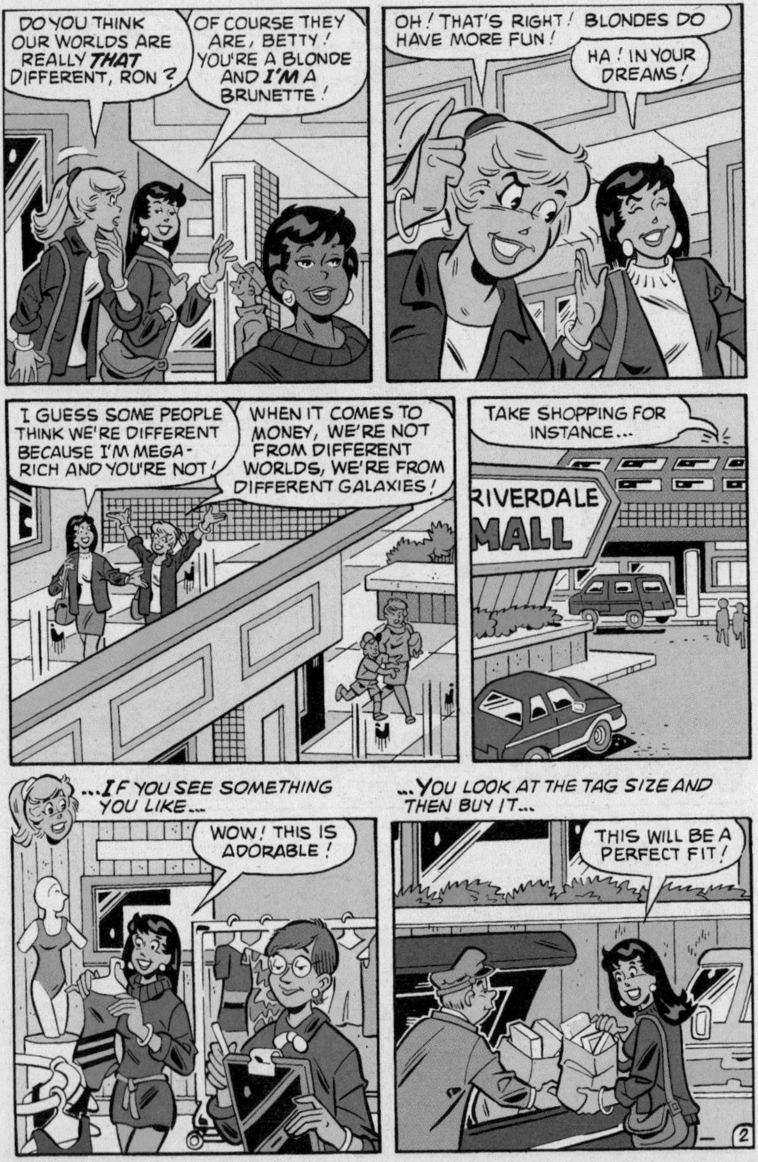
DO YOU THINK OUR WORLDS ARE REALLY THAT DIFFERENT, RON ?
OF COURSE THEY ARE, BETTY ! YOU'RE A BLONDE AND I'M A BRUNETTE !
OH ! THAT'S RIGHT ! BLONDES DO HAVE MORE FUN !
HA ! IN YOUR DREAMS !
I GUESS SOME PEOPLE THINK WE'RE DIFFERENT BECAUSE I'M MEGA-RICH AND YOU'RE NOT !
WHEN IT COMES TO MONEY, WE'RE NOT FROM DIFFERENT WORLDS, WE'RE FROM DIFFERENT GALAXIES !
TAKE SHOPPING FOR INSTANCE...
RIVERDALE MALL
...IF YOU SEE SOMETHING YOU LIKE...
WOW ! THIS IS ADORABLE !
...YOU LOOK AT THE TAG SIZE AND THEN BUY IT...
THIS WILL BE A PERFECT FIT !
2

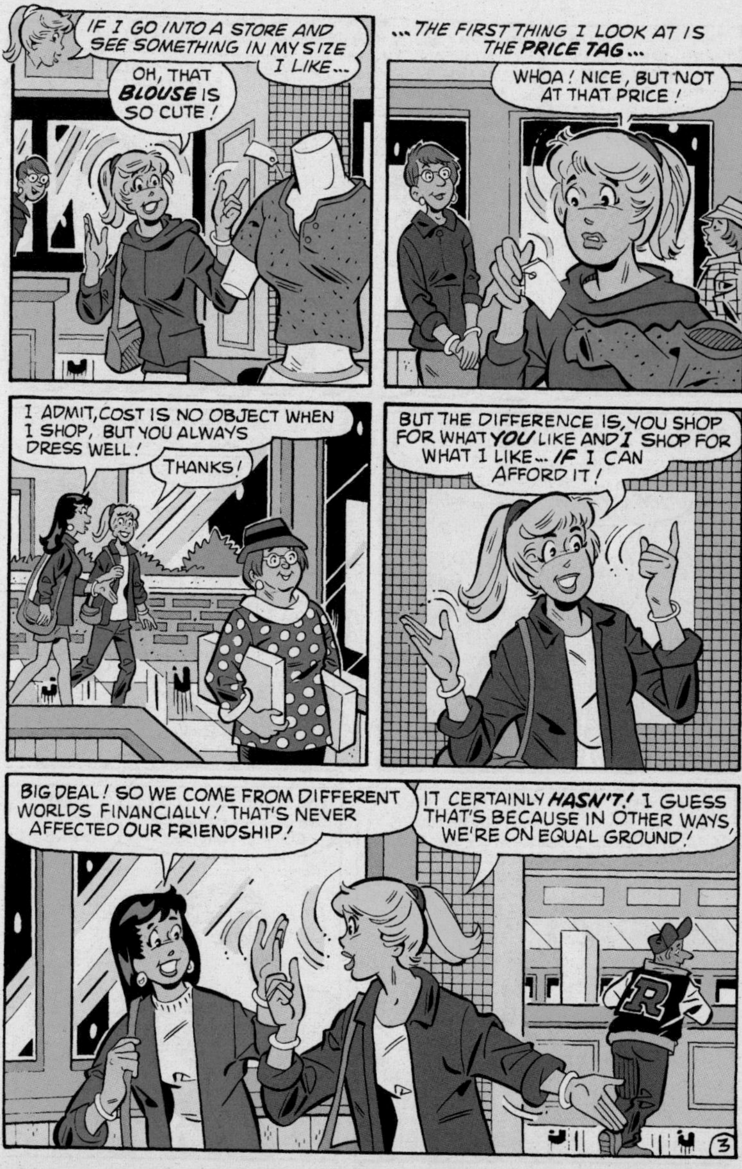
IF I GO INTO A STORE AND SEE SOMETHING IN MY SIZE I LIKE...
OH, THAT BLOUSE IS SO CUTE!
...THE FIRST THING I LOOK AT IS THE PRICE TAG...
WHOA! NICE, BUT NOT AT THAT PRICE!
I ADMIT, COST IS NO OBJECT WHEN I SHOP, BUT YOU ALWAYS DRESS WELL!
THANKS!
BUT THE DIFFERENCE IS, YOU SHOP FOR WHAT YOU LIKE AND I SHOP FOR WHAT I LIKE... IF I CAN AFFORD IT!
BIG DEAL! SO WE COME FROM DIFFERENT WORLDS FINANCIALLY! THAT'S NEVER AFFECTED OUR FRIENDSHIP!
IT CERTAINLY HASN'T! I GUESS THAT'S BECAUSE IN OTHER WAYS, WE'RE ON EQUAL GROUND!
3

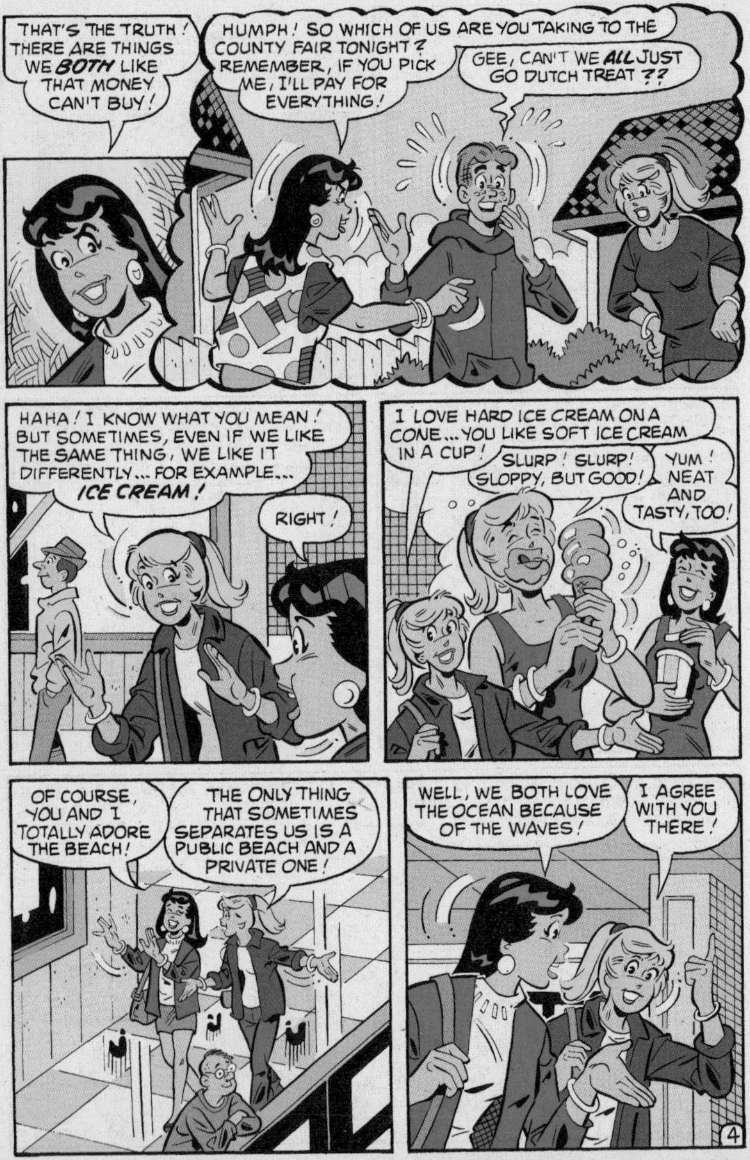
THAT'S THE TRUTH! THERE ARE THINGS WE BOTH LIKE THAT MONEY CAN'T BUY!
HUMPH! SO WHICH OF US ARE YOU TAKING TO THE COUNTY FAIR TONIGHT? REMEMBER, IF YOU PICK ME, I'LL PAY FOR EVERYTHING!
GEE, CAN'T WE ALL JUST GO DUTCH TREAT??
HAHA! I KNOW WHAT YOU MEAN! BUT SOMETIMES, EVEN IF WE LIKE THE SAME THING, WE LIKE IT DIFFERENTLY... FOR EXAMPLE... ICE CREAM!
RIGHT!
I LOVE HARD ICE CREAM ON A CONE... YOU LIKE SOFT ICE CREAM IN A CUP!
SLURP! SLURP! SLOPPY, BUT GOOD!
YUM! NEAT AND TASTY, TOO!
OF COURSE, YOU AND I TOTALLY ADORE THE BEACH!
THE ONLY THING THAT SOMETIMES SEPARATES US IS A PUBLIC BEACH AND A PRIVATE ONE!
WELL, WE BOTH LOVE THE OCEAN BECAUSE OF THE WAVES!
I AGREE WITH YOU THERE!
4

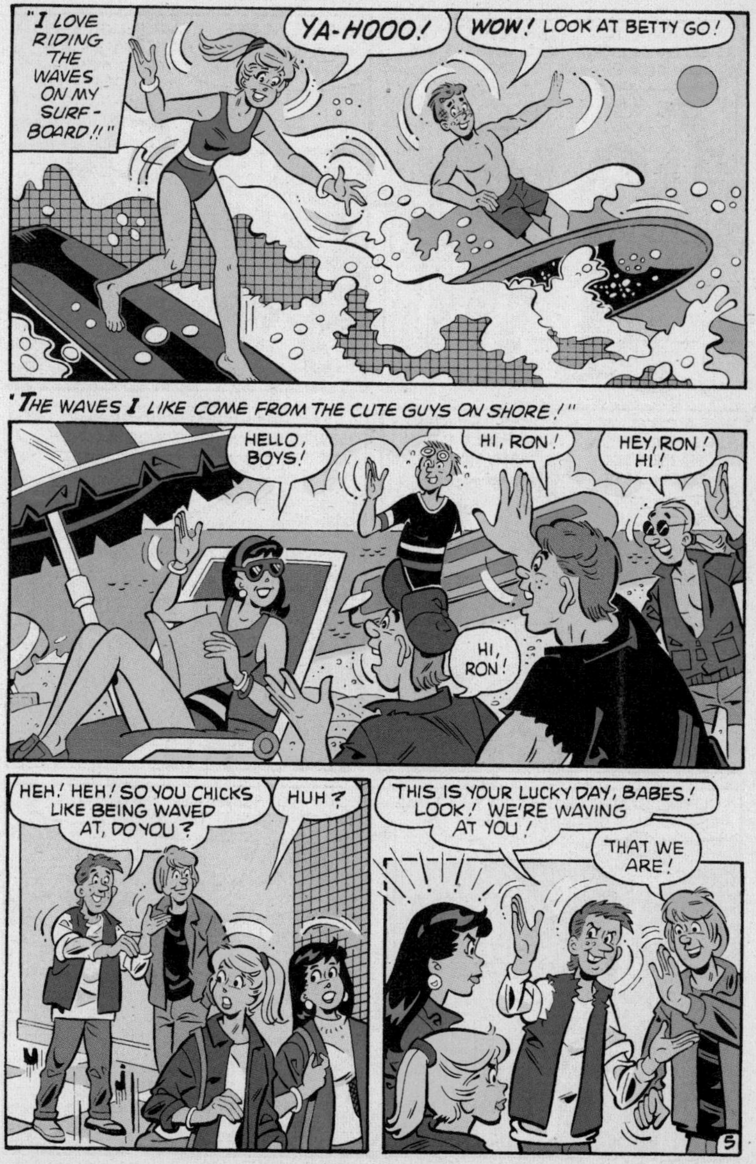
"I LOVE RIDING THE WAVES ON MY SURF-BOARD!!"
YA-HOOO!
WOW! LOOK AT BETTY GO!
"THE WAVES I LIKE COME FROM THE CUTE GUYS ON SHORE!"
HELLO, BOYS!
HI, RON!
HEY, RON! HI!
HI, RON!
HEH! HEH! SO YOU CHICKS LIKE BEING WAVED AT, DO YOU?
HUH?
THIS IS YOUR LUCKY DAY, BABES! LOOK! WE'RE WAVING AT YOU!
THAT WE ARE!
5

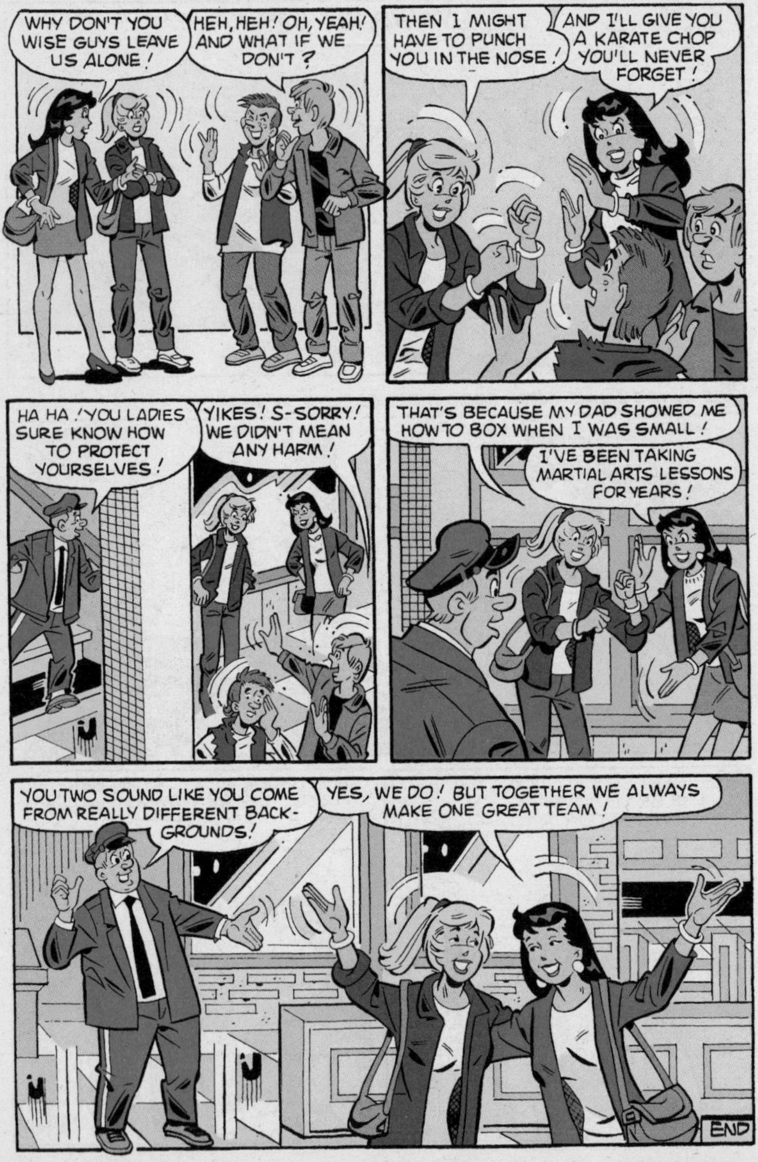

WHY DON'T YOU WISE GUYS LEAVE US ALONE!
HEH, HEH! OH, YEAH! AND WHAT IF WE DON'T?
THEN I MIGHT HAVE TO PUNCH YOU IN THE NOSE!
AND I'LL GIVE YOU A KARATE CHOP YOU'LL NEVER FORGET!
HA HA! YOU LADIES SURE KNOW HOW TO PROTECT YOURSELVES!
YIKES! S-SORRY! WE DIDN'T MEAN ANY HARM!
THAT'S BECAUSE MY DAD SHOWED ME HOW TO BOX WHEN I WAS SMALL!
I'VE BEEN TAKING MARTIAL ARTS LESSONS FOR YEARS!
YOU TWO SOUND LIKE YOU COME FROM REALLY DIFFERENT BACK-GROUNDS!
YES, WE DO! BUT TOGETHER WE ALWAYS MAKE ONE GREAT TEAM!
END

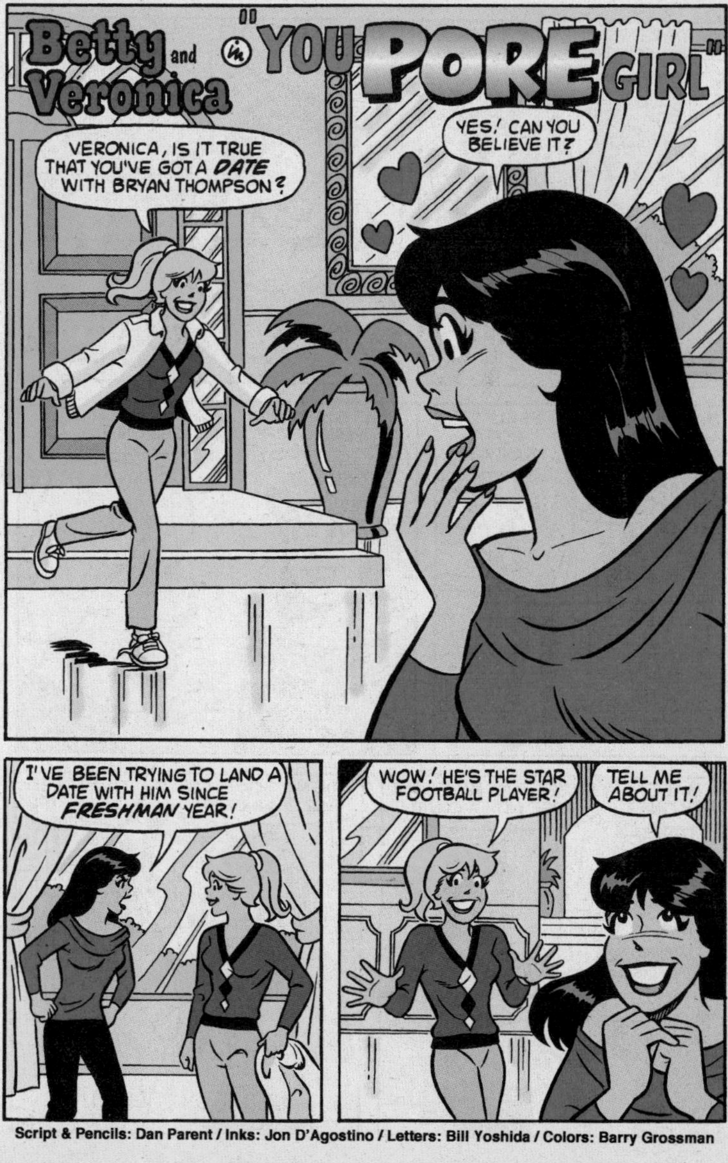
Betty and Veronica in "YOU PORE GIRL"
VERONICA, IS IT TRUE THAT YOU'VE GOT A DATE WITH BRYAN THOMPSON?
YES! CAN YOU BELIEVE IT?
I'VE BEEN TRYING TO LAND A DATE WITH HIM SINCE FRESHMAN YEAR!
WOW! HE'S THE STAR FOOTBALL PLAYER!
TELL ME ABOUT IT!

Script & Pencils: Dan Parent / Inks: Jon D'Agostino / Letters: Bill Yoshida / Colors: Barry Grossman

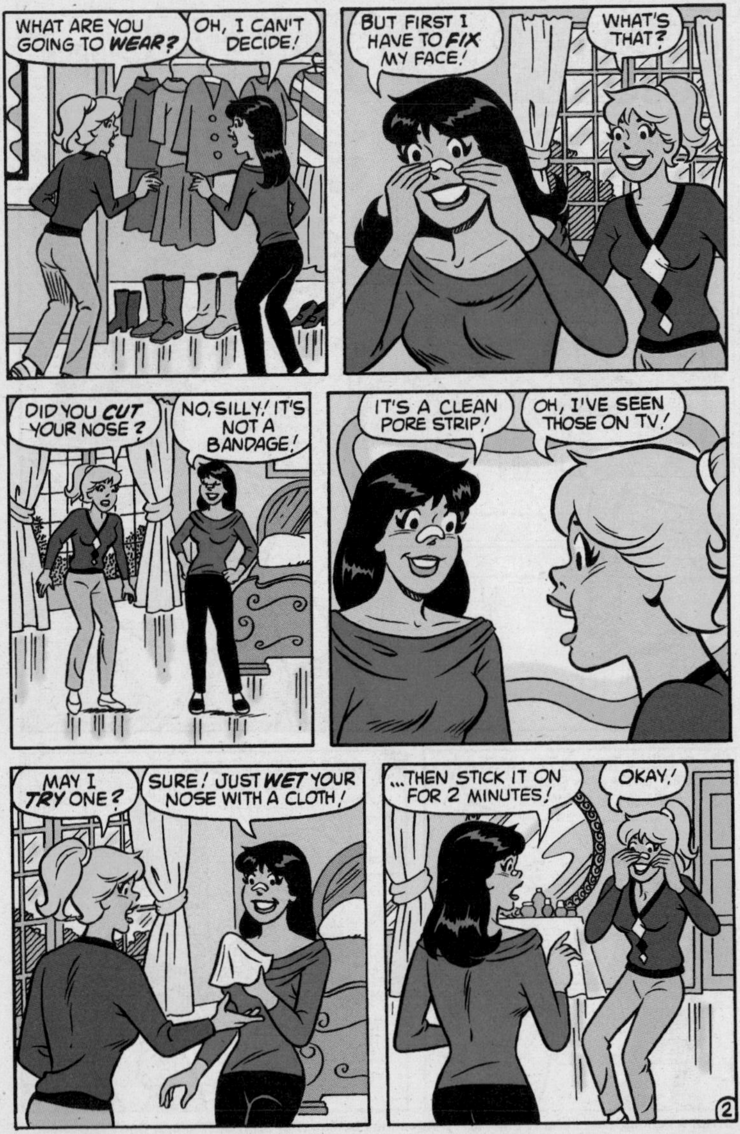
WHAT ARE YOU GOING TO WEAR?
OH, I CAN'T DECIDE!
BUT FIRST I HAVE TO FIX MY FACE!
WHAT'S THAT?
DID YOU CUT YOUR NOSE?
NO, SILLY! IT'S NOT A BANDAGE!
IT'S A CLEAN PORE STRIP!
OH, I'VE SEEN THOSE ON TV!
MAY I TRY ONE?
SURE! JUST WET YOUR NOSE WITH A CLOTH!
...THEN STICK IT ON FOR 2 MINUTES!
OKAY!
2

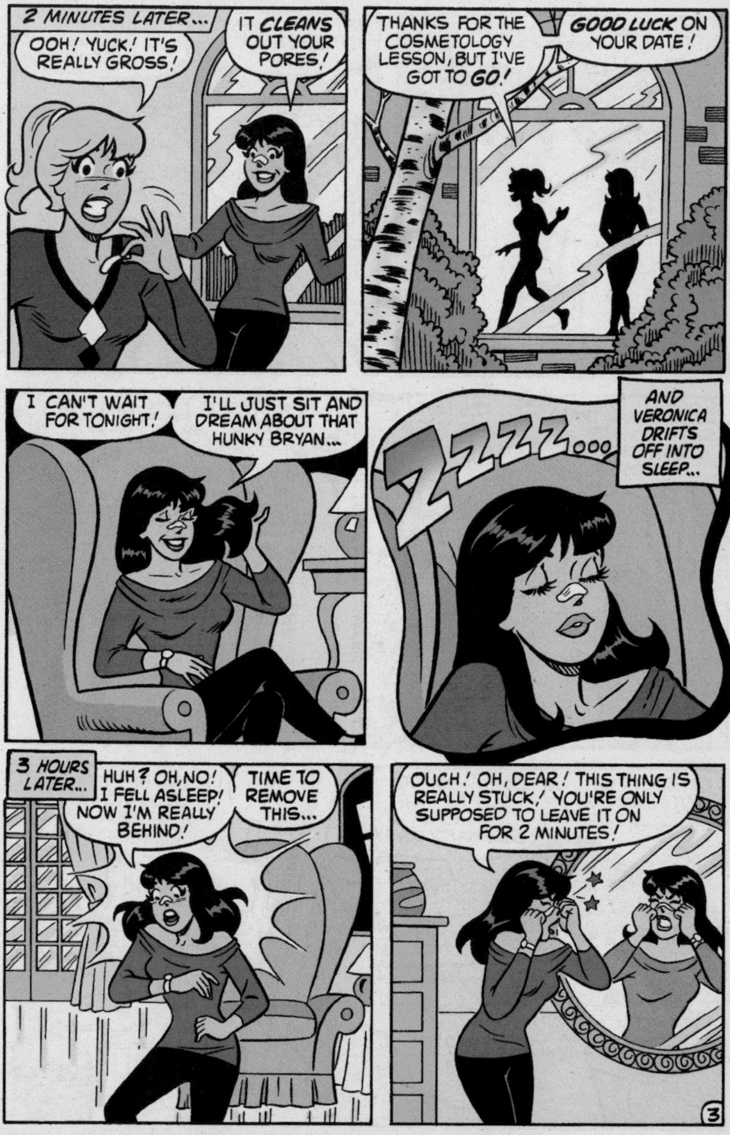
2 MINUTES LATER...
OOH! YUCK! IT'S REALLY GROSS!
IT CLEANS OUT YOUR PORES!
THANKS FOR THE COSMETOLOGY LESSON, BUT I'VE GOT TO GO!
GOOD LUCK ON YOUR DATE!
I CAN'T WAIT FOR TONIGHT!
I'LL JUST SIT AND DREAM ABOUT THAT HUNKY BRYAN...
ZZZZooo
AND VERONICA DRIFTS OFF INTO SLEEP...
3 HOURS LATER...
HUH? OH, NO! I FELL ASLEEP! NOW I'M REALLY BEHIND!
TIME TO REMOVE THIS...
OUCH! OH, DEAR! THIS THING IS REALLY STUCK! YOU'RE ONLY SUPPOSED TO LEAVE IT ON FOR 2 MINUTES!
3

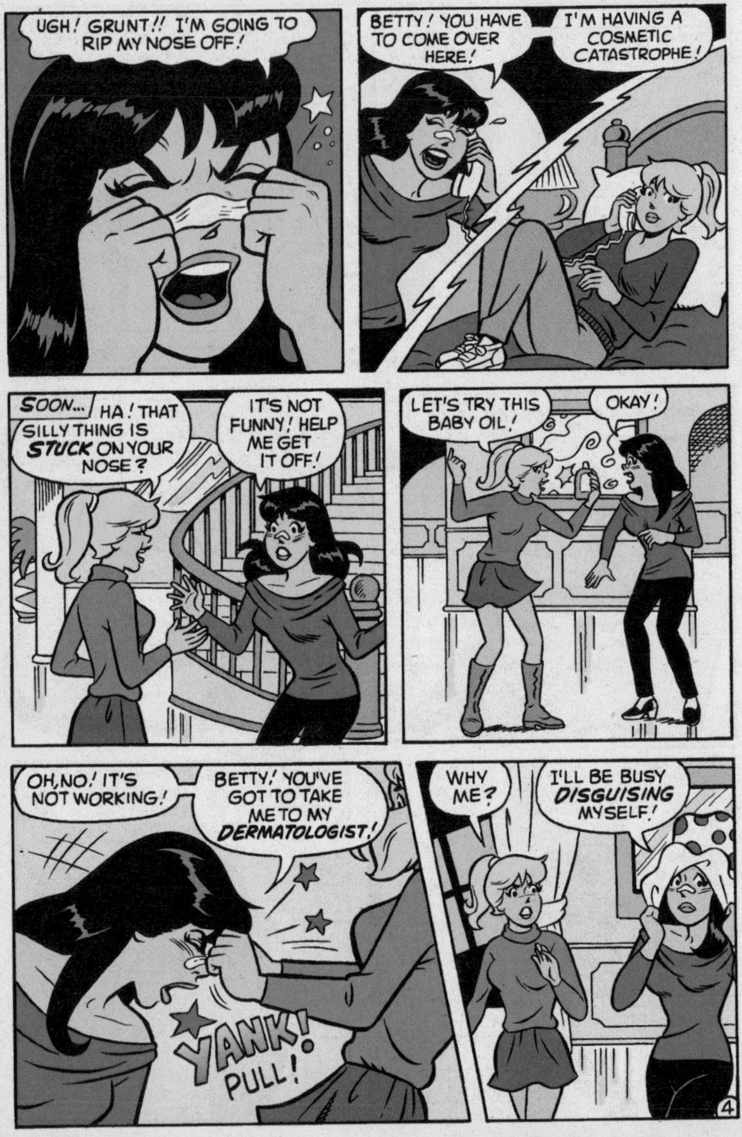
UGH! GRUNT!! I'M GOING TO RIP MY NOSE OFF!
BETTY! YOU HAVE TO COME OVER HERE!
I'M HAVING A COSMETIC CATASTROPHE!
SOON...
HA! THAT SILLY THING IS STUCK ON YOUR NOSE?
IT'S NOT FUNNY! HELP ME GET IT OFF!
LET'S TRY THIS BABY OIL!
OKAY!
OH, NO! IT'S NOT WORKING!
BETTY! YOU'VE GOT TO TAKE ME TO MY DERMATOLOGIST!
YANK!
PULL!
WHY ME?
I'LL BE BUSY DISGUISING MYSELF!
4

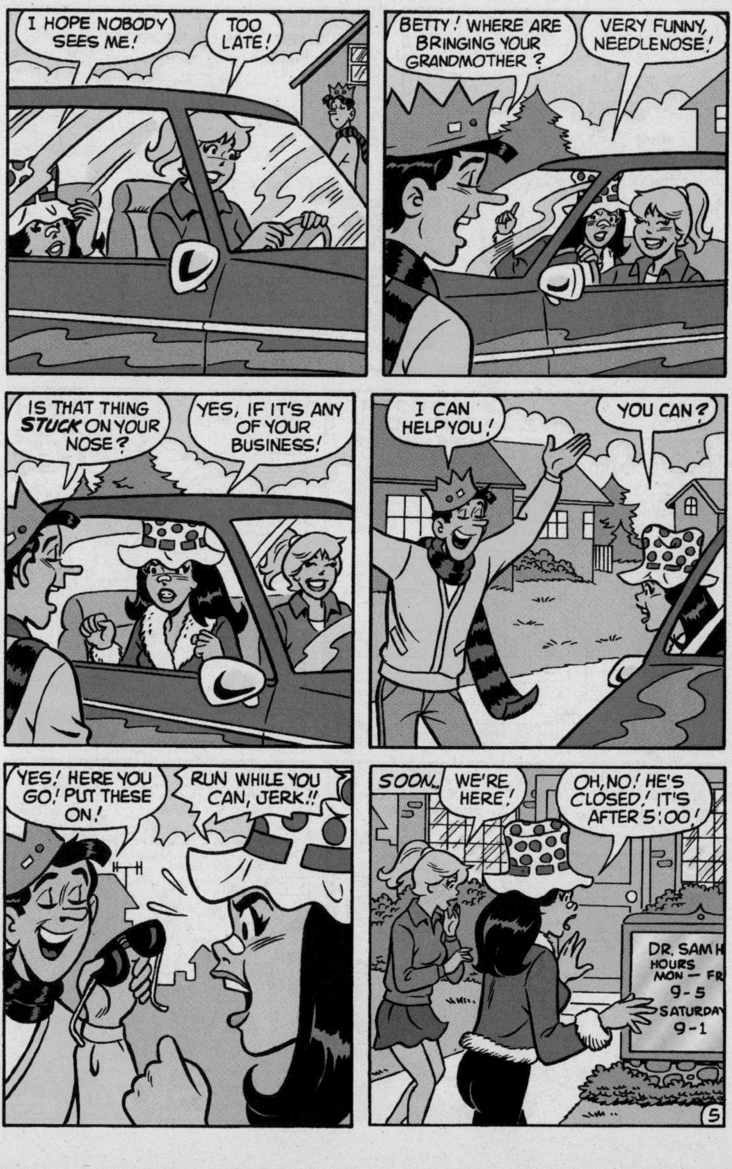

I HOPE NOBODY SEES ME!
TOO LATE!
BETTY! WHERE ARE BRINGING YOUR GRANDMOTHER?
VERY FUNNY, NEEDLENOSE!
IS THAT THING STUCK ON YOUR NOSE?
YES, IF IT'S ANY OF YOUR BUSINESS!
I CAN HELP YOU!
YOU CAN?
YES! HERE YOU GO! PUT THESE ON!
RUN WHILE YOU CAN, JERK!!
SOON...
WE'RE HERE!
OH, NO! HE'S CLOSED! IT'S AFTER 5:00!
DR. SAM H
HOURS
MON — FR
9-5
SATURDA
9-1
5

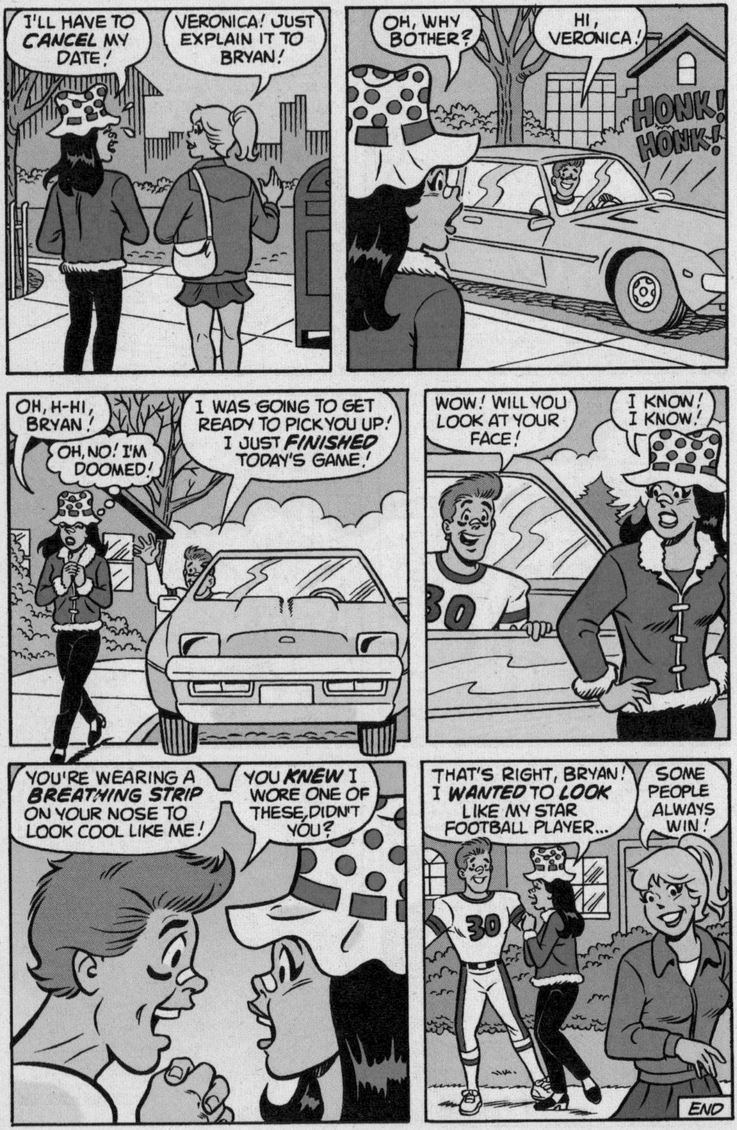
I'LL HAVE TO CANCEL MY DATE!
VERONICA! JUST EXPLAIN IT TO BRYAN!
OH, WHY BOTHER?
HI, VERONICA!
HONK! HONK!
OH, H-HI, BRYAN!
OH, NO! I'M DOOMED!
I WAS GOING TO GET READY TO PICK YOU UP! I JUST FINISHED TODAY'S GAME!
WOW! WILL YOU LOOK AT YOUR FACE!
I KNOW! I KNOW!
YOU'RE WEARING A BREATHING STRIP ON YOUR NOSE TO LOOK COOL LIKE ME!
YOU KNEW I WORE ONE OF THESE, DIDN'T YOU?
THAT'S RIGHT, BRYAN! I WANTED TO LOOK LIKE MY STAR FOOTBALL PLAYER...
SOME PEOPLE ALWAYS WIN!
END

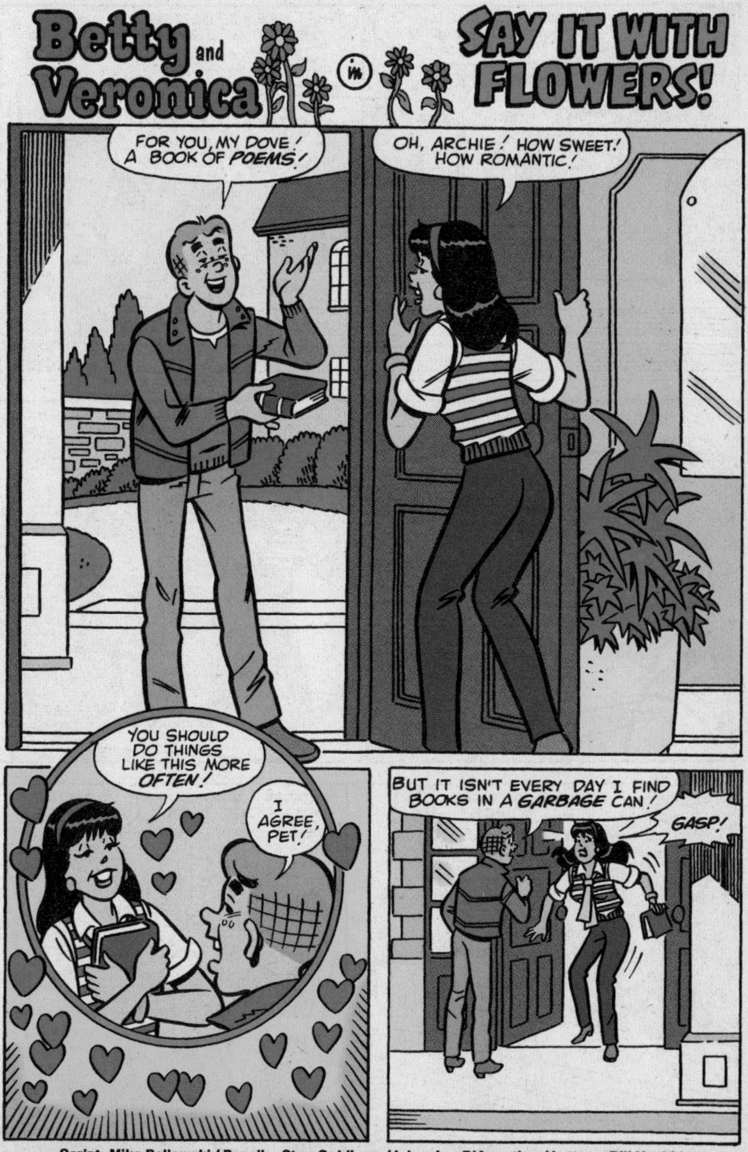
Betty and Veronica in
SAY IT WITH FLOWERS!
FOR YOU, MY DOVE! A BOOK OF POEMS!
OH, ARCHIE! HOW SWEET! HOW ROMANTIC!
YOU SHOULD DO THINGS LIKE THIS MORE OFTEN!
I AGREE, PET!
BUT IT ISN'T EVERY DAY I FIND BOOKS IN A GARBAGE CAN!
GASP!

Script: Mike Pellowski / Pencils: Stan Goldberg / Inks: Jon D'Agostino / Letters: Bill Yoshida

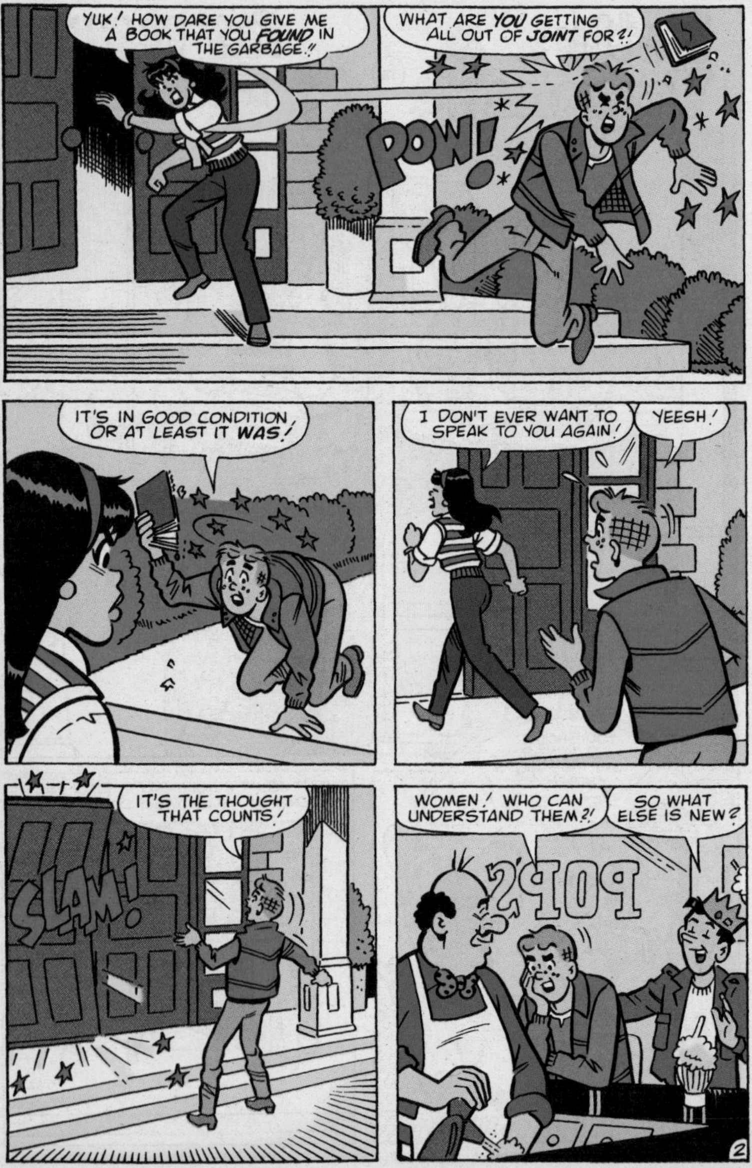
YUK! HOW DARE YOU GIVE ME A BOOK THAT YOU FOUND IN THE GARBAGE!!
WHAT ARE YOU GETTING ALL OUT OF JOINT FOR?!
POW!
IT'S IN GOOD CONDITION, OR AT LEAST IT WAS!
I DON'T EVER WANT TO SPEAK TO YOU AGAIN!
YEESH!
IT'S THE THOUGHT THAT COUNTS!
SLAM!
WOMEN! WHO CAN UNDERSTAND THEM?!
SO WHAT ELSE IS NEW?
POP'S
2

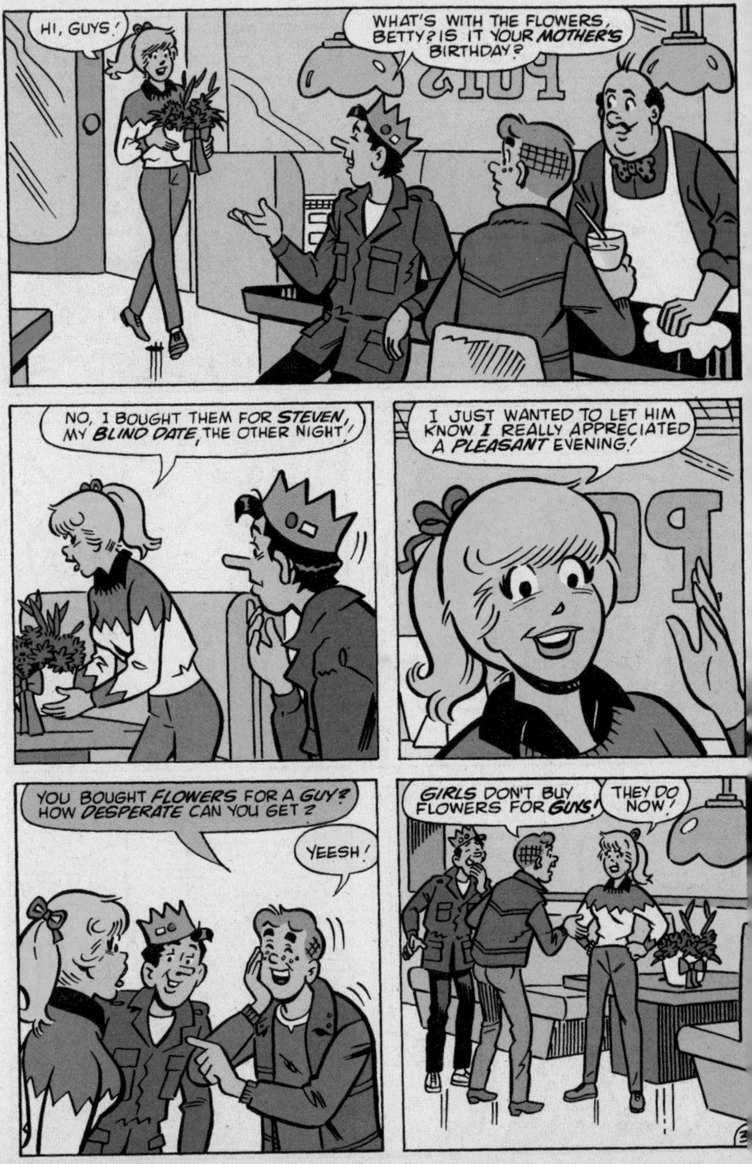
HI, GUYS!
WHAT'S WITH THE FLOWERS, BETTY? IS IT YOUR MOTHER'S BIRTHDAY?
NO, I BOUGHT THEM FOR STEVEN, MY BLIND DATE, THE OTHER NIGHT!
I JUST WANTED TO LET HIM KNOW I REALLY APPRECIATED A PLEASANT EVENING!
YOU BOUGHT FLOWERS FOR A GUY? HOW DESPERATE CAN YOU GET?
YEESH!
GIRLS DON'T BUY FLOWERS FOR GUYS!
THEY DO NOW!
3

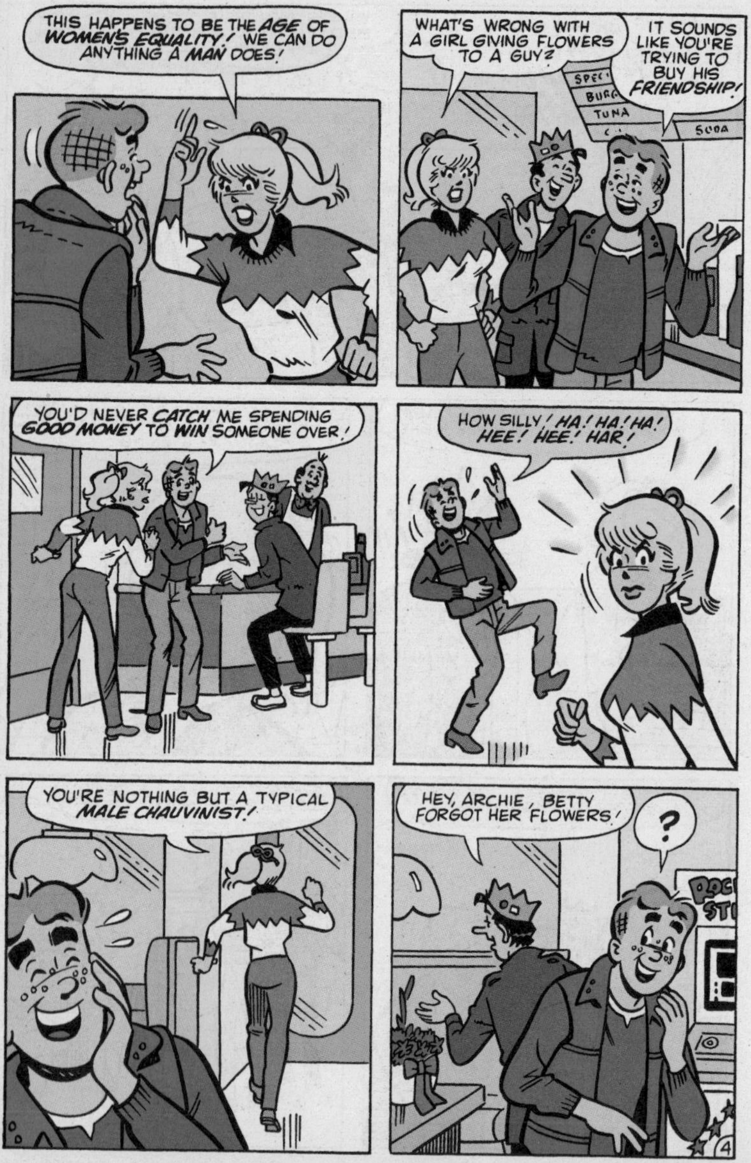
THIS HAPPENS TO BE THE AGE OF WOMEN'S EQUALITY! WE CAN DO ANYTHING A MAN DOES!
WHAT'S WRONG WITH A GIRL GIVING FLOWERS TO A GUY?
IT SOUNDS LIKE YOU'RE TRYING TO BUY HIS FRIENDSHIP!
TUNA
SODA
YOU'D NEVER CATCH ME SPENDING GOOD MONEY TO WIN SOMEONE OVER!
HOW SILLY! HA! HA! HA! HEE! HEE! HAR!
YOU'RE NOTHING BUT A TYPICAL MALE CHAUVINIST!
HEY, ARCHIE, BETTY FORGOT HER FLOWERS!
?
4

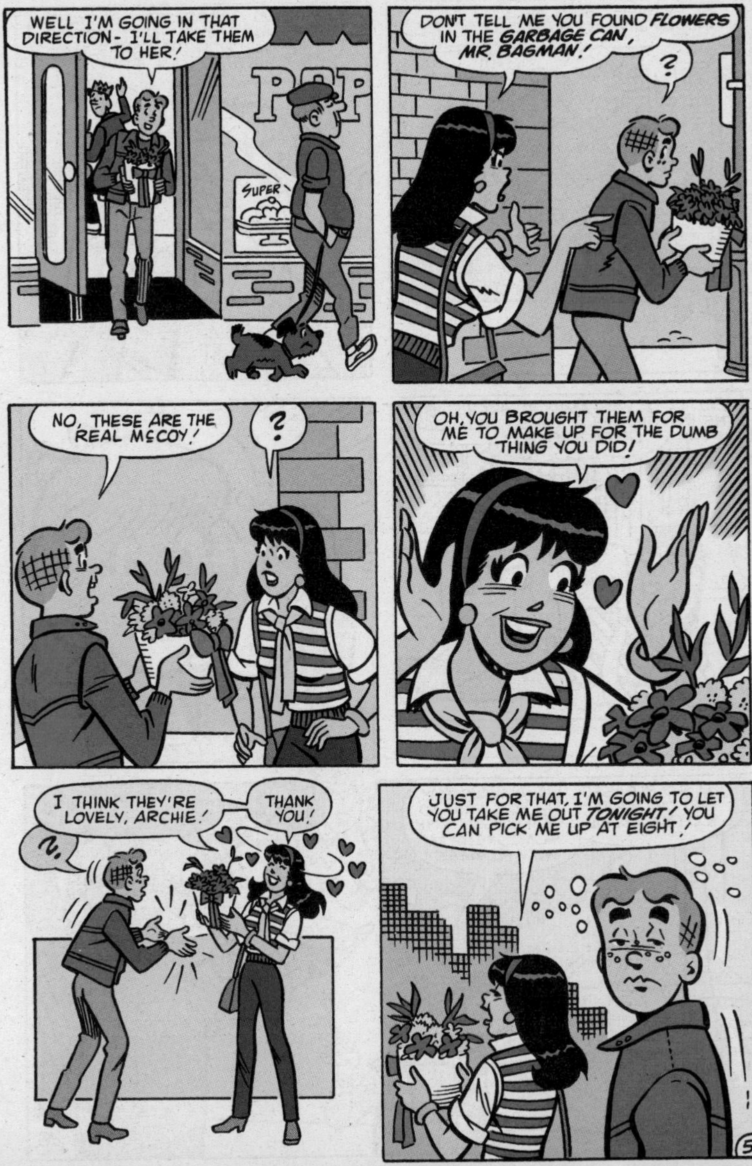
WELL I'M GOING IN THAT DIRECTION - I'LL TAKE THEM TO HER!
POP
SUPER
DON'T TELL ME YOU FOUND FLOWERS IN THE GARBAGE CAN, MR. BAGMAN!
?
NO, THESE ARE THE REAL McCOY!
?
OH, YOU BROUGHT THEM FOR ME TO MAKE UP FOR THE DUMB THING YOU DID!
I THINK THEY'RE LOVELY, ARCHIE!
THANK YOU!
?
JUST FOR THAT, I'M GOING TO LET YOU TAKE ME OUT TONIGHT! YOU CAN PICK ME UP AT EIGHT!
5

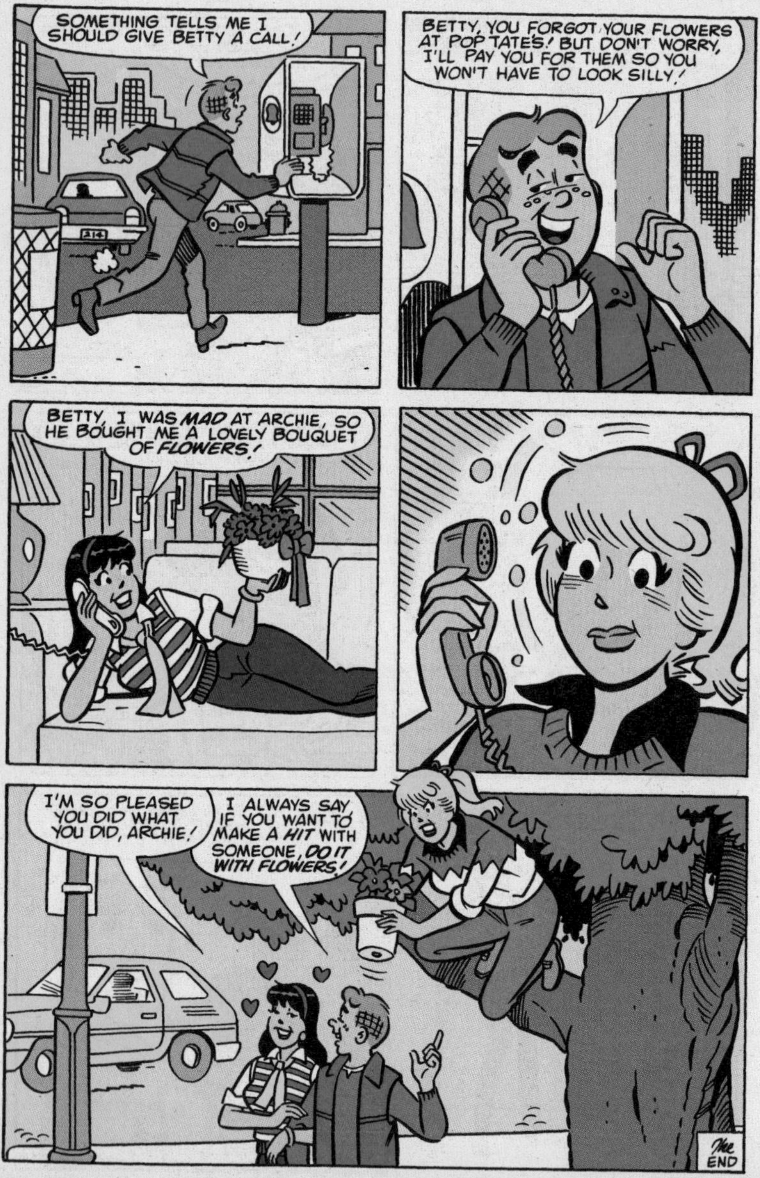
SOMETHING TELLS ME I SHOULD GIVE BETTY A CALL!
BETTY, YOU FORGOT YOUR FLOWERS AT POP TATE'S! BUT DON'T WORRY, I'LL PAY YOU FOR THEM SO YOU WON'T HAVE TO LOOK SILLY!
BETTY, I WAS MAD AT ARCHIE, SO HE BOUGHT ME A LOVELY BOUQUET OF FLOWERS!
I'M SO PLEASED YOU DID WHAT YOU DID, ARCHIE!
I ALWAYS SAY, IF YOU WANT TO MAKE A HIT WITH SOMEONE, DO IT WITH FLOWERS!
The END

Betty IN "THE BODYGUARD"

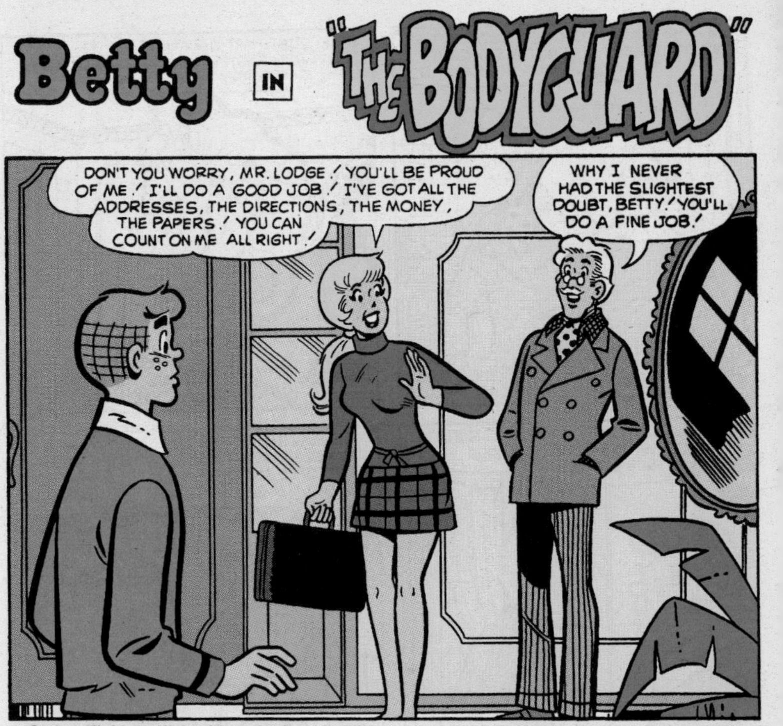
DON'T YOU WORRY, MR. LODGE! YOU'LL BE PROUD OF ME! I'LL DO A GOOD JOB! I'VE GOT ALL THE ADDRESSES, THE DIRECTIONS, THE MONEY, THE PAPERS! YOU CAN COUNT ON ME ALL RIGHT!
WHY I NEVER HAD THE SLIGHTEST DOUBT, BETTY! YOU'LL DO A FINE JOB!

Script: Kathleen Webb / Pencils: Stan Goldberg / Inks: Jon D'Agostino / Letters: Bill Yoshida

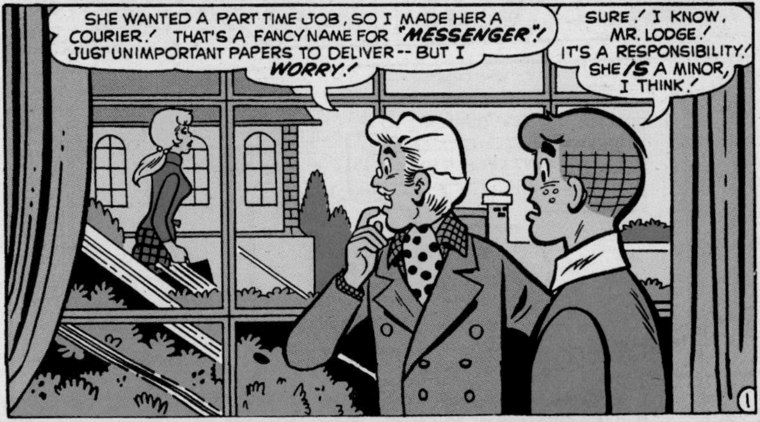
SHE WANTED A PART TIME JOB, SO I MADE HER A COURIER! THAT'S A FANCY NAME FOR "MESSENGER"! JUST UNIMPORTANT PAPERS TO DELIVER -- BUT I WORRY!
SURE! I KNOW, MR. LODGE! IT'S A RESPONSIBILITY! SHE IS A MINOR, I THINK!
1

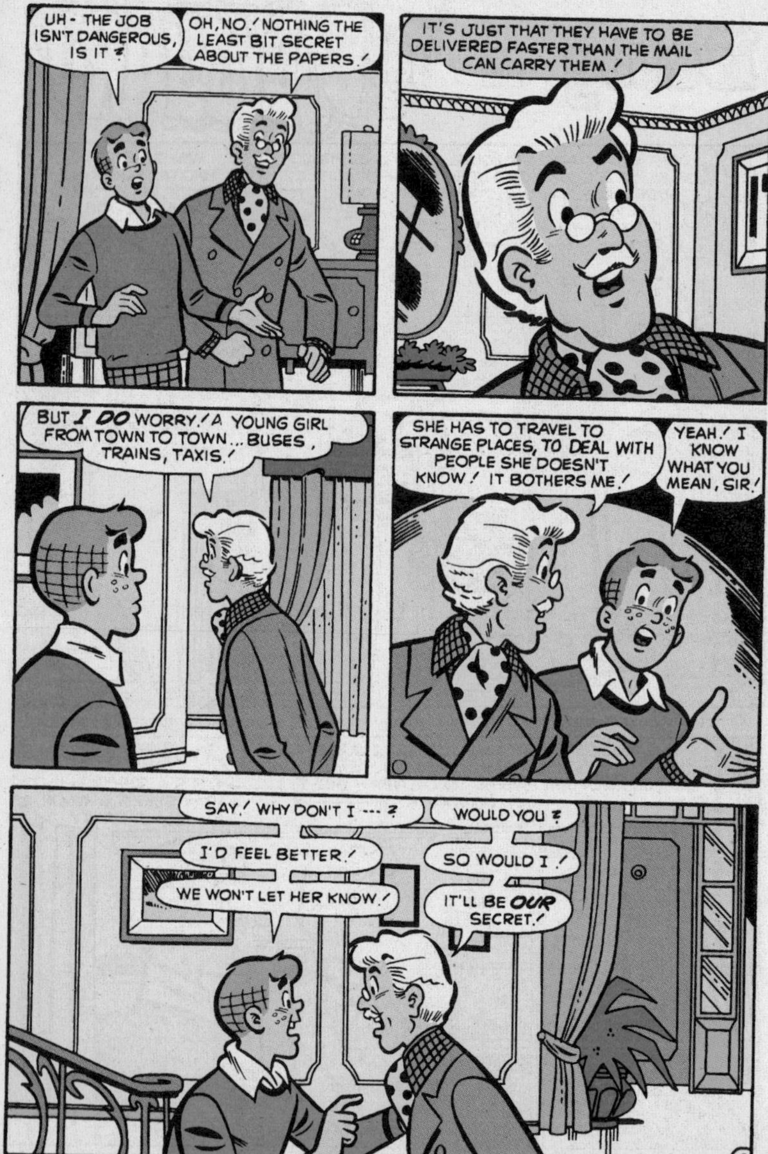

UH - THE JOB ISN'T DANGEROUS, IS IT ?
OH, NO.! NOTHING THE LEAST BIT SECRET ABOUT THE PAPERS.!
IT'S JUST THAT THEY HAVE TO BE DELIVERED FASTER THAN THE MAIL CAN CARRY THEM.!
BUT I DO WORRY.! A YOUNG GIRL FROM TOWN TO TOWN... BUSES, TRAINS, TAXIS.!
SHE HAS TO TRAVEL TO STRANGE PLACES, TO DEAL WITH PEOPLE SHE DOESN'T KNOW.! IT BOTHERS ME.!
YEAH.! I KNOW WHAT YOU MEAN, SIR.!
SAY.! WHY DON'T I --- ?
WOULD YOU ?
I'D FEEL BETTER.!
SO WOULD I.!
WE WON'T LET HER KNOW.!
IT'LL BE OUR SECRET.!
2

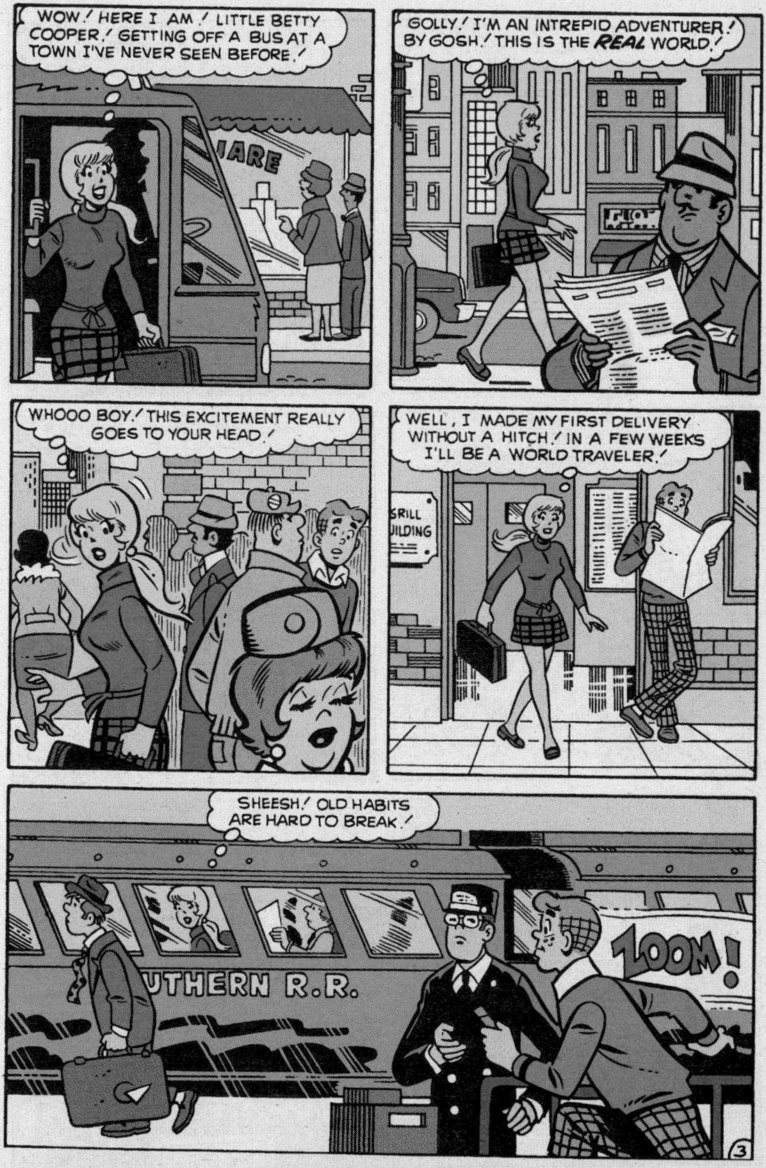
WOW! HERE I AM! LITTLE BETTY COOPER! GETTING OFF A BUS AT A TOWN I'VE NEVER SEEN BEFORE!
GOLLY! I'M AN INTREPID ADVENTURER! BY GOSH! THIS IS THE REAL WORLD!
WHOOO BOY! THIS EXCITEMENT REALLY GOES TO YOUR HEAD!
WELL, I MADE MY FIRST DELIVERY WITHOUT A HITCH! IN A FEW WEEKS I'LL BE A WORLD TRAVELER!
SHEESH! OLD HABITS ARE HARD TO BREAK!
UTHERN R.R.
ZOOM!
3

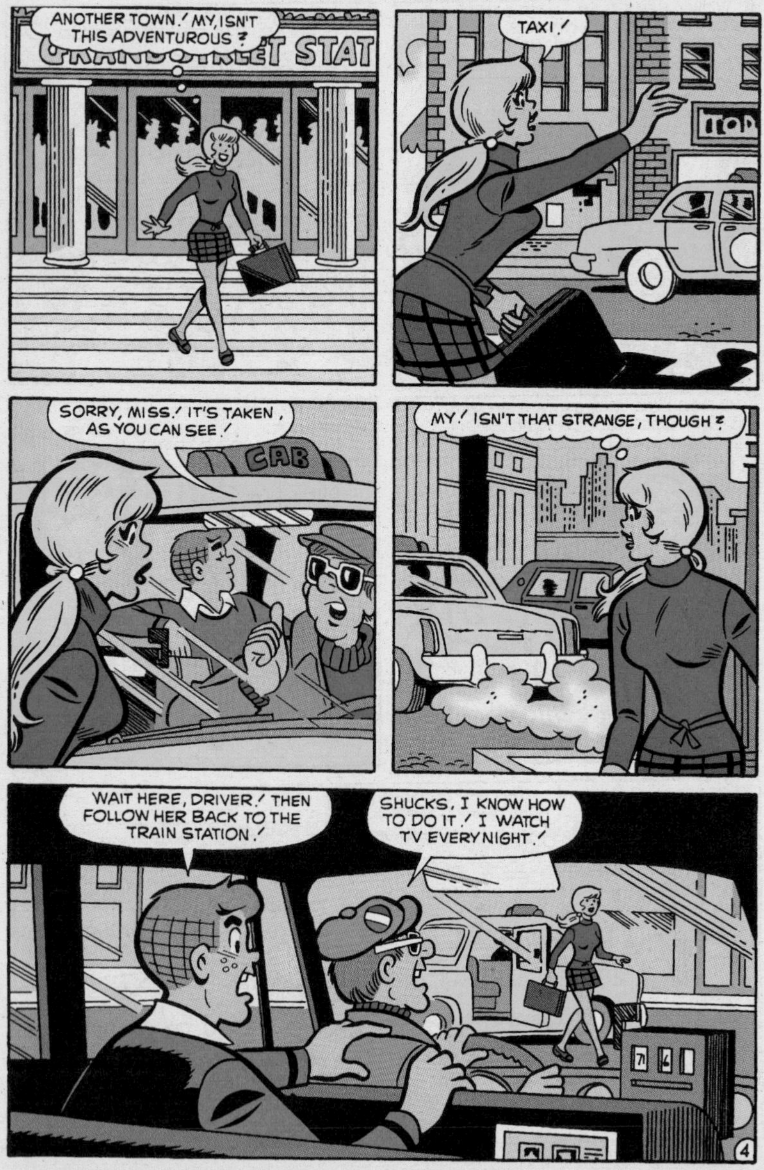
ANOTHER TOWN! MY, ISN'T THIS ADVENTUROUS?
TAXI!
SORRY, MISS! IT'S TAKEN, AS YOU CAN SEE!
CAB
MY! ISN'T THAT STRANGE, THOUGH?
WAIT HERE, DRIVER! THEN FOLLOW HER BACK TO THE TRAIN STATION!
SHUCKS, I KNOW HOW TO DO IT! I WATCH TV EVERY NIGHT!
4

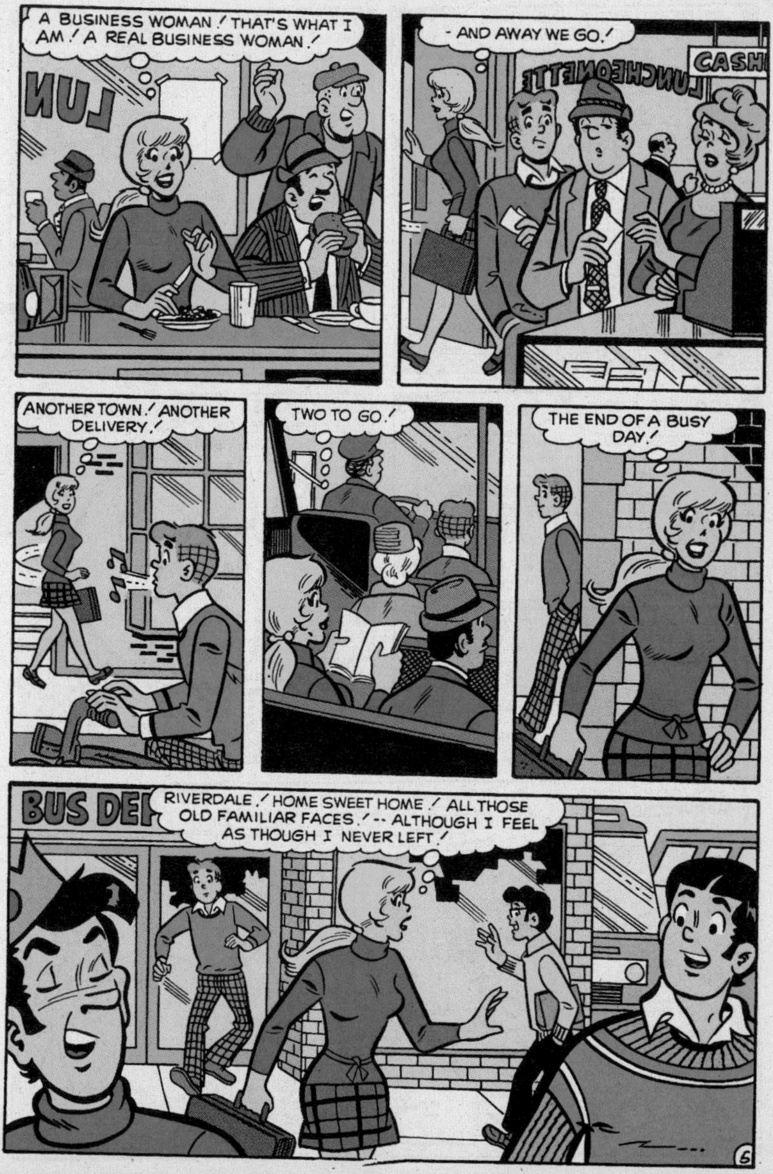
A BUSINESS WOMAN! THAT'S WHAT I AM! A REAL BUSINESS WOMAN!
LUN
- AND AWAY WE GO!
CASH
LUNCHEONETTE
ANOTHER TOWN! ANOTHER DELIVERY!
TWO TO GO!
THE END OF A BUSY DAY!
BUS DEP
RIVERDALE! HOME SWEET HOME! ALL THOSE OLD FAMILIAR FACES! -- ALTHOUGH I FEEL AS THOUGH I NEVER LEFT!
6

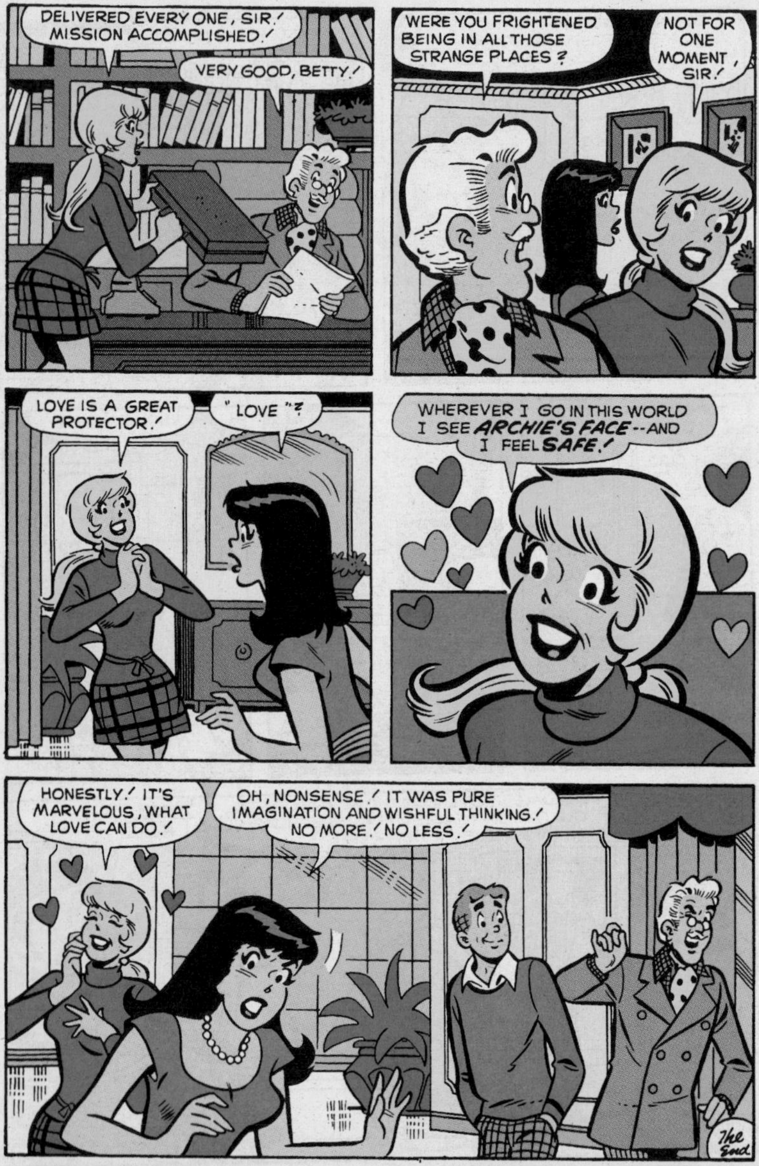
DELIVERED EVERY ONE, SIR! MISSION ACCOMPLISHED!
VERY GOOD, BETTY!
WERE YOU FRIGHTENED BEING IN ALL THOSE STRANGE PLACES?
NOT FOR ONE MOMENT, SIR!
LOVE IS A GREAT PROTECTOR!
"LOVE"?
WHEREVER I GO IN THIS WORLD I SEE ARCHIE'S FACE--AND I FEEL SAFE!
HONESTLY! IT'S MARVELOUS, WHAT LOVE CAN DO!
OH, NONSENSE! IT WAS PURE IMAGINATION AND WISHFUL THINKING! NO MORE! NO LESS!
The End

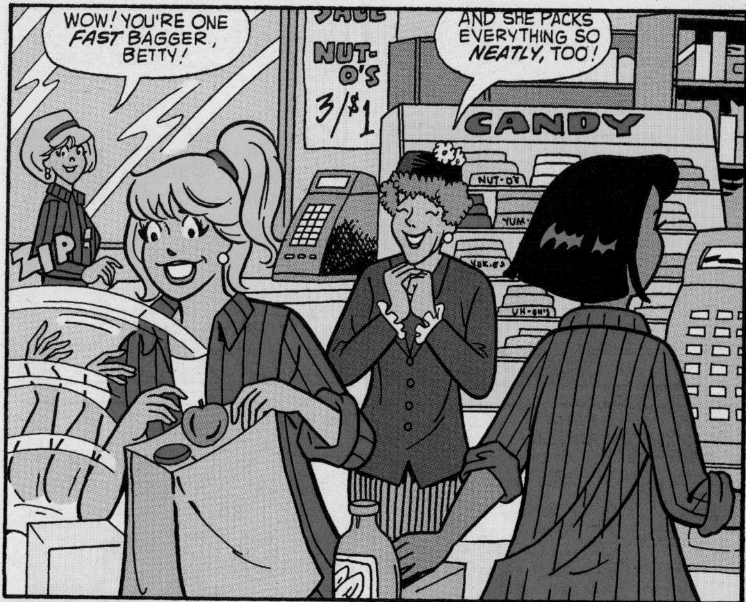
WOW! YOU'RE ONE FAST BAGGER, BETTY!
NUT-O'S 3/$1
CANDY
AND SHE PACKS EVERYTHING SO NEATLY, TOO!
ZIP

Betty and Veronica in IT'S in the BAG!!

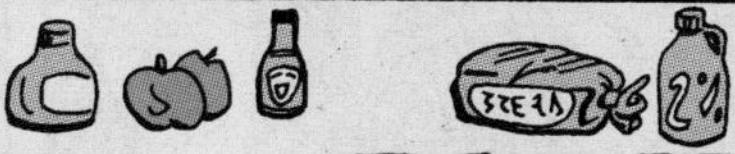

Script & Pencils: Dan Parent / Inks: Alison Flood / Letters: Bill Yoshida / Colors: Barry Grossman

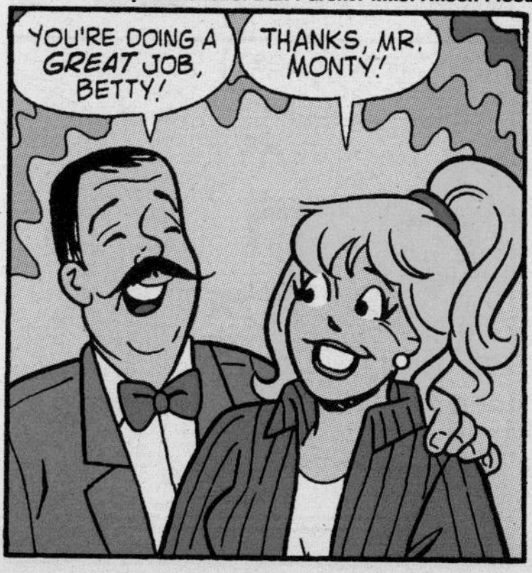
YOU'RE DOING A GREAT JOB, BETTY!
THANKS, MR. MONTY!

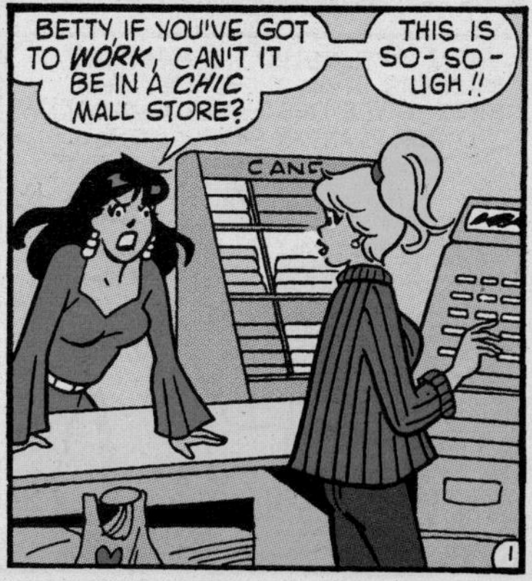
BETTY, IF YOU'VE GOT TO WORK, CAN'T IT BE IN A CHIC MALL STORE?
THIS IS SO- SO- UGH!!
1

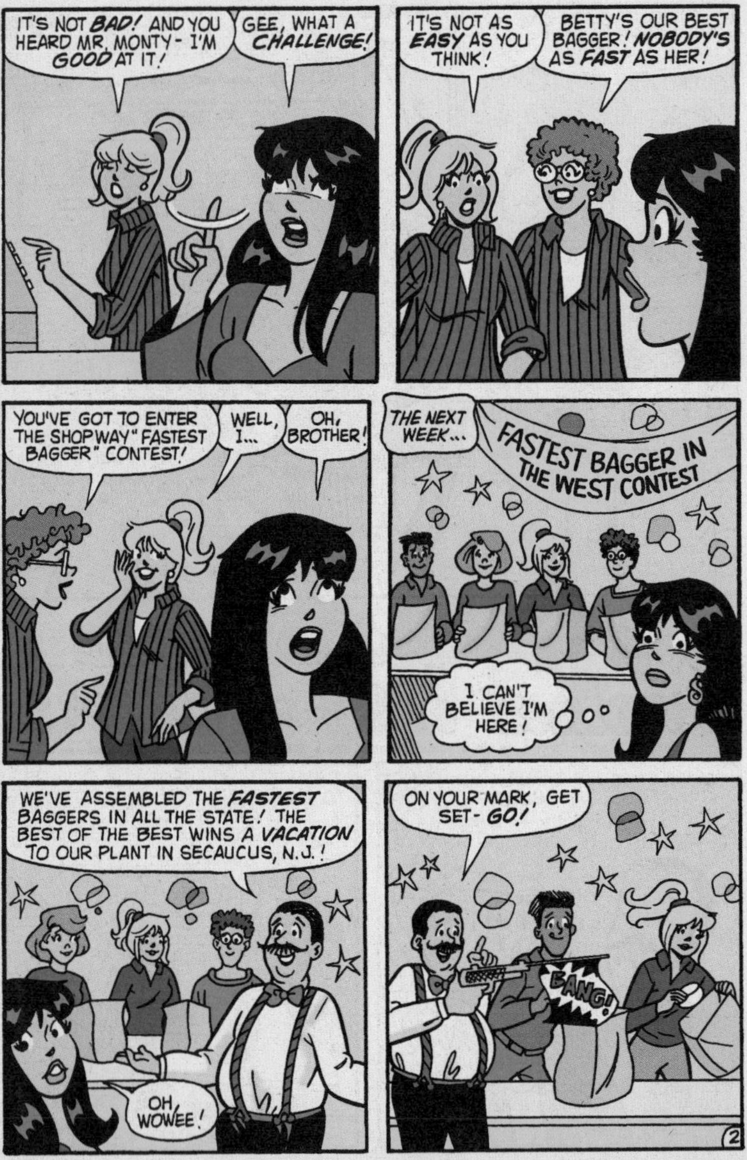
IT'S NOT BAD! AND YOU HEARD MR. MONTY - I'M GOOD AT IT!
GEE, WHAT A CHALLENGE!
IT'S NOT AS EASY AS YOU THINK!
BETTY'S OUR BEST BAGGER! NOBODY'S AS FAST AS HER!
YOU'VE GOT TO ENTER THE SHOPWAY "FASTEST BAGGER" CONTEST!
WELL, I...
OH, BROTHER!
THE NEXT WEEK...
FASTEST BAGGER IN THE WEST CONTEST
I CAN'T BELIEVE I'M HERE!
WE'VE ASSEMBLED THE FASTEST BAGGERS IN ALL THE STATE! THE BEST OF THE BEST WINS A VACATION TO OUR PLANT IN SECAUCUS, N.J.!
OH, WOWEE!
ON YOUR MARK, GET SET- GO!
BANG!
2

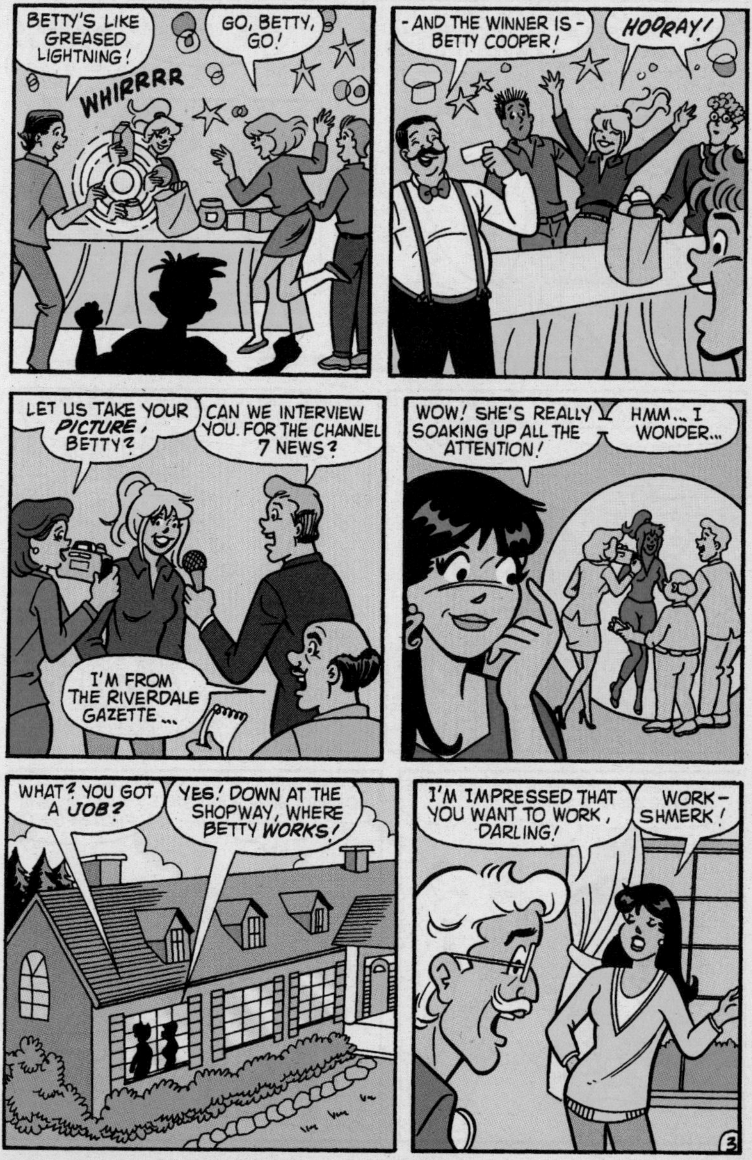

BETTY'S LIKE GREASED LIGHTNING!
GO, BETTY, GO!
WHIRRRR
- AND THE WINNER IS - BETTY COOPER!
HOORAY!
LET US TAKE YOUR PICTURE, BETTY?
CAN WE INTERVIEW YOU. FOR THE CHANNEL 7 NEWS?
I'M FROM THE RIVERDALE GAZETTE...
WOW! SHE'S REALLY SOAKING UP ALL THE ATTENTION!
HMM... I WONDER...
WHAT? YOU GOT A JOB?
YES! DOWN AT THE SHOPWAY, WHERE BETTY WORKS!
I'M IMPRESSED THAT YOU WANT TO WORK, DARLING!
WORK-SHMERK!
3

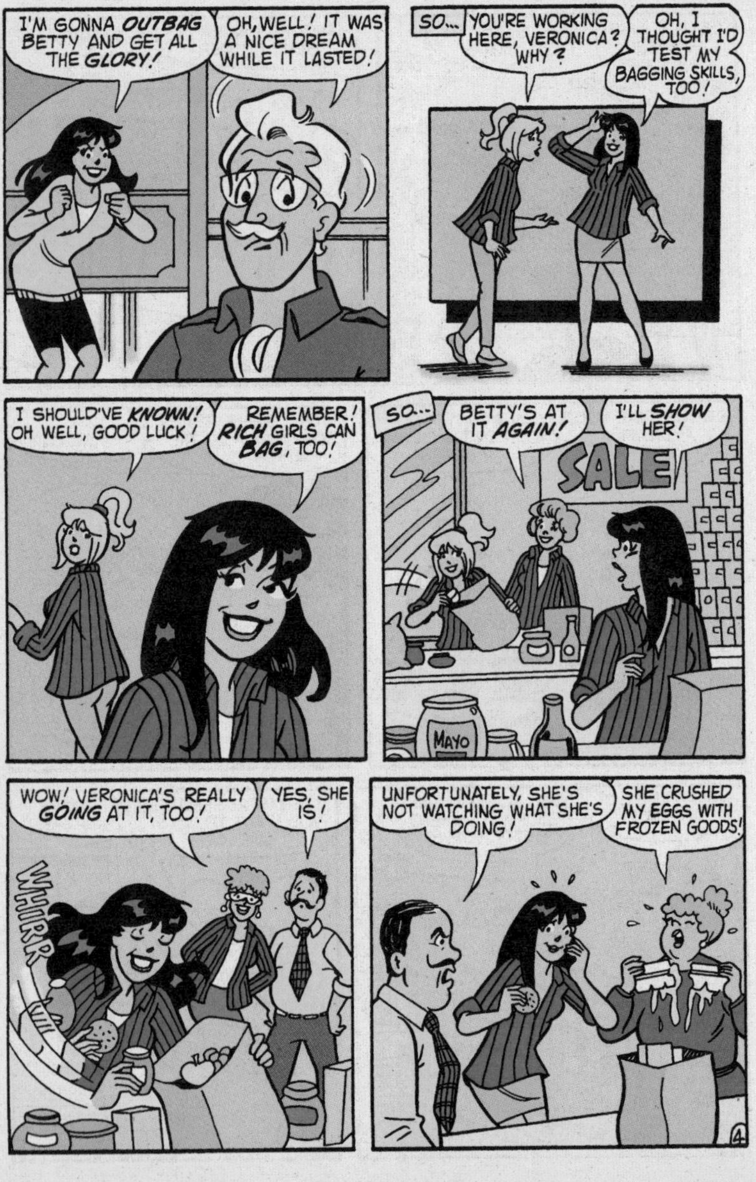
I'M GONNA OUTBAG BETTY AND GET ALL THE GLORY!
OH, WELL! IT WAS A NICE DREAM WHILE IT LASTED!
SO...
YOU'RE WORKING HERE, VERONICA? WHY?
OH, I THOUGHT I'D TEST MY BAGGING SKILLS, TOO!
I SHOULD'VE KNOWN! OH WELL, GOOD LUCK!
REMEMBER! RICH GIRLS CAN BAG, TOO!
SO...
BETTY'S AT IT AGAIN!
I'LL SHOW HER!
SALE
MAYO
WOW! VERONICA'S REALLY GOING AT IT, TOO!
YES, SHE IS!
WHIRR
UNFORTUNATELY, SHE'S NOT WATCHING WHAT SHE'S DOING!
SHE CRUSHED MY EGGS WITH FROZEN GOODS!
4

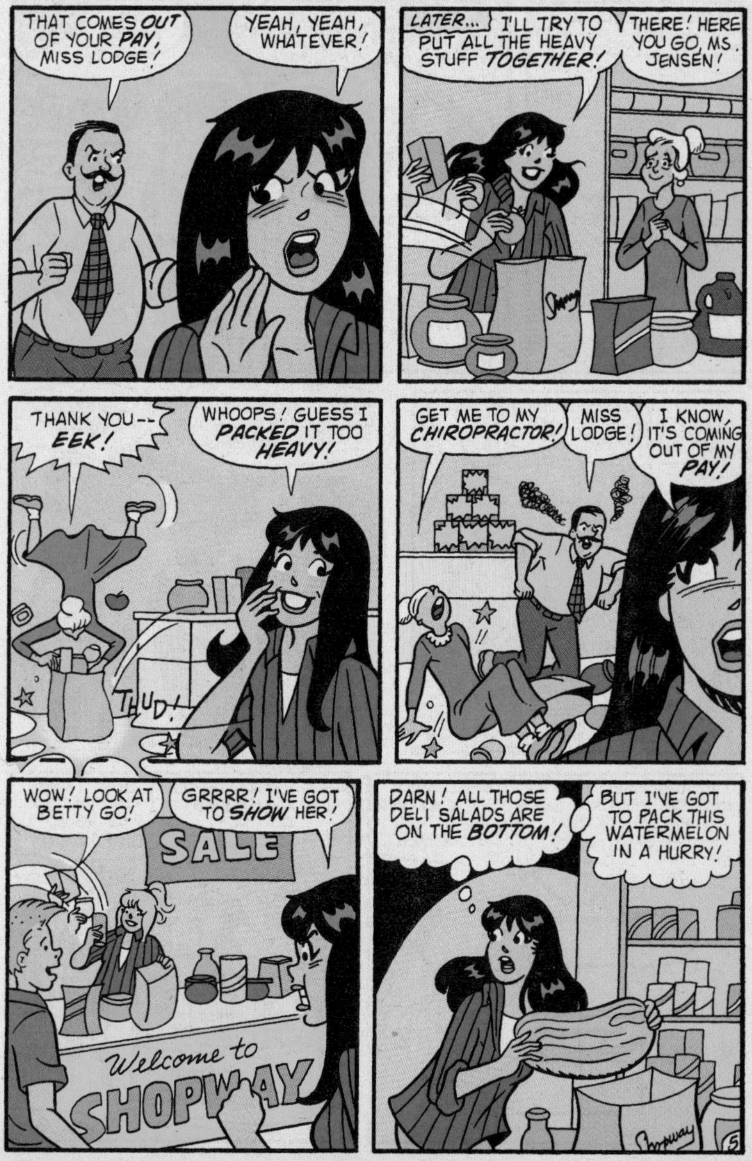
THAT COMES OUT OF YOUR PAY, MISS LODGE!
YEAH, YEAH, WHATEVER!
LATER...
I'LL TRY TO PUT ALL THE HEAVY STUFF TOGETHER!
THERE! HERE YOU GO, MS. JENSEN!
THANK YOU-- EEK!
WHOOPS! GUESS I PACKED IT TOO HEAVY!
THUD!
GET ME TO MY CHIROPRACTOR!
MISS LODGE!
I KNOW, IT'S COMING OUT OF MY PAY!
WOW! LOOK AT BETTY GO!
GRRRR! I'VE GOT TO SHOW HER!
SALE
Welcome to SHOPWAY
DARN! ALL THOSE DELI SALADS ARE ON THE BOTTOM!
BUT I'VE GOT TO PACK THIS WATERMELON IN A HURRY!
Shopway
5

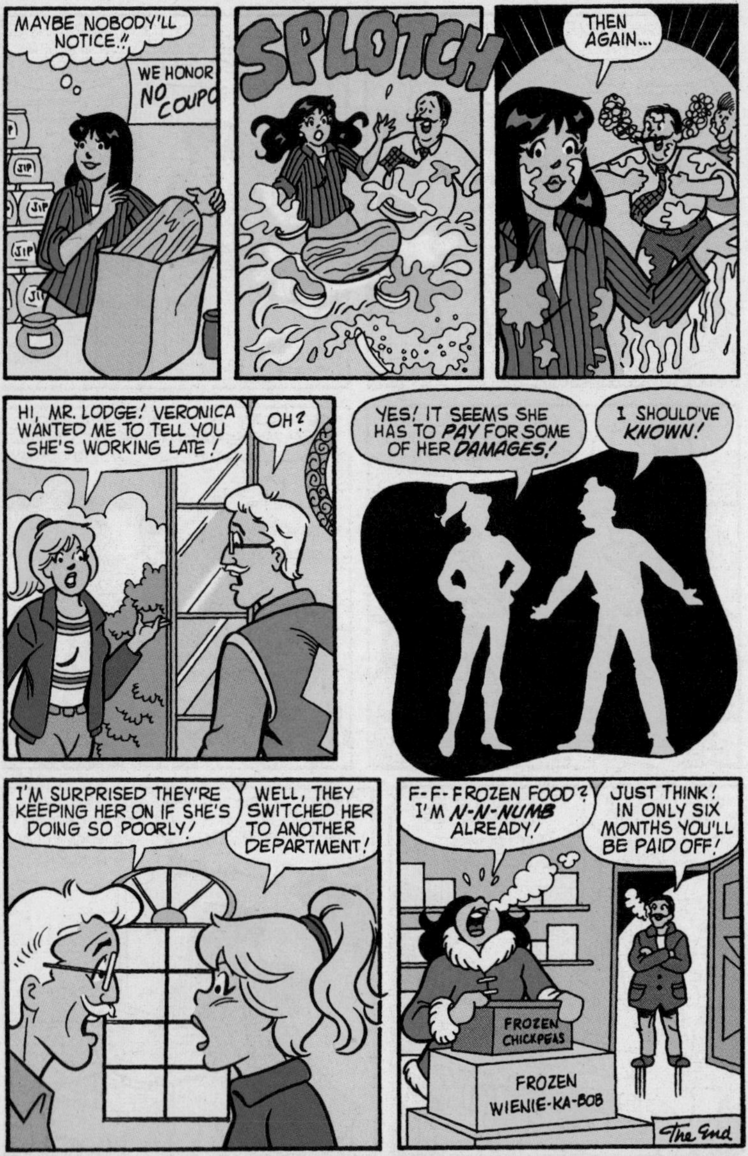
MAYBE NOBODY'LL NOTICE!!
WE HONOR NO COUPO
JIP
SPLOTCH
THEN AGAIN...
HI, MR. LODGE! VERONICA WANTED ME TO TELL YOU SHE'S WORKING LATE!
OH?
YES! IT SEEMS SHE HAS TO PAY FOR SOME OF HER DAMAGES!
I SHOULD'VE KNOWN!
I'M SURPRISED THEY'RE KEEPING HER ON IF SHE'S DOING SO POORLY!
WELL, THEY SWITCHED HER TO ANOTHER DEPARTMENT!
F-F-FROZEN FOOD? I'M N-N-NUMB ALREADY!
JUST THINK! IN ONLY SIX MONTHS YOU'LL BE PAID OFF!
FROZEN CHICKPEAS
FROZEN WIENIE-KA-BOB
The End

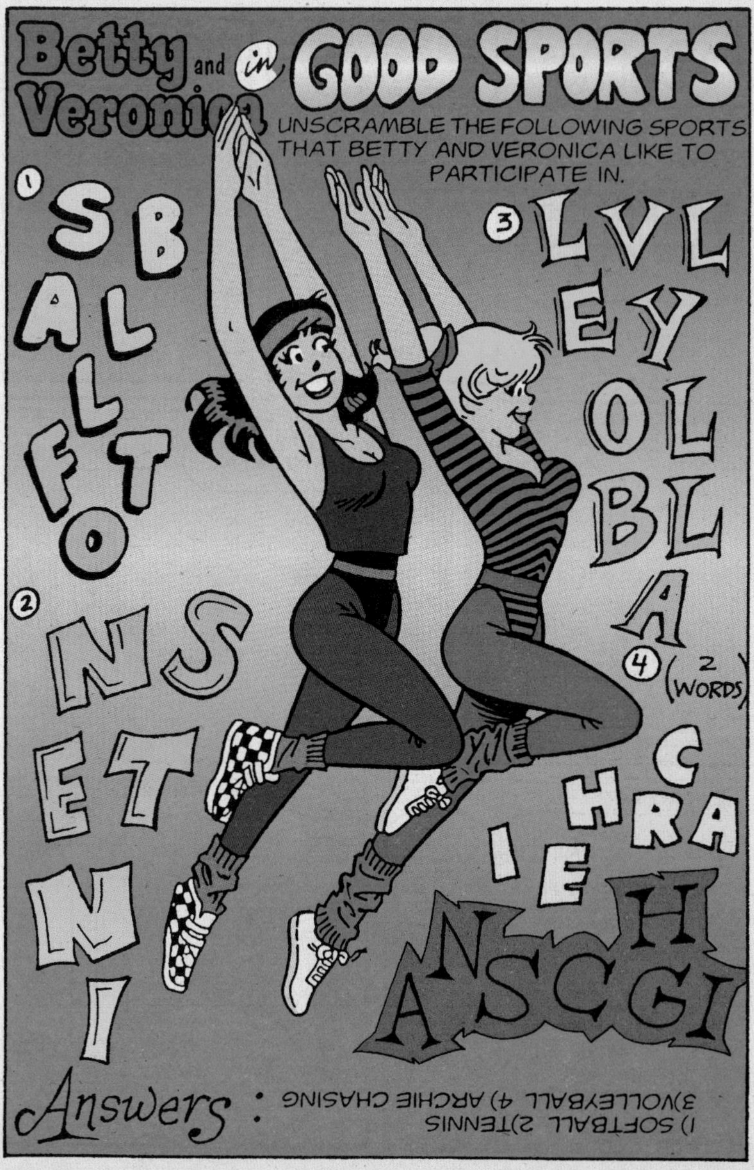
Betty and Veronica in GOOD SPORTS
UNSCRAMBLE THE FOLLOWING SPORTS THAT BETTY AND VERONICA LIKE TO PARTICIPATE IN.
1 S B A L L F L T O
2 N S E T N I
3 L V L E Y O L B L A
4 (2 WORDS) C H R A I E H N A S C G I
Answers :
1) SOFTBALL 2) TENNIS
3) VOLLEYBALL 4) ARCHIE CHASING

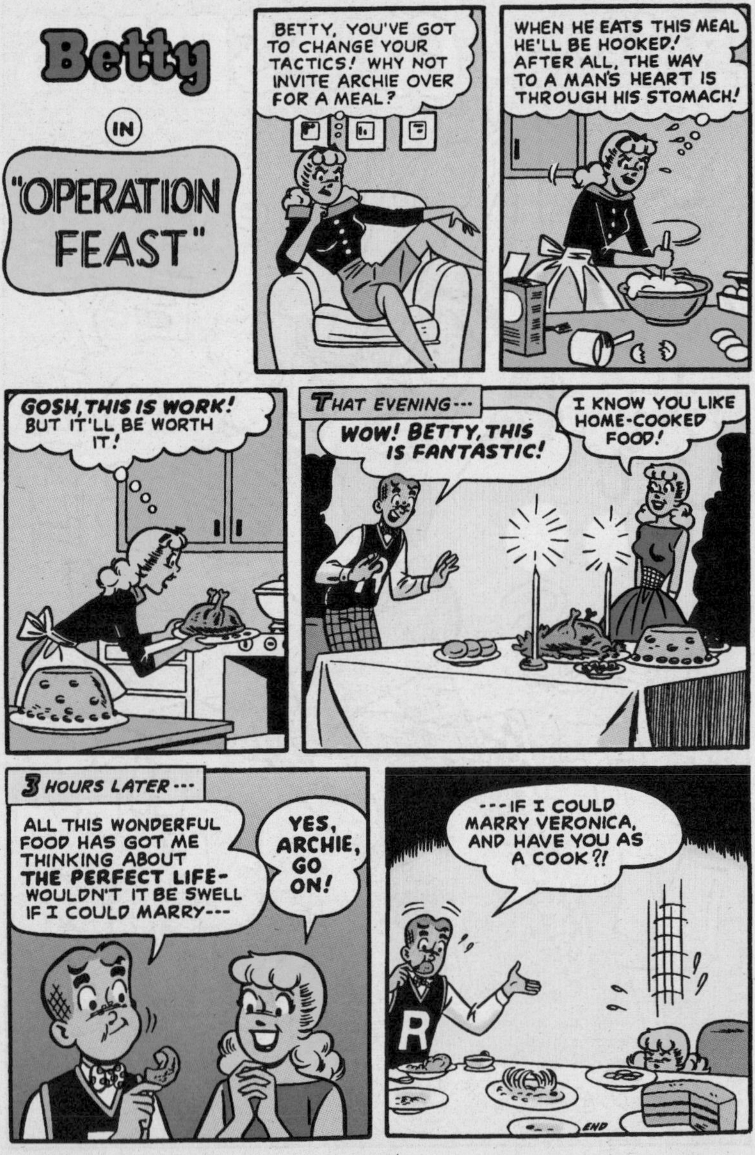

Betty
IN
"OPERATION FEAST"
BETTY, YOU'VE GOT TO CHANGE YOUR TACTICS! WHY NOT INVITE ARCHIE OVER FOR A MEAL?
WHEN HE EATS THIS MEAL HE'LL BE HOOKED! AFTER ALL, THE WAY TO A MAN'S HEART IS THROUGH HIS STOMACH!
GOSH, THIS IS WORK! BUT IT'LL BE WORTH IT!
THAT EVENING---
WOW! BETTY, THIS IS FANTASTIC!
I KNOW YOU LIKE HOME-COOKED FOOD!
3 HOURS LATER---
ALL THIS WONDERFUL FOOD HAS GOT ME THINKING ABOUT THE PERFECT LIFE- WOULDN'T IT BE SWELL IF I COULD MARRY---
YES, ARCHIE, GO ON!
---IF I COULD MARRY VERONICA, AND HAVE YOU AS A COOK?!
END

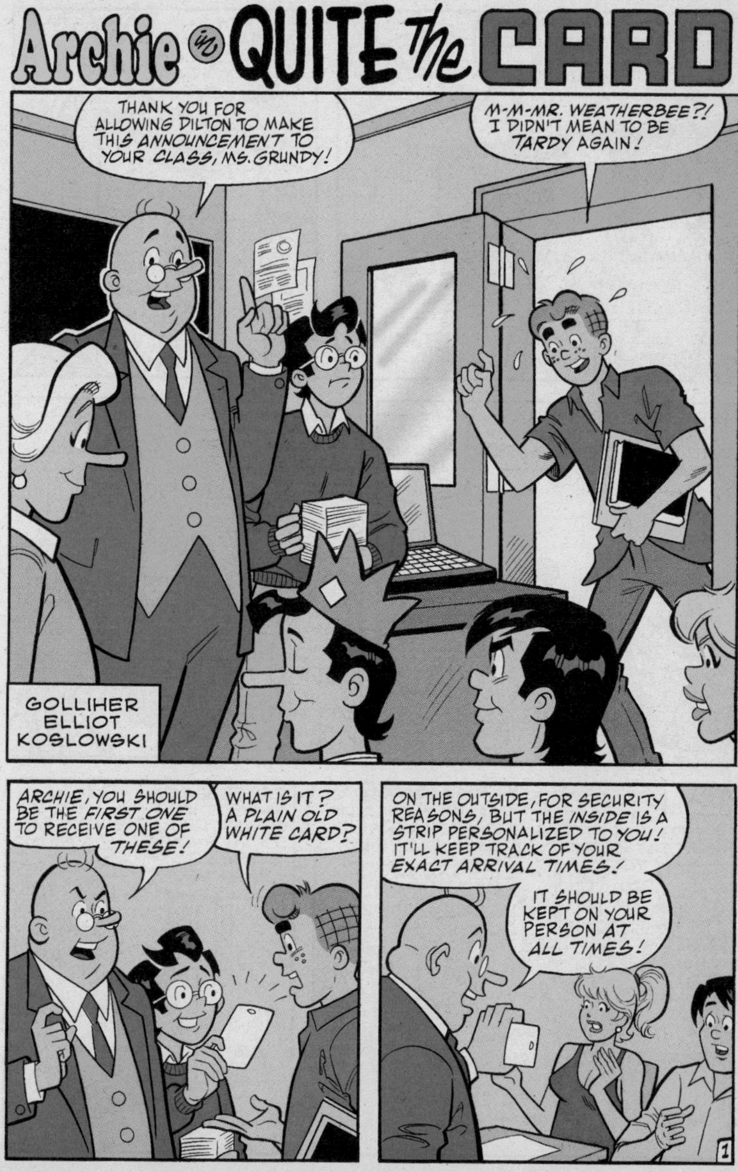
Archie in QUITE the CARD
THANK YOU FOR ALLOWING DILTON TO MAKE THIS ANNOUNCEMENT TO YOUR CLASS, MS. GRUNDY!
M-M-MR. WEATHERBEE?! I DIDN'T MEAN TO BE TARDY AGAIN!
GOLLIHER ELLIOT KOSLOWSKI
ARCHIE, YOU SHOULD BE THE FIRST ONE TO RECEIVE ONE OF THESE!
WHAT IS IT? A PLAIN OLD WHITE CARD?
ON THE OUTSIDE, FOR SECURITY REASONS, BUT THE INSIDE IS A STRIP PERSONALIZED TO YOU! IT'LL KEEP TRACK OF YOUR EXACT ARRIVAL TIMES!
IT SHOULD BE KEPT ON YOUR PERSON AT ALL TIMES!
1

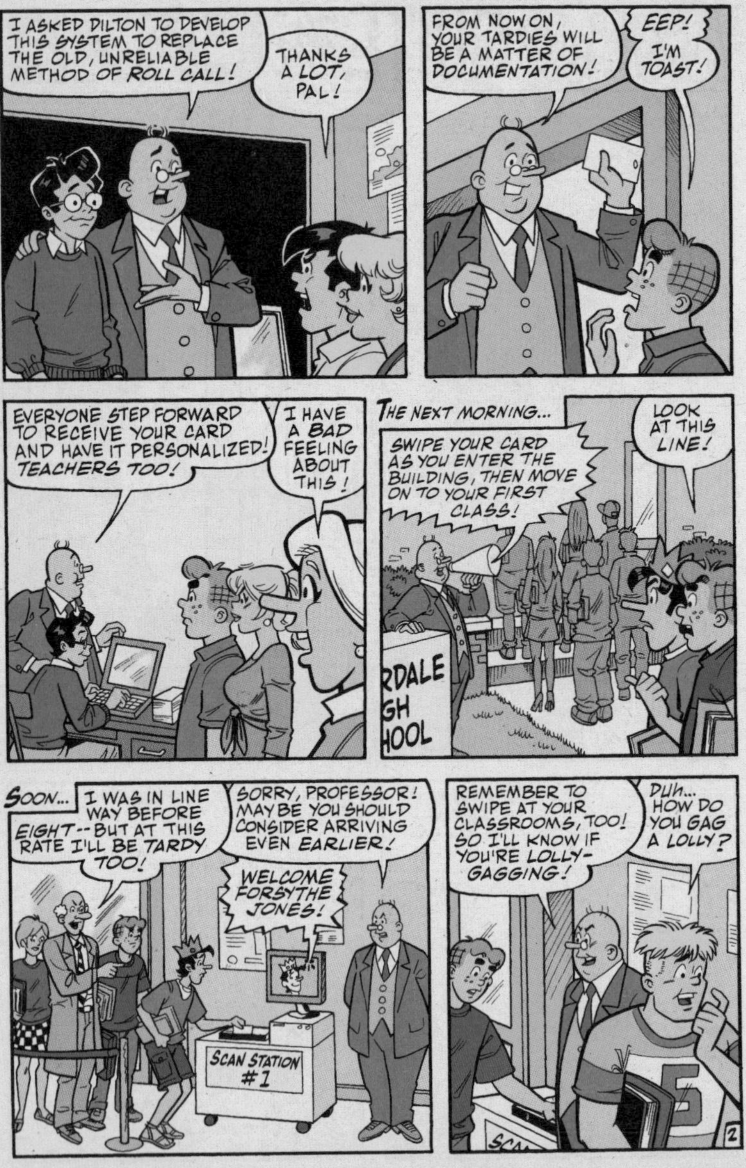

I ASKED DILTON TO DEVELOP THIS SYSTEM TO REPLACE THE OLD, UNRELIABLE METHOD OF ROLL CALL!
THANKS A LOT, PAL!
FROM NOW ON, YOUR TARDIES WILL BE A MATTER OF DOCUMENTATION!
EEP! I'M TOAST!
EVERYONE STEP FORWARD TO RECEIVE YOUR CARD AND HAVE IT PERSONALIZED! TEACHERS TOO!
I HAVE A BAD FEELING ABOUT THIS!
THE NEXT MORNING...
SWIPE YOUR CARD AS YOU ENTER THE BUILDING, THEN MOVE ON TO YOUR FIRST CLASS!
LOOK AT THIS LINE!
RDALE
GH
HOOL
SOON...
I WAS IN LINE WAY BEFORE EIGHT--BUT AT THIS RATE I'LL BE TARDY TOO!
SORRY, PROFESSOR! MAYBE YOU SHOULD CONSIDER ARRIVING EVEN EARLIER!
WELCOME FORSYTHE JONES!
SCAN STATION #1
REMEMBER TO SWIPE AT YOUR CLASSROOMS, TOO! SO I'LL KNOW IF YOU'RE LOLLY-GAGGING!
DUH... HOW DO YOU GAG A LOLLY?
5
2

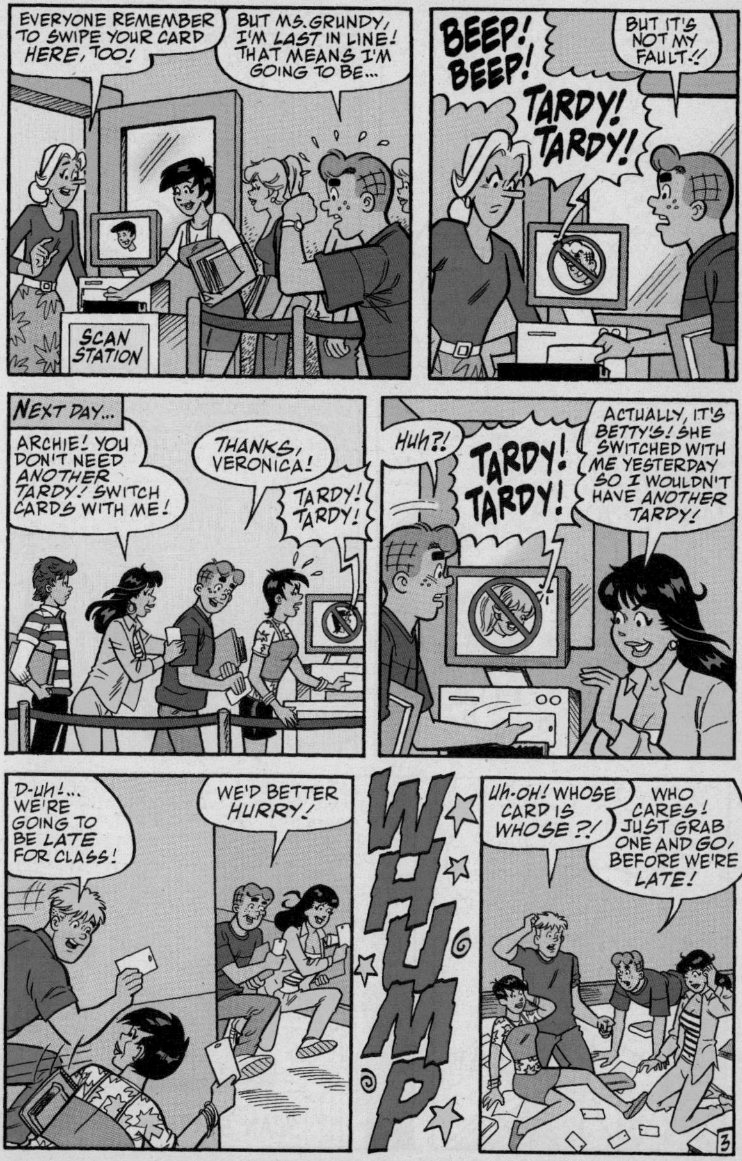

EVERYONE REMEMBER TO SWIPE YOUR CARD HERE, TOO!
BUT MS. GRUNDY, I'M LAST IN LINE! THAT MEANS I'M GOING TO BE...
SCAN STATION
BEEP! BEEP!
TARDY! TARDY!
BUT IT'S NOT MY FAULT!!
NEXT DAY...
ARCHIE! YOU DON'T NEED ANOTHER TARDY! SWITCH CARDS WITH ME!
THANKS, VERONICA!
TARDY! TARDY!
HUH?!
TARDY! TARDY!
ACTUALLY, IT'S BETTY'S! SHE SWITCHED WITH ME YESTERDAY SO I WOULDN'T HAVE ANOTHER TARDY!
D-UH!... WE'RE GOING TO BE LATE FOR CLASS!
WE'D BETTER HURRY!
WHUMP
UH-OH! WHOSE CARD IS WHOSE?!
WHO CARES! JUST GRAB ONE AND GO, BEFORE WE'RE LATE!
3

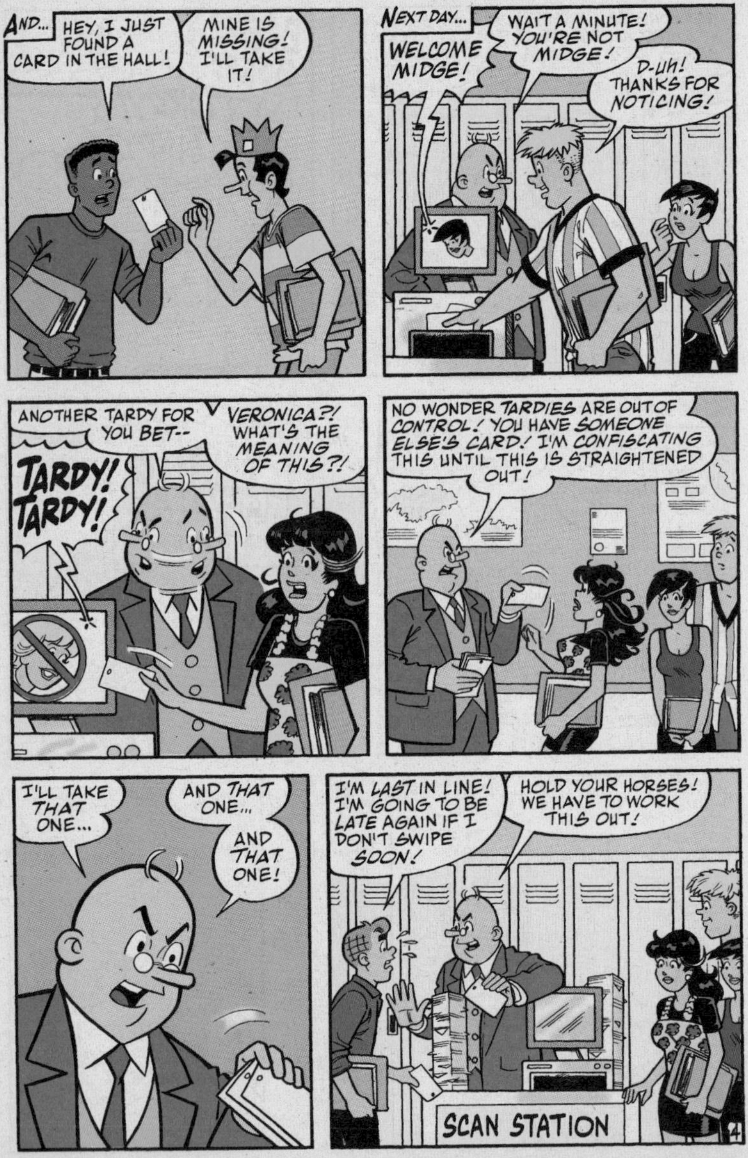
AND...
HEY, I JUST FOUND A CARD IN THE HALL!
MINE IS MISSING! I'LL TAKE IT!
NEXT DAY...
WELCOME MIDGE!
WAIT A MINUTE! YOU'RE NOT MIDGE!
D-uh! THANKS FOR NOTICING!
ANOTHER TARDY FOR YOU BET--
TARDY! TARDY!
VERONICA?! WHAT'S THE MEANING OF THIS?!
NO WONDER TARDIES ARE OUT OF CONTROL! YOU HAVE SOMEONE ELSE'S CARD! I'M CONFISCATING THIS UNTIL THIS IS STRAIGHTENED OUT!
I'LL TAKE THAT ONE...
AND THAT ONE...
AND THAT ONE!
I'M LAST IN LINE! I'M GOING TO BE LATE AGAIN IF I DON'T SWIPE SOON!
HOLD YOUR HORSES! WE HAVE TO WORK THIS OUT!
SCAN STATION
4

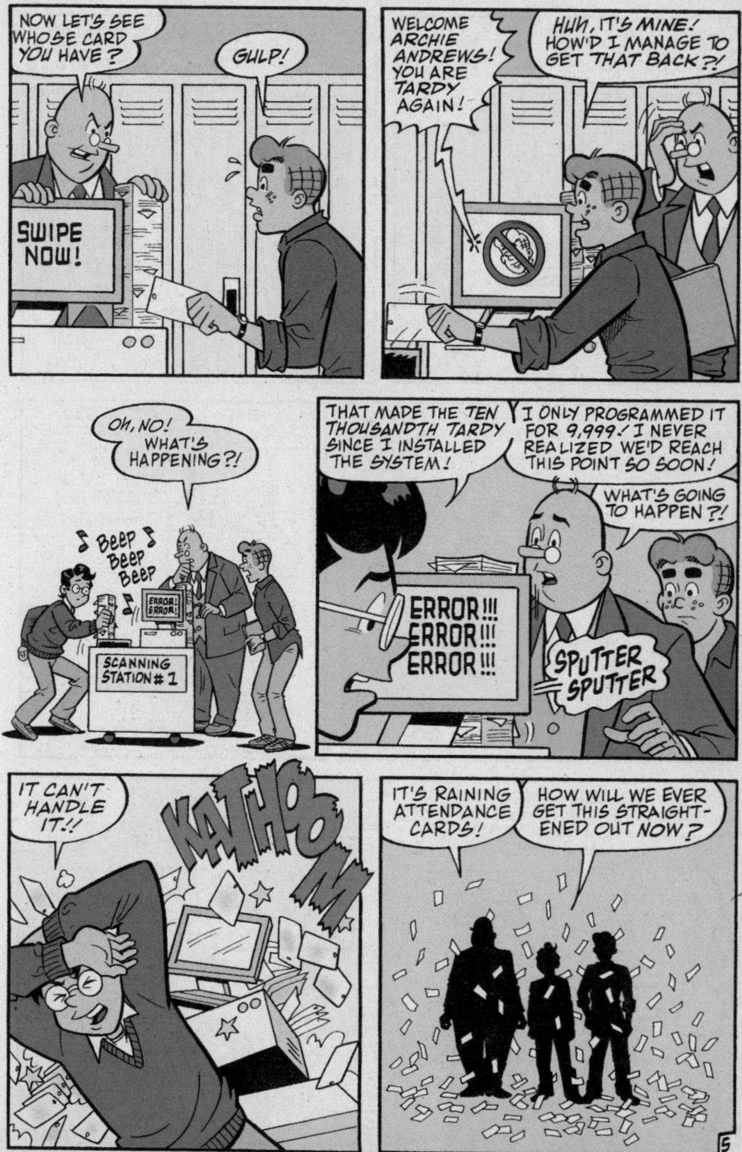
NOW LET'S SEE WHOSE CARD YOU HAVE?
GULP!
SWIPE NOW!
WELCOME ARCHIE ANDREWS! YOU ARE TARDY AGAIN!
HUH, IT'S MINE! HOW'D I MANAGE TO GET THAT BACK?!
OH, NO! WHAT'S HAPPENING?!
Beep Beep Beep
ERROR! ERROR!
SCANNING STATION #1
THAT MADE THE TEN THOUSANDTH TARDY SINCE I INSTALLED THE SYSTEM!
I ONLY PROGRAMMED IT FOR 9,999! I NEVER REALIZED WE'D REACH THIS POINT SO SOON!
WHAT'S GOING TO HAPPEN?!
ERROR!!! ERROR!!! ERROR!!!
SPUTTER SPUTTER
IT CAN'T HANDLE IT!!
KATHOOM
IT'S RAINING ATTENDANCE CARDS!
HOW WILL WE EVER GET THIS STRAIGHT-ENED OUT NOW?

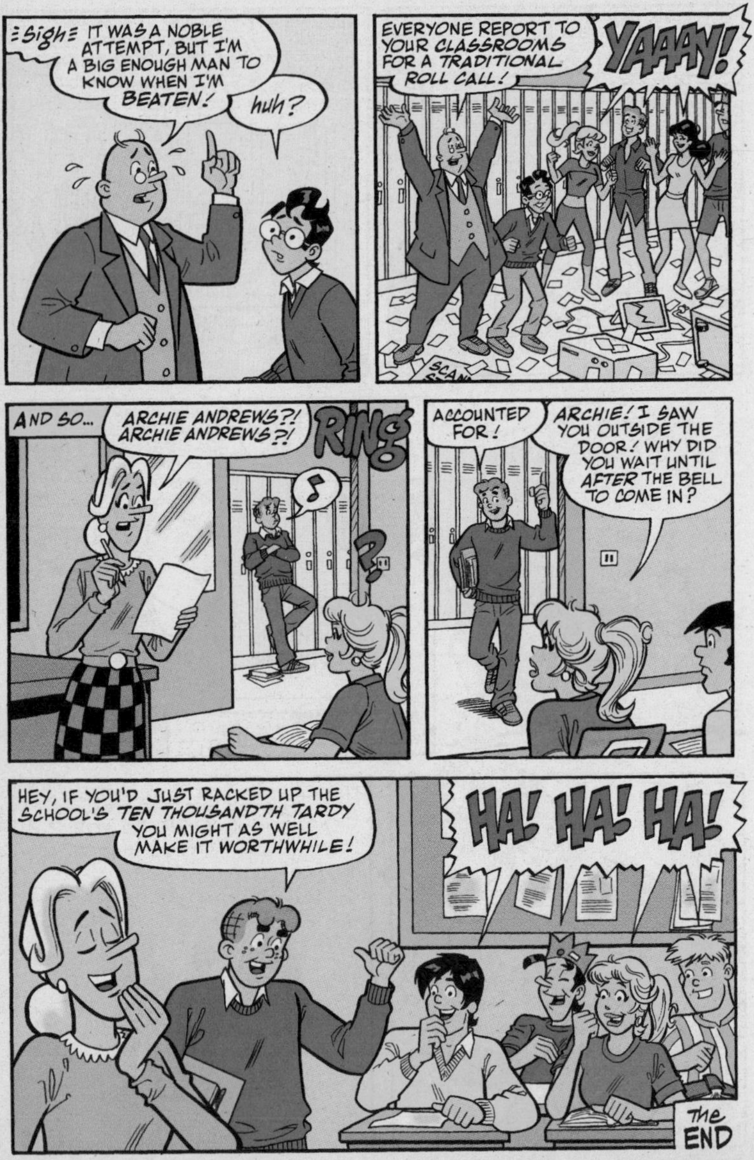

SIGH IT WAS A NOBLE ATTEMPT, BUT I'M A BIG ENOUGH MAN TO KNOW WHEN I'M BEATEN!
huh?
EVERYONE REPORT TO YOUR CLASSROOMS FOR A TRADITIONAL ROLL CALL!
YAAAY!
AND SO...
ARCHIE ANDREWS?! ARCHIE ANDREWS?!
RING
ACCOUNTED FOR!
ARCHIE! I SAW YOU OUTSIDE THE DOOR! WHY DID YOU WAIT UNTIL AFTER THE BELL TO COME IN?
HEY, IF YOU'D JUST RACKED UP THE SCHOOL'S TEN THOUSANDTH TARDY YOU MIGHT AS WELL MAKE IT WORTHWHILE!
HA! HA! HA!
The END

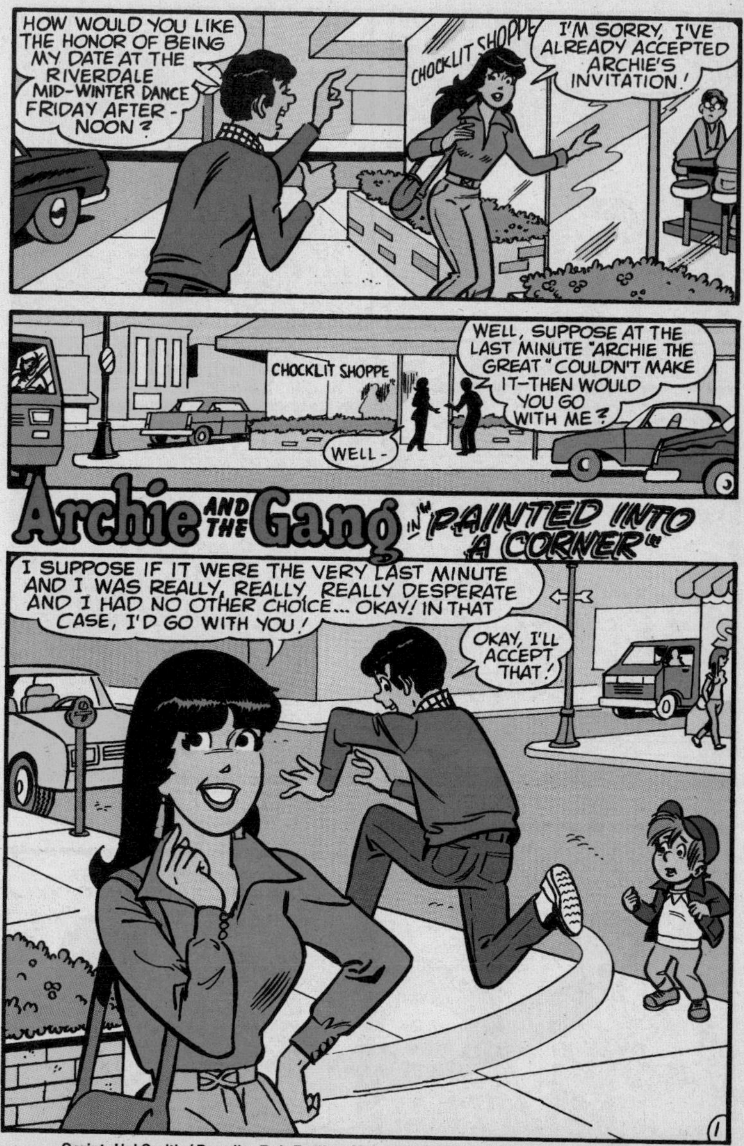
HOW WOULD YOU LIKE THE HONOR OF BEING MY DATE AT THE RIVERDALE MID-WINTER DANCE FRIDAY AFTER-NOON ?
CHOCKLIT SHOPPE
I'M SORRY, I'VE ALREADY ACCEPTED ARCHIE'S INVITATION !
CHOCKLIT SHOPPE
WELL, SUPPOSE AT THE LAST MINUTE "ARCHIE THE GREAT" COULDN'T MAKE IT—THEN WOULD YOU GO WITH ME ?
WELL -
Archie AND THE Gang IN "PAINTED INTO A CORNER"
I SUPPOSE IF IT WERE THE VERY LAST MINUTE AND I WAS REALLY, REALLY, REALLY DESPERATE AND I HAD NO OTHER CHOICE... OKAY! IN THAT CASE, I'D GO WITH YOU !
OKAY, I'LL ACCEPT THAT !
1

Script: Hal Smith / Pencils: Bob Bolling / Inks: Mike Esposito / Letters: Bill Yoshida

NOW, LET'S SEE, HOW CAN I BE SURE THAT "CARROT-TOP" WON'T BE ABLE TO MAKE IT?

I'VE GOT IT.... A BRILLIANT PLAN TO TIE HIM UP FRIDAY AFTERNOON!

AND SO, THURSDAY, REGGIE PUTS HIS PLAN INTO ACTION...

FIRST, HE PICKS A FIGHT WITH ARCHIE IN FRONT OF WITNESSES AND GETS ARCHIE TO CALL HIM A NAME!

TAKE A HIKE, NERD-FACE!

THEN, AROUND 3 P.M., HE PRETENDS TO MAKE UP WITH ARCHIE AND SENDS HIM ON A WILD GOOSE CHASE...

THIS REALLY FOXY BLONDE WANTS TO MEET YOU AT THE BASEBALL DIAMOND BEHIND THE SCHOOL!

THEN HE SETS THE SCENE...

MR. WEATHERBEE, MY LOCKER DOOR'S STUCK! COULD YOU HELP ME OPEN IT? IT'S 3:02 AND I'M LATE FOR A DATE!

VERY WELL!

A FEW MINUTES LATER, HE SPRAY-PAINTS THE NAME ARCHIE CALLED HIM ON HIS LOCKER!

IS "NERD-FACE" THE BEST NAME HE COULD THINK OF?

REGGIE IS A NERD FACE

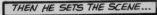

②

THEN HE HIDES THE SPRAY-GUN IN ARCHIE'S CAR...

...AND DRIVES AROUND THE BLOCK BACK INTO THE PARKING LOT JUST AS MR. WEATHERBEE IS LEAVING...

SIR! I'M GLAD I CAUGHT YOU! I LEFT A BOOK IN ENGLISH CLASS! COULD YOU UNLOCK THE DOOR SO I COULD GET IT?

OH, VERY WELL! BUT THIS IS THE LAST TIME!

...HE MAKES SURE MR. WEATHERBEE SEES THE LOCKER...

OH, NO! LOOK AT WHAT SOMEONE DID BETWEEN 3:02 AND 3:31! HEY! THAT'S THE NAME ARCHIE CALLED ME!

REGGIE IS A NERD FACE

...JUST AS ARCHIE RETURNS...

REGGIE, I DON'T SEE ANY... WHAT HAPPENED HERE?

DON'T PLAY INNOCENT! I KNOW IT WAS YOU!

SIR! I'LL BET YOU'LL FIND THE SPRAY-CAN IN ARCHIE'S CAR!

REGGIE A NERD FACE

DO YOU MIND, ARCHIE?

NO, SIR! I DIDN'T DO THIS!

REGGIE IS A NERD FACE

I'M SORRY, ARCHIE, BUT THIS LOOKS INCRIMINATING! WE'LL TAKE THIS MATTER UP TOMORROW IN STUDENT COURT!

3

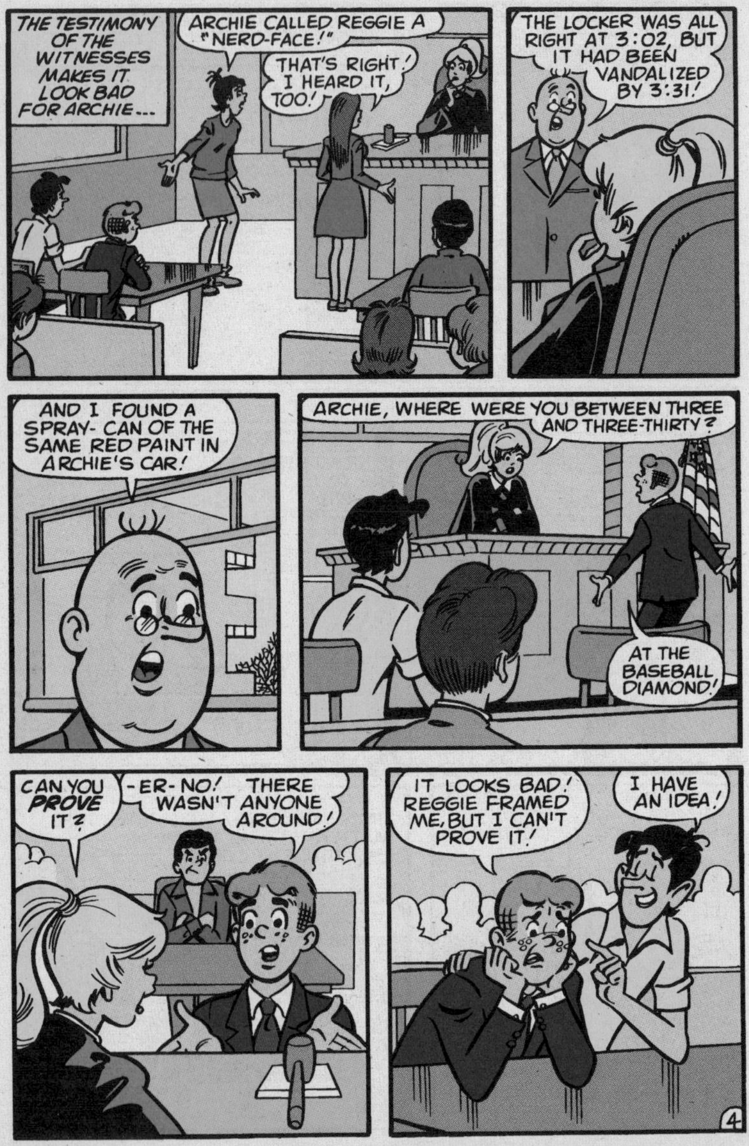
THE TESTIMONY OF THE WITNESSES MAKES IT LOOK BAD FOR ARCHIE...
ARCHIE CALLED REGGIE A "NERD-FACE!"
THAT'S RIGHT! I HEARD IT, TOO!
THE LOCKER WAS ALL RIGHT AT 3:02, BUT IT HAD BEEN VANDALIZED BY 3:31!
AND I FOUND A SPRAY- CAN OF THE SAME RED PAINT IN ARCHIE'S CAR!
ARCHIE, WHERE WERE YOU BETWEEN THREE AND THREE-THIRTY?
AT THE BASEBALL DIAMOND!
CAN YOU PROVE IT?
-ER- NO! THERE WASN'T ANYONE AROUND!
IT LOOKS BAD! REGGIE FRAMED ME, BUT I CAN'T PROVE IT!
I HAVE AN IDEA!
4

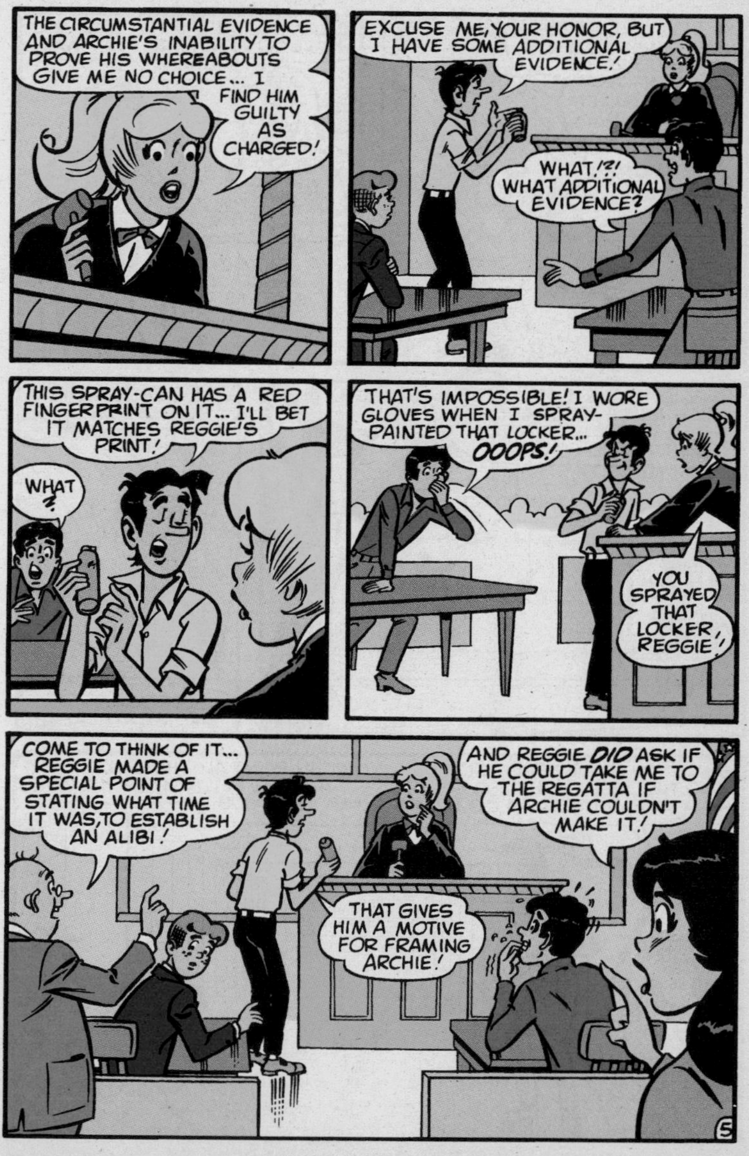
THE CIRCUMSTANTIAL EVIDENCE AND ARCHIE'S INABILITY TO PROVE HIS WHEREABOUTS GIVE ME NO CHOICE... I
FIND HIM GUILTY AS CHARGED!
EXCUSE ME, YOUR HONOR, BUT I HAVE SOME ADDITIONAL EVIDENCE!
WHAT!?! WHAT ADDITIONAL EVIDENCE?
THIS SPRAY-CAN HAS A RED FINGERPRINT ON IT... I'LL BET IT MATCHES REGGIE'S PRINT!
WHAT?
THAT'S IMPOSSIBLE! I WORE GLOVES WHEN I SPRAY-PAINTED THAT LOCKER...
OOOPS!
YOU SPRAYED THAT LOCKER, REGGIE!
COME TO THINK OF IT... REGGIE MADE A SPECIAL POINT OF STATING WHAT TIME IT WAS, TO ESTABLISH AN ALIBI!
AND REGGIE DID ASK IF HE COULD TAKE ME TO THE REGATTA IF ARCHIE COULDN'T MAKE IT!
THAT GIVES HIM A MOTIVE FOR FRAMING ARCHIE!
5

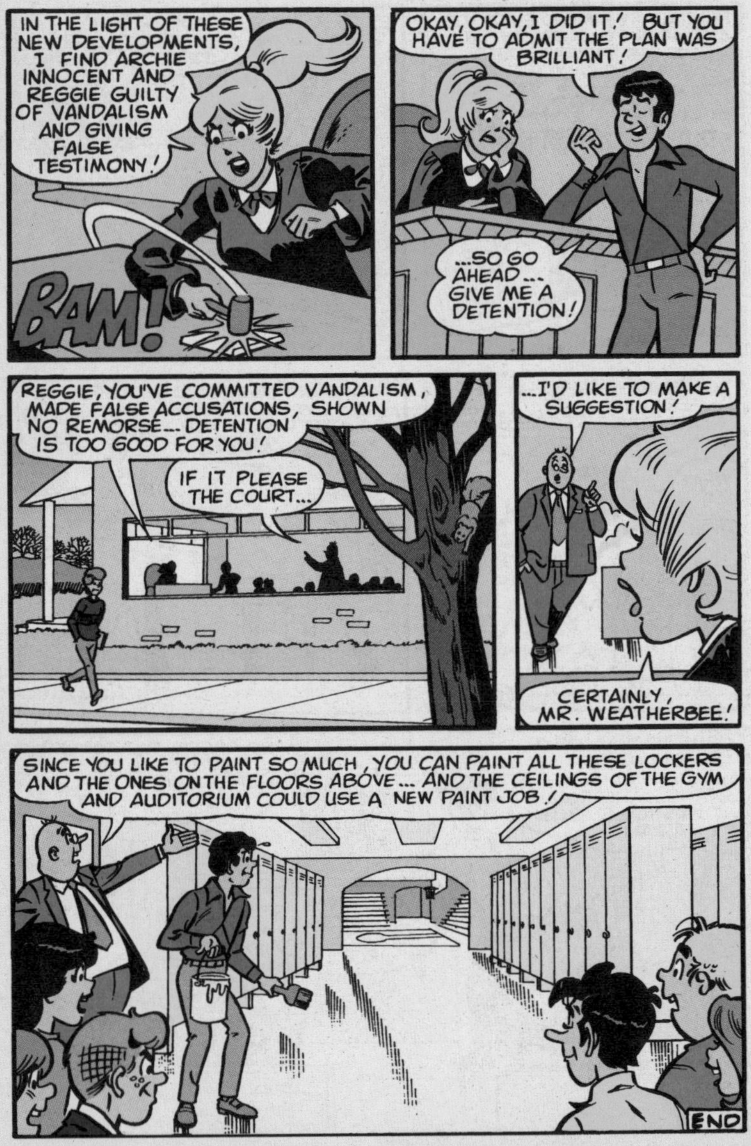
IN THE LIGHT OF THESE NEW DEVELOPMENTS, I FIND ARCHIE INNOCENT AND REGGIE GUILTY OF VANDALISM AND GIVING FALSE TESTIMONY!
BAM!
OKAY, OKAY, I DID IT! BUT YOU HAVE TO ADMIT THE PLAN WAS BRILLIANT!
...SO GO AHEAD... GIVE ME A DETENTION!
REGGIE, YOU'VE COMMITTED VANDALISM, MADE FALSE ACCUSATIONS, SHOWN NO REMORSE... DETENTION IS TOO GOOD FOR YOU!
IF IT PLEASE THE COURT...
...I'D LIKE TO MAKE A SUGGESTION!
CERTAINLY, MR. WEATHERBEE!
SINCE YOU LIKE TO PAINT SO MUCH, YOU CAN PAINT ALL THESE LOCKERS AND THE ONES ON THE FLOORS ABOVE... AND THE CEILINGS OF THE GYM AND AUDITORIUM COULD USE A NEW PAINT JOB!
END

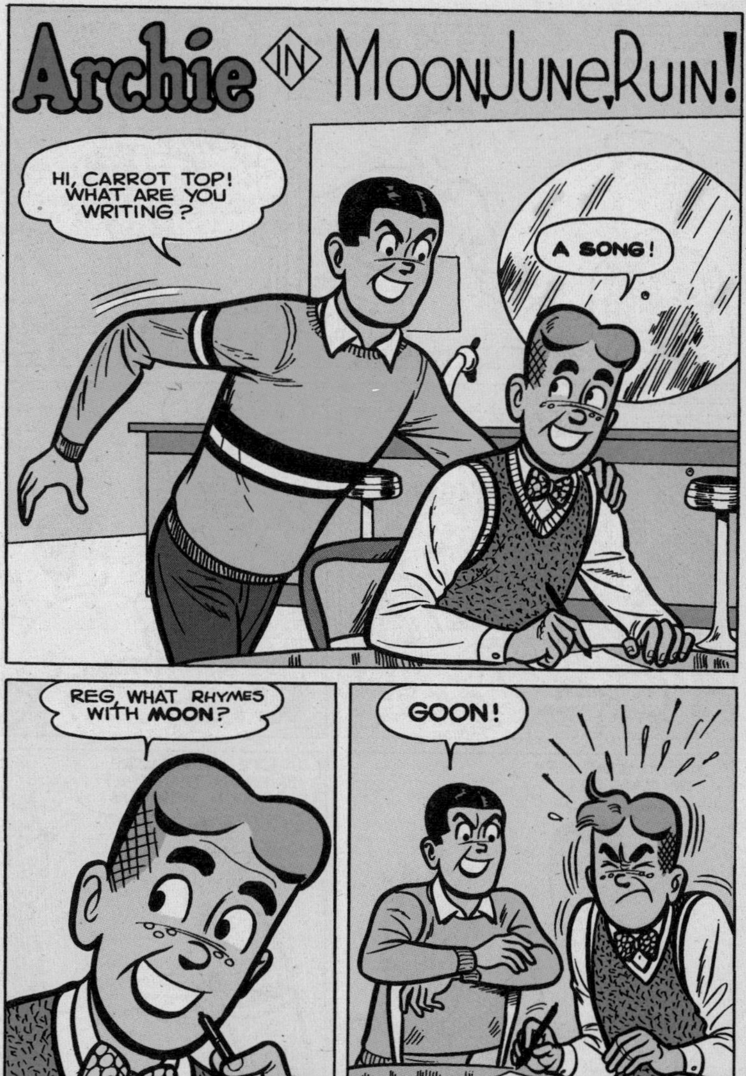
Archie IN MoonJuneRuin!
HI, CARROT TOP! WHAT ARE YOU WRITING?
A SONG!
REG, WHAT RHYMES WITH MOON?
GOON!

Script: Frank Doyle / Art & Letters: Bill Vigoda

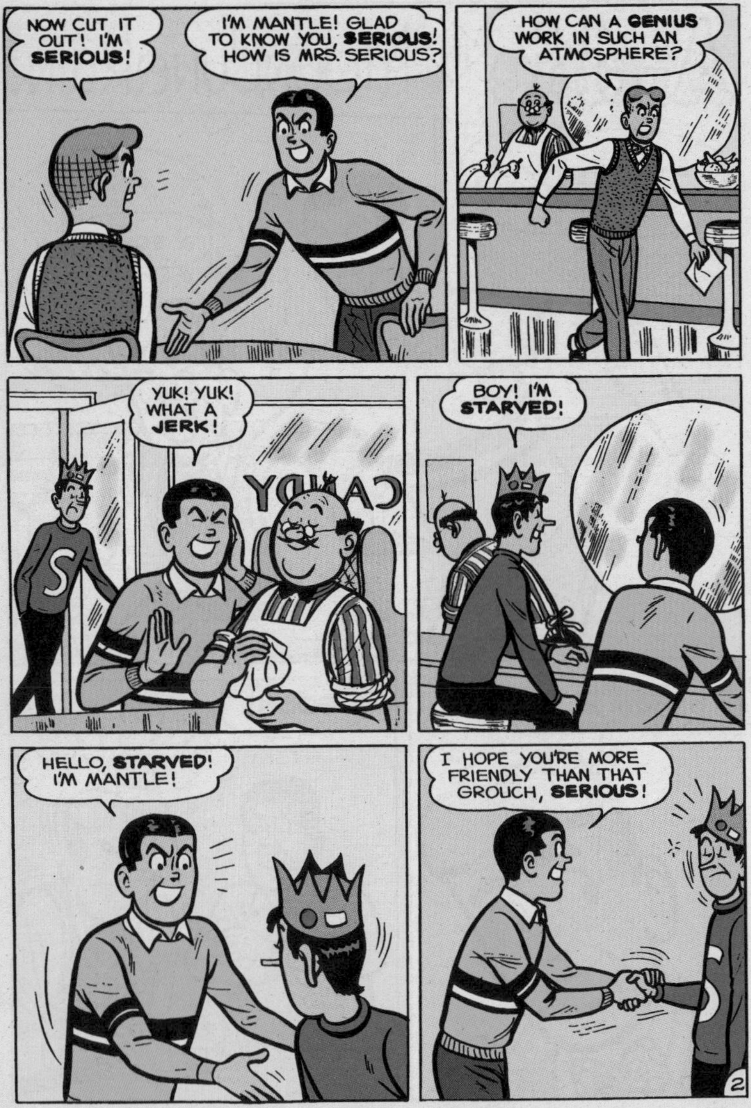
NOW CUT IT OUT! I'M SERIOUS!
I'M MANTLE! GLAD TO KNOW YOU, SERIOUS! HOW IS MRS. SERIOUS?
HOW CAN A GENIUS WORK IN SUCH AN ATMOSPHERE?
YUK! YUK! WHAT A JERK!
CANDY
BOY! I'M STARVED!
HELLO, STARVED! I'M MANTLE!
I HOPE YOU'RE MORE FRIENDLY THAN THAT GROUCH, SERIOUS!
2

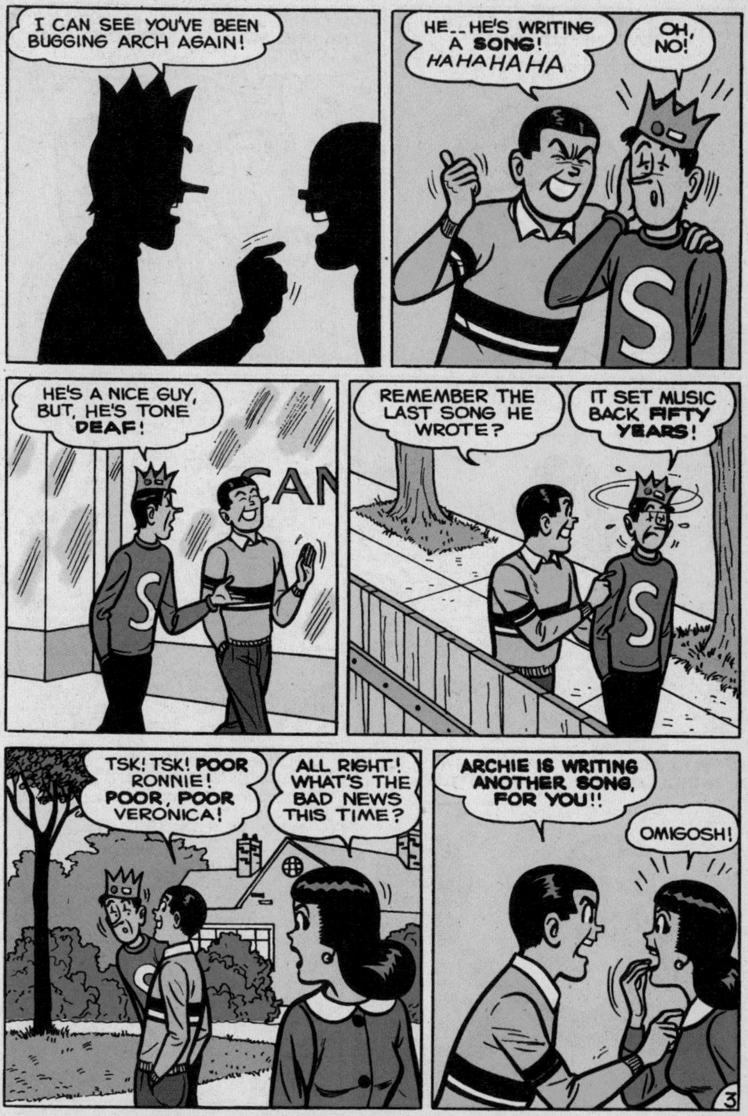
I CAN SEE YOU'VE BEEN BUGGING ARCH AGAIN!
HE_-HE'S WRITING A SONG! HAHAHAHA
OH, NO!
HE'S A NICE GUY, BUT, HE'S TONE DEAF!
CAN
REMEMBER THE LAST SONG HE WROTE?
IT SET MUSIC BACK FIFTY YEARS!
TSK! TSK! POOR RONNIE! POOR, POOR VERONICA!
ALL RIGHT! WHAT'S THE BAD NEWS THIS TIME?
ARCHIE IS WRITING ANOTHER SONG, FOR YOU!!
OMIGOSH!
3

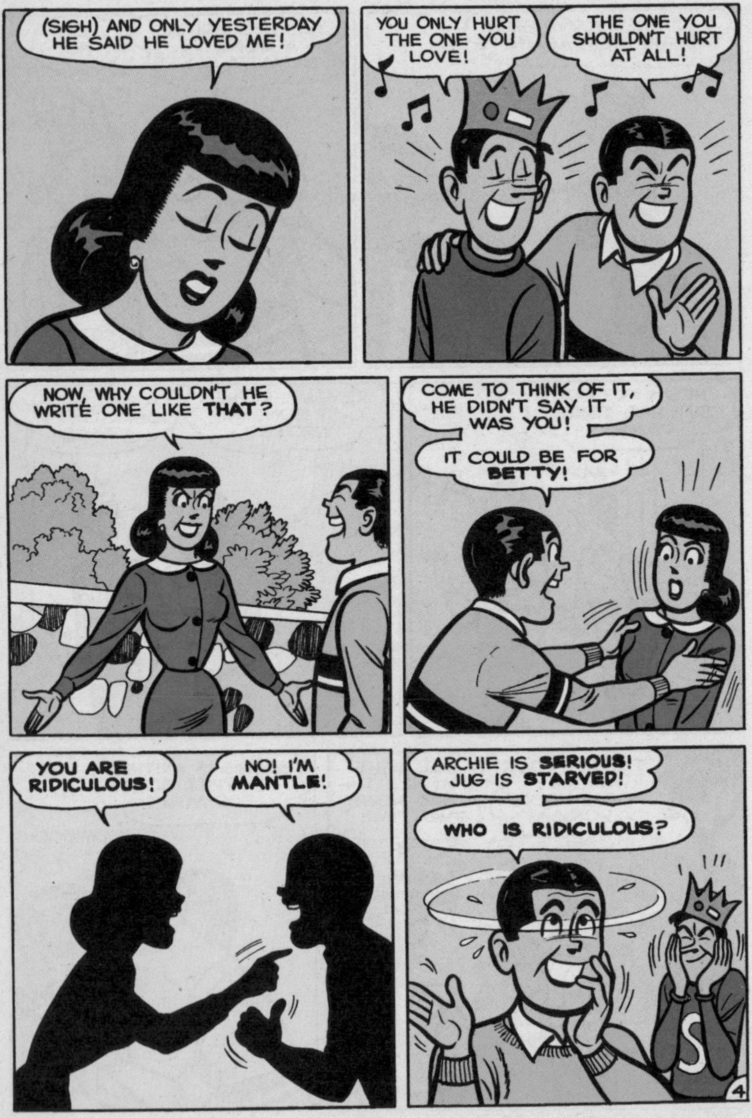
(SIGH) AND ONLY YESTERDAY HE SAID HE LOVED ME!
YOU ONLY HURT THE ONE YOU LOVE!
THE ONE YOU SHOULDN'T HURT AT ALL!
NOW, WHY COULDN'T HE WRITE ONE LIKE THAT?
COME TO THINK OF IT, HE DIDN'T SAY IT WAS YOU!
IT COULD BE FOR BETTY!
YOU ARE RIDICULOUS!
NO! I'M MANTLE!
ARCHIE IS SERIOUS! JUG IS STARVED!
WHO IS RIDICULOUS?
4

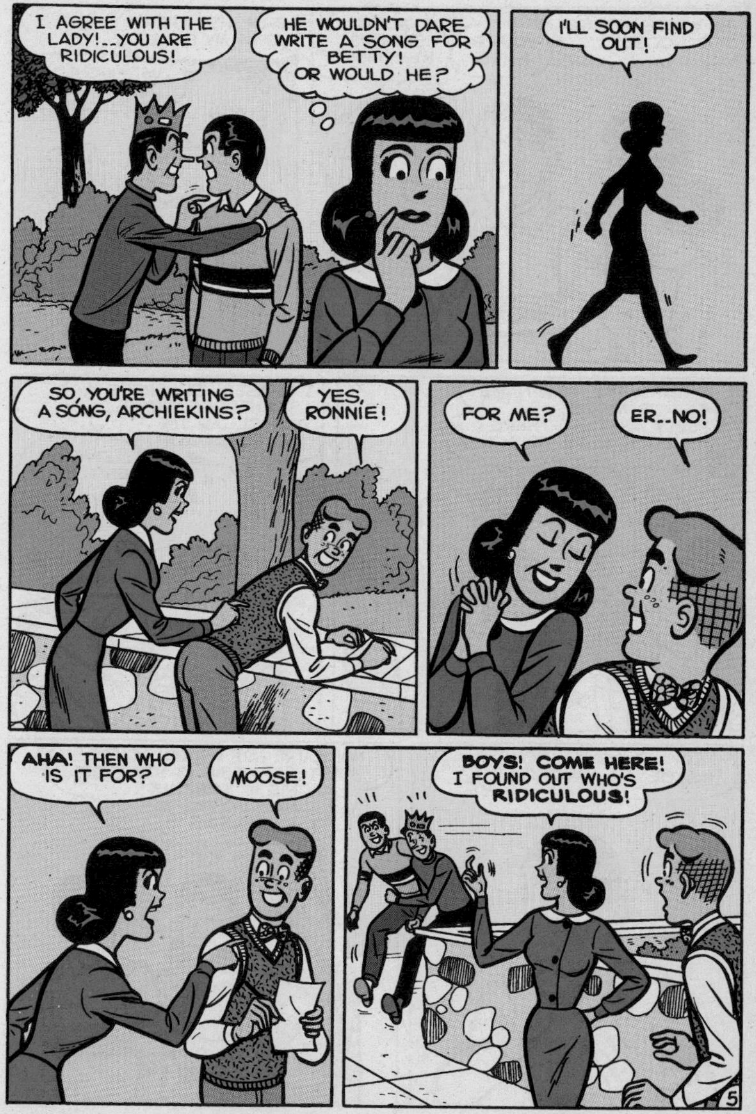

I AGREE WITH THE LADY!..YOU ARE RIDICULOUS!
HE WOULDN'T DARE WRITE A SONG FOR BETTY! OR WOULD HE?
I'LL SOON FIND OUT!
SO, YOU'RE WRITING A SONG, ARCHIEKINS?
YES, RONNIE!
FOR ME?
ER..NO!
AHA! THEN WHO IS IT FOR?
MOOSE!
BOYS! COME HERE! I FOUND OUT WHO'S RIDICULOUS!
5

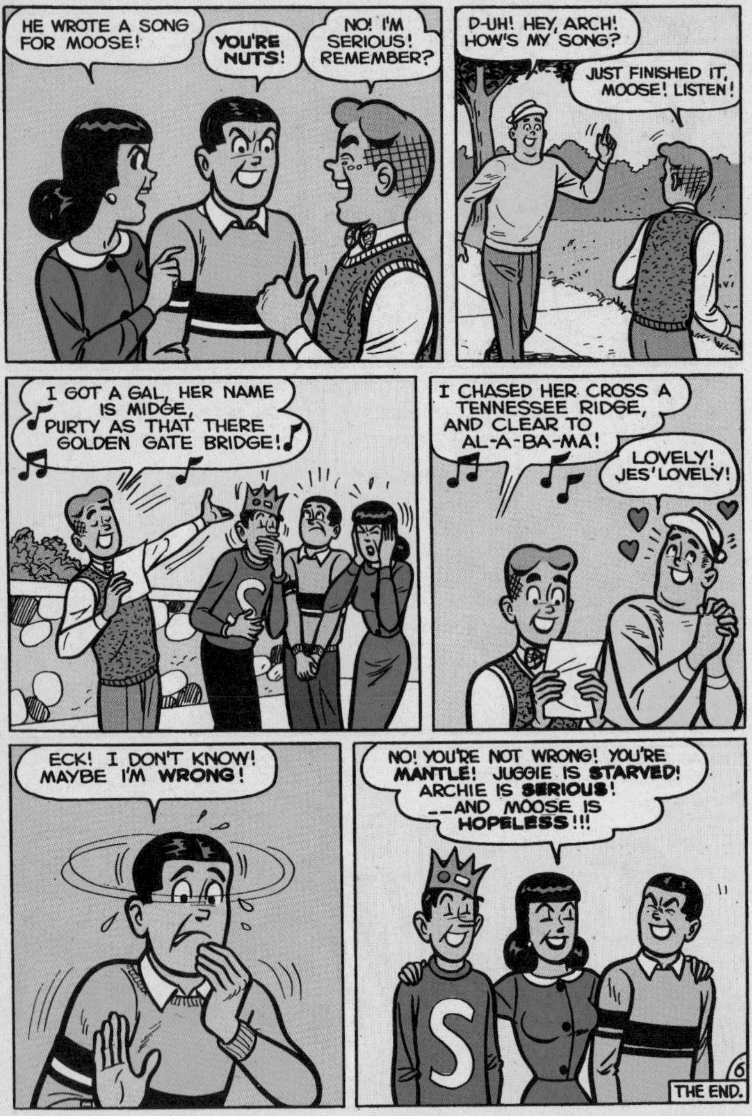
HE WROTE A SONG FOR MOOSE!
YOU'RE NUTS!
NO! I'M SERIOUS! REMEMBER?
D-UH! HEY, ARCH! HOW'S MY SONG?
JUST FINISHED IT, MOOSE! LISTEN!
I GOT A GAL, HER NAME IS MIDGE, PURTY AS THAT THERE GOLDEN GATE BRIDGE!
I CHASED HER CROSS A TENNESSEE RIDGE, AND CLEAR TO AL-A-BA-MA!
LOVELY! JES' LOVELY!
ECK! I DON'T KNOW! MAYBE I'M WRONG!
NO! YOU'RE NOT WRONG! YOU'RE MANTLE! JUGGIE IS STARVED! ARCHIE IS SERIOUS! --AND MOOSE IS HOPELESS!!!
6
THE END.

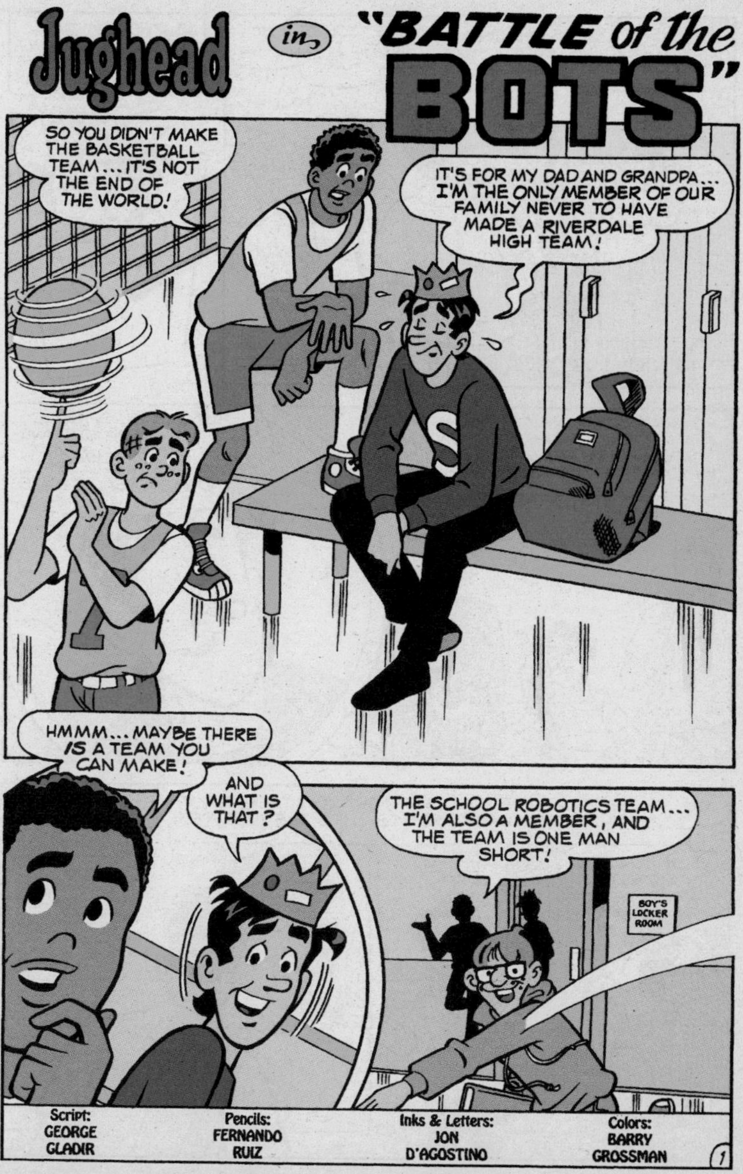
Jughead in "BATTLE of the BOTS"
SO YOU DIDN'T MAKE THE BASKETBALL TEAM... IT'S NOT THE END OF THE WORLD!
IT'S FOR MY DAD AND GRANDPA... I'M THE ONLY MEMBER OF OUR FAMILY NEVER TO HAVE MADE A RIVERDALE HIGH TEAM!
HMMM... MAYBE THERE IS A TEAM YOU CAN MAKE!
AND WHAT IS THAT?
THE SCHOOL ROBOTICS TEAM... I'M ALSO A MEMBER, AND THE TEAM IS ONE MAN SHORT!
BOY'S LOCKER ROOM

Script: GEORGE GLADIR | Pencils: FERNANDO RUIZ | Inks & Letters: JON D'AGOSTINO | Colors: BARRY GROSSMAN

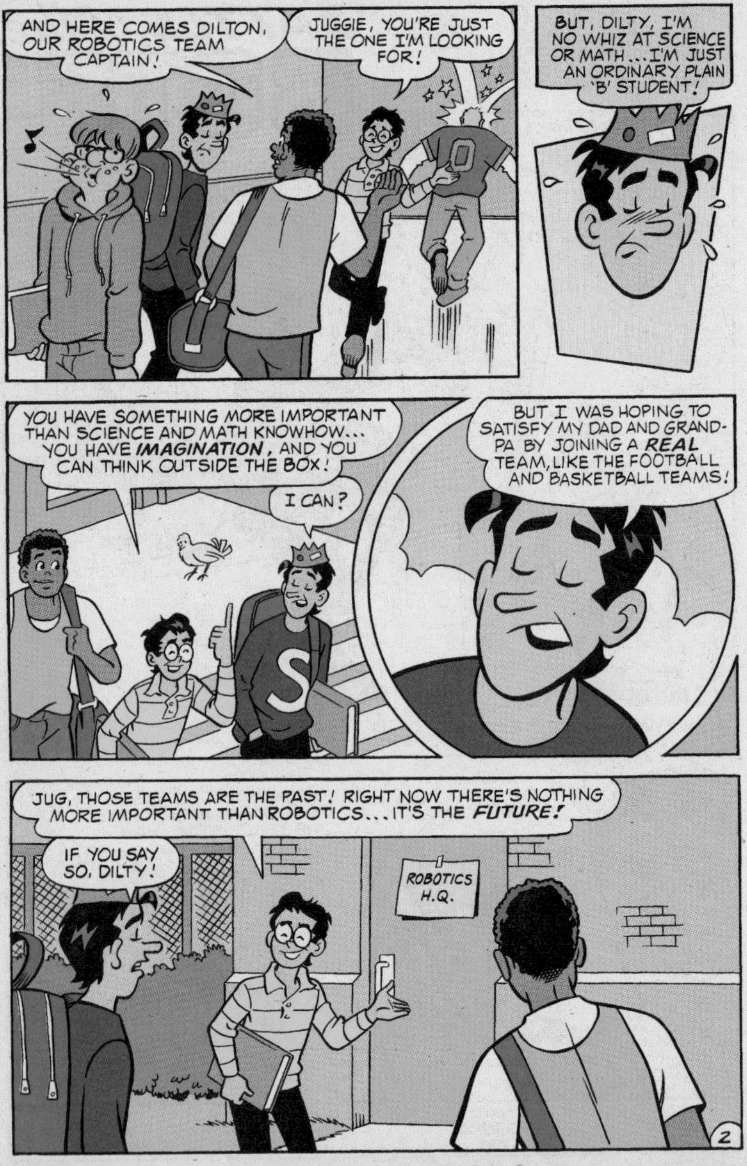

AND HERE COMES DILTON, OUR ROBOTICS TEAM CAPTAIN!
JUGGIE, YOU'RE JUST THE ONE I'M LOOKING FOR!
BUT, DILTY, I'M NO WHIZ AT SCIENCE OR MATH... I'M JUST AN ORDINARY PLAIN 'B' STUDENT!
YOU HAVE SOMETHING MORE IMPORTANT THAN SCIENCE AND MATH KNOWHOW... YOU HAVE IMAGINATION, AND YOU CAN THINK OUTSIDE THE BOX!
I CAN?
BUT I WAS HOPING TO SATISFY MY DAD AND GRAND-PA BY JOINING A REAL TEAM, LIKE THE FOOTBALL AND BASKETBALL TEAMS!
JUG, THOSE TEAMS ARE THE PAST! RIGHT NOW THERE'S NOTHING MORE IMPORTANT THAN ROBOTICS... IT'S THE FUTURE!
IF YOU SAY SO, DILTY!
ROBOTICS H.Q.

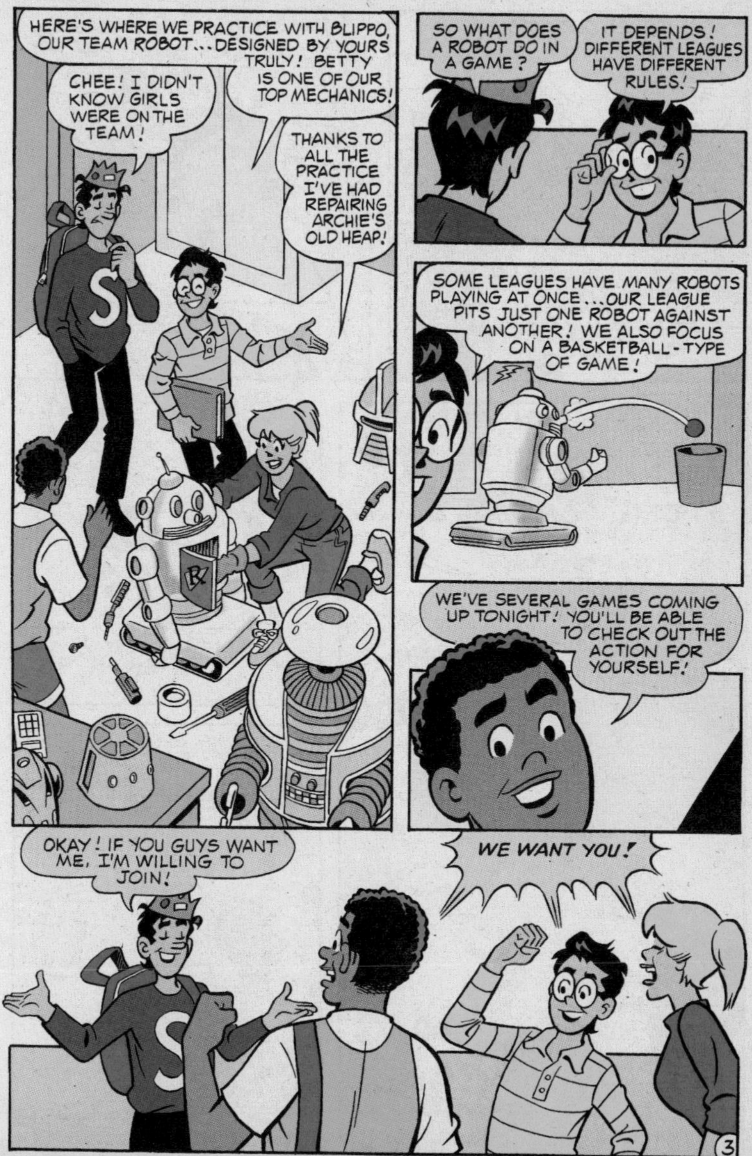

HERE'S WHERE WE PRACTICE WITH BLIPPO, OUR TEAM ROBOT... DESIGNED BY YOURS TRULY! BETTY IS ONE OF OUR TOP MECHANICS!
CHEE! I DIDN'T KNOW GIRLS WERE ON THE TEAM!
THANKS TO ALL THE PRACTICE I'VE HAD REPAIRING ARCHIE'S OLD HEAP!
SO WHAT DOES A ROBOT DO IN A GAME?
IT DEPENDS! DIFFERENT LEAGUES HAVE DIFFERENT RULES!
SOME LEAGUES HAVE MANY ROBOTS PLAYING AT ONCE... OUR LEAGUE PITS JUST ONE ROBOT AGAINST ANOTHER! WE ALSO FOCUS ON A BASKETBALL-TYPE OF GAME!
WE'VE SEVERAL GAMES COMING UP TONIGHT! YOU'LL BE ABLE TO CHECK OUT THE ACTION FOR YOURSELF!
OKAY! IF YOU GUYS WANT ME, I'M WILLING TO JOIN!
WE WANT YOU!
3

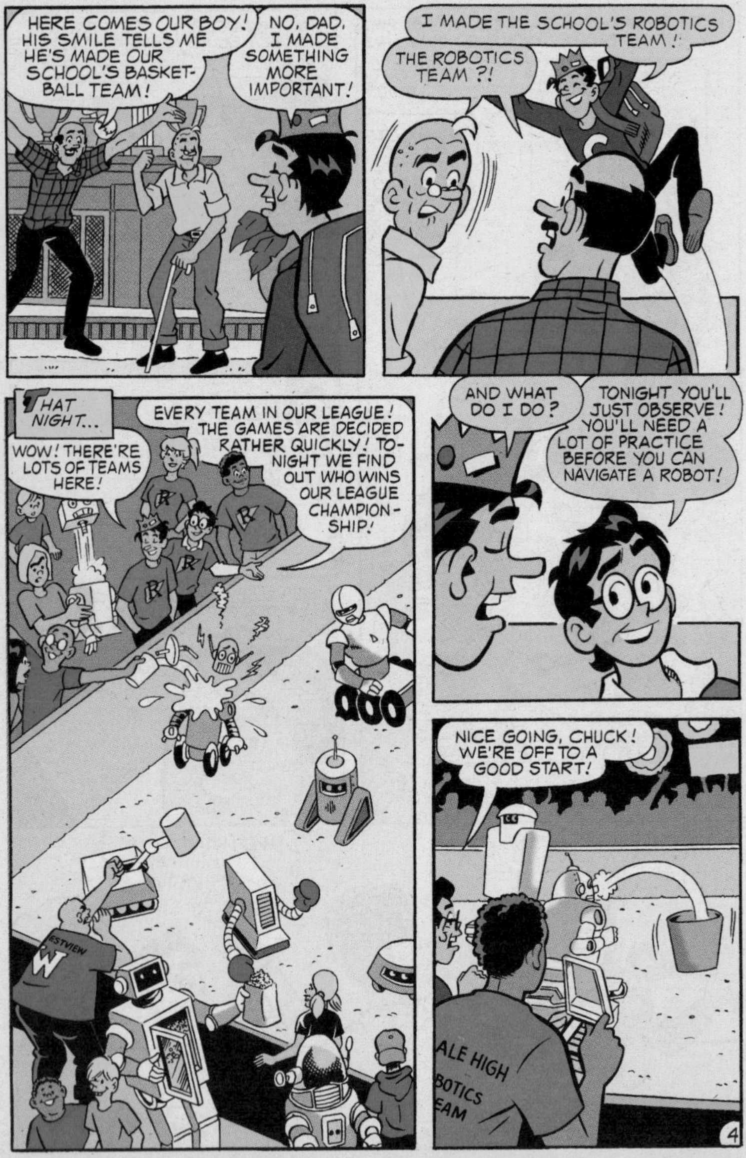

HERE COMES OUR BOY! HIS SMILE TELLS ME HE'S MADE OUR SCHOOL'S BASKET-BALL TEAM!
NO, DAD, I MADE SOMETHING MORE IMPORTANT!
I MADE THE SCHOOL'S ROBOTICS TEAM!
THE ROBOTICS TEAM?!
THAT NIGHT...
WOW! THERE'RE LOTS OF TEAMS HERE!
EVERY TEAM IN OUR LEAGUE! THE GAMES ARE DECIDED RATHER QUICKLY! TO-NIGHT WE FIND OUT WHO WINS OUR LEAGUE CHAMPION-SHIP!
AND WHAT DO I DO?
TONIGHT YOU'LL JUST OBSERVE! YOU'LL NEED A LOT OF PRACTICE BEFORE YOU CAN NAVIGATE A ROBOT!
NICE GOING, CHUCK! WE'RE OFF TO A GOOD START!
ALE HIGH
BOTICS
EAM

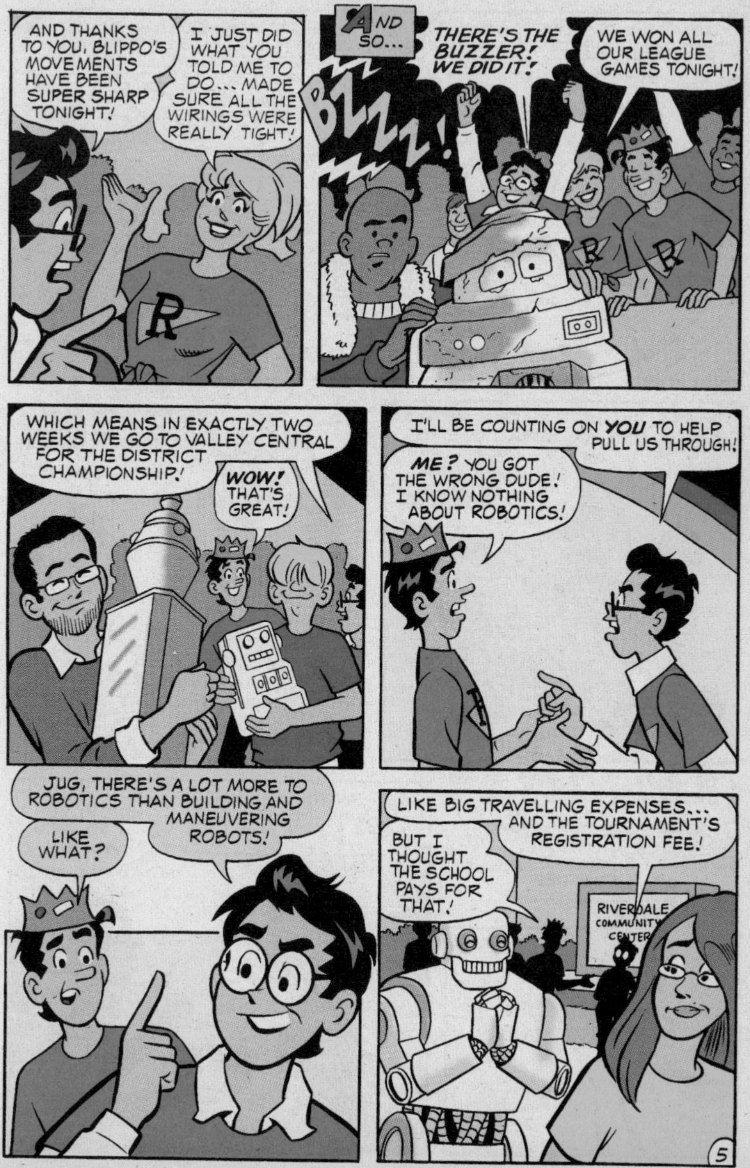
AND THANKS TO YOU, BLIPPO'S MOVEMENTS HAVE BEEN SUPER SHARP TONIGHT!
I JUST DID WHAT YOU TOLD ME TO DO... MADE SURE ALL THE WIRINGS WERE REALLY TIGHT!
AND SO...
BZZZZ!
THERE'S THE BUZZER! WE DID IT!
WE WON ALL OUR LEAGUE GAMES TONIGHT!
WHICH MEANS IN EXACTLY TWO WEEKS WE GO TO VALLEY CENTRAL FOR THE DISTRICT CHAMPIONSHIP!
WOW! THAT'S GREAT!
I'LL BE COUNTING ON YOU TO HELP PULL US THROUGH!
ME? YOU GOT THE WRONG DUDE! I KNOW NOTHING ABOUT ROBOTICS!
JUG, THERE'S A LOT MORE TO ROBOTICS THAN BUILDING AND MANEUVERING ROBOTS!
LIKE WHAT?
LIKE BIG TRAVELLING EXPENSES... AND THE TOURNAMENT'S REGISTRATION FEE!
BUT I THOUGHT THE SCHOOL PAYS FOR THAT!
RIVERDALE COMMUNITY CENTER
5

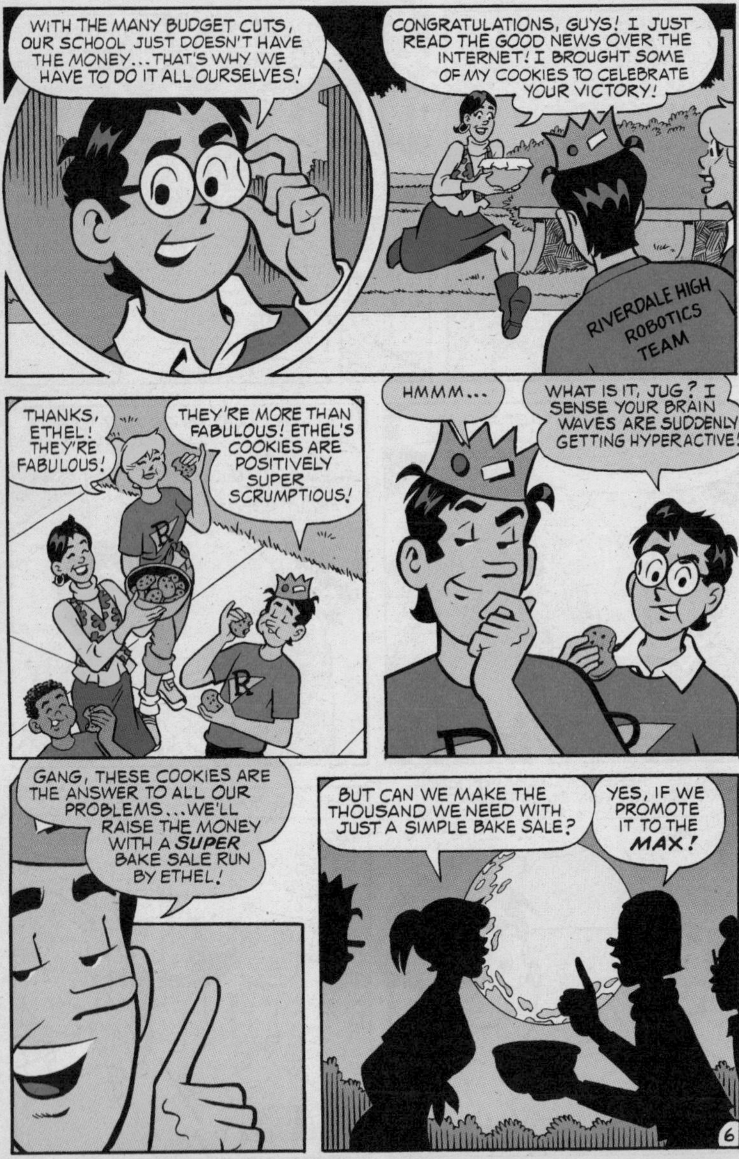
WITH THE MANY BUDGET CUTS, OUR SCHOOL JUST DOESN'T HAVE THE MONEY... THAT'S WHY WE HAVE TO DO IT ALL OURSELVES!
CONGRATULATIONS, GUYS! I JUST READ THE GOOD NEWS OVER THE INTERNET! I BROUGHT SOME OF MY COOKIES TO CELEBRATE YOUR VICTORY!
RIVERDALE HIGH ROBOTICS TEAM
THANKS, ETHEL! THEY'RE FABULOUS!
THEY'RE MORE THAN FABULOUS! ETHEL'S COOKIES ARE POSITIVELY SUPER SCRUMPTIOUS!
HMMM...
WHAT IS IT, JUG? I SENSE YOUR BRAIN WAVES ARE SUDDENLY GETTING HYPERACTIVE!
GANG, THESE COOKIES ARE THE ANSWER TO ALL OUR PROBLEMS... WE'LL RAISE THE MONEY WITH A *SUPER* BAKE SALE RUN BY ETHEL!
BUT CAN WE MAKE THE THOUSAND WE NEED WITH JUST A SIMPLE BAKE SALE?
YES, IF WE PROMOTE IT TO THE ***MAX!***

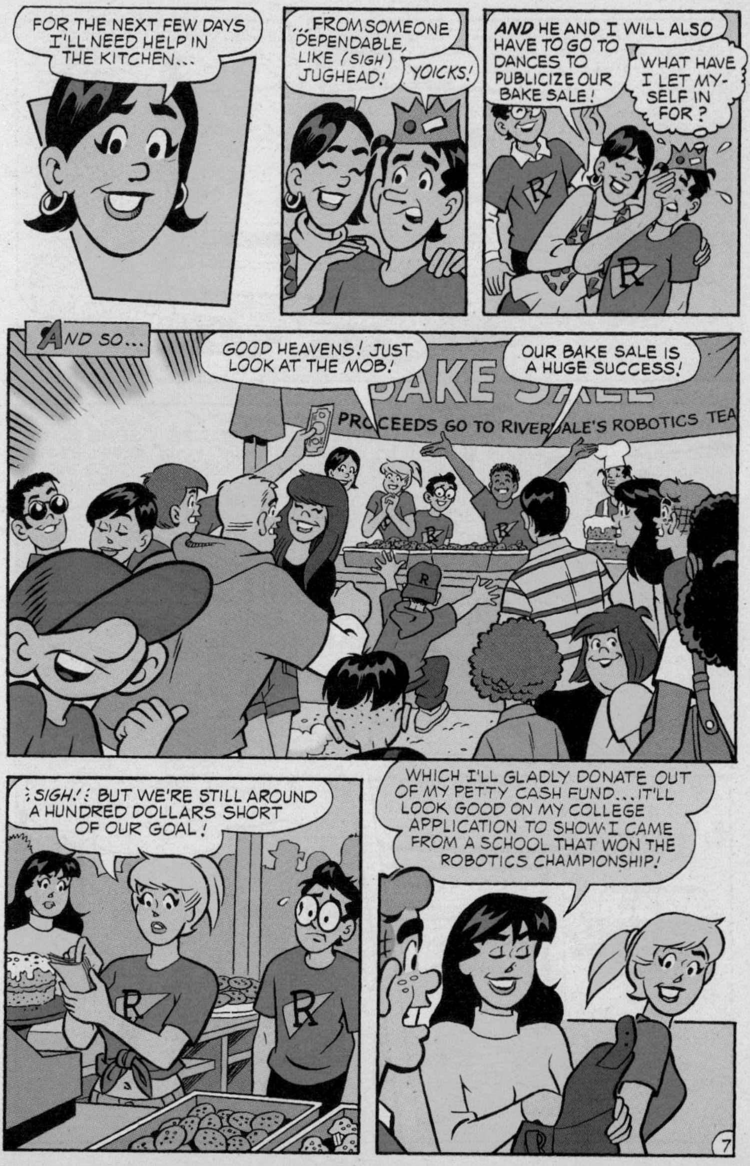

FOR THE NEXT FEW DAYS I'LL NEED HELP IN THE KITCHEN...
...FROM SOMEONE DEPENDABLE, LIKE (SIGH) JUGHEAD!
YOICKS!
AND HE AND I WILL ALSO HAVE TO GO TO DANCES TO PUBLICIZE OUR BAKE SALE!
WHAT HAVE I LET MY-SELF IN FOR?
AND SO...
GOOD HEAVENS! JUST LOOK AT THE MOB!
OUR BAKE SALE IS A HUGE SUCCESS!
PROCEEDS GO TO RIVERDALE'S ROBOTICS TEA
:SIGH!: BUT WE'RE STILL AROUND A HUNDRED DOLLARS SHORT OF OUR GOAL!
WHICH I'LL GLADLY DONATE OUT OF MY PETTY CASH FUND... IT'LL LOOK GOOD ON MY COLLEGE APPLICATION TO SHOW I CAME FROM A SCHOOL THAT WON THE ROBOTICS CHAMPIONSHIP!

AND MR. LODGE CONTRIBUTED ONE OF HIS COMPANY'S VANS TO TAKE US TO VALLEY CENTRAL!

ETHEL WOULD LIKE TO JOIN US!

OKAY, JUST SO LONG AS SHE DOESN'T HAVE TO SIT ON MY LAP!

DON'T GO GIVING ME IDEAS, HANDSOME!

DILT, WHAT'S WITH THE DIFFERENT-SIZED PIPE SECTIONS YOU BROUGHT ALONG?

OH, JUST SOME EXTRA SUPPLIES IN CASE THEY'RE NEEDED!

WELL, HERE WE ARE, GANG!

VALLEY CENTRAL

DISTRICT ROBOTIC CHAMPIONSHIP TODAY

QUICK! YOUR GAME WITH MORTON HIGH IS ABOUT TO BEGIN!

ROBOT WARS

8

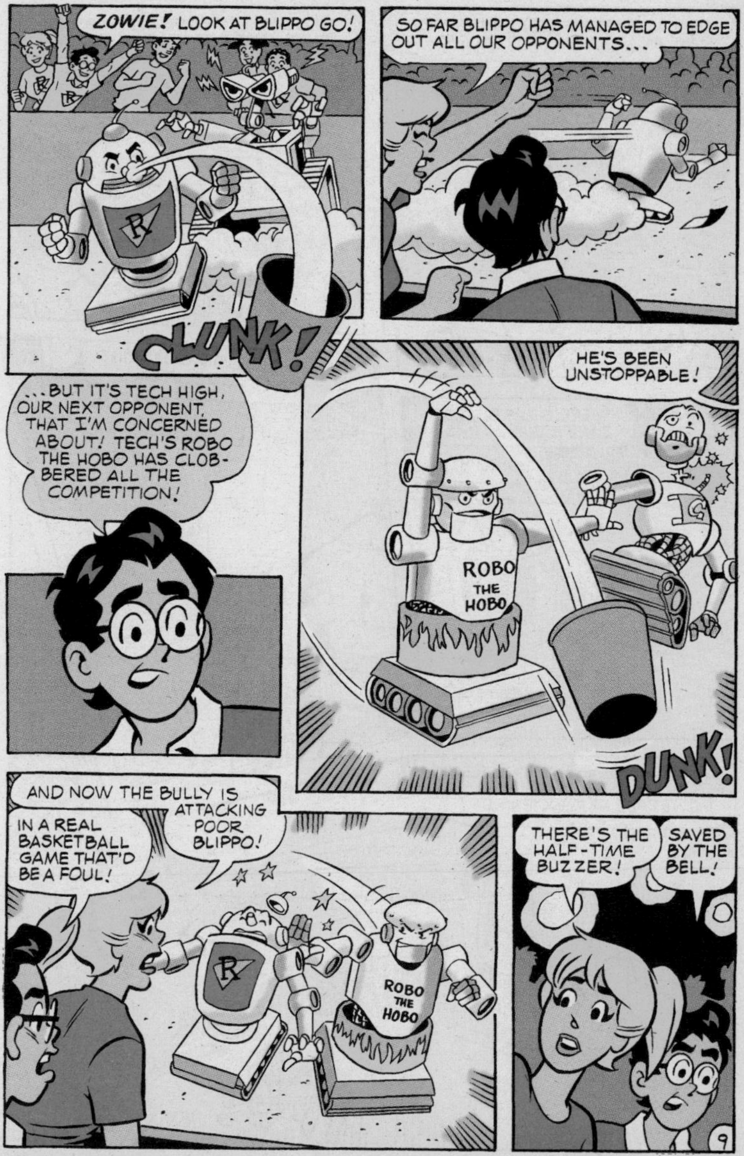

ZOWIE! LOOK AT BLIPPO GO!
CLUNK!
SO FAR BLIPPO HAS MANAGED TO EDGE OUT ALL OUR OPPONENTS...
...BUT IT'S TECH HIGH, OUR NEXT OPPONENT, THAT I'M CONCERNED ABOUT! TECH'S ROBO THE HOBO HAS CLOBBERED ALL THE COMPETITION!
HE'S BEEN UNSTOPPABLE!
ROBO THE HOBO
DUNK!
AND NOW THE BULLY IS ATTACKING POOR BLIPPO!
IN A REAL BASKETBALL GAME THAT'D BE A FOUL!
ROBO THE HOBO
THERE'S THE HALF-TIME BUZZER!
SAVED BY THE BELL!

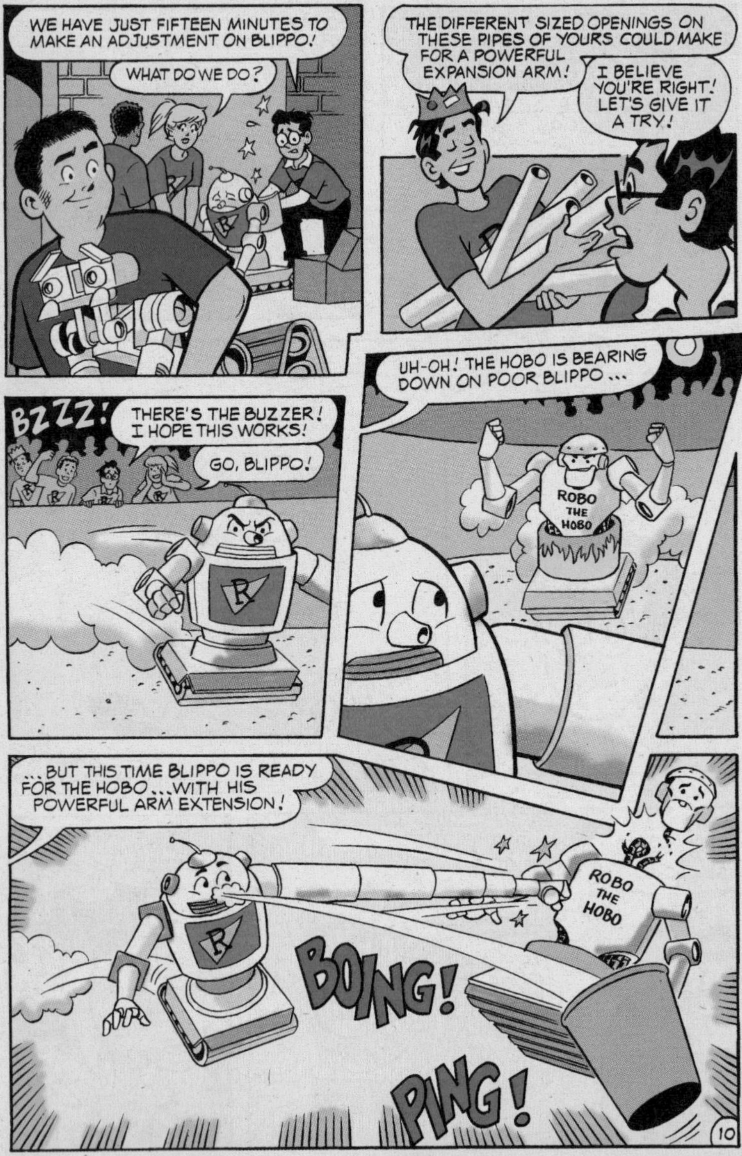

WE HAVE JUST FIFTEEN MINUTES TO MAKE AN ADJUSTMENT ON BLIPPO!
WHAT DO WE DO?
THE DIFFERENT SIZED OPENINGS ON THESE PIPES OF YOURS COULD MAKE FOR A POWERFUL EXPANSION ARM!
I BELIEVE YOU'RE RIGHT! LET'S GIVE IT A TRY!
BZZZ!
THERE'S THE BUZZER! I HOPE THIS WORKS!
GO, BLIPPO!
UH-OH! THE HOBO IS BEARING DOWN ON POOR BLIPPO...
ROBO THE HOBO
...BUT THIS TIME BLIPPO IS READY FOR THE HOBO...WITH HIS POWERFUL ARM EXTENSION!
ROBO THE HOBO
BOING!
PING!
10

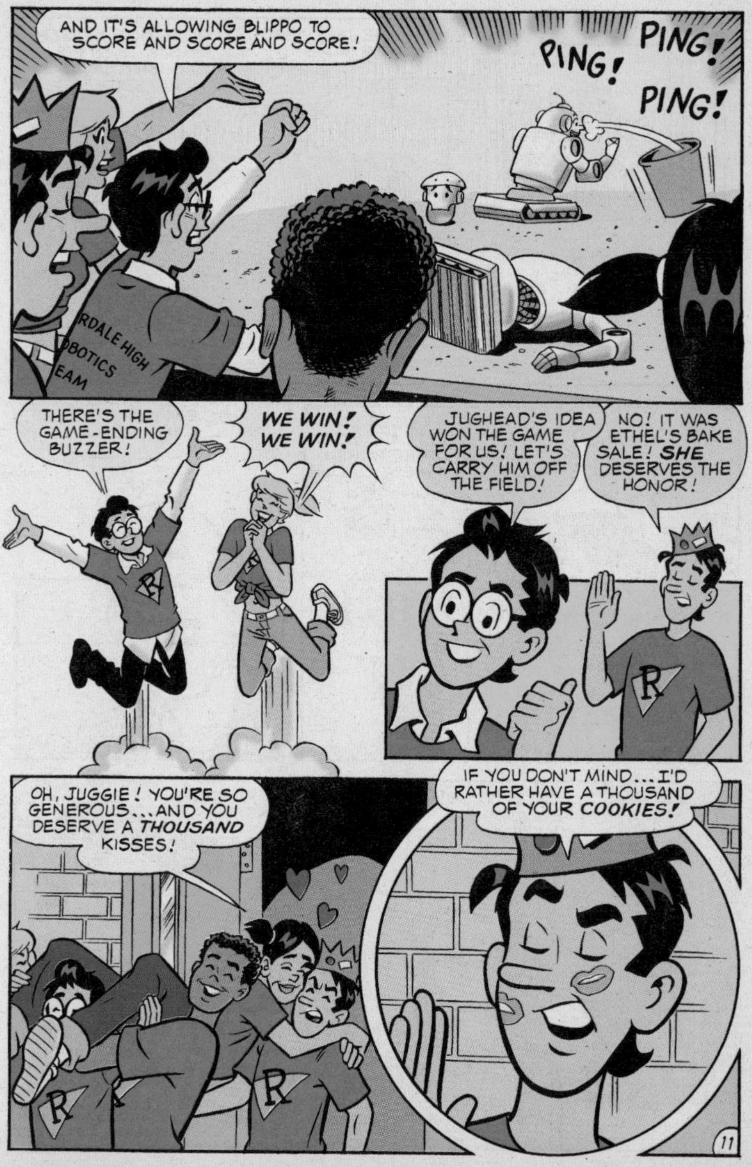
AND IT'S ALLOWING BLIPPO TO SCORE AND SCORE AND SCORE!
PING!
PING!
PING!
RDALE HIGH OBOTICS EAM
THERE'S THE GAME-ENDING BUZZER!
WE WIN! WE WIN!
JUGHEAD'S IDEA WON THE GAME FOR US! LET'S CARRY HIM OFF THE FIELD!
NO! IT WAS ETHEL'S BAKE SALE! SHE DESERVES THE HONOR!
OH, JUGGIE! YOU'RE SO GENEROUS...AND YOU DESERVE A THOUSAND KISSES!
IF YOU DON'T MIND... I'D RATHER HAVE A THOUSAND OF YOUR COOKIES!
11

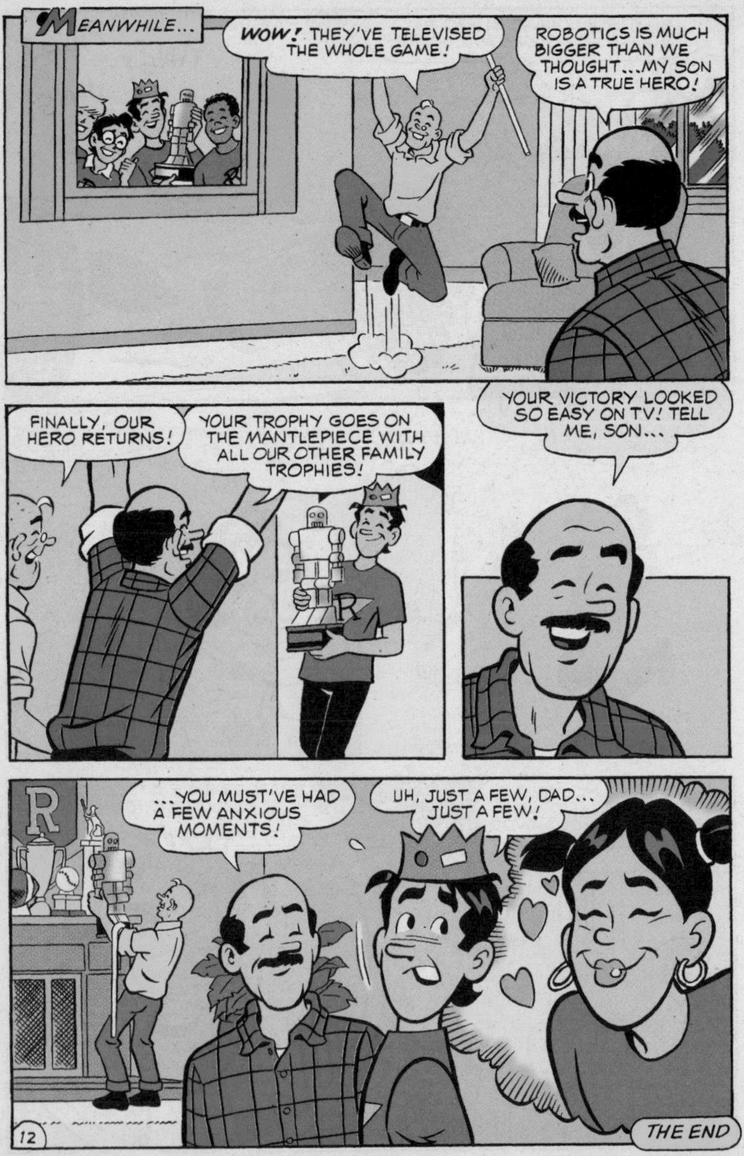
MEANWHILE...
WOW! THEY'VE TELEVISED THE WHOLE GAME!
ROBOTICS IS MUCH BIGGER THAN WE THOUGHT...MY SON IS A TRUE HERO!
FINALLY, OUR HERO RETURNS!
YOUR TROPHY GOES ON THE MANTLEPIECE WITH ALL OUR OTHER FAMILY TROPHIES!
YOUR VICTORY LOOKED SO EASY ON TV! TELL ME, SON...
...YOU MUST'VE HAD A FEW ANXIOUS MOMENTS!
UH, JUST A FEW, DAD... JUST A FEW!
12
THE END

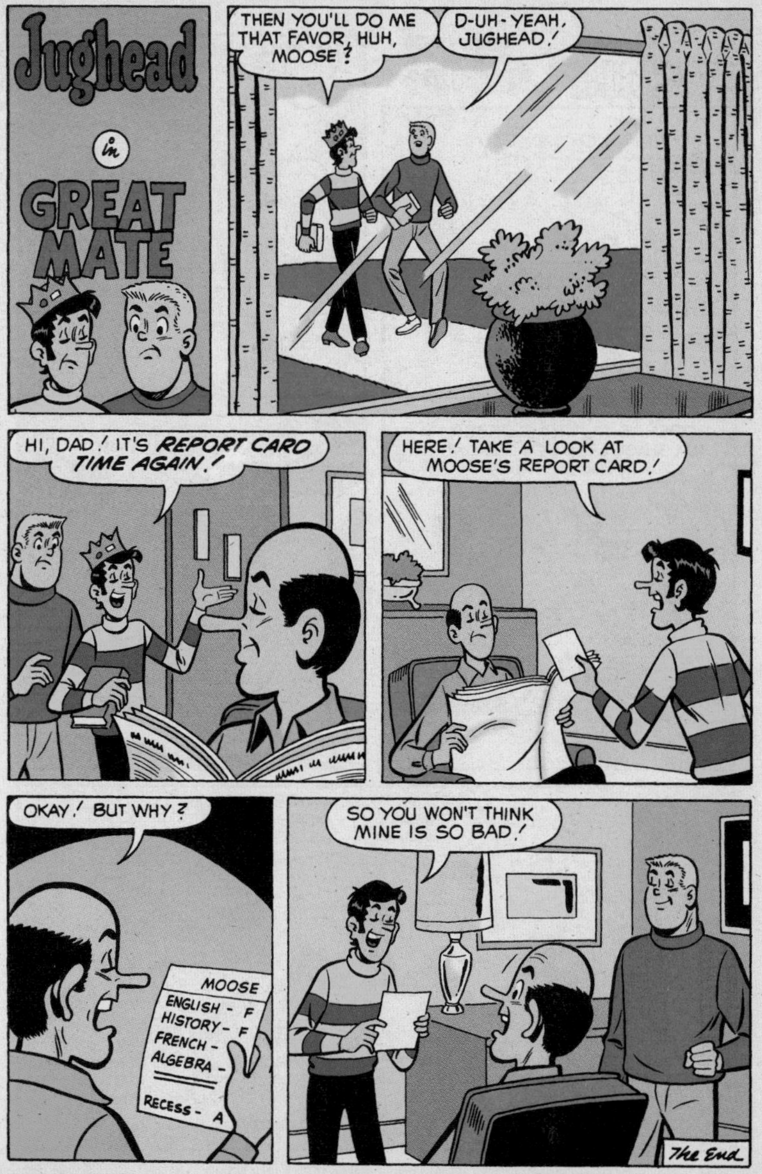
Jughead
in
GREAT MATE
THEN YOU'LL DO ME THAT FAVOR, HUH, MOOSE ?
D-UH-YEAH, JUGHEAD !
HI, DAD ! IT'S REPORT CARD TIME AGAIN !
HERE ! TAKE A LOOK AT MOOSE'S REPORT CARD !
OKAY ! BUT WHY ?
MOOSE
ENGLISH - F
HISTORY - F
FRENCH -
ALGEBRA -
RECESS - A
SO YOU WON'T THINK MINE IS SO BAD !
The End

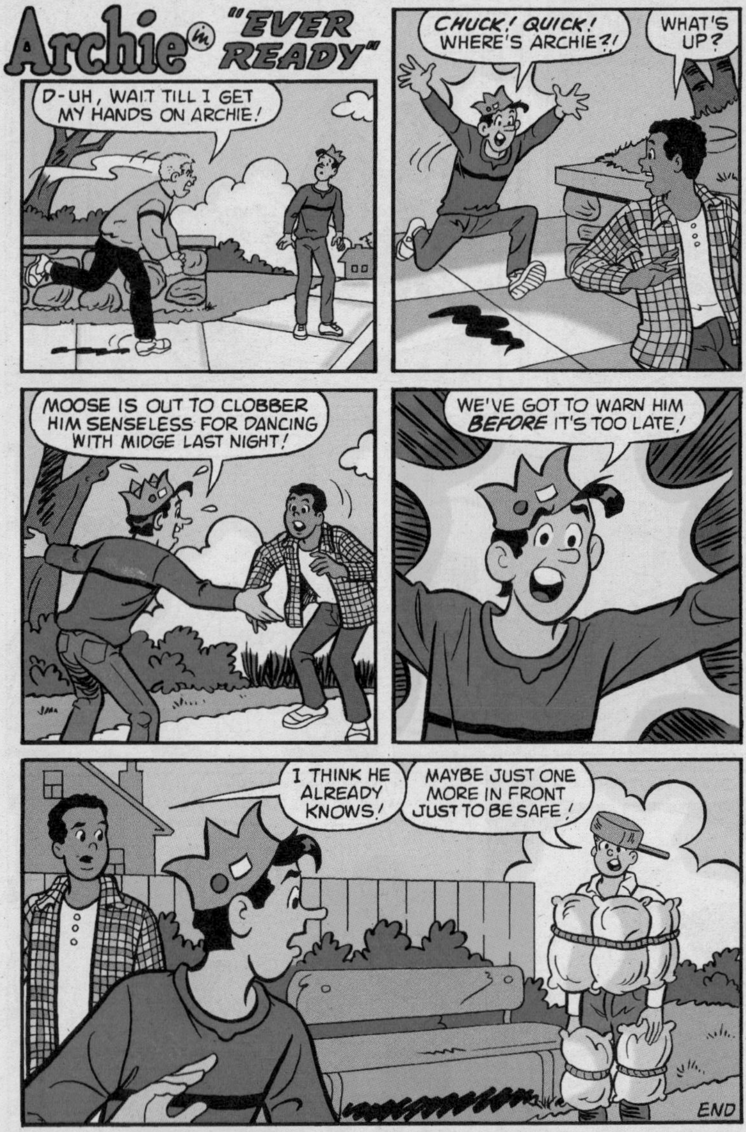
Archie in "EVER READY"
D-UH, WAIT TILL I GET MY HANDS ON ARCHIE!
CHUCK! QUICK! WHERE'S ARCHIE?!
WHAT'S UP?
MOOSE IS OUT TO CLOBBER HIM SENSELESS FOR DANCING WITH MIDGE LAST NIGHT!
WE'VE GOT TO WARN HIM BEFORE IT'S TOO LATE!
I THINK HE ALREADY KNOWS!
MAYBE JUST ONE MORE IN FRONT JUST TO BE SAFE!
END

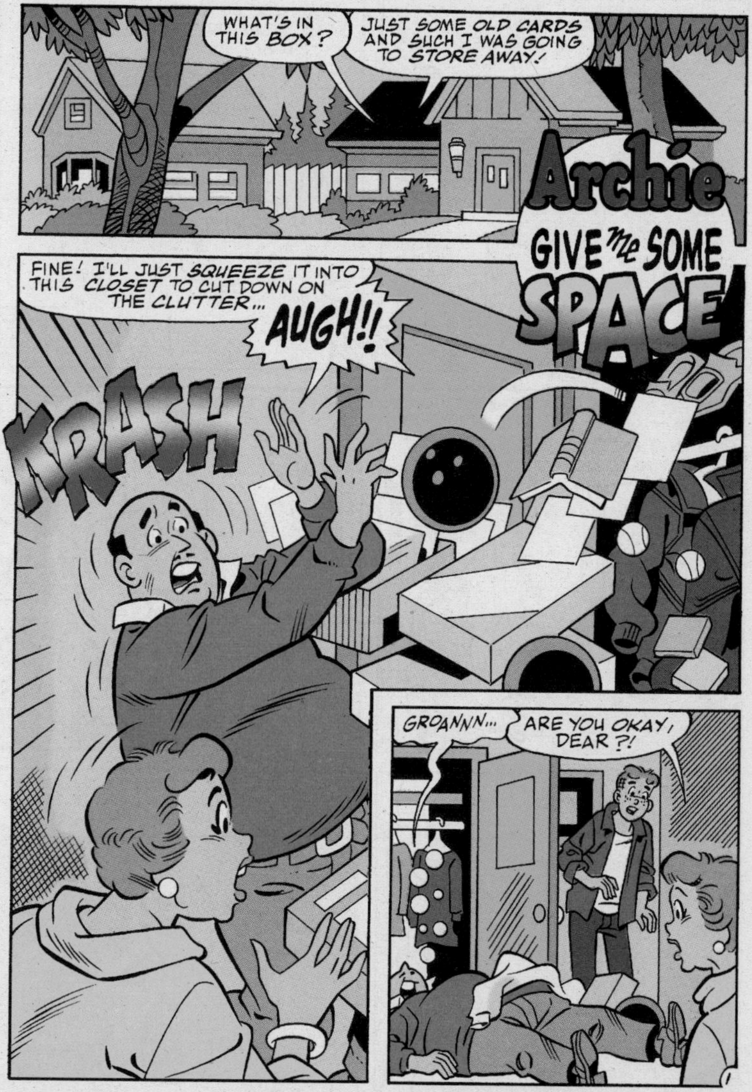
WHAT'S IN THIS BOX?
JUST SOME OLD CARDS AND SUCH I WAS GOING TO STORE AWAY!
Archie
GIVE me SOME SPACE
FINE! I'LL JUST SQUEEZE IT INTO THIS CLOSET TO CUT DOWN ON THE CLUTTER... AUGH!!
KRASH
GROANNN...
ARE YOU OKAY, DEAR?!

SCRIPT: BILL GOLLIHER PENCILS: PAT KENNEDY INKS: BOB SMITH
COLORS: BARRY GROSSMAN LETTERS: JACK MORELLI

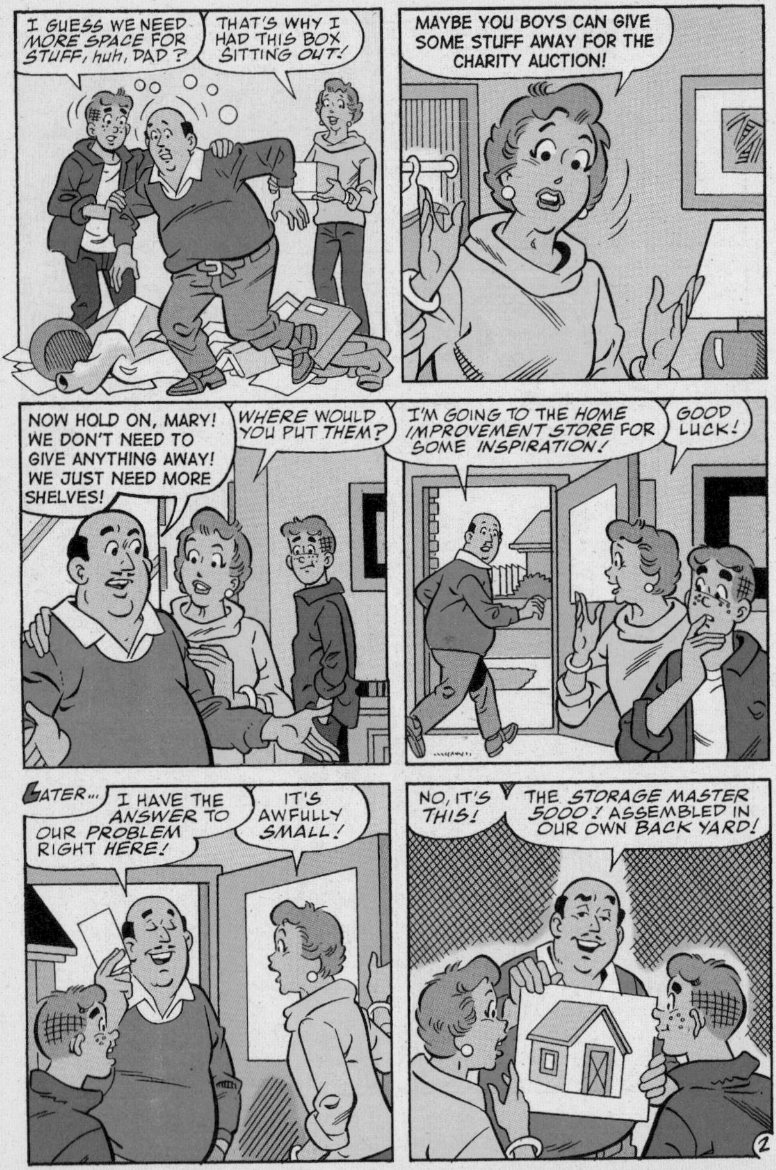
I GUESS WE NEED MORE SPACE FOR STUFF, huh, DAD?
THAT'S WHY I HAD THIS BOX SITTING OUT!
MAYBE YOU BOYS CAN GIVE SOME STUFF AWAY FOR THE CHARITY AUCTION!
NOW HOLD ON, MARY! WE DON'T NEED TO GIVE ANYTHING AWAY! WE JUST NEED MORE SHELVES!
WHERE WOULD YOU PUT THEM?
I'M GOING TO THE HOME IMPROVEMENT STORE FOR SOME INSPIRATION!
GOOD LUCK!
LATER...
I HAVE THE ANSWER TO OUR PROBLEM RIGHT HERE!
IT'S AWFULLY SMALL!
NO, IT'S THIS!
THE STORAGE MASTER 5000! ASSEMBLED IN OUR OWN BACK YARD!
2

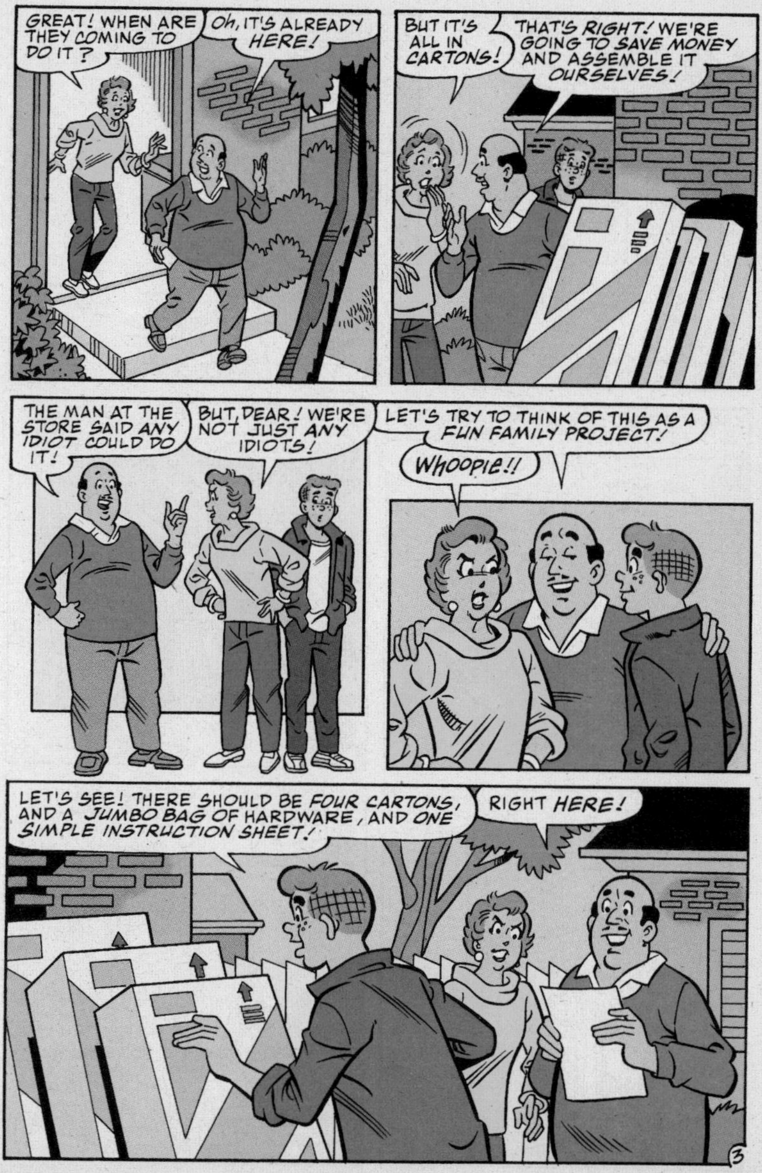
GREAT! WHEN ARE THEY COMING TO DO IT?
Oh, IT'S ALREADY HERE!
BUT IT'S ALL IN CARTONS!
THAT'S RIGHT! WE'RE GOING TO SAVE MONEY AND ASSEMBLE IT OURSELVES!
THE MAN AT THE STORE SAID ANY IDIOT COULD DO IT!
BUT, DEAR! WE'RE NOT JUST ANY IDIOTS!
LET'S TRY TO THINK OF THIS AS A FUN FAMILY PROJECT!
Whoopie!!
LET'S SEE! THERE SHOULD BE FOUR CARTONS, AND A JUMBO BAG OF HARDWARE, AND ONE SIMPLE INSTRUCTION SHEET!
RIGHT HERE!
3

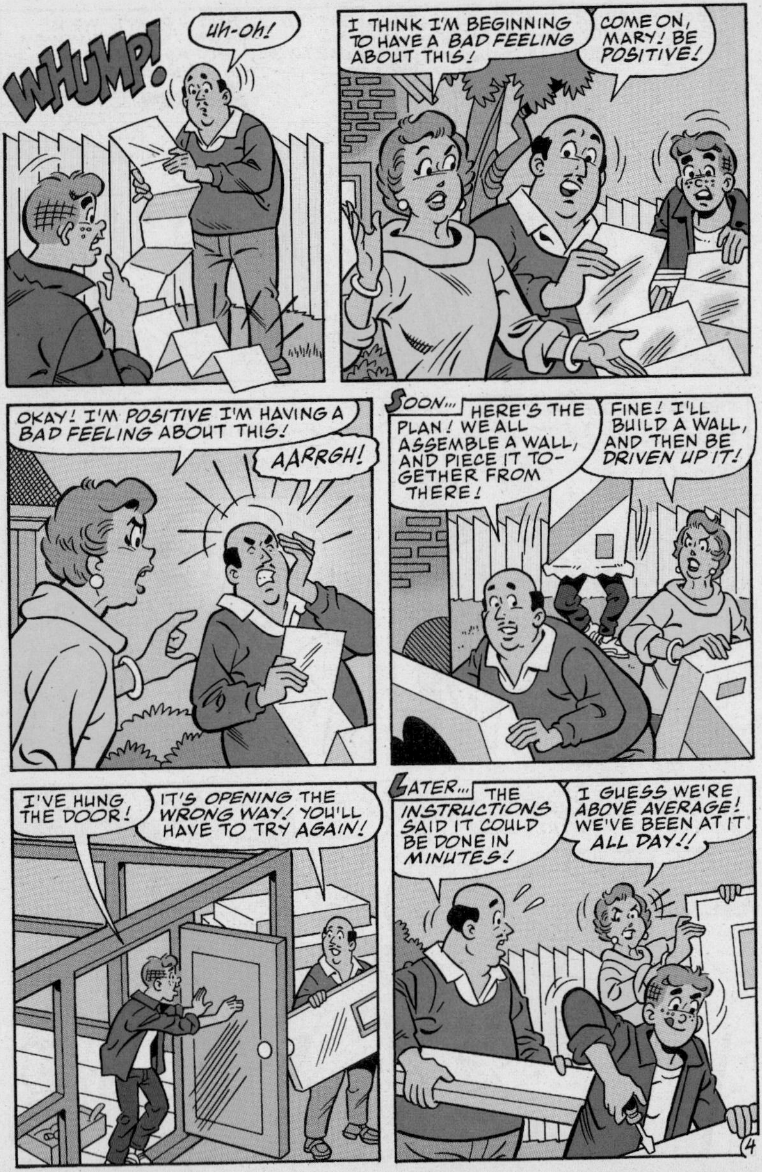
WHUMP!
Uh-oh!
I THINK I'M BEGINNING TO HAVE A BAD FEELING ABOUT THIS!
COME ON, MARY! BE POSITIVE!
OKAY! I'M POSITIVE I'M HAVING A BAD FEELING ABOUT THIS!
AARRGH!
SOON...
HERE'S THE PLAN! WE ALL ASSEMBLE A WALL, AND PIECE IT TOGETHER FROM THERE!
FINE! I'LL BUILD A WALL, AND THEN BE DRIVEN UP IT!
I'VE HUNG THE DOOR!
IT'S OPENING THE WRONG WAY! YOU'LL HAVE TO TRY AGAIN!
LATER...
THE INSTRUCTIONS SAID IT COULD BE DONE IN MINUTES!
I GUESS WE'RE ABOVE AVERAGE! WE'VE BEEN AT IT ALL DAY!!
4

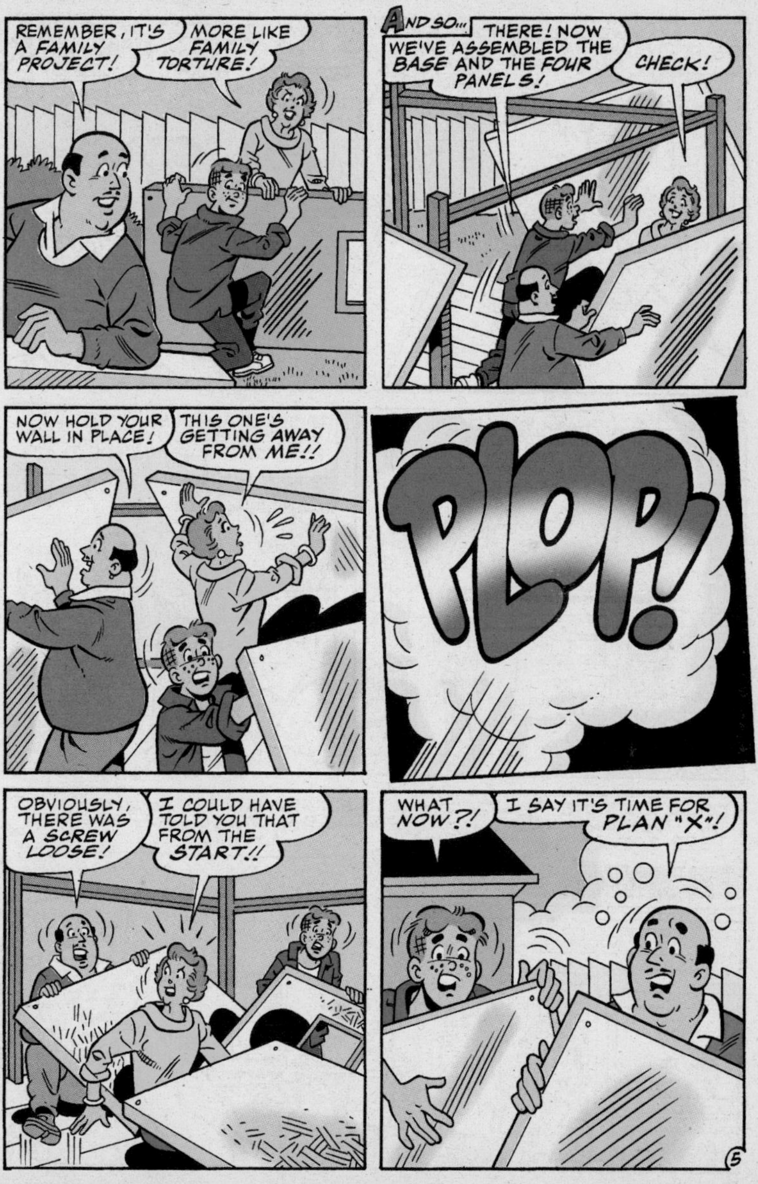
REMEMBER, IT'S A FAMILY PROJECT!
MORE LIKE FAMILY TORTURE!
AND SO...
THERE! NOW WE'VE ASSEMBLED THE BASE AND THE FOUR PANELS!
CHECK!
NOW HOLD YOUR WALL IN PLACE!
THIS ONE'S GETTING AWAY FROM ME!!
PLOP!
OBVIOUSLY, THERE WAS A SCREW LOOSE!
I COULD HAVE TOLD YOU THAT FROM THE START!!
WHAT NOW?!
I SAY IT'S TIME FOR PLAN "X"!
5

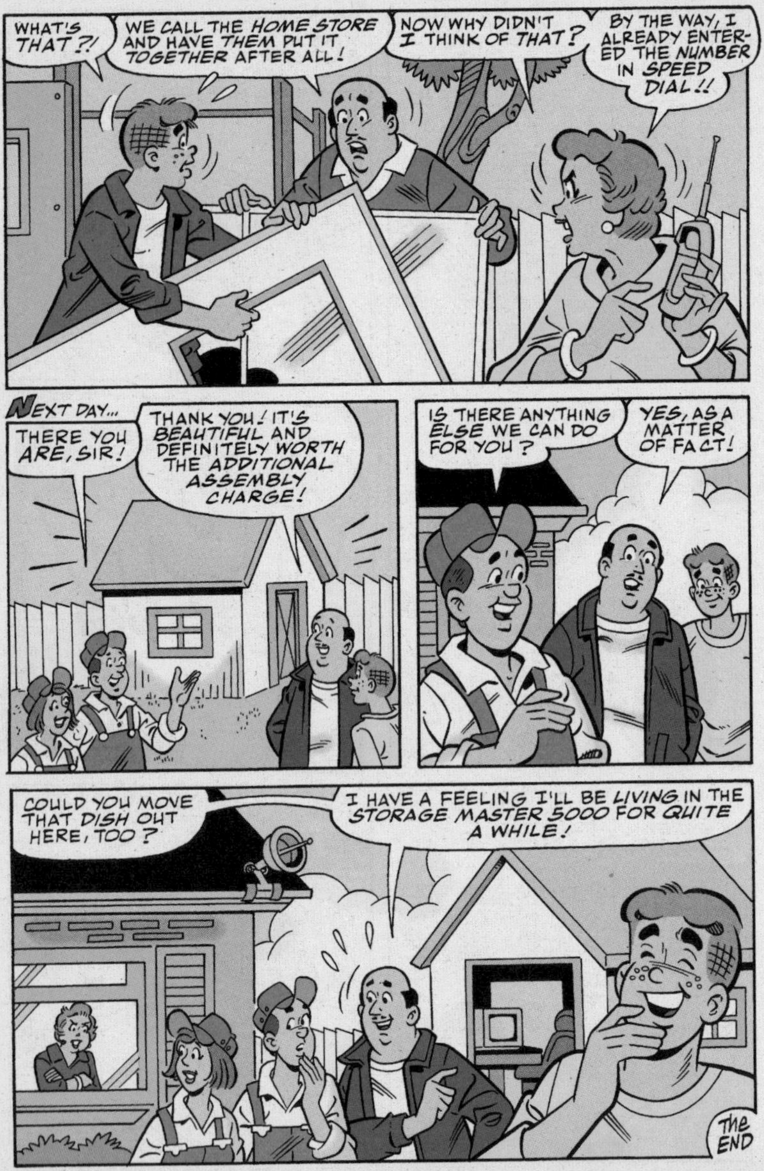
WHAT'S THAT ?!
WE CALL THE HOME STORE AND HAVE THEM PUT IT TOGETHER AFTER ALL!
NOW WHY DIDN'T I THINK OF THAT?
BY THE WAY, I ALREADY ENTERED THE NUMBER IN SPEED DIAL!!
NEXT DAY...
THERE YOU ARE, SIR!
THANK YOU! IT'S BEAUTIFUL AND DEFINITELY WORTH THE ADDITIONAL ASSEMBLY CHARGE!
IS THERE ANYTHING ELSE WE CAN DO FOR YOU?
YES, AS A MATTER OF FACT!
COULD YOU MOVE THAT DISH OUT HERE, TOO?
I HAVE A FEELING I'LL BE LIVING IN THE STORAGE MASTER 5000 FOR QUITE A WHILE!
THE END

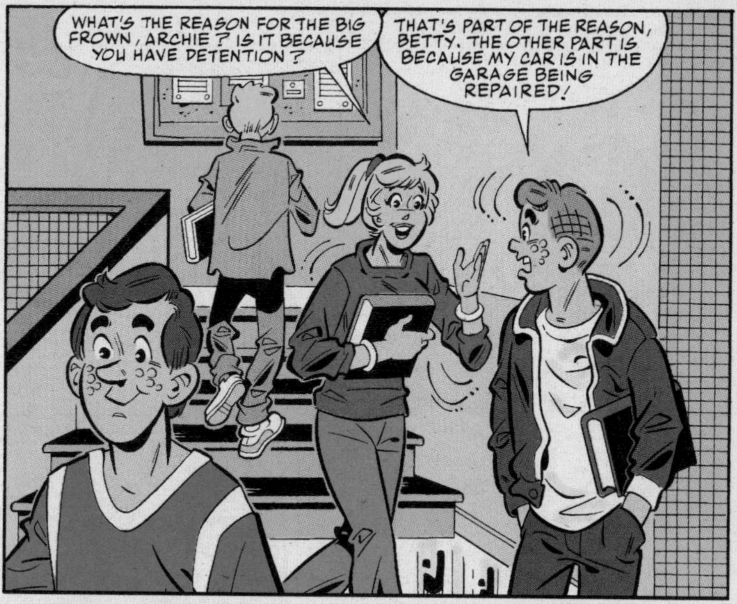
WHAT'S THE REASON FOR THE BIG FROWN, ARCHIE? IS IT BECAUSE YOU HAVE DETENTION?
THAT'S PART OF THE REASON, BETTY. THE OTHER PART IS BECAUSE MY CAR IS IN THE GARAGE BEING REPAIRED!

SCRIPT: MIKE PELLOWSKI PENCILS: TIM KENNEDY INKS: KEN SELIG
COLORS: BARRY GROSSMAN LETTERS: MINDY EISMAN

Archie in BUS BOY

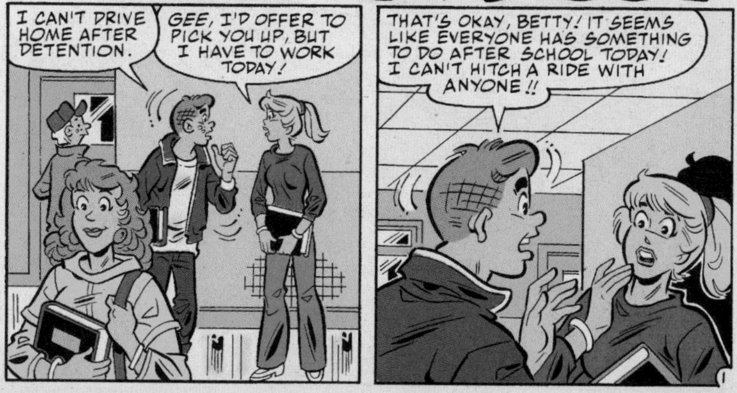
I CAN'T DRIVE HOME AFTER DETENTION.
GEE, I'D OFFER TO PICK YOU UP, BUT I HAVE TO WORK TODAY!
THAT'S OKAY, BETTY! IT SEEMS LIKE EVERYONE HAS SOMETHING TO DO AFTER SCHOOL TODAY! I CAN'T HITCH A RIDE WITH ANYONE!!

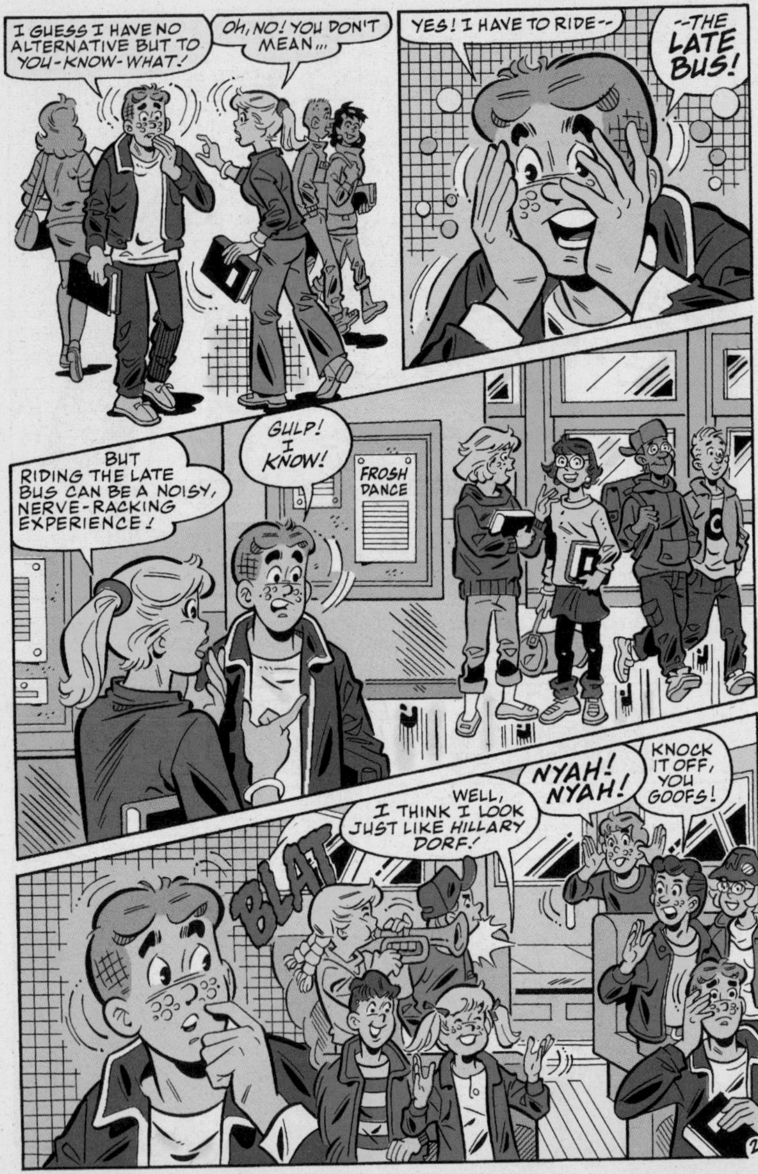
I GUESS I HAVE NO ALTERNATIVE BUT TO YOU-KNOW-WHAT!
Oh, NO! YOU DON'T MEAN...
YES! I HAVE TO RIDE--
--THE LATE BUS!
BUT RIDING THE LATE BUS CAN BE A NOISY, NERVE-RACKING EXPERIENCE!
GULP! I KNOW!
FROSH DANCE
BLAT
WELL, I THINK I LOOK JUST LIKE HILLARY DORF!
NYAH! NYAH!
KNOCK IT OFF, YOU GOOFS!

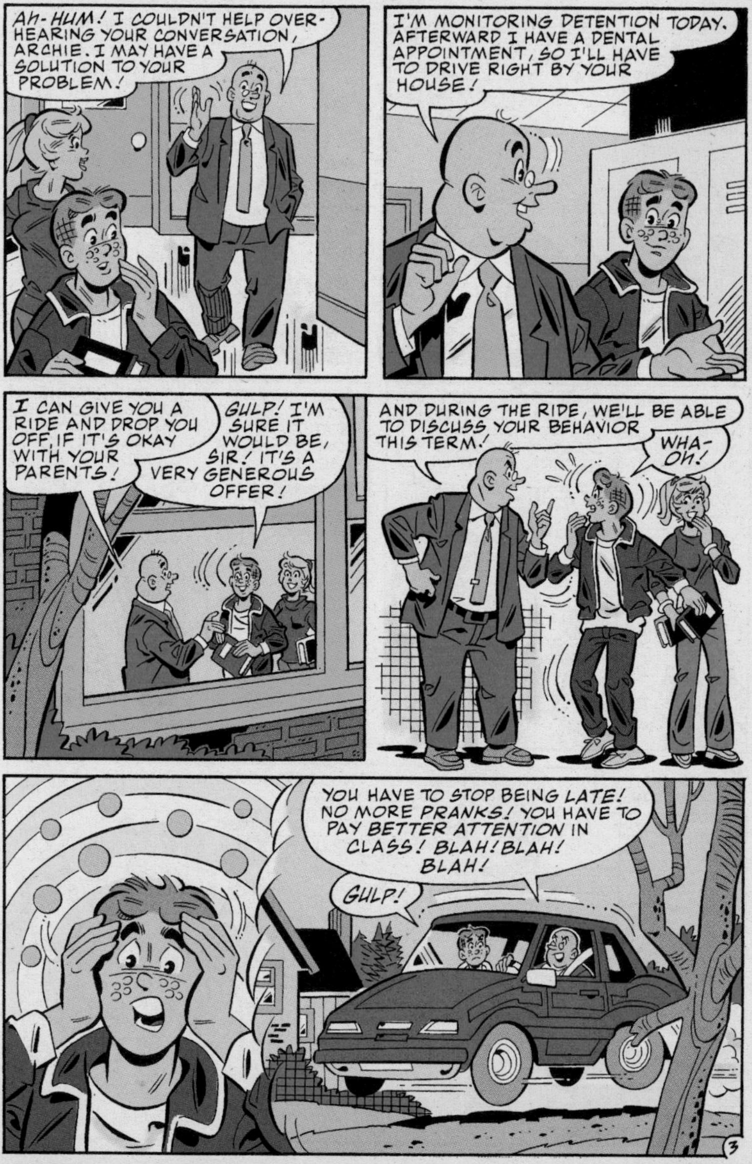

AH-HUM! I COULDN'T HELP OVER-HEARING YOUR CONVERSATION, ARCHIE. I MAY HAVE A SOLUTION TO YOUR PROBLEM!
I'M MONITORING DETENTION TODAY. AFTERWARD I HAVE A DENTAL APPOINTMENT, SO I'LL HAVE TO DRIVE RIGHT BY YOUR HOUSE!
I CAN GIVE YOU A RIDE AND DROP YOU OFF, IF IT'S OKAY WITH YOUR PARENTS!
GULP! I'M SURE IT WOULD BE, SIR! IT'S A VERY GENEROUS OFFER!
AND DURING THE RIDE, WE'LL BE ABLE TO DISCUSS YOUR BEHAVIOR THIS TERM!
WHA-OH!
YOU HAVE TO STOP BEING LATE! NO MORE PRANKS! YOU HAVE TO PAY BETTER ATTENTION IN CLASS! BLAH! BLAH! BLAH!
GULP!

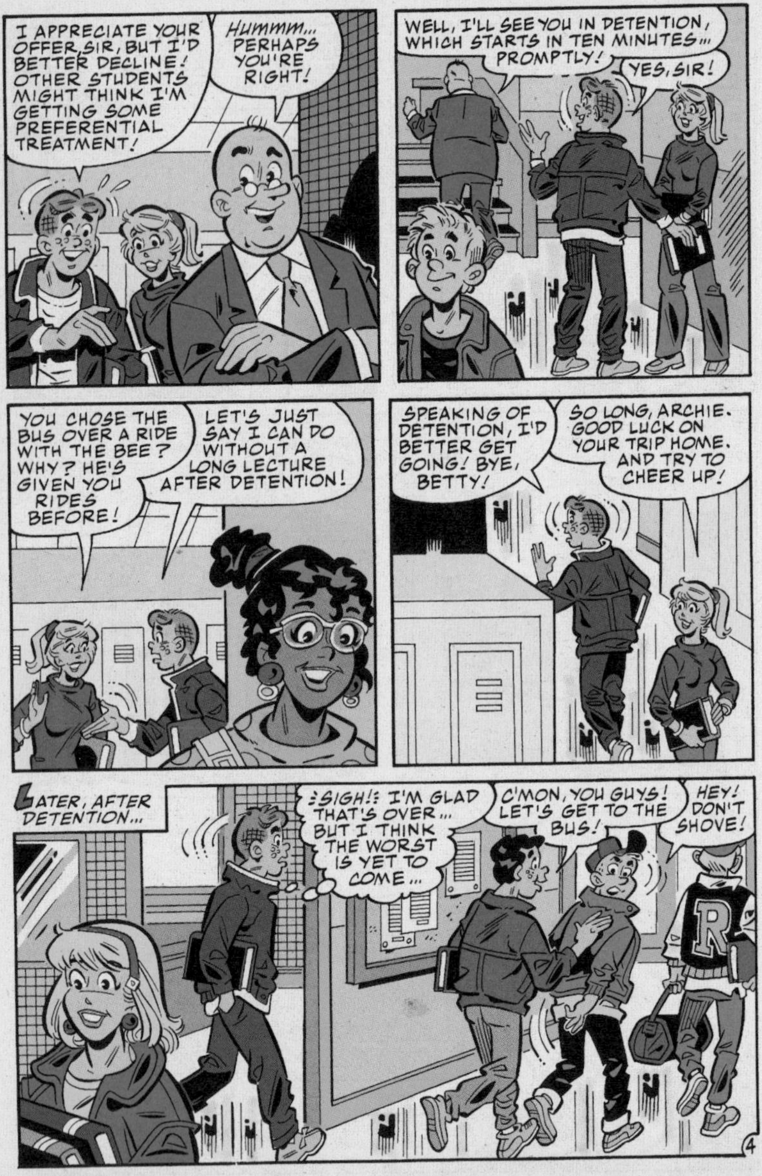
I APPRECIATE YOUR OFFER, SIR, BUT I'D BETTER DECLINE! OTHER STUDENTS MIGHT THINK I'M GETTING SOME PREFERENTIAL TREATMENT!
HUMMM... PERHAPS YOU'RE RIGHT!
WELL, I'LL SEE YOU IN DETENTION, WHICH STARTS IN TEN MINUTES... PROMPTLY!
YES, SIR!
YOU CHOSE THE BUS OVER A RIDE WITH THE BEE? WHY? HE'S GIVEN YOU RIDES BEFORE!
LET'S JUST SAY I CAN DO WITHOUT A LONG LECTURE AFTER DETENTION!
SPEAKING OF DETENTION, I'D BETTER GET GOING! BYE, BETTY!
SO LONG, ARCHIE. GOOD LUCK ON YOUR TRIP HOME. AND TRY TO CHEER UP!
LATER, AFTER DETENTION...
:SIGH!: I'M GLAD THAT'S OVER... BUT I THINK THE WORST IS YET TO COME...
C'MON, YOU GUYS! LET'S GET TO THE BUS!
HEY! DON'T SHOVE!
R
4

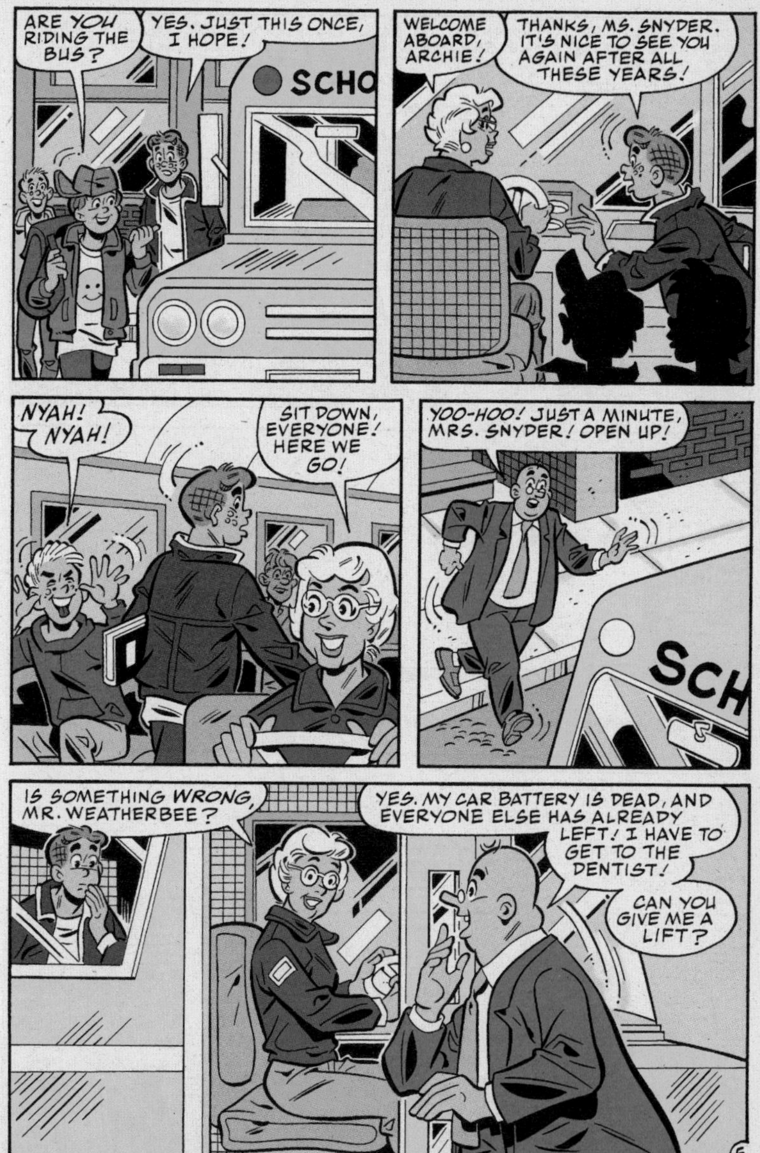
ARE YOU RIDING THE BUS?
YES. JUST THIS ONCE, I HOPE!
SCHO
WELCOME ABOARD, ARCHIE!
THANKS, MS. SNYDER. IT'S NICE TO SEE YOU AGAIN AFTER ALL THESE YEARS!
NYAH! NYAH!
SIT DOWN, EVERYONE! HERE WE GO!
YOO-HOO! JUST A MINUTE, MRS. SNYDER! OPEN UP!
SCH
IS SOMETHING WRONG, MR. WEATHERBEE?
YES. MY CAR BATTERY IS DEAD, AND EVERYONE ELSE HAS ALREADY LEFT! I HAVE TO GET TO THE DENTIST!
CAN YOU GIVE ME A LIFT?

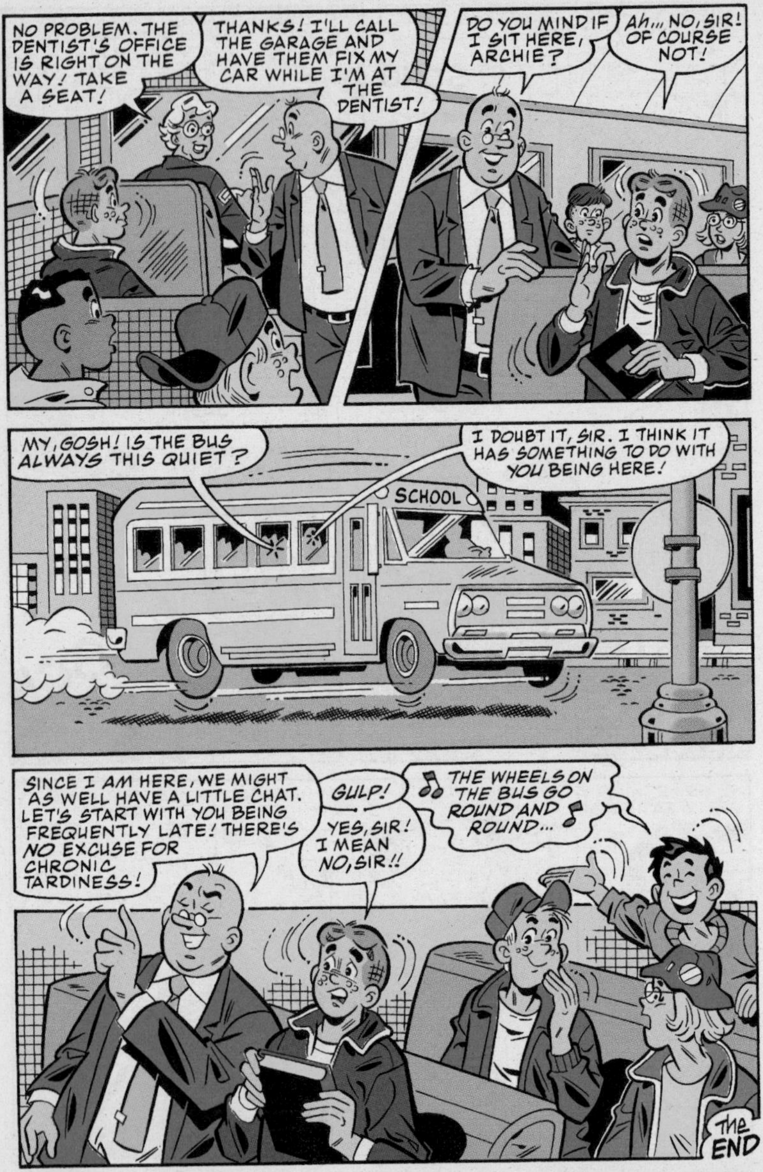
NO PROBLEM. THE DENTIST'S OFFICE IS RIGHT ON THE WAY! TAKE A SEAT!
THANKS! I'LL CALL THE GARAGE AND HAVE THEM FIX MY CAR WHILE I'M AT THE DENTIST!
DO YOU MIND IF I SIT HERE, ARCHIE?
Ah... NO, SIR! OF COURSE NOT!
MY, GOSH! IS THE BUS ALWAYS THIS QUIET?
I DOUBT IT, SIR. I THINK IT HAS SOMETHING TO DO WITH YOU BEING HERE!
SCHOOL
SINCE I AM HERE, WE MIGHT AS WELL HAVE A LITTLE CHAT. LET'S START WITH YOU BEING FREQUENTLY LATE! THERE'S NO EXCUSE FOR CHRONIC TARDINESS!
GULP!
YES, SIR! I MEAN NO, SIR!!
THE WHEELS ON THE BUS GO ROUND AND ROUND...
THE END

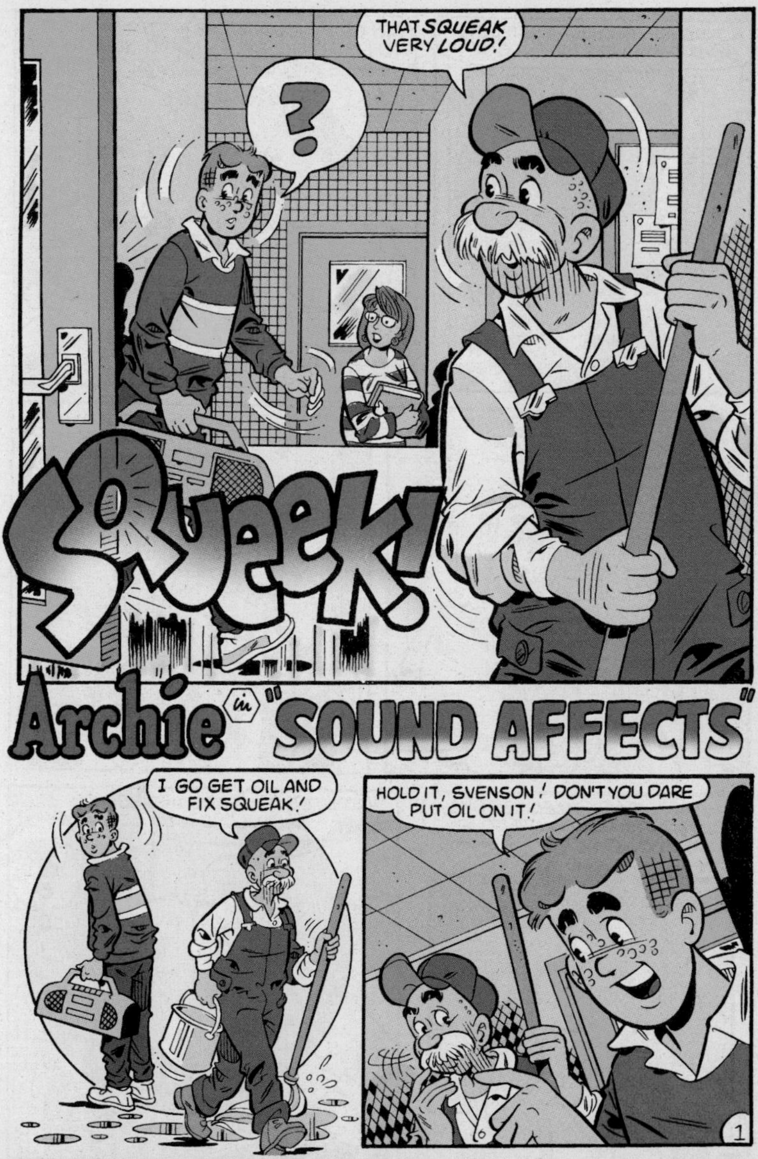

THAT SQUEAK VERY LOUD!
?
SQUEEK!
Archie in "SOUND AFFECTS"
I GO GET OIL AND FIX SQUEAK!
HOLD IT, SVENSON! DON'T YOU DARE PUT OIL ON IT!
1

Script: Frank Doyle / Pencils: Tim Kennedy / Inks: Ken Selig / Letters: Bill Yoshida

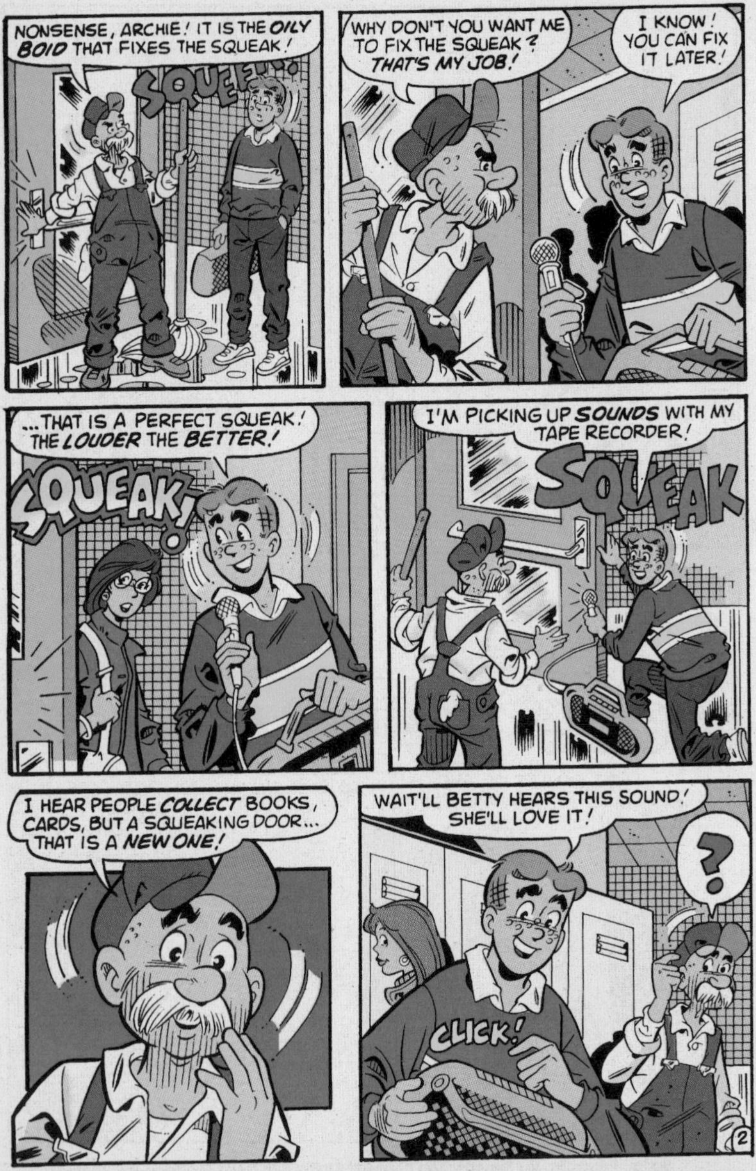
NONSENSE, ARCHIE! IT IS THE OILY BOID THAT FIXES THE SQUEAK!
SQUEE...
WHY DON'T YOU WANT ME TO FIX THE SQUEAK? THAT'S MY JOB!
I KNOW! YOU CAN FIX IT LATER!
...THAT IS A PERFECT SQUEAK! THE LOUDER THE BETTER!
SQUEAK!
I'M PICKING UP SOUNDS WITH MY TAPE RECORDER!
SQUEAK
I HEAR PEOPLE COLLECT BOOKS, CARDS, BUT A SQUEAKING DOOR... THAT IS A NEW ONE!
WAIT'LL BETTY HEARS THIS SOUND! SHE'LL LOVE IT!
?
CLICK!
2

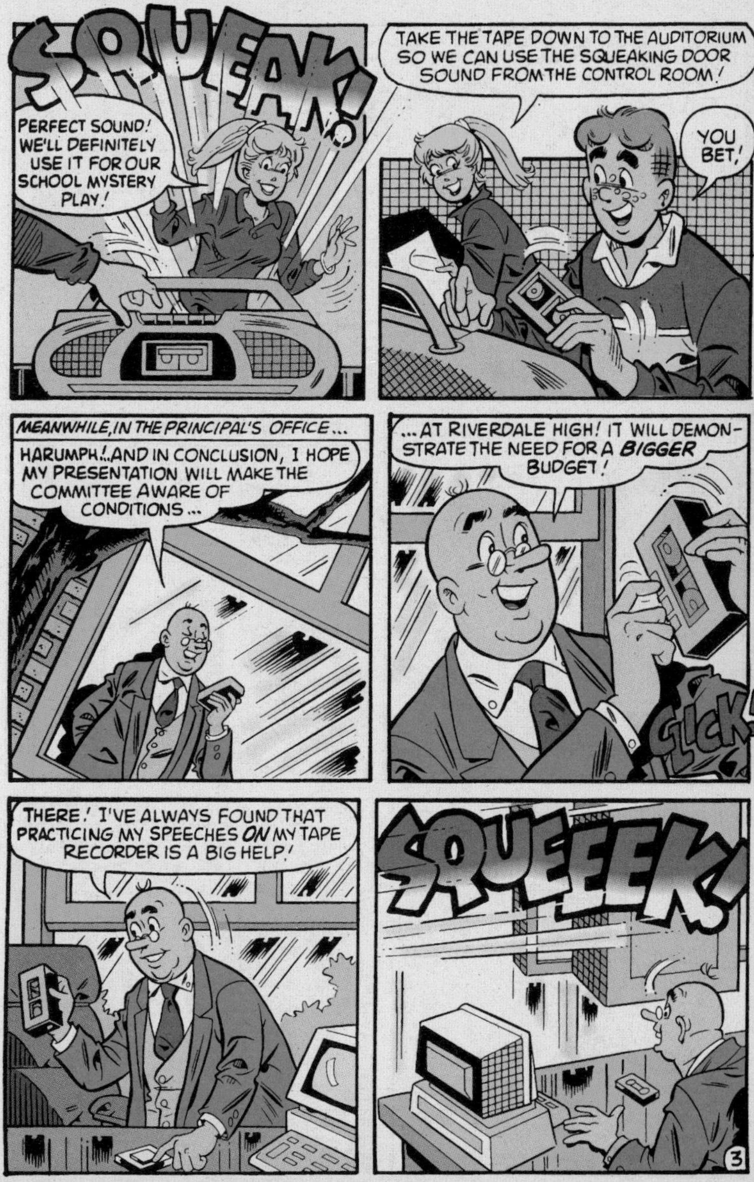
SQUEAK!
PERFECT SOUND! WE'LL DEFINITELY USE IT FOR OUR SCHOOL MYSTERY PLAY!
TAKE THE TAPE DOWN TO THE AUDITORIUM SO WE CAN USE THE SQUEAKING DOOR SOUND FROM THE CONTROL ROOM!
YOU BET!
MEANWHILE, IN THE PRINCIPAL'S OFFICE...
HARUMPH!..AND IN CONCLUSION, I HOPE MY PRESENTATION WILL MAKE THE COMMITTEE AWARE OF CONDITIONS...
...AT RIVERDALE HIGH! IT WILL DEMONSTRATE THE NEED FOR A BIGGER BUDGET!
CLICK!
THERE! I'VE ALWAYS FOUND THAT PRACTICING MY SPEECHES ON MY TAPE RECORDER IS A BIG HELP!
SQUEEEK!
3

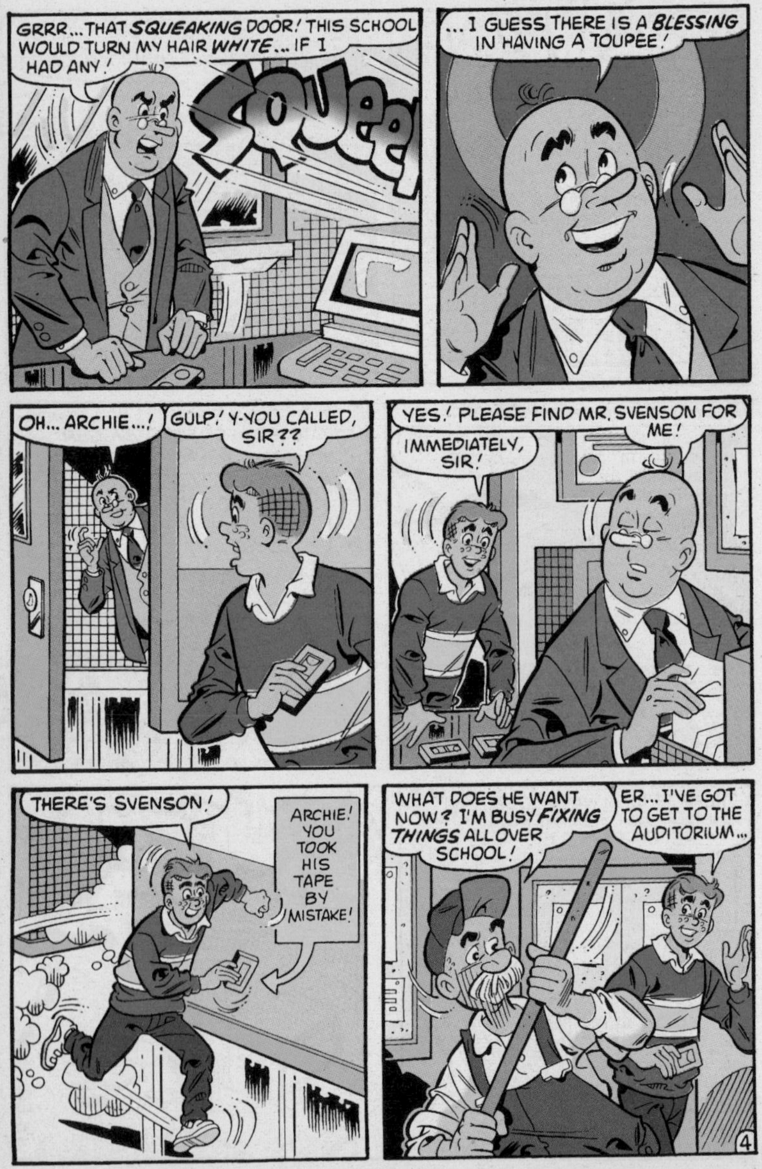
GRRR... THAT SQUEAKING DOOR! THIS SCHOOL WOULD TURN MY HAIR WHITE... IF I HAD ANY!
SQUEE
... I GUESS THERE IS A BLESSING IN HAVING A TOUPEE!
OH... ARCHIE...!
GULP! Y-YOU CALLED, SIR??
YES! PLEASE FIND MR. SVENSON FOR ME!
IMMEDIATELY, SIR!
THERE'S SVENSON!
ARCHIE! YOU TOOK HIS TAPE BY MISTAKE!
WHAT DOES HE WANT NOW? I'M BUSY FIXING THINGS ALL OVER SCHOOL!
ER... I'VE GOT TO GET TO THE AUDITORIUM...
4

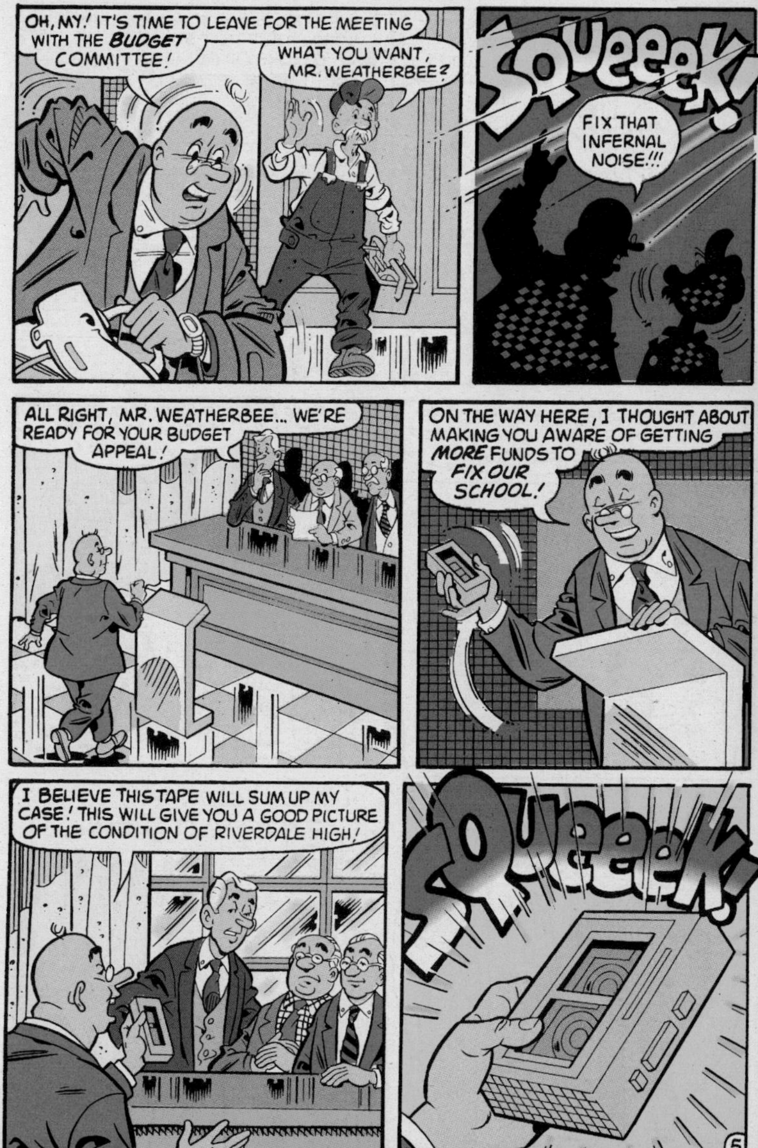

OH, MY! IT'S TIME TO LEAVE FOR THE MEETING WITH THE BUDGET COMMITTEE!
WHAT YOU WANT, MR. WEATHERBEE?
SQUEEEK!
FIX THAT INFERNAL NOISE!!!
ALL RIGHT, MR. WEATHERBEE... WE'RE READY FOR YOUR BUDGET APPEAL!
ON THE WAY HERE, I THOUGHT ABOUT MAKING YOU AWARE OF GETTING MORE FUNDS TO FIX OUR SCHOOL!
I BELIEVE THIS TAPE WILL SUM UP MY CASE! THIS WILL GIVE YOU A GOOD PICTURE OF THE CONDITION OF RIVERDALE HIGH!
SQUEEEK!

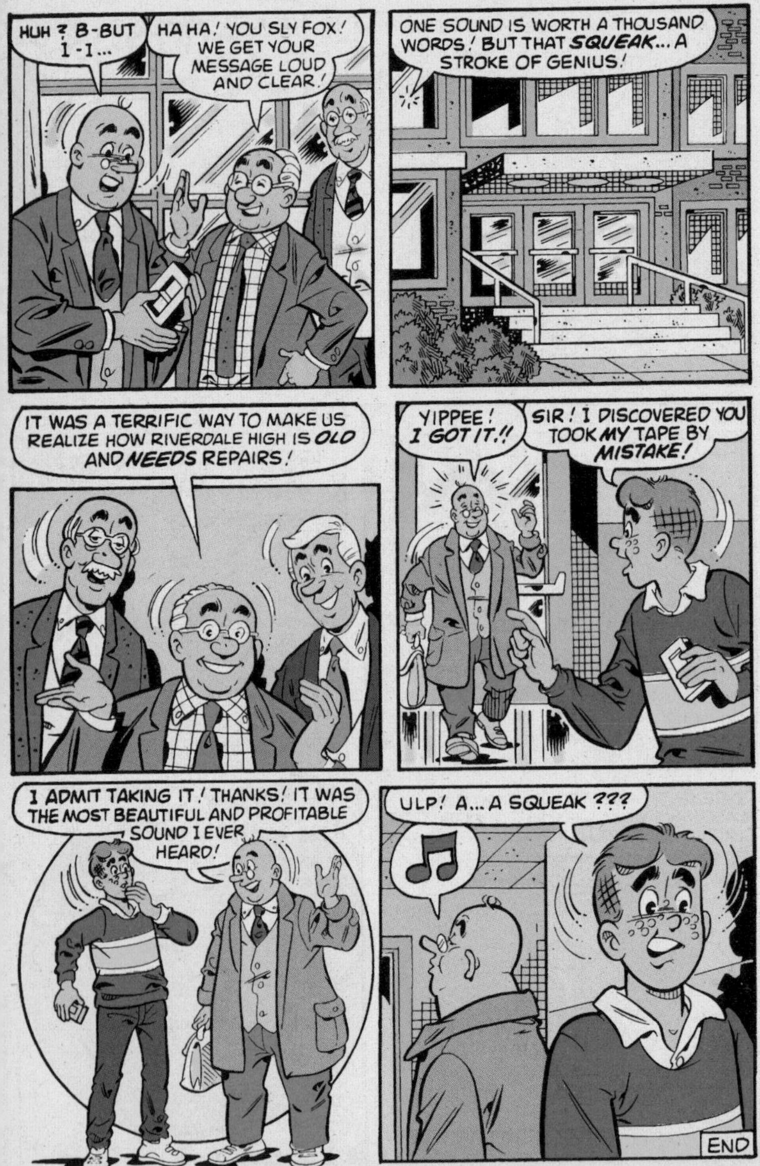
HUH ? B-BUT I-I...
HA HA! YOU SLY FOX! WE GET YOUR MESSAGE LOUD AND CLEAR!
ONE SOUND IS WORTH A THOUSAND WORDS! BUT THAT SQUEAK... A STROKE OF GENIUS!
IT WAS A TERRIFIC WAY TO MAKE US REALIZE HOW RIVERDALE HIGH IS OLD AND NEEDS REPAIRS!
YIPPEE! I GOT IT.!!
SIR! I DISCOVERED YOU TOOK MY TAPE BY MISTAKE!
I ADMIT TAKING IT! THANKS! IT WAS THE MOST BEAUTIFUL AND PROFITABLE SOUND I EVER HEARD!
ULP! A... A SQUEAK ???
END

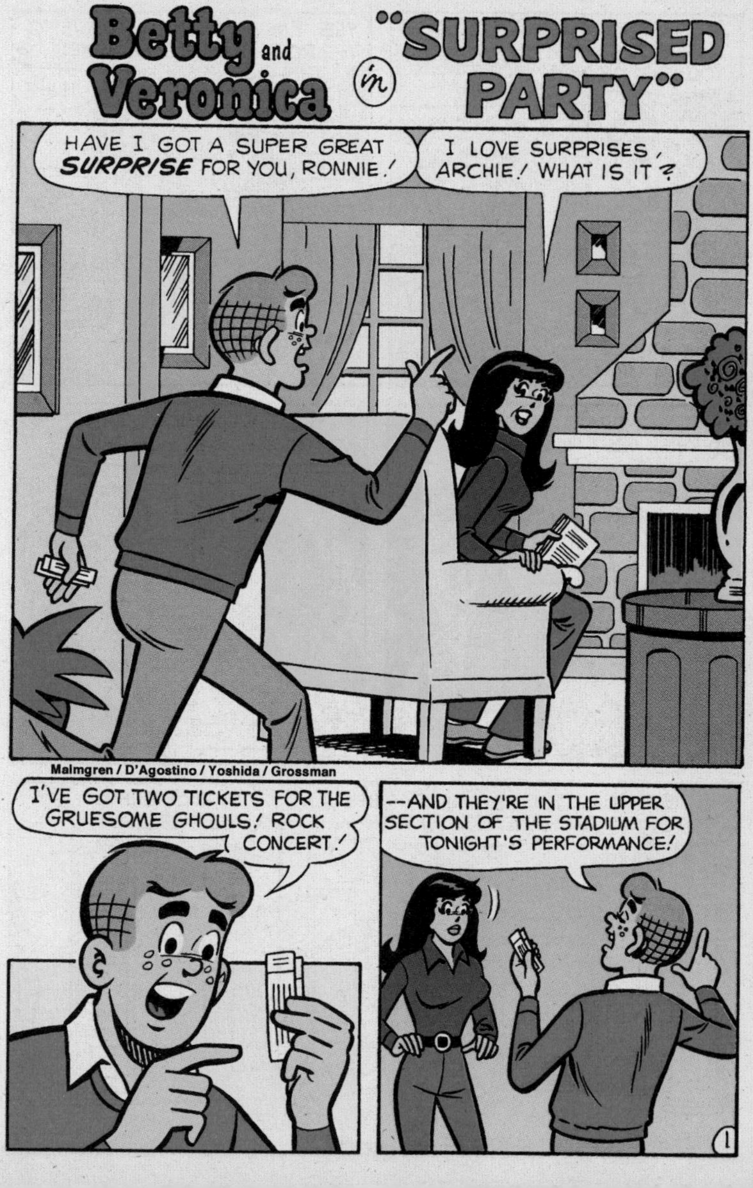
Betty and Veronica in "SURPRISED PARTY"
HAVE I GOT A SUPER GREAT SURPRISE FOR YOU, RONNIE!
I LOVE SURPRISES, ARCHIE! WHAT IS IT?
Malmgren / D'Agostino / Yoshida / Grossman
I'VE GOT TWO TICKETS FOR THE GRUESOME GHOULS! ROCK CONCERT!
--AND THEY'RE IN THE UPPER SECTION OF THE STADIUM FOR TONIGHT'S PERFORMANCE!
1

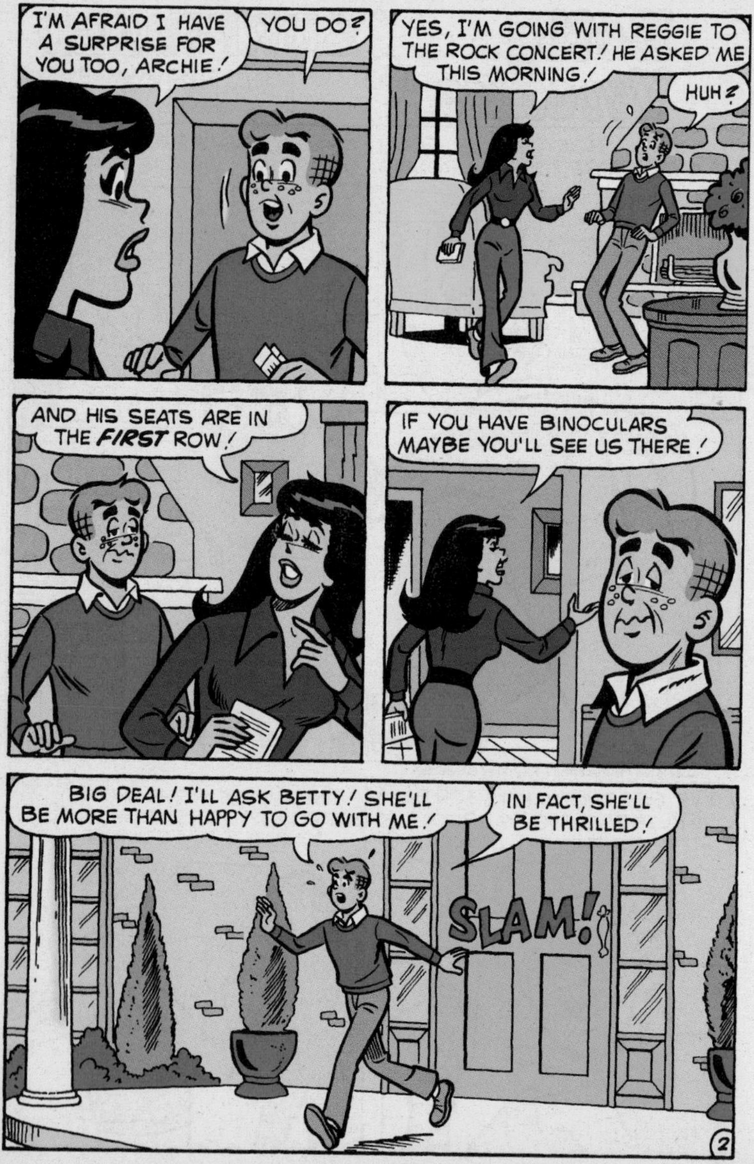
I'M AFRAID I HAVE A SURPRISE FOR YOU TOO, ARCHIE!
YOU DO?
YES, I'M GOING WITH REGGIE TO THE ROCK CONCERT! HE ASKED ME THIS MORNING!
HUH?
AND HIS SEATS ARE IN THE FIRST ROW!
IF YOU HAVE BINOCULARS MAYBE YOU'LL SEE US THERE!
BIG DEAL! I'LL ASK BETTY! SHE'LL BE MORE THAN HAPPY TO GO WITH ME!
IN FACT, SHE'LL BE THRILLED!
SLAM!
2

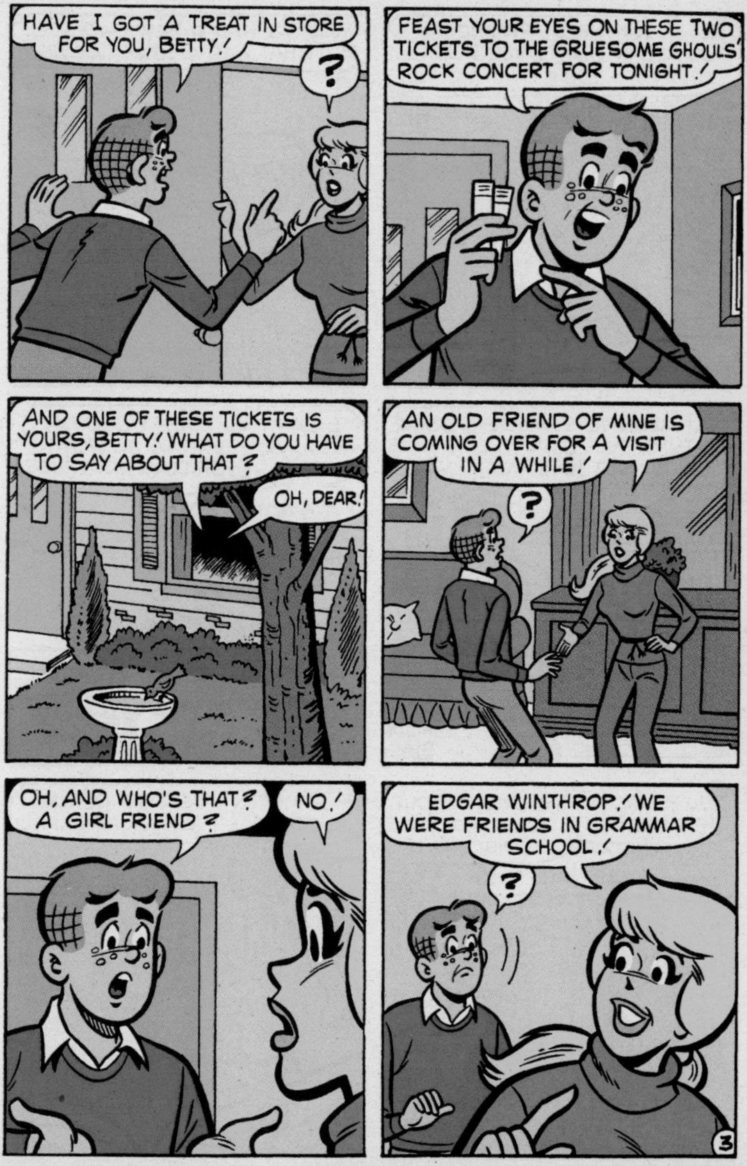
HAVE I GOT A TREAT IN STORE FOR YOU, BETTY!
?
FEAST YOUR EYES ON THESE TWO TICKETS TO THE GRUESOME GHOULS' ROCK CONCERT FOR TONIGHT!
AND ONE OF THESE TICKETS IS YOURS, BETTY! WHAT DO YOU HAVE TO SAY ABOUT THAT?
OH, DEAR!
AN OLD FRIEND OF MINE IS COMING OVER FOR A VISIT IN A WHILE!
?
OH, AND WHO'S THAT? A GIRL FRIEND?
NO!
EDGAR WINTHROP! WE WERE FRIENDS IN GRAMMAR SCHOOL!
?

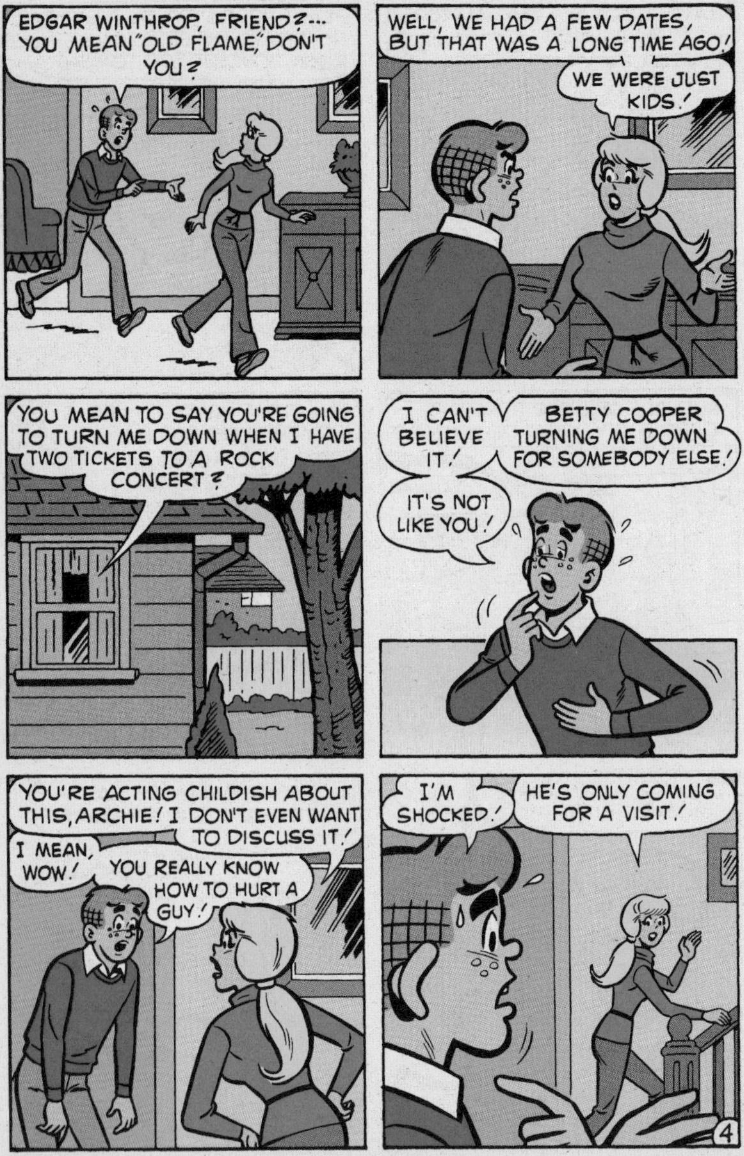
EDGAR WINTHROP, FRIEND?... YOU MEAN "OLD FLAME," DON'T YOU?
WELL, WE HAD A FEW DATES, BUT THAT WAS A LONG TIME AGO!
WE WERE JUST KIDS!
YOU MEAN TO SAY YOU'RE GOING TO TURN ME DOWN WHEN I HAVE TWO TICKETS TO A ROCK CONCERT?
I CAN'T BELIEVE IT!
BETTY COOPER TURNING ME DOWN FOR SOMEBODY ELSE!
IT'S NOT LIKE YOU!
YOU'RE ACTING CHILDISH ABOUT THIS, ARCHIE! I DON'T EVEN WANT TO DISCUSS IT!
I MEAN, WOW!
YOU REALLY KNOW HOW TO HURT A GUY!
I'M SHOCKED!
HE'S ONLY COMING FOR A VISIT!
4

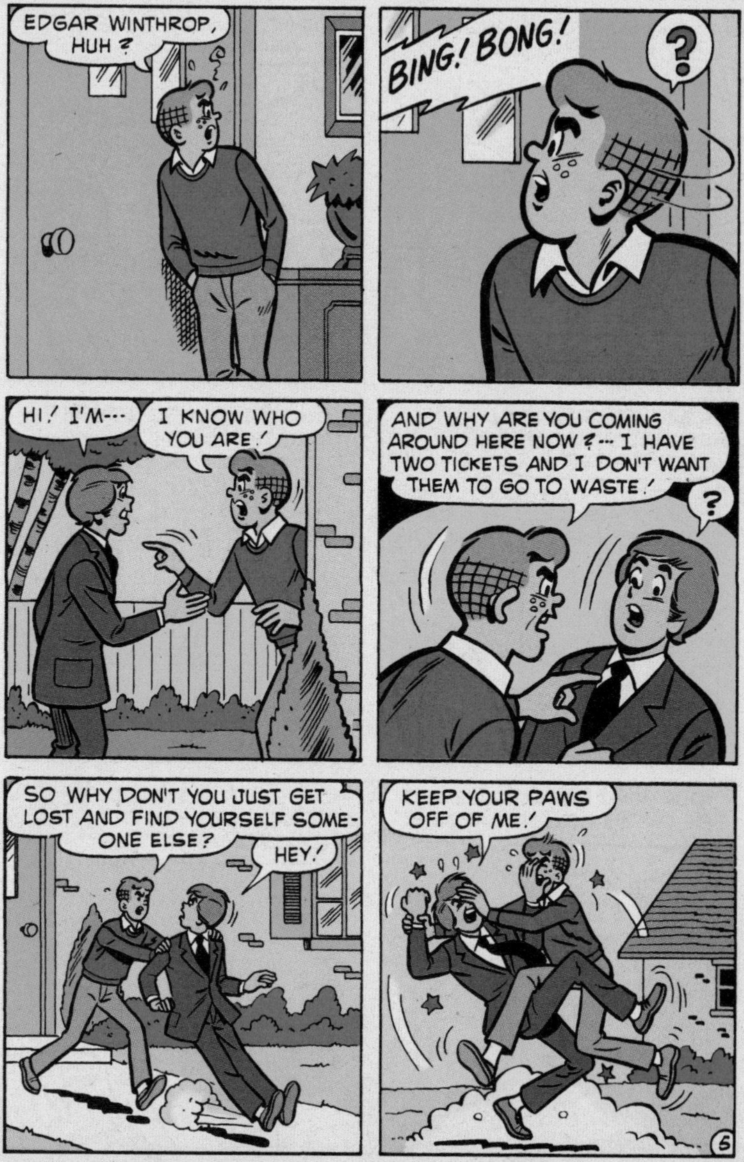
EDGAR WINTHROP, HUH ?
BING! BONG!
?
HI! I'M---
I KNOW WHO YOU ARE!
AND WHY ARE YOU COMING AROUND HERE NOW ?--- I HAVE TWO TICKETS AND I DON'T WANT THEM TO GO TO WASTE!
?
SO WHY DON'T YOU JUST GET LOST AND FIND YOURSELF SOME-ONE ELSE?
HEY!
KEEP YOUR PAWS OFF OF ME!
5

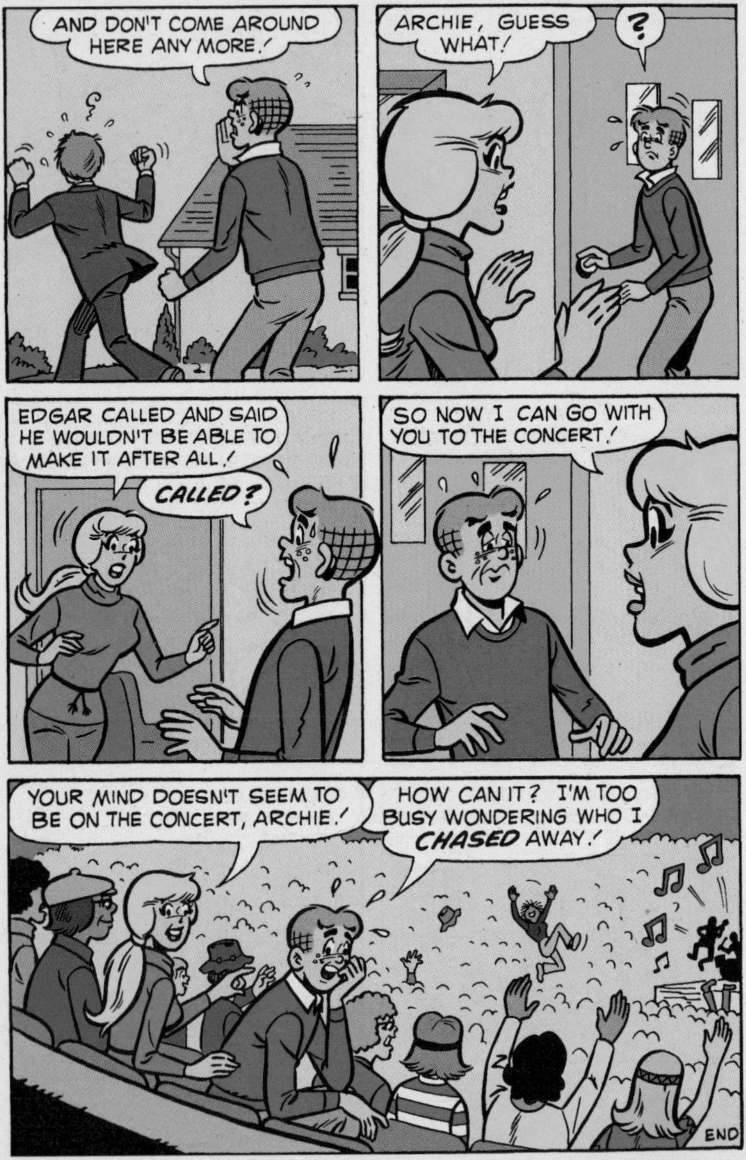
AND DON'T COME AROUND HERE ANY MORE.!
ARCHIE, GUESS WHAT!
?
EDGAR CALLED AND SAID HE WOULDN'T BE ABLE TO MAKE IT AFTER ALL.!
CALLED?
SO NOW I CAN GO WITH YOU TO THE CONCERT.!
YOUR MIND DOESN'T SEEM TO BE ON THE CONCERT, ARCHIE.!
HOW CAN IT? I'M TOO BUSY WONDERING WHO I CHASED AWAY.!
END

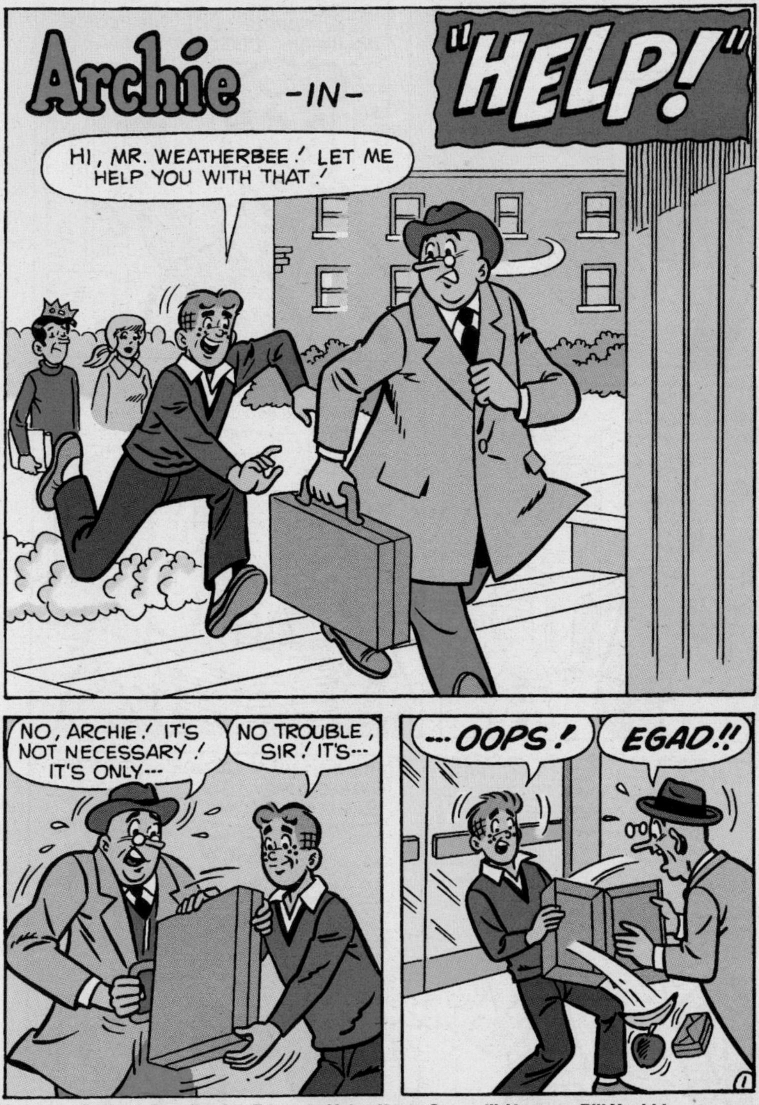
Archie -IN- "HELP!"
HI, MR. WEATHERBEE! LET ME HELP YOU WITH THAT!
NO, ARCHIE! IT'S NOT NECESSARY! IT'S ONLY---
NO TROUBLE, SIR! IT'S---
---OOPS!
EGAD!!
1

Script & Pencils: Joe Edwards / Inks: Henry Scarpelli / Letters: Bill Yoshida

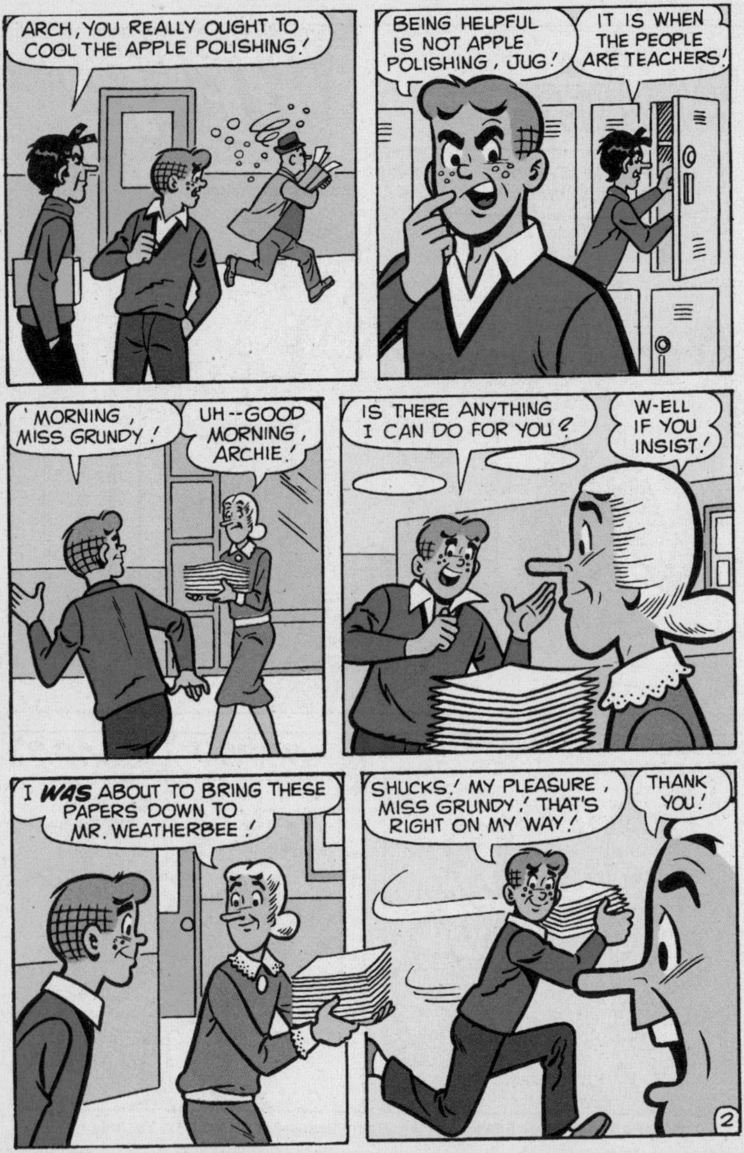

ARCH, YOU REALLY OUGHT TO COOL THE APPLE POLISHING!
BEING HELPFUL IS NOT APPLE POLISHING, JUG!
IT IS WHEN THE PEOPLE ARE TEACHERS!
'MORNING, MISS GRUNDY!
UH--GOOD MORNING, ARCHIE!
IS THERE ANYTHING I CAN DO FOR YOU?
W-ELL IF YOU INSIST!
I WAS ABOUT TO BRING THESE PAPERS DOWN TO MR. WEATHERBEE!
SHUCKS! MY PLEASURE, MISS GRUNDY! THAT'S RIGHT ON MY WAY!
THANK YOU!
2

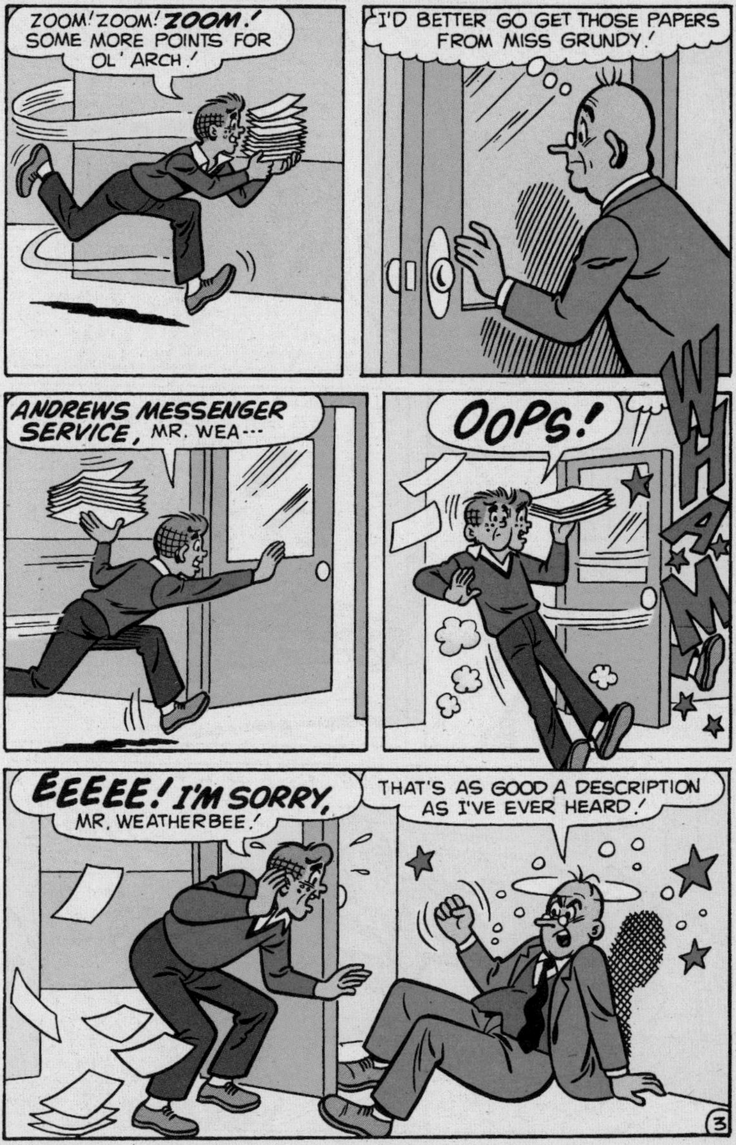
ZOOM! ZOOM! ZOOM! SOME MORE POINTS FOR OL' ARCH!
I'D BETTER GO GET THOSE PAPERS FROM MISS GRUNDY!
ANDREWS MESSENGER SERVICE, MR. WEA---
OOPS!
WHAM
EEEEE! I'M SORRY, MR. WEATHERBEE!
THAT'S AS GOOD A DESCRIPTION AS I'VE EVER HEARD!
3

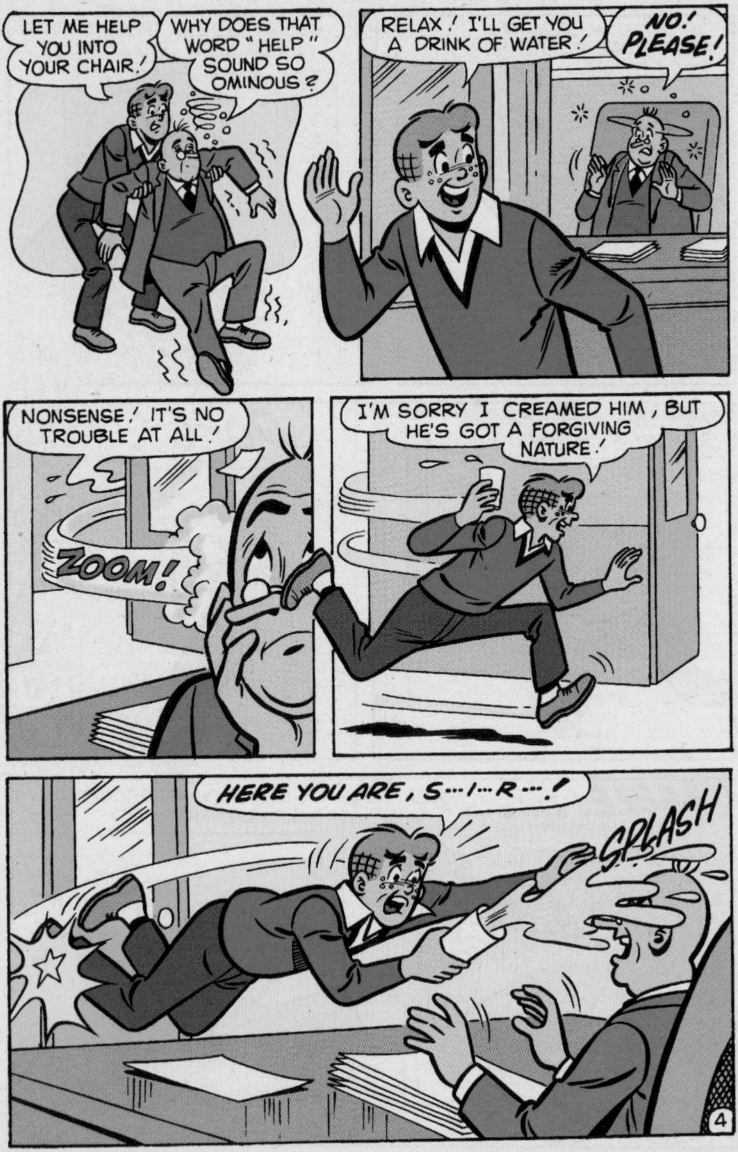
LET ME HELP YOU INTO YOUR CHAIR.!
WHY DOES THAT WORD " HELP " SOUND SO OMINOUS ?
RELAX.! I'LL GET YOU A DRINK OF WATER.!
NO! PLEASE!
NONSENSE.! IT'S NO TROUBLE AT ALL.!
ZOOM!
I'M SORRY I CREAMED HIM , BUT HE'S GOT A FORGIVING NATURE.!
HERE YOU ARE, S---I---R---!
SPLASH
4

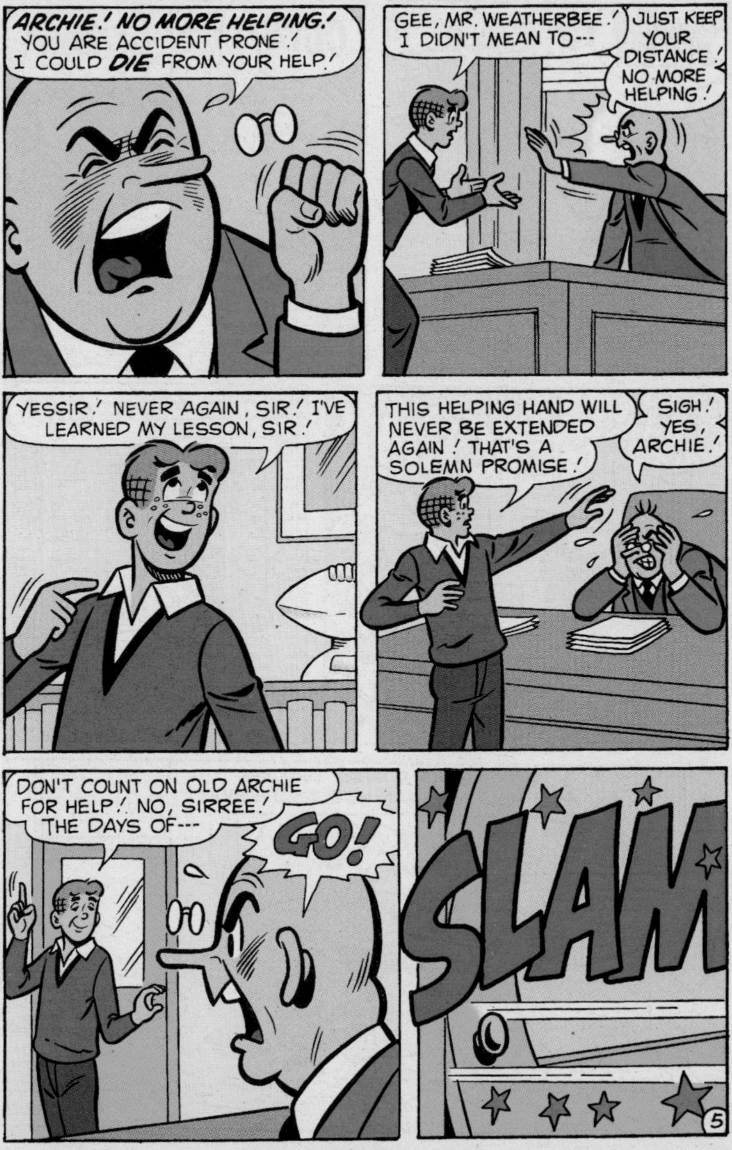
ARCHIE! NO MORE HELPING! YOU ARE ACCIDENT PRONE! I COULD DIE FROM YOUR HELP!
GEE, MR. WEATHERBEE! I DIDN'T MEAN TO---
JUST KEEP YOUR DISTANCE! NO MORE HELPING!
YESSIR! NEVER AGAIN, SIR! I'VE LEARNED MY LESSON, SIR!
THIS HELPING HAND WILL NEVER BE EXTENDED AGAIN! THAT'S A SOLEMN PROMISE!
SIGH! YES, ARCHIE!
DON'T COUNT ON OLD ARCHIE FOR HELP! NO, SIRREE! THE DAYS OF---
GO!
SLAM
5

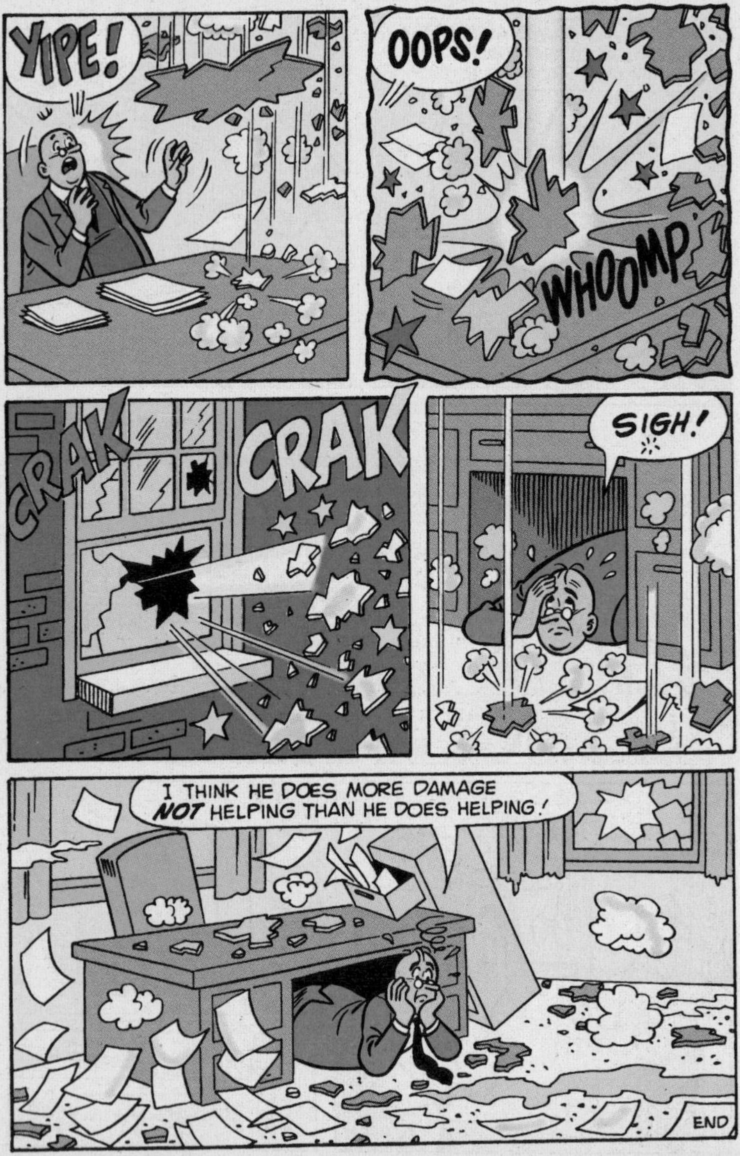
YIPE!
OOPS!
WHOOMP
CRAK
CRAK
SIGH!
I THINK HE DOES MORE DAMAGE *NOT* HELPING THAN HE DOES HELPING!
END

Archie WON'T GO!

THIS ONE'S GOING TO BE **TOUGH!** YOU'LL HAVE TO SUBSTITUTE EACH LETTER IN THE BOXES FOR THE PRECEDING LETTER IN THE ALPHABET! FOR EXAMPLE: A=Z, B=A, AND Z=Y... OKAY?! IF YOU SUCCEED, YOU'LL FIND OUT WHERE ARCHIE REFUSES TO GO ON HIS VACATION! YEP... THE ANSWERS ARE BELOW!! HAVE FUN!!

T I P Q Q J O H G P S D M P U I F T X
J U I W F S P O J D
B N V E X S F T U
M J O H N B U D I
F T B V O U Q I P
F C F T I P V T F
J O I P I P L V T
O K U I F S J W
F S E B M F E P
H B O E L F O O
F M T I P X J D
F T L B U J O
H T B U V S O

I'M NOT GOIN'!

ANSWERS ↑

SHOPPING FOR CLOTHES WITH VERONICA • MUD WRESTLING MATCHES • AUNT PHOEBE'S HOUSE IN HOHOKUS, NJ • THE RIVERDALE DOG AND KENNEL SHOW • ICE SKATING • SATURN

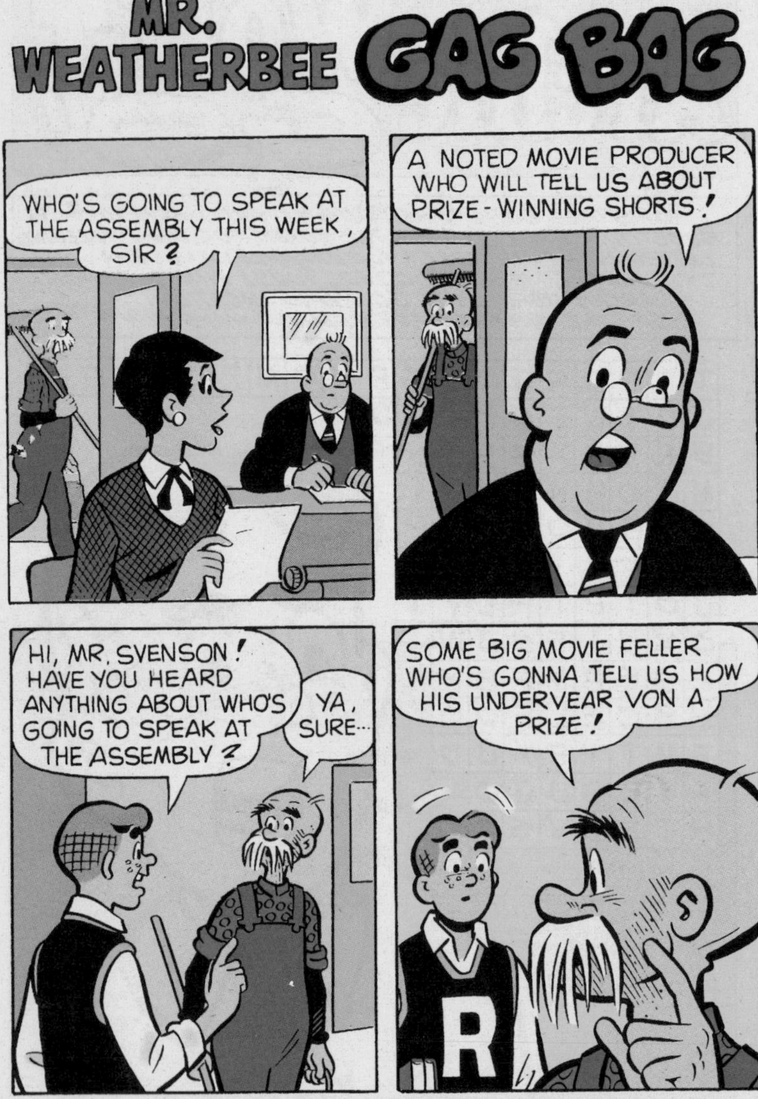
MR. WEATHERBEE GAG BAG
WHO'S GOING TO SPEAK AT THE ASSEMBLY THIS WEEK, SIR?
A NOTED MOVIE PRODUCER WHO WILL TELL US ABOUT PRIZE-WINNING SHORTS!
HI, MR. SVENSON! HAVE YOU HEARD ANYTHING ABOUT WHO'S GOING TO SPEAK AT THE ASSEMBLY?
YA, SURE...
SOME BIG MOVIE FELLER WHO'S GONNA TELL US HOW HIS UNDERVEAR VON A PRIZE!
R

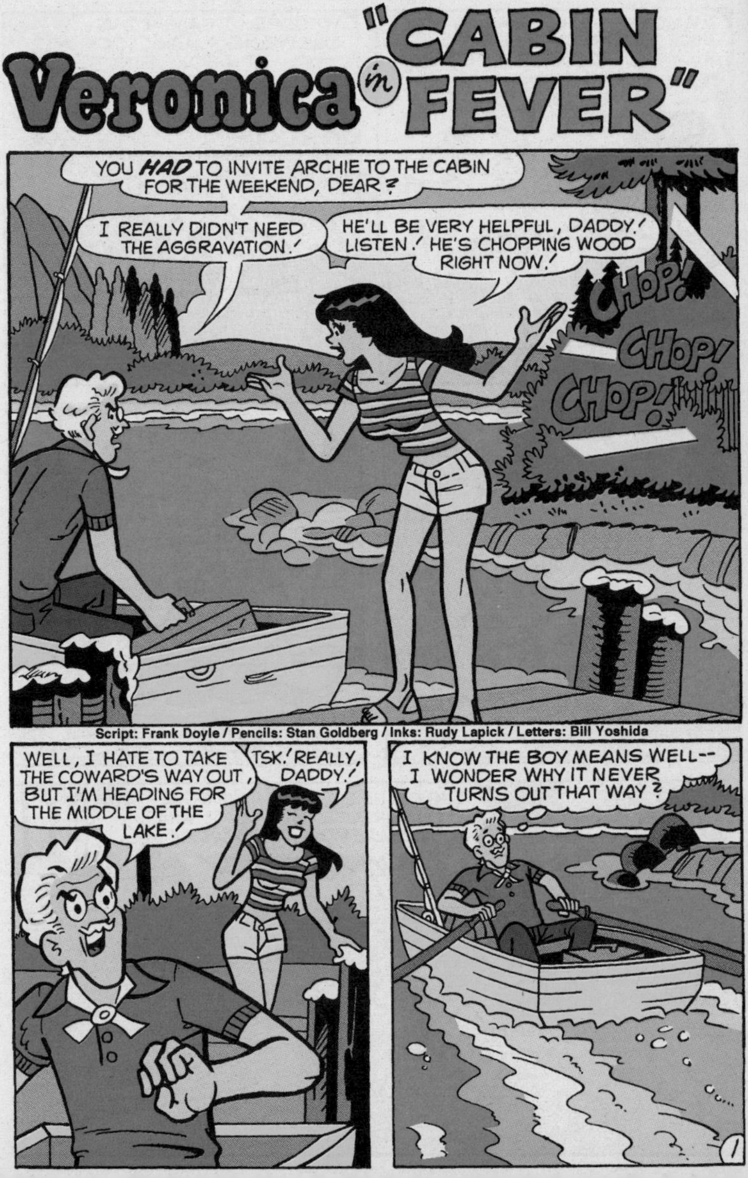
Veronica in "CABIN FEVER"
YOU HAD TO INVITE ARCHIE TO THE CABIN FOR THE WEEKEND, DEAR?
I REALLY DIDN'T NEED THE AGGRAVATION!
HE'LL BE VERY HELPFUL, DADDY! LISTEN! HE'S CHOPPING WOOD RIGHT NOW!
CHOP! CHOP! CHOP!
Script: Frank Doyle / Pencils: Stan Goldberg / Inks: Rudy Lapick / Letters: Bill Yoshida
WELL, I HATE TO TAKE THE COWARD'S WAY OUT, BUT I'M HEADING FOR THE MIDDLE OF THE LAKE!
TSK! REALLY, DADDY!
I KNOW THE BOY MEANS WELL-- I WONDER WHY IT NEVER TURNS OUT THAT WAY?
1

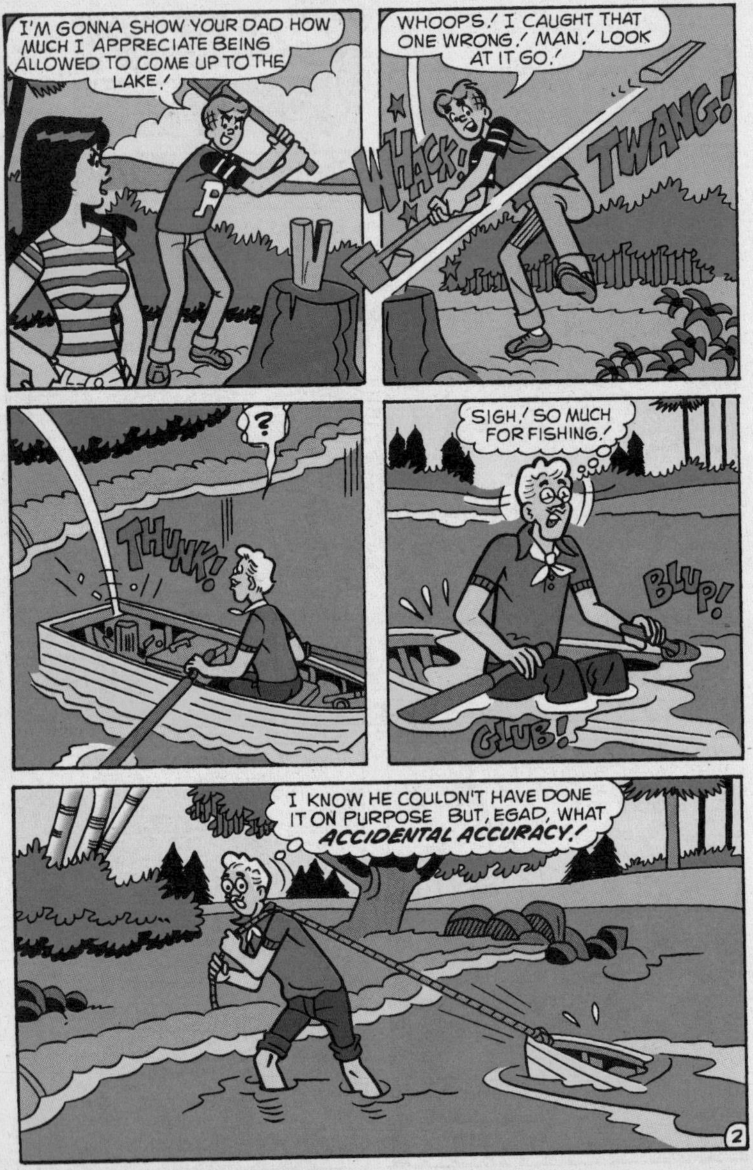
I'M GONNA SHOW YOUR DAD HOW MUCH I APPRECIATE BEING ALLOWED TO COME UP TO THE LAKE!
WHOOPS! I CAUGHT THAT ONE WRONG! MAN! LOOK AT IT GO!
WHACK!
TWANG!
?
THUNK!
SIGH! SO MUCH FOR FISHING!
BLUP!
GLUB!
I KNOW HE COULDN'T HAVE DONE IT ON PURPOSE BUT, EGAD, WHAT ACCIDENTAL ACCURACY!
2

UGH! NEVER A DULL MOMENT WHEN THAT BOY IS AROUND!

ALWAYS SOMETHING TO DO!--SOMETHING IN THE *"REPAIR"* LINE!

UGH!

WELL, IF I'M GOING TO GET IT DONE, I'D BETTER GO GET SOME TOOLS!

HMM! NO MORE WOOD TO SPLIT! WHAT CAN I DO NOW?

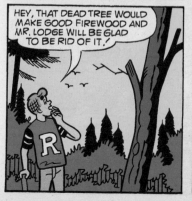

HEY, THAT DEAD TREE WOULD MAKE GOOD FIREWOOD AND MR. LODGE WILL BE GLAD TO BE RID OF IT!

BUT THIS IS A JOB FOR A CHAIN SAW!

3

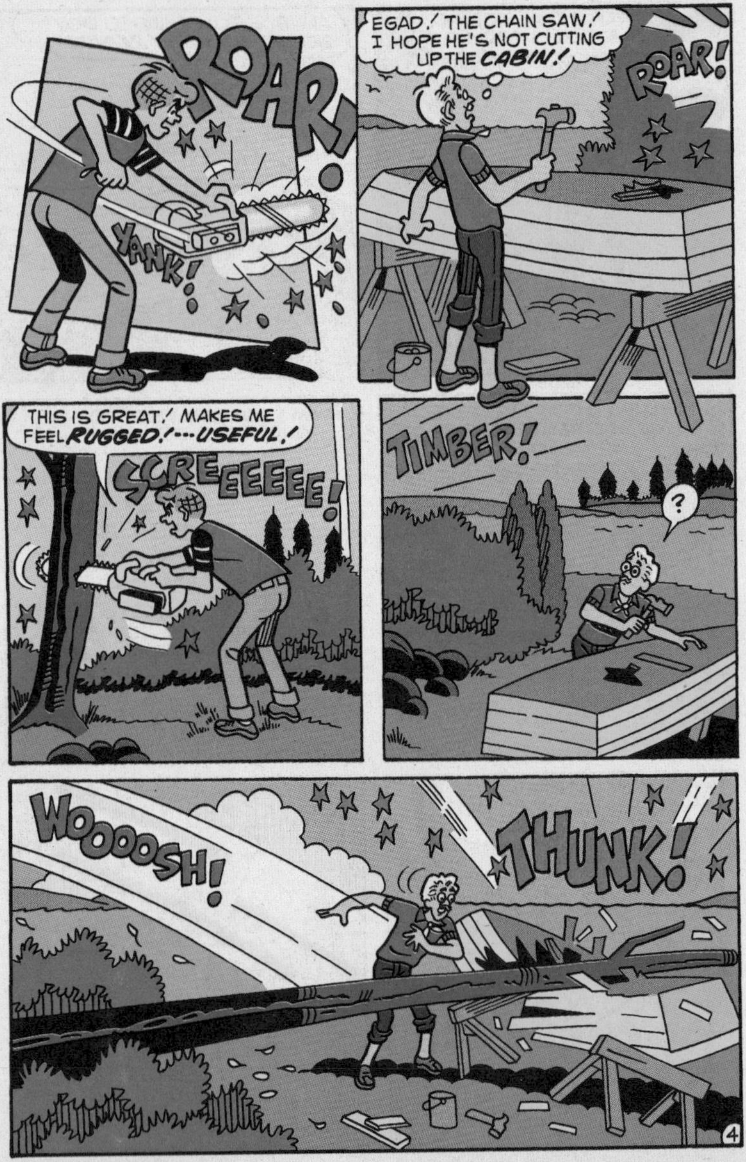
ROAR!
YANK!
EGAD! THE CHAIN SAW! I HOPE HE'S NOT CUTTING UP THE CABIN!
ROAR!
THIS IS GREAT! MAKES ME FEEL RUGGED!---USEFUL!
SCREEEEEEE!
TIMBER!
?
WOOOOOSH!
THUNK!

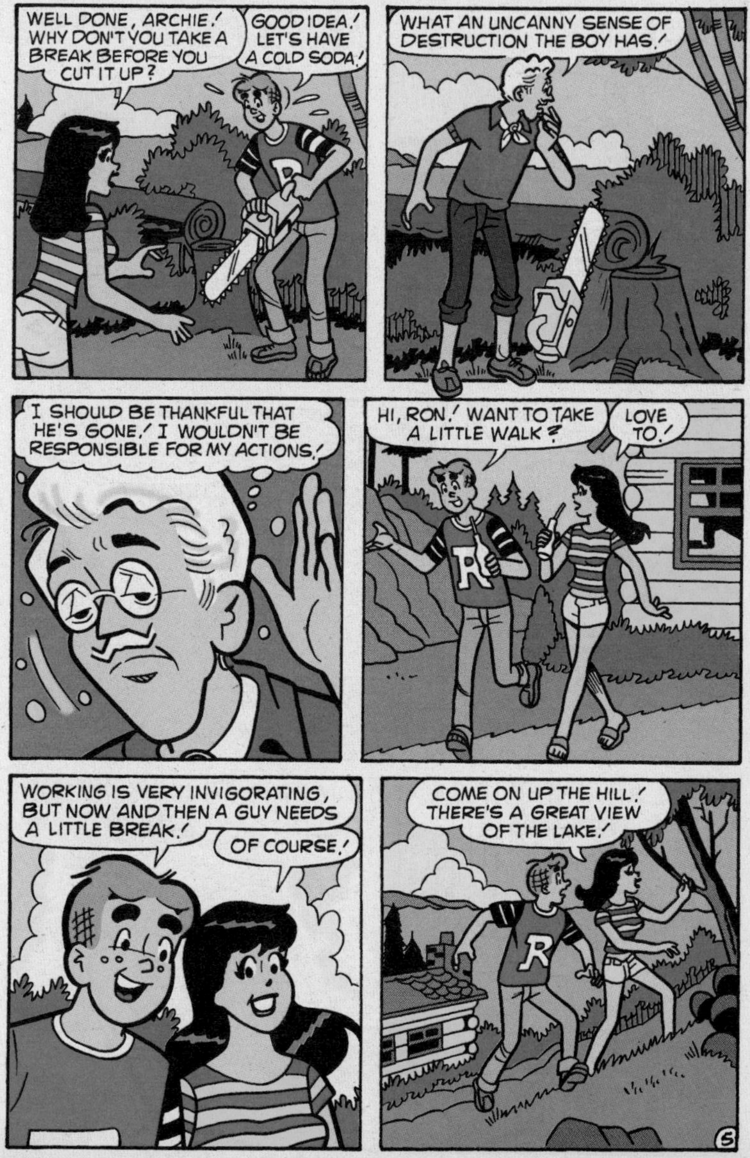
WELL DONE, ARCHIE! WHY DON'T YOU TAKE A BREAK BEFORE YOU CUT IT UP?
GOOD IDEA! LET'S HAVE A COLD SODA!
WHAT AN UNCANNY SENSE OF DESTRUCTION THE BOY HAS!
I SHOULD BE THANKFUL THAT HE'S GONE! I WOULDN'T BE RESPONSIBLE FOR MY ACTIONS!
HI, RON! WANT TO TAKE A LITTLE WALK?
LOVE TO!
WORKING IS VERY INVIGORATING, BUT NOW AND THEN A GUY NEEDS A LITTLE BREAK!
OF COURSE!
COME ON UP THE HILL! THERE'S A GREAT VIEW OF THE LAKE!
5

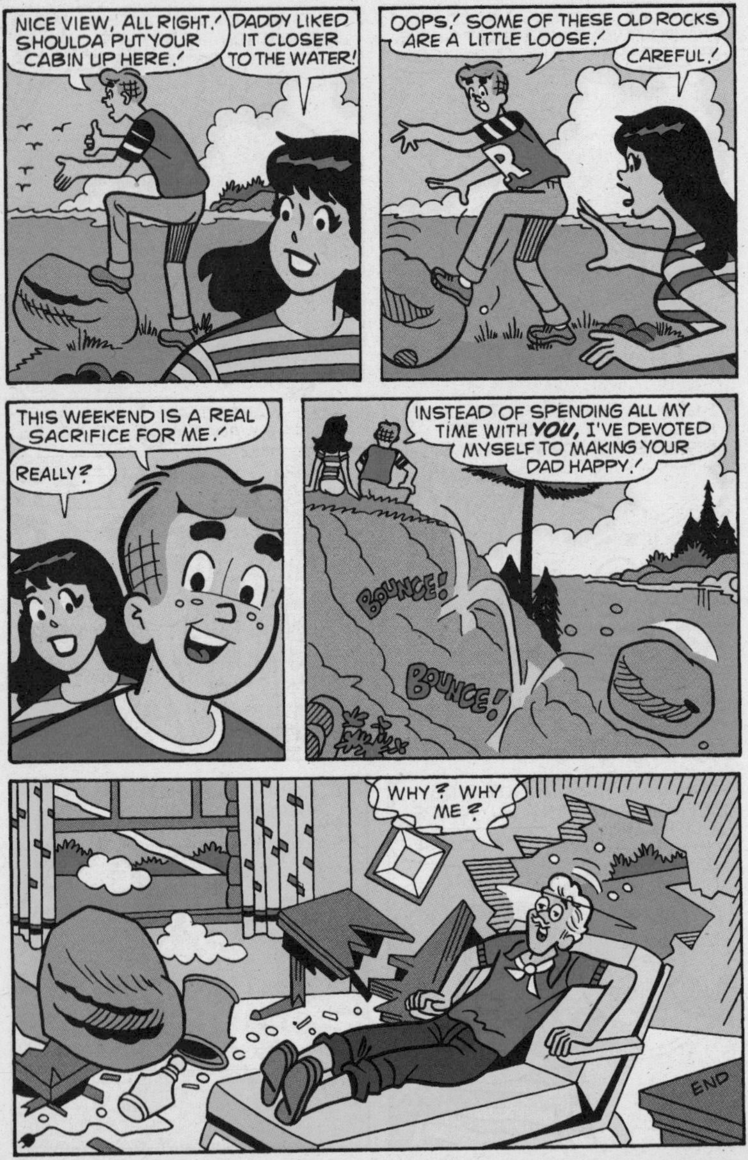
NICE VIEW, ALL RIGHT.! SHOULDA PUT YOUR CABIN UP HERE.!
DADDY LIKED IT CLOSER TO THE WATER!
OOPS.! SOME OF THESE OLD ROCKS ARE A LITTLE LOOSE.!
CAREFUL.!
THIS WEEKEND IS A REAL SACRIFICE FOR ME.!
REALLY?
INSTEAD OF SPENDING ALL MY TIME WITH **YOU,** I'VE DEVOTED MYSELF TO MAKING YOUR DAD HAPPY.!
BOUNCE!
BOUNCE!
WHY? WHY ME?
END

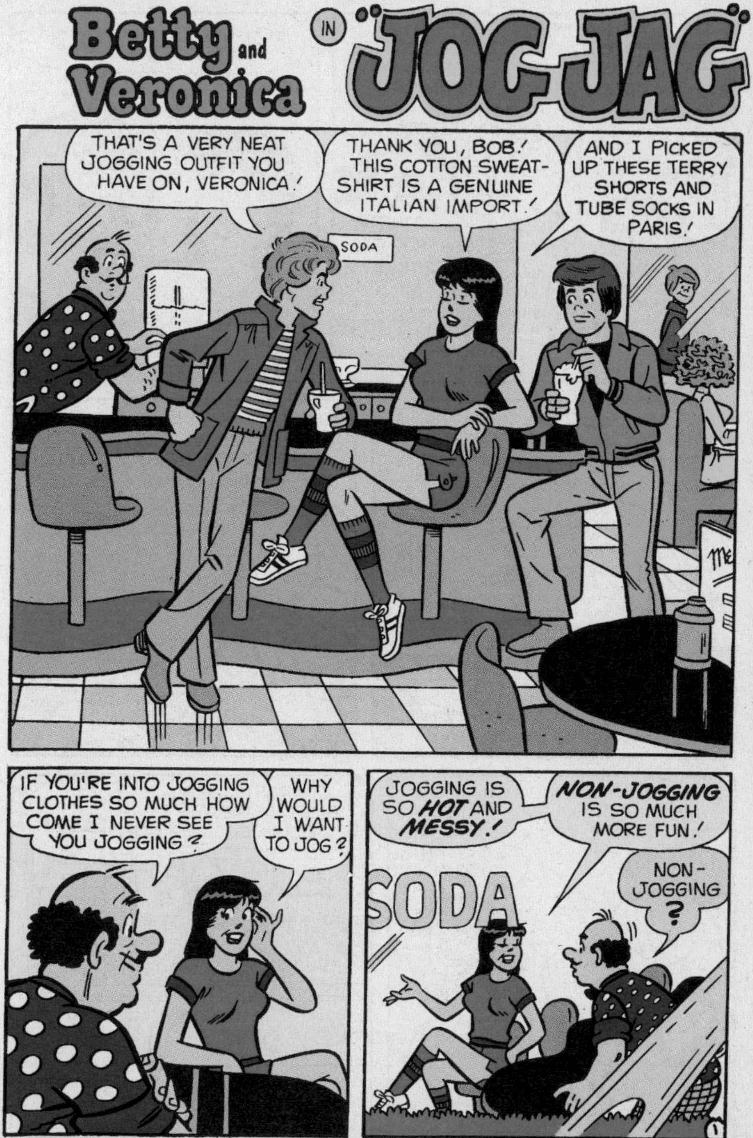
Betty and Veronica
IN "JOG JAG"
THAT'S A VERY NEAT JOGGING OUTFIT YOU HAVE ON, VERONICA!
THANK YOU, BOB! THIS COTTON SWEAT-SHIRT IS A GENUINE ITALIAN IMPORT!
AND I PICKED UP THESE TERRY SHORTS AND TUBE SOCKS IN PARIS!
SODA
IF YOU'RE INTO JOGGING CLOTHES SO MUCH HOW COME I NEVER SEE YOU JOGGING?
WHY WOULD I WANT TO JOG?
JOGGING IS SO *HOT* AND *MESSY*!
NON-JOGGING IS SO MUCH MORE FUN!
SODA
NON-JOGGING?
1

Script: Frank Doyle / Pencils: Dan DeCarlo / Inks: Rudy Lapick / Letters: Bill Yoshida / Colors: Barry Grossman

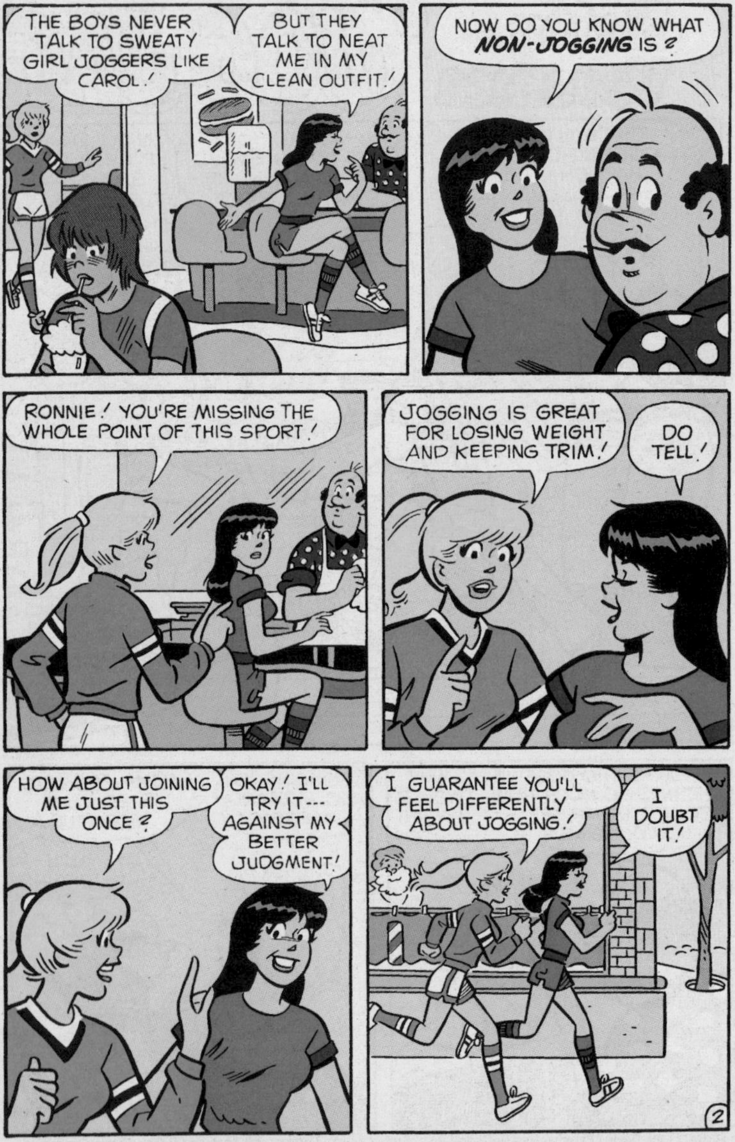
THE BOYS NEVER TALK TO SWEATY GIRL JOGGERS LIKE CAROL!
BUT THEY TALK TO NEAT ME IN MY CLEAN OUTFIT!
NOW DO YOU KNOW WHAT NON-JOGGING IS?
RONNIE! YOU'RE MISSING THE WHOLE POINT OF THIS SPORT!
JOGGING IS GREAT FOR LOSING WEIGHT AND KEEPING TRIM!
DO TELL!
HOW ABOUT JOINING ME JUST THIS ONCE?
OKAY! I'LL TRY IT--- AGAINST MY BETTER JUDGMENT!
I GUARANTEE YOU'LL FEEL DIFFERENTLY ABOUT JOGGING!
I DOUBT IT!
2

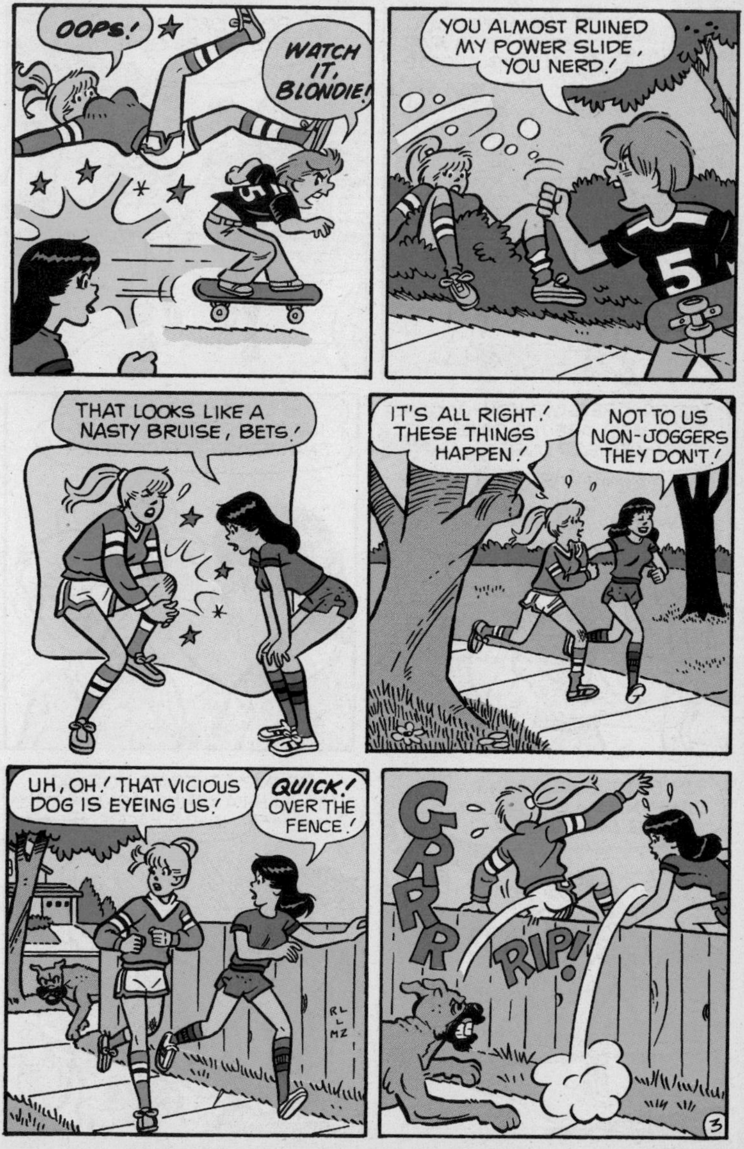
OOPS!
WATCH IT, BLONDIE!
YOU ALMOST RUINED MY POWER SLIDE, YOU NERD!
THAT LOOKS LIKE A NASTY BRUISE, BETS!
IT'S ALL RIGHT! THESE THINGS HAPPEN!
NOT TO US NON-JOGGERS THEY DON'T!
UH, OH! THAT VICIOUS DOG IS EYEING US!
QUICK! OVER THE FENCE!
GRRR
RIP!
3

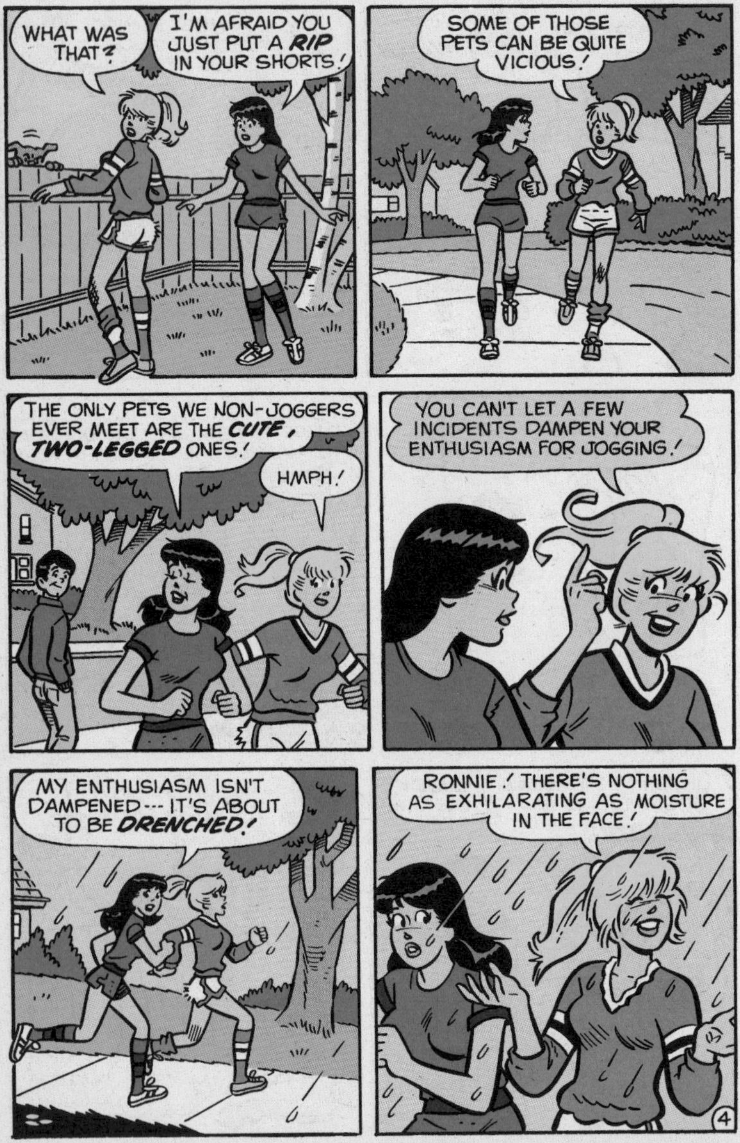
WHAT WAS THAT?
I'M AFRAID YOU JUST PUT A RIP IN YOUR SHORTS!
SOME OF THOSE PETS CAN BE QUITE VICIOUS!
THE ONLY PETS WE NON-JOGGERS EVER MEET ARE THE CUTE, TWO-LEGGED ONES!
HMPH!
YOU CAN'T LET A FEW INCIDENTS DAMPEN YOUR ENTHUSIASM FOR JOGGING!
MY ENTHUSIASM ISN'T DAMPENED--- IT'S ABOUT TO BE DRENCHED!
RONNIE! THERE'S NOTHING AS EXHILARATING AS MOISTURE IN THE FACE!
4

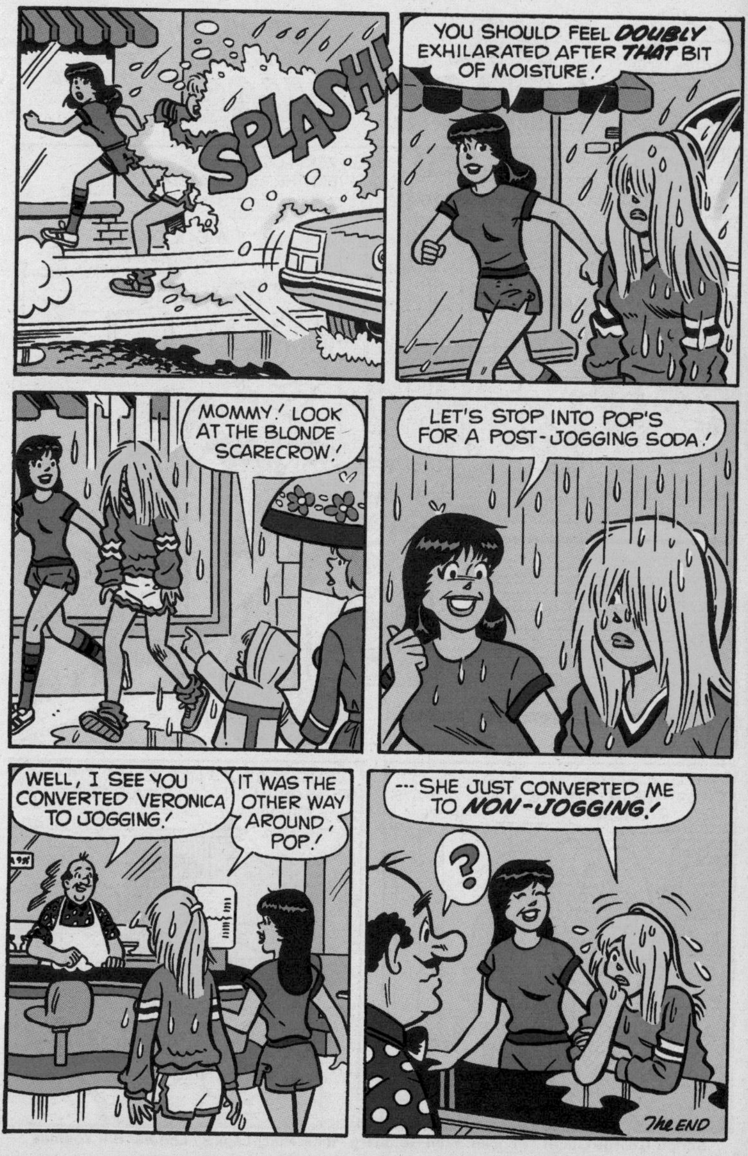
SPLASH!
YOU SHOULD FEEL DOUBLY EXHILARATED AFTER THAT BIT OF MOISTURE!
MOMMY! LOOK AT THE BLONDE SCARECROW!
LET'S STOP INTO POP'S FOR A POST-JOGGING SODA!
WELL, I SEE YOU CONVERTED VERONICA TO JOGGING!
IT WAS THE OTHER WAY AROUND, POP!
--- SHE JUST CONVERTED ME TO NON-JOGGING!
?
THE END

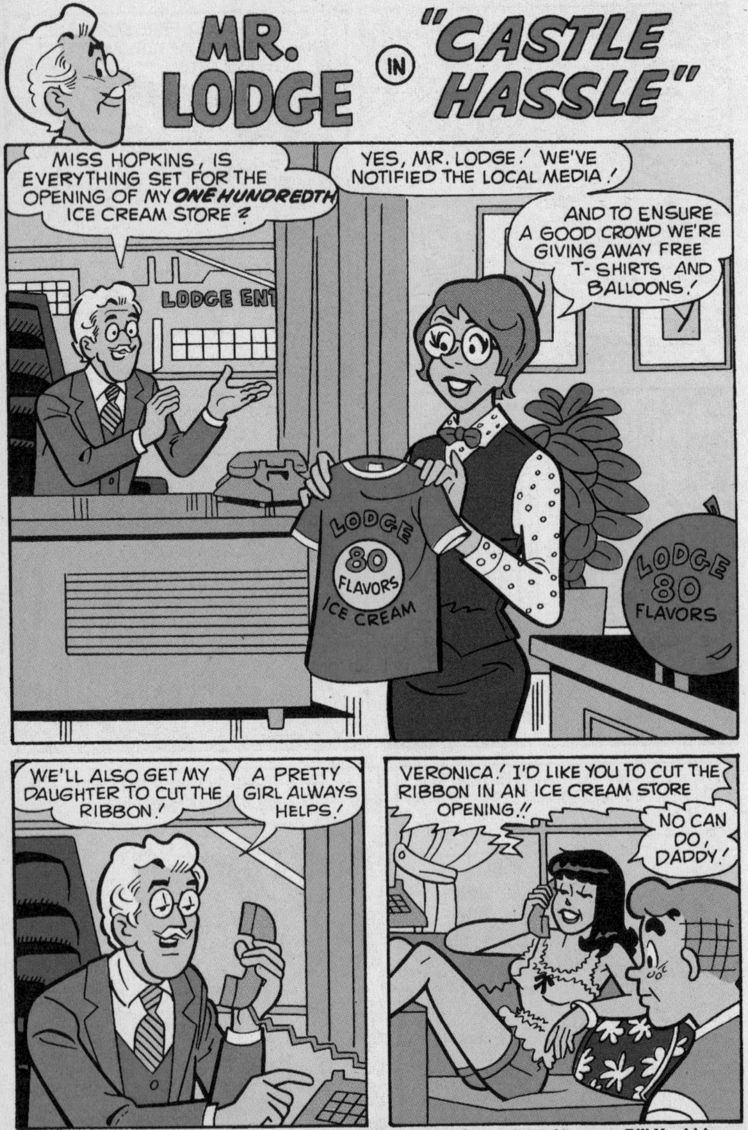
MR. LODGE IN "CASTLE HASSLE"
MISS HOPKINS, IS EVERYTHING SET FOR THE OPENING OF MY ONE HUNDREDTH ICE CREAM STORE?
YES, MR. LODGE! WE'VE NOTIFIED THE LOCAL MEDIA!
AND TO ENSURE A GOOD CROWD WE'RE GIVING AWAY FREE T-SHIRTS AND BALLOONS!
LODGE ENT
LODGE 80 FLAVORS ICE CREAM
LODGE 80 FLAVORS
WE'LL ALSO GET MY DAUGHTER TO CUT THE RIBBON!
A PRETTY GIRL ALWAYS HELPS!
VERONICA! I'D LIKE YOU TO CUT THE RIBBON IN AN ICE CREAM STORE OPENING!!
NO CAN DO, DADDY!

Script: George Gladir / Pencils: Stan Goldberg / Inks: Rudy Lapick / Letters: Bill Yoshida

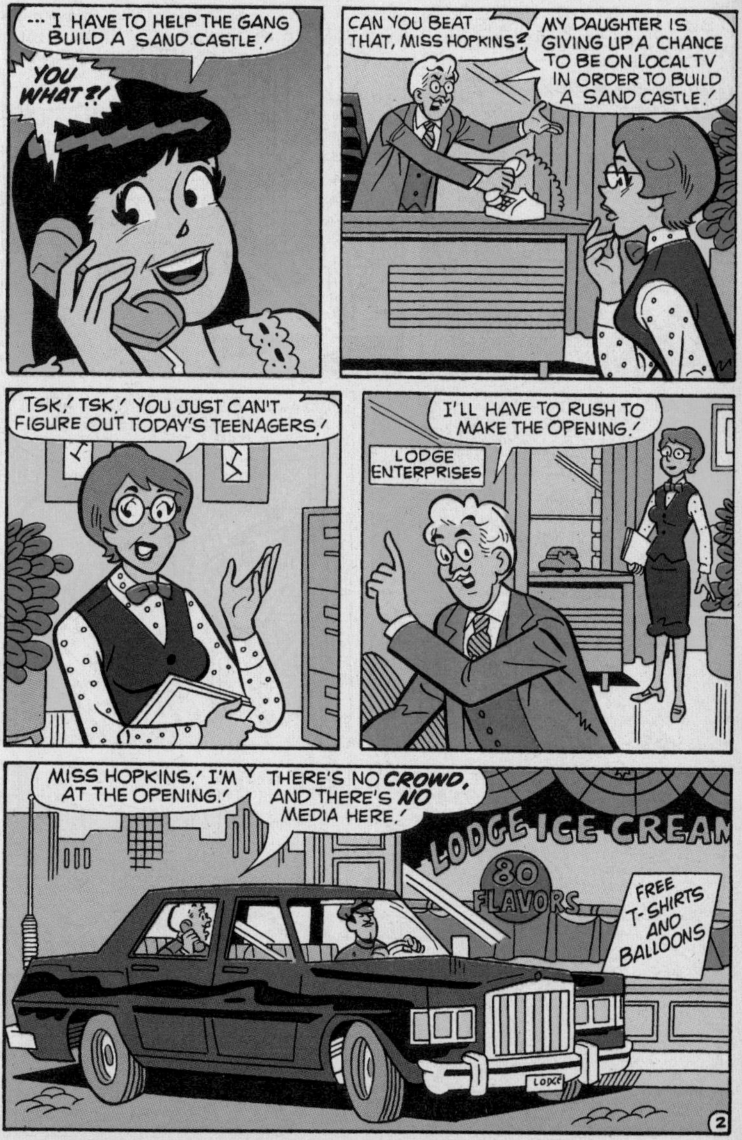

--- I HAVE TO HELP THE GANG BUILD A SAND CASTLE!
YOU WHAT?!
CAN YOU BEAT THAT, MISS HOPKINS?
MY DAUGHTER IS GIVING UP A CHANCE TO BE ON LOCAL TV IN ORDER TO BUILD A SAND CASTLE!
TSK! TSK! YOU JUST CAN'T FIGURE OUT TODAY'S TEENAGERS!
I'LL HAVE TO RUSH TO MAKE THE OPENING!
LODGE ENTERPRISES
MISS HOPKINS! I'M AT THE OPENING!
THERE'S NO CROWD, AND THERE'S NO MEDIA HERE!
LODGE ICE CREAM
80 FLAVORS
FREE T-SHIRTS AND BALLOONS
LODGE
2

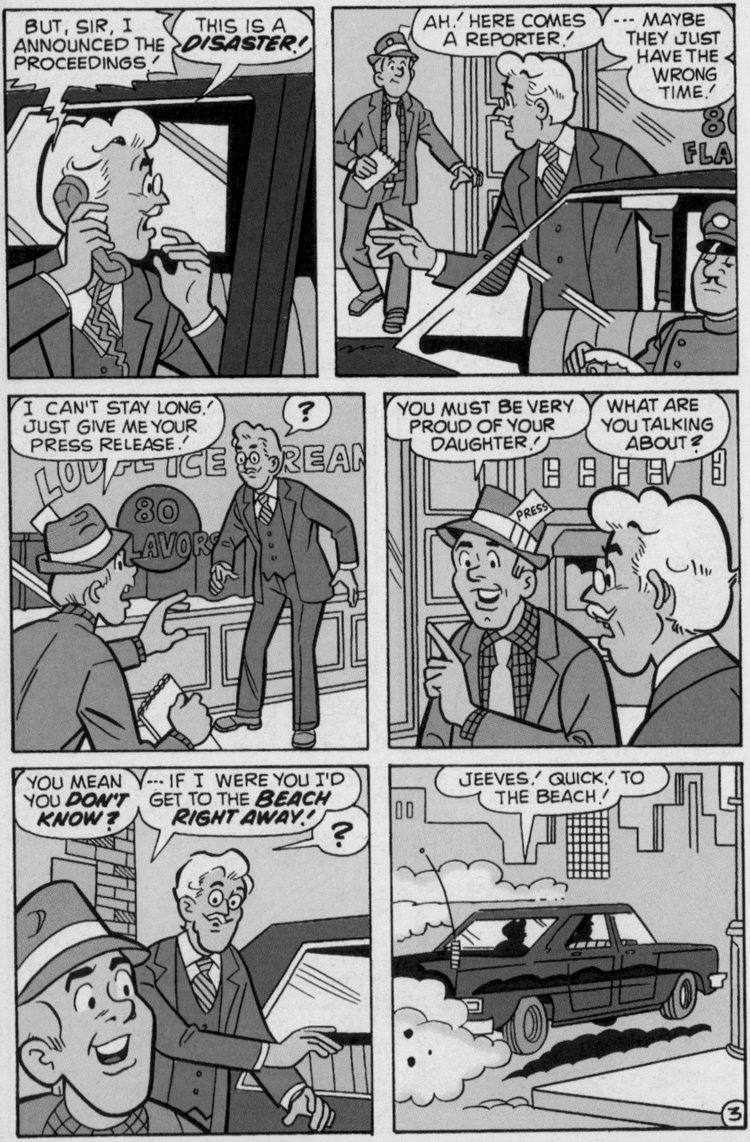
BUT, SIR, I ANNOUNCED THE PROCEEDINGS!
THIS IS A DISASTER!
AH! HERE COMES A REPORTER!
--- MAYBE THEY JUST HAVE THE WRONG TIME!
I CAN'T STAY LONG! JUST GIVE ME YOUR PRESS RELEASE!
?
YOU MUST BE VERY PROUD OF YOUR DAUGHTER!
WHAT ARE YOU TALKING ABOUT?
PRESS
YOU MEAN YOU DON'T KNOW?
--- IF I WERE YOU I'D GET TO THE BEACH RIGHT AWAY!
?
JEEVES! QUICK! TO THE BEACH!
3

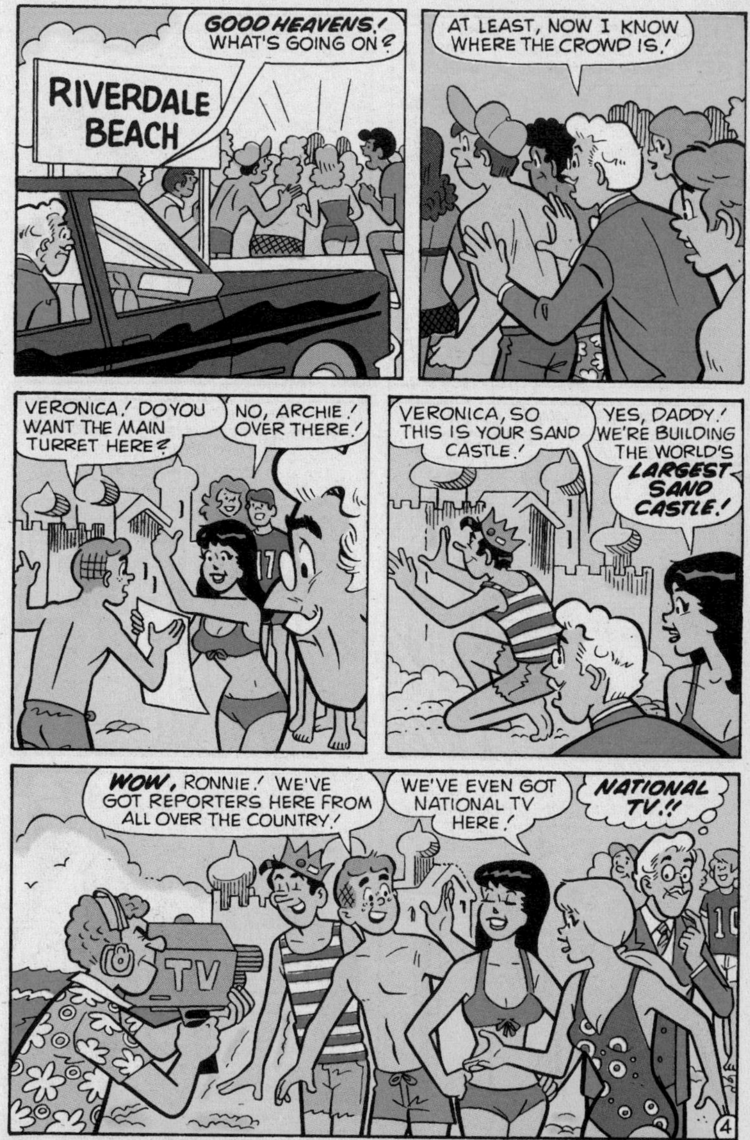

GOOD HEAVENS! WHAT'S GOING ON?
RIVERDALE BEACH
AT LEAST, NOW I KNOW WHERE THE CROWD IS!
VERONICA! DO YOU WANT THE MAIN TURRET HERE?
NO, ARCHIE! OVER THERE!
VERONICA, SO THIS IS YOUR SAND CASTLE!
YES, DADDY! WE'RE BUILDING THE WORLD'S LARGEST SAND CASTLE!
WOW, RONNIE! WE'VE GOT REPORTERS HERE FROM ALL OVER THE COUNTRY!
WE'VE EVEN GOT NATIONAL TV HERE!
NATIONAL TV!!
TV
4

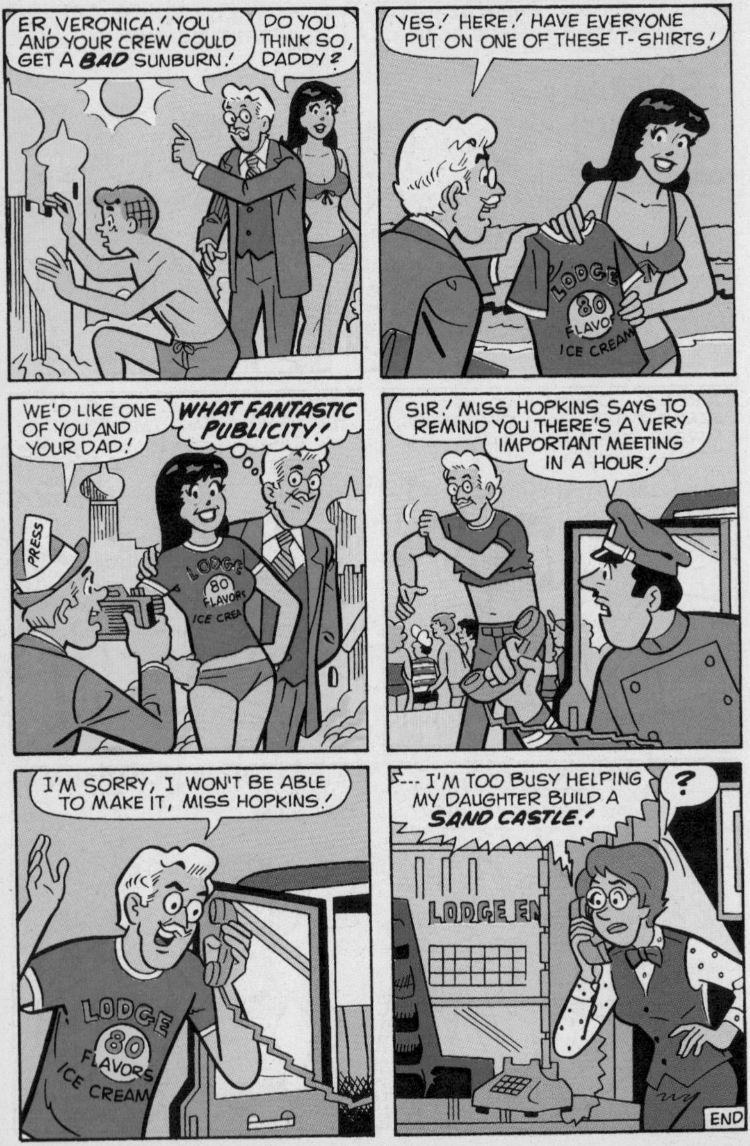
ER, VERONICA! YOU AND YOUR CREW COULD GET A BAD SUNBURN!
DO YOU THINK SO, DADDY?
YES! HERE! HAVE EVERYONE PUT ON ONE OF THESE T-SHIRTS!
LODGE 80 FLAVORS ICE CREAM
WE'D LIKE ONE OF YOU AND YOUR DAD!
WHAT FANTASTIC PUBLICITY!
PRESS
SIR! MISS HOPKINS SAYS TO REMIND YOU THERE'S A VERY IMPORTANT MEETING IN A HOUR!
I'M SORRY, I WON'T BE ABLE TO MAKE IT, MISS HOPKINS!
LODGE 80 FLAVORS ICE CREAM
--- I'M TOO BUSY HELPING MY DAUGHTER BUILD A SAND CASTLE!
?
LODGE EN
END

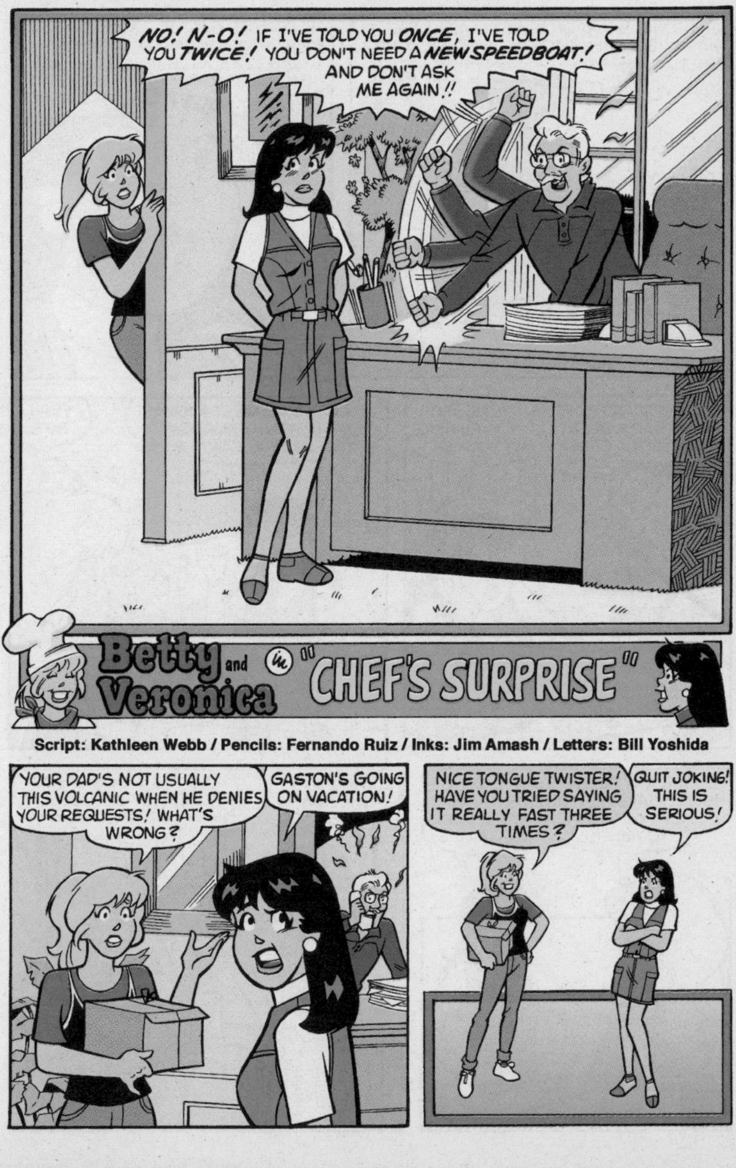

NO! N-O! IF I'VE TOLD YOU ONCE, I'VE TOLD YOU TWICE! YOU DON'T NEED A NEW SPEEDBOAT! AND DON'T ASK ME AGAIN!!
Betty and Veronica in "CHEF'S SURPRISE"
Script: Kathleen Webb / Pencils: Fernando Ruiz / Inks: Jim Amash / Letters: Bill Yoshida
YOUR DAD'S NOT USUALLY THIS VOLCANIC WHEN HE DENIES YOUR REQUESTS! WHAT'S WRONG?
GASTON'S GOING ON VACATION!
NICE TONGUE TWISTER! HAVE YOU TRIED SAYING IT REALLY FAST THREE TIMES?
QUIT JOKING! THIS IS SERIOUS!

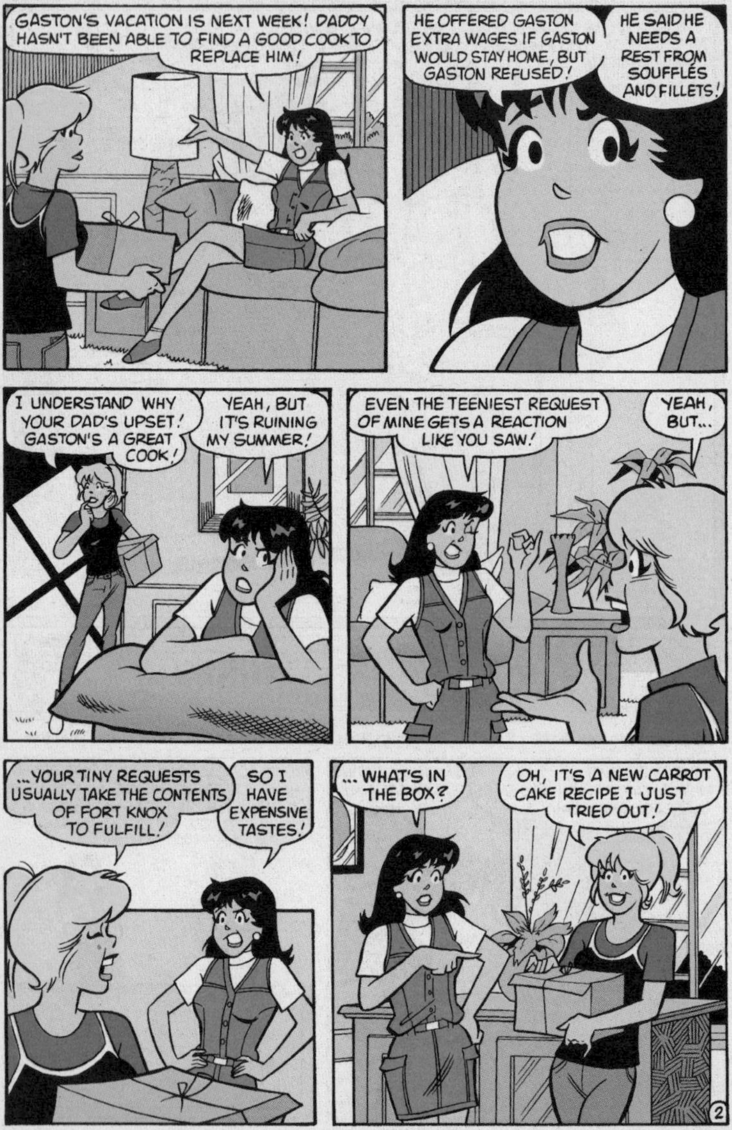
GASTON'S VACATION IS NEXT WEEK! DADDY HASN'T BEEN ABLE TO FIND A GOOD COOK TO REPLACE HIM!
HE OFFERED GASTON EXTRA WAGES IF GASTON WOULD STAY HOME, BUT GASTON REFUSED!
HE SAID HE NEEDS A REST FROM SOUFFLÉS AND FILLETS!
I UNDERSTAND WHY YOUR DAD'S UPSET! GASTON'S A GREAT COOK!
YEAH, BUT IT'S RUINING MY SUMMER!
EVEN THE TEENIEST REQUEST OF MINE GETS A REACTION LIKE YOU SAW!
YEAH, BUT...
...YOUR TINY REQUESTS USUALLY TAKE THE CONTENTS OF FORT KNOX TO FULFILL!
SO I HAVE EXPENSIVE TASTES!
... WHAT'S IN THE BOX?
OH, IT'S A NEW CARROT CAKE RECIPE I JUST TRIED OUT!
2

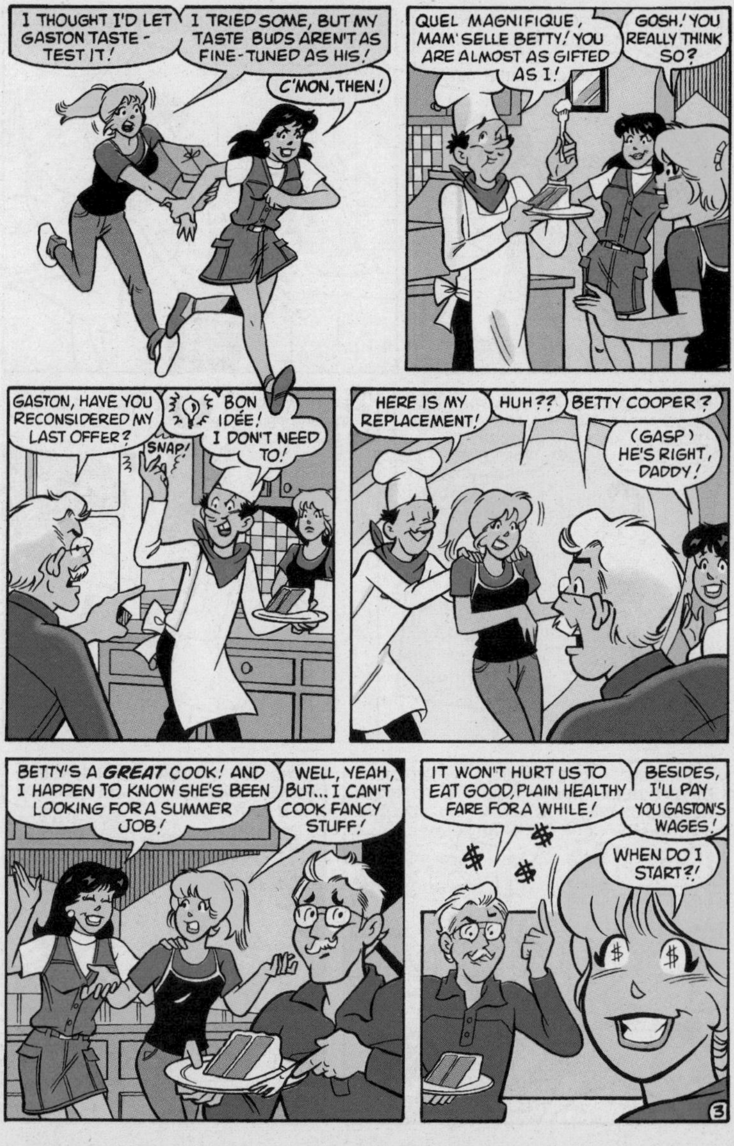
I THOUGHT I'D LET GASTON TASTE-TEST IT!
I TRIED SOME, BUT MY TASTE BUDS AREN'T AS FINE-TUNED AS HIS!
C'MON, THEN!
QUEL MAGNIFIQUE, MAM'SELLE BETTY! YOU ARE ALMOST AS GIFTED AS I!
GOSH! YOU REALLY THINK SO?
GASTON, HAVE YOU RECONSIDERED MY LAST OFFER?
BON IDÉE! I DON'T NEED TO!
SNAP!
HERE IS MY REPLACEMENT!
HUH??
BETTY COOPER?
(GASP) HE'S RIGHT, DADDY!
BETTY'S A GREAT COOK! AND I HAPPEN TO KNOW SHE'S BEEN LOOKING FOR A SUMMER JOB!
WELL, YEAH, BUT... I CAN'T COOK FANCY STUFF!
IT WON'T HURT US TO EAT GOOD, PLAIN HEALTHY FARE FOR A WHILE!
BESIDES, I'LL PAY YOU GASTON'S WAGES!
WHEN DO I START?!
3

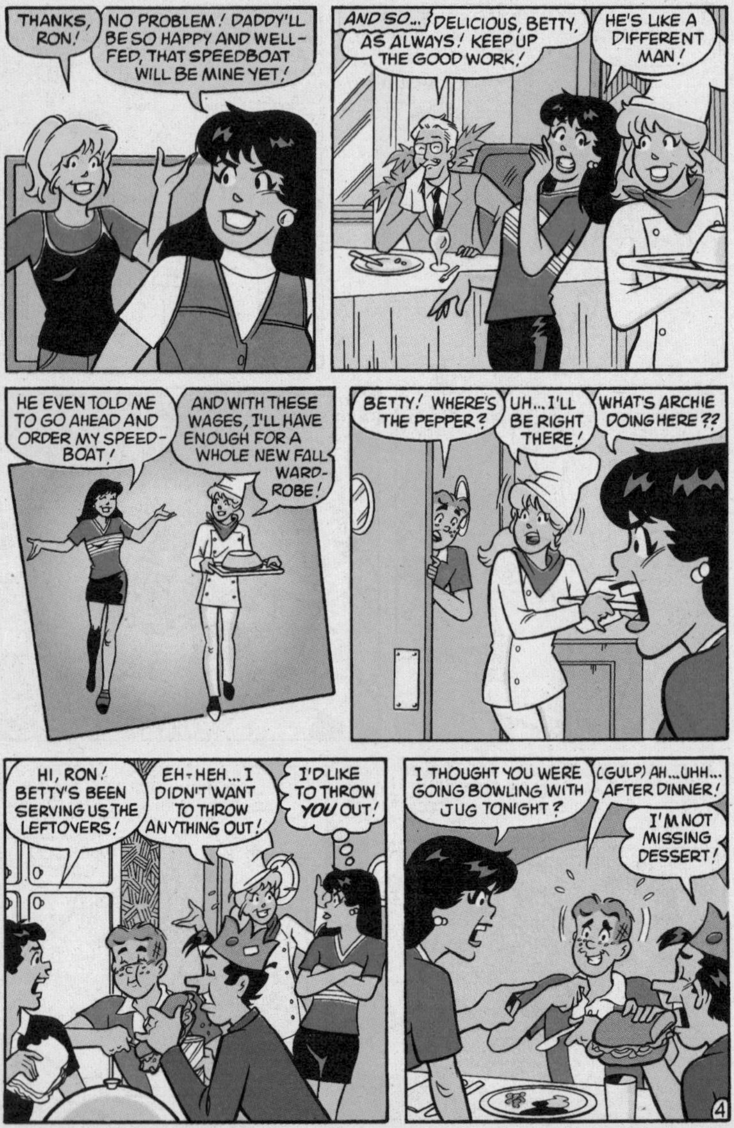
THANKS, RON!
NO PROBLEM! DADDY'LL BE SO HAPPY AND WELL-FED, THAT SPEEDBOAT WILL BE MINE YET!
AND SO...
DELICIOUS, BETTY, AS ALWAYS! KEEP UP THE GOOD WORK!
HE'S LIKE A DIFFERENT MAN!
HE EVEN TOLD ME TO GO AHEAD AND ORDER MY SPEED-BOAT!
AND WITH THESE WAGES, I'LL HAVE ENOUGH FOR A WHOLE NEW FALL WARD-ROBE!
BETTY! WHERE'S THE PEPPER?
UH... I'LL BE RIGHT THERE!
WHAT'S ARCHIE DOING HERE??
HI, RON! BETTY'S BEEN SERVING US THE LEFTOVERS!
EH-HEH... I DIDN'T WANT TO THROW ANYTHING OUT!
I'D LIKE TO THROW YOU OUT!
I THOUGHT YOU WERE GOING BOWLING WITH JUG TONIGHT?
(GULP) AH... UHH... AFTER DINNER!
I'M NOT MISSING DESSERT!
4

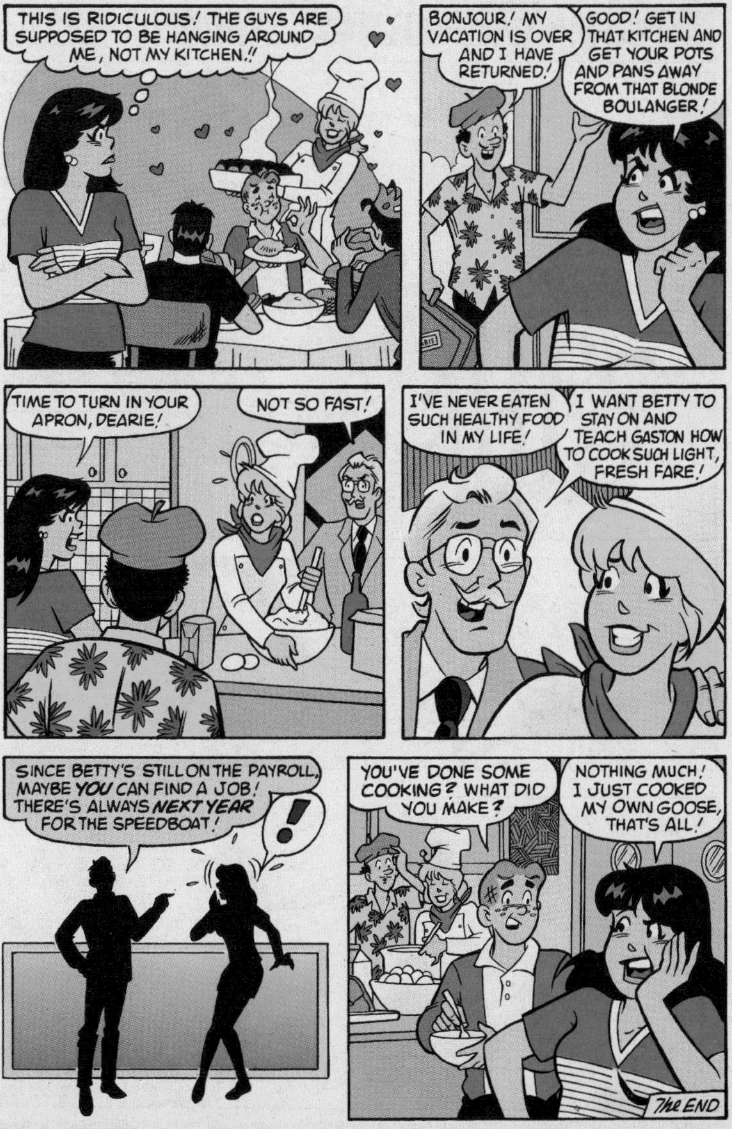
THIS IS RIDICULOUS! THE GUYS ARE SUPPOSED TO BE HANGING AROUND ME, NOT MY KITCHEN.!!
BONJOUR! MY VACATION IS OVER AND I HAVE RETURNED!
GOOD! GET IN THAT KITCHEN AND GET YOUR POTS AND PANS AWAY FROM THAT BLONDE BOULANGER!
PARIS
TIME TO TURN IN YOUR APRON, DEARIE!
NOT SO FAST!
I'VE NEVER EATEN SUCH HEALTHY FOOD IN MY LIFE!
I WANT BETTY TO STAY ON AND TEACH GASTON HOW TO COOK SUCH LIGHT, FRESH FARE!
SINCE BETTY'S STILL ON THE PAYROLL, MAYBE YOU CAN FIND A JOB! THERE'S ALWAYS NEXT YEAR FOR THE SPEEDBOAT!
!
YOU'VE DONE SOME COOKING? WHAT DID YOU MAKE?
NOTHING MUCH! I JUST COOKED MY OWN GOOSE, THAT'S ALL!
The END

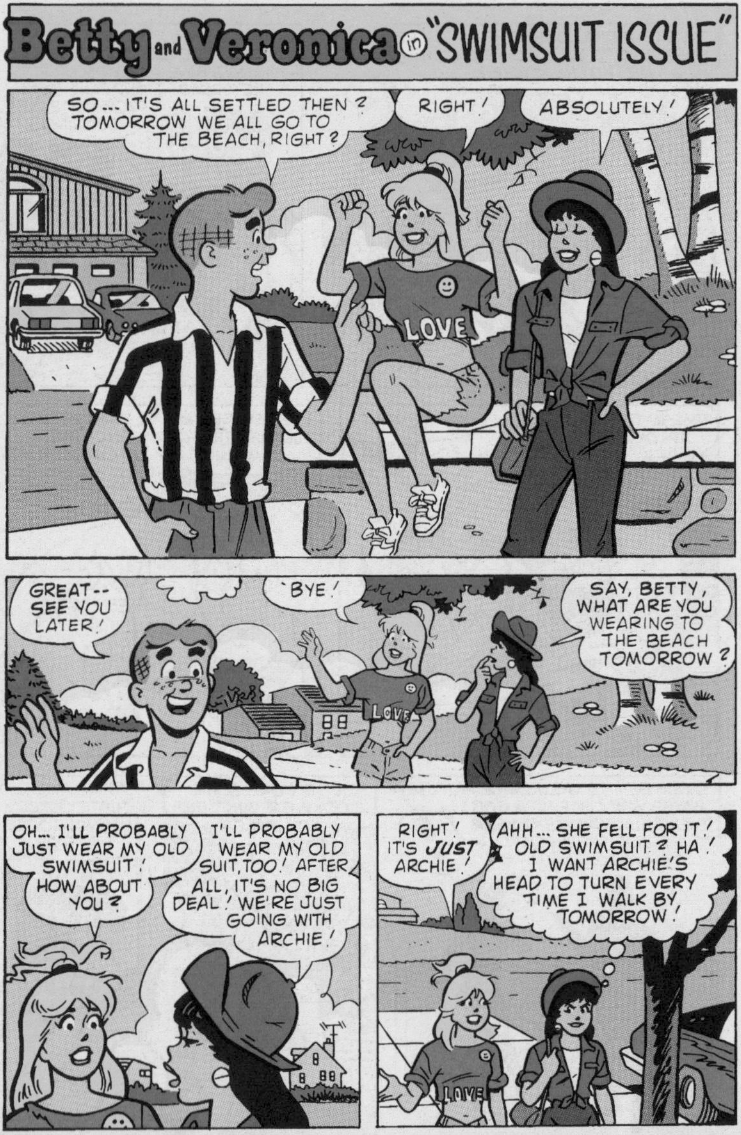
Betty and Veronica in "SWIMSUIT ISSUE"
SO... IT'S ALL SETTLED THEN ? TOMORROW WE ALL GO TO THE BEACH, RIGHT ?
RIGHT!
ABSOLUTELY!
LOVE
GREAT-- SEE YOU LATER!
'BYE!
SAY, BETTY, WHAT ARE YOU WEARING TO THE BEACH TOMORROW ?
OH... I'LL PROBABLY JUST WEAR MY OLD SWIMSUIT! HOW ABOUT YOU ?
I'LL PROBABLY WEAR MY OLD SUIT, TOO! AFTER ALL, IT'S NO BIG DEAL! WE'RE JUST GOING WITH ARCHIE!
RIGHT! IT'S *JUST* ARCHIE!
AHH... SHE FELL FOR IT! OLD SWIMSUIT ? HA! I WANT ARCHIE'S HEAD TO TURN EVERY TIME I WALK BY, TOMORROW!

Script: Mike Pellowski / Pencils: Dan DeCarlo / Inks: Jimmy DeCarlo / Letters: Bill Yoshida / Colors: Barry Grossman

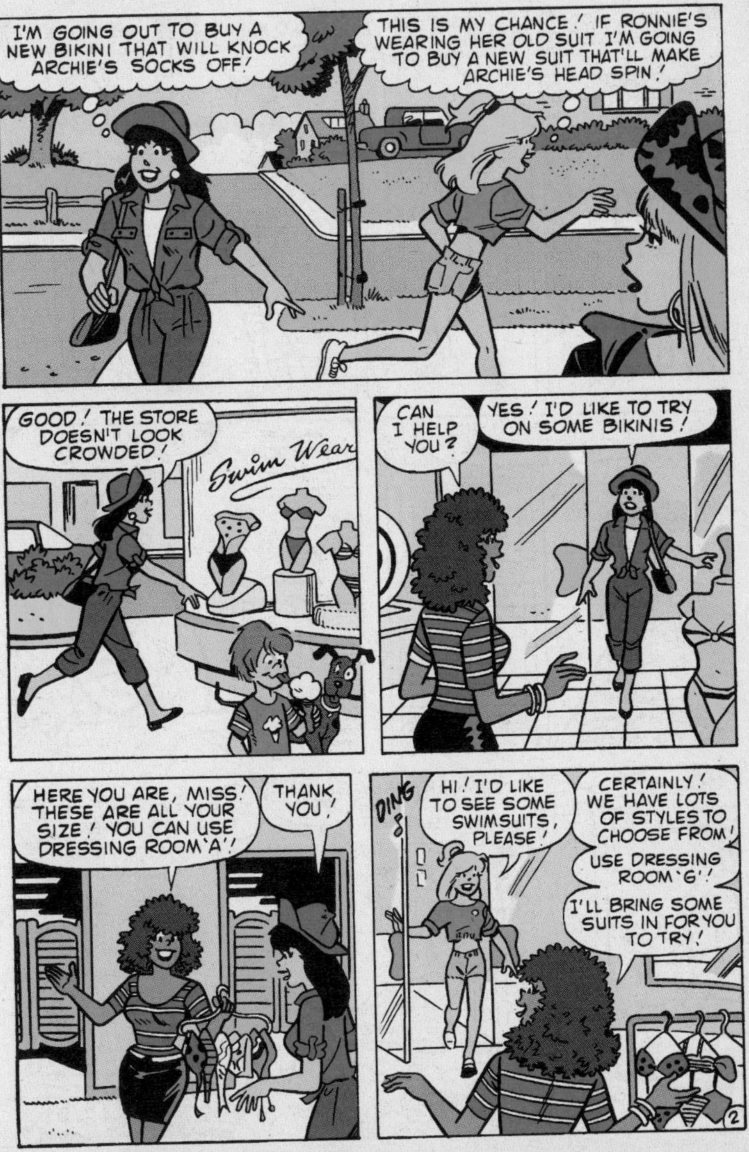
I'M GOING OUT TO BUY A NEW BIKINI THAT WILL KNOCK ARCHIE'S SOCKS OFF!
THIS IS MY CHANCE! IF RONNIE'S WEARING HER OLD SUIT I'M GOING TO BUY A NEW SUIT THAT'LL MAKE ARCHIE'S HEAD SPIN!
GOOD! THE STORE DOESN'T LOOK CROWDED!
Swim Wear
CAN I HELP YOU?
YES! I'D LIKE TO TRY ON SOME BIKINIS!
HERE YOU ARE, MISS! THESE ARE ALL YOUR SIZE! YOU CAN USE DRESSING ROOM 'A'!
THANK YOU!
DING
HI! I'D LIKE TO SEE SOME SWIMSUITS, PLEASE!
CERTAINLY! WE HAVE LOTS OF STYLES TO CHOOSE FROM!
USE DRESSING ROOM 'G'!
I'LL BRING SOME SUITS IN FOR YOU TO TRY!
2

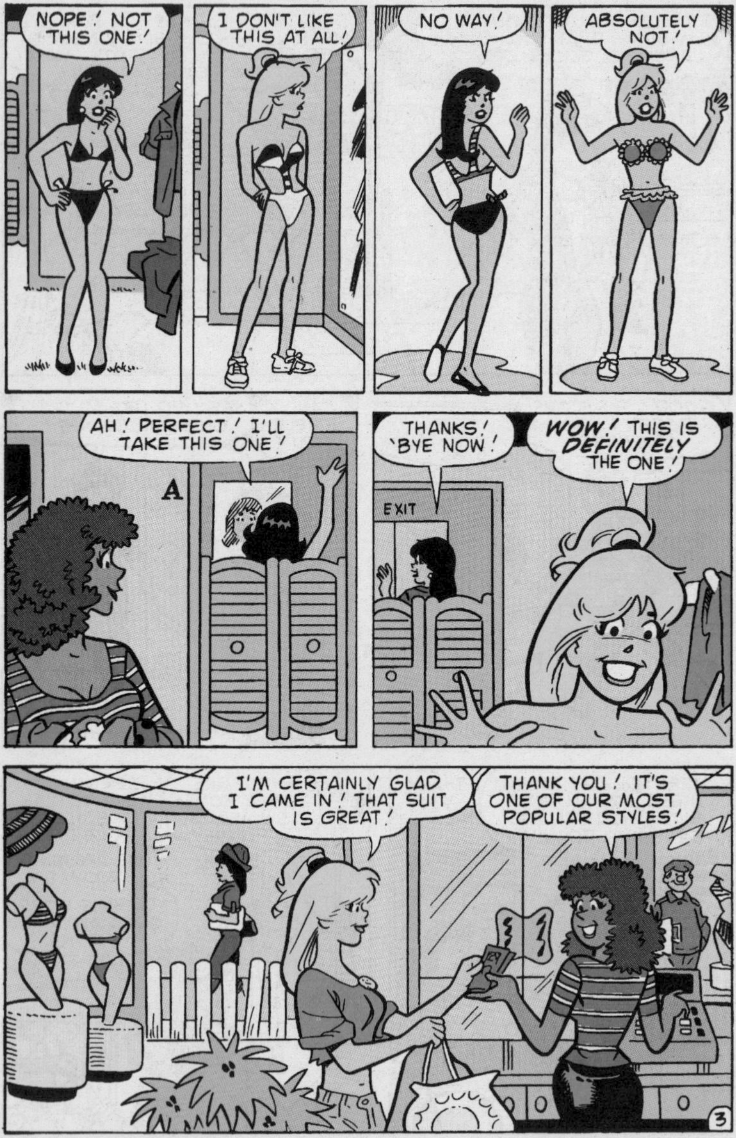
NOPE! NOT THIS ONE!
I DON'T LIKE THIS AT ALL!
NO WAY!
ABSOLUTELY NOT!
AH! PERFECT! I'LL TAKE THIS ONE!
A
THANKS! 'BYE NOW!
EXIT
WOW! THIS IS DEFINITELY THE ONE!
I'M CERTAINLY GLAD I CAME IN! THAT SUIT IS GREAT!
THANK YOU! IT'S ONE OF OUR MOST POPULAR STYLES!
3

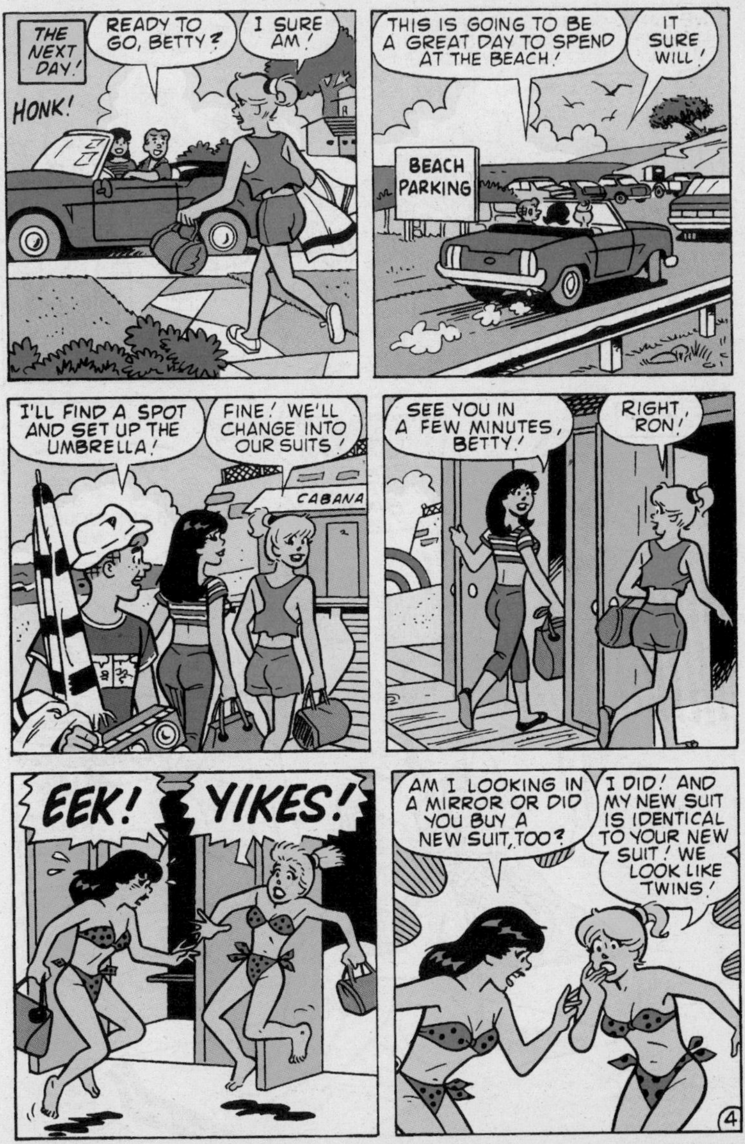
THE NEXT DAY!
HONK!
READY TO GO, BETTY?
I SURE AM!
THIS IS GOING TO BE A GREAT DAY TO SPEND AT THE BEACH!
IT SURE WILL!
BEACH PARKING
I'LL FIND A SPOT AND SET UP THE UMBRELLA!
FINE! WE'LL CHANGE INTO OUR SUITS!
CABANA
SEE YOU IN A FEW MINUTES, BETTY!
RIGHT, RON!
EEK!
YIKES!
AM I LOOKING IN A MIRROR OR DID YOU BUY A NEW SUIT, TOO?
I DID! AND MY NEW SUIT IS IDENTICAL TO YOUR NEW SUIT! WE LOOK LIKE TWINS!
4

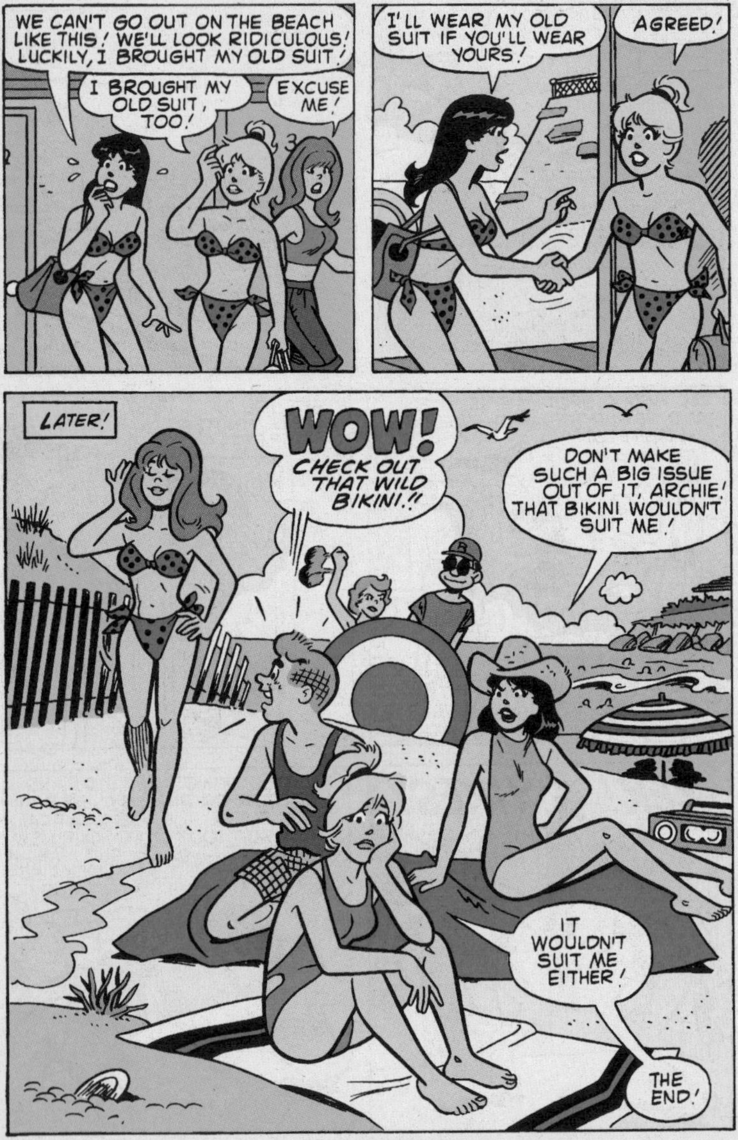
WE CAN'T GO OUT ON THE BEACH LIKE THIS! WE'LL LOOK RIDICULOUS! LUCKILY, I BROUGHT MY OLD SUIT!
I BROUGHT MY OLD SUIT, TOO!
EXCUSE ME!
I'LL WEAR MY OLD SUIT IF YOU'LL WEAR YOURS!
AGREED!
LATER!
WOW! CHECK OUT THAT WILD BIKINI!!
DON'T MAKE SUCH A BIG ISSUE OUT OF IT, ARCHIE! THAT BIKINI WOULDN'T SUIT ME!
IT WOULDN'T SUIT ME EITHER!
THE END!

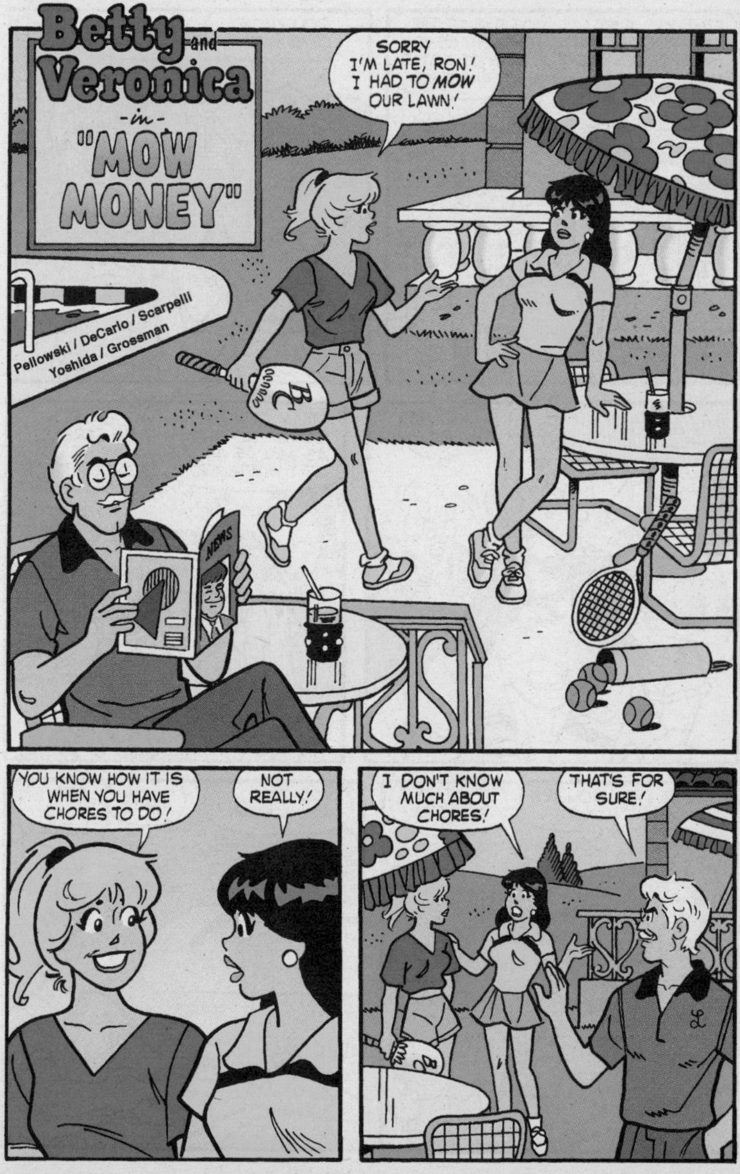
Betty and Veronica
-in-
"MOW MONEY"
Pellowski / DeCarlo / Scarpelli
Yoshida / Grossman
SORRY I'M LATE, RON! I HAD TO MOW OUR LAWN!
NEWS
YOU KNOW HOW IT IS WHEN YOU HAVE CHORES TO DO!
NOT REALLY!
I DON'T KNOW MUCH ABOUT CHORES!
THAT'S FOR SURE!

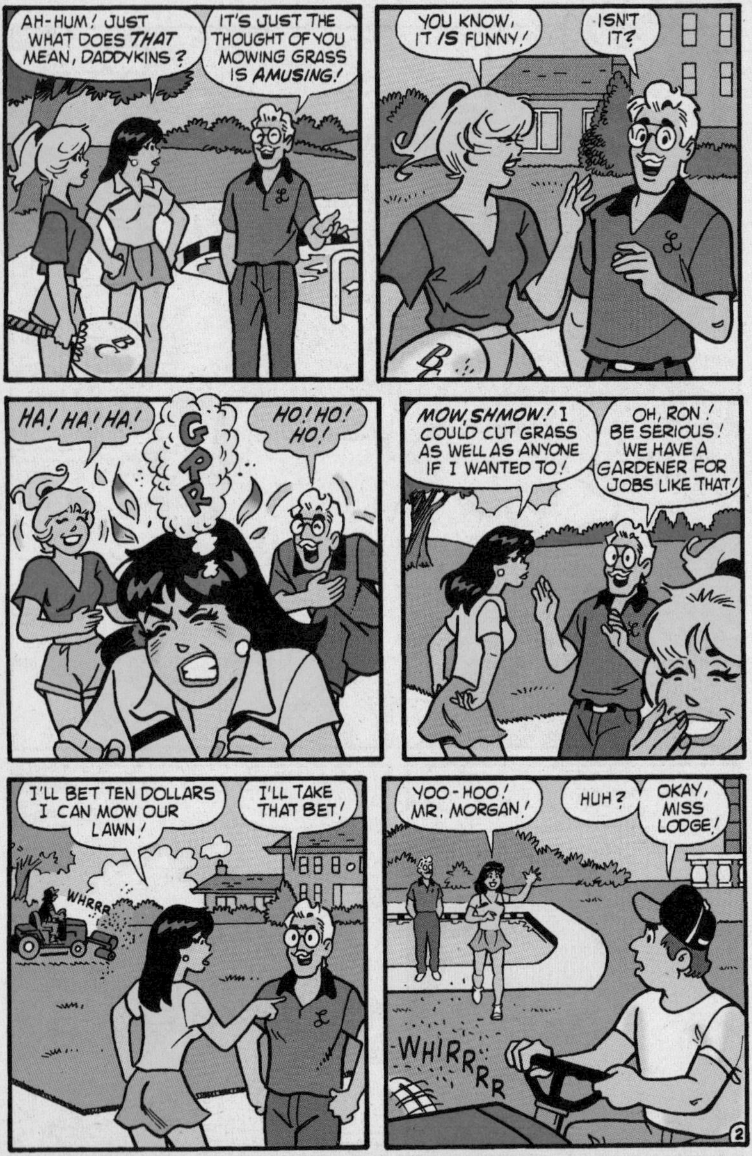
AH-HUM! JUST WHAT DOES THAT MEAN, DADDYKINS?
IT'S JUST THE THOUGHT OF YOU MOWING GRASS IS AMUSING!
YOU KNOW, IT IS FUNNY!
ISN'T IT?
HA! HA! HA!
GRR
HO! HO! HO!
MOW, SHMOW! I COULD CUT GRASS AS WELL AS ANYONE IF I WANTED TO!
OH, RON! BE SERIOUS! WE HAVE A GARDENER FOR JOBS LIKE THAT!
I'LL BET TEN DOLLARS I CAN MOW OUR LAWN!
I'LL TAKE THAT BET!
WHRRR
YOO-HOO! MR. MORGAN!
HUH?
OKAY, MISS LODGE!
WHIRRRR
2

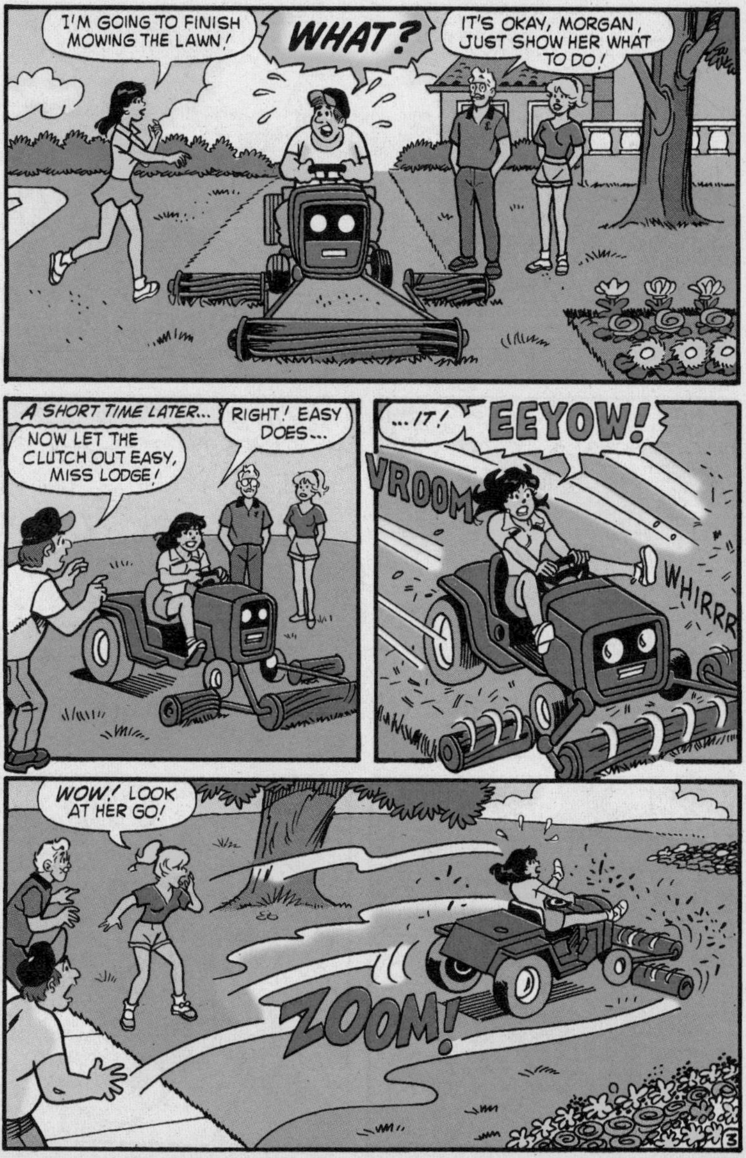

I'M GOING TO FINISH MOWING THE LAWN!
WHAT?
IT'S OKAY, MORGAN, JUST SHOW HER WHAT TO DO!
A SHORT TIME LATER...
NOW LET THE CLUTCH OUT EASY, MISS LODGE!
RIGHT! EASY DOES...
...IT!
EEYOW!
VROOM
WHIRRR
WOW! LOOK AT HER GO!
ZOOM!

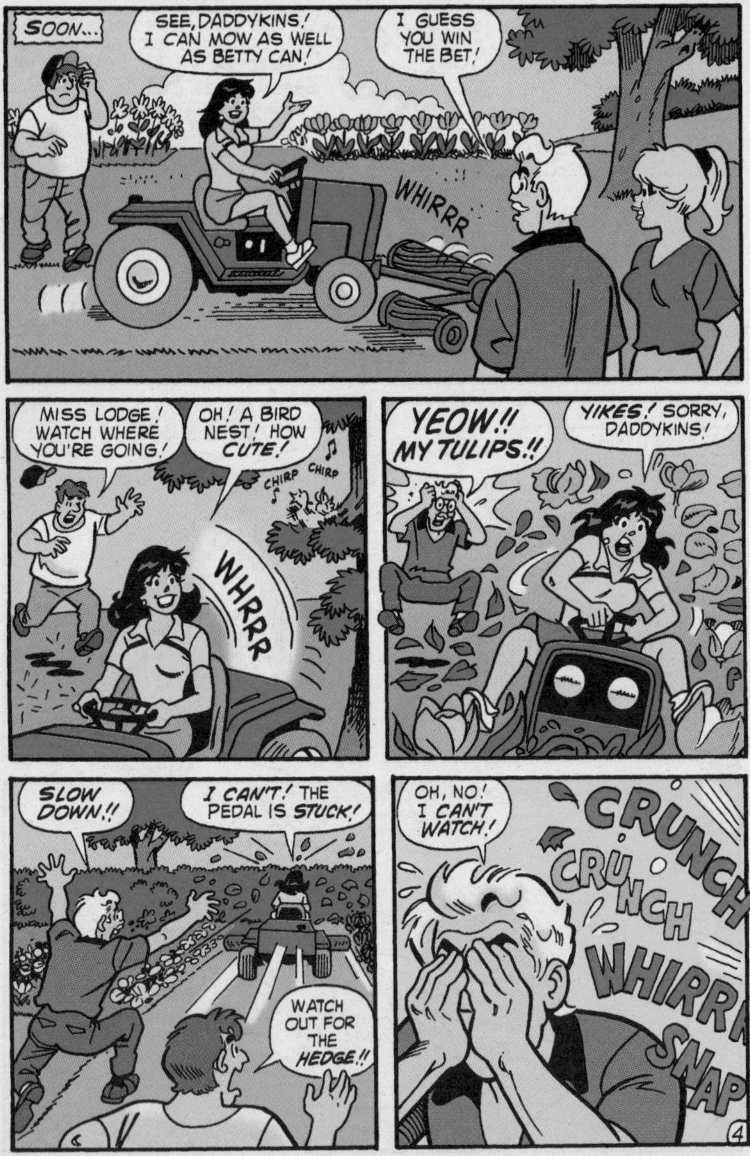
SOON...
SEE, DADDYKINS! I CAN MOW AS WELL AS BETTY CAN!
I GUESS YOU WIN THE BET!
WHIRRR
MISS LODGE! WATCH WHERE YOU'RE GOING!
OH! A BIRD NEST! HOW CUTE!
CHIRP CHIRP
WHRRR
YEOW!! MY TULIPS!!
YIKES! SORRY, DADDYKINS!
SLOW DOWN!!
I CAN'T! THE PEDAL IS STUCK!
WATCH OUT FOR THE HEDGE!!
OH, NO! I CAN'T WATCH!
CRUNCH
CRUNCH
WHIRRR
SNAP
4

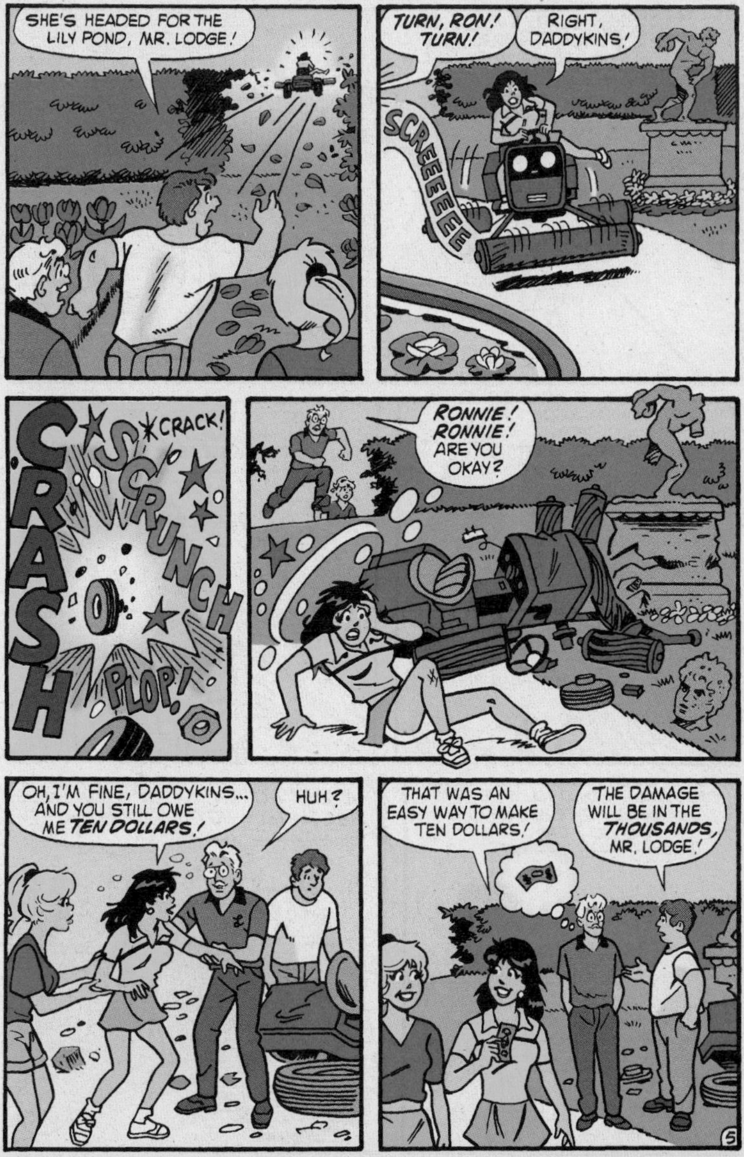
SHE'S HEADED FOR THE LILY POND, MR. LODGE!
TURN, RON! TURN!
RIGHT, DADDYKINS!
SCREEEEEEE
CRASH
CRACK!
SCRUNCH
PLOP!
RONNIE! RONNIE! ARE YOU OKAY?
OH, I'M FINE, DADDYKINS... AND YOU STILL OWE ME TEN DOLLARS!
HUH?
THAT WAS AN EASY WAY TO MAKE TEN DOLLARS!
THE DAMAGE WILL BE IN THE THOUSANDS, MR. LODGE!
5

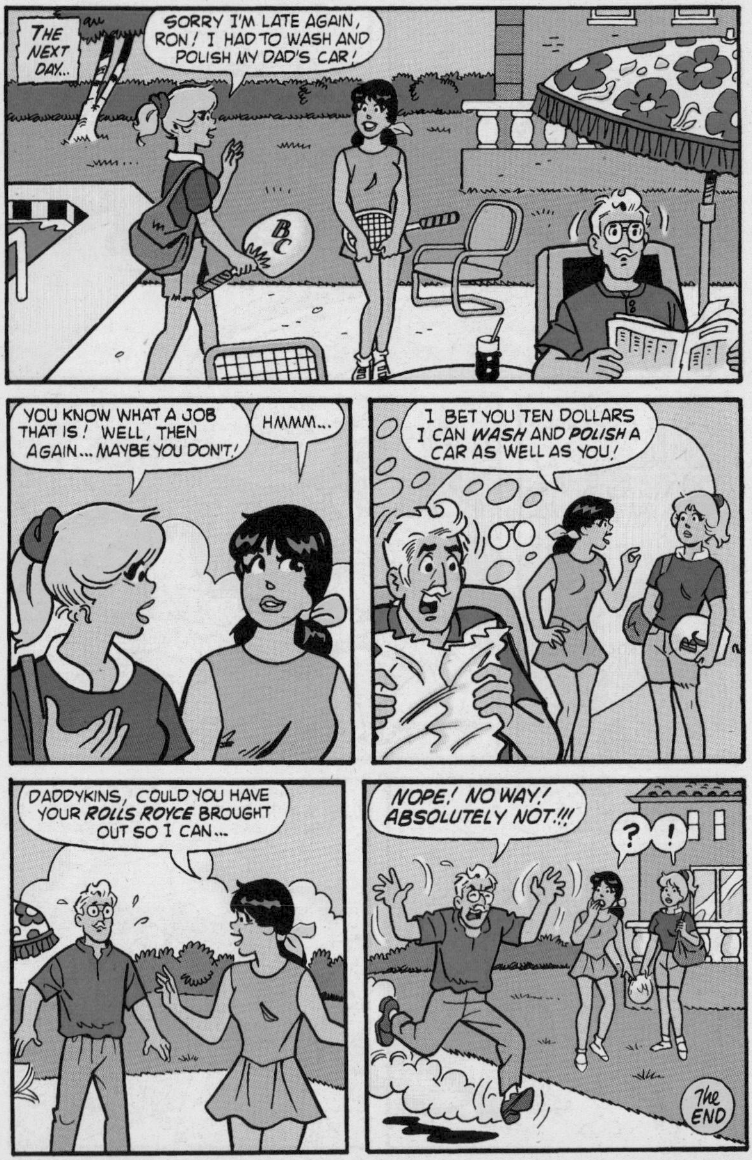
THE NEXT DAY...
SORRY I'M LATE AGAIN, RON! I HAD TO WASH AND POLISH MY DAD'S CAR!
BC
YOU KNOW WHAT A JOB THAT IS! WELL, THEN AGAIN... MAYBE YOU DON'T!
HMMM...
I BET YOU TEN DOLLARS I CAN WASH AND POLISH A CAR AS WELL AS YOU!
DADDYKINS, COULD YOU HAVE YOUR ROLLS ROYCE BROUGHT OUT SO I CAN...
NOPE! NO WAY! ABSOLUTELY NOT!!!
?
!
The END

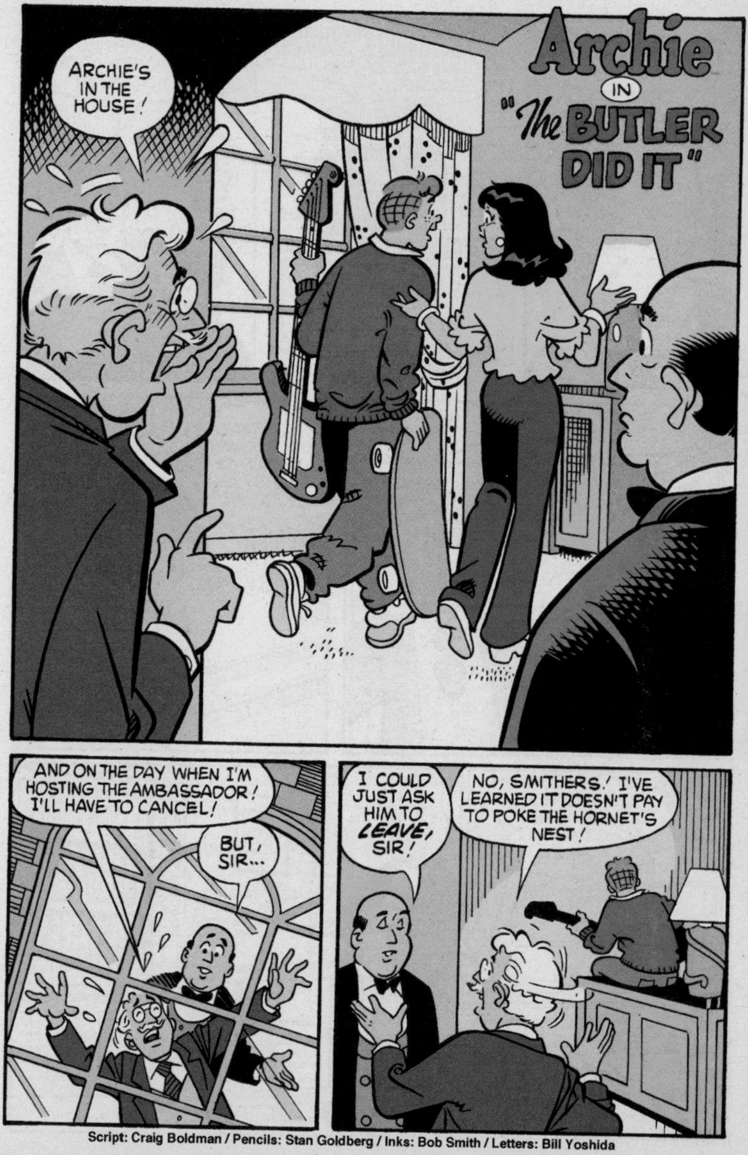
Archie
IN
"The BUTLER DID IT"
ARCHIE'S IN THE HOUSE!
AND ON THE DAY WHEN I'M HOSTING THE AMBASSADOR! I'LL HAVE TO CANCEL!
BUT, SIR...
I COULD JUST ASK HIM TO LEAVE, SIR!
NO, SMITHERS! I'VE LEARNED IT DOESN'T PAY TO POKE THE HORNET'S NEST!

Script: Craig Boldman / Pencils: Stan Goldberg / Inks: Bob Smith / Letters: Bill Yoshida

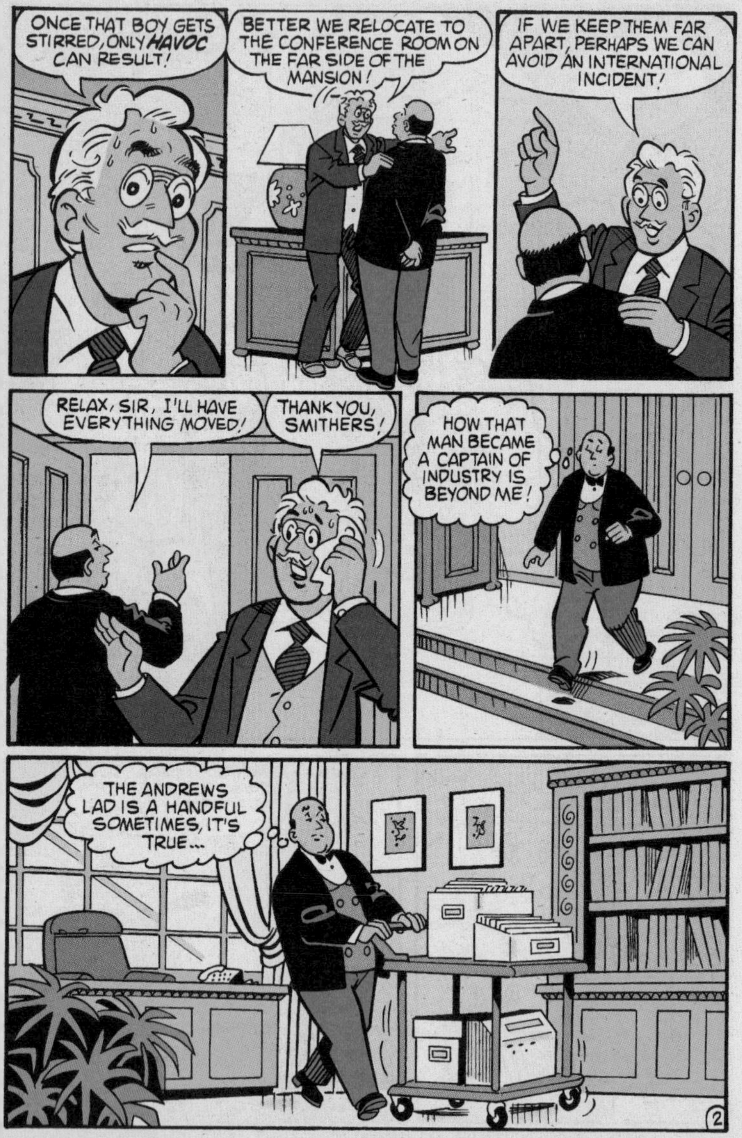
ONCE THAT BOY GETS STIRRED, ONLY HAVOC CAN RESULT!
BETTER WE RELOCATE TO THE CONFERENCE ROOM ON THE FAR SIDE OF THE MANSION!
IF WE KEEP THEM FAR APART, PERHAPS WE CAN AVOID AN INTERNATIONAL INCIDENT!
RELAX, SIR, I'LL HAVE EVERYTHING MOVED!
THANK YOU, SMITHERS!
HOW THAT MAN BECAME A CAPTAIN OF INDUSTRY IS BEYOND ME!
THE ANDREWS LAD IS A HANDFUL SOMETIMES, IT'S TRUE...
2

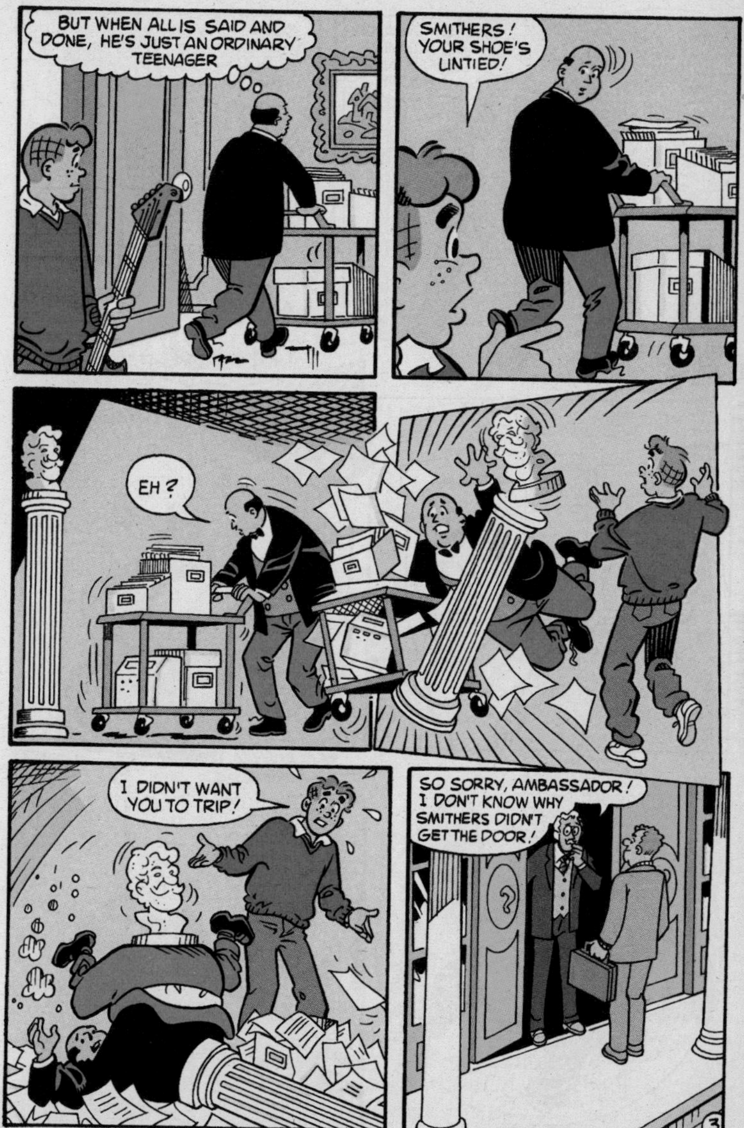
BUT WHEN ALL IS SAID AND DONE, HE'S JUST AN ORDINARY TEENAGER
SMITHERS! YOUR SHOE'S UNTIED!
EH?
I DIDN'T WANT YOU TO TRIP!
SO SORRY, AMBASSADOR! I DON'T KNOW WHY SMITHERS DIDN'T GET THE DOOR!
3

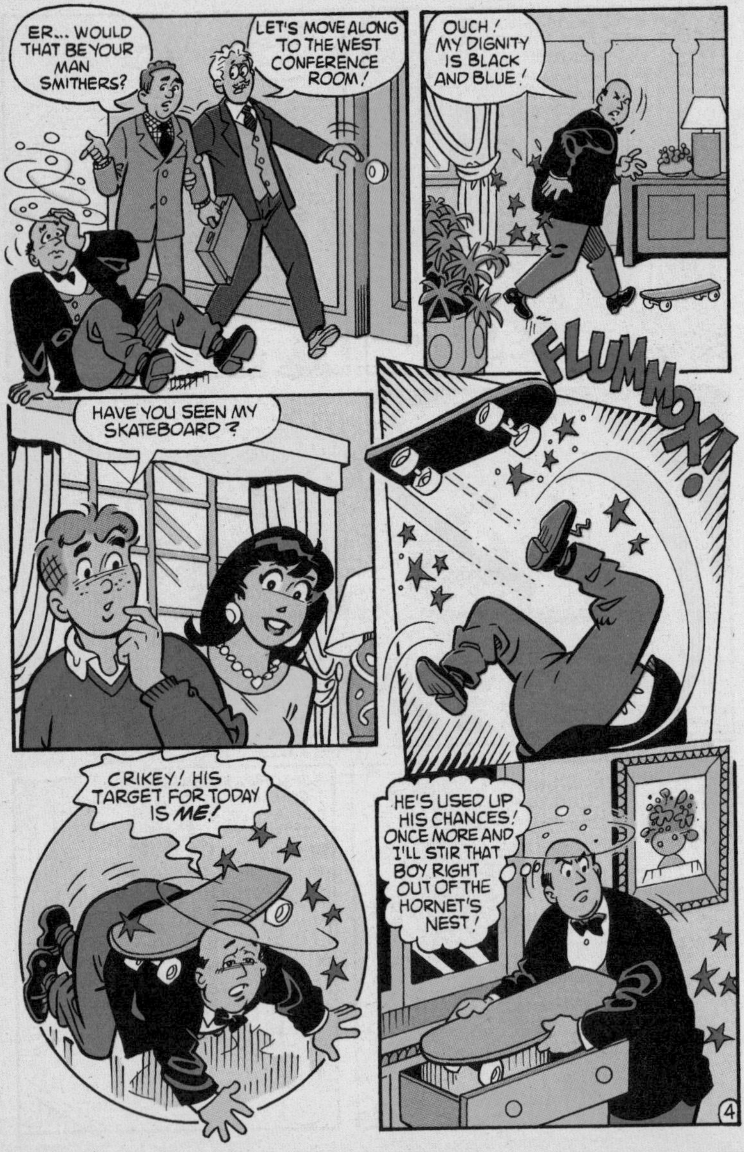
ER... WOULD THAT BE YOUR MAN SMITHERS?
LET'S MOVE ALONG TO THE WEST CONFERENCE ROOM!
OUCH! MY DIGNITY IS BLACK AND BLUE!
HAVE YOU SEEN MY SKATEBOARD?
FLUMMOX!
CRIKEY! HIS TARGET FOR TODAY IS ME!
HE'S USED UP HIS CHANCES! ONCE MORE AND I'LL STIR THAT BOY RIGHT OUT OF THE HORNET'S NEST!
4

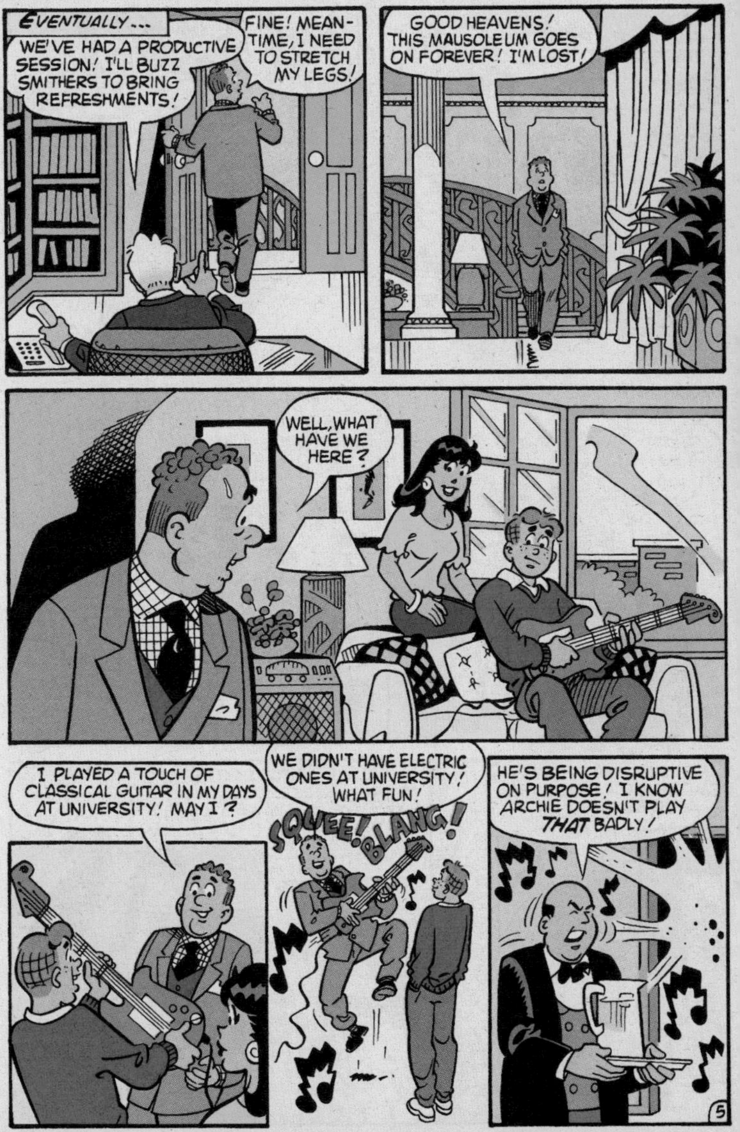
EVENTUALLY...
WE'VE HAD A PRODUCTIVE SESSION! I'LL BUZZ SMITHERS TO BRING REFRESHMENTS!
FINE! MEAN-TIME, I NEED TO STRETCH MY LEGS!
GOOD HEAVENS! THIS MAUSOLEUM GOES ON FOREVER! I'M LOST!
WELL, WHAT HAVE WE HERE?
I PLAYED A TOUCH OF CLASSICAL GUITAR IN MY DAYS AT UNIVERSITY! MAY I?
WE DIDN'T HAVE ELECTRIC ONES AT UNIVERSITY! WHAT FUN!
SQUEE! BLANG!
HE'S BEING DISRUPTIVE ON PURPOSE! I KNOW ARCHIE DOESN'T PLAY THAT BADLY!
5

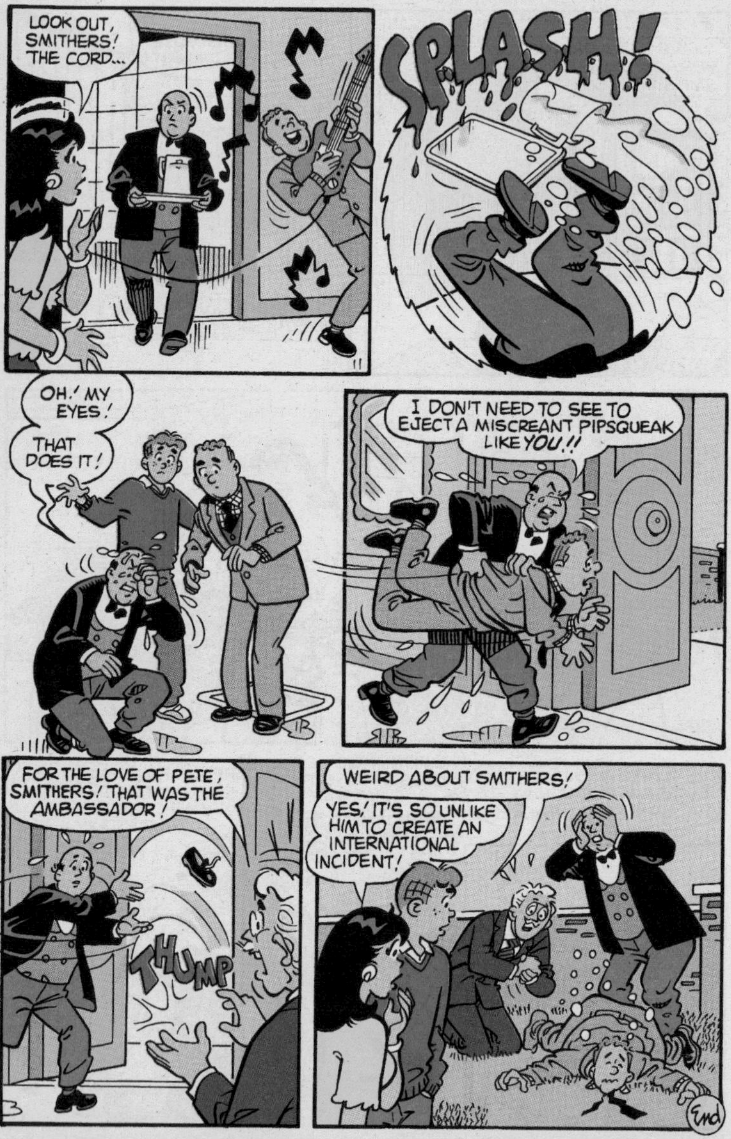
LOOK OUT, SMITHERS! THE CORD...
SPLASH!
OH.! MY EYES!
THAT DOES IT!
I DON'T NEED TO SEE TO EJECT A MISCREANT PIPSQUEAK LIKE YOU!!
FOR THE LOVE OF PETE, SMITHERS! THAT WAS THE AMBASSADOR!
THUMP
WEIRD ABOUT SMITHERS!
YES! IT'S SO UNLIKE HIM TO CREATE AN INTERNATIONAL INCIDENT!
End

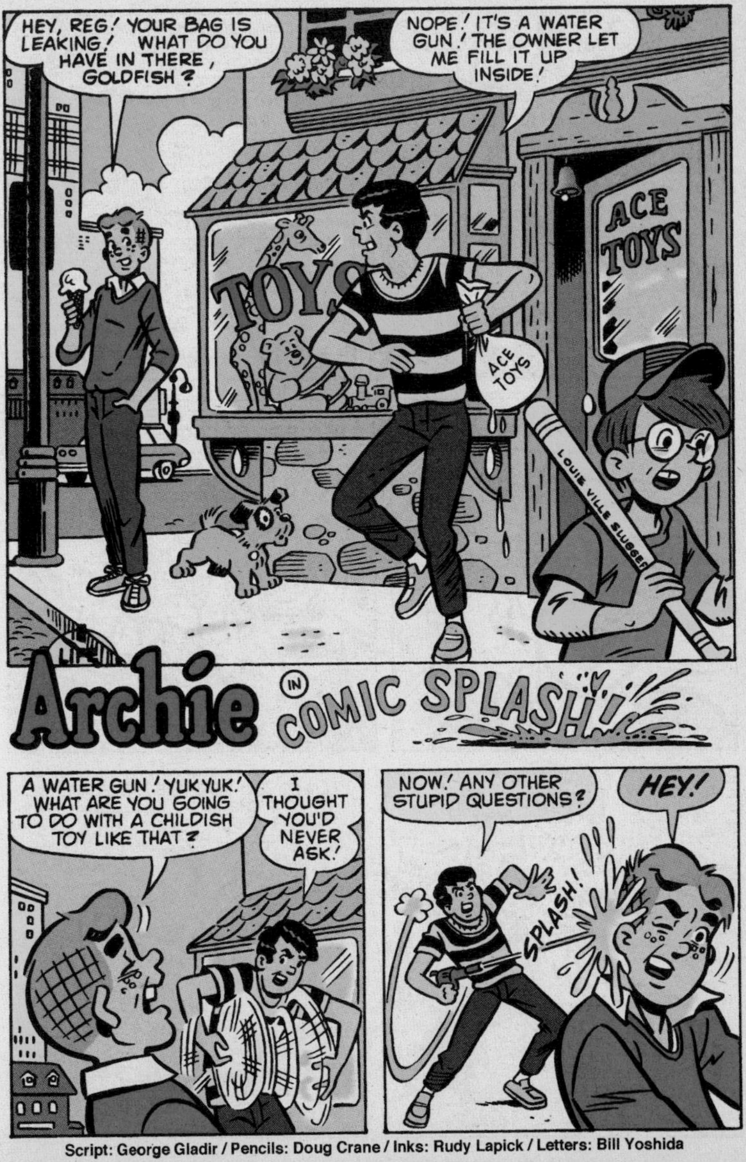
HEY, REG! YOUR BAG IS LEAKING! WHAT DO YOU HAVE IN THERE, GOLDFISH?
NOPE! IT'S A WATER GUN! THE OWNER LET ME FILL IT UP INSIDE!
TOYS
ACE TOYS
ACE TOYS
LOUIE VILLE SLUGGER
Archie
IN
COMIC SPLASH!
A WATER GUN! YUK YUK! WHAT ARE YOU GOING TO DO WITH A CHILDISH TOY LIKE THAT?
I THOUGHT YOU'D NEVER ASK!
NOW! ANY OTHER STUPID QUESTIONS?
HEY!
SPLASH!

Script: George Gladir / Pencils: Doug Crane / Inks: Rudy Lapick / Letters: Bill Yoshida

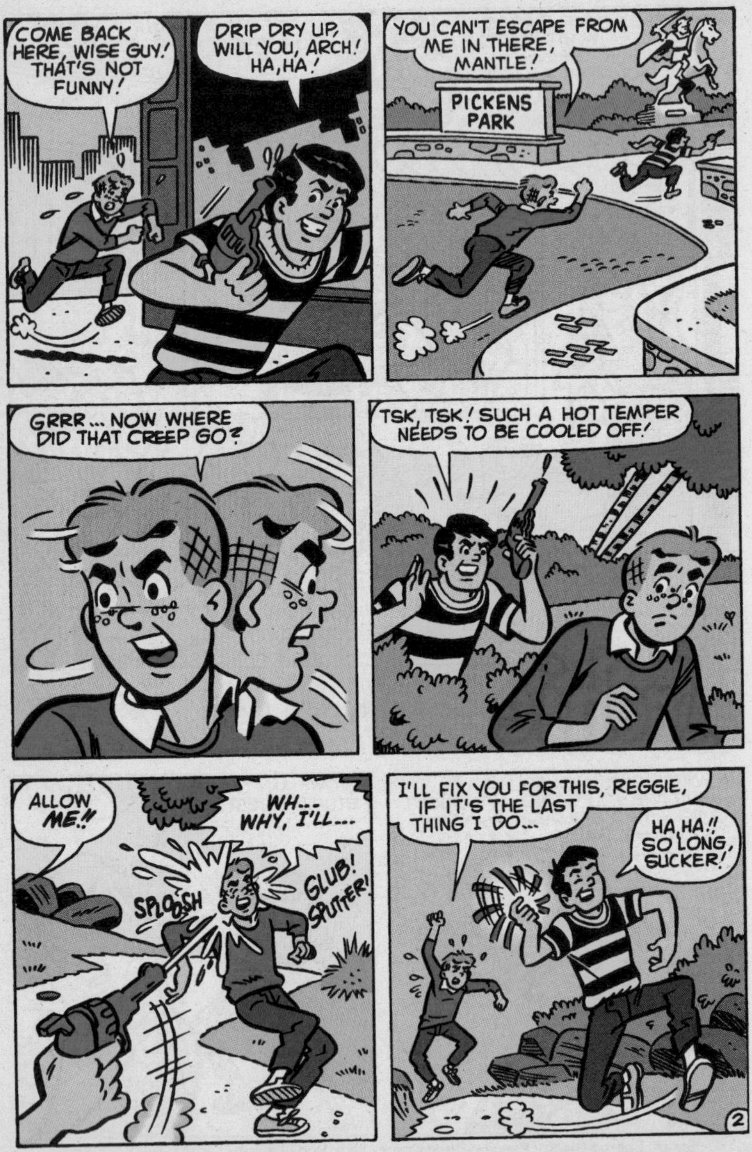
COME BACK HERE, WISE GUY! THAT'S NOT FUNNY!
DRIP DRY UP, WILL YOU, ARCH! HA, HA!
YOU CAN'T ESCAPE FROM ME IN THERE, MANTLE!
PICKENS PARK
GRRR... NOW WHERE DID THAT CREEP GO?
TSK, TSK! SUCH A HOT TEMPER NEEDS TO BE COOLED OFF!
ALLOW ME!!
WH... WHY, I'LL...
SPLOOSH
GLUB! SPUTTER!
I'LL FIX YOU FOR THIS, REGGIE, IF IT'S THE LAST THING I DO...
HA, HA!! SO LONG, SUCKER!
2

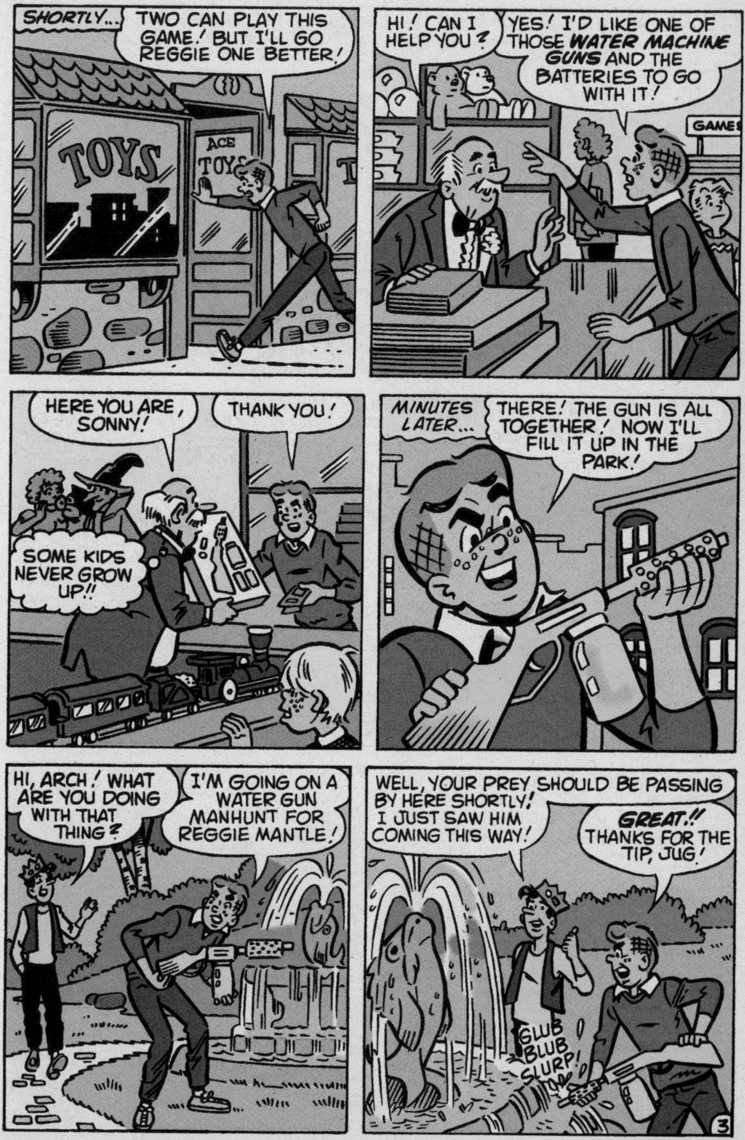
SHORTLY...
TWO CAN PLAY THIS GAME! BUT I'LL GO REGGIE ONE BETTER!
TOYS
ACE TOYS
HI! CAN I HELP YOU?
YES! I'D LIKE ONE OF THOSE WATER MACHINE GUNS AND THE BATTERIES TO GO WITH IT!
GAMES
HERE YOU ARE, SONNY!
THANK YOU!
SOME KIDS NEVER GROW UP!!
MINUTES LATER...
THERE! THE GUN IS ALL TOGETHER! NOW I'LL FILL IT UP IN THE PARK!
HI, ARCH! WHAT ARE YOU DOING WITH THAT THING?
I'M GOING ON A WATER GUN MANHUNT FOR REGGIE MANTLE!
WELL, YOUR PREY SHOULD BE PASSING BY HERE SHORTLY! I JUST SAW HIM COMING THIS WAY!
GREAT!! THANKS FOR THE TIP, JUG!
GLUB BLUB SLURP!
3

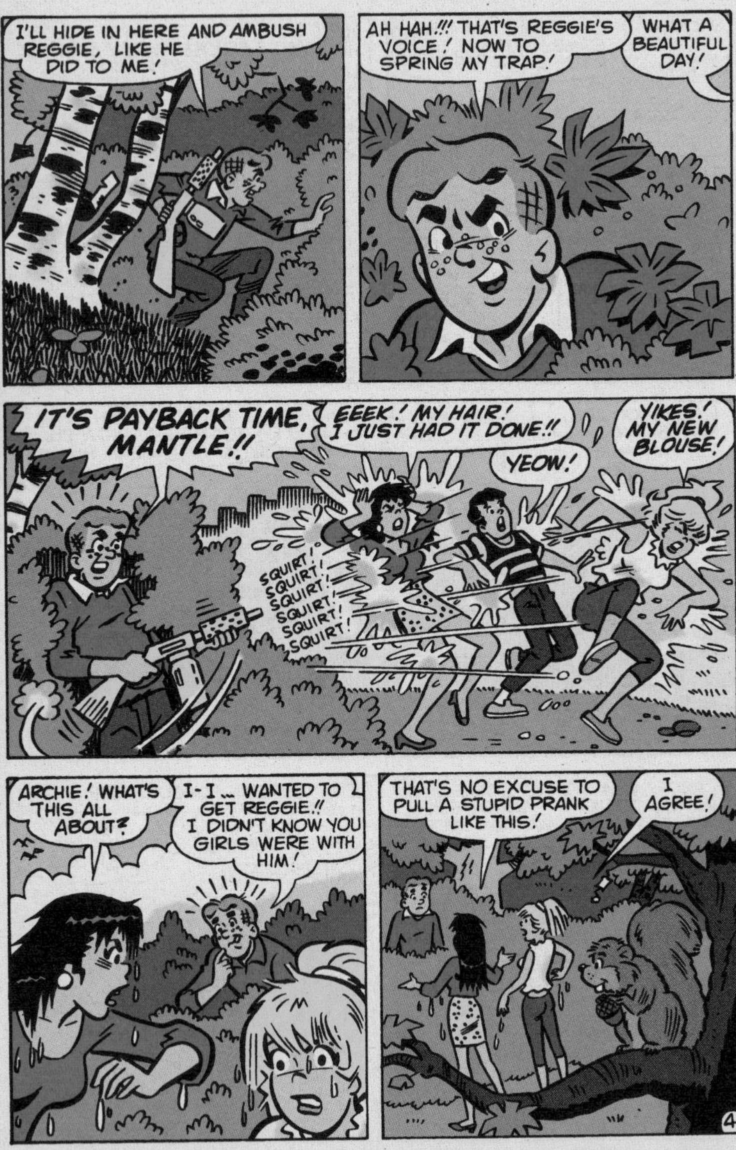
I'LL HIDE IN HERE AND AMBUSH REGGIE, LIKE HE DID TO ME!
AH HAH!!! THAT'S REGGIE'S VOICE! NOW TO SPRING MY TRAP!
WHAT A BEAUTIFUL DAY!
IT'S PAYBACK TIME, MANTLE!!
EEEK! MY HAIR! I JUST HAD IT DONE!!
YIKES! MY NEW BLOUSE!
YEOW!
SQUIRT! SQUIRT! SQUIRT! SQUIRT! SQUIRT! SQUIRT!
ARCHIE! WHAT'S THIS ALL ABOUT?
I-I... WANTED TO GET REGGIE!! I DIDN'T KNOW YOU GIRLS WERE WITH HIM!
THAT'S NO EXCUSE TO PULL A STUPID PRANK LIKE THIS!
I AGREE!
4

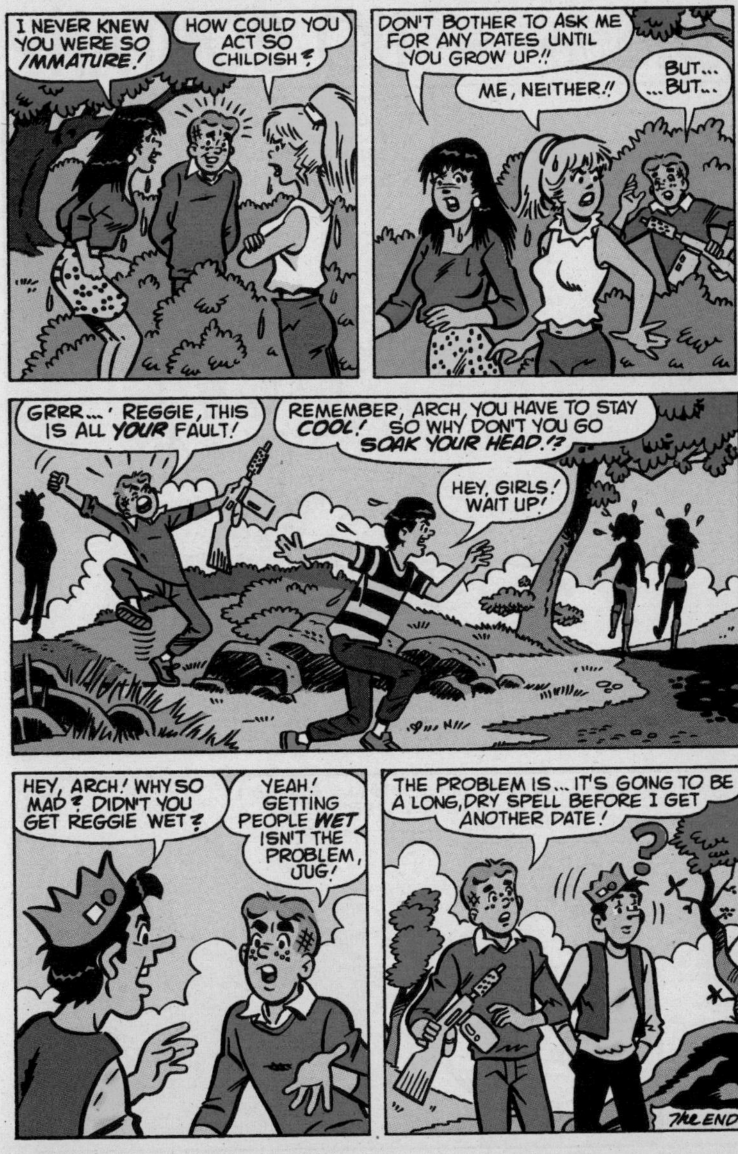
I NEVER KNEW YOU WERE SO IMMATURE!
HOW COULD YOU ACT SO CHILDISH?
DON'T BOTHER TO ASK ME FOR ANY DATES UNTIL YOU GROW UP!!
ME, NEITHER!!
BUT... ...BUT...
GRRR...' REGGIE, THIS IS ALL YOUR FAULT!
REMEMBER, ARCH, YOU HAVE TO STAY COOL! SO WHY DON'T YOU GO SOAK YOUR HEAD!?
HEY, GIRLS! WAIT UP!
HEY, ARCH! WHY SO MAD? DIDN'T YOU GET REGGIE WET?
YEAH! GETTING PEOPLE WET ISN'T THE PROBLEM, JUG!
THE PROBLEM IS... IT'S GOING TO BE A LONG, DRY SPELL BEFORE I GET ANOTHER DATE!
THE END

Archie in NO COMPANY

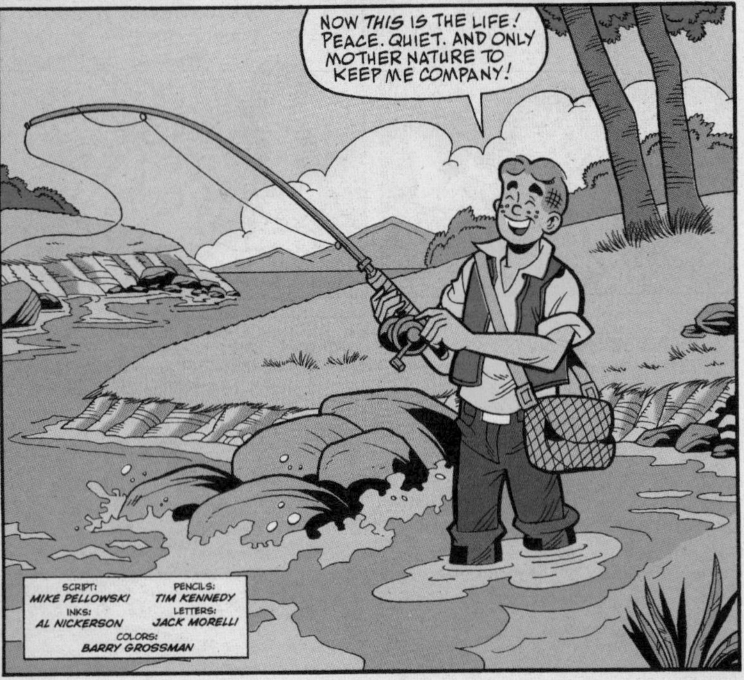

NOW THIS IS THE LIFE! PEACE. QUIET. AND ONLY MOTHER NATURE TO KEEP ME COMPANY!
SCRIPT: MIKE PELLOWSKI PENCILS: TIM KENNEDY INKS: AL NICKERSON LETTERS: JACK MORELLI COLORS: BARRY GROSSMAN

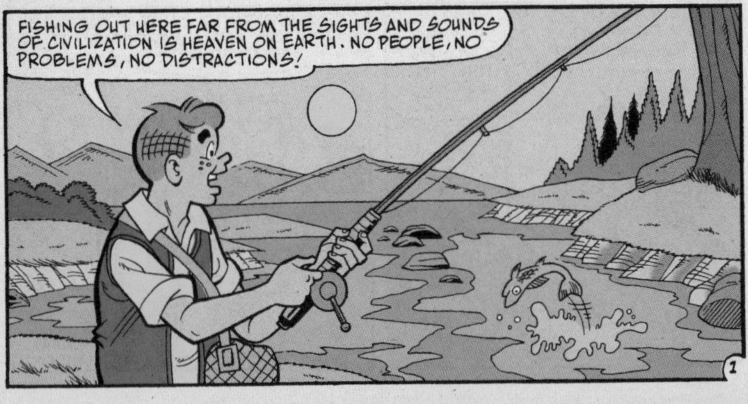

FISHING OUT HERE FAR FROM THE SIGHTS AND SOUNDS OF CIVILIZATION IS HEAVEN ON EARTH. NO PEOPLE, NO PROBLEMS, NO DISTRACTIONS!

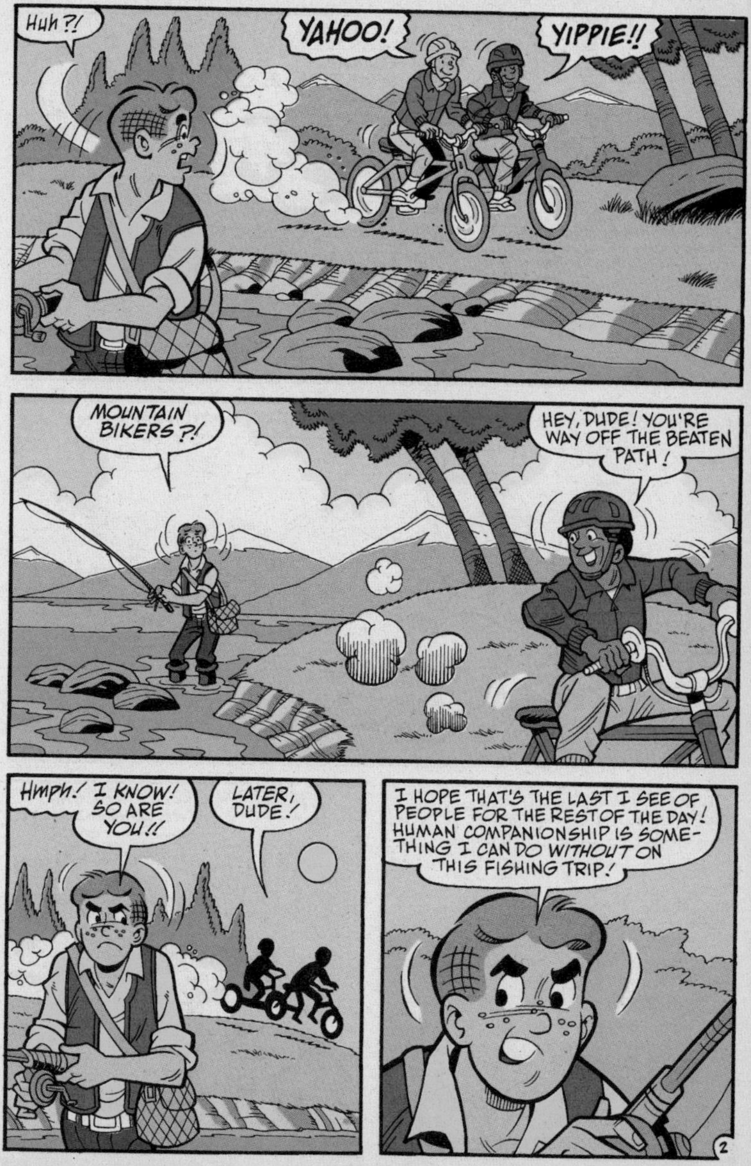
Huh?!
YAHOO!
YIPPIE!!
MOUNTAIN BIKERS?!
HEY, DUDE! YOU'RE WAY OFF THE BEATEN PATH!
Hmph! I KNOW! SO ARE YOU!!
LATER, DUDE!
I HOPE THAT'S THE LAST I SEE OF PEOPLE FOR THE REST OF THE DAY! HUMAN COMPANIONSHIP IS SOMETHING I CAN DO WITHOUT ON THIS FISHING TRIP!
2

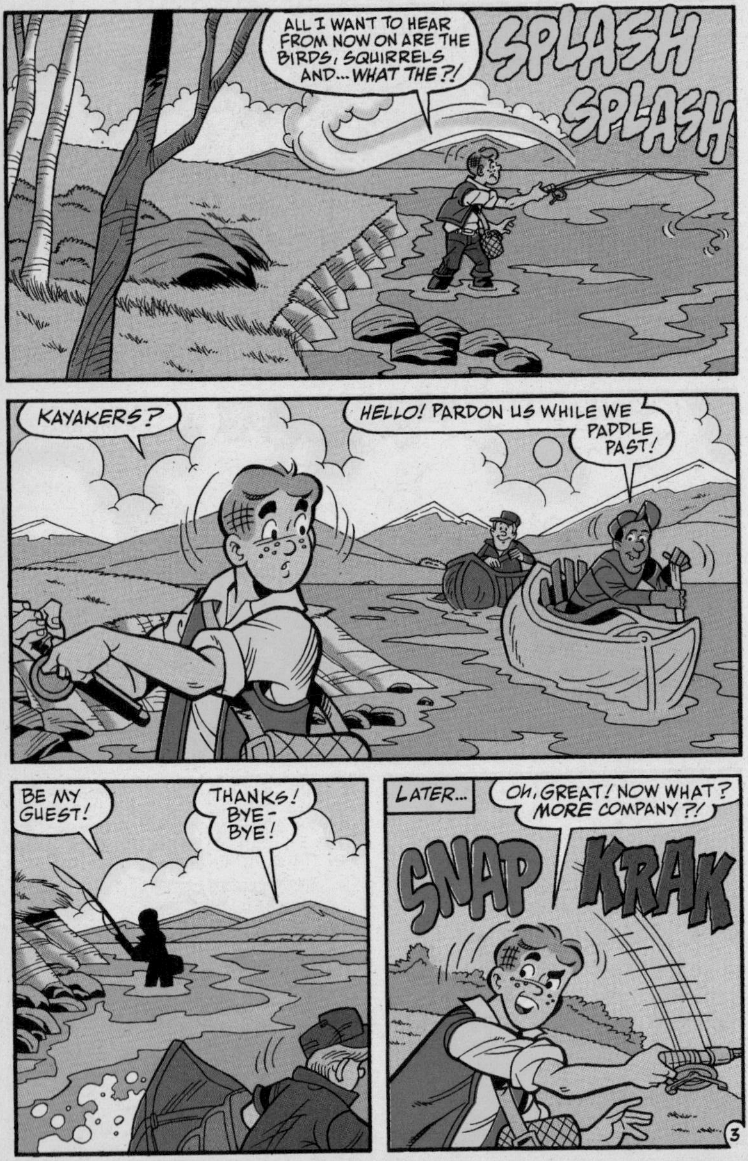
ALL I WANT TO HEAR FROM NOW ON ARE THE BIRDS, SQUIRRELS AND... WHAT THE?!
SPLASH
SPLASH
KAYAKERS?
HELLO! PARDON US WHILE WE PADDLE PAST!
BE MY GUEST!
THANKS! BYE-BYE!
LATER...
OH, GREAT! NOW WHAT? MORE COMPANY?!
SNAP
KRAK
3

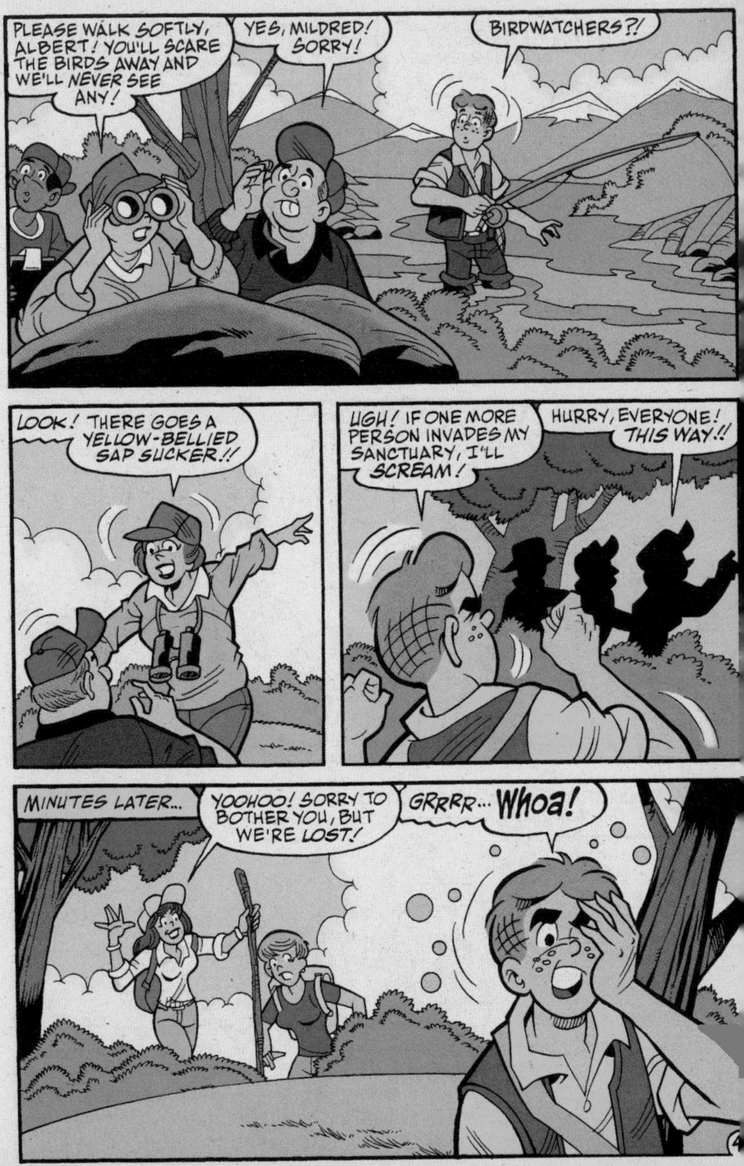
PLEASE WALK SOFTLY, ALBERT! YOU'LL SCARE THE BIRDS AWAY AND WE'LL NEVER SEE ANY!
YES, MILDRED! SORRY!
BIRDWATCHERS?!
LOOK! THERE GOES A YELLOW-BELLIED SAP SUCKER!!
UGH! IF ONE MORE PERSON INVADES MY SANCTUARY, I'LL SCREAM!
HURRY, EVERYONE! THIS WAY!!
MINUTES LATER...
YOOHOO! SORRY TO BOTHER YOU, BUT WE'RE LOST!
GRRRR... Whoa!

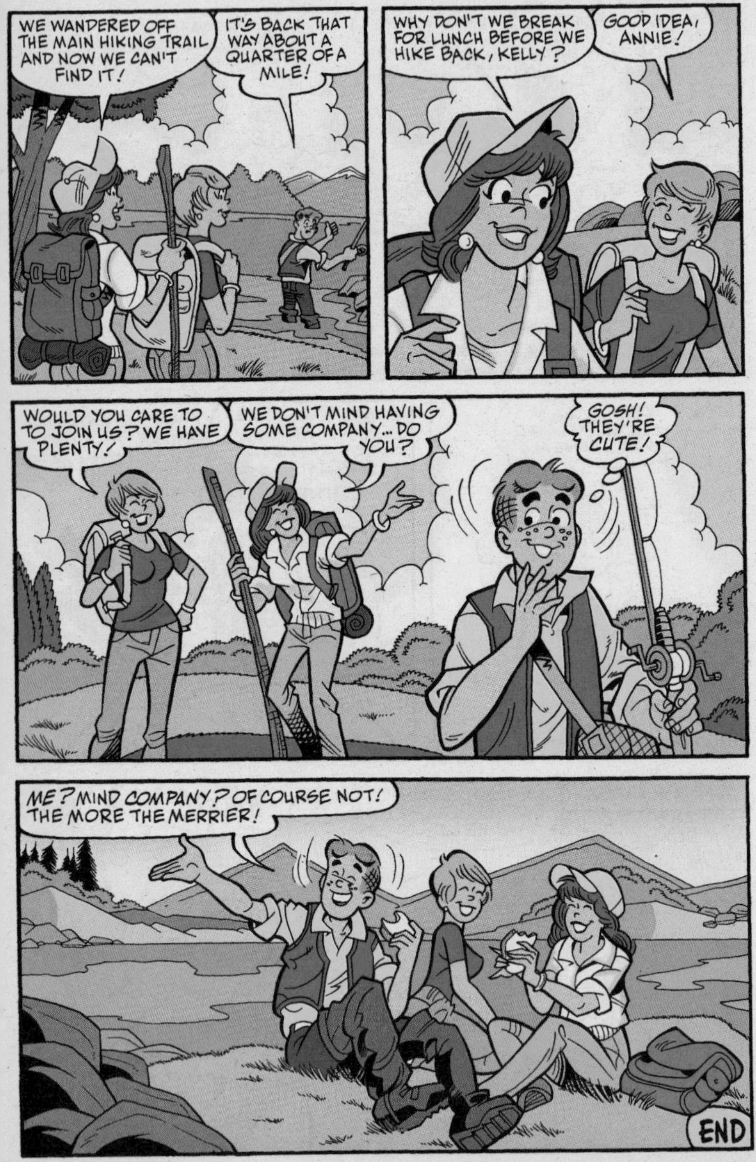
WE WANDERED OFF THE MAIN HIKING TRAIL AND NOW WE CAN'T FIND IT!
IT'S BACK THAT WAY ABOUT A QUARTER OF A MILE!
WHY DON'T WE BREAK FOR LUNCH BEFORE WE HIKE BACK, KELLY?
GOOD IDEA, ANNIE!
WOULD YOU CARE TO TO JOIN US? WE HAVE PLENTY!
WE DON'T MIND HAVING SOME COMPANY... DO YOU?
GOSH! THEY'RE CUTE!
ME? MIND COMPANY? OF COURSE NOT! THE MORE THE MERRIER!
END

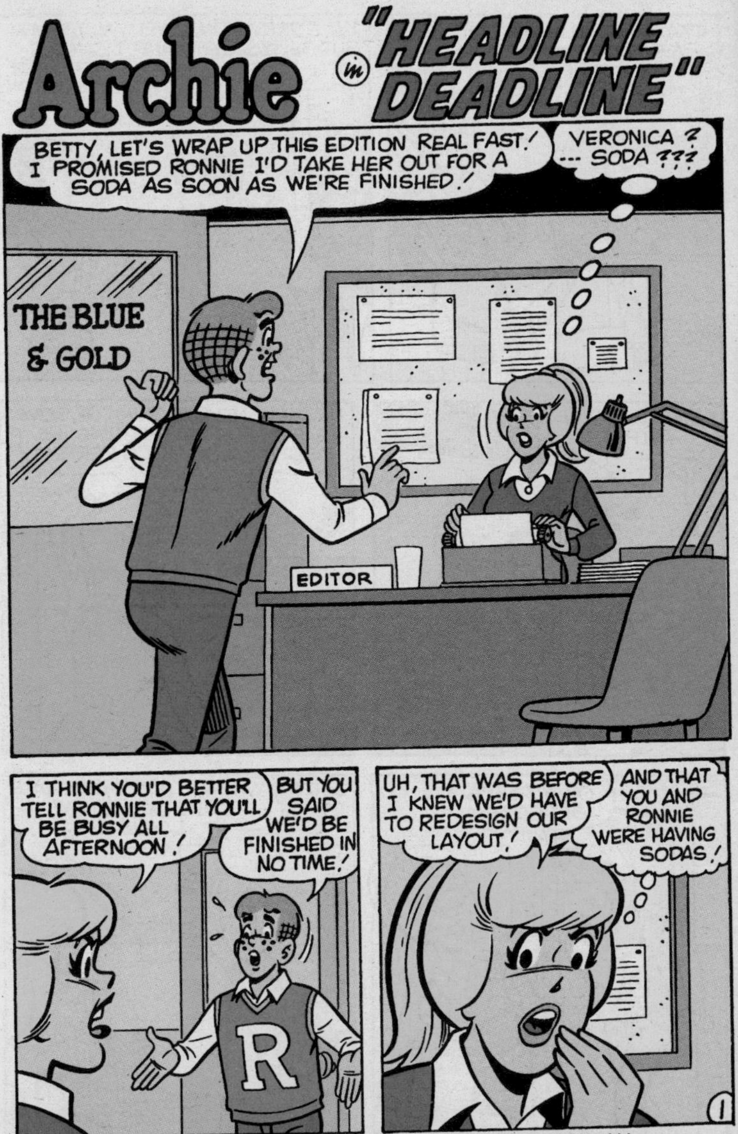
Archie in "HEADLINE DEADLINE"
BETTY, LET'S WRAP UP THIS EDITION REAL FAST! I PROMISED RONNIE I'D TAKE HER OUT FOR A SODA AS SOON AS WE'RE FINISHED!
VERONICA ? --- SODA ???
THE BLUE & GOLD
EDITOR
I THINK YOU'D BETTER TELL RONNIE THAT YOU'LL BE BUSY ALL AFTERNOON!
BUT YOU SAID WE'D BE FINISHED IN NO TIME!
UH, THAT WAS BEFORE I KNEW WE'D HAVE TO REDESIGN OUR LAYOUT!
AND THAT YOU AND RONNIE WERE HAVING SODAS!
1
Script & Pencils: Dick Malmgren / Inks: Jon D'Agostino / Letters: Bill Yoshida

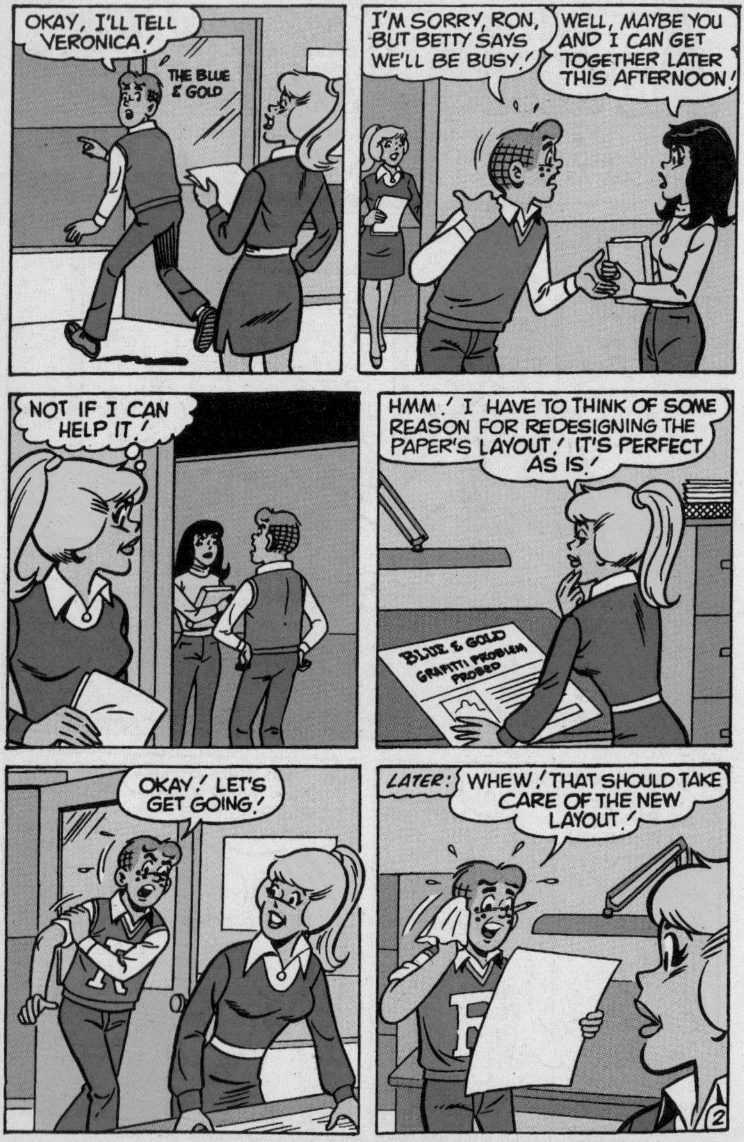
OKAY, I'LL TELL VERONICA!
THE BLUE & GOLD
I'M SORRY, RON, BUT BETTY SAYS WE'LL BE BUSY!
WELL, MAYBE YOU AND I CAN GET TOGETHER LATER THIS AFTERNOON!
NOT IF I CAN HELP IT!
HMM! I HAVE TO THINK OF SOME REASON FOR REDESIGNING THE PAPER'S LAYOUT! IT'S PERFECT AS IS!
BLUE & GOLD
GRAFITTI PROBLEM PROBED
OKAY! LET'S GET GOING!
LATER:
WHEW! THAT SHOULD TAKE CARE OF THE NEW LAYOUT!
2

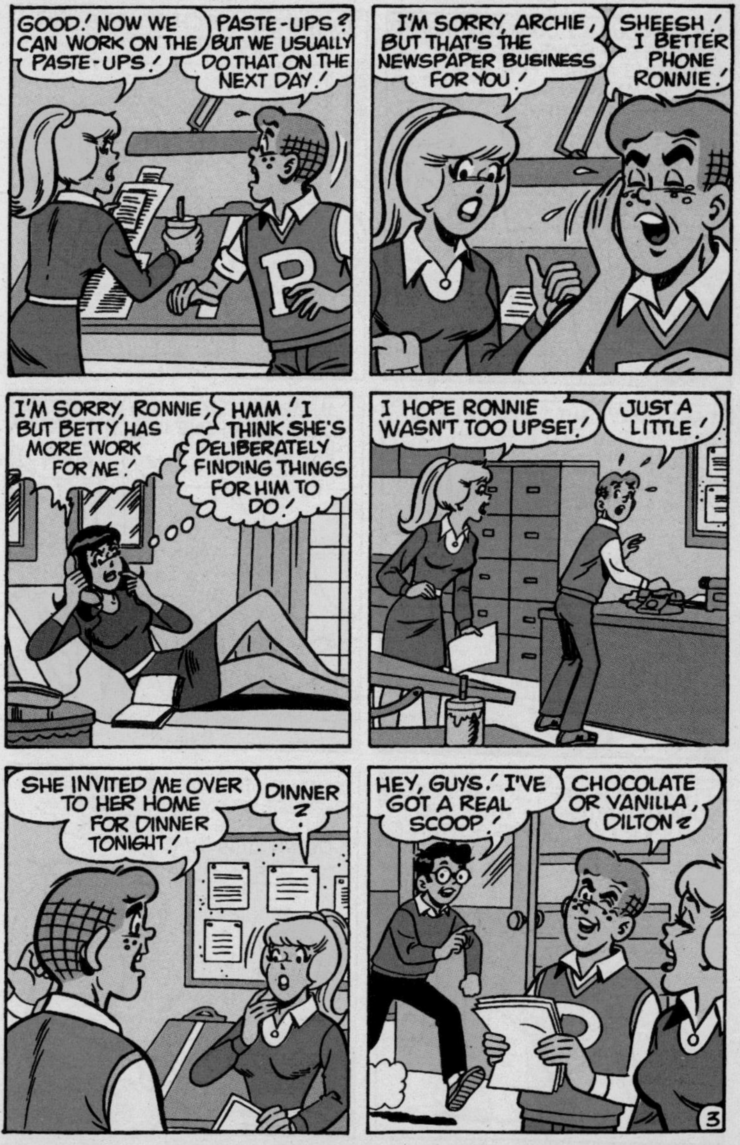
GOOD! NOW WE CAN WORK ON THE PASTE-UPS!
PASTE-UPS? BUT WE USUALLY DO THAT ON THE NEXT DAY!
I'M SORRY, ARCHIE, BUT THAT'S THE NEWSPAPER BUSINESS FOR YOU!
SHEESH! I BETTER PHONE RONNIE!
I'M SORRY, RONNIE, BUT BETTY HAS MORE WORK FOR ME!
HMM! I THINK SHE'S DELIBERATELY FINDING THINGS FOR HIM TO DO!
I HOPE RONNIE WASN'T TOO UPSET!
JUST A LITTLE!
SHE INVITED ME OVER TO HER HOME FOR DINNER TONIGHT!
DINNER?
HEY, GUYS! I'VE GOT A REAL SCOOP!
CHOCOLATE OR VANILLA, DILTON?
3

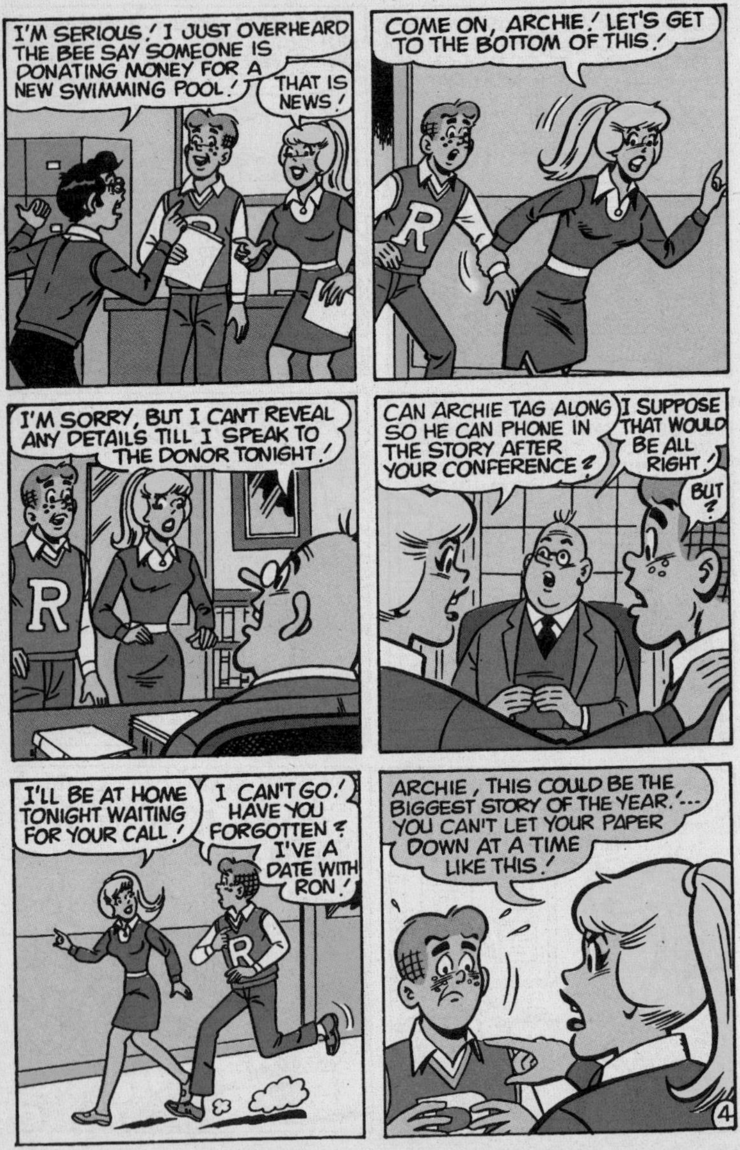
I'M SERIOUS! I JUST OVERHEARD THE BEE SAY SOMEONE IS DONATING MONEY FOR A NEW SWIMMING POOL!
THAT IS NEWS!
COME ON, ARCHIE! LET'S GET TO THE BOTTOM OF THIS!
I'M SORRY, BUT I CAN'T REVEAL ANY DETAILS TILL I SPEAK TO THE DONOR TONIGHT!
CAN ARCHIE TAG ALONG SO HE CAN PHONE IN THE STORY AFTER YOUR CONFERENCE?
I SUPPOSE THAT WOULD BE ALL RIGHT!
BUT?
I'LL BE AT HOME TONIGHT WAITING FOR YOUR CALL!
I CAN'T GO! HAVE YOU FORGOTTEN? I'VE A DATE WITH RON!
ARCHIE, THIS COULD BE THE BIGGEST STORY OF THE YEAR!... YOU CAN'T LET YOUR PAPER DOWN AT A TIME LIKE THIS!
4

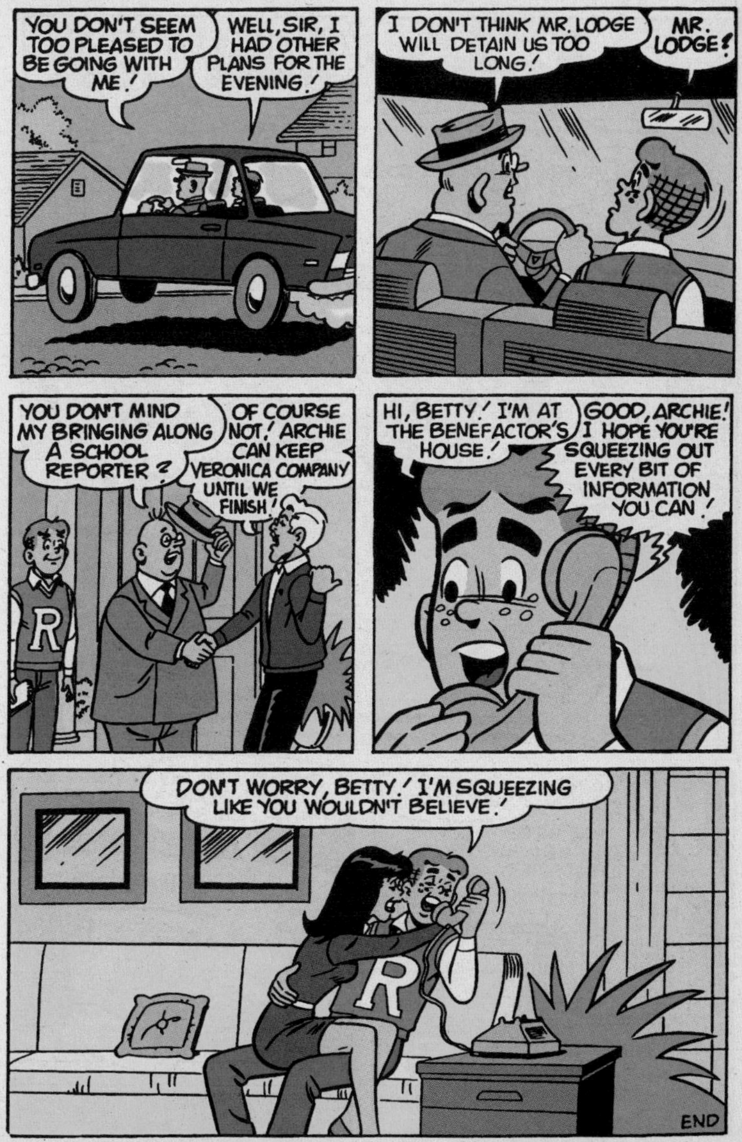
YOU DON'T SEEM TOO PLEASED TO BE GOING WITH ME.!
WELL, SIR, I HAD OTHER PLANS FOR THE EVENING.!
I DON'T THINK MR. LODGE WILL DETAIN US TOO LONG.!
MR. LODGE?!
YOU DON'T MIND MY BRINGING ALONG A SCHOOL REPORTER?
OF COURSE NOT! ARCHIE CAN KEEP VERONICA COMPANY UNTIL WE FINISH!
HI, BETTY! I'M AT THE BENEFACTOR'S HOUSE!
GOOD, ARCHIE! I HOPE YOU'RE SQUEEZING OUT EVERY BIT OF INFORMATION YOU CAN!
DON'T WORRY, BETTY! I'M SQUEEZING LIKE YOU WOULDN'T BELIEVE!
END

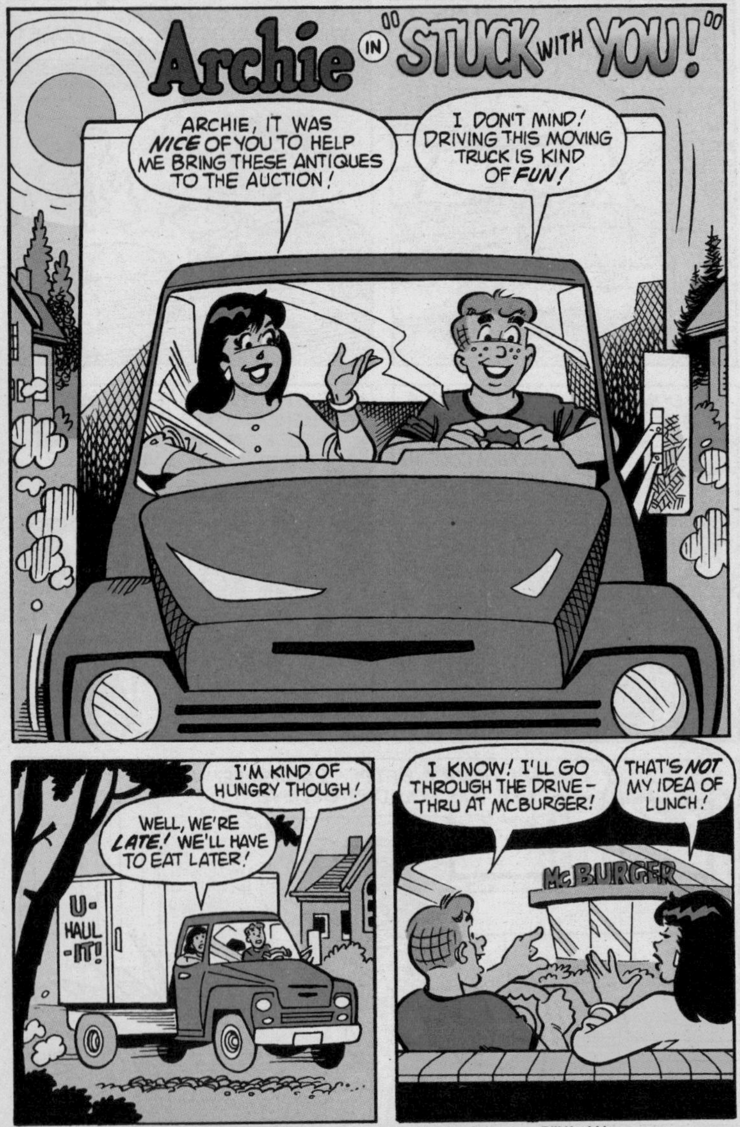
Archie IN "STUCK WITH YOU!"
ARCHIE, IT WAS NICE OF YOU TO HELP ME BRING THESE ANTIQUES TO THE AUCTION!
I DON'T MIND! DRIVING THIS MOVING TRUCK IS KIND OF FUN!
I'M KIND OF HUNGRY THOUGH!
WELL, WE'RE LATE! WE'LL HAVE TO EAT LATER!
U-HAUL-IT!
I KNOW! I'LL GO THROUGH THE DRIVE-THRU AT MCBURGER!
THAT'S NOT MY IDEA OF LUNCH!
McBURGER

Script: Dan Parent / Pencils: Stan Goldberg / Inks: Bob Smith / Letters: Bill Yoshida

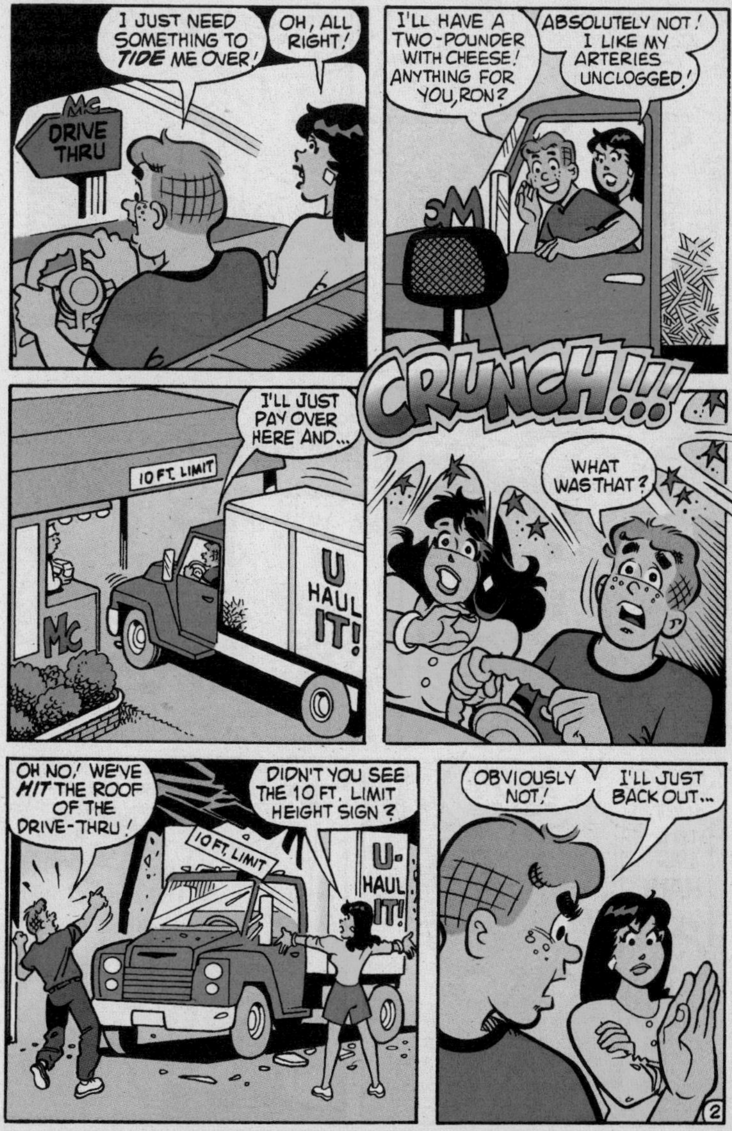
I JUST NEED SOMETHING TO *TIDE* ME OVER!
OH, ALL RIGHT!
MC DRIVE THRU
I'LL HAVE A TWO-POUNDER WITH CHEESE! ANYTHING FOR YOU, RON?
ABSOLUTELY NOT! I LIKE MY ARTERIES UNCLOGGED!
I'LL JUST PAY OVER HERE AND...
10 FT. LIMIT
U HAUL IT!
CRUNCH!!!!
WHAT WAS THAT?
OH NO! WE'VE *HIT* THE ROOF OF THE DRIVE-THRU!
DIDN'T YOU SEE THE 10 FT. LIMIT HEIGHT SIGN?
10 FT. LIMIT
U-HAUL IT!
OBVIOUSLY NOT!
I'LL JUST BACK OUT...

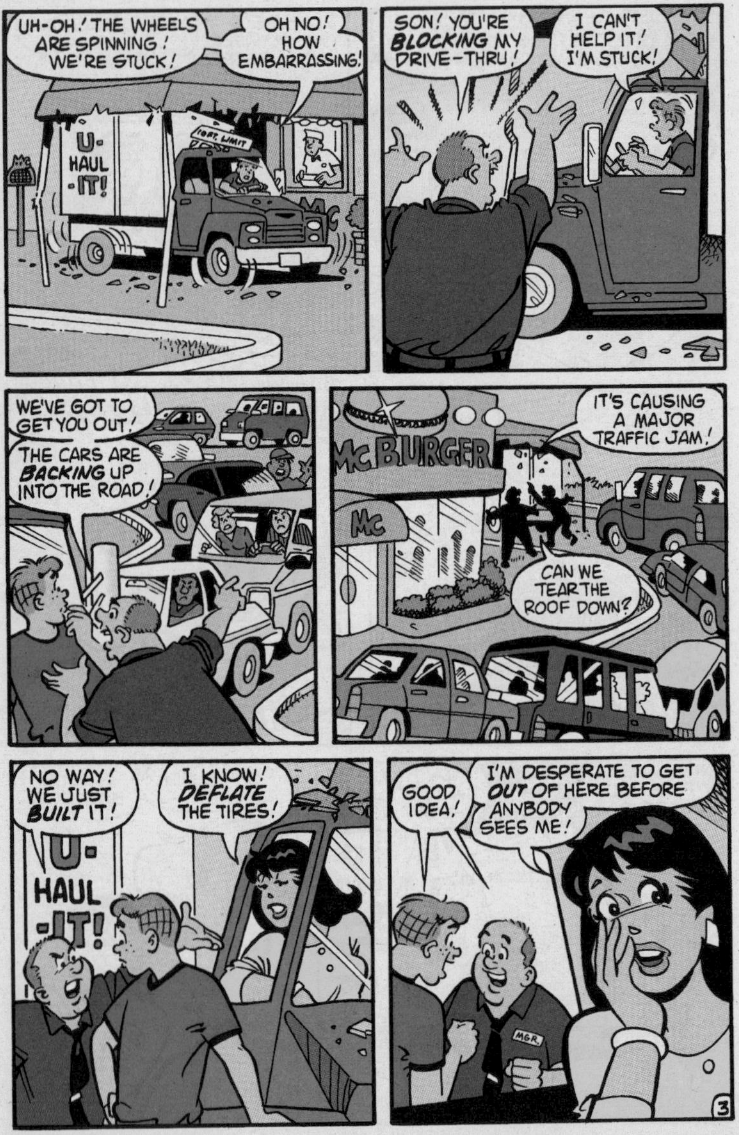
UH-OH! THE WHEELS ARE SPINNING! WE'RE STUCK!
OH NO! HOW EMBARRASSING!
U-HAUL-IT!
SON! YOU'RE BLOCKING MY DRIVE-THRU!
I CAN'T HELP IT! I'M STUCK!
WE'VE GOT TO GET YOU OUT!
THE CARS ARE BACKING UP INTO THE ROAD!
McBURGER
Mc
IT'S CAUSING A MAJOR TRAFFIC JAM!
CAN WE TEAR THE ROOF DOWN?
NO WAY! WE JUST BUILT IT!
I KNOW! DEFLATE THE TIRES!
U-HAUL-IT!
GOOD IDEA!
I'M DESPERATE TO GET OUT OF HERE BEFORE ANYBODY SEES ME!
MGR.
3

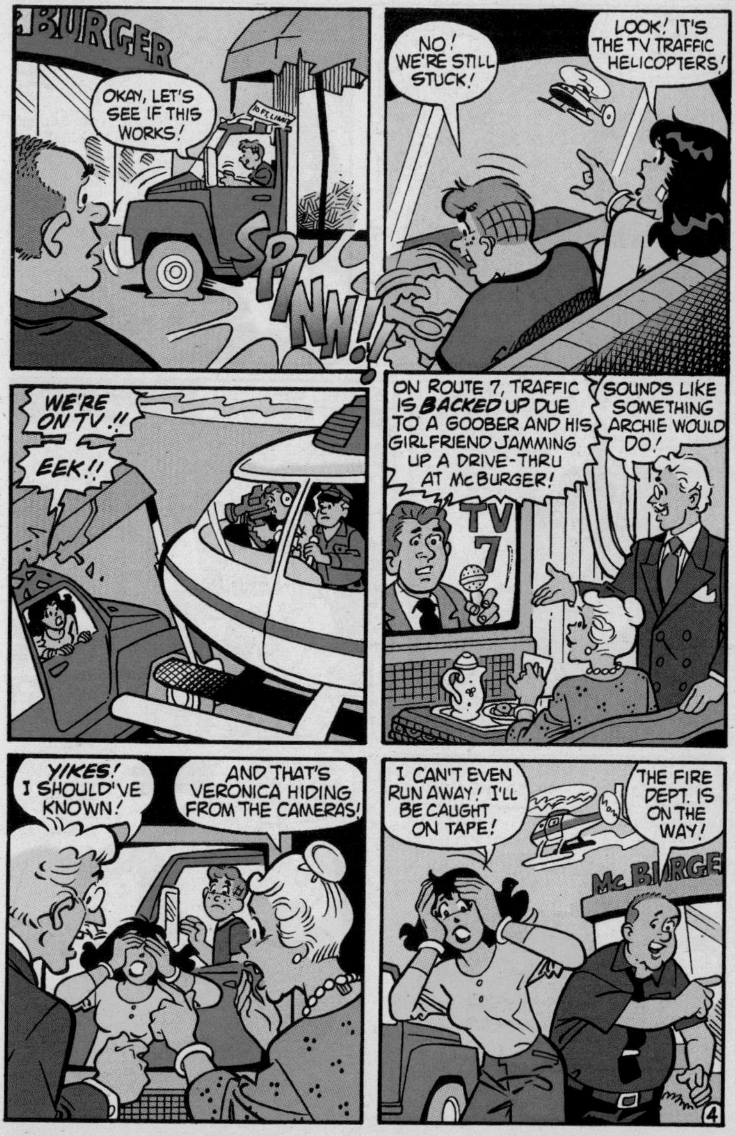

BURGER
OKAY, LET'S SEE IF THIS WORKS!
SPINN!!
NO! WE'RE STILL STUCK!
LOOK! IT'S THE TV TRAFFIC HELICOPTERS!
WE'RE ON TV!!
EEK!!
ON ROUTE 7, TRAFFIC IS BACKED UP DUE TO A GOOBER AND HIS GIRLFRIEND JAMMING UP A DRIVE-THRU AT McBURGER!
SOUNDS LIKE SOMETHING ARCHIE WOULD DO!
TV 7
YIKES! I SHOULD'VE KNOWN!
AND THAT'S VERONICA HIDING FROM THE CAMERAS!
I CAN'T EVEN RUN AWAY! I'LL BE CAUGHT ON TAPE!
THE FIRE DEPT. IS ON THE WAY!
4

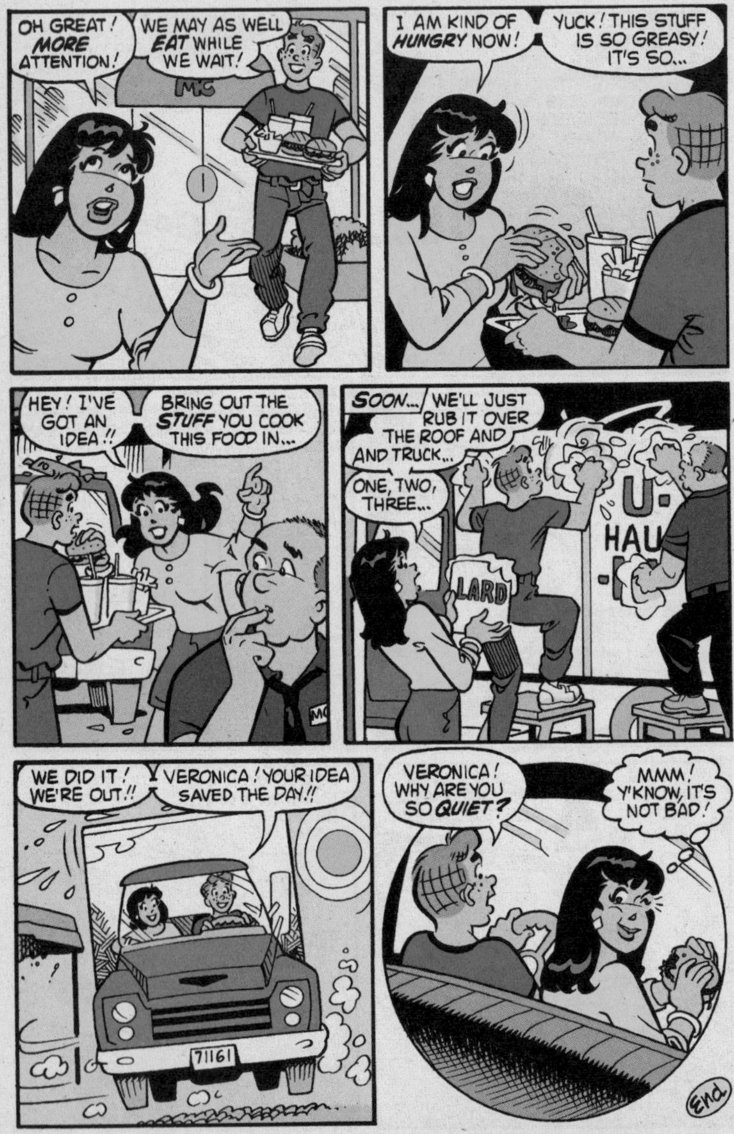

OH GREAT! MORE ATTENTION!
WE MAY AS WELL EAT WHILE WE WAIT!
MC
I AM KIND OF HUNGRY NOW!
YUCK! THIS STUFF IS SO GREASY! IT'S SO...
HEY! I'VE GOT AN IDEA!!
BRING OUT THE STUFF YOU COOK THIS FOOD IN...
MC
SOON...
WE'LL JUST RUB IT OVER THE ROOF AND AND TRUCK...
ONE, TWO, THREE...
LARD
U-HAU
WE DID IT! WE'RE OUT!!
VERONICA! YOUR IDEA SAVED THE DAY!!
71161
VERONICA! WHY ARE YOU SO QUIET?
MMM! Y'KNOW, IT'S NOT BAD!
End

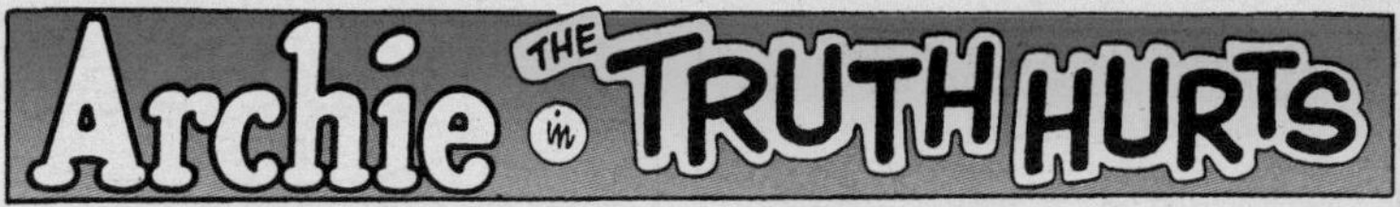
Archie in THE TRUTH HURTS

Script: George Gladir / Pencils: Stan Goldberg / Inks: Rudy Lapick / Letters: Bill Yoshida

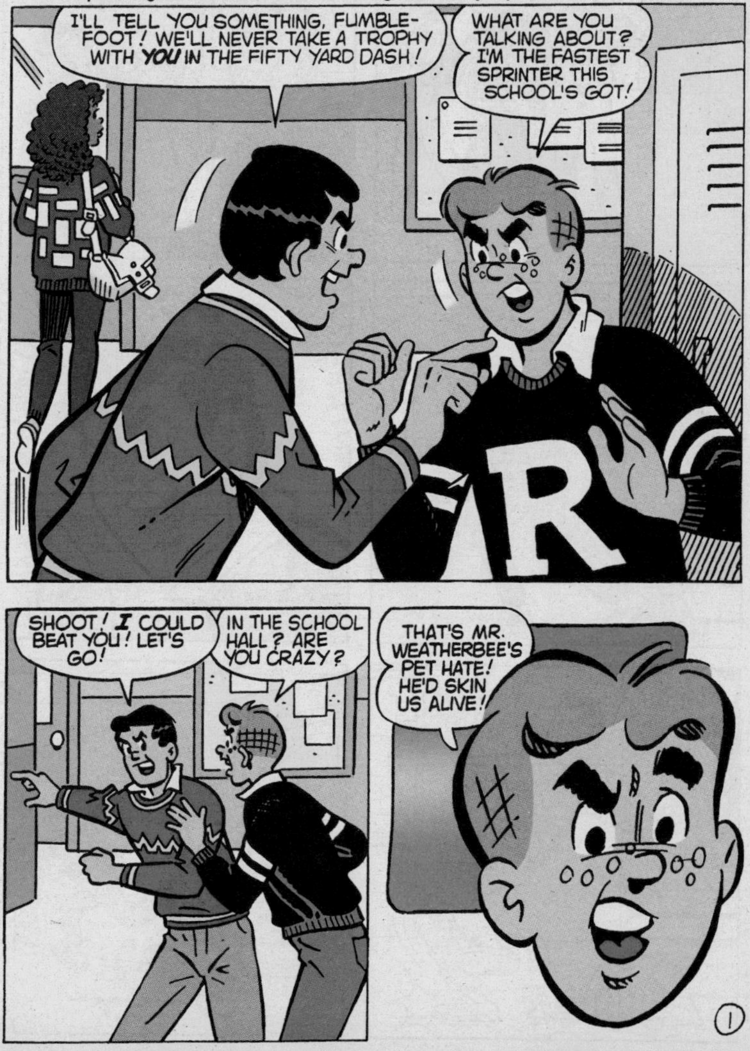
I'LL TELL YOU SOMETHING, FUMBLE-FOOT! WE'LL NEVER TAKE A TROPHY WITH YOU IN THE FIFTY YARD DASH!
WHAT ARE YOU TALKING ABOUT? I'M THE FASTEST SPRINTER THIS SCHOOL'S GOT!
SHOOT! I COULD BEAT YOU! LET'S GO!
IN THE SCHOOL HALL? ARE YOU CRAZY?
THAT'S MR. WEATHERBEE'S PET HATE! HE'D SKIN US ALIVE!

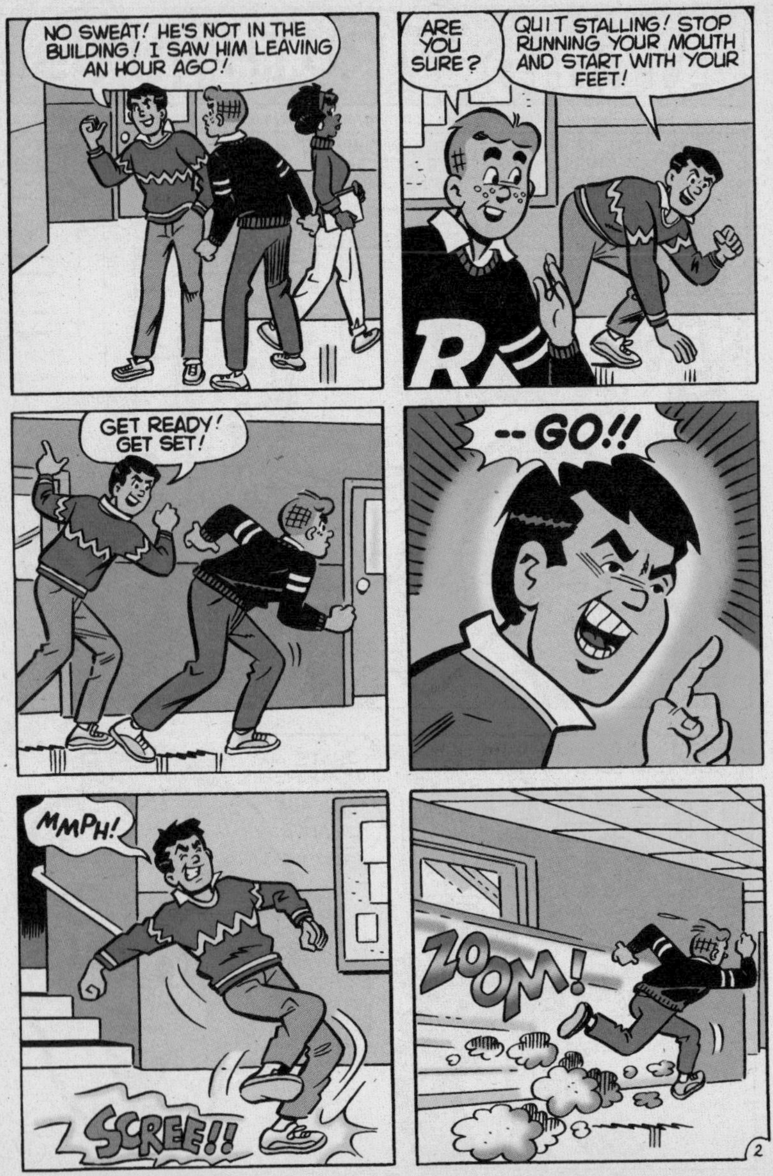
NO SWEAT! HE'S NOT IN THE BUILDING! I SAW HIM LEAVING AN HOUR AGO!
ARE YOU SURE?
QUIT STALLING! STOP RUNNING YOUR MOUTH AND START WITH YOUR FEET!
GET READY! GET SET!
--GO!!
MMPH!
SCREE!!
ZOOM!

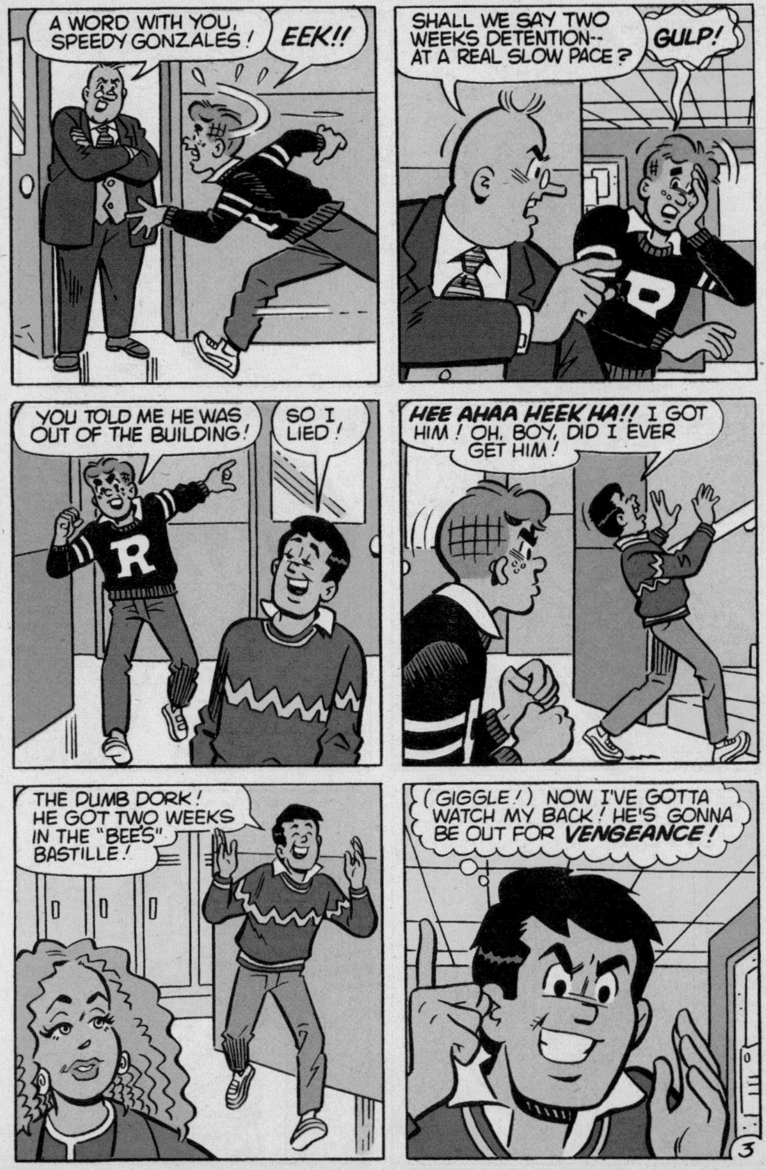
A WORD WITH YOU, SPEEDY GONZALES!
EEK!!
SHALL WE SAY TWO WEEKS DETENTION-- AT A REAL SLOW PACE?
GULP!
YOU TOLD ME HE WAS OUT OF THE BUILDING!
SO I LIED!
HEE AHAA HEEK HA!! I GOT HIM! OH, BOY, DID I EVER GET HIM!
THE DUMB DORK! HE GOT TWO WEEKS IN THE "BEE'S" BASTILLE!
(GIGGLE!) NOW I'VE GOTTA WATCH MY BACK! HE'S GONNA BE OUT FOR VENGEANCE!
3

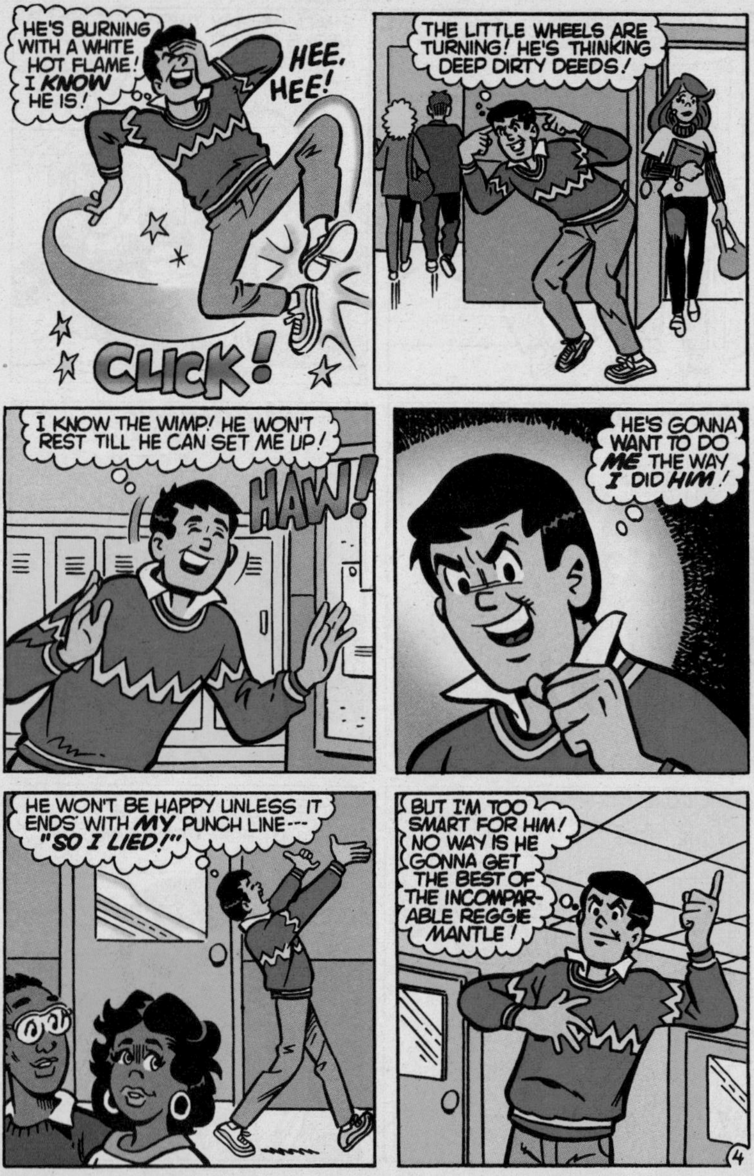
HE'S BURNING WITH A WHITE HOT FLAME! I KNOW HE IS!
HEE, HEE!
CLICK!
THE LITTLE WHEELS ARE TURNING! HE'S THINKING DEEP DIRTY DEEDS!
I KNOW THE WIMP! HE WON'T REST TILL HE CAN SET ME UP!
HAW!
HE'S GONNA WANT TO DO ME THE WAY I DID HIM!
HE WON'T BE HAPPY UNLESS IT ENDS WITH MY PUNCH LINE--- "SO I LIED!"
BUT I'M TOO SMART FOR HIM! NO WAY IS HE GONNA GET THE BEST OF THE INCOMPARABLE REGGIE MANTLE!
4

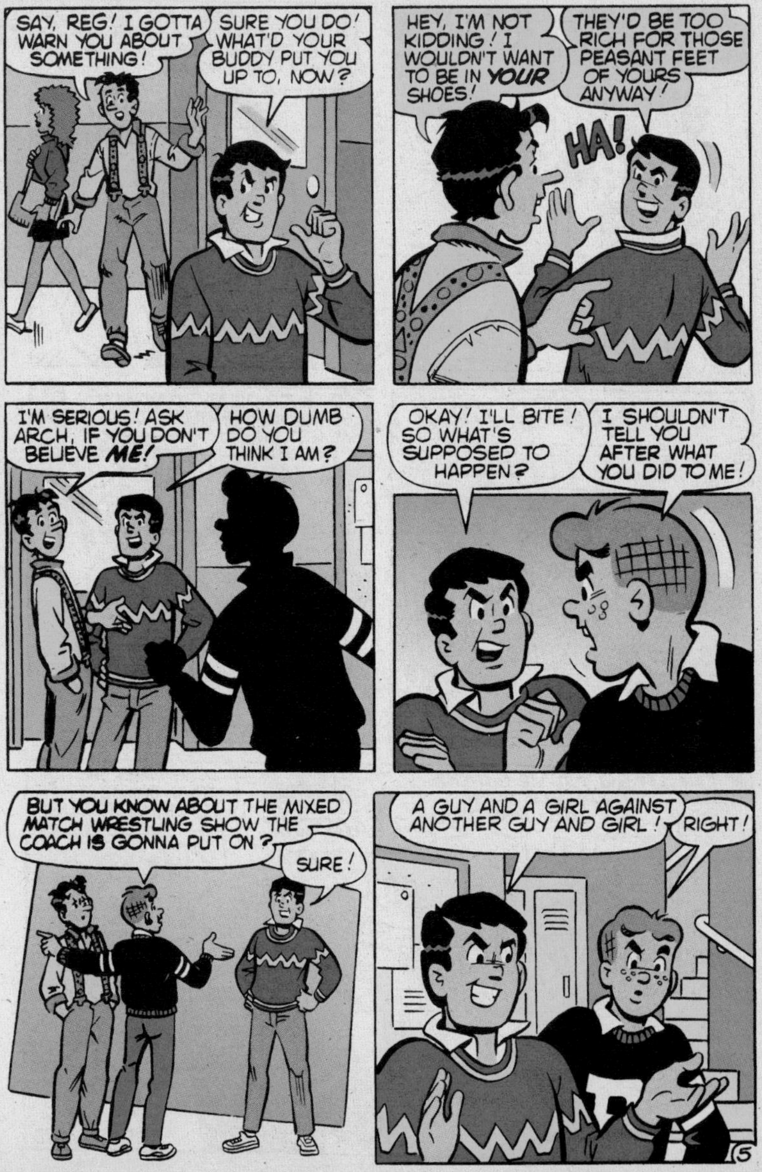

SAY, REG! I GOTTA WARN YOU ABOUT SOMETHING!
SURE YOU DO! WHAT'D YOUR BUDDY PUT YOU UP TO, NOW?
HEY, I'M NOT KIDDING! I WOULDN'T WANT TO BE IN YOUR SHOES!
THEY'D BE TOO RICH FOR THOSE PEASANT FEET OF YOURS ANYWAY!
HA!
I'M SERIOUS! ASK ARCH, IF YOU DON'T BELIEVE ME!
HOW DUMB DO YOU THINK I AM?
OKAY! I'LL BITE! SO WHAT'S SUPPOSED TO HAPPEN?
I SHOULDN'T TELL YOU AFTER WHAT YOU DID TO ME!
BUT YOU KNOW ABOUT THE MIXED MATCH WRESTLING SHOW THE COACH IS GONNA PUT ON?
SURE!
A GUY AND A GIRL AGAINST ANOTHER GUY AND GIRL!
RIGHT!

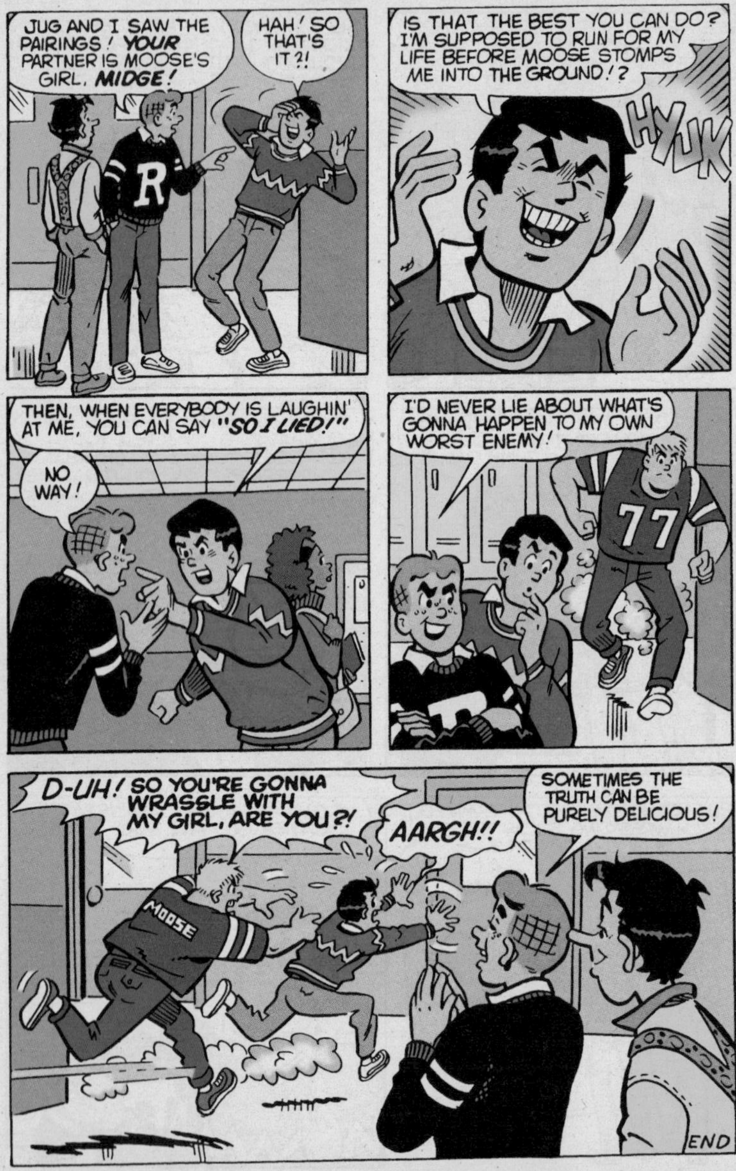
JUG AND I SAW THE PAIRINGS! YOUR PARTNER IS MOOSE'S GIRL, MIDGE!
HAH! SO THAT'S IT?!
IS THAT THE BEST YOU CAN DO? I'M SUPPOSED TO RUN FOR MY LIFE BEFORE MOOSE STOMPS ME INTO THE GROUND!?
HYUK
THEN, WHEN EVERYBODY IS LAUGHIN' AT ME, YOU CAN SAY "SO I LIED!"
NO WAY!
I'D NEVER LIE ABOUT WHAT'S GONNA HAPPEN TO MY OWN WORST ENEMY!
77
D-UH! SO YOU'RE GONNA WRASSLE WITH MY GIRL, ARE YOU?!
MOOSE
AARGH!!
SOMETIMES THE TRUTH CAN BE PURELY DELICIOUS!
END

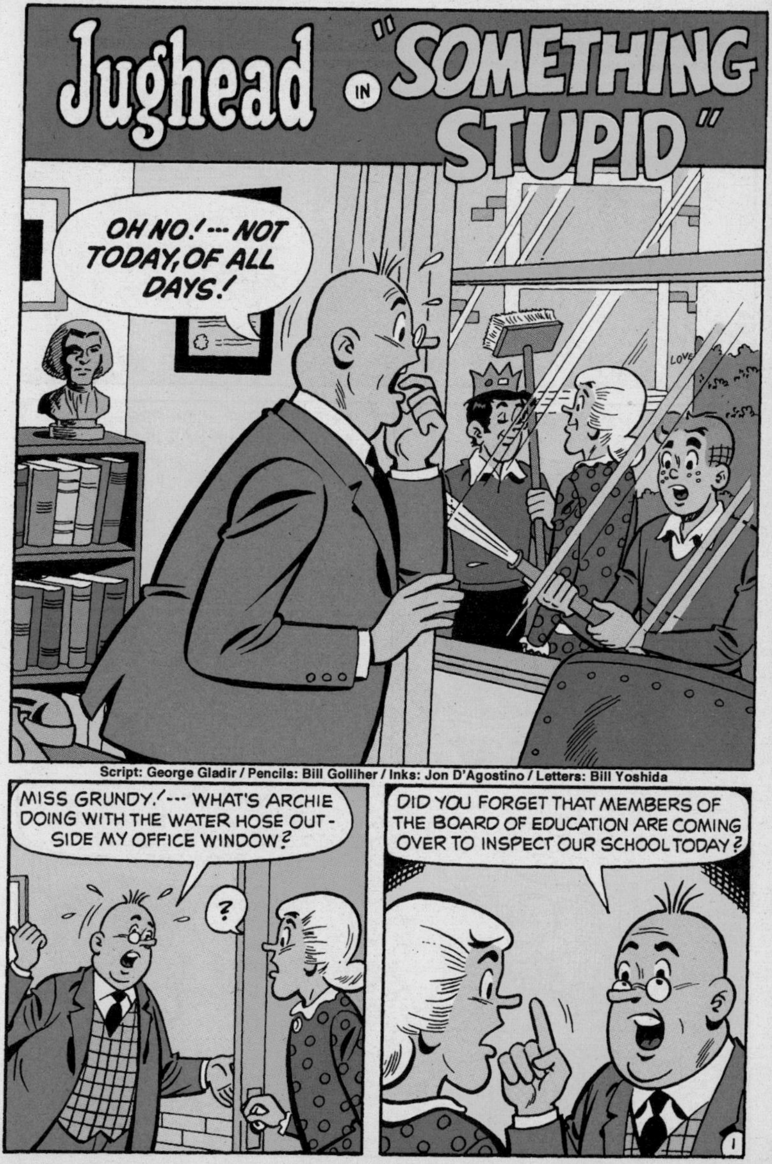

Jughead
IN
"SOMETHING STUPID"
OH NO! --- NOT TODAY, OF ALL DAYS!
LOVE
Script: George Gladir / Pencils: Bill Golliher / Inks: Jon D'Agostino / Letters: Bill Yoshida
MISS GRUNDY! --- WHAT'S ARCHIE DOING WITH THE WATER HOSE OUT-SIDE MY OFFICE WINDOW?
?
DID YOU FORGET THAT MEMBERS OF THE BOARD OF EDUCATION ARE COMING OVER TO INSPECT OUR SCHOOL TODAY?
1

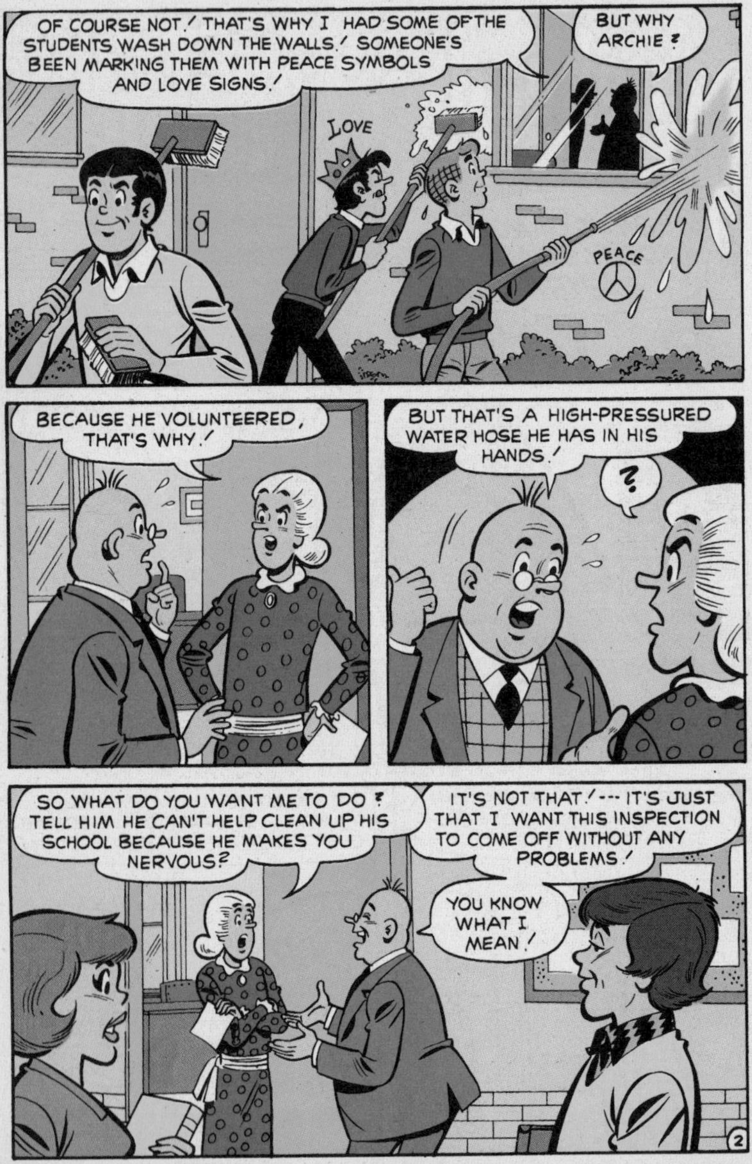
OF COURSE NOT! THAT'S WHY I HAD SOME OF THE STUDENTS WASH DOWN THE WALLS! SOMEONE'S BEEN MARKING THEM WITH PEACE SYMBOLS AND LOVE SIGNS!
BUT WHY ARCHIE?
LOVE
PEACE
BECAUSE HE VOLUNTEERED, THAT'S WHY!
BUT THAT'S A HIGH-PRESSURED WATER HOSE HE HAS IN HIS HANDS!
?
SO WHAT DO YOU WANT ME TO DO? TELL HIM HE CAN'T HELP CLEAN UP HIS SCHOOL BECAUSE HE MAKES YOU NERVOUS?
IT'S NOT THAT! --- IT'S JUST THAT I WANT THIS INSPECTION TO COME OFF WITHOUT ANY PROBLEMS!
YOU KNOW WHAT I MEAN!
2

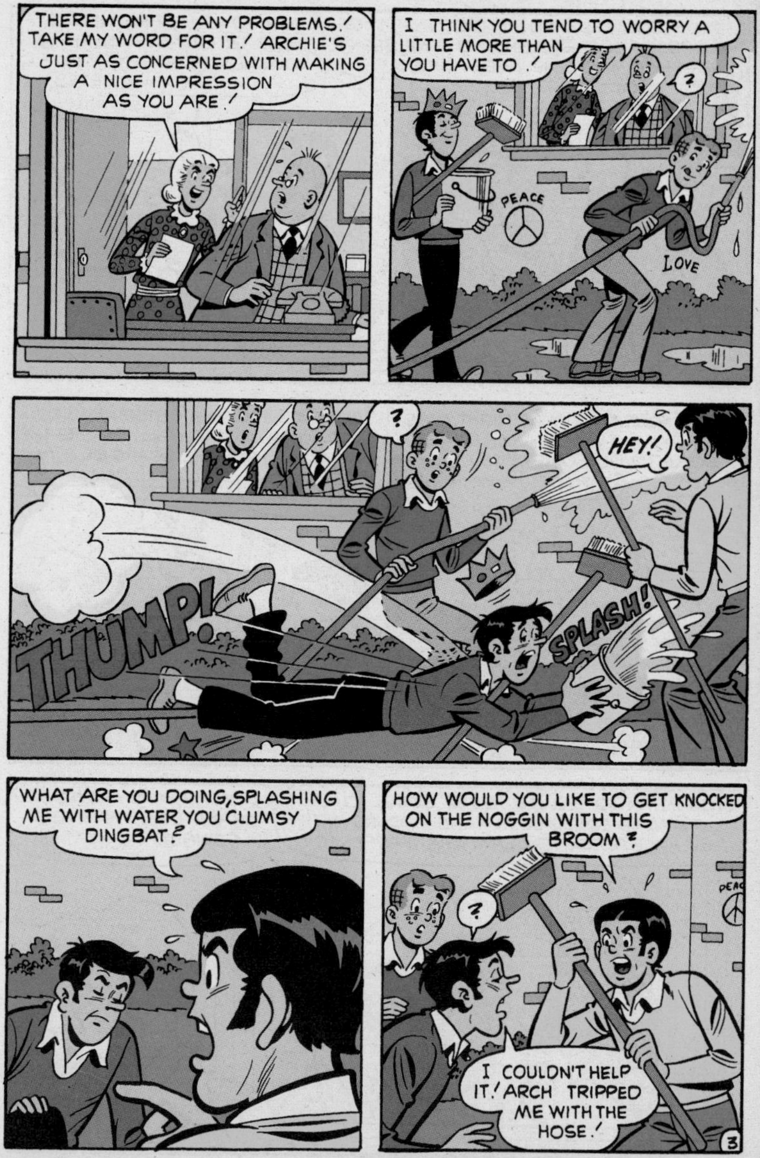
THERE WON'T BE ANY PROBLEMS! TAKE MY WORD FOR IT! ARCHIE'S JUST AS CONCERNED WITH MAKING A NICE IMPRESSION AS YOU ARE!
I THINK YOU TEND TO WORRY A LITTLE MORE THAN YOU HAVE TO!
?
PEACE
LOVE
?
HEY!
THUMP!
SPLASH!
WHAT ARE YOU DOING, SPLASHING ME WITH WATER YOU CLUMSY DINGBAT?
HOW WOULD YOU LIKE TO GET KNOCKED ON THE NOGGIN WITH THIS BROOM?
?
I COULDN'T HELP IT! ARCH TRIPPED ME WITH THE HOSE!
3

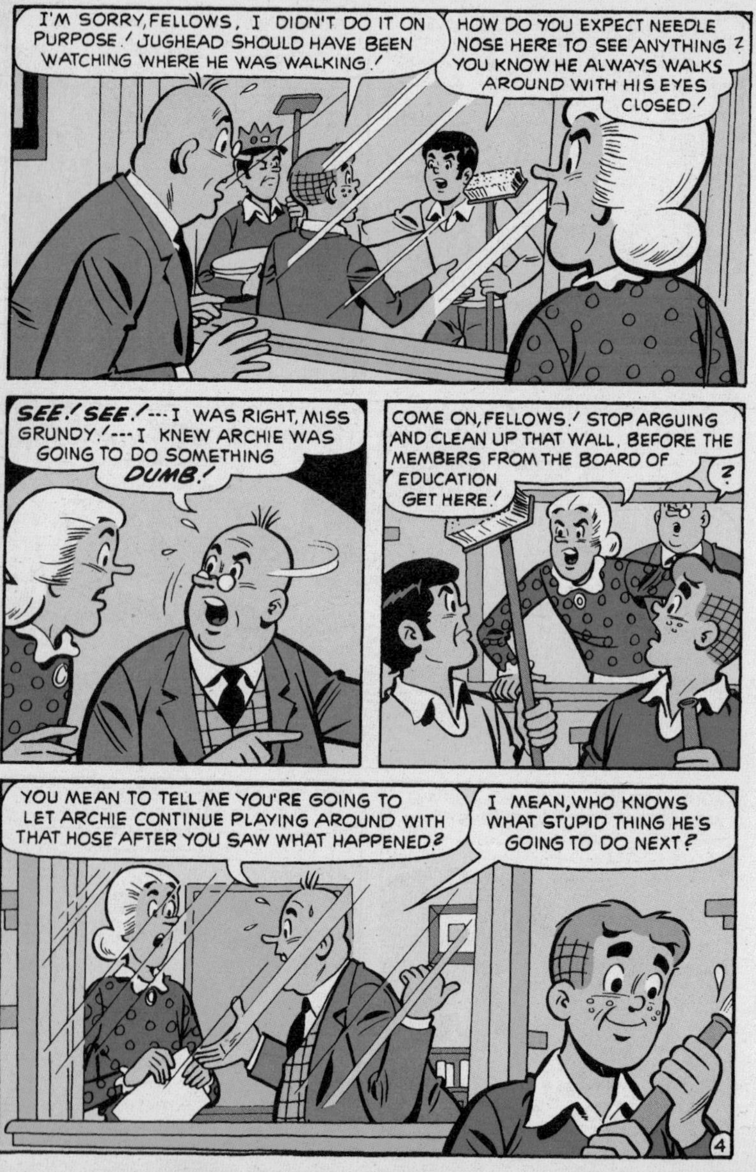
I'M SORRY, FELLOWS, I DIDN'T DO IT ON PURPOSE! JUGHEAD SHOULD HAVE BEEN WATCHING WHERE HE WAS WALKING!
HOW DO YOU EXPECT NEEDLE NOSE HERE TO SEE ANYTHING? YOU KNOW HE ALWAYS WALKS AROUND WITH HIS EYES CLOSED!
SEE! SEE! --- I WAS RIGHT, MISS GRUNDY! --- I KNEW ARCHIE WAS GOING TO DO SOMETHING DUMB!
COME ON, FELLOWS! STOP ARGUING AND CLEAN UP THAT WALL, BEFORE THE MEMBERS FROM THE BOARD OF EDUCATION GET HERE!
?
YOU MEAN TO TELL ME YOU'RE GOING TO LET ARCHIE CONTINUE PLAYING AROUND WITH THAT HOSE AFTER YOU SAW WHAT HAPPENED?
I MEAN, WHO KNOWS WHAT STUPID THING HE'S GOING TO DO NEXT?
4

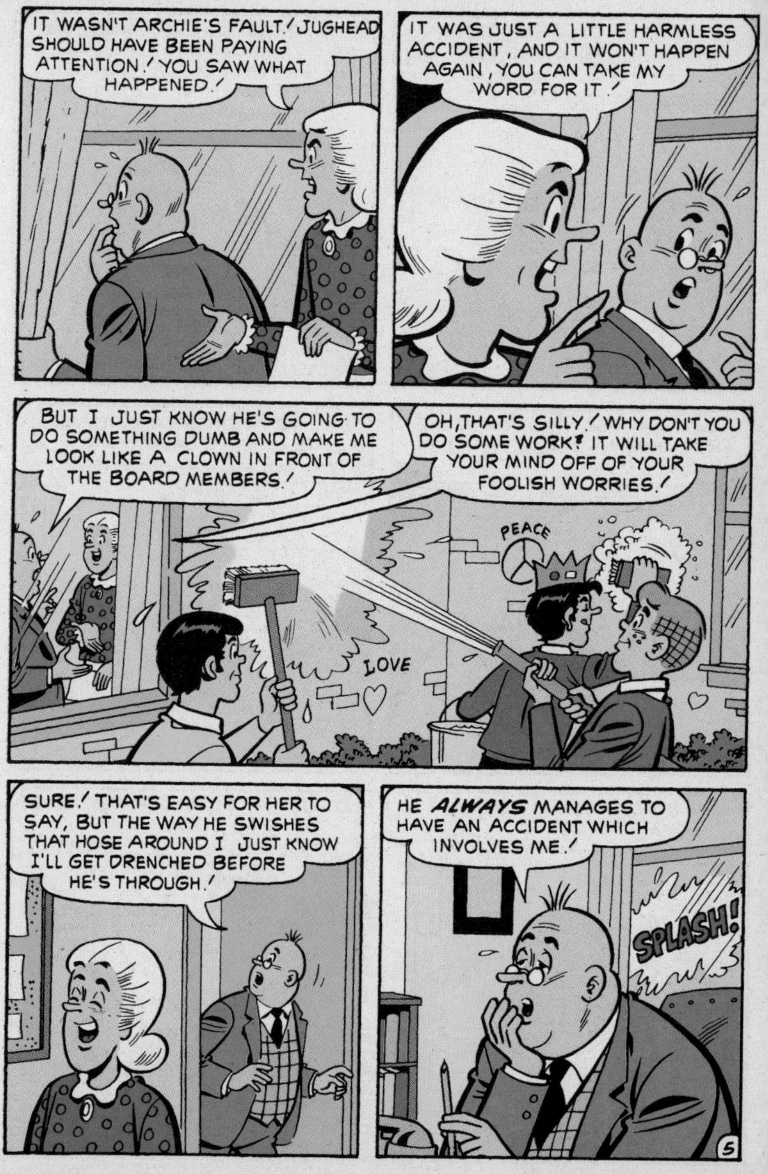
IT WASN'T ARCHIE'S FAULT! JUGHEAD SHOULD HAVE BEEN PAYING ATTENTION! YOU SAW WHAT HAPPENED!
IT WAS JUST A LITTLE HARMLESS ACCIDENT, AND IT WON'T HAPPEN AGAIN, YOU CAN TAKE MY WORD FOR IT!
BUT I JUST KNOW HE'S GOING TO DO SOMETHING DUMB AND MAKE ME LOOK LIKE A CLOWN IN FRONT OF THE BOARD MEMBERS!
OH, THAT'S SILLY! WHY DON'T YOU DO SOME WORK? IT WILL TAKE YOUR MIND OFF OF YOUR FOOLISH WORRIES!
PEACE
LOVE
SURE! THAT'S EASY FOR HER TO SAY, BUT THE WAY HE SWISHES THAT HOSE AROUND I JUST KNOW I'LL GET DRENCHED BEFORE HE'S THROUGH!
HE ALWAYS MANAGES TO HAVE AN ACCIDENT WHICH INVOLVES ME!
SPLASH!
5

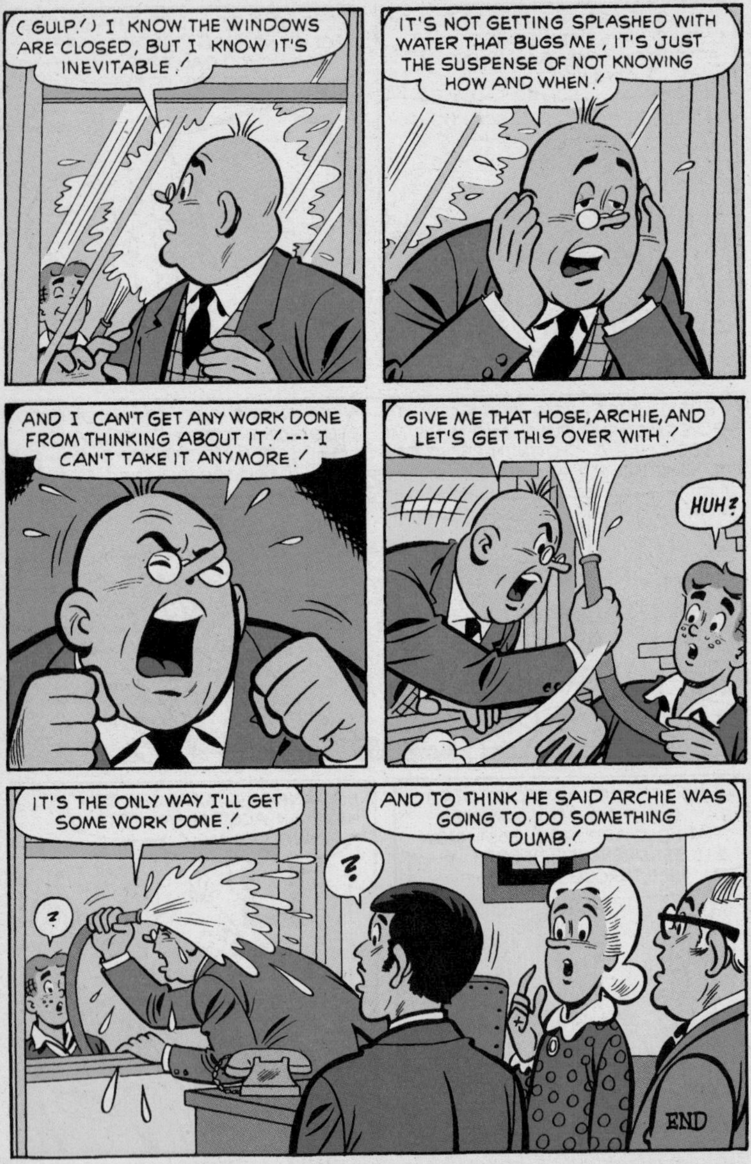

(GULP.') I KNOW THE WINDOWS ARE CLOSED, BUT I KNOW IT'S INEVITABLE.'
IT'S NOT GETTING SPLASHED WITH WATER THAT BUGS ME, IT'S JUST THE SUSPENSE OF NOT KNOWING HOW AND WHEN.'
AND I CAN'T GET ANY WORK DONE FROM THINKING ABOUT IT.' --- I CAN'T TAKE IT ANYMORE.'
GIVE ME THAT HOSE, ARCHIE, AND LET'S GET THIS OVER WITH.'
HUH?
IT'S THE ONLY WAY I'LL GET SOME WORK DONE.'
?
?
AND TO THINK HE SAID ARCHIE WAS GOING TO DO SOMETHING DUMB.'
END

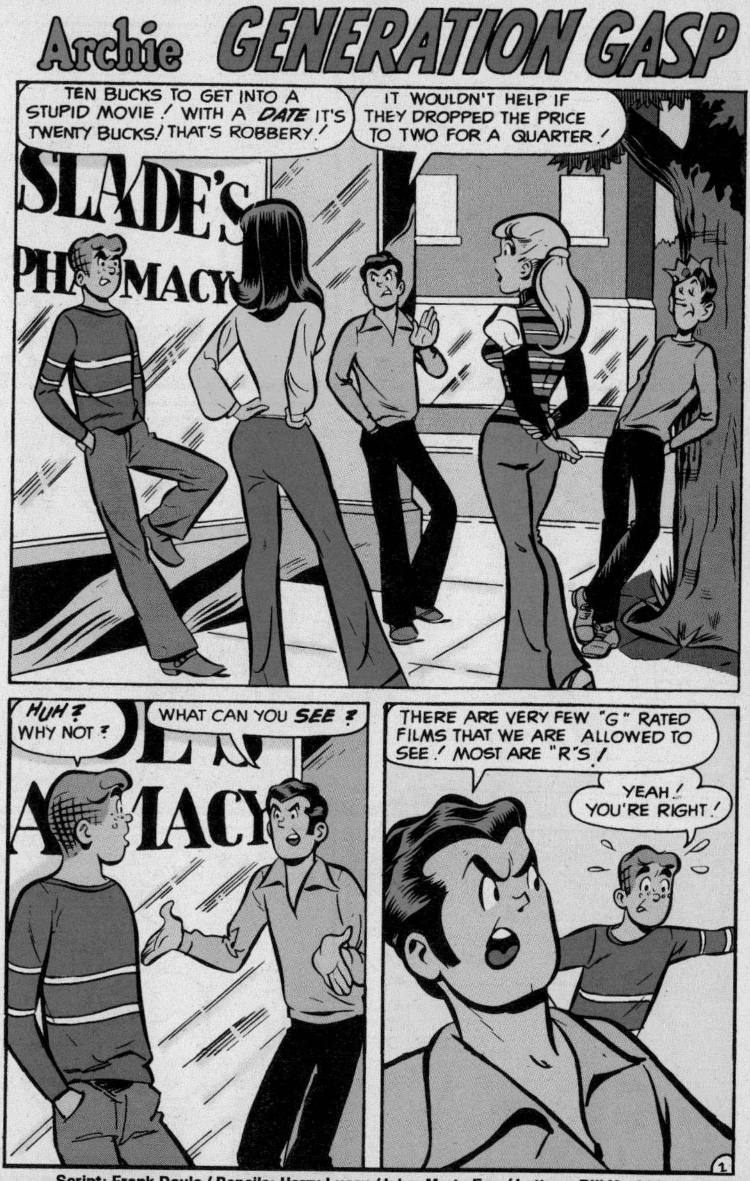

Archie
GENERATION GASP
TEN BUCKS TO GET INTO A STUPID MOVIE! WITH A DATE IT'S TWENTY BUCKS! THAT'S ROBBERY!
IT WOULDN'T HELP IF THEY DROPPED THE PRICE TO TWO FOR A QUARTER!
SLADE'S
PHARMACY
HUH? WHY NOT?
WHAT CAN YOU SEE?
THERE ARE VERY FEW "G" RATED FILMS THAT WE ARE ALLOWED TO SEE! MOST ARE "R"S!
YEAH! YOU'RE RIGHT!
1

Script: Frank Doyle / Pencils: Harry Lucey / Inks: Marty Epp / Letters: Bill Yoshida

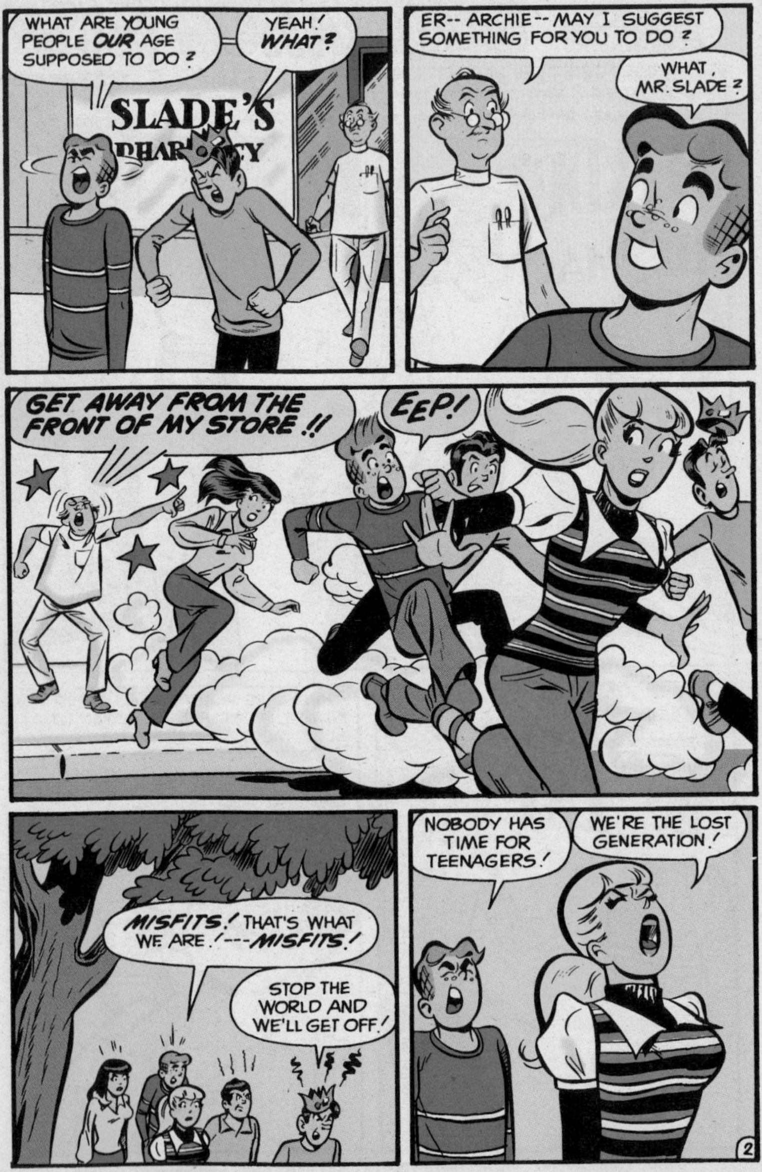
WHAT ARE YOUNG PEOPLE OUR AGE SUPPOSED TO DO?
YEAH! WHAT?
SLADE'S
ER-- ARCHIE-- MAY I SUGGEST SOMETHING FOR YOU TO DO?
WHAT, MR. SLADE?
GET AWAY FROM THE FRONT OF MY STORE!!
EEP!
MISFITS! THAT'S WHAT WE ARE!---MISFITS!
STOP THE WORLD AND WE'LL GET OFF!
NOBODY HAS TIME FOR TEENAGERS!
WE'RE THE LOST GENERATION!
2

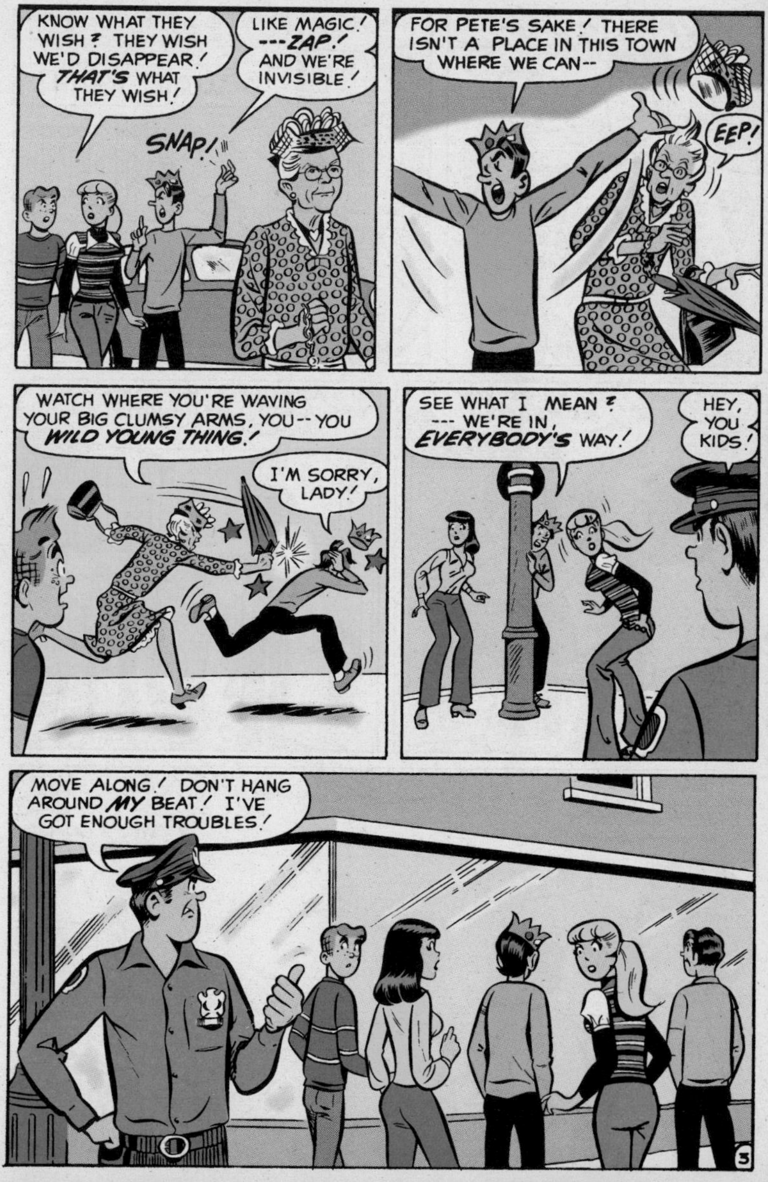
KNOW WHAT THEY WISH? THEY WISH WE'D DISAPPEAR! THAT'S WHAT THEY WISH!
LIKE MAGIC! ---ZAP! AND WE'RE INVISIBLE!
SNAP!
FOR PETE'S SAKE! THERE ISN'T A PLACE IN THIS TOWN WHERE WE CAN--
EEP!
WATCH WHERE YOU'RE WAVING YOUR BIG CLUMSY ARMS, YOU-- YOU WILD YOUNG THING!
I'M SORRY, LADY!
SEE WHAT I MEAN? --- WE'RE IN, EVERYBODY'S WAY!
HEY, YOU KIDS!
MOVE ALONG! DON'T HANG AROUND MY BEAT! I'VE GOT ENOUGH TROUBLES!
3

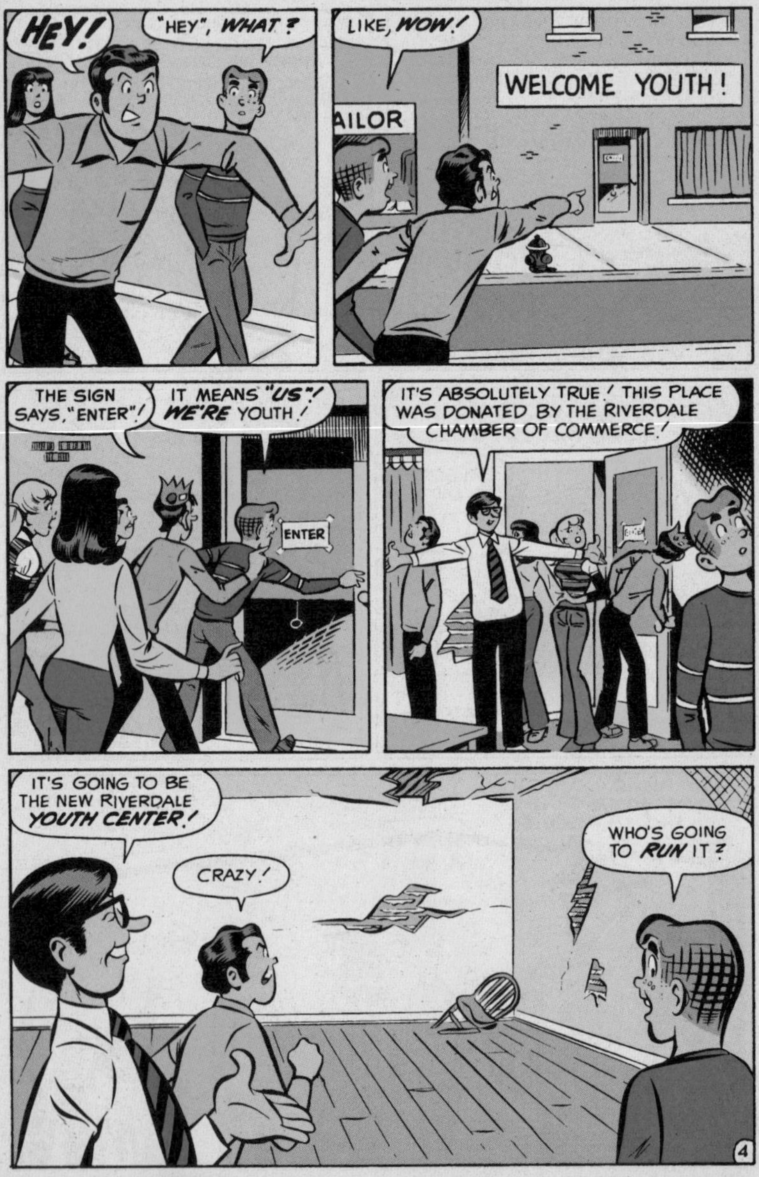
HEY!
"HEY", WHAT ?
LIKE, WOW!
AILOR
WELCOME YOUTH!
THE SIGN SAYS, "ENTER"!
IT MEANS "US"! WE'RE YOUTH!
ENTER
IT'S ABSOLUTELY TRUE! THIS PLACE WAS DONATED BY THE RIVERDALE CHAMBER OF COMMERCE!
IT'S GOING TO BE THE NEW RIVERDALE YOUTH CENTER!
CRAZY!
WHO'S GOING TO RUN IT?
4

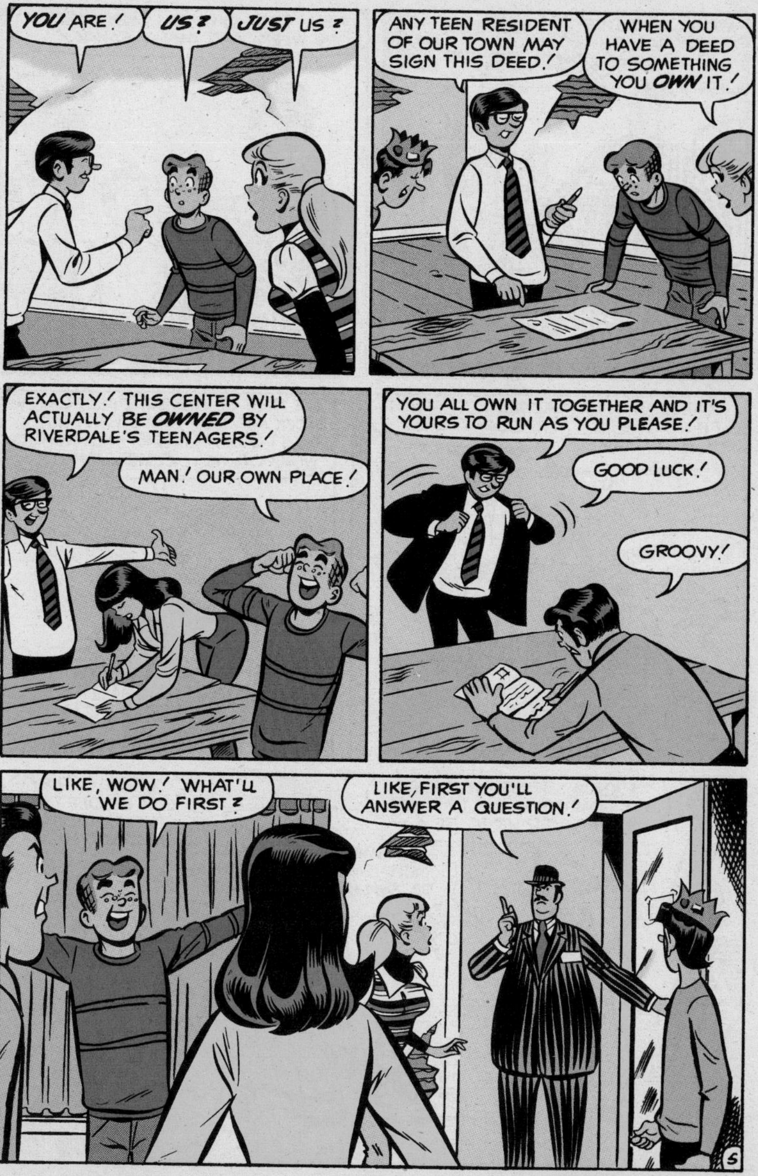
YOU ARE!
US?
JUST US?
ANY TEEN RESIDENT OF OUR TOWN MAY SIGN THIS DEED!
WHEN YOU HAVE A DEED TO SOMETHING YOU OWN IT!
EXACTLY! THIS CENTER WILL ACTUALLY BE OWNED BY RIVERDALE'S TEENAGERS!
MAN! OUR OWN PLACE!
YOU ALL OWN IT TOGETHER AND IT'S YOURS TO RUN AS YOU PLEASE!
GOOD LUCK!
GROOVY!
LIKE, WOW! WHAT'LL WE DO FIRST?
LIKE, FIRST YOU'LL ANSWER A QUESTION!

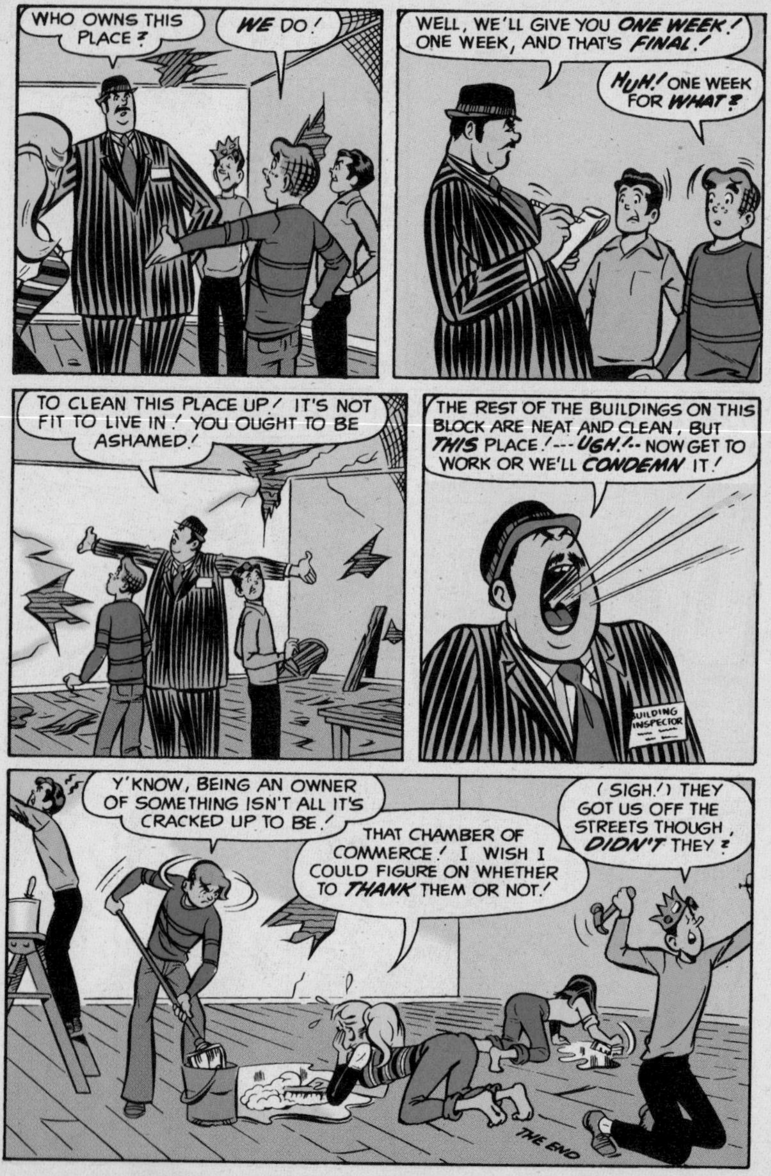
WHO OWNS THIS PLACE ?
WE DO!
WELL, WE'LL GIVE YOU ONE WEEK! ONE WEEK, AND THAT'S FINAL!
HUH! ONE WEEK FOR WHAT ?
TO CLEAN THIS PLACE UP! IT'S NOT FIT TO LIVE IN! YOU OUGHT TO BE ASHAMED!
THE REST OF THE BUILDINGS ON THIS BLOCK ARE NEAT AND CLEAN, BUT THIS PLACE! --- UGH! -- NOW GET TO WORK OR WE'LL CONDEMN IT!
BUILDING INSPECTOR
Y'KNOW, BEING AN OWNER OF SOMETHING ISN'T ALL IT'S CRACKED UP TO BE!
THAT CHAMBER OF COMMERCE! I WISH I COULD FIGURE ON WHETHER TO THANK THEM OR NOT!
(SIGH!) THEY GOT US OFF THE STREETS THOUGH, DIDN'T THEY ?
THE END

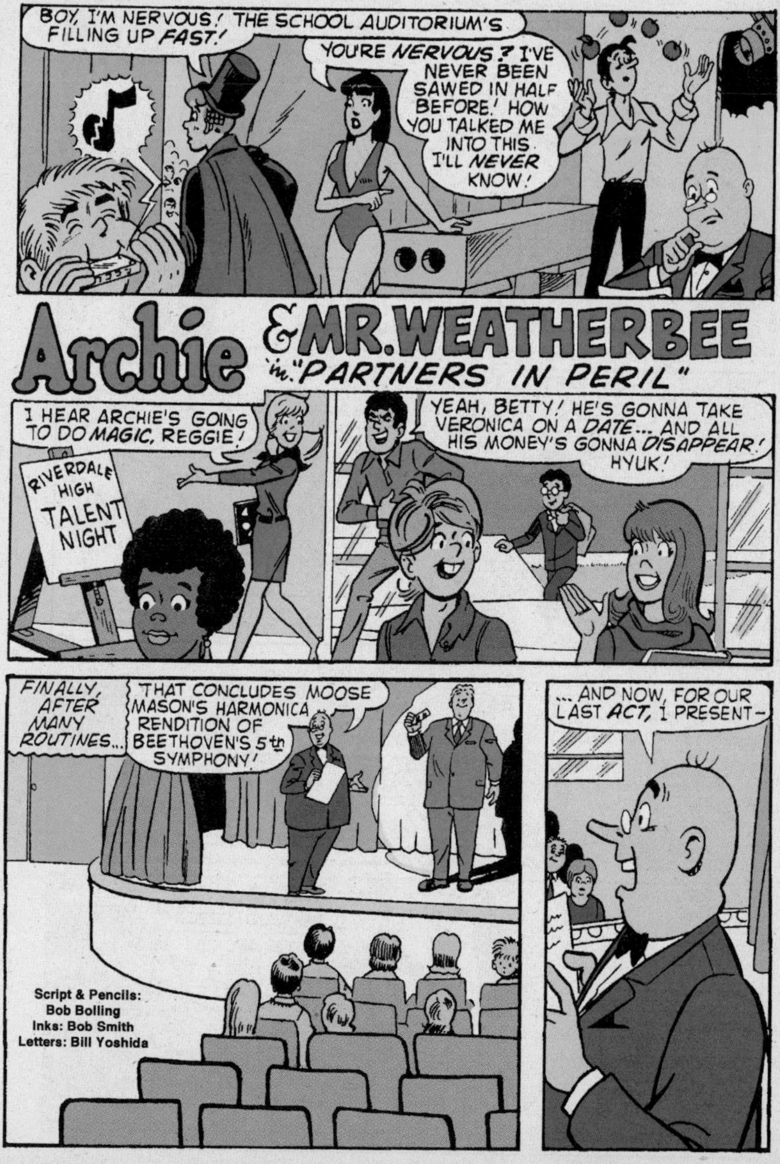

BOY, I'M NERVOUS! THE SCHOOL AUDITORIUM'S FILLING UP FAST!
YOU'RE NERVOUS? I'VE NEVER BEEN SAWED IN HALF BEFORE! HOW YOU TALKED ME INTO THIS I'LL NEVER KNOW!
Archie & MR. WEATHERBEE
"in" "PARTNERS IN PERIL"
I HEAR ARCHIE'S GOING TO DO MAGIC, REGGIE!
RIVERDALE HIGH TALENT NIGHT
YEAH, BETTY! HE'S GONNA TAKE VERONICA ON A DATE... AND ALL HIS MONEY'S GONNA DISAPPEAR! HYUK!
FINALLY, AFTER MANY ROUTINES...
THAT CONCLUDES MOOSE MASON'S HARMONICA RENDITION OF BEETHOVEN'S 5th SYMPHONY!
Script & Pencils: Bob Bolling
Inks: Bob Smith
Letters: Bill Yoshida
... AND NOW, FOR OUR LAST ACT, I PRESENT–

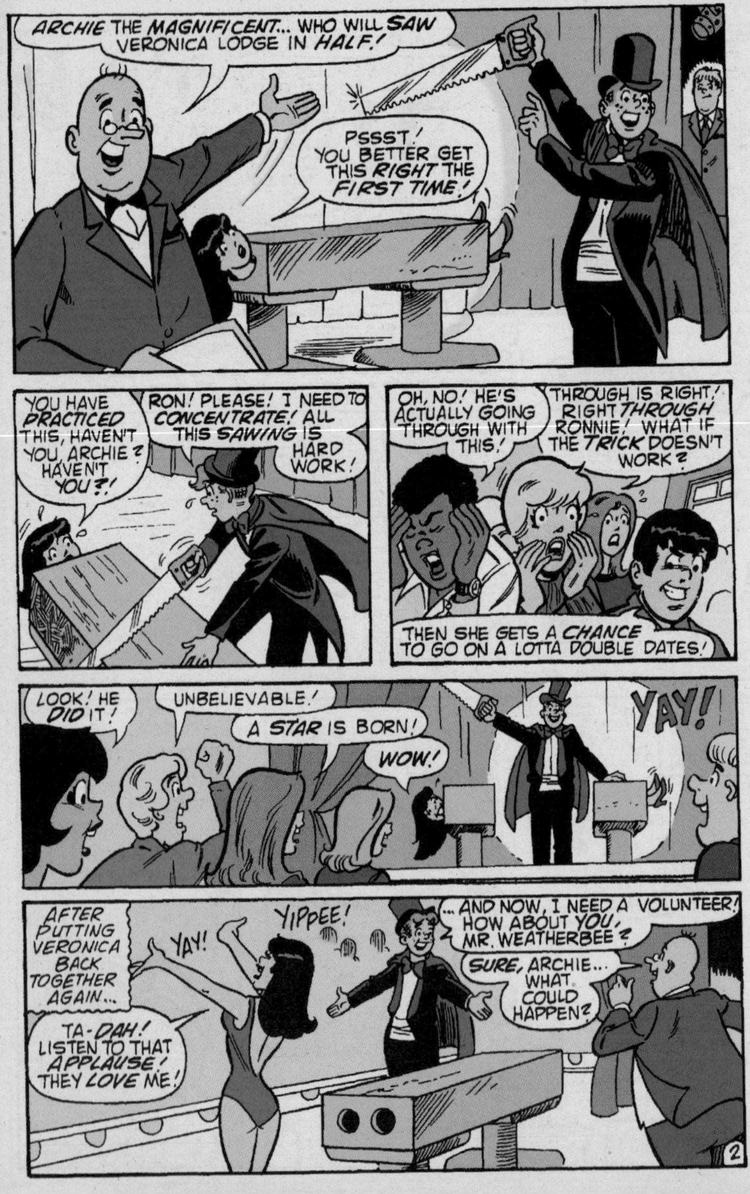

ARCHIE THE MAGNIFICENT... WHO WILL SAW VERONICA LODGE IN HALF!
PSSST! YOU BETTER GET THIS RIGHT THE FIRST TIME!
YOU HAVE PRACTICED THIS, HAVEN'T YOU, ARCHIE? HAVEN'T YOU?!
RON! PLEASE! I NEED TO CONCENTRATE! ALL THIS SAWING IS HARD WORK!
OH, NO! HE'S ACTUALLY GOING THROUGH WITH THIS!
THROUGH IS RIGHT! RIGHT THROUGH RONNIE! WHAT IF THE TRICK DOESN'T WORK?
THEN SHE GETS A CHANCE TO GO ON A LOTTA DOUBLE DATES!
LOOK! HE DID IT!
UNBELIEVABLE!
A STAR IS BORN!
WOW!
YAY!
AFTER PUTTING VERONICA BACK TOGETHER AGAIN...
YAY!
YIPPEE!
... AND NOW, I NEED A VOLUNTEER! HOW ABOUT YOU, MR. WEATHERBEE?
SURE, ARCHIE... WHAT COULD HAPPEN?
TA-DAH! LISTEN TO THAT APPLAUSE! THEY LOVE ME!
2

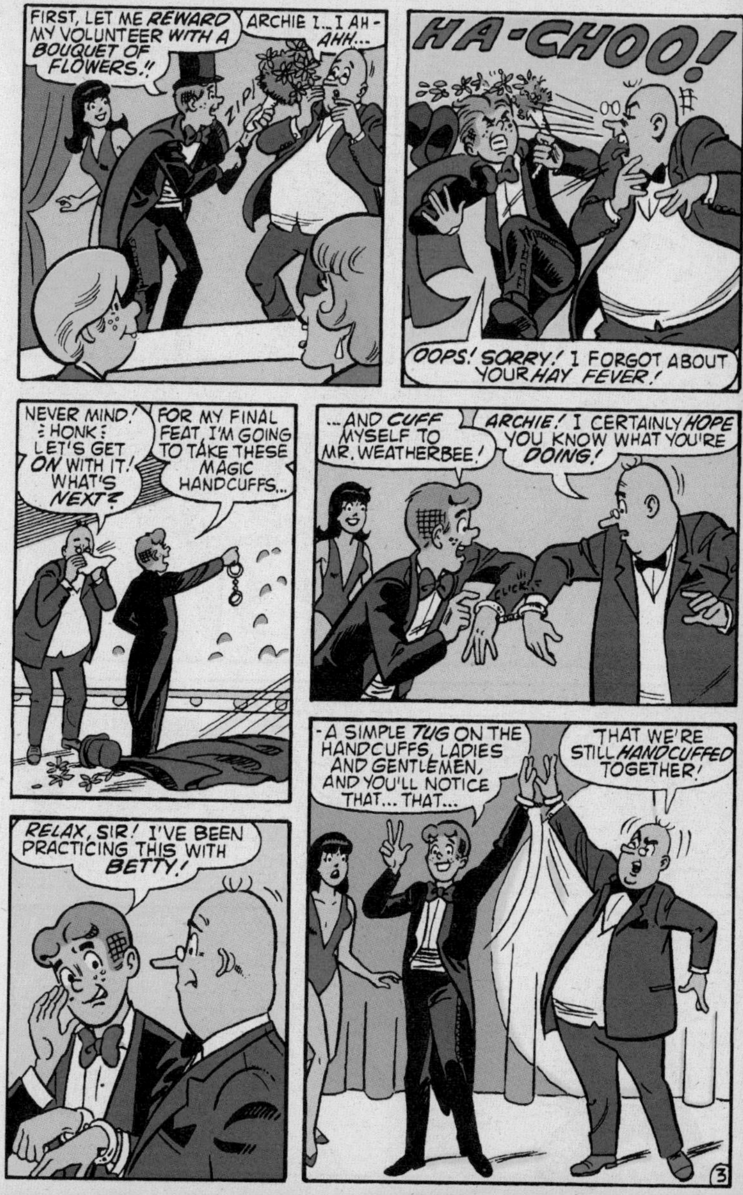
FIRST, LET ME REWARD MY VOLUNTEER WITH A BOUQUET OF FLOWERS.!!
ARCHIE I... I AH- AHH...
ZIP!
HA-CHOO!
OOPS! SORRY! I FORGOT ABOUT YOUR HAY FEVER!
NEVER MIND! :HONK: LET'S GET ON WITH IT! WHAT'S NEXT?
FOR MY FINAL FEAT, I'M GOING TO TAKE THESE MAGIC HANDCUFFS...
...AND CUFF MYSELF TO MR. WEATHERBEE!
ARCHIE! I CERTAINLY HOPE YOU KNOW WHAT YOU'RE DOING!
CLICK!
RELAX, SIR! I'VE BEEN PRACTICING THIS WITH BETTY!
-A SIMPLE TUG ON THE HANDCUFFS, LADIES AND GENTLEMEN, AND YOU'LL NOTICE THAT... THAT...
THAT WE'RE STILL HANDCUFFED TOGETHER!
3

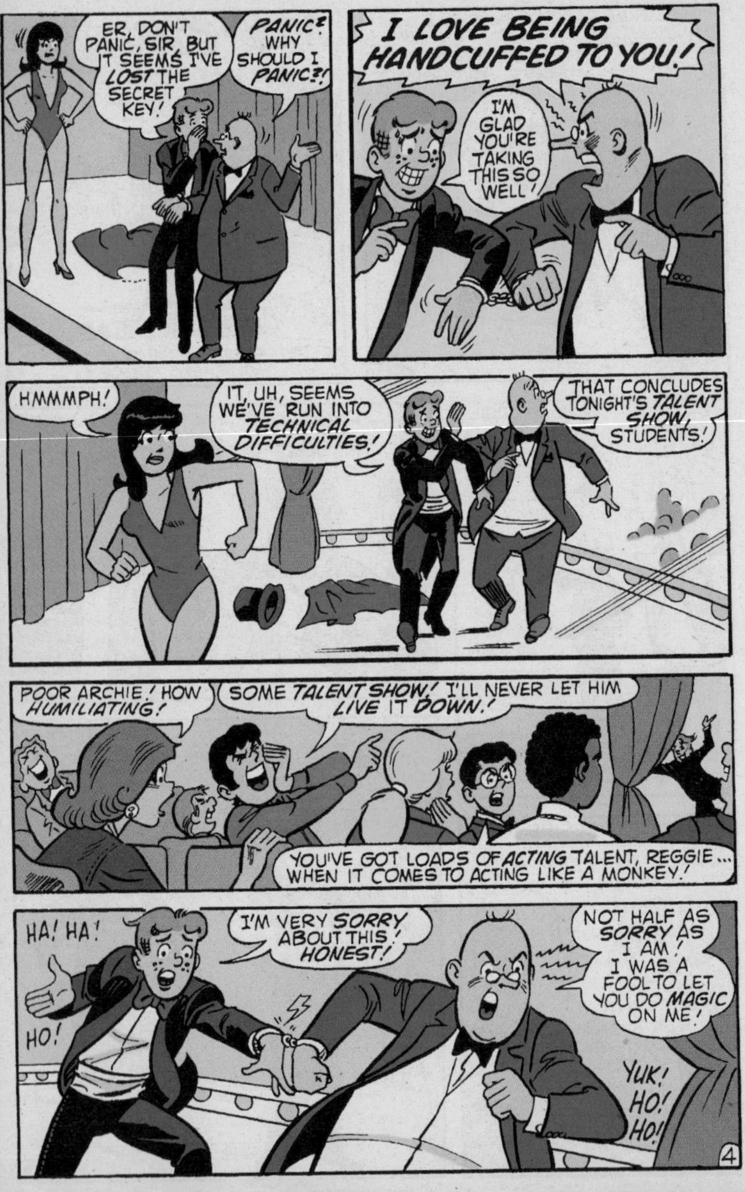
ER, DON'T PANIC, SIR, BUT IT SEEMS I'VE LOST THE SECRET KEY!
PANIC? WHY SHOULD I PANIC?!
I LOVE BEING HANDCUFFED TO YOU!
I'M GLAD YOU'RE TAKING THIS SO WELL!
HMMMPH!
IT, UH, SEEMS WE'VE RUN INTO TECHNICAL DIFFICULTIES!
THAT CONCLUDES TONIGHT'S TALENT SHOW, STUDENTS!
POOR ARCHIE! HOW HUMILIATING!
SOME TALENT SHOW! I'LL NEVER LET HIM LIVE IT DOWN!
YOU'VE GOT LOADS OF ACTING TALENT, REGGIE... WHEN IT COMES TO ACTING LIKE A MONKEY!
HA! HA!
HO!
I'M VERY SORRY ABOUT THIS! HONEST!
NOT HALF AS SORRY AS I AM! I WAS A FOOL TO LET YOU DO MAGIC ON ME!
YUK! HO! HO!
4

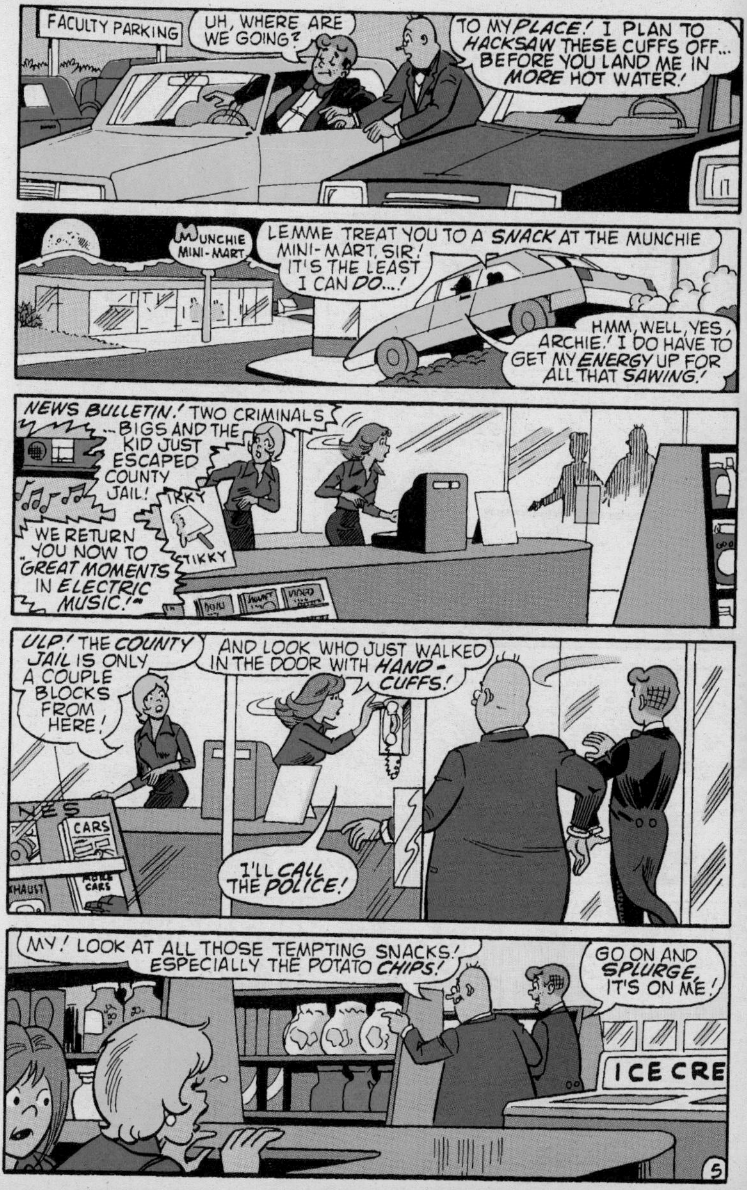
FACULTY PARKING
UH, WHERE ARE WE GOING?
TO MY PLACE! I PLAN TO HACKSAW THESE CUFFS OFF... BEFORE YOU LAND ME IN MORE HOT WATER!
MUNCHIE MINI-MART
LEMME TREAT YOU TO A SNACK AT THE MUNCHIE MINI-MART, SIR! IT'S THE LEAST I CAN DO...!
HMM, WELL, YES, ARCHIE! I DO HAVE TO GET MY ENERGY UP FOR ALL THAT SAWING!
NEWS BULLETIN! TWO CRIMINALS ...BIGS AND THE KID JUST ESCAPED COUNTY JAIL!
WE RETURN YOU NOW TO "GREAT MOMENTS IN ELECTRIC MUSIC!"
TIKKY TIKKY
ULP! THE COUNTY JAIL IS ONLY A COUPLE BLOCKS FROM HERE!
AND LOOK WHO JUST WALKED IN THE DOOR WITH HAND-CUFFS!
I'LL CALL THE POLICE!
CARS
MORE CARS
MY! LOOK AT ALL THOSE TEMPTING SNACKS! ESPECIALLY THE POTATO CHIPS!
GO ON AND SPLURGE, IT'S ON ME!
ICE CRE

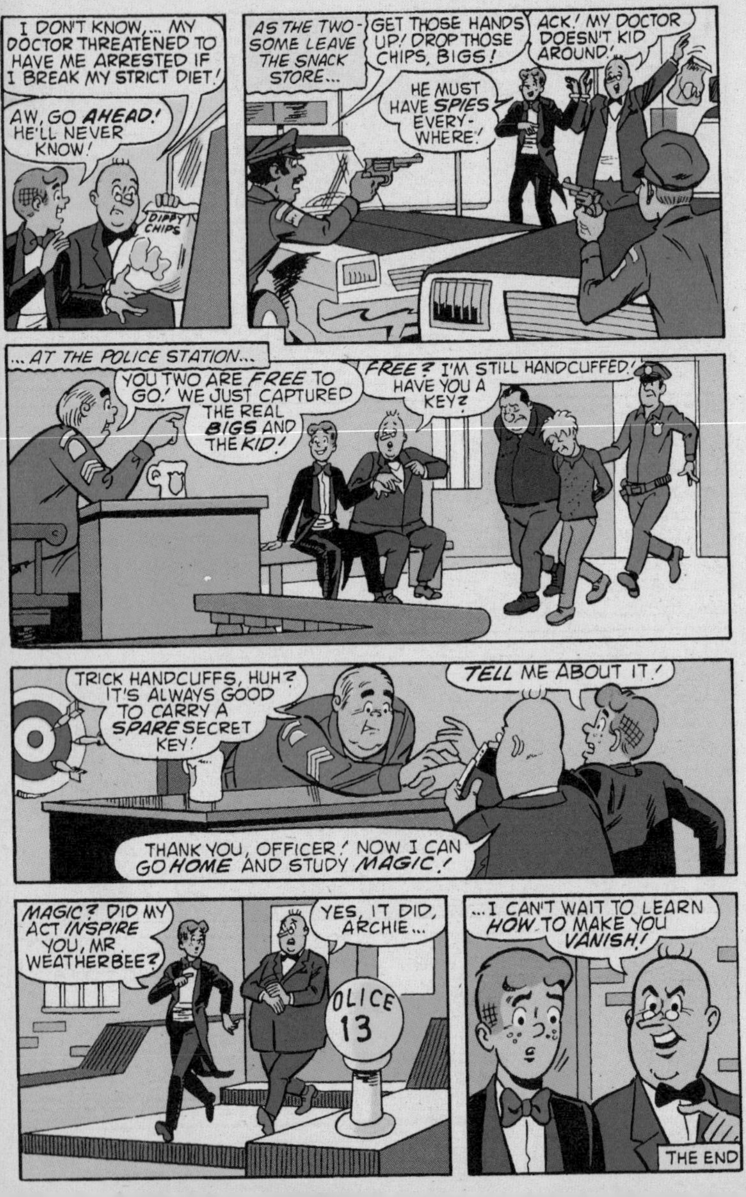
I DON'T KNOW,... MY DOCTOR THREATENED TO HAVE ME ARRESTED IF I BREAK MY STRICT DIET!
AW, GO AHEAD! HE'LL NEVER KNOW!
DIPPY CHIPS
AS THE TWO-SOME LEAVE THE SNACK STORE...
GET THOSE HANDS UP! DROP THOSE CHIPS, BIGS!
ACK! MY DOCTOR DOESN'T KID AROUND!
HE MUST HAVE SPIES EVERY-WHERE!
...AT THE POLICE STATION...
YOU TWO ARE FREE TO GO! WE JUST CAPTURED THE REAL BIGS AND THE KID!
FREE? I'M STILL HANDCUFFED! HAVE YOU A KEY?
TRICK HANDCUFFS, HUH? IT'S ALWAYS GOOD TO CARRY A SPARE SECRET KEY!
TELL ME ABOUT IT!
THANK YOU, OFFICER! NOW I CAN GO HOME AND STUDY MAGIC!
MAGIC? DID MY ACT INSPIRE YOU, MR. WEATHERBEE?
YES, IT DID, ARCHIE...
OLICE 13
...I CAN'T WAIT TO LEARN HOW TO MAKE YOU VANISH!
THE END

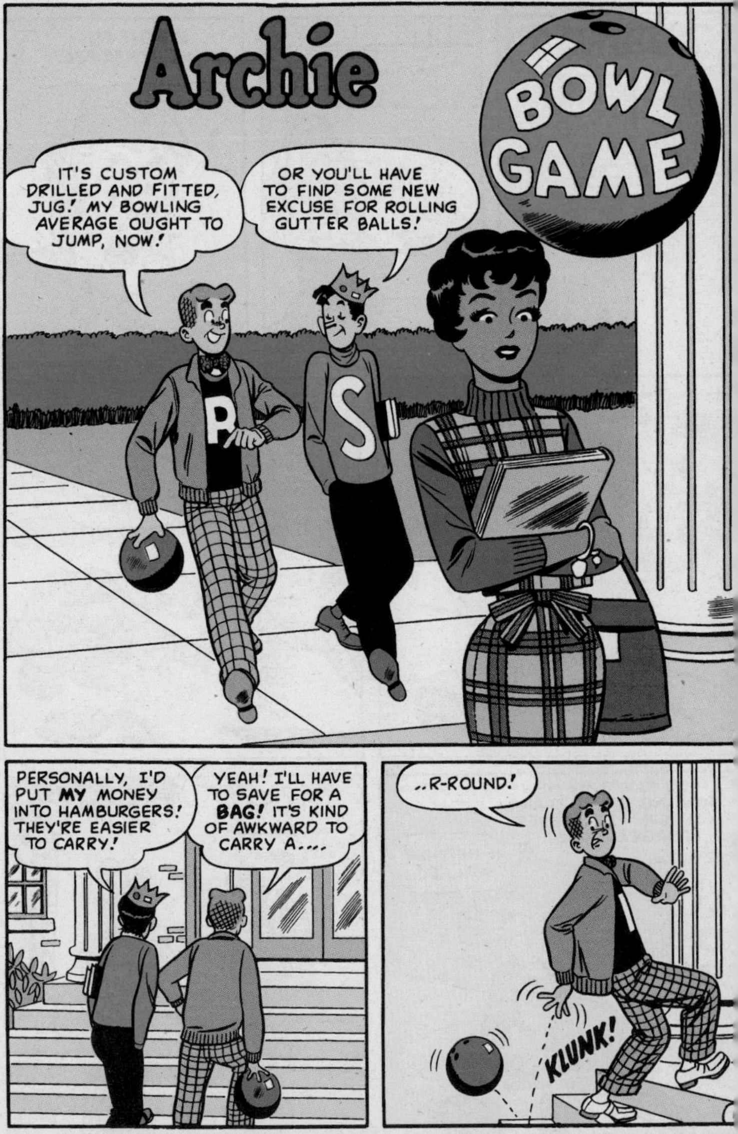
Archie
BOWL GAME
IT'S CUSTOM DRILLED AND FITTED, JUG! MY BOWLING AVERAGE OUGHT TO JUMP, NOW!
OR YOU'LL HAVE TO FIND SOME NEW EXCUSE FOR ROLLING GUTTER BALLS!
PERSONALLY, I'D PUT MY MONEY INTO HAMBURGERS! THEY'RE EASIER TO CARRY!
YEAH! I'LL HAVE TO SAVE FOR A BAG! IT'S KIND OF AWKWARD TO CARRY A....
..R-ROUND!
KLUNK!

Script: Frank Doyle / Art & Letters: Harry Lucey

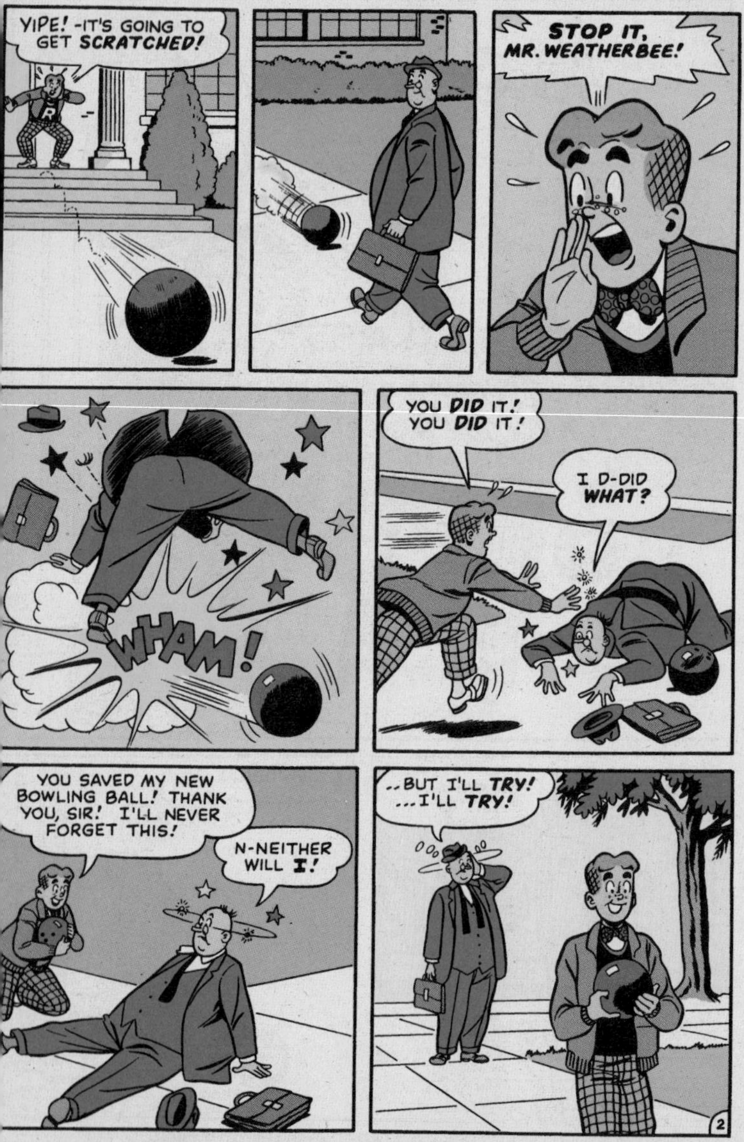

YIPE! -IT'S GOING TO GET SCRATCHED!
STOP IT, MR. WEATHERBEE!
WHAM!
YOU DID IT! YOU DID IT!
I D-DID WHAT?
YOU SAVED MY NEW BOWLING BALL! THANK YOU, SIR! I'LL NEVER FORGET THIS!
N-NEITHER WILL I!
..BUT I'LL TRY! ...I'LL TRY!
2

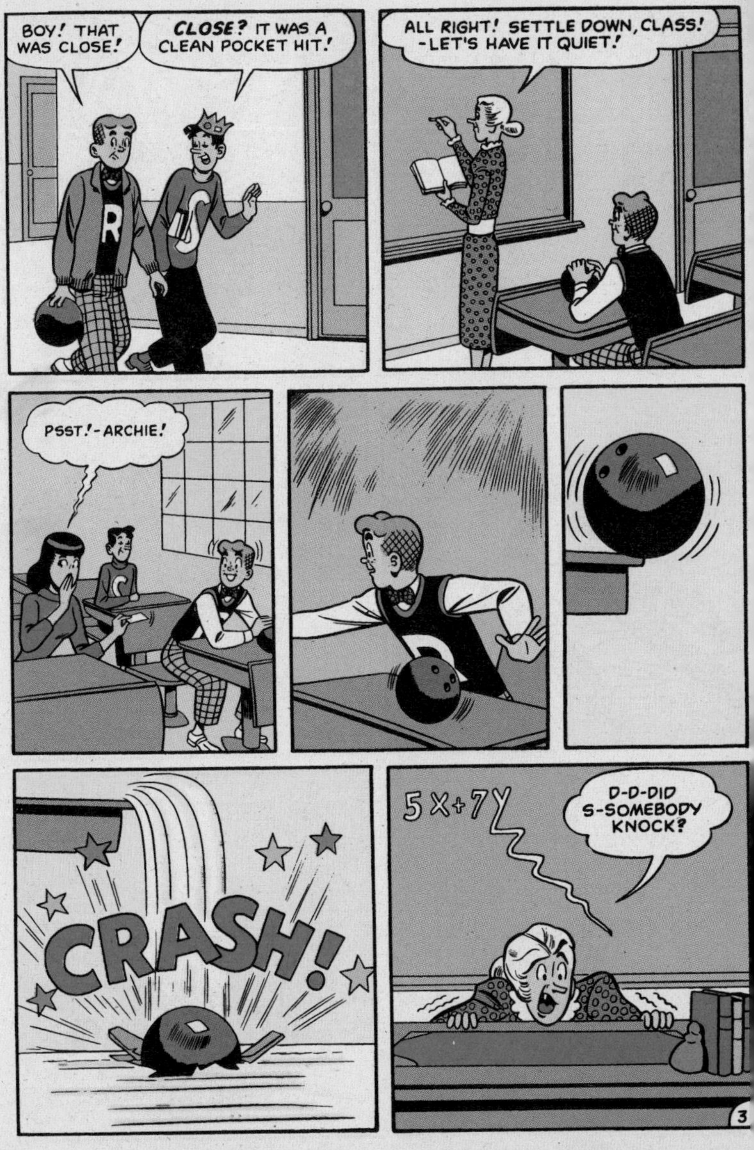
BOY! THAT WAS CLOSE!
CLOSE? IT WAS A CLEAN POCKET HIT!
ALL RIGHT! SETTLE DOWN, CLASS! -LET'S HAVE IT QUIET!
PSST!-ARCHIE!
CRASH!
5X+7Y
D-D-DID S-SOMEBODY KNOCK?

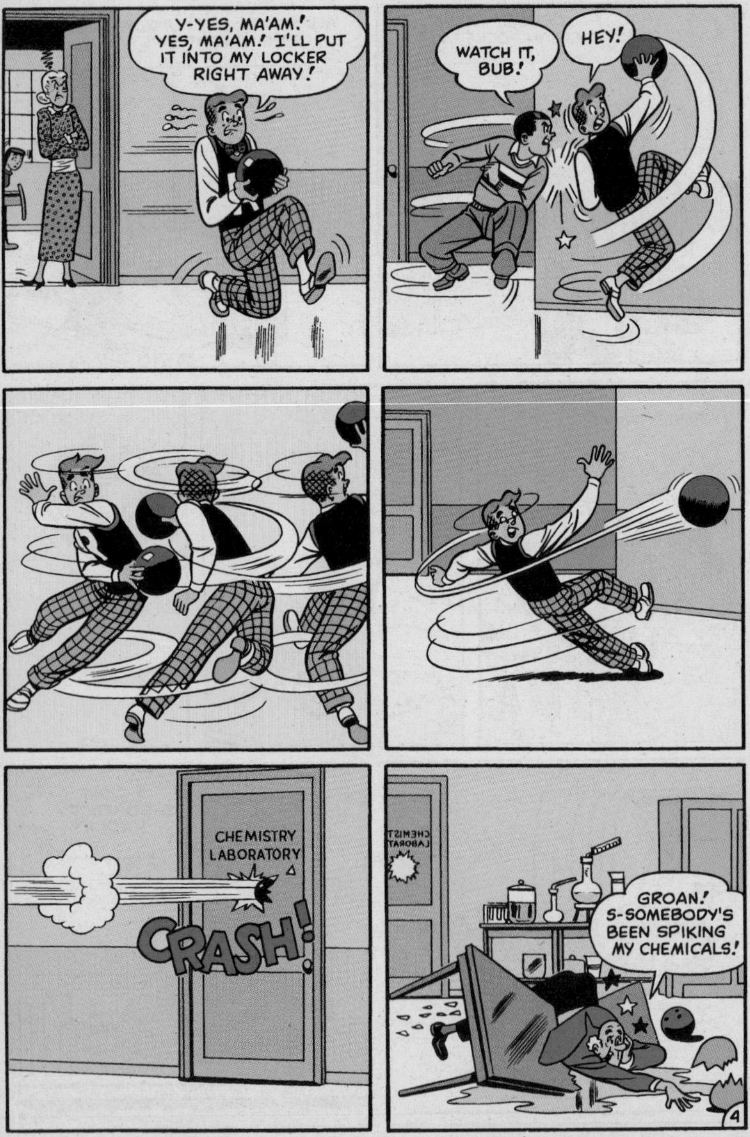
Y-YES, MA'AM! YES, MA'AM! I'LL PUT IT INTO MY LOCKER RIGHT AWAY!
WATCH IT, BUB!
HEY!
CHEMISTRY LABORATORY
CRASH!
GROAN! S-SOMEBODY'S BEEN SPIKING MY CHEMICALS!
4

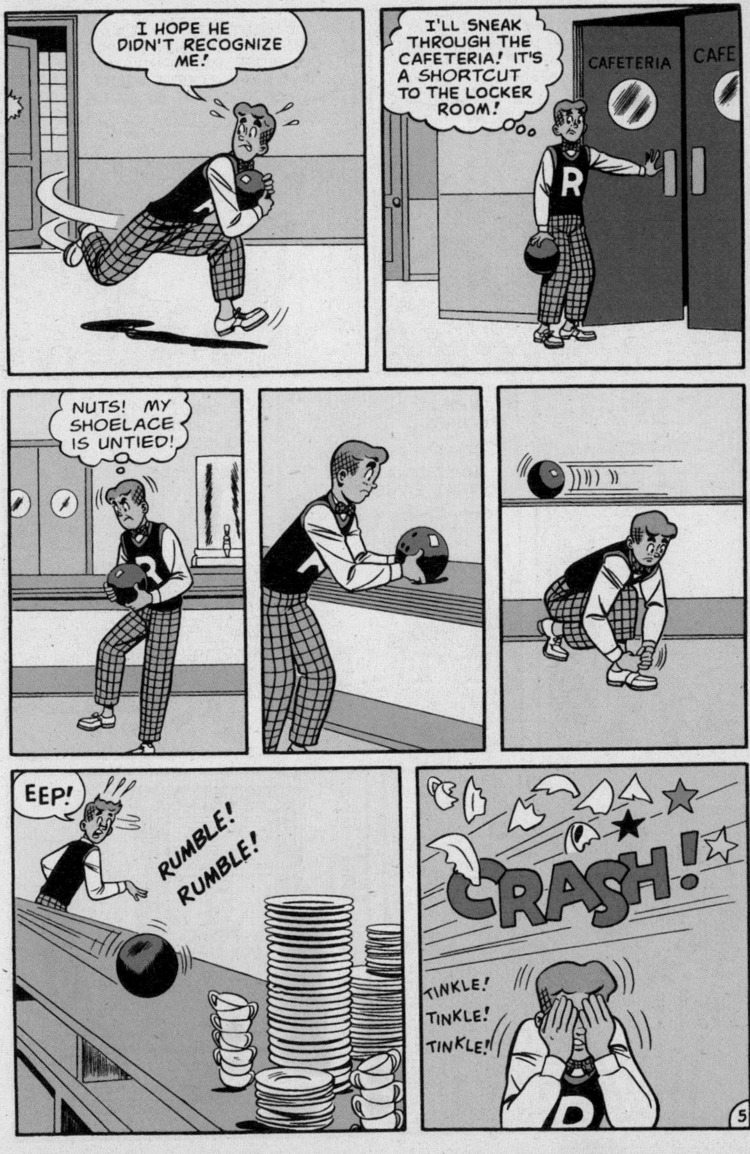
I HOPE HE DIDN'T RECOGNIZE ME!
I'LL SNEAK THROUGH THE CAFETERIA! IT'S A SHORTCUT TO THE LOCKER ROOM!
CAFETERIA
CAFE
NUTS! MY SHOELACE IS UNTIED!
EEP!
RUMBLE! RUMBLE!
CRASH!
TINKLE! TINKLE! TINKLE!

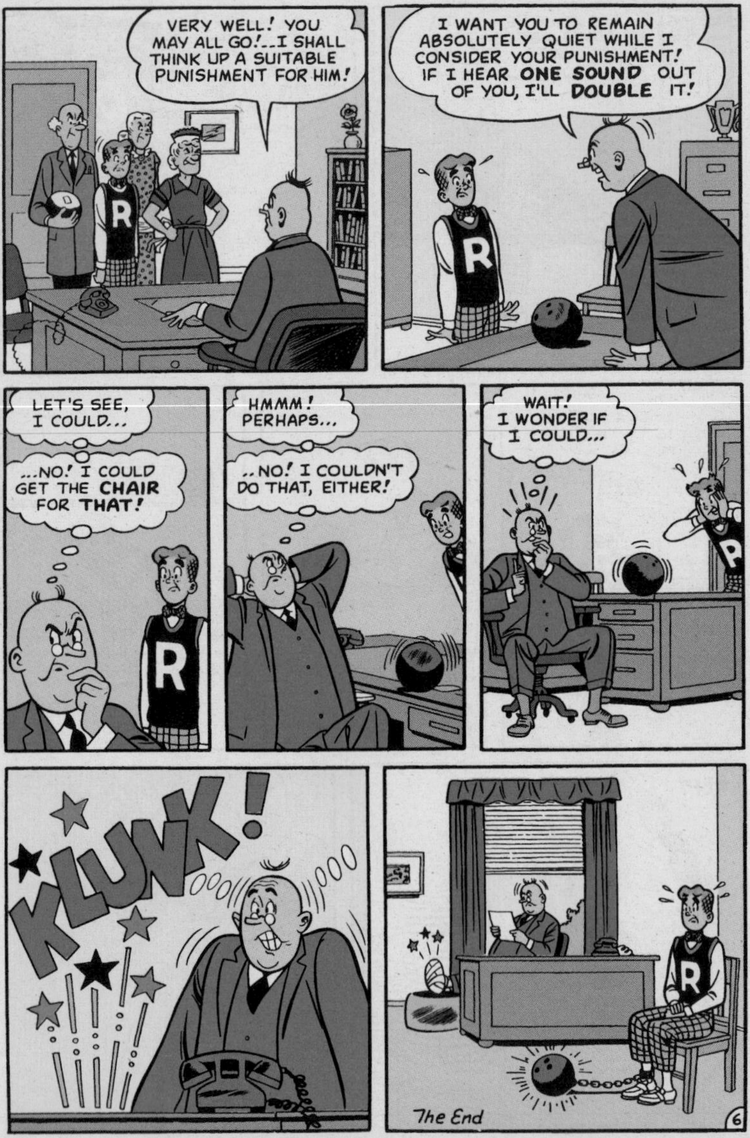
VERY WELL! YOU MAY ALL GO!..I SHALL THINK UP A SUITABLE PUNISHMENT FOR HIM!
I WANT YOU TO REMAIN ABSOLUTELY QUIET WHILE I CONSIDER YOUR PUNISHMENT! IF I HEAR ONE SOUND OUT OF YOU, I'LL DOUBLE IT!
LET'S SEE, I COULD...
...NO! I COULD GET THE CHAIR FOR THAT!
HMMM! PERHAPS...
..NO! I COULDN'T DO THAT, EITHER!
WAIT! I WONDER IF I COULD...
KLUNK!
The End
6

Betty and Veronica in Walk the Walk

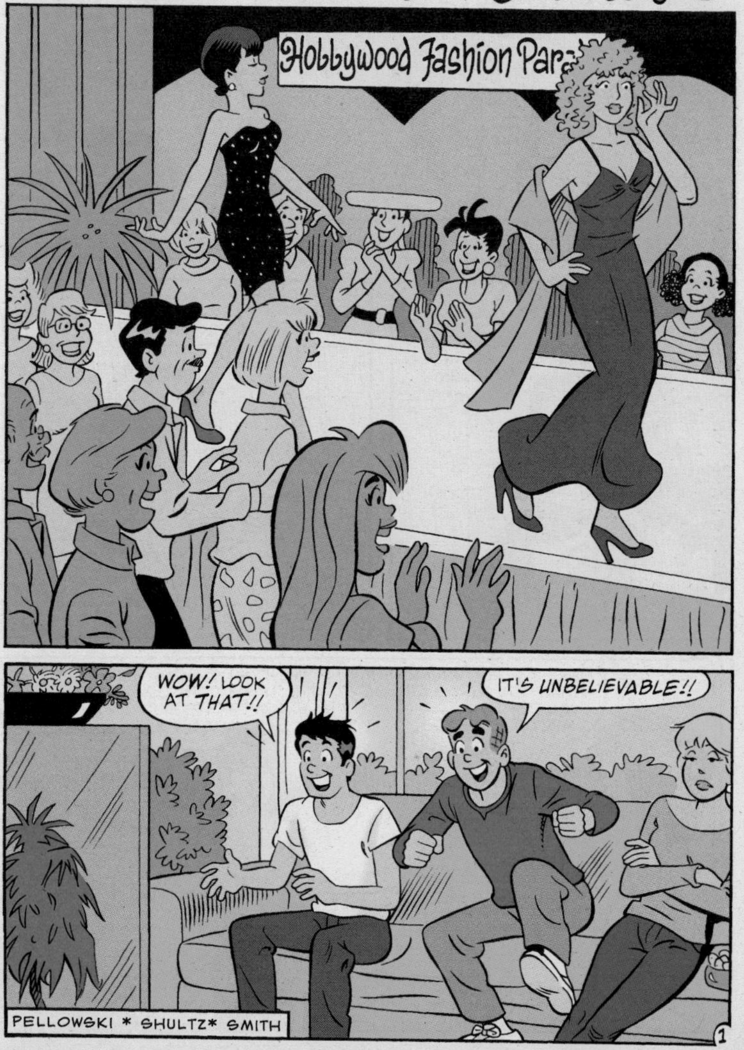

Hobbywood Fashion Par
WOW! LOOK AT THAT!!
IT'S UNBELIEVABLE!!
PELLOWSKI * SHULTZ* SMITH

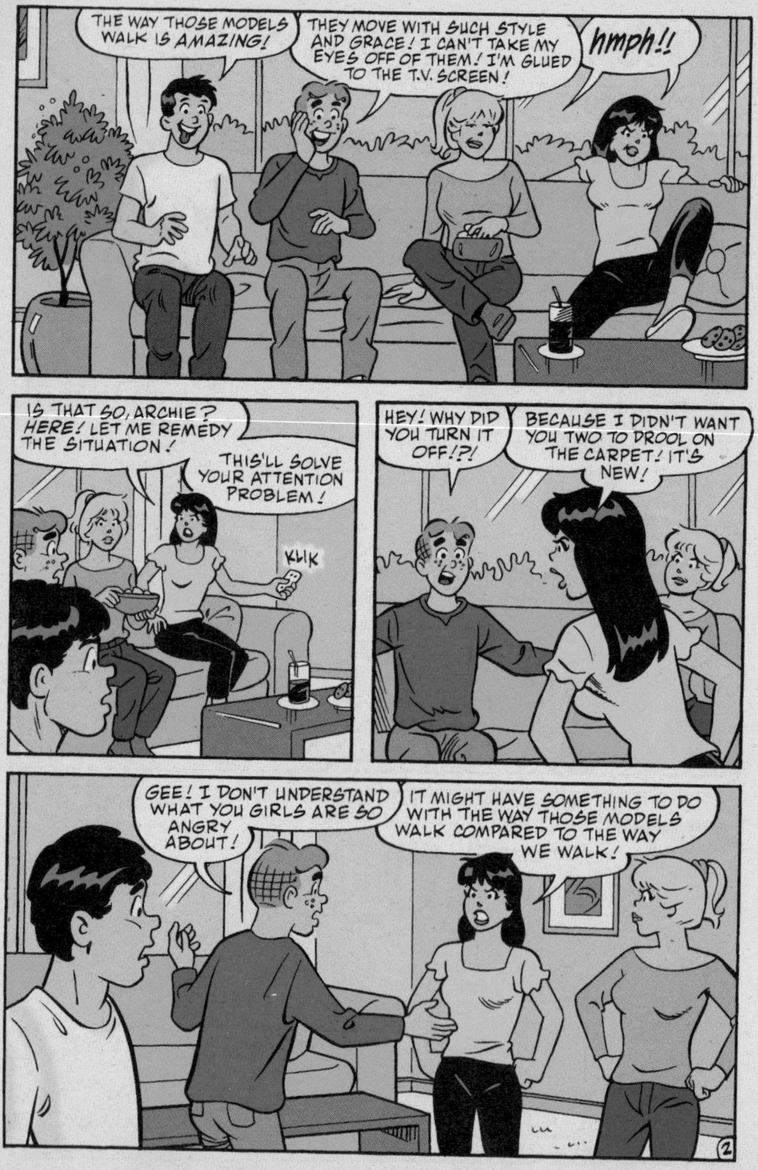
THE WAY THOSE MODELS WALK IS AMAZING!
THEY MOVE WITH SUCH STYLE AND GRACE! I CAN'T TAKE MY EYES OFF OF THEM! I'M GLUED TO THE T.V. SCREEN!
hmph!!
IS THAT SO, ARCHIE? HERE! LET ME REMEDY THE SITUATION!
THIS'LL SOLVE YOUR ATTENTION PROBLEM!
KLIK
HEY! WHY DID YOU TURN IT OFF!?!
BECAUSE I DIDN'T WANT YOU TWO TO DROOL ON THE CARPET! IT'S NEW!
GEE! I DON'T UNDERSTAND WHAT YOU GIRLS ARE SO ANGRY ABOUT!
IT MIGHT HAVE SOMETHING TO DO WITH THE WAY THOSE MODELS WALK COMPARED TO THE WAY WE WALK!
2

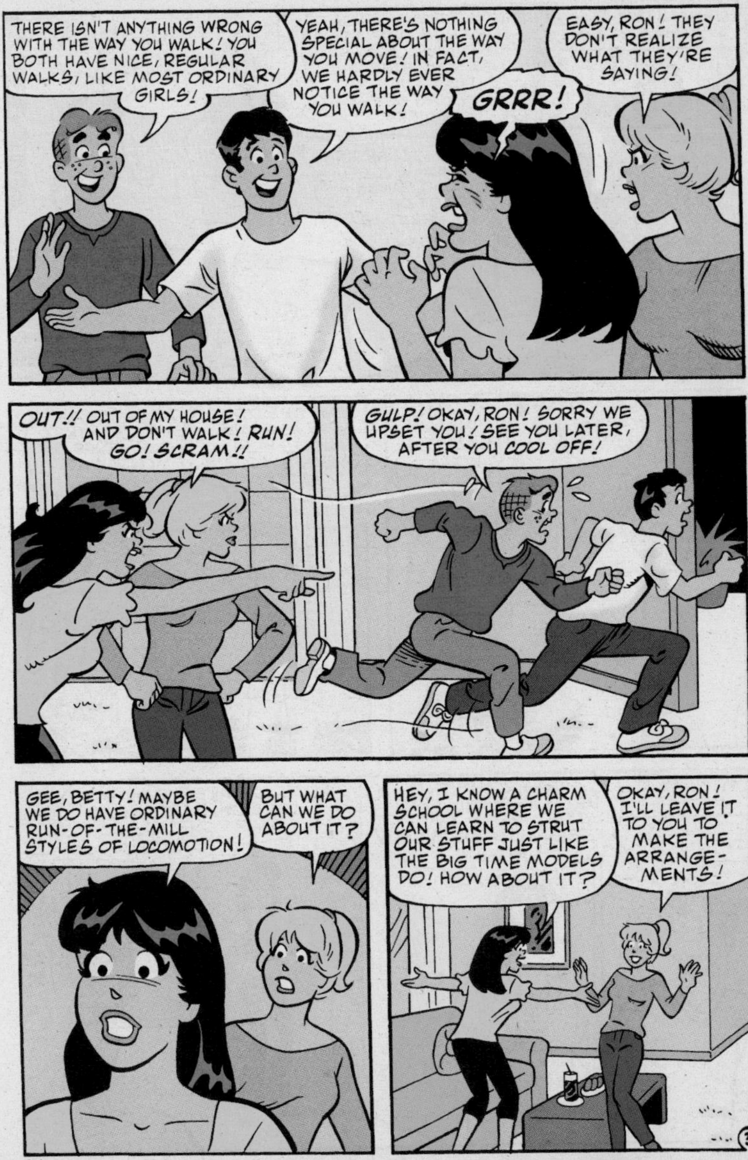
THERE ISN'T ANYTHING WRONG WITH THE WAY YOU WALK! YOU BOTH HAVE NICE, REGULAR WALKS, LIKE MOST ORDINARY GIRLS!
YEAH, THERE'S NOTHING SPECIAL ABOUT THE WAY YOU MOVE! IN FACT, WE HARDLY EVER NOTICE THE WAY YOU WALK!
EASY, RON! THEY DON'T REALIZE WHAT THEY'RE SAYING!
GRRR!
OUT!! OUT OF MY HOUSE! AND DON'T WALK! RUN! GO! SCRAM!!
GULP! OKAY, RON! SORRY WE UPSET YOU! SEE YOU LATER, AFTER YOU COOL OFF!
GEE, BETTY! MAYBE WE DO HAVE ORDINARY RUN-OF-THE-MILL STYLES OF LOCOMOTION!
BUT WHAT CAN WE DO ABOUT IT?
HEY, I KNOW A CHARM SCHOOL WHERE WE CAN LEARN TO STRUT OUR STUFF JUST LIKE THE BIG TIME MODELS DO! HOW ABOUT IT?
OKAY, RON! I'LL LEAVE IT TO YOU TO MAKE THE ARRANGE-MENTS!
3

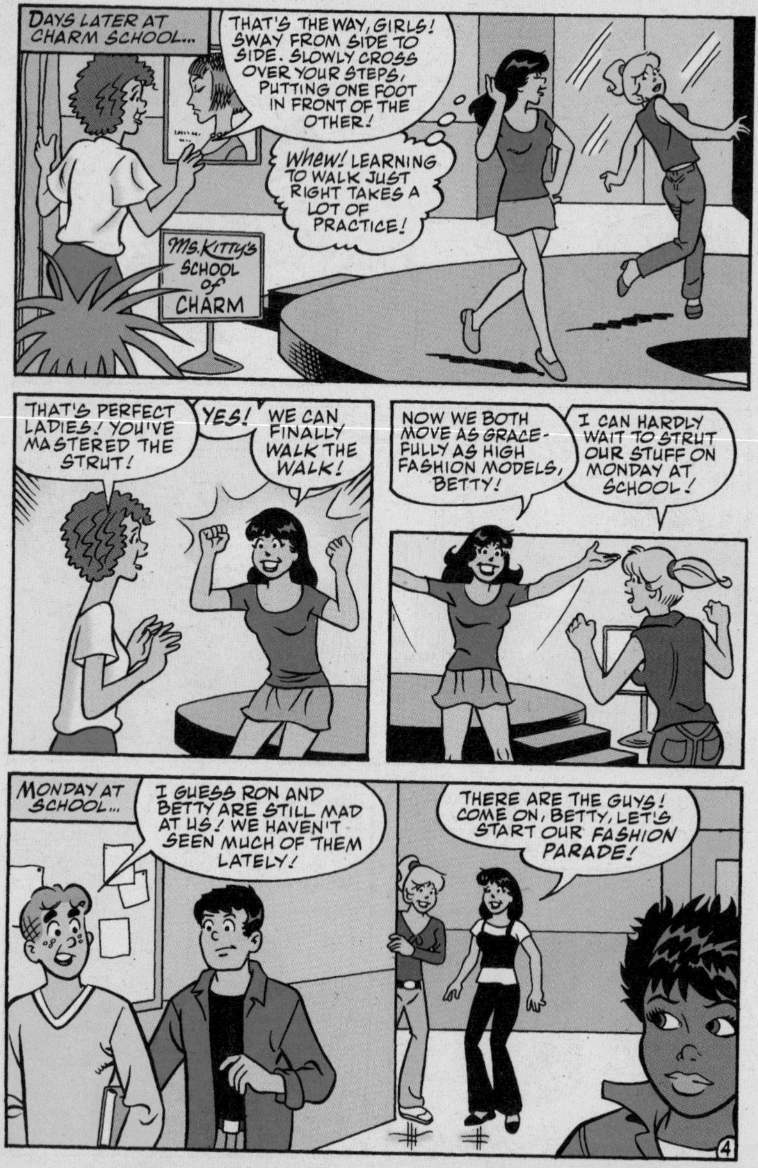
DAYS LATER AT CHARM SCHOOL...
THAT'S THE WAY, GIRLS! SWAY FROM SIDE TO SIDE. SLOWLY CROSS OVER YOUR STEPS, PUTTING ONE FOOT IN FRONT OF THE OTHER!
WHEW! LEARNING TO WALK JUST RIGHT TAKES A LOT OF PRACTICE!
MS. KITTY'S SCHOOL of CHARM
THAT'S PERFECT LADIES! YOU'VE MASTERED THE STRUT!
YES!
WE CAN FINALLY WALK THE WALK!
NOW WE BOTH MOVE AS GRACEFULLY AS HIGH FASHION MODELS, BETTY!
I CAN HARDLY WAIT TO STRUT OUR STUFF ON MONDAY AT SCHOOL!
MONDAY AT SCHOOL...
I GUESS RON AND BETTY ARE STILL MAD AT US! WE HAVEN'T SEEN MUCH OF THEM LATELY!
THERE ARE THE GUYS! COME ON, BETTY, LET'S START OUR FASHION PARADE!
4

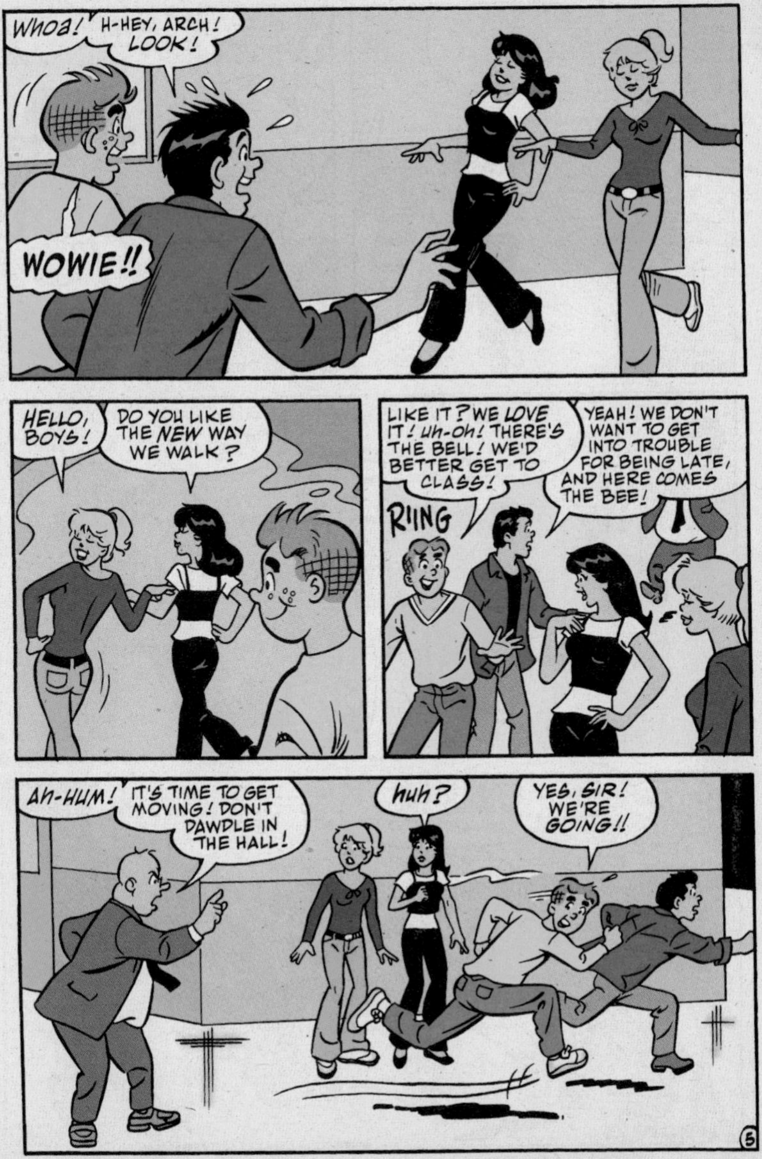
Whoa!
H-HEY, ARCH! LOOK!
WOWIE!!
HELLO, BOYS!
DO YOU LIKE THE NEW WAY WE WALK?
LIKE IT? WE LOVE IT! uh-oh! THERE'S THE BELL! WE'D BETTER GET TO CLASS!
RIING
YEAH! WE DON'T WANT TO GET INTO TROUBLE FOR BEING LATE, AND HERE COMES THE BEE!
Ah-HUM!
IT'S TIME TO GET MOVING! DON'T DAWDLE IN THE HALL!
huh?
YES, SIR! WE'RE GOING!!

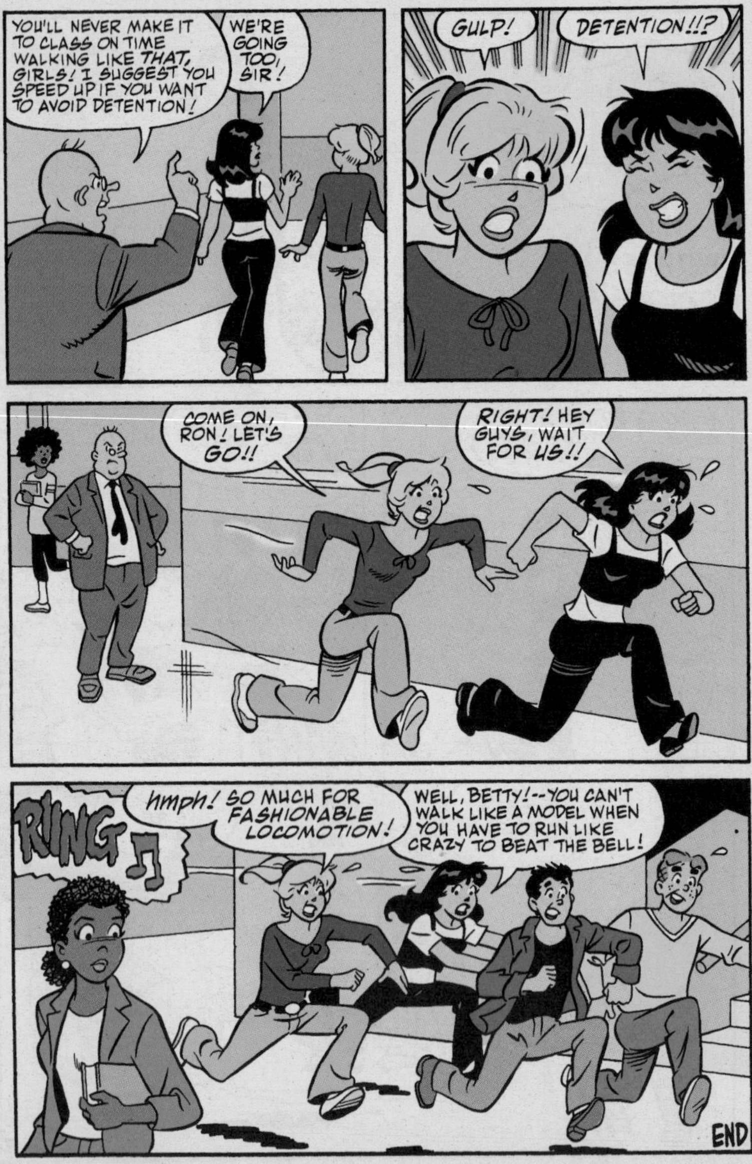
YOU'LL NEVER MAKE IT TO CLASS ON TIME WALKING LIKE THAT, GIRLS! I SUGGEST YOU SPEED UP IF YOU WANT TO AVOID DETENTION!
WE'RE GOING TOO, SIR!
GULP!
DETENTION!!?
COME ON, RON! LET'S GO!!
RIGHT! HEY GUYS, WAIT FOR US!!
RING
hmph! SO MUCH FOR FASHIONABLE LOCOMOTION!
WELL, BETTY!--YOU CAN'T WALK LIKE A MODEL WHEN YOU HAVE TO RUN LIKE CRAZY TO BEAT THE BELL!
END

MISS GRUNDY

GROUP EFFORT

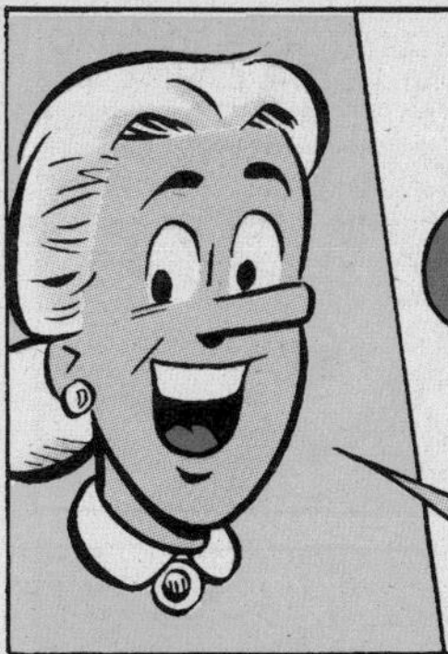
SEE IF YOU CAN MATCH THE GROUPS OF ANIMALS BELOW TO THE INDIVIDUAL MEMBERS!

1. HERD	A. WOLVES
2. SCHOOL	B. COWS
3. FLOCK	C. BEES
4. PACK	D. SEAGULLS
5. SWARM	E. FISH

ANSWERS: 1-B, 2-E, 3-D 4-A, 5-C

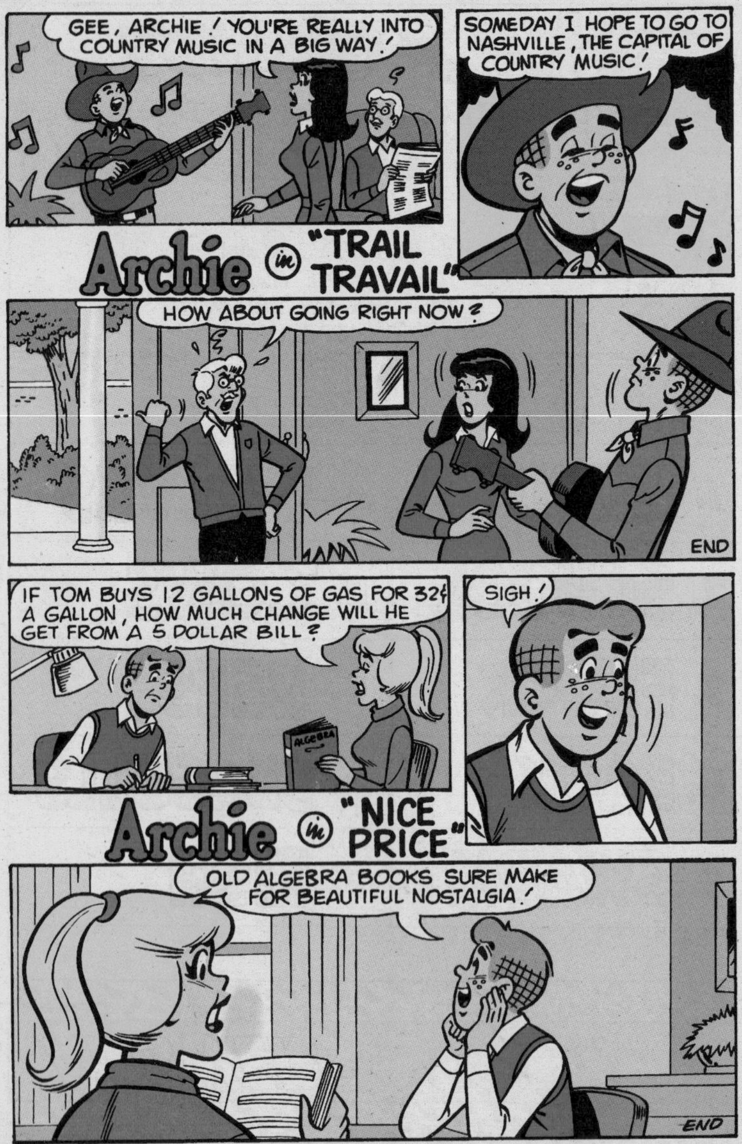
GEE, ARCHIE! YOU'RE REALLY INTO COUNTRY MUSIC IN A BIG WAY!
SOMEDAY I HOPE TO GO TO NASHVILLE, THE CAPITAL OF COUNTRY MUSIC!
Archie in "TRAIL TRAVAIL"
HOW ABOUT GOING RIGHT NOW?
END
IF TOM BUYS 12 GALLONS OF GAS FOR 32¢ A GALLON, HOW MUCH CHANGE WILL HE GET FROM A 5 DOLLAR BILL?
ALGEBRA
SIGH!
Archie in "NICE PRICE"
OLD ALGEBRA BOOKS SURE MAKE FOR BEAUTIFUL NOSTALGIA!
END